DEAN R. KOONTZ

THREE COMPLETE NOVELS

DEAN R. KOONTZ

THREE COMPLETE NOVELS

THE SERVANTS OF TWILIGHT

DARKFALL

PHANTOMS

WINGS BOOKS
NEW YORK
AVENEL, NEW JERSEY

This edition contains the complete and unabridged texts of the original
editions. They have been completely reset for this volume.
This omnibus was originally published in separate volumes under
the titles:
The Servants of Twilight, copyright © 1984 by NKUI, Inc.
(Previously published as *Twilight* under the pseudonym Leigh Nichols.)
The author gratefully acknowledges the permission to quote
from *Something Wicked This Way Comes* © 1962 by Ray Bradbury,
permission granted by Simon & Schuster, Inc.,
1230 Avenue of the Americas, New York, New York, 10020.
Darkfall, copyright © 1984 by Dean R. Koontz.
Phantoms, copyright © 1983 by Dean R. Koontz.
All rights reserved.

This 1991 edition is published by Wings Books,
distributed by Outlet Book Company, Inc., a Random House Company,
40 Engelhard Avenue, Avenel, New Jersey 07001,
by arrangement with The Berkley Publishing Group.

Printed and bound in the United States of America

Library of Congress Cataloging-in-Publication Data
Koontz, Dean R. (Dean Ray), 1945–
Three complete novels / Dean R. Koontz.
p.   cm.
Contents: The Servants of twilight—Phantoms—Darkfall.
ISBN 0-517-06487-1
I. Title.
PS3561.O55A6 1991
813′.54—dc20
91-17863
CIP
8 7 6 5 4

Book design by Clair Moritz

CONTENTS

THE SERVANTS OF TWILIGHT

This book is dedicated to very special people,

George and Jane Smith

—and to their lovely offspring, Diana Summers, and to their cats. May they have all the success and happiness they so well deserve. (I mean, of course, George and Jane and Diana, not the cats.) And may they have much fun catching mice and singing on backyard fences. (That is, the cats, not George, Jane and Diana.)

PART ONE

THE HAG

An' all us other children, when
   the supper things is done,
We sit around the kitchen fire
   an' has the mostest fun
A-list-nin' to the witch-tales
   that Annie tells about,
An' the Gobble'uns that gits you
If you
   Don't
     Watch
      Out!
       —*Little Orphant Annie,*
       James Whitcomb Riley

. . . the Dust Witch came, mumbling. A moment later,
looking up, Will saw her. Not dead! he thought. Carried
off, bruised, fallen, yes, but now back, and mad! Lord, yes,
mad, looking *especially* for *me*!
       —*Something Wicked This Way Comes,*
       Ray Bradbury

CHAPTER 1

IT BEGAN IN sunshine, not on a dark and stormy night.

She wasn't prepared for what happened, wasn't on guard. Who would have expected trouble on a lovely Sunday afternoon like that?

The sky was clear and blue. It was surprisingly warm, for the end of February, even in southern California. The breeze was gentle and scented with winter flowers. It was one of those days when everyone seemed destined to live forever.

Christine Scavello had gone to South Coast Plaza in Costa Mesa to do some shopping, and she had taken Joey with her. He liked the big mall. He was fascinated by the stream that splashed through one wing of the building, down the middle of the public promenade and over a gentle waterfall. He was also intrigued by the hundreds of trees and plants that thrived indoors, and he was a born people-watcher. But most of all he liked the carousel in the central courtyard. In return for one ride on the carousel, he would tag along happily and quietly while Christine spent two or three hours shopping.

Joey was a good kid, the best. He never whined, never threw tantrums or complained. Trapped in the house on a long, rainy day, he could entertain himself for hour after hour and not once grow bored or restless or crabby the way most kids would.

To Christine, Joey sometimes seemed to be a little old man in a six-year-old

4

boy's small body. Occasionally he said the most amazingly grown-up things, and he usually had the patience of an adult, and he was often wiser than his years.

But at other times, especially when he asked where his daddy was or why his daddy had gone away—or even when he *didn't* ask but just stood there with the question shimmering in his eyes—he looked so innocent, fragile, so heart-breakingly vulnerable that she just had to grab him and hug him.

Sometimes the hugging wasn't merely an expression of her love for him, but also an evasion of the issue that he had raised. She had never found a way to tell him about his father, and it was a subject she wished he would just drop until *she* was ready to bring it up. He was too young to understand the truth, and she didn't want to lie to him —not *too* blatantly, anyway—or resort to cutesy euphemisms.

He had asked about his father just a couple of hours ago, on the way to the mall. She had said, "Honey, your daddy just wasn't ready for the responsibility of a family."

"Didn't he like me?"

"He never even *knew* you, so how could he not like you? He was gone before you were born."

"Oh, yeah? How could I have been borned if he wasn't here?" the boy had asked skeptically.

"That's something you'll learn in sex education class at school," she had said, amused.

"When?"

"Oh, in about six or seven more years, I guess."

"That's a long time to wait." He had sighed. "I'll bet he didn't like me and that's why he went away."

Frowning, she had said, "You put that thought right out of your mind, sugar. It was *me* your daddy didn't like."

"You? He didn't like you?"

"That's right."

Joey had been silent for a block or two, but finally he had said, "Boy, if he didn't like you, he musta been just plain *dumb.*"

Then, apparently sensing that the subject made her uneasy, he had changed it. A little old man in a six-year-old boy's small body.

The fact was that Joey was the result of a brief, passionate, reckless, and *stupid* affair. Sometimes, looking back on it, she couldn't believe that she had been so naive . . . or so desperate to prove her womanhood and independence. It was the only relationship in Christine's life that qualified as a "fling," the only time she had ever been swept away. For that man, for no other man before or since, for *that* man alone, she had put aside her morals and principles and common sense, heeding only the urgent desires of her flesh. She had told herself that it was Romance with a capital R, not just love but the Big Love, even Love At First Sight. Actually she had just been weak, vulnerable, and eager to make a fool of herself. Later, when she realized that Mr. Wonderful had lied to her and used her with cold, cynical disregard for her feelings, when she discovered that she had given herself to a man who was utterly without respect for her and who lacked even a minimal sense of responsibility, she had been deeply ashamed. Eventually she realized there was a point at which shame and remorse became self-indulgent and nearly as lamentable as the sin that had occasioned those emotions, so she put the shabby episode behind her and vowed to forget it.

Except that Joey kept asking who his father was, where his father was, why his father had gone away. And how did you tell a six-year-old about your libidinous urges, the treachery of your own heart, and your regrettable capacity for occasionally making a complete fool of yourself? If it could be done, she hadn't seen the way. She was just going to have to wait until he was grown up enough to understand that adults could sometimes be just as dumb and confused as little kids. Until then, she stalled him with vague answers and evasions that satisfied neither of them.

She only wished he wouldn't look quite so lost, quite so small and vulnerable when he asked about his father. It made her want to cry.

She was haunted by the vulnerability she perceived in him. He was never ill, an extremely healthy child, and she was grateful for that. Nevertheless, she was always reading magazine and newspaper articles about childhood diseases, not merely polio and measles and whooping cough—he had been immunized for those and more—but horrible, crippling, incurable illnesses, often rare although no less frightening for their rarity. She memorized the early-warning signs of a hundred exotic maladies and was always on the watch for those symptoms in Joey. Of course, like any active boy, he suffered his share of cuts and bruises, and the sight of his blood always scared the hell out of her, even if it was only one drop from a shallow scratch. Her concern about Joey's health was almost an obsession, but she never quite allowed it to actually *become* an obsession, for she was aware of the psychological problems that could develop in a child with an overly protective mother.

That Sunday afternoon in February, when death suddenly stepped up and grinned at Joey, it wasn't in the form of the viruses and bacteria about which Christine worried. It was just an old woman with stringy gray hair, a pallid face, and gray eyes the shade of dirty ice.

When Christine and Joey left the mall by way of Bullock's Department Store, it was five minutes past three. Sun glinted off automobile chrome and windshield glass from one end of the broad parking lot to the other. Their silver-gray Pontiac Firebird was in the row directly in front of Bullock's doors, the twelfth car in the line, and they were almost to it when the old woman appeared.

She stepped out from between the Firebird and a white Ford van, directly into their path.

She didn't seem threatening at first. She was a bit odd, sure, but nothing worse than that. Her shoulder-length mane of thick gray hair looked windblown, although only a mild breeze washed across the lot. She was in her sixties, perhaps even early seventies, forty years older than Christine, but her face wasn't deeply lined, and her skin was baby-smooth; she had the unnatural puffiness that was often associated with cortisone injections. Pointed nose. Small mouth, thick lips. A round, dimpled chin. She was wearing a simple turquoise necklace, a long-sleeved green blouse, green skirt, green shoes. On her plump hands were eight rings, all green: turquoise, malachite, emeralds. The unrelieved green suggested a uniform of some kind.

She blinked at Joey, grinned, and said, "My heavens, aren't you a handsome young man?"

Christine smiled. Unsolicited compliments from strangers were nothing new to Joey. With his dark hair, intense blue eyes, and well-related features, he was a strikingly good-looking child.

"Yes, sir, a regular little movie star," the old woman said.

"Thank you," Joey said, blushing.

Christine got a closer look at the stranger and had to revise her initial impression of grandmotherliness. There were specks of lint on the old woman's badly wrinkled skirt, two small food stains on her blouse, and a sprinkling of dandruff on her shoulders. Her stockings bagged at the knees, and the left one had a run in it. She was holding a smoldering cigarette, and the fingers of her right hand were yellow with nicotine. She was one of those people from whom kids should never accept candy or cookies or any other treat—not because she seemed the type to poison or molest children (which she did not), but because she seemed the type to keep a dirty kitchen. Even on close inspection, she didn't appear dangerous, just unkempt.

Leaning toward Joey, grinning down at him, paying no attention whatever to Christine, she said, "What's your name, young man? Can you tell me your name?"

"Joey," he said shyly.

"How old are you, Joey?"

"Six."

"Only six and already pretty enough to make the ladies swoon!"

Joey fidgeted with embarrassment and clearly wished he could bolt for the car. But he stayed where he was and behaved courteously, the way his mother had taught him.

The old woman said, "I'll bet a dollar to a doughnut that I know your birthday."

"I don't have a doughnut," Joey said, taking the bet literally, solemnly warning her that he wouldn't be able to pay off if he lost.

"Isn't that cute?" the old woman said to him. "So perfectly, wonderfully cute. But I *know*. You were born on Christmas Eve."

"Nope," Joey said. "Febroonary second."

"February second? Oh, now, don't joke around with me," she said, still ignoring Christine, still grinning broadly at Joey, wagging one nicotine-yellowed finger at him. "Sure as shootin', you were born December twenty-fourth."

Christine wondered what the old woman was leading up to.

Joey said, "Mom, you tell her. Febroonary second. Does she owe me a dollar?"

"No, she doesn't owe you anything, honey," Christine said. "It wasn't a real bet."

"Well," he said, "if I'd lost, I couldn't've given her any doughnut anyway, so I guess it's okay if she don't give me a dollar."

Finally the old woman raised her head and looked at Christine.

Christine started to smile but stopped when she saw the stranger's eyes. They were hard, cold, angry. They were neither the eyes of a grandmother nor those of a harmless old bag lady. There was power in them—and stubbornness and flinty resolve. The woman wasn't smiling any more, either.

What's going on here?

Before Christine could speak, the woman said, "He *was* born on Christmas Eve, wasn't he? Hmmm? Wasn't he?" She spoke with such urgency, with such force that she sprayed spittle at Christine. She didn't wait for an answer, either, but hurried on: "You're lying about February second. You're just trying to hide, both of you, but I know the truth. I *know*. You can't fool me. Not *me.*"

Suddenly she seemed dangerous, after all.

Christine put a hand on Joey's shoulder and urged him around the crone, toward the car.

But the woman stepped sideways, blocking them. She waved her cigarette at Joey, glared at him, and said, "I know who you are. I know *what* you are, everything about you, everything. Better believe it. Oh, yes, yes, I know, yes."

A nut, Christine thought, and her stomach twisted. Jesus. A crazy old lady, the kind who might be capable of anything. God, please let her be harmless.

Looking bewildered, Joey backed away from the woman, grabbed his mother's hand and squeezed tight.

"Please get out of our way," Christine said, trying to maintain a calm and reasonable tone of voice, wanting very much not to antagonize.

The old woman refused to move. She brought the cigarette to her lips. Her hand was shaking.

Holding Joey's hand, Christine tried to go around the stranger.

But again the woman blocked them. She puffed nervously on her cigarette and blew smoke out her nostrils. She never took her eyes off Joey.

Christine looked around the parking lot. A few people were getting out of a car two rows away, and two young men were at the end of this row, heading in the other direction, but no one was near enough to help if the crazy woman became violent.

Throwing down her cigarette, hyperventilating, eyes bulging, looking like a big malicious toad, the woman said, "Oh, yeah, I know your ugly, vicious, hateful secrets, you little fraud."

Christine's heart began to hammer.

"Get out of our way," she said sharply, no longer trying to remain —or even *able* to remain—calm.

"You can't fool me with your play-acting—"

Joey began to cry.

"—and your phony cuteness. Tears won't help, either."

For the third time, Christine tried to go around the woman—and was blocked again.

The harridan's face hardened in anger. "I know exactly what you are, you little monster."

Christine shoved, and the old woman stumbled backward.

Pulling Joey with her, Christine hurried to the car, feeling as if she were in a nightmare, running in slow-motion.

The car door was locked. She was a compulsive door-locker.

She wished that, for once, she had been careless.

The old woman scuttled in behind them, shouting something that Christine couldn't hear because her ears were filled with the frantic pounding of her heart and with Joey's crying.

"Mom!"

Joey was almost jerked out of her grasp. The old woman had her talons hooked in his shirt.

"Let go of him, damn you!" Christine said.

"Admit it!" the old woman shrieked at him. "Admit what you are!"

Christine shoved again.

The woman wouldn't let go.

Christine struck her, open-handed, first on the shoulder, then across the face.

The old woman tottered backward, and Joey twisted away from her, and his shirt tore.

Somehow, even with shaking hands, Christine fitted the key into the lock, opened the car door, pushed Joey inside. He scrambled across to the passenger's seat, and she got behind the wheel and pulled the door shut with immense relief. Locked it.

The old woman peered in the driver's-side window. "Listen to me!" she shouted. "Listen!"

Christine jammed the key in the ignition, switched it on, pumped the accelerator. The engine roared.

With one milk-white fist, the crazy woman thumped the roof of the car. Again. And again.

Christine put the Firebird in gear and backed out of the parking space, moving slowly, not wanting to hurt the old woman, just wanting to get the hell away from her.

The lunatic followed, shuffling along, bent over, holding on to the door handle, glaring at Christine. "He's got to die. He's got to die."

Sobbing, Joey said, "Mom, don't let her get me!"

"She won't get you, honey," Christine said, her mouth so dry that she was barely able to get the words out.

The boy huddled against his locked door, eyes streaming tears but open wide and fixed on the contorted face of the stringy-haired harpy at his mother's window.

Still in reverse, Christine accelerated a bit, turned the wheel, and nearly backed into another car that was coming slowly down the row. The other driver blew his horn, and Christine stopped just in time, with a harsh bark of brakes.

"He's got to die!" the old woman screamed. She slammed the side of one pale fist into the window almost hard enough to break the glass.

This can't be happening, Christine thought. Not on a sunny Sunday. Not in peaceful Costa Mesa.

The old woman struck the window again.

"He's got to die!"

Spittle sprayed the glass.

Christine had the car in gear and was moving away, but the old woman held on. Christine accelerated. Still, the woman kept a grip on the door handle, slid and ran and stumbled along with the car, ten feet, twenty, thirty feet, faster, faster still. Christ, was she human? Where did such an old woman find the strength and tenacity to hold on like this? She leered in through the side window, and there was such ferocity in her eyes that it wouldn't have surprised Christine if, in spite of her size and age, the hag had torn the door off. But at last she let go with a howl of anger and frustration.

At the end of the row, Christine turned right. She drove too fast through the parking lot, and in less than a minute they were away from the mall, on Bristol Street, heading north.

Joey was still crying, though more softly than before.

"It's all right, sweetheart. It's okay now. She's gone."

She drove to MacArthur Boulevard, turned right, went three blocks, repeatedly glancing in the rearview mirror to see if they were being followed, even though she knew there wasn't much chance of that. Finally she pulled over to the curb and stopped.

She was shaking. She hoped Joey wouldn't notice.

Pulling a Kleenex from the small box on the console, she said, "Here you are, honey. Dry your eyes, blow your nose, and be brave for Mommy. Okay?"

"Okay," he said, accepting the tissue. Shortly, he was composed.

"Feeling better?" she asked.

"Yeah. Sorta."

"Scared?"

"I was."

"But not now?"

He shook his head.

"You know," Christine said, "she really didn't mean all those nasty things she said to you."

He looked at her, puzzled. His lower lip trembled, but his voice was steady. "Then why'd she say it if she didn't mean it?"

"Well, she couldn't help herself. She was a sick lady."

"You mean . . . like sick with the flu?"

"No, honey. I mean . . . mentally ill . . . disturbed."

"She was a real Looney Tune, huh?"

He had gotten that expression from Val Gardner, Christine's business partner. This was the first time she'd heard him use it, and she wondered what other, less socially acceptable words he might have picked up from the same source.

"Was she a real Looney Tune, Mom? Was she crazy?"

"Mentally disturbed, yes."

He frowned.

She said, "That doesn't make it any easier to understand, huh?"

"Nope. 'Cause what does crazy really mean, anyway, if it doesn't mean being locked up in a rubber room? And even if she was a crazy old lady, why was she so mad at me? Huh? I never even saw her before."

"Well . . ."

How do you explain psychotic behavior to a six-year-old? She could think of no way to do it without being ridiculously simplistic; however, in this case, a simplistic answer was better than none.

"Maybe she once had a little boy of her own, a little boy she loved very much, but maybe he wasn't a good little boy like you. Maybe he grew up to be very bad and did a lot of terrible things that broke his mother's heart. Something like that could . . . unbalance her a little."

"So now maybe she hates *all* little boys, whether she knows them or not," he said.

"Yes, perhaps."

"Because they remind her of her own little boy? Is that it?"

"That's right."

He thought about it for a moment, then nodded. "Yeah. I can sorta see how that could be."

She smiled at him and mussed his hair. "Hey, I'll tell you what—let's stop at Baskin-Robbins and get an ice cream cone. I think their flavor of the month is peanut butter and chocolate. That's one of your favorites, isn't it?"

He was obviously surprised. She didn't approve of too much fat in his diet, and she planned his meals carefully. Ice cream wasn't a frequent indulgence. He seized the moment and said, "Could I have one scoop of that and one scoop of lemon custard?"

"*Two* scoops?"

"It's Sunday," he said.

"Last time I looked, Sunday wasn't so all-fired special. There's one of them every week. Or has that changed while I wasn't paying attention?"

"Well . . . but . . . see, I've just had . . ." He screwed up his face, thinking hard. He worked his mouth as if chewing on a piece of taffy, then said, "I've just had a . . . a traumamatatic experience."

"Traumatic experience?"

"Yeah. That's it."

She blinked at him. "Where'd you get a big word like that? Oh. Of course. Never mind. Val."

According to Valerie Gardner, who was given to theatrics, just getting up in

the morning was a traumatic experience. Val had about half a dozen traumatic experiences every day—and thrived on them.

"So it's Sunday, and I had this traumatic experience," Joey said, "and I think maybe what I better do is, I better have two scoops of ice cream to make up for it. You know?"

"I know I'd better not hear about *another* traumatic experience for at least ten years."

"What about the ice cream?"

She looked at his torn shirt. "Two scoops," she agreed.

"Wow! This is some terrific day, isn't it? A real Looney Tune *and* a double-dip ice cream!"

Christine never ceased to be amazed by the resiliency of children, especially the resiliency of this child. Already, in his mind, he had transmuted the encounter with the old woman, had changed it from a moment of terror to an adventure that was not quite—but almost—as good as a visit to an ice cream parlor.

"You're some kid," she said.

"You're some mom."

He turned on the radio and hummed along happily with the music, all the way to Baskin-Robbins.

Christine kept checking the rearview mirror. No one was following them. She was sure of that. But she kept checking anyway.

CHAPTER 2

AFTER A LIGHT dinner at the kitchen table with Joey, Christine went to her desk in the den to catch up on paperwork. She and Val Gardner owned a gourmet shop called Wine & Dine in Newport Beach, where they sold fine wines, specialty foods from all over the world, high quality cooking utensils, and slightly exotic appliances like pasta-makers and expresso machines. The store was in its sixth year of operation and was solidly established; in fact, it was returning considerably more profit than either Christine or Val had ever dared hope when they'd first opened their doors for business. Now, they were planning to open a second outlet this summer, then a third store in West Los Angeles sometime next year. Their success was exciting and gratifying, but the business demanded an ever-increasing amount of their time. This wasn't the first weekend evening that she had spent catching up on paperwork.

She wasn't complaining. Before Wine & Dine, she had worked as a waitress, six days a week, holding down two jobs at the same time: a four-hour lunch shift in a diner and a six-hour dinner shift at a moderately expensive French restaurant, Chez Lavelle. Because she was a polite and attentive waitress who hustled her butt off, the tips had been good at the diner and excellent at Chez Lavelle, but after a few years the work numbed and aged her: the sixty-hour weeks; the busboys who often came to work so high on drugs that she had to cover for them and do two jobs instead of one; the lecherous guys who ate lunch at the diner and who could be gross and obnoxious and frighteningly persistent, but who had to be turned down with coquettish good humor for the sake of business. She spent so many hours on her feet that, on her day off, she did nothing but sit with her aching legs raised on an ottoman while she read the Sunday papers with special attention to the financial section, dreaming of one day owning her *own* business.

But because of the tips and because she lived frugally—even doing without a car for two years—she had eventually managed to put enough aside to pay for a one-week cruise to Mexico aboard a luxury liner, the *Aztec Princess,* and had accumulated a nest egg large enough to provide half the cash with which she and Val had launched their gourmet shop. Both the cruise and the shop had radically changed her life.

And if spending too many evenings doing paperwork was better than working as a waitress, it was immeasurably better than the two years of her life that had preceded her jobs at the diner and Chez Lavelle. The Lost Years. That was how she thought of that time, now far in the past: the bleak, miserable, sad and stupid Lost Years.

Compared to *that* period of her life, paperwork was a pleasure, a delight, a veritable *carnival* of fun . . .

She had been at her desk more than an hour when she realized that Joey had been exceptionally quiet ever since she'd come into the den. Of course, he was never a noisy child. Often he played by himself for hours, hardly making a sound. But after the unnerving encounter with the old woman this afternoon, Christine was still a little jumpy, and even this perfectly ordinary silence suddenly seemed strange and threatening. She wasn't exactly frightened. Just anxious. If anything happened to Joey . . .

She put down her pen and switched off the softly humming adding machine. She listened.

Nothing.

In an echo chamber of memory, she could hear the old woman's voice: *He's got to die, he's got to die* . . .

She rose, left the den, quickly crossed the living room, went down the hall to the boy's bedroom.

The door was open, the light on, and he was there, safe, playing on the floor with their dog, Brandy, a sweet-faced and infinitely patient golden retriever.

"Hey, Mom, wanna play *Star Wars* with us? I'm Han Solo, and Brandy's my buddy, Chewbacca the Wookie. You could be the princess if you want."

Brandy was sitting in the middle of the floor, between the bed and the sliding closet doors. He was wearing a baseball cap emblazoned with the words RETURN OF THE JEDI, and his long furry ears hung out from the sides of it. Joey had also strapped a bandoleer of plastic bullets around the pooch, plus a holster containing a futuristic-looking plastic gun. Panting, eyes bright, Brandy was taking it all in stride; he even seemed to be smiling.

"He makes a great Wookie," Christine said.

"Wanna play?"

"Sorry, Skipper, but I've got an awful lot of work to do. I just stopped by to see if . . . if you were okay."

"Well, what happened is that we almost got vaporized by an empire battle cruiser," Joey said. "But we're okay now."

Brandy snuffled in agreement.

She smiled at Joey. "Watch out for Darth Vader."

"Oh, yeah, sure, *always.* We're being super careful cause we know he's in this part of the galaxy somewhere."

"See you in a little while."

She took only one step toward the door before Joey said, "Mom? Are you afraid that crazy old lady's going to show up again?"

Christine turned to him. "No, no," she said, although that was precisely what had been in her mind. "She can't possibly know who we are or where we live."

Joey's eyes were even a more brilliant shade of blue than usual; they met her own eyes unwaveringly, and there was disquiet in them. "I told her my name, Mom. Remember? She asked me, and so I told her my name."

"Only your first name."

He frowned. "Did I?"

"You just said, 'Joey.' "

"Yeah. That's right."

"Don't worry, honey. You'll never see her again. That's all over and done with. She was just a sad old woman who—"

"What about our license plate?"

"What about it?"

"Well, see, if she got the number, maybe there's some way she can use it. To find out who we are. Like they sometimes do on those detective shows on TV."

That possibility disconcerted her, but she said, "I doubt it. I think only policemen can track down a car's owner from the license number."

"But just maybe," the boy said worriedly.

"We pulled away from her so fast she didn't have time to memorize the number. Besides, she was hysterical. She wasn't thinking clearly enough to study the license plate. Like I told you, it's all over and done with. Really. Okay?"

He hesitated a moment, then said, "Okay. But, Mom, I been thinking . . ."

"What?"

"That crazy old lady . . . could she've been . . . a witch?"

Christine almost laughed, but she saw that he was serious. She suppressed all evidence of her amusement, put on a sober expression that matched the grave look on his face, and said, "Oh, I'm sure she wasn't a witch."

"I don't mean like Broom Hilda. I mean a *real* witch. A real witch wouldn't need our license number, you know? She wouldn't need anything. She'd sniff us out. There's no place in the whole universe where you can hide when there's a witch after you. Witches have magic powers."

He was either already certain that the old woman was a witch or was rapidly convincing himself of it. Either way, he was scaring himself unnecessarily because, after all, they really never would see her again.

Christine remembered the way that strange woman had clung to the car, jerking at the handle of the locked door, keeping pace with them as they pulled away, screeching crazy accusations at them. Her eyes and face had radiated both fury and a disturbing power that made it seem as if she might really be able to stop the Firebird with her bare hands. A witch? That a child might think she had supernatural powers was certainly understandable.

"A real witch," Joey repeated, a tremor in his voice.

Christine was aware that she had to snip this line of thought right away, before he became obsessed with witches. Last year, for almost two months, he had been certain that a magical white snake—like one he'd seen in a movie—was hiding in his room, waiting for him to go to sleep, so that it could slither out and bite him. She'd had to sit with him each evening until he'd fallen asleep. Frequently, when he awakened in the middle of the night, she had to take him into her own bed in order to settle him down. He'd gotten over the snake thing the same day that she'd made up her mind to take him to a child psychologist; later, she'd cancelled the appointment. After a few weeks had passed, when she'd been sure that mentioning the snake wouldn't get him started on it again, she asked what had happened to it. He looked embarrassed and said, "It was only 'magination, Mom. I sure was acting like a dumb little kid, huh?" He'd never mentioned the white snake again. He possessed a healthy, rampaging imagination, and it was up to her to rein it in when it got out of control. Like now.

Although she had to put an end to this witch stuff, she couldn't just tell him there was no such thing. If she tried that approach, he would think she was just babying him. She would have to go along with his assumption that witches were real, then use the logic of a child to make him see that the old woman in the parking lot couldn't possibly have been a witch.

She said, "Well, I can understand how you might wonder about her being a witch. Whew! I mean, she did look a little bit like a witch is supposed to look, didn't she?"

"More than a little bit."

"No, no, just a little bit. Let's be fair to the poor old lady."

"She looked *exactly* like a mean witch," he said. "Exactly. Didn't she, Brandy?"

The dog snorted as if he understood the question and was in full agreement with his young master.

Christine squatted, scratched the dog behind the ears, and said, "What do you know about it, fur-face? You weren't even there."

Brandy yawned.

To Joey, Christine said, "If you really think about it, she didn't look all that much like a witch."

"Her eyes were creepy," the boy insisted, "bugging out of her head like they did. You saw them, sort of wild, Jeez, and her frizzy hair just like a witch's hair."

"But she didn't have a big crooked nose with a wart on the tip of it, did she?"

"No," Joey admitted.

"And she wasn't dressed in black, was she?"

"No. But all in *green,*" Joey said, and from his tone of voice it was clear that the old woman's outfit had seemed as odd to him as it had to Christine.

"Witches don't wear green. She wasn't wearing a tall, pointed black hat, either."

He shrugged.

"And she didn't have a cat with her," Christine said.

"So?"

"A witch never goes anywhere without her cat."

"She doesn't?"

"No. It's her familiar."

"What's that mean?"

"The witch's familiar is her contact with the devil. It's through the familiar, through the cat, that the devil gives her magic powers. Without the cat, she's just an ugly old woman."

"You mean like the cat watches her and makes sure she doesn't do something the devil wouldn't like?"

"That's right."

"I didn't see any cat," Joey said, frowning.

"There wasn't a cat because she wasn't a witch. You've got nothing to worry about, honey."

His face brightened. "Boy, that's a relief! If she'd been a witch, she might've turned me into a toad or something."

"Well, life as a toad might not be so bad," she teased. "You'd get to sit on a lily pad all day, just taking it easy."

"Toads eat flies," he said, grimacing, "and I can't even stand to eat *veal.*"

She laughed, leaned forward, and kissed his cheek.

"Even if she was a witch," he said, "I'd probably be okay because I've got Brandy, and Brandy wouldn't let any old cat get anywhere near."

"You can rely on Brandy," Christine agreed. She looked at the clown-faced dog and said, "You're the nemesis of all cats and witches, aren't you, fur-face?"

To her surprise, Brandy thrust his muzzle forward and licked her under the chin.

"Yuck," she said. "No offense, fur-face, but I'm not sure whether kissing you is any better than eating flies."

Joey giggled and hugged the dog.

Christine returned to the den. The mound of paperwork seemed to have grown taller while she was gone.

She had no sooner settled into the chair behind the desk than the telephone rang. She picked it up.

"Hello?"

No one answered.

"Hello?" she said again.

"Wrong number," a woman said softly and hung up.

Christine put the receiver down and went back to work. She didn't give the call a second thought.

CHAPTER 3

//////

SHE WAS AWAKENED by Brandy's barking, which was unusual because Brandy hardly ever barked. Then she heard Joey's voice.

"Mom! Come quick! *Mommy!*"

He wasn't merely calling her; he was *screaming* for her.

As she threw back the covers and got out of bed, she saw the glowing red numbers on the digital alarm clock. It was 1:20 A.M.

She plunged across the room, through the open door, into the hall, headed toward Joey's room, flipping up light switches as she went.

Joey was sitting in bed, pressing back against the headboard as if he were trying to pass through it and slip magically into the wall behind it, where he could hide. His hands were filled with twisted lumps of sheet and blanket. His face was pale.

Brandy was at the window, forepaws up on the sill. He was barking at something in the night beyond the glass. When Christine entered the room, the dog stopped barking, padded to the bed, and looked inquiringly at Joey, as if seeking guidance.

"Someone was out there," the boy said. "Looking in. It was that crazy old lady."

Christine went to the window. There wasn't much light. The yellowish glow of the streetlamp at the corner didn't reach quite this far. Although a moon ornamented the sky, it wasn't a full moon, and it cast only a weak, milky light that frosted the sidewalks, silvered the cars parked along the street, but revealed few of the night's secrets. For the most part, the lawn and shrubbery lay in deep darkness.

"Is she still out there?" Joey asked.

"No," Christine said.

She turned away from the window, went to him, sat on the edge of his bed. He was still pale. Shaking.

She said, "Honey, are you sure—"

"She was there!"

"Exactly what did you see?"

"Her face."

"The old woman?"

"Yeah."

"You're sure it was her, not somebody else?"

He nodded. "Her."

"It's so dark out there. How could you see well enough to—"

"I saw somebody at the window, just sort of a shadow in the moonlight, and then what I did was I turned on the light, and it was her. I could see. It was *her.*"

"But, honey, I just don't think there's any way she could have followed us. I *know* she didn't. And there's no way she could've learned where we live. Not this soon, anyway."

He said nothing. He just stared down at his fisted hands and slowly let go of the sheet and blanket. His palms were sweaty.

Christine said, "Maybe you were dreaming, huh?"

He shook his head vigorously.

She said, "Sometimes, when you wake up from a nightmare, just a few seconds, you can be sort of confused about what's real and what's just part of the dream. You know? It's all right. It happens to everybody now and then."

He met her eyes. "It wasn't like that, Mom. Brandy started barking, and then I woke up, and there was the crazy old lady at the window. If it was just a dream . . . then what was Brandy barking at? He don't bark just to hear himself. Never does. You know how he is."

She stared at Brandy, who had plopped down on the floor beside the bed, and she began to feel uneasy again. Finally she got up and went to the window.

Out in the night, there were a lot of places where the grip of darkness was firm, places where a prowler could hide and wait.

"Mom?"

She looked at him.

He said, "This isn't like before."

"What do you mean?"

"This isn't a 'maginary white snake under my bed. This is *real* stuff. Cross my heart and hope to die."

A sudden gust of wind soughed through the eaves and rattled a loose rain gutter.

"Come on," she said, holding out a hand to him.

He scrambled out of bed, and she took him into the kitchen.

Brandy followed. He stood in the doorway for a moment, his bushy tail thumping against both jambs, then came in and curled up in the corner.

Joey sat at the table in his blue pajamas with the words SATURN PATROL, in red, streaking across his chest. He looked anxiously at the windows over the sink, while Christine telephoned the police.

The two police officers stood on the porch and listened politely while Christine, in the open front door with Joey at her side, told them her story—what little there was to tell. The younger of the two men, Officer Statler, was dubious and quick to conclude that the prowler was merely a phantom of Joey's imagination, but the older man, Officer Templeton, gave them the benefit of the doubt. At Templeton's insistence, he and Statler spent ten minutes searching the property with their long-handled flashlights, probing the shrubbery, circling the house, checking out the garage, even looking in the neighbors' yards. They didn't find anyone.

Returning to the front door where Christine and Joey waited, Templeton seemed somewhat less willing to believe their story than he had been a few minutes ago. "Well, Mrs. Scavello, if that old woman was around here, she's gone now. Either she wasn't up to much of anything . . . or maybe she was scared away when she saw the patrol car. Maybe both. She's probably harmless."

"Harmless? She sure didn't seem harmless this afternoon at South Coast Plaza," Christine said. "She seemed dangerous enough to me."

"Well . . ." He shrugged. "You know how it is. An old lady . . . maybe a little senile . . . saying things she really didn't mean."

"I don't think that's the case."

Templeton didn't meet her eyes. "So . . . if you see her again or if you have any other trouble, be sure to give us a call."

"You're leaving?"

"Yes, ma'am."

"You're not going to do anything else?"

He scratched his head. "Don't see what else we *can* do. You said you don't know this woman's name or where she lives, so we can't go have a chat with her. Like I said, if she shows up again, you call us soon as you spot her, and we'll come back."

With a nod of his head, he turned away and went down the walk, toward the street, where his partner waited.

A minute later, as Christine and Joey stood at the living room windows, watching the patrol car drive away, the boy said, "She was out there, Mom. Really, really. This isn't like the snake."

She believed him. What he had seen at the window could have been a figment of his imagination or an image left over from a nightmare—but it hadn't been that. He had seen what he thought he'd seen: the old woman herself, in the flesh. Christine didn't know why she was so sure of that, but she was. Dead sure.

She gave him the option of spending the rest of the night in her room, but he was determined to be brave.

"I'll sleep in my bed," he said. "Brandy'll be there. Brandy'll smell that old witch coming a mile away. But . . . could we sorta leave a lamp on?"

"Sure," she said, though she had only recently weaned him away from the need for a night light.

In his room she closed the draperies tight, leaving not even a narrow crack through which someone might be able to see him. She tucked him in, kissed him goodnight, and left him in Brandy's care.

Back in her own bed once more, with the lights out, she stared at the tenebrous ceiling. She was unable to sleep. She kept expecting a sudden sound —glass shattering, a door being forced—but the night remained peaceful.

Only the February wind, with an occasional violent gust, marred the nocturnal stillness.

In his room Joey switched off the lamp that his mother had left on for him. The darkness was absolute.

Brandy jumped onto the bed, where he was never supposed to be (one of Mom's rules: no dog in bed), but Joey didn't push him off. Brandy settled down and was welcome.

Joey listened to the night wind sniffing and licking at the house, and it sounded like a living thing. He pulled the blanket all the way up to his nose, as if it were a shield that would protect him from all harm.

After a while he said, "She's still out there somewhere."

The dog lifted his square head.

"She's waiting, Brandy."

The dog raised one ear.

"She'll be back."

The dog growled in the back of his throat.

Joey put one hand on his furry companion. "You know it, too, don't you, boy? You know she's out there, don't you?"

Brandy woofed softly.

The wind moaned.

The boy listened.

The night ticked toward dawn.

CHAPTER 4

IN THE MIDDLE of the night, unable to sleep, Christine went downstairs to Joey's room to look in on him. The lamp she had left burning was off now, and the bedroom was tomb-black. For a moment fear pinched off her breath. But when she snapped on the light, she saw that Joey was in bed, asleep, safe.

Brandy was comfortably ensconced in the bed, too, but he woke when she turned on the light. He yawned and licked his chops, and gave her a look that was rich with canine guilt.

"You know the rules, fuzzy-butt," she whispered. "On the floor."

Brandy got off the bed without waking Joey, slunk to the nearest corner, and curled up on the floor. He looked at her sheepishly.

"Good dog," she whispered.

He wagged his tail, sweeping the carpet around him.

She switched off the light and started back toward her own room. She had gone only a step or two when she heard movement in the boy's room, and she knew it was Brandy returning to the bed. Tonight, however, she just didn't care all that much whether he got dog hairs on the sheets and blankets. Tonight, the only thing that seemed to matter was that Joey was safe.

She returned to her bed and dozed fitfully, tossing and turning, murmuring in her sleep as night crept toward dawn. She dreamed of an old woman with a green face, green hair, and long green fingernails that hooked wickedly into sharp claws.

Monday morning came at last, and it was sunny. Too damned sunny. She woke early, and light speared through her bedroom windows, making her wince. Her eyes were grainy, sensitive, bloodshot.

She took a long, hot shower, steaming away some of her weariness, then dressed for work in a maroon blouse, simple gray skirt, and gray pumps.

Stepping to the full-length mirror on the bathroom door, she examined herself critically, although staring at her reflection always embarrassed her. There was no mystery about her shyness; she knew her embarrassment was a result of the things she had been taught during the Lost Years, between her eighteenth and twentieth birthdays. During that period she had struggled to throw off all vanity and a large measure of her individuality because gray-faced uniformity was what had been demanded of her back then. They had expected her to be humble, self-effacing, and plain. Any concern for her appearance, any slightest pride in her looks, would have brought swift disciplinary action from her superiors. Although she had put those grim lonely years and events behind her, they still had a lingering effect on her that she could not deny.

Now, almost as a test of how completely she had triumphed over the Lost Years, she fought her embarrassment and resolutely studied her mirror image with as much vanity as she could summon from a soul half-purged of it. Her figure was good, though she didn't have the kind of body that, displayed in a bikini, would ever sell a million pin-up posters. Her legs were slender and well shaped. Her hips flared just right, and she was almost *too* small in the waist, though that smallness made her bustline—which was only average—seem larger than it was. She sometimes wished she were as busty as Val, but Val said that very large breasts were more of a curse than a blessing, that it was like carrying around a pair of saddlebags, and that some evenings her shoulders ached with the strain of that burden. Even if what Val said was true and not just a white lie told out of sympathy for those less amply endowed, Christine nevertheless wished she had big boobs, and she knew that this desire, this hopeless vanity, was a blatant reaction to—and rejection of—all that she had been taught in that gray and dreary place where she had lived between the ages of eighteen and twenty.

By now, her face was flushed, but she forced herself to remain in front of the mirror a minute more, until she had determined that her hair was properly combed and that her makeup was evenly applied. She knew she was pretty. Not gorgeous. But she had a good complexion, a delicate chin and jawline, a good nose. Her eyes were her best feature, large and dark and clear. Her hair was dark, too, almost black. Val said she would trade her big boobs for hair like that any day, but Christine *knew* that was only talk. Sure, her hair looked good when the weather was right, but as soon as the humidity rose past a certain point, it got either lank and flat or fizzy and curly, and then she looked like either Vampira or Gene Shalit.

At last, blushing furiously but feeling that she had triumphed over the excessive self-effacement that had been hammered into her years ago, she turned away from the mirror.

She went to the kitchen to make coffee and toast, and found Joey already at the breakfast table. He wasn't eating, just sitting there, face turned away from her, staring out the window at the sun-splashed rear lawn.

Taking a paper filter from a box and fitting it into the basket of the dripolator, Christine said, "What can I get for you for breakfast, Skipper?"

He didn't answer.

Spooning coffee into the filter, she said, "How about cereal and peanut butter toast? English muffins? Maybe you even feel like an egg."

He still didn't answer. Sometimes—not often—he could be cranky in the morning, but he always could be teased into a better mood. By nature, he was too mild-mannered to remain sullen for long.

Switching on the dripolator and pouring water into the top of it, she said, "Okay, so if you don't want cereal or toast or an egg, maybe I could fix some spinach, brussel sprouts, and broccoli. They're all your favorites, aren't they?"

He didn't rise to the bait. Just stared out the window. Unmoving. Silent.

"Or I could put one of your old shoes in the microwave and cook it up nice and tender for you. How about that? Nothing's quite as tasty as an old shoe for breakfast. Mmmmmmmm! Really sticks to your ribs."

He said nothing.

She got the toaster out of the cupboard, put it on the counter, plugged it in —then suddenly realized that the boy wasn't merely being cranky. Something was wrong.

Staring at the back of his head, she said, "Honey?"

He made a wretched, stifled little sound.

"Honey, what's wrong?"

At last he turned away from the window and looked at her. His tousled hair hung down in his eyes, which were possessed by a haunted look, a bleak expression so stark for a six-year-old that it made Christine's heart beat faster. Bright tears glistened on his cheeks.

She quickly went to him and took his hand. It was cold.

"Sweetheart, what is it? Tell me."

He wiped at his reddened eyes with his free hand. His nose was runny, and he blotted it on his sleeve.

He was so *pale*.

Whatever was wrong, it wasn't simply a standard complaint, no ordinary childhood trauma. She sensed that much and her mouth went dry with fear.

He tried to speak, couldn't get out even one word, pointed to the kitchen door, took a deep shuddery breath, began to shake, and finally said, "The p-p-porch."

"What about the porch?"

He wasn't able to tell her.

Frowning, she went to the door, hesitated, opened it. She gasped, rocked by the sight that awaited her.

Brandy. His furry, golden body lay at the edge of the porch, near the steps. But his head was immediately in front of the door, at her feet. The dog had been decapitated.

CHAPTER 5

fffff

CHRISTINE AND JOEY sat on the beige sofa in the living room. The boy was no longer crying, but he still looked stunned.

The policeman filling out the report, Officer Wilford, sat on one of the Queen Anne armchairs. He was tall and husky, with rough features, bushy eyebrows, an air of rugged self-sufficiency: the kind of man who probably felt at home only outdoors and especially in the woods and mountains, hunting and fishing. He perched on the very edge of the chair and held his notebook on his knees, an amusingly prim posture for a man his size; apparently he was concerned about rumpling or soiling the furniture.

"But who let the dog out?" he inquired, after having asked every other question he could think of.

"Nobody," Christine said. "He let himself out. There's a pet portal in the bottom of the kitchen door."

"I saw it," Wilford said. "Not big enough for a dog that size."

"I know. It was here when we bought the house. Brandy hardly ever used it, but if he wanted out badly enough, and if there wasn't anyone around to let him out, he could put his head down, wriggle on his belly, and squeeze through that little door. I kept meaning to have it closed up because I was afraid he might get stuck. If only I *had* closed it up, he might still be alive."

"The witch got him," Joey said softly.

Christine put an arm around her son.

Wilford said, "So you think maybe they used meat or dog biscuits to lure him outside?"

"No," said Joey adamantly, answering for his mother, clearly offended by the suggestion that a gluttonous impulse had led to the dog's death. "Brandy went out there to protect me. He knew the old witch was still hanging around, and he went to get her, but what happened was . . . she got him first."

Christine was aware that Wilford's suggestion was probably the correct explanation, but she also knew that Joey would find it easier to accept Brandy's death if he could believe that his dog had died in a noble cause. She said, "He was a very brave dog, very brave, and we're proud of him."

Wilford nodded. "Yes, I'm sure you've got every reason to be proud. It's a darned shame. A golden retriever's such a handsome breed. Such a gentle face and sweet disposition."

"The witch got him," Joey repeated, as if numbed by that terrible realization.

"Maybe not," Wilford said. "Maybe it wasn't the old woman."

Christine frowned at him. "Well, of course it was."

"I understand how upsetting the incident was at South Coast Plaza yesterday," Wilford said. "I understand how you'd be inclined to link the old woman to this thing with the dog. But there's no solid proof, no real reason to think they *are* linked. It might be a mistake to assume they are."

"But the old woman was at Joey's window last night," Christine said exasperatedly. "I told you that. I told the officers who were here last night, too. Doesn't anyone listen? She was at Joey's window, looking in at him, and Brandy was barking at her."

"But she was gone when you got there," Wilford said.

"Yes," Christine said. "But—"

Smiling down at Joey, Wilford said, "Son, are you absolutely, positively sure it was the old lady there at your window?"

Joey nodded vigorously. "Yeah. The witch."

"Because, see, when you looked up and noticed someone at the window, it would have been perfectly natural for you to figure it was the old woman. After all, she'd already given you one bad scare earlier in the day, so she was on your mind. Then, when you switched the light on and got a glimpse of who it was there at the window, maybe you had the old woman's face so firmly fixed in your mind that you would've seen her no matter who it *really* was."

Joey blinked, unable to follow the policeman's reasoning. He just stubbornly repeated himself: "It was her. The witch."

To Christine, Officer Wilford said, "I'd be inclined to think the prowler was the one who later killed the dog—but that it wasn't the old woman who was the prowler. You see, most always, when a dog's been poisoned—and it happens more often than you think—it's not the work of some total stranger. It's someone within a block of the house where the dog lived. A neighbor. What I figure is, some neighbor was prowling around, looking for the dog, not looking for your little boy at all, when Joey saw them at the window. Later they found the dog and did what they'd come to do."

"That's ridiculous," Christine said. "We've got good neighbors here. None of them would kill our dog."

"Happens all the time," Wilford said.

"Not in *this* neighborhood."

"Any neighborhood," Wilford insisted. "Barking dogs, day after day, night after night . . . they drive some people a little nuts."

"Brandy hardly ever barked."

"Well, now, 'hardly ever' to you might seem like 'all the time' to one of your neighbors."

"Besides, Brandy wasn't poisoned. It was a hell of a lot more violent than that. You saw. Crazy-violent. Not something any neighbor would do."

"You'd be surprised what neighbors will do," Wilford said. "Sometimes they even kill each other. Not unusual at all. It's a strange world we're living in."

"You're wrong," she said hotly. "It was the old woman. The dog and the face at the window—they were both connected with that old woman."

He sighed. "You may be right."

"I *am* right."

"I was only suggesting that we keep our minds open," he said.

"Good idea," she said pointedly.

He closed his notebook. "Well, I guess I've got all the details I need."

Christine got up as the officer rose from his chair. She said, "What now?"

"We'll file a report, of course, including your statement, and we'll give you an open case number."

"What's an open case number?"

"If anything else should happen, if this old woman should show up again, you give the case number when you call us, and the officers answering your call will know the story before they get here; they'll know what to look for on the way, so if maybe the woman leaves before they arrive, they'll spot her in passing and be able to stop her."

"Why didn't they give us a case number after what happened last night?"

"Oh, they wouldn't open a file just for one report of a prowler," Wilford explained. "Last night, you see, no crime had been committed—at least so far as we could tell. No evidence of any sort of crime. But this is . . . a little worse."

"A *little* worse?" she said, remembering Brandy's severed head, the dead glassy eyes gazing up at her.

"An unfortunate choice of words," he said. "I'm sorry. It's just that, compared to a lot of other things we see on this job, a dead dog isn't so—"

"Okay, okay," Christine said, increasingly unable to conceal her anger and impatience. "You'll call us and give us an open case number. But what else are you going to do?"

Wilford looked uncomfortable. He rolled his broad shoulders and scratched at his thick neck. "The description you've given us is the only thing we've got to go on, and that's not much. We'll run it through the computer and try to work backwards to a name. The machine'll spit out the name of anyone who's been in trouble with us before and who fits at least seven of the ten major points of standard physical comparison. Then we'll pull mug shots of whatever other photos we have in the files. Maybe the computer'll give us several names, and we'll have photos of more than one old woman. Then we'll bring all the pictures over here for you to study. As soon as you tell us we've found her . . . well, then we can go have a talk with her and find out what this is all about. You see, it really isn't hopeless, Mrs. Scavello."

"What if she hasn't been in trouble with you before and you don't *have* a file on her?"

Moving to the front door, Wilford said, "We have data-sharing arrangements with every police agency in Orange, San Diego, Riverside, and Los Angeles Counties. We can reach their computers through our own. Instant access. Datalink, they call it. If she's in any of their files, we'll find her just as quickly as if she were in our own."

"Yeah, sure, but what if she's never been in trouble anywhere?" Christine asked anxiously.

Opening the front door, Wilford said, "Oh, don't worry, we'll probably turn up something. We almost always do."

"That's not good enough," she said, and she would have said it even if she had believed him, which she didn't. They wouldn't turn up anything.

"I'm sorry, Mrs. Scavello, but it's the best we can do."

"Shit."

He scowled. "I understand your frustration, and I want to assure you we won't file this away and forget about it. But we can't work miracles."

"Shit."

His scowl deepened. His bushy eyebrows drew together in a single thick bar. "Lady, it's none of my business, but I don't think you should use words like that in front of your little boy."

She stared at him, astonished. Astonishment turned to anger. "Yeah? And what're you—a born-again Christian?"

"In fact, I am, yes. And I believe it's extremely important for us to set good examples for our young ones, so they'll grow up in God's image. We've got to—"

"I don't *believe* this," Christine said. "You're telling me that I'm setting a bad example because I used a four-letter word, a harmless word—"

"Words aren't harmless. The devil beguiles and persuades with words. Words are the—"

"What about the example *you're* setting for my son? Huh? By your every act, you're teaching him that the police really can't protect anyone, that they really can't help anyone, that they can't do much more than come around afterwards and pick up the pieces."

"I wish you didn't see it that way," Wilford said.

"How the hell else am I supposed to see it?"

He sighed. "We'll call you with the case number." Then he turned away from the door, away from her and Joey, and moved stiffly down the walkway.

After a moment, she hurried in his wake, caught up with him, put a hand on his shoulder. "Please."

He stopped, turned to her. His face was hard, his eyes cold.

She said, "I'm sorry. I really am. I'm just distraught. I don't know what to think. All of a sudden I don't know where to turn."

"I understand," he said, as he had said a couple of times before, but there was no understanding in his granite face.

Glancing back to make sure Joey was still in the doorway, still too far away to hear, she said, "I'm sorry I flew off the handle at you. And I guess you're right about watching my language around Joey. Most of the time I do watch it, believe me, but today I'm not thinking straight. That crazy woman told me that my little boy had to die. That's what she said. *He's got to die,* she said. And now the dog's dead, poor old fur-face. *God,* I liked that mutt a lot. He's dead and gone, and Joey saw a face at the window in the middle of the night, and all of a sudden the world's turned upside-down, and I'm scared, really scared, because I think somehow that crazy woman followed us, and I think she's going to do it, or at least *try* to do it, try to kill my little boy. I don't know why. There can't *be* a reason. Not a reason that makes any sense. But that doesn't make any difference, does it? Not these days. These days, the newspapers are full of stories about punks and child molesters and lunatics of all kinds who don't *need* a reason to do what they do."

Wilford said, "Mrs. Scavello, please, you've got to keep control of yourself. You're being melodramatic. I won't say hysterical, but definitely melodramatic. It's not as bad as you're making out. We'll get to work on this, just like I told you. Meanwhile, you put your trust in God, and you'll be all right, you and your boy."

She couldn't reach this man. Not ever. Not in a million years. She couldn't make him feel her terror, couldn't make him understand what it would mean to her if she lost Joey. It was hopeless, after all.

She could barely remain on her feet. All the strength went out of her.

He said, "I sure am glad, though, to hear you say you'll watch your language around the boy. The last couple generations in this country, we've been raising anti-social, know-it-all snots who have no respect for anything. If we're ever going to have us a good, peaceful, God-loving and God-fearing society, then we got to raise 'em up by the right example."

She said nothing. She felt as if she were standing here with someone from another country—maybe even from another planet—who not only didn't speak her language but who had no capacity to learn. There was no way he could ever grasp her problems, appreciate her concerns. In every way that counted, they were thousands of miles apart, and there was no road between them.

Wilford's flinty eyes sparked with the passion of a true believer as he said: "And I also recommend you don't go around without a bra in front of the boy, the way you are now. A woman built like you, even wearing a loose blouse like that, certain ways you turn or stretch . . . it's bound to be . . . arousing."

She stared at him in disbelief. Several cutting remarks came to mind, any one of which would have stopped him dead, but for some reason she couldn't seem to summon the words to her lips. Of course, her reticence was in part the result of having had a mother who would have made General George Patton look soft-hearted, a mother who had insisted on good manners and unfailing politeness. There were also the lessons of the Church, deeply ingrained in her, which said you were supposed to turn the other cheek. She told herself she had broken loose from all of that, had left it far behind, but now her inability to put Wilford in his place was indisputable proof that, to her dismay, she was still to some degree a prisoner of her past.

Wilford went right on babbling, oblivious of her fury. "Maybe the boy doesn't even notice now, but in a couple of years he'll notice for sure, and a boy shouldn't be having those kinds of thoughts about his own mother. You'd be leading him in the way of the devil."

If she hadn't been so weak, if she hadn't been weighed down by the terrible awareness of her and Joey's helplessness, Christine would have laughed in his face. But right now there was no laughter in her.

Wilford said, "Well, okay then. I'll be talking to you. Trust in God, Mrs. Scavello. Trust in God."

She wondered what he'd say if she told him it wasn't *Mrs.* Scavello. What would he do if she told him Joey had been born out of wedlock, a bastard child? Would he work on the case a little less eagerly? Would he be at all concerned about preserving the life of an illegitimate little boy?

God damn all hypocrites.

She wanted to hit Wilford, kick him and hit him and take out her frustration on him, but she only watched as he got into the patrol car where his partner waited for him. He looked back at her, raised one hand, and gave her a curt little wave through the window.

She returned to the front door.

Joey was waiting for her.

She wanted to say something reassuring to him. He looked as if he needed that. But even if she'd been able to find the words, she wouldn't have been able to deceive him by speaking them. Right now, until they knew what the hell was happening, it was probably better to be scared. If he was frightened, he would be careful, watchful.

She felt disaster coming.

Was she being melodramatic?

No.

Joey felt it coming, too. She could see a dreadful anticipation in his eyes.

CHAPTER 6

🖋🖋

SHE STEPPED INTO the house, closed the door, locked it.

She ruffled Joey's hair. "You okay, honey?"

"I'm gonna miss Brandy," he said in a shaky voice, trying to be a brave little man but not quite succeeding.

"Me too," Christine said, remembering how funny Brandy had looked in the role of Chewbacca the Wookie.

Joey said, "I thought . . ."

"What?"

"Maybe it would be a good idea . . ."

"Yeah?"

". . . a good idea to get another dog soon."

She hunkered down to his level. "You know, that's a very mature idea. Very wise, I think."

"I don't mean I want to forget Brandy."

"Of course not."

"I couldn't ever forget him."

"We'll always remember Brandy. He'll always have a special place in our hearts," she said. "And I'm sure he'd understand about us getting another dog right away. In fact, I'm sure that's what he'd want us to do."

"So I'll still be protected," Joey said.

"That's right. Brandy would want you to be protected."

In the kitchen, the telephone rang.

"Tell you what," she said, "I'll just answer the phone, and then we'll make arrangements for burying Brandy."

The phone rang again.

"We'll find a nice pet cemetery or something, and we'll lay Brandy to rest with all the right honors."

"I'd like that," he said.

The phone rang a third time.

Heading toward the kitchen, she said, "Then later we'll look for a puppy." She picked up the phone just as it completed a fifth ring. "Hello?"

A woman said, "Are you part of it?"

"Excuse me?"

"Are you part of it—or don't you know what's happening?" the woman asked.

Although the voice was vaguely familiar, Christine said, "I think you've got the wrong number."

"You *are* Miss Scavello, aren't you?"

"Yes. Who's this?"

"I've got to know if you're part of it. Are you one of *them?* Or are you an innocent? I've got to know."

Suddenly Christine recognized the voice, and a chill crept up her spine.

The old woman said, "Do you know what your son really is? Do you know the evil in him? Do you know why he's got to die?"

Christine slammed the phone down.

Joey had followed her into the kitchen. He was standing just this side of the door to the dining room, chewing on a thumbnail. In his striped shirt and jeans and somewhat tattered sneakers, he looked pathetically small, defenseless.

The phone began to ring again.

Ignoring it, Christine said, "Come on, Skipper. Stay with me. Stay close to me."

She led him out of the kitchen, through the dining room and living room, upstairs to the master bedroom.

He didn't ask what was wrong. From the look on his face, she thought he probably knew.

The phone kept ringing.

In the bedroom she pulled the top drawer out of the highboy, rummaged under a stack of folded sweaters, and came up with a wicked-looking pistol, a selective double-action Astra Constable .32 automatic with a snub-nosed barrel. She had purchased it years ago, before Joey was born, when she'd begun living alone, and she had learned how to use it. The gun had given her a much-needed sense of security—as it did now, once again.

The phone rang and rang.

When Joey had come into her life, especially when he had begun to walk, she'd been afraid that, in his ceaseless curiosity, he would find the weapon and play with it. Protection against burglars had to be weighed against the more likely—and more frightening—possibility that Joey would hurt himself. She had unloaded the gun, had put the empty magazine in a dresser drawer, and had buried the gun itself beneath the sweaters in the highboy, and fortunately had never needed it since then.

Until now.

The shrill ringing of the telephone became louder and more irritating by the moment.

Pistol in hand, Christine went to the dresser and located the empty magazine. She hurried to the closet where she kept a box of ammunition on the top shelf, all the way at the back. With trembling and clumsy fingers, she pushed cartridges into the magazine until it was full, then slapped it into the butt of the pistol hard enough to lock it in place.

Joey watched in wide-eyed fascination.

At last the telephone stopped ringing.

The sudden silence had the force of a blow. It briefly stunned Christine.

Joey was the first to speak. Still chewing on a thumbnail, he said, "Was it the witch on the phone?"

There was no point in hiding it from him and no point in telling him the old woman wasn't really a witch. "Yeah. It was her."

"Mommy . . . I'm scared."

For the past several months, ever since he had overcome his fear of the imaginary white snake that had disturbed his sleep, he had called her "Mom" instead of "Mommy" because he was trying to be more grown-up. His reversion to "Mommy" was an indication of just how badly frightened he was.

"It'll be all right. I'm not going to let anything happen to . . . either of us. If we're just careful, we'll be okay."

She kept expecting to hear a knock at the door or see a face at the window. Where had the old woman been calling from? How long would it take her to get here now that the cops were gone, now that she had a clear shot at Joey?

"What're we gonna do?" he asked.

She put the loaded gun on top of the six-drawer highboy and dragged two suitcases from the back of the closet. "I'm going to pack a bag for each of us and then we're getting out of here."

"Where're we going?"

She threw one of the suitcases onto her bed and opened it. "I don't know for sure, sweetheart. Anywhere. To a hotel, probably. We'll go someplace where that crazy old hag won't be able to find us no matter how hard she looks."

"Then what?"

As she folded clothes into the open suitcase, she said, "Then we'll find someone who can help us . . . *really* help us."

"Not like the cops?"

"Not like the cops."

"Who?"

"I'm not sure. Maybe . . . a private detective."

"Like Magnum on TV?"

"Maybe not exactly like Magnum," Christine said.

"Like who, then?"

"We need a big firm that can provide us with bodyguards and everything while they're tracking down that old woman. A first-rate organization."

"Like in them old movies?"

"What old movies are those?"

"You know. Where they're in real bad trouble, and they say, 'We'll hire Pinkelton.' "

"Pinkerton," she corrected. "Yeah. Something like Pinkerton. I can afford to hire people like that and, by God, I'm going to hire them. We're not just going to be a couple of sitting ducks the way the cops would have us."

"I'd feel a whole bunch safer if we just went and hired Magnum," Joey said.

She didn't have time to explain to a six-year-old that Magnum wasn't a real private eye. She said, "Well, maybe you're right. Maybe we will hire Magnum."

"Yeah?"

"Yeah."

"He'll do a good job," Joey said soberly. "He always does."

At her direction, Joey took the empty suitcase and headed toward his room. She followed, carrying the suitcase that she had already packed—and the pistol.

She decided they wouldn't go to a hotel first. They'd go straight to a detective agency and not waste any time dealing with this.

Her mouth was sandpaper-dry. Her heart thudded. She was breathing hard and fast.

In her mind a terrible vision rose, an image of a bloody and decapitated body sprawled on the back porch. But in the vision, it wasn't Brandy she saw in gory ruin. It was Joey.

CHAPTER 7

/////

CHARLIE HARRISON WAS proud of his accomplishments. He had started with nothing, just a poor kid from the shabby side of Indianapolis. Now, at thirty-six, he was owner of a thriving business—full owner since the retirement of the company's founder, Harvey Klemet—and was living the good life in southern California. If he wasn't exactly on top of the world yet, he was at least eighty percent of the way there, and the view from his current elevation was quite satisfying.

The offices of Klemet-Harrison were not remotely like the seedy quarters of private investigators in novels and films. These rooms, on the fifth floor of a five-story building on a quiet street in Costa Mesa, were comfortably and tastefully decorated.

The reception lounge made a good first impression on new clients. It was plushly carpeted, and the walls were covered with a subtle grass cloth. The furniture was new—and not from the low end of the manufacturer's line, either. The walls weren't adorned only with cheap prints; there were three Eyvind Earle serigraphs worth more than fifteen hundred dollars apiece.

Charlie's private office was even somewhat plusher than the reception area, yet it avoided the ponderous and solemn look favored by attorneys and many other professionals. Bleached-wood paneling reached halfway up the walls. There were bleached-wood shutters on the windows, a contemporary desk by Henredon, armchairs covered in an airy green print from Brunschwig & Fils. On the walls were two large, light-filled paintings by Martin Green, undersea scenes of ethereal plant life fluttering gracefully in mysterious currents and tides. A few large plants, mostly ferns and pothos, hung from the ceiling or rested on rosewood stands. The effect was almost subtropical yet cool and rich.

But when Christine Scavello walked through the door, Charlie suddenly felt that the room was woefully inadequate. Yes, it was light and well-balanced and expensive and truly exquisite; nevertheless, it seemed hopelessly heavy, clunky, and even garish when compared to this striking woman.

Coming out from behind his desk, he said, "Ms. Scavello, I'm Charlie Harrison. I'm so pleased to meet you."

She accepted his hand and said she was pleased to meet him, too.

Her hair was thick, shiny, dark-dark brown, almost black. He wanted to run his fingers through it. He wanted to put his face in her hair and smell it.

Unaccustomed to having such a strong and immediate reaction to anyone, Charlie reined himself in. He looked at her more closely, as dispassionately as possible. He told himself that she wasn't perfect, certainly not breathtakingly beautiful. Pretty, yes, but not a total knockout. Her brow was somewhat too high, and her cheekbones seemed a little heavy, and her nose was slightly pinched.

Nevertheless, with a breathless and ingratiating manner that wasn't like him, he said, "I apologize for the condition of the office," and was surprised and dismayed to hear himself make such a statement.

She looked puzzled. "Why should you apologize? It's lovely."

He blinked. "You really think so?"

"Absolutely. It's unexpected. Not at all what I thought a private detective's office would look like. But that just makes it even more interesting, appealing."

Her eyes were huge and dark. Clear, direct eyes. Each time he met them, his breath caught for an instant.

"Did it myself," he said, deciding the room didn't look so bad, after all. "Didn't use an interior decorator."

"You've got a real flair for it."

He showed her to a chair and noticed, as she sat down, that she had lovely legs and perfectly shaped ankles.

But I've seen other legs as lovely, other ankles as well shaped, he thought with some bafflement, and I haven't ever before been swept away by this adolescent longing, haven't felt this ridiculously sudden surge in hormone levels.

Either he was hornier than he thought, or he was reacting to more than her appearance.

Perhaps her appeal was as much in the way she walked and shook hands and carried herself (with an easy, graceful minimum of movement), and in her voice (soft, earthy, feminine, yet unaffected, with a note of strength), and in the way she met his eyes (forthrightly), as it was in the way she looked. In spite of the circumstances in which he was meeting her, in spite of the fact that she had a serious problem about which she must be worried, she possessed an uncommon inner tranquility that intrigued him.

That doesn't quite explain it either, he thought. Since when have I ever wanted to jump into bed with a woman because of her uncommon inner tranquility?

All right, so he wasn't going to be able to analyze this feeling, not yet. He would just have to go with it and try to understand it later.

Stepping behind his desk, sitting down, he said, "Maybe I shouldn't have told you I'm interested in interior design. Maybe that's really the wrong image for a private detective."

"On the contrary," she said, "what it tells me is that you're observant, perceptive, probably quite sensitive, and you have an excellent eye for details. Those are the qualities I'd hope for in any man in your line of work."

"Right! Exactly," he said, beaming at her, delighted by her approval.

He was stricken by an almost irresistible urge to kiss her brow, her eyes, the bridge of her nose, the tip of her nose, her cheeks, her chin, and last of all her sculpted lips.

But all he did was say, "Well, Ms. Scavello, what can I do for you?"

She told him about the old woman.

He was shocked, intrigued, and sympathetic, but he was also uneasy because you never knew what to expect from flaky types like this old woman. Anything might happen, and it probably would. Furthermore, he knew how difficult it was to track down and deal with any perpetrator of this type of irrational harassment. He much preferred people with clear, understandable motivations. Understandable motivations were what made his line of work possible: greed, lust, envy, jealousy, revenge, love, hate—they were the raw material of his industry. Thank God for the weaknesses and imperfections of mankind, for otherwise he would have been without work. He was also uneasy because he was afraid he might fail Christine Scavello, and if he failed her, she would walk out of his life forever. And if she walked out of his life forever, he would have to be satisfied with only dreams of her, and he was just too damn old for dreams of that kind.

When Christine finished recounting the events of this morning—the murder of the dog, the call from the old woman—Charlie said, "Where's your son now?"

"Out in your waiting room."

"All right. He's safe there."

"I'm not sure he's safe anywhere."

"Relax. It's not the end of the world. It's really not."

He smiled at her to show her that it wasn't the end of the world. He wanted to make her smile back at him because he was certain that her smile would make her lovely face even lovelier, but she didn't seem to have a smile in her.

He said, "All right, about this old woman . . . You've given me a pretty detailed description of her." He had made notes as she talked. Now he glanced at them. "But is there anything else about her that might help us make an identification?"

"I've told you everything I remember."

"What about scars? Did she have any scars?"

"No."

"Did she wear glasses?"

"No."

"You said she was in her late sixties or early seventies—"

"Yes."

"—yet her face was hardly lined."

"That's right."

"Unnaturally smooth, somewhat puffy, you said."

"Her skin, yes. I had an aunt who took cortisone injections for arthritis. Her face was like this woman's face."

"So you think she's being treated for some form of arthritis?"

Christine shrugged. "I don't know. Could be."

"Was she wearing a copper bracelet or any copper rings?"

"Copper?"

"It's only a wives' tale, of course, but a lot of people think copper jewelry helps arthritis. I had an aunt with arthritis, too, and she wore a copper necklace, two copper bracelets on each wrist, a couple of copper rings, and even a copper ankle bracelet. She was a thin little bird of a woman, weighed down with crummy-looking jewelry, and she swore by it, said it did her a world of good, but she never moved any easier and never had any relief from the pain."

"This woman didn't have any copper jewelry. Lots of other jewelry, like I said, but nothing copper."

He stared at his notes. Then: "She didn't tell you her name—"

"No."

"—but was she wearing a monogram, like maybe on her blouse—"

"No."

"—or were her initials spelled out on one of her rings?"

"I don't think so. If they were, I didn't notice."

"And you didn't see where she came from?"

"No."

"If we knew what kind of car she got out of—"

"I've no idea. We were almost to our car, and she just stepped out from beside it."

"What kind of car was parked next to yours?"

She frowned, trying to remember.

While she thought, Charlie studied her face, looking for imperfections. Nothing in this world was free of imperfections. Everything had at least one flaw. Even a bottle of Lafitte Rothschild could have a bad cork or too much tannic acid. Not even a Rolls Royce had an unblemished paint job. Reese's Peanut Butter Cups were unquestionably delicious—but they made you fat. However, no matter how carefully he studied Christine Scavello's face, he could find nothing whatsoever wrong with it. Oh, yes, well, the pinched nose, and the heavy cheekbones, and the too-high brow, but in her case those didn't strike him as imperfections; they were merely . . . well, deviations from the ordinary definition of beauty, minor deviations that gave her character, a look of her own—

And what the hell is wrong with me? he wondered. I've got to stop mooning over her as if I were a lovesick schoolboy.

On one hand, he liked the way he felt; it was a fresh, exhilarating feeling. On the other hand, he *didn't* like it because he didn't understand it, and it was his nature to want to understand everything. That was why he'd become a detective—to find answers, to *understand.*

She blinked, looked up at him. "I remember. It wasn't a car parked next to us. It was a van."

"A paneled van? What kind?"

"White."

"I mean, what make?"

She frowned again, trying to recall.

"Old or new?" he asked.

"New. Clean, sparkling."

"Did you notice any dents, scrapes?"

"No. And it was a Ford."

"Good. Very good. Do you know what year?"

"No."

"A recreational vehicle, was it? With one of those round windows on the side or maybe a painted mural?"

"No. Very utilitarian. Like a van somebody would use for work."

"Was there a company name on the side?"

"No."

"Any message at all painted on it?"

"No. It was just plain white."

"What about the license plate?"

"I didn't see it."

"You passed by the back of the van. You noticed it was a Ford. The license plate would've been right there."

"I guess. But I didn't look at it."

"If it becomes necessary, we can probably get it out of you with hypnosis. At least now we have a little something to start with."

"*If* she got out of the van."

"For starters, we'll assume she did."

"And that's probably a mistake."

"And maybe it isn't."

"She could've come from anywhere in the parking lot."

"But since we have to start somewhere, we might as well begin with the van," he said patiently.

"She might've come from another row of cars altogether. We might just be wasting time. I don't want to waste time. *She* isn't wasting time. I have an awful feeling we don't *have* much time."

Her nervous, fidgety movements escalated into uncontrollable shivers that shook her entire body. Charlie realized that she had been maintaining her composure only with considerable effort.

"Easy," he said. "Easy now. Everything'll work out fine. We won't let anything happen to Joey."

She was pale. Her voice quavered when she spoke: "He's so sweet. He's such a sweet little boy. He's the center of my life . . . the center of everything. If anything happened to him . . ."

"Nothing's going to happen to him. I guarantee you that."

She began to cry. She didn't sob or wail or get hysterical. She just took deep, shuddery breaths, and her eyes grew watery, and tears slipped down her cheeks.

Pushing his chair back from the desk, getting up, wanting to comfort her, feeling awkward and inadequate, Charlie said, "I think you need a drink."

She shook her head.

"It'll help," he said.

"I don't drink much," she said shakily, and the tears poured from her even more copiously than before.

"Just one drink."

"Too early," she said.

"It's past eleven-thirty. Almost lunchtime. Besides, this is medicinal."

He went to the bar that stood in the corner by one of the two big windows. He opened the lower doors, took out a bottle of Chivas Regal and one glass, put them on the marble-topped counter, poured two ounces of Scotch.

As he was capping the bottle, he happened to look out the window beside him—and froze. A white Ford van, clean and sparkling, with no advertising on it, was parked across the street. Looking over the tops of the uppermost fronds of an enormous date palm that rose almost to his fifth-floor window, Charlie saw a man in dark clothing leaning against the side of the van.

Coincidence.

The man seemed to be eating. Just a workman stopped on a quiet side street to grab an early lunch. That's all. Surely, it couldn't be anything more than that.

Coincidence.

Or maybe not. The man down there also seemed to be watching the front of this building. He appeared to be having a bite of lunch and running a stakeout at the same time. Charlie had been involved in dozens of stakeouts over the years. He knew what a stakeout looked like, and this sure as hell looked like one, although it was a bit obvious and amateurish.

Behind him, Christine said, "Is something wrong?"

He was surprised by her perspicacity, by how sharply attuned to him she was, especially since she was still highly agitated, still crying.

He said, "I hope you like Scotch."

He turned away from the window and took the drink to her.

She accepted it without further protestations. She held the glass in both hands but still couldn't keep it from shaking. She sipped rather daintily at the whiskey.

Charlie said, "Drink it straight down. Two swallows. Get it inside you where it can do some good."

She did as he said, and he could tell that she really didn't drink much because she grimaced at the bitterness of the Scotch, even though Chivas was about the smoothest stuff ever to come out of a distillery.

He took the empty glass from her, carried it back to the bar, rinsed it out in the small sink, and set it on the drainboard.

He looked out the window again.

The white truck was still there.

So was the man in the dark pants and shirt, eating his lunch with studied casualness.

Returning to Christine, Charlie said, "Feel better?"

Some color had crept back into her face. She nodded. "I'm sorry for coming apart on you like that."

He sat half on the edge of his desk, keeping one foot on the floor. He smiled at her. "You have nothing to apologize for. Most people, if they'd had the scare you've had, would've come through the door blubbering incoherently, and they'd *still* be blubbering incoherently. You're holding up quite well."

"I don't *feel* as if I'm holding up." She took a handkerchief from her purse and blew her nose. "But I guess you're right. One crazy old lady isn't the end of the world."

"Exactly."

"One crazy old lady can't be *that* hard to deal with."

"That's the spirit," he said.

But he thought: One crazy old lady? Then who's the guy with the white truck?

CHAPTER 8

〰️〰️

GRACE SPIVEY SAT on a hard oak chair, her ice-gray eyes shining in the gloom.

Today was a red day in the spirit world, one of the reddest days she had ever known, and she was dressed entirely in red in order to be in harmony with it, just as she had dressed entirely in green yesterday, when the spirit world had been going through a green phase. Most people weren't aware that the spirit world around them changed color from day to day; of course, most people couldn't see the supernatural realm as clearly as Grace could see it when she really tried; in fact, most of them couldn't see it at all, so there was no way they could possibly understand Grace's manner of dress. But for Grace, who was a psychic and a medium, it was essential to be in harmony with the color of the spirit world, for then she could more easily receive clairvoyant visions of both the past and future. These visions were sent to her by benign spirits and were transmitted on brilliantly colored beams of energy, beams that, today, were all shades of red.

If she had tried to explain this to most people, they would have thought her insane. A few years ago her own daughter had committed Grace to a hospital for psychiatric evaluation; but Grace had slipped out of that trap, had disowned her daughter, and had been more cautious ever since.

Today she wore dark red shoes, a dark red skirt, and a lighter red, two-tone, striped blouse. All her jewelry was red: a double strand of crimson beads and matching bracelets on each wrist; a porcelain brooch as bright as fire; two ruby rings; one ring with four dazzling ovals of highly polished carnelian; four other rings with cheap red glass, vermilion enamel, and scarlet porcelain. Whether precious, semi-precious, or fake, all the stones in her rings glinted and sparkled in the flickering candlelight.

The quivering flames, adance upon the points of the wicks, caused strange shadows to writhe over the basement walls. The room was large, but it seemed small because the candles were grouped at one end of it, and three-quarters of the chamber lay beyond the reach of their inconstant amber light. There were eleven candles in all, each fat and white, each fitted in a brass holder with an ornate drip guard, and each brass candlestick was gripped firmly by one of Grace's followers, all of whom were waiting eagerly for her to speak. Of the eleven, six were men and five were women. Some were young, some middle-aged, some old. They sat on the floor, forming a semicircle around the chair on which Grace sat, their faces gleaming and queerly distorted in the fluttering, shimmering, eldritch glow.

These eleven did not constitute the entire body of her followers. More than fifty others were in the room overhead, waiting anxiously to hear what transpired during this session. And more than a thousand others were elsewhere, in a hundred different places, engaged upon work that Grace had assigned to them.

However, these eleven at her feet were her most trusted, valued, and capable lieutenants. They were the ones she most cherished.

She even knew and remembered their names, although it wasn't easy for her to remember names (or much of anything else) these days, not as easy as it had been before the Gift had been given to her. The Gift filled her, filled her mind, and crowded out so many things that she had once taken for granted—such as the ability to remember names and faces. And the ability to keep track of time. She never knew what time it was any more; even when she looked at a clock, it frequently had no meaning for her. Seconds, minutes, hours, and days now seemed like ridiculously arbitrary measurements of time; perhaps they were still useful to ordinary men and women, but she was beyond the need of them. Sometimes, when she thought only a day had passed, she discovered that an entire week was missing. It was scary but also curiously exhilarating, for it made her constantly aware that she was special, that she was Chosen. The Gift had also crowded out sleep. Some nights she didn't sleep at all. Most nights she slept one hour, never more than two, but she didn't seem to *need* sleep any more, so it didn't matter how little she got. The Gift crowded out everything that might interfere with the great and sacred work she must accomplish.

Nevertheless, she remembered the names of these eleven people because they were the purest members of her flock. They were the best of the best, largely untainted souls who were the most worthy of carrying out the demanding tasks ahead of them.

One other man was in the basement. His name was Kyle Barlowe. He was thirty-two, but he looked older—older, somber, mean, and dangerous. He had lank brown hair, thick but without luster. His high forehead ended in a heavy shelf of bone under which his deeply set brown eyes were watchful and shrewd. He had a large nose, but it wasn't regal or proud; it had been broken more than once and was lumpy. His cheekbones and jawbone were heavy, crudely formed, like the plate of bone from which his forehead had been carved. Although his features were for the most part over-sized and graceless, his lips were thin, and they were so bloodless and pale that they seemed even thinner than they actually were; as a result, his mouth appeared to be nothing more than a slash in his face. He was an extraordinarily big man, six-eleven, with a bull's neck, slab shoulders, well-muscled chest and arms. He looked as if he could break a man in half—and as if he frequently did exactly that, strictly for the fun of it.

In fact, for the past three years, since Kyle had become one of Grace's followers and then a member of her inner circle and then her most trusted assistant, he hadn't raised a hand against anyone. Before Grace had found and saved him, he had been a moody, violent, and brutal man. But those days were gone. Grace had been able to see beyond Kyle Barlowe's forbidding exterior, had glimpsed the good soul that lay beneath. He had gone astray, yes, but he had been eager (even if he hadn't realized it himself) to return to the good and righteous path. All he needed was someone to show him the way. Grace had shown him, and he had followed. Now, his huge, powerful arms and his marble-hard fists would harm no virtuous man or woman but would smite only those who were the enemies of God and, even then, only when Grace *told* him to smite them.

Grace knew the enemies of God when she saw them. The ability to recognize a hopelessly corrupt soul in the first instant upon encountering it—that was but one small part of the Gift that God had bestowed upon her. One split second of eye contact was usually all Grace needed in order to determine if a person was habitually sinful and beyond redemption. She had the Gift. No one else. Just her, the Chosen. She heard evil in the voices of the wicked; she saw evil in their eyes. There was no hiding from her.

Some people, given the Gift, would have doubted it, would have wondered if they were wrong or even crazy. But Grace never doubted herself or questioned her sanity. Never. She knew she was special, and she knew she was always right in these matters because God had told her that she was right.

The day was rapidly coming when she would finally call upon Kyle (and upon some of the others) to strike down many of those disciples of Satan. She would point to the evil ones, and Kyle would destroy them. He would be the hammer of God. How wonderful that day would be! Sitting in the basement of her church, on the hard oak chair, in front of her innermost circle of believers, Grace shivered with anticipatory pleasure. It would be so fine, so satisfying to watch the big man's hard muscles bunch and flex and bunch again as he brought the wrath of God to the infidels and Satanists.

Soon. The time was coming. The Twilight.

Now, the candlelight flickered, and Kyle said softly, "Are you ready, Mother Grace?"

"Yes," she said.

She closed her eyes. For a moment she saw nothing, only darkness, but then she quickly established contact with the spirit world, and lights appeared behind her eyes, bursts and squiggles and fountains and spots and shifting-heaving-writhing shapes of light, some brilliant and some dim, all shades of red, naturally, because they were spirits and spectral energies, and this was a red day in their plane of existence. It was the reddest day Grace had ever known.

The spirits swarmed on all sides of her, and she moved off among them as if she were drifting away into a world that was painted on the backs of her own eyelids. At first she drifted slowly. She felt her mind and spirit separating from her body, gradually leaving the flesh behind. She was still aware of the temporal plane in which her body existed—the odor of burning candles, the hard oak chair beneath her, an occasional rustle or murmur from one of her disciples—but eventually all that faded. She accelerated until she was rushing, then flying, then rocketing through the light-spotted void, faster and faster, with exhilarating, now sickening, now terrifying speed—

Sudden stillness.

She was deep in the spirit world, hanging motionless, as if she were an asteroid suspended in a distant corner of space. She was no longer able to see, hear, smell, or feel the world she had left behind. Across an infinite night, red-hued spirits of all descriptions moved in every direction, some fast and some slow, some purposefully and some erratically, on adventures and holy errands that Grace could not begin to comprehend.

Grace thought about the boy, Joey Scavello. She knew what he really was, and she knew he had to die. But she didn't know if the time had come to dispose of him. She had made this journey into the spirit world for the sole purpose of inquiring as to when and how she should deal with the boy.

She hoped she would be told to kill him. She wanted so much to kill him.

CHAPTER 9

✐✐✐✐

THE DOUBLE SHOT of Chivas Regal seemed to have calmed Christine Scavello, although not entirely. She finally leaned back in her chair, and her hands were no longer knotted together, but she was still tense and noticeably shaky.

Charlie continued to sit on the edge of his desk with one foot on the floor. "At least until we know who this old woman is and what kind of person we're dealing with, I think we should put two armed bodyguards with Joey around the clock."

"All right. Do it."

"Does the boy go to school?"

"Pre-school. He starts regular school next fall."

"We'll keep him out of pre-school until this blows over."

"It won't just blow over," she said edgily.

"Well, of course, I didn't mean we were just going to wait it out. I meant to say that we'll keep him out of pre-school until we put a stop to this thing."

"Will two bodyguards be enough?"

"Actually, it'll be six. Three pairs working in eight-hour shifts."

"Still, it'll only be two men during any one shift, and I—"

"Two can handle it. They're well trained. However, this can all get pretty expensive. If—"

"I can afford it," she said.

"My secretary can give you a fee sheet—"

"Whatever's needed. I can pay."

"What about your husband?"

"What about him?"

"Well, what's he think about all this?"

"I don't have a husband."

"Oh. I'm sorry if—"

"No need for sympathy. I'm not a widow, and I wasn't divorced, either." Here was the forthrightness he had seen in her; this refusal to be evasive was refreshing. "I've never been married."

"Ah," he said.

Although Charlie was sure his voice contained not the slightest note of disapproval, Christine stiffened as if he had insulted her. With a sudden, irrational, quiet yet steel-hard anger that startled him, she said, "What're you trying to tell me? That you've got to approve of your client's morality before you accept a case?"

He gaped at her, astonished and confused by her abrupt change of attitude. "Well of course not! I only—"

"Because I'm not about to sit here like a criminal on trial—"

"Wait, wait, wait. What's wrong? Huh? What'd I say? Good heavens, why should I care if you've been married or not?"

"Fine. Glad you feel that way. Now, how are you going to track down that old woman?"

Anger, like a smouldering fire, remained in her eyes and voice.

Charlie couldn't understand why she was so sensitive and defensive about her son's lack of a legal father. It was unfortunate, yes, and she probably wished the situation were otherwise. But it really wasn't a terrible social stigma these days. She acted as if she were living in the 1940s instead of the '80s.

"I really mean it," he said. "I don't care."

"Terrific. Congratulations on your open-mindedness. If it was up to me, you'd get a Nobel Prize for humanitarianism. Now can we drop the subject?"

What the hell is *wrong* with her? he wondered. He was *glad* there was no husband. Couldn't she sense his interest in her? Couldn't she see through his tissue-thin professional demeanor? Couldn't she see how she got to him? Most women had a sixth sense for that sort of thing.

He said, "If I rub you the wrong way or something, I can turn this case over to one of my junior men—"

"No, I—"

"They're all quite reliable, capable. But I assure you I didn't mean to disparage or ridicule you—or whatever the heck you think I did. I'm not like that cop this morning, the one who chewed you out about using four-letter words."

"Officer Wilford."

"I'm not like Wilford. I'm easy. Okay? Truce?"

She hesitated, then nodded. The stiffness left her. The anger faded and was replaced by embarrassment.

She said, "Sorry I snapped at you, Mr. Harrison—"

"Call me Charlie. And you can snap at me anytime." He smiled. "But we have to talk about Joey's father because maybe he's connected with this."

"With the old woman?"

"Maybe."

"Oh, I doubt it."

"Maybe he wants custody of his son."

"Then why not just come and ask?"

Charlie shrugged. "People don't always approach a problem from a logical point of view."

She shook her head. "No. It's not Joey's . . . father. As far as I know, he isn't even aware that Joey exists. Besides, that old woman was saying Joey had to *die.*"

"I still think we have to consider the possibility and talk about his father, even if that's painful for you. We can't leave any possibility unexplored."

She nodded. "It's just that . . . when I got pregnant with Joey, it nearly destroyed Evelyn . . . my mother. She had expected so much of me . . . She made me feel terribly guilty, made me wallow in guilt." She sighed. "I guess, because of the way my mother treated me, I'm still overly sensitive about Joey's . . . illegitimacy."

"I understand."

"No. You don't. You can't."

He waited and listened. He was a good and patient listener. It was part of his job.

She said, "Evelyn . . . Mother . . . doesn't like Joey much. Won't have much to do with him. She blames *him* for his illegitimacy. She sometimes even treats him as if . . . as if he's wicked or evil or something. It's wrong, it's sick, it doesn't make sense, but it's so much like Mother to blame *him* because *my* life didn't turn out exactly the way she planned it for me."

"If she actively dislikes Joey, is it possible that your mother might be behind this thing with the old woman?" he asked.

That thought clearly startled her. But she shook her head. "No. Surely not. It isn't Evelyn's style. She's direct. She tells you what she thinks, even if she knows she's going to hurt you, even if she knows every word she speaks is going to be like a nail going into you. She wouldn't be asking her friends to harass my boy. That's ludicrous."

"She might not be involved directly. But maybe she's talked about you and Joey to other people, and maybe this old woman at the mall was one of those people. Maybe your mother said intemperate things about the boy, not realizing this old woman was unbalanced, not realizing the old woman would take what your mother said the wrong way, take it too literally and actually act upon it."

Scowling, Christine said, "Maybe . . ."

"I know it's far-fetched, but it *is* possible."

"Okay. Yeah. I suppose so."

"So tell me about your mother."

"I assure you, she couldn't be involved with this."

"Tell me anyway," he coaxed.

She sighed and said, "She's a dragon lady, my mother. You can't understand, and I can't really make you understand, because you had to live with her to know what she's like. She kept me under her thumb . . . intimidated . . . browbeaten . . . all those years . . ."

* * *

. . . all those years.

Her mind drifted back, against her will, and she became aware of a pressure on her chest and began to have some difficulty drawing her breath, for the predominant feeling associated with her childhood was one of suffocation.

She saw the rambling Victorian house in Pomona that had been passed from her Grandma Giavetti to Evelyn, where they had lived from the time Christine was a year old, where Evelyn still lived, and the memory of it was an unwelcome weight. Although she knew it to be a white house with pale yellow trim and awnings, with charming gingerbread ornamentation and many windows to admit the sun, in her mind's eye she always saw it crouched in shadows, with Halloween-bare trees crowding close to it, beneath a threatening gray-black sky. She could hear the grandfather clock ticking monotonously in the parlor, an ever-present sound that in those days had seemed always to be mocking her with its constant reminder that the misery of her childhood stretched almost to eternity and would be counted out in millions and millions of leaden seconds. She could see again, in every room, heavy over-stuffed pieces of furniture pressed too close to one another, and she supposed that her memory made the ticking clock louder and more maddeningly intrusive than it had actually been, and that in reality the furniture hadn't been quite so large and clunky and ugly and dark as it was in recollection.

Her father, Vincent Scavello, had found that house, that life, as oppressive as it was in Christine's memory, and he had left them when she was four and her brother, Tony, was eleven. He never came back, and she never saw him again. He was a weak man with an inferiority complex, and Evelyn made him feel even more inadequate because she set such high standards for everyone. Nothing he did could satisfy her. Nothing *anyone* did—especially not Christine or Tony—was half as good as Evelyn expected of them. Because he couldn't measure up to her expectations, Vincent developed a drinking problem, and that only made her nag him more, and finally he just left. Two years later, he was dead. In a way he committed suicide, though not with a gun—nothing so dramatic as that; it was just a case of drunken driving; he ran head-on into a bridge abutment at seventy miles an hour.

Evelyn went to work the day after Vincent walked out, not only supported her family but did a good job of it, living up to her own high standards. That made things even worse for Christine and Tony. "You've got to be the best at what you do, and if you aren't the best there's no use doing it at all," Evelyn said—at least a thousand times.

Christine had one especially clear memory of an entire, tense evening spent at the kitchen table, after Tony brought home a report card with a D in math, a failure that, in Evelyn's eyes, was in no way mitigated by the fact that he had received an A in every other subject. This would have been bad enough, but that same day he had been mildly reprimanded by the school principal for smoking in the boys' washroom. It was the first time he tried a cigarette, and he didn't like it and didn't intend to smoke again; it was just an experiment, hardly unusual for a fourteen-year-old boy, but Evelyn was furious. That night the lecture had gone on for almost three hours, with Evelyn alternately pacing, sitting at the table with her head in her hands, shouting, weeping, pleading, pounding the table. "You're a Giavetti, Tony, more of a Giavetti than a Scavello. You might carry your father's name, but by God, there's more of *my* blood in you; there must be. I couldn't bear to think half your blood is poor weak Vincent's, because if that was true, God knows what would become of you. I won't have it! I won't! I work my fingers to the bone to give you every chance, every opportunity, and I won't have you spitting in my face, which is what this is, goofing off in school, goofing off in math class—it's just the same as spitting in my face!" The anger gave way to tears, and she got up from the table, pulled a handful of Kleenex from the box on the kitchen counter, noisily blew her nose. "What good does it do for me to worry about you, to care what happens to you? *You* don't care. There's that few drops of your father's blood in you, that loafer's blood, and it only takes a few drops to contaminate you. Like a disease. Scavello Disease. But you're also a Giavetti, and Giavettis always work harder and study harder, which is only right, only fitting, because God didn't intend for us to loaf and drink our lives away, like some I could mention. You've got to get As in school, and even if you don't like math, you've got to just work harder until you're perfect in it, because you *need* math in this world, and your father, God pity him, was lousy with figures, and I won't have you being like poor weak Vincent; that scares me. I don't want my son being a bum, and I'm afraid I see a bum in you, just like your father, weakness in you. Now, you're also a *Giavetti,* and don't you forget it. Giavettis always do their best, and their best is always as good as *anyone* could do, and don't you tell me that you're already spending most of your time studying, and don't tell me about your weekend job at the grocery store. Work is good for you. I got you that job because you show me a teenage boy who *doesn't* have a part-time job and I'll show you a future bum. Why, even with your job and your studying and the things you do around here, you should still have plenty of free time, too much, way too much. You should maybe even be working a night or two during the week at the market. There's *always* more time if you want to find it; God made the whole world in six days, and don't tell me you aren't God because if you listened to your catechism lessons you'd know you were made in His image, and remember you're a Giavetti, which means you were made in His image just a little more than some other people I could name, like Vincent Scavello, but I won't. Look at *me!* I work all day, but I cook good meals for you, too, and with Christine I keep this big house immaculate, absolutely immaculate, God as my witness, and though I may be tired sometimes and feel like I just can't go on, I *do* go on, for you, for *you* I go on, and your clothes are always nicely pressed—Aren't they?—and your socks are always mended—Tell me *once* you ever had to wear a sock with a hole in it!—so if I do all this and not drop dead and not even *complain,* then you can be the kind of son to make me proud, and by God you're *going* to be! And as for *you,* Christine . . ."

Evelyn never ceased lecturing them. Always, every day, holidays, birthdays —there was no day free of her lectures. Christine and Tony sat captive, not daring to answer back because that brought the most withering scorn and the worst punishment—and encouraged even *more* lecturing. She pushed them relentlessly, demanded the greatest possible accomplishments in everything they did, which wasn't necessarily a bad thing; it might even have been good for them. However, when they *did* achieve the best grade possible, win the highest award being given, move up to the first seats in their sections of the school orchestra, when they did all that and more, much more, it never satisfied their mother. The best wasn't good enough for Evelyn. When they achieved the best, reached the pinnacle, she chastised them for not having gotten there sooner, set new goals for them, and suggested they were trying her patience and running out of time in which to make her proud of them.

When she felt lecturing wasn't sufficient, she used her ultimate weapon— tears. She wept and blamed herself for their failures. "Both of you are going to come to a bad end, and it'll be my fault, all my fault, because I didn't know how to reach you, how to make you see what was important. I didn't do enough for you, I didn't know how to help you overcome the Scavello blood that's in you, and I should have known, should have done better. What good am I as a mother? No good, no mother at all."

. . . all those years ago . . .

But it seemed like yesterday.

Christine couldn't tell Charlie Harrison everything about her mother and that claustrophobic childhood of shadowy rooms and heavy Victorian furniture and heavy Victorian guilt, for she would have needed hours to explain. Besides, she wasn't looking for pity, and she was not by nature the kind of person given to sharing the intimate details of her life with others—not even with friends, let alone strangers like this man, nice as he might be. She only alluded to her past with a few sentences, but from his expression, she thought he sensed and understood more than she told him; perhaps the pain of it was in her eyes and face, more easily read than she supposed.

"Those years were worse for Tony than for me," she told the detective. "Mainly because, on top of everything else that Evelyn expected of him, she also wanted him to be a priest. The Giavettis had produced two priests in her generation, and they were the most revered members of the family."

In addition to the Giavettis' tradition of service to the Church, Evelyn was a religious woman, and even without that family history, she would have pushed Tony toward the priesthood. She pushed successfully, too, for he went straight from parochial school into the seminary. He had no choice. By the time he was twelve, Evelyn had him brainwashed, and it was impossible for him to imagine being anything *but* a priest.

"Evelyn expected Tony to be a parish priest," Christine told Charlie Harrison. "Maybe eventually a monsignor, perhaps even a bishop. Like I said, she had high standards. But when Tony took his vows, he asked to be assigned to missionary work, and he was—in Africa. Mother was so upset! See, in the Church, like in government, the way you usually move up through the hierarchy is largely through astute politicking. But you can't be a constant, visible presence in the corridors of power when you're stuck in some remote African mission. Mother was furious."

The detective said, "Did he choose missionary work because he knew she'd be against it?"

"No. The problem was Mother saw the priesthood as a way for Tony to bring honor to her and the family. But to Tony, the priesthood was an opportunity to serve. He took his vows seriously."

"Is he still in Africa?"

"He's dead."

Startled, Charlie Harrison said, "Oh. I'm sorry. I—"

"It's not a recent loss," she assured him. "Eleven years ago, when I was a high school senior, Tony was killed by terrorists, African revolutionaries. For a while Mother was inconsolable, but gradually her grief gave way to a . . . sick anger. She was actually angry with Tony for getting himself killed—as if he'd run away like my father before him. She made me feel I ought to make up for how Daddy and Tony had failed her. In my own grief and confusion and guilt . . . I said I wanted to become a nun, and Evelyn . . . Mother leaped at the idea. So, after high school, at her urging, I entered the convent . . . and it was a disaster . . ."

So much time had passed, yet she could still vividly remember the way the novice's habit had felt when she'd first worn it: the unexpected weight of it; the surprisingly coarse texture of the black fabric; the way she had continually caught the flowing skirts on doorknobs, furniture, and everything else that she passed, unaccustomed as she was to such voluminous clothes. Being trapped within that venerable uniform, sleeping within a narrow stone cubicle on a simple cot, day after day spent within the dreary and ascetically furnished confines of the convent—it all stayed with her in spite of her efforts to forget. Those Lost Years had been so similar to the suffocating life in the Victorian house in Pomona that, like thoughts of childhood, any recollection of her convent days was apt to put pressure on her chest and make breathing difficult.

"A nun?" Charlie Harrison said, unable to conceal his astonishment.

"A nun," she said.

Charlie tried to picture this vibrant, sensuous woman in a nun's habit. He simply couldn't do it. His imagination rebelled.

At least he understood why she projected an uncommon inner tranquility. Two years in a nunnery, two years of long daily sessions of meditation and prayer, two years isolated from the turbulent currents of everyday life were bound to have a lasting effect.

But none of this explained why she exerted such an instant, powerful attraction on him, or why he felt like a randy teenager in her company. That was still a mystery—a pleasant mystery, but a mystery nonetheless.

She said, "I hung on for two years, trying to convince myself I had a vocation in the sisterhood. No good. When I left the convent, Evelyn was crushed. Her entire family had failed her. Then, a couple of years later, when I got pregnant with Joey, Evelyn was horrified. Her only daughter, who might've been a nun, instead turned out to be a loose woman, an unwed mother. She piled the guilt on me, smothered me in it."

She looked down, paused for a moment to compose herself.

Charlie waited. He was as good at waiting as he was at listening.

Finally she said, "By that time, I was a fallen-away Catholic. I'd pretty much lost my religion . . . or been driven away from it. Didn't go to Mass any more. But I was still enough of a Catholic to abhor the idea of abortion. I kept Joey, and I've never regretted it."

"Your mother's never had a change of heart?"

"No. We speak to each other, but there's a vast gulf between us. And she won't have much to do with Joey."

"That's too bad."

"Ironically, almost from the day I got pregnant, my life turned around. Everything's gotten better and better since then. I was still carrying Joey when I went into business with Val Gardner and started Wine & Dine. By the time Joey was a year old, I was supporting my mother. I've had a lot of success, and it doesn't matter at all to her; it isn't good enough for her, not when I *could* have been a nun, and not when I *am* an unwed mother. She still heaps guilt on me each time I see her."

"Well, now I can understand why you're sensitive about it."

"So sensitive that . . . when all this started with the old woman yesterday . . . well, in the back of my mind I sort of wondered if maybe it was meant to be."

"What do you mean?"

"Maybe I'm meant to lose Joey. Maybe it's inevitable. Even . . . predestined."

"I don't follow you."

She fidgeted, managed to look angry and dispirited and frightened and embarrassed all at the same time. She cleared her throat and took a deep breath and said, "Well, uh, maybe . . . just maybe . . . it's God's way of punishing me for failing as a nun, for breaking my mother's heart, for drifting away from the Church after once having been so close to it."

"But that's . . ."

"Ridiculous?" she suggested.

"Well, yes."

She nodded. "I know."

"God isn't spiteful."

"I know," she said sheepishly. "It's silly. Illogical. Just plain dumb. Yet . . . it gnaws at me. Silly things can be true sometimes." She sighed and shook her head. "I'm proud of Joey, fiercely proud, but I'm not proud of being an unwed mother."

"You were going to tell me about the father . . . in case he might have something to do with this. What was his name?"

"He told me his name was Luke—actually Lucius—Under."

"Under what?"

"That was his last name. Under. Lucius Under, but he told me to call him Luke."

"Under. It's an unusual name."

"It's a *phony* name. He was probably thinking about getting me out of my underwear when he made it up," she said angrily, and then she blushed. Clearly, she was embarrassed by these personal revelations, but she forged ahead. "It happened aboard a cruise ship to Mexico, one of those Love Boat-type excursions." She laughed without humor when she spoke of love in this context. "After I left the sisterhood and spent a few years working as a waitress, that trip was the first treat I gave myself. I met a man only a few hours out of L.A. Very handsome . . . charming. Said his name was Luke. One thing led to another. He must have seen how vulnerable I was because he moved in like a shark. I was so different then, you see, so timid, very much the little ex-nun, a virgin, utterly inexperienced. We spent five days together on that ship, and I think most of it was in my cabin . . . in bed. A few weeks later, when I learned I was pregnant, I tried to contact him. I wasn't after support, you understand. I just thought he had a right to know about his son." Another sour laugh. "He'd given me an address and phone number, but they were phony. I considered tracking him down through the cruise line, but it would've been so . . . humiliating." She smiled ruefully. "Believe me, I've led a tame life ever since. Even before I knew I was pregnant, I felt . . . *soiled* by this man, that tawdry shipboard affair. I didn't want to feel like that again, so I've been . . . well, not exactly a sexual recluse . . . but cautious. Maybe that's the ex-nun in me. And it's definitely the ex-nun in me that feels I need to be punished, that maybe God will punish me through Joey."

He didn't know what to tell her. He was accustomed to providing physical, emotional, and mental comfort for his clients, but spiritual comfort wasn't something he knew how to supply.

"I'm a little crazy on the subject," she said. "And I'll probably drive *you* a little crazy with all my worrying. I'm always scared that Joey'll get sick or be hurt in an accident. I'm not just talking about ordinary motherly concern. Sometimes . . . I'm almost *obsessed* with worry about him. And then yesterday this old crone shows up and tells me that my little boy is evil, says he's got to die, comes prowling around the house in the middle of the night, kills our dog . . . Well, God, I mean, she seems so relentless, so inevitable."

"She's not," Charlie said.

"So now that you know a little something about Evelyn . . . my mother . . . do you still think she could be involved in this?"

"Not really. But it's still possible the old woman heard your mother talking about you, talking about Joey, and that's how *she* fixated on you."

"I think it was probably just pure chance. We were in the wrong place at the wrong time. If we hadn't been at the mall yesterday, if it had been some other woman with her little boy, that old hag would have fixated on them instead."

"I imagine you're right," he said.

He got up from the desk.

"But don't you worry about this crazy person," he said. "We'll find her."

He went to the window.

"We'll put a stop to this harassment," he said. "You'll see."

He looked out, over the top of the date palm. The white van was still parked across the street. The man in dark clothes was still leaning against the front fender, but he was no longer eating lunch. He was just waiting there, arms folded on his chest, ankles crossed, watching the front entrance of the building.

"Come here a minute," Charlie said.

Christine came to the window.

"Could that be the van that was parked beside your car at the mall?"

"Yeah. One like that."

"But could this be the *same* one?"

"You think I was followed this morning?"

"Would you have noticed if you had been?"

She frowned. "I was in such a state . . . so nervous, upset . . . I might not have realized I was being tailed, not if it was done with at least some circumspection."

"Then it could be the same van."

"Or just a coincidence."

"I don't believe in coincidences."

"But if it's the same van, if I *was* followed, then who's the man leaning against it?"

They were too far above the stranger to get a good look at his face. They could tell very little about him from this distance. He might have been old or young or middle-aged.

"Maybe he's the old woman's husband. Or her son," Charlie said.

"But if he's following me, he'd have to be as crazy as she is."

"Probably."

"The whole family can't be nuts."

"No law against it," he said.

He went to his desk and placed an in-house telephone call to Henry Rankin, one of his best men. He told Rankin about the van across the street. "I want you to walk past it, get the license number, and take a look at that guy over there, so you'll recognize him later. Glom anything else you can without being conspicuous about it. Be sure to come and go by the back entrance, and circle all the way around the block, so he won't have any idea where you came from."

"No sweat," Rankin said.

"Once you've got the number, get on the line to the DMV and find out who holds the registration."

"Yes, sir."

"Then you report to me."

"I'm leaving now."

Charlie hung up. He went to the window again.

Christine said, "Let's hope it's just a coincidence."

"On the contrary—let's hope it's the same van. It's the best lead we could've asked for."

"But if it is the same van, and if that guy's with it—"

"He's with it, all right."

"—then it's not just the old woman who's a threat to Joey. There're *two* of them."

"Or more."

"Huh?"

"Might be another one or two we don't know about."

A bird swooped past the window.

The palm fronds stirred in the unseasonably warm breeze.

Sunshine silvered the windows of the cars parked along the street.

At the van, the stranger waited.

Christine said, "What the *hell* is going on?"

CHAPTER 10

IN THE WINDOWLESS basement, eleven candles held the insistent shadows at bay.

The only noise was Mother Grace Spivey's increasingly labored breathing as she settled deeper into a trance. The eleven disciples made no sound whatsoever.

Kyle Barlowe was silent, too, and perfectly still even though he was uncomfortable. The oak chair on which he sat was too small for him. That wasn't the fault of the chair, which would have provided adequate seating for anyone else in the room. But Barlowe was so big that, to him, most furniture seemed to have been designed and constructed for use by dwarves. He liked deep-seated, over-stuffed easy chairs and old-fashioned wing-backed armchairs but only if the wings were angled wide enough to accommodate his broad shoulders. He liked king-sized beds, La-Z-Boy recliners, and ancient claw-foot bathtubs that were so large they didn't force him to sit with his legs drawn up as if he were a baby taking a bath in a basin. His apartment in Santa Ana was furnished to his dimensions, but when he wasn't at home he was usually uncomfortable to one degree or another.

However, as Mother Grace slipped deeper into her trance, Barlowe became increasingly eager to hear what message she would bring from the spirit world, and gradually he ceased to notice that he seemed to be perched on a child's playroom chair.

He adored Mother Grace. She had told him about the coming of Twilight, and he had believed every word. Twilight. Yes, it made sense. The world was long overdue for Twilight. By warning him that it was coming, by soliciting his help to prepare mankind for it, Mother Grace had given him an opportunity to redeem himself before it was too late. She had saved him, body and soul.

Until he met her, he had spent most of his twenty-nine years in the single-minded pursuit of self-destruction. He'd been a drunkard, a barroom brawler, a dope addict, a rapist, even a murderer. He'd been promiscuous, bedding at least one new woman every week, most of them junkies or prostitutes or both.

He'd contracted gonorrhea seven or eight times, syphilis twice, and it was amazing he hadn't gotten both diseases more often than that.

On rare occasions, he had been sober and clear-headed enough to be disgusted or even frightened by his lifestyle. But he had rationalized his behavior by telling himself that self-loathing and anti-social violence were simply the natural responses to the thoughtless—and sometimes intentional—cruelty with which most people treated him.

To the world at large, he was a freak, a lumbering giant with a Neanderthaloid face that would scare off a grizzly bear. Little children were usually frightened of him. People of all ages stared, some openly and some surreptitiously. A few even laughed at him when they thought he wasn't looking, joked about him behind his back. He usually pretended not to be aware of it—unless he was in a mood to break arms and kick ass. But he was *always* aware, and it hurt. Certain teenagers were the worst, especially certain girls, who giggled and laughed openly at him; now and then, when they were at a safe distance, they even taunted him. He had never been anything but an outsider, shunned and alone.

For many years, his violent and self-destructive life had been easy to justify to himself. Bitterness, hatred, and rage had seemed to be essential armor against society's cruelty. Without his reckless disregard for personal well-being and without his diligently nurtured lust for revenge, he would have felt defenseless. The world insisted on making an outcast of him, insisted on seeing him as either a seven-foot buffoon with a monkey's face or a threatening monster. Well, he wasn't a buffoon, but he didn't mind playing the monster for them; he didn't mind showing them just how viciously, shockingly monstrous he could be when he really put his mind to it. *They* had made him what he was. He wasn't responsible for his crimes. He was bad because they had *made* him bad. For most of his life, that's what he had told himself.

Until he met Mother Grace Spivey.

She showed him what a self-pitying wretch he was. She made him see that his justifications for sinful and self-indulgent behavior were pitifully flimsy. She taught him that an outcast could gain strength, courage, and even pride from his condition. She helped him see Satan within himself and helped him throw the devil out.

She helped him understand that his great strength and his singular talent for destruction were to be used only to bring terror and punishment to the enemies of God.

Now, sitting in front of Mother Grace as she drifted in a trance, Kyle Barlowe regarded her with unqualified adoration. He didn't see that her untrimmed mane of gray hair was frizzy, knotted, and slightly greasy; to him, in the flickering golden light, her shining hair was a holy nimbus framing her face, a halo. He didn't see that her clothes were badly wrinkled; he didn't notice the threads and lint and dandruff and food stains that decorated her. He saw only what he wanted to see, and he wanted to see salvation.

She groaned. Her eyelids fluttered but did not open.

Still sitting on the floor and holding their candles steady, the eleven disciples of the inner council became tense, but none of them spoke or made any sound that might break the fragile spell.

"Oh God," Mother Grace said as if she had just seen something awesome or perhaps terrifying. "Oh God oh God oh *God!*"

She winced. She shuddered. She licked her lips nervously.

Sweat broke out on her brow.

She was breathing harder than before. She gasped, open-mouthed, as if she were drowning. Then she drew breath through clenched teeth, with a cold hissing sound.

Barlowe waited patiently.

Mother Grace raised her hands, grabbed at the empty air. Her rings gleamed in the candlelight. Then her hands fell back into her lap, fluttered briefly like dying birds, and were still.

At last she spoke in a weak, strained, tremulous voice that was barely recognizable as her own. "Kill him."

"Who?" Barlowe asked.

"The boy."

The eleven disciples stirred, looked at one another meaningfully, and the movement of their candles caused shadows to twist and flap and shift all over the room.

"You mean Joey Scavello?" Barlowe asked.

"Yes. Kill him," Mother Grace said from a great distance. *"Now."*

For reasons that neither Barlowe nor Mother Grace understood, he was the only person who could communicate with her when she was in a trance. If others spoke to her, she wouldn't hear them. She was the only contact they had with the spirit world, the sole conduit for all messages from the other side, but it was Barlowe, through his careful and patient questioning, who made certain that those messages were always clear and fully detailed. More than anything else, it was this function, this precious gift that convinced him he was one of God's chosen people, just as Mother Grace said he was.

"Kill him . . . kill him," she chanted softly in a raspy voice.

"You're sure this boy is the one?" Barlowe asked.

"Yes."

"There's no doubt?"

"None."

"How can he be killed?"

Mother Grace's face was slack now. Lines had appeared in her usually creaseless skin. Her pale flesh hung like wrinkled, lifeless cloth.

"How can we destroy him?" Barlowe inquired again.

Her mouth hung open wide. Breath rattled in her throat. Saliva glistened at one corner of her lips, welled up, and drooled slowly onto her chin.

"Mother Grace?" Barlowe prodded.

Her voice was even fainter than before: "Kill him . . . any way you choose."

"With a gun, a knife? Fire?"

"Any weapon . . . will succeed . . . but only if . . . you act soon."

"How soon?"

"Time is running out. Day by day . . . he becomes . . . more powerful . . . less vulnerable."

"When we kill him, is there a ritual we must follow?" Barlowe asked.

"Only that . . . once dead . . . his heart . . ."

"What about his heart?"

"Must be . . . cut *out,*" she said, her voice becoming somewhat stronger, sharper.

"And then?"

"It will be black."

"His heart will be black?"

"As coal. And rotten. And you will see . . ."

She sat up straighter in her chair. The sweat from her brow was trickling down her face. Tiny beads of perspiration had popped out on her upper lip.

Like a pair of stricken moths, her white hands fluttered in her lap. Color returned to her face, although her eyes remained closed. She was no longer drooling, but spittle still shone on her chin.

"What will we see when we cut his heart out?" Barlowe asked.

"Worms," she said with disgust.

"In the boy's heart?"

"Yes. And beetles. Squirming."

A few of the disciples murmured to one another. It didn't matter. Nothing could disturb Mother Grace's trance now. She was thoroughly caught up in it, swept away by her visions.

Leaning forward in his chair, his big hands clamped on his meaty thighs, Barlowe said, "What must we do with the heart once we've cut it out of him?"

She chewed on her lip so hard he was afraid she would draw blood. She raised her spastic hands again and worked them in the empty air as if she could wring the answer from the ether.

Then: "Plunge the heart into . . ."

"Into what?" Barlowe asked.

"A bowl of holy water."

"From a church?"

"Yes. The water will remain cool . . . but the heart . . . will boil, turn to dark steam . . . and evaporate."

"And then we can be certain the boy is dead?"

"Yes. Dead. Forever dead. Unable to return through another incarnation."

"Then there's hope?" Barlowe asked, hardly daring to believe that it was so.

"Yes," she said thickly. "Hope."

"Praise God," Barlowe said.

"Praise God," the disciples said.

Mother Grace opened her eyes. She yawned, sighed, blinked, and looked around in confusion. "Where's this? What's wrong? I feel all clammy. Did I miss the six o'clock news? I mustn't miss the six o'clock news. I've got to know what Lucifer's people have been up to."

"It's only a few minutes till noon," Barlowe said. "The six o'clock news is hours away."

She stared at him with that familiar, blurry-eyed, muddle-headed look that always marked her return from a deep trance. "Who're you? Do I know you? I don't think I do."

"I'm Kyle, Mother Grace."

"Kyle?" she said as if she'd never heard of him. A suspicious glint entered her eyes.

"Just relax," he said. "Relax and think about it. You've had a vision. You'll remember it in a moment. It'll come back to you."

He held out both of his large, calloused hands. Sometimes, when she came out of a trance, she was so frightened and lost that she needed friendly contact. Usually, when she gripped his hands, she drew from his great reservoir of physical strength and soon regained her senses, as if he were a battery that she was tapping.

But today she pulled away from him. She frowned. She wiped at her spittle-damp chin. She looked around at the candles, at the disciples, clearly baffled by them. "God, I'm so thirsty," she said.

One of the disciples hurried to get her a drink.

She looked at Kyle. "What do you want from me? Why'd you bring me here?"

"It'll all come back to you," he said patiently, smiling reassuringly.

"I don't like this place," she said, her voice thin and querulous.

"It's your church."

"Church?"

"The basement of your church."

"It's dark," she whined.

"You're safe here."

She pouted as if she were a child, then scowled, then said, "I don't like the dark. I'm afraid of the dark." She hugged herself. "What've you got me here in the dark for?"

One of the disciples got up and turned on the lights.

The others blew out the candles.

"Church?" Mother Grace said again, looking at the paneled basement walls and at the exposed ceiling beams. She was trying hard to get a handle on her situation, but she was still disoriented.

There was nothing Barlowe could do to help her. Sometimes, she needed as long as ten minutes to shake off the confusion that always followed a journey into the spirit world.

She stood up.

Barlowe stood, too, towering over her.

She said, "I gotta pee real bad. *Real* bad." She grimaced and put one hand on her abdomen. "Isn't there anywhere to pee in this place? Huh? I got to *pee.*"

Barlowe motioned to Edna Vanoff, a short stout woman who was a member of the inner council, and Edna led Mother Grace to the lavatory at the far end of the basement. The old woman was unsteady; she leaned against Edna as she walked, and she continued to look around in bewilderment.

In a loud voice that carried the length of the room, Mother Grace said, "Oh, boy, I gotta pee so bad I think I'm gonna bust."

Barlowe sighed wearily and sat down on the too-small, too-hard wooden chair.

The most difficult thing for him—and for the other disciples—to understand and accept was Mother Grace's bizarre behavior after a vision. At times like this she didn't seem at all like a great spiritual leader. Instead, she seemed as if she were nothing more than a befuddled, crazy old woman. In ten minutes, at most, she would have regained her wits, as she always did; soon she would be the same intense, sharp-minded, clear-eyed woman who had converted him from a life of sin. Then no one would doubt her insight, power, and holiness; no one would question the truth of her exalted mission. However, just for these few disconcerting minutes, even though he had seen her in this dismaying condition many times before and knew it wouldn't last, Barlowe nevertheless felt uneasy, sick with uncertainty.

He doubted her.

And hated himself for doubting.

He supposed that God put Mother Grace through these sorry, undignified spells of disorientation for the very purpose of testing the faith of her followers. It was God's way of making certain that only Mother Grace's most devoted disciples remained with her, thereby insuring a strong church during the difficult days ahead. Yet, every time she was like this, Barlowe was badly shaken by the way she looked and acted.

He glanced at the members of the inner council, who were still sitting on the floor. All of them looked troubled, and all of them were praying. He figured they were praying for the strength not to doubt Mother Grace the way he was doubting her. He closed his eyes and began to pray, too.

They were going to need all the strength, faith, and confidence they could find within themselves, for killing the boy wasn't going to be easy. He wasn't an ordinary child. Mother Grace had adamantly made that clear. He would possess awesome powers of his own, and perhaps he would even be able to destroy them the moment they dared lift a hand against him. But for the sake of all mankind, they had to try to kill him.

Barlowe hoped Mother Grace would permit him to strike the mortal blow. Even if it meant his own death, he wanted to be the one who actually drew the boy's blood because whoever killed the boy (or died in the attempt) was assured of a place in Heaven, close to the throne of God. Barlowe was convinced that this was true. If he used his tremendous physical strength and his pent-up rage to strike out at this evil child, he would be making amends for all the times he had harmed the innocent in the days before Mother Grace had converted him.

Sitting on the hard oak chair, eyes closed, praying, he slowly curled his big hands into fists. He began to breathe faster. Eagerness was apparent in the hunch of his shoulders and in the bunching of muscles in his neck and jaws. Tremors passed through him. He was impatient to do God's work.

CHAPTER 11

LESS THAN TWENTY minutes after he had left, Henry Rankin returned to Charlie Harrison's office with the Department of Motor Vehicles' report on the white van's license number.

Rankin was a small man, five-three, slender, with an athletic grace and bearing. Christine wondered if he had ever been a jockey. He was well dressed in a pair of black Bally loafers, a light gray suit, white shirt, and a blue knit tie, with a blue display handkerchief carefully folded in the breast pocket of his jacket. He didn't look anything like Christine's conception of a private investigator.

After Rankin was introduced to Christine, he handed Charlie a sheet of paper and said, "According to the DMV, the van belongs to a printing company called The True Word."

Come to think of it, Charlie Harrison didn't look much like a private investigator, either. She expected a PI to be tall. Charlie wasn't short like Henry Rankin, but he was only about five-ten or five-eleven. She expected a PI to be built like a truck, to look as if he could ram through a brick wall. Charlie was lean, and although he looked as if he could take care of himself well enough, he would never ram through a wall, brick or otherwise. She expected a PI to seem at least a little bit dangerous, with a violent aspect to his eyes and perhaps a tight-lipped, cruel mouth. Charlie appeared to be intelligent, efficient, capable—but not dangerous. He had an unremarkable, though generally handsome face framed by thick blond hair that was neatly combed. His eyes were his best features, gray-green, clear, direct; they were warm, friendly eyes, but there was no violence in them, at least none that she could detect.

In spite of the fact that neither Charlie nor Rankin looked like Magnum or Sam Spade or Philip Marlowe, Christine sensed she had come to the right place. Charlie Harrison was friendly, self-possessed, plain-spoken. He walked, turned, and performed every task with an unusual economy of motion, and his gestures, too, were neat and precise. He projected an aura of competence and trustworthiness. She suspected that he seldom, if ever, failed to do his job well. He made her feel secure.

Few people had that effect on her. Damned few. Especially men. In the past, when she had relied upon men, her faith had not always—or even usually— been well placed. However, instinct told her that Charlie Harrison was differ- ent from most other men and that she would not regret placing her trust in him.

Charlie looked up from the paper Rankin had given him. "The True Word, huh? Anything on it in our files?"

"Nothing."

Charlie looked at Christine. "You ever hear of them?"

"No."

"You ever have any brochures or stationery or anything printed for that gourmet shop of yours?"

"Sure. But that's not the printer we use."

"Okay," Charlie said, "we'll have to find out who owns the company, try to get a list of their employees, start checking everyone out."

"Can do," Henry Rankin said.

To Christine, Charlie said, "You might have to talk with your mother about this, Ms. Scavello."

"I'd rather not," she said. "Not unless it becomes absolutely necessary."

"Well . . . all right. But it probably *will* become necessary. For now . . . you might as well go on to work. It'll take us awhile to dig into this."

"What about Joey?"

"He can stay here with me this afternoon," Charlie said. "I want to see what'll happen if you leave without the boy. Will the guy in the van follow you —or will he wait for Joey to come out? Which of you is he most interested in?"

He'll wait for Joey, Christine thought grimly. Because it's Joey he wants to kill.

Sherry Ordway, the receptionist at Klemet-Harrison, wondered if she and Ted, her husband, had made a mistake. Six years ago, after three years of marriage, they had decided they didn't really want children, and Ted had had a vasectomy. With no children, they could afford a better house and better furniture and a nicer car, and they were free to travel, and the evenings were always peaceful and perfect for curling up with a book—or with each other. Most of their friends were tied down with families, and every time Sherry and Ted saw someone else's child being rude or downright malevolent, they con- gratulated themselves on the wisdom of avoiding parenthood. They relished their freedom, and Sherry never regretted remaining childless. Until now. As she answered the telephone and typed letters and did filing, she watched Joey Scavello, and she began to wish (just a little) that he was hers.

He was such a good kid. He sat in one of the armchairs in the waiting area, dwarfed by it, his feet off the floor. He spoke when spoken to, but he didn't interrupt anyone or call attention to himself. He leafed through some of the magazines, looking at pictures, and he hummed softly to himself, and he was just about the cutest thing she'd ever seen.

She had just finished typing a letter and had been surreptitiously watching the boy as, with much frowning and tongue-biting, he checked the knots in the laces of his sneakers and retied one of them. She was about to ask him if he would like another of her butterscotch Life Savers when the telephone rang.

"Klemet-Harrison," Sherry said.

A woman said, "Is Joey Scavello there? He's just a little boy, six years old. You can't miss him if he's there; he's such a charmer."

Surprised that anyone would be calling the boy, Sherry hesitated.

"This is his grandmother," the woman said. "Christine told me she was bringing Joey to your office."

"Oh. His grandmother. Why, yes, of course, they're here right now. Mrs. Scavello is in Mr. Harrison's office at the moment. She's not available, but I'm sure—"

"Well, it's Joey I really want to talk to. Is he in with Mr. Harrison, too?"

"No. He's right here with me."

"Do you think I could speak to him for a moment?" the woman said. "If it's not too much trouble."

"Oh, it's no trouble—"

"I won't tie up your line for long."

"Sure. Just a minute," Sherry said. She held the phone away from her face and said, "Joey? It's for you. Your grandmother."

"Grandma?" he said, and seemed to be amazed.

He came to the desk. Sherry gave him the phone, and he said hello, but didn't say anything else. He went stiff, his small hand clenching the handset so tightly that his knuckles looked as if they would pierce the skin that sheathed them. He stood there, wide-eyed, listening. The blood drained out of his face. His eyes filled with tears. Suddenly, with a gasp and shudder, he slammed the phone down.

Sherry jumped in surprise. "Joey? What's wrong?"

His mouth became soft and tremulous.

"Joey?"

"It was . . . h-her."

"Your grandmother."

"No. The w-witch."

"Witch?"

"She said . . . she's gonna . . . c-c-cut my heart out."

Charlie sent Joey into his office with Christine, closed the door after them, and remained in the lounge to question Sherry.

She looked distraught. "I shouldn't have let her talk to him. I didn't realize—"

"It wasn't your fault," Henry Rankin said.

"Of course it wasn't," Charlie told her.

"What sort of woman—"

"That's what we're trying to find out," Charlie said. "I want you to think about the call and answer a few questions."

"There wasn't much said."

"She claimed to be his grandmother?"

"Yes."

"She said she was Mrs. Scavello?"

"Well . . . no. She didn't give her name. But she knew he was here with his mother, and I never suspected . . . I mean, well, she *sounded* like a grandmother."

"Exactly what did she sound like?" Henry asked.

"God, I don't know . . . a very pleasant voice," Sherry said.

"She speak with an accent?" Charlie asked.

"No."

"Doesn't have to've been a real obvious accent to be of help to us," Henry said. "Almost everyone speaks with at least a mild accent of some kind."

"Well, if it was there, I didn't notice it," Sherry said.

"Did you hear anything in the background?" Charlie asked.

"Like what?"

"Any noise of any kind?"

"No."

"If she was calling from an outdoor pay phone, for instance, there would've been traffic noises, street noises of some kind."

"There wasn't anything like that."

"Any noises that might help us figure the kind of place she *was* calling from?"

"No. Just her voice," Sherry said. "She sounded so *nice.*"

CHAPTER 12

AFTER HER VISION, Mother Grace dismissed all her disciples except Kyle Barlowe and Edna Vanoff. Then, using the phone in the church basement, she placed a call to the detective agency where Joey Scavello and his mother had gone, and she spoke briefly with the boy. Kyle wasn't sure he saw the sense of it, but Mother Grace was pleased.

"Killing him isn't sufficient," she said. "We must terrify and demoralize him, too. Through the boy, we'll bring fear and despair to Satan himself. We'll make the devil understand, at last, that the Good Lord will never permit him to rule the earth, and then he'll finally abandon his schemes and hopes of glory."

Kyle loved to hear her talk like that. When he listened to Mother Grace, he knew that he was a vital part of the most important events in the history of the world. Awe and humility made his knees weak.

Grace led Kyle and Edna to the far end of the basement, where a wood-paneled wall contained a cleverly concealed door. Beyond the door lay a room measuring twenty by twenty-six feet. It was full of guns.

Early in her mission, Mother Grace had received a vision in which she had been warned that, when Twilight came, she must be prepared to defend herself with more than just prayer. She had taken the vision very seriously indeed. This was not the church's only armory.

Kyle had been here many times before. He enjoyed the coolness of the room, the vague scent of gun oil. Most of all he took pleasure from the realization that terrible destruction waited quietly on these shelves, like a malevolent genie in a bottle, needing only a hand to pull the cork.

Kyle liked guns. He liked to turn a gun over and over in his enormous hands, sensing the power in it the way a blind man sensed the meaning in lines of Braille.

Sometimes, when his sleep was particularly deep and dark, he dreamed about holding a large gun in both hands and pointing it at people. It was a .357 Magnum, with a bore that seemed as big as a cannon's, and when it roared it was like the voice of a dragon. Each time it bucked in his hands, it gave him a jolt of intense pleasure.

For a while he had worried about these night-fantasies because he had thought it meant the devil hadn't been driven out of him, after all. But he came to see that the people in the dreams were God's enemies and that it was *good* for him to fantasize their destruction. Kyle was destined to be an instrument of divine justice. Grace had told him so.

Now, in the armory, Mother Grace went to the shelves along the wall to the left of the door. She took down a box, opened it, removed the plastic-wrapped revolver that lay within, and put the weapon on a work table. The gun she had chosen was a Smith & Wesson .38 Chiefs Special, a snub-barreled piece that packed a lot of wallop. She took another one from the shelf, removed it from its box, and placed it beside the first.

Edna Vanoff removed the weapons from their plastic wrappings.

Before the day was done, the boy would be dead, and it might be one of these two weapons that destroyed him.

Mother Grace removed a Remington 20-gauge shotgun from one of the shelves and brought it to the work table.

Kyle's excitement grew.

CHAPTER 13

JOEY SAT IN Charlie's chair, behind the big desk, sipping Coca-Cola that Charlie had poured for him.

Christine was in the client's chair once more. She was shaken. A couple of times, Charlie saw her put her fingernail between her teeth and almost bite it before she realized she'd be biting acrylic.

He was upset that they had been reached and disturbed *here,* in his offices. They had come to him for help, for protection, and now both of them were frightened again.

Sitting on the edge of his desk, looking at Joey, he said, "If you don't want to talk about the phone call, I'll understand. But I'd really like to ask you some questions."

To his mother, Joey said, "I thought we were going to hire Magnum."

Christine said, "Honey, you've forgotten that Magnum's in Hawaii."

"Oh, yeah. Jeez, that's right," the boy said. He looked troubled. "Magnum would've been the best one to help us."

For a moment Charlie didn't know what the boy was talking about, and then he remembered the television show, and he smiled.

Joey took a long drink of his Coke, studying Charlie over the rim of the glass. Finally he said, "I guess you'll be okay."

Charlie almost laughed. "You won't be sorry you came to us, Joey. Now . . . what did the woman on the phone say to you?"

"She said . . . 'You can't hide from me.' "

Charlie heard fear ooze into the boy's voice, and he quickly said, "Well, she's wrong about that. If we have to hide you from her, we can. Don't you worry about that. What else did she say?"

"She said she knew what I was."

"What do you think she meant by that?"

The boy looked baffled. "I don't know."

"What else did she say?"

"She said . . . she'd cut my heart out."

A strangled sound came from Christine. She stood, nervously clutching her purse. "I think I ought to take Joey . . . away somewhere."

"Maybe eventually," Charlie said soothingly. "But not just yet."

"I think now's the time. Before . . . anything happens. We could go to San Francisco. Or farther. I've never been to the Caribbean. This is a good time of the year for the Caribbean, isn't it?"

"Give me at least twenty-four hours," Charlie said.

"Yeah? Twenty-four hours? And what if that hag catches up with us? No. We should leave today."

"And how long do you intend to stay away?" Charlie asked. "A week? A month? A year?"

"Two weeks should be long enough. You'll find her in two weeks."

"Not necessarily."

"Then how long?"

Understanding and sympathizing with Christine's concern, wanting to be gentle with her, knowing that he had to be blunt instead, Charlie said, "Clearly, she's got some sort of fixation on Joey, some sort of obsession about him. It's Joey that keeps her motor running, so to speak. Without him around, she might pull in her horns. She might evaporate on us. We might never find her if Joey isn't here to bring her out. Do you intend to go on vacation *forever?*"

"Are you saying you intend to use my son as *bait?*"

"No. Not exactly. We'd never put him right in the jaws of a trap. We'll use him more as a lure."

"That's outrageous!"

"But it's the only way we'll get her. If he's not around, there'll be no reason for her to show herself." He went to Christine and put a hand on her shoulder. "He'll be guarded at all times. He'll be safe."

"Like hell he will."

"I swear to you—"

"You've already got the van's license number," she said.

"That might not be enough. It might not lead anywhere."

"You've got the name of the company that owns it. The True Word."

"That might not be enough, either. And if it's not enough, if it doesn't lead us anywhere, then Joey has to be around so the old woman has a reason to risk exposing herself."

"Seems like *we're* the ones taking the risks."

"Trust me," he said softly.

She met his eyes.

He said, "Sit down. Come on. Give me a chance. Later, if I see any indication—the *slightest* indication—that we might not be able to handle the situation, I'll send you and Joey out of town for a while. But please . . . not just yet."

She looked past him at her son, who had put down his glass of Coke and was sitting on the edge of Charlie's big chair. She seemed to realize that her fear was directly transmitted to the boy, and she sat down and composed herself as Charlie requested.

He sat on the edge of his desk again. "Joey, don't worry about the witch. I know just how to deal with witches. Leave the worrying to me. Now . . . you were on the phone, and she said she wanted to cut . . . cut you. What did she say after that?"

The boy screwed up his face, trying to remember. "Not much . . . just something about some judges."

"Judges?"

"Yeah. She said something like . . . God wants her to bring some judge men to me."

"Judgment?" Charlie asked.

"Yeah," the boy said. "She said she was bringing these judge men to see me. She said God wasn't gonna let me escape from her." He looked at his mother. "Why does God want that old witch to get me?"

"He doesn't want her to get you, honey. She was lying. She's crazy. God has nothing to do with this."

Frowning, Charlie said, "Maybe, in a roundabout way, He does. When Henry said the van was owned by a printing company called The True Word, I wondered if maybe it was a religious printing company. 'The True Word'— meaning the holy word, scripture, the *Bible*. Maybe what we've got on our hands here is a religious fanatic."

"Or two," she said, glancing at the window, obviously remembering the man with the white van.

Or more than two, Charlie thought uneasily.

During the past couple of decades, when it had become fashionable to distrust and disparage all of society's institutions (as if there had been no wisdom at all in the creation of them), a lot of religious cults had sprung up, eager to fill the power vacuum. Some of them were honest, earnest off-shoots of long-established religions, and some were crackpot organizations established for the benefit of their founders, to enrich them, or to spread their gospels of madness and violence and bigotry. California was more tolerant of unusual and controversial views than any other state in the union; therefore, California was home to more cults, both good and bad, than anywhere else. It wouldn't be surprising if, for some bizarre reason, one of these cults had gone looking for scapegoats or sacrifices and had settled on an innocent six-year-old boy. Crazy, yes, but not particularly surprising.

Charlie hoped that wasn't the explanation for what had happened to the Scavellos. No one was harder to deal with than a religious fanatic on a holy mission.

Then, as Charlie turned away from Christine, as he looked back at the boy, something odd happened. Something frightening.

For a moment the boy's smooth young skin seemed to become translucent, then almost entirely transparent. Incredibly, the skull was visible beneath the skin. Charlie could see hollow dark eye sockets glaring at him. Worms writhing deep in those calcimine pits. A bony smile. Gaping black holes where the nose should have been. Joey's face was still there, though it was like a vague photograph superimposed over the skeletal countenance. A presentiment of death.

Shocked, Charlie stood and coughed.

The brief vision left him almost as soon as it came, shimmering before him for no more than a split second.

And he told himself it was his imagination, though nothing like this had ever happened to him before.

An icy snake of fear uncoiled in his stomach.

Just imagination. Not a vision. There *weren't* such things as visions. Charlie didn't believe in the supernatural, in psychic phenomena or any of that clap-trap. He was a *sensible* man and prided himself on his solid, dependable nature.

To cover his surprise and fear, but also to put the grisly sight out of mind, he said, "Uh, okay then, I think now you should just go on to work, Christine. As much as you can, try to carry on as if this were an ordinary day. I know it won't be easy. But you've got to get on with your business and your life while we're sorting this out for you. Henry Rankin will go with you. I've already talked to him about it."

"You mean . . . he'll come along as my bodyguard?"

"I know he's not a big man," Charlie said, "but he's a martial arts expert, and he carries a gun, and if I had to choose any man from among my staff to entrust with my own life, I think it would be Henry."

"I'm sure he's competent. But I don't really need a bodyguard. I mean, it's *Joey* the woman wants."

"And getting at you is an indirect way of getting at him," Charlie said. "Henry goes with you."

"What about me?" Joey said. "Am I going to pre-school?" He looked at his Mickey Mouse watch. "I'm already late."

"No pre-school today," Charlie said. "You'll stay with me."

"Yeah? Am I gonna help you do some investigating?"

Charlie smiled. "Sure. I could use a bright young assistant."

"Wow! You hear him, Mom? I'm gonna be like Magnum."

Christine forced a smile, and even though it was false it made her face lovelier than ever. Charlie longed to see a real, warm, genuine smile take possession of her.

She kissed her son goodbye, and Charlie could see that it was difficult, even painful, for her to leave the boy under these circumstances.

He walked her to the door while, behind them, Joey picked up his Coke again.

She said, "Should I come back here after I leave work?"

"No. We'll bring him to the store at . . . what . . . five o'clock?"

"That'll be fine."

"Then you and Joey'll go home with bodyguards. They'll stay the night. Two of them in the house with you. And I'll probably have a man stationed out on the street, watching for people who don't belong in the neighborhood."

Charlie opened the door between his office and the reception lounge, but suddenly Joey called out to his mother, and she turned back.

"What about the dog?" the boy said, getting up, coming out from around Charlie's desk.

"We'll look for one tomorrow, honey."

During the past few minutes, the boy had not been visibly frightened. Now, he became tense and uneasy again. "Today," he said. "You promised. You said we'd get another dog today."

"Honey—"

"I got to have a dog today, before it gets dark," the boy said plaintively. "I just got to, Mom. I got to."

"I can take him to buy a dog," Charlie said.

"You have work to do," she said.

"This is not a hole-in-the-wall operation, dear lady. I've got a staff to do the leg work. My job, for the time being, is to look after Joey, and if getting him a dog is part of looking after him, then I'll take him to get a dog. No problem. Is there any pet store you'd prefer?"

"We got Brandy at the pound," Joey said. "Rescued him from certain death."

"Did you?" Charlie said, amused.

"Yeah. They was gonna put Brandy to sleep. Only it wasn't just sleep, see. What it was . . . well, it was sleep, yeah, but it was a whole lot worse than just sleep."

"I can take him to the pound," Charlie told Christine.

"We'll rescue another one!" Joey said.

"If it's not too much trouble," Christine said.

"Sounds like fun," Charlie said.

She looked at him with evident gratitude, and he winked at her, and she smiled a halfway *real* smile this time, and Charlie wanted to kiss her, but he didn't.

"Not a German shepherd," Christine said. "They sort of scare me. Not a boxer either."

"What about a Great Dane?" Charlie asked, teasing her. "Or maybe a St. Bernard or a Doberman?"

"Yeah!" Joey said excitedly. "A Doberman!"

"How about a big, fierce Alsatian with three-inch-long teeth?" Charlie said.

"You're incorrigible," Christine said, but she smiled again, and it was that smile he was trying so hard to elicit.

"We'll get a good dog," Charlie said. "Don't worry. Trust me."

"Maybe I'll call him Pluto," Joey said.

Charlie looked askance. "Why would you want to call me Pluto?"

Joey giggled. "Not *you*. The new dog."

"Pluto," Charlie said, mulling it over. "Not bad."

For that one shining moment, it seemed as if all was right with the world. It seemed there was no such thing as death. And for the first time, Charlie had the feeling that the three of them somehow *belonged* together, that their destinies were linked, that they had more of a future together than just their investigator-client relationship. It was a nice, warm feeling. Too bad it couldn't last.

CHAPTER 14

Two REVOLVERS AND two shotguns lay on the work table in the armory. All four weapons had been loaded. Boxes of spare ammunition stood beside the firearms.

Mother Grace had sent Edna Vanoff on another errand. She and Kyle were alone.

Kyle picked up the shotgun. "I'll lead the attack."

"No," Mother Grace said.

"No? But you've always told me I'd be allowed to—"

"The boy won't be easy to kill," Mother Grace said.

"So?"

"He isn't fully human. Demonic blood flows in his veins."

"He doesn't frighten me," Kyle said.

"He should. His powers are great and growing every day."

"But I've got the power of Almighty God behind me."

"Nevertheless, this first attack will almost surely fail."

"I'm prepared to die," he said.

"I know, dear boy. I know. But I mustn't risk losing you at the very beginning of this battle. You're too valuable. You're my link between this world and the spirit realm."

"I'm also the hammer," he said petulantly.

"I'm aware of your strength."

She took the shotgun away from him, returned it to the table.

He felt a terrible need to strike out at something—as long as he was striking out in the name of God, of course. He no longer needed to wreak pain and destruction on the innocent merely for the satisfaction of it. Those days were gone forever. But he longed to be a soldier for God. His chest tightened and his stomach twisted with his need.

He had been looking forward to the attack tonight. Anticipation had rubbed his nerves raw. "The hammer of God," he reminded her.

"And in time you'll be used," she assured him.

"When?"

"When there's a real chance of destroying the child."

"Huh? If there's no chance of destroying him tonight, then why go after the little bastard? Why not wait?"

"Because, if we're lucky, we might at least hurt him, wound him," Mother Grace said. "And that will shake his confidence. Right now, the little beast believes that we can never really cause him harm. If he begins to think he's vulnerable, then he'll *become* more vulnerable. We must first weaken his self-confidence. Do you see?"

Reluctantly, Kyle nodded.

"And if we're very fortunate," Grace said, "if God is with us and the devil is off guard, we might be able to kill the mother. Then the boy will be alone. The dog is already gone. If the mother is removed, as well, the boy will have no one, and his confidence will collapse, and he'll become extremely vulnerable."

"Then let me kill the mother," Kyle pleaded.

She smiled at him and shook her head. "Dear boy, when God wants you to be His hammer, I'll tell you. Until then, you must be patient."

Charlie stood at the window with a pair of high-power binoculars that doubled as a camera. He focused on the man standing by the white van on the street below.

The stranger was about six feet tall, thin, pale, with a tightly compressed mouth, a narrow nose, and thick dark eyebrows that grew together in the center of his face. He was an intense-looking man, and he couldn't keep his hands still. One hand tugged at his shirt collar. The other hand smoothed his hair, then pinched one ear lobe. Scratched his chin. Picked lint from his jacket. Smoothed his hair again. He would never pass for an ordinary workman taking a leisurely lunch break.

Charlie snapped several pictures of him.

When Christine Scavello and Henry drove away in the woman's gray Firebird, the watcher almost got in the van to follow them. But he hesitated, looked around, puzzled, and finally decided to stay where he was.

Joey stood beside Charlie. He was just tall enough to see out the window. "He's waiting for me, huh?"

"Looks that way."

"Why don't we go out there and shoot him?" Joey asked.

Charlie laughed. "Can't go around shooting people. Not in California, anyway. Maybe if this was *New York* . . ."

"But you're a private eye," Joey said. "Don't you have a license to kill?"

"That's James Bond."

"You know him, too?" Joey asked.

"Not really. But I know his brother," Charlie said.

"Yeah? I never heard of his brother. What's his name?"

"Municipal Bond," Charlie said.

"That's a weird name," Joey said, not getting the joke.

He's only six, Charlie reminded himself. Sometimes the kid behaved as if he were a few years older, and he expressed himself with clarity that you didn't expect of a pre-schooler.

The boy looked out the window again. For a moment he was silent as Charlie snapped two final photographs of the man at the white van, and then he said, "I don't see why we can't shoot him. He'd shoot me if he got the chance."

"Oh, I don't think he'd really go that far," Charlie said, trying to discourage the boy from frightening himself.

But with an equanimity and a steadiness of voice that, given the circumstances, were beyond his years, Joey said, "Oh, yeah. He would. He'd shoot me if he could get away with it. He'd shoot me and cut my heart out, that's what he'd do."

Five stories below, the watcher smoothed his hair with one pale, long-fingered hand.

PART TWO

ﾟﾟﾟﾟ

THE ATTACK

Is the end of the world a-coming?
Is that the devil they hear humming?
Are those doomsday bells a-ringing?
Is that the Devil they hear singing?

Or are their dark fears exaggerated?
Are these doom-criers addlepated?

Those who fear the coming of all Hells
are those who should be feared themselves.
— *The Book of Counted Sorrows*

A fanatic does what he thinks the Lord
would do if He knew the facts of the case.
—Finley Peter Dunne

CHAPTER 15

WINE & DINE was located in an attractive, upscale, brick-and-timber shopping center, half a block from Newport Beach's yacht harbor. Even on a Monday, the shop was busy, with a steady flow of customers through the imported foods section and almost as many in the wine department. At any one time there were at least two or three people browsing in the cookware department, inspecting the pots and pans, imported ice cream machines, food processors, and other kitchen tools. During the afternoon, in addition to food and wine and small culinary implements, Christine and Val and their clerk, Tammy, sold two top-of-the-line pasta makers, an expensive set of cutlery, one Cuisinart, a beautiful copper buffet warmer with three serving compartments, and an ornate copper and brass cappuccino machine that was priced at nine hundred dollars.

Although the shop had done uncannily well almost from the day they had opened the doors, and although it had actually become profitable in the third week of operation (an unheard-of situation for a new business), Christine was still surprised and delighted every day that the cash register kept ringing. Six and a half years of dependable profitability had still not made her blasé about success.

The hustle and bustle of Wine & Dine made Monday afternoon pass a lot faster than she had thought possible when, reluctantly, she had left Joey with

Charlie Harrison. The crazy old woman was in the back of her mind, of course. Several times she thought of Brandy's decapitated corpse on the back porch, and she felt weak and dry-mouthed for a few minutes. And Henry Rankin was ever-present, helping bag purchases, putting price tags on some new merchandise, assisting them wherever he could, pretending to be an employee, but surreptitiously keeping an eye on the customers, prepared to tackle one of them if Christine appeared to be threatened. Nevertheless, in spite of the bloody images of the dog that haunted her, and in spite of the constant reminder of danger that Henry's presence provoked, the hours flitted past, and it was a relief to be kept busy.

Val Gardner was a help, too. With some misgivings, Christine had told her the situation, although she had expected Val to pester her with questions all day long and drive her half crazy by five o'clock. Val seemed to thrive on the smallest adversity, claiming to be "traumatized" by even such minor setbacks as a leaky bathroom faucet or a run in her stockings. Val found drama and even tragedy in a head cold or a broken fingernail, but she was never really upset or depressed by any of the little twists of fate that brought on her histrionics; she just enjoyed being the heroine of her own soap opera, dramatizing her life, making it more colorful for herself. And if she was temporarily without a trauma to brighten her day, she could make do with the problems of her friends, taking them upon herself as if she were a combination of Dear Abby and Atlas with the world on her shoulders. But she was a well-meaning woman, with a good sense of humor, honest, hardworking. And now, somewhat to Christine's surprise, Val was sensitive enough to avoid dwelling on the crazy woman and the threats on Joey's life; she held her tongue even though she must have been eaten up by a thousand nibbling questions.

At five o'clock, Charlie Harrison showed up with Joey and two guys who looked as if they were on their way to a casting call for a new Hercules movie. They were the bodyguards who would be on duty until another team replaced them at midnight.

The first was Pete Lockburn, who was six-three, with curly blond hair, a solemn face, and watchful eyes. The shoulders of his suit jacket looked as if they were padded out with a couple of railroad ties, but it was only Pete himself under there. The other was Frank Reuther, a black man, every bit as formidable as Lockburn, handsome, with the biggest hands Christine had ever seen. Both Lockburn and Reuther were neatly dressed in suits and ties, and both were soft-spoken and polite, yet you would somehow never mistake them for Baptist ministers or advertising account executives. They looked as if they wrestled grizzly bears and broke full-grown oak trees in half just to keep in shape.

Val stared at them, amazed, and a new look of concern took possession of her face when she turned to Christine. "Oh, Chris, baby, listen, I guess maybe it didn't really hit me until your army here showed up. I mean, this is really *serious,* isn't it?"

"Really serious," Christine agreed.

The two men Grace chose for the mission were Pat O'Hara and Kevin Baumberg. O'Hara was a twenty-four-year-old Irishman, husky, slightly overweight, a convert from Catholicism. Baumberg was a short, stocky man with a thick black beard. He had walked away from a lifetime of Judaism—as well as from a family and a prosperous jewelry store—to help Mother Grace prepare the world for Twilight, the coming of the Antichrist. She selected them for the assassination attempt because they symbolized two important things: the universal appeal of her message, and the brotherhood of all good men, which was the only power that had a chance of delaying or preventing the end of the world.

A few minutes after five o'clock, O'Hara and Baumberg carried a couple of laundry bags out of the church basement in Anaheim. They climbed a set of concrete steps into a macadam parking lot.

The early winter night, sailing across the sky like a vast black armada, had already driven most of the light toward the western horizon. A few threatening clouds had come in from the sea, and the air was cool and damp.

O'Hara and Baumberg put the laundry bags into the trunk of a white Chrysler sedan that belonged to the church. The bags contained two shotguns, two revolvers, and ammunition that had been blessed by Mother Grace.

Tense, frightened, preoccupied with thoughts of mortality, neither man felt like talking. In silence, they drove out of the parking lot and into the street, where a newborn wind suddenly stirred the curbside trees and blew dry leaves along the gutters.

CHAPTER 16

As TAMMY DEALT with the last customers of the day, Charlie said to Christine, "Any problems? Anybody cause any trouble?"

"No. It was peaceful."

Henry Rankin said, "What did you dig up on The True Word?"

"It'll take too long to tell you," Charlie said. "I want to take Christine and Joey home, make sure their house is secure, get them settled in for the night. But I brought your car. It's outside, and on the front seat there's a copy of the file to date. You can read it later and get caught up."

"You need me any more tonight?" Henry asked.

"Nope," Charlie said.

And Joey said, "Mom, come on. Come out to the car. I want to show you something really neat."

"In a second, honey."

Although both Lockburn and Reuther were, at least physically, the kind of men about whom most women fantasized, Val Gardner hardly gave either of them a second glance. She zeroed in on Charlie as soon as he was finished talking to Henry Rankin, and she turned up her charm until it was as hot as a gas flame.

"I've always wanted to meet a detective," Val said breathlessly. "It must be such an exciting life."

"Actually, it's usually boring," Charlie said. "Most of our work is research or stakeout, hour after hour of boredom."

"But once in a while . . . ," Val said teasingly.

"Well, sure, now and then there's some fireworks."

"I'll bet those are the moments you *live* for," Val said.

"No one looks forward to being shot at or punched in the face by the husband in a nasty divorce case."

"You're just being modest," Val said, shaking a finger at him, winking as cute as she knew how.

And she sure knows how, Christine thought. Val was an extremely attractive woman, with auburn hair, luminous green eyes, and a striking figure. Christine envied her lush good looks. Although a few men had told Christine that she was beautiful, she never really believed those who paid the compliment. She had never been attractive in her mother's eyes; in fact, her mother had referred to her as a "plain" child, and although she knew her mother's standards were absurdly high and that her mother's opinions were not always rational or fair, Christine still had an image of herself as a *somewhat* pretty woman, in the most modest sense, more suited to being a nun than a siren. Sometimes, when Val was dressed in her finest and being coquettish, Christine felt like a boy beside her.

To Charlie, Val said, "I'll bet you're the kind of man who needs a little danger in his life to spice it up, the kind of man who knows how to *deal* with danger."

"You're romanticizing me, I'm afraid," Charlie said.

But Christine could see that he enjoyed Val's attentions.

Joey said, "Mom, please, come on. Come out to the car. We got a dog. A real beauty. Come see him."

"From the pound?" Christine asked Charlie, cutting in on Val's game.

"Yeah," he said. "I tried to get Joey to go for a hundred-and-forty-pound mastiff named Killer, but he wouldn't listen to me."

Christine grinned.

"Come on and see him, Mom," Joey said. *"Please."* He took her hand and pulled on it, urging her toward the door.

"Do you mind closing up by yourself, Val?" Christine asked.

"I'm not by myself. I've got Tammy," Val said. "You go on home." She looked wistfully at Charlie, obviously wishing she had more time to work on him. Then, to Christine: "And if you don't want to come in tomorrow, don't worry about it."

"Oh," Christine said, "I'll be here. It'll help the day pass. I'd have gone crazy if I hadn't been able to work this afternoon."

"Nice meeting you," Charlie said to Val.

"Hope to see you again," she said, giving him a hundred-kilowatt smile.

Pete Lockburn and Frank Reuther left the shop first, surveying the promenade in front of the rows of stores, suspiciously studying the parking lot. Christine was self-conscious in their company. She didn't think of herself as important enough to need bodyguards. The presence of these two hired guns made her feel awkward and strangely pretentious, as if she were putting on airs.

Outside, the sky to the east was black. Overhead, it was deep blue. To the west, over the ocean, there was a gaudy orange-yellow-red-maroon sunset back-lighting an ominous bank of advancing storm clouds. Although the day had been warm for February, the air was already chilly. Later, it would be downright cold. In California, a warm winter day was not an infrequent gift of nature, but nature's generosity seldom extended to the winter nights.

A dark green Chevrolet, a Klemet-Harrison company car, was parked next to Christine's Firebird. There was a dog in the back seat, peering out the window at them, and when Christine saw it her breath caught in her throat.

It was Brandy. For a second or two, she stood in shock, unable to believe her eyes. Then she realized it *wasn't* Brandy, of course, but another golden retriever virtually the same size and age and coloration as Brandy.

Joey ran ahead and pulled open the door, and the dog leaped out, emitting one short, deep, happy-sounding bark. He sniffed at the boy's legs and then jumped up, putting paws on his shoulders, almost knocking him to the ground.

Joey laughed, ruffled the dog's fur. "Isn't he neat, Mom? Isn't he something?"

She looked at Charlie, whose grin was almost as big as Joey's. Still thirty feet away from the boy, out of his hearing, she spoke softly, with evident irritation: "Don't you think some other breed would've been a better choice?"

Charlie seemed baffled by her accusatory tone. "You mean it's too big? Joey told me it was the same size as the dog . . . you lost."

"Not only the same size. It's the same *dog.*"

"You mean Brandy was a golden retriever?"

"Didn't I tell you?"

"You never mentioned the breed."

"Oh. Well, didn't Joey mention it?"

"He never said a word."

"This dog's an exact double for Brandy," Christine said worriedly. "I don't know if that's such a good idea—psychologically, I mean."

Turning to them, holding the retriever by its collar, Joey confirmed her intuition when he said, "Mom, you know what I'm gonna call him? Brandy! Brandy the Second!"

"I see what you mean," Charlie said to Christine.

"He's trying to deny that Brandy was ever killed," she said, "and that's not healthy."

As the parking lot's sodium-vapor lamps came on, casting yellowish light into the deepening twilight, she went to her son and stooped beside him.

The dog snuffled at her, checking her out, cocked its head, looked at her as if it was trying to figure how she fit in, and finally put one paw on her leg, as if seeking her assurance that she would love it as much as its new young master did.

Sensing that she was already too late to take the dog back and get another breed, unhappily aware that Joey was already attached to the animal, she decided at least to stop him from calling the dog Brandy. "Honey, I think it'd be a good idea to come up with another name."

"I like Brandy," he said.

"But using that name again . . . it's like an insult to the first Brandy."

"It is?"

"Like you're trying to forget our Brandy."

"*No!*" he said fiercely. "I couldn't ever forget." Tears came to his eyes again.

"This dog should have his own name," she insisted gently.

"I really like the name Brandy."

"Come on. Think of another name."

"Well . . ."

"How about . . . Prince."

"Yuck. But maybe . . . Randy."

She frowned and shook her head. "No, honey. Think of something else. Something totally different. How about . . . something from *Star Wars?* Wouldn't it be neat to have a dog named Chewbacca?"

His face brightened. "Yeah! Chewbacca! That'd be great."

As if it had understood every word, as if voicing approval, the dog barked once and licked Christine's hand.

Charlie said, "Okay, let's put Chewbacca in your Firebird. I want to get out of here. You and Joey and I will ride in the Chevy, and Frank will drive. Pete'll follow us in your car, with Chewbacca. And by the way, we still have company."

Christine looked in the direction that Charlie indicated. The white van was at the far end of the parking lot, half in the yellowish light from the tall lampposts, half in shadow. The driver wasn't visible beyond the black windshield, but she knew he was in there, watching.

CHAPTER 17

/////

NIGHT HAD FALLEN.

The storm clouds were still rolling in from the west. They were blacker than the night itself. They rapidly blotted out the stars.

In the white Chrysler, O'Hara and Baumberg cruised slowly, studying the well-maintained, expensive houses on both sides of the street. O'Hara was driving, and his hands kept slipping on the steering wheel because he was plagued by a cold sweat. He knew he was an agent of God in this matter because Mother Grace had told him so. He knew that what he was doing was good and right and absolutely necessary, but he still couldn't picture himself as an assassin, holy or otherwise. He knew that Baumberg felt the same way because the ex-jeweler was breathing too fast for a man who hadn't yet exerted himself. The few times that Baumberg had spoken, his voice had been shaky and higher-pitched than usual.

They weren't having doubts about their mission or about Mother Grace. Both of them had a deep and abiding faith in the old woman. Both of them would do what they were told. O'Hara knew the boy must die, and he knew why, and he believed in the reason. Murdering this particular child did not disturb him. He knew Baumberg felt the same way. They were sweat-damp and nervous merely because they were scared.

Along the tree-shrouded street, several houses were dark, and one of those might serve their purpose. But it was early in the evening, and a lot of people were still on their way back from work. O'Hara and Baumberg didn't want to select a house, break in, and then be discovered and perhaps trapped by some guy coming home with a briefcase in one hand and Chinese take-out in the other.

O'Hara was prepared to kill the boy and the boy's mother and any bodyguards hired to protect the boy, for all of them were in the service of Lucifer. Grace had convinced him of that. But O'Hara wasn't prepared to kill just any innocent bystander who happened to get in his way. Therefore, they would have to choose the house carefully.

What they were looking for was a place where a few days' worth of newspapers were piled up on the porch, or where the mailbox was overflowing, or where there was some other sign that the occupants were away from home. It had to be in this block, and they probably wouldn't find what they were looking for. In that case they'd have to shift to another plan of attack.

They had almost reached the north end of the block when Baumberg said, "There. What about that place?"

It was a two-story Spanish house, light beige stucco with a tile roof, half hidden by large trees, banks of veronica, and rows of azaleas. The streetlight shone on a real estate company's sign that stood on the lawn, near the sidewalk. The house was for sale, and no lights glowed in any of its rooms.

"Maybe it's unoccupied," Baumberg said.

"No such luck," O'Hara said.

"It's worth taking a look."

"I guess so."

O'Hara drove to the next block and parked at the curb. Carrying an airline flight bag that he had packed at the church, he got out of the car, accompanied Baumberg to the Spanish house, hurried up a walkway bordered by flourishing begonias, and stopped at a gated atrium entrance. Here they were in deep shadow. O'Hara was confident they wouldn't be spotted from the street.

A cold wind soughed in the branches of the benjaminas and rustled the shiny-leafed veronicas, and it seemed to O'Hara that the night itself was watching them with hostile intent. Could it be that some demonic entity had followed them and was with them now, at home in these shadows, an emissary of Satan, waiting to catch them off guard and tear them to pieces?

Mother Grace had said Satan would do anything he could to wreck their mission. Grace saw these things. Grace knew. Grace spoke the truth. Grace *was* the truth.

His heart hammering, Pat O'Hara gazed blindly into the most impenetrable pockets of darkness, expecting to catch a glimpse of some lurking monstrosity. But he saw nothing out of the ordinary.

Baumberg stepped away from the wrought-iron atrium gate, onto the lawn, then into a planting bed filled with azaleas and dark-leafed begonias that, in the gloom, appeared to be utterly black. He peered in a window and said softly, "No drapes . . . and I don't think there's any furniture, either."

O'Hara went to another window, put his face to the pane, squinted, and found the same signs of vacancy.

"Bingo," Baumberg said.

They had found what they were looking for.

At the side of the house, the entrance to the rear lawn was also gated, but that gate wasn't locked. As Baumberg pushed it open, the wrought-iron barrier squealed on unoiled hinges.

"I'll go back to the car and get the laundry bags," Baumberg said, and he slipped away through the night's black curtains.

O'Hara didn't think it was a good idea to split up, but Baumberg was gone before he could protest. Alone, it was more difficult to hold fear at bay, and fear was the food of the devil. Fear drew the Beast. O'Hara looked around at the throbbing darkness and told himself to remember that his faith was his armor. Nothing could harm him as long as he trusted the armor of his belief in Grace and God. But it wasn't easy.

Sometimes he longed for the days before his conversion, when he hadn't known about the approach of Twilight, when he hadn't realized that Satan was loose upon the earth and that the Antichrist had been born. He had been blissfully ignorant. The only things he had feared were cops, doing time in prison, and cancer because cancer had killed his old man. Now he was afraid of everything between sunset and dawn, for it was in the dark hours that evil was boldest. These days, his life was shaped by fear, and at times the burden of Mother Grace's truth was almost too much to bear.

Still carrying the airline flight bag, O'Hara continued to the rear of the house, deciding not to wait for Baumberg. He'd show the devil that he was not intimidated.

CHAPTER 18

JOEY WANTED TO ride up front with Pete Lockburn, to whom he chattered ceaselessly and enthusiastically all the way home.

Christine sat in back with Charlie, who occasionally turned to look through the rear window. Frank Reuther followed in Christine's Pontiac Firebird, and a few cars back of Reuther, the white van continued to trail them, easily identified even at night because one of its headlights was slightly brighter than the other.

Charlie said, "I can't figure that guy out. Is he so dumb he thinks we don't notice him? Does he really think he's being discreet?"

"Maybe he doesn't care if we see him," Christine said. "They seem so . . . arrogant."

Charlie turned away from the rear window and sighed. "You're probably right."

"What've you found out about the printing company—The True Word?" Christine asked.

"Like I suspected, The True Word prints religious material—booklets, pamphlets, tracts of all kinds. It's owned by the Church of the Twilight."

"Never heard of them," Christine said. "Some crackpot cult?"

"As far as I'm concerned, yeah. Totally fruitcake."

"Mustn't be a big group, or I'd probably have heard of them."

"Not big, but rich," Charlie said. "Maybe a thousand of them."

"Dangerous?"

"They haven't been involved in any big trouble. But the potential is there, the fanaticism. We've had a run-in with them on behalf of another client. About seven months ago. This guy's wife ran off, joined the cult, took their two kids with her—a three- and a four-year-old. These twilight weirdos wouldn't tell him where his wife was, wouldn't let him see his kids. The police weren't too much help. Never are in these cases. Everyone's so worried about treading on religious liberties. Besides, the kids hadn't been kidnapped; they were with their mother. A mother can take her kids anywhere she pleases, as long as she's not violating a custody agreement in a divorce situation, which wasn't the case here. Anyway, we found the kids, snatched them away, returned them to the father. We couldn't do anything about the wife. She was staying with the cult voluntarily."

"They live communally? Like those people at Jonestown a few years ago?"

"Some of them do. Others have their own homes and apartments—but only if Mother Grace allows them that privilege."

"Who's Mother Grace?"

He opened a briefcase, took an envelope and a penlight from it. He handed her the envelope, switched on the light, and said, "Have a look."

The envelope contained an eight-by-ten glossy. It was a picture of the old

woman who had harassed them in the parking lot. Even in a black-and-white photograph, even in two dimensions, the old woman's eyes were scary; there was a mad gleam in them. Christine shivered.

CHAPTER 19

ALONG THE BACK of the house were windows to the dining room, kitchen, breakfast nook, and family room. A pair of French doors led into the family room. O'Hara tried them, even though he was sure they'd be locked; they were.

The patio was bare. No flowerpots. No lawn furniture. The swimming pool had been drained, perhaps for repainting.

Standing by the French doors, O'Hara looked at the house to the north of this one. A six-foot cinder block wall separated this property from the next; therefore, he could see only the second story of that other house. It was dark. To the south, beyond another wall, the second story of another house was visible, but this one was filled with light. At least no one was looking out any of the windows.

The rear of the property was walled, also, but the house in that direction was evidently a single-story model, for it couldn't be seen from the patio on which O'Hara stood.

He took a flashlight from the airline flight bag and used it to examine the panes of glass in the French doors and in one of the windows. He moved quickly, afraid of being seen. He was looking for wires, conductive alarm tape, and photo-electric cells—anything that would indicate the house was equipped with a burglar alarm. It was the kind of neighborhood where about a third of the houses would be wired. He found no indication that this place was part of that one-third.

He switched the flashlight off, fumbled in the flight bag, and withdrew a compact, battery-powered electronic device the size of a small transistor radio. An eighteen-inch length of wire extended from one end of it, terminating in a suction cup as large as the lid of a mayonnaise jar. He fixed the suction cup to a pane in one of the French doors.

Again, he had the creepy feeling that something dangerous was moving in on him, and a chill quivered down his spine as he turned to peer into the shadow-draped rear yard. The wind clattered through the thick, somewhat brittle leaves of a huge ficus, hissed in the fronds of two palms, and caused smaller shrubs to sway and flutter as if they were alive. But it was the empty swimming pool that drew O'Hara's attention and became the focus of his fear. He suddenly got the idea that something large and hideous was hiding in the pool, crouched down in that concrete pit, listening to him, waiting for the opportune moment in which to make its move. Something that had coalesced out of the darkness. Something that had risen up from the pits of Hell. Something sent to stop them from killing the boy. Underlying the myriad sounds produced by the wind, he thought he could hear a sinister, wet, slithering sound coming from the pool, and he was suddenly cold clear through to his bones.

Baumberg returned with the two laundry bags, startling O'Hara.

"Do you feel it, too?" Baumberg asked.

"Yes," O'Hara said.

"It's out there. The Beast himself. Or one of his messengers."

"In the pool," O'Hara said.

Baumberg stared at the black pit in the center of the lawn. Finally he nodded. "Yeah. I feel it. Down there in the pool."

It can only hurt us if we begin to doubt Mother Grace's power to protect us, O'Hara told himself. It can only stop us if we lose our faith or if we let our fear of it overwhelm us.

That was what Mother Grace had told them.

Mother Grace was never wrong.

O'Hara turned to the French doors again. The suction cup was still firmly affixed to one of the panes. He switched on the small device to which the suction cup was connected, and a glass-covered dial lit up in the center of the instrument case. The device was a sonic-wave detector that would tell them if the house was equipped with a wireless alarm system that protected the premises by detecting motion. The lighted dial did not move, which meant there was no radio wave activity of any kind within the family room, beyond the French doors.

Before Mother Grace had converted him, O'Hara had been a busy and professional burglar, and he had been damned good at his trade. Because Grace had a propensity for seeking converts from among those who had fallen the furthest from God, the Church of the Twilight could tap a wealth of skills and knowledge not available to the average church whose members were from the law-abiding segments of the population. Sometimes that was a blessing.

He popped the suction cup off the glass, switched off the wave detector, and returned it to the flight bag. He withdrew a roll of strapping tape and a pair of scissors. He cut several strips of tape and applied them to the pane of glass nearest the door handle. When the glass was completely covered, he struck it hard with one fist. The pane shattered, but with little sound, and the fragments all stuck to the tape. He pulled the pieces out of the frame, put them aside, reached through, fumbled for the deadbolt, unlocked it, opened the door.

He was now pretty sure there was no alarm, but he had one last thing to check for. He got down on his knees on the patio, reached across the threshold, and pulled up the carpet from the tack strip. There was no alarm mat under the carpet, just ordinary quilted padding.

He put the carpet back in place. He and Baumberg went into the house, taking the laundry bags and the flight bag with them.

O'Hara closed and locked the French doors.

He looked out at the rear lawn. It was peaceful now.

"It isn't out there any more," Baumberg said.

"No," O'Hara said.

Baumberg peered across the unlighted family room, into the breakfast area and the dark kitchen beyond. He said, "Now it's inside with us."

"Yes," O'Hara said. He had felt the hostile presence within the house the moment they'd crossed the threshold.

"I wish we could turn on some lights," Baumberg said uneasily.

"The house is supposed to be deserted. The neighbors would notice lights and maybe call the cops."

Overhead, from an upstairs room, a floorboard creaked.

Before converting to Mother Grace's faith, in the days when he had been a thief, stealing his way along the road to hell, O'Hara would have figured the creaking was merely a settling noise, one of the many meaningless sounds that an empty house produced as joints expanded and contracted in response to the humidity—or lack of it—in the air. But tonight he knew it was no settling sound.

O'Hara's old friends and some in his family said that he had become paranoid since joining the Church of the Twilight. They just didn't understand. His behavior seemed paranoid only because he had seen the truth as Mother Grace taught it, and his old friends and family had not been saved. His eyes had been opened; their eyes were still blind.

More creaking noise overhead.

"Our faith is a shield," Baumberg said shakily. "We don't dare doubt that."

"Mother has provided us with armor," O'Hara said.

Creeeeeaaak.

"We're doing God's work," Baumberg said, challenging the darkness that filled the house.

O'Hara switched on the flashlight, shielding it with one hand to provide just enough light to guide them but not enough to be seen from outside.

Baumberg followed him to the stairs and up to the second floor.

CHAPTER 20

///////

"HER NAME'S GRACE SPIVEY," Charlie said as their car moved through the increasingly blustery February night.

Christine couldn't take her eyes from the photograph. The old woman's black-and-white gaze was strangely hypnotic, and a cold radiation seemed to emanate from it.

In the front seat, Joey was talking to Pete Lockburn about Steven Spielberg's *E.T.,* which Joey had seen four times and which Lockburn seemed to have seen more often than that. Her son's voice sounded far away, as if he were on a distant mountain, already lost to her.

Charlie switched off the penlight.

Christine was relieved when shadow fell across the photograph, breaking the uncanny hold it had on her. She put it in the envelope, returned the envelope to Charlie. "She's head of this cult?"

"She *is* the cult. It's primarily a personality cult. Her religious message isn't anything special or unique; the whole thing's in the way she delivers it. If anything happened to Grace, her followers would drift away and the church would probably collapse."

"How can a crazy old woman like that draw any followers? She sure didn't seem charismatic to me."

"But she is," Charlie said. "I've never spoken to her myself, but Henry Rankin has. He handled that case I mentioned, the two little kids whose mother took them with her into the cult. And he told me Grace has a certain undeniable magnetism, a very forceful personality. And although her message isn't particularly new, it's dramatic and exciting, just the sort of thing that a certain type of person would respond to with enthusiasm."

"What *is* her message?"

"She says we're living in the last days of the world."

"Every religious crackpot from here to Maine has made that proclamation at one time or another."

"Of course."

"So there must be more to it. What else does she say?"

Charlie hesitated, and she sensed that he dreaded having to tell her the rest. "Charlie?"

He sighed. "Grace says the Antichrist has already been born."

"I've heard that one, too. There's one cult around that says the Antichrist is the King of Spain."

"That's a new one to me."

"Others say the Antichrist will be the man who takes over the Russian government after the current Premier."

"Sounds a bit more reasonable than laying it on the King of Spain."

"I wouldn't be surprised if there's a cult somewhere that thinks Burt Reynolds or Stephen King or Rodney Dangerfield is the Antichrist."

Charlie didn't smile at her little joke. "We're living in weird times," he said.

"We're approaching the end of a millennium," Christine said. "For some reason, that brings all the nuts out of the trees. They say that, last time, when the year 1000 was approaching, there were all sorts of bizarre cults, decadence, and violence associated with people's fears of the end of the world. I guess it's going to be that way as we approach 2000. Hell, it's already started."

"It sure has," he said softly.

She perceived that he still hadn't told her everything Grace Spivey professed to believe. Even in the dim light that came through the car windows, she could see that he was deeply disturbed.

"Well?" she prodded him.

"Grace says we're in the Twilight, that period just before the son of Satan takes power over the earth and rules for a thousand years. How well do you know the Bible—especially the prophecies?"

"I was very familiar with it at one time," she said. "But not any more. In fact, I can't remember much of anything."

"Join the club. But from what I understand of Grace Spivey's preaching, the Bible says that the Antichrist will rule for a thousand years, bringing mankind indescribable suffering, after which the battle of Armageddon will transpire, and God will at last descend to destroy Satan forever. She says that God has given her one last chance to avoid the devil's thousand-year dominion. She says He's ordered her to try to save mankind by organizing a church of righteous people who will stop the Antichrist before he reaches a position of power."

"If I didn't know there were people—fanatical and maybe *dangerous* people —who believed in this kind of nonsense, I'd find it amusing. And how do they think their little band of righteous people is going to combat the awesome power of Satan—presuming you believe in the awesome power of Satan in the first place?"

"Which I don't. But as far as I'm aware, their battle plans are a secret known only to those who've become members of the church. But I suspect I know what they've got in mind."

"And what's that?"

He hesitated. Then: "They intend to kill him."

"The Antichrist?"

"Yes."

"Just like that?"

"I don't imagine they think it'll be easy."

"I should say not!" Christine said, smiling in spite of the situation. "What kind of devil would allow himself to be killed with ease? Anyway, the logic's inconsistent. The Antichrist would be a supernatural figure. Supernatural beings can't be killed."

"I know that Roman Catholicism has a tradition of justifying points of doctrine through logical processes," Charlie said. "St. Thomas Aquinas and his writings, for instance. But these people we're dealing with are fringe types. Fanatics. Consistency of logic isn't something religious fanatics require of one another." He sighed. "Anyway, assuming that you believe in all this mythology as presented by the Bible—and as interpreted by Grace—maybe it isn't such lousy logic. After all, Jesus was supposed to have been a supernatural being, the son of God, yet He was killed by the Romans."

"That's different," she said. "According to the Christ story, that was His mission, His purpose, His destiny—to allow Himself to be killed to save us from the worst consequences of our sins. Right? But I hardly think the Antichrist would be as altruistic."

"You're thinking logically again. If you want to understand Grace and the Church of the Twilight, you've got to put logic behind you."

"Okay. So who does she say is the Antichrist?"

"When we pulled those two little kids out of the cult," Charlie said, "Grace still hadn't identified the Antichrist. She hadn't found him yet. But now I think perhaps she has."

"So? Who?" Christine asked, but before Charlie could respond, the answer hit her with the force of a sledgehammer blow.

Up front, Joey was still talking with Pete Lockburn, oblivious of the conversation between his mother and Charlie Harrison.

Nevertheless, Christine lowered her voice to a whisper. "Joey? My God, does that crazy woman think my little boy is the Antichrist?"

"I'd almost bet on it."

Christine could hear the old woman's hate-filled voice, rising from a dark pool of memory: *He's got to die; he's got to die.*

"But why him? Why Joey? Why didn't she fixate on some other child?"

"Maybe it's like you said: You were just at the wrong place at the wrong time," Charlie said. "If some other woman with another child had been in the South Coast Plaza parking lot at that same time last Sunday, Grace would now be after another little boy instead of Joey."

Christine knew that he was probably right, but the thought dizzied her. It was a stupid, cruel, malignant lunacy. What kind of world were they living in if an innocent shopping trip to the mall made them eligible for martyrdom?

"But . . . how do we ever stop her?" Christine asked.

"If she actually resorts to violence, we deflect it. If we can't deflect it, then . . . well, we blow her people away before they touch Joey. There's no question of legal responsibility. You've hired us to protect you, and we have legal sanction to resort to violent force, if that's necessary and unavoidable, to fulfill our obligation."

"No. I mean . . . how do we change her mind? How do we get her to admit that Joey's just a little boy? How do we get her to go away?"

"I don't know. I would imagine a fanatic like this is about as single-minded as anyone can be. I don't think it would be easy to make her change her mind about anything, let alone anything as important to her as this."

"But you said she's got a thousand followers."

"Maybe even a few more than that by now."

"If she keeps sending them after Joey, we can't kill them all. Sooner or later, one of them will get through our defenses."

"I'm not going to let this drag on," he assured her. "I'm not going to give them a lot of chances to hurt Joey. I'll make Grace change her mind, back off, go away."

"How?"

"I don't know yet."

An image of the harpy in the parking lot returned to Christine—the wind-blown hair, the bulging eyes, the lint-specked and food-stained clothes—and she felt despair clutching at her. "There's no way to change her mind."

"There's a way," Charlie insisted. "I'll find it."

"She'll never stop."

"I have an appointment with an excellent psychologist in the morning. Dr. Denton Boothe. He's especially interested in cult psychology. I'm going to discuss the case with him, give him our profile on Grace, ask him to work with us to find her weak spot."

Christine didn't see much promise in that approach. But then she didn't see much promise in any approach.

Charlie took her hand as the car sped through the windy darkness. "I won't let you down."

But for the first time she wondered if his promises were empty.

CHAPTER 21

⸉⸉⸉⸉⸉

ON THE SECOND floor of the empty house, O'Hara and Baumberg stood by the windows in the large master bedroom.

They still felt the menacing presence of an evil entity watching over them. They tried to ignore it, holding steadfast to their faith and to their determination to complete the task Mother Grace had given them.

Outside, the rear yard lay in darkness, scoured by a rising wind. From up here they could see into the swimming pool. No beast crouched within that concrete concavity. Not now. Now it was in the house with them.

Beyond this property was another lawn and another house, a sprawling, one-story, ranch-style place with a shake-shingle roof and a swimming pool of its own. The pool held water and was lit from the bottom, a glimmering blue-green jewel in the shape of a kidney.

O'Hara had taken a pair of night binoculars from the flight bag at his feet. They made use of available light to produce an enhanced image of a dark landscape. Through them, he had a pretty good view of all the properties that butted up against the rear of the lots along this street. Those houses faced out onto another street, parallel to this one.

"Which is the Scavello place?" Baumberg asked.

O'Hara slowly turned to his right, looking farther north. "Not the house behind this one. The next one, with the rectangular pool and the swings."

"I don't see any swings," Baumberg said.

O'Hara handed him the binoculars. "To the left of the pool. A child's swing set and a jungle gym."

"Just two doors away," Baumberg said.

"Yeah."

"No lights on."

"They aren't home yet."

"Maybe they won't come home."

"They'll come," O'Hara said.

"If they don't?"

"We'll go looking for them."

"Where?"

"Wherever God sends us."

Baumberg nodded.

O'Hara opened one of the laundry bags and withdrew a shotgun.

CHAPTER 22

AS THEY TURNED into Christine's block and came within sight of her house, Charlie said, "See that camper?"

Across the street, a pickup truck was parked at the curb. A camper shell was attached to the bed of the truck. It was just an ordinary camper; she had noticed it but hadn't given it a second thought. Suddenly it seemed sinister.

"Is that them, too?" she asked.

"No. That's *us,*" Charlie said. "I've got a man in there, keeping an eye on every vehicle that comes along the street. He's got a camera with infra-red film, so he can record license plate numbers even in the dark. He's also got a portable telephone, so he can call your place, the police, or get in touch with me in a hurry."

Pete Lockburn parked the green Chevy in front of the Scavello house, while Frank Reuther pulled Christine's Firebird into the driveway.

The white Ford van, which had been following them, passed by. They watched it in silence as its driver took it into the next block, found a parking space, and switched off its lights.

"Amateurs," Pete Lockburn said scornfully.

"Arrogant bastards," Christine said.

Reuther climbed out of the Firebird, leaving the dog in it, and came to their car.

As Charlie put down the window to talk to Frank, he asked Christine for her house keys. When she produced them from her purse, he gave them to Frank. "Check the place out. Make sure nobody's waiting in there."

"Right," Frank said, unbuttoning his suit jacket to provide quick access to the weapon in his shoulder holster. He headed up the walk to the front door.

Pete got out of the Chevy and stood beside it, surveying the night-shrouded street. He left his coat unbuttoned, too.

Joey said, "Is this where the bad guys show up?"

"Let's hope not, honey."

There were a lot of trees and not many streetlights, and Charlie began to feel uneasy about sitting here at the curb, so he got out of the Chevy, too, warning

Christine and Joey to stay where they were. He stood at his side of the car, his back toward Pete Lockburn, taking responsibility for the approaches in his direction.

Occasionally a car swung around the corner, entered the block, drove past or turned into the driveway of another house. Each time he saw a new pair of headlights, Charlie tensed and put his right hand under his coat, on the butt of the revolver in his shoulder holster.

He was cold. He wished he'd brought an overcoat.

Sheet lightning pulsed dully in the western sky. A far-off peal of thunder made him think of the freight trains that had rumbled past the shabby little house in which he'd grown up, back in Indiana, in what now seemed like another century.

For some reason, those trains had never been a symbol of freedom and escape, as they might have been to other boys in his situation. To young Charlie, lying in his narrow bed in his narrow room, trying to forget his father's latest outburst of drunken violence, the sound of those trains had always reminded him that he lived on the wrong side of the tracks. The clattering-growling wheels had been the voice of poverty, the sound of need and fear and desperation.

He was surprised that this low thunder could bring back, with such disturbing clarity, the rumbling of those train wheels. Equally surprising was that the memory of those trains could evoke childhood fears and recall to mind the feeling of being trapped that had been such an integral part of his youth.

In that regard, he had a lot in common with Christine. His childhood had been blighted by physical abuse, hers by psychological abuse. Both of them had lived under the fist, one literally, one figuratively, and as children they had felt trapped, claustrophobic.

He looked down at the side window of the Chevy, saw Joey peering out at him. He gave a thumbs-up sign. The boy returned it, grinning.

Having been a target of abuse as a boy, Charlie was especially sensitive to children who were victims of violence. Nothing made him angrier than adults who battered children. Crimes against defenseless children gave him a cold, greasy, sick feeling and filled him with a hatred and a bleak despair that nothing else could engender.

He would not let them harm Joey Scavello.

He would not fail the boy. He didn't *dare* fail because, having failed, he very likely wouldn't be able to live with himself.

It seemed quite a long time before Frank came back. He was still watchful but a bit more relaxed than when he'd gone inside. "Clean, Mr. Harrison. I looked in the back yard, too. Nobody around."

They took Christine and Joey and Chewbacca inside, surrounding the woman and the boy as they moved, allowing no clear line of fire.

Christine had said that she was successful, but Charlie hadn't expected such a large, well-furnished house. The living room had a huge fireplace surrounded by a carved mantel and oak bookshelves extending to the corners. An enormous Chinese carpet provided the focus for a pleasing mix of Oriental and European antiques and antique reproductions of high quality. Along one wall was an eight-panel, hand-carved rosewood screen with a double triptych depicting a waterfall and bridge and ancient Japanese village, all rendered in intricately fitted pieces of soapstone.

Joey wanted to go to his room and play a game with his new dog, and Frank Reuther went with him.

At Charlie's suggestion, Pete Lockburn went through the house, from bottom to top and back again, checking to be sure all doors and windows were locked, shutting all the draperies, so no one could see inside.

Christine said, "I guess I'd better see what I can find for supper. Probably hot dogs. That's the only thing I have plenty of."

"Don't bother," Charlie said. "I've got a man bringing a lot of takeout at seven o'clock."

"You think of everything."

"Let's hope so."

CHAPTER 23

O'HARA TRAINED HIS binoculars on an upstairs window of the Scavello house, then on the next window, and the next, eventually scanning the first floor as well. Light shone in every room, but all the draperies were drawn tight.

"Maybe she came home but sent the boy somewhere else for the night," Baumberg said.

"The boy's there," O'Hara said.

"How do you know?"

"Can't you *feel* him over there?"

Baumberg squinted through the window.

"Feel him," O'Hara said in a hushed and frightened voice.

Baumberg groped for the awareness that had terrified his partner.

"The darkness," O'Hara said. "Feel the special darkness of the boy, the terrible darkness that rolls off him like fog off the ocean."

Baumberg strained his senses.

"The evil," O'Hara said, his voice reduced to a hoarse whisper. "Feel it."

Baumberg placed his hands against the cool glass, pressed his forehead to it, stared intently at the Scavello house. After a while he *did* feel it, just like O'Hara said. The darkness. The evil. It poured forth from that house like atomic radiation from a block of plutonium. It streamed through the night, through the glass in front of Baumberg, contaminating him, a malignant energy that produced no heat or light, that was bleak and black and frigid.

O'Hara abruptly lowered his binoculars, turned away from the window, put his back toward the Scavello house, as if the evil energy pouring from it was more than he could bear.

"It's time," Baumberg said, picking up a shotgun and a revolver.

"No," O'Hara said. "Let them settle in. Let them relax. Give them a chance to lower their guard."

"When?"

"We'll leave here at . . . eight-thirty."

CHAPTER 24

6:45 P.M.

Christine watched as Charlie unplugged the telephone in her study and replaced it with a device that he had brought with him. It looked like a cross between a phone, an answering machine, and a briefcase-sized electronic calculator.

Charlie picked up the receiver, and Christine could hear the dial tone even though she was a few feet away.

Replacing the handset in the cradle, he said, "If someone calls, we'll come in here to answer it."

"That'll record the conversation?"

"Yeah. But it's primarily a tracer phone. It's like the equipment the police have when you call their emergency number."

"911?"

"Yeah. When you call 911, they know what number and address you're calling from because, as soon as they pick up their receiver and establish a connection with you, that information prints out at their end." He indicated what looked like a short, blank length of adding machine tape that was sticking out of a slot in the device he'd put on her desk. "We'll have the same information about anyone who phones here."

"So if this Grace Spivey calls, we'll not only have a recording of her voice, but we'll have proof the call was made on her phone—or one that belongs to her church."

"Yep. It probably wouldn't be admissible as court evidence, but it ought to help get the police interested if we can prove she's making threats against Joey."

7:00 P.M.

The take-out food arrived precisely on the hour, and Christine noticed that Charlie was quietly pleased by how prompt his man was.

The five of them ate at the dining room table—beef ribs, barbecued chicken, baked potatoes, and cole slaw—while Charlie told funny stories about cases his agency had handled. Joey listened, spellbound, even though he didn't always understand or appreciate the details of the anecdotes.

Christine watched her son watching Charlie. More poignantly than ever, she realized what the boy had been missing by not having a father or any other male authority figure to admire and from whom he could learn.

Chewbacca, the new dog, ate from a dish in the corner of the room, then stretched out and put his head down on his paws, waiting for Joey. Obviously, he had belonged to a family that had cared for him and had trained him well. He was going to fit in quickly and easily. Christine was still disconcerted by his resemblance to Brandy, but she was beginning to think it would work out anyway.

At 7:20, the intermittent, distant sound of thunder suddenly grew louder. A blast split the night sky, and the windows rattled.

Startled, Christine dropped her fork. For an instant she thought a bomb had gone off outside the house. When she realized it was only thunder, she felt silly, but a glance at the others told her that they, too, had been briefly startled and frightened by the noise.

A few fat raindrops struck the roof, the windows.

At 7:35, Frank Reuther finished eating and left the table to make a complete circuit of the house, re-examining all the doors and windows that Pete had checked earlier.

A light but steady rain was falling.

At 7:47, finished eating, Joey challenged Pete Lockburn to a game of Old Maid, and Pete accepted. They went off to the boy's room, the dog padding friskily and eagerly behind them.

Frank pulled a chair up to one of the living room windows and studied the rain-swept street through a narrow chink in the draperies.

Charlie helped Christine gather up the paper plates and napkins, which they carried to the kitchen, where the sound of the rain was louder, booming off the patio cover at the back of the house.

"What now?" Christine asked, stuffing the plates into the garbage can.

"We get through the night."

"Then?"

"If the old woman doesn't call tonight and give us something to use against her, then tomorrow I'll talk to Dr. Boothe, the psychologist I mentioned. He has a special interest in religious neuroses and psychoses. He's developed some successful deprogramming procedures to rehabilitate people who've been brainwashed by some of these weird cults. He knows how these cult leaders think, so maybe he can help us find Grace Spivey's weak spot. I'm also going to try to talk to the woman herself, face to face."

"How're you going to arrange that?"

"Call the Church of the Twilight and ask for an appointment with her."

"You think she'll actually see you?"

He shrugged. "The boldness of it might intrigue her."

"Can't we go to the cops now?"

"With what?"

"You've got proof Joey and I are being followed."

"Following someone isn't a crime."

"That Spivey woman called your office and threatened Joey."

"We haven't any proof it was Grace Spivey. And only Joey heard the threat."

"Maybe if we explain to the cops how this madwoman thinks Joey is the Antichrist—"

"That's only a theory."

"Well . . . maybe we could find someone who used to belong to the cult, someone who's left it, and then they could substantiate this Antichrist nonsense."

"People don't leave the Church of the Twilight," Charlie said.

"What do you mean?"

"When we were hired to pull those two little kids out of the cult, we first figured we'd dig up someone who'd been a follower of Grace Spivey's but wasn't any more, someone who'd become disillusioned and could tell us where the kids might be and how we might best be able to snatch them. But we couldn't find anybody who'd quit the church. Once they join up, they seem committed for life."

"There're always going to be a few disgruntled, disillusioned—"

"Not with the Church of the Twilight."

"What kind of hold does that crazy old woman have on them?"

"Hard as iron and tight as a vise," Charlie said.

Lightning pulsed so brilliantly that it was visible through the tiny spaces between the slats of the Levolor blinds.

Thunder crashed, reverberating in the windows, and the rain came down harder than ever.

At 8:15, after giving some final instructions to Lockburn and Reuther, Charlie left.

He insisted that Christine lock the door behind him before he would even walk away from the front porch.

She pulled aside the curtain on the window next to the door and watched him hurry toward the green Chevy, splashing through dark puddles, buffeted by the wet wind, hurrying in and out of dense night shadows that appeared to flap and billow like black draperies.

Frank Reuther suggested she get away from the window, and she took his advice, though reluctantly. Somehow, as long as she could still see Charlie Harrison, she felt safe. But the moment she dropped the curtain and turned away from the window, a crushing awareness of Joey's vulnerability (and her own) settled over her.

She knew Pete and Frank were well trained, competent, and trustworthy, but neither of them gave her the feeling of security that she got from Charlie.

8:20.

She went to Joey's room. He and Pete were sitting on the floor, playing Old Maid.

"Hey, Mom, I'm winning," Joey said.

"He's a real card shark," Pete said. "If this ever gets back to the guys in the office, I'll never live it down."

Chewbacca lay in the corner, watching his master, tongue lolling.

Christine could almost believe that Chewbacca was actually Brandy, that there had never been a decapitation, that Pete and Frank were just a couple of family friends, that this was merely an ordinary, quiet evening at home. Almost. But not quite.

She went into her study and sat at her desk, looking at the two covered windows, listening to the rain. It sounded like thousands of people chanting so far away that you couldn't make out their words but could hear only the soft, blended roar of many ardent voices.

She tried to work but couldn't concentrate. She took a book from the shelves, a light novel, but she couldn't even keep her attention focused on that.

For a moment she considered calling her mother. She needed a shoulder to cry on. But of course Evelyn wouldn't provide the comfort and commiseration she needed.

She wished her brother were still alive. She wished she could call him and ask him to come be with her. But Tony was gone forever. Her father was gone forever, too, and although she had barely known him, she missed him now in a way she never had before.

If only Charlie were here . . .

In spite of Frank and Pete and the unnamed man watching the house from the camper outside, she felt terribly alone.

She stared at the tracer phone on her desk. She wished the crazy old woman would call and threaten Joey. At least they would have sufficient evidence to interest the police.

But the phone didn't ring.

The only sounds were those of the storm.

At 8:40, Frank Reuther came into the study, smiled at her, and said, "Don't mind me. Just making the rounds."

He went to the first window, held the drape aside, checked the lock, peered into the darkness for a second, then let the drape fall back into place.

Like Pete Lockburn, Frank had taken off his jacket and had rolled up his shirt sleeves. His shoulder holster hung under his left arm. The butt of his revolver caught the light for an instant and gleamed blackly.

For a moment Christine felt as if, through some inexplicable interchange of fantasy and reality, she was trapped in a '30s gangster movie.

Frank pulled aside the drape at the second window—and cried out in surprise.

The shotgun blast was louder than the clashing armies of the thunder storm.

The window exploded inward.

Christine leaped up as a shower of glass and blood cascaded over her.

Before he had time to reach for his own gun, Frank was lifted off his feet by the force of the blast and pitched backward.

Christine's chair fell over with a bang.

The bodyguard collapsed across the desk in front of her. His face was gone. The shotgun pellets had hammered his skull into bloody ruin.

Outside, the gunman fired again.

Stray pellets found the ceiling light, pulverizing it, bringing down more glass, some plaster, and darkness. The desk lamp already had been knocked to the floor when Frank Reuther had fallen against it. The room was in darkness except for what little light came through the open doorway from the hall.

The pellet-shredded draperies were seized by an intrusive gust of wind. Tattered fragments lashed at one another, fluttered and whirled in the air, like the rotted burial garments of an animated corpse in a carnival funhouse.

Christine heard someone screaming, thought it was Joey, realized it was a woman, then discovered it was her own voice.

A squall of rain burst through the ribboned drapes. But the rain wasn't the only thing trying to get inside. Frank Reuther's killer was also clambering through the shattered window.

Christine ran.

CHAPTER 25

IN AN ADRENALINE-HOT, fear-scorched, dreamlike fever, with the urgent yet weirdly slow-motion time sense of a nightmare, Christine ran from her study to the living room. The short journey required only a few seconds, but it *seemed* as if the distance from one end of her house to the other was a hundred miles and that hours passed during her panicky progress from one room to another. She knew she was awake, yet she felt as if she were asleep. This was reality yet unreal.

When she reached the living room, Pete Lockburn and Joey were just entering from the direction of the boy's bedroom. Lockburn's revolver was in his hand.

Chewbacca came behind them, ears flattened, tail down, barking loudly.

A shotgun blast tore the lock out of the front door. Even as the wood chips were still flying, a man burst into the house. He crouched in the foyer that opened into the living room, holding a shotgun in front of him, eyes wide, face white with anger or terror or both, an incongruously ordinary-looking man, short and husky, with a thick black beard jeweled with raindrops. He saw Christine first and leveled his weapon at her.

Joey screamed.

A hard, ear-shattering explosion rocked the room, and Christine was certain that she was in the last milliseconds of her life.

But it was the intruder who was hit. His shirt blossomed with an ugly red flower of blood.

Pete Lockburn had fired first. Now he fired again.

A spray of blood erupted from the intruder's shoulder. The stranger's shotgun spun out of his hands, and he stumbled backwards. Lockburn's third shot caught him in the neck, catapulting him off his feet. Already dead, he was pitched into a small foyer table; his head slammed backwards, striking a mirror above the table, cracking it, and then he collapsed in a gory heap.

As Joey bolted into Christine's arms, she shouted to Lockburn: "There's another man! The study—"

Too late. The gunman who had killed Frank Reuther was already in the living room.

Lockburn whirled. Fast but not fast enough. The shotgun roared. Pete Lockburn was blown away.

Although he had been their dog less than a day, Chewbacca knew where his loyalties ought to lie. Snarling, teeth bared, he leapt at the gunman, bit the intruder's left leg, sank his fangs in deep and held on tight.

The man cried out, raised the shotgun, slammed the heavy butt down on top of the retriever's golden head. The dog yelped and crumpled in a heap.

"No!" Joey said, as if the loss of a second pet was worse than the prospect of his own slaughter.

Sobbing in pain, obviously frightened, the gunman said, "God help me, God help me, God help me," and he turned the 20-gauge on Christine and Joey.

She saw that he, like the bearded man, did not really appear to be mad or degenerate or evil. The ferocity of the terror that gripped him was the most unusual thing about him. Otherwise, he was quite ordinary. Young, in his early twenties. Slightly overweight. Fair-skinned, with a few freckles and rain-soaked reddish hair that was plastered to his head. His ordinariness was the very thing that made him so scary; if *this* man could become a mindless killer under the influence of Grace Spivey, then the old woman could corrupt any-one; no one could be trusted; anyone might be an assassin in her thrall.

He pulled the trigger.

There was only a dry click.

He had forgotten that both barrels were empty.

Whimpering and squealing as if *he* were the one in danger, the killer fum-bled in his jacket pocket and withdrew a pair of shotgun shells.

With a strength and agility born of terror, Christine scooped Joey up and ran, not toward the front door and the street beyond, for they would surely die out there, but toward the stairs and the master bedroom, where she had left her purse—the purse in which she'd been carrying her own pistol. Joey clung desperately to her, and he seemed to weigh nothing at all; she was briefly possessed with a more-than-human power, and the stairs succumbed to her pumping legs. Then, almost at the top, she stumbled, nearly fell, grabbed at the banister, cried out in despair.

But it was a good thing she had stumbled, for, in that same moment, the gunman below opened fire, discharging both barrels. Two waves of buckshot smashed into the railing at the top of the stairs, reducing the oak handrail to splinters, tearing plaster from the wall, blowing out the ceiling light up there, at the very place she would have been if she hadn't misstepped.

As the killer reloaded yet again, Christine plunged ahead, into the upstairs hall. For a moment she hesitated, clutching Joey, swaying, disoriented. This was her own house, more familiar to her than any place in the world, but tonight it was alien; the angles and proportions and lighting in the rooms seemed wrong, different. The hallway, for instance, appeared infinitely long, with distorted walls like a passageway in a carnival maze. She blinked and tried to repress the heart-hammering panic that twisted her perceptions; she hurried forward and made it to the master bedroom door.

Behind her, from the stairway, came the sound of the killer's footsteps as he raced after her, favoring his bitten leg.

She stepped into the bedroom, slammed the door behind her, latched it, put Joey down. Her purse was on the nightstand. She grabbed it just as the assassin reached the door and rattled the knob. Her fingers were too frantic; for a moment she couldn't work the zipper. Then she had her purse open, the gun in hand.

Joey had crawled into a corner, beside the highboy. He cringed, trying to make himself even smaller than he was.

The bedroom door shook and partially dissolved in a storm of buckshot. A hole opened on the right side of it. One hinge was torn out of the frame; it spun into the air, bounced off a wall, clattered across the top of the dresser.

Holding her pistol in both hands, painfully aware that she wasn't holding it steady, Christine swung toward the door.

Another blast ruined the lock, and the door swung inward, hanging on only one hinge.

The young, red-haired killer stood in the doorway, looking even more terrified than Christine felt. He was gibbering senselessly. His hands were shaking worse than hers. Snot hung from one of his nostrils, but he seemed unaware of it.

She pointed the pistol at him, pulled the trigger.

Nothing happened.

The safety was on.

The assassin seemed startled to find her armed. His shotgun was empty again. He dropped it and pulled a revolver from the waistband of his trousers.

She heard herself saying, "No, no, no, no, no," in a chant of pure fear as she fumbled for the two safeties on the pistol. She snapped off both of them, pulled the trigger again and again and again.

The thunder of her own gunfire, booming off the walls around her, was the sweetest sound she'd ever heard.

The intruder went to his knees as the bullets ripped into him, then sprawled on his face. The revolver fell out of his limp hand.

Joey was crying.

Christine cautiously approached the body. Blood was soaking into the carpet around it. With one foot she prodded the man. He was dead weight.

She went to the door, looked into the shadowy hall, which was littered with fragments of the stairway railing and splinters of glass from the light fixture that had been struck by shotgun pellets. The carpet was spotted with blood from the dead gunman's bitten leg; he had left a trail from the head of the stairs.

She listened. No one moved or spoke downstairs. There were no footsteps.

Had there been just two assassins?

She wondered how many bullets she had left. The magazine held ten. She thought she had fired five. Five left.

Joey's sobbing subsided. "M-Mom?"

"Sshhh," she said.

They both listened.

Wind. Thunder. Rain on the roof, tapping the windows.

Four men dead. That realization hit her, and she felt nausea uncoiling in her stomach. The house was a slaughtering pen, a graveyard.

Wind-stirred, a tree branch scraped against the house.

Inside, the funereal silence deepened.

Finally she looked at Joey.

He was bleached white. His hair hung in his face. His eyes looked haunted. In a moment of terror, he had bitten his lip, and a thread of blood had sewn a curving red seam down his chin, along his jawline, and part of the way down his neck. As always, she was shocked by the sight of his blood. However, considering what had almost happened to him, this injury could be borne.

The cemetery stillness lost its cold grip on the night. Outside, along the street, there were shouts, not of anger but of fear and curiosity, as neighbors at last ventured out of their homes. In the distance, a siren swelled.

PART THREE

THE HOUNDS

Satan hasn't a single salaried helper;
the Opposition employs a million.
—Mark Twain

The hounds, the hounds
come baying at his heels.
The hounds, the hounds!
The breath of death he feels.
—*The Book of Counted Sorrows*

CHAPTER 26

As THE AUTHORITIES went about their work, Christine and Joey waited in the kitchen because that was one of the few rooms in the house that wasn't splashed with blood.

Christine had never seen so many policemen in one place before. Her house was crowded with uniformed men, plainclothes detectives, police lab technicians, a police photographer, a coroner and his assistant. Initially, she had welcomed the lawmen because their presence gave her a feeling of security, at last. But after a while she wondered if one of them might be a follower of Mother Grace and the Church of the Twilight. That notion didn't seem far-fetched. In fact, the logical assumption was that a militant religious cult, determined to force its views upon society at large, would make a special point of planting its people in various law-enforcement agencies and converting those who were already employed in that capacity. She remembered Officer Wilford, the born-again Christian who had disapproved of her language and manner of dress, and she wondered if perhaps Grace Spivey had been the midwife of his "rebirth."

Paranoia.

But considering the situation, perhaps a measure of paranoia was not a sign of mental illness; maybe, instead, it was prudent, a necessity for survival.

As rain continued to spatter the windows and as thunder shoved its way roughly through the night outside, she watched the cops warily, regarded each unusual move with suspicion. She realized that she couldn't go through the rest of her life distrusting everyone; that would require a constant watchfulness and a level of tension that would utterly drain her physical, emotional, and mental energies. It would be like living a life entirely on a high wire. For the moment, however, she couldn't relax; she remained on guard, alert, her muscles half tensed, ready to spring at anyone who made a threatening move toward Joey.

Again, the boy's resiliency surprised her. When the police had first arrived, he had seemed to be in shock. His eyes had been glazed, and he hadn't been willing or able to speak. The sight of so much bloody violence and the threat of death had left a mark on him that, for a while, had seemed disturbingly profound. She knew this experience would scar him for life; there was no escaping that. But for a time she had been afraid that the harrowing events of the past couple of hours would render him catatonic or precipitate some other dangerous form of psychological withdrawal. But eventually he had come out of it, and she had encouraged him by getting his battery-powered Pac-Man game and playing it with him. The electronic Pac-Man musical theme and the beeping sounds made by the cookie-gobbling yellow circle on the game board made a bizarre counterpoint to the grimness of murder and the seriousness of the homicide investigation being conducted around them.

Joey's recovery had also been helped by Chewbacca's miraculous recovery from the blow to the head that one of the assassins had delivered with the butt of a shotgun. The dog had been knocked unconscious, and his scalp had been skinned a bit, but the mild bleeding had stopped in response to pressure which Christine applied with antiseptic pads. There were no signs of concussion. Now the pooch was almost as good as new, and he stayed close to them, lying on the floor by Joey's chair, occasionally rising and looking up at the Pac-Man game, cocking his head, trying to figure out what the noisy device was.

She was no longer so sure that this dog's strong resemblance to Brandy was a bad thing. To endure the horror and turmoil, Joey needed reminders of more placid times, and he needed a sense of continuity that, like a bridge, would let him cross this period of chaos with his wits intact. Chewbacca, largely because of his resemblance to Brandy, could serve both those functions.

Charlie Harrison was in and out of the kitchen every ten or fifteen minutes, checking up on them and on the two new bodyguards he had stationed with them. One man, George Swarthout, sat on a tall stool by the kitchen phone, drinking coffee, watching Joey, watching the police who came in and out, watching Christine as she watched the police. The other, Vince Fields, was outside on the patio, guarding the rear approach to the house. It wasn't likely that any of Grace Spivey's people would launch a second attack while the house was swarming with cops, but the possibility couldn't be ruled out altogether. After all, kamikaze missions had a certain popularity with religious fanatics.

On each of his visits to the kitchen, Charlie kidded with Joey, played a game of Pac-Man, scratched behind Chewbacca's ears, and did whatever he could to lift the boy's spirits and keep his mind off the carnage in the rest of the house. When the police wanted to question Christine, Charlie stayed with Joey and sent her into another room, so the boy wouldn't have to listen to such gruesome talk. They wanted to question Joey, too, but Charlie managed their interrogation of the boy and kept it to a minimum. Christine realized that it wasn't easy for him to be such a rock, such a font of good spirits; he had lost two of his men, not only employees but friends. She was grateful that he seemed determined to conceal his own horror, tension, and grief for Joey's sake.

At eleven o'clock, just as Joey was tiring of Pac-Man, Charlie came in, pulled up a chair to the kitchen table, sat down, and said, "Those suitcases you packed this morning—"

"Still in my car."

"I'll have them put in mine. Go pack whatever else you might need for . . . say . . . a week. We'll be leaving here as soon as you're ready."

"Where are we going?"

"I'd rather not tell you just now. We could be overheard."

Had he, too, considered the possibility that one of Grace Spivey's people might be working as a cop? Christine wasn't sure whether his paranoia made her feel better or worse.

Joey said, "We gonna hole up in a hideout somewhere?"

"Yep," Charlie said. "That's exactly what we're going to do."

Joey frowned. "The witch has magic radar. She'll find us."

"Not where I'm taking you," Charlie said. "We've had a sorcerer cast a spell on the place so she can't detect it."

"Yeah?" Joey said, leaning forward, fascinated. "You know a sorcerer?"

"Oh, don't worry, he's a good guy," Charlie said. "He doesn't do black magic or anything like that."

"Well, sure," the boy said. "I wouldn't figure a private eye would work with an *evil* sorcerer."

Christine had a hundred questions for Charlie, but she didn't think it was a good idea to ask any of them in front of Joey and perhaps disturb his fragile equilibrium. She went upstairs, where the coroner was overseeing the removal of the red-haired killer's body, and she packed another suitcase. Downstairs, in Joey's room, she packed a second case for him, then, after a brief hesitation, stuffed some of his favorite toys in another bag.

She was gripped and shaken by the unsettling feeling that she would never see this house again.

Joey's bed, the *Star Wars* posters on his wall, his collection of plastic action figures and spaceships seemed slightly faded, as if they were not really here, as if they were objects in a photograph. She touched the bedpost, touched an E.T. doll, put a hand to the cool surface of the blackboard that stood in one corner, and she could feel those things beneath her fingers, but still, somehow, they didn't seem real any more. It was a strange, cold, augural feeling that left a hollowness within her.

No, she thought. I'll be back. Of course I will.

But the feeling of loss remained with her as she walked out of her son's room.

Chewbacca was taken out first and put into the green Chevy.

Then, in raincoats, shepherded by Charlie and his men, they left the house, and Christine shuddered when the cold, stinging rain struck her face.

Newspapermen, television camera teams, and a van from an all-news radio station awaited them. Powerful camera lights snapped on as soon as Christine and Joey appeared. Reporters jostled one another for the best position, and all of them spoke at once:

"Mrs. Scavello—"

"—a moment, please—"

"—just one question—"

She squinted as the lights lanced painfully at her eyes.

"—who would want to kill you and—"

"—is this a drug case—"

She held Joey tightly. Kept moving.

"—do you—"

"—can you—"

Microphones bristled at her.

"—have you—"

"—will you—"

A kaleidoscope of strange faces formed and reformed in front of her, some in shadow, some unnaturally pale and bright in the backsplash of the camera lights.

"—tell us what it feels like to live through—"

She got a glimpse of the familiar face of a man from KTLA's "Ten O'clock News."

"—tell us—"

"—what—"

"—how—"

"—why—"

"—terrorists or whatever they were?"

Cold rain trickled under the collar of her coat.

Joey was squeezing her hand very hard. The newsmen were scaring him.

She wanted to scream at them to get away, stay away, shut up.

They crowded closer.

Jabbered at her.

She felt as if she were making her way through a pack of hungry animals.

Then, in the crush and babble, an unfamiliar and unfriendly face loomed: a man in his fifties, with gray hair and bushy gray eyebrows. He had a gun.

No!

Christine couldn't get her breath. She felt a terrible weight on her chest.

It couldn't be happening again. Not so soon. Surely, they wouldn't attempt murder in front of all these witnesses. This was madness.

Charlie saw the weapon and pushed Christine and Joey out of the way.

At that same instant, a newswoman also saw the threat and tried to chop the gun out of the assailant's hand, but took a bullet in the thigh for her trouble.

Madness.

People screamed, and cops yelled, and everyone dropped to the rain-soaked ground, everyone but Christine and Joey, who ran toward the green Chevy, flanked by Vince Fields and George Swarthout. She was twenty feet from the car when something tugged at her, and pain flashed along her right side, just above the hip, and she knew she had been shot, but she didn't go down, didn't even stumble on the rain-slick sidewalk, just plunged ahead, gasping for breath, heart pounding so hard that each beat hurt her, and she held on to Joey, didn't look back, didn't know if the gunman was pursuing them, but heard a tremendous volley of shots, and then someone shouting, "Get me an ambulance!"

She wondered if Charlie had shot the assailant.

Or had Charlie been shot instead?

That thought almost brought her to a stop, but they were already at the Chevy.

George Swarthout yanked open the rear door of the car and shoved them inside, where Chewbacca was barking excitedly.

Vince Fields ran around to the driver's door.

"On the floor!" Swarthout shouted. "Stay down!"

And then Charlie was there, piling in after them, half on top of them, shielding them.

The Chevy's engine roared, and they pulled away from the curb with a shrill screeching of tires, rocketed down the street, away from the house, into the night and the rain, into a world that couldn't have been more completely hostile if it had been an alien planet in another galaxy.

CHAPTER 27

KYLE BARLOWE DREADED taking the news to Mother Grace, although he supposed she had already learned about it through a vision.

He entered the back of the church and stood there for a while, filling the doorway between the narthex and the nave, his broad shoulders almost touching both jambs. He was gathering strength from the giant brass cross above the altar, from the Biblical scenes depicted in the stained-glass windows, from the reverent quietude, from the sweet smell of incense.

Grace sat alone, on the left side of the church, in the second pew from the front. If she heard Barlowe enter, she gave no indication that she knew he was with her. She stared straight ahead at the cross.

At last Barlowe walked down the aisle and sat beside her. She was praying. He waited for her to finish. Then he said, "The second attempt failed, too."

"I know," she said.

"What now?"

"We follow them."

"Where?"

"Everywhere." She spoke softly at first, in a whisper he could barely hear, but gradually her voice rose and gained power and conviction, until it echoed eerily off the shadow-hung walls of the nave. "We give them no peace, no rest, no haven, no quarter. We must be pitiless, relentless, unsleeping, unshakable. We will be hounds. The hounds of Heaven. We will bay at their heels, lunge for their throats, and bring them to ground, sooner or later, here or there, when God wills it. We shall win. I am sure of it."

She had been staring intently at the cross as she spoke, but now she turned her colorless gray eyes on him, and as always he felt her gaze penetrating to the core of him, to his very soul.

He said, "What do you want me to do?"

"For now, go home. Sleep. Prepare yourself for the morning."

"Aren't we going after them again tonight?"

"First, we must find them."

"How?"

"God will lead. Now go. Sleep."

He stood, stepped into the aisle. "Will you sleep, too? You need your rest," he said worriedly.

Her voice had faded to a reedy whisper once more, and there was exhaustion in it. "I can't sleep, dear boy. An hour a night. Then I wake, and my mind is filled with visions, with messages from the angels, contacts from the spirit world, with worries and fears and hopes, with glimpses of the promised land, scenes of glory, with the awful weight of the responsibilities God has settled upon me." She wiped at her mouth with the back of one hand. "How I wish I *could* sleep, how I *long* for sleep, for surcease from all these demands and anxieties! But He has transformed me so that I can function without sleep during this crisis. I will not sleep well again until the Lord wills it. For reasons I don't understand, He needs me awake, *insists* upon it, gives me the strength to endure without sleep, keeps me alert, almost *too* alert." Her voice was shaking, and Barlowe imagined it was both awe and fear that put the tremor in it. "I tell you, dear Kyle, it's both glorious and terrible, wonderful and fright- ful, exhilarating and exhausting to be the instrument of God's will."

She opened her purse, withdrew a handkerchief, and blew her nose. Sud- denly she noticed that the hankie was stained brown and yellow, disgustingly knotted and crusted with dried snot.

"Look at this," she said, indicating the handkerchief. "It's horrible. I used to be so neat. So clean. My husband, bless his soul, always said my house was cleaner than a hospital operating room. And I was always very conscious of grooming; I dressed well. And I *never* would have carried a revolting handker- chief like this, never, not before the Gift was given to me and crowded out so many ordinary thoughts." Tears glimmered in her gray eyes. "Sometimes . . . I'm frightened . . . grateful to God for the Gift, yes . . . grateful for what I've gained . . . but frightened about what I've lost . . ."

He wanted to understand what it must be like for her, to be the instrument of God's will, but he couldn't comprehend her state of mind or the mighty forces working within her. He did not know what to say to her, and he was depressed that he couldn't comfort her.

She said, "Go home, sleep. Tomorrow, perhaps, we'll kill the boy."

CHAPTER 28

✐✐✐✐

IN THE CAR, speeding through the storm-sodden streets, Charlie insisted on having a look at Christine's wound, although she said it wasn't serious. He was relieved to discover that she was right; she had only been grazed; the bullet had left a shallow furrow, two inches long, just above her hip. It was more of an abrasion than a wound, mostly cauterized by the heat of the bullet; the slug wasn't in her, and there was only minor bleeding. Nevertheless, they stopped at an all-night market, where they picked up alcohol and iodine and bandages, and Charlie dressed the wound while Vince, behind the wheel, got them on the road again. They switched from street to street, doubled back, circled through the rain-lashed darkness, like a flying insect reluctant to light anywhere for fear of being swatted, crushed.

They took every possible precaution to insure that they weren't followed, and they didn't arrive at the safe-house in Laguna Beach until almost one o'clock in the morning. It was halfway up a long street, with (in daylight) a view of the ocean; a small place, almost a bungalow, two bedrooms and one bath; quaint, about forty years old but beautifully maintained, with a trellised front porch, gingerbread shutters; shrouded in bougainvillaea that grew up one wall and most of the way across the roof. The house belonged to Henry

Rankin's aunt, who was vacationing in Mexico, and there was no way Grace Spivey or anyone from the Church of the Twilight could know about it.

Charlie wished they had come here earlier, that he had never allowed Christine and Joey to return to their own house. Of course, he'd had no way of knowing that Grace Spivey would take such drastic and violent action so soon. Killing a dog was one thing, but dispatching assassins armed with shotguns, sending them boldly into a quiet residential neighborhood . . . well, he hadn't imagined she was *that* crazy. Now he had lost two of his men, two of his *friends.* An emotional acid, part grief and part self-reproach, ate at him. He had known Pete Lockburn for nine years, Frank Reuther for six, and liked both of them a great deal. Although he knew he wasn't at fault for what had happened, he couldn't help blaming himself; he felt as bleak as a man could feel without contemplating suicide.

He tried to conceal the depth of his grief and rage because he didn't want to upset Christine further. She was distraught about the murders and seemed determined to hold herself, in part, accountable. He tried to reason with her: Frank and Pete knew the risk when they took the job; if she hadn't hired Klemet-Harrison, the bodies now on the way to the morgue would be hers and Joey's, so she'd done the right thing by seeking help. Regardless of the arguments he presented, she couldn't shake off her dark sense of responsibility.

Joey had fallen asleep in the car, so Charlie carried him through the slanting rain, through the drizzling night quiet of the Laguna hills, into the house. He put him down on the bed in the master bedroom, and the boy didn't even stir, only murmured softly and sighed. Together, Charlie and Christine undressed him and put him under the covers.

"I guess it won't hurt if he misses brushing his teeth just one night," she said worriedly.

Charlie couldn't suppress a smile, and she saw him smiling, and she seemed to realize how ironic it was to be fretting about cavities only hours after the boy had escaped three killers.

She blushed and said, "I guess, if God spared him from the bullets, He'll spare him from tooth decay, huh?"

"It's a good bet."

Chewbacca curled up at the side of the bed and yawned heartily. He'd had a rough day, too.

Vince Fields came to the doorway and said, "Where do you want me, boss?"

Charlie hesitated, remembering Pete and Frank. He had put them in the line of fire. He didn't want to put Vince in the line of fire, too. But, of course, it was ridiculous of him to think that way. He couldn't tell Vince to hide in the back of the closet where it was safe. It was Vince's job to *be* in the line of fire if necessary; Vince knew that, and Charlie knew that, and they both knew it was Charlie's job to give the orders, regardless of the consequences. So what was he waiting for? Either you had the guts to accept the risks in this job, or you didn't.

He cleared his throat and said, "Uh . . . I want you right here, Vince. Sitting on a chair. Beside the bed."

Vince sat down.

Charlie took Christine to the small tidy kitchen, where George Swarthout had made a large pot of coffee and had poured cups for himself and Vince. Charlie sent George to the living room windows, to keep watch on the street, poured some of the coffee for himself and Christine.

"Miriam—Henry's aunt—is a brandy drinker. Would you like a slug in that coffee?"

"Might be a good idea," Christine said.

He found the brandy in the cabinet by the refrigerator and laced both cups of coffee.

They sat across from each other at a small table by a window that looked out on a rain-hammered garden where, at the moment, only shadows bloomed.

He said, "How's your hip?"

"Just a twinge."

"Sure?"

"Positive. Listen, what happens now? Will the police make arrests?"

"They can't. The assailants are all dead."

"But the woman who sent them isn't dead. She's a party to attempted murder. A conspirator. She's as guilty as they were."

"We've no proof Grace Spivey sent them."

"If all three of them are members of her church—"

"That would be an important lead. The problem is, how do we prove they were church members?"

"The police could question their friends, their families."

"Which they would definitely do . . . if they could *find* their friends and families."

"What do you mean?"

"None of those three gunmen was carrying identification. No wallets, no credit cards, no driver's licenses, no nothing."

"Fingerprints. Couldn't they be identified by their fingerprints?"

"Of course, the police will be following up on that. But unless those men were in the army or have criminal records or once held a security job that required them to be fingerprinted, their prints won't be on file anywhere."

"So we might *never* know who they were?"

"Maybe not. And until we can identify them, there's no way to trace them back to Grace Spivey."

She scowled as she drank some of her coffee and brandy, mulling over the situation, trying to see what they might have missed, trying to come up with a way to link the killers with the Church of the Twilight. Charlie could tell her that she was wasting her time, that Grace Spivey had been too careful, but she had to reach that conclusion on her own.

Finally she said, "The man who attacked us in front of the house . . . was he the one who was driving the van?"

"No. He's not the man I watched through binoculars."

"But if he was in that van, even as a passenger, maybe it's still parked down the street from my house."

"Nope. The police looked for it. No white van anywhere in the neighborhood. Nothing at all that would point to The True Word or to the Church of the Twilight."

"What about their weapons?"

"Those are being checked out, too. But I expect they weren't purchased legitimately. There'll be no way to find out who bought them."

Her face soured by frustration, she said, "But we know Grace Spivey threatened Joey, and we know one of her people has been following us in a van. After what happened tonight, isn't that reason enough for the cops to at least go talk to her?"

"Yes. And they will."

"When?"

"Now. If they haven't already. But she'll deny everything."

"They'll keep a watch on her?"

"Nope. No point in it, anyway. They might be able to watch her, but they can't keep tabs on everyone who's a member of her church. That would require a lot more manpower than they have. Besides, it'd be unconstitutional."

"Then we're right back where we started," she said miserably.

"No. Eventually, maybe not right away but in time, one of those nameless dead men or one of their guns or the pictures I took of the man in the van will give us a concrete connection with Grace Spivey. These people aren't perfect. Somewhere, they've overlooked a detail, made a mistake, and we'll capitalize on it. They'll make other mistakes, too, and sooner or later we'll have enough evidence to nail them."

"Meanwhile?"

"You and Joey will lay low."

"Here?"

"For the time being."

"They'll find us."

"No."

"They will," she said grimly.

"Not even the police know where you are."

"But your people know."

"We're on *your* side."

She nodded, but he could see that she still had something to say, something she really didn't want to say but something she couldn't contain, either.

"What is it? What're you thinking?" he prodded.

"Isn't it possible that one of your people belongs to the Church of the Twilight?"

The question startled him. He hand-picked his people, knew them, liked them, trusted them. "Impossible."

"After all, your agency had a run-in with Spivey. You rescued those two little children from her cult, snatched them away from their mother. I'd think maybe Grace Spivey would be wary of you, wary enough to plant someone in your organization. She could've converted one of your men."

"No. Impossible. The first time she tried to contact one of them, he'd report it to me immediately."

"Maybe it's one of your new employees, someone who was a Spivey disciple before he ever came to work for you. Have you hired anyone new since you snatched those kids?"

"A few people. But our employees have to undergo a rigorous background investigation before we hire them—"

"Membership in the church could be hidden, kept secret."

"It'd be difficult."

"I notice you've stopped saying 'impossible.' "

She'd made him uneasy. He liked to believe that he always thought of everything, prepared for every contingency. But he hadn't thought of this, primarily because he knew his people too well to entertain the notion that any of them was weak-minded enough to sign up with a crackpot cult. Then again, people were strange, especially these days, and the only thing about them that could surprise you was if they *never* surprised you.

He sipped his coffee and said, "I'll have Henry Rankin run entirely new checks on everyone who's joined us since the Spivey case. If something was missed the first time, Henry'll find it. He's the best there is."

"And you're sure you can trust Henry?"

"Jesus, Christine, he's like my brother!"

"Remember Cain and Abel."

"Listen, Christine, a little suspicion, a touch of paranoia—that's good. I encourage it. Makes you more cautious. But you can go too far. You've got to trust someone. You can't handle this alone."

She nodded, looked down at her half-finished coffee and brandy. "You're right. And I guess it's not very charitable of me to worry about how trustworthy your people are when two of them have already died for me."

"They didn't die for you," he said.

"Yes, they did."

"They only—"

"Died for me."

He sighed and said nothing more. She was too sensitive a woman not to feel some guilt about Pete Lockburn and Frank Reuther. She would just have to work it out by herself—the same way he would.

"All right," she said. "So while Joey and I are lying low, what'll you be doing?"

"Before we left your house, I called the rectory at the church."

"Her church?"

"Yeah. She wasn't in. But I asked her secretary to arrange a meeting for tomorrow. I made her promise to call Henry Rankin tonight, no matter how late, and let him know when I'm to be there."

"Walking into the lion's den."

"It's not quite that dramatic or dangerous."

"What do you expect to gain by talking to her?"

"I don't know. But it seems the next logical step."

She shifted in her chair, picked up her coffee, put it down without taking a drink, and chewed nervously on her lower lip. "I'm afraid that . . ."

"What?"

"I'm afraid, if you go to her . . . somehow she'll make you tell her where we are."

"I'm not that easy," he said.

"But she might use drugs or torture or—"

"Believe me, Christine, I can handle myself and I can handle this old woman and her pack of crazies."

She stared at him for a long time.

Her eyes were mesmerizingly beautiful.

At last she said, "You can. I know it. You can handle them. I have a lot of faith in you, Charlie Harrison. It's an . . . instinct. I feel good about you. I know you're capable. I don't doubt you. Really I don't. But I'm still scared."

At 1:30, someone from Klemet-Harrison brought Charlie's gray Mercedes to the house in Laguna Beach, so he could drive himself home when he was ready. At 2:05, grainy-eyed and bone-weary, he looked at his watch, said, "Well, I guess I'll be going," and went to the sink to rinse out his coffee cup.

When he put his cup in the rack to dry and turned, she was standing at the kitchen window, beside the door, staring out at the dark lawn. She was hugging herself.

He went to her. "Christine?"

She turned, faced him.

"You okay?" he asked.

She nodded, being brave. "Just a chill."

Her teeth chattered when she spoke.

On impulse, he put his arms around her. Without a hint of reservation, she came against him, allowed herself to be held, her head on his shoulder. Then her arms slipped around him, too, and they were linked, and nothing had ever been better than hugging her. Her hair was against his cheek, her hands on his back, her body molded to him, her warmth piercing him, the scent of her filling him. The embrace had the electrifying quality of a new and longed-for experience and, at the same time, it was a comfortable, familiar sharing. It was difficult to believe he had known her less than one day. He seemed to have *wanted* her much longer than that—and, of course, he had, though until he'd seen her he hadn't known it was her that he had wanted for so many years.

He could have kissed her then. He had the desire and the nerve to put a hand under her chin and lift her face and press his lips to hers, and he knew she wouldn't resist, might even welcome it. But he did no more than hug her because he sensed the time wasn't exactly right for the commitment that a passionate kiss implied. Now, it would be a kiss that she sought partly out of fear, partly out of a desperate need to be reassured. When at last he did kiss her, he wanted it to be for other reasons entirely: desire, affection, love. He wanted the start to be perfect for them.

When she finally let go of him, she seemed self-conscious. She smiled shyly and said, "Sorry. Didn't mean to get shaky on you. I've got to be strong. I know it. There's no room for weakness in this situation."

"Nonsense," he said gently. "I needed a hug, too."

"You did?"

"Everyone could use a teddy bear now and then."

She smiled at him.

He hated to leave her. All the way out to the car, with the wind tearing at his coat and the rain battering his bare head, he wanted to turn around and go back in there and tell her that something special was happening between them, something that shouldn't happen this fast, something like you saw in the movies but never in real life. He wanted to tell her now, even if it was the wrong time, because in spite of all his reassuring talk, he didn't know for sure that he would be able to handle Spivey and her crazies; there was a possibility, however slim, that he would never get another chance, never see Christine Scavello again.

He lived in the hills of North Tustin, and he was almost halfway home, cruising a lonely stretch of Irvine Boulevard, thinking about Frank Reuther and Pete Lockburn, when the events of the past few hours became too much to handle, and he was suddenly short of breath. He had to pull to the berm and stop. There were orange groves on one side of the roadway, strawberry fields on the other side, and darkness all around. At this hour, there was no traffic. Slumped back in his seat, he stared at the rain-spattered windshield where the water made ghostly, speckled patterns in the backsplash of his own headlight beams, brief-lived patterns erased by the metronomically thumping windshield wipers. It was unnerving and dispiriting to realize that human lives could be erased as suddenly and easily as those rain patterns on the glass. He wept.

In all its years of operation, Klemet-Harrison had lost only one other man in the line of duty. He had been killed in an automobile accident while he was working, although it was unconnected to his assignment and could have taken place as easily on his own time. A few men had been shot at over the years, mostly by estranged husbands who were determined to harass their wives in spite of court orders restraining them from doing so; and a couple of guys had even been hit. But until now no one had been *murdered,* for God's sake. The private investigation business was far less violent, far less dangerous than it was portrayed on television and in the movies. Sometimes you got roughed up a bit or had to rough up someone else, and there was always the *potential* for violence, but the potential was rarely realized.

Charlie wasn't afraid for himself, but he was afraid for his men, the people who worked for him and relied upon him. When he had taken this case, maybe he had gotten them into something he shouldn't have. Maybe, by signing on to protect Christine and Joey, he had also signed death warrants for himself and his associates. Who knew what to expect when you were dealing with religious fanatics? Who knew how far they would go?

On the other hand, everyone who worked with him knew the risks, even though they usually expected better odds than these. And what kind of detective agency would they be, what kind of bodyguards would they be if they walked away from the first really nasty case they handled? And how could he back down on his word to Christine Scavello? He wouldn't be able to face himself in the morning if he left her defenseless. Besides, he was more certain than ever that he was, with irrational but not entirely involuntary haste, falling in love with her.

In spite of the rain booming on the roof and the thumping of the windshield wipers, the night was unbearably silent in the oppressively humid car; there was a dearth of *meaningful* sound, just the random noises of the storm which, by their very randomness, reminded him of the chasm of chaos above which his life and all other lives unfolded. That was a thought on which he preferred not to dwell at the moment.

He pulled back onto the road, accelerated, and sent up twin plumes of spray from a deep puddle, heading toward the hills, and home.

CHAPTER 29

//////

CHRISTINE HADN'T EXPECTED to be able to sleep. She stretched out on the bed where Joey lay like a stone, but she figured she would just wait there with her eyes closed, resting, until he woke. She must have dropped off instantly.

She came around once during the night and realized the rain had stopped. The silence was profound.

George Swarthout was sitting in a chair in the corner, reading a magazine in the soft glow of a table lamp with a mother-of-pearl shade. She wanted to speak to him, wanted to know if everything was all right, but she hadn't the strength to sit up or even talk. She closed her eyes and drifted down into darkness again.

She came fully awake before seven o'clock, feeling fuzzy-headed after only four and a half hours of sleep. Joey was snoring softly. She left George watching over her son, went into the bathroom, and took a long, hot shower, wincing when water got under the bandage on her hip and elicited a stinging pain from her still-healing wound.

She finally stepped out of the shower, toweled dry, applied a new bandage, and was pulling on her clothes when she sensed that Joey was in trouble, right now, terrible trouble; she felt it in her bones. She thought she heard him scream above the rumbling of the bathroom's exhaust fan. Oh Jesus *no*. He was being slaughtered out there in the bedroom, hacked to pieces by some Bible-thumping maniac. Her stomach tightened, and her skin goose-pimpled, and in spite of the moaning bathroom fan she thought she heard something else, a thump, a clubbing sound. They must be beating him, too, stabbing and beating him, and her lungs blocked up, and she knew it, *knew* Joey was dead, my God, and in a wild panic she pulled up the zipper on her jeans, didn't even finish buttoning her blouse, stumbled out of the bathroom, shoeless, with her wet hair hanging in glossy clumps.

She had imagined everything.

The boy was safe.

He was awake, sitting up in bed, listening wide-eyed as George Swarthout told him a story about a magic parrot and the King of Siam.

Later, worried that her mother would hear about their problems on the news or read about them in the papers, she called, but then wished she hadn't. Evelyn listened to all the details, was properly shocked, but instead of offering much sympathy, she launched into an interrogation that surprised and angered Christine.

"What did you do to these people?" Evelyn wanted to know.

"What people?"

"The people at this church."

"I didn't do anything to them, Mother. They're trying to do it to *us*. Didn't you hear what I said?"

"They wouldn't pick on you for no reason," Evelyn said.

"They're crazy, Mother."

"Can't all of them be crazy, a whole churchful of people."

"Well, they are. They're bad people, Mother, real bad people."

"Can't all of them be bad. Not *religious* people like that. Can't all of them be after you just for the fun of it."

"I told you why they're after us. They've got this crazy idea that Joey—"

"That's what you *told* me," Evelyn said, "but that can't be it. Not really. There must be something else. Must be something you did that made them angry. But even if they're angry, I'm sure they're not trying to kill anybody."

"Mother, I *told* you, they came with guns, and men were killed—"

"Then the people who had guns weren't these church people," Evelyn said. "You've got it all wrong. It's someone else."

"Mother, I haven't got it all wrong. I—"

"Church people don't use guns, Christine."

"These church people do."

"It's someone else," Evelyn insisted.

"But—"

"You have a grudge against religion," Evelyn said. "Always have. A grudge against the Church."

"Mother, I don't hold any grudges—"

"That's why you're so quick to blame this on religious people when it's plainly the work of someone else, maybe political terrorists like on the news all the time, or maybe you're involved in something you shouldn't be and now it's getting out of hand, which wouldn't surprise me. Are you involved in something, Christine, like drugs, which they're always killing themselves over, like you see on TV, dealers shooting each other all the time—is it anything like that, Christine?"

She imagined she could hear the grandfather clock ticking monotonously in the background. Suddenly, she couldn't breathe well.

The conversation progressed in that fashion until Christine couldn't stand any more. She said she had to go, and she hung up before her mother could protest. Evelyn hadn't even said, "I love you," or "be careful," or "I'm worried about you," or "I'll do anything I can to help."

Her mother might as well be dead; their relationship certainly was.

At seven-thirty, Christine made breakfast for George, Vince, Joey, and herself. She was buttering toast when the rain began to fall again.

The morning was so drab, the clouds so low, the light so dim and gray that it might have been the end rather than the beginning of the day, and the rain came out of that somber sky with gutter-flooding force. Fog still churned outside, and without any sun it probably would hang on all day, barely dissipate, and get blindingly thick tonight. This was the time of year when relentless trains of storms could assault California, moving in from the Pacific, pounding the coastal areas until creeks swelled over their banks and reservoirs topped out and hillsides began to slide, carrying houses into the bottoms of the canyons with deadly swiftness. From the look of it, they were probably in the process of being run over by one of those storm trains right now.

The prospect of a long stretch of bad weather made the threat from the Church of the Twilight even more frightening. When winter rains closed in like this, streets were flooded, and freeways jammed up beyond belief, and mobility was curtailed, and California seemed to shrink, the mountains contracting toward the coast, squeezing the land in between. When the rainy season was at its worst, California acquired a claustrophobic aspect that you never read about in tourist brochures or see on postcards. In weather like this, Christine always felt a little trapped, even when she wasn't being hounded by well-armed lunatics.

When she took a plate of bacon and eggs to Vince Fields, where he was stationed by the front door, she said, "You guys must be tired. How long can you keep this up?"

He thanked her for the food, glanced at his watch, and said, "We only have about an hour to go. The replacement team will be here by then."

Of course. A replacement team. A new shift. That should have been obvious to her, but it hadn't been. She had grown accustomed to Vince and George, had learned to trust them. If either of them had been a member of the Church of the Twilight, she and Joey would have been dead by now. She wanted them to stay, but they couldn't remain awake and on guard forever. Foolish of her not to have understood that.

Now she had to worry about the new men. One of *them* might have sold his soul to Grace Spivey.

She returned to the kitchen. Joey and George Swarthout were having breakfast at the semicircular pine table which could accommodate only three chairs. She sat down in front of her own plate, but suddenly she wasn't hungry any more. She picked at her food and said, "George, the next shift of bodyguards—"

"Be here soon," he said around a mouthful of eggs and toast.

"Do you know who Charlie . . . who Mr. Harrison is sending?"

"You mean their names?"

"Yes, their names."

"Nope. Could be any of several fellas. Why?"

She didn't know why she would feel better if she knew their names. She wasn't familiar with Charlie's staff. Their names would mean nothing to her.

She wouldn't be able to tell that they were Grace Spivey's people just by their names. She wasn't being rational.

"If you know any of our people and would prefer to have them work a shift here, you should tell Mr. Harrison," George said.

"No. I don't know anybody. I just . . . well . . . never mind. It wasn't important."

Joey seemed to sense the nature of her fear. He stopped teasing Chewbacca with a piece of bacon, put one small hand on Christine's arm, as if to reassure her the way he'd seen Charlie do, and said, "Don't worry, Mom. They'll be good guys. Whoever Charlie sends, they'll be real good."

"The best," George agreed.

To George, Joey said, "Hey, tell Mom the story about the talking giraffe and the princess who didn't have a horse."

"I doubt if it's exactly your mother's kind of story," George said, smiling.

"Then tell me again," Joey said. "Please?"

As George told the fairytale—which seemed to be of his own creation—Christine's attention drifted to the rainy day beyond the window. Somewhere out there, two of Charlie's men were coming, and she was increasingly certain that at least one of them would be a disciple of the Spivey creature.

Paranoia. She knew that half her problem was psychological. She was worrying unnecessarily. Charlie had warned her not to go off the deep end. She wouldn't be much good to either Joey or herself if she started seeing boogeymen in every shadow. It was just the damned lousy weather, closing in on them, the rain and the morning fog, weaving a shroud around them. She felt trapped, suffocated, and her imagination was working overtime.

She was aware of all that.

It didn't matter.

She couldn't talk herself out of her fear. She knew that something bad was going to happen when the two men showed up.

CHAPTER 30

AT EIGHT O'CLOCK Tuesday morning, Charlie met Henry Rankin in front of the Church of the Twilight: a Spanish-style structure with stained-glass windows, red tile roof, two bell towers, and a broad expanse of steps leading up to six massive carved oak doors. Rain slanted at the doors, streamed off the steps, making oily puddles on the cracked and canted sidewalk. The doors needed to be refinished, and the building needed new stucco; it was shabby and neglected, but that was in keeping with the neighborhood, which had been deteriorating for decades. The church had once been the home of a Presbyterian congregation, which had fled ten blocks north, to a new site, where there weren't so many abandoned stores, adult bookshops, failing businesses, and crumbling houses.

"You look wiped out," Henry said. He stood at the foot of the church steps, holding a big black umbrella, frowning as Charlie approached under an umbrella of his own.

"Didn't get to bed until three-thirty," Charlie said.

"I tried to make this appointment for later," Henry said. "This was the only time she would see us."

"It's all right. If I'd had more time, I'd have just lain there, staring at the ceiling. Did the police talk to her last night?"

Henry nodded. "I spoke with Lieutenant Carella this morning early. They questioned Spivey, and she denied everything."

"They believe her?"

"They're suspicious, if only because they've had their own problems with more than a few of these cults."

Each time a car passed in the street, its tires hissed on the wet pavement with what sounded like serpentine anger.

"Have they been able to put a name to any of those three dead men?"

"Not yet. As for the guns, the serial numbers are from a shipment that was sent from the wholesaler in New York to a chain of retail sporting goods outlets in the Southwest, two years ago. The shipment never arrived. Hijacked. So these guns were bought on the black market. No way to trace who sold or purchased them."

"They cover their tracks well," Charlie said.

It was time to talk to Grace Spivey. He wasn't looking forward to it. He had little patience for the psychotic babble in which these cult types frequently spoke. Besides, after last night, anything was possible; they might even risk committing murder on their own doorstep.

He looked at his car, by the curb, where one of his men, Carter Rilbeck, was waiting behind the wheel. Carter would wait for them and send for help if they weren't out in half an hour. In addition, both Charlie and Henry were packing revolvers in shoulder holsters.

The rectory was to the left of the church, set back from the street, beyond an unkempt lawn, between two coral trees in need of trimming, ringed by shrubbery that hadn't been thinned or shaped in months. Like the church, the rectory was in ill-repair. Charlie supposed that if you really believed the end of the world was imminent—as these Twilighters claimed to believe—then you didn't waste time on such niceties as gardening and house painting.

The rectory porch had a creaking floor, and the doorbell made a thin, harsh, irregular sound, more animal than mechanical.

The curtain covering the window in the center of the door was abruptly drawn aside. A florid-faced, overweight woman with protuberant green eyes stared at them for a long moment, then let the curtain fall into place, unlocked the door, and ushered them into a drab entry hall.

When the door was closed and the susurrous voice of the storm faded somewhat, Charlie said, "My name is—"

"I know who you are," the woman replied curtly. She led them back down the hall to a chamber on the right, where the door was ajar. She opened the door all the way and indicated that they were to enter. She didn't come with them, didn't announce them, just closed the door after them, leaving them to their own introductions. Evidently, common courtesy was not an ingredient in the bizarre stew of Christianity and doomsday prophecy that Spivey's followers had cooked up for themselves.

Charlie and Henry were in a room twenty feet long and fifteen feet wide, sparsely and cheaply furnished. Filing cabinets lined one wall. In the center were a simple metal table on which lay a woman's purse and an ashtray, one metal folding chair behind the table, and two chairs in front of it. Nothing else. No draperies at the windows. No tables or cabinets or knick-knacks. There were no lamps, either, just the ceiling fixture, which cast a yellowish glow that, blending with the gray storm light coming through the tall windows, gave the room a muddy look.

Perhaps the oddest thing of all was the complete lack of religious objects: no paintings portraying Christ, no plastic statues of Biblical figures or angels, no needlepoint samplers bearing religious messages, none of the sacred objects— or kitsch, depending on your point of view—that you expected to find among cult fanatics. There had been none in the hallway, either, or in any of the rooms they had passed.

Grace Spivey was standing at the far end of the room, at a window, her back to them, staring out at the rain.

Henry cleared his throat.

She didn't move.

Charlie said, "Mrs. Spivey?"

Finally she turned away from the window and faced them. She was dressed all in yellow: pale yellow blouse, a gay yellow polka-dot scarf knotted at her neck, deep yellow skirt, yellow shoes. She was wearing yellow bracelets on each wrist and half a dozen rings set with yellow stones. The effect was ludicrous. The brightness of her outfit only accentuated the paleness of her puffy face, the withered dullness of her age-spotted skin. She looked as if she were possessed by senile whimsy and thought of herself as a twelve-year-old girl on the way to a friend's birthday party.

Her gray hair was wild, but her eyes were wilder. Even from across the room, those eyes were riveting and strange.

She was curiously rigid, shoulders drawn up tight, arms straight down at her sides, hands curled into tight fists.

"I'm Charles Harrison," Charlie said because he'd never actually met the woman before, "and this is my associate, Mr. Rankin."

As unsteady as a drunkard, she took two steps away from the window. Her face twisted, and her white skin became even whiter. She cried out in pain, almost fell, caught herself in time, and stood swaying as if the floor were rolling under her.

"Is something wrong?" Charlie asked.

"You'll have to help me," she said.

He hadn't figured on anything like this. He had expected her to be a strong woman with a vital, magnetic personality, a take-charge type who would keep them off balance from the start. Instead it was she who was off balance, and quite literally.

She was standing in a partial crouch now, as if pain were bending her in half. She was still stiff, and her hands were still fisted.

Charlie and Henry went to her.

"Help me to that chair before I fall," she said weakly. "It's my feet."

Charlie looked down at her feet and was shocked to see blood on them. He took her left arm, and Henry took her right, and they half carried her to the chair that stood behind the metal table. As she sat down, Charlie realized there was a bleeding wound on the bridge of each foot, just above the tongue of each shoe, twin holes, as if she had been stabbed, not by a knife but by something with a very narrow blade—perhaps an ice pick.

"Can I get you a doctor?" he asked, disconcerted to find himself being so solicitous to her.

"No," she said. "No doctor. Please sit down."

"But—"

"I'll be all right. I'll be fine. God watches over me, you know. God is good to me. Sit. Please."

Confused, they went to the two chairs on the other side of the table, but before either of them could sit, the old woman opened her fisted hands and held her palms up to them. "Look," she said in a demanding whisper. "Look at *this!* Behold *this!*"

The gruesome sight stopped Charlie from sitting down. In each of the woman's palms, there was another bleeding hole, like those in her feet. As he stared at her wounds, the blood began to ooze out faster than before.

Incredibly, she was smiling.

Charlie glanced at Henry and saw the same question in his friend's eyes that he knew must be in his own: *What the hell is going on here?*

"It's for you," the old woman said excitedly. She leaned toward them, stretching her arms across the table, holding her hands out to them, urging them to look.

"For us?" Henry said, baffled.

"What do you mean?" Charlie asked.

"A sign," she said.

"Sign?"

"A holy sign."

Charlie stared at her hands.

"Stigmata," she said.

Jesus. The woman belonged in an institution.

A chill worked its way assiduously up Charlie's spine and curled at the base of his neck, flicking its icy tail.

"The wounds of Christ," she said.

What have we walked into? Charlie wondered.

Henry said, "I better call a doctor."

"No," she said softly but authoritatively. "These wounds ache, yes, but it's a sweet pain, a good pain, a cleansing pain, and they won't become infected; they'll heal well on their own. Don't you understand? These are the wounds Christ endured, the holes made by the nails that pinned Him to the cross."

She's mad, Charlie thought, and he looked uneasily at the door, wondering where the florid-faced woman had gone. To get some other crazies? To organize a death squad? A human sacrifice? They had the nerve to call *this* Christianity?

"I know what you're thinking," Grace Spivey said, her voice growing louder, stronger. "You don't think I look like a prophet. You don't think God would work through an old, crazy-looking woman like me. But that *is* how He works. Christ walked with the outcasts, befriended the lepers, the prostitutes, the thieves, the deformed, and sent them forth to spread His word. Do you know why? Do you *know?*"

She was speaking so loudly now that her voice rebounded from the walls, and Charlie was reminded of a television evangelist who spoke in hypnotic rhythms and with the projection of a well-trained actor.

"Do you know why God chooses the most unlikely messengers?" she demanded. "It's because He wants to test you. *Anyone* could bring himself to believe the preachings of a pretty-boy minister with Robert Redford's face and Richard Burton's voice! But only the *righteous,* only those who truly *want* to believe in the Word . . . only those with enough *faith* will recognize and accept the Word regardless of the messenger!"

Her blood was dripping on the table. Her voice had risen until it vibrated in the window glass.

"God is testing you. Can you hear His message regardless of what you think of the messenger? Is your soul pure enough to allow you to *hear?* Or is there corruption within you that makes you deaf?"

Both Charlie and Henry were speechless. There was a mesmerizing quality to her tirade that was numbing and demanding of attention.

"Listen, listen, listen!" she said urgently. "Listen to what I *tell* you. God visited these stigmata upon me the moment you rang the doorbell. He has given you a *sign,* and that can mean only one thing: You aren't yet in Satan's thrall, and the Lord is giving you a chance to *redeem* yourselves. Apparently you don't realize what the woman is, what her *child* is. If you knew and still protected them, God wouldn't be offering you redemption. Do you know what they are? Do you *know?"*

Charlie cleared his throat, blinked, freed himself from the fuzziness that had briefly affected his thoughts. "I know what *you* think they are," Charlie said.

"It's not what I think. It's what I know. It's what God has told me. The boy is the Antichrist. The mother is the black Madonna."

Charlie hadn't expected her to be so direct. He was sure she would deny any interest in Joey, just as she had denied it to the police. He was startled by her forthrightness and didn't know what to make of it.

"I know you're not recording this conversation," she said. "We have instruments that would have detected a recorder. I would have been alerted. So I can speak freely. The boy has come to rule the earth for a thousand years."

"He's just a six-year-old boy," Charlie said, "like any other six-year-old boy."

"No," she said, still holding her hands up to reveal the blood seeping from her wounds. "No, he is more, worse. He must die. We must kill him. It is God's wish, God's work."

"You can't really mean—"

She interrupted him. "Now that you have been told, now that God has made the truth clear to you, you must cease protecting them."

"They're my clients," Charlie said. "I—"

"If you persist in protecting them, you're damned," the old woman said worriedly, begging them to accept redemption.

"We have an obligation—"

"Damned, don't you see? You'll rot in Hell. All hope lost. Eternity spent in suffering. You must listen. You must learn."

He looked into her fevered eyes, which challenged him with berserk intensity. His pity for her was mixed with a disgust that left him unable and unwilling to debate with her. He realized it had been pointless to come. The woman was beyond the reach of reason.

He was now more afraid for Christine and Joey than he had been last night, when one of Grace Spivey's followers had been shooting at them.

She raised her bleeding palms an inch or two higher. "This sign is for you, for *you,* to convince you that I am, in fact, a herald bearing a true message. Do you see? Do you believe now? Do you *understand?"*

Charlie said, "Mrs. Spivey, you shouldn't have done this. Neither of us is a gullible man, so it's all been for nothing."

Her face darkened. She curled her hands into fists again.

Charlie said, "If you used a nail that was at all rusty or dirty, I hope you'll go immediately to your doctor and get tetanus shots. This could be very serious."

"You're lost to me," she said in a voice as flat as the table to which she lowered her bleeding hands.

"I came here to try to reason with you," Charlie said. "I see that's not possible. So just let me warn you—"

"You belong to Satan now. You've had your chance—"

"—if you don't back off—"

"—and you've thrown your chance away—"

"—if you don't leave the Scavellos alone—"

"—and now you'll pay the terrible price!"

"—I'll dig into this and hang on. I'll keep at it come Hell or high water, until I've seen you put on trial, until I've seen your church lose its tax exemption, until everyone knows you for what you really are, until your followers lose their faith in you, and until your insane little cult is crushed. I mean it. I can be as relentless as you, as determined. I can finish you. Stop while you have a chance."

She glared at him.

Henry said, "Mrs. Spivey, will you put an end to this madness?"

She said nothing. She lowered her eyes.

"Mrs. Spivey?"

No response.

Charlie said, "Come on, Henry. Let's get out of here."

As they approached the door, it opened, and an enormous man entered the room, ducking his head to avoid rapping it on the frame. He had to be almost seven feet tall. He had a face from a nightmare. He didn't seem real; only images from the movies were suitable to describe him, Charlie thought. He was like a Frankenstein monster with the hugely muscled body of Conan the Barbarian, a shambling hulk spawned by a bad script and a low budget. He saw Grace Spivey weeping, and his face knotted with a look of despair and rage that made Charlie's blood turn to icy slush. The giant reached out, grabbed Charlie by the coat, and nearly hauled him off the floor.

Henry drew his gun, and Charlie said, "Hold it, hold it," because although the situation was bad it wasn't necessarily lethal.

The big man said, "What'd you do to her? What'd you do?"

"Nothing," Charlie said. "We were—"

"Let them go," Grace Spivey said. "Let them pass, Kyle."

The giant hesitated. His eyes, like hard bright sea creatures hiding deep under a suboceanic shelf, regarded Charlie with a pure malignant fury that would have given nightmares to the devil himself. At last he let go of Charlie, lumbered toward the table at which the woman sat. He spotted blood on her hands and wheeled back toward Charlie.

"She did it to herself," Charlie said, edging toward the door. He didn't like the wheedling note in his own voice, but at the moment there didn't seem to be room for pride. To give in to a macho urge would be ironclad proof of feeble-mindedness. "We didn't touch her."

"Let them go," Grace Spivey repeated.

In a low, menacing voice, the giant said, "Get out. Fast."

Charlie and Henry did as they were told.

The florid-faced woman with the protruding green eyes was waiting at the front of the rectory. As they hurried down the hallway, she opened the door. The instant they stepped onto the porch, she slammed the door behind them and locked it.

Charlie went out into the rain without putting up his umbrella. He turned his face toward the sky. The rain felt fresh and clean, and he let it hammer at him because he felt soiled by the madness in the house.

"God help us," Henry said shakily.

They walked out to the street.

Dirty water was churning to the top of the gutter. It formed a brown lake out toward the intersection, and bits of litter, like a flotilla of tiny boats, sailed on the wind-chopped surface.

Charlie turned and looked back at the rectory. Now its grime and deterioration seemed like more than ordinary urban decay; the rot was a reflection of the minds of the building's occupants. In the dust-filmed windows, in the peeling paint and sagging porch and badly cracked stucco, he saw not merely ruin but the physical world's representation of human madness. He had read a lot of science fiction as a child, still read some now and then, so maybe that was why he thought of the Law of Entropy, which held that the universe and all things within it moved in only one basic direction—toward decay, collapse, dissolution, and chaos. The Church of the Twilight seemed to embrace entropy as the ultimate expression of divinity, aggressively promulgating madness, unreason, and chaos, reveling in it.

He was scared.

CHAPTER 31

/////

AFTER BREAKFAST, CHRISTINE called Val Gardner and a couple of other people, assured them that she and Joey were all right, but didn't tell any of them where she was. Thanks to the Church of the Twilight, she no longer entirely trusted her friends, not even Val, and she resented that sad development.

By the time she finished making her phone calls, two new bodyguards arrived to relieve Vince and George. One of them, Sandy Breckenstein, was tall and lean, about thirty, with a prominent Adam's apple; he brought to mind Ichabod Crane in the old Disney cartoon version of *The Legend of Sleepy Hollow.* Sandy's partner was Max Steck, a bull of a man with big-knuckled hands, a massive chest, a neck almost as thick as his head—and a smile as sweet as any child's.

Joey took an immediate liking to both Sandy and Max and was soon running back and forth from one end of the small house to the other, trying to keep company with both of them, jabbering away, asking them what it was like to be a bodyguard, telling them his charmingly garbled version of George Swarthout's story about the giraffe who could talk and the princess who didn't have a horse.

Christine was not as quick as Joey to place her confidence in her new protectors. She was friendly but cautious, watchful.

She wished she had a weapon of her own. She didn't have her pistol any more. The police had kept it last night until they could verify that it was properly registered. She couldn't very well take a knife from the kitchen drawer and walk around with it in her hand; if either Sandy or Max *was* a follower of Grace Spivey, the knife might not forestall violence but precipitate it. And if neither of them was a Twilighter, she would only offend and alienate them by such an open display of distrust. Her only weapons were wariness and her wits, which wouldn't be terribly effective if she found herself confronted by a maniac with a .357 Magnum.

However, when trouble paid a visit, shortly after nine o'clock, it did not come from either Sandy or Max. In fact, it was Sandy, keeping watch from a chair by a living room window, who saw that something was wrong and called their attention to it.

When Christine came in from the kitchen to ask him if he wanted more coffee, she found him studying the street outside with visible tension. He had risen from the chair, leaned closer to the window, and was holding the binoculars to his eyes.

"What is it?" she asked. "Who's out there?"

He watched for a moment longer, then lowered the binoculars. "Maybe nobody."

"But you think there is."

"Go tell Max to keep a sharp eye at the back," Sandy said, his Adam's apple bobbling. "Tell him the same van has cruised by the house three times."

Her heartbeat accelerated as if someone had thrown a switch. "A white van?"

"No," he said. "Midnight blue Dodge with a surfing mural on the side. Probably it's nothing. Just somebody who's not familiar with the neighborhood, trying to find an address. But . . . uh . . . better tell Max, anyway."

She hurried into the kitchen, which was at the back of the house, and she tried to deliver the news to Max Steck calmly, but her voice had a tremor in it, and she couldn't control her hands, which made nervous, meaningless, butterfly gestures in the air.

Max checked the lock on the kitchen door, even though he had tested it himself when he'd first come on duty. He closed the blinds entirely on one window. He closed them halfway on the other.

Chewbacca had been lying in one corner, dozing. He raised his head and snorted, sensing the new tension in the air.

Joey was sitting at the table by the garden window, busily using his crayons to fill in a picture in a coloring book. Christine moved him away from the window, took him into the corner, near the humming refrigerator, out of the line of fire.

With the short attention span and emotional adaptability of a six-year-old, he had pretty much forgotten about the danger that had forced them to hide out in a stranger's house. Now it all came back to him, and his eyes grew big. "Is the witch coming?"

"It's probably nothing to worry about, honey."

She stooped down, pulled up his jeans, and tucked in his shirt, which had come half out of his waistband. His fear made her heart ache, and she kissed him on the cheek.

"Probably just a false alarm," she said. "But Charlie's men don't take any chances, you know."

"They're super," he said.

"They sure are," she said.

Now that it looked as if they might actually have to put their lives on the line for her and Joey, she felt guilty about being suspicious of them.

Max shoved the small table away from the window, so he wouldn't have to lean over it to look out.

Chewbacca made an interrogatory whining sound in the back of his throat, and began to pad around in a circle, his claws ticking on the kitchen tile.

Afraid that the dog would get in Max's way at a crucial moment, she called to it, and then so did Joey. The animal couldn't have learned its new name yet, but it responded to tone of voice. It came to Joey and sat beside him.

Max peered through a chink between two of the slats in the blind and said, "This damn fog sure is hanging on this morning."

Christine realized that, in the fog and obscuring rain, the garden—with its azaleas, bushy oleander, veronicas, carefully shaped miniature orange trees, lilacs, bougainvillaea-draped arbor, and other shrubbery—would make it easy for someone to creep dangerously close to the house before being spotted.

In spite of his mother's reassurances, Joey looked up at the ceiling, toward the sound of rain on the roof, which was loud in this one-story house, and he said, "The witch is coming. She's coming."

CHAPTER 32

DR. DENTON BOOTHE, both a psychologist and psychiatrist, was living proof that the heirs of Freud and Jung didn't have all the answers, either. One wall in Boothe's office was covered with degrees from the country's finest universities, awards from his colleagues in half a dozen professional organizations, and honorary doctorates from institutions of learning in four countries. He had written the most widely adopted and highly praised textbook on general psychology in thirty years, and his position as one of the most knowledgeable experts in the specialty of abnormal psychology was unchallenged. Yet Boothe, for all his knowledge and expertise, wasn't without problems of his own.

He was fat. Not just pleasantly plump. *Fat.* Shockingly, grossly overweight. When Charlie encountered Denton Boothe ("Boo" to friends), after not having seen him for a few weeks, he was always startled by the man's immensity; he never seemed to remember him as being *that* fat. Boothe stood five-eleven, Charlie's height, but he weighed four hundred pounds. His face did a good imitation of the moon. His neck was a post. His fingers were like sausages. Sitting, he overflowed chairs.

Charlie couldn't understand why Boothe, who could uncover and treat the neuroses even of those patients highly resistant to treatment, could not deal with his own compulsive eating. It was a puzzlement.

But his unusual size and the psychological problems underlying it did nothing to change the fact that he was a delightful man, kind and amusing and quick to laugh. Although he was fifteen years older than Charlie and infinitely better educated, they had hit it off on first encounter and had been friends for several years, getting together for dinner once or twice a month, exchanging gifts at Christmas, making an effort to keep in touch that, sometimes, surprised both of them.

Boo welcomed Charlie and Henry into his office, part of a corner suite in a glass high-rise in Costa Mesa, and insisted on showing them his latest antique bank. He collected animated banks with clockwork mechanisms that made a little adventure out of the deposit of each coin. There were at least two dozen of them displayed at various points in the office. This one was an elaborate affair the size of a cigar humidor; standing on the lid were hand-painted metal figurines of two bearded gold prospectors flanking a comically detailed donkey. Boo put a quarter in the hand of one prospector and pushed a button on the side of the bank. The prospector's hand came up, holding the coin out to the second prospector, but the donkey's hinged head lowered, and its jaws clamped shut on the quarter, which the prospector relinquished. The donkey raised its head again, and the quarter dropped down its gullet and into the bank underneath, while both prospectors shook their heads in dismay. The name on the donkey's saddlebags was Uncle Sam.

"It was made in 1903. So far as anyone knows, there are only eight working models in the world," Boo said proudly. "It's titled 'The Tax Collector,' but I call it 'There Is No Justice in a Jackass Universe.' "

Charlie laughed, but Henry looked baffled.

They adjourned to a corner of the room where large comfortable armchairs were grouped around a glass-topped coffee table. Boo's chair groaned softly as he settled into it.

Being a corner office, the room had two exterior walls that were largely glass. Because this building faced away from the other high-rise structures in Costa Mesa, toward one of the few remaining tracts of agricultural land in this part of the county, there seemed to be nothing outside but a gray void composed of churning clouds, gauzy veils of lingering fog, and rain that streamed down the glass walls in a vertical river. The effect was disorienting, as if Boothe's office didn't exist in this world but in an alternate reality, another dimension.

"You say this is about Grace Spivey?" Boothe asked.

He had a special interest in religious psychoses and had written a book about the psychology of cult leaders. He found Grace Spivey intriguing and intended to include a chapter about her in his next book.

Charlie told Boo about Christine and Joey, about their encounter with Grace at South Coast Plaza and the attempts on their lives.

The psychologist, who didn't believe in being solemn with patients, who used cajolery and humor as part of his therapy, whose face seldom played host to a frown, was now scowling. He said, "This is bad. Very bad. I've always known Grace is a true believer, not just a phony, mining the religious rackets for a buck. She's always been convinced that the world really was coming to an end. But I never believed she was sunk this deep in psychotic fantasy." He sighed and looked out at his twelfth-floor view of the storm. "You know, she talks a lot about her 'visions,' uses them to whip her followers into a frenzy. I've always thought that she doesn't really have them, that she merely *pretends* to have them because she realizes they're a good tool for making converts and keeping disciples in line. By using the visions, she can have God tell her people to do the things *she* wants them to do, things they might not accept if they didn't think the orders were coming straight down from Heaven."

"But if she's a true believer," Henry said, "how would she justify fakery to herself?"

"Oh, easily, easily," the psychologist said, looking away from the rain-filled February morning. "She'd justify it by saying she was only telling her followers things that God would've told them, anyway, if He actually *had* appeared to her in visions. The second possibility, which is more disturbing, is that she actually *is* seeing and hearing God."

"You don't mean literally seeing Him," Henry said, surprised.

"No, no," Boo said, waving one pudgy hand. He was an agnostic, flirting with atheism. He sometimes told Charlie that, considering the miserable state of the world, God must be on extended vacation in Albania, Tahiti, Cleveland or some other remote corner of the universe, where the news just wasn't getting to Him. He said, "I mean that she's seeing and hearing God, but, of course, He's merely a figment of her own sick mind. Psychotics, if they're far enough over the line, often have visions, sometimes of a religious nature and sometimes not. But I wouldn't have thought Grace had gone that far 'round the bend."

Charlie said, "She's so far gone that they don't even have Taco Bells where she's at."

Boo laughed, not as heartily as Charlie would have liked, but he *did* laugh, which was better than the scowl that made Charlie nervous. Boo had no pretensions about his profession and held nothing sacred; he was as likely to use the term "fruitcake" as "mentally disturbed." He said, "But if Grace has slipped her moorings altogether, then there's something about this situation that's hard to explain."

To Henry, Charlie said, "He loves to explain things. A born pedant. He'll explain beer to you while you're trying to drink it. And don't ask him to explain the meaning of life, or we'll be here until our retirement funds start to pay off."

Boothe remained uncharacteristically solemn. "It isn't the meaning of life that puzzles me right now. You say Grace has gone 'round the bend, and it certainly sounds as if you may be correct. But you see, if she really believes all this Antichrist stuff, and she's willing to kill an innocent child, then she's evidently a paranoid schizophrenic with apocalyptic fantasies and delusions of grandeur. But it's hard to imagine someone in that condition would be able to function as an authority figure or conduct the business of her cult."

"Maybe someone else is running the cult," Henry said. "Maybe she's just a figurehead now. Maybe someone else is using her."

Boothe shook his head. "It's damned difficult to use a paranoid schizophrenic the way you're suggesting. They're too unpredictable. But if she's really turned violent, has begun to *act* on her doomsday prophecies, she doesn't *have* to be crazy. Could be another explanation."

"Such as?" Charlie asked.

"Such as . . . maybe her followers are disillusioned with her. Maybe the cult is falling apart, and she's resorting to these drastic measures to renew her disciples' excitement and keep them faithful."

"No," Charlie said. "She's nuts." He told Boo about his macabre meeting with Grace just a short while ago.

Boothe was startled. "She actually drove nails into her hands?"

"Well, we didn't see her do it," Charlie admitted. "Maybe one of her followers wielded the hammer. But she obviously cooperated."

Boo shifted, and his chair creaked. "There's another possibility. The spontaneous appearance of crucifixion stigmata on the hands and feet of psychotics with religious persecution complexes is a rare phenomenon but not entirely unheard of."

Henry Rankin was astonished. "You mean they were *real?* You mean . . . *God* did that to her?"

"Oh, no, I don't mean to imply this was a genuine holy sign or anything of that sort. God had nothing to do with it."

"I'm glad to hear you say that," Charlie told him. "I was afraid you were suddenly going mystical on me. And if there are two things I'd never expect you to do, one is to go mystical on me, and the other is to become a ballet dancer."

The worried look on the fat man's face did not soften.

Charlie said, "Jesus, Boo, I'm already scared, but if the situation worries *you* this much, I'm not half as frightened as I ought to be."

Boothe said, "I *am* worried. As for the stigmata phenomenon, there is some evidence that, in a Messianic frenzy, a psychotic may exert a control on his body . . . on tissue structure . . . an almost, well, psychic control that medical science can't explain. Like those Indian holy men who walk on hot coals or lie on nails and *prevent* injury by an act of will. Grace's wounds would be the other side of that coin."

Henry, who liked everything to be reasonable and orderly and predictable, who expected the universe to be as neat and well-pressed as his own wardrobe, was clearly disturbed by talk of psychic abilities. He said, "They can make themselves bleed just by *thinking* about it?"

"They probably don't even have to think about it, at least not consciously," Boo said. "The stigmata are the result of a strong unconscious desire to be a religious figure or symbol, to be venerated, or to be a part of something bigger than self, something cosmic." He folded his hands on his ample stomach. "For instance . . . how much do you know about the supposed miracle at Fatima?"

"Not much," Charlie said.

"The Virgin Mary appeared to a lot of people there, thousands of people," Henry said, "back in the twenties, I think."

"A stunning and moving divine visitation—or one of the most incredible cases of mass hysteria and self-hypnosis ever recorded," Boo said, clearly favoring the second explanation. "Hundreds of people reported seeing the Virgin Mary and described a turbulent sky seething with all the colors of the rainbow. Among those in the huge crowd, two people developed crucifixion stigmata; one man's hands began to bleed, and nail holes appeared in a woman's feet. Several people claimed to have spontaneously acquired tiny punctures in a ring around their heads, as if from a crown of thorns. There's a documented case of an onlooker weeping tears of blood; subsequent medical examination showed no eye damage whatsoever, no possible source of blood. In short, the mind is still largely an uncharted sea. There are mysteries in here"—he tapped his head with one thick finger—"that we may never understand."

Charlie shivered. It was creepy to think Grace had descended so far into madness that she could make her body bleed spontaneously for the sole purpose of lending substance to her sick fantasies.

"Of course," Boo said, "you're probably right about the hammer and nails. Spontaneous crucifixion stigmata are rare. Grace probably did it to herself—or had one of her people do it."

The rain streamed down the walls of glass, and a miserably wet black bird swooped close, seeking escape from the cold downpour, then darted away an instant before crashing through the window.

Considering what Boothe had told them about tears of blood and mentally-inflicted stigmata, Charlie said, "I think I've stumbled across the meaning of life."

"What's that?" Boo asked.

"We're all just actors in a cosmic horror film in God's private movie theater."

"Could be," Boo said. "If you read your Bible, you'll see that God can think up more horrible punishments than anything Tobe Hooper or Steven Spielberg or Alfred Hitchcock ever dreamed of."

WITH HIS BINOCULARS, Sandy Breckenstein had gotten the license plate number the third time the blue Dodge van with the surfing murals had driven by the house. While Christine Scavello had hurried into the kitchen to report the presence of a suspicious vehicle to Max, Sandy had phoned Julie Gethers, the police liaison at Klemet-Harrison, and had asked her to get a make on the Dodge.

While he waited for a response from Julie, he stood tensely by the window, binoculars in hand.

Within five minutes, the van made a fourth pass, heading up the hill this time.

Sandy used the binoculars and saw, indistinctly, two men behind the rain-washed windshield.

They seemed to be studying this house in particular.

Then they were gone. Sandy almost wished they'd parked out front. At least there he could keep an eye on them. He didn't like having them out of sight.

While Sandy stood at the window, chewing on his lip, wishing he had become a certified public accountant like his father, Julie at HQ made contact with the Department of Motor Vehicles and then with the Orange County Sheriff's Department. Thanks to computerization at both agencies, the information was obtained quickly, and she returned Sandy's call in twelve minutes. According to the DMV, the blue van was registered to Emanuel Luis Spado of Anaheim. According to the Sheriff's office, which shared hot sheet data with all other police agencies in the county, Mr. Spado had reported his vehicle stolen as of six o'clock this morning.

As soon as he had that information, Sandy went into the kitchen to share it with Max, who was equally uneasy about it.

"It's trouble," Max said bluntly.

Christine Scavello, who had moved her son out of the line of fire, into the corner by the refrigerator, said, "But it doesn't belong to the church."

"Yeah, but it could've been someone from the church who stole it," Sandy said.

"To put distance between the church and any attack they might make on us here," Max explained.

"Or it could just be coincidence that someone in a stolen van is cruising this street," the woman said, though she sounded as if she didn't believe it.

"Never met a coincidence I liked," Max said, keeping a watch on the garden behind the house.

"Me either," Sandy said.

"But how did they find us?" Christine demanded.

"Beats me," Sandy said.

"Damned if I know," Max said. "We took every precaution."

They all knew the most likely explanation: Grace Spivey had an informer planted at Klemet-Harrison. None of them wanted to say it. The possibility was too unnerving.

"What'd you tell them at HQ?" Max asked.

"To send help," Sandy said.

"You think we should wait for it?"

"No."

"Me neither. We're sitting ducks here. This place was a good idea only as long as we figured they'd never find it. Now, our best chance is to get out, get moving, before they know we've spotted them. They won't be expecting us to suddenly pull up and light out."

Sandy agreed. He turned to Christine. "Get your coats on. You can take only two suitcases, 'cause you'll have to carry them both. Max and I can't be tied down with luggage on the way to the car; we've got to keep our hands free."

The woman nodded. She looked stricken. The boy was pale and waxy. Even the dog seemed to be worried; it sniffed the air, cocked its head, and made a peculiar whining noise.

Sandy didn't feel so good himself. He knew what had happened to Frank Reuther and Pete Lockburn.

CHAPTER 34

THUNDER SHOOK the window-walls.

Rain fell harder than ever.

Heat streamed from the ceiling vents, but Charlie couldn't get rid of a chill that made his hands clammy.

Denton Boothe said, "I've talked with people who knew Grace before this religious fanaticism. Many of them mention how close she and her husband were. Married forty-four years, she idolized the man. Nothing was too good for her Albert. She kept his house exactly as he liked it, cooked only his favorite foods, did everything the way he preferred. The only thing she was never able to give him was the thing he would have liked the most—a son. At his funeral, when she broke down, she kept saying, over and over, 'I never gave him a son.' It's conceivable that, to Grace, a male child—*any* male child—is a symbol of her failure to give her husband what he most desired. While he was alive, she could make up for that failure by treating him like a king, but once he was gone she had no way to atone for her barrenness, and perhaps she began to hate little boys. Hate them, then fear them, then fantasize that one of them was the Antichrist, here to destroy the world. It's an understandable if regrettable progression for psychosis."

Henry said, "If I recall, they did adopt a daughter—"

"The one who had Grace committed for psychiatric evaluation when this Twilight business first came up," Charlie said.

"Yes," Boo said. "Grace sold her house, liquidated investments, and put the money into this church. It was irrational, and the daughter was correct in seeking to preserve her mother's estate. But Grace came through the psychiatric evaluation with flying colors—"

"How?" Charlie wondered.

"Well, she was cunning. She knew what the psychiatric examiner was looking for, and she had sufficient control of herself to hide all those attitudes and tendencies that would have set off the alarm bells."

"But she *was* liquidating property to form a church," Henry said. "Surely the doctor could see that wasn't the act of a rational person."

"On the contrary. Provided she understood the risks of her actions and had a firm grip on all the potential consequences, or at least as long as she convinced the examining doctor that she had a firm grip, the mere fact that she wanted to give everything to God's work would not be sufficient to declare her mentally incompetent. We have religious liberty in this country, you know. It's an important constitutional freedom, and the law steps respectfully around it in cases like this."

"You've got to help me, Boo," Charlie said. "Tell me how this woman thinks. Give me a handle on her. Show me how to turn her off, how to make her change her mind about Joey Scavello."

"This kind of psychopathic personality is *not* frightened, shaky, about to collapse. Just the opposite. With a cause she believes in, supported by delusions of grandeur that are intensely religious in nature . . . well, despite appearances to the contrary, she's a rock, utterly resistant to pressure and stress. She lives in a reality that she made for herself, and she's made it so well that there's probably no way you can shake it or pull it apart or cause her to lose faith in it."

"Are you saying I can't change her mind?"

"I would think it's impossible."

"Then how do I make her back off? She's a flake; there must be an easy way to handle her."

"You're not listening—or you don't want to hear what I'm telling you. You mustn't make the mistake of assuming that, just because she's psychotic, she's vulnerable. This sort of mental problem carries with it a peculiar strength, an ability to withstand rejection, failure, and all forms of stress. You see, Grace evolved her psychotic fantasy for the sole purpose of protecting herself from those things. It's a way of armoring herself against the cruelties and disappointments of life, and it's damned good armor."

Charlie said, "Are you telling me she has no weaknesses?"

"Everyone has weaknesses. I'm just telling you that, in Grace's case, finding them won't be easy. I'll have to look over my file on her, think about it awhile . . . Give me a day at least."

"Think fast," Charlie said, getting to his feet, "I've got a few hundred homicidal religious fanatics breathing down my neck."

At the door, as they were leaving his office, Boo said, "Charlie, I know you put quite a lot of faith in me sometimes—"

"Yeah, I've got a Messiah complex about you."

Ignoring the joke, still unusually somber, Boo said, "I just don't want you to pin a lot of hope on what I might be able to come up with. In fact, I might not be able to come up with anything. Right now, I'd say there's only one answer, one way to deal with Grace if you want to save your clients."

"What's that?"

"Kill her," Boo said without a smile.

"You certainly aren't one of those bleeding-heart psychiatrists who always want to give mass murderers a second chance at life. Where'd you get your degree—Attila the Hun School of Head-Shrinking?"

He very much wanted Boo to joke with him. The psychiatrist's grim reaction to the story of his meeting with Grace this morning was so out of character that it unsettled Charlie. He needed a laugh. He needed to be told there was a silver lining somewhere. Boo's gray-faced sobriety was almost scarier than Grace Spivey's flamboyant ranting.

But Boo said, "Charlie, you know me. You know I can find something humorous in *anything*. I chuckle at dementia praecox in certain situations. I am amused by certain aspects of death, taxes, leprosy, American politics, and cancer. I've even been known to smile at reruns of 'Laverne & Shirley' when my grandchildren have insisted I watch with them. But I see nothing to laugh at here. You are a dear friend, Charlie. I'm frightened for you."

"You don't really mean I should kill her."

"I know you couldn't commit cold-blooded murder," Boothe said. "But I'm afraid Grace's death is the only thing that might redirect these cultists' attention away from your clients."

"So it'd be helpful if I *was* capable of cold-blooded murder."

"Yes."

"Helpful if I had just a *little* killer in me."

"Yes."

"Jesus."

"A difficult state of affairs," Boo agreed.

CHAPTER 35

HHHH

THE HOUSE HAD no garage, just a carport, which meant they had to expose themselves while getting in the green Chevy. Sandy didn't like it, but there was no other choice except to stay in the house until reinforcements arrived, and his gut instinct told him that would be a mistake.

He left the house first, by the side door, stepping directly into the open carport. The roof kept the rain from falling straight down on him, and lattice-work covered with climbing honeysuckle kept it from slanting in through the long side of the stall, but the chilly wind drove sheets of rain through the open end of the structure and threw it in his face.

Before giving the all-clear signal for Christine and Joey to come outside, he went to the end of the carport, into the driveway, because he wanted to make sure no one was lurking in front of the house. He wore a coat but went without an umbrella in order to keep his hands free, and the rain beat on his bare head, stung his face, trickled under his collar. No one was at the front door or along the walk or crouching by the shrubbery, so he called back to the woman to get into the car with the boy.

He took a few more steps along the driveway in order to have a look up and down the street, and he saw the blue Dodge van. It was parked a block and a half up the hill, on the other side of the street, facing down toward the house. Even as he spotted it, the van swung away from the curb and headed toward him.

Sandy glanced back and saw that Christine, lugging two suitcases and accompanied by the dog, had just reached the car, where the boy had opened the rear door for her. "Wait!" he shouted to them.

He looked back at the street. The van was coming fast now. Too damned fast.

"Into the house!" Sandy shouted.

The woman must have been wound up tight because she didn't even hesitate, didn't ask what was wrong, just dropped the suitcases, grabbed her son, and headed back the way she'd come, toward the open door in which Max now stood.

The rest of it happened in a few seconds, but terror distorted Sandy Breckenstein's time sense, so that it seemed as though minutes passed in an unbearably extended panic.

First, the van surprised him by angling all the way across the street and entering the driveway of the house that was two doors uphill from this one. But it wasn't stopping there. It swung out of that driveway almost as soon as it entered, not back into the street but onto the grass. It roared across the lawn in front of that house, coming this way, tearing up grass, casting mud and chunks of sod in its wake, squashing flowers, knocking over a birdbath, engine screaming, tires spinning for a moment but then biting in again, surging forward with maniacal intent.

What the hell—

The passenger door of the van flew open, and the man on that side threw himself out, struck the lawn, and rolled.

Sandy thought of rats deserting a doomed ship.

The van plowed through the picket fence between the lawn and the next property.

Behind Sandy, Max yelled, "What's happening?"

Now only one house separated the Dodge from this property.

Chewbacca was barking furiously.

The driver gave the van more gas. It was coming fast, like an express train, like a rocket.

The intent was clear. Crazy as it seemed, the van was going to ram the house in which they'd been hiding.

"Get out!" Sandy shouted back toward Christine and Joey and Max. "Out of the house, away from here, *fast!*"

Max plunged out of the house, and the three of them—and the dog—fled toward the back yard, which was the only way they could go.

Uphill, the Dodge swerved to avoid a jacaranda in the neighboring yard and struck the fence between this property and that one.

Sandy had already turned away from the van. He was already running back along the side of the house.

Behind him, the picket fence gave way with a sound like cracking bones.

Sandy raced through the carport, past the car, leaping over the abandoned suitcases, yelling at the others to hurry, for God's sake *hurry,* screaming at them to get out of the way, urging them into the rear lawn, and then toward the back fence, beyond which lay a narrow alley.

But they didn't get all the way to the rear of the small lot before the van rammed into the house with a tremendous crash. A split second later, an ear-pulverizing explosion shook the rain-choked day, and for a moment it sounded as if the sky itself was falling, and the earth rose violently, fell.

The van had been packed full of explosives!

The blast picked Sandy up and pitched him, and he felt a wave of hot air smash over him, and then he was tumbling across the lawn, through a row of azaleas, into the board fence by the alleyway, jarring his right shoulder, and he saw fire where the house had been, fire and smoke, shooting up in a dazzling column, and there was flying debris, a lot of it—chunks of masonry, splintered boards, roofing shingles, lath and plaster, glass, the padded back of an armchair that was leaking stuffing, the cracked lid of a toilet seat, sofa cushions, a piece of carpeting—and he tucked his head down and prayed that he wouldn't be struck by anything heavy or sharp.

As debris pummeled him, he wondered if the driver of the van had leaped out as the man on the passenger's side had done. Had he jumped free at the last moment—or had he been so committed to murdering Joey Scavello that he had remained behind the wheel, piloting the Dodge all the way into the house? Maybe he was now sitting in the rubble, flesh stripped from his bones, his skeletal hands still clutching the fire-blackened steering wheel.

The explosion was like a giant hand that slammed Christine in the back. Briefly deafened by the blast, she was thrown away from Joey, knocked down. In a temporary but eerie silence, she rolled through a muddy flower bed, crushing dense clusters of bright red and purple impatiens, aware of billowing waves of superheated air that seemed to vaporize the falling rain for a moment. She cracked a knee painfully against the low brick edging that ringed the planting area, tasted dirt, and came to rest against the side of the arbor, which was thickly entwined with bougainvillaea. Still in silence, cedar shingles and shattered pieces of stucco and unidentifiable rubble fell on her and on the garden around her. Then her hearing began to return when the toaster, which she had so recently used when making breakfast, clanged onto the grass and noisily hopped along for some distance, as if it were a living thing, trailing its cord like a tail. An enormously heavy object, perhaps a roof beam or a large chunk of masonry, slammed down into the roof of the ten-foot-long, tunnel-like arbor, collapsing it. The wall against which she was leaning sagged inward, and torn bougainvillaea runners drooped over her, and she realized how close she had come to being killed.

"Joey!" she shouted.

He didn't answer.

She pushed away from the ruined arbor, onto her hands and knees, then staggered to her feet, swaying.

"Joey!"

No answer.

Foul-smelling smoke poured across the lawn from the demolished house; combined with the lingering fog and the wind-whipped rain, it reduced visibility to a few feet. She couldn't see her boy, and she didn't know where to look, so she struck off blindly to her left, finding it difficult to breathe because of the acrid smoke and because of her own panic, which was like a vise squeezing her chest. She came upon the scorched and mangled door of the refrigerator, forced her way between two miniature orange trees, one of which was draped in a tangled bed sheet, and walked across the rear door of the house, which was lying flat on the grass, thirty feet from the frame in which it had once stood. She saw Max Steck. He was alive, trying to extricate himself from the thorny trailers of several rose bushes, among which he had been tossed. She moved past him, still calling Joey, still getting no answer, and then, among all the other rubble, her gaze settled on a strangely unnerving object. It was Joey's E.T. doll, one of his favorite toys, which had been left behind in the house. The blast had torn off both of the doll's legs and one of its arms. Its face was scorched. Its round little belly was ripped open, and stuffing bulged out of the rent. It was only a doll, but somehow it seemed like a harbinger of death, a warning of what she would find when she finally located Joey. She began to run, keeping the fence in sight, circling the property, frantically searching for her son, tripping, falling, pushing up again, praying that she would find him whole, alive.

"Joey!"

Nothing.

"Joey!"

Nothing.

The smoke stung her eyes. It was hard to see.

"Joooeeeeey!"

Then she spotted him. He was lying at the back of the property, near the gate to the alley, face down on the rain-soaked grass, motionless. Chewbacca was standing over him, nuzzling his neck, trying to get a response out of him, but the boy wouldn't respond, couldn't, just lay there, still, so very still.

CHAPTER 36

SHE KNELT AND nudged the dog out of the way.

She put her hands on Joey's shoulders.

For a moment she was afraid to turn him over, afraid that his face had been smashed in or his eyes punctured by flying debris.

Sobbing, coughing as another tide of smoke lapped out from the burning ruins behind them, she finally rolled him gently onto his back. His face was unmarked. There were smears of dirt but no cuts or visible fractures, and the rain was swiftly washing even the dirt away. She could see no blood. Thank God.

His eyelids fluttered. Opened. His eyes were unfocused.

He had merely been knocked unconscious.

The relief that surged through her was so powerful that it made her feel buoyant, as if she were floating inches off the ground.

She held him, and when his eyes finally cleared, she checked him for concussion by holding up three fingers in front of his face and asking him how many he saw.

He blinked and looked confused.

"How many fingers, honey?" she repeated.

He wheezed a few times, getting smoke out of his lungs, then said, "Three. Three fingers."

"Now how many?"

"Two."

Having freed himself from the thorn-studded rose bushes, Max Steck joined them.

To Joey, Christine said, "Do you know who I am?"

He seemed puzzled, not because he had trouble finding the answer but because he couldn't figure out why she was asking the question. "You're Mom," he said.

"And what's your name?"

"Don't you know my name?"

"I want to see if you know it," she said.

"Well, sure, I know it," he said. "Joey. Joseph. Joseph Anthony Scavello."

No concussion.

Relieved, she hugged him tight.

Sandy Breckenstein crouched beside them, coughing smoke out of his lungs. His forehead was cut above his left eye, and blood sheathed one side of his face, but he wasn't seriously hurt.

"Can the boy be moved?" Breckenstein asked.

"He's fine," Max Steck said.

"Then let's get out of here. They may come nosing around to see if the explosives took care of us."

Max unlatched the gate, pushed it open.

Chewbacca dashed through, into the alleyway, and the rest of them followed.

It was a narrow alley, with the back yards of houses on both sides of it, as well as a garage here and there, and lots of garbage cans awaiting pickup. There were no gutters or drains, and water streamed down the width of the one-lane passage, rushing toward storm culverts at the bottom of the hill.

As the four of them sloshed into the middle of the shallow stream, trying to decide which way to go, another gate opened two doors up the hill, and a tall man in a hooded yellow rain slicker came out of another yard. Even in the rain and the gloom, Christine could see that he was carrying a gun.

Max brought up his revolver, gripping it in both hands, and shouted, "Drop it!"

But the stranger opened fire.

Max fired, too, three shots in quick succession, and he was a much better marksman than his enemy. The would-be assassin was hit in the leg and fell even as the sound of the shots roared up the hillside. He rolled, splashing through the rivulet, his yellow rain slicker flapping like the wings of an enormous and brightly colored bird. He collided with two garbage cans, knocked them over, half-disappeared under a spreading mound of refuse. The gun flew out of his hand, spun along the macadam.

They didn't even wait to see if the man was dead or alive. There might be other Twilighters nearby.

"Let's get out of this neighborhood," Max said urgently. "Get to a phone, call this in, get a backup team out here."

With Sandy and Chewbacca leading the way and Max bringing up the rear, they ran down the hill, slipping and sliding a bit on the slick macadam but avoiding a fall.

Christine looked back a couple of times.

The wounded man had not gotten up from the garbage in which he'd landed.

No one was pursuing them.

Yet.

They turned right at the first corner, raced along a flat street that ran across the side of the hill, past a startled mailman who jumped out of their way. A ferocious wind sprang up, as if giving chase. As they fled, the wind-shaken trees tossed and shuddered around them, and the brittle branches of palms clattered noisily, and an empty soda can tumbled along at their heels.

After two blocks, they left the flat street and turned into another steeply sloped avenue. Overhanging trees formed a tunnel across the roadway and added to the gloom of the sunless day, so that it almost seemed like evening rather than morning.

Breath burned in Christine's throat. Her eyes still stung from the smoke they had left behind them, and her heart was beating so hard and fast that her chest ached. She didn't know how much farther she could go at this pace. Not far.

She was surprised that Joey's little legs could pump this fast. The rest of them weren't keeping back much on account of the boy; he could hold his own.

A car was coming up the hill, headlights stabbing out before it, cutting through the thinning mist and the deep shadows cast by the huge trees.

Christine was suddenly sure that Grace Spivey's people were behind those lights. She grabbed Joey by one shoulder, turned him in another direction.

Sandy shouted at her to stay with him, and Max shouted something she couldn't make out, and Chewbacca began barking loudly, but she ignored them.

Didn't they see death coming?

She heard the car's engine growing louder behind her. It sounded feral, hungry.

Joey stumbled on a canted section of sidewalk, went down, skidding into someone's front yard.

She threw herself on him to protect him from the gunfire she expected to hear at any second.

The car drew even with them. The sound of its laboring engine filled the world.

She cried out, *"No!"*

But the car went by without stopping. It hadn't been Grace Spivey's people, after all.

Christine felt foolish as Max Steck helped her to her feet. The entire world wasn't after them. It only seemed that way.

CHAPTER 37

〽〽〽

IN DOWNTOWN LAGUNA BEACH, in an Arco Service Station they took shelter from the storm and from Grace Spivey's disciples. After Sandy Breckenstein showed the manager his PI license and explained enough of the situation to gain cooperation, they were allowed to bring Chewbacca into the service bay, as long as they tied him securely to a tool rack. Sandy didn't want to let the dog outside, not only because it would get wet—it was already soaked and shivering—but because there was a possibility, however insignificant, that Spivey's people might be cruising around town, looking for them, and might spot the dog.

While Max stayed with Christine and Joey at the rear of the service bays, away from doors and windows, Sandy used the pay phone in the small, glassed-in sales room. He called Klemet-Harrison. Charlie wasn't in the office. Sandy spoke with Sherry Ordway, the receptionist, and explained enough of their situation to make her understand the seriousness of it, but he wouldn't tell her where they were or at what number they could be reached. He doubted that Sherry was the informant who was reporting to the Church of the Twilight, but he could not be absolutely sure where her loyalties might lie.

He said, "Find Charlie. I'll only talk to him."

"But how's he going to know where to reach you?" Sherry asked.

"I'll call back in fifteen minutes."

"If I can't get hold of him in fifteen minutes—"

"I'll call back every fifteen minutes until you do," he said, and hung up.

He returned to the humid service bays, which smelled of oil and grease and gasoline. A three-year-old Toyota was up on one of the two hydraulic racks, and a fox-faced man in gray coveralls was replacing the muffler. Sandy told Max and Christine that it was going to take awhile to reach Charlie Harrison.

The pump jockey, a young blond guy, was mounting new tires on a set of custom chrome wheels, and Joey was watching, fascinated by the specialized power tools, obviously bubbling over with questions but trying not to bother the man with more than a few of them. The poor kid was soaked to the skin, muddy, bedraggled, yet he wasn't complaining or whining as most children would have been doing in these circumstances. He was a damned good kid, and he seemed able to find a positive side to any situation; in this case, getting to watch tires being mounted appeared to be sufficient compensation for the ordeal he had just been through.

Seven months ago, Sandy's wife, Maryann, had given birth to a boy. Troy Franklin Breckenstein. Sandy hoped his son would turn out to be as well-behaved as Joey Scavello.

Then he thought: If I'm going to wish for anything, maybe I'd better wish that I live long enough to see Troy grow up, whether or not he's well-behaved.

When fifteen minutes had passed, Sandy returned to the sales room out front, went to the phone by the candy machine, and called Sherry Ordway at HQ. She had beeped Charlie on his telepage, but he hadn't yet called in.

The rain bounced off the macadam in front of the station, and the street began to disappear under a deep puddle, and the pump jockey finished another tire, and Sandy was jumpier than ever when he called the office a third time.

Sherry said, "Charlie's at the police lab with Henry Rankin, trying to find out if forensics discovered anything about those bodies at the Scavello house that would help him tie them to Grace Spivey."

"That sounds like a long shot."

"I guess it's the best he has," Sherry said.

That was more bad news.

She gave him the number where Charlie could be reached, and he jotted it down in a small notebook he carried.

He dialed the forensics lab, asked for Charlie, and had him on the line right away. He told him about the attack on Miriam Rankin's house, laying it out in more detail than he'd given Sherry Ordway.

Charlie had heard the worst of it from Sherry, but he still sounded shocked and dismayed by how quickly Spivey had located the Scavellos.

"They're both all right?" he asked.

"Dirty and wet, but unhurt," Sandy assured him.

"So we've got a turncoat among us," Charlie said.

"Looks that way. Unless you were followed when you left their house last night."

"I'm sure we weren't. But maybe the car we used had a bug on it."

"Could be."

"But probably not," Charlie said. "I hate to admit it, but we've probably got a mole in our operation. Where are you calling from?"

Instead of telling him, Sandy said, "Is Henry Rankin with you?"

"Yeah. Right here. Why? You want to talk to him?"

"No. I just want to know if he can hear this."

"Not your side of it."

"If I tell you where we are, it's got to stay with you. Only you," Sandy said.

He quickly added: "It's not that I have reason to suspect Henry of being Spivey's plant. I don't. I trust Henry more than most. The point is, I don't really trust *anyone* but you. You, me—and Max, because if it was Max, he'd already have snuffed the kid."

"If we do have a bad apple," Charlie said, "it's most likely a secretary or bookkeeper or something like that."

"I know," Sandy said. "But I've got a responsibility to the woman and the kid. And my own life's on the line here, too, as long as I'm with them."

"Tell me where you are," Charlie said. "I'll keep it to myself, and I'll come alone."

Sandy told him.

"This weather . . . better give me forty-five minutes," Charlie said.

"We're not going anywhere," Sandy said.

He hung up and went out to the garage to be with the others.

When the rains had first come, yesterday evening, there had been a brief period of lightning, but none in the past twelve hours. Most California storms were much quieter than those in other parts of the country. Lightning was not a common accompaniment of the rains here, and wildly violent electrical storms were rare. But now, with its hills grown dangerously soggy and with the threat of mudslides at hand, with its streets awash, with its coastline hammered by wind-whipped waves almost twice as high as usual, Laguna Beach was suddenly assaulted by fierce bolts of lightning as well. With a crash of accompanying thunder that shook the walls of the building, a cataclysmic bolt stabbed to earth somewhere nearby, and the gray day was briefly, flickeringly bright. With strobelike effect, the light pulsed through the open doors of the garage and through the dirty high-set windows, bringing a moment of frenzied life to the shadows, which twisted and danced for a second or two. Another bolt quickly followed with an even harder clap of thunder, and loose windows rattled in their frames, and then a third bolt smashed down, and the wet macadam in front of the station glistened and flashed with scintillant reflections of nature's bright anger.

Joey had drifted away from his mother, toward the open doors of the garage bays. He winced at the crashes of thunder that followed each lightning strike, but he seemed pretty much unafraid. When the skies calmed for a moment, he looked back at his mother and said, "Wow! God's fireworks, huh, Mom? Isn't that what you said it is?"

"God's fireworks," Christine agreed. "Better get away from there."

Another bolt arced across the sky, and the day outside seemed to leap as the murderous current jolted through it. This one was worse than all the others, and the blast from it not only rattled windows and made the walls tremble, but seemed to shake the ground as well, and Sandy even felt it in his *teeth*.

"Wow!" the boy said.

"Honey, get away from that open door," Christine said.

The boy didn't move, and in the next instant he was silhouetted by a chain of lightning strikes far brighter and more violent than anything yet, so dazzling and shocking in their power that the pump jockey was startled enough to drop a lug wrench. The dog whimpered and tried to hide under the tool rack, and Christine scurried to Joey, grabbed him, and brought him back from the open doorway.

"Aw, Mom, it's pretty," he said.

Sandy tried to imagine what it would be like to be young again, so young that you hadn't yet realized how much there was to fear in this world, so young that the word "cancer" had no definition, so young that you hadn't any real grip on the meaning of death or the inevitability of taxes or the horror of nuclear war or the treacherous nature of the clot-prone human circulatory system. What would it be like to be that young again, so young that you could watch storm lightning with delight, unaware that it might find its way to you and fry your brains in one ten-thousandth of a second? Sandy stared at Joey Scavello and frowned. He felt old, only thirty-two but terribly old.

What bothered him was that he couldn't remember *ever* having been that young and free of fear, though surely he had been just as innocent of death when he was six. They said that animals lived their lives with no sense of mortality, and it seemed terribly unjust that men didn't have the same luxury. Human beings couldn't escape the knowledge of their death; consciously or subconsciously, it was with them every hour of every day. If Sandy could have had a word with this religious fanatic, this Grace Spivey, he would have wanted to know how she could have such faith in—and devotion for—a God who created human beings only to let them die by one horrible means or another.

He sighed. He was getting morbid, and that wasn't like him. At this rate he would need more than his usual bottle of beer before bed tonight—like a *dozen* bottles. Still . . . he would like to ask Grace Spivey that question.

CHAPTER 38

HHHH

SHORTLY BEFORE NOON, Charlie arrived in Laguna Beach, where he found Sandy, Max, Christine, Joey and the dog waiting for him in the service station.

Joey ran to him, met him just inside the garage doors, shouting, "Hey, Charlie, you shoulda seen the house go boom, just like in a war movie or somethin'!"

Charlie scooped him up and held him. "I expected you to be mad at us for slipping up. I thought you'd insist on hiring Magnum again."

"Heck, no," the boy said. "Your guys were great. Anyway, how could you've known it was gonna turn into a war movie?"

How indeed?

Charlie carried Joey to the rear of the garage, where the others stood in the shadows between shelves of spare parts and stacks of tires.

Sandy had told him that the woman and the boy were all right, and of course he believed Sandy, but his stomach finally unknotted only now that he saw them with his own eyes. The wave of relief that washed through him was a physical and not just emotional force, and he was reminded—though he didn't *need* reminding—of just how important these two people had become to him in such a short period of time.

They were a miserable-looking group, pretty much dried out by now, but rumpled and mud-streaked, hair lank and matted. Max and Sandy looked rough, angry, and dangerous, the kind of men who cleared out a bar just by walking into it.

It was a tribute to Christine's beauty, and an indication of its depth, that she looked almost as good now as when she was scrubbed and fresh and neatly groomed. Charlie remembered how it had felt to hold her, last night in the kitchen of Miriam Rankin's little house, just before he'd gone home, and he wanted to hold her again, felt a warm melting *need* to hold her, but in front of his men he could do nothing but put Joey down, take her hand in both of his, and say, "Thank God you're all right."

Her lower lip quivered. For a moment she looked as if she would lean against him and cry. But she kept control of herself and said, "I keep telling myself it's just a nightmare . . . but I can't wake up."

Max said, "We ought to get them out of here *now,* out of Laguna."

"I agree," Charlie said. "I'll take them right now, in my car. After we've left, you two call the office, tell Sherry where you are, and have a car sent out. Go back up the hill to Miriam's house—"

"There's not anything left of it," Sandy said.

"That was one hell of a blast," Max confirmed. "The van must've been packed wall to wall with explosives."

"There might not be anything left of the house," Charlie said, "but the cops and fire department are still up there. Sherry's been checking into it with the Laguna Beach police, and I talked with her on the phone, coming down here. Report to the cops, help them any way you can, and find out what they've come up with."

"Did they find the guy in the alley, the one I shot?" Max asked.

"Nope," Charlie said. "He got away."

"He'd have to've crawled. I shot him in the leg."

"Then he crawled," Charlie said. "Or there was a third man around who helped him escape."

"Third?" Sandy said.

"Yeah," Charlie said. "Sherry says the second man stayed with the van all the way into the house."

"Jesus."

"They *are* kamikazes," Christine said shakily.

"There mustn't have been anything left of him but a lot of little pieces," Max said and would have said more, but Charlie stopped him by nodding toward the boy, who was listening, mouth agape.

They were silent, contemplating the van driver's violent demise. The rain on the roof was like the solemn drums in a funeral cortege.

Then the mechanic switched on a power wrench, and all of them jumped at the sudden, clangorous noise.

When the mechanic switched the wrench off, Charlie looked at Christine and said, "Okay, let's get out of here."

Suspiciously studying everything that moved in the rain-battered day, Max and Sandy accompanied them to the gray Mercedes in front of the service station. Christine sat up front with Charlie, and Joey got in back with Chewbacca.

Sitting behind the steering wheel, speaking to Sandy and Max through the open window, Charlie said, "You did a damned fine job."

"Almost lost them," Sandy said, turning aside the praise.

"Point is—you didn't," Charlie said. "And you're safe, too."

If another of his men had died so soon after the deaths of Pete and Frank, he wasn't sure how he could have handled it. From here on, only he would know where Christine and Joey were. His men would be working on the case, trying to link the Church of the Twilight to these murders and attempted murders, but only he would know the whereabouts of their clients until Grace Spivey was somehow stopped. That way, the old woman's spies wouldn't be able to find Christine and Joey, and Charlie wouldn't have to worry about losing another man. His own life was the only one he would be risking.

He put up his window, locked all the doors with the master switch, and drove away from the service station.

Laguna was actually a lovely, warm, clean, vital beach town, but today it seemed drab, cloaked in rain and gray mist and mud. It made Charlie think of graveyards, and it seemed to close in around them like the descending lid of a coffin. He breathed a bit easier when they were out of town, heading north on the Pacific Coast Highway.

Christine turned and looked at Joey, who was sitting quietly in the back of the car. Brandy . . . no, *Chewbacca* was lying on the seat, his big furry head in the boy's lap. Joey was listlessly petting the dog and staring out the window at the ocean, which was choppy and wind-tossed in front of a dense wall of ash-gray fog moving shoreward from half a mile out. His face was almost expressionless, almost blank, but not quite. There was a subtle expression, something she had never seen on his face before, and she couldn't read it. What was he thinking? Feeling? She had already asked him twice if he was all right, and he had said he was. She didn't want to nag him, but she was worried.

She wasn't merely concerned about his physical safety, although that fear gnawed at her. She was also worried about his mental condition. If he did survive Grace Spivey's demented crusade against him, what emotional scars would he carry with him for the rest of his life? It was impossible that he would come through these experiences unmarked. There would have to be psychological consequences.

Now he continued to stroke the dog's head but in a hypnotic fashion, as if not fully aware that the animal was there with him, and he stared at the ocean beyond the window.

Charlie said, "The police want me to bring you in for more questioning."

"The hell with them," Christine said.

"They're more inclined to help now—"

"It took all these deaths to get their attention."

"Don't write them off. Sure, we'll do a better job of protecting you than they can, and we might turn up something that'll help them nail Grace Spivey for all this. But now that they've got a homicide investigation under way, they'll do most of the work leading up to the indictments and convictions. They'll be the ones to stop her."

"I don't trust the cops," she said flatly. "Spivey probably has people planted there."

"She can't have infiltrated every police force in the country. She doesn't have that many followers."

"Not every police force," Christine said. "Just those in the towns where she carries on her fund raising and seeks out her converts."

"The Laguna Beach police want to talk to you, too, of course, about what happened this morning."

"To hell with them, too. Even if none of them belongs to the Church of the Twilight, Spivey might be expecting me to show up at police headquarters; she might have people watching, waiting to cut us down the minute we step out of the car." She had a sudden terrible thought and said: "You're not taking us to any police station, are you?"

"No," he said. "I only said they want to talk to you. I didn't say I thought it was a good idea."

She sagged back against the seat. *"Are* there any good ideas?"

"Got to keep your chin up."

"I mean, what're we going to do now? We have no clothes, nothing but what we've got on our backs. My purse and credit cards. That's not much. We've got nowhere to stay. We don't dare go to our friends or anywhere else we're known. They've got us on the run like a couple of wild animals."

"It's not quite that bad," he said. "Hunted animals don't have the luxury of fleeing in a Mercedes Benz."

She appreciated his attempt to make her smile, but she couldn't find the will to do so.

The *thump-thump-thump* of the windshield wipers sounded like a strange, inhuman heartbeat.

Charlie said, "We'll go into L.A., I think. The Church of the Twilight does some work in the city, but most of its activities are centered in Orange and San Diego Counties. There're fewer of Grace's people floating around in L.A., so there'll be less chance of anyone accidentally spotting us. In fact, almost no chance at all."

"They're everywhere," she said.

"Be optimistic," he said. "Remember little ears."

She glanced back at Joey, a pang of guilt cutting through her at the realization that she might be frightening him. But he seemed not to have been paying attention to the conversation in the front seat. He still stared out the window, not at the ocean any longer but at the array of shops along the highway in Corona Del Mar.

"In L.A., we'll buy suitcases, clothes, toiletries, whatever you need," Charlie said.

"Then?"

"We'll have dinner."

"Then?"

"Find a hotel."

"What if one of her people works at the hotel?"

"What if one of her people is mayor of Peking?" Charlie said. "We'd better not go to China, either."

She found a weak smile for him, after all. It wasn't much, but it was all she had in her, and she was surprised she could respond even that well.

"I'm sorry," she said.

"For what? Being human? Human and afraid?"

"I don't want to get hysterical."

"Then don't."

"I won't."

"Good. Because there *are* favorable developments."

"Such as?"

"One of the three dead men from last night—the red-head you shot—has been identified. His name's Pat O'Hara. They were able to get positive ID on him because he's a professional burglar with three arrests and one conviction on his record."

"Burglar?" she said, baffled by this unexpected introduction of a more ordinary criminal element.

"The cops have done better than come up with a name for him. They can also tie him to Grace."

She sat up straight, startled. "How?"

"His family and friends say he joined the Church of the Twilight eight months ago."

"Then there it is!" she said, excited. "There's what they need to go after Grace Spivey."

"Well, they've gone back to the church to talk to her again, of course."

"That's all? Just *talk* to her?"

"At this point, they don't have any proof—"

"O'Hara was one of hers!"

"But there's no proof he was acting on her say-so."

"They all do what she tells them, exactly what she tells them."

"But Grace claims her church believes in free will, that none of her people is any more *controlled* than Catholics or Presbyterians, no more brainwashed than any Jew in any synagogue."

"Bullshit," she said softly but with feeling.

"True," he said. "But it's damned hard to prove it, especially since we can't put our hands on any ex-members of the church who might tell us what it's like in there."

Some of her excitement drained away. "Then what good does it do us to have O'Hara identified as a Twilighter?"

"Well, it gives some substance to your claims that Grace is harassing you. The cops take your story a whole lot more seriously now than they first did, and that can't hurt."

"We need more than that."

"There's a little something else."

"What?"

"O'Hara—or maybe it was the other guy who came with him—left something outside your house. An airline flight bag. There were burglary tools in it, but there were other things, too. A large plastic jar full of a colorless liquid that turned out to be ordinary water. They don't know why it was there, what purpose it was meant to serve. More of interest was a small brass cross—and a copy of the Bible."

"Doesn't that prove they were there on some crackpot religious mission?"

"Doesn't prove it, no, but it's interesting, anyway. It's one more knot in the hangman's noose, one more little thing that helps build a case against Grace Spivey."

"At this rate we'll have her in court by the turn of the century," Christine said sourly.

They were traveling MacArthur Boulevard now, climbing and descending a series of hills that took them past Fashion Island, past hundreds of million-dollar homes, a marshy area of backwater from Newport Bay, and fields of tall grass that bent with the driving rain and then stood straight up and quivered as the erratic storm wind abruptly changed directions. In spite of the fact that it was midday, most of the cars in the oncoming lane had their headlights on.

Christine said, "The police know what Grace Spivey teaches—about the coming of Twilight, doomsday, the Antichrist?"

"Yes. They know all of it," Charlie said.

"They know she thinks the Antichrist is already among us?"

"Yes."

"And they know that she's spent the past few years searching for him?"

"Yes."

"And that she intends to kill him when she finds him?"

"She's never said as much in a speech or in any of the religious literature she's had published."

"But that *is* what she intends. We know it."

"What we know and what we can prove are two different things."

"The police should be able to see that this is why she's fixated on Joey and—"

"Last night, when the police questioned her, she denied knowing you and Joey, denied the scene at South Coast Plaza. She says she doesn't understand what you have against her, why you're trying to smear her. She said she hadn't found the Antichrist yet and didn't even think she was close. They asked her what she would do if she ever found him, and she said she'd direct prayers against him. They asked if she would try to kill him, and she pretended to be outraged by the very idea. She said she was a woman of God, not a criminal. She said prayer would be enough. She said she'd chain the devil in prayers, bind him up with prayers, drive him back to Hell with nothing but prayer."

"And of course they believed her."

"No. I talked to a detective this morning, read the report of their session with her. They think she's unbalanced, probably dangerous, and ought to be considered the primary suspect in the attempts on your lives."

She was surprised.

He said, "You see? You've got to be more positive. Things *are* happening. Not as fast as you'd like, no, because there are procedures the police must follow, rules of evidence, constitutional rights that must be respected—"

"Sometimes it seems like the only people who have constitutional rights are the criminals among us."

"I know. But we've got to work within the system as best we can."

They passed the Orange County Airport and got on the San Diego Freeway, heading north toward Los Angeles.

Christine glanced back at Joey. He was no longer staring out the window or petting the dog. He was slumped down in a corner of the back seat, eyes closed, mouth open, breathing softly and deeply. The motion of the car had lulled him to sleep.

To Charlie, she said, "What worries me is that while *we* have to work within the system, slowly and carefully, that Spivey bitch doesn't have any rules holding her back. She can move fast and be brutal. While we're treading carefully around her rights, she'll kill us all."

"She might self-destruct first," he said.

"What do you mean?"

"I went to the church this morning. I met her. She's completely around the bend, Christine. Utterly irrational. Coming apart at the seams."

He told her about his meeting with the old woman, about the bloody stigmata on her hands and feet.

If he intended to reassure her by painting a picture of Grace Spivey as a babbling lunatic teetering on the edge of collapse, he failed. The intensity of the old woman's madness only made her seem more threatening, more predictable, more relentless than ever.

"Have you reported this to the cops?" Christine asked. "Have you told them that she threatened Joey to your face?"

"No. It would just be my word against hers."

He told her about his discussion with Denton Boothe, his friend the psychologist. "Boo says a psychotic of this sort has surprising strength. He says we shouldn't expect her to collapse and solve this problem for us—but then *he* didn't see her. If he'd been there with me and Henry, in her office, when she held up her bleeding hands, he'd know she can't hold it together much longer."

"Did he have any suggestions, any ideas about how to stop her?"

"He said the best way was to kill her," Charlie said, smiling.

Christine didn't smile.

He glanced away from the rain-swept freeway long enough to gauge her reaction, then said, "Of course, Boo was joking."

"Was he really?"

"Well . . . no . . . he sort of meant it . . . but he knew it wasn't an option we could seriously consider."

"Maybe it *is* the only answer."

He looked at her again, his brow creased with worry. "I hope *you're* joking."

She said nothing.

"Christine, if you could somehow get her with a gun, if you killed her, you'd only wind up in prison. The state would take Joey away from you. You'd lose him anyway. Killing Grace Spivey isn't the answer."

She sighed and nodded. She didn't want to argue about it.

But she wondered . . .

Maybe she would end up in prison, and maybe they would take Joey away from her, but at least he would still be *alive.*

When Charlie pulled the Mercedes off the freeway at the Wilshire Boulevard ramp, on the west side of L.A., Joey woke and yawned noisily and wanted to know where they were.

"Westwood," Charlie said.

"I never been to Westwood," Joey said.

"Oh?" Charlie said. "I thought you were a man of the world. I thought you'd been everywhere."

"How could I have been everywhere?" the boy asked. "I'm only six."

"Plenty old enough to've been everywhere," Charlie said. "Why, by the time I was six, I'd been all the way from my home in Indiana clear to Peoria."

"Is that a dirty word?" the boy asked suspiciously.

Charlie laughed and saw that Christine was laughing, too. "Peoria? No, that's not a dirty word; it's a place. I guess you aren't a man of the world after all. A man of the world would know Peoria as well as he'd know Paris."

"Mom, what's he talking about?"

"He's just being silly, honey."

"That's what I thought," the boy said. "Lots of detectives act that way sometimes. Jim Rockford's silly like that sometimes, too."

"That's where I picked it up," Charlie said. "From good old Jim Rockford."

They parked the car in the underground garage beside the Westwood Playhouse, across the street from UCLA, and went shopping for clothes and necessities in Westwood Village, putting everything on credit cards. In spite of the circumstances, in spite of the weather, it was a rather pleasant excursion. There were overhangs or awnings in front of all the stores, and they could always find a dry place to tie Chewbacca while they went inside to browse. The incredible downpour, which was the main topic of conversation among all the salesclerks, helped explain Joey's and Christine's rumpled and bedraggled appearance; no one looked at them askance. Charlie made jokes about some of the clothes they tried on, and Joey held his nose as if detecting a pungent odor when Charlie pretended to consider a loud orange sportshirt, and after a while it almost seemed as if they were an ordinary family on an ordinary outing in a world where all the religious fanatics were over in the Middle East somewhere, fighting over their oil and their mosques. It was nice to think that the three of them were a unit, sharing special bonds, and Charlie felt another surge of that domestic yearning that had never come upon him until he had met Christine Scavello.

They made two trips back to the car to put their purchases in the trunk. When Christine and Joey had everything they needed, they went to a couple of stores to outfit Charlie, as well. Because he didn't want to risk returning to his own house, where he might pick up a tail, he bought a suitcase, toiletries, and three days worth of clothes.

Several times they saw people on the street who seemed to be watching them or were otherwise suspicious, but in each instance the danger proved to be imaginary, and gradually they relaxed a bit. They were still watchful, alert, but they no longer felt as if there were armed maniacs lurking around every corner.

They finished shopping just as the stores were closing, and by the time they found a cozy-looking restaurant—nothing fancy but with lots of satiny-looking dark wood and stained-glass windows, and a menu rich with fattening specialties like potato skins stuffed with cheese and bacon—it was almost five-thirty. It was early for dinner, but they hadn't eaten lunch, and they were starved.

They ordered drinks, and then Christine took Joey to the ladies' room with her, where both of them washed up a bit and changed into some of the new clothes they'd bought.

While they were thus engaged, Charlie used a pay phone to ring the office. Sherry was still at her desk, and she put him through to Henry Rankin, who'd been awaiting his call, but Henry didn't have much news to report. From the results of lab tests, the police believed the stolen blue Dodge van had been carrying a couple of cases of a moldable plastic explosive favored by more than one branch of the United States armed forces, but they couldn't possibly work back to the point at which the stuff had been purchased or stolen. Henry's Aunt Miriam had been reached in Mexico, was shocked at the news that her house was gone, but didn't blame Henry. She didn't seem disposed to return early from her trip, partly because there wasn't anything left to salvage from the rubble anyway, partly because insurance would cover the loss, partly because she had always taken bad news well, but mainly because she had encountered an interesting man in Acapulco. His name was Ernesto. Those were the only recent developments.

"I'll check in twice a day to see how the case is progressing and to make suggestions," Charlie said.

"If I have any news about Aunt Miriam and Ernesto, I'll save that for you, too."

"I'd appreciate it."

They were both silent a moment, neither of them in a mood to carry the joke any further.

Finally Henry said, "You think it's wise for you to try to protect them all by yourself?"

"It's the only way."

"I find it hard to believe Spivey has someone planted here, but I'm putting everyone under the microscope, looking for the disease. If one of them's a Twilighter, I'll find him."

"I know you will," Charlie said. He wasn't going to mention that another operative, Mike Specklovitch, was checking up on Henry, at Charlie's orders, while Henry was checking up on everyone else. He felt guilty about that betrayal of trust, even though it was unavoidable.

"Where are you now?" Henry asked.

"The Australian outback," Charlie said.

"What? Oh. None of my business, huh?"

"I'm sorry, Henry."

"That's all right. You're playing it the only way you possibly can," Henry said, but he sounded slightly wounded by Charlie's distrust.

Depressed about the way this case was fracturing the much-valued camaraderie among his employees, Charlie hung up and returned to the table. The waitress was just putting down his vodka martini. He ordered another one even before sipping the first, then took a look at the menu.

Christine returned from the ladies' room in tan corduroy jeans and a green blouse, carrying a bag filled with their old clothes and a few toiletries. Joey wore blue jeans and a cowboy shirt of which he was particularly proud. Their outfits were in need of a steam iron, but they were cleaner and fresher than the clothes they had been wearing since fleeing Miriam Rankin's doomed house in Laguna Beach. Indeed, regardless of the wrinkles in her blouse, Christine looked no worse than stunning, and Charlie's heart lifted again at the sight of her.

By the time they left the restaurant, carrying two hamburgers for Chewbacca, night had settled in completely, and the rain had let up. A light drizzle was falling, and the humid air was oppressively heavy, but it no longer seemed as if they should start building an ark. The dog smelled the burgers, sensed they were for him, and insisted on being fed before they got back to the garage. He gobbled both sandwiches right there in front of the restaurant, and Christine said, "You know, he even has Brandy's manners."

"You always said Brandy had no manners," Joey reminded her.

"That's what I mean."

Now that the storm seemed to be subsiding, the sidewalks along Westwood Boulevard were filling up with students from UCLA on their way to dinner or a movie, window-shoppers, and theater-goers killing some time before heading to the Playhouse. Californians have little or no tolerance for rain, and after a storm like this one, they always burst forth, eager to be out and around, in an almost festive mood. Charlie was sorry it was time to leave; the Village seemed like an oasis of sanity in a deranged world, and he was thankful for the respite it had provided.

The parking garage had been almost full when they'd arrived this afternoon, and they'd had to leave the car on the lowest level. Now, as they took the elevator down to the bottom of the structure, they were all in a better state of mind than they would have thought possible only a few hours ago. There was nothing like good food, a couple of drinks, and several hours of walking freely on public streets without being shot at to convince you that God was in His heaven and that all was right with the world.

But it was a short-lived feeling. It ended when the elevator doors opened.

The lights immediately beyond the doors were all burned out. There were lights glowing some distance to the left and others to the right, revealing rows of cars and drab concrete walls and massive roof-supporting pillars, but directly in front of the elevator, there was darkness.

How likely was it that three or four lights would be out all at the same time?

That unsettling question flashed into Charlie's mind the moment the doors slid open, and before he could react, Chewbacca began to bark at the shadows beyond the doors. The dog was shockingly ferocious, as if possessed by a sudden black rage, yet he didn't rush out of the elevator to pursue the object of his anger, and that was a sure sign that something very bad was waiting out there for them.

Charlie reached toward the elevator's control board.

Something whizzed into the cab and slammed into the back wall, two inches from Christine's head. A bullet. It tore a hole through the metal panel. The sound of the shot was almost like an afterthought.

"Down!" Charlie shouted, and hit the CLOSE DOOR button, and another shot slammed into the doors as they started to roll shut, and he punched the button for the top floor, and Chewbacca was still barking, and Christine was screaming, and then the doors were completely shut, and the cage was on its way up, and Charlie thought he heard a last futile shot as they rose out of the concrete depths.

The killers hadn't planned on the dog reacting so quickly and noisily. They had expected Christine and Joey to come out of the elevator, and they hadn't been prepared to hit their quarry within the cab itself. Otherwise, the shots would have been more carefully placed, and Joey or his mother—or both—would already be dead.

With any luck, the only gunmen were those on the lowest level of the garage. But if they had planned for this contingency, for the possibility that their prey would be forewarned and would not get out of the elevator, then they might have stationed others on the upper floor. The cab might stop rising at any level, and the doors might open, and another hit squad might be waiting there.

But how did they find us? Charlie asked himself desperately as Christine picked herself up from the floor. In Christ's name, *how?*

He was still packing his own gun, which he'd taken to the Church of the Twilight this morning, and he drew it, aimed at the doors in front of them.

The cab didn't stop until it reached the top floor of the garage. The doors opened. Yellowish lights. Gray concrete walls. Gleaming cars parked in narrow spaces. But no men with guns.

"Come on!" Charlie said.

They ran because they knew the men on the bottom floor of the garage must be coming up quickly behind them.

CHAPTER 39

THEY RAN TO Hilgarde Avenue, then beyond it, away from UCLA and the commercial area of Westwood, into an expensive and quiet residential neighborhood. Charlie welcomed each convocation of shadows, but dreaded the pools of light surrounding every streetlamp, because here they were the only people on the sidewalks and easily spotted. They turned several times, seeking concealment in the upper-class warren of lushly landscaped streets. Gradually he began to think they had lost their pursuers, though he knew he wouldn't feel entirely safe for a long time to come.

Although the rain had subsided to little more than a light mist, and although they were all wearing raincoats, they were wet and cold again by the time Charlie began looking for transportation. Automobiles were parked along the street, and he moved down the block, under the dripping coral trees and palms, stealthily trying doors, hoping no one was watching from any of the houses. The first three cars were locked up tight, but the driver's door on the fourth, a two-year-old yellow Cadillac, opened when he tried it.

He motioned Christine and Joey into the car. "Hurry."

She said, "Are the keys in it?"

"No."

"Are you stealing it or what?"

"Yes. Get in."

"I don't want you breaking the law and winding up in prison because of me and—"

"Get in!" he said urgently.

The velour-covered bench seat in front accommodated the three of them, so Christine put Joey in the middle, apparently afraid to let him get even as far away as the rear seat. The dog got in back, shaking the rain off his coat and spraying everyone in the process.

The glove compartment contained a small, detachable flashlight that came with the car and that was kept, except when needed, in a specially designed niche where its batteries were constantly recharged. Charlie used it to look under the dashboard, below the steering wheel, where he located the ignition wires. He hot-wired the Cadillac, and the engine turned over without hesitation.

No more than two minutes after he had opened the car door, they pulled away from the curb. For the first block, he drove without headlights. Then, confident they had gotten away unnoticed, he snapped on the lights and headed up toward Sunset Boulevard.

Christine said, "What if the cops stop us?"

"They won't. The owner probably won't report it stolen until morning. And even if he discovers it's gone ten minutes from now, it won't make the police hot sheets for a while."

"But they might stop us for speeding—"

"I don't intend to speed."

"—or some other traffic violation—"

"What do you think I am—a stunt driver?"

"Are you?" Joey asked.

"Oh, sure, better than Evel Knievel," Charlie said.

"Who?" the boy asked.

"God, I'm getting old," Charlie said.

"Are we gonna get in a car chase like on TV?" Joey asked.

"I hope not," Charlie said.

"Oh, I'd like that," the boy said.

Charlie checked the rearview mirror. There were two cars behind him. He couldn't tell what make they were or anything about them. They were just pairs of headlights in the darkness.

Christine said, "But sooner or later, the car *will* end up on the hot sheets—"

"We'll have parked it somewhere and taken another car by then," Charlie said.

"Steal another one?"

"I'm sure not going to Hertz or Avis," he said. "A rental car can be traced. They might find us that way."

Jesus, listen to me, he thought. Pretty soon I'm going to be like Ray Milland in *Lost Weekend,* imagining a threat in every corner, seeing giant bugs crawling out of the walls.

He turned left at the next corner.

So did both of the cars behind him.

"How did they find us?" Christine asked.

"Must've planted a transmitter on my Mercedes."

"When would they've done that?"

"I don't know. Maybe when I was at their church this morning."

"But you said you left a man in your car while you went in there, someone who could call for help if you didn't come back out when you were supposed to."

"Yeah. Carter Rilbeck."

"So he'd have seen them trying to plant a transmitter."

"Unless, of course, he's one of them," Charlie said.

"Do you think he could be?"

"Probably not. But maybe they planted the bug before that. As soon as they knew you'd hired me."

At Hilgarde, he turned right.

So did both of the cars behind him.

To Christine, he said, "Or maybe Henry Rankin is a Twilighter, and when I called him from the restaurant awhile ago, maybe he got a trace on the line and found out where I was."

"You said he's like a brother."

"He is. But Cain was like a brother to Abel, huh?"

He turned left on Sunset Boulevard, with UCLA on the left now and Bel Air on the hills to the right.

Only one of the cars followed him.

She said, "You sound as if you've become as paranoid as I am."

"Grace Spivey gives me no choice."

"Where are we going?" she asked.

"Farther away."

"Where?"

"I'm not sure yet."

"We spent all that time buying clothes and things, and now a lot of it's gone," she said.

"We can outfit ourselves again tomorrow."

"I can't go home; I can't go to work; I can't take shelter with any of my friends—"

"I'm your friend," Charlie said.

"We don't even have a car now," she said.

"Sure we do."

"A stolen car."

"It's got four wheels," he said. "It runs. That's good enough."

"I feel like we're the cowboys in one of those old movies where the Indians trap them in a box canyon and keep pushing them farther and farther toward the wall."

"Remember who always won in those movies," Charlie said.

"The cowboys," Joey said.

"Exactly."

He had to stop for a red traffic light because, as luck would have it, a police cruiser was stopped on the other side of the intersection. He didn't like sitting there, vulnerable. He used the rearview mirror and the side mirror to keep a watch on the car that had followed them, afraid that someone would get out of it while they were immobilized here—someone with a shotgun.

In a weary voice that dismayed Charlie, Christine said, "I wish I had your confidence."

So do I, he thought wryly.

The light changed. He crossed the intersection. Behind him, the unknown car fell back a bit.

He said, "Everything'll seem better in the morning."

"And where will we be in the morning?" she asked.

They had come to an intersection where Wilshire Boulevard lay in front of them. He turned right, toward the freeway entrance, and said, "How about Santa Barbara?"

"Are you serious?"

"It's not that far. A couple hours. We could be there by nine-thirty, get a hotel room."

The unknown car had turned right at Wilshire, too, and was still on his tail.

"L.A.'s a big city," she said. "Don't you think we'd be just as safe hiding out here?"

"We probably would," he said. "But I wouldn't *feel* as safe, and I've got to settle us down somewhere that feels right to me, so I can relax and think about the case from a calmer perspective. I can't function well in a constant panic. They won't expect us to go as far away from my operations as Santa Barbara. They'll expect me to hang around, at least as close as L.A., so I know we'll be safe up there."

He drove onto the entrance ramp of the San Diego Freeway, heading north. Checked the rearview mirror. Didn't see the other car yet. Realized he was holding his breath.

She protested. "You didn't bargain for this much trouble, this much inconvenience."

"Sure I did," he said. "I thrive on it."

"Of course you do."

"Ask Joey. He knows all about us private detectives. He knows we just *love* danger."

"They do, Mom," the boy said. "They love danger."

Charlie looked at the rearview mirror again. No other car had come onto the freeway behind him. They weren't being followed.

They drove north into the night, and after a while the rain began to fall heavily again, and there was fog. At times, because of the mist and rain that obscured the landscape and the road ahead, it seemed as if they weren't driving through the real world at all but through some haunted and insubstantial realm of spirits and dreams.

CHAPTER 40

KYLE BARLOWE'S SANTA ANA apartment was furnished to suit his dimensions. There were roomy La-Z-Boy recliners, a big sectional sofa with a deep seat, sturdy end tables, and a solidly built coffee table on which a man could prop his feet without fear of the thing collapsing. He had searched a long time, in countless used furniture stores, before he'd found the round table in the dining alcove; it was plain and somewhat battered, maybe not too attractive, but it was a little higher than most dining tables and gave him the kind of leg room he required. In the bathroom stood a very old, very large claw-foot tub, and in the bedroom he had one big dresser that he'd picked up for forty-six bucks and a king-size bed with an extra-long custom mattress that accommodated him, though with not an inch to spare. This was the one place in the world in which he could be truly comfortable.

But not tonight.

He could not be comfortable when the Antichrist was still alive. He could not relax, knowing that two assassination attempts had failed within the past twelve hours.

He paced from the small kitchen to the living room, into the bedroom, back to the living room again, pausing to look out windows. Main Street was eerily lit by sickly yellow streetlamps, as well as by red and blue and pink and purple neon, all bleeding together, disguising the true colors of every object, giving the shadows fuzzy electric edges. Passing cars spewed up phosphorescent plumes of water that splashed back to the pavement, like rhinestone sequins. The falling rain looked silvery and molten, though the night was far from hot.

He tried watching television. Couldn't get interested in it.

He couldn't keep still. He sat down, got up right away, sat in another chair, got up, went into the bedroom, stretched out on the bed, heard an odd noise at the window, got up to investigate, realized it was only rainwater falling through the downspout, returned to bed, decided he didn't want to lie down, returned to the living room.

The Antichrist was still alive.

But that wasn't the only thing that was making him nervous. He tried to believe nothing else was bothering him, tried to pretend he was only worried about the Scavello boy, but finally he had to admit to himself that another thing was chewing at him.

The old need. Such a fierce need. The NEED. He wanted—

No!

It didn't matter what he wanted. He couldn't have it. He couldn't surrender to the NEED. He didn't dare.

He dropped to his knees in the middle of the living room and prayed to God to help him resist the weakness in him. He prayed hard, prayed with all his might, with all his attention and devotion, prayed with such teeth-grinding intensity that he began to sweat.

He still felt the old, despicable terrifying urge to mangle someone, to pummel and twist and claw, to hurt somebody, to *kill.*

In desperation, he got up and went into the kitchen, to the sink, and turned on the cold water. He put the stopper in the drain. He got ice cubes from the refrigerator and added them to the growing pool. When the sink was almost full, he turned the spigot off and lowered his head into the freezing water, forced himself to stay there, holding his breath, face submerged, skin stinging, until he finally had to come up, gasping for air. He was shivering, and his teeth were chattering, but he still felt the violence building in him, so he put his head under again, waiting until his lungs were bursting, came up sputtering and spitting, and now he was frigid, quaking uncontrollably, but still the urge to do violence swelled unchecked.

Satan was here now. Must be. Satan was here and dredging up the old feelings, pushing Kyle's face in them, tempting him, trying to get him to toss away his last chance at salvation.

I won't!

He stormed through the apartment, trying to detect exactly where Satan was. He looked in closets, opened cabinets, pulled aside the draperies to check behind them. He didn't actually expect to *see* Satan, but he was sure he would at least sense the devil's presence somewhere, invisible though the demon might be. But there was nothing to be found. Which only meant the devil was clever at concealing himself.

When he finally gave up searching for Satan, he was in the bathroom, and he caught a glimpse of himself in the mirror: eyes wild, nostrils dilated, jaw muscles popping, lips bloodless and skinned back over his crooked yellow teeth. He thought of the Phantom of the Opera. He thought of Frankenstein's monster and a hundred other tortured, unhuman faces from a hundred other films he had seen on "Chiller Theater."

The world hated him, and he hated the world, all of them, the ones who laughed, who pointed, the women who found him repulsive, all the—

No. God. Please. Don't let me think about these things. Get my mind off this subject. Help me. Please.

He couldn't look away from his Boris Karloff-Lon Chaney-Rhondo Hatten face, which filled the age-spotted mirror.

He never missed those old horror movies when they were on TV. Many nights he sat alone in front of his black-and-white set, riveted by the ghastly images, and when each picture ended, he went into the bathroom, to this very mirror, and looked at himself and told himself that he wasn't *that* ugly, wasn't *that* frightening, not as bad as the creatures that crept out of primeval swamps or came from beyond the stars or escaped from mad scientists' laboratories. By comparison, he was almost ordinary. At worst, pathetic. But he could never believe himself. The mirror didn't lie. The mirror showed him a face made for nightmares.

He smiled at himself in the mirror, tried to look amiable. The result was awful. The smile was a leer.

No woman would ever have him unless he paid, and even some whores turned him down. Bitches. All of them. Rotten, stinking, heartless bitches. He wanted to make one of them hurt. He wanted to bring his pain to one of them, hammer his pain into some woman and leave it in her, so that for a short while, at least, there would be no pain in him.

No. That was bad thinking. Evil thinking.

Remember Mother Grace.

Remember the Twilight and salvation and life everlasting.

But he wanted. He needed.

He found himself at the door of his apartment without being able to recall how he'd gotten there. He had the door half open. He was on his way out to find a prostitute. Or someone to beat up. Or both.

No!

He slammed the door, locked it, put his back to it, and looked frantically around his living room.

He had to act quickly to save himself.

He was losing his battle against temptation. He was whimpering now, shuddering and mewling. He knew that in a second or two he would open the door again, and this time he would leave, go hunting . . .

In panic, he rushed to a small bookshelf, pulled out one of the inspirational volumes from his collection of a hundred such titles, tore out a fistful of pages and threw them onto the floor, tore out more pages, and more, until only the covers of the book remained, and then he ripped those apart, too. It felt good to mutilate something. He was gasping and shuddering like a horse in distress, and he seized another book, tore it to pieces, pitched the fragments behind him, grabbed another book, demolished it, then another, another . . .

When he regained his senses, he was on the floor, weeping softly. Twenty ruined books, thousands of ripped pages, were heaped around him. He sat up, pulled out his handkerchief, wiped his eyes. Got to his knees, stood. He wasn't shaking any more. The NEED was gone.

Satan had lost.

Kyle had not surrendered to temptation, and now he knew why God wanted men like him to fight the battle of the Twilight. If God built His army strictly of men who had never sinned, how could He know that they would be able to resist the devil's entreaties? But by choosing men like me, Kyle thought, men with no resistance to sin, by giving us a second chance at salvation, by making us prove ourselves, God has acquired an army of *tempered* soldiers.

He looked up at the ceiling but didn't see it. Instead he saw the sky beyond, saw into the heart of the universe. He said, "I'm worthy. I've climbed out of the sewer of sin, and I've proved I'll never sink back down. If what You want is for me to handle the boy for You, I'm worthy now. Give me the boy. Let me have the boy. Let me."

He felt the NEED surging in him again, the desire to choke and rend and crush, but this time it was a purer emotion, the clean white holy desire to be God's gladiator.

It occurred to him that God was asking him to do the very thing he most wanted to avoid. He didn't *want* to kill again. He didn't *want* to harm people any more. He was finally gaining a small measure of respect for himself, finally saw the dim but real possibility that he might one day live in peace with the rest of the world—and now God wanted him to kill, wanted him to use his rage against selected targets.

Why? he asked in sudden, silent misery. Why do *I* have to be the one? I used to thrive on the NEED, but now it scares me, and it *should* scare me. Why must I be used this way; why not in some other way?

That was what Mother Grace called "wrong-thought," and he tried to wipe it out of his mind. You never challenged God like that. You just accepted what He wanted. God was mysterious. Sometimes He was harsh, and you couldn't understand why He demanded so much of you. Like why He wanted you to kill . . . or why He'd made you a freak in the first place when He could just as easily have made you handsome.

No. That was more wrong-thought.

Kyle cleaned up the ravaged books. He poured a glass of milk. He sat down by his telephone. He waited for Grace to call and say that it was time for him to be the hammer of God.

PART FOUR

THE CHASE

Everything that deceives also enchants.
—Plato

There's no escape
From death's embrace,
though you lead it on
a merry chase.

The dogs of death
enjoy the chase.
Just see the smile
on each hound's face.

The chase can't last;
the dogs must feed.
It will come to pass
with terrifying speed.
—*The Book of Counted Sorrows*

CHAPTER 41

IN VENTURA, THEY abandoned the yellow Cadillac. They searched along another residential street until Charlie found a dark blue Ford LTD whose owner had been unwise enough to leave the keys in the ignition. He drove the LTD only two miles before stopping again, in a poorly lit parking lot behind a movie theater, where he removed the license plates and tossed them in the trunk. He took the plates off a Toyota parked nearby and put those on the LTD.

With a little luck, the Toyota's owner wouldn't notice that his plates were missing until tomorrow, perhaps later. Once he did notice, he might not bother reporting the incident to the police, at least not immediately. Anyway, the police wouldn't put stolen plates on the hot sheet the way they would if the entire car was stolen, wouldn't have every cop in the state looking for just a pair of tags, and wouldn't be likely to connect this small crime with the bigger theft of the LTD. They'd treat the plate-nabbing report as just a case of vandalism. Meanwhile, the stolen LTD would have new tags and a new identity, and it would, in effect, cease to be a hot car.

They left Ventura, heading north, and reached Santa Barbara at 9:50 Tuesday night.

Santa Barbara was one of Charlie's favorite getaway places when the pressures of work became overwhelming. He usually stayed at either the Biltmore

141

or the Montecito Inn. This time, however, he chose a slightly shabby motel, The Wile-Away Lodge, at the east end of State Street. Considering his well-known taste for the finer things in life, this was about the last place anyone would look for him.

There was a kitchenette unit available, and Charlie took it for a week, signing the name Enoch Flint to the register and paying cash in advance, so he wouldn't have to show the clerk a credit card.

The room had turquoise draperies, burnt-orange carpet, and bedspreads in a loud purple and yellow pattern; either the decorator had been limited by a tight budget and had bought whatever was available within a certain price range—or he had been a blind beneficiary of the Equal Opportunity Employment Act. The pair of queen-size beds had mattresses that were too soft and lumpy. A couch converted into a third bed, which looked even less comfortable. The furniture was mismatched and well used. The bathroom had an age-yellowed mirror, lots of cracked floor tiles, and a vent fan that wheezed asthmatically. In the kitchen alcove, out of sight from the bedroom, there were four chairs and a table, a sink with a leaky faucet, a battered refrigerator, a stove, cheap plates and cheaper silverware, and an electric percolator with complimentary packets of coffee, Sanka, sugar, and non-dairy creamer. It wasn't much, but it was cleaner than they had expected.

While Christine put Joey to bed, Charlie brewed a pot of Sanka.

When she came into the kitchenette a few minutes later, Christine said, "Mmmmm, that smells heavenly."

He poured two cups for them. "How's Joey?"

"He was asleep before I finished tucking him in. The dog's on the bed with him, and I usually don't allow that, but, what the hell, I figure any day that starts out with a bomb attack and goes downhill from there is a day you should be allowed to have your dog on your bed."

They sat at the kitchen table, by a window that presented a view of one end of the motel parking lot and a small swimming pool ringed by a wrought-iron fence in need of paint. The wet macadam and the parked cars were splashed with orange neon light from the motel's sign. The storm was winding down again.

The coffee was good, and the conversation was better. They talked about everything that came to mind—politics, movies, books, favorite vacation spots, work, music, Mexican food—everything but Grace Spivey and the Twilight. They seemed to have an unspoken agreement to ignore their current circumstances. They desperately needed a respite.

But, to Charlie, their conversation was much more than that; it was a chance to learn about Christine. With the obsessive curiosity of a man in love, he wanted to know every detail of her existence, every thought and opinion, no matter how mundane.

Maybe he was only flattering himself, but he suspected that his romantic interest in her was matched by her interest in him. He hoped that was the case. More than anything, he wanted her to want him.

By midnight, he found himself telling her things he had never told anyone before, things he had long wanted to forget. They were events he thought had lost the power to hurt him, but as he spoke of them he realized the pain had been there all the while.

He talked about being poor in Indianapolis, when there wasn't always enough food or enough heat in the winter because the welfare checks were used first for wine, beer, and whiskey. He spoke of being unable to sleep for fear that the rats infesting their tumble-down shack would get up on the bed with him and start chewing on his face.

He told her about his drunken, violent father, who had beaten his mother as regularly as if that were a husband's duty. Sometimes the old man had beaten his son, too, usually when he was too drunk and unsteady to do much damage. Charlie's mother had been weak and foolish, with her own taste for booze; she hadn't wanted a child in the first place, and she had never interfered when her husband struck Charlie.

"Are your mother and father still alive?" Christine asked.

"Thank God, no! Now that I've done well, they'd be camping on my doorstep, pretending they'd been the best parents a kid ever had. But there was never any love in that house, never any affection."

"You've come a long way up the ladder," Christine said.

"Yeah. Especially considering I didn't expect to live long."

She was looking out at the parking lot and swimming pool. He turned his eyes to the window, too. The world was so quiet and motionless that they might have been the only people in it.

He said, "I always thought my father would kill me sooner or later. The funny thing is, even way back then, I wanted to be a private detective because I saw them on TV—Richard Diamond and Peter Gunn—and I knew they were never afraid of anything. I was always afraid of everything, and more than anything else I wanted not to be afraid."

"And now, of course, you're fearless," she said with irony.

He smiled. "How simple it seems when you're just a kid."

A car pulled into the lot, and both of them stared at it until the doors opened and a young couple got out with two small children.

Charlie poured more Sanka for both of them and said, "I used to lie in bed, listening to the rats, praying that both my parents would die before they got a chance to kill me, and I became real angry with God because He didn't answer that prayer. I couldn't understand why He would let those two go on victimizing a little kid like me. I couldn't defend myself. Why wouldn't God protect the defenseless? Then, when I got a little older, I decided God couldn't answer my prayers because God was good and wouldn't ever kill anyone, not even moral rejects like my folks. So I started praying just to get out of that place. 'Dear God, this is Charlie, and all I want is to some day get out of here and live in a decent house and have money and not be scared all the time.' "

He suddenly recalled a darkly comic episode he hadn't thought about in years, and he laughed sharply at the bizarre memory.

She said, "How can you laugh about it? Even though I know things turned out pretty well for him, I still feel *terrible* for that little boy back there in Indianapolis. As if he's still there."

"No, no. It's just . . . I remembered something else, something that *is* funny in a grim sort of way. After a while, after I'd been praying to God for maybe a year, I got tired of how long it took for a prayer to be answered, and I went over to the other side for a while."

"Other side?"

Staring out the window as a squall of rain whirled through the darkness, he said, "I read this story about a man who sold his soul to the devil. He just one day wished for something he really needed, said that he'd sell his soul for it, and *poof,* the devil showed up with a contract to sign. I decided the devil was much more prompt and efficient than God, so I started praying to the devil at night."

"I assume he never showed up with a contract."

"Nope. He turned out to be as inefficient as God. But then one night it occurred to me that my parents were sure to wind up in Hell, and if I sold my soul to the devil I'd wind up in Hell, too, right there with my folks, for all eternity, and I was so frightened I got out of bed in the dark, and I prayed with all my might for God to save me. I told Him I understood he had a big backlog of prayers to answer, and I said I realized it might take awhile to get around to mine, and I groveled and begged and pleaded for Him to forgive me for doubting Him. I guess I made some noise because my mother came in my room to see what was up. She was as drunk as I'd ever seen her. When I told her I was talking to God, she said, 'Yeah? Well, tell God your daddy's out with a whore somewhere again, and ask Him to make the bastard's cock fall off.' "

"Good heavens," Christine said, laughing but shocked. He knew she wasn't shocked by the word or by his decision to tell her this story; she was shaken, instead, by what his mother's casual crudity revealed about the house in which he'd been raised.

Charlie said, "Now, I was only ten years old, but I'd lived all my life in the worst part of town, and my parents would never be mistaken for Ozzie and Harriet, so even then I knew what she was talking about, and I thought it was the funniest thing I'd ever heard. Every night after that, when I'd be saying my prayers, sooner or later I'd think of what my mother had wanted God to do to my father, and I'd start to laugh. I couldn't finish a prayer without laughing. After a while, I just stopped talking to God altogether, and by the time I was twelve or thirteen I knew there probably wasn't any God or devil and that, even if there was, you have to make your own good fortune in this life."

She told him more about her mother, the convent, the work that had gone into Wine & Dine. Some of her stories were almost as sad as parts of his youth, and others were funny, and all of them were the most fascinating stories he had ever heard because they were *her* stories.

Once in a while, one of them would say they ought to be getting some sleep, and they both really were exhausted, but they kept talking anyway, through two pots of Sanka. By 1:30 in the morning, Charlie realized that a compelling desire to know each other better was not the only reason they didn't want to go to bed. They were also afraid to sleep. They often glanced out the window, and he realized they both expected to see a white Ford van pull into the motel parking lot.

Finally he said, "Look, we can't stay up all night. They can't find us here. No way. Let's go to bed. We need to be rested for what's ahead."

She looked out the window. She said, "If we sleep in shifts, one of us will always be awake to keep a guard."

"It's not necessary. There's no way they could have followed us."

She said, "I'll take the first shift. You go sleep, and I'll wake you at . . . say four-thirty."

He sighed. "No. I'm wide awake. You sleep."

"You'll wake me at four-thirty, so I can take over?"

"All right."

They took their dirty coffee cups to the sink, rinsed them—then were some-how holding each other and kissing gently, softly. His hands moved over her, lightly caressing, and he was stirred by the exquisite shape and texture of her. If Joey had not been in the same room, Charlie would have made love to her, and it would have been the best either of them had ever known. But all they could do was cling to each other in the kitchenette, until at last the frustration outweighed the pleasure. Then she kissed him three times, once deeply and twice lightly on the corners of his mouth, and she went to bed.

When all the lights were out, he sat at the table by the window and watched the parking lot.

He had no intention of waking Christine at four-thirty. Half an hour after she joined Joey in bed, when Charlie was sure she was asleep, he went silently to the other bed.

Waiting for sleep to overtake him, he thought again of what he'd told Christine about his childhood, and for the first time in more than twenty-five years, he said a prayer. As before, he prayed for the safety and deliverance of a little boy, though this time it was not the boy in Indianapolis, whom he had once been, but a boy in Santa Barbara who by chance had become the focus of a crazy old woman's hatred.

Don't let Grace Spivey do this, God. Don't let her kill an innocent innocent child in Your name. There can be no greater blasphemy than that. If You really exist, if You really care, then surely this is the time to do one of Your miracles. Send a flock of ravens to pluck out the old woman's eyes. Send a mighty flood to wash her away. Something. At least a heart attack, a stroke, something to stop her.

As he listened to himself pray, he realized why he had broken the silence between God and himself after all these years. It was because, for the first time in a long time, on the run from the old woman and her fanatics, he felt like a child, unable to cope, in need of help.

CHAPTER 42

IN KYLE BARLOWE'S dream he was being murdered; a faceless adversary was stabbing him repeatedly, and he knew he was dying, yet it didn't hurt and he wasn't afraid. He didn't fight back, just surrendered, and in that acquiescence he discovered the most profound sense of peace he had ever known. Although he was being killed, it was a pleasant dream, not a nightmare, and a part of him somehow knew that not *all* of him was being killed, just the *bad* part of him, just the old Kyle who had hated the world, and when that part of him was finally disposed of, he would be like everyone else, which is the only thing he had ever wanted in life. To be like everyone else . . .

The telephone woke him. He fumbled for it in the darkness.

"Hello?"

"Kyle?" Mother Grace.

"It's me," he said, sleep instantly dispelled.

"Much has been happening," she said.

He looked at the illuminated dial of the clock. It was 4:06 in the morning. He said, "What? What's been happening?"

"We've been burning out the infidels," she said cryptically.

"I wanted to *be* there if anything was going to happen."

"We've burned them out and salted the earth so they can't return," she said, her voice rising.

"You promised me. I wanted to *be* there."

"I haven't needed you—until now," Mother Grace said.

He threw off the covers, sat up on the edge of the bed, grinning at the darkness. "What do you want me to do?"

"They've taken the boy away. They're trying to hide him from us until his powers increase, until he's untouchable."

"Where have they taken him?" Kyle asked.

"I don't know for sure. As far as Ventura. I know that much. I'm waiting for more news or for a vision that'll clarify the situation. Meanwhile, we're going north."

"Who?"

"You, me, Edna, six or eight of the others."

"After the boy?"

"Yes. You must pack some clothes and come to the church. We're leaving within the hour."

"I'll be there right away," he said.

"God bless you," she said, and she hung up.

Barlowe was scared. He remembered the dream, remembered how *good* it had felt in that dream, and he thought he knew what it meant: He was losing his taste for violence, his thirst for blood. But that was no good because, now, for the first time in his life, he had an opportunity to use that talent for violence in a good cause. In fact his salvation depended upon it.

He must kill the boy. It was the right thing. He must not entirely lose the bitter hatred that had motivated him all his life.

The hour was late; Twilight drew near. And now Grace needed him to be the hammer of God.

CHAPTER 43

//////

WEDNESDAY MORNING, RAIN was no longer falling, and the sky was only half obscured by clouds.

Charlie got up first, showered, and was making coffee by the time Christine and Joey woke.

Christine seemed surprised that they were still alive. She didn't have a robe, so she wrapped a blanket around herself and came into the kitchen looking like an Indian squaw. A beautiful Indian squaw. "You didn't wake me for guard duty," she said.

"This isn't the marines," Charlie said, smiling, determined to avoid the panic that had infected them yesterday.

When they were *too* keyed up, they didn't act; they only *reacted*. And that was the kind of behavior that would eventually get them killed.

He had to think; he had to plan. He couldn't do either if he spent all his time looking nervously over his shoulder. They were safe here in Santa Barbara, as long as they were just a little cautious.

"But we were all asleep at the same time," Christine said.

"We needed our rest."

"But I was sleeping so deeply . . . they could've broken in here, and the first thing I would've known about it was when the shooting started."

Charlie looked around, frowning. "Where's the camera? Are we filming a Sominex commercial?"

She sighed, smiled. "You think we're safe?"

"Yes."

"Really?"

"We made it through the night, didn't we?"

Joey came into the kitchen, barefoot, in his underpants, his hair tousled, his face still heavy with sleep. He said, "I dreamed about the witch."

Charlie said, "Dreams can't hurt you."

The boy was solemn this morning. There was no sparkle in his bright blue eyes. "I dreamed she used her magic to turn you into a bug, and then she just stepped on you."

"Dreams don't mean anything," Charlie said. "I once dreamed I was President of the United States. But you don't see any Secret Service men hanging around me, do you?"

"She killed . . . in the *dream* she killed my mom, too," Joey said.

Christine hugged him. "Charlie's right, honey. Dreams don't mean anything."

"Nothing I've *ever* dreamed about has ever happened," Charlie said.

The boy went to the window. He stared out at the parking lot. He said, "She's out there somewheres."

Christine looked at Charlie. He knew what she was thinking. The boy had thus far been amazingly resilient, bouncing back from every shock, recovering from every horror, always able to smile one more time. But maybe he had exhausted his resources; maybe he wasn't going to bounce back very well any more.

Chewbacca padded into the kitchenette, stopped at the boy's side, and growled softly.

"See?" Joey said. "Chewbacca knows. Chewbacca knows she's out there somewheres."

The boy's usual verve was gone. It was disturbing to see him so gray-faced and bereft of spirit.

Charlie and Christine tried to kid him into a better mood, but he was having none of it.

Later, at nine-thirty, they ate breakfast in a nearby coffee shop. Charlie and Christine were starved, but they repeatedly had to urge Joey to eat. They were in a booth by one of the big windows, and Joey kept looking out at the sky, where a few strips of blue seemed like gaily colored ropes holding the drab clouds together. He looked as glum as a six-year-old could look.

Charlie wondered why the boy's eyes were drawn repeatedly to the sky. Was he expecting the witch to come sailing in on her broom?

Yes, in fact, that was probably just what he was worried about. When you were six years old, it wasn't always possible to distinguish between real and imaginary dangers. At that age you *believed* in the monster-that-lives-in-the-closet, and you are convinced that something even worse was crouching under your bed. To Joey, it probably made as much sense to search for broomsticks in the sky as to look for white Ford vans on the highway.

Chewbacca had been left in the car outside the coffee shop. When they were finished with breakfast, they brought him an order of ham and eggs, which he devoured eagerly.

"Last night it was hamburgers, this morning ham and eggs," Christine said.

"We've got to find a grocery store and buy some real dog food before this mutt gets the idea that he's *always* going to eat this well."

They went shopping again for clothes and personal effects in a mall just off East State Street. Joey tried on some clothes, but listlessly, without the enthusiasm he had shown yesterday. He said little, smiled not at all.

Christine was obviously worried about him. So was Charlie.

They were finished shopping before lunch. The last thing they bought was a small electronic device at Radio Shack. It was the size of a pack of cigarettes, a product of the paranoid '70s and '80s that would not have had any buyers in a more trusting era: a tap detector that could tell you if your telephone line was being monitored by a recorder or a tracing mechanism of any kind.

In a phone booth near the side entrance of Sears, Charlie unscrewed the earpiece on the handset, screwed on another earpiece that came with the tap detector. He removed the mouthpiece, used a car key to short the inhibitor that made it impossible to place a long-distance call without operator assistance, and dialed Klemet-Harrison in Costa Mesa, toll-free. If his equipment indicated a tap, he'd be able to hang up in the first fraction of a second after the connection was made and, most likely, cut the line before anyone had a chance even to determine that the call was from another area code.

The number rang twice, then there was a click on the line.

The meter in Charlie's hand gave no indication of a tap.

But instead of Sherry Ordway's familiar voice, the call was answered by a telephone company recording: "The number you have dialed is no longer in service. Please consult your directory for the correct number or dial the operator for . . ."

Charlie hung up.

Tried it again.

He got the same response.

With a presentiment of disaster chewing at him, he dialed Henry Rankin's home number. It was picked up on the first ring, and again the meter indicated no tap, but this time the voice was not a recording.

"Hello?" Henry said.

Charlie said, "It's me, Henry. I just called the office—"

"I've been waiting here by the phone, figuring you'd try me sooner or later," Henry said. "We got trouble, Charlie. We got lots of trouble."

From outside the booth, Christine couldn't hear what Charlie was saying, but she could tell something bad had happened. When he finally hung up and opened the folding door, he was ashen.

"What's wrong?" she asked.

He glanced at Joey and said, "Nothing's wrong. I talked to Henry Rankin. They're still working on the case, but there's nothing new to report yet."

He was lying for Joey's sake, but the boy sensed it just as Christine did, and said, "What'd she do now? What'd the witch do now?"

"Nothing," Charlie said. "She can't find us, so she's throwing tantrums down there in Orange County. That's all."

"What's a tantrum?" Joey asked.

"Don't worry about it. We're okay. Everything's ticking along as planned. Now let's go back to the car, find a supermarket, and stock up on groceries."

Walking through the open-air mall and all the way out to the car, Charlie looked around uneasily, with a visible tension he hadn't shown all morning.

Christine had begun to accept his assurances that they were safe in Santa

Barbara, but now fear crawled up out of her subconscious and took possession of her once more.

As if it were an omen of renewed danger, the weather worsened again. The sky began to clot up with black clouds.

They found a supermarket, and as they shopped, Joey moved down the aisles ahead of them. Ordinarily, he scampered ahead, searching for items on their shopping list, eager to help. Today he moved slowly and studied the shelves with little interest.

When the boy was far enough away, Charlie said softly, "Last night my offices were torched."

"Torched?" Christine said. There was suddenly a greasy, roiling feeling in her stomach. "You mean . . . burned?"

He nodded, taking a couple of cans of Mandarin orange slices from the shelf and putting them in the shopping cart. "Everything's . . . lost . . . furniture, equipment, all the files . . . gone." He paused while two women with carts moved past them. Then: "The files were in fire-proof cabinets, but someone got the drawers open anyway, pulled out all the papers, and poured gasoline on them."

Shocked, Christine said, "But in a business like yours, don't you have burglar alarms—"

"Two systems, each independent of the other, both with backup power sources in case of a blackout," Charlie said.

"But that sounds fool-proof."

"It was supposed to've been, yeah. But her people got through somehow."

Christine felt sick. "You think it was Grace Spivey."

"I know it was Grace. You haven't heard everything that happened last night. Besides, it had to be her because there's such a quality of rage about it, such an air of desperation, and she must be angry and desperate right now because we've given her the slip. She doesn't know where we've gone, can't get her hands on Joey, so she's striking out wherever she can, flailing away in a mad frenzy."

She remembered the Henredon desk in his office, the Martin Green paintings, and she said, "Oh, dammit, Charlie, I'm so sorry. Because of me, you've lost your business and all your—"

"It can all be replaced," he said, although she could see that the loss disturbed him. "The important files are on microfilm and stored elsewhere. They can be recreated. We can find new offices. Insurance will cover most everything. It's not the money or the inconvenience that bothers me. It's the fact that, for a few days at least, until Henry gets things organized down there, my people won't be able to keep after Grace Spivey—and we won't have them behind us, supporting us. Temporarily, we're pretty much on our own."

That *was* a disturbing thought.

Joey came back with a can of pineapple rings. "Can I have these, Mom?"

"Sure," she said, putting the can in the cart. If it would have brought a smile to his small glum face, she'd have allowed him to get a whole package of Almond Joys or some other item he was usually not permitted to have.

Joey went off to scout the rest of the aisle ahead.

To Charlie, Christine said, "You mentioned that something else happened last night . . ."

He hesitated. He put two jars of applesauce in the cart. Then, with a look of sympathy and concern, he said, "Your house was also torched."

Instantly, without conscious intent, she began to catalogue what she had lost, the sentimental as well as the truly valuable things that this act of arson

had stolen from her: all Joey's baby pictures; the fifteen-thousand-dollar oriental carpet in the living room, which was the first expensive thing she'd owned,
her first gesture of self-indulgence after the years of self-denial her mother had
demanded of her; photographs of Tony, her long-dead brother; her collection
of Lalique crystal . . .

For an awful moment she almost burst into tears, but then Joey returned to
say that the dairy case was at the end of this aisle and that he would like some
cottage cheese to go with the pineapple rings. And Christine realized that
losing the oriental carpets, the paintings, and even the old photographs was of
little importance as long as she still had Joey. He was the only thing in her life
that was irreplaceable. No longer on the verge of tears, she told him to get the
cottage cheese.

When Joey moved away again, Charlie said, "My house, too."

For a moment she wasn't sure she understood. "Burned?"

"To the ground," he said.

"Oh my God."

It was too much. Christine felt like a plague-carrier. She had brought disaster to everyone who was trying to help her.

"Grace is desperate, you see," Charlie said excitedly. "She doesn't know
where we've gone, and she really thinks that Joey is the Antichrist, and she's
afraid she's failed in her God-given mission. She's furious and frightened, and
she's striking out blindly. The very fact that she's done these things means
we're safe here. Better than that, it means she's rapidly destroying herself.
She's gone too far. She's stepped way, way over the line. The cops can't help
but connect those three torchings with the murders at your place and with the
bomb at Miriam Rankin's house in Laguna. This is now the biggest story in
Orange County, maybe the biggest story in the whole state. She can't go
around blowing up houses, burning them down. She's brought *war* to Orange
County, for Christ's sake, and no one's going to tolerate that. The cops are
going to come down hard on her now. They're going to be grilling her and
everyone in her church. They'll go over her affairs with a microscope. She'll
have made a mistake last night; she'll have left incriminating evidence. Somewhere. Somehow. One little mistake is all the cops need. They'll seize on it and
pull her alibi apart. She's done for. It's only a matter of time. All we've got to
do is lie low here for a few days, stay in the motel, and wait for the Church of
the Twilight to fall apart."

"I hope you're right," she said, but she wasn't going to get her hopes up.
Not again.

Joey returned with the cottage cheese and stayed close to them for a while,
until they entered an aisle that contained a small toy section, where he drifted
away to look at the plastic guns.

Charlie said, "We'll finish shopping, get a bunch of magazines, a deck of
cards, a few games, whatever we need to keep us occupied for the rest of the
week. After we've taken everything back to the room, I'll get rid of the car—"

"But I thought it wouldn't turn up on any hot sheets for a few days yet.
That's what you said."

He was trying not to look grim, but he couldn't keep the worry out of either
his face or his voice. He took a package of Oreos from the cookie section and
put them in the cart. "Yeah, well, according to Henry, the cops have already
found the yellow Cadillac we abandoned in Ventura, and they've already
linked it with the stolen LTD and the missing plates. They lifted fingerprints
from the Caddy, and because my prints are on file with my PI license application, they made a quick connection."

"But from what you said, I didn't think they ever worked that fast."

"Ordinarily, no. But we had a piece of bad luck."

"Another one?"

"That Cadillac belongs to a state senator. The police didn't treat this like they would an ordinary stolen car report."

"Are we jinxed or what?"

"Just a bit of bad luck," he said, but he was clearly unnerved by this development.

Across the aisle from the cookies were potato chips, corn chips, and other snack foods, just the stuff she tried to keep Joey away from. But now she put potato chips, cheese puffs, and Fritos in the cart. She did it partly because she wanted to cheer Joey up—but also because it seemed foolish to deny themselves anything when the time left to them might be very short.

"So now the cops aren't just looking for the LTD," she said. "They're looking for you, too."

"There's worse," he said, his voice little more than a whisper.

She stared at him, not sure she wanted to hear what he had to tell her. During the last couple of days, she'd had the feeling they were all caught in a vise. For the past few hours, the jaws of the vise had loosened a bit, but now Grace Spivey was turning the handle tight again.

He said, "They found my Mercedes in the garage in Westwood. A phone tip sent them to it. In the trunk . . . they found a dead body."

Stunned, Christine said, "Who?"

"They don't know yet. A man. In his thirties. No identification. He'd been shot twice."

"Spivey's people killed him and put him in your car?" she asked, keeping an eye on Joey as he checked out the toy guns at the end of the aisle.

"Yeah. That's what I figure. Maybe he was in the garage when they attacked us. Maybe he saw too much and had to be eliminated, and they realized they could use his body to put the police on my tail. Now Grace doesn't have just her thousand or two thousand followers out looking for us; she's got every cop in the state helping with the search."

They were at a standstill now, speaking softly but intently, no longer pretending to be interested only in groceries.

"But surely the police don't think *you* killed him."

"They have to assume I'm involved somehow."

"But won't they realize it's related to the church, to that crazy woman—"

"Sure. But they might think the guy in my trunk is one of her people and that I've eliminated him. Or even if they do suspect I'm being framed, they've still got to talk to me. They've still got to put a warrant out for me."

The whole world was after them now. It seemed hopeless. Like a toxic chemical, despair settled into her bones, leeching her strength. She just wanted to lie down, close her eyes, and sleep for a while.

Charlie said, "Come on. Let's get the shopping done, take everything back to the motel, and then dump the car. I want to hole up inside before some cop spots our license plates or recognizes me."

"Do you think the police know we headed for Santa Barbara after we left Ventura?"

"They can't know for sure. But they've got to figure we were running from L.A., moving north, so Santa Barbara's a good bet."

As they went up and down the remaining aisles, as they checked out and paid for the groceries, Christine found it difficult to breathe. She felt as if a spotlight were trained on them. She kept waiting for sirens and alarms.

Joey became even more lethargic and solemn than before. He sensed that they were hiding something from him, and maybe it wasn't good to withhold the truth, but she decided it would be worse to tell him that the witch had burned down their house. That would convince him they were never going back, never going home again, which might be more than he could handle.

It was almost more than *she* could handle.

Because maybe it was the truth. Maybe they'd never be able to go home again.

CHAPTER 44

CHARLIE DROVE THE LTD into the motel lot, parked in the slot in front of their unit—and saw movement at the small window in the kitchenette. It might have been his imagination, of course. Or it might have been the maid. He didn't think it was either.

Instead of switching the engine off, he immediately threw the LTD into reverse and began backing out of the parking space.

Christine said, "What's wrong?"

"Company," he said.

"What? Where?"

In the rear seat, in a voice that was the essence of terror, Joey said, "The witch."

In front of them, as they backed away from it, the door to their unit began to open.

How the hell did they find us so soon? Charlie wondered.

Not wanting to waste the time required to turn the car around, he kept it in reverse and backed rapidly toward the avenue in front of the motel.

Out in the street, a white van appeared and swung to the curb, blocking the exit from the Wile-Away Lodge.

Charlie saw it in the rearview mirror, jammed on the brakes to avoid hitting it.

He heard gunfire. Two men with automatic weapons had come out of the motel room.

"Get down!"

Christine looked back at Joey. "Get on the floor!" she told him.

"You too," Charlie said, tramping on the accelerator again, pulling on the steering wheel, angling away from the van behind them.

She popped her seatbelt and crouched down, keeping her head below the windows.

If a bullet came through the door, she'd be killed anyway.

There wasn't anything Charlie could do about that. Except get the hell out of there.

Chewbacca barked, an ear-rupturing sound in the closed car.

Charlie reversed across the lot, nearly sideswiping a Toyota, clipping one corner of the wrought-iron fence that encircled the swimming pool. There was no other exit to the street, but he didn't care. He'd make an exit of his own. He drove backwards, over the sidewalk and over the curb. The undercarriage scraped, and Charlie prayed the fuel tank hadn't been torn open, and the LTD slammed to the pavement with a jolt. The engine didn't cut out. *Thank God.* His heart pounding as fast as the sedan's six cylinders, Charlie kept his foot on the accelerator, roaring backwards into State Street, tires screaming and smoking, nearly hitting a VW that was coming up the hill, causing half a dozen other vehicles to brake and wheel frantically out of his path.

The white Ford van pulled away from the motel exit, which it had been blocking, drove into the street again, and tried to ram them. The truck's grille looked like a big grinning mouth, a shark's maw, as it bore down on them. Two men were visible beyond the windshield. The van clipped the right front fender of the LTD, and there was a tortured cry of shredding metal, a shattering of glass as the car's right headlight was pulverized. The LTD rocked from the blow, and Joey cried out, and the dog bleated, and Charlie almost bit his tongue.

Christine started to rise to see what was happening, and Charlie shouted at her to stay down as he shifted gears and drove forward, east on State, swinging wide around the back of the white van. It tried to ram him in reverse, but he got past it in time.

He expected the crumpled fender to obstruct the tire and eventually bring them to a stop, but it didn't. There were a few clanging-tinkling sounds as broken pieces of the car fell away, but there was no grinding noise of the sort that an impacted tire or an obstructed axle would make.

He heard more gunfire. Bullets thudded into the car, but none of them entered the passenger compartment. Then the LTD was moving fast, pulling out of range.

Charlie was grinding his teeth so hard that his jaws hurt, but he couldn't stop.

Ahead, at the corner, on the cross-street, another white Ford van appeared on their right, swiftly moving out from the shadows beneath a huge oak.

Jesus, they're everywhere!

The new van streaked toward the intersection, intent on blocking Charlie. To stay out of its way, he pulled recklessly into oncoming traffic. A Mustang swung wide of the LTD, and behind the Mustang a red Jaguar jumped the curb and bounced into the parking lot of a Burger King to avoid a collision.

The LTD had reached the intersection. The car was responding too sluggishly, though Charlie pressed the accelerator all the way to the floor.

From the right, the second van was still coming. It couldn't block him now; it was too late for that, so it was going to try to ram him instead.

Charlie was still in the wrong lane. The driver of an oncoming Pontiac braked too suddenly, and his car went into a slide. It turned sideways, came straight at them, a juggernaut.

Charlie eased up on the accelerator but didn't hit the brakes because he would lose his flexibility if he stopped completely and would only be delaying the moment of impact.

In a fraction of a second, he considered all his options. He couldn't swing left into the cross-street because it was crowded with traffic. He couldn't go right because the car was bearing down on him from that direction. He couldn't throw the car into reverse because there was lots of traffic behind him, and, besides, there was no time to shift gears and back up. He could only go forward as the Pontiac slid toward him, go forward and try to dodge the hurtling mass of steel that suddenly loomed as large as a mountain.

A strip of rubber peeled off one of the Pontiac's smoking tires, spun into the air, like a flying snake.

In another fraction of a second, the situation changed: The Pontiac was no longer coming at him broadside, but was continuing to turn, turn, turn, until it had swiveled one hundred and eighty degrees from its original position. Now its back end pointed at the LTD, and, though it was still sliding, it was a smaller target than it had been. Charlie wrenched the steering wheel to the right, then left again, arcing around the careening Pontiac, which shrieked past with no more than an inch to spare.

The van rammed them. Fortunately, it caught only the last couple inches of the LTD. The bumper was torn off with a horrendous sound, and the whole car shuddered and was pushed sideways a couple of feet. The steering wheel abruptly had a mind of its own; it tore itself out of Charlie's grasp, spun through his clutching hands, burning his palms, and he cried out in pain but got hold of it again. Cursing, blinking back the tears of pain that briefly blurred his vision, he got the car pointed eastward again, stood on the accelerator, and kept going. When they were through the intersection, he swung back into his own lane. He hammered the horn, encouraging the cars in front of him to get out of his way.

The second white van—the one that had ripped away their bumper—had gotten out of the mess at the intersection and had followed them. At first it was two cars back of them, then one; then it was right behind the LTD.

With the subsidence of gunfire, both Christine and Joey sat up again.

The boy looked out the rear window at the van and said, "It's the witch! I can see her! I can *see* her!"

"Sit down and put your seatbelt on," Charlie told him. "We might be making some sudden stops and turns."

The van was thirty feet back but closing.

Twenty feet.

Chewbacca was barking again.

Belted in, Joey held the dog close and quieted it.

Traffic in front of them was closing up, slowing down.

Charlie checked the rearview mirror.

The van was only fifteen feet back of them.

Ten feet.

"They're going to ram us while we're moving," Christine said.

Barely touching the brakes, Charlie whipped the car to the right, into a narrow cross-street, leaving the heavy traffic and commercial development of State Street behind. They were in an older residential neighborhood: mostly bungalows, a few two-story houses, lots of mature trees, cars parked on one side.

The van followed, but it dropped back a bit because it couldn't make the turn as quickly as the LTD. It wasn't as maneuverable as the car. That's what Charlie was counting on.

At the next corner he turned left, cutting his speed as little as possible, almost standing the LTD on two wheels, almost losing control in a wild slide, but somehow holding on, nearly clipping a car parked too close to the intersection. A block later he turned right, then left, then right, then right again, weaving through the narrow streets, putting distance between them and the van.

When they were not just one but *two* corners ahead of the van, when their pursuers could no longer see which way they were turning, Charlie stopped making random turns and began choosing their route with some deliberation, street by street, heading back toward State, then across the main thoroughfare and into the parking lot of another shopping center.

"We're not stopping here?" Christine said.

"Yeah."

"But—"

"We've lost them."

"For the moment, maybe. But they—"

"There's something I have to check on," Charlie said.

He parked out of sight of the traffic on State Street, between two larger vehicles, a camper and a pickup truck.

Apparently, when the second white van had grazed the back of the LTD, tearing off the rear bumper, it had also damaged the exhaust pipe and perhaps the muffler. Acrid fumes were rising through the floorboards, into the car. Charlie told them to crank their windows down an inch or two. He didn't want to turn off the engine if he could help it; he wanted to be ready to move out at a moment's notice; but the fumes were just too strong, and he had to shut the car down.

Christine unhooked her seatbelt and turned to Joey. "You okay, honey?"

The boy didn't answer.

Charlie looked back at him.

Joey was slumped down in the corner. His small hands were fisted tight. His chin was tucked down. His face was bloodless. His lips trembled, but he was too scared to cry, scared speechless, paralyzed with fear. At Christine's urging, he finally looked up, and his eyes were haunted, forty years too old for his young face.

Charlie felt sick and sad and weary at the sight of the boy's eyes and the tortured soul they revealed. He was also angry. He had the irrational urge to get out of the car right now, stalk back to State Street, find Grace Spivey, and put a few bullets in her.

The bitch. The stupid, crazy, pitiful, hateful, raving, disgusting old *bitch!*

The dog mewled softly, as if aware of its young master's state of mind.

The boy produced a similar sound and turned his eyes down to the dog, which put its head in his lap.

As if by magic, the witch had found them. The boy had said that you couldn't hide from a witch, no matter what you did, and now it seemed that he was correct.

"Joey," Christine said, "are you all right, honey? Speak to me, baby. Are you okay?"

Finally the boy nodded. But he still wouldn't—or couldn't—speak. And there was no conviction in his nod.

Charlie understood how the boy felt. It was difficult to believe that everything could have gone so terribly wrong in the span of just a few minutes.

There were tears in Christine's eyes. Charlie knew what she was thinking. She was afraid that Joey had finally snapped.

And maybe he had.

CHAPTER 45

THE CHURNING BLACK-GRAY clouds at last unleashed the pent-up storm that had been building all morning. Rain scoured the shopping center parking lot and pounded on the battered LTD. Sheet lightning pulsed across large portions of the dreary sky.

Good, Charlie thought, looking out at the water-blurred world.

The storm—especially the static caused by the lightning—gave them a little more cover. They needed all the help they could get.

"It has to be in here," he said, opening Christine's purse, dumping the contents on the seat between them.

"But I don't see how it could be," she said.

"It's the only place they could have hidden it," he insisted, frantically stirring through the contents of the purse, searching for the most likely object in which a tiny transmitter might have been concealed. "It's the only thing that's come with us all the way from L.A. We left behind the suitcases, my car . . . this is the only place it could've been hidden."

"But no one could've gotten hold of my purse—"

"It might've been planted a couple of days ago, when you weren't suspicious or watchful, before all this craziness began," he said, aware that he was grasping at straws, trying to keep his desperation out of his voice but not entirely succeeding.

If we aren't unwittingly carrying a transmitter, he thought, then how the hell did they find us so quickly? How the *hell?*

He looked out at the parking lot, turned and glanced out of the back window. No white vans. Yet.

Joey was staring out the side window. His lips were moving, but he wasn't making a sound. He looked wrung-out. A few raindrops slanted in through the narrow gap at the top of the window, struck the boy's head, but he didn't seem to notice.

Charlie thought of his own miserable childhood, the beatings he had endured at the hands of his father, the loveless face of his drunken mother. He thought about the other helpless children, all over the world, who became victims because they were too small to fight back, and a renewed, powerful current of anger energized him again.

He picked up a green malachite compact from the pile of stuff that had been in Christine's purse, opened it, lifted out the powder puff, took out the cake of powder, dropped them both in the litter bag that hung on the dashboard. He quickly examined the compact, but he couldn't see anything unusual about it. He hammered it against the steering wheel a couple of times, smashed it, examined the pieces, saw nothing suspicious.

Christine said, "If we *have* been carrying a transmitter, something they've been able to home in on, it'd need a strong power source, wouldn't it?"

"A battery," he said, taking apart her tube of lipstick.

"But surely it couldn't operate off a battery *that* small."

"You'd be surprised what modern technology has made possible. Microminiaturization. You'd be surprised."

Although all four of the windows were down an inch or two, letting in a bit of fresh air, the glass was steaming up. He couldn't see the parking lot, and that made him uneasy, so he started the engine again and switched on the defroster, in spite of the exhaust fumes that seeped in from the damaged muffler and tailpipe.

The purse contained a gold fountain pen and a Cross ballpoint. He took them both apart.

"But how far would something like that broadcast?" Christine asked.

"Depends on its sophistication."

"More specifically?"

"A couple of miles."

"That's all?"

"Maybe five miles if it was really good."

"Not all the way to L.A.?"

"No."

Neither of the pens was a transmitter.

Christine said, "Then how'd they find us all the way up here in Santa Barbara?" While he carefully examined her wallet, a penlight, a small bottle of Excedrin, and several other items, he said, "Maybe they have contacts in various police agencies, and maybe they learned about the stolen Caddy turning up in Ventura. Maybe they figured we were headed toward Santa Barbara, so they came up here and started cruising around, just hoping to strike it lucky, just driving from street to street in their vans, monitoring their receivers, until they got close enough to pick up the signal from the transmitter."

"But we could have gone a hundred other places," Christine said. "I just don't see why they would've zeroed in on Santa Barbara so quickly."

"Maybe they weren't just looking for us here. Maybe they had search teams working in Ventura and Ojai and a dozen other towns."

"What are the odds of their finding us just by cruising around in a city this size, waiting to pick up our transmitter's signal?"

"Not good. But it could happen. It *must* have happened that way. How else would they find us?"

"The witch," Joey said from the back seat. "She has . . . magic powers . . . witch powers . . . stuff like that." Then he lapsed into moody silence again, staring out at the rain.

Charlie was almost ready to accept Joey's childish explanation. The old woman was inhumanly relentless and seemed to possess an uncanny gift for tracking down her prey.

But of course it wasn't magic. There was a logical explanation. A hidden, miniaturized transmitter made the most sense. But whether it was a transmitter or something else, they must figure it out, apply reason and common sense until they found the answer, or they were never going to lose the old bitch and her crazies.

The windows had unsteamed.

As far as Charlie could see, there were still no white vans in the parking lot.

He had looked through everything in the purse without finding the electronic device that he had been sure would be there. He began to examine the purse itself, seeking lumps in the lining.

"I think we should get moving again," Christine said nervously.

"In a minute," Charlie said, using her nail file to rip out the well-stitched seams in the handles of her purse.

"The exhaust fumes are making me sick," she said.

"Open your window a little more."

He found nothing but cotton padding inside the handles of the purse.

"No transmitter," she said.

"It's still got to be the answer."

"But if not in my purse . . . where?"

"Somewhere," he said, frowning.

"You said yourself that it *had* to be in the purse."

"I was wrong. Somewhere else . . ." He tried to think. But he was too worried about the white vans to think clearly.

"We've got to get moving," Christine said.

"I know," he said.

He released the emergency brake, put the car in gear, and drove away from the shopping center, splashing through large puddles.

"Where now?" Christine asked.

"I don't know."

CHAPTER 46

FOR A WHILE they drove aimlessly through Santa Barbara and neighboring Montecito, mostly staying away from main thoroughfares, wandering from one residential area to another, just keeping on the move.

Here and there, at an intersection, a confluence of overflowing gutters formed a lake that made passage difficult or impossible. The dripping trees looked limp, soggy. In the rain and mist, all the houses, regardless of color or style, seemed gray, drab.

Christine was afraid that Charlie had run out of ideas. Worse, she was afraid he had run out of hope. He didn't want to talk. He drove in silence, staring morosely at the storm-swept streets. Until now she hadn't fully realized how much she had come to depend upon his good humor, positive outlook, and bulldog determination. He was the glue holding her together. She never thought she would say such a thing about a man, any man, but she had to say it about Charlie: Without him, she would be lost.

Joey would speak when spoken to, but he didn't have much to say, and his voice was frail and distant like the voice of a ghost.

Chewbacca was equally lethargic and taciturn.

They listened to the radio, changing from a rock station to a country station, to one that played swing and other jazz. The music, regardless of type, sounded flat. The commercials were all ludicrous: When you were running from a pack of lunatics who wanted to kill you and your little boy, who *cared* whether one brand of motor oil, Scotch, blue jeans, or toilet tissue was better than another brand? The news was all weather, and none of it good: flooding in half a dozen towns between L.A. and San Diego; high waves smashing into the living rooms of expensive homes in Malibu; mud slides in San Clemente, Laguna Beach, Pacific Palisades, Montecito, and points north along the stormy coastline.

Christine's personal world had fallen apart, and now the rest of the world seemed dead set on following her example.

When Charlie finally stopped thinking and started talking, Christine was so relieved she almost wept.

He said, "The main thing we've got to do is get away from Santa Barbara, find a safe place to hide out, and lie low until Henry can get the organization functioning again. We can't do anything to help ourselves until all my men are focused on Grace Spivey, putting pressure on her and on the others in that damned church."

"So how do we get out of town?" she asked. "This car's hot."

"Yeah. Besides, it's falling apart."

"Do we steal another set of wheels?"

"No," he said. "The first thing we need is cash. We're running out of money, and we don't want to use credit cards everywhere we go because that leaves a trail. Of course, it doesn't matter if we use cards *here* because they already know we're in Santa Barbara, so we'll start milking our plastic for all the cash in it."

When at last Charlie swung into action, he moved with gratifying speed.

First they went to a telephone booth, searched the yellow pages, and made a note of the addresses of the nearest Wells Fargo and Security Pacific bank offices. In Orange County, Charlie had his accounts at the former, Christine at the latter.

At one Security Pacific office, Christine used her Visa card to get a cash advance of one thousand dollars, which was the maximum allowable. At another branch, she obtained a five-hundred-dollar advance on her Mastercard. At a third office, using her American Express Card she bought two thousand dollars worth of traveller's checks in twenty- and hundred-dollar denominations. Then, outside the same bank, she used her automatic teller card to obtain more cash. She was permitted to withdraw three hundred dollars at a time from the computerized teller, and she was allowed to make such withdrawals twice a day. Therefore, she was able to add six hundred bucks to the fifteen hundred that she had gotten from Visa and Mastercard. Counting the two thousand in traveller's checks, she had put together a bankroll of forty-one hundred dollars.

"Now let's see what I can add to that," Charlie said, setting out in search of a Wells Fargo office.

"But this ought to be enough for quite a while," she said.

"Not for what I've got in mind," he said.

"What is it you've got in mind?"

"You'll see."

Charlie always carried a blank check in his wallet. At the nearest Wells Fargo branch, after presenting an array of ID and after speaking at length with the manager, he withdrew $7,500 of the $8,254 in his personal checking account.

He was worried that the police might have informed his bank of the warrant for his arrest and that the Wells Fargo computer would direct any teller to call the authorities the moment he showed up to withdraw money. But luck was with him. The cops weren't moving quite as fast as Grace Spivey and her followers.

At other banks, he obtained cash advances on his Visa, Mastercard, Carte Blanche, and American Express cards.

Twice, in their travels back and forth across town, they saw police cruisers, and Charlie tried to duck out of their way. When it wasn't possible to duck, he held his breath, sure that the end had come, but they were not stopped. He knew they were swiftly running out of luck. At any moment a cop was going to notice their license plate number—or Spivey's people were going to make contact again.

Where was the transmitter if not in Christine's purse? There *had* to be a transmitter somewhere. It was the only explanation.

Minute by minute, his uneasiness grew until, at last, he found himself sheathed in a cold sweat.

By late afternoon, they had put together a kitty of more than fourteen thousand dollars.

Rain was still falling.

Darkness was settling in early.

"That's it," Christine said. "Even if there was some way to squeeze out a few hundred dollars more, the banks are all closed. So now what?"

They stopped at a small shopping center, where they bought a new purse for Christine, a briefcase in which Charlie could carry the neat stacks of cash they had amassed, and a newspaper.

A headline on the bottom half of the front page caught his attention: CULT LEADER SOUGHT IN WAKE OF ARSON, BOMBINGS.

He showed the story to Christine. Standing under an awning in front of a dress shop, they read the piece all the way through, while rain hissed and pattered and gurgled in the settling twilight. Their names—and Joey's—were mentioned repeatedly, and the article said Charlie was wanted for questioning in a related homicide investigation, but fortunately there were no pictures.

"So the police aren't just looking for me," Charlie said. "They want to talk to Grace Spivey, too. That's some consolation, anyway."

"Yeah, but they won't be able to pin anything on her," Christine said. "She's too slippery, too clever."

"A witch isn't scared of cops," Joey said grimly.

"Don't be pessimistic," Charlie told them. "If you'd seen her with those holes in her hands, if you'd heard her raving, you'd know she's teetering right on the edge. Wouldn't surprise me if she *bragged* about what she'd done next time the cops talk to her."

Christine said, "Listen, they're probably looking for her down in Orange County, or maybe in L.A., but not up here. Why don't we call the cops—anonymously, of course—and tell them she's in the neighborhood?"

"Excellent idea," he said.

He made the call from a pay phone and kept it brief. He spoke with a desk sergeant named Pulaski and told him that the incident at the Wile-Away Lodge, earlier in the day, had involved Grace Spivey and the Church of the Twilight. He described the white vans and warned Pulaski that the Twilighters were armed with automatic weapons. He hung up without answering any of the sergeant's questions.

When they were in the car once more, Charlie opened the paper to the classified ads, found the "For Sale" section under the heading "Automobiles," and began reading.

The house was small but beautifully kept. It was a Cape Cod-style structure, unusual for California, pale blue with white shutters and white window frames. The lamps at the end of the walk and those on the porch pillars were brass ship's lamps with flame-shaped bulbs. It looked like a warm, snug haven against the storm and against all the other vicissitudes of life.

Charlie had a sudden longing for his own home, back in North Tustin. Belatedly, he felt the terrible impact of the news that Henry had given him this morning: His house, like Christine's, had been burned to the ground. He had told himself insurance would cover the loss. He had told himself there was no use crying over spilt milk. He had told himself that he had more important things to worry about than what he had lost in the fire. But now, no matter *what* he told himself, he could not dispel the dull ache that took possession of his heart. Standing here in the chilly February darkness, dripping rainwater, weary and worried, burdened by his responsibility for the safety of Christine and Joey (a crushing weight that grew heavier by the hour), he was overcome by a poignant yearning for his favorite chair, for the familiar books and furnishings of his den.

Stop it, he told himself angrily. There's no time for sentiment or self-pity. Not if we're going to stay alive.

His house was rubble.

His favorite chair was ashes.

His books were smoke.

With Christine, Joey, and Chewbacca, Charlie climbed the porch steps of the Cape Cod house and rang the bell.

The door was opened by a white-haired, sixtyish man in a brown cardigan sweater.

Charlie said, "Mr. Madigan? I called a little while ago about—"

"You're Paul Smith," Madigan said.

"Yes," Charlie said.

"Come in, come in. Oh, you've got a dog. Well, just tie him up there on the porch."

Looking past Madigan at the light beige carpet in the living room, Charlie said, "Afraid we'll track up your carpet. Is that the station wagon there in the driveway?"

"That's it," Madigan said. "Wait a moment, and I'll get the keys."

They waited in silence on the porch. The house was on a hill above Santa Barbara. Below, the city twinkled and shimmered in the darkness, beyond curtains of blowing rain.

When Madigan returned, he was wearing a raincoat, hood, and high-top galoshes. The amber light from the porch lamps softened the wrinkles in his face; if they had been making a movie and looking for a gentle grandfatherly type, Madigan would have been perfect casting. He assumed Christine and Joey were Charlie's wife and son, and he expressed concern about them being out in such foul weather.

"Oh, we're originally from Seattle," Christine lied. "We're used to duck weather like this."

Joey had retreated even further into his private world. He didn't speak to Madigan, didn't smile when the old man teased him. However, unless you knew what an outgoing boy he usually was, his silence and solemnity seemed like nothing worse than shyness.

Madigan was eager to sell the Jeep wagon, though he didn't realize how obvious his eagerness was. He thought he was being cool, but he kept pointing out the low mileage (32,000), the like-new tires, and other attractive features.

After they had talked awhile, Charlie understood the man's situation. Madigan had retired a year ago and had quickly discovered that Social Security and a modest pension were insufficient to support the lifestyle that he and his wife had maintained previously. They had two cars, a boat, the Jeep wagon, and two snowmobiles. Now they had to choose between boating and winter sports, so they were getting rid of the Jeep and snowmobiles. Madigan was bitter. He complained at length about all the taxes the government had sucked out of his pockets when he'd been a younger man. "If they'd taken just ten percent less," he said, "I'd have had a pension that would've let me live like a king the rest of my life. But they took it and peed it away. Excuse me, Mrs. Smith, but that's exactly what they did: peed it away."

The only light was from two lamps on the garage, but Charlie could see no visible body damage on the wagon, no sign of rust or neglect. The engine caught at once, didn't sputter, didn't knock.

"We can take it for a spin if you'd like," Madigan said.

"That won't be necessary," Charlie said. "Let's talk a deal."

Madigan's expression brightened. "Come on in the house."

"Still don't want to track up your carpet."

"We'll go in by the kitchen door."

They tied Chewbacca to one of the posts on the back porch, wiped their feet, shook the rain off their coats, and went inside.

The pale-yellow kitchen was cheery and warm.

Mrs. Madigan was cleaning and chopping vegetables on a cutting board beside the sink. She was gray-haired, round-faced, as much a Norman Rockwell type as her husband. She insisted on pouring coffee for Charlie and Christine, and she mixed up a cup of hot chocolate for Joey, who wouldn't speak or smile for her, either.

Madigan asked twenty percent too much for the Jeep, but Charlie agreed to the price without hesitation, and the old man had trouble concealing his surprise.

"Well . . . fine! If you come back tomorrow with a cashier's check—"

"I'd like to pay cash and take the Jeep tonight," Charlie said.

"Cash?" Madigan said, startled. "Well . . . um . . . I guess that'd be okay. But the paperwork—"

"Do you still owe the bank anything, or do you have the pink slip?"

"Oh, it's free and clear. I have the pink slip right here."

"Then we can take care of the paperwork tonight."

"You'll have to have an emissions test run before you'll be able to apply for registration in your name."

"I know. I can handle that first thing in the morning."

"But if there's some problem—"

"You're an honest man, Mr. Madigan. I'm sure you've sold me a first-rate machine."

"Oh, it is! I've taken good care of her."

"That's good enough for me."

"You'll need to talk to your insurance agent—"

"I will. Meanwhile, I'm covered for twenty-four hours."

The haste with which Charlie wanted to proceed, combined with the offer of cash on the spot, not only surprised Madigan but made him uneasy and somewhat suspicious. However, he was being paid eight or nine hundred more than he had expected to get, and that was enough to insure his cooperation.

Fifteen minutes later, they left in the Jeep wagon, and there was no way that Grace Spivey or the police could trace the sale to them if they didn't bother to file an application for registration.

Though rain was still falling, though an occasional soft pulse of lightning backlit the clouds, the night seemed less threatening than it had before they'd made their deal with Madigan.

"Why did it have to be a Jeep?" Christine asked as they found the freeway and drove north on 101.

"Where we're going," Charlie said, "we'll need four-wheel-drive."

"Where's that?"

"Eventually . . . the mountains."

"Why?"

"I know a place where we can hide until Henry or the police find a way to stop Grace Spivey. I'm part owner of a cabin in the Sierras, up near Tahoe."

"That's so far away . . ."

"But it's the perfect place. Remote. It's a sort of time-sharing arrangement with three other owners. Each of us has several weeks there every year, and when none of us is using it, we rent it out. It was supposed to be a ski chalet, but it's hardly occupied during the worst of the winter because the road into it was never paved. It was planned to be the first of twenty chalets, and the county had promised to pave the road, but everything fell through after the first one was built. So now, there's still just a one-lane dirt track that's never plowed, and getting in there in the winter isn't easy. Bad investment, as it turned out, but now maybe I'll get my money's worth."

"We keep running, running . . . I'm not used to running away from problems."

"But there's nothing we can do here. It's all up to Henry and my other men. We've just got to stay out of sight, stay alive. And no one will ever look for us up in the mountains."

From the back seat, in a low voice filled with weariness and resignation, Joey said, "The witch will. She'll come after us. She'll find us. We can't hide from the witch."

CHAPTER 47

As usual, Grace could not sleep.

After leaving Santa Barbara and driving north for a while—ten of them in two white vans and one blue Oldsmobile—they had finally stopped at a motel in Soledad. They had lost the boy. Grace was certain he was still heading into the northern part of the state—she felt it in her bones—but she didn't know *where* in the north. She had to stop and wait for news—or holy guidance.

Before they checked into the motel, she had tried to put herself into a trance, and Kyle had done everything he could to help her, but she hadn't been able to break through the barrier between this world and the next. Something lay in her way, a wall she had never encountered before, a malignant and inhibiting force. She had been sure that Satan was there, in the back of the van, preventing her from entering the spirit realm. All her prayers had not been sufficient to dispel the devil and bring her close to God, as she had desired.

Defeated, they had stopped for the night at the motel and had taken dinner together in the coffee shop, most of them too weary and too scared to eat much or to talk. Then they had all gone to their separate rooms, like monks to cells, to pray and think and rest.

But sleep eluded Grace.

Her bed was firm and comfortable, but she was distracted by voices from the spirit realm. Even though she was not in a trance, they spoke to her from beyond, called out warnings that she could not quite understand, asked questions she could not quite discern. This was the first time since she had received the Gift that she was unable to commune with the spirit world, and she was both frustrated and afraid. She was afraid because she knew what this meant: The devil's power on earth was increasing rapidly; the Beast's confidence had grown to such an extent that he could now boldly interfere between Grace and her God.

Twilight was coming faster than expected.

The gates of Hell were swinging open.

Although she could no longer understand the spirit voices, although their cries were muffled and distorted, she detected an urgency in all of them, and she knew the abyss loomed ahead.

Maybe if she rested, got a little sleep, she would be stronger and better equipped to break through the barrier between this world and the next. But there was no rest. Not in these desperate times.

She had lost five pounds in the last few days, and her eyes stung from lack of sleep. She longed for sleep. But the incomprehensible spirit voices continued to assault her, a steady stream of them, a torrent, a flood of other-worldly messages. Their urgency infected her, pushed her to the brink of panic.

Time was running out. The boy was growing stronger.

Too little time to do all that was necessary.

Too little time. Maybe no time at all . . .

She was overwhelmed not only by voices but by visions, as well. As she lay in her bed, staring at the dark ceiling, the shadows abruptly came to life, and the folds of the night were transmuted into leathery black wings, and something hideous descended from the ceiling—*No!*—fell atop her, flapping and hissing, spitting in her face, something slimy and cold—*oh God, no, please!*—with breath that reeked of sulfur. She gagged and flailed and tried to cry out for help, but her voice failed her the way she had failed God. Her arms were pinned. She kicked. Her legs were pinned. She writhed. She bucked. Hard hands pawed at her. Pinched her. Struck her. An oily tongue lapped her face. She saw eyes of crimson fire glaring down at her, a grinning mouth full of viciously sharp teeth, a stoved-in nose, a nightmare visage that was partly human, partly porcine, partly like the face of a bat. She was finally able to speak but only in a whisper. She frantically called out some of the names of God, of saints, and those holy words had an effect on the shadow-demon; it shrank from her, and its eyes grew less bright, and the stench of its breath faded, and, mercifully, it rose from her, swooped up toward the ceiling, whirled away into a tenebrous corner of the room.

She sat up. Threw back the tangled covers. Scrambled to the edge of the bed. Reached for the nightstand lamp. Her hands were shaking. Her heart was hammering so hard that pain spread across her chest, and it seemed her breastbone would fracture. She finally switched on the bedside lamp. No demon crouched in the room.

She turned on the other lamps, went into the bathroom.

The demon wasn't there, either.

But she knew it had been real, yes, terribly real, knew it wasn't just imagination or lunacy. Oh, yes. She knew. She knew the truth. She knew the awful truth—

—but what she *didn't* know was how she had gotten from the bathroom to the floor at the foot of the queen-size bed, where she next found herself. Apparently she had passed out in the bathroom and had crawled to the bed. But she couldn't remember anything. When she came to, she was naked, on her belly, weeping softly, clawing at the carpet.

Shocked, embarrassed, confused, she found her pajamas and pulled them on —and became aware of the serpent under the bed. Hissing. It was the most wicked sound she had ever heard. It slithered out from beneath the bed, big as a boa constrictor, but with the supremely evil head of a rattlesnake, the multi-faceted eyes of an insect, and venom-dripping fangs as big as hooked fingers.

Like the serpent in the Garden of Eden, this one spoke: "Your God cannot protect you any more. Your God has abandoned you."

She shook her head frantically: *no, no, no, no!*

With a sickening sinuosity, it coiled itself. Its head reared up. Its jaws fell open. It struck, biting her in the neck—

—and then, without knowing how she had come to be there, she found herself sitting, some time later, on a stool in front of the dresser mirror, staring into her own bloodshot, watery eyes. She shivered. Her eyes, even the flat reflection of them, contained something she didn't want to see, so she looked elsewhere in the mirror, at the reflection of her age-wrinkled throat, where she expected to find the mark of the serpent. There was no wound. Impossible. The mirror must be lying. She put one hand to her throat. She could not feel a wound, either. And she had no pain. The serpent hadn't bitten her, after all. Yet she remembered so clearly . . .

She noticed an ashtray in front of her. It was overflowing with cigarette butts. She was holding a smouldering cigarette in her right hand. She must have been sitting here an hour or more, smoking constantly, staring into the mirror—yet she couldn't remember any of it. What was happening to her?

She stubbed out the cigarette she'd been holding and looked into the mirror again, and she was shocked. She seemed to *see* herself for the first time in years. She saw that her hair was wild, frizzy, tangled, unwashed. She saw how sunken her eyes were, ringed with crepe-like flesh that had an unhealthy purplish tint. Her teeth, my God, they looked as if they hadn't been brushed in a couple of weeks; they were yellow, caked with plaque! In addition to banishing sleep, the Gift had driven many other things out of her life; she was aware of that. However, until now, she hadn't been so painfully aware that the Gift—the visions, the trances, the communications with spirits—had caused her to *completely* neglect personal hygiene. Her pajamas were spotted with food and cigarette ashes. She raised her hands and looked at them with amazement. Her fingernails were too long, chipped, dirty. There were traces of dirt in her knuckles.

She had always valued cleanliness, neatness.

What would her Albert say if he could see her now?

For one devastating moment, she wondered if her daughter had been correct in having her hospitalized for psychiatric evaluation. She wondered if she was not a visionary after all, not a genuine religious leader, but simply a disturbed old woman, senile, plagued by bizarre hallucinations and delusions, deranged. Was the Scavello boy really the Antichrist? Or just an innocent child? Was Twilight actually coming? Or was her fear of the devil only a foolish old woman's demented fantasy? She was suddenly, gut-twistingly sure that her "holy mission" was, in fact, merely the crusade of a pitiful schizophrenic.

No. She shook her head violently. *No!*

These despicable doubts were planted by Satan.

This was her Gethsemane. Jesus had endured an agony of doubt in the Garden of Gethsemane, near the brook of Kedron. *Her* Gethsemane was in a more humble location: a nondescript motel in Soledad, California. But it was every bit as important a turning point for her as Jesus's experience in the garden had been for Him.

She was being tested. She must hold on to her faith in both God and herself. She opened her eyes. Looked in the mirror again. She still saw madness in her eyes. *No!*

She picked up the ashtray and threw it at her reflection, smashing the mirror. Glass and cigarette butts rained over the dresser and the floor around it.

Immediately she felt better. The devil had been in the mirror. She had smashed the glass *and* the devil's hold on her. Self-confidence flooded into her once more.

She had a sacred mission.

She must not fail.

CHAPTER 48

CHARLIE STOPPED AT a motel shortly before midnight. They got one room with two king-size beds. He and Christine took turns sleeping. Although he was positive they couldn't have been followed, although he felt safer tonight than he had felt last night, he now believed that a watch must be kept at all times.

Joey slept fitfully, repeatedly waking from nightmares, shivering in a cold sweat. In the morning he looked paler than ever, and he spoke even less than before.

The rain had subsided to a light drizzle.

The sky was low, gray, bleak, and ominous.

After breakfast, when Charlie pointed the station wagon north again, toward Sacramento, Christine rode in the back seat with the boy. She read to him from some of the story books and comics they had bought yesterday. He listened but asked no questions, showed little interest, never smiled. She tried to engage him in a card game, but he didn't want to play.

Charlie was increasingly worried about Joey, increasingly frustrated and angry, too. He had promised to protect them and put a stop to Spivey's harassment. Now all he could do for them was help them run, tails between their legs, toward an uncertain future.

Even Chewbacca seemed depressed. The dog lay in the cargo area behind the rear seat, rarely stirring, rising only a few times to look out one of the windows at the soot-colored day, then slumping back down, out of sight.

They arrived in Sacramento before ten o'clock in the morning, located a large sporting goods store, and bought a lot of things they would need for the mountains: insulated sleeping bags in case the heating system in the cabin was not strong enough to completely compensate for winter's deep-freeze temperatures; rugged boots; ski suits—white for Joey, blue for Christine, green for Charlie; gloves; tinted goggles to guard against snow-blindness; knitted toboggan caps; snowshoes; weatherproof matches in watertight cans; an ax; and a score of other items. He also bought a Remington 30-gauge shotgun, and a Winchester Model 100 automatic rifle chambered for a .308 cartridge, which was a light but powerful weapon; he stocked up on plenty of ammunition, too.

He was sure Spivey wouldn't find them in the mountains.

Positive.

But just in case . . .

After a quick and early lunch at McDonalds, Charlie connected the electronic tap detector to a pay phone and called Henry Rankin. The line wasn't bugged, and Henry didn't have much news. The Orange County and Los Angeles papers were still filled with stuff about the Church of the Twilight. The cops were still looking for Grace Spivey. They were still looking for Charlie, too, and they were getting impatient; they were beginning to suspect he hadn't turned himself in because he actually was guilty of the murder about which they wanted to question him. They couldn't understand that he was avoiding them because Spivey might have followers within the police department; they refused even to consider such a possibility. Meanwhile, Henry was busy getting the company back on its feet and was, for the time being, headquartering the agency in his own house. By tomorrow they would again be working full-steam on the Spivey case.

At a service station, they used the rest rooms to change into the winter clothing they had purchased. The mountains were not far away.

In the Jeep wagon once more, Charlie headed east toward the Sierras, while Christine continued to sit in back, reading to Joey, talking to him, trying hard —but without much success—to draw him out of his shell.

The rain stopped.

The wind grew stronger.

Later, there were snow flurries.

CHAPTER 49

/////

MOTHER GRACE RODE in the Oldsmobile. Eight disciples followed in the two white vans. They were on Interstate 5 now, in the heart of California's farm country, passing between immense flat fields, where crops flourished even in the middle of winter.

Kyle Barlowe drove the Olds, now anxious and edgy, now bored and drowsy, sometimes oppressed by the tedium of the long drive and the rain-grayed landscape.

Although the church's sources of information—in various police departments and elsewhere—had no news about Joey Scavello and his mother, they headed north from Soledad because Grace said the boy and his protectors had gone that way. She claimed to have received a vision in the night.

Barlowe was pretty sure she'd had no vision and that she was just guessing. He knew her too well to be fooled. He understood her moods. If she'd really had a vision, she would be . . . euphoric. Instead, she was sullen, silent, grim. He suspected she was at a loss but didn't want to tell them that she was no longer in contact with the spirit world.

He was worried. If Grace had lost the ability to talk with God, if she could not journey to the other side to commune with angels and with the spirits of the dead, did that mean she was no longer God's chosen messenger? Did it mean that her mission no longer had His blessing? Or did it mean that the devil's power on earth had grown so dramatically that the Beast could interfere between Grace and God? If the latter were true, Twilight was very near, and the Antichrist would soon reveal himself, and a thousand-year reign of evil would begin.

He glanced at Grace. She was staring ahead, through the rain, at the arrow-straight highway, lost in thought. She looked older than she had last week. She had aged ten years in a few days. She seemed positively ancient. Her skin looked lifeless, brittle, gray.

Her face wasn't the only thing that was gray. All her clothes were gray, too. For reasons Barlowe didn't fully understand, she always dressed in a single color; he thought it had a religious significance, something to do with her visions, but he wasn't sure. He was accustomed to her monochromatic costumes, but this was the first time he had ever seen her in gray. Yellow, blue, fire-red, apple-red, blood-red, green, white, purple, violet, orange, pink, rose— yes, she had worn all of those, but always bright colors, never anything as somber as this.

She hadn't *expected* to dress in gray; this morning, after leaving the motel, they'd had to go shopping to buy her gray shoes, gray slacks, a gray blouse and sweater because she had owned no gray clothes. She had been in great distress, almost hysterical, until she'd changed into a completely gray outfit. "It's a gray day in the spirit world," she had said. "The energy is all gray. I'm not synchronized. I'm not in tune, not in touch. I've got to get in touch!" She had wanted jewelry, too, because she liked jewelry a lot, but it wasn't easy to find gray rings and bracelets and brooches. Most jewelry was bright. She'd finally had to settle for just a string of gray beads. Now it was odd to see her without a single ring on her pale, leathery hands.

A gray day in the spirit world.

What did that mean? Was that good or bad?

Judging from Grace's demeanor, it was bad. Very bad. Time was running out. That's what Grace had said this morning, but she hadn't been willing to elaborate. Time was running out, and they were lost, driving north on just a hunch.

He was scared. He still worried that it would be a terrible thing for him to kill anyone, that it would be backsliding into his old ways, even if he was doing it for God. He was proud of himself for resisting the violent impulses which he had once embraced, proud of the way he had begun to fit into society, just a little bit, and he was afraid that one murder would lead to another. Was it right to kill—even for God? He knew that was wrong-thought, but he couldn't shake it. And sometimes, when he looked at Grace, he had the unsettling notion that perhaps he had been wrong about her all along, that perhaps she wasn't God's agent—and that was *more* wrong-thought. The thing was . . . Grace had taught him that there were such things as moral values, and now he could not avoid applying them to everything he did.

Anyway, if Grace *was* right about the boy—and surely she was—then time was running out, but there was nothing to be done but drive, wait for her to regain contact with the spirit world, and call the church in Anaheim once in a while to learn if there was any news that might help.

Barlowe put his foot down a little harder on the accelerator. They were already doing over seventy, which was maybe about as fast as they ought to push it in the rain, even on this long straight highway. But they were Chosen, weren't they? God *was* watching over them, wasn't He? Barlowe accelerated until the needle reached 80 on the speedometer. The two vans accelerated behind him, staying close.

CHAPTER 50

THE JEEP WAGON was, as Madigan had promised, in fine shape. It gave them no trouble at all, and they reached Lake Tahoe on Thursday afternoon.

Christine was weary, but Joey had perked up a bit. He was showing some interest in the passing scenery, and that was a welcome change. He didn't seem any happier, just more alert, and she realized that, until today, he had never seen snow before, except in magazine pictures, on TV, and in the movies. There was plenty of snow in Tahoe, all right. The trees were crusted and burdened with it; the ground was mantled with it. Fresh flurries sifted down from the steely sky, and according to the news on the radio, the flurries would build into a major storm during the night.

The lake, which straddled the state line, was partly in California and partly in Nevada. On the California side of the town of South Lake Tahoe, there were a great many motels—some of them surprisingly shabby for such a lovely and relatively expensive resort area—lots of touristy shops and liquor stores and restaurants. On the Nevada side, there were several large hotels, casinos, gambling in just about every form, but not as much glitz as in Las Vegas. Along the northern shore, there was less development, and the man-made structures were better integrated with the land than they were along the southern shore. On *both* sides of the border, and both in the north and south, there was some of the most beautiful scenery on the face of the earth, what many Europeans have called "America's Switzerland": snow-capped peaks that were dazzling even on a cloudy day; vast, primeval forests of pine, fir, spruce, and other evergreens; a lake that, in its ice-free summer phase, was the cleanest, clearest, and most colorful in the world, iridescent blues and glowing greens, a lake so pure you could see the bottom as far as sixty and eighty feet down.

They stopped at a market on the north shore, a large but rustic building shadowed by tamarack and spruce. They still had most of the groceries they'd bought in Santa Barbara yesterday, the stuff they'd never had a chance to put in the refrigerator and cupboards at the Wile-Away Lodge. They'd disposed of the perishables, of course, and that was what they stocked up on now: milk, eggs, cheese, ice cream, and frozen foods of all kinds.

At Charlie's request, the cashier packed the frozen food in a sturdy cardboard box with a lid, separate from the goods that were not frozen. In the parking lot, Charlie carefully poked a few holes in the box. He had purchased nylon clothesline in the market, and with Christine's assistance, he threaded the rope through the holes and looped it around the box and secured it to the luggage rack on top of the Jeep. The temperature was below freezing; nothing carried on the roof would thaw on the way to the cabin.

As they worked (with Chewbacca watching interestedly from inside the Jeep), Christine noticed that a lot of the cars in the market lot were fitted with ski racks. She had always wanted to learn to ski. She often promised herself that she would take lessons with Joey one day, the two of them beginning and learning together, just as soon as he seemed old enough. It would have been fun. Now it was probably just one more thing they would never get to do together . . .

That was a damned grim thought. Uncharacteristically grim.

She knew she had to keep her spirits up, if only for Joey's sake. He would sense her pessimism and would crawl away even deeper into the psychological hole he seemed to be digging for himself.

But she couldn't shake off the gloom that weighed her down. Her spirits had sunk, and there seemed to be no way to get them afloat again.

She told herself to enjoy the crisp, clean mountain air. But it just seemed painfully, bitingly cold. If a wind sprang up, the weather would be insufferable.

She told herself that the snow was beautiful and that she should enjoy it. It looked wet, cold, and forbidding.

She looked at Joey. He was standing beside her, watching as Charlie tied the final knot in the clothesline. He was more like a little old man than a child. He didn't make a snowball. He didn't stick out his tongue and catch snowflakes. He didn't run and slide on the icy portions of the parking lot. He didn't do any of the things a small boy could be expected to do when setting foot on a snowy landscape for the first time in his life.

He's just tired, and so am I, Christine told herself. It's been a long day. Neither of us has had a restful night since last Saturday. Once we've had a good supper, once we've each gotten eight solid hours in the sack without nightmares and without waking up a dozen times to the imagined sound of footsteps . . . *then* we'll feel better. Sure we will. Sure.

But she couldn't convince herself either that she would feel better tomorrow or that their circumstances would improve. In spite of all the distance they'd driven and the remoteness of the haven toward which they were making their way, she did not feel safe. It wasn't just that there were a couple of thousand religious fanatics who, more than anything else, wanted them dead. That was bad enough. But there was also something curiously suffocating about the huge trees rising on all sides and pressing close from every direction, something claustrophobic about the way the mountains walled them in, an indefinable menace in the stark shadows and the gray winter light of this high fastness. She would never feel safe here.

But it wasn't just the mountains. She wouldn't have felt safer anywhere else.

They left the main road that circled the lake, turned onto a two-lane blacktop that rose up a series of steep slopes, past expensive homes and getaway chalets that were tucked back in among the densely packed and massive trees. If there hadn't been light in those houses, glowing warmly in the purple-black shadows beneath the trees, you wouldn't have known most of them were there. Even on the day-side of eventide, lights were needed here.

Snow was piled high on both sides of the road, and in some places new drifts reduced traffic to a single lane. Not that there were many other vehicles around: They passed only two—another Jeep Wagon with a plow on the front, and a Toyota Land Rover.

Near the end of the paved road, Charlie decided it would be a good idea to put the chains on the tires. Although a plow had been through recently, the drifts were inching farther across the pavement here than on the lower slopes, and there were bigger patches of ice. He pulled into a driveway, which ran across the face of the mountain and was level, stopped, and got the chains from the back. He required twenty minutes to complete the job, and he was unhappily aware of how fast the sunlight was fading from behind the snow-spitting clouds.

With chains clanking, they drove on, and soon the paved road ended in a one-lane dirt track. This, too, was plowed for the first half mile, but because it was narrower than the lower road, it tended to drift shut faster. Nevertheless, slowly but steadily, the Jeep clawed its way upward.

Charlie didn't attempt to keep a conversation going. There was no point in making the effort. Ever since they'd left Sacramento earlier in the day, Christine had become steadily less communicative. Now, she was almost as silent and withdrawn as Joey.

He was dismayed by the change in her, but he understood why she was having difficulty staving off depression. The mountains, which usually conveyed an uplifting feeling of openness and freedom, now seemed paradoxically restraining, oppressive. Even when they passed through a broad meadow and the trees fell back from the roadway, the mood of the landscape didn't change.

Christine was probably wondering if coming here had been a serious mistake.

Charlie was wondering, too.

But there had been nowhere else to go. With Grace's people looking for them, with the police searching for them throughout California, unable to trust the authorities or even Charlie's own employees, they hadn't much choice but to go to ground in a place where no one would spot them, which meant a place with few people.

Charlie told himself that they had done the wisest thing, that they had been cautious in the purchase of the Jeep, that they had planned well and had moved with admirable speed and flexibility, that they were in control of their destiny. They would probably be here only a week or so, until Grace Spivey was brought to heel either by his own men or the police.

But in spite of what he told himself, he felt as if they were out of control, fleeing in near-panic. The mountain seemed not a haven but a trap. He felt as if they had walked out on a gangplank.

He tried to stop thinking about it. He knew he wasn't being entirely rational. For the moment, his emotions had the upper hand. Until he could think calmly again, it was best to put Grace Spivey out of his mind as much as possible.

There were considerably fewer houses and cabins along the dirt lane than there had been along the paved road, and after a third of a mile there were none visible at all.

At the end of the first half mile, the dirt road was no longer plowed. It vanished under several feet of snow. Charlie stopped the Jeep, pulled on the emergency brake, and switched off the engine.

"Where's the cabin?" Christine asked.

"Half a mile from here."

"What now?"

"We walk."

"In snowshoes?"

"Yep. That's why we bought 'em."

"I've never used them before."

"You can learn."

"Joey—"

"We'll take turns carrying him. Then he can stay at the cabin while you and I come back for—"

"Stay there by himself?"

"He'll have the dog, and he'll be perfectly safe. Spivey can't have known we were coming here; she's not around anywhere."

Joey didn't object. He didn't even appear to hear what they'd said. He was staring out the window, but he couldn't be looking at anything because the glass was fogged by his breath.

Charlie got out of the station wagon and winced as the winter air bit at his face. It had grown considerably colder since they had left the market down by the lake. The snowflakes were enormous and falling faster than before. They spun down from the lowering sky on a gently shifting breeze that became a little less gentle, more insistent, even as he paused for a moment to look around at the forest. The trees shouldered against one another and seemed to be crouching, ready to pounce, at the edges of the meadow.

For some reason he thought of an old fairytale: *Little Red Riding Hood.* He could still remember the spooky illustration in the storybook he'd had when he'd been a child, a picture of Red making her way through a gloomy, wolf-haunted forest.

That made him think of Hansel and Gretel, lost in the woods.

And *that* made him think of witches.

Witches who baked children in ovens and ate them.

Jesus, he had never realized how gruesome some fairytales were!

The snowflakes had grown slightly smaller and were falling faster by the second.

Softly, softly, the wind began to howl.

Christine was surprised by how quickly she learned to walk in the cumbersome snowshoes, and she realized how difficult—and perhaps impossible—the journey would have been without them, especially with the heavy backpacks they carried. In some places, the wind had almost scoured the meadow bare, but in other places, wherever the land presented even the slightest windbreak, drifts had piled up eight, ten, or twelve feet deep, even deeper. And of course snow had filled in every gully and hole and basin in the land. If you were to attempt to cross an unseen depression without snowshoes, you might find yourself sinking down into a deep well of snow out of which it would be difficult or impossible to climb.

The gray afternoon light, which had a disconcerting artificial quality, played tricks with snow-glare and shadow, giving a false sense of distance, distorting shapes. Sometimes it even caused a mounting ridge of snow to look like a depression until she reached it and realized she must climb instead of descend as she'd expected.

Joey found it more difficult to adapt to snowshoes than she did, even though he had a small pair suitable for a child. Because the day was fast fading and because they didn't want to finish unloading the Jeep entirely in the dark, they didn't have time for him to learn snowshoeing right now. Charlie picked him up and carried him.

Chewbacca was a big dog but still light enough so he didn't break through the crust on top of the snow. He also had an instinct for avoiding places where the crust was thin or nonexistent, and he could often find his way around the deepest snow, moving from one wind-scoured spot to another. Three times he sank in; once he was able to dig his way up and out by himself, but twice he had to be helped.

From the abandoned Jeep, they went up a slope for three hundred yards, until they reached the end of the meadow. They followed the snow-hidden road into the trees, bearing right along the top of a broad ridge, with a table of forested land on their right and a tree-choked valley on their left. Even though nightfall was still perhaps an hour away, the valley dropped down through shades of gray and blue and purple, finally into blackness, and there were no spots of light down there, so she supposed there were no dwellings.

By now she knew that Charlie was a considerably more formidable man than either his size or general appearance would indicate, but she was nevertheless surprised by his stamina. Her own backpack was beginning to feel like a truckload of cement blocks, but though Charlie's pack was bigger and heavier than hers, he did not seem to be bothered by it. In addition, he carried Joey without complaint and stopped only once in the first quarter-mile to put the boy down and relieve cramping muscles.

After a hundred yards, the road angled away from the rim of the valley, moving across the mountain instead of uphill, but then turned and sloped upward again in another fifty yards. The trees became thicker and bigger and bushier, and in places the sheltered lane was so deep in shadow that night might as well have come already. In time they arrived at the foot of another meadow, broader than the one where they'd parked the Jeep, and about four hundred yards long.

"There's the cabin!" Charlie said, the words bursting out of him with plumes of crystallized breath.

Christine didn't see it.

He stopped, put Joey down again, and pointed. "There. At the far end, just in front of the tree line. There's a windmill beside it."

She saw the windmill first because her eye caught the movement of the spinning blades. It was a tall, skeletal mill, nothing picturesque about it, more like an oil derrick than anything a Dutchman would recognize, very business-like and somewhat ugly.

Both the cabin and the mill blended well with the trees behind them, although she supposed they would be more visible earlier in the day.

"You didn't tell me there was a windmill," she said. "Does that mean electric light?"

"Sure does." His cheeks, nose, and chin were pink from the cold, and he sniffed to clear a runny nose. "And plenty of hot water."

"Electric heat?"

"Nope. There's a limit to what a power mill can provide, even in a place as windy as this."

The jacket snap at Joey's throat had come undone, and his scarf was loose. Christine stooped to make adjustments. His face was more red than pink, and his eyes were tearing from the cold.

"We're almost there, Skipper."

He nodded.

After catching their breath, they started uphill once more, with Chewbacca bounding ahead as if he understood that the cabin was their final destination.

The place was constructed of redwood that had silvered slightly in the harsh weather. Though the cedar-shingled roof was steeply sloped, some snow clung to it anyway. The windows were frosted. Snow had drifted over the front steps and onto the porch.

They took off their snowshoes and gloves.

Charlie retrieved a spare key from a cleverly hidden recess in one of the porch posts. Ice cracked away from the door as he pulled it open, and the frozen hinges squealed briefly.

They went inside, and Christine was surprised by how lovely the cabin was. The downstairs consisted of one enormous room, with a kitchen occupying the far end, a long pine dining table just this side of the kitchen, and then a living area with a polished oak floor, braided rag rugs, comfortable dark green sofas and armchairs, brass lamps, paneled walls, draperies in a Scottish-plaid pattern that was dominated by greens to complement the sofas and chairs, and a massive rock fireplace almost as big as a walk-in closet. Half the downstairs was open all the way to the second-floor ceiling, and was overlooked by a gallery. Up there, three closed doors led to three other rooms: "Two bedrooms and a bath," Charlie said. The effect was rustic yet quite civilized.

A tiled area separated the front door from the oak floor of the living room, and that was where they removed their snow-crusted boots. Then they took an inspection tour of the cabin. There was some dust on the furniture, and the air smelled musty. There was no electricity because the breakers were all thrown in the fuse box, which was out in the battery room below the windmill, but Charlie said he would go out there and remedy the situation in a few minutes. Beside each of the three fireplaces—the big one in the living room and a smaller one in each of the bedrooms—were stacks of split logs and kindling, which Charlie used to start three fires. All the fireplaces were equipped with Heatolators, so the cabin would be reasonably warm even in the bitter heart of winter.

"At least no one's broken in and wrecked things," he said.

"Is that a problem?" Christine asked.

"Not really. During the warmer months, when the road's open all the way, there's nearly always somebody staying here. When the road is snowed shut and there's no one here to look after the place, most would-be looters wouldn't even know there was a cabin this far into the woods. And the ones who *do* know . . . well . . . they probably figure the trek isn't worth what little they'd find to carry away. Still, first time you arrive each spring, you wonder if you're going to discover the place has been wrecked."

The fires were building nicely, and the vents of the Heatolator in the downstairs mantel were spewing welcome draughts of warm air into the big main room. Chewbacca had already settled down on the hearth there, head on his paws.

"Now what?" Christine asked.

Opening one of the backpacks and removing a flashlight from it, Charlie said, "Now you and Joey take everything out of these bags while I go out and see about getting us some electricity."

She and Joey carried the backpacks into the kitchen while Charlie pulled his boots on again. By the time he had gone out to the windmill, they were stashing canned goods in the cabinets, and it almost seemed as if they were an ordinary family on an ordinary skiing holiday, getting settled in for a week of fun. Almost. She tried to instill a holiday mood in Joey by whistling happy songs and making little jokes and pretending that she was actually going to enjoy this adventure, but either the boy saw through her charade or he wasn't even paying attention to her, for he seldom responded and never smiled.

With the monotonous humming-churning of the windmill's propellers above him, Charlie used a shovel to clear the snow from the wooden doors that protected the steps that led down to the room under the windmill. He descended two flights of steps that went rather deeply into the ground; the battery room was below the frost line. When he reached the bottom, he was in a hazy-blue darkness that robbed the whiteness from the snowflakes sifting down around him, so they looked as if they were bits of gray ash. He took the flashlight from his coat pocket and snapped it on. A heavy metal door stood in front of him. The cabin key worked this lock, too, and in a moment he was in the battery room, where everything appeared to be in order: cables; twenty heavy-duty, ten-year storage batteries lined up side by side on two sturdy benches; a concrete pallet holding all the machinery; a rack of tools.

A foul odor assaulted him, and he immediately knew the cause of it, knew he would have to deal with it, but first he went to the fuse box and pushed all the breakers from OFF to ON. That done, the wall switch by the door brought light to the two long fluorescent bulbs in the ceiling. The light revealed three dead, decaying mice, one in the middle of the room, the other two in the corner by the first battery bench.

It was necessary to leave tins of poisoned bait here, especially during the winter when mice were most likely to come seeking shelter, for if the rodents were left to their own devices they would eat the insulation from all the cables and wires, leaving a ruined electrical system by the time spring arrived.

The mouse in the middle of the small chamber had been dead a long time. The process of decomposition had pretty much run its course in the tiny corpse. There were bones, fur, scraps of leathery skin, little else.

The two in the corner were more recent casualties. The small bodies were bloated and putrescent. Their eye sockets were alive with squirming maggots. They had been dead only a few days.

Queasy, Charlie went outside, got the shovel, returned, scooped up all three of the creatures, took them out to the woods behind the mill, and pitched them off into the trees. Even when he had disposed of them, even though a blustery wind was huffing up the mountainside and scrubbing the world clean as it passed, Charlie couldn't get the stink of death out of his nostrils. Oddly, the smell stayed with him all the way back to the battery room, where, of course, it still hung on the damp musty air.

He didn't have time for a really thorough inspection of the equipment, but he wanted to give it a quick once-over to be sure the mice had died before they had done any serious damage. The wires and cables were lightly nibbled in a few places, but there didn't seem to be any reason to worry that they'd lose their lights to rodent sabotage.

He had almost satisfied himself as to the system's integrity when he heard a strange, threatening noise behind him.

CHAPTER 51

THE DAY WAS melting into darkness. Color was seeping out of the landscape through which they drove, leaving the trees and hills and everything else as gray as the surface of the highway.

Kyle Barlowe switched on the headlights and hunched over the steering wheel of the Oldsmobile, grinning.

Now. Now they had something real to go on. Now they had a solid lead. Information. A logical plan. They weren't just going on a hunch and a prayer any more. They were no longer driving blind, heading north merely because it seemed like a good idea. They knew where the boy was, where he *must* be. *Now* they had a destination, and now Barlowe was beginning to believe in Mother Grace's leadership again.

She was in the seat beside him, slumped against the door, briefly lost in one of those short but mile-deep sleeps that came to her with decreasing frequency. Good. She needed her rest. The confrontation was coming. The showdown. When they were face to face with the devil, she would need all the energy she could muster.

And if Grace *wasn't* God's messenger, why had this vital information been conveyed to them? This proved she was right, meant well, told the truth, and should be obeyed.

For the moment his doubts had receded.

Barlowe looked in the rearview mirror. The two vans were still behind him. Crusaders. Crusaders on wheels instead of horseback.

CHAPTER 52

WHEN CHARLIE HEARD the strange noises behind him, he dropped into a defensive crouch as he turned. He expected to see Grace Spivey standing in the doorway to the battery room, but the disturbance had no human source. It was a rat.

The filthy thing was between him and the doorway, but he was sure it hadn't come in from the snow because part of what he had heard was the thump it made as it scurried out from under some machinery. It was hissing, squeaking, glaring at him with bloody eyes, as if threatening to prevent his escape.

It was a damned big rat, but in spite of its size, which indicated that it had once been well fed, it didn't look healthy now. Its pelt wasn't smooth, but oily and matted and dull. There was something dark and crusted at its ears, probably blood, and there was bloody foam dripping from its mouth. It had been the poison. Now, pain-wracked and delirious, it might be a bold and vicious opponent.

And there was another, even less pleasant possibility to consider. Maybe it *hadn't* been the poison. Maybe the foam at its mouth was an indication of rabies. Could rodents carry rabies just as easily as dogs and cats? Every year in the California mountains, the state's vector control officers turned up a few rabid animals. Sometimes, portions of state parks were even put off limits until it could be ascertained whether there was a rabies epidemic.

This rat was most likely affected by the poison, not rabies. But if he was wrong, and if the rat bit him . . .

He wished he had brought the shovel back into the battery room after disposing of the three dead mice. He had no weapon except his revolver, and that was too powerful for this small job, like going hunting for pheasant with a cannon.

He straightened up from his crouch, and his movement agitated the rat. It came at him.

He jumped back against the wall.

It was coming fast, screeching. If it ran up his leg—

He kicked, catching it squarely with the reinforced toe of his boot. The kick threw it across the room, and it struck the wall, shrieking, and dropped to the floor on its back.

Charlie reached the door and was through it before the rat got on its feet. He climbed the stairs, picked up the shovel that was leaning against the base of the mill, and went back down.

The rat was just inside the open door to the battery room. It was making a continuous racket, a wailing-hissing-whining noise that Charlie found bone-chilling. It rushed him again.

He swung the shovel like a mallet, struck the rat, again, a third time, until it stopped making noise, then looked at it, saw it quivering, struck it again, harder, and then it was still and silent, obviously dead, and he slowly lowered the shovel, breathing hard.

How could a rat that size have gotten into the closed battery room?

Mice, yes, that was understandable, because mice needed only the smallest chink or crevice to get inside. But this rat was bigger than a dozen mice; it would require a hole at least three or four inches in diameter, and because the ceiling of the small room was of reinforced concrete, the walls of cinder block and mortar, there was no way the beast could have chewed open an entrance. And the door to the room was metal, inviolable and unviolated.

Could it have been locked in this past autumn, when the last vacationers closed up the place, or when the real estate management firm had come up to "winterize" the cabin? No. It would have eaten the poison bait and would have been dead months ago. It had been poisoned recently; therefore, it had only recently gotten into the battery room.

He circled the chamber, searching for the rat's passage, but all he found were a couple of small chinks in the mortar where a mouse—but never anything larger—might have squirmed through after first gaining access to the air space between the double-thick block walls.

It was a mystery, and as he stood staring at the dead rat, he had the creepy feeling that the brief and violent encounter between him and this disgusting creature was more than it appeared to be, that it *meant* something, that the rat was a symbol of something. Of course, he had grown up with the terror of rats, which had infested the shack in which he had spent his childhood, so they would always have a powerful effect on him. And he couldn't help thinking of old horror comics and horror movies in which there'd been scenes in ancient graveyards with rats skulking about. Death. That's what rats usually symbolized. Death, decay, the revenge of the tomb. So maybe this was an omen. Maybe it was a warning that death—in the form of Grace Spivey—was going to come after them up here on the mountain, a warning to be prepared.

He shook himself. No. He was letting his imagination run away with him. Like in his office, on Monday, when he'd looked at Joey and thought he had seen only a bare skull where the boy's face should have been. That had been imagination—and this, too. He didn't believe in such things as omens. Death wouldn't find them here. Grace Spivey wouldn't discover where they had gone. Couldn't. Not in a thousand years.

Joey was not going to die.

The boy was safe.

They were all safe.

Christine didn't want to leave Joey alone in the cabin while she and Charlie returned to the Jeep for more of their supplies. She knew Grace Spivey wasn't near. She knew the cabin was safe, that nothing would happen in the short time she was gone. Nevertheless, she was terrified that they would find her little boy dead when they got back.

But Charlie couldn't carry everything by himself; it was wrong of her to expect him to do it. And Joey couldn't come along because he would slow them down too much now that the last of the daylight was rapidly fading and the storm was getting dangerously fierce. She had to go, and Joey had to stay. No choice.

She told herself it might even be good for him to be left alone with Chewbacca for a while, for it would be a demonstration of her and Charlie's confidence in the safety of their chosen hiding place. He might regain some self-assurance and hope from the experience.

Yet, after she hugged him, kissed him, reassured him, and left him on the green sofa in front of the fireplace, she almost could not find the strength to turn and leave. When she closed the cabin door and watched as Charlie locked it, she was nearly overcome by fear so strong it made her sick to her stomach. Moving off the porch, descending the snow-covered steps, she felt an aching weakness in her legs that was almost incapacitating. Each step away from the cabin was like a step taken on a planet with five times the gravity of this world.

The weather had deteriorated dramatically since they had come up the mountain from where they had parked the Jeep, and the extreme hostility of the elements gradually began to occupy her thoughts and push her fear toward the back of her mind. The wind was a steady twenty to thirty miles an hour, gusting to at least fifty at times, racing across the mountain with a banshee shriek, shaking the enormous trees. The snowflakes were no longer large and fluffy, but small, hard-driven by the wind, mounting up on the ground at a startling rate. They had not worn ski masks earlier, on the way up to the cabin, but Charlie had insisted they wear them on the way down. And although she initially objected because the mask felt smothering, she was glad she had it, for the temperature had fallen drastically and now must be around zero or lower, even without taking into account the wind-chill factor. With the protection of the mask, icy needles of wind still managed to prick and numb her face; without it, she would surely have suffered frostbite.

When they reached the station wagon, daylight was fading as if the world was in a pot onto which a giant lid was being lowered. Snow was already drifted around the Jeep's tires, and the lock was half frozen and stubborn when Charlie tried the key in it.

They stuffed their backpacks full of cans and boxes of food, canned matches, ammunition for the guns, and other things. Charlie strung the three tightly rolled sleeping bags on a length of clothesline and tied one end of the line around his waist so he could drag the bags behind him; they were lightweight, made of a cold-resistant vinyl that would slide well on the snow, and he said he was sure they wouldn't give him much trouble. She carried the rifle, which was equipped with a shoulder strap, and Charlie carried the shotgun. Neither of them could handle a single additional item without buckling under the load, yet there was still more in the station wagon.

"We'll come back for it," Charlie said, shouting to be heard above the roaring wind.

"It's almost dark," she protested, having realized how easily you could become lost at night, in a blinding snowstorm.

"Tomorrow," he said. "We'll come back tomorrow."

She nodded, and he locked the Jeep, although the foul weather was surely a sufficient deterrent to thieves. No self-respecting criminal, in the habit of living an easy life off the labors of others, would be out on a night like this.

They headed back toward the cabin, moving with considerably less speed than they had on the way down, slowed by the weight of what they carried, by the wind that hammered at them, and by the fact that they were now climbing instead of descending. Walking in snowshoes had been surprisingly easy—until now. As they made their way up the first meadow, the muscles in Christine's thighs began to pull, then those in her calves, and she knew that she would be stiff and sore in the morning.

The wind whipped up the snow that was already on the ground, dressed itself in crystalline cloaks and robes that flapped and swirled, formed whirling funnels that danced through the twilight. In the swiftly dying light, the snow devils seemed like spirits, cold ghosts roaming the lonely reaches of the top of the world.

The hills felt steeper than when she and Charlie had first made this trip with Joey and the dog. Her snowshoes were certainly twice as large as they had been then . . . and ten times heavier.

Darkness fell when they were in the woods, before they even reached the upper meadow. They were in no danger of getting lost because the snow-covered ground had a vague natural luminosity, and the clear swath of the road provided an unmistakable route through the otherwise densely packed trees.

However, by the time they reached the upper meadow, the storm's fury eliminated the advantage of the snow's slight phosphorescence. New snow was falling so heavily, and the wind was kicking up such thick clouds of old snow that, had there not been lights on at the cabin, they would without doubt have become disoriented and would have been in serious risk of wandering aim-lessly, back and forth, around in circles, until they collapsed and died, less than four hundred yards from safety. The dim, diffuse, amber glow at the cabin windows was a welcome beacon. On those occasions when the gale-driven snow temporarily blocked that beacon, Christine had to resist panic, stop and wait until she glimpsed her target again, for when she kept on without being able to see the lights, she always headed off in the wrong direction within a few steps. Although she stayed close to Charlie, she frequently could not see him, either; visibility sometimes declined to no more than two or three feet.

The aching in her leg muscles grew worse, and the throbbing in her shoulders and back became unbearable, and the night's chill somehow found its way through all her layers of clothes, but though she cursed the storm she also welcomed it. For the first time in days, she was beginning to feel safe. This wasn't just a storm; it was a damned *blizzard!* They were shut off from the world now. Isolated. By morning they would be snowbound. The storm was the best security they could have. At least for the next day or so, Grace Spivey would not be able to reach them even if, by some miracle, she learned their whereabouts.

When they finally reached the cabin, they found Joey in a better mood than when they'd left. There was color in his face again. He was energetic and talkative for the first time in a couple of days. He even smiled. The change in him was startling and, for a moment, mysterious, but then it became clear that he took the same comfort from the storm as Christine did. He said, "We'll be okay now, huh, Mom? A witch can't fly a broom in a blizzard, can she, huh?"

"Nope," Christine assured him as she took off the backpack she'd been carrying. "All the witches are grounded tonight."

"FWA rules," Charlie said.

Joey looked at him quizzically. "What's . . . FWA?"

"Federal Witch Administration," Charlie said, pulling off his boots. "That's the government agency that licenses witches."

"You gotta have a license to be a witch?" the boy asked.

Charlie feigned surprise. "Oh, sure, what'd you think—just anybody can be a witch? First, when a girl wants to be a witch, she's got to prove she has a mean streak in her. For instance, your mom would never qualify. Then a would-be witch has got to be ugly because witches are always ugly, and if a pretty lady like your mom wants to be a witch she's got to go have plastic surgery to *make* herself ugly."

"Wow," Joey said softly, wide-eyed. "Really?"

"But that's not the worst of it," Charlie said. "The hardest thing if you want to be a witch is finding those tall, pointy black hats."

"It is?"

"Well, just think about it once. You've gone shopping with your mom when she was buying clothes. You ever see any of those tall, pointy black hats in any stores you were ever in?"

The boy frowned, thinking about it.

"No, you haven't," Charlie said as he carried one of the heavy backpacks into the kitchen. "Nobody sells those hats because nobody wants witches coming in their stores all the time. Witches smell like the wings of bats and tails of newts and salamander tongue and all those other weird things they're always cooking in their cauldrons. Nothing will chase off a storekeeper's customers faster than a witch who reeks of boiled pig's snout."

"Yuck," Joey said.

"Exactly," Charlie said.

Christine was so happy and relieved to see Joey acting like a six-year-old again that she had trouble holding back tears. She wanted to put her arms around Charlie, squeeze him tight, and thank him for his strength, for his way with children, for just being the man he was.

Outside, the wind howled and huffed and wailed and whistled.

Night hugged the cabin. Snow dressed it.

In the living room fireplace, the big logs sputtered and crackled.

They worked together to make dinner. Afterwards, they sat on the floor in the living room, where they played Old Maid and Tic-Tac-Toe, and Charlie told knock-knock jokes that Joey found highly amusing.

Christine felt snug. Secure.

CHAPTER 53

IN SOUTH LAKE TAHOE, the snowmobile shop was about to close when Grace Spivey, Barlowe, and the eight others arrived. They had come from just down the street, where they had all purchased ski suits and other insulated winter clothing. They had changed into their new gear and now looked as if they belonged in Tahoe. To the surprise and delight of the owner of Mountain Country Sportmobile—a portly man whose name was Orley Treat and who said his friends called him "Skip"—they purchased four Skidoos and two custom-designed flatbed trailers to haul them.

Kyle Barlowe and a churchman named George Westvec did most of the talking because Westvec knew a lot about snowmobiles, and Barlowe had a knack for getting the best price possible on anything he bought. His great size, forbidding appearance, and air of barely controlled violence gave him an advantage in any bargaining session, of course, but his negotiating skills were not limited to intimidation. He had a first-rate businessman's knack of sensing an adversary's strengths, weaknesses, limits, and intentions. This was something he had learned about himself only after Grace had converted him from a life of self-hatred and sociopathic behavior, and it was a discovery that was as gratifying as it was surprising. He was in Mother Grace's everlasting debt not only because she had saved his soul but because she had provided him the opportunity to discover and explore the talents which, without her, he would never have known were there, within himself.

Orley Treat, who was too beefy to have such a boyish nickname as "Skip," kept trying to figure out who they were. He kept asking questions of Grace and Barlowe and the others, such as whether they belonged to a club of some kind or whether they were all related.

Keeping in mind that the police were still interested in talking to Grace about certain recent events in Orange County, worried that one of the disciples would inadvertently say too much to Treat, Barlowe sent everyone but George Westvec to scout the nearby motels along the main road and find one with sufficient vacancies to accommodate them.

When they paid for the snowmobiles with stacks of cash, Treat gaped at their money in disbelief. Barlowe saw greed in the man's eyes, and figured Treat had already thought of a way to doctor his books and hide this cash from the IRS. Even though his curiosity had an almost physically painful grip on him, Treat stopped prying into their business because he was afraid of queering the deal.

The white Ford vans weren't equipped with trailer hitches, but Treat said he could arrange to have the welding done overnight. "They'll be ready first thing in the morning . . . say . . . ten o'clock."

"Earlier," Grace said. "Much earlier than that. We want to haul these up to the north shore come first light."

Treat smiled and pointed to the showroom windows, beyond which wind-driven snow was falling heavily in the sodium-glow of the parking lot lights. "Weatherman's calling for maybe eighteen inches. Stormfront won't pass until four or five o'clock tomorrow morning, so the road crews won't have the highway open around to the north shore until ten, even eleven o'clock. No point you folks starting out earlier."

Grace said, "If you can't have the hitches on our trucks and the Skidoos ready to go by four-thirty in the morning, the deal's off."

Barlowe knew she was bluffing because this was the only place they could get the machines they needed. But judging from the tortured expression on Treat's face, he took her threat seriously.

Barlowe said, "Listen, Skip, it's only a couple of hours worth of welding. We're willing to pay extra to have it done tonight."

"But I've got to prep the Skidoos and—"

"Then prep them."

"But I was just closing for the day when you—"

"Stay open a couple more hours," Barlowe said. "I know it's inconvenient. I appreciate that. I really do. But, Skip, how often do you sell four snowmobiles and two trailers in one clip?"

Treat sighed. "Okay, it'll be ready for pickup at four-thirty in the morning. But you'll never get up to the north shore at that hour."

Grace, George Westvec, and Barlowe went outside, where the others were waiting.

Edna Vanoff stepped forward and said, "We've found a motel with enough spare rooms to take us, Mother Grace. It's just a quarter of a mile up the road here. We can walk it easy."

Grace looked up into the early-night sky, squinting as the snow struck her face and frosted her eyebrows. Long tangled strands of wet frizzy gray hair escaped the edges of her knitted hat, which she had pulled down over her ears. "Satan brought this storm. He's trying to delay us. Trying to keep us from reaching the boy until it's too late. But God will get us through."

CHAPTER 54

BY NINE-THIRTY JOEY was asleep. They put him to bed between clean sheets, under a heavy blue and green quilt. Christine wanted to stay in the bedroom with him, even though she wasn't ready for bed, but Charlie wanted to talk to her and plan for certain contingencies.

He said, "You'll be all right by yourself, won't you, Joey?"

"I guess so," the boy said. He looked tiny, elfin, under the huge quilt and with his head propped on an enormous feather pillow.

"I don't want to leave him alone," Christine said.

Charlie said, "No one can get him here unless they come up from downstairs, and we'll be downstairs to stop them."

"The window—"

"It's a second-story window. They'd have to put a ladder up against the house to reach it, and I doubt they'd be carrying a ladder."

She frowned at the window, undecided.

Charlie said, "We're socked in here, Christine. Listen to that wind. Even if they knew we were in these mountains, even if they knew about this particular cabin—which they don't—they wouldn't be able to make it up here tonight."

"I'll be okay, Mom," Joey said. "I got Chewbacca. And like Charlie said, it's against FWA rules for witches to fly in a storm."

She sighed, tucked the covers in around her son, and kissed him goodnight. Joey wanted to give Charlie a goodnight kiss, too, which was a new experience for Charlie, and as he felt the boy's lips smack his cheek, a flood of emotions washed through him: a poignant sense of the child's profound vulnerability; a fierce desire to protect him; an awareness of the purity of the kid's affection; a heart-wrenching impression of innocence and sweet simplicity; a touching and yet quite frightening realization of the complete trust the boy had in him. The moment was so warm, so disarming and satisfying, that Charlie couldn't understand how he could have come to be thirty-six without having started a family of his own.

Maybe it had been his destiny to be here, waiting for Christine and Joey, when they needed him. If he'd had his own family, he wouldn't have been able to go to the wall for the Scavellos as he had done; these recent deeds, all beyond the call of duty, would have fallen to one of his men—who might not have been as clever or as committed as Charlie was. When Christine had walked into his office, he had been rocked by her beauty and by a feeling that they were meant to meet, one way or another, that they would have found each other in a different fashion if Grace Spivey hadn't acted to bring them together now. Their relationship seemed . . . inevitable. And now it seemed equally inevitable and right that he should be Joey's protector, that he should one day soon become the child's legal father, that each night he should hear this small boy say, "Goodnight, Daddy," instead of "Goodnight, Charlie."

Destiny.

That was a word and a concept to which he had never given much thought. If anyone had asked him last week if he believed in destiny, he would probably have said he did not. Now, it seemed a simple, natural, and undeniable truth that all men and women had a destiny to fulfill and that his lay with this woman and this child.

They closed the heavy draperies at the bedroom window, and left a lamp on with a towel draped over the shade to soften the light. Joey fell asleep while they were arranging the towel. Chewbacca had curled up on the bed, too. Christine quietly motioned for the dog to get down, but it just stared mournfully at her. Charlie whispered that Chewbacca could stay where he was, and finally he and Christine retreated from the room with exaggerated stealth, leaving the door ajar an inch or two.

As they went downstairs she looked back a couple of times, as if having second thoughts about leaving the boy alone, but Charlie held her arm and steered her firmly to the table. They sat and had coffee and talked, while the wind moaned in the eaves and grainy snow tapped at the windows or hissed along the glass.

Charlie said, "Now, once this storm is past and the roads are open farther down the mountain, I'll want to go into the market to use the pay phone, call Henry Rankin, see what's up. I'll be going in every two days, at least, maybe even every day, and when I'm gone I think you and Joey ought to hole up in the battery room, under the windmill. It—"

"No," she said quickly. "If you go down the mountain, we go with you."

"It'll get tiring if it has to be done every day."

"I can handle it."

"But maybe Joey can't."

"We won't stay here alone," she said adamantly.

"But with the police looking for us, we'll be more noticeable as a group, more easily—"

"We go with you everywhere," she said. "Please. *Please.*"

He nodded. "All right."

He got a map that he had purchased at the sporting goods store in Sacramento, spread it out on the table, and showed her their back door escape route, which they would use if, against all odds, Spivey's people showed up, and if there was enough time to escape. They would go farther up the mountain, to the top of the next ridge, turn east into the valley that lay that way, find the stream at the bottom of the valley, and follow it south toward the lake. It was a journey of four or five miles—which would seem like a hundred in the snow-blanketed wilderness. But there would be good landmarks all the way and little chance of getting lost as long as they had the map and a compass.

Gradually, their conversation drifted away from Grace Spivey, and they talked about themselves, exploring each other's past, likes and dislikes, hopes and dreams, getting a better fix on each other than they'd had an opportunity to do thus far. In time they moved away from the table, switched off all the lights, and sat on the big sofa in front of the stone hearth, with nothing but the softly flickering firelight to hold back the shadows. Their conversation became more intimate, and more was said with fewer words, and finally even their silences conveyed a richness of information.

Charlie couldn't remember the first kiss; he just suddenly realized that they had been touching and kissing with increasing ardor for some time, and then his hand was on her breast, and he could feel her erect nipple through her blouse, hot upon the center of his palm. Her tongue moved within his mouth, and it was very hot, too, and her lips were searing, and when he touched her face with his fingertips the contact was so electrifying that it seemed as if sparks and smoke should issue from it. He had never wanted or needed a woman a fraction as much as he did Christine, and judging from the way her body arched against him and the way her muscles tensed, she wanted and needed him with a passion equal to his own. He knew that, in spite of their circumstances, in spite of the less than ideal trysting place that fate had provided, they would make love tonight; it was inevitable.

Her blouse was unbuttoned now. He lowered his mouth to her breasts.

"Charlie . . . ," she said softly.

He licked her swollen nipples, first one, then the other, lovingly.

"No," she said, but she did not push him away with any conviction, only half heartedly, wanting to be convinced.

"I love you," he said, meaning it. In just a few days, he had fallen in love with her exquisitely composed face, with her body, with her complex mind and wit, with her courage in the face of adversity, with her indomitable spirit, with the way she walked, with the way her hair looked in the wind . . .

"Joey . . . ," she said.

"He's sleeping."

"He might wake up . . ."

Charlie kissed her throat, felt the throbbing of her pulse against his lips. Her heart was beating fast. So was his.

"He might come out to the gallery . . . look down and see us," she said.

He led her away from the firelight, to a long, deep sofa that was under the gallery overhang, out of sight. The shadows were deep and purple.

"We shouldn't," she said, but she kept kissing his neck, his chin, lips, cheeks, and eyes. "Even here . . . if he wakes up . . ."

"He'll call to us first," Charlie said, breathless, aching with need. "He won't just come down into a dark living room."

She kissed his nose, each corner of his mouth, planted a chain of kisses along his jaw line, kissed his ear.

His hands moved over her body, and he thrilled to the perfect form and texture of her. Each sweet concavity and convexity, each enticing angle, the swell of breasts and hips, the taut flatness of belly, the ripeness of buttocks, the sleek roundness of thigh and calf—all of her seemed, to the millimeter, a precise definition of ideal femininity.

"All right," she said weakly. "But silently . . ."

"Not a sound," he promised.

"Not a sound."

"Not one small sound . . ."

The wind moaned at the window above the sofa, but he gave voice to his own intense pleasure only in his mind.

It's the wrong moment, she thought hazily. The wrong place. The wrong time. The wrong everything.

Joey. Might. Wake up.

But although it should matter, it didn't seem to, not much, not enough for her to resist.

He had said he loved her, and she had said she loved him, and she knew they had both meant it, that it was true, real. She didn't know for sure how long she had loved him, but if she thought about it hard enough she would probably be able to fix the precise moment in which respect and admiration and affection had been transformed into something better and more powerful. After all, she had known him only a few days; the moment of love's birth should not be difficult to pin down in that brief span of time. Of course, at the moment, she couldn't think hard about anything, or clearly; she was swept away, though such a condition was out of character for her.

In spite of their protestations of love, it wasn't merely love that induced her to cast caution aside and take the risk of being overheard in the midst of their passion: it was good, healthy lust, too. She had never wanted a man as much as she wanted Charlie. Suddenly she *had* to have him within her, couldn't *breathe* until he took her. His body was lean, the muscles hard and well defined; his sculpted shoulders, his rocklike biceps, smooth broad chest—everything about him excited her to an extent that she had never been excited before. Every nerve in her body was many times more sensitive than before; each kiss and touch, each stroke he took within her, was so explosively pleasurable that it bordered on pain, astonishing pleasure, pleasure that filled her and drove out everything else, every other thought, until she clung mindlessly to him, amazed at the abandon with which she embraced him, unable to understand or resist the primitive rutting fever that possessed her.

The need to be quiet, the oath of silence, had a strangely powerful erotic effect. Even when Charlie climaxed, he did not cry out, but gripped her hips and held her against him and arched his back and opened his mouth but remained mute, and somehow, by containing the cry he also contained his energy and virility, for he didn't lose his erection, not even for a moment, and they paused only to change positions, remaining welded together, but sliding around on the sofa until she was on top, and then she rode him with a pneumatic fluidity and a sinuous rhythm that was unlike anything he had ever known before, and he lost track of time and place, lost *himself* in the soft, silken, silent song of flesh and motion.

She had never in her life been so lacking in self-consciousness while making love. For long moments she forgot where she was, even who she was; she became an animal, a mindlessly copulating organism intent on taking pleasure, oblivious of all else. Only once was the hypnotic rhythm of their lovemaking interrupted, and that was when she was suddenly stricken by the feeling that Joey had come downstairs and was standing in the shadows, watching them, but when she lifted her head from Charlie's chest and looked around, she saw nothing but the shadowy forms of the furniture, backlit by the dying fire, and she knew she was only imagining things. Then love-lust-sex seized her again with a power that was startling and even scary, and she gave herself to the act, was unable to do anything else, was lost, utterly.

Before they were done, Charlie had been shaken by three orgasms, and he had lost count of the number of times she had climaxed, but he didn't need a scorecard to know that neither of them had ever experienced anything like this in the past. When it was over, he was still trembling, and he felt drugged. They lay for a time, neither speaking, until they gradually became aware of the wind howling outside and realized that the dying fire had allowed a chill to creep back into the room. Then, reluctantly, they dressed and went upstairs, where they prepared the second bedroom for her.

"I should sleep with Joey and let you have this bed," she said.

"No. You'll only wake him if you go in there now. The poor kid needs his rest."

"But where will you sleep?" she asked.

"In the gallery."

"On the floor?"

"I'll put a sleeping bag at the head of the stairs."

For a moment anxiety replaced the dreaminess in her eyes. "I thought you said there was no way they could get here tonight even if—"

He put a finger to her lips. "There isn't any way. No way at all. But it wouldn't do for Joey to find me sleeping in your bed in the morning, would it? And most of the sofas downstairs are too soft for sleeping. So if I'm going to use a sleeping bag, I might as well put it at the head of the stairs."

"And keep a gun at your side?"

"Of course. Even though I won't need it. I really won't, you know. So let's get you tucked in."

When she was under the covers, he kissed her goodnight and backed out of the room, leaving her door ajar.

In the gallery, he looked at his watch and was startled to see how late it was. Could they have been making love for almost two hours? No. Surely not. There had been something frighteningly, deliciously animalistic about their coupling; they had indulged with an abandon and an intensity that stole the meaning from time, but he had never thought of himself as a rampaging stud, and he could not believe that he had performed so insatiably for so long. Yet his watch had never run fast before; surely it couldn't have gained an extra hour or more in just the past thirty minutes.

He realized he was standing there, alone, outside her bedroom door, grinning like the Cheshire cat, full of self-satisfaction.

He built up the fire downstairs, carried a sleeping bag to the gallery and unrolled it, switched off the landing light, and slipped into the bedroll. He listened to the storm raging outside, but not for long. Sleep came like a great dark tide.

In the dream, he was tucking Joey into bed, straightening the covers, fluffing the boy's pillow, and Joey wanted to give him a goodnight kiss, and Charlie leaned over, but the boy's lips were hard and cold on his cheek, and when he looked down he saw the boy no longer had a face but just a bare skull with two staring eyes that seemed horribly out of place in that otherwise calcimine countenance. Charlie hadn't felt lips against his cheek but a fleshless mouth, cold teeth. He recoiled in terror. Joey threw back the covers and sat up in bed. He was a normal little boy in every respect except for having only a skull instead of a complete head. The skull's protuberant eyes fixed on Charlie, and the boy's small hands began unbuttoning his Space Raiders pajamas, and when his shallow little chest was revealed it began to split open, and Charlie tried to turn and run but couldn't, couldn't close his eyes either, couldn't look away, could only watch as the child's chest cracked apart and from it streamed a horde of red-eyed rats like the one in the battery room, ten and then a hundred and then a thousand rats, until the boy had emptied himself and had collapsed into a pile of skin, like a deflated balloon, and then the rats surged forward toward Charlie—

—and he woke, sweating, gasping, a scream frozen in his throat. Something was holding him down, constraining his arms and legs, and for a moment he thought it was rats, that they had followed him out of the dream, and he

thrashed in panic until he realized he was in a zippered sleeping bag. He found the zipper, pulled the bag open, freed himself, and crawled until he came to a wall in the darkness, sat with his back to it, listening to his thunderous heartbeat, waiting for it to subside.

When at last he had control of himself, he went into Joey's room, just to reassure himself. The boy was sleeping peacefully. Chewbacca raised his furry head and yawned.

Charlie looked at his watch, saw that he had slept about four hours. Dawn was nearing.

He returned to the gallery.

He couldn't stop shaking.

He went downstairs and made some coffee.

He tried not to think about the dream, but he couldn't help it. He had never before had such a vivid nightmare, and the shattering power of it led him to believe that it had been less a dream than a clairvoyant experience, a foreshadowing of events to come. Not that rats were going to burst out of Joey. Of course not. The dream had been symbolic. But what it meant was that Joey was going to die. Not wanting to believe it, devastated by the very idea that he would fail to protect the boy, he was nevertheless unable to dismiss it as only a dream; he knew; he felt it in his bones: *Joey was going to die.* Maybe they were all going to die.

And now he understood why he and Christine had made love with such intensity, with such abandon and fiercely animalistic need. Deep down, they both had known that time was running out; subconsciously, they had felt death approaching, and they had tried to deny it in that most ancient and fundamental of life-affirming rituals, the ceremony of flesh, the dance done lying down.

He got up from the table, left his half-finished coffee, and went to the front door. He wiped at the frosted glass until he could look out at the snow-covered porch. He couldn't see much of anything, just a few whirling flakes and darkness. The worst of the storm had passed. And Spivey was out there. Somewhere. That's what the dream had meant.

CHAPTER 55

By DAWN THE storm had passed.

Christine and Joey were up early. The boy was not as ebullient as he had been last night. In fact he was sinking back into gloom and perhaps despair, but he helped his mother and Charlie make breakfast, and he ate well.

After breakfast, Charlie suited up and went outside, alone, to sight-in the rifle that he had purchased yesterday in Sacramento.

More than a foot of new snow had fallen during the night. The drifts that sloped against the cabin were considerably higher than they had been yesterday, and a couple of first-floor windows were drifted over. The boughs of the evergreens dropped lower under the weight of the new snow, and the world was so silent it seemed like a vast graveyard.

The day was cold, gray, bleak. At the moment no wind blew.

He had fashioned a target out of a square of cardboard and two lengths of twine. He tied the target around the trunk of a Douglas Fir that stood a few yards downhill from the windmill, then backed off twenty-five yards and stretched out on his belly in the snow. Using one of the rolled-up sleeping bags as a makeshift bench rest, he aimed for the center of the target and fired three rounds, pausing between each to make sure the cross hairs were still lined up on the bull's-eye.

The Winchester Model 100 was fitted with a 3-power telescope sight which brought the target right up to him. He was firing 180-grain soft-point bullets, and he saw each of them hit home.

The shots cracked the morning stillness all across the mountain and echoed back from distant valleys.

He got up, went to the target, and measured the point of average impact, which was the center point of the three hits. Then he measured the distance from the point of impact to the point of aim (which was the bull's-eye where he had lined up the cross hairs), and that figure told him how much adjustment the scope required. The rifle was pulling low and to the right. He corrected the elevation dial first, then the windage dial, then sprawled in the snow again and fired another group of three. This time he was gratified to see that every shot found the center of the target.

Because a bullet does not travel in a straight line but in a curving trajectory, it twice crosses the line of sight—once as it is rising and once as it is falling. With the rifle and ammunition he was using, Charlie could figure that any round he fired would first cross the line of sight at about twenty-five yards, then rise until it was about two and a half inches high of the mark at one hundred yards, then fall and cross the line of sight a second time at about two hundred yards. Therefore, the Winchester was now sighted-in for two hundred yards.

He didn't want to have to kill anyone.

He hoped killing wouldn't be necessary.

But now he was ready.

Christine and Charlie put on their snowshoes and backpacks and went down the mountain to the lower meadow to finish unloading the Jeep.

Charlie was carrying the rifle, slung over one shoulder.

She said, "You're not expecting trouble?"

"No. But what's the use of having the gun if I don't always keep it close by?"

She felt better about leaving Joey alone this morning than she had last night, but she still wasn't happy about it. His high spirits had been short-lived. He was withdrawing again, retreating into his own inner world, and this change was even more frightening than it had been the last time it happened because, after his recovery yesterday evening, she had thought he was permanently back with them. If he withdrew into silence and despair again, perhaps he would slip even deeper than before, and perhaps this time he would not come out again. It *was* possible for a once perfectly normal, outgoing child to become autistic, cutting off most or all interaction with the real world. She'd read about such cases, but she'd never worried about it as much as she worried about diseases and accidents because Joey had always been such an open, joyous, communicative child. Autism had been something that could happen to other people's children, never to her extroverted little boy. But now . . . This morning he spoke little. He didn't smile at all. She wanted to stay with him every minute, hug him a lot, but she remembered that being left alone for a while last evening had convinced him that the witch must not be near, after all. Being left to his own resources this morning might have that same salutary effect again.

Christine didn't glance back as she and Charlie headed downhill, away from the cabin. If Joey was watching from a window, he might interpret a look back as an indication that she was afraid for him, and her own fear would then feed his.

Her breath took frosty form and wreathed her head. The air was bitterly cold, but because there was no wind, they didn't need to wear ski masks.

At first she and Charlie didn't speak, just walked, finding their way through the new soft snow, sinking in now and then in spite of the snowshoes, searching for a firmer crust, squinting because the glare of the snow was fatiguing to the eyes even under a sunless sky like this one. However, as they reached the woods at the base of the meadow, Charlie said, "Uh . . . about last night—"

"Me first," she said quickly, speaking softly because the air was so still that a whisper carried as well as a shout. "I've been sort of . . . well, a little embarrassed all morning."

"About what happened last night?"

"Yes."

"You're sorry it happened?"

"No, no."

"Good. Because I'm sure not sorry."

She said, "I just want you to know . . . that the way I was last night . . . so eager . . . so aggressive . . . so . . . ."

"Passionate?"

"It was more than passion, wouldn't you say?"

"I'd say."

"My God, I was like . . . an animal or something. I couldn't get enough of you."

"It was great for my ego," he said, grinning.

"I didn't know your ego was deflated."

"Wasn't. But I never thought of myself as God's gift to women, either."

"But after last night you do, huh?"

"Absolutely."

Twenty yards into the woods, they stopped and looked at each other and kissed gently.

She said, "I just want you to understand that I've *never* been like that before."

He feigned surprise and disappointment. "You mean you're *not* sex crazy?"

"Only with you."

"That's because I'm God's gift to women, I guess."

She didn't smile. "Charlie, this is important to me—that you understand. Last night . . . I don't know what got into me."

"*I* got into you."

"Be serious. Please. I don't want you to think I've been like that with other men. I haven't. Not ever. I did things with you last night that I've never done before. I didn't even know I *could* do them. I was really like a wild animal. I mean . . . I'm no prude but—"

"Listen," he said, "if you were an animal last night, then I was a *beast*. It's not like me to completely surrender control of myself like that, and it certainly isn't like me to be that . . . well, demanding . . . rough. But I'm not embarrassed by the way I was, and you shouldn't be, either. We've got something special, something unique, and that's why we both felt able to let go the way we did. At times it was maybe crude—but it was also pretty terrific, wasn't it?"

"God, yes."

They kissed again, but it was a brief kiss interrupted by a distant growling-buzzing.

Charlie cocked his head, listening.

The sound grew louder.

"Plane?" she said, looking up at the narrow band of sky above the tree-flanked lane.

"Snowmobiles," Charlie said. "There was a time when the mountains were always quiet, serene. Not any more. Those damned snowmobiles are every-where, like fleas on a cat."

The roar of engines grew louder.

"They wouldn't come up this far?" she asked worriedly.

"Might."

"Sounds like they're almost on top of us."

"Probably still pretty far off. Sound is deceptive up here; it carries a long way."

"But if we do run into some snowmobilers—"

"We'll say we're renting the cabin. My name's . . . Bob . . . mmm . . . Henderson. You're Jane Henderson. We live in Seattle. Up here to do some cross-country skiing and just get away from it all. Got it?"

"Got it," she said.

"Don't mention Joey."

She nodded.

They started downhill again.

The sound of snowmobile engines grew louder, louder—and then cut out one at a time, until there was once again only the deep enveloping silence of the mountains and the soft crunch and squeak of snowshoes in the snow.

When they reached the next break in the tree line, at the top of the lower meadow, they saw four snowmobiles and eight or ten people gathered around the Jeep, almost three hundred yards below. They were too far away for Christine to see what they looked like, or even whether they were men or women; they were just small, dark figures against the dazzling whiteness of the snowfield. The station wagon was half buried in drifted snow, but the strangers were busily cleaning it off, trying the doors.

Christine heard faint voices but couldn't understand the words. The sound of breaking glass clinked through the crisp cold air, and she realized these were not ordinary snowmobile enthusiasts.

Charlie pulled her backward, into the darkness beneath the trees, off to the left of the trail, and both of them nearly fell because snowshoes were not designed for dodging and running. They stood under a gigantic hemlock. Its spreading branches began about seven feet above the ground, casting shadows and shedding needles on the thin skin of snow that covered the earth beneath it. Charlie leaned against the enormous trunk of the tree and peered around it, past a couple of other hemlocks, between a few knobcone pines, toward the meadow and the Jeep. He unsnapped the binocular case that was clipped to his belt, took out the binoculars.

"Who are they?" Christine asked as she watched Charlie focus the glasses. Certain that she already knew the answer to her question but not wanting to believe it, not having the strength to believe it. "Not just a group of people who like winter sports; that's for sure. They wouldn't go around busting the win-dows out of abandoned vehicles."

"Maybe it's a bunch of kids," he said, still focusing. "Just out looking for a little trouble."

"Nobody goes out in deep snow, comes this far up a mountain, just looking for trouble," she said.

Charlie took two steps away from the hemlock, held the binoculars with both hands, peering downhill. At last he said, "I recognize one of them. The big guy who came into her office at the rectory, just as Henry and I were leaving. She called him Kyle."

"Oh Jesus."

The mountain wasn't a haven, after all, but a dead end. A trap.

Suddenly the loneliness of the snow-blasted slopes and forests made their retreat to the cabin appear short-sighted, foolish. It seemed like such a good idea to get away from people, where they would not be spotted, but they had also removed themselves from all chance of help, from everyone who might have come to their assistance if they were attacked. Here, in these cold high places, they could be slaughtered and buried, and no one but their murderers would ever know what had happened to them.

"Do you see . . . *her?*" Christine asked.

"Spivey? I think . . . yeah . . . the only one still sitting in a snowmobile. I'm sure that's her."

"But *how* could they find us?"

"Somebody who knew I was part owner of the cabin. Somebody remembered it and told Spivey's people."

"Henry Rankin?"

"Maybe. Very few people know about this place."

"But still . . . so quickly!"

Charlie said, "Six . . . seven . . . nine of them. No. Ten. Ten of them."

We're going to die, she thought. And for the first time since leaving the convent, since losing her religion, she wished that she had not turned entirely away from the Church. Suddenly, by comparison with the insanity of Spivey's cult beliefs, the ancient and compassionate doctrines of the Roman Catholic Church were immeasurably appealing and comforting, and she wished she could turn to them now without feeling like a hypocrite, wished she could beg God for help and ask the Blessed Virgin for her divine intercession. But you couldn't just reject the Church, put it entirely out of your life—then go running back when you needed it, and expect to be embraced without first making penance. God required your faith in the good times as well as the bad. If she died at the hands of Spivey's fanatics, she would do so without making a final confession to a priest, without the last rites or a proper burial in consecrated ground, and she was surprised that those things mattered to her and seemed important after all these years during which she had discounted their value.

Charlie put the binoculars back into the case, snapped it shut. He unslung the rifle from his shoulder.

He said, "You head back to the cabin. Fast as you can. Stay in the trees until you reach the bend in the trail. After that they can't see you from the lower meadow. Get Joey suited up. Pack some food in your knapsack. Do whatever you can to get ready."

"You're staying here? Why?"

"To kill a few of them," he said.

He unzipped one of the pockets in his insulated jacket. It was filled with loose cartridges. When he exhausted the rounds already in the rifle, he would be able to reload quickly.

She hesitated, afraid to leave him.

"Go!" he said. "Hurry! We haven't much time."

Heart racing, she nodded, turned, and made her way through the trees, heading upslope, shuffling as fast as the snowshoes would allow, which wasn't nearly fast enough, repeatedly raising her arms to push branches out of her way. She was thankful that the huge trees blocked the sun and prevented much undergrowth because it would have tangled in the snowshoes and snagged her ski suit and held her back.

Successful rifle shooting requires two things: the steadiest possible position for the gunman, and the letting-off of the trigger at exactly the right time and with the easiest possible pull. Very few riflemen—hunters, military men, whatever—are any good at all. Too many of them try to shoot off-hand when a better position is available, or they exert all the pull on the trigger in one swift movement that throws their aim entirely off.

A rifleman shoots best from a prone position, especially when he is aiming down a slope or into a basin. After taking off his snowshoes, Charlie moved to the perimeter of the forest, to the very edge of the meadow, and dropped to the ground. The snow was only about two inches deep here, for the wind came across the meadow from the west and scoured the land, pushing most of the snow eastward, packing it in drifts along that flank of the woods. The slope was steep at this point, and he was looking down at the people below, where they were still milling around the Jeep station wagon. He raised the rifle, resting it on the heel of the palm of his left hand; his left arm was bent, and the left elbow was directly under the rifle. In this position the rifle wouldn't wobble, for it was well supported by the bones of the forearm, which served as a pillar between the ground and the weapon.

He aimed at the dark figure in the lead snowmobile, though there were better targets, for he was almost certain it was Grace Spivey. Her head was above the vehicle's windscreen, which was one less thing to worry about: no chance of the shot being deflected by the Plexiglas. If he could take her out, the others might lose their sense of commitment and come apart psychologically. It ought to be devastating for a fanatic to see his little tin God die right in front of his eyes.

His gloved finger was curled around the trigger, but he didn't like the feel, couldn't get the right sense of it, so he stripped the glove off with his teeth, put his bare finger on the trigger, and that was a great deal better. He had the cross hairs lined up on the center of Grace Spivey's forehead because, at this distance, the bullet would fall past the sight line by the time it hit its target and would come in about an inch lower. With luck—right between her eyes. Without luck but with skill, it would still take her in the face or throat.

In spite of the sub-zero air, he was perspiring. Inside his ski suit, sweat trickled down from his armpits.

Could you call this self-defense? None of them had a gun on him at the moment. He wasn't in imminent danger of his life. Of course, if he didn't eliminate a few of them before they got closer, they would overwhelm him. Yet he hesitated. He had never before done anything this . . . cold blooded. A small inner voice told him that, if he resorted to an ambush of this sort, he would be no better than the monsters against which he found himself pitted. But if he didn't resort to it, he would eventually die—as would Christine and Joey.

The cross hairs were on Spivey's forehead.

Charlie squeezed the trigger but didn't take up all the pull in one tug because the initial pressure would throw the rifle off target just a little, so he kept the trigger mostly depressed, on the wire-edge of firing, until he brought the cross hairs back onto target, and then, almost as an after-thought but with a clean quick squeeze, he took up the last few ounces of pull. The rifle fired, and he flinched but not in anticipation of the blast, only in delayed reaction to it, by which time it was too late for the bullet to be deflected, for it was already out of the barrel. An anticipatory flinch was what you had to avoid, and the two-stage pull always fooled the subconscious a little, just enough that the muzzle blast was a slight surprise.

There was another surprise, a bad one, when he thought he saw Spivey lean forward in the snowmobile, reaching for something, lowering her profile, just as he let off the shot. Now, lining up the scope again, he couldn't see her, which meant either that he had hit her and that she had collapsed below the windscreen of the snowmobile—*or* that she had, indeed, bent down at the penultimate moment, saved by fate, and was now crouching out of the line of fire.

He immediately brought the rifle around on one of the others.

A man standing by the Jeep. Just turning this way in reaction to the shot. Not gifted with split-second reactions, confused, not fully aware of the danger.

Charlie fired. This time he was rewarded by the sight of his target pitching back, sprawling in the snow, dead or mortally wounded.

Moving at the edge of the woods, Christine had reached the bend in the open land and, out of sight of those below, had moved out onto the easier ground, when she heard a shot and then, a second or two later, another. She wanted to go back to Charlie, wanted to be there helping him, knew she couldn't do a damn thing for him. She didn't even have time to *look* back. Instead she doubled her efforts, huffing out a fog of breath, trying to walk lightly on the snow, breaking through the crust because of her haste, searching frantically for wind-scoured stretches of ground where she could make better time.

But what if something happened to Charlie? What if he was never able to rejoin her and Joey?

She wasn't an outdoors type. She wouldn't know how to survive in these wintry wastes. If they had to leave the cabin without Charlie, they'd get lost in the wilderness, either starve or freeze to death.

Then, as if nature was intent on honing Christine's fear to a razor's edge, as if in mocking glee, snow flurries began to fall again.

When the first man was hit and went down, most of the others dived for cover alongside the Jeep wagon, but two men started toward the snowmobiles, making perfect targets of themselves, and Charlie lined up on one of them. This shot, too, was well placed, taking the man high in the chest, pitching him completely over one of the snowmobiles, and when he went down in a drift he stayed there, unmoving.

The other man dropped, making a hard target of himself. Charlie fired anyway. He couldn't tell if he had scored this time because his prey was now hidden by a mound of snow.

He reloaded.

He wondered if any of them were hunters or ex-military men with enough savvy to have pinpointed his position. He considered moving along the tree line, finding another good vantage point, and he knew the shadows under the trees would probably cover his movement. But he had a hunch that most of

them were not experienced in this sort of thing, were not cut out for guerrilla warfare, so he stayed where he was, waiting for one of them to make a mistake.

He didn't have to wait long. One of those who had taken shelter by the Jeep proved too curious for his own good. When half a minute had passed with no gunfire, the Twilighter rose slightly to look around, still in a half-crouch, ready to drop, probably figuring that a half-crouch made him an impossible target when, in fact, he was giving Charlie plenty at which to aim. Most likely, he also figured he could fall flat and hug the ground again at the slightest sound, but he was hit and dead before the sound of the shot could have reached him.

Three down. Seven left. Six—if he had also killed Spivey.

For the first time in his life, Charlie Harrison was glad that he had served in Vietnam. Fifteen years had passed, but battlefield cunning had not entirely deserted him. He felt the heart-twisting terror of both the hunter and the hunted, the battle stress that was like no other kind of stress, but he still knew how to *use* that tension, how to take advantage of that stress to keep himself alert and sharp.

The others remained very still, burrowing into the snow, hugging the Jeep and the snowmobiles. Charlie could hear them shouting to one another, but none of them dared move again.

He knew they would remain pinned down for five or ten minutes, and maybe he should get up now, head back to the cabin, use that lead time. But there was a chance that if he outwaited them he would get another clear shot the next time they regained a little confidence. For the moment, anyway, there was no danger of *losing* any advantage by staying put, so he remained at the perimeter of the woods. He reloaded again. He stared down at them, exhilarated by his marksmanship but wishing he wasn't so proud of it, savagely delighted that he had brought down three of them but also ashamed of that delight.

The sky looked hard, metallic. Light snow flurries were falling.

No wind yet. Good. Wind would interfere with his shooting.

Below, Spivey's people had stopped talking. Preternatural silence returned to the mountain.

Time ticked by.

They were scared of him down there.

He dared to hope.

CHAPTER 56

AT THE CABIN, Christine found Joey standing in the living room. His face was ashen. He had heard the shooting. He knew. "It's her."

"Honey, get your ski suit on, your boots. We're going out soon."

"Isn't it?" he said softly.

"We've got to be ready to leave as soon as Charlie comes."

"Isn't it her?"

"Yes," Christine said. Tears welled up in the boy's eyes, and she held him. "It'll be okay. Charlie will take care of us."

She was looking into his eyes, but he was not looking into hers. He was looking *through* her, into a world other than this one, a place of his own, and the emptiness in his eyes sent a chill up her spine.

She had hoped that he could dress himself while she stuffed things into her backpack, but he was on the verge of catatonia, just standing there, face slack, arms slack. She grabbed his ski suit and dressed him, pulling it on over the sweater and jeans he already wore. She pulled two pair of thick socks onto his small feet, put his boots on for him, laced them up. She put his gloves and ski mask on the floor by the door, so she wouldn't forget them when it was time to leave.

As she went into the kitchen and began choosing food and other items for the backpack, Joey came with her, stood beside her. Abruptly he shook off his trance, and his face contorted with fear, and he said, "Brandy? Where's Brandy?"

"You mean Chewbacca, honey."

"Brandy. I mean *Brandy!*"

Shocked, Christine stopped packing, stooped beside him, put a hand to his face. "Honey . . . don't do this . . . don't worry your mommy like this. You remember. I know you do. You remember . . . Brandy's dead."

"No."

"The witch—"

"*No!*"

"—killed him."

He shook his head violently. "No. No! Brandy!" He called desperately for his dead dog. "Brandy! *Braaannndeeeee!*"

She held him. He struggled. "Honey, please, please . . ."

At that moment Chewbacca padded into the kitchen to see what all the commotion was about, and the boy wrenched free of Christine, seized the dog joyfully, hugged the furry head. "Brandy! See? It's Brandy. He's still here. You lied. Brandy's not hurt. Brandy's okay. Nothin' wrong with good old Brandy."

For a moment Christine couldn't breathe or move because pain immobilized her, not physical pain but emotional pain, deep and bitter. Joey was slipping away. She thought he had accepted Brandy's death, that all of this had been settled when she'd forced him to name the dog Chewbacca instead of Brandy Two. But now . . . When she spoke his name, he didn't respond or look at her, just murmured and cooed to the dog, stroked it, hugged it. She shouted his name; still he didn't respond.

She should never have let him keep this look-alike. She should have made him take it back to the pound, should have made him choose another mutt, anything but a golden retriever.

Or maybe not. Maybe there was nothing she could have done to save his sanity. No six-year-old could be expected to hold himself together when his whole world was crumbling around him. Many adults would have cracked sooner. Although she had tried to pretend otherwise, the boy's emotional and mental problems had been inevitable.

A good psychiatrist would be able to help him. That's what she told herself. His retreat from reality wasn't permanent. She had to believe that was true. She had to *believe*. Or there was no point in going on from here.

She lived for Joey. He was her world, her *meaning*. Without him . . .

The worst thing was that she didn't have time to hold and cuddle and talk to him now, which was something he desperately needed and something she needed, as well. But Spivey was coming, and time was running out, so she had to ignore Joey, turn away from him when he needed her most, get control of herself, and ram things into the backpack. Her hands shook, and tears streamed down her face. She had never felt worse. Now, even if Charlie saved Joey's life, she might still lose her boy and be left with only the living but empty shell of him. But she kept on working, yanking open cupboard doors, looking for things they would need when they went into the woods.

She was filled with the blackest hatred for Spivey and the Church of the Twilight. She didn't just want to kill them. She wanted to torture them first. She wanted to make the old bitch scream and beg for mercy; the disgusting, filthy, rotten, crazy old *bitch!*

Softly, cooingly, Joey said, "Brandy . . . Brandy . . . Brandy," and stroked Chewbacca.

CHAPTER 57

SEVEN MINUTES PASSED before any of Spivey's people dared rise up to test whether Charlie was still sighting down on them.

He was, and he opened fire. But though this was the opportunity he had been waiting for, he was sloppy, too tense and too eager. He jerked the trigger instead of squeezing it, threw the sights off target, and missed.

Instantly, there was return fire. He had figured they were armed, but he hadn't been absolutely sure until now. Two rifles opened up, and the fire was directed toward the upper end of the meadow. But the first rounds entered the woods fifty yards to the left of him; he heard them cracking through the trees. The next shots hit closer, maybe thirty-five yards away, still to his left, but the gunmen kept shooting, and the shots grew closer. They knew in general— though not precisely—where he was, and they were trying to elicit a reaction that would pinpoint his location.

As the shots came closer, he put his head down, pressed into the thinning shadows at the edge of the forest. He heard bullets slamming through the branches directly overhead. Scraps of bark, a spray of needles, and a couple pine cones rained down around him, and a few bits and pieces even fell on his back, but if the riflemen below were also hoping for a lucky hit, they would be disappointed. The fire slowly moved off to his right, which indicated they knew only that the shots had come from above and did not know for sure which corner of the meadow harbored their assailant.

Charlie raised his head, lifted the rifle again, brought his eye to the scope— and discovered, with a start, that their shooting had another purpose, too. It was meant to cover two Twilighters who were running pell-mell for the forest at the east end of the meadow.

"Shit!" he said, quickly trying to line up a shot on one of the two. But they were moving fast, in spite of the drifting snow, kicking up clouds of crystalline flakes. Just as he got the cross hairs on one of them, both men plunged into the darkness between the trees and were gone.

The Twilighters down by the Jeep stopped firing.

Charlie wondered how long it would take the two in the woods to work their way up through the trees and come in behind him. Not long. There wasn't a lot of underbrush in these forests. Five minutes. Less.

He could still do some damage, even if those remaining in the meadow did not show themselves. He brought one of the snowmobiles into the bull's-eye in his scope and pumped two rounds through the front of it, hoping to smash something vital. If he could put them on foot, he would slow them down, make the chase more fair. He targeted another snowmobile, pumped two slugs into the engine. The third machine was half hidden by the other two, offering less of a target, and he fired five times at that one, reloading the rifle as needed, and all his shooting finally made it possible for them to pinpoint him. They began blasting from below, but this time all the shots were coming within a few yards of him.

The fourth snowmobile was behind the Jeep, out of reach, so there was nothing more he could do. He put on the glove he had stripped off a few minutes ago, then slithered on his belly, deeper into the woods, until he found a big hemlock trunk to put between himself and the incoming bullets. He had taken off his snowshoes earlier, when he had needed to be in a prone position to get the most from his rifle. Now he put them on again, working as rapidly as possible, trying to make as little noise as he could, listening intently for any sounds made by the two men coming up through the eastern arm of the forest.

He had expected to hear or see them by this time, but now he realized they would be extremely cautious. They would figure he had seen them making a break for the trees, and they would be sure he was lying in wait for them. And they knew he enjoyed the advantage of familiarity with the terrain. They would move slowly, from one bit of cover to the next, thoroughly studying every tree and rock formation and hollow that lay ahead of them, afraid of an ambush. They might not be here for another five or even ten minutes, and once they got here they'd waste another ten minutes, at least, searching the area until they were sure he had pulled back. That gave him, Christine, and Joey maybe a twenty- or twenty-five-minute lead.

As fast as he could, he moved through the woods, heading toward the upper meadow and the cabin.

Snow flurries were still falling.

A wind had risen.

The sky had darkened and lowered. It was still morning, but it felt like late afternoon. Hell, it felt later than that, much later; it felt like the end of time.

Chewbacca stayed beside Joey, as if he sensed that his young master needed him, but the boy no longer paid attention to the dog. Joey was lost in an inner world, oblivious of this one.

Biting her lip, repressing her concern for her son, Christine had finished stuffing provisions into her backpack, had made a pile of everything that ought to go into Charlie's pack, and had loaded the shotgun by the time he returned to the cabin. His face was flushed from the bitter air, and his eyebrows were white with snow, but for a moment his eyes were the coldest thing about him.

"What happened?" she asked as he came across the living room to the dining table, leaving clumps of melting snow in his wake.

"I blew them away. Like ducks in a barrel, for God's sake."

Helping him off with his backpack and spreading it on the table, she said, "All of them?"

"No. I either killed or badly wounded three men. And I might've nipped a fourth, but I doubt it."

She began frantically tucking things into the waterproof vinyl pack. "Spivey?"

"I don't know. Maybe. Maybe I hit her. I don't know."

"They're still coming?"

"They will be. We've got maybe a twenty minute head start."

The pack was half full. She paused, a can of matches in her hand. Staring hard at him, she said. "Charlie? What's wrong?"

He wiped at the melting snow trickling down from his eyebrows. "I . . . I've never done anything like that. It was . . . slaughter. In the war, of course, but that was different. That was war."

"So is this."

"Yeah. I guess so. Except . . . when I was shooting them . . . I *liked* it. And even in the war, I never liked it."

"Nothing wrong with that," she said, continuing to stuff things into the backpack. "After what they've put us through, I'd like to shoot a few of them, too. God, would I ever!"

Charlie looked at Joey. "Get your gloves and mask on, Skipper."

The boy didn't respond. He was standing by the table, his face expressionless, his eyes dead.

"Joey?" Charlie said.

The boy didn't react. He was staring at Christine's hands as she jammed various items into the second backpack, but he didn't really seem to be watching her.

"What's wrong with him?" Charlie asked.

"He . . . he just . . . went away," Christine said, fighting back the tears that she had only recently been able to overcome.

Charlie went to the boy, put a hand under his chin, lifted his head. Joey looked up, toward Charlie but not at him, and Charlie spoke to him but without effect. The boy smiled vaguely, humorlessly, a ghastly smile, but even that wasn't meant for Charlie; it was for something he had seen or thought of in the world where he had gone, something that was light-years away. Tears shimmered in the corners of the boy's eyes, but the eerie smile didn't leave his face, and he didn't sob or make a sound.

"Damn," Charlie said softly.

He hugged the boy, but Joey didn't respond. Then Charlie picked up the first backpack, which was already full, and he put his arms through the straps, shrugged it into place, buckled it across his chest.

Christine finished with the second pack, made sure all the flaps were securely fastened, and took that burden upon herself.

Charlie put Joey's gloves and ski mask on for him. The boy offered little or no assistance.

Picking up the loaded shotgun, Christine followed Charlie, Joey, and Chewbacca out of the cabin. She looked back inside before she closed the door. A pile of logs blazed in the fireplace. One of the brass lamps was on, casting a circle of soft amber light. The armchairs and sofas looked comfortable and enticing.

She wondered if she would ever sit in a chair again, ever see another electric light. Or would she die out there in the woods tonight, in a grave of drifted snow?

She closed the door and turned to face the gray, frigid fastness of the mountains.

Carrying Joey, Charlie led Christine around the cabin and into the forest behind it. Until they were into the screen of trees, he kept glancing around nervously at the open meadow behind them, expecting to see Spivey's people come into sight at the far end of it.

Chewbacca stayed a few yards ahead of them, anticipating their direction with some sixth sense. He struggled a bit with the snow until he reached the undrifted ground within the forest, and then he pranced ahead with an eager sprightliness, unhindered by rock formations, fallen timber, or anything else.

There was some brush at the edge of the forest, but then the trees closed ranks and the brush died away. The land rose, and the earth became rocky and difficult, except for a shallow channel that, in spring, was probably filled with run-off from the melting snowpack, pouring down from higher elevations. They stayed in the channel, heading north and west, which was the direction they needed to go. Their snowshoes were strapped to their backpacks because, for the next few hours, they would be mostly under the huge trees, where the mantle of snow was not particularly deep. In fact, in places, the boughs of the densely grown evergreens were so tightly interlaced that the ground beneath them was bare or virtually so.

Nevertheless, there was sufficient snow for them to leave a clear trail. He could have stopped and tried brushing away their tracks, but he didn't bother. Waste of time. The signs he would leave by trying to eradicate their footprints would be just as obvious as the footprints themselves, for the wind couldn't gain much force in the deepest part of the forest, at least not down here at floor level, and it would not soften and obliterate the brush marks. They could only press on, keep moving, and hope to outrun their pursuers. Perhaps later, if and when they crossed any stretches of open land, the increasing wind might be strong enough to help them out, obscure their passage.

If.

If they ever made it through this part of the woods and onto a stretch of open ground.

If they weren't brought down by Spivey's hounds in the next half hour or forty-five minutes.

If.

The woods were shadowy, and they soon found that the narrow eye holes of the ski masks limited their vision even further. They tripped and stumbled because they didn't see everything in their path, and at last they had to take the masks off. The sub-zero air nipped at them, but they would just have to endure it.

Charlie became acutely aware that their lead on Spivey's people was dwindling. They had been at the cabin almost five minutes. So they were now just fifteen minutes ahead of the pack, maybe even less. And because he couldn't move as fast as he wanted while carrying Joey, Charlie had little doubt that their lead was narrowing dangerously, minute by minute.

The land rose more steeply; he began to breathe harder, and he heard Christine panting behind him. His calves and thighs were knotted, beginning to ache already, and his arms were weary with the burden of the boy. The convenient channel began to curve eastward, which wasn't the way they needed to go. It was still heading more north than east, so they could continue to follow it for a short while, but soon he would have to put the boy down in order to make his way over considerably less hospitable terrain. If they were going to escape, Joey would have to walk on his own.

But what if he wouldn't walk? What if he just stood there, staring, empty-eyed?

CHAPTER 58

GRACE CROUCHED WITHIN the snowmobile, staying down out of the line of fire, though her old bones protested against her cramped position.

It was a black day in the spirit world. This morning, discovering this disturbing development, she thought she would not be able to dress in harmony with the spectral energies. She had no black clothes. There had never been a black day prior to this. Never. Fortunately, Laura Panken, one of her disciples, had a black ski suit, and they were nearly the same size, so Grace swapped her gray suit for Laura's black outfit.

But now she almost wished she weren't in contact with the saints and with the souls of the dead. The spectral energies radiating from them were uniformly unsettling, tinged with fear.

Grace was also assaulted with clairvoyant images of death and damnation, but these didn't come from God; they had another source, a taint of brimstone. With emotionally unsettling visions, Satan was trying to destroy her faith, to terrorize her. He wanted her to turn, run, abandon the mission. She knew what the Father of Lies was up to. She knew. Sometimes, when she looked at the faces of those around her, she didn't see their real countenances but, instead, rotting tissue and maggot-ridden flesh, and she was shaken by these visions of mortality. The devil, as wise as he was evil, knew she would never give in to temptation, so he was trying to shatter her faith with a hammer of fear.

It wouldn't work. Never. She was strong.

But Satan kept trying. Sometimes, when she looked at the stormy sky, she saw *things* in the clouds: grinning goat heads, monstrous pig faces with protruding fangs. There were voices in the wind, too. Hissing, sinister voices made false promises, told lies, spoke of perverse pleasures, and their hypnotic descriptions of these unspeakable acts were rich in images of the mutant beauty of wickedness.

While she was crouched in the snowmobile, hiding from the rifleman at the top of the meadow, Grace suddenly saw a dozen huge cockroaches, each as large as her hand, crawling over the floor of the machine, over her boots, inches from her face. She almost leapt up in revulsion. That was what the devil wanted; he hoped she would present a better target and make an easy job of it for Charlie Harrison. She swallowed hard, choked on her revulsion, and remained pressed down in the small space.

She saw that each cockroach had a human head instead of the head of an insect. Their tiny faces, filled with pain and self-disgust and terror, looked up at her, and she knew these were damned souls who had been crawling through Hell until, moments ago, Satan had transported them here, to show her how he tortured his subjects, to prove his cruelty had no limits. She was so afraid that she almost lost control of her bladder. Staring at the beetles with human faces, she was supposed to wonder how God could permit the existence of Hell. That's what the devil meant for her to do. Yes. She was supposed to wonder if, by permitting Satan's cruelty, God was indeed cruel Himself. She was supposed to doubt the virtue of her Maker. This vision was intended to bring despair and fear deep into her heart.

Then she saw that one beetle had the face of her dead husband, Albert. No.

Albert was a good man. Albert had not gone to Hell. It was a lie. The tiny face peered up, screaming yet making no sound. No. Albert was a sweet man, sinless, a saint. Albert in Hell? Albert damned for eternity? God wouldn't do such a thing. She was looking forward to being with Albert again, in Heaven, but if Albert had gone the other way . . .

She felt herself teetering on the edge of madness.

No. No, no, no. Satan was lying. Trying to drive her crazy.

He'd like that. Oh, yes. If she was insane, she wouldn't be able to serve her God. If she even questioned her sanity, she would also be questioning her mission, her Gift, and her relationship with God. She must not doubt herself. She was sane, and Albert was in Heaven, and she had to repress all doubts, give herself completely to blind faith.

She closed her eyes and would not look at the things crawling on her boots. She could feel them, even through the heavy leather, but she gritted her teeth and listened to the rifle fire and prayed, and when eventually she opened her eyes, the cockroaches were gone.

She was safe for a while. She had pushed the devil away.

The rifle fire had stopped, too. Now, Pierce Morgan and Denny Rogers, the two men who had been sent into the woods to circle around behind Charlie Harrison, called from the upper end of the meadow. The way was clear. Harrison was gone.

Grace climbed out of the snowmobile and saw Morgan and Rogers at the top of the meadow, waving their arms. She turned to the body of Carl Rainey, the first man shot. He was dead, a big hole in his chest. The wind was drifting snow over his outflung arms. She knelt beside him.

Kyle eventually came to her. "O'Conner is dead, too. And George Westvec." His voice quaked with anger and grief.

She said, "We knew some of us would be sacrificed. Their deaths were not in vain."

The others gathered around: Laura Panken, Edna Vanoff, Burt Tully. They looked as angry and determined as they did frightened. They would not turn and run. They *believed.*

Grace said, "Carl Rainey . . . is in Heaven now, in the arms of God. So are . . ." She had trouble remembering first names for O'Conner and Westvec, hesitated, once again wishing that the Gift did not drive so much else out of her mind. "So are . . . George Westvec and . . . Ken . . . Ken . . . uh . . . Kevin . . . *Kevin* O'Conner . . . all in Heaven."

Gradually the snow knitted a shroud over Rainey's corpse.

"Will we bury them here?" Laura Panken asked.

"Ground's frozen," Kyle said.

"Leave them. No time for burials," Grace said. "The Antichrist is within our reach, but his power grows by the hour. We can't delay."

Two of the Skidoos were out of commission. Grace, Edna, Laura, and Burt Tully rode in the remaining two, while Kyle followed them on foot to the top of the meadow where Morgan and Rogers were waiting.

A sadness throbbed through Grace. Three men dead.

They moved forward, proceeding in fits and starts, only when the way ahead had been scouted, wary of running into another ambush.

The wind had picked up. The snow flurries grew thicker. The sky was all the shades of death.

Soon she would be face to face with the child, and her destiny would be fulfilled.

PART FIVE

THE KILL

Pestilence, disease, and war
haunt this sorry place.
And nothing lasts forever;
that's a truth we have to face.

We spend vast energy and time
plotting death for one another.
No one, nowhere, is ever safe.
Not father, child, or mother.
—*The Book of Counted Sorrows*

By the pricking of my thumbs,
something wicked this way comes.
—*Macbeth,*
William Shakespeare

Nothing saddens God more than the
death of a child.
—Dr. Tom Dooley

CHAPTER 59

CHRISTINE SAID, "That's good. That's my boy," as Joey followed Charlie up through the trees, heading for a broad set-back in the slope, halfway to the ridge line.

She had been afraid that he wouldn't walk on his own, would just stand like a zombie. But perhaps he was not as detached from reality as he seemed; he didn't talk, didn't meet her eyes, seemed numb with fear, but apparently he was still enough in tune with this world to understand that he had to keep moving to avoid the witch.

His small legs were not strong, and his bulky ski suit hindered him a bit, and the ground was extremely steep in places, but he kept going, grabbing at rocks and at a few clumps of sparse brush to steady himself and pull himself along. He walked with increasing difficulty, crawled in some places, and Christine, following behind, often had to lift him over fallen timber or help him across a slippery, ice-crusted outcropping of rock. They couldn't move as fast with the boy as they could have without him, but at least they were covering some ground; if they'd had to carry him, they would have been brought to a complete halt.

Frequently, Chewbacca moved ahead of them, loping and scrabbling up the forested slopes as if he were not a dog at all but a wolf, at home in these primeval regions. Often, the retriever stopped above them and looked back, panting, with one ear raised in an almost comical expression. And the boy, seeing him, seemed to take heart and move forward with renewed effort, so Christine supposed she ought to be grateful the animal was with them, even if its resemblance to Brandy might have contributed to Joey's mental deterioration.

Indeed, she had begun to worry about the dog's chances of survival. Its coat was heavy, yes, but silky, not like the thick fur of a wolf or any other animal indigenous to these climes. Already, snow had frozen to the tips of the long hairs on its flanks and belly, as well as to part of its tail and to the furry tips of its ears. It didn't seem bothered yet, or too cold, but how would it feel an hour from now? Two hours? The pads of its feet were not made for this rugged terrain, either. It was a house pet, after all, accustomed to the easy life of suburbia. Soon its feet would be bruised and cut, and it would begin to limp, and instead of racing ahead it would be lagging behind.

If Chewbacca couldn't make it, if the poor mutt died out here, what would *that* do to Joey?

Kill him?

Maybe. Or send him irretrievably far off into his own silent, inner world.

For a couple of minutes, Christine heard a distant growling-buzzing below and behind them, and she knew it must be the snowmobiles roaring into the upper meadow, closing in on the cabin. That grim fact must have penetrated Joey's fog, too, because for a few minutes he made a gallant effort, moved faster, clawing and scrambling upward. When the sound of the snowmobiles died, however, so did his energy, and he resumed a slower, more labored pace.

They reached the set-back in the ridge and paused for breath, but none of them spoke because speaking required energy they could put to better use. Besides, there was nothing to talk about except how soon they might be caught and killed.

Several yards away, something broke from a vine-entangled clump of gnarled dogwood and dashed across the forest floor, startling them.

Charlie unslung his rifle.

Chewbacca stiffened, gave a short, sharp yip.

It was only a gray fox.

It vanished in the shadows.

Christine supposed it was on the trail of game, a squirrel or a snow rabbit or something. Life must be hard up here, in the winter. However, her sympathies lay not with the fox but with the prey. She knew what it was like to be hunted.

Charlie slung the rifle over his shoulder again, and they started climbing once more.

Above the set-back, on the last slope before the ridge line, the trees thinned out, and there was more snow on the ground, although not enough to require snowshoes. Charlie found a deer path, which followed the route of least resistance toward the flat top of the ridge. Where the track passed unavoidably through deep snow that might have given Joey trouble, the deer had cleared the way—there must have been dozens of them through here since the last big storm, tamping the snow with their hooves—and the boy was able to proceed with only a little slipping and sliding.

Chewbacca became excited by the scent of the deer that had come this way before them, whimpered and growled in the back of his throat, but didn't bark. She realized he hadn't once barked since leaving the cabin. Even when startled by the fox, he had made only a small sound that couldn't have carried far, as if he sensed that a bark would have been a beacon for the witch. Or maybe he just didn't have enough energy to climb and bark at the same time.

Each upward step not only put ground between them and their pursuers but seemed to take them into worse weather. It was as if winter were a geographic reality rather than an atmospheric condition, a real place rather than a season, and they were walking deeper into its frigid kingdom.

The sky seemed only inches higher than the treetops. The flurries had changed to heavy snow that slanted down between the pines and firs. By the time they reached the crest of the ridge, where there were no trees at all, Christine could see that a new storm had moved in and that, judging by this early stage, it was going to be even worse than last night's storm. The temperature was well below zero, and the wind was beginning to churn up from the valleys, driven by the rising thermals, blowing harder and gusting more fiercely even as they stood there, trying to catch their breath. Within a couple of hours, the mountain would be a white hell. And now they were without the warm refuge of the cabin.

Charlie didn't immediately lead them down into the next valley. He turned and, standing at the edge of the ridge, stared thoughtfully back the way they had come. Something was on his mind, a plan of some sort. Christine could tell that much, and she hoped it was a good plan. They were outnumbered and outgunned. They needed to be damned clever if they were going to win.

She stooped beside Joey. His nose was running, and the mucous had frozen to his upper lip and to one cheek. She wiped his face with her gloved hand, cleaning him as best she could, and she kissed each of his eyes, held him close, keeping his back to the wind.

He did not speak.

His eyes looked *through* hers, as before.

Grace Spivey, I will kill you, Christine thought, looking back the way they had come, into the woods. For what you've done to my little boy, I will blow your goddamned head off.

Squinting as the stinging wind blew snow into his face, Charlie surveyed the top of the ridge and decided it was just the place for an ambush. It was a long, treeless expanse, running roughly north and south, as narrow as fifteen feet in some places, as wide as thirty feet in others, mostly swept free of snow by the gales that punished its exposed contours. Rock formations, smoothed and carved by centuries of wind, thrust up all along the crest, providing a score of superb hiding places from which he could observe the ascending Twilighters.

At the moment there was no sign of Spivey's people. Of course, he could not see particularly far down into the shadowed woods. Although the trees were not as densely grown on the slope immediately under him as they were on the lower hills, nevertheless they appeared to close up into a wall no more than a hundred or a hundred and twenty yards below. Beyond that point, an army could have been approaching, and he would have been unable to see it. And the wind, whistling and moaning across the top of the ridge, evoked a noisy hissing and rustling from the branches of the enormous trees, masking any sounds that pursuers might have made.

Instinctively, however, Charlie sensed that the cultists were still at least twenty minutes behind, maybe even farther back. Climbing toward the top of the ridge, slowed down by Joey, Charlie had been sure they were losing precious lead time. But now he remembered that Spivey's gang would ascend cautiously, wary of another ambush, at least for the first quarter or half a mile, until their confidence returned. Besides, they had probably stopped to have a look in the cabin and had wasted a few minutes there. He had plenty of time to arrange a little welcoming party for them.

He went to Christine and Joey, knelt beside them.

The boy was still detached, almost catatonic, even unaware of the dog rubbing affectionately against his leg.

To Christine, Charlie said, "We'll head down into the next valley, as far as we can go in five minutes, find a place for you to get out of the weather a little. Then I'll come straight back here and wait for them."

"No."

"I should be able to pick off at least one before they dive for cover."

"No," Christine said, shaking her head adamantly. "If you're going to wait here for them, we wait with you."

"Impossible. Once I'm finished shooting, I want to be able to clear out fast, make a run for it. If you're here with me, we'll have to move slow. We'll lose too much of our lead on them."

"I don't think we should separate."

"It's the only way."

"It scares me."

"I've got to keep picking them off if I can."

She bit her lip. "It still scares me."

"It won't be dangerous for me."

"Like hell it won't."

"No. Really. I'll be above them when I start shooting. I'll be well concealed. They won't know where the fire's coming from until it's too late, until I've already pulled out. I'll have all the advantages."

"Maybe they won't even follow us up here."

"They will."

"It's not an easy hike."

"We made it. They can, too."

"But Spivey's an old woman. She isn't up to this sort of thing."

"So they'll leave her behind at the cabin with a couple of guards, and the rest of them will come after us. I have to make it hard for them, Christine. I have to kill all of them if I can. I swear to you, an ambush won't be dangerous. I'll shoot one or two of them and slip away before they even have a chance to spot my location and return my fire."

She said nothing.

"Come on," he said. "We're wasting time."

She hesitated, nodded, and got up. "Let's go."

She was one hell of a woman. He didn't know many *men* who would have come this far without complaint, as she had done, and he didn't think he knew any other woman who would consent to being left alone in the middle of this frozen forest under these circumstances, regardless of how necessary the separation might be. She had as much emotional strength and stability as she had beauty.

Not far north along the ridge line, he found where the deer trail continued, and they followed it down into the next valley. The path made two switchback turns to avoid the steepest slopes and take full advantage of the friendliest contours of the land. Charlie hoped to lead them most of the way to the bottom before turning back to set the trap for Spivey's people. In five minutes, however, because the deer trail added distance as well as ease to the journey downward, they had not reached the floor of the valley, were not even halfway there.

He found a place where the trail turned a corner and passed under a rocky overhang, creating a protected hollow, not a full-fledged cave but the next best thing, out of the wind and out of what little snow sifted down through the trees. At the far end of the niche, opposite the curve in the trail, the hillside bulged out, forming a wall, so that the natural shelter was enclosed on three of its four sides.

"Wait here for me," Charlie said. "Better break off some of the dead branches toward the center of that big spruce over there, start a fire."

"But you'll only be gone . . . what . . . twenty or twenty-five minutes? Doesn't seem like it's worth the effort to build a fire just for that long."

"We've been moving ever since we left the cabin," he said. "We've continuously generated body heat. But sitting here, unmoving, you'll start to notice the cold more."

"We're wearing insulated—"

"Doesn't matter. You'll probably still need the fire. If you don't, Joey will. He doesn't have an adult's physical resources."

"All right. Or . . . we could keep moving, heading down along the deer trail, until you catch up with us."

"No. It's too easy to get lost in these woods. There might be branches in the trail. You might even pass one without seeing it, but I might see it, and then I wouldn't know for sure which way you went."

She nodded.

He said, "Build the fire here, on the trail, but just out beyond the overhang. That way the smoke won't collect under here with you, but you'll still be able to feel the heat."

"Won't they see the smoke?" Christine asked.

"No. They're still beyond the ridge, with no clear view of the sky." He quickly unstrapped the snowshoes from his backpack. "Doesn't matter if they see it, anyway. I'll be between you and them, and I hope to take out at least one of them, maybe two, and make them lie low for at least ten minutes. By the time they get started again, this fire'll be out, and we'll be on down in the valley." He hurriedly slipped off his backpack, dropped it, kept only his rifle and pocketsful of ammunition. "Now I've got to get back up there."

She kissed him.

Joey seemed unaware of his departure.

He headed back the way they had come, along the narrow deer path, not exactly running, but hurrying, because it was going to take longer to go up than it had to come down, and he didn't have a lot of time to waste.

Leaving Christine and Joey alone in the forest was the most difficult thing he had ever done.

Joey and Chewbacca waited under the rocky overhang while Christine went into the trees to collect dead wood for a fire. Underneath the huge spreading branches that were green and healthy, close to the trunks, the evergreens provided a lot of dead branches thick with old pine cones and crisp brown needles that would make excellent tinder. These were all dry because the upper, living branches stopped the snow far above. Furthermore, the weight of those snow-bent upper branches had cracked and splintered the dead wood underneath, so she found it relatively easy to wrench and break off the kindling she needed. She swiftly assembled a big pile of it.

In short order, with a squirt of lighter fluid and a single match, she had a roaring blaze in front of the cul-de-sac where she and Joey and the dog took shelter. As soon as she felt the warmth of the fire, she realized how deeply the cold had sunk into her bones in spite of all the winter clothing she wore, and she knew it would have been dangerous to wait here, unmoving, without the fire.

Joey slumped back against a wall of rock and stared at the fire with a blank expression, with eyes that looked like two flat ovals of polished glass, empty of everything except the reflection of the leaping flames.

The dog settled down and began to lick one paw, then the other. Christine wasn't sure if its feet were just bruised or cut, but she could see that it was hurting a little, even though it didn't whine or whimper.

Around them the stone began to absorb the heat from the bonfire, and because the wind didn't reach into the cul-de-sac, the air was soon surprisingly warm.

Sitting next to Joey, Christine pulled off her gloves, zipped open one of the pockets in her insulated jacket, and took out a box of shotgun shells. She opened the box and put it beside the gun, which was already loaded. That was in case Charlie never came back . . . and in case someone else did.

CHAPTER 60

BY THE TIME Charlie reached the top of the ridge, he was short of breath, and a stabbing pain thrust rhythmically through his thighs and calves. His back and shoulders and neck ached as if the heavy pack was still strapped to him, and he repeatedly had to shift the rifle from hand to hand because the muscles in both arms were weary and aching, too.

He was not out of shape; back in Orange County, when life had been normal, he had gone to the gym twice a week, and he had run five miles every other morning. If *he* was beginning to tire, what must Christine and Joey feel like? Even if he could kill a couple more of Spivey's fanatics, how much longer could Christine and Joey go on?

He tried to put that question out of his mind. He didn't want to think about it because he suspected the answer would not be encouraging.

Running in a crouch because the wind along the ridge had grown violent enough to stagger him, he crossed the narrow rocky plateau. Snow was falling so thickly now that, on the treeless summit, visibility was reduced to fifteen or twenty yards, considerably less when the wind gusted. He had never seen such snow in his life; it seemed as if it were not just coming down in flakes but in cold-welded agglomerations of flakes, in clumps and wads. If he hadn't known exactly where he was going, he might have become disoriented, might have wasted precious time floundering back and forth on the ridge, but he moved unerringly to a jumble of weather-smoothed boulders along the crest and flopped down on his stomach at a place he had chosen earlier.

Here, he could lie at the very lip of the slope, in a gap between two lumpy outcroppings in a long series of granite formations, and look straight down a winding section of the deer trail that he and Christine and Joey had climbed and along which the Twilighters were certain to ascend. He inched forward, peered down into the trees, and was startled by movement hardly more than a hundred yards below. He quickly brought the rifle up, looked through the telescopic sight, and saw two people.

Jesus.

They were here already.

But only two? Where were the others?

He saw that this pair was moving up toward a blind spot in the trail, and he figured they must be the last in the party. The others, ahead of these two, had already gone around the bend and would soon reappear higher on the path.

Of the two who were in sight, the first was of average size, wearing dark clothing. The second was a strikingly tall man in a blue ski suit over which he was wearing a hooded brown parka, his face framed in a fringe of fur lining.

The giant in the parka must be the man Charlie had seen in Spivey's rectory office, the monster Kyle. Charlie shuddered. Kyle gave him the creeps every bit as much as Mother Grace did.

Charlie had expected to have to wait here awhile, ten minutes or even longer, before they came into sight, but now they were almost on top of him. They must be climbing without pause, without scouting the way ahead, reckless, unafraid of an ambush. If he'd been a couple of minutes slower getting here, he would have walked right into them as they came over the crest.

The deer trail turned a corner. The two Twilighters moved out of sight behind a rock, around a stand of interlaced pines and fir.

His heart racing, he shifted his sights to the point at which the trail emerged from those trees. He saw an open stretch of about eight yards in which he would be able to draw down on his targets. The distance between him and them would be only about seventy yards, which meant each round would be approximately one and three-quarters inches high when it impacted, so he would need to aim for the lower part of the chest in order to put a slug through the heart. Depending on how close together the bastards were, as many as three of them might have moved into that clear area before the first would be drawing close to the next blind spot. But he didn't think he would be able to pick off all three, partly because each would be in the way of the other; one target would have to fall to give him a good line on the next. They were also sure to leap for cover as the first shot slammed through the woods. He might bring down the second one during that mad rush for shelter, but the third would be hidden before he could realign his sights.

He would hope for two.

The first appeared, stepping out of shadows into a gray fall of light that splashed down in a gap among the trees. He put the cross hairs on target, and he saw it was a woman. A rather pretty young woman. He hesitated. A second Twilighter appeared, and Charlie swung the scope on that target. Another woman, less pretty and not as young as the first.

Very clever. They were putting the females first in hope of foiling an ambush. They were counting on his having compunctions about killing women, compunctions *they* did not have. It was almost amusing. *They* were the churchfolk, and they believed they were God's agents and that he was an infidel, yet they saw no contradiction in the fact that *his* moral code might be more demanding and inviolable than theirs.

Their plan might have worked, too, if he hadn't served in Vietnam. But fifteen years ago he had lost two close friends, had almost died himself, when a village woman had come to greet them, smiling, and then had blown herself up when they stopped to talk with her. These were not the first fanatics he had ever dealt with, although the others had been motivated by politics rather than religion. No difference, really. Both politics and religion could sometimes be a poison. And he knew that the mindless hatred and the thirst for violence that infected a true believer could turn a woman into a rabid killer every bit as deadly as any *man* with a mission. Institutionalized madness and savagery knew no limitations as to gender.

He had Joey and Christine to consider. If he spared these women, they would kill the woman he loved and her son.

They'll kill me, too, he thought.

He was repelled by the need to shoot her, but he brought his sights back to the first woman, put the cross hairs on her chest. Fired.

She was lifted off her feet and pitched off the deer path. Dead, she slammed into the bristling branches of a black spruce, bringing a small avalanche of snow off its boughs and onto her head.

Then a bad thing happened.

Christine had just put more fuel on the fire and had settled down beside Joey again, under the rock overhang, when she heard the first rifle blast echo down through the forest.

Chewbacca raised his head, his ears pricking up.

Other shots were fired a second or so after the first, but they weren't from Charlie's rifle. There was a steady chatter of shots, a thunderous metallic *ack-ack-ack-ack* which she recognized from old movies, the blood-freezing voice of an automatic weapon, maybe a machine gun. It was a cold, ugly, terrifying sound, filling the forest, and she thought that, if Death laughed, *this* was how he would sound.

She knew Charlie was in trouble.

Charlie didn't even have time to line up the second shot before the machine gun chattered, scaring the hell out of him. For a moment the racket of automatic fire echoed and reechoed from a hundred points along the mountain, and it was difficult to tell where it came from. But the events of the past few days had shown that his hard-learned war skills had not been forgotten, and he quickly determined that the gunman was not on the slope below but on the ridge with him, north of his position.

They *had* sent a scout ahead, and the scout had laid a trap.

Pressing hard against the ground, trying to become one with the stone, Charlie wondered why the trap hadn't been sprung earlier. Why hadn't he been gunned down the moment he'd come onto the top of the ridge? Maybe the scout had been inattentive, looking the wrong way. Or maybe the heavy snow had closed around Charlie at just the right time, granting him a temporary cloak of invisibility. That was probably part of the explanation, anyway, because he remembered a particularly thick and whirling squall of snow just as he'd come over the crest.

The machine gun fell silent for a moment.

He heard a series of metallic clinks and a grating noise, and he figured the gunner was replacing the weapon's empty magazine.

Before Charlie could rise up and have a look, the man began to fire again. Bullets ricocheted off the boulders among which Charlie was nestled, spraying chips of granite, and he realized that none of the other shots had been nearly this close. The gunner had been pumping rounds into the rocks north of Charlie. Now the piercing whine of the ricochets moved away, south along the ridge line, and he knew the Twilighter was firing blind, unsure of his target's position.

There was, after all, a chance Charlie could get off the ridge alive.

He got his feet under him, still hiding behind the boulders, keeping low. He shuffled around a bit until he was facing north.

The gunner stopped firing.

Was he just pausing to study the terrain, moving to another position? Or was he changing magazines again?

If the former were the case, then the man was still armed and dangerous; if the latter, he was temporarily defenseless.

Charlie couldn't hear the noises he had heard when the magazine had been changed before, but he couldn't squat here and wait forever, so he jumped up anyway, straight up, and *there* was his nemesis, only twenty feet away, standing in the snow. It was a man in brown insulated pants and a dark parka, *not* changing the machine gun's magazine but squinting at the ridge plateau beyond Charlie—until Charlie popped up and caught his attention. He cried out and swung the muzzle of the machine gun toward Charlie.

But Charlie had the element of surprise on his side and got off a round first. It struck the Twilighter in the throat.

The man appeared to take a great jump backwards, swinging his automatic weapon straight up and letting off a useless burst of fire at the snow-filled sky as he collapsed. His neck had been ripped apart, his spinal cord severed, and his head nearly taken off. Death had been instantaneous.

And in the instant Death embraced the machine gunner, as the sound of Charlie's shot split the cold air, he saw that there was a second man on the ridge, thirty feet behind the first and over to the right, near the rocky crest. This one had a rifle, and he fired even as Charlie recognized the danger.

As if battered by a sledgehammer, Charlie was spun around and knocked down. He struck the ground hard and lay behind the boulders, out of sight of the rifleman, out of the line of fire, safe but not for long. His left arm, left shoulder, and the left side of his chest suddenly felt cold, very cold, and numb. Although there was no pain yet, he knew he had been hit. Solidly hit. It was bad.

CHAPTER 61

THE SCREAMS BROUGHT Christine out of the cul-de-sac, past the dying fire, onto the trail.

She looked up toward the ridge. She couldn't see all the way to the top of the valley wall, of course. It was too far. The snow and the trees blocked her view.

The screaming went on and on. God, it was awful. In spite of the distance and the muffling effect of the forest, it was a horrible, bloodcurdling shriek of pain and terror. She shivered, and not because of the cold air.

It sounded like Charlie.

No. She was letting her imagination run away with her. It could have been anyone. The sound was too far away, too distorted by the trees for her to be able to say that it was Charlie.

It went on for half a minute or maybe even longer. It *seemed* like an hour. Whoever he was, he was screaming his guts out up there, one scream atop the other, until *she* wanted to scream, too. Then it subsided, faded, as if the screamer suddenly had insufficient energy to give voice to his agony.

Chewbacca came out onto the trail and looked up toward the top of the valley.

Silence settled in.

Christine waited.

Nothing.

She returned to the sheltered niche, where Joey sat in a stupor, and picked up the shotgun.

It was a shoulder wound. Serious. His entire arm was numb, and he couldn't move his hand. Damned serious. Maybe mortal. He wouldn't know until he could get out of his jacket and thermal underwear and have a look at it—or until he began to pass out. If he lost consciousness in this bitter cold, he would die, regardless of whether the Twilighters came along to finish him off.

As soon as he realized he was hit, Charlie screamed, not because the pain was so bad (for there was no pain yet), and not because he was scared (though he was *damned* scared), but because he wanted the man who had shot him to *know* that he was hit. He shrieked as a man might if he were watching his own entrails pour out of a grievous wound in his stomach, screamed as if he knew he were dying, and as he screamed he turned onto his back, stretched out flat in the snow, pushed the rifle aside because it was of little use to him now that he no longer had two good hands. He unzipped his jacket, pulled the revolver out of his shoulder holster. Keeping the gun in his good right hand, he tucked that arm under him, so his body concealed the weapon. His useless left arm was flung out at his side, the hand turned with the palm up, limp. He began to punctuate his screams with desperate gasping sounds; then he let the screams subside, though putting an even more horrible groan into them. Finally he went silent.

The wind died down for a moment, as if cooperating with Charlie. The mountain was tomb-quiet.

He heard movement beyond the boulders that screened him from the gunman. Boots on snow-free stone. A few quick footsteps. Then wary silence. Then a few more footsteps.

He was counting on this man being an amateur, like the guy with the machine gun. A pro would be shooting when he came around the granite formation. But an amateur would want to believe the screams, would be congratulating himself on a good kill, and would be vulnerable.

Footsteps. Closer. Very close now.

Charlie opened his eyes wide and stared straight up at the gray sky. The rock formation kept some of the falling snow out of his way, but flakes still dropped onto his face, onto his eyelashes, and he needed all of his will power to keep from blinking.

He let his mouth sag open, but he held his breath because it would spiral up in a frosty plume and thus betray him.

A second passed. Five seconds. Ten.

In another half minute or so, he would need to breathe.

His eyes were beginning to water.

Suddenly this seemed like a bad plan. Stupid. He was going to die here. He had to think of something better, more clever.

Then the Twilighter appeared, edging around the hump of granite.

Charlie stared fixedly at the sky, playing dead; therefore, he couldn't see what the stranger looked like; he was aware of him only peripherally. But he felt sure that his performance as a corpse was convincing, and well it should have been, for he had provided a liberal display of his own blood as stage dressing.

The gunman stepped closer, stood directly over him, looking down, grinning.

Charlie had to strain not to focus on him, had to continue to look straight through him. It wasn't easy. The eye was naturally drawn toward movement.

The stranger still had a rifle and was still on his feet, better armed and more agile than Charlie. If he realized Charlie was still alive, he could finish the job in a fraction of a second.

A beat.

Another.

Irrationally, Charlie thought: *He'll hear my heart!*

That irrational terror gave rise to a more realistic fear—the possibility that the gunman would see Charlie's pulse beating in his neck or temple. Charlie almost panicked at that thought, almost moved. But he realized that his coat and the attached hood concealed both his neck and his temples; he would not be betrayed by his own throbbing blood flow.

Then the Twilighter stepped past him, to the lip of the ridge, and shouted down to his fellow churchmen on the slope below. "I got him! I got the son of a bitch!"

The moment the gunman's attention was elsewhere, Charlie rolled slightly to the left, freeing his right hand, which had been under his buttocks, bringing up the revolver.

The Twilighter gasped, began to turn.

Charlie shot him twice. Once in the side. Once in the head.

The man went over the brink, crashed through some brush, rolled down between the trees, and came to a stop against the broad trunk of a pine, dead before he even had a chance to scream.

Turning onto his stomach, Charlie pulled himself to the edge of the ridge and looked down. Some of Spivey's people had come out of hiding in response to the rifleman's shout of triumph. Apparently, not all of them realized their enemy was still alive. Most likely they thought the two subsequent shots had been fired by their own man, to make sure Charlie was dead, and they probably figured the body toppling off the crest was Charlie's. They didn't dive for cover again until he shouted, "Bastards," and squeezed off two rounds from the revolver. Then, like a pack of rats smelling a cat, they scuttled into safe dark places.

He loosed the remaining two rounds in the revolver, not expecting to hit anyone, not even taking aim, intending only to frighten them and force them to lie low for a while.

"I got both of them!" he shouted. "They're both dead. How come they're both dead if God's on *your* side?"

No one below responded.

The shouting winded him. He waited a moment, drawing several deep breaths, not wanting them to hear any weakness in his voice. Then he shouted again: "Why don't you stand up and let God stop the bullets when I shoot at you?"

No answer.

"That would prove something, wouldn't it?"

No answer.

He took several long, slow breaths.

He tried flexing his left hand, and the fingers moved, but they were still numb and stiff.

Wondering whether he had killed enough of them to make them turn back, he did a little arithmetic. He had killed two on the ridge top, one on the trail, three down in the meadow where they had huddled around the Jeep and the snowmobiles. Six dead. Six of ten. How many did that leave in the woods below him? Three? He thought he'd seen three others down there: another woman, Kyle, and the man who had been in front of Kyle, toward the end of the line. But wouldn't at least one of them have stayed behind with Mother Grace? Surely she wouldn't have remained alone at the cabin. And she wouldn't have been able to come up here, on such an arduous hike. Would she? Or was she there among the trees right now, only sixty or seventy yards away, crouching in the shadows like an evil old troll?

"I'm going to wait right here," he shouted.

He fished half a dozen cartridges out of a jacket pocket and, hampered by having only one good hand, reloaded the revolver.

"Sooner or later, you're going to have to move," Charlie called down to them. "You'll have to stretch your muscles, or you'll cramp up." His voice sounded eerie in the snowy stillness. "You'll cramp up, and you'll slowly start freezing to death."

The anesthetizing shock of being shot was beginning to wear off. His nerves began to respond, and the first dull pain crept into his shoulder and arm.

"Any time you're ready," he shouted, "let's test your faith. Let's see if you *really* believe God is on your side. Any time you're ready, just stand up and let me take a shot at you, and let's see if God turns the bullets away."

He waited half a minute, until he was sure they weren't going to respond, and then he holstered his revolver and eased away from the crest. They wouldn't know he had left. They might suspect, but they couldn't be sure. They would be pinned down for half an hour, maybe longer, before they finally decided to risk continuing their ascent. At least he hoped to God they would. He needed every minute he could get.

With the dull pain in his shoulder rapidly growing sharper, he belly-crawled all the way across the flat top of the ridge, moving like a crippled crab, and didn't stand up until he had reached the place where the land sloped down and the deer trail headed off through the trees.

When he tried to rise, he found his legs were surprisingly weak; they crumpled under him, and he dropped back to the ground, jarring his injured arm — Christ!—and felt a big black wave roaring toward him. He held his breath and closed his eyes and waited until the wave had passed, refusing to be carried away by it. The pain was not dull any longer; it was a stinging, burning, *gnawing* pain, as if a living creature had burrowed into his shoulder and was now eating its way out. It was bad enough when he was perfectly still, but the slightest movement made it ten times worse. However, he couldn't just lie here. Regardless of the pain, he had to get up, return to Christine. If he was going to die, he didn't want to be alone in these woods when his time came. Christ, that was inexcusably negative thinking, wasn't it? Mustn't think about dying. The thought is father to the deed, right? The pain was bad, but that didn't mean the wound was mortal. He hadn't come this far to give up so easily. There was a chance. Always a chance. He had been an optimist all his life. He had survived two abusive, drunken parents. He had survived poverty. He had survived the war. He would survive this, too, dammit. He crawled off the plateau, onto the deer trail. Just over the edge of the crest, he grabbed a branch on a spruce and pulled himself upright at last, leaning on the trunk of the tree for support.

He wasn't dizzy, and that was a good sign. After he had taken several deep breaths and had stood there against the tree for a minute, his legs became less rubbery. The pain from the wound did not subside, but he found that he was gradually adjusting to it; he either had to adjust or escape it by surrendering consciousness, which was a luxury he could not afford.

He moved away from the tree, gritting his teeth as the fire in his shoulder blazed up a bit higher, and he descended along the deer path, moving faster than he had thought he could, though not as fast as he had come down the first time, when Christine and Joey had been with him. He was in a hurry, but he was also cautious, afraid of slipping, falling, and further injuring his shoulder and arm. If he fell on his left side, he would probably pass out from the subsequent explosion of pain, and then he might not come around again until Spivey's people were standing over him, poking him with the barrel of a gun.

Sixty or seventy yards below the ridge, he realized he should have brought the machine gun with him. Perhaps there were a couple of spare magazines of ammunition on the dead gunner's body. That would even the odds a bit. With a machine gun, he might be able to set up another ambush and wipe out all of them this time.

He stopped and looked back, wondering if he should return for the weapon. The rising trail behind him looked steeper than he remembered it. In fact the climb appeared as challenging as the most difficult face on Mount Everest. He breathed harder just looking up at it. As he studied it, the path seemed to grow even steeper. Hell, it looked *vertical.* He didn't have the strength to go back, and he cursed himself for not thinking of the machine gun while he was up there; he realized he wasn't as clearheaded as he thought.

He continued downward.

Twenty yards farther along the trail, the forest seemed to spin around him. He halted and planted his legs wide, as if he could bring the carrousel of trees to a stop just by digging in his heels. He *did* slow it down, but he couldn't stop it altogether, so he finally proceeded cautiously, putting one foot in front of the other with the measured deliberation of a drunkard trying to prove sobriety to a cop.

The wind had grown stronger, and it made quite a racket in the huge trees. Some of the tallest creaked as the higher, slenderer portions of their trunks swayed in the inconstant gusts. The woody branches clattered together, and the shaken evergreen needles clicked-rustled-hissed. The creaking grew louder until it sounded like a thousand doors opening on unoiled hinges, and the clicking and rustling and hissing grew louder, too, thunderous, until the noise was painful, until he felt as if he were inside a drum, and he staggered, stumbled, nearly fell, realized that most of the sound wasn't coming from the wind in the trees but from his own body, realized he was hearing his own blood roar in his ears as his heart pounded faster and faster. Then the forest began to spin again, and as it spun it pulled darkness down from the sky like thread from a spool, more and more darkness, and now the whirling forest didn't seem like a carrousel but like a loom, weaving the threads of darkness into a black cloth, and the cloth billowed around him, settled over him, and he couldn't see where he was going, stumbled again, and fell—

Pain!

A bright blast.

Darkness.

Blackness.

Deeper than night.

Silence . . .

He was crawling through pitch blackness, frantically searching for Joey. He had to find the boy soon. He had learned that Chewbacca wasn't an ordinary dog but a robot, an evil construction, packed full of explosives. Joey didn't know the truth. He was probably playing with the dog right this minute. Any second now, Spivey would press the plunger, and the dog would blow up, and Joey would be dead. He crawled toward a gray patch in the darkness, and then he was in a bedroom, and he saw Joey sitting up in bed. Chewbacca was there, too, sitting up just like a person, holding a knife in one paw and fork in the other. The boy and the dog were both eating steak. Charlie said, "For God's sake, what're you eating?" And the boy said, "It's delicious." Charlie got to his feet beside the bed and took the meat away from the boy. The dog snarled. Charlie said, "Don't you see? The meat's been poisoned. They've poisoned you." "No," Joey said, "it's good. You should try some." "Poison! It's poison!" Then Charlie remembered the explosives that were hidden in the dog, and he started to warn Joey, but it was too late. The explosion came. Except it wasn't the dog that exploded. It was Joey. His chest blew open, and a horde of rats surged out of it, just like the rat in the battery room under the windmill, and they rushed at Charlie. He staggered backward, but they surged up his legs. They were all over him, scores of rats, and they bit him, and he fell, dragged down by their numbers, and his blood poured out of him, and it was cold blood, cold instead of warm, and he screamed—

—and woke, gagging. He could feel cold blood all over his face, and he wiped at it, looked at his hand. It wasn't actually blood; it was snow.

He was lying on his back in the middle of the deer path, looking up at the trees and at a section of gray sky from which snow fell at a fierce rate. With considerable effort, he sat up. His throat was full of phlegm. He coughed and spat.

How long had he been unconscious?

No way to tell.

As far as he could see, the trail leading up toward the crest of the ridge was deserted. Spivey's people hadn't yet come after him. He couldn't have been out for long.

The pain in his arm and shoulder had sent questing tendrils across his back and chest, up his neck, into his skull. He tried to raise his arm and had some success, and he could move his hand a little without making the pain any worse.

He squirmed to the nearest tree and attempted to pull himself up, but he couldn't do it. He waited a moment, tried again, failed again.

Christine. Joey. They were counting on him.

He would have to crawl for a while. Just till his strength returned. He tried it, on hands and knees, putting most of his weight on his right arm, but demanding some help from his left, and to his surprise he was able to shuffle along at a decent pace. Where the angle of the slope allowed him to accept gravity's assistance, he slid down the trail, sometimes as far as four or five yards, before coming to a stop.

He wasn't sure how far he had to go before reaching the rocky overhang under which he had left Christine and Joey. It might be around the next bend —or it might be hundreds of yards away. He had lost his ability to judge distance. But he hadn't lost his sense of direction, so he crabbed down toward the valley floor.

A few minutes or a few seconds later, he realized he had lost his rifle. It had probably come off his shoulder when he'd fallen. He ought to go back for it. But maybe it had slipped off the trail, into some underbrush or into a jumble of rocks. It might not be easy to find. He still had his revolver. And Christine had the shotgun. Those weapons would have to be sufficient.

He crawled farther down the trail and came to a fallen tree that barred his

way. He didn't remember that it had been here earlier, though it might have been, and he wondered if he had taken a wrong turn somewhere. But on the first two trips, he hadn't noticed any branches in the trail, so how could he have gone wrong? He leaned against the log—

—and he was in a dentist's office, strapped into a chair. He had grown a hundred teeth in his left shoulder and arm, and as luck would have it all of them were in need of root canal work. The dentist opened the door and came in, and it was Grace Spivey. She had the biggest, nastiest drill he had ever seen, and she wasn't even going to use it on the teeth in his shoulder; she was going to bore a hole straight through his heart—

—and his heart was pounding furiously when he woke and found himself slumped against the fallen log.

Christine.

Joey.

Mustn't fail them.

He climbed over the log, sat on it, wondered if he dared to try walking, decided against it, and slipped down to his knees again. He crawled.

In a while his arm felt better.

It felt *dead*. That was better.

The pain subsided.

He crawled.

If he stopped for a moment and curled up and closed his eyes, the pain would go away altogether. He knew it would.

But he crawled.

He was thirsty and hot in spite of the frigid air. He paused and scooped up some snow and put it in his mouth. It tasted coppery, foul. He swallowed anyway because his throat felt as if it were afire, and the wretched-tasting snow was at least cool.

Now all he needed before moving on again was a moment's rest. The day wasn't bright; nevertheless, the gray light striking down between the trees hurt his eyes. If he could just close them for a moment, shut out the gray glare for a few seconds . . .

CHAPTER 62

CHRISTINE DIDN'T WANT to leave Joey and Chewbacca alone under the overhang, but she had no choice because she knew Charlie was in trouble. It wasn't just the extended gunfire that had worried her. It was partly the screaming, which had stopped some time ago, and partly the fact that he was taking so long. But mainly it was just a hunch. Call it woman's intuition: she *knew* Charlie needed her.

She told Joey she wouldn't go far, just up the trail a hundred yards or so, to see if there was any sign of Charlie. She hugged the boy, asked him if he would be all right, thought he nodded in response, but couldn't get any other reaction from him.

"Don't go anywhere while I'm gone," she said.

He didn't answer.

"Don't you leave here. Understand?"

The boy blinked. He still wasn't focusing on her.

"I love you, honey."

The boy blinked again.

"You watch over him," she told Chewbacca.

The dog snorted.

She took the shotgun and went out onto the trail, past the dying fire. She glanced back. Joey wasn't even looking at her. He was leaning against the rock wall, shoulders hunched, head bowed, hands in his lap, staring at the ground in front of him. Afraid to leave him, but also afraid that Charlie needed her, she turned away and headed up the deer path.

The heat from the fire had done her some good. Her bones and muscles didn't feel as stiff as they had awhile ago; there wasn't so much soreness when she walked.

The trees protected her from most of the wind, but she knew it was blowing furiously, for it made a wild and ghoulish sound as it raged through the highest branches. In those places where the forest parted to reveal patches of leaden sky, the snow came down so thick and fast that it almost seemed like rain.

She had gone no more than eighty yards, around two bends in the trail, when she saw Charlie. He was lying face-down in the middle of the path, head turned to one side.

No.

She stopped a few feet from him. She dreaded going closer because she knew what she would find.

He was motionless.

Dead.

Oh, Jesus, he was dead. They had killed him. She had loved him, and he had loved her, and now he had died for her, and she was sick with the thought of it. The somber, sullen colors of the day seeped into her, and she was filled with a cold grayness, a numbing despair.

But grief had to allow room for fear, as well, because now she and Joey were on their own, and without Charlie she didn't think they would make it out of the mountains. At least not alive. His death was an omen of their own fate.

She studied the woods around her, decided that she was alone with the body. Evidently, Charlie had been hurt up on the ridge top and had managed to come this far under his own steam. Spivey's fanatics were apparently still on the other side of the ridge.

Or maybe he had killed them all.

Slipping the shotgun strap over her shoulder, she went to him, reluctant to examine him more closely, not certain she had the strength to look upon his cold dead face. She knelt beside him—and realized that he was breathing.

Her own breath caught in her throat, and her heart seemed to miss a beat or two.

He was alive.

Unconscious but alive.

Miracles did happen.

She wanted to laugh but repressed the urge, superstitiously afraid that the gods would be displeased by her joy and would take Charlie from her, after all. She touched him. He murmured but didn't come around. She turned him onto his back, and he grumbled at her without opening his eyes. She saw the torn shoulder of his jacket and realized he had been shot. Around the wound, lumps of dark and frozen blood adhered to the shredded fabric. It was bad, but at least he wasn't dead.

"Charlie?"

When he didn't reply, she touched his face and spoke his name again, and finally his eyes opened. For a moment they were out of focus, but then he fixed on her and blinked, and she saw that he was aware, sluggish and perhaps fuzzy-headed but not delirious.

"Lost it," he said.

"What?"

"The rifle."

"Don't worry about it," she said.

"Killed three of them," he said thickly.

"Good."

"Where are they?" he asked worriedly.

"I don't know."

"Must be near."

"I don't think so."

He tried to sit up.

Apparently, a dark current of pain crackled through him, for he winced and held his breath, and for a moment she thought he was going to pass out again.

He was too pale, corpse-white.

He squeezed her hand until the pain subsided a bit.

He said, "Still others coming," and this time he managed to sit up when he tried.

"Can you move?"

"Weak . . ."

"We've got to get out of here."

"Was . . . crawling."

"Can you walk?"

"Not by myself."

"If you lean on me?"

"Maybe."

She helped him to his feet, gave him support, and encouraged him to descend the path. They made slow, halting progress at first, then went a bit faster, and a couple of times they slipped and almost fell, but eventually they reached the overhang.

Joey didn't react to their arrival. But as Christine helped Charlie ease to the ground, Chewbacca came over, wagging his tail, and licked Charlie's face.

The rock walls had absorbed a lot of heat from the fire, which was now little more than embers, and warmth radiated from the stone on all sides.

"Nice," Charlie said.

His voice was too dreamy to suit Christine.

"Light-headed?" she asked.

"A little."

"Dizzy?"

"Was. Not now."

"Blurred vision?"

"Nothing like that."

She said, "I want to see that wound," and she began taking off his jacket.

"No time," he said, putting a hand on hers, stopping her from tending to him.

"I'll be quick about it."

"No *time!*" he insisted.

"Listen," she said, "right now, with all the pain you're in, you can't move fast."

"A damned turtle."

"And you're losing your strength."

"Feel like . . . a little kid."

"But we have a pretty extensive first-aid kit, so maybe we can patch you up and alleviate some of the pain. Then maybe you can get on your feet and get moving faster. If so, we'll be damned glad we took the time."

He thought about it, nodded. "Okay. But . . . keep your ears open. They might not be . . . far away."

She removed his quilted jacket, unbuttoned his shirt, slipped it off his injured shoulder, then unsnapped and pulled back the top of his insulated underwear, which was sticky with blood and sweat. There was an ugly hole in him, high in the left side of his chest, just below the shoulder bones. The sight of it gave her the feeling that live snakes were writhing in her stomach. The worst of the bleeding had stopped, but the flesh immediately around the wound was swollen, an angry shade of red. The skin color faded to purple farther away from the hole, then to a dead-pale white.

"Lot of blood?" he asked.

"There was."

"Now?"

"Still bleeding a little."

"Spurting?"

"No. If an artery had been hit, you'd be dead by now."

"Lucky," he said.

"Very."

An exit wound scarred his back. The flesh looked just as bad on that side, and she thought she saw splinters of bone in the torn and bloody meat of him.

"Bullet's not in you," she said.

"That's a plus."

The first-aid kit was in his backpack. She got it out, opened a small bottle of boric acid solution and poured it into the wound. It foamed furiously for a moment, but it didn't sting as iodine or Merthiolate would have; with a slightly dreamy, detached air, Charlie watched it bubble.

She hastily packed some snow into a tin cup and set it to melt on the hot coals of the burnt-out fire.

He overcame his dreaminess, shook his head as if to clear it, and said "Hurry."

"Doing the best I can," she said.

When the boric acid had finished working, she quickly dusted both the entry and exit wounds with a yellowish antibiotic powder, then with a mild, white anesthetizing powder. Now there was almost no bleeding at all. Taking off her gloves so she could work faster and better, she used cotton pads, gauze pads, and a two-inch-wide roll of gauze to fashion an unsatisfactory and somewhat amateurish bandage, but she fixed it in place with so much white adhesive tape that she knew it would stay put.

"Listen!" he said.

She was very still.

They listened, but there was only the wind in the trees.

"Not them," she said.

"Not yet."

"Chewbacca will warn us if anyone's coming."

The dog was lying beside Joey, at ease.

The icy air had already leeched the stored-up warmth in the stone. Beneath

the rocky overhang, the sheltered niche was growing cold again. Charlie was shivering violently.

She hurriedly dressed him, pulled up the zipper on his jacket, tugged his hood in place and tied it under his chin, then fetched the cupful of melted snow from the embers. The first-aid kit contained Tylenol, which was not nearly a strong enough pain-suppressant for his needs, but it was all they had. She gave him two tablets, hesitated, then a third. At first he had a bit of trouble swallowing, and that worried her, but he said it was just that his mouth and throat were so dry, and by the time he took the third tablet he seemed better.

He wouldn't be able to carry his backpack; they would have to abandon it.

She shook a few items out of her own bag in order to get the first-aid kit into it, secured all the flaps. She slipped her arms through the loops, buckled the last strap across her chest.

She was frantic to get moving. She didn't need a wrist watch to know they were running out of time.

CHAPTER 63

KYLE BARLOWE WAS a big man but not graceless. He could move stealthily and sure-footedly when he put his mind to it. Ten minutes after Harrison killed Denny Rogers and threw his body down from the crest of the ridge, Barlowe moved cautiously from the tangle of dead brush where he had been hiding, and slipped across the face of the slope to a spot where shadows lay like frozen pools of night. From the shadows he dashed catlike to a huge fallen tree, from there to a jagged snout of rock poking up from the hillside. He neither climbed nor descended the slope, moved only laterally, away from the area over which Harrison held dominion, leaving the others pinned down but, with luck, not for long.

After another ten minutes, when he was certain that he was well out of Harrison's sight, Barlowe became less circumspect, rushed boldly up the slope to the crest, crawled over it. He moved through a gap between two rock formations and stood up on the flat, wind-abraded top of the ridge.

He had a Smith & Wesson .357 Magnum in a shoulder holster. He unzipped his jacket long enough to get the revolver.

The snow was coming down so hard that he couldn't see more than twenty feet, sometimes not even that far. The limited visibility didn't worry him. In fact, he figured it was a gift from God. He already knew the spot from which Harrison had been firing on them; he wouldn't have any difficulty finding it. But in the meantime the snow would screen him from Harrison—if the detective was still on the ridge, which was doubtful.

He moved southward, directly into the raging wind. It stung and numbed his face, made him squint. His eyes watered and his nose dripped. But it couldn't stagger him or knock him down; it would have more easily felled one of the massive trees along the ridge line.

In fifty yards he found Morgan Pierce's body. The staring but unseeing eyes did not look human, for they were sheathed by milky cataracts that were actually thin films of crazed ice. The eyebrows and lashes and mustache were frosted. The wind was industriously packing snow in the angles formed by the dead man's arms, legs, and bent neck.

Barlowe was surprised to see that Harrison had not taken Pierce's Uzi, a compact Israeli-made gun. He picked it up, hoping it hadn't been damaged by the snow. He decided he'd better not rely on the Uzi until he had a chance to test it, so he slung it over his shoulder and kept the .357 in his right hand.

Staying close to the granite outcroppings along the eastern crest of the ridge, he crept toward the place from which Harrison had shot at them, from which he had pitched Denny Rogers down the slope. The .357 thrust out in front of him, Barlowe eased around the boulder that formed the northern wall of Harrison's roost—and was not surprised to discover the detective was gone.

The nook between rock formations was somewhat protected from the wind; therefore, some snow had settled and remained within the niche. Brass glinted in the snow: several expended cartridges.

Barlowe also noticed blood on the rocks that formed the walls of that sheltered space: dark, frozen stains on the grayish granite.

He stooped, stared at the cartridges poking out of the white-mantled floor. He brushed away the soft, dry layer of new flakes that had fallen in the past half an hour or so, pushing the expended cartridges aside as well, and he found a lot more blood on the older layer of snow underneath. Denny Rogers' blood? Or was some of it Harrison's? Maybe Rogers *had* wounded the bastard.

He turned away from the eastern crest, stepped across the narrow ridge top, and began searching for the place at which the deer path continued into the next valley. Because the Antichrist and his guardians had followed the trail this far, it was logical to assume they'd continue to follow it down the far side of the ridge. The new snow didn't cling to the wind-blasted plateau, but it was piling up just over the edge of the crest, where the wind didn't hit as hard and where brush and rocks gave it drift points against which it could build, and it obscured the entrance to the deer path. He almost missed the trail, had to kick through a drift, but then saw both deer tracks and human footprints in the more meager carpet of snow under the trees.

He went down the slope a few yards, until he found what he had hoped for: spots of blood. There was no way this could be Denny Rogers' blood. No doubt about it now: Harrison was hurt.

CHAPTER 64

MMM

CHARLIE WAS IMPRESSED but not surprised by how quickly and surely Christine took charge. She got them out on the trail and moving down toward the valley again.

Joey and Chewbacca followed them. The boy said nothing, shuffled along as if he felt they were wasting their time trying to escape. But he didn't stop, didn't fall back, stayed close. The dog took his cue from his master, padding along in silence, his head drooping, his eyes downcast.

Charlie expected to hear shouting on the trail behind them. Minute by minute, he was increasingly sure that gunfire would break out.

But the snow fell, the wind whooped, the trees creaked and rustled, and

Spivey's people did not appear. He must have put a damned good scare into them with that last ambush. They must have stayed where he'd left them for at least half an hour, afraid to crawl out of hiding, and when they *had* begun to move, they must have proceeded to the ridge top with extreme caution.

It was too much to hope they had given up and turned back. They would never give up. He had learned that much about them, anyway. Denton Boothe, his fat psychologist friend, had been right: Only death would stop this breed of fanatic.

As it wound down the lower half of the valley wall, the deer trail took a more wandering route than before. They were not going to reach the bottom as fast as they had anticipated.

During the first twenty minutes, Charlie didn't need much help. For the most part the path was gentle and undemanding. A few times he had to grab a tree or put one hand against a pillar of rock to keep his balance, and twice, when the land sloped too steeply, he leaned on Christine, but he didn't hang on her constantly. In fact he got along considerably better than he had thought possible when they'd started out.

Although the Tylenol and the antibiotic powder had taken the edge off the pain in his shoulder and arm, it was still bad. In fact, even softened by the drugs, it was so intense that he would have expected to be incapacitated by it, but he discovered he had more tolerance for pain than he had thought; he was adapting to it, grinding his teeth into calcium sand and cutting permanent lines of agony in his face, but adapting.

After twenty minutes, however, his strength began to ebb, and he needed Christine's help more often. They reached the valley floor in twenty-five minutes, by which time he was beginning to get slightly dizzy again. Five minutes later, when they came to the edge of a broad meadow, where twin hammers of snow and wind pounded the land, he had to stop and rest while still in the shelter of the woods. He sat under a pine and leaned against the trunk.

Joey sat beside him but said nothing, didn't even acknowledge his presence. Charlie was too weary to attempt to elicit a word or a smile from the boy.

Chewbacca licked his paws. They were bleeding a little.

Christine sat, too, and took out the map that Charlie had spread on the table at the cabin, yesterday, when he'd insisted on showing her how they would get out of the mountains if Spivey's people arrived and tried to corner them. Christ, how unlikely such a situation had seemed then, and how terribly inevitable it seemed now!

Christine had to fold and refold the map, keeping it small while she studied it, because the wind occasionally broke out of the meadow and lashed between the trees, reaching some distance into the dense forest to slap and poke and grab at everything in its path.

Beyond the perimeter of the woods, a fierce blizzard raged across the valley floor. The wind was from the southwest, roaring like an express train from one end of the valley to the other, harrying sheets of snow in front of it. The snow was so thick that, most of the time, you could see only about a third of the way across the meadow, where the world appeared to end in a blank white wall. But occasionally the wind subsided for a few seconds or briefly changed directions, and the hundreds of opaque curtains of snow fluttered and parted at the same instant, and in the distance you could see more trees crowding the other side of the meadow, and then the far wall of the somewhat narrow valley, and beyond that another faraway ridge crest where ice and rock shone like chrome even in the sunless gloom.

According to the map, a little creek cut through the middle of the meadow and ran the length of the valley. She looked up, squinted at the white maelstrom beyond the forest, but she couldn't see the creek out there, not even when the snow parted. She figured it was frozen over and covered with snow. If they followed the creek (instead of crossing the meadow into the next arm of the woods), they would eventually come to the upper end of a narrow draw that sloped down toward the lake, for this was a high valley that funneled southwest, and they were still far above Tahoe. Yesterday, when he had first brought out the map, Charlie had said they would follow this route if they had to leave the cabin and take to the wilds, but that had been before he was shot. It was a three- or four-mile hike to civilization from here, not a discouragingly long way—*if* you were in good physical condition. However, now that he was wounded and weak, and with a full-scale blizzard moving in, there was absolutely no hope of getting down to the lake by that route. In their circumstances, three or four miles was a journey every bit as epic as a trek across China.

She desperately searched the map for some other way out or for some indication of shelter, and after consulting the key several times to interpret the cartographer's symbols, she discovered the caves. They were along this same side of the valley, half a mile northeast of here. Judging by the map, the caves were a point of interest for those hardy hikers who were curious about ancient Indian wall paintings and who had a mania for collecting arrowheads. Christine could not determine whether it was just one or two small caves or an extensive network of them, but she figured they would be at least large enough to serve as a place to hide from both Spivey's fanatics and the murderous weather.

She moved closer to Charlie, put her head to his in order to be heard above the cacophonous wind, and told him what she had in mind. He was in complete agreement, and his confidence in her plan gave her more faith in it. She stopped worrying about whether going to the caves was a wise decision, and she *started* worrying about whether they would be able to make it there through the storm.

"We could walk northeast through the woods, following the base of the valley wall," she told Charlie, "but that would leave a trail."

"Whereas, if we went out into the meadow before heading up the valley, if we traveled out there in the open, the storm would obliterate our tracks in no time."

"Yes."

"Spivey's people would lose us right here," he said.

"Exactly. Of course, to reach the caves, we'd have to re-enter the woods farther north, but there's not a chance in a million that they'd pick up our trail again. For one thing, they'll be expecting us to head *down* the valley, southwest, toward the lake, 'cause civilization is that direction."

"Right." He licked his cracked lips. "There's nothing at all northeast of us but . . . more wilderness."

"They won't look for us in that neighborhood—will they?" Christine asked.

"I doubt it," he said. "Let's get moving."

"Walking out there in the open, in the wind and snow . . . isn't going to be easy," she said.

"I'm all right. I can make it."

He didn't *look* as if he could make it. He didn't look as if he could even get up. His eyes were watery and bloodshot. His face was gaunt and shockingly pale, and his lips were bloodless.

"But you've got to . . . look out for Joey," Charlie said. "Better cut a piece of line . . . put him on a tether."

That was a good suggestion. Out in the open field, visibility was only a dozen yards in the best moments, declining to less than four yards when the wind whipped up and the snow squalled. It would be easy for Joey to wander a few steps off course, and once they were separated, they would find it difficult if not impossible to locate each other again. She cut a length of rope from the coil that hung on her backpack and made a tether that allowed the boy six feet of play; she linked them, waist to waist.

Charlie repeatedly, nervously looked back the way they had come.

Christine was more disturbed by the fact that Chewbacca, too, was watching the trail along which they'd come. He was still lying down, still relatively calm, but his ears had perked up, and he was growling softly in the back of his throat.

She helped Charlie and Joey put on their ski masks because they would need them now, whether or not the eye holes restricted their vision. She put on her own mask, replaced her hood, pulled the drawstring tight under her chin.

Joey rose without being told. She decided that was a good sign. He still seemed lost, detached, uninterested in what was happening around him, but at least on a subconscious level he knew it was time to go, which meant he wasn't *completely* beyond reach.

Christine helped Charlie get to his feet.

He looked bad.

This last half mile to the caves was going to be sheer torture for him. But there was nothing else they could do.

Keeping one hand on Charlie's good arm, ready to provide support if he needed it, tethered to Joey, she led them into the meadow. The wind was a raging beast. The air temperature was at least twenty below zero. The snowflakes were not really flakes any more; they had shrunk to tiny, crystal pellets that bounced off Christine's insulated clothing with a sharp ticking sound. If Hell was cold instead of hot, this was what it must be like.

CHAPTER 65

ASHES AND HALF-BURNED black branches were all that remained of the fire that had recently flourished in the middle of the deer path. Kyle Barlowe kicked at the charred detritus, scattering it.

He stepped under the rocky overhang and looked at the abandoned backpack. There were scraps of paper in one corner of the rocky niche, wrappers from prepackaged gauze bandages.

"You were right," Burt Tully said. "The man's been hurt."

"Bad enough so he can't carry his pack any more," Barlowe said, turning away from the abandoned gear.

"But I'm still not sure we should go after him, just the four of us," Tully said. "We need reinforcements."

"There's no time to go for them," Kyle Barlowe said.

"But he . . . he's killed so many of us."

"Are you turning yellow on us?"

"No, no," Tully said, but he looked scared.

"You're a soldier now," Barlowe said. "With God's protection."

"I know. It's just . . . this guy . . . Harrison . . . he's damned *good.*"

"Not as good as he was before Denny shot him."

"But *he* shot Denny! He must still have a lot on the ball."

Impatiently, Kyle said, "You saw the place farther back on the trail, where he fell. There was *more* blood there, where she came and helped him."

"But reinforcements—"

"Forget it," Kyle said, pushing past him.

He had his doubts, too, and he wondered if he was being sharp with Burt only to push his own second-thoughts out of his mind.

Edna Vanoff and Mother Grace were waiting on the trail.

The old woman didn't look well. Her eyes were bloodshot, deeply sunken, pinched half shut by the sooty flesh that ringed them. She stood round-shouldered, bent at the waist, the very image of exhaustion.

Barlowe was amazed that she had come this far. He had wanted her to stay back at the cabin, with guards, but she had insisted on going farther into the mountains with them. He knew she was a vital woman, possessed of considerable strength and stamina for her age, but he was surprised by her unflagging progress through the woods. Occasionally they had to help her over a rough spot, and once he had even carried her for thirty yards or so, but for the most part she had made it on her own.

"How long ago did they leave this place?" Grace asked him, her voice as cracked and bloodless as her lips.

"Hard to say. Fire's cold, but in this weather the embers would cool off real fast."

Burt Tully said, "If Harrison is as badly wounded as we think, they can't be making good time. We must be closing on them. We can afford to go slowly, be careful, and make sure we don't walk into another ambush."

Grace said, "No, if they're close, let's hurry, get it over with."

She turned, took one step, stumbled, fell.

Barlowe lifted her to her feet. "I'm worried about you, Mother."

She said, "I'm fine."

But Edna Vanoff said, "Mother, you look . . . wrung out."

"Maybe we should rest here a few minutes," Burt said.

"No!" Mother Grace said. Her bloodshot eyes transfixed them, each in turn. "Not a few minutes. Not even *one* minute. We don't dare give the boy a second more than we have to. I've told you . . . each second he lives, his power increases. I've told you a thousand times!"

Barlowe said, "But Mother, if anything happens to you, the rest of us won't be able to go on."

He flinched from the penetrating power of her eyes. And now her voice had a special quality that entered it only when she was having a vision, a piercing resonance that vibrated in his bones: "If I fail, you *must* go on. You *will* go on. It's blasphemy to say your allegiance is to me rather than to God. You *will* go on until your own legs fail, until you can't *crawl* another foot. And then you will *still* go on, or God will have no pity on you. No pity and no mercy. If you fail Him in this, He will let your souls be conscripted into the armies of *Hell.*"

Some people were not swayed when Mother Grace spoke to them in this manner. Some heard nothing but the ranting of an old fool. Some fled as if she were threatening them. Some laughed. But Kyle Barlowe had always been humbled. He was still enthralled by her voice.

But will I be enthralled and obedient when she finally tells me to kill the boy? Or will I resist the violence that I used to thrive upon? Wrong-thought.

They left the rocky overhang, headed down the deer trail, Barlowe leading, Edna Vanoff second, Mother Grace third, and Burt Tully bringing up the rear. The howling of the wind seemed like a great demonic voice, and to Barlowe it was a constant reminder of the malignant forces that were even now conspiring to take control of the earth.

CHAPTER 66

〃〃〃

CHRISTINE WAS BEGINNING to think they would never get out of the meadow alive.

This was worse than a blizzard. It was a white-out, with the wind so strong it would have been a hurricane in a tropical climate, and with the snow coming down so hard and so fast that she couldn't see more than two or three feet ahead. The world had vanished; she was moving through a nightmare landscape without detail, a world composed solely of snow and gray light; she could not see the forest on any side. She couldn't always see Joey when he ranged to the end of the tether. It was terrifying. And although the light was gray and diffuse, there was an all-pervading glare that made her eyes burn, and she realized that the threat of snow-blindness was very real. What would they do if they had to feel their way through the meadow, sightless, seeking the northeast end of the valley by instinct alone? She knew the answer: They would die. She paused every thirty steps to look at the compass, sheltering it in her gloved hands, and although she tried to move always in a straight line, she found, on several occasions, that they were heading in the wrong direction, and she had to correct their course.

Even if they didn't get disoriented and lost, they could die out here if they didn't move fast enough, for it was colder than she had ever thought it could be, so cold that she wouldn't have been surprised if she had suddenly frozen solid, upright, in mid-stride.

She was worried sick about Joey, but he stayed on his feet and plodded along at her side long after she expected him to drop. His quasi-catatonic withdrawal was, ironically, of benefit to him in these circumstances; having tuned out the real world, he was less affected by the cold and wind than he otherwise might have been. Even so, the elements would take their toll of him in time. She would soon have to get him off the meadow, into the comparative shelter of the forest, whether or not they reached the area in which the caves were situated.

Charlie fared worse than the boy. He stumbled frequently, went to his knees a couple of times. After five minutes, he occasionally leaned on Christine for support. After ten minutes, he needed her more than occasionally. After fifteen, he required her support constantly, and they were slowed to little more than a shuffle.

She couldn't tell either him or Joey that she was soon going to head toward the woods, for the wind made conversation impossible. When she faced into the wind, her words were driven back into her throat even as she spoke them, and when she faced away from it, her words were torn like fragile cloth and scattered in meaningless syllables.

For long minutes she lost sight of Chewbacca, and several times she was certain she'd never see the dog again, but he always reappeared, bedraggled and obviously weak, but alive. His fur was crusted with ice, and when he appeared out of the surging rivers of snow, he seemed like a revenant journeying back from the far side of the grave.

The wind swept broad areas of the meadow almost clean of snow, leaving just a few well-packed inches in some places, but drifts piled up against even the smallest windbreaks and filled in gullies and depressions, creating traps that could not be seen or avoided. They had abandoned Charlie's snowshoes with his backpack, partly because his wounded shoulder prevented him from carrying them any longer and partly because he was no longer sufficiently surefooted to use them. As a result, she and Joey couldn't use their snowshoes to go across the drifts because they had to follow a route Charlie could negotiate with them. At times she found herself suddenly wading in snow up to her knees, then up to mid-thigh and getting deeper, and she had to backtrack and find a way around the drift, which wasn't easy when she couldn't see where the hell she was going. At other times, she stepped into holes that the snow had filled in; with no warning at all, from one step to the other, she was waist-deep.

She was afraid there might be an abrupt drop-off or a really deep sinkhole somewhere in the meadow. Sinkholes were not uncommon in mountain country like this; they had passed a few earlier in the day, seemingly bottomless holes, some ancient and ringed with water-smoothed limestone. If she took one misplaced step and plunged down into snow over her head, Charlie might not be able to get her out again, even if she didn't break a leg in the process. By the same token, she wasn't sure she could extricate them from a similar trap if they fell into it.

She became so concerned about this danger that she stopped and untied the tether from her waist. She was afraid of dragging Joey into a chasm with her. She coiled the line around her right hand; she could always let go, let it unravel, if she actually did sink into a trap.

She told herself that the things we fear most never happen to us, that it's always something else that brings us down, something totally unexpected— like Grace Spivey's chance encounter with them in the South Coast Plaza parking lot last Sunday afternoon. But when they were well into the meadow, when she was almost ready to lead them back toward the eastern forest again, the worst happened, after all.

Charlie had just found new reserves of strength and had let go of her arm when she put her foot down into suddenly deep snow and realized she had found the very thing she feared. She tried to throw herself backward, but she had been leaning forward to begin with, bent by the wind, and her momentum was all forward, and she couldn't change her balance in time. Unleashing a loud scream that the wind softened to a quiet cry, she dropped into snow over her head, struck bottom eight feet down, crumpling, with her left leg twisted painfully under her.

She looked up, saw the snow caving in above her. It was filling the hole she'd made when she'd fallen through it.

She was going to be buried alive.

She had read newspaper stories about workmen buried alive, suffocated or crushed to death, in caved-in ditches, no deeper than this. Of course, snow wasn't as heavy as dirt or sand, so she wouldn't be crushed, and she would be able to claw her way through it, and even if she couldn't get all the way out, she would still be able to breathe under the snow, for it wasn't as compact and suffocating as earth, but that realization did not alleviate her panic.

She jackknifed onto her feet an instant after hitting bottom, in spite of the pain in her leg, and she clawed for firm handholds, for the hidden side of the gully or pit into which she had stepped. But she couldn't find it. Just snow. Soft, yielding snow, infuriatingly insubstantial.

She was still screaming. A clump of snow fell into her open mouth, choking her. The pit was caving in above her, on all sides, pouring down around her, up to her shoulders, then up to her chin, *Jesus,* and she kept pushing the snow away from her head, desperate to keep her face and arms free, but it closed over her faster than she could dig it away.

Above, Charlie's face appeared. He was lying on the ground, leaning over the edge of the drop, looking down at her. He was shouting something. She couldn't understand what he was saying.

She flailed at the snow, but it weighed down on her, an ever-increasing cascade, pouring in from the drift all around, until at last her aching arms were virtually pinned at her sides. *No!* And still the snow collapsed inward, up to her chin again, up to her mouth. She sealed her lips, closed her eyes, sure that she was going under altogether, that it would cover her head, that Charlie would never be able to get her out, that this would be her grave. But then the cave-in ceased before her nose was buried.

She opened her eyes, looked up from the bottom of a white funnel, toward Charlie. The walls of snow were still, but at any moment they might tremble and continue to collapse on top of her.

She was rigid, afraid to move, breathing hard.

Joey. What about Joey?

She had released the tether (and Joey) as soon as she'd felt herself going into the pit. She hoped Charlie had stopped Joey before he, too, had plunged over the edge. In his trancelike state, the boy would not necessarily have halted just because she had gone under. If he had fallen into the drift, they would probably never find him. The snow would have closed over him, and they wouldn't be able to locate him by listening to his screams, not in this howling wind, not when his cries would be muffled by a few feet of snow.

She wouldn't have believed her heart could beat this fast or hard without bursting.

Above, Charlie reached down with his good arm, his hand open, making a come-to-me gesture with his fingers.

If she dug her arms free of the snow that now pinned them, she could grab hold of him, and together they could try to work her up and out of the hole. But in freeing her arms, she might trigger another avalanche that would cover her head with a couple of feet of snow. She had to be careful, move slowly and deliberately.

She twisted her right arm back and forth under the snow, packing the snow away from it, making a hollow space, then turned her palm up and clawed at the stuff with her fingers, loosening it, letting it slide back into the hollow by her arm, and in seconds she had made a tunnel up to the surface. She snaked her arm through the tunnel, and it came into sight, unhampered from fingertips to above the elbow. She reached straight up, gripped Charlie's extended hand. Maybe she would make it, after all. She clawed her other arm free, grabbed Charlie's wrist.

The snow around her shifted. Just a little.

Charlie began to pull, and she heaved herself up.

The white walls started falling in again. The snow sucked at her as if it were quicksand. Her feet left the ground as Charlie hauled her up, and she kicked out, frantically searching for the wall of the gully, struck it, tried to dig her feet in against it and use it to shove herself toward the top. He eased backwards, pulling her farther up. This must be agony for him, as the strain passed through his good arm and shoulder into his wounded shoulder, sapping whatever strength he had left. But it was working. Thank God. The sucking snow was letting go of her. She was now high enough to risk holding on to Charlie's arm with only one hand, while she grabbed at the brink of the gully with the other. Ice and frozen earth gave way under her clutching fingers, but she grabbed again, and this time she gripped something solid. With both Charlie and solid earth to cling to, she was able to lever herself up and out and onto her back, gasping, whimpering, with the unnerving feeling that she was escaping the cold maw of a living creature and had nearly been devoured by a beast composed of ice and snow.

Suddenly she realized that the shotgun, which had been slung from her shoulder when she'd fallen into the trap, had slipped off, or the strap had broken. It must still be in the pit. But the hole had closed up behind her when Charlie had pulled her out. It was lost.

It didn't matter. Spivey's people wouldn't be following them through the blizzard.

She got onto her hands and knees and crawled away from the snow trap, looking for Joey. He was there, on the ground, curled on his side, in a fetal position, knees drawn up, head tucked down.

Chewbacca was with him, as if he knew the boy needed his warmth, though the animal seemed to have no warmth to give. His coat was crusted with snow and ice, and there was ice on his ears. He looked at her with soulful brown eyes full of confusion, suffering, and fear.

She was ashamed she had blamed him, in part, for Joey's withdrawal and that she had wished she'd never seen him. She put one hand on his large head, and, even as weak as he was, he nuzzled her affectionately.

Joey was alive, conscious, but hurting bad. Impacted snow clogged his ski mask. If she didn't get him out of this wind soon, he would be frost-bitten. His eyes were even more distant than before.

She tried to get him to stand, but he couldn't. Although she was exhausted and shaky, although her left leg still hurt from the fall she had taken, she would have to carry him.

She dug the compass out of her pocket, studied it, and turned to face east-northeast, toward the section of woodland where the caves ought to be. She could see only five or six feet, and then the storm fell like a heavy drapery.

Surprised by the extent of her own stamina, she scooped Joey up, held him in both arms. A mother's instinct was to save her child, regardless of the cost to herself, and her maternal desperation had loosed some last meager store of adrenaline.

Charlie moved in beside her. He was on his feet, but he looked bad, almost as terrible as Joey.

"Got to get into the forest!" she shouted. "Out of this wind!"

She didn't think he could have heard her, not with the banshee storm shrieking across the meadow, but he nodded as if he understood her intention, and they moved into the white-out, trusting in the compass to lead them to the comparative shelter of the mammoth trees, shuffling with exaggerated caution to avoid falling into another snow trap.

Christine looked back at Chewbacca. The dog was getting up to follow, but creakily. Even if he could regain his feet, there was almost no chance that he would make it to the trees with them. This would probably be the last glimpse she ever had of him; the storm would swallow him just as the snow-filled pit had tried to swallow her.

Each step was an ordeal.

Wind. Snow. Cruel cold.

Dying would be easier than going on.

That thought scared her and gave her the will to take a few more steps.

One good thing: There was no doubt that their trail would be completely erased. The raging wind and arctic-fierce snowfall would make it impossible for Spivey's fanatics to follow them.

Snow dropped from the sky as if it were being dumped out of huge bins, came hurtling down in sheets and clumps.

Another step. Another.

As if plating them with suits of armor, the wind welded the snow to their arms and legs and backs and chests, until their clothes were the same color as the landscape around them.

Something ahead. A dark shape. It materialized in the storm, then was blotted out by an even more furious squall of snow. It appeared again. Didn't fade away this time. And another one. Huge blobs of darkness, shadowy formations rising up beyond snowy curtains. Gradually they became clearer, better defined. Yes. A tree. Several trees.

They trudged at least fifty yards into the forest before they found a place where the interlacing branches of the evergreens were so thick overhead that a significant amount of snow was shut out. Visibility improved. They were free of the wind's brutal fists, as well.

Christine stopped, put Joey down, peeled off his snow-caked ski mask. Her heart twisted when she saw his face.

CHAPTER 67

🖋️

KYLE BARLOWE, Burt Tully, and Edna Vanoff gathered around Grace at the edge of the forest, under the last of the evergreens. The wind licked at them from the meadow, as if hungry for their warmth. With her gloves off, Grace held her arms out, palms spread toward the meadow beyond the trees, receiving psychic impressions. The others waited silently for her to decide what to do next.

Out on the open floor of the valley, the fulminating blizzard was like an endless chain of dynamite detonations, a continuous roar, the violent waves of wind like concussions, the snow as thick as smoke. It was appropriate weather for the end of the world.

"They went this way," Mother Grace said.

Barlowe already knew their quarry had left the forest here, for their tracks told him as much. Which direction they had gone after heading into the open was another question; although they had left here only a short while ago, their footprints had not survived much past the perimeter of the woods. He waited for Mother Grace to tell him something he could not discern for himself.

Worriedly studying the snow-lashed field in front of them, Burt Tully said, "We can't go out there. We'd die out there."

Suddenly Grace lowered her hands and backed away from the meadow, farther into the trees.

They moved with her, alarmed by the look of terror on her face.

"Demons," she said hoarsely.

"Where?" Edna asked.

Grace was shaking. "Out there . . ."

"In the storm?" Barlowe asked.

"Hundreds . . . thousands . . . waiting for us . . . hiding in the drifts . . . waiting to rise up . . . and destroy us . . ."

Barlowe looked out at the open fields. He could see nothing but snow. He wished he had Mother Grace's Gift. There were malevolent spirits near, and he could not detect them, and that made him feel frighteningly vulnerable.

"We must wait here," Grace said, "until the storm passes."

Burt Tully was clearly relieved.

Barlowe said, "But the boy—"

"Grows stronger," Grace admitted.

"And Twilight?"

"Grows near."

"If we wait—"

"We might be too late," she said.

Barlowe said, "Won't God protect us if we go into the meadow? Aren't we armored with His might and mercy?"

"We must wait," was the only answer she gave him. "And pray."

Then Kyle Barlowe knew how late it really was. So late that they must be more vigilant than they had ever been before. So late that they could no longer be bold. Satan was now as strong and real a presence in this world as God Himself. Maybe the scales had not yet tipped in the devil's direction, but the balance was delicate.

CHAPTER 68

IIIII

CHRISTINE PEELED OFF the boy's ice-crusted ski mask, and Charlie had to look away from the child's face when it was revealed.

I've failed them, he thought.

Despair flooded into him and brought tears to his eyes.

He was sitting on the ground, with his back to a tree. He rested his head against the trunk, too, closed his eyes, took several deep breaths, trying to stop shaking, trying to think positively, trying to convince himself that everything would turn out all right, failing. He had been an optimist all his life, and this recent acquaintance with soul-shaking doubt was devastating.

The Tylenol and the anaesthetic powder had only slight effect on his pain, but even that minimal relief was fading. The pain in his shoulder was gaining strength again, and it was beginning to creep outward, as before, across his chest and up his neck and into his head.

Christine was talking softly and encouragingly to Joey, though she must have wanted to weep at the sight of him, as Charlie had done.

He steeled himself and looked at the boy again.

The child's face was red, lumpy, and badly misshapen from hives caused by the fierce cold. His eyes were nearly swollen shut; the edges of them were caked with a gummy, mucous-like substance, and the lashes were matted with the same stuff. His nostrils were mostly swollen shut, so he was breathing through his mouth, and his lips were cracked, puffy, bleeding. Most of his face was flushed an angry red, but two spots on his cheeks and one on the tip of his nose were gray-white, which might indicate frostbite, though Charlie hoped to God it wasn't.

Christine looked at Charlie, and her own despondency was evident in her troubled eyes if not in her voice. "Okay. We've got to move on. Got to get Joey out of this cold. We've got to find those caves."

"I don't see any sign of them," Charlie said.

"They must be near," she said. "Do you need help getting up?"

"I can make it," he said.

She lifted Joey. The boy didn't hold on to her. His arms hung down, limp. She glanced at Charlie.

Charlie sighed, gripped the tree, and got laboriously to his feet, quite surprised when he made it all the way up.

But he was even more surprised when, a second later, Chewbacca appeared, cloaked in snow and ice, head hung low, a walking definition of misery. When he had last seen the dog, out in the meadow, Charlie had been sure the animal would collapse and die in the storm.

"My God," Christine said when she saw the dog, and she looked as startled as Charlie was.

It's important, Charlie thought. The dog pulling through—that means we're *all* going to survive.

He wanted very much to believe it. He tried hard to convince himself. But they were a long way from home.

The way things had been going for them, Christine figured they would be unable to find the caves and would simply wander through the forest until they dropped from exhaustion and exposure to the cold. But fate finally had a bit of luck in store for them, and they found what they were looking for in less than ten minutes.

The trees thinned out in the neighborhood of the caves because the land became extremely rocky. It sloped up in uneven steps of stone, in humps and knobs and ledges and set-backs. Because there were fewer trees, more snow found its way in here, and there were some formidable drifts at the base of the slope and at many points higher up, where a set-back or a narrower ledge provided accommodation. But there was more wind, too, whistling down from the tops of the surrounding trees, and large areas of rock were swept bare of snow. She could see the dark mouths of three caves in the lower formations, where she and Charlie might be able to climb, and there were half a dozen others visible in the upper formations, but those were out of reach. There might be more openings, now drifted shut and hidden, because this portion of the valley wall appeared to be a honeycomb of tunnels, caves, and caverns.

She carried Joey to a jumble of boulders at the bottom of the slope and put him down, out of the wind.

Chewbacca limped after them and slumped wearily beside his master. It was astonishing that the dog had made it all this way, but it was clear he would not be able to go much farther.

With a grateful sigh and a gasp of pain, Charlie lowered himself to the ground beside Joey and the dog.

The look of him scared Christine as much as Joey's tortured face. His bloodshot eyes were fevered, two hot coals in his burnt-out face. She was afraid she was going to wind up alone out here with the bodies of the only two people she loved, caretaker of a wilderness graveyard that would eventually become her own final resting place.

"I'll look in these caves," she told Charlie, shouting to be heard now that they were more or less in the open again. "I'll see which is the best for us."

He nodded, and Joey didn't react, and she turned away from them, clambered over the rocky terrain toward the first dark gap in the face of the slope.

She wasn't sure if this part of the valley wall was limestone or granite, but it didn't matter because, not being a spelunker, she didn't know which kind of rock made for the safest caves, anyway. Besides, even if these were unsafe, she would have to make use of them; she had nowhere else to go.

The first cave had a low, narrow entrance. She took the flashlight out of her backpack and went into that hole in the ground. She was forced to crawl on her hands and knees, and in some places the passage was tight enough to require some agile squirming. After ten or twelve feet, the tunnel opened into a room about fifteen feet on a side, with a low ceiling barely high enough to allow her to stand up. It was big enough to house them, but far from ideal. Other passages led off the room, deeper into the hillside, perhaps to larger chambers, but none of them was of sufficient diameter to let her through. She went out into the wind and snow again.

The second cave wasn't suitable, either, but the third was as close to ideal as she could expect to find. The initial passageway was high enough so she didn't have to crawl to enter, wide enough so she didn't have to squeeze. There was a small drift at the opening, but she stamped through it with no difficulty. Five feet into the hillside, the passage turned sharply to the right, and in another six feet it turned just as sharply back to the left, a double baffle that kept the wind out. The first chamber was about twenty feet wide and thirty or thirty-five feet long, as much as twelve to fifteen feet high at the near end, with a smooth floor, walls that were fractured and jagged in some places and water-smoothed in others.

To her right, another chamber opened off this one. It was smaller, with a lower ceiling. There were several stalactites and stalagmites that looked as if they had been formed from melted gray wax, and in a few places they met at the middle of the room to form wasp-waisted pillars. She shone the flashlight beam around, saw a passage at the far end of the second room and guessed it led to yet a third cavern, but that was all she needed to know.

The first room had everything they required. Toward the back, the floor rose and the ceiling dropped down, and in the last five feet the floor shelved up abruptly, forming a ledge five feet deep and twenty feet wide, only four feet below the ceiling. Exploring this raised niche with her flashlight, Christine discovered a two-foot-wide hole in the rock above it, boring up into darkness, and she realized she had found a huge, natural fireplace with its own flue. The hole must lead into another cave farther up the hillside, and either that chamber or another beyond it would eventually vent to the outside; smoke would rise naturally toward the distant promise of open air.

Having a fire was important. They hadn't brought their sleeping bags with them because such bulky items would have slowed them down and because they had expected to reach the lake before nightfall, in which case they wouldn't have required bedrolls. The blizzard and the bullet hole in Charlie's shoulder had changed their plans drastically, and now without sleeping bags to ward off the night chill and help conserve body heat, a fire was essential.

She wasn't worried about the smoke giving away their position. The forest would conceal it, and once it rose above the trees, it would be lost in the white whirling skirts of the storm. Besides, Spivey's fanatics would almost certainly be searching southwest, toward the end of the valley that led to civilization.

The chamber boasted one other feature that, at first, added to its appeal. One wall was decorated with a seven-foot-tall drawing, an Indian totem of a bear, perhaps a grizzly. It had been etched into the rock with a corrosive yellow dye of some sort. It was either crude or highly stylized; Christine didn't know enough about Indian totems to make the fine distinction. All she knew for sure was that drawings like this were usually meant to bring good luck to the occupants of the cave; the image of the bear supposedly embodied a real spirit that would provide protection. Initially, that seemed like a good thing. She and Charlie and Joey needed all the protection they could get. But as she paused a moment to study the sulfur-yellow bear, she got the feeling there was something threatening about it. That was ridiculous, of course, an indication of her shaky state of mind, for it was nothing but a drawing on stone. Nevertheless, on reappraisal, she decided she would have preferred another drab gray wall in place of the totem.

But she wasn't going to look for another cave just because she didn't like the decor of this one. The natural fireplace more than outweighed the previous occupants' taste in art. With a fire for heat and light, the cave would provide almost as much shelter as the cabin they had left behind. It would not be as comfortable, of course, but at the moment, she wasn't as concerned about comfort as she was worried about keeping her son, Charlie, and herself alive.

In spite of the stone floor that served as chair and bed, Charlie was delighted with the cave, and at the moment it seemed as luxurious as any hotel suite he'd ever occupied. Just being out of the wind and snow was an incomparable blessing.

For more than an hour, Christine gathered dead wood and crisp dry evergreen branches with which to make a fire and keep it going until morning. She returned to the cave again and again with armloads of fuel, making one stack for the logs and larger pieces of wood, another for the small stuff that would serve as tinder.

Charlie marveled at her energy. Could such stamina spring entirely from a mother's instinct to preserve her offspring's life? There seemed no other explanation. She should have collapsed long ago.

He knew he should switch the flashlight off each time she went outside, turn it on again only so she would be able to see when she came in with more wood, for he was concerned the batteries would go dead. But he left it burning, anyway, because he was afraid Joey would react badly to being plunged into total darkness.

The boy was in bad shape. His breathing was labored. He lay motionless, silent, beside the equally depleted dog.

As he listened to Joey's ragged breathing, Charlie told himself that finding the cave was another good sign, an indication their luck was improving, that they would recover their strength in a day or two and then head down toward the lake. But another, grimmer voice within him wondered if the cave was, instead, a tomb, and although he didn't want to consider that depressing possibility, he couldn't tune it out.

He listened, as well, to the drip-drip-drip of water in an adjacent chamber. The cold stone walls and hollow spaces amplified the humble sound and made it seem both portentous and strange, like a mechanical heartbeat or, perhaps, the tapping of one clawed finger on a sheet of glass.

The fire cast flickering orange light on the yellow bear totem, making it shimmer, and on drab stone walls. Welcome heat poured from the blazing pile of wood. The natural flue worked as Christine had hoped, drawing the smoke up into higher caverns, leaving their air untainted. In fact, the drying action of the fire took some of the dampness out of the air and eliminated most of the vaguely unpleasant, musty odor that had been in the dank chamber since she had first entered.

For a while they just basked in the warmth, doing nothing, saying nothing, even trying not to think.

In time Christine took off her gloves, lowered the hood of her jacket, then finally took off the jacket itself. The cave wasn't exactly toasty, and drafts circulated through it from adjacent caverns, but her flannel shirt and long insulated underwear were now sufficient. She helped Charlie and Joey out of their jackets, too.

She gave Charlie more Tylenol. She lifted his bandage, dusted in more powdered antibiotics and more of the anaesthetic as well.

He said he wasn't in much pain.

She knew he was lying.

The hives that afflicted Joey began, at last, to recede. The swelling subsided, and his misshapen face slowly regained its proper proportions. His nostrils opened, and he no longer needed to breathe through his mouth, although he continued to wheeze slightly, as if there was some congestion in his lungs.

Please, God, not pneumonia, Christine thought.

His eyes opened wider, but they were still frighteningly empty. She smiled at him, made a couple of funny faces, trying to get a reaction out of him, all to no avail. As far as she could tell he didn't even see her.

Charlie didn't think he was hungry until Christine began to heat beans and Vienna sausages in the aluminum pot that was part of their compact mess kit. The aroma made his mouth water and his stomach growl, and suddenly he was shaking with hunger.

Once he began to eat, however, he filled up fast. His stomach bloated, and he found it increasingly difficult to swallow. The very act of chewing exacerbated the pain in his head, which doubled back along the lines of pain in his neck and all the way into the shoulder wound, making that ache worse, too. Finally the food lost its flavor, then seemed bitter. He ate about a fourth of what he first thought he could put away, and even the meager meal didn't rest well in his belly.

"You can't get more of it down?" Christine asked.

"I'll have more later."

"What's wrong?"

"Nothing."

"Do you feel nauseous?"

"No, no. I'm okay. Just tired."

She studied him in silence for a moment, and he forced a smile for her sake, and she said, "Well . . . whenever you're ready for more, I'll reheat it."

As the fluttering fire made shadows leap and cavort on the walls, Charlie watched her feed Joey. The boy was willing to eat and able to swallow, but she had to mash up the sausages and beans, and spoon the stuff into his mouth as if she were feeding an infant instead of a six-year-old.

A grim sense of failure settled over Charlie once more.

The boy had fled from an intolerable situation, from a world of pure hostility, into a fantasy that he found more congenial. How far had he retreated into that inner world of his? Too far ever to come back?

Joey would take no more food. His mother was unhappy about how little he had eaten, but she couldn't force him to swallow even one more mouthful.

She fed the dog, too, and he had a better appetite than his master. Charlie wanted to tell her that they couldn't waste food on Chewbacca. If this storm was followed by another, if the weather didn't clear for a few days, they would have to ration what little provisions they had left, and they would regret every morsel that had been given to the dog. But he knew she admired the animal's courage and perseverance, and she felt its presence helped prevent Joey from slipping all the way down into deep catatonia. He didn't have the heart to tell her to stop feeding it. Not now. Not yet. Wait until morning. Maybe the weather would have changed by then, and maybe they would head southwest to the lake.

Joey's breathing worsened for a moment; his wheezing grew alarmingly loud and ragged.

Christine quickly changed the child's position, used her folded jacket to prop up his head. It worked. The wheezing softened.

Watching the boy, Charlie thought: Are you hurting as bad as I am, little one? God, I hope not. You don't deserve this. What you *do* deserve is a better bodyguard than I've been, and that's for damned sure.

Charlie's own pain was far worse than he let Christine know. The new dose of Tylenol and powdered anaesthetic helped, but not quite as much as the first dose. The pain in his shoulder and arm no longer felt like a live thing trying to chew its way out of him. *Now* it felt as if little men from another planet were inside him, breaking his bones into smaller and smaller splinters, popping open his tendons, slicing his muscles, and pouring sulfuric acid over everything. What they wanted to do was gradually hollow him out, use acid to burn away everything inside him, until only his skin remained, and then they would inflate the limp and empty sack of skin and put him on exhibit in a museum back on their own world. That's how it felt, anyway. Not good. Not good at all.

Later, Christine went out to the mouth of the cave to get some snow to melt for drinking water, and discovered that night had fallen. They hadn't been able to hear the wind from within the cave, but it was still raging. Snow slanted down from the darkness, and the frigid, turbulent air hammered the valley wall with arctic fury.

She returned to the cave, put the pan of snow by the fire to melt, and talked with Charlie for a while. His voice was weak. He was in more pain than he wanted her to know, but she allowed him to think he was deceiving her because there wasn't anything she could do to make him more comfortable. In less than an hour, in spite of his pain, he was asleep, as were Joey and Chewbacca.

She sat between her son and the man she loved, with her back to the fire, looking toward the front of the cave, watching the shadows and the reflections of the flames as they danced a frantic gavotte upon the walls. With one part of her mind she listened for unusual sounds, and with another part she monitored the respiration of the man and the boy, afraid that one of them might suddenly cease breathing.

The loaded revolver was at her side. To her dismay, she had learned that Charlie had no more spare cartridges in his jacket pockets. The box of ammo was in his backpack, which they had abandoned at the rocky overhang where she had patched his shoulder. She was furious with herself for having forgotten it. The rifle and shotgun were gone. The handgun was their only protection, and she had only the six shells that were in it.

The totem bear glowed on the wall.

At 8:10, as Christine finished adding fuel to the fire, Charlie began to groan in his sleep and toss his head on the pillow she had made from his folded jacket. He had broken out in a greasy sweat.

A hand against his forehead was enough to tell her that he had a fever. She watched him for a while, hoping he would quiet down, but he only got worse. His groans became soft cries, then less soft. He began to babble. Sometimes it was wordless nonsense. Sometimes he spat out words and disjointed, meaningless sentences.

At last he became so agitated that she got two more Tylenol tablets from the bottle, poured a cupful of water, and attempted to wake him. Although sleep seemed to be providing no comfort for him, he wouldn't come around at first, and when he finally did open his eyes they were bleary and unfocused. He was delirious and didn't seem to know who she was.

She made him take the pills, and he greedily swallowed the water, washing them down. He was asleep again even as she took the cup from his lips.

He continued to groan and mutter for a while, and although he was sweating heavily, he also began to shiver. His teeth chattered. She wished they had some blankets. She piled more wood on the fire. The cave was relatively warm, but she figured it couldn't be *too* warm right now.

Around 10:00, Charlie grew quiet again. He stopped tossing his head, stopped sweating, slept peacefully.

At least, she *told* herself it was sleep that had him. But she was afraid it might be a coma.

Something squeaked.

Christine grabbed the revolver and bolted to her feet as if the squeak had been a scream.

Joey and Charlie slept undisturbed.

She listened closely, and the squeak came again, more than one short sound this time, a whole series of squeaks, a shrill though distant chittering.

It wasn't a sound of stone or earth or water, not a dead sound. Something else, something *alive*.

She picked up the flashlight. Heart pumping furiously, holding the revolver out in front of her, she edged toward the sound. It seemed to be coming from the cavern that adjoined this one.

Soft as they were, the shrill cries nevertheless lifted the hairs on the back of her neck because they were so eerie, alien.

At the entrance of the next chamber, she stopped, probing ahead with the beam of the flashlight. She saw the waxy-looking stalactites and stalagmites, the damp rock walls, but nothing out of the ordinary. The noises now seemed to be coming from farther away, from a third cavern or even a fourth.

As she cocked her head and listened more intently, Christine suddenly understood what she was hearing. Bats. A lot of them, judging by their cries.

Evidently, they always nested in another chamber, elsewhere in the mountain, always entered and exited by another route, for there was no sign of them here, no bat corpses or droppings. Okay. She didn't mind sharing the caves with them, just as long as they kept to their own neighborhood.

She returned to Charlie and Joey and sat down between them, put the gun aside, switched off the flashlight.

Then she wondered what would happen if Spivey's people showed up, blocked off the entrance to this cave, and left them no option but to head deeper into the mountain in search of another way out, a back door to safety. What if she and Charlie and Joey were forced to flee from cave to cave and eventually had to pass through that chamber in which the bats nested? It would probably be knee-deep in bat shit, and there would be hundreds—maybe *thousands*—of them hanging overhead, and a few of them or even *all* of them might have rabies, because bats were excellent carriers of rabies—

Stop it! she told herself angrily.

She had enough to worry about already. Spivey's lunatics. Joey. Charlie's wound. The weather. The long journey back to civilization. She couldn't add bats to the list. That was crazy. There was only a chance in a million that they would ever have to go nearer the bats.

She tried to relax.

She put more wood on the fire.

The squeaking faded.

The caves became silent again except for Joey's labored breathing and the crackle of the fire.

She was getting drowsy.

She tried every trick she could think of to keep herself awake, but sleep continued to close in on her.

She was afraid to let herself go under. Joey might take a turn for the worse while she was dozing. Or Charlie might need her, and she wouldn't know.

Besides, someone ought to stand guard.

Spivey's people might come in the night.

No. The storm. Witches weren't allowed to fly on their brooms in storms like this.

She smiled, remembering the way Charlie had joked with Joey.

The flickering firelight was mesmerizing . . .

Someone ought to stand guard, anyway.

Just a quick nap.

Witches . . .

Someone . . . ought to . . .

It was one of those nightmares in which she knew she was asleep, knew that what was happening was not real, but that didn't make it any less frightening. She dreamed that all the caves in the valley wall were connected in an elaborate maze, and that Grace Spivey and her religious terrorists had entered this particular cave from other chambers farther along the hillside. She dreamed they were preparing a human sacrifice, and the sacrifice was Joey. She was trying to kill them, but each time she shot one of them, the corpse divided into two *new* fanatics, so by murdering them she was only adding to their numbers. She became increasingly frantic and terrified, increasingly outnumbered, until all the caves within the valley wall were swarming with Spivey's people, like a horde of rats or cockroaches. And then, aware that she was dreaming, she began to suspect that Grace Spivey's followers were not only in the caves of the dream but in the *real* caves in the real world beyond sleep, and they were conducting a human sacrifice in *both* the nightmare and in reality, and if she didn't wake up and stop them, they were going to kill Joey for real, kill him while she slept. She struggled to free herself of sleep's iron grip, but she could not do it, could not wake up, and now in the dream they were going to cut the boy's throat. And in reality, beyond the dream?

CHAPTER 69

WHEN CHRISTINE WOKE in the morning, Joey was eating a chocolate bar and petting Chewbacca.

She watched him for a moment, and she realized tears were streaming down her cheeks. This time, however, she was crying because she was happy.

He seemed to be returning from his self-imposed psychological exile. He was in better physical shape, too. Maybe he was going to be all right. Thank God.

The swelling was gone from his face, replaced by a better—though not really healthy—color, and he was no longer having difficulty breathing. His eyes were still blank, and he continued to be withdrawn, but not nearly as far-off and pathetic as he had been yesterday.

The fact that he had gone to the supplies, had rummaged through them, and had found the candy for himself was encouraging. And he had apparently added wood to the fire, for it was burning brightly, though after being untended during the night it should have cooled down to just a bank of hot coals.

She crawled to him and hugged him, and he hugged her, too, though weakly. He didn't speak, wouldn't be bribed or teased or encouraged into uttering a single word. And he still wouldn't meet her eyes directly, as if he were not entirely aware that she was here with him; however, she had the feeling that, when she looked away from him, his intense blue eyes turned toward her and lost their slightly glazed and dreamy quality. She wasn't positive. She couldn't catch him at it. But she dared to hope that he was returning to her, slowly feeling his way back from the edge of autism, and she knew she must not rush him or push him too hard.

Chewbacca had not perked up as much as his young master, though he was a bit less weak and stringy looking than he had been last night. The pooch seemed to grow healthier and more energetic even as Christine watched the boy pet him, responding to each pat and scratch and stroke as if Joey's small hands had healing power. There was sometimes a wonderful, mysterious, deep sharing, an instant bonding in the relationships between children and their animals.

Joey held his candy bar out in front of him, turned it back and forth, and seemed to be staring at it. He smiled vaguely.

Christine had never wanted anything more than she had wanted to see him smile, and a smile came to her own face in sympathy with his.

Behind her, Charlie woke with a start, and she went to him. She saw at once that, unlike Joey and the dog, he had not improved. The delirium had left him, but in all other ways his condition had grown worse. His face was the color and texture of bread dough, greasy with sweat. His eyes appeared to have collapsed back into his skull, as if the supporting bones and tissues beneath them had crumpled under the weight of things he had seen. Forceful shivers shook him, and at times they grew into violent tremors only one step removed from convulsions.

He was partially dehydrated from the fever. His tongue clove to the roof of his mouth when he tried to speak.

She helped him sit up and take more Tylenol with a cup of water. "Better?"

"A little," he said, speaking only slightly louder than a whisper.

"How's the pain?"

"Everywhere," he said.

Thinking he was confused, she said, "I mean the pain in your shoulder."

"Yeah. That's what . . . I mean. It's no longer . . . just in my shoulder. It feels like . . . it's *everywhere* now . . . all through me . . . head to foot . . . everywhere. What time is it?"

She checked her watch. "Good heavens! Seven-thirty. I must've slept hours without stirring an inch, and on this hard floor."

"How's Joey?"

"See for yourself."

He turned his head and looked just as Joey fed a last morsel of chocolate to Chewbacca.

Christine said, "He's mending, I think."

"Thank God."

With her fingers, she combed Charlie's damp hair back from his forehead.

When they'd made love at the cabin, she had thought him by far the most beautiful man she had ever known. She had been thrilled by the contour of each masculine muscle and bone. And even now, when he was shrunken and pale and weak, he seemed beautiful to her: His face was so sensitive, his eyes so caring. She wanted to lie beside him, put her arms around him, hold him close, but she was afraid of hurting him.

"Can you eat something?" she asked.

He shook his head.

"You should," she said. "You've got to build up your strength."

He blinked his rheumy eyes as if trying to clear his vision. "Maybe later. Is it . . . still snowing?"

"I haven't been outside yet this morning."

"If it's cleared up . . . you've got to leave at once . . . without me."

"Nonsense."

"This time of year . . . the weather might clear for only . . . a day . . . or even just . . . a few hours. You've got to . . . take advantage of good weather . . . the moment it comes . . . get out of the mountains . . . before the next storm."

"Not without you."

"Can't walk," he said.

"You haven't tried."

"Can't. Hardly . . . can talk."

Even the effort at conversation weakened him. His breathing grew more labored word by word.

His condition frightened her, and the notion of leaving him alone seemed heartless.

"You couldn't tend the fire here, all by yourself," she protested.

"Sure. Move me . . . closer to it. Within arm's reach. And pile up . . . enough wood . . . to last a couple of days. I'll be . . . okay."

"You won't be able to prepare and heat your food—"

"Leave me a couple . . . candy bars."

"That's not enough."

He scowled at her and, for a moment, managed to put more volume in his voice, forced a steely tone: "You've *got* to go without me. It's the only way, dammit. It's best for you and Joey . . . and it's best for me, too, because I'm . . . not going to get out of here . . . without the help of a medical evacuation team."

"All right," she said. "Okay."

He sagged, exhausted by that short speech. When he spoke again, his voice was not only a whisper but a *quavering* whisper that sometimes faded out altogether on the ends of words. "When you get down . . . to the lake . . . you can send help back . . . for me."

"Well, it's all moot until I find out whether the storm has let up or not," she said. "I better go have a look."

As she began to get up, a man's voice called to them from the mouth of the cave, beyond the double baffle of the entrance passage: "We know you're in there! You can't hide from us! We know!"

Spivey's hounds had found them.

CHAPTER 70

HHH

ACTING INSTINCTIVELY, NOT hesitating to consider the danger of her actions, Christine snatched up the loaded revolver and sprinted across the cave toward the Z-shaped passage that led outside.

"No!" Charlie said.

She ignored him, came to the first bend in the passage, turned right without checking to see if anyone was there, saw only the close rock walls and a vague spot of gray light at the next turn, beyond which lay the last straight stretch of tunnel and then the open hillside. She rushed forth with reckless abandon because that was probably the last thing Spivey's people would expect of her, but also because she couldn't possibly proceed in any other fashion; she was not entirely in control of herself. The crazy, vicious, stupid bastards had driven her out of her home, and put her on the run, had cornered her here in a hole in the ground, and now they were going to kill her baby.

The unseen man shouted again: *"We know you're in there!"*

She had never before in her life been hysterical, but she was hysterical now, and she knew it, couldn't help it. In fact, she didn't care that she was hysterical because it felt *good*, damned good, just to let go, to give in to blind rage and a savage desire to spill *their* blood, to make *them* feel some pain and fear.

With the same irrational disregard for danger that she had shown when turning the first blind corner in the passageway, she now turned the second, and ahead of her was the last stretch of the tunnel, then open air, and a figure silhouetted in the gray morning light, a man in a parka with a hood pulled up on his head. He was holding a rifle—no, a machine gun—but he was pointing it more or less at the ground, not directly ahead into the tunnel, because he wasn't expecting her to rush straight out at him and make such an easy target of herself, not in a million years, but that was just what she was doing, like a crazy kamikaze, and to hell with the consequences. She took him by surprise, and as he started to raise the muzzle of the machine gun to cover her, she fired once, twice, three times, hitting him every time, because he was so close that it was almost impossible to miss him.

The first shot jolted him, seemed to lift him off his feet, and the second shot flung him backwards, and the third shot knocked him down. The machine gun flew out of his hands, and for a moment Christine had a hope of getting hold of it, but by the time she stepped out of the cave, that immensely desirable weapon was clattering down the rocky slope.

She saw that the snow had stopped falling, that the wind was no longer blowing, and that there were three people on the slope behind the man she had killed. One of the three, an incredibly big man, off to her left, was already diving for cover, reacting to the shots that had wasted his buddy, though that first body had just hit the ground and bounced and was not yet still. The other two Twilighters weren't as quick as the giant. A short stocky woman stood directly in front of Christine, no more than ten or twelve feet away, a perfect target, and Christine reflexively pulled off a shot, and that woman went down, too, her face exploding like a punctured balloon full of red water.

Although Christine had plunged along the passageway and out of the cave in silence, she began to scream now, uncontrollably, shouting invectives at them, yelling so loud that her throat hurt and her voice cracked, then screaming louder still. She was using words she had never used before, and she was shocked by what she heard spewing from her own lips, yet was unable to stop, because her rage had reduced her to inarticulate noises and mindless obscenities.

And as she screamed her lungs out, even as she saw the stocky woman's face exploding, Christine turned on the third Twilighter, the one to her right, twenty feet away, and she saw at once that it was Grace Spivey.

"*You!*" she shouted, her hysteria stoked by the sight of the crone. "*You!* You crazy old bitch!"

How could a woman of her age have the stamina to climb these ridges and battle the life-sapping weather of the high Sierras? Did her madness give her strength? Yes, probably. Her madness blocked all doubt, all weariness, just as it had shielded her from pain when she had punctured her hands and feet to fake crucifixion stigmata.

God help us, Christine thought.

The hag stood unmoving, unbent, arrogant, defiant, as if daring Christine to pull the trigger, and even from this distance, Christine felt the strange and riveting power of the old woman's eyes. Immune to the hypnotic effect of that mad gaze, she fired a shot, the revolver bucking in her hands. She missed even though the distance was not great, squeezed the trigger again, was surprised when she missed a second time at such close range, tried a third shot but discovered she was out of ammunition.

Oh, Jesus.

No more bullets. No other weapons. Jesus. Nothing but her bare hands.

Okay, I can do it, I can do it, bare hands, all right, I'll strangle the bitch, I'll tear her goddamned head off.

Sobbing, cursing, shrieking, carried forward on a crashing wave of terror, she started toward Spivey. But the other Twilighter, the giant, began shooting at her from behind some boulders, where he had taken cover. Shots exploded and then ricocheted off the rocks around her with a piercing whine. She sensed bullets cutting the air near her head. She realized she couldn't help Joey if she was dead, so she stopped, turned back toward the cave.

Another shot. Sharp chips of stone sprayed up from the point of impact.

She was still hysterical, but all that manic energy was suddenly redirected, away from rage and blood lust, toward the survival instinct. With the sound of gunfire behind her, she stumbled back to the cave. The giant left his hiding place and came after her. Slugs whacked into the stone beside her, and she expected to take one in the back. Then she was through the entrance to the caves, into the first stretch of the Z-shaped passageway, out of sight of the gunman, and she thought she was safe. But one last shot ricocheted around the corner from the first length of the tunnel and slammed into her right thigh, kicking her off her feet. She went down, landing hard on her shoulder, and saw darkness reach up for her.

Refusing to succumb to the numbing effect of the shock that followed being hit, gasping for breath, desperately fending off the welling darkness that pooled up behind her eyes, Christine dragged herself along the passageway.

She didn't think they would come straight in after her. They couldn't know that she possessed only one gun or that she was out of ammunition. They would be wary.

But they *would* come. Cautiously. Slowly.

Not slowly enough.

They were relentless, like a posse in a Western movie.

Sweating in spite of the cold air, heaving and pulling her leg along as if it were a hunk of concrete, she hitched herself into the cave, where Charlie and Joey waited in the capering light of the fire.

"Oh, Christ, you've been shot," Charlie said.

Joey said nothing. He was standing by the ledge on which the fire was burning, and the pulsing light gave his face a bloody cast. He was sucking on one thumb, watching her with enormous eyes.

"Not bad," she said, trying not to let them see how scared she was. She pulled herself up against the wall, standing on one leg.

She put one hand on her thigh, felt sticky blood. She refused to look at it. If it was bleeding heavily, she'd need a tourniquet. But there wasn't time for first aid. If she paused to apply a tourniquet, Spivey or the giant might just walk in and blow her brains out.

She wasn't dizzy yet, and she was no longer in imminent danger of passing out, but she was beginning to feel weak.

She was still holding the empty, useless gun. She dropped it.

"Pain?" Charlie asked.

"No." That much was true; she felt little or no pain at the moment, but she knew it would come soon.

Outside, the giant was yelling: "Give us the boy! We'll let you live if you'll just give us the boy."

Christine ignored him. "I got two of the bastards," she told Charlie.

"How many are left?" he asked.

"Two more," she said, giving no additional details, not wanting Joey to know that Grace Spivey was one of the two.

Chewbacca had gotten to his feet and was growling in the back of his throat. Christine was surprised the dog could stand up, but he was far from recovered; he looked sick and wobbly. He wouldn't be able to do much fighting or protect Joey.

She spotted the knife from the mess kit, which lay between Joey and Charlie, at the far end of the room. She asked Joey to bring it to her, but he only stared, unmoving, and would not be coaxed into helping.

"No more ammo?" Charlie asked.

"None."

From outside: *"Give us the boy!"*

Charlie tried to inch toward the knife, but he was too weak and too tortured by pain to accomplish the task. The effort made him wheeze, and the wheezing developed into a wracking cough, and the cough left him limp with exhaustion —and with bloody saliva on his lips.

Christine had a frantic sense of time running out like sand pouring from the bottom of a funnel.

"Give us the Antichrist!"

Although Christine couldn't move fast, she began to make her way to the other end of the room, following the wall and bracing herself against it, hopping on her uninjured leg. If she could get to the knife, then return to this end of the chamber, she could wait just this side of the passageway, around the corner, and when they came in she might be able to lurch forward and stab one of them.

She finally reached the supplies and bent down and picked up the knife — and realized how short the blade was. She turned it over and over in her hand, trying to convince herself that it was just the weapon she needed. But it would have to penetrate a parka and the clothes underneath before doing any damage, and it wasn't long enough. If she had a chance to stab at their faces . . . but they would have guns, and she didn't have much hope of carrying out a successful frontal assault.

Damn.

She threw the knife down in disgust.

"Fire," Charlie said.

At first she didn't understand.

He raised one hand to his mouth and wiped at the bloody saliva that he continued to cough up. "Fire. It's . . . a good . . . weapon."

Of course. Fire. Better than a knife with a stubby little blade.

Suddenly she thought of something that, used in conjunction with a burning brand, would be almost as effective as a gun.

In her wounded leg, a dull pain had begun to throb in time with her rapid pulse, but she gritted her teeth and stooped down beside the pile of supplies. Stooping was not easy, an involved and painful maneuver, and she dreaded having to stand up again, even though she had the wall against which to support herself. She poked through the items she had emptied out of the backpack yesterday, and in a few seconds she turned up the squeeze-can of lighter fluid, which they had bought in case they had trouble starting a fire in the fireplace at the cabin. She stashed the can in the right-hand pocket of her pants.

When she stood, the stone floor rolled under her. She grabbed the edge of the raised hearth and waited until the dizziness passed.

She turned to the fire, snatched a burning branch from between two larger logs, afraid it would sputter out when she removed it from the blaze, but the branch continued to burn, a bright torch.

Joey did not move or speak, but he watched with interest. He was depending on her. His life was entirely in her hands now.

She hadn't heard any shouting from outside in quite some time. That silence wasn't welcome. It might mean Spivey and the giant were on their way inside, already in the Z-shaped passage . . .

She embarked upon a return trip around the room, past Charlie, toward the passageway through which the Twilighters might come at any moment, taking the long route because in her condition it was safest. She was agonizingly aware of the precious seconds she was wasting, but she couldn't risk going straight across the room because if she fell she might pass out or extinguish the torch. She held the burning brand in her left hand, using the other to steady herself against the wall, limping instead of hopping because limping was faster, daring to use the injured leg a little, though pain shot all through her when she put much weight on her right foot. And although the pain still throbbed in sympathy with her pounding pulse, it was no longer dull; it was a burning-stinging-stabbing-pinching-twisting pain that was getting worse with each punishing beat of her heart.

She briefly wondered how much blood she was losing, but she told herself it didn't matter. If she wasn't losing a lot, she might be able to take one last stand against the Twilighters. If she was losing too much, if it was pouring from a major vein or spurting from a nicked artery, there was no use checking on it, anyway, because a tourniquet would not save her, not out here, miles from the nearest medical assistance.

By the time she made her way to the far end of the chamber and stopped next to the mouth of the entrance tunnel, she was light-headed and nauseated. She gagged and tasted vomit at the back of her throat, but she managed to choke it down. The rippling light of the fire, lapping at the walls, imparted an amorphous feeling to the cave, as if the chamber's dimensions and contours were in a constant state of flux, as if the stone were not stone at all but some strange plastic that continuously melted and reformed: the walls receded, now drew closer, too close, now receded again; a convexity of rock suddenly appeared where there had been a concavity; the ceiling bulged downward until it almost touched her head, then snapped back to its former height; the floor churned and rose and then slid down until it seemed it would drop out from under her completely.

In desperation she closed her eyes, squeezed them tight, bit her lip, and breathed deeply until she felt less faint. When she opened her eyes again, the chamber was solid, unchanging. She felt relatively stable, but she knew it was a fragile stability.

She pressed against the wall, into a shallow depression to one side of the passageway. Holding the torch in her left hand, she fumbled in her pocket with her right hand and withdrew the squeeze-can of lighter fluid. Gripping it with three fingers and her palm, she used her thumb and forefinger to screw off the cap, uncovering the rigid plastic nozzle. She was ready. She had a plan. A good plan. It *had* to be good because it was the only plan she could come up with.

The big man would probably be the first into the cave. He would have a gun, probably the same semi-automatic rifle he had been using outside. The weapon would be thrust out in front of him, pointed straight ahead, waist-high. That was the problem: dousing him before he could turn the muzzle on her and pull the trigger. Which was something he could do in—what?—maybe two seconds. Maybe one. The element of surprise was her best and only hope. He might be expecting gunfire, knives—but not *this*. If she squirted him with lighter fluid the instant he appeared, he might be sufficiently startled to lose a full second of reaction time, might lose another second or so in shock as he smelled the fluid and realized he had been sprayed with something highly flammable. That was all the time she would need to set him afire.

She held her breath, listened.

Nothing.

Even if she didn't get any fuel on the giant's skin, only managed to douse his parka, he would almost certainly drop the rifle in horror and panic, and slap at the fire.

She took a deep breath, held it, listened again.

Still nothing.

If she was able to squirt his face, it wouldn't be panic alone that caused him to drop the gun. He would be rocked by intense pain as his skin blistered and peeled off, and as fire ate into his eyes.

Smoke roiled up from her torch and fanned out along the ceiling, seeking escape from the confining rock.

At the other end of the room, Charlie, Joey, and Chewbacca waited in silence. The weary dog had slumped back on his hindquarters.

Come on, Spivey! *Come on,* damn you.

Christine did not have unqualified faith in her ability to use the lighter fluid and the torch effectively. She figured, at best, there was only one chance in ten that she could pull it off, but she wanted them to come anyway, right now, so she could get it over with. The waiting was worse than the inevitable confrontation.

Something cracked, snapped, and Christine jumped, but it was only the fire at the other end of the room, a branch crumbling in the flames.

Come on.

She wanted to peek around the corner, into the passageway, and end this suspense. She didn't dare. She'd lose the advantage of surprise.

She thought she could hear the soft ticking of her watch. It must have been imagination, but the sound counted off the seconds, anyway: *tick, tick, tick . . .*

If she doused the big man and set him afire without getting herself shot, she would then have to handle Spivey. The old woman was sure to have a gun of her own.

Tick, tick . . .

If the hag was right behind the giant, maybe the flash of fire and all the screaming would disconcert her. The old woman might be confused enough for Christine to be able to strike again with more lighter fluid.

Tick, tick . . .

The natural flue sucked away the smoke from the main fire, but the smoke from Christine's torch rose to the ceiling and formed a noxious cloud. Now the cloud was slowly settling down into the room, fouling the air they had to breathe, hitching a ride on every vagrant current but not moving away fast enough. The stink wasn't bad yet, but in a few minutes they would start choking. The caverns were so drafty that there was little chance of suffocation, though an ordeal by smoke would only further weaken them. Yet she couldn't extinguish the torch; it was her only weapon.

Something better happen soon, she thought. Damned soon.

Tick, tick, tick . . .

Distracted by the problem of the smoke and by the imaginary but nonetheless maddening sound of time slipping away, Christine almost didn't react to the *important* sound when it came. A single click, a scraping noise. It passed before Christine realized it had to be Spivey or the big man.

She waited, tense, torch raised high, the can of lighter fluid extended in front of her, fingers poised to depress and pump the sides of the container.

More scraping noises.

A soft metallic sound.

Christine leaned forward from the shallow depression in which she had taken refuge, praying her bad leg would hold up—

—and abruptly realized the noises hadn't come from the Z-shaped passageway but from the chamber that adjoined this one, from deeper in the hillside.

She glimpsed a hooded flashlight in the next cave, the beam spearing past a stalactite. Then it winked out.

No. This wasn't possible!

She saw movement at the brink of darkness where the other cavern joined this one. An incredibly tall, broad-shouldered, hideously ugly man stepped from the gloom, into the edge of the wavering firelight, twelve or fourteen feet from Christine.

Too late, she understood that Spivey was coming at them through the network of caverns rather than through the more easily defended entrance tunnel. But how? How could they know which caves led toward this one? Did they have maps of the caves? Or did they trust to luck? How could they be *that* lucky?

It was crazy.

It wasn't *fair.*

Christine lurched forward, one step, two, out of the shadows in which she had been hiding.

The giant saw her. He brought up his rifle.

She squirted the lighter fluid at him.

He was too far away. The flammable liquid arced out seven or eight feet, but then curved down and spattered onto the stone floor, two or three feet short of him.

It must have been instantly clear to him that she wouldn't be attacking with such a crude weapon unless she had no more ammunition for the gun.

"Drop it," he said coldly.

Her great plan suddenly seemed pathetic, foolish.

Joey. He was depending on her. She was his last defense. She tottered one step closer.

"Drop it!"

Before he could shoot, her bad leg gave out. She collapsed.

With despair and anguish hanging heavily on the single word, Charlie said, "Christine!"

The can of lighter fluid spun across the floor, away from her and Charlie and Joey, coming to rest in an inaccessible corner.

She landed on her wounded thigh and screamed as a hand grenade of pain went off in her leg.

Even as she was collapsing, the torch fell from her hand and landed on the trail of fluid that she had squirted at the huge, ugly man. A line of fire whooshed up, briefly filling the cave with dazzling light, then fluttered and went out, causing no harm to anyone.

Snarling, teeth bared, Chewbacca charged the big man, but the dog was too weak to be effective. He got jawsful of parka, but the giant raised the semiautomatic rifle in both hands and brought it down butt-first into the dog's skull. Chewbacca emitted a short, sharp yelp and slumped at the giant's feet, either unconscious or dead.

Christine clung to consciousness, though tides of blackness lapped at her.

Grinning like a creature out of an old Frankenstein movie, the big man advanced into the room.

Christine saw Joey backing into the corner at the far end of the cave.

She had failed him.

No! There must be something she could do, Jesus, some decisive action she could still take, something that would dramatically turn the tables, something that would save them. There *must* be something. But she couldn't think of anything.

CHAPTER 71

THE HUGE MAN stepped farther into the cave. It was the monster Charlie had met at Spivey's rectory, the giant with the twisted face. The one the hag had called Kyle.

As he watched Kyle swagger into the chamber, and as he watched Christine cower from the grotesque intruder, Charlie was filled with equal measures of fear and self-loathing. He was afraid because he knew he was going to die in this dank and lonely hole, and he loathed himself for his weakness and incompetence and ineffectual performance. His parents had been weak and ineffectual, had retreated into a haze of alcohol to console themselves for their inability to cope with life, and from the time he was very young Charlie had promised himself that he would never be like them. He had spent a lifetime learning to be strong, always strong. He *never* backed away from a challenge, largely because his parents had *always* backed away. And he seldom lost a battle. He *hated* losing, his parents were losers, not him, not Charlie Harrison of Klemet-Harrison. Losers were weak in body and mind and spirit, and weakness was the greatest sin. But he couldn't deny his current circumstances; there was no escaping the fact that he was now half paralyzed with pain, weak as a kitten, and struggling to retain consciousness. There was no dodging the truth, which was that he had brought Christine and Joey to this place and this condition with the promise that he would help them, and his promise had been empty. They needed him, and he couldn't do anything for them, and now he was going to end his life by failing those he loved, which didn't make him a lot different from his alky father and his hate-riddled, drunken mother.

A part of him knew that he was being too hard on himself. He had done his best. No one could have done more. But he was *always* too hard on himself, and he wouldn't relent now. What mattered was not what he had *meant* to do but what he had, in fact, done. And what he had done was bring them face to face with Death.

Behind Kyle, another figure moved out of the archway between this chamber and the next. A woman. For a moment she was in shadows, then revealed in the Halloween-orange light of the fire. Grace Spivey.

With effort, Charlie turned his stiff neck, blinked to clear his blurry vision, and looked at Joey. The boy was in the corner, back to the wall, hands down at his sides with his palms pressing hard against the stone behind him, as if he could will his way into the rock and out of this room. His eyes seemed to bulge. Tears glistened on his face. There was no question that he had been pulled back from the fantasy into which he had tried to escape, no doubt that his attention was now fully commanded by this world, by the chilling reality of Grace Spivey's hateful presence.

Charlie tried to raise his arms because if he could raise his arms he might be able to sit up, and if he could sit up he might be able to stand, and if he could stand he could fight. But he couldn't raise his arms, neither of them, not an inch.

Spivey paused to look down at Christine.

"Don't hurt him," Christine said, reduced to begging. "For God's sake, don't hurt my little boy."

Spivey didn't reply. Instead, she turned toward Charlie and shuffled slowly across the room. In her eyes was a look of maniacal hatred and triumph.

Charlie was terrified and repelled by what he saw in those eyes, and he looked away from her. He searched frantically for something that could save them, for a weapon or a course of action they had overlooked.

He was suddenly certain that there was still a way out, that they were not doomed, after all. It wasn't just wishful thinking, and it wasn't just a fever dream. He knew his own feelings better than that; he trusted his hunches, and this one was as real and as reliable as any he'd ever had before. *There was still a way out.* But where, how, *what?*

When Christine stared into Grace Spivey's eyes, she felt as if an ice-cold hand had plunged through her chest and had seized her heart in an arctic grip. For a moment she couldn't blink her eyes, couldn't swallow, couldn't breathe, couldn't *think.* The old woman was mad, yes, a raving lunatic, but there was power in her eyes, a perverse strength, and now Christine saw how Spivey might be able to make and hold converts to her insane crusade. Then the hag turned away from her, and Christine could breathe again, and she became aware, once more, of the searing pain in her leg.

Spivey stopped in front of Charlie and stared down at him.

She's purposefully ignoring Joey, Christine thought. He's the reason she has come all this way and has risked being shot, the reason she has struggled into these mountains through two blizzards, and now she's ignoring him just to savor the moment, relish the triumph.

Christine had nurtured a black hatred for Spivey; but now it was blacker than black. It pushed everything else out of her heart; for just a few seconds it drove out even her love for Joey and became all-fulfilling, consuming.

Then the madwoman turned toward Joey, and the hatred in Christine receded as conflicting waves of love, terror, remorse, and horror swept through her.

Something else swept through her, as well: the resurging feeling that there was still something that could be done to bring Spivey and the giant to their knees, if only she could think clearly.

At last Grace came face to face with the boy.

She became aware of the dark aura that surrounded him and radiated from him, and she was much afraid, for she might be too late. Perhaps the power of the Antichrist had grown too strong, and perhaps the child was now invulnerable.

There were tears on his face. He was still pretending to be only an ordinary six-year-old, small and scared and defenseless. Did he really think that she would be deceived by his act, that he had any chance at all of instilling doubt in her at this late hour? She had had moments of doubt before, as in that motel in Soledad, but those periods of weakness had been short-lived and were all behind her now.

She took a few steps toward him.

He tried to squeeze farther back into the corner, but he was already jammed so tightly into the junction of the rock walls that he almost seemed to be a boy-shaped extrusion of them.

She stopped when she was only six or eight feet from him, and she said, "You will not inherit the earth. Not for a thousand years and not even for one minute. I have come to stop you."

The child didn't answer.

She sensed that his powers had not yet grown too strong for her, and her confidence soared. He was still afraid of her. She had reached him in time.

She smiled. "Did you really think you could run away from me?"

His gaze strayed past her, and she knew he was looking at the battered dog.

"Your hellhound won't help you now," she said.

He began to shake, and he worked his mouth in an effort to speak, and she could see him form the word "Mommy," but he was unable to make even the slightest sound.

From a sheath attached to her belt, she withdrew a long-bladed hunting knife. It was sharply pointed and had been stropped until it was as keen as a razor.

Christine saw the knife and tried to bolt up from the floor, but the savage pain in her leg thwarted her, and she collapsed back onto the stone even as the giant was bringing the muzzle of the rifle around to cover her.

Speaking to Joey, Spivey said, "I was chosen for this task because of the way I dedicated myself to Albert all those years, because I knew how to give myself completely, unstintingly. That's how I've dedicated myself to this holy mission —without reservation or hesitation, with every ounce of my strength and will power. There was never any chance you would escape from me."

Desperately trying to reach Spivey, trying to touch her on an emotional level, Christine said, "Please, listen, *please,* you're wrong, all wrong. He's just a little boy, my little boy, and I love him, and he loves me." She was babbling, suddenly inarticulate, and she was furious with herself for being unable to find words that would convince. "Oh God, if you could only see how sweet and loving he is, you'd know you're all confused about him. You can't take him away from me. It would be so . . . *wrong.*"

Ignoring Christine, talking to Joey, Spivey held the knife out and said, "I've spent many hours praying over this blade. And one night I saw the spirit of one of Almighty God's angels come down from the heavens and through the window of my bedroom, and that spirit still resides here, within this consecrated instrument, and when it cuts into you, it will be not just the blade rending your flesh but the angelic spirit, as well."

The woman was stark raving mad, and Christine knew that an appeal to logic and reason would be as hopeless as an appeal to the emotions had been, but she had to try it, anyway. With growing desperation, she said, "Wait! Listen. You're wrong. Don't you see? Even if Joey was what you say—which he isn't, that's just crazy—but even if he *was,* even if God wanted him dead, then why wouldn't *God* destroy him? If He wanted my little boy dead, why wouldn't He strike him with lightning or cancer or let him be hit by a car? God wouldn't need *you* to deal with the Antichrist."

Spivey answered Christine this time but didn't turn to face her; the old woman's gaze remained on Joey. She spoke with a fervency that was scary, her voice rising and falling like that of a tent revivalist, but with more energy than any Elmer Gantry, with a rabid excitement that turned some words into animalistic growls, and with a soaring exaltation that gave other phrases a lilting songlike quality. The effect was terrifying and hypnotic, and Christine imagined that this was the same mysterious, powerful effect that Hitler and Stalin had had on crowds:

"When evil appears to us, when we see it at work in this troubled, troubled world, we can't merely fall to our *knees* and beg God to deliver us from it. Evil and vile temptation are a *test* of our faith and virtue, a *challenge* that we must face every day of our lives, in order to prove ourselves *worthy* of salvation and ascendance into Heaven. We cannot expect *God* to remove the yoke from us, for it is a yoke that *we* put upon *ourselves* in the first place. It is our sacred responsibility to *confront* evil and triumph over it, *on our own,* with those resources that Almighty God has given us. *That* is how we earn a place at His right hand, in the company of *angels."*

At last the old woman turned away from Joey and faced Christine, and her eyes were more disturbing than ever. She continued her harangue:

"And you reveal your own ignorance and your *damning* lack of faith when you attribute cancer and death and other afflictions to our *Lord,* God of Heaven and earth. It was not *He* who brought evil to the earth and afflicted mankind with ten thousand scourges. It was *Satan,* the abominable *serpent,* and it was *Eve,* in the blessed garden of peace, who brought the knowledge of *sin* and *death* and *despair* to the *thousand* generations that followed. We brought evil upon ourselves, and now that the *ultimate* evil walks the earth in this child's body, it is our responsibility to deal with it ourselves. It is the *test of tests,* and the hope of all mankind rests with our ability to meet it!"

The old woman's fury had left Christine speechless, devoid of hope.

Spivey turned to Joey again and said, "I smell your putrescent heart. I feel your radiant evil. It's a coldness that cuts right into my bones and vibrates there. Oh, I know you, all right. I *know* you."

Fighting off panic that threatened to leave her as emotionally and mentally incapacitated as she was physically helpless, Christine wracked her mind for a plan, an idea. She was willing to try anything, no matter how pointless it seemed, *anything,* but she could think of nothing.

She saw that, in spite of his condition, Charlie had pulled himself into a sitting position. Weak as he was, overwhelmed by pain, any movement must have been an ordeal for him. He wouldn't have pulled himself up without reason—would he? Maybe he had thought of the course of action which continued to elude Christine. That's what she wanted to believe. That's what she hoped with all her heart.

Spivey reversed her grip on the knife, held the handle toward the ugly giant. "It's time, Kyle. The boy's appearance is deceptive. He looks small and weak, but he'll be strong, he'll resist, and although I am Chosen, I'm not *physically* strong, not any more. It's up to you."

An odd expression took possession of Kyle's face. Christine expected a look of triumph, eagerness, maniacal hatred, but instead he appeared . . . not worried, not confused, but a little of both . . . and hesitant.

Spivey said, "Kyle, it's time for you to be the hammer of God."

Christine shuddered. She scrambled across the floor toward the giant, so frightened that she could ignore the pain in her leg. She grabbed for the hem of his parka, hoping to unbalance him, topple him, and get the gun away from him, a hopeless plan considering his size and strength, but she didn't even have a chance to try it because he swung the butt of his rifle at her, just as he'd swung it at the dog. It slammed into her shoulder, knocking her back, onto her side, and all the air was driven from her lungs. She gasped for breath and put one hand to her damaged shoulder and began to cry.

With tremendous effort, nearly blacking out from the pain, Charlie sat up because he thought he might see the situation differently from a new position and might, finally, spot a solution they had overlooked. However, he still could not think of anything that would save them.

Kyle took the knife from Grace and gave her the rifle.

The old woman stepped out of the giant's way.

Kyle turned the knife over and over in his hand, staring at it with a slightly baffled expression. The blade glinted in the goblin light of the fire.

Charlie tried to pull himself up the five-foot-high face of the ledge that formed the hearth, with the notion of grabbing a burning log and throwing it. From the corner of her eye, Spivey saw him struggling with the dead weight of his own shattered body, and she pointed the rifle at him. She might as well have saved herself the trouble; he didn't have sufficient strength to reach the fire, anyway.

Kyle Barlowe looked at the knife in his hand, then at the boy, and he wasn't sure which scared him more.

He had used knives before. He'd cut people before, even killed them. It had been easy, and he had vented some of the rage that periodically built in him like a head of steam in a boiler. But he was not the same man that he had been then. He could control his emotions now. He understood himself at last. The old Kyle had hated everyone he met, whether he knew them or not, because inevitably they rejected him. But the new Kyle realized that his hatred did more harm to him than to anyone else. In fact, he now knew that he had not always been rejected because of his ugliness, but often because of his surliness and anger. Grace had given him purpose and acceptance, and in time he had discovered affection, and after affection had come the first indications of an ability to love and be loved. And now, if he used the knife, if he killed the boy, he might be launching himself on an inevitable slide back down to the depths from which he'd climbed. He feared the knife.

But he was afraid of the boy, too. He knew Grace had psychic power, for he had seen her do things that no ordinary person could have done. Therefore, she must be right when she said the boy was the Antichrist. If he failed to kill the demonic child, he would be failing God, Grace, and all mankind.

But wasn't he being asked to throw away his soul in order to gain salvation? Kill in order to be blessed? Did that make sense?

"Please don't hurt my little boy. *Please,*" Christine Scavello said.

Kyle looked down at her, and his quandary deepened. She didn't *look* like the dark Madonna, with the power of Satan behind her. She was hurt, scared, begging for mercy. He had hurt her, and he felt a pang of guilt at the injury he'd caused.

Sensing that something was wrong, Mother Grace said, "Kyle?"

Turning to the boy, Kyle drew his knife hand back, so he would have all the power of his muscles behind the first blow. If he took the last few steps in a crouch, swung the knife in low, rammed the blade into the boy's guts, it would all be over in a few seconds.

The child was still crying, and his bright blue eyes were transfixed by the point of the knife in Kyle's hand. His face was twisted into a wretched mask of terror, and sweat had broken out all over his pasty skin. His small body was slightly bent as if in anticipation of the pain to come.

"Strike him!" Mother Grace urged.

Questions raced through Kyle's mind. How can God be merciful and still make me bear the burden of my monstrous face? What kind of god would let me be saved from a meaningless life of violence and pain and hatred—just to force me to kill again? If God rules the world, why does He allow so much suffering and pain and misery? And how could it be any worse if Satan ruled?

"The devil is putting doubt in your mind!" Grace said. "That's where it's coming from, Kyle. Not from within you! From the devil!"

"No," he told her. "You taught me to always think about doing the right thing, to *care* about doing the right thing, and now I'm going to take a minute here, just a minute to *think!*"

"Don't think, just *do!*" she said. "Or get out of my way and let me use this gun. How can you fail me now? After all I've done, how can you fail?"

She was right. He owed her everything. He would still be peddling dope, living in the gutter, consumed by hatred, if not for her. If he failed her now, where was his honor, his gratitude? In failing her, wouldn't he be sliding back into his old life almost as surely as if he used the knife as she demanded?

"Please," Christine Scavello said. "Oh, God, please don't hurt my baby."

"Send him back to Hell forever!" Grace shouted.

Kyle felt as if he were being torn apart. He had been making moral judgments and value decisions for only a few years, not long enough for it to be an unconscious habit, not long enough to deal easily with a dilemma like this. He realized that tears were spilling down his cheeks.

The boy's gaze rose from the point of the blade.

Kyle met the child's eyes and was jolted by them.

"Kill him!" Grace said.

Kyle was shaking violently.

The boy was shaking, too.

Their gazes had not merely locked but . . . *fused* . . . so it seemed to Kyle that he could see not only through his own eyes but through the eyes of the boy, as well. It was an almost magical empathy, as if he were both himself and the child, both assailant and victim. He felt large and dangerous . . . yet small and helpless at the same time. He was suddenly dizzy and increasingly confused. His vision swam out of focus for a moment. Then he saw—or imagined that he saw—himself looming over the child, literally saw himself from the boy's point of view, as if *he* were Joey Scavello. It was a stunning moment of insight, strange and disorienting, almost a clairvoyant experience. Looking up at himself from the boy's eyes, he was shocked by his appearance, by the savagery in his own face, by the madness of this attack. A chill swept up his spine, and he could not get his breath. This unflattering vision of himself was the psychic equivalent of a blow to the head with a ball-peen hammer, psychologically concussive. He blinked, and the moment of insight passed, and he was just himself again, though with a terrible headache and a lingering dizziness. Finally, he knew what he must do.

To Christine's surprise, the giant turned away from Joey and threw the knife into the flames beyond Charlie. Sparks and embers flew up like a swarm of fireflies.

"No!" Grace Spivey shouted.

"I'm through killing," the big man said, tears pouring copiously down his cheeks, softening the hard and dangerous look of him much as rain on a windowpane blurs and softens the view beyond.

"No," Spivey repeated.

"It's wrong," he said. "Even if I'm doing it for you . . . it's wrong."

"The devil put this thought in your mind," the old woman warned.

"No, Mother Grace. *You* put it there."

"The devil!" she insisted frantically. "The devil put it there!"

The giant hesitated, blotting his face with his big hands.

Christine held her breath and watched the confrontation with both hope and dread. If this Frankensteinian creature actually turned against his master, he might be a formidable ally, but at the moment he did not seem sufficiently stable to deliver them from their crisis. Though he had thrown the knife away, he appeared confused, in a mental and emotional turmoil, and even slightly unsteady on his feet. When he put his hands to his head and squinted through his tears, he seemed in pain, almost as if he had been blackjacked. He might, at any moment, turn on Joey and kill him, after all.

"The devil put this doubt in your mind," Grace Spivey insisted, advancing on the giant, shouting at him. "The devil, the devil, the *devil!*"

He took his tear-wet hands from his face and blinked at the old woman. "If it was the devil, then he's not all bad. Not all bad if he wants me never to kill again." He staggered toward the passageway that led out of the caves, stopped just his side of it, and leaned wearily against the wall, as if he needed a moment to recover from some exhausting task.

"Then *I'll* do it," Spivey said furiously. She had been clutching the semi-automatic rifle by its shoulder strap. Now she took it in both hands. "You're my Judas, Kyle Barlowe. Judas. You've failed me. But God won't fail me. And I won't fail God the way you have, no, not me, not the Chosen, not *me!*"

Christine looked at Joey. He still stood in the corner, with his back against the stone, his arms raised now, his small pale palms flattened and turned outward, as if warding off the bullets that Grace Spivey would fire at him. His eyes were huge and frightened and fixed on the old woman as though she had hypnotized him. Christine wanted to shout at him to run, but it was pointless because Spivey was in his way and would surely stop him. Besides, where could he go? Outside, in the subzero air, where he would quickly succumb to exposure? Deeper in the caves, where Spivey would easily follow and soon find him? He was trapped, small and defenseless, with nowhere to hide.

Christine looked at Charlie, who was weeping with frustration at his own inability to help, and she tried to launch herself up at Grace Spivey, but she was defeated by her wounded leg and damaged shoulder, and finally, in desperation, she looked back at Kyle and said, "Don't let her do it! For God's sake, don't let her hurt him!"

The giant only blinked stupidly at Christine. He seemed shellshocked, in no condition to wrest the rifle out of Spivey's hands.

"Please, please, stop her," Christine begged him.

"*You* shut up!" Grace warned, taking one threatening step toward Christine. Then, to Joey, she said, "And don't you try using those eyes on me. It won't work with me. You can't get at me that way, not *any* way, not me. I can resist."

The old woman was having some difficulty figuring how to fire the gun, and when she finally got a round off, it went high, smashed into the wall above Joey's head, almost striking the ceiling, the explosive report crashing back and forth in that confined area, one deafening echo laminated atop another. The thunderous noise and the recoil surprised Spivey, jolting her frail body. She stumbled backwards two steps, fired again without meaning to, and that second bullet *did* strike the ceiling and ricocheted around the room.

Joey was screaming.

Christine was shouting, looking for something to throw, a weapon no matter how crude, but she could find nothing. The pain in her wounded leg was like a bolt fastening her to the stone, and she could only beat her hand on the floor in frustration.

The old woman moved in on Joey, holding the rifle awkwardly though with evident determination to finish the job this time. But something was wrong. She was either out of ammunition or the gun had jammed, for she began to struggle with the weapon angrily.

As the echoes of the second shot faded, a mysterious sound arose from deeper in the mountain, adding to the confusion, rising up from other caverns, a strange and frightening racket that Christine could almost but not quite identify.

The gun *had* jammed. Spivey managed to eject an expended cartridge that had been wedged in the chamber. The brass cylinder popped into the air, reflecting the firelight, and hit the floor with a faint clink and ping.

Wicka-wicka-wicka-wicka: The strange, leathery, flapping sound drew nearer, approaching from deeper in the mountain. The cool air vibrated with it.

Spivey half turned away from Joey to look at the entrance to the adjoining cave, through which she and the giant had entered a few minutes ago. "No!" she said, and she seemed to know what was coming.

And in that instant Christine knew, too.

Bats.

A thunderous, flapping, whirling tornado of bats.

An instant later they swarmed out of the adjoining caverns and into this room, a hundred of them, two hundred, more, rising to the vaulted ceiling, screeching, industriously working their leathery wings, darting back and forth, a seething multitude of frenziedly whirling shadows at the upper reaches of the firelight.

The old woman stared at them. She was speaking, but her words were lost in the drumlike roar of the swarm.

As one, the bats stopped shrieking. Only the rustling-fluttering-hissing of wings sounded now. Their silence was so unnatural that it seemed worse than their screams.

No, Christine thought. *Oh, no!*

In the pall of this frightening assemblage, Spivey's maniacal self-confidence shattered. She fired two rounds at the nightmare flock, a senseless and, in fact, dangerous assault.

Whether provoked by the gunfire or otherwise motivated, the bats swooped down as if they were a single creature, a cloud of tiny black killing machines, all claws and teeth, and fell upon Grace Spivey. They slashed at her insulated ski suit, got tangled in her hair, sank their claws into her and hung on. She staggered across the cavern, flailing her arms and whirling about, as if performing a macabre dance, or as if she thought she could take flight with them. Squealing, gagging, retching, she collided with one wall, rebounded from it, and still the beasts clung to her, darted, nipped.

Kyle Barlowe took two tentative steps toward her, halted, looking not so much afraid as bewildered.

Christine did not want to look, but she could not help it. She was transfixed by the horrible battle.

Spivey appeared to be wearing a garment composed of hundreds of flapping black rags. Her face vanished entirely beneath that tattered cloth. But for the flutter and scrape and tick of their wings, the bats maintained their eerie silence, though they moved even more frantically now, with malign intent. They tore her to pieces.

CHAPTER 72

AT LAST THE bats were still.

Spivey was motionless, too.

For perhaps a minute, the bats were a living, black funeral shroud covering the body, quivering slightly like wind-rustled cloth. By the second, their unnatural silence grew more remarkable and unnerving. They did not quite look, behave, or seem like ordinary bats. Besides the astonishing timeliness of their appearance and the purposefulness of their attack, they had a quality—an *air* —that was indefinably strange. Christine saw some of the small, dark, evil heads lift up, turn left and right and left again, crimson eyes blinking, and it seemed as if they were awaiting an order from the leader of their flock. Then, as if the order came in a voice only they could hear, they rose as one, in a sudden fluttering cloud, and flew back into other caverns.

Kyle Barlowe and Charlie were silent, stunned.

Christine would not look at the dead woman.

And she could not look away from her son. He was alive—unbelievably, amazingly, miraculously alive. After all the terror and pain they had been through, after death had seemed inevitable, she had difficulty believing this last-minute reprieve was real. Irrationally, she felt that if she looked away from Joey, even for a moment, he would be dead when she looked back again, and their extraordinary salvation would prove to be a delusion, a dream.

More than anything, she wanted to hold him, touch his hair, his face, hug him tight, feel the beat of his heart and the warmth of his breath on her neck. But her injuries prevented her from going to him, and he appeared to be in a state of shock that rendered him temporarily oblivious of her.

Far away in other caves, the bats must have begun to resume their familiar perches, for they squeaked again as if contesting with one another for favored positions. The eerie sound of them, which soon faded into silence once more, sent a chill through Christine, a chill that intensified when she saw her half-mesmerized son cock his head as if in understanding of the shrill language of those nightmare creatures. He was disturbingly pale. His mouth curved into what appeared to be a vague smile, but then Christine decided it was actually a grimace of disgust or horror engendered by the scene that he had just witnessed and that had left him in this semiparalytic stupor.

As the renewed cries of the bats gradually faded, fear uncoiled in Christine, though not because of what had happened to Grace Spivey. And she was not afraid that the bats would return and kill again. In fact, somehow, she knew they would not, and it was precisely that impossible knowledge that frightened her. She did not want to consider where it came from, to ponder just *how* she knew. She did not want to think about what it might mean.

Joey was alive. Nothing else mattered. The sound of the gun had drawn the bats, and by a stroke of luck—or through God's mercy—they had limited their attack to Grace Spivey. Joey was alive. *Alive.* She felt tears of joy suddenly burning in her eyes. Joey was alive. She must concentrate on that wonderful twist of fate, for it was from here that their future began, and she was determined that it would be a bright future full of love and happiness, with no sadness, no fear, and above all no *doubts.*

Doubt could eat at you, destroy happiness, turn love to bitterness. Doubt could even come between a mother and her much-loved son, producing an unbridgeable chasm, and she simply could not allow that to happen.

Nevertheless, unbidden and unwanted, a memory came to her: Tuesday, Laguna Beach, the Arco station service bay where they had waited for Charlie after barely escaping the bomb that destroyed Miriam Rankin's house; she and Joey and the two bodyguards standing by the stacks of tires, with the world outside caught in a fierce electrical storm so powerful that it seemed to signal the end of the world; Joey moving to the open garage doors, fascinated by the lightning, one devastating bolt after another, unlike anything Christine had seen before, especially in southern California where lightning was uncommon; Joey regarding it without fear, as if it were only fireworks, as if . . . as if he knew it could not harm him. As if it were a *sign?* As if the preternatural ferocity of the storm was somehow a message that he understood and took hope from?

No. Nonsense.

She had to push such stupid thoughts out of her mind. That was just the kind of craziness that could infect you merely from association with the likes of Grace Spivey. My God, the old woman had been like a plague carrier, spreading irrationality, infecting everyone with her paranoid fantasies.

But what about the bats? Why had they come at exactly the right moment? Why had they attacked only Grace Spivey?

Stop it, she told herself. You're just . . . making something out of nothing. The bats came because they were frightened by the first two shots that the old woman fired. The sound was so loud it scared them, brought them out. And then . . . when they got here . . . well, she shot at them and made them angry. Yes. Of course. That was it.

Except . . . If the first pair of shots scared the bats, why didn't the third and fourth shots scare them again? Why didn't they fly away? Why did they attack her and dispose of her so . . . *conveniently?*

No.

Nonsense.

Joey was staring at the floor, still anemically pale, but he was beginning to emerge from his semi-catatonic state. He was nervously chewing on one finger, very much like a little boy who knew he had done something that would upset his mother. After a few seconds, he raised his head, and his eyes met Christine's. He tried to smile through his tears, but his mouth was still soft and loose with shock, with fear. He had never looked sweeter or more in need of a mother's love, and his weakness and vulnerability gave her heart a twist.

His vision clouded by pain, weak from infection and loss of blood, Charlie wondered if everything that had happened in the cave had actually transpired only in his fevered imagination.

But the bats were real. Their bloody handiwork lay only a few feet away, undeniable.

He assured himself that the bizarre attack on Grace Spivey had a rational, natural explanation, but he was not entirely convinced by his own assurances. Maybe the bats were rabid; that might explain why they had not fled from the sound of the gun but had, instead, been drawn to it, for all rabid animals were especially sensitive to—and easily angered by—bright lights and loud noises. But why had they bitten and clawed only Grace, leaving Joey, Christine, Barlowe, and Charlie himself untouched?

He looked at Joey.

The boy had come out of his quasi-autistic trance. He had moved to Chewbacca. He was kneeling by the dog, sobbing, wanting to touch the motionless animal, but afraid, making little gestures of helplessness with his hands.

Charlie remembered when, last Monday in his office, he had looked at Joey and had seen a fleshless skull instead of a face. It had been a brief vision, lasting only the blink of an eye, and he had shoved the memory of it to the back of his mind. If he had worried about it at all, it was because he had thought it might mean Joey was going to die; but he hadn't really believed in visions or clairvoyant revelations, so he hadn't worried much. Now he wondered if the vision had been real. Maybe it had not meant that Joey would die; maybe it had meant that Joey *was* death.

Surely such thoughts were proof only of the seriousness of his fever. Joey was Joey—nothing more, nothing worse, nothing strange.

But Charlie remembered the rat in the battery cellar, too, and the dream he had later that same night, in which rats—messengers of death—had poured forth from the boy's chest.

This is nuts, he told himself. I've been a detective too long. I don't trust anyone any more. Now I'm looking for deception and corruption in even the most innocent hearts.

Petting the dog, Joey began to speak, the words coming in groups, in breathless rushes, between sobs: "Mom, is he dead? Is Chewbacca dead? Did . . . that bad man . . . did he kill Chewbacca?"

Charlie looked at Christine. Her face was wet with tears, and her eyes brimmed with a new flood. She seemed temporarily speechless. Contrasting emotions fought for possession of her lovely face: horror over the bloodiness of Spivey's death, surprise at their own survival, and joy at the sight of her unharmed child.

Seeing her joy, Charlie was ashamed that he had regarded the boy with suspicion. Yet . . . he was a detective, and it was a detective's job to be suspicious.

He watched Joey closely, but he didn't detect the radiant evil of which Spivey spoke, didn't feel that he was in the presence of something monstrous. Joey was still a six-year-old boy. Still a good-looking kid with a sweet smile. Still able to laugh and cry and worry and hope. Charlie had seen what had happened to Grace Spivey, yet he was not in the least afraid of Joey because, dammit, he could not just suddenly start believing in devils, demons, and the Antichrist. He'd always had a layman's interest in science, and he'd been an advocate of the space program from the time he was a kid himself; he always had believed that logic, reason, and science—the secular equivalent of Christianity's Holy Trinity—would one day solve all of mankind's problems and all the mysteries of existence, including the source and meaning of life. And science could probably explain what had happened here, too; a biologist or zoologist, with special knowledge of bats, would most likely find their behavior well within the range of normality.

As Joey continued to crouch over Chewbacca, petting him, weeping, the dog's tail stirred, then swished across the floor.

Joey cried, "Mom, look! He's alive!"

Christine saw Chewbacca roll off his side, get to his feet, shake himself. He had appeared to be dead. Now he was not even dizzy. He pranced up onto his hind feet, put his forepaws up on his young master's shoulders, and began licking Joey's face.

The boy giggled, ruffled the dog's fur. "How ya doin', Chewbacca? Good dog. Good old Chewbacca."

Chewbacca? Christine wondered. Or Brandy?

Brandy had been decapitated by Spivey's people, had been buried with honors in a nice pet cemetery in Anaheim. But if they went back to that cemetery now and opened the grave, what would they find? Nothing? An empty wooden box? Had Brandy been resurrected and had he found his way to the pound just in time for Charlie and Joey to adopt him again?

Garbage, Christine told herself angrily. Junk thought. Stupid.

But she could not get those sick thoughts out of her head, and they led to other irrational considerations.

Seven years ago . . . the man on the cruise ship . . . Lucius Under . . . Luke.

Who had he *really* been?

What had he been?

No, no, no. Impossible.

She squeezed her eyes shut and put one hand to her head. She was so tired. Exhausted. She did not have the strength to resist those fevered speculations. She felt contaminated by Spivey's craziness, dizzy, disconnected, sort of the way victims of malaria must feel.

Luke. For years she had tried to forget him; now she tried to remember. He'd been about thirty, lean, well muscled. Blond hair streak-bleached by the sun. Clear blue eyes. A bronze tan. White, perfectly even teeth. An ingratiating smile, an easy manner. He had been a charming but not particularly original mix of sophistication and simplicity, worldliness and innocence, a smooth-talker who knew how to get what he wanted from women. She'd thought of him as a surfer, for God's sake; that's what he had seemed like, the epitome of the young California surfer.

Even with her strength draining away through her wound and leaving her increasingly light-headed, even though her exhaustion and loss of blood had put her in a feeble state of mind that left her highly susceptible to Spivey's insane accusations, she could not believe that Luke had been Satan. The devil in the guise of a surfer boy? It was too banal to be believable. If Satan were real, if he wanted a son, if he wanted her to bear that son, why wouldn't he simply have come to her in the night in his real form? She could not have resisted him. Why wouldn't he have taken her forthrightly, with much flapping of his wings and lashing of his tail?

Luke had drunk beer, and he'd had a passion for potato chips. He had urinated and showered and brushed his teeth like any other human being. Sometimes his conversation had been downright tedious, dumb. Wouldn't the devil at least have been unfailingly witty?

Surely, Luke had been Luke, nothing more, nothing less.

She opened her eyes.

Joey was giggling and hugging Chewbacca, so happy. So ordinary.

Of course, she thought, the devil might take a perverse pleasure in using me, *particularly* me, to carry his child.

After all, she was a former nun. Her brother had been a priest—and a martyr. She had fallen away from her faith. She had been a virgin when she'd given herself to the man on the cruise ship. Wasn't she a perfect means by which the devil could make a mockery of the *first* virgin birth?

Madness. She hated herself for doubting her child, for giving any credence whatsoever to Spivey's babbling.

And yet . . . hadn't her whole life changed for the better as soon as she had become pregnant with the boy? She had been uncommonly healthy—no colds, no headaches—and happy and successful in business. As if she were . . . *blessed.*

Finally satisfied that his dog was all right, Joey disentangled himself from Chewbacca and came to Christine. Rubbing at his red eyes, sniffling, he said, "Mom, is it over? Are we going to be okay? I'm still scared."

She didn't want to look into his eyes, but to her surprise she found nothing frightening in them, nothing to make her blood run cold.

Brandy . . . no, *Chewbacca* came to her and nuzzled her hand.

"Mommy," Joey said, kneeling beside her, "I'm scared. What'd they do to you? What'd they do? Are you going to die? Don't die, please, don't die, Mommy, please."

She put a hand to his face.

He was afraid, trembling. But that was better than an autistic trance.

He slid against her, and after only a moment's hesitation, she held him with her good arm. Her Joey. Her son. Her *child.* The feel of him, snuggling against her, was marvelous, indescribably wonderful. The contact was better than any medicine could have been, for it revitalized her, cleared her head, and dissipated the sick images and insane fears that were Grace Spivey's perverse legacy. Hugging her child, feeling him cling to her in need of love and reassurance, she was cured of Spivey's mad contagion. This boy was the fruit of her womb, a life she had given to the world, and nothing was more precious to her than he was—and always would be.

Kyle Barlowe had slid down to the floor, his back against the wall, and had buried his face in his hands to avoid staring at Mother Grace's hideous remains. But the dog came to Kyle, nuzzled him, and Kyle looked up. The mutt licked his face; its tongue was warm, its nose cold, like the tongue and nose of any dog. It had a clownish face. How could he ever have imagined that such a dog was a hound from Hell?

"I loved her like a mother, and she changed my life, so I stayed with her even when she went wrong, went bad, even when she started . . . to do really crazy things," Kyle said, startled by the sound of his own voice, surprised to hear himself explaining his actions to Christine Scavello and Charlie Harrison. "She had . . . this power. No denying that. She was . . . like in the movies . . . clairvoyant. You know? Psychic. That's how she could follow you and the boy . . . not because God was guiding her . . . and not because the boy was the son of Satan . . . but because she was just . . . clairvoyant." This was not something he had known until he heard himself speaking it. In fact, even now, he did not seem to know what he was going to say until the words came from him. "She had visions. I guess they weren't religious like I thought. Not from God. Not really. Maybe she knew that all along. Or maybe she misunderstood. Maybe she actually believed she *was* talking with God. I don't think she meant to do bad, you know. She could've misinterpreted her visions, couldn't she? But there's a big difference between being psychic and being Joan of Arc, huh? A big difference."

Charlie listened to Kyle Barlowe wrestle with his conscience, and he was curiously soothed by the ugly giant's deep, remorseful voice. The soothing effect was partly due to the fact that Barlowe was helping them understand these recent events in a light less fantastic than that shed by Armageddon; he was showing them how it might be paranormal without being supernatural or cataclysmic. But Charlie was also affected and relaxed by the odd, soft, rumbling tones and cadences of the big man's voice, by a slight smokiness in the air, and by some indefinable quality of light or heat that made him receptive to this message, as a hypnotist's subject is receptive to suggestions of all kinds.

Kyle said, "Mother Grace meant well. She just got confused there toward the end. Confused. And, God help me, I went along with her even though I had my doubts. Almost went too far. Almost . . . God help me . . . almost used the knife on that little boy. See, what it is . . . I think maybe your Joey . . . maybe he has a little psychic ability of his own. You know? Have you ever noticed it? Any indications? I think he must be a little like Mother Grace herself, a little bit clairvoyant or something, even if he doesn't know it, even if the power hasn't become obvious yet . . . and *that* was what she sensed in him . . . but she misunderstood it. That must be it. That must explain it.. Poor Grace. Poor, sweet Grace. She meant well. Can you believe that? She meant well, and so did I, and so did everyone in the church. She meant well."

Chewbacca left Kyle and came to Charlie, and he let the dog nuzzle him affectionately. He noticed blood in its ears, and blood matting the fur *on* its ears, which meant Barlowe had hit it very hard with the butt of the rifle, terribly hard indeed, and yet it seemed completely recovered. Surely it had suffered a severe concussion. Yet it was not dizzy or disoriented.

The dog looked into his eyes.

Charlie frowned.

"She meant well. She meant well," Kyle said, and he put his face in his hands and began to cry.

Cuddling with his mother, Joey said, "Mommy, he scares me. What's he talkin' about? He scares me."

"It's all right," Christine said.

"He scares me."

"It's okay, Skipper."

To Charlie's surprise, Christine found the strength to sit up and hitch backward a couple of feet, until she was leaning against the wall. She had seemed too exhausted to move, even to speak. Her face looked better, too, not quite so pale.

Still sniffling, wiping at his nose with his sleeve, wiping his eyes with one small fist, Joey said, "Charlie? You okay?"

Although Spivey and her people no longer posed any threat, Charlie was still quite certain that he would die in this cave. He was in bad shape, and it would be hours yet before help could be summoned and could reach them. He would not last that long. Yet he tried to smile at Joey, and in a voice so weak it frightened him, he said, "I'm okay."

The boy left his mother and came to Charlie. He said, "Magnum couldn't've done better than you did."

Joey sat down beside Charlie and put a hand on him. Charlie flinched, but it was all right, perfectly all right, and then for a couple of minutes he lost consciousness, or perhaps he merely dropped off to sleep. When Charlie came to, Joey was with his mother again, and Kyle Barlowe seemed to be getting ready to leave. "What's wrong?" Charlie asked. "What's happening now?"

Christine was obviously relieved to see him conscious once more. She said, "There's no way you and I can make it out of here on our feet. We'll have to be carried in litters. Mr. Barlowe is going for help."

Barlowe smiled reassuringly. It was a ghastly expression on his cruelly formed face. "The snow's stopped falling, and there's no wind. If I stay to the forest trails, I should be able to make it down to civilization in a few hours.

Maybe I can get a mountain rescue team back here before nightfall. I'm sure I can."

"Are you taking Joey with you?" Charlie asked. He noticed that his voice was stronger than before; speaking did not require as much effort as it had done a few minutes ago. "Are you getting him out?"

"No," Christine said. "Joey's staying with us."

"I'll move faster without him," Barlowe said. "Besides, the two of you need him to put wood on the fire every now and then."

Joey said, "I'll take care of them, Mr. Barlowe. You can count on me. Chewbacca and me."

The dog barked softly, once, as if in affirmation of the boy's pledge.

Barlowe favored the boy with another malformed smile, and Joey grinned at him in return. Joey had accepted the giant's conversion with considerably greater alacrity than Charlie had, and his trust seemed to be reciprocated and well placed.

Barlowe left them.

They sat in silence for a moment.

They did not even glance at Grace Spivey's corpse, as if it were only another formation of stone.

Clenching his teeth, preparing for an agonizing and most likely fruitless ordeal, Charlie tried pulling himself up into a sitting position. Although he had possessed insufficient strength to do it before, he now found the task remarkably easy. The pain from the bullet wound in his shoulder had dramatically subsided, much to his surprise, and was now only a dull ache which he could endure with little trouble. His other injuries provided a measure of discomfort, but they were not as bothersome or as sapping of his energy as they had been. He felt somewhat . . . revitalized . . . and he knew that he would be able to hold onto life until the rescue team had arrived and had gotten them off the mountain, to a hospital.

He wondered if he felt better because of Joey. The boy had come to him, had laid a hand on him, and he had slept for a couple of minutes, and when he had regained consciousness he was . . . partially healed. Was that one of the child's powers? If so, it was an imperfect power, for Charlie had not been entirely or even mostly healed; the bullet wound had not knitted up; his bruises and lacerations had not faded; he felt only a little bit better. The very imperfection of the healing power—*if* it existed at all—seemed to argue for the psychic explanation that Barlowe had offered them. The inadequacy of it indicated that it was a power of which Joey was unaware, a paranormal ability expressed in an entirely unconscious manner. Which meant he was just a little boy with a special gift. Because if he was the Antichrist, he would possess unlimited and miraculous power, and he would quickly and entirely heal both his mother and Charlie. Wouldn't he? Sure. Sure he would.

Chewbacca returned to Charlie.

There was still blood crusted in the dog's ears.

Charlie stared into its eyes.

He petted it.

The bullet wound in Christine's leg had stopped bleeding, and the pain had drained out of it. She felt clear-headed. With each passing minute she developed a greater appreciation of their survival, which was (she now saw) a tribute—*not* to the intervention of supernatural forces, but—to their incredible determination and endurance. Confidence returned to her, and she began to believe, once more, in the future.

For a few minutes, when she had been bleeding and helpless, when Spivey had been looming over Joey, Christine had surrendered to an uncharacteristic despair. She had been in such a bleak mood that, when the angry bats had responded to the gunfire and had attacked Spivey, Christine had even briefly wondered if Joey was, after all, what Spivey had accused him of being. Good heavens! Now, with Barlowe on his way for help, with the worst of her pain gone, with a growing belief in the likelihood of her and Charlie's survival, watching Joey as he fumblingly added a few branches to the fire, she could not imagine how such dark and foolish fears could have seized her. She had been so exhausted and so weak and so despondent that she had been susceptible to Spivey's insane message. Though that moment of hysteria was past and equilibrium restored, she was chilled by the realization that even *she* had been, however briefly, fertile ground for Spivey's lunacy.

How easily it could happen: one lunatic spreads her delusions to the gullible, and soon there is a hysterical mob, or in this case a cult, believing itself to be driven by the best intentions and, therefore, armored against doubt by steely self-righteousness. *There* was evil, she realized: not in her little boy but in mankind's fatal attraction to easy, even if irrational, answers.

From across the room, Charlie said, "You trust Barlowe?"

"I think so," Christine said.

"He could have another change of heart on the way down."

"I think he'll send help," she said.

"If he changes his mind about Joey, he wouldn't even have to come back. He could just leave us here, let cold and hunger do the job for him."

"He'll come back, I bet," Joey said, dusting his small hands together after adding the branches to the fire. "I think he's one of the good guys, after all. Don't you, Mom? Don't you think he's one of the good guys?"

"Yeah," Christine said. She smiled. "He's one of the good guys, honey."

"Like us," Joey said.

"Like us," she said.

Hours later, but well before nightfall, they heard the helicopter.

"The chopper will have skis on it," Charlie said. "They'll land in the meadow, and the rescue team will walk in from there."

"We're going home?" Joey asked.

Christine was crying with relief and happiness. "We're going home, honey. You better get your jacket and gloves, start getting dressed."

The boy ran to the pile of insulated sportswear in the corner.

To Charlie, Christine said, "Thank you."

"I failed you," he said.

"No. We had a bit of luck there at the end . . . Barlowe's indecision, and then the bats. But we wouldn't have gotten that far if it hadn't been for you. You were great. I love you, Charlie."

He hesitated to reply in kind, for any embrace of her was also an embrace of the boy; there was no escaping that. And he was not entirely comfortable with the boy, even though he was trying hard to believe that Barlowe's explanation was the right one.

Joey went to Christine, frowning. The drawstring on his hood was too loose, and he could not undo the clumsy knot he had put it in. "Mommy, why'd they have to put a *shoe*lace under my chin like this?"

Smiling, Christine helped him. "I thought you were getting really good at tying shoelaces."

"I am," the boy said proudly. "But they gotta be on my *feet.*"

"Well, I'm afraid we can't think of you as a big boy until you're able to tie a shoelace no matter *where* they put it."

"Jeez. Then I guess I'll never be a big boy."

Christine finished retying the hood string. "Oh, you'll get there one day, honey."

Charlie watched as she hugged her son. He sighed. He shook his head. He cleared his throat. He said, "I love you, too, Christine. I really do."

Two days later, in the hospital in Reno, after enduring the attention of uncountable doctors and nurses, after several interviews with the police and one with a representative of the press, after long phone conversations with Henry Rankin, after two nights of much-needed drug-induced sleep, Charlie was left to find unassisted rest on the third night. He had no difficulty getting to sleep, but he dreamed.

He dreamed of making love to Christine, and it was not a fantasy of sex but more a memory of their lovemaking at the cabin. He had never given himself so completely as he had to her that night, and the next day she had gone out of her way to tell him that she had done things with him that she had never contemplated doing with another man. Now, in the dream, they coupled with that same startling fervor and energy, casting aside all inhibitions. But in the dream, as it had been in reality, there was also something . . . *savage* about it, something fierce and animalistic, as if the sex they shared were more than an expression of love or lust, as if it were a . . . ceremony, a bonding, which was somehow committing him totally to Christine and, therefore, to Joey as well. As Christine straddled him, as he thrust like a bull deep within her, the floor under them began to split open—and here the dream departed from reality—and the couch began to slip into a widening aperture, and although both he and Christine recognized the danger, they could not do anything about it, could not cease their rutting even to save themselves, but continued to press flesh to flesh as the crack in the floor grew ever wider, as they became aware of something in the darkness below, something that was *hungry* for them, and Charlie wanted to pull away from her, flee, wanted to scream, but could not, could only cling to her and thrust within her, as the couch collapsed through the yawning hole, the cabin floor vanishing above them. And they fell away into—

He sat up in the hospital bed, gasping.

The patient in the other bed grunted softly but did not rouse from his deep sleep.

The room was dark except for a small light at the foot of each bed and vague moonglow at the window.

Charlie leaned back against the headboard.

Gradually, his rapid heartbeat and frantic breathing subsided.

He was damp with sweat.

The dream had brought back all his doubts about Joey. Val Gardner had flown up from Orange County and had taken Joey home with her this afternoon, and Charlie had been genuinely sorry to see the kid go. The boy had been so cute, so full of good humor and unconsciously amusing banter, that the hospital staff had taken him to their hearts, and his frequent visits had made the time pass more quickly and agreeably for Charlie. But now, courtesy of his nightmare, which was courtesy of his subconscious, he was in an emotional turmoil again.

Charlie had always thought of himself as a good man, a man who always did the right thing, who tried to help the innocent and punish the guilty. That was why he had wanted to spend his life playing Mr. Private Investigator. Sam Spade, Philip Marlowe, Lew Archer, Charlie Harrison: moral men, admirable men, maybe even heroes. So. So what if? What if *Joey* had called forth those bats? What if Chewbacca was Brandy, dead twice and resurrected by his master both times? What if Joey was less the unaware psychic that Barlowe believed and more the . . . more the demon that Spivey claimed? Crazy. But what if? What was a good man supposed to do in such a case? What was the right course of action?

Weeks later, on a Sunday evening in April, Charlie went to the pet cemetery where Brandy had been buried. He arrived after closing time, well after dark, and he took a pick and shovel with him.

The small grave with its little marker was right at the top of a knoll, where Christine had said it was, between two Indian laurels, where the grass looked silver in the light of a three-quarter moon.

BRANDY
BELOVED DOG
PET AND FRIEND

Charlie stood beside the plot, staring down at it, not really wanting to proceed, but aware that he had no choice. He would not be at peace until he knew the truth.

The night-mantled graveyard full of eternally slumbering cats, dogs, hamsters, parrots, rabbits, and guinea pigs was preternaturally silent. The mild breeze was cool. The branches of the trees stirred slightly, but with only an infrequent rustle.

Reluctantly, he stripped off his lightweight jacket, put his flashlight aside, and set to work. The bullet wound in his shoulder had healed well, more quickly than the doctors had expected, but he was not yet back in shape, and his muscles began to ache from his labors. Suddenly his spade produced a hollow *thunk-clonk* when it struck the lid of a solidly made though unfinished and unadorned pine box, a little more than two feet below ground. A few minutes later he had bared the entire coffin; in the moonlight it was visible as a pale, undetailed rectangle surrounded by black earth.

Charlie knew that the cemetery offered two basic methods of burial: with or without coffin. In either case, the animal was wrapped in cloth and tucked into a zippered canvas bag. Evidently, Christine and Joey had opted for the full treatment, and one of those zippered bags now lay within this box.

But did the bag contain Brandy's remains—or was it empty?

He perceived no stench of decomposition, but that was to be expected if the canvas sack was moisture-proof and tightly sealed.

He sat at the edge of the grave for a moment, pretending that he needed to catch his breath. Actually, he was just delaying. He dreaded opening the dog's casket, not because he was sickened by the thought of uncovering a maggot-riddled golden retriever but because he was sickened by the thought of *not* uncovering one.

Maybe he should stop right now, refill the grave, and go away. Maybe it did not matter *what* Joey Scavello was.

After all, there were those theologians who argued that the devil, being a fallen angel and therefore inherently good, was not evil in any degree but merely *different* from God.

He suddenly remembered something that he had read in college, a line from

Samuel Butler, a favorite of his: *An apology for the devil—it must be remembered that we have heard only one side of the case. God has written all the books.*

The night smelled of damp earth.

The moon watched.

At last he pried the lid off the small casket.

Inside was a zippered sack. Hesitantly, he stretched out on the ground beside the grave, reached down into it, and put his hands on the bag. He played a macabre game of blindman's buff, exploring the contours of the thing within, and gradually convinced himself that it was the corpse of a dog about the size of a full-grown golden retriever.

All right. This was enough. Here was the proof he had needed. God knows *why* he had thought he needed it, but here it was. He had felt that he was being . . . *commanded* to discover the truth; he had not been driven only by curiosity, but by an obsessive compulsion that seemed to come from outside of him, a motivating urge that some might have said was the hand of God pushing him along, but which he preferred not to analyze or define. The past few weeks had been shaped by that urge, by an inner voice compelling him to make a journey to the pet cemetery. At last he had succumbed, had committed himself to this silly scheme, and what he had found was not proof of a hellborn plot but, instead, merely evidence of his own foolishness. Although there was no one in the pet cemetery to see him, he flushed with embarrassment. Brandy had not come back from the grave. Chewbacca was an altogether different dog. It had been stupid to suspect otherwise. This was sufficient evidence of Joey's innocence; there was no point in opening the bag and forcing himself to confront the disgusting remains.

He wondered what he would have done if the grave had been empty. Would he then have had to kill the boy, destroy the Antichrist, save the world from Armageddon? What utter balderdash. He could not have done any such thing, not even if God had appeared to him in flowing white robes, with a beard of fire, and with the death order written on tablets of stone. His own parents had been child-beaters, child-abusers, and he the victim. That was the one crime that most outraged him—a crime against a child. Even if the grave had been empty, even if that emptiness had convinced him that Spivey was right about Joey, Charlie could not have gone after the boy. He could not outdo his own sick parents by *killing* a child. For a while, maybe, he would be able to live with the deed because he would feel sure that Joey was *more* than just a little boy, was in fact an evil being. But as time went on, doubts would arise. He would begin to think that he had imagined the inexplicable behavior of the bats, and the empty grave would have less significance, and all the other signs and portents would seem to have been self-delusion. He would begin to tell himself that Joey wasn't demonic, only gifted, not possessed of supernatural powers but merely psychic abilities. He would inevitably determine that he had killed nothing evil, that he had destroyed a special but altogether innocent child. And then, at least for him, Hell on earth would be reality, anyway.

He lay face-down on the cool, damp ground.

He stared into the dog's grave.

The canvas-wrapped lump was framed by the pale pine boards. It was a perfectly black bundle that might have contained anything, but which his hands told him contained a dog, so there was no need to open it, no need whatsoever.

The tab of the bag's zipper was caught in a moonbeam. Its silvery glint was like a single, cold, staring eye.

Even if he opened the bag and found only rocks, or even if he found something worse, something unimaginably horrible that was proof positive of Joey's sulphurous origins, he could not act as God's avenger. What allegiance did he owe to a god who allowed so much suffering in the world to begin with? What of his own suffering as a child, the terrible loneliness and the beatings and the constant fear he had endured? Where had God been then? Could life be all that much worse just because there had been a change in the divine monarchy?

He remembered Denton Boothe's mechanical coin bank: *There is No Justice in a Jackass Universe.*

Maybe a change would bring justice.

But, of course, he did not believe the world was ruled by either God or the devil, anyway. He did not *believe* in divine monarchies.

Which made his presence here even more ridiculous.

The zipper tab glinted.

He rolled onto his back so he'd be unable to see the zipper shine.

He got to his feet, picked up the coffin lid. He would put it in place and fill in the grave and go home and be sensible about this situation.

He hesitated.

Damn.

Cursing his own compulsion, he put the lid down. He reached into the grave, instead, and heaved out the bag. He ran the zipper the length of the sack, and it made an insectlike sound.

He was shaking.

He peeled back the burial cloth.

He switched on his flashlight, gasped.

What the hell—?

With a trembling hand, he directed the flashlight beam at the small headstone and, in the quaverous light, read the inscription again, then threw the light on the contents of the bag once more. For a moment he did not know what to make of his discovery, but gradually the mists of confusion cleared, and he turned away from the grave, away from the decomposing corpse that produced a vile stench, and he stifled the urge to be thoroughly sick.

When the nausea subsided, he began to shake, but with laughter rather than fear. He stood there in the still of the night, on a knoll in a pet cemetery, a grown man who had been in the fanciful grip of a childish superstition, feeling like the butt of a cosmic joke, a good joke, one that tickled the hell out of him even though it made him feel like a prime jackass. The dog in Brandy's grave was an Irish setter, not a golden retriever, not Brandy at all, which meant the people in charge of this place had screwed up royally, had buried Brandy in the wrong grave and had unknowingly planted the setter in *this* hole. One canvas-wrapped dog is like another, and the undertaker's mix-up seemed not only understandable but inevitable. If the mortician was careless or if, more likely, he nipped at the bottle now and then, the odds were high that a lot of dogs in the graveyard were buried under the wrong markers. After all, burying the family dog was not exactly as serious a matter as burying Grandma or Aunt Emma; the precautions were not quite as meticulous. Not quite! To locate Brandy's true resting place, he would have to track down the identity of the setter and rob a second grave, and as he looked out at the hundreds upon hundreds of low markers, he knew it was an impossible task. Besides, it did not matter. The pet mortician's screw-up was like a dash of cold water in the face; it brought Charlie to his senses. He suddenly saw himself as a parody of the hero in one of those old E.C. Horror Comics, haunting a cemetery in pursuit of

. . . Of what? Dracula Dog? He laughed so hard that he had to sit down before he fell down.

They said the Lord worked in mysterious ways, so maybe the devil worked in mysterious ways, too, but Charlie simply could not believe that the devil was *so* mysterious, so subtle, so elaborately devious, so downright *silly* as to muddy the trail to Brandy's grave by causing a mixup in a pet cemetery's mortuary. A devil like that might try to buy a man's soul by offering him a fortune in baseball trading cards, and such a demon was not to be taken seriously.

How and why *had* he taken this so seriously. Had Grace Spivey's religious mania been like a contagion? Had he picked up a mild case of end-of-the-world fever?

His laughter had a purging effect, and by the time it had run its course, he felt better than he had in weeks.

He used the blade of the shovel to push the dead dog and the canvas bag back into the grave. He threw the lid of the coffin on top of it, shoveled the hole full of dirt, tamped it down, wiped the shovel blade clean in the grass, and returned to his car.

He had not found what he expected, and perhaps he had not even found the truth, but he had more or less found what he had *hoped* to find —a way out, an acceptable answer, something he could live with, absolution.

Early May in Las Vegas was a pleasant time, with the fierce heat of summer still to come, but with the chill winter nights gone for another year. The warm dry air blew away whatever memories still lingered of the nightmare chase in the High Sierras.

On the first Wednesday morning of the month, Charlie and Christine were to be married in a gloriously gaudy, hilariously tasteless nonsectarian wedding chapel next door to a casino, which vastly amused both of them. They did not see their wedding as a solemn occasion, but as the beginning of a joyous adventure that was best begun with laughter, rather than with pomp and circumstance. Besides, once they made up their minds to marry, they were suddenly in a frenzy to get it done, and no place but Vegas, with its liberal marriage laws, could meet their timetable.

They came into Vegas the night before and took a small suite at Bally's Grand, and within a few hours the city seemed to be sending them omens that indicated a happy future together. On their way to dinner, Christine put four quarters into a slot machine, and although it was the first time she had ever played one, she pulled off a thousand-dollar jackpot. Later, they played a little blackjack, and they won nearly another thousand apiece. In the morning, exiting the coffee shop after a superb breakfast, Joey found a silver dollar that someone had dropped, and as far as he was concerned his good fortune far exceeded that of his mother and Charlie: "A whole *dollar!*"

They had brought Joey with them because Christine could not bear to leave him. Their recent ordeal, the near loss of the boy, still weighed heavily on her, and when he was out of her sight for more than a couple of hours, she grew nervous. "In time," she told Charlie, "I'll be able to relax a bit more. But not yet. In time, we'll be able to go away together by ourselves, just the two of us, and leave Joey with Val. I promise. But not yet. Not quite yet. So if you want to marry me, you're going to have to take my son along on the honeymoon. How's *that* for romance?"

Charlie didn't mind. He liked the boy. Joey was a good companion, well-behaved, inquisitive, bright, and affectionate.

Joey served as best man at the ceremony and was delighted with his role. He guarded the ring with stern-faced solemnity and, at the proper moment, gave it to Charlie with a grin so wide and warm it threatened to melt the gold in which the diamond was set.

When it was official, when they had left the chapel to the recorded strains of Wayne Newton singing "Joy to the World," they decided to forgo the complimentary limousine and walk back to the hotel. The day was warm, blue, clear (but for a few scattered white clouds), and beautiful, even with the honky-tonk of Las Vegas Boulevard crowding close on both sides.

"What about the wedding lunch?" Joey demanded as they walked.

"You just had breakfast two hours ago," Charlie said.

"I'm a growin' boy."

"True."

"What sounds like a good wedding lunch to you?" Christine asked.

Joey thought about that for a few steps, then said, "Big Macs and Baskin-Robbins!"

"You know what happens to you when you eat too many Big Macs?" Christine said.

"What?" the boy asked.

"You grow up to look like Ronald McDonald."

"That's right," Charlie said. "Big red nose, funny orange hair, and big red lips."

Joey giggled. "Gee, I wish Chewbacca was here."

"I'm sure Val's taking good care of him, honey."

"Yeah, but he's missing all the jokes."

They strolled along the sidewalk, Joey between them, and even at this hour a few of the big signs and marquees were flashing.

"Will I grow up with big funny clown's feet, too?" Joey asked.

"Absolutely," Charlie said. "Size twenty-eight."

"Which will make it impossible to drive a car," Christine said.

"Or dance," Charlie said.

"I don't want to dance," Joey said. "I don't like *girls.*"

"Oh, in a few years, you'll like them," Christine said.

Joey frowned. "That's what Chewbacca says, but I just don't believe it."

"Oh, so Chewbacca talks, does he?" Christine teased.

"Well . . ."

"And he's an authority on girls, yet!"

"Well, okay, if you want to make a big deal of it," Joey said, "I gotta admit I just *pretend* he talks."

Charlie laughed and winked at his new wife over their son's head.

Joey said, "Hey, if I eat too many Big Macs, will I grow up with big funny clown *hands,* too?"

"Yep," Charlie said. "So you won't be able to tie your own shoes."

"Or pick your nose," Christine said.

"I don't pick my nose anyway," the boy said indignantly. "You know what Val told me about picking my nose?"

"No. What did Val tell you?" Christine asked, and Charlie could see she was a little afraid of the answer because the boy was always learning the wrong kind of language from Val.

Joey squinted in the desert sun, as if struggling to remember exactly what Val had said. Then: "She told me the only people who pick their noses are bums, Looney Tunes, IRS agents, and her ex-husband."

Charlie and Christine glanced at each other and laughed. It was so good to laugh.

Joey said, "Hey, if you guys wanta be, you know . . . ummm . . . alone . . . then you can leave me in the hotel playroom. I don't mind. It looks great in there. They got all kinds of neat games and stuff. Hey, maybe you guys want to play some more cards or them slot machines where Mom made money last night."

"I think we'll probably quit gambling while we're ahead, honey."

"Oh," the boy said, "I think you should play, Mom! You'll win, I bet. You'll win a lot more. Really. I know you will. I just *know* you will."

The sun came out from behind one of the scattered white clouds, and its light fell full-strength across the pavement, sparkled on the chrome and glass of the passing cars, made the plush hotels and casinos look brighter and cleaner than they really were, and made the air itself shimmer fantastically.

It ended in sunshine, not on a dark and stormy night.

DARKFALL

Because the original door prize was
too hard to accomplish, this book is
dedicated to some good neighbors—
Oliviero and Becky Migneco,
Jeff and Bonnie Paymar
—with the sincere hope that a mere
dedication is an acceptable substitute.

(At least this way, there's much less
chance of a lawsuit!)

I owe special thanks to Mr. Owen West
for giving me the opportunity to publish
this variation on a theme under my by-line.

PROLOGUE

I

Wednesday, December 8, 1:12 A.M.

PENNY DAWSON WOKE and heard something moving furtively in the dark bedroom.

At first she thought she was hearing a sound left over from her dream. She had been dreaming about horses and about going for long rides in the country, and it had been the most wonderful, special, thrilling dream she'd ever had in all of her eleven-and-a-half dream-filled years. When she began to wake up, she struggled against consciousness, tried to hold on to sleep and prevent the lovely fantasy from fading. But she heard an odd sound, and it scared her. She told herself it was only a horse sound or just the rustle of straw in the stable in her dream. Nothing to be alarmed about. But she couldn't convince herself; she couldn't tie the strange sound to her dream, and she woke up all the way.

The peculiar noise was coming from the other side of the room, from Davey's bed. But it wasn't ordinary, middle-of-the-night, seven-year-old-boy, pizza-and-ice-cream-for-dinner noise. It was a sneaky sound. Definitely sneaky.

What was he doing? What trick was he planning this time?

Penny sat up in bed. She squinted into the impenetrable shadows, saw nothing, cocked her head, and listened intently.

A rustling, sighing sound disturbed the stillness.

Then silence.

She held her breath and listened even harder.

Hissing. Then a vague, shuffling, scraping noise.

The room was virtually pitch-black. There was one window, and it was beside her bed; however, the drape was drawn shut, and the alleyway outside was especially dark tonight, so the window provided no relief from the gloom.

The door was ajar. They always slept with it open a couple of inches, so Daddy could hear them more easily if they called for him in the night. But there were no lights on in the rest of the apartment, and no light came through the partly open door.

Penny spoke softly: "Davey?"

He didn't answer.

"Davey, is that you?"

Rustle-rustle-rustle.

"Davey, stop it."

No response.

Seven-year-old boys were a trial sometimes. A truly monumental pain.

She said, "If you're playing some stupid game, you're going to be real sorry."

A dry sound. Like an old, withered leaf crunching crisply under someone's foot.

It was nearer now than it had been.

"Davey, don't be weird."

Nearer. Something was coming across the room toward the bed.

It wasn't Davey. He was a giggler; he would have broken up by now and would have given himself away.

Penny's heart began to hammer, and she thought: Maybe this is just another dream, like the horses, only a bad one this time.

But she knew she was wide awake.

Her eyes watered with the effort she was making to peer through the darkness. She reached for the switch on the cone-shaped reading lamp that was fixed to the headboard of her bed. For a terribly long while, she couldn't find it. She fumbled desperately in the dark.

The stealthy sounds now issued from the blackness beside her bed. The thing had reached her.

Suddenly her groping fingers found the metal lampshade, then the switch. A cone of light fell across the bed and onto the floor.

Nothing frightening was crouched nearby. The reading lamp didn't cast enough light to dispel all the shadows, but Penny could see there wasn't anything dangerous, menacing, or even the least bit out of place.

Davey was in his bed, on the other side of the room, Davey tangled in his covers, sleeping beneath large posters of Chewbacca the Wookie, from *Star Wars,* and E.T.

Penny didn't hear the strange noise any more. She knew she hadn't been imagining it, and she wasn't the kind of girl who could just turn off the lights and pull the covers over her head and forget about the whole thing. Daddy said she had enough curiosity to kill about a thousand cats. She threw back the covers, got out of bed, and stood very still in her pajamas and bare feet, listening.

Not a sound.

Finally she went over to Davey and looked at him more closely. Her lamp's light didn't reach this far; he lay mostly in shadows, but he seemed to be sound asleep. She leaned very close, watching his eyelids, and at last she decided he wasn't faking it.

The noise began again. Behind her.

She whirled around.

It was under the bed now. A hissing, scraping, softly rattling sound, not particularly loud, but no longer stealthy, either.

The thing under the bed knew she was aware of it. It was making noise on purpose, teasing her, trying to scare her.

No! she thought. That's silly.

Besides, it wasn't a *thing,* wasn't a boogeyman. She was too old for boogeymen. That was more Davey's speed.

This was just a . . . a mouse. Yes! That was it. Just a mouse, more scared than she was.

She felt somewhat relieved. She didn't like mice, didn't want them under her bed, for sure, but at least there was nothing *too* frightening about a lowly mouse. It was grody, creepy, but it wasn't big enough to bite her head off or anything major like that.

She stood with her small hands fisted at her sides, trying to decide what to do next.

She looked up at Scott Baio, who smiled down at her from a poster that hung on the wall behind her bed, and she wished he were here to take charge of the situation. Scott Baio wouldn't be scared of a mouse; not in a million years. Scott Baio would crawl right under the bed and grab that miserable rodent by its tail and carry it outside and release it, unharmed, in the alley behind the apartment building, because Scott Baio wasn't just brave—he was good and sensitive and gentle, too.

But Scott wasn't here. He was out there in Hollywood, making his TV show.

Which left Daddy.

Penny didn't want to wake her father until she was absolutely, positively, one hundred percent sure there actually was a mouse. If Daddy came looking for a mouse and turned the room upside-down and then didn't find one, he'd treat her as if she were a *child,* for God's sake. She was only two months short of her twelfth birthday, and there was nothing she loathed more than being treated like a child.

She couldn't see under the bed because it was very dark under there and because the covers had fallen over the side; they were hanging almost to the floor, blocking the view.

The thing under the bed—the *mouse* under the bed!—hissed and made a gurgling-scraping noise. It was almost like a voice. A raspy, cold, nasty little voice that was telling her something in a foreign language.

Could a mouse make a sound like that?

She glanced at Davey. He was still sleeping.

A plastic baseball bat leaned against the wall beside her brother's bed. She grabbed it by the handle.

Under her own bed, the peculiar, unpleasant hissing-scratching-scrabbling continued.

She took a few steps toward her bed and got down on the floor, on her hands and knees. Holding the plastic bat in her right hand, she extended it, pushed the other end under the drooping blankets, lifted them out of the way, and pushed them back onto the bed where they belonged.

She still couldn't see anything under there. That low space was cave-black.

The noises had stopped.

Penny had the spooky feeling that something was peering at her from those oily black shadows . . . something more than just a mouse . . . worse than just a mouse . . . something that knew she was only a weak little girl . . . something smart, not just a dumb animal, something at least as smart as she was, something that knew it could rush out and gobble her up alive if it really wanted to.

Cripes. No. Kid stuff. Silliness.

Biting her lip, determined not to behave like a helpless child, she thrust the fat end of the baseball bat under the bed. She probed with it, trying to make the mouse squeal or run out into the open.

The other end of the plastic club was suddenly seized, held. Penny tried to pull it loose. She couldn't. She jerked and twisted it. But the bat was held fast.

Then it was torn out of her grip. The bat vanished under the bed with a thump and a rattle.

Penny exploded backwards across the floor—until she bumped into Davey's bed. She didn't even remember moving. One instant she was on her hands and knees beside her own bed; the next instant she banged her head against the side of Davey's mattress.

Her little brother groaned, snorted, blew out a wet breath, and went right on sleeping.

Nothing moved under Penny's bed.

She was ready to scream for her father now, ready to risk being treated like a child, more than ready, and she did scream, but the word reverberated only in her mind: *Daddy, Daddy, Daddy!* No sound issued from her mouth. She had been stricken temporarily dumb.

The light flickered. The cord trailed down to an electrical outlet in the wall behind the bed. The thing under the bed was trying to unplug the lamp.

"Daddy!"

She made some noise this time, though not much; the word came out as a hoarse whisper.

And the lamp winked off.

In the lightless room she heard movement. Something came out from under the bed and started across the floor.

"Daddy!"

She could still only manage a whisper. She swallowed, found it difficult, swallowed again, trying to regain control of her half-paralyzed throat.

A creaking sound.

Peering into the blackness, Penny shuddered, whimpered.

Then she realized it was a familiar creaking sound. The door to the bed-room. The hinges needed oiling.

In the gloom, she detected the door swinging open, sensed more than saw it: a slab of darkness moving through more darkness. It had been ajar. Now, almost certainly, it was standing wide open. The hinges stopped creaking.

The eerie rasping-hissing sound moved steadily away from her. The thing wasn't going to attack, after all. It was going away.

Now it was in the doorway, at the threshold.

Now it was in the hall.

Now at least ten feet from the door.

Now . . . gone.

Seconds ticked by, slow as minutes.

What had it been?

Not a mouse. Not a dream.

Then what?

Eventually, Penny got up. Her legs were rubbery.

She groped blindly, located the lamp on Davey's headboard. The switch clicked, and light poured over the sleeping boy. She quickly turned the cone-shaped shade away from him.

She went to the door, stood on the threshold, listened to the rest of the apartment. Silence. Still shaky, she closed the door. The latch clicked softly.

Her palms were damp. She blotted them on her pajamas.

Now that sufficient light fell on her bed, she returned and looked beneath it. Nothing threatening crouched under there.

She retrieved the plastic baseball bat, which was hollow, very lightweight, meant to be used with a plastic Whiffle Ball. The fat end, seized when she'd shoved it under the bed, was dented in three places where it had been gripped and squeezed. Two of the dents were centered around small holes. The plastic had been punctured. But . . . by what? Claws?

Penny squirmed under the bed far enough to plug in her lamp. Then she crossed the room and switched off Davey's lamp.

Sitting on the edge of her own bed, she looked at the closed hall door for a while and finally said, "Well."

What had it been?

The longer she thought about it, the less real the encounter seemed. Maybe the baseball bat had merely been caught in the bed's frame somehow; maybe the holes in it had been made by bolts or screws protruding from the frame. Maybe the hall door had been opened by nothing more sinister than a draft.

Maybe . . .

At last, itchy with curiosity, she got up, went into the hall, snapped on the light, saw that she was alone, and carefully closed the bedroom door behind her.

Silence.

The door to her father's room was ajar, as usual. She stood beside it, ear to the crack, listening. He was snoring. She couldn't hear anything else in there, no strange rustling noises.

Again, she considered waking Daddy. He was a police detective. Lieutenant Jack Dawson. He had a gun. If something *was* in the apartment, he could blast it to smithereens. On the other hand, if she woke him and they found nothing, he would tease her and speak to her as if she were a child, Jeez, even worse than that, as if she were an *infant.* She hesitated, then sighed. No. It just wasn't worth the risk of being humiliated.

Heart pounding, she crept along the hall to the front door and tried it. It was still securely locked.

A coat rack was fixed to the wall beside the door. She took a tightly rolled umbrella from one of the hooks. The metal tip was pointed enough to serve as a reasonably good weapon.

With the umbrella thrust out in front of her, she went into the living room, turned on all the lights, looked everywhere. She searched the dining alcove and the small L-shaped kitchen, as well.

Nothing.

Except the window.

Above the sink, the kitchen window was open. Cold December air streamed through the ten-inch gap.

Penny was sure it hadn't been open when she'd gone to bed. And if Daddy had opened it to get a breath of fresh air, he'd have closed it later; he was conscientious about such things because he was always setting an example for

Davey, who *needed* an example because he wasn't conscientious about much of anything.

She carried the kitchen stool to the sink, climbed onto it, and pushed the window up farther, far enough to lean out and take a look. She winced as the cold air stung her face and sent icy fingers down the neck of her pajamas. There was very little light. Four stories beneath her, the alleyway was blacker than black at its darkest, ash-gray at its brightest. The only sound was the soughing of the wind in the concrete canyon. It blew a few twisted scraps of paper along the pavement below and made Penny's brown hair flap like a banner; it tore the frosty plumes of her breath into gossamer rags. Otherwise, nothing moved.

Farther along the building, near the bedroom window, an iron fire escape led down to the alley. But here at the kitchen, there was no fire escape, no ledge, no way that a would-be burglar could have reached the window, no place for him to stand or hold on while he pried his way inside.

Anyway, it hadn't been a burglar. Burglars weren't small enough to hide under a young lady's bed.

She closed the window and put the stool back where she'd gotten it. She returned the umbrella to the coat rack in the hall, although she was somewhat reluctant to give up the weapon. Switching off the lights as she went, refusing to glance behind into the darkness that she left in her wake, she returned to her room and got back into bed and pulled up the covers.

Davey was still sleeping soundly.

Night wind pressed at the window.

Far off, across the city, an ambulance or police siren made a mournful song.

For a while, Penny sat up in bed, leaning against the pillows, the reading lamp casting a protective circle of light around her. She was sleepy, and she wanted to sleep, but she was afraid to turn out the light. Her fear made her angry. Wasn't she almost twelve years old? And wasn't twelve too old to fear the dark? Wasn't she the woman of the house now, and hadn't she *been* the woman of the house for more than a year and a half, ever since her mother had died? After about ten minutes, she managed to shame herself into switching off the lamp and lying down.

She couldn't switch her mind off as easily.

What had it been?

Nothing. A remnant of a dream. Or a vagrant draft. Just that and nothing more.

Darkness.

She listened.

Silence.

She waited.

Nothing.

She slept.

II

Wednesday, 1:34 A.M.

VINCE VASTAGLIANO WAS halfway down the stairs when he heard a shout, then a hoarse scream. It wasn't shrill. It wasn't a piercing scream. It was a startled, guttural cry that he might not even have heard if he'd been upstairs; nevertheless, it managed to convey stark terror. Vince paused with one hand on the stair railing, standing very still, head cocked, listening intently, heart suddenly hammering, momentarily frozen by indecision.

Another scream.

Ross Morrant, Vince's bodyguard, was in the kitchen, making a late-night snack for both of them, and it was Morrant who had screamed. No mistaking the voice.

There were sounds of struggle, too. A crash and clatter as something was knocked over. A hard thump. The brittle, unmelodic music of breaking glass.

Ross Morrant's breathless, fear-twisted voice echoed along the downstairs hallway from the kitchen, and between grunts and gasps and unnerving squeals of pain, there were words: "No . . . no . . . please . . . Jesus, no . . . help . . . someone help me . . . oh, my God, my God, please . . . *no!*"

Sweat broke out on Vince's face.

Morrant was a big, strong, mean son of a bitch. As a kid he'd been an ardent street fighter. By the time he was eighteen, he was taking contracts, doing murder for hire, having fun and being paid for it. Over the years he gained a reputation for taking any job, regardless of how dangerous or difficult it was, regardless of how well-protected the target was, and he always got his man. For the past fourteen months, he had been working for Vince as an enforcer, collector, and bodyguard; during that time, Vince had never seen him scared. He couldn't imagine Morrant being frightened of anyone or anything. And Morrant begging for mercy . . . well, that was simply inconceivable; even now, hearing the bodyguard whimper and plead, Vince *still* couldn't conceive of it; it just didn't seem real.

Something screeched. Not Morrant. It was an ungodly, inhuman sound. It was a sharp, penetrating eruption of rage and hatred and alien need that belonged in a science fiction movie, the hideous cry of some creature from another world.

Until this moment, Vince had assumed that Morrant was being beaten and tortured by other *people,* competitors in the drug business, who had come to waste Vince himself in order to increase their market share. But now, as he listened to the bizarre, ululating wail that came from the kitchen, Vince wondered if he had just stepped into the Twilight Zone. He felt cold all the way to his bones, queasy, disturbingly fragile, and alone.

He quickly descended two more steps and looked along the hall toward the front door. The way was clear. He could probably leap down the last of the stairs, race along the hallway, unlock the front door, and get out of the house before the intruders came out of the kitchen and saw him. Probably. But he harbored a small measure of doubt, and because of that doubt he hesitated a couple of seconds too long.

In the kitchen Morrant shrieked more horribly than ever, a final cry of bleak despair and agony that was abruptly cut off.

Vince knew what Morrant's sudden silence meant. The bodyguard was dead.

Then the lights went out from one end of the house to the other. Apparently someone had thrown the master breaker switch in the fuse box, down in the basement.

Not daring to hesitate any longer, Vince started down the stairs in the dark, but he heard movement in the unlighted hallway, back toward the kitchen, coming in this direction, and he halted again. He wasn't hearing anything as ordinary as approaching footsteps; instead, it was a strange, eerie hissing-rustling-rattling-grumbling that chilled him and made his skin crawl. He sensed that something monstrous, something with pale dead eyes and cold clammy hands was coming toward him. Such a fantastic notion was wildly out of character for Vince Vastagliano, who had the imagination of a tree stump, but he couldn't dispel the superstitious dread that had come over him.

Fear brought a watery looseness to his joints.

His heart, already beating fast, now thundered.

He would never make it to the front door alive.

He turned and clambered up the steps. He stumbled once in the blackness, almost fell, regained his balance. By the time he reached the master bedroom, the noises behind him were more savage, closer, louder—and hungrier.

Vague shafts of weak light came through the bedroom windows, errant beams from the streetlamps outside, lightly frosting the eighteenth century Italian canopy bed and the other antiques, gleaming on the beveled edges of the crystal paperweights that were displayed along the top of the writing desk that stood between the two windows. If Vince had turned and looked back, he would have been able to see at least the bare outline of his pursuer. But he didn't look. He was afraid to look.

He got a whiff of a foul odor. Sulphur? Not quite, but something like it.

On a deep, instinctual level, he knew what was coming after him. His conscious mind could not—or would not—put a name to it, but his subconscious knew what it was, and that was why he fled from it in blind panic, as wide-eyed and spooked as a dumb animal reacting to a bolt of lightning.

He hurried through the shadows to the master bath, which opened off the bedroom. In the cloying darkness he collided hard with the half-closed bathroom door. It crashed all the way open. Slightly stunned by the impact, he stumbled into the large bathroom, groped for the door, slammed and locked it behind him.

In that last moment of vulnerability, as the door swung shut, he had seen nightmarish, silvery eyes glowing in the darkness. Not just two eyes. A dozen of them. Maybe more.

Now, something struck the other side of the door. Struck it again. And again. There were several of them out there, not just one. The door shook, and the lock rattled, but it held.

The creatures in the bedroom screeched and hissed considerably louder than before. Although their icy cries were utterly alien, like nothing Vince had ever heard before, the meaning was clear; these were obviously bleats of anger and disappointment. The things pursuing him had been certain that he was within their grasp, and they had chosen not to take his escape in a spirit of good sportsmanship.

The *things*. Odd as it was, that was the best word for them, the only word: *things*.

He felt as if he were losing his mind, yet he could not deny the primitive perceptions and instinctive understanding that had raised his hackles. *Things*.

Not attack dogs. Not any animal he'd ever seen or heard about. This was something out of a nightmare; only something from a nightmare could have reduced Ross Morrant to a defenseless, whimpering victim.

The creatures scratched at the other side of the door, gouged and scraped and splintered the wood. Judging from the sound, their claws were sharp. Damned sharp.

What the hell *were* they?

Vince was always prepared for violence because violence was an integral part of the world in which he moved. You couldn't expect to be a drug dealer and lead a life as quiet as that of a schoolteacher. But he had never anticipated an attack like this. A man with a gun—yes. A man with a knife—he could handle that, too. A bomb wired to the ignition of his car—that was certainly within the realm of possibility. But this was madness.

As the things outside tried to chew and claw and batter their way through the door, Vince fumbled in the darkness until he found the toilet. He put the lid down on the seat, sat there, and reached for the telephone. When he'd been twelve years old, he had seen, for the first time, the telephone in his uncle Gennaro Carramazza's bathroom, and from that moment it had seemed to him that having a phone in the can was the ultimate symbol of a man's importance, proof that he was indispensable and wealthy. As soon as he'd been old enough to get an apartment of his own, Vince had had a phone installed in every room, including the john, and he'd had one in every master bath in every apartment and house since then. In terms of self-esteem, the bathroom phone meant as much to him as his white Mercedes Benz. Now, he was glad he had the phone right here because he could use it to call for help.

But there was no dial tone.

In the dark he rattled the disconnect lever, trying to command service.

The line had been cut.

The unknown things in the bedroom continued to scratch and pry and pound on the door.

Vince looked up at the only window. It was much too small to provide an escape route. The glass was opaque, admitting almost no light at all.

They won't be able to get through the door, he told himself desperately. They'll eventually get tired of trying, and they'll go away. Sure they will. Of course.

A metallic screech and clank startled him. The noise came from within the bathroom. From this side of the door.

He got up, stood with his hands fisted at his sides, tense, looking left and right into the deep gloom.

A metal object of some kind crashed to the tile floor, and Vince jumped and cried out in surprise.

The doorknob. Oh, Jesus. They had somehow dislodged the knob and the lock!

He threw himself at the door, determined to hold it shut, but he found it was still secure; the knob was still in place; the lock was firmly engaged. With shaking hands, he groped frantically in the darkness, searching for the hinges, but they were also in place and undamaged.

Then what had clattered to the floor?

Panting, he turned around, putting his back to the door, and he blinked at the featureless black room, trying to make sense of what he'd heard.

He sensed that he was no longer safely alone in the bathroom. A many-legged quiver of fear slithered up his back.

The grille that covered the outlet from the heating duct—*that* was what had fallen to the floor.

He turned, looked up at the wall above the door. Two radiant silver eyes glared at him from the duct opening. That was all he could see of the creature. Eyes without any division between whites and irises and pupils. Eyes that shimmered and flickered as if they were composed of fire. Eyes without any trace of mercy.

A rat?

No. A rat couldn't have dislodged the grille. Besides, rats had red eyes— didn't they?

It hissed at him.

"No," Vince said softly.

There was nowhere to run.

The thing launched itself out of the wall, sailing down at him. It struck his face. Claws pierced his cheeks, sank all the way through, into his mouth, scraped and dug at his teeth and gums. The pain was instant and intense.

He gagged and nearly vomited in terror and revulsion, but he knew he would strangle on his own vomit, so he choked it down.

Fangs tore at his scalp.

He lumbered backward, flailing at the darkness. The edge of the sink slammed painfully into the small of his back, but it was nothing compared to the white-hot blaze of pain that consumed his face.

This couldn't be happening. But it was. He hadn't just stepped into the Twilight Zone; he had taken a giant leap into Hell.

His scream was muffled by the unnameable thing that clung to his head, and he couldn't get his breath. He grabbed hold of the beast. It was cold and greasy, like some denizen of the sea that had risen up from watery depths. He pried it off his face and held it at arm's length. It screeched and hissed and chattered wordlessly, wriggled and twisted, writhed and jerked, bit his hand, but he held onto it, afraid to let go, afraid that it would fly straight back at him and go for his throat or for his eyes this time.

What *was* it? Where did it come from?

Part of him wanted to see it, had to see it, needed to know what in God's name it was. But another part of him, sensing the extreme monstrousness of it, was grateful for darkness.

Something bit his left ankle.

Something else started climbing his right leg, ripping his trousers as it went.

Other creatures had come out of the wall duct. As blood ran down his forehead from his scalp wounds and clouded his vision, he realized that there were many pairs of silvery eyes in the room. Dozens of them.

This had to be a dream. A nightmare.

But the pain was real.

The ravenous intruders swarmed up his chest, up his back and onto his shoulders, all of them the size of rats but not rats, all of them clawing and biting. They were all over him, pulling him down. He went to his knees. He let go of the beast he was holding, and he pounded at the others with his fists.

One of them bit off part of his ear.

Wickedly pointed little teeth sank into his chin.

He heard himself mouthing the same pathetic pleas that he had heard from Ross Morrant. Then the darkness grew deeper and an eternal silence settled over him.

PART ONE

Wednesday, 7:53 A.M.–3:30 P.M.

Holy men tell us life is a mystery.
They embrace that concept happily.
But some mysteries bite and bark
and come to get you in the dark.
  —*The Book of Counted Sorrows*

A rain of shadows, a storm, a squall!
Daylight retreats; night swallows all.
If good is bright, if evil is gloom,
high evil walls the world entombs.
Now comes the end, the drear, Darkfall.
  —*The Book of Counted Sorrows*

CHAPTER 1

I

THE NEXT MORNING, the first thing Rebecca said to Jack Dawson was, "We have two stiffs."

"Huh?"

"Two corpses."

"I know what stiffs are," he said.

"The call just came in."

"Did you order two stiffs?"

"Be serious."

"*I* didn't order two stiffs."

"Uniforms are already on the scene," she said.

"Our Shift doesn't start for seven minutes."

"You want me to say we won't be going out there because it was thoughtless of them to die this early in the morning?"

"Isn't there at least time for polite chit-chat?" he asked.

"No."

"See, the way it should be . . . you're supposed to say, 'Good morning, Detective Dawson.' And then I say, 'Good morning, Detective Chandler.' Then you say, 'How're you this morning?' And then I wink and say—"

She frowned. "It's the same as the other two, Jack. Bloody and strange. Just

286

like the one Sunday and the one yesterday. But this time it's *two* men. Both with crime family connections from the sound of it."

Standing in the grubby police squad room, half out of his heavy gray overcoat, a smile incompletely formed, Jack Dawson stared at her in disbelief. He wasn't surprised that there had been another murder or two. He was a homicide detective; there was *always* another murder. Or two. He wasn't even surprised that there was another *strange* murder; after all, this was New York City. What he couldn't believe was her attitude, the way she was treating him —this morning of all mornings.

"Better put your coat back on," she said.

"Rebecca—"

"They're expecting us."

"Rebecca, last night—"

"Another weird one," she said, snatching up her purse from the top of a battered desk.

"Didn't we—"

"We've sure got a sick one on our hands this time," she said, heading for the door. "Really sick."

"Rebecca—"

She stopped in the doorway and shook her head. "You know what I wish sometimes?"

He stared at her.

She said, "Sometimes I wish I'd married Tiny Taylor. Right now, I'd be up there in Connecticut, snug in my all-electric kitchen, having coffee and Danish, the kids off to school for the day, the twice-a-week maid taking care of the housework, looking forward to lunch at the country club with the girls . . ."

Why is she doing this to me? he wondered.

She noticed that he was still half out of his coat, and she said, "Didn't you hear me, Jack? We've got a call to answer."

"Yeah. I—"

"We've got two more stiffs."

She left the squad room, which was colder and shabbier for her departure.

He sighed.

He shrugged back into his coat.

He followed her.

II

JACK FELT GRAY and washed out, partly because Rebecca was being so strange, but also because the day itself was gray, and he was always sensitive to the weather. The sky was flat and hard and gray. Manhattan's piles of stone, steel, and concrete were all gray and stark. The bare-limbed trees were ash-colored; they looked as if they had been severely scorched by a long-extinguished fire.

He got out of the unmarked sedan, half a block off Park Avenue, and a raw gust of wind hit him in the face. The December air had a faint tomb-dank smell. He jammed his hands into the deep pockets of his overcoat.

Rebecca Chandler got out of the driver's side and slammed the door. Her long blond hair streamed behind her in the wind. Her coat was unbuttoned; it flapped around her legs. She didn't seem bothered by the chill or by the omnipresent grayness that had settled like soot over the entire city.

Viking woman, Jack thought. Stoical. Resolute. And just look at that profile!

Hers was the noble, classic, feminine face that seafarers had once carved on the prows of their ships, ages ago, when such beauty was thought to have sufficient power to ward off the evils of the sea and the more vicious whims of fate.

Reluctantly, he took his eyes from Rebecca and looked at the three patrol cars that were angled in at the curb. On one of them, the red emergency beacons were flashing, the only spot of vivid color in this drab day.

Harry Ulbeck, a uniformed officer of Jack's acquaintance, was standing on the steps in front of the handsome, Georgian-style, brick townhouse where the murders had occurred. He was wearing a dark blue regulation greatcoat, a woolen scarf, and gloves, but he was still shivering.

From the look on Harry's face, Jack could see it wasn't the cold weather bothering him. Harry Ulbeck was chilled by what he had seen inside the townhouse.

"Bad one?" Rebecca asked.

Harry nodded. "The worst, Lieutenant."

He was only twenty-three or twenty-four, but at the moment he appeared years older; his face was drawn, pinched.

"Who're the deceased?" Jack asked.

"Guy named Vincent Vastagliano and his bodyguard, Ross Morrant."

Jack drew his shoulders up and tucked his head down as a vicious gust of wind blasted through the street. "Rich neighborhood," he said.

"Wait till you see inside," Harry said. "It's like a Fifth Avenue antique shop in there."

"Who found the bodies?" Rebecca asked.

"A woman named Shelly Parker. She's a real looker. Vastagliano's girlfriend, I think."

"She here now?"

"Inside. But I doubt she'll be much help. You'll probably get more out of Nevetski and Blaine."

Standing tall in the shifting wind, her coat still unbuttoned, Rebecca said, "Nevetski and Blaine? Who're they?"

"Narcotics," Harry said. "They were running a stakeout on this Vastagliano."

"And he got killed right under their noses?" Rebecca asked.

"Better not put it quite like that when you talk to them," Harry warned. "They're touchy as hell about it. I mean, it wasn't just the two of them. They were in charge of a six-man team, watching all the entrances to the house. Had the place sealed tight. But somehow somebody got in anyway, killed Vastagliano *and* his bodyguard, and got out again without being seen. Makes poor Nevetski and Blaine look like they were sleeping."

Jack felt sorry for them.

Rebecca didn't. She said, "Well, damnit, they won't get any sympathy from me. It sounds as if they *were* screwing around."

"I don't think so," Harry Ulbeck said. "They were really shocked. They swear they had the house covered."

"What else would you expect them to say?" Rebecca asked sourly.

"Always give a fellow officer the benefit of the doubt," Jack admonished her.

"Oh, yeah?" she said. "Like hell. I don't believe in blind loyalty. I don't expect it; don't give it. I've known good cops, more than a few, and if I *know* they're good, I'll do anything to help them. But I've also known some real jerks who couldn't be trusted to put their pants on with the fly in front."

Harry blinked at her.

She said, "I won't be surprised if Nevetski and Blaine are two of those types, the ones who walk around with zippers up their butts."

Jack sighed.

Harry stared at Rebecca, astonished.

A dark, unmarked van pulled to the curb. Three men got out, one with a camera case, the other two with small suitcases.

"Lab men're here," Harry said.

The new arrivals hurried along the sidewalk, toward the townhouse. Something about their sharp faces and squinted eyes made them seem like a trio of stilt-legged birds eagerly rushing toward a new piece of carrion.

Jack Dawson shivered.

The wind shook the day again. Along the street, the stark branches of the leafless trees rattled against one another. That sound brought to mind a Halloween-like image of animated skeletons engaged in a macabre dance.

III

THE ASSISTANT MEDICAL examiner and two other men from the pathology lab were in the kitchen, where Ross Morrant, the bodyguard, was sprawled in a mess of blood, mayonnaise, mustard, and salami. He had been attacked and killed while preparing a midnight snack.

On the second floor of the townhouse, in the master bathroom, blood patterned every surface, decorated every corner: sprays of blood, streaks of it, smears and drops; bloody handprints on the walls and on the edge of the tub.

Jack and Rebecca stood at the doorway, peering in, touching nothing. Everything had to remain undisturbed until the lab men were finished.

Vincent Vastagliano, fully clothed, lay jammed between the tub and sink, his head resting against the base of the toilet. He had been a big man, somewhat flabby, with dark hair and bushy eyebrows. His slacks and shirt were blood-soaked. One eye had been torn from its socket. The other was open wide, staring sightlessly. One hand was clenched; the other was open, relaxed. His face, neck, and hands were marked by dozens of small wounds. His clothes had been ripped in at least fifty or sixty places, and through those narrow rents in the fabric, other dark and bloody injuries could be seen.

"Worse than the other three," Rebecca said.

"Much."

This was the fourth hideously disfigured corpse they'd seen in the past four days. Rebecca was probably right: There was a psychopath on the loose.

But this wasn't merely a crazed killer who slaughtered while in the grip of a psychotic rage or fugue. This lunatic was more formidable than that, for he seemed to be a psychopath with a purpose, perhaps even a holy crusade: All four of his victims had been in one way or another involved in the illegal drug trade.

Rumors were circulating to the effect that a gang war was getting underway, a dispute over territories, but Jack didn't put much faith in that explanation. For one thing, the rumors were . . . strange. Besides, these didn't look like gangland killings. They certainly weren't the work of a professional assassin; there was nothing clean, efficient, or professional about them. They were savage killings, the product of a badly, darkly twisted personality.

Actually, Jack would have preferred tracking down an ordinary hit man. This was going to be tougher. Few criminals were as cunning, clever, bold, or difficult to catch as a maniac with a mission.

"The number of wounds fits the pattern," Jack said.

"But they're not the same kind of wounds we've seen before. Those were stabbings. These definitely aren't punctures. They're too ragged for that. So maybe this one isn't by the same hand."

"It is," he said.

"Too soon to say."

"It's the same case," he insisted.

"You sound so certain."

"I *feel* it."

"Don't get mystical on me like you did yesterday."

"I never."

"Oh, yes, you did."

"We were only following up viable leads yesterday."

"In a voodoo shop that sells goat's blood and magic amulets."

"So? It was still a viable lead," he said.

They studied the corpse in silence.

Then Rebecca said, "It almost looks as if something bit him about a hundred times. He looks . . . *chewed.*"

"Yeah. Something small," he said.

"Rats?"

"This is really a nice neighborhood."

"Yeah, sure, but it's also just one big happy city, Jack. The good and the bad neighborhoods share the same streets, the same sewers, the same rats. It's democracy in action."

"If those're rat bites, then the damned things came along and nibbled at him after he was already dead; they must've been drawn by the scent of blood. Rats are basically scavengers. They aren't bold. They aren't aggressive. People don't get attacked by packs of rats in their own homes. You ever heard of such a thing?"

"No," she admitted. "So the rats came along after he was dead, and they gnawed on him. But it was only rats. Don't try to make it anything mystical."

"Did I *say* anything?"

"You really bothered me yesterday."

"We were only following viable leads."

"Talking to a sorceror," she said disdainfully.

"The man wasn't a sorcerer. He was—"

"Nuts. That's what he was. Nuts. And you stood there listening for more than half an hour."

Jack sighed.

"These are rat bites," she said, "and they've disguised the real wounds. We'll have to wait for the autopsy to learn the cause of death."

"I'm already sure it'll be like the others. A lot of small stab wounds under those bites."

"You're probably right," she said.

Queasy, Jack turned away from the dead man.

Rebecca continued to look.

The bathroom door frame was splintered, and the lock on the door was broken.

As Jack examined the damage, he spoke to a beefy, ruddy-faced patrolman who was standing nearby. "You found the door like this?"

"No, no, Lieutenant. It was locked tight when we got here."

Surprised, Jack looked up from the ruined door. "Say *what?*"

Rebecca turned to face the patrolman. "Locked?"

The officer said, "See, this Parker broad . . . uh, I mean, this Miss Parker . . . she had a key. She let herself into the house, called for Vastagliano, figured he was still sleeping, and came upstairs to wake him. She found the bathroom door locked, couldn't get an answer, and got worried he might've had a heart attack. She looked under the door, saw his hand, sort of out-stretched, and all that blood. She phoned it in to 911 right away. Me and Tony —my partner—were the first here, and we broke down the door in case the guy might still be alive, but one look told us he wasn't. Then we found the other guy in the kitchen."

"The bathroom door was locked from inside?" Jack asked.

The patrolman scratched his square, dimpled chin. "Well, sure. Sure, it was locked from inside. Otherwise, we wouldn't have had to break it down, would we? And see here? See the way it works? It's what the locksmiths call a 'privacy set.' It *can't* be locked from outside the bathroom."

Rebecca scowled. "So the killer couldn't possibly have locked it after he was finished with Vastagliano?"

"No," Jack said, examining the broken lock more closely. "Looks like the victim locked himself in to avoid whoever was after him."

"But he was wasted anyway," Rebecca said.

"Yeah."

"In a locked room."

"Yeah."

"Where the biggest window is only a narrow slit."

"Yeah."

"Too narrow for the killer to escape that way."

"Much too narrow."

"So how was it done?"

"Damned if I know," Jack said.

She scowled at him.

She said, "Don't go mystical on me again."

He said, "I never."

"There's an explanation."

"I'm sure there is."

"And we'll find it."

"I'm sure we will."

"A *logical* explanation."

"Of course."

IV

THAT MORNING, SOMETHING bad happened to Penny Dawson when she went to school.

The Wellton School, a private institution, was in a large, converted, four-story brownstone on a clean, tree-lined street in a quite respectable neighborhood. The bottom floor had been remodeled to provide an acoustically perfect music room and a small gymnasium. The second floor was given over to classrooms for grades one through three, while grades four through six received their instruction on the third level. The business offices and records room were on the fourth floor.

Being a sixth grader, Penny attended class on the third floor. It was there, in the bustling and somewhat overheated cloakroom, that the bad thing happened.

At that hour, shortly before the start of school, the cloakroom was filled with chattering kids struggling out of heavy coats and boots and galoshes. Although snow hadn't been falling this morning, the weather forecast called for precipitation by mid-afternoon, and everyone was dressed accordingly.

Snow! The first snow of the year. Even though city kids didn't have fields and country hills and woods in which to enjoy winter's games, the first snow of the season was nevertheless a magic event. Anticipation of the storm put an edge on the usual morning excitement. There was much giggling, name-calling, teasing, talk about television shows and homework, joke-telling, riddle-making, exaggerations about just how much snow they were supposed to be in for, and whispered conspiracy, the rustle of coats being shed, the slap of books on benches, the clank and rattle of metal lunchboxes.

Standing with her back to the whirl of activity, stripping off her gloves and then pulling off her long woolen scarf, Penny noticed that the door of her tall, narrow, metal locker was dented at the bottom and bent out slightly along one edge, as if someone had been prying at it. On closer inspection, she saw the combination lock was broken, too.

Frowning, she opened the door—and jumped back in surprise as an avalanche of paper spilled out at her feet. She had left the contents of her locker in a neat, orderly arrangement. Now, everything was jumbled together in one big mess. Worse than that, every one of her books had been torn apart, the pages ripped free of the bindings; some pages were shredded, too, and some were crumpled. Her yellow, lined tablet had been reduced to a pile of confetti. Her pencils had been broken into small pieces.

Her pocket calculator was smashed.

Several other kids were near enough to see what had tumbled out of her locker. The sight of all that destruction startled and silenced them.

Numb, Penny crouched, reached into the lower section of the locker, pulled out some of the rubbish, until she uncovered her clarinet case. She hadn't taken the instrument home last night because she'd had a long report to write and hadn't had time to practice. The latches on the black case were busted.

She was afraid to look inside.

Sally Wrather, Penny's best friend, stooped beside her. "What happened?"

"I don't know."

"You didn't do it?"

"Of course not. I . . . I'm afraid my clarinet's broken."

"Who'd do something like that? That's downright *mean.*"

Chris Howe, a sixth-grade boy who was always clowning around and who could, at times, be childish and obnoxious and utterly impossible—but who could also be cute because he looked a little like Scott Baio—crouched next to Penny. He didn't seem to be aware that something was wrong. He said, "Jeez, Dawson, I never knew you were such a *slob.*"

Sally said, "She didn't—"

But Chris said, "I'll bet you got a family of big, grody cockroaches in there, Dawson."

And Sally said, "Oh, blow it out your ears, Chris."

He gaped at her in surprise because Sally was a petite, almost fragile-looking redhead who was usually very soft-spoken. When it came to standing up for her friends, however, Sally could be a tiger. Chris blinked at her and said, "Huh? *What* did you say?"

"Go stick your head in the toilet and flush twice," Sally said. "We don't need your stupid jokes. Somebody trashed Penny's locker. It isn't funny."

Chris looked at the rubble more closely. "Oh. Hey, I didn't realize. Sorry, Penny."

Reluctantly, Penny opened the damaged clarinet case. The silver keys had been snapped off. The instrument had also been broken in two.

Sally put a hand on Penny's shoulder.

"Who did it?" Chris asked.

"We don't know," Sally said.

Penny stared at the clarinet, wanting to cry, not because it was broken (although that was bad enough), but because she wondered if someone had smashed it as a way of telling her she wasn't wanted here.

At Wellton School, she and Davey were the only kids who could boast a policeman for a father. The other children were the offspring of attorneys, doctors, businessmen, dentists, stockbrokers, and advertising executives. Having absorbed certain snobbish attitudes from their parents, there were those in the student body who thought a cop's kids didn't really *belong* at an expensive private school like Wellton. Fortunately, there weren't many of that kind. Most of the kids didn't care what Jack Dawson did for a living, and there were even a few who thought it was special and exciting and better to be a cop's kid than to have a banker or an accountant for a father.

By now, everyone in the cloakroom realized that something big had happened, and everyone had fallen silent.

Penny stood, turned, and surveyed them.

Had one of the snobs trashed her locker?

She spotted two of the worst offenders—a pair of sixth-grade girls, Sissy Johansen and Cara Wallace—and suddenly she wanted to grab hold of them, shake them, scream in their faces, tell them how it was with her, make them understand.

I didn't ask *to come to your damned school. The only reason my dad can afford it is because there was my mother's insurance money and the out-of-court settlement with the hospital that killed her. You think I wanted my mother dead just so I could come to Wellton? Cripes. Holy cripes! You think I wouldn't give up Wellton in a snap if I could only have my mother back? You creepy, snot-eating nerds! Do you think I'm glad my mother's dead, for God's sake? You stupid creeps! What's wrong with you?*

But she didn't scream at them.

She didn't cry, either.

She swallowed the lump in her throat. She bit her lip. She kept control of herself, for she was determined not to act like a child.

After a few seconds, she was relieved she hadn't snapped at them, for she began to realize that even Sissy and Cara, snotty as they could be sometimes, were not capable of anything as bold and as vicious as the trashing of her locker and the destruction of her clarinet. No. It hadn't been Sissy or Cara or any of the other snobs.

But if not them . . . who?

Chris Howe had remained crouched in front of Penny's locker, pawing through the debris. Now he stood up, holding a fistful of mangled pages from her textbooks. He said, "Hey, look at this. This stuff hasn't just been torn up. A lot of it looks like it's been *chewed.*"

"Chewed?" Sally Wrather said.

"See the little teeth marks?" Chris asked.

Penny saw them.

"Who would chew up a bunch of books?" Sally asked.

Teeth marks, Penny thought.

"Rats," Chris said.

Like the punctures in Davey's plastic baseball bat.

"Rats?" Sally said, grimacing. "Oh, yuck."

Last night. The thing under the bed.

"Rats . . ."

". . . rats . . ."

". . . rats."

The word swept around the room.

A couple of girls squealed.

Several kids slipped out of the cloakroom to tell the teachers what had happened.

Rats.

But Penny knew it hadn't been a rat that had torn the baseball bat out of her hand. It had been . . . something else.

Likewise, it hadn't been a rat that had broken her clarinet. Something else. Something else.

But what?

V

JACK AND REBECCA found Nevetski and Blaine downstairs, in Vincent Vastagliano's study. They were going through the drawers and compartments of a Sheraton desk and a wall of beautifully crafted oak cabinets.

Roy Nevetski looked like a high school English teacher, circa 1955. White shirt. Clip-on bow tie. Gray vee-neck sweater.

By contrast, Nevetski's partner, Carl Blaine, looked like a thug. Nevetski was on the slender side, but Blaine was stocky, barrel-chested, slab-shouldered, bull-necked. Intelligence and sensitivity seemed to glow in Roy Nevetski's face, but Blaine appeared to be about as sensitive as a gorilla.

Judging from Nevetski's appearance, Jack expected him to conduct a neat search, leaving no marks of his passage; likewise, he figured Blaine to be a slob, scattering debris behind, leaving dirty pawprints in his wake. In reality, it was the other way around. When Roy Nevetski finished poring over the contents of a drawer, the floor at his feet was littered with discarded papers, while Carl Blaine inspected every item with care and then returned it to its original resting place, exactly as he had found it.

"Just stay the hell out of our way," Nevetski said irritably. "We're going to pry into every crack and crevice in this fuckin' joint. We aren't leaving until we find what we're after." He had a surprisingly hard voice, all low notes and rough edges and jarring metallic tones, like a piece of broken machinery. "So just step back."

"Actually," Rebecca said, "now that Vastagliano's dead, this is pretty much out of your hands."

Jack winced at her directness and all-too-familiar coolness.

"It's a case for Homicide now," Rebecca said. "It's not so much a matter for Narcotics any more."

"Haven't you ever heard of inter-departmental cooperation, for Christ's sake?" Nevetski demanded.

"Haven't *you* ever heard of common courtesy?" Rebecca asked.

"Wait, wait, wait," Jack said quickly, placatingly. "There's room for all of us. Of course there is."

Rebecca shot a malevolent look at him.

He pretended not to see it. He was very good at pretending not to see the looks she gave him. He'd had a lot of practice at it.

To Nevetski, Rebecca said, "There's no reason to leave the place like a pig sty."

"Vastagliano's too dead to care," Nevetski said.

"You're just making it harder for Jack and me when we have to go through all this stuff ourselves."

"Listen," Nevetski said, "I'm in a hurry. Besides, when I run a search like this, there's no fuckin' reason for anyone else to double-check me. I never miss anything."

"You'll have to excuse Roy," Carl Blaine said, borrowing Jack's placating tone and gestures.

"Like hell," Nevetski said.

"He doesn't mean anything by it," Blaine said.

"Like hell," Nevetski said.

"He's extraordinarily tense this morning," Blaine said. In spite of his brutal face, his voice was soft, cultured, mellifluous. "Extraordinarily tense."

"From the way he's acting," Rebecca said, "I thought maybe it was his time of the month."

Nevetski glowered at her.

There's nothing so inspiring as police camaraderie, Jack thought.

Blaine said, "It's just that we were conducting a tight surveillance on Vastagliano when he was killed."

"Couldn't have been *too* tight," Rebecca said.

"Happens to the best of us," Jack said, wishing she'd shut up.

"Somehow," Blaine said, "the killer got past us, both going in and coming out. We didn't get a glimpse of him."

"Doesn't make any goddamned sense," Nevetski said, and he slammed a desk drawer with savage force.

"We saw the Parker woman come in here around twenty past seven," Blaine said. "Fifteen minutes later, the first black-and-white pulled up. That was the first we knew anything about Vastagliano being snuffed. It was embarrassing. The captain won't be easy on us."

"Hell, the old man'll have our balls for Christmas decorations."

Blaine nodded agreement. "It'd help if we could find Vastagliano's business records, turn up the names of his associates, customers, maybe collect enough evidence to make an important arrest."

"We might even wind up heroes," Nevetski said, "although right now I'd settle for just getting my head above the shit line before I drown."

Rebecca's face was lined with disapproval of Nevetski's incessant use of obscenity.

Jack prayed she wouldn't chastise Nevetski for his foul mouth.

She leaned against the wall beside what appeared to be (at least to Jack's unschooled eye) an original Andrew Wyeth oil painting. It was a farm scene rendered in intricate and exquisite detail.

Apparently oblivious of the exceptional beauty of the painting, Rebecca said, "So this Vincent Vastagliano was in the dope trade?"

"Does McDonald's sell hamburgers?" Nevetski asked.

"He was a blood member of the Carramazza family," Blaine said.

Of the five mafia families that controlled gambling, prostitution, and other rackets in New York, the Carramazzas were the most powerful.

"In fact," Blaine said, "Vastagliano was the nephew of Gennaro Carramazza himself. His uncle Gennaro gave him the Gucci route."

"The what?" Jack asked.

"The uppercrust clientele in the dope business," Blaine said. "The kind of people who have twenty pairs of Gucci shoes in their closet."

Nevetski said, "Vastagliano didn't sell shit to school kids. His uncle wouldn't have let him do anything *that* seamy. Vince dealt strictly with show business and society types. Highbrow muckety-mucks."

"Not that Vince Vastagliano was one of them," Blaine quickly added. "He was just a cheap hood who moved in the right circles only because he could provide the nose candy some of those limousine types were looking for."

"He was a scumbag," Nevetski said. "This house, all those antiques—this wasn't *him*. This was just an image he thought he should project if he was going to be the candyman to the jet set."

"He didn't know the difference between an antique and a K-Mart coffee table," Blaine said. "All these books. Take a closer look. They're old textbooks, incomplete sets of outdated encyclopedias, odds and ends, bought by the yard from a used-book dealer, never meant to be read, just dressing for the shelves."

Jack took Blaine's word for it, but Rebecca, being Rebecca, went to the bookcases to see for herself.

"We've been after Vastagliano for a long time," Nevetski said. "We had a hunch about him. He seemed like a weak link. The rest of the Carramazza family is as disciplined as the fuckin' Marine Corps. But Vince drank too much, whored around too much, smoked too much pot, even used cocaine once in a while."

Blaine said, "We figured if we could get the goods on him, get enough evidence to guarantee him a prison term, he'd crack and cooperate rather than do hard time. Through him, we figured to finally lay our hands on some of the wiseguys at the heart of the Carramazza organization."

Nevetski said, "We got a tip that Vastagliano would be contacting a South American cocaine wholesaler named Rene Oblido."

"Our informant said they were meeting to discuss new sources of supply. The meeting was supposed to be yesterday or today. It wasn't yesterday—"

"And for damned sure, it won't happen today, not now that Vastagliano is nothing but a pile of bloody garbage." Nevetski looked as if he would spit on the carpet in disgust.

"You're right. It's screwed up," Rebecca said, turning away from the bookshelves. "It's over. So why not split and let us handle it?"

Nevetski gave her his patented glare of anger.

Even Blaine looked as if he were finally about to snap at her.

Jack said, "Take your time. Find whatever you need. You won't be in our way. We've got a lot of other things to do here. Come on, Rebecca. Let's see what the M.E.'s peopie can tell us."

He didn't even glance at Rebecca because he knew she was giving him a look pretty much like the one Blaine and Nevetski were giving her.

Reluctantly, Rebecca went into the hall.

Before following her, Jack paused at the door, looking back at Nevetski and Blaine. "You notice anything odd about this one?"

"Such as?" Nevetski asked.

"Anything," Jack said. "Anything out of the ordinary, strange, weird, unexplainable."

"I can't explain how the hell the killer got in here," Nevetski said irritably. *That's* damned strange."

"Anything else?" Jack asked. "Anything that would make you think this is more than just your ordinary drug-related homicide?"

They looked at him blankly.

He said, "Okay, what about this woman, Vastagliano's girlfriend or whatever she is . . ."

"Shelly Parker," Blaine said. "She's waiting in the living room if you want to talk to her."

"Have you spoken with her yet?" Jack asked.

"A little," Blaine said. "She's not much of a talker."

"A real sleazebag is what she is," Nevetski said.

"Reticent," Blaine said.

"An uncooperative sleazebag."

"Self-contained, very composed," Blaine said.

"A two-dollar pump. A bitch. A scuz. But gorgeous."

Jack said, "Did she mention anything about a Haitian?"

"A what?"

"You mean . . . someone from Haiti? The island?"

"The island," Jack confirmed.

"No," Blaine said. "Didn't say anything about a Haitian."

"What fuckin' Haitian are we talking about?" Nevetski demanded.

Jack said, "A guy named Lavelle. Baba Lavelle."

"Baba?" Blaine said.

"Sounds like a clown," Nevetski said.

"Did Shelly Parker mention him?"

"No."

"How's this Lavelle fit in?"

Jack didn't answer that. Instead, he said, "Listen, did Miss Parker say anything to you about . . . well . . . did she say anything at all that seemed *strange?*"

Nevetski and Blaine frowned at him.

"What do you mean?" Blaine said.

Yesterday, they'd found the second victim: a black man named Freeman Coleson, a middle-level dope dealer who distributed to seventy or eighty street pushers in a section of lower Manhattan that had been conferred upon him by the Carramazza family, which had become an equal opportunity employer in order to avoid ill-feeling and racial strife in the New York underworld. Coleson had turned up dead, leaking from more than a hundred small stab wounds, just like the first victim on Sunday night. His brother, Darl Coleson, had been panicky, so nervous he was pouring sweat. He had told Jack and Rebecca a story about a Haitian who was trying to take over the cocaine and heroin trade. It was the weirdest story Jack had ever heard, but it was obvious that Darl Coleson believed every word of it.

If Shelly Parker had told a similar tale to Nevetski and Blaine, they wouldn't have forgotten it. They wouldn't have needed to ask what sort of "strange" he was talking about.

Jack hesitated, then shook his head. "Never mind. It's not really important."

If it's not important, why did you bring it up?

That would be Nevetski's next question. Jack turned away from them before

Nevetski could speak, kept moving, through the door, into the hall, where Rebecca was waiting for him.

She looked angry.

VI

LAST WEEK, ON Thursday evening, at the twice-a-month poker game he'd been attending for more than eight years, Jack had found himself defending Rebecca. During a pause in the game, the other players—three detectives: Al Dufresne, Witt Yardman, and Phil Abrahams—had spoken against her.

"I don't see how you put up with her, Jack," Witt said.

"She's a cold one," Al said.

"A regular ice maiden," Phil said.

As the cards snapped and clicked and softly hissed in Al's busy hands, the three men dealt out insults:

"She's colder than a witch's tit."

"About as friendly as a Doberman with one fierce damned toothache and a bad case of constipation."

"Acts like she don't ever have to breathe or take a piss like the rest of humanity."

"A real ball-buster," Al Dufresne said.

Finally Jack said, "Ah, she's not so bad once you know her."

"A ball-buster," Al repeated.

"Listen," Jack said, "if she was a guy, you'd say she was just a hard-nosed cop, and you'd even sort of admire her for it. But 'cause she's a hard-nosed *female* cop, you say she's just a cold bitch."

"I know a ball-buster when I see one," Al said.

"A ball-*crusher,*" Witt said.

"She's got her good qualities," Jack said.

"Yeah?" Phil Abrahams said. "Name one."

"She's observant."

"So's a vulture."

"She's smart. She's efficient," Jack said.

"So was Mussolini. He made the trains run on time."

Jack said, "And she'd never fail to back up her partner if things got hairy out there on the street."

"Hell's bells, *no* cop would fail to back up a partner," Al said.

"Some would," Jack said.

"Damned few. And if they did, they wouldn't be cops for long."

"She's a hard worker," Jack said. "Carries her weight."

"Okay, okay," Witt said, "so maybe she can do the job well enough. But why can't she be a human being, too?"

"I don't think I ever heard her laugh," Phil said.

Al said, "Where's her heart? Doesn't she have a heart?"

"Sure she does," Witt said. "A little stone heart."

"Well," Jack said, "I suppose I'd rather have Rebecca for a partner than any of you brass-plated monkeys."

"Is that so?"

"Yeah. She's more sensitive than you give her credit for."

"Oh, ho! *Sensitive!*"

"Now it comes out!"

"He's not just being chivalrous."

"He's *sweet* on her."

"She'll have your balls for a necklace, old buddy."

"From the look of him, I'd say she's already had 'em."

"Any day now, she'll be wearing a brooch made out of his—"

Jack said, "Listen, you guys, there's nothing between me and Rebecca except—"

"Does she go in for whips and chains, Jack?"

"Hey, I'll bet she does! Boots and dog collars."

"Take off your shirt and show us your bruises, Jack."

"Neanderthals," Jack said.

"Does she wear a leather bra?"

"Leather? Man, that broad must wear *steel.*"

"Cretins," Jack said.

"I *thought* you've been looking poorly the last couple months," Al said. "Now I know what it is. You're pussy-whipped, Jack."

"Definitely pussy-whipped," Phil said.

Jack knew there was no point in resisting them. His protestations would only amuse and encourage them. He smiled and let the wave of good-natured abuse wash over him, until they were at last tired of the game.

Eventually, he said, "Alright, you guys have had your fun. But I don't want any stupid rumors starting from this. I want you to understand there's nothing between Rebecca and me. I think she *is* a sensitive person under all those calluses. Beneath that cold-as-an-alligator pose she works so hard at, there's some warmth, tenderness. That's what I think, but I don't know from personal experience. Understand?"

"Maybe there's nothing between you two," Phil said, "but judging by the way your tongue hangs out when you talk about her, it's obvious you wish there *was.*"

"Yeah," Al said, "when you talk about her, you drool."

The taunting started all over again, but this time they were much closer to the truth than they had been before. Jack didn't know from personal experience that Rebecca was sensitive and special, but he sensed it, and he wanted to be closer to her. He would have given just about anything to be with her—not merely *near* her; he'd been near her five or six days a week, for almost ten months—but really *with* her, sharing her innermost thoughts, which she always guarded jealously.

The biological pull was strong, the stirring in the gonads; no denying it. After all, she was quite beautiful. But it wasn't her beauty that most intrigued him.

Her coolness, the distance she put between herself and everyone else, made her a challenge that no male could resist. But that wasn't the thing that most intrigued him, either.

Now and then, rarely, no more than once a week, there was an unguarded moment, a few seconds, never longer than a minute, when her hard shell slipped slightly, giving him a glimpse of another and very different Rebecca beyond the familiar cold exterior, someone vulnerable and unique, someone worth knowing and perhaps worth holding on to. *That* was what fascinated Jack Dawson: that brief glimpse of warmth and tenderness, the dazzling radiance she always cut off the instant she realized she had allowed it to escape through her mask of austerity.

Last Thursday, at the poker game, he had felt that getting past Rebecca's elaborate psychological defenses would always be, for him, nothing more than a fantasy, a dream forever unattainable. After ten months as her partner, ten months of working together and trusting each other and putting their lives in each other's hands, he felt that she was, if anything, more of a mystery than ever. . . .

Now, less than a week later, Jack knew what lay under her mask. He knew from personal experience. *Very* personal experience. And what he had found was even better, more appealing, more special than what he had hoped to find. She was wonderful.

But this morning there was absolutely no sign of the inner Rebecca, not the slightest hint that she was anything more than the cold and forbidding Amazon that she assiduously impersonated.

It was as if last night had never happened.

In the hall, outside the study where Nevetski and Blaine were still looking for evidence, she said, "I heard what you asked them—about the Haitian."

"So?"

"Oh, for God's sake, Jack!"

"Well, Baba Lavelle *is* our only suspect so far."

"It doesn't bother me that you asked about him," she said. "It's the *way* you asked about him."

"I used English, didn't I?"

"Jack—"

"Wasn't I polite enough?"

"Jack—"

"It's just that I don't understand what you mean."

"Yes, you do." She mimicked him, pretending she was talking to Nevetski and Blaine: " 'Has either of you noticed anything *odd* about this one? Anything out of the ordinary? Anything *strange?* Anything *weird?* ' "

"I was just pursuing a lead," he said defensively.

"Like you pursued it yesterday, wasting half the afternoon in the library, reading about voodoo."

"We were at the library less than an hour."

"And then running up there to Harlem to talk to that sorcerer."

"He's not a sorcerer."

"That *nut.*"

"Carver Hampton isn't a nut," Jack said.

"A real nut case," she insisted.

"There was an article about him in that book."

"Being written about in a book doesn't automatically make him respectable."

"He's a priest."

"He's not. He's a fraud."

"He's a voodoo priest who practices only white magic, good magic. A *Houngon.* That's what he calls himself."

"I can call myself a fruit tree, but don't expect me to grow any apples on my ears," she said. "Hampton's a charlatan. Taking money from the gullible."

"His religion may seem exotic—"

"It's foolish. That shop he runs. Jesus. Selling herbs and bottles of goat's blood, charms and spells, all that other nonsense—"

"It's not nonsense to him."

"Sure it is."

"He believes in it."

"Because he's a nut."

"Make up your mind, Rebecca. Is Carver Hampton a nut or a fraud? I don't see how you can have it both ways."

"Okay, okay. Maybe this Baba Lavelle *did* kill all four of the victims."

"He's our only suspect so far."

"But he didn't use voodoo. There's no such thing as black magic. He stabbed them, Jack. He got blood on his hands, just like any other murderer."

Her eyes were intensely, fiercely green, always a shade greener and clearer when she was angry or impatient.

"I never said he killed them with magic," Jack told her. "I didn't say I believe in voodoo. But you saw the bodies. You saw how strange—"

"Stabbed," she said firmly. "Mutilated, yes. Savagely and horribly disfigured, yes. Stabbed a hundred times or more, yes. But *stabbed*. With a knife. A real knife. An ordinary knife."

"The medical examiner says the weapon used in those first two murders would've had to've been no bigger than a penknife."

"Okay. So it was a penknife."

"Rebecca, that doesn't make sense."

"Murder never makes sense."

"What kind of killer goes after his victims with a penknife, for God's sake?"

"A lunatic."

"Psychotic killers usually favor dramatic weapons—butcher knives, hatchets, shotguns . . ."

"In the movies, maybe."

"In reality, too."

"This is just another psycho like all the psychos who're crawling out of the walls these days," she insisted. "There's nothing special or strange about him."

"But how does he overpower them? If he's only wielding a penknife, why can't his victims fight him off or escape?"

"There's an explanation," she said doggedly. "We'll find it."

The house was warm, getting warmer; Jack took off his overcoat.

Rebecca left her coat on. The heat didn't seem to bother her any more than the cold.

"And in every case," Jack said, "the victim has fought his assailant. There are always signs of a big struggle. Yet none of the victims seems to have managed to wound his attacker; there's never any blood but the victim's own. That's damned strange. And what about Vastagliano—murdered in a locked bathroom?"

She stared at him suddenly but didn't respond.

"Look, Rebecca, I'm not saying it's voodoo or anything the least bit supernatural. I'm not a particularly superstitious man. My point is that these murders might be the work of someone who *does* believe in voodoo, that there might be something ritualistic about them. The condition of the corpses certainly points in that direction. I didn't say voodoo works. I'm only suggesting that the killer might *think* it works, and his belief in voodoo might lead us to him and give us some of the evidence we need to convict him."

She shook her head. "Jack, I know there's a certain streak in you . . ."

"What certain streak is that?"

"Call it an excessive degree of open-mindedness."

"How is it possible to be excessively open-minded? That's like being *too* honest."

"When Darl Coleson said this Baba Lavelle was taking over the drug trade by using voodoo curses to kill his competition, you listened . . . well . . . you listened as if you were a child, enraptured."

"I didn't."

"You did. Then the next thing I know, we're off to Harlem to a voodoo shop!"

"If this Baba Lavelle really is interested in voodoo, then it makes sense to assume that someone like Carver Hampton might know him or be able to find out something about him for us."

"A nut like Hampton won't be any help at all. You remember the Holderbeck case?"

"What's that got to do with—"

"The old lady who was murdered during the seance?"

"Emily Holderbeck. I remember."

"You were *fascinated* with that one," she said.

"I never claimed there was anything supernatural about it."

"Absolutely fascinated."

"Well, it was an incredible murder. The killer was so bold. The room was dark, sure, but there were eight people present when the shot was fired."

"But it wasn't the facts of the case that fascinated you the most," Rebecca said. "It was the medium that interested you. That Mrs. Donatella with her crystal ball. You couldn't get enough of her ghost stories, her so-called psychic experiences."

"So?"

"Do you believe in ghosts, Jack?"

"You mean, do I believe in an afterlife?"

"Ghosts."

"I don't know. Maybe. Maybe not. Who can say?"

"*I* can say. I don't believe in ghosts. But your equivocation proves my point."

"Rebecca, there are millions of perfectly sane, respectable, intelligent, level-headed people who believe in life after death."

"A detective's a lot like a scientist," she said. "He's got to be logical."

"He doesn't have to be an *atheist,* for God's sake!"

Ignoring him, she said, "Logic is the best tool we have."

"All I'm saying is that we're on to something strange. And since the brother of one of the victims thinks voodoo is involved—"

"A good detective has to be reasonable, methodical."

"—we should follow it up even if it seems ridiculous."

"A good detective has to be tough-minded, realistic."

"A good detective also has to be imaginative, flexible," he countered. Then, abruptly changing the subject, he said, "Rebecca, what about last night?"

Her face reddened. She said, "Let's go have a talk with the Parker woman," and she started to turn away from him.

He took hold of her arm, stopped her. "I thought something very special happened last night."

She said nothing.

"Did I just imagine it?" he asked.

"Let's not talk about it now."

"Was it really awful for you?"

"Later," she said.

"Why're you treating me like this?"

She wouldn't meet his eyes; that was unusual for her. "It's complicated, Jack."

"I think we've got to talk about it."

"Later," she said. "Please."

"When?"

"When we have the time."

"When will that be?" he persisted.

"If we have time for lunch, we can talk about it then."

"We'll make time."

"We'll see."

"Yes, we will."

"Now, we've got work to do," she said, pulling away from him.

He let her go this time.

She headed toward the living room, where Shelly Parker waited.

He followed her, wondering what he'd gotten himself into when he'd become intimately involved with this exasperating woman. Maybe she was a nut case herself. Maybe she wasn't worth all the aggravation she caused him. Maybe she would bring him nothing but pain, and maybe he would come to regret the day he'd met her. At times, she certainly seemed neurotic. Better to stay away from her. The smartest thing he could do was call it quits right now. He could ask for a new partner, perhaps even transfer out of the Homicide Division; he was tired of dealing with death all the time, anyway. He and Rebecca should split, go their separate ways both personally and professionally, before they got too tangled up with each other. Yes, that was for the best. That was what he should do.

But as Nevetski would say: *Like hell.*

He wasn't going to put in a request for a new partner.

He wasn't a quitter.

Besides, he thought maybe he was in love.

VII

AT FIFTY-EIGHT, NAYVA ROONEY looked like a grandmother but moved like a dockworker. She kept her gray hair in tight curls. Her round, pink, friendly face had bold rather than delicate features, and her merry blue eyes were never evasive, always warm. She was a stocky woman but not fat. Her hands weren't smooth, soft, grandmotherly hands; they were strong, quick, efficient, with no trace of either the pampered life or arthritis, but with a few calluses. When Nayva walked, she looked as if nothing could stand in her way, not other people and not even brick walls; there was nothing dainty or graceful or even particularly feminine about her walk; she strode from place to place in the manner of a no-nonsense army sergeant.

Nayva had been cleaning the apartment for Jack Dawson since shortly after Linda Dawson's death. She came in once a week, every Wednesday. She also did some babysitting for him; in fact, she'd been here last evening, watching over Penny and Davey, while Jack had been out on a date.

This morning, she let herself in with the key that Jack had given her, and she went straight to the kitchen. She brewed a pot of coffee and poured a cup for herself and drank half of it before she took off her coat. It was a bitter day, indeed, and even though the apartment was warm, she found it difficult to rid herself of the chill that had seeped deep into her bones during the six-block walk from her own apartment.

She started cleaning in the kitchen. Nothing was actually dirty. Jack and his two young ones were clean and reasonably orderly, not at all like *some* for whom Nayva worked. Nonetheless, she labored diligently, scrubbing and polishing with the same vigor and determination that she brought to really grimy jobs, for she prided herself on the fact that a place positively *gleamed* when she was finished with it. Her father—dead these many years and God rest his soul —had been a uniformed policeman, a foot patrolman, who took no graft whatsoever, and who strived to make his beat a safe one for all who lived or toiled within its boundaries. He had taken considerable pride in his job, and he'd taught Nayva (among other things) two valuable lessons about work: first, there is always satisfaction and esteem in a piece of work well done, regardless of how menial it might be; second, if you cannot do a job well, then there's not much use in doing it at all.

Initially, other than the noises Nayva made as she cleaned, the only sounds in the apartment were the periodic humming of the refrigerator motor, occasional thumps and creaks as someone rearranged the furniture in the apartment above, and the moaning of the brisk winter wind as it pressed at the windows.

Then, as she paused to pour a little more coffee for herself, an odd sound came from the living room. A sharp, short squeal. An animal sound. She put down the coffee pot.

Cat? Dog?

It hadn't seemed like either of those; like nothing familiar. Besides, the Dawsons had no pets.

She started across the kitchen, toward the door to the dining alcove and the living room beyond.

The squeal came again, and it brought her to a halt, froze her, and suddenly she was uneasy. It was an ugly, angry, brittle cry, again of short duration but piercing and somehow menacing. This time it didn't sound as much like an animal as it had before.

It didn't sound particularly human, either, but she said, "Is someone there?"

The apartment was silent. Almost too silent, now. As if someone were listening, waiting for her to make a move.

Nayva wasn't a woman given to fits of nerves and certainly not to hysteria. And she had always been confident that she could take care of herself just fine, thank you. But suddenly she was stricken by an uncharacteristic twinge of fear.

Silence.

"Who's there?" she demanded.

The shrill, angry shriek came again. It was a hateful sound.

Nayva shuddered.

A rat? Rats squealed. But not like this.

Feeling slightly foolish, she picked up a broom and held it as if it were a weapon.

The shriek came again, from the living room, as if taunting her to come see what it was.

Broom in hand, she crossed the kitchen and hesitated at the doorway.

Something was moving around in the living room. She couldn't see it, but she could hear an odd, dry-paper, dry-leaf rustling and a scratching-hissing noise that sometimes sounded like whispered words in a foreign language.

With a boldness she had inherited from her father, Nayva stepped through the doorway. She edged past the tables and chairs, looking beyond them at the living room, which was visible through the wide archway that separated it from the dining alcove. She stopped beneath the arch and listened, trying to get a better fix on the noise.

From the corner of her eye, she saw movement. The pale yellow drapes fluttered, but not from a draft. She wasn't in a position to see the lower half of the drapes, but it was clear that something was scurrying along the floor, brushing them as it went.

Nayva moved quickly into the living room, past the first sofa, so that she could see the bottom of the drapes. Whatever had disturbed them was nowhere in sight. The drapes became still again.

Then, behind her, she heard a sharp little squeal of anger.

She whirled around, bringing up the broom, ready to strike.

Nothing.

She circled the second sofa. Nothing behind it. Looked in back of the armchair, too. Nothing. Under the end tables. Nothing. Around the bookcase, on both sides of the television set, under the sideboard, behind the drapes. Nothing, nothing.

Then the squeal came from the hallway.

By the time she got to the hall, there wasn't anything to be seen. She hadn't flicked on the hall light when she'd come into the apartment, and there weren't any windows in there, so the only illumination was what spilled in from the kitchen and living room. However, it was a short passageway, and there was absolutely no doubt that it was deserted.

She waited, head cocked.

The cry came again. From the kids' bedroom this time.

Nayva went down the hall. The bedroom was more than half dark. There was no overhead light; you had to go into the room and snap on one of the lamps in order to dispel the gloom. She paused for a moment on the threshold, peering into the shadows.

Not a sound. Even the furniture movers upstairs had stopped dragging and heaving things around. The wind had slacked off and wasn't pressing at the windows right now. Nayva held her breath and listened. If there was anything here, anything *alive,* it was being as still and alert as she was.

Finally, she stepped cautiously into the room, went to Penny's bed, and clicked on the lamp. That didn't burn away all the shadows, so she turned toward Davey's bed, intending to switch on that lamp, as well.

Something hissed, moved.

She gasped in surprise.

The thing darted out of the open closet, through shadows, under Davey's bed. It didn't enter the light, and she wasn't able to see it clearly. In fact, she had only a vague impression of it: something small, about the size of a large rat; sleek and streamlined and slithery like a rat.

But it sure didn't sound like a rodent of any kind. It wasn't squeaking or squealing now. It hissed and . . . *gabbled* as if it were whispering urgently to itself.

Nayva backed away from Davey's bed. She glanced at the broom in her hands and wondered if she should poke it under the bed and rattle it around until she drove the intruder out in the open where she could see exactly what it was.

Even as she was deciding on a course of action, the thing scurried out from the foot of the bed, through the dark end of the room, into the shadowy hallway; it moved *fast.* Again, Nayva failed to get a good look at it.

"Damn," she said.

She had the unsettling feeling that the critter—whatever in God's name it might be—was just toying with her, playing games, teasing.

But that didn't make sense. Whatever it was, it was still only a dumb animal, one kind of dumb animal or another, and it wouldn't have either the wit or the desire to lead her on a merry chase merely for the fun of it.

Elsewhere in the apartment, the thing shrieked, as if calling to her.

Okay, Nayva thought. Okay, you nasty little beast, whatever you may be, look out because here I come. You may be fast, and you may be clever, but I'll track you down and have a look at you even if it's the last thing I do in this life.

CHAPTER 2

I

THEY HAD BEEN questioning Vince Vastagliano's girlfriend for fifteen minutes. Nevetski was right. She was an uncooperative bitch.

Perched on the edge of a Queen Anne chair, Jack Dawson leaned forward and finally mentioned the name that Darl Coleson had given him yesterday. "Do you know a man named Baba Lavelle?"

Shelly Parker glanced at him, then quickly looked down at her hands, which were folded around a glass of Scotch, but in that unguarded instant, he saw the answer in her eyes.

"I don't know anyone named Lavelle," she lied.

Rebecca was sitting in another Queen Anne chair, legs crossed, arms on the chair arms, looking relaxed and confident and infinitely more self-possessed than Shelly Parker. She said, "Maybe you don't *know* Lavelle, but maybe you've heard of him. Is that possible?"

"No," Shelly said.

Jack said, "Look, Ms. Parker, we know Vince was dealing dope, and maybe we could hang a related charge on you—"

"I had nothing to do with that!"

"—but we don't intend to charge you with anything—"

"You can't!"

"—if you cooperate."

"You have nothing on me," she said.

"We can make life very difficult for you."

"So can the Carramazzas. I'm not talking about them."

"We aren't asking you to talk about them," Rebecca said. "Just tell us about this Lavelle."

Shelly said nothing. She chewed thoughtfully on her lower lip.

"He's a Haitian," Jack said, encouraging her.

Shelly stopped biting her lip and settled back on the white sofa, trying to look nonchalant, failing. "What kind of neese is he?"

Jack blinked at her. "Huh?"

"What kind of neese is this Lavelle?" she repeated. "Japanese, Chinese, Vietnamese . . . ? You said he was Asian."

"*Haitian.* He's from Haiti."

"Oh. Then he's no kind of neese at all."

"No kind of neese at all," Rebecca agreed.

Shelly apparently detected the scorn in Rebecca's voice, for she shifted nervously, although she didn't seem to understand exactly what had elicited that scorn. "Is he a black dude?"

"Yes," Jack said, "as you know perfectly well."

"I don't hang around with black dudes," Shelly said, lifting her head and squaring her shoulders and assuming an affronted air.

Rebecca said, "We heard Lavelle wants to take over the drug trade."

"I wouldn't know anything about that."

Jack said, "Do you believe in voodoo, Ms. Parker?"

Rebecca sighed wearily.

Jack looked at her and said, "Bear with me."

"This is pointless."

"I promise not to be excessively open-minded," Jack said, smiling. To Shelly Parker, he said, "Do you believe in the power of voodoo?"

"Of course not."

"I thought maybe that's why you won't talk about Lavelle—because you're afraid he'll get you with the evil eye or something."

"That's all a bunch of crap."

"Is it?"

"All that voodoo stuff—crap."

"But you *have* heard of Baba Lavelle?" Jack said.

"No, I just told you—"

"If you didn't know anything about Lavelle," Jack said, "you would've been surprised when I mentioned something as off-the-wall as voodoo. You would've asked me what the hell voodoo had to do with anything. But you weren't surprised, which means you know about Lavelle."

Shelly raised one hand to her mouth, put a fingernail between her teeth, almost began to chew on it, caught herself, decided the relief provided by biting them was not worth ruining a forty-dollar nail job.

She said, "All right, all right. I know about Lavelle."

Jack winked at Rebecca. "See?"

"Not bad," Rebecca admitted.

"Clever interrogational technique," Jack said. *"Imagination."*

Shelly said, "Can I have more Scotch?"

"Wait till we've finished questioning you," Rebecca said.

"I'm not *drunk,"* Shelly said.

"I didn't say you were," Rebecca told her.

"I never get potted," Shelly said. "I'm not a lush."

She got up from the sofa, went to the bar, picked up a Waterford decanter, and poured more Scotch for herself.

Rebecca looked at Jack, raised her eyebrows.

Shelly returned and sat down. She put the glass of Scotch on the coffee table without taking a sip of it, determined to prove that she had all the will power she needed.

Jack saw the look Shelly gave Rebecca, and he almost winced. She was like a cat with her back up, spoiling for a fight.

The antagonism in the air wasn't really Rebecca's fault this time. She hadn't been as cold and sharp with Shelly as it was in her power to be. In fact, she had been almost pleasant until Shelly had started the "neese" stuff. Apparently, however, Shelly had been comparing herself with Rebecca and had begun to feel that she came off second-best. *That* was what had generated the antagonism.

Like Rebecca, Shelly Parker was a good-looking blonde. But there the resemblance ended. Rebecca's exquisitely shaped and harmoniously related features bespoke sensitivity, refinement, breeding. Shelly, on the other hand, was a parody of seductiveness. Her hair had been elaborately cut and styled to achieve a carefree, abandoned look. She had flat, wide cheekbones, a short upper lip, a pouting mouth. She wore too much makeup. Her eyes were blue, although slightly muddy, dreamy; they were not as forthright as Rebecca's eyes. Her figure was *too* well developed; she was rather like a wonderful French pastry made with far too much butter, too many eggs, mounds of whipped cream and sugar; too rich, soft. But in tight black slacks and a purple sweater, she was definitely an eye-catcher.

She was wearing a lot of jewelry: an expensive watch; two bracelets; two rings; two small pendants on gold chains, one with a diamond, the other with what seemed to be an emerald the size of a large pea. She was only twenty-two, and although she had not been gently used, it would be quite a few years before men stopped buying jewelry for her.

Jack thought he knew why she had taken an instant disliking to Rebecca. Shelly was the kind of woman a lot of men wanted, fantasized about. Rebecca, on the other hand, was the kind of woman men wanted, fantasized about, *and married.*

He could imagine spending a torrid week in the Bahamas with Shelly Parker; oh, yes. But only a week. At the end of a week, in spite of her sexual energy and undoubted sexual proficiency, he would most certainly be bored with her. At the end of a week, conversation with Shelly would probably be less rewarding than conversation with a stone wall. Rebecca, however, would never be boring; she was a woman of infinite layers and endless revelations. After twenty years of marriage, he would surely still find Rebecca intriguing.

Marriage? Twenty years?

God, just listen to me! he thought, astonished. Have I been bitten, or have I been *bitten?*

To Shelly, he said, "So what *do* you know about Baba Lavelle?"

She sighed. "I'm not telling you anything about the Carramazzas."

"We're not asking for anything about them. Just Lavelle."

"And then forget about me. I walk out of here. No phony detention as a material witness."

"You weren't a witness to the killings. Just tell us what you know about Lavelle, and you can go."

"All right. He came from nowhere a couple months ago and started dealing coke and smack. I don't mean penny ante stuff, either. In a month, he'd organized about twenty street dealers, supplied them, and made it clear he expected to expand. At least that's what Vince told me. I don't know first-hand 'cause I've never been involved with drugs."

"Of course not."

"Now, nobody but nobody deals in this city without an arrangement with Vince's uncle. At least that's what I've heard."

"That's what I've heard, too," Jack said dryly.

"So some of Carramazza's people passed word to Lavelle to stop dealing until he'd made arrangements with the family. Friendly advice."

"Like Dear Abby," Jack said.

"Yeah," Shelly said. She didn't even smile. "But he didn't stop like he was told. Instead, the crazy nigger sent word to Carramazza, offering to split the New York business down the middle, half for each of them, even though Carramazza already has *all* of it."

"Rather audacious of Mr. Lavelle," Rebecca said.

"No, it was smartass is what it was," Shelly said. "I mean, Lavelle is a nobody. Who ever heard of him before this? According to Vince, old man

Carramazza figured Lavelle just hadn't understood the first message, so he sent a couple of guys around to make it plainer."

"They were going to break Lavelle's legs?" Jack asked.

"Or worse," Shelly said.

"There's always worse."

"But something happened to the messengers," Shelly said.

"Dead?"

"I'm not sure. Vince seemed to think they just never came back again."

"That's dead," Jack said.

"Probably. Anyway, Lavelle warned Carramazza that he was some sort of voodoo witch doctor and that not even the family could fight him. Of course, everyone laughed about that. And Carramazza sent five of his best, five big mean bastards who know how to watch and wait and pick the right moment."

"And something happened to them, too?" Rebecca asked.

"Yeah. Four of them never came back."

"What about the fifth man?" Jack asked.

"He was dumped on the sidewalk in front of Gennaro Carramazza's house in Brooklyn Heights. Alive. Badly bruised, scraped, cut up—but alive. Trouble was, he might as well have been dead."

"Why's that?"

"He was ape-shit."

"What?"

"Crazy. Stark, raving mad," Shelly said, turning the Scotch glass around and around in her long-fingered hands. "The way Vince heard it, this guy must've seen what happened to the other four, and whatever it was it drove him clear out of his skull, absolutely ape-shit."

"What was his name?"

"Vince didn't say."

"Where is he now?"

"I guess Don Carramazza's got him somewhere."

"And he's still . . . crazy?"

"I guess so."

"Did Carramazza send a third hit squad?"

"Not that I heard of. I guess, after that, this Lavelle sent a message to old man Carramazza: 'If you want war, then it's war.' And he warned the family not to underestimate the power of voodoo."

"No one laughed this time," Jack said.

"No one," Shelly confirmed.

They were silent for a moment.

Jack looked at Shelly Parker's downcast eyes. They weren't red. The skin around them wasn't puffy. There was no indication that she had wept for Vince Vastagliano, her lover.

He could hear the wind outside.

He looked at the windows. Snowflakes tapped the glass.

He said, "Ms. Parker, do you believe that all of this *has* been done through . . . voodoo curses or something like that?"

"No. Maybe. Hell, I don't know. After what's happened these last few days, who can say? One thing I believe in for sure: I believe this Baba Lavelle is one smart, creepy, badass dude."

Rebecca said, "We heard a little of this story yesterday, from another victim's brother. Not so much detail as you've given us. He didn't seem to know where we could find Lavelle. Do you?"

"He used to have a place in the Village," Shelly said. "But he's not there any more. Since all this started going down, nobody can find him. His street dealers are still working for him, still getting supplies, or so Vince said, but no one knows where Lavelle has gone."

"The place in the Village where he used to be," Jack said. "You happen to know the address?"

"No. I told you, I'm not really involved in this drug business. Honest, I don't know. I only know what Vince told me."

Jack glanced at Rebecca. "Anything more?"

"Nope."

To Shelly, he said, "You can go."

At last she swallowed some Scotch, then put the glass down, got to her feet, and straightened her sweater. "Christ, I swear, I've had it with wops. No more wops. It always turns out bad with them."

Rebecca gaped at her, and Jack saw a flicker of anger in her eyes, and then she said, "I hear some of the neese are pretty nice guys."

Shelly screwed up her face and shook her head. "Neese? Not for me. They're all little guys, aren't they?"

"Well," Rebecca said sarcastically, "so far you've ruled out blacks, wops, and neese of all descriptions. You're a very choosy girl."

Jack watched the sarcasm sail right over Shelly's head.

She smiled tentatively at Rebecca, misapprehending, imagining that she saw a spark of sisterhood. She said, "Oh, yeah. Hey, look, even if I say so myself, I'm not exactly your average girl. I've got a lot of fine points. I can afford to be choosy."

Rebecca said, "Better watch out for spics, too."

"Yeah?" Shelly said. "I never had a spic for a boyfriend. Bad?"

"Sherpas are worst," Rebecca said.

Jack coughed into his hand to stifle his laughter.

Picking up her coat, Shelly frowned. "Sherpas? Who're they?"

"From Nepal," Rebecca said.

"Where's that?"

"The Himalayas."

Shelly paused halfway into her coat. "Those mountains?"

"Those mountains," Rebecca confirmed.

"That's the other side of the world, isn't it?"

"The other side of the world."

Shelly's eyes were wide. She finished putting on her coat. She said, "Have you traveled a lot?"

Jack was afraid he'd draw blood if he bit his tongue any harder.

"I've been around a little," Rebecca said.

Shelly sighed, working on her buttons. "I haven't traveled much myself. Haven't been anywhere but Miami and Vegas, once. I've never even seen a Sherpa let alone slept with one."

"Well," Rebecca said, "if you happen to meet up with one, better walk away from him fast. No one'll break your heart faster or into more pieces than a Sherpa will. And by the way, I guess you know not to leave the city without checking with us first."

"I'm not going anywhere," Shelly assured them.

She took a long, white, knit scarf from a coat pocket and wrapped it around her neck as she started out of the room. At the doorway, she looked back at Rebecca. "Hey . . . uh . . . Lieutenant Chandler, I'm sorry if maybe I was a little snappy with you."

"Don't worry about it."

"And thanks for the advice."

"Us girls gotta stick together," Rebecca said.

"Isn't that the truth!" Shelly said.

She left the room.

They listened to her footsteps along the hallway.

Rebecca said, "Jesus, what a dumb, egotistical, racist bitch!"

Jack burst out laughing and plopped down on the Queen Anne chair again. "You sound like Nevetski."

Imitating Shelly Parker's voice, Rebecca said, " 'Even if I say so myself, I'm not exactly your average girl. I've got a lot of fine points.' *Jesus,* Jack! The only fine points I saw on that broad were the two on her chest!"

Jack fell back in the chair, laughing harder.

Rebecca stood over him, looking down, grinning. "I *saw* the way you were drooling over her."

"Not me," he managed between gales of laughter.

"Yes, you. Positively drooling. But you might as well forget about her, Jack. She wouldn't have you."

"Oh?"

"Well, you've got a bit of Irish blood in you. Isn't that right? Your grandmother was Irish, right?" Imitating Shelly Parker's voice again, she said, " 'Oh, there's nothing worse than those damned, Pope-kissing, potato-sucking Irish.' "

Jack howled.

Rebecca sat on the sofa. She was laughing, too. "And you've got some British blood, too, if I remember right."

"Oh, yes," he said, gasping. "I'm a tea-swilling limey, too."

"Not as bad as a Sherpa," she said.

They were convulsed with laughter when one of the uniformed cops looked in from the hallway. "What's going on?" he asked.

Neither of them were able to stop laughing and tell him.

"Well, show some respect, huh?" he said. "We have two dead men here."

Perversely, that admonition made everything seem even funnier.

The patrolman scowled at them, shook his head, and went away.

Jack knew it was precisely *because* of the presence of death that Shelly Parker's conversation with Rebecca had seemed so uproariously funny. After having encountered four hideously mutilated bodies in as many days, they were desperately in need of a good laugh.

Gradually, they regained their composure and wiped the tears from their eyes. Rebecca got up and went to the windows and stared out at the snow flurries. For a couple of minutes, they shared a most companionable silence, enjoying the temporary but nonetheless welcome release from tension that the laughter had provided.

This moment was the sort of thing Jack couldn't have explained to the guys at the poker game last week, when they'd been putting Rebecca down. At times like this, when the other Rebecca revealed herself—the Rebecca who had a sly sense of humor and a gimlet eye for life's absurdities—Jack felt a special kinship with her. Rare as those moments were, they made the partnership workable and worthwhile—and he hoped that eventually this secret Rebecca would come into the open more often. Perhaps, someday, if he had enough patience, the other Rebecca might even replace the ice maiden altogether.

As usual, however, the change in her was short-lived. She turned away from the window and said, "Better go talk with the M.E. and see what he's found."

"Yeah," Jack said. "And let's try to stay glum-faced from now on, Chandler. Let's show them we really *do* have the proper respect for death."

She smiled at him, but it was only a vague smile now.

She left the room.

He followed.

II

As NAYVA ROONEY stepped into the hall, she closed the door to the kids' bedroom behind her, so that the rat—or whatever it was—couldn't scurry back in there.

She searched for the intruder in Jack Dawson's bedroom, found nothing, and closed the door on that one, too.

She carefully inspected the kitchen, even looked in cupboards. No rat. There were two doors in the kitchen; one led to the hall, the other to the dining alcove. She closed them both, sealing the critter out of that room, as well.

Now, it simply had to be hiding in the dining alcove or the living room.

But it wasn't.

Nayva looked everywhere. She couldn't find it.

Several times she stopped searching just so she could hold her breath and listen. Listen. . . . Not a sound.

Throughout the search, in all the rooms, she hadn't merely looked for the elusive little beast itself but also for a hole in a partition or in the baseboard, a breach big enough to admit a largish rat. She discovered nothing of that sort.

At last, she stood in the archway between the living room and the hall. Every lamp and ceiling light was blazing. She looked around, frowning, baffled.

Where had it gone? It still had to be here—didn't it?

Yes. She was sure of it. The thing was still here.

She had the eerie feeling that she was being watched.

III

THE ASSISTANT MEDICAL examiner on the case was Ira Goldbloom, who looked more Swedish than Jewish. He was tall, fair-skinned, with hair so blond it was almost white; his eyes were blue with a lot of gray speckled through them.

Jack and Rebecca found him on the second floor, in the master bedroom. He had completed his examination of the bodyguard's corpse in the kitchen, had taken a look at Vince Vastagliano, and was getting several instruments out of his black leather case.

"For a man with a weak stomach," he said, "I'm in the wrong line of work."

Jack saw that Goldbloom did appear paler than usual.

Rebecca said, "We figure these two are connected with the Charlie Novello homicide on Sunday and the Coleson murder yesterday. Can you make the link for us?"

"Maybe."

"Only maybe?"

"Well, yeah, there's a chance we can tie them together," Goldbloom said. "The number of wounds . . . the mutilation factor . . . there are several similarities. But let's wait for the autopsy report."

Jack was surprised. "But what about the wounds? Don't they establish a link?"

"The number, yes. Not the type. Have you looked at these wounds?"

"At a glance," Jack said, "they appear to be bites of some kind. Rat bites, we thought."

"But we figured they were just obscuring the *real* wounds, the stab wounds," Rebecca said.

Jack said, "Obviously, the rats came along after the men were already dead. Right?"

"Wrong," Goldbloom said. "So far as I can tell from a preliminary examination, there aren't any stab wounds in either victim. Maybe tissue bisections will reveal wounds of that nature underneath some of the bites, but I doubt it. Vastagliano and his bodyguard were savagely bitten. They bled to death from those bites. The bodyguard suffered at least three torn arteries, major vessels: the external carotid, the left brachial, and the femoral artery in the left thigh. Vastagliano looks like he was chewed up even worse."

Jack said, "But rats aren't that aggressive, damnit. You just don't get attacked by packs of rats in your own home."

"I don't think these were rats," Goldbloom said. "I mean, I've seen rat bites before. Every now and then, a wino will be drinking in an alley, have a heart attack or a stroke, right there behind the garbage bin, where nobody finds him for maybe two days. Meanwhile, the rats get at him. So I know what a rat bite looks like, and this just doesn't seem to match up on a number of points."

"Could it have been . . . dogs?" Rebecca asked.

"No. For one thing, the bites are too small. I think we can rule out cats, too."

"Any ideas?" Jack asked.

"No. It's weird. Maybe the autopsy will pin it down for us."

Rebecca said, "Did you know the bathroom door was locked when the uniforms got here? They had to break it down."

"So I heard. A locked room mystery," Goldbloom said.

"Maybe there's not much of a mystery to it," Rebecca said thoughtfully. "If Vastagliano was killed by some kind of animal, then maybe the thing was small enough to get under the door."

Goldbloom shook his head. "It would've had to've been *real* small to manage that. No. It was bigger. A good deal bigger than the crack under the door."

"About what size would you say?"

"As big as a large rat."

Rebecca thought for a moment. Then: "There's an outlet from a heating duct in there. Maybe the thing came through the duct."

"But there's a grille over the duct," Jack said. "And the vents in the grille are narrower than the space under the door."

Rebecca took two steps to the bathroom, leaned through the doorway, looked around, craning her neck. She came back and said, "You're right. And the grille's firmly in place."

"And the little window is closed," Jack said.

"And locked," Goldbloom said.

Rebecca brushed a shining strand of hair from her forehead. "What about the drains? Could a rat come up through the tub drain?"

"No," Goldbloom said. "Not in modern plumbing."

"The toilet?"

"Unlikely."

"But possible?"

"Conceivable, I suppose. But, you see, I'm sure it wasn't just one animal."

"How many?" Rebecca asked.

"There's no way I can give you an exact count. But . . . I would think, whatever they were, there had to be at least . . . a dozen of them.

"Good heavens," Jack said.

"Maybe two dozen. Maybe more."

"How do you figure?"

"Well," Goldbloom said, "Vastagliano was a big man, a strong man. He'd be able to handle one, two, three rat-size animals, no matter what sort of things they were. In fact, he'd most likely be able to deal with half a dozen of them. Oh, sure, he'd get bitten a few times, but he'd be able to take care of himself. He might not be able to kill all of them, but he'd kill a few and keep the rest at bay. So it looks to me as if there were so many of these things, such a horde of them, that they simply overwhelmed him."

With insect-quick feet, a chill skittered the length of Jack's spine. He thought of Vastagliano being borne down onto the bathroom floor under a tide of screeching rats—or perhaps something even worse than rats. He thought of the man harried at every flank, bitten and torn and ripped and scratched, attacked from all directions, so that he hadn't the presence of mind to strike back effectively, his arms weighed down by the sheer numbers of his adversaries, his reaction time affected by a numbing horror. A painful, bloody, lonely death. Jack shuddered.

"And Ross, the bodyguard," Rebecca said. "You figure he was attacked by a lot of them, too?"

"Yes," Goldbloom said. "Same reasoning applies."

Rebecca blew air out through clenched teeth in an expression of her frustration. "This just makes the locked bathroom even more difficult to figure. From what I've seen, it looks as if Vastagliano and his bodyguard were both in the kitchen, making a late-night snack. The attack started there, evidently. Ross was quickly overwhelmed. Vastagliano ran. He was chased, couldn't get to the front door because they cut him off, so he ran upstairs and locked himself in the bathroom. Now, the rats—or whatever—weren't in there when he locked the door, so how did they *get* in there?"

"And out again," Goldbloom reminded her.

"It almost has to be plumbing, the toilet."

"I rejected that because of the numbers involved," Goldbloom said. "Even if there weren't any plumbing traps designed to stop a rat, and even if it held its breath and swam through whatever water barriers there were, I just don't buy that explanation. Because what we're talking about here is a whole pack of creatures slithering in that way, one behind the other, like a commando team, for God's sake. Rats just aren't that smart or that . . . determined. *No* animal is. It doesn't make sense."

The thought of Vastagliano wrapped in a cloak of swarming, biting rats had caused Jack's mouth to go dry and sour. He had to work up some saliva to unstick his tongue. Finally he said, "Another thing. Even if Vastagliano and his bodyguard were overwhelmed by scores of these . . . these *things,* they'd still have killed a couple—wouldn't they? But we haven't found a single dead rat or a single dead anything else—except, of course, dead people."

"And no droppings," Goldbloom said.

"No what?"

"Droppings. Feces. If there were dozens of animals involved, you'd find droppings, at least a few, probably piles of droppings."

"If you find animal hairs—"

"We'll definitely be looking for them," Goldbloom said. "We'll vacuum the floor around each body, of course, and analyze the sweepings. If we could find a few hairs, that would clear up a lot of the mystery." The assistant medical examiner wiped one hand across his face, as if he could pull off and cast away his tension, his disgust. He wiped so hard that spots of color actually did rise in his cheeks, but the haunted look was still in his eyes. "There's something else that disturbs me, too. The victims weren't . . . eaten. Bitten, ripped, gouged . . . all of that . . . but so far as I can see, not an ounce of flesh was consumed. Rats would've eaten the tender parts: eyes, nose, earlobes, testicles. . . . They'd have torn open the body cavities in order to get to the soft organs. So would any other predator or scavenger. But there was nothing like that in this case. These things killed purposefully, efficiently, methodically . . . and then just went away without devouring a scrap of their prey. It's unnatural. Uncanny. What motive or force was driving them? And *why?*"

IV

AFTER TALKING WITH Ira Goldbloom, Jack and Rebecca decided to question the neighbors. Perhaps one of them had heard or seen something important last night.

Outside Vastagliano's house, they stood on the sidewalk for a moment, hands in their coat pockets.

The sky was lower than it had been an hour ago. Darker, too. The gray clouds were smeared with others that were soot-dark.

Snowflakes drifted down; not many; they descended lazily, except when the wind gusted, and they seemed like fragments of burnt sky, cold bits of ash.

Rebecca said, "I'm afraid we'll be pulled off this case."

"You mean . . . off these two murders or off the whole business?"

"Just these two. They're going to say there's no connection."

"There's a connection," Jack said.

"I know. But they're going to say Vastagliano and Ross are unrelated to the Novello and Coleson cases."

"I think Goldbloom will tie them together for us."

She looked sour. "I hate to be pulled off a case, damnit. I like to finish what I start."

"We won't be pulled off."

"But don't you see? If some sort of animal did it . . ."

"Yes?"

"Then how can they possibly classify it as murder?"

"It's murder," he said emphatically.

"But you can't charge an animal with homicide."

He nodded. "I see what you're driving at."

"Damn."

"Listen, if these were animals that were trained to kill, then it's still homicide; the trainer is the murderer."

"If these were dog bites that Vastagliano and Ross died from," Rebecca said, "then maybe you might just be able to sell that theory. But what animal — what animal as small as these apparently were—can be trained to kill, to obey all commands? Rats? No. Cats? No. Gerbils, for God's sake?"

"Well, they train ferrets," Jack said. "They use them for hunting sometimes. Not game hunting where they're going after the meat, but just for sport, 'cause the prey is generally a ragged mess when the ferret gets done with it."

"Ferrets, huh? I'd like to see you convince Captain Gresham that someone's prowling the city with a pack of killer ferrets to do his dirty work for him."

"Does sound far-fetched," Jack admitted.

"To say the least."

"So what does that leave us with?"

She shrugged.

Jack thought about Baba Lavelle.

Voodoo?

No. Surely not. It was one thing to propose that Lavelle was making the murders look strange in order to frighten his adversaries with the threat of voodoo curses, but it was quite something else to imagine that the curses actually worked.

Then again . . . What about the locked bathroom? What about the fact that Vastagliano and Ross hadn't been able to kill even one of their attackers? What about the lack of animal droppings?

Rebecca must have known what he was thinking, for she scowled and said, "Come on. Let's talk to the neighbors."

The wind suddenly woke, breathed, raged. Spitting flecks of snow, it came along the street as if it were a living beast, a very cold and angry wind.

V

MRS. QUILLEN, PENNY'S teacher at Wellton School, was unable to understand why a vandal would have wrecked only one locker.

"Perhaps he intended to ruin them all but had second thoughts. Or maybe he started with yours, Penny dear, then heard a sound he couldn't place, thought someone was coming, got frightened, and ran. But we keep the school locked up tight as a drum at night, of course, and there's the alarm system, too. However did he get in and out?"

Penny knew it wasn't a vandal. She knew it was something a whole lot stranger than that. She knew the trashing of her locker was somehow connected with the eerie experience she'd had last night in her room. But she didn't know how to express this knowledge without sounding like a child afraid of boogeymen, so she didn't try to explain to Mrs. Quillen those things which, in truth, she couldn't even explain to herself.

After some discussion, much sympathy, and even more bafflement, Mrs. Quillen sent Penny to the basement where the supplies and spare textbooks were kept on well-ordered storage shelves.

"Get replacements for everything that was destroyed, Penny. All the books, new pencils, a three-ring notebook with a pack of filler, and a new tablet. And don't dawdle, please. We'll be starting the math lesson in a few minutes, and you know that's where you need to work the hardest."

Penny went down the front stairs to the ground floor, paused at the main doors to look through the beveled glass windows at the swirling puffs of snow, then hurried back the hall to the rear of the building, past the deserted gymnasium, past the music room where a class was about to begin.

The cellar door was at the very end of the hallway. She opened it and found the light switch. A long, narrow flight of stairs led down.

The ground-floor hallway, through which she'd just passed, had smelled of chalk dust that had escaped from classrooms, pine-scented floor wax, and the dry heat of the forced-air furnace. But as she descended the narrow steps, she noticed that the smells of the cellar were different from those upstairs. She detected the mild lime-rich odor of concrete dust. Insecticide lent a pungent note to the air; she knew they sprayed every month to discourage silverfish from making a meal of the books stored here. And, underlying everything else, there was a slightly damp smell, a vague but nonetheless unpleasant mustiness.

She reached the bottom of the stairs. Her footsteps rang sharply, crisply on the concrete floor and echoed hollowly in a far corner.

The basement extended under the entire building and was divided into two chambers. At the opposite end from the stairs lay the furnace room, beyond a heavy metal fire door that was always kept closed. The largest of the two rooms was on this side of the door. A work table occupied the center, and freestanding metal storage shelves were lined up along the walls, all crammed full of books and supplies.

Penny took a folding carry-all basket from a rack, opened it, and collected the items she needed. She had just located the last of the textbooks when she heard a strange sound behind her. *That* sound. The hissing-scrabbling-muttering noise that she had heard last night in her bedroom.

She whirled.

As far as she could see, she was alone.

The problem was that she couldn't see everywhere. Deep shadows coiled under the stairs. In one corner of the room, over by the fire door, a ceiling light was burned out. Shadows had claimed that area. Furthermore, each unit of metal shelving stood on six-inch legs, and the gap between the lowest shelf and the floor was untouched by light. There were a lot of places where something small and quick could hide.

She waited, frozen, listening, and ten long seconds elapsed, then fifteen, twenty, and the sound didn't come again, so she wondered if she'd really heard it or only imagined it, and another few seconds ticked away as slowly as minutes, but then something thumped overhead, at the top of the stairs: the cellar door.

She had left the door standing open.

Someone or something had just pulled it shut.

With the basket of books and supplies in one hand, Penny started toward the foot of the stairs but stopped abruptly when she heard other noises up there on the landing. Hissing. Growling. Murmuring. The tick and scrape of movement.

Last night, she had tried to convince herself that the thing in her room hadn't actually been there, that it had been only a remnant of a dream. Now she knew it was more than that. But just what was it? A ghost? Whose ghost? Not her mother's ghost. She maybe wouldn't have minded if her mother had been hanging around, sort of watching over her. Yeah, that would have been okay. But, at best, this was a malicious spirit; at worst, a dangerous spirit. Her mother's ghost would never be malicious like this, not in a million years. Besides, a ghost didn't follow you around from place to place. No, that wasn't how it worked. *People* weren't haunted. *Houses* were haunted, and the ghosts doing the haunting were bound to one place until their souls were finally at rest; they couldn't leave that special place they haunted, couldn't just roam all over the city, following one particular young girl.

Yet the cellar door had been drawn shut.

Maybe a draft had closed it.

Maybe. But something was moving around on the landing up there where she couldn't see it. Not a draft. Something strange.

Imagination.

Oh, yeah?

She stood by the stairs, looking up, trying to figure it out, trying to calm herself, carrying on an urgent conversation with herself:

—*Well, if it's not a ghost, what is it?*
—*Something bad.*
—*Not necessarily.*
—*Something very, very bad.*
—*Stop it! Stop scaring yourself. It didn't try to hurt you last night, did it?*
—*No.*
—*So there. You're safe.*
—*But now it's back.*

A new sound jolted her out of her interior dialogue. Another thump. But this was different from the sound the door had made when it had been pushed shut. And again: *thump!* Again. It sounded as if something was throwing itself against the wall at the head of the stairs, bumping mindlessly like a summer moth battering against a window.

Thump!

The lights went out.

Penny gasped.

The thumping stopped.

In the sudden darkness, the weird and unsettlingly eager animal sounds rose on all sides of Penny, not just from the landing overhead, and she detected movement in the claustrophobic blackness. There wasn't merely one unseen, unknown creature in the cellar with her; there were many of them.

But what *were* they?

Something brushed her foot, then darted away into the subterranean gloom.

She screamed. She was loud but not loud enough. Her cry hadn't carried beyond the cellar.

At the same moment, Mrs. March, the music teacher, began pounding on the piano in the music room directly overhead. Kids began to sing up there. *Frosty the Snowman.* They were rehearsing for a Christmas show which the entire school would perform for parents just prior to the start of the holiday vacation.

Now, even if Penny could manage a louder scream, no one would hear her, anyway.

Likewise, because of the music and singing, she could no longer hear the things moving in the darkness around her. But they were still there. She had no doubt that they were there.

She took a deep breath. She was determined not to lose her head. She wasn't a *child.*

They won't hurt me, she thought.

But she couldn't convince herself.

She shuffled cautiously to the foot of the stairs, the carry-all in one hand, her other hand out in front of her, feeling her way as if she were blind, which she might as well have been.

The cellar had two windows, but they were small rectangles set high in the wall, at street level, with no more than one square foot of glass in each of them. Besides, they were dirty on the outside; even on a bright day, those grimy panes did little to illuminate the basement. On a cloudy day like today, with a storm brewing, the windows gave forth only a thin, milky light that traveled no more than a few inches into the cellar before expiring.

She reached the foot of the stairs and looked up. Deep, deep blackness.

Mrs. March was still hammering on the piano, and the kids were still singing about the snowman that had come to life.

Penny raised one foot, found the first step.

Overhead, at the top of the stairs, a pair of eyes appeared only a few inches above the landing floor, as if disembodied, as if floating in the air, although they must have been attached to an animal about the size of a cat. It wasn't a cat, of course. She wished it were. The eyes were as large as a cat's eyes, too, and very bright, not merely reflective like the eyes of a cat, but so unnaturally bright that they glowed like two tiny lanterns. The color was odd, too: white, moon-pale, with the faintest trace of silvery blue. Those cold eyes glared down at her.

She took her foot off the first step.

The creature above slipped off the landing, onto the highest step, edging closer.

Penny retreated.

The thing descended two more steps, its advance betrayed only by its unblinking eyes. Darkness cloaked its form.

Breathing hard, her heart pounding louder than the music above, she backed up until she collided with a metal storage shelf. There was nowhere to turn, nowhere to hide.

The thing was now a third of the way down the stairs and still coming.

Penny felt the urge to pee. She pressed back against the shelves and squeezed her thighs together.

The thing was halfway down the stairs. Moving faster.

Overhead, in the music room, they had really gotten into the spirit of *Frosty the Snowman,* a lilt in their voices, belting it out with what Mrs. March always called "gusto."

From the corner of her eye, Penny saw something in the cellar, off to the right: a wink of soft light, a flash, a glow, movement. Daring to look away from the creature that was descending the stairs in front of her, she glanced into the unlighted room—and immediately wished she hadn't.

Eyes.

Silver-white eyes.

The darkness was full of them. Two eyes shone up at her from the floor, hardly more than a yard away, regarding her with a cold hunger. Two more eyes were little farther than a foot behind the first pair. Another four eyes gleamed frostily from a point at least three feet above the floor, in the center of the room, and for a moment she thought she had misjudged the height of these creatures, but then she realized two of them had climbed onto the worktable. Two, four, six *pair* of eyes peered malevolently at her from various shelves along the far wall. Three more pair were at floor level near the fire door that led to the furnace room. Some were perfectly still; some were moving restlessly back and forth; some were creeping slowly toward her. None of them blinked. Others were moving out from the space under the stairs. There were about twenty of the things: forty brightly glowing, vicious, unearthly eyes.

Shaking, whimpering, Penny tore her own gaze away from the demonic horde in the cellar and looked at the stairs again.

The lone beast that had started slinking down from the landing no more than a minute ago had now reached the bottom. It was on the last step.

VI

BOTH TO THE east and to the west of Vincent Vastagliano's house, the neighbors were established in equally large, comfortable, elegantly furnished homes that might as well have been isolated country manors instead of townhouses. The city did not intrude into these stately places, and none of the occupants had seen or heard anything unusual during the night of blood and murder.

In less than half an hour, Jack and Rebecca had exhausted that line of inquiry and had returned to the sidewalk. They kept their heads tucked down to present as small a target as possible to the wind, which had grown steadily more powerful. It was now a wicked, icy, lashing whip that snatched litter out of the gutters and flung it through the air, shook the bare trees with almost enough violence to crack the brittle limbs, snapped coattails with sharp reports, and stung exposed flesh.

The snow flurries were falling in greater numbers now. In a few minutes, they would be coming down too thick to be called flurries any more. The street was still bare black macadam, but soon it would boast a fresh white skin.

Jack and Rebecca headed back toward Vastagliano's place and were almost there when someone called to them. Jack turned and saw Harry Ulbeck, the young officer who had earlier been on watch at the top of Vastagliano's front steps; Harry was leaning out of one of the three black-and-whites that were parked at the curb. He said something, but the wind ripped his words into meaningless sounds. Jack went to the car, bent down to the open window, and said, "Sorry, Harry, I didn't hear what you said," and his breath smoked out of him in cold white plumes.

"Just came over the radio," Harry said. "They want you right away. You and Detective Chandler."

"Want us for what?"

"Looks as if it's part of this case you're working on. There's been more killing. More like this here. Maybe even worse . . . even bloodier."

VII

THEIR EYES WEREN'T at all like eyes should be. They looked, instead, like slots in a furnace grate, providing glimpses of the fire beyond. A silver-white fire. These eyes contained no irises, no pupils, as did human and animal eyes. There was just that fierce glow, the white light from within them, pulsing and flickering.

The creature on the stairs moved down from the last step, onto the cellar floor. It edged toward Penny, then stopped, stared up at her.

She couldn't move back even one more inch. Already, one of the metal shelves pressed painfully across her shoulder blades.

Suddenly she realized the music had stopped. The cellar was silent. Had been silent for some time. Perhaps for as long as half a minute. Frozen by terror, she hadn't reacted immediately when *Frosty the Snowman* was concluded.

Belatedly she opened her mouth to scream for help, but the piano started up again. This time the tune was *Rudolph the Red-Nosed Reindeer,* which was even louder than the first song.

The thing at the foot of the stairs continued to glare at her, and although its eyes were utterly different from the eyes of a tiger, she was nevertheless reminded of a picture of a tiger that she'd seen in a magazine. The eyes in that photograph and these strange eyes looked absolutely nothing alike, yet they had something in common: They were the eyes of predators.

Even though her vision was beginning to adjust somewhat to the darkness, Penny still couldn't see what the creatures looked like, couldn't tell whether they were well-armed with teeth and claws. There were only the menacing, unblinking eyes, adance with white flame.

In the cellar to her right, the other creatures began to move, almost as one, with a single purpose.

She swung toward them, her heart racing faster than ever, her breath caught in her throat.

From the gleam of silvery eyes, she could tell they were leaping down from the shelves where they'd perched.

They're coming for me.

The two on the work table jumped to the floor.

Penny screamed as loud as she could.

The music didn't stop. Didn't even miss a beat.

No one had heard her.

Except for the one at the foot of the stairs, all the creatures had gathered into a pack. Their blazing eyes looked like a cache of diamonds spread on black velvet.

None of them advanced on her. They waited.

After a moment she turned to the stairs again.

Now, the beast at the bottom of the stairs moved, too. But it didn't come toward her. It darted into the cellar and joined the others of its kind.

The stairs were clear, though dark.

It's a trick.

As far as she could see, there was nothing to prevent her from climbing the stairs as fast as she could.

It's a trap.

But there was no need for them to set a trap. She was *already* trapped. They could have rushed her at any time. They could have killed her if they'd wanted to kill her.

The flickering ice-white eyes watched her.

Mrs. March pounded on the piano.

The kids sang.

Penny bolted away from the shelves, dashed to the stairs, and clambered upward. Step by step she expected the things to bite her heels, latch onto her, and drag her down. She stumbled once, almost fell back to the bottom, grabbed the railing with her free hand, and kept going. The top step. The landing. Fumbling in the dark for the doorknob, finding it. The hallway. Light, safety. She slammed the door behind her. Leaned on it. Gasping.

In the music room, they were still singing *Rudolph the Red-Nosed Reindeer.*

The corridor was deserted.

Dizzy, weak in the legs, Penny slid down and sat on the floor, her back against the door. She let go of the carry-all. She had been gripping it so tightly that the handle had left its mark across her palm. Her hand ached.

The song ended.

Another song began. *Silver Bells.*

Gradually, Penny regained her strength, calmed herself, and was able to think clearly. What *were* those hideous little things? Where did they come from? What did they want from her?

Thinking clearly wasn't any help. She couldn't come up with a single acceptable answer.

A lot of really dumb answers kept occurring to her, however: goblins, gremlins, ogres. . . . Cripes. It couldn't be anything like that. This was real life, not a fairy tale.

How could she ever tell anyone about her experience in the cellar without seeming childish or, worse, even slightly crazy? Of course, grown-ups didn't like to use the term "crazy" with children. You could be as nuts as a walnut tree, babble like a loon, chew on furniture, set fire to cats, and talk to brick walls, and as long as you were still a kid, the worst they'd say about you—in public, at least—was that you were "emotionally disturbed," although what they meant by that was "crazy." If she told Mrs. Quillen or her father or any other adult about the things she had seen in the school basement, everyone would think she was looking for attention and pity; they'd figure she hadn't yet adjusted to her mother's death. For a few months after her mother passed away, Penny *had* been in bad shape, confused, angry, frightened, a problem to her father and to herself. She had needed help for a while. Now, if she told them about the things in the basement, they would think she needed help again. They would send her to a "counselor," who would actually be a psychologist or some other kind of head doctor, and they'd do their best for her, give her all sorts of attention and sympathy and treatment, but they simply wouldn't *believe* her—until, with their own eyes, they saw such things as she had seen.

Or until it was too late for her.

Yes, they'd all believe *then*—when she was dead.

She had no doubt whatsoever that the fiery-eyed things would try to kill her, sooner or later. She didn't know *why* they wanted to take her life, but she sensed their evil intent, their hatred. They hadn't harmed her yet, true, but they were growing bolder. Last night, the one in her bedroom hadn't damaged anything except the plastic baseball bat she'd poked at it, but by this morning, they had grown bold enough to destroy the contents of her locker. And now, bolder still, they had revealed themselves and had threatened her.

What next?

Something worse.

They enjoyed her terror; they fed on it. But like a cat with a mouse, they would eventually grow tired of the game. And then . . .

She shuddered.

What am I going to do? she wondered miserably. *What am I going to do?*

VIII

THE HOTEL, ONE of the best in the city, overlooked Central Park. It was the same hotel at which Jack and Linda had spent their honeymoon, thirteen years ago. They hadn't been able to afford the Bahamas or Florida or even the Catskills. Instead, they had remained in the city and had settled for three days at this fine old landmark, and even *that* had been an extravagance. They'd had a memorable honeymoon, nevertheless, three days filled with laughter and good conversation and talk of their future and lots of loving. They'd promised themselves a trip to the Bahamas on their tenth anniversary, something to look forward to. But by the time that milestone rolled around, they had two kids to think about and a new apartment to get in order, and they renegotiated the promise, rescheduling the Bahamas for their fifteenth anniversary. Little more than a year later, Linda was dead. In the eighteen months since her funeral, Jack had often thought about the Bahamas, which were now forever spoiled for him, and about this hotel.

The murders had been committed on the sixteenth floor, where there were now two uniformed officers—Yeager and Tufton—stationed at the elevator alcove. They weren't letting anyone through except those with police ID and those who could prove they were registered guests with lodgings on that level.

"Who were the victims?" Rebecca asked Yeager. "Civilians?"

"Nope," Yeager said. He was a lanky man with enormous yellow teeth. Every time he paused, he probed at his teeth with his tongue, licked and pried at them. "Two of them were pretty obviously professional muscle."

"You know the type," Tufton said as Yeager paused to probe again at his teeth. "Tall, big hands, big arms; you could break ax handles across their necks, and they'd think it was just a sudden breeze."

"The third one," Yeager said, "was one of the Carramazzas." He paused; his tongue curled out, over his upper teeth, swept back and forth. "One of the immediate family, too." He scrubbed his tongue over his lowers. "In fact—" Probe, probe. "—it's Dominick Carramazza."

"Oh, shit!" Jack said. "Gennaro's *brother?*"

"Yeah, the godfather's little brother, his favorite brother, his right hand," Tufton said quickly, before Yeager started to answer. Tufton was a fast-spoken man with a sharp face, an angular body, and quick movements, brisk and efficient gestures. Yeager's slowness must be a constant irritant to him, Jack thought. "And they didn't just kill him. They tore him up bad. There isn't any mortician alive who can put Dominick back together well enough for an open-casket funeral, and you know how important funerals are to these Sicilians."

"There'll be blood in the streets now," Jack said wearily.

"Gang war like we haven't seen in years," Tufton agreed.

Rebecca said, "Dominick . . . ? Wasn't he the one who was in the news all summer?"

"Yeah," Yeager said. "The D.A. thought he had him nailed for—"

When Yeager paused to swab his yellowed teeth with his big pink tongue, Tufton quickly said, "Trafficking in narcotics. He's in charge of the entire Carramazza narcotics operation. They've been trying to put him in the stir for twenty years, maybe longer, but he's a fox. He always walks out of the court-room a free man."

"What was he doing here in the hotel?" Jack wondered.

"I think he was hiding out," Tufton said.

"Registered under a phony name," Yeager said.

Tufton said, "Holed up here with those two apes to protect him. They must've known he was targeted, but he was hit anyway."

"Hit?" Yeager said scornfully. He paused to tend to his teeth and made an unpleasant sucking sound. Then: "Hell, this was more than just a hit. This was total devastation. This was crazy, totally off the wall; that's what *this* was. Christ, if I didn't know better, I'd say these three here had been *chewed,* just chewed to pieces."

The scene of the crime was a two-room suite. The door had been broken down by the first officers to arrive. An assistant medical examiner, a police photographer, and a couple of lab technicians were at work in both rooms.

The parlor, decorated entirely in beige and royal blue, was elegantly ap-pointed with a stylish mixture of French provincial and understated contem-porary furniture. The room would have been warm and welcoming if it hadn't been thoroughly splattered with blood.

The first body was sprawled on the parlor floor, on its back, beside an overturned, oval-shaped coffee table. A man in his thirties. Tall, husky. His dark slacks were torn. His white shirt was torn, too, and much of it was stained crimson. He was in the same condition as Vastagliano and Ross: savagely bitten, mutilated.

The carpet around the corpse was saturated with blood, but the battle hadn't been confined to that small portion of the room. A trail of blood, weaving and erratic, led from one end of the parlor to the other, then back again; it was the route the panicked victim had taken in a futile attempt to escape from and slough off his attackers.

Jack felt sick.

"It's a damned slaughterhouse," Rebecca said.

The dead man had been packing a gun. His shoulder holster was empty. A silencer-equipped .38 pistol was at his side.

Jack interrupted one of the lab technicians who was moving slowly around the parlor, collecting blood samples from various stains. "You didn't touch the gun?"

"Of course not," the technician said. "We'll take it back to the lab in a plastic bag, see if we can work up any prints."

"I was wondering if it'd been fired," Jack said.

"Well, that's almost a sure thing. We've found four expended shell casings."

"Same caliber as this weapon?"

"Yep."

"Find any of the loads?" Rebecca asked.

"All four," the technician said. He pointed: "Two in that wall, one in the door frame over there, and one right through the upholstery button on the back of that armchair."

"So it looks as if he didn't hit whatever he was shooting at," Rebecca said.

"Probably not. Four shell casings, four slugs. Everything's been neatly accounted for."

Jack said, "How could he have missed four times in such close quarters?"

"Damned if I know," the technician said. He shrugged and went back to work.

The bedroom was even bloodier than the parlor. Two dead men shared it.

There were two living men, as well. A police photographer was snapping the bodies from every angle. An assistant medical examiner named Brendan Mulgrew, a tall, thin man with a prominent Adam's apple, was studying the positions of both corpses.

One of the victims was on the king-size bed, his head at the foot of it, his bare feet pointed toward the headboard, one hand at his torn throat, the other hand at his side, the palm turned up, open. He was wearing a bathrobe and a suit of blood.

"Dominick Carramazza," Jack said.

Looking at the ruined face, Rebecca said, "How can you tell?"

"Just barely."

The other dead man was on the floor, flat on his stomach, head turned to one side, face torn to ribbons. He was dressed like the one in the parlor: white shirt open at the neck, dark slacks, a shoulder holster.

Jack turned away from the gouged and oozing flesh. His stomach had gone sour; an acid burning etched its way up from his gut to a point under his heart. He fumbled in his coat pocket for a roll of Tums.

Both of the victims in the bedroom had been armed. But guns had been of no more help to them than to the man in the parlor.

The cadaver on the floor was still clutching a silencer-equipped pistol, which was as illegal as a howitzer at a presidential press conference. It was like the gun on the floor in the first room.

The man on the bed hadn't been able to hold on to his weapon. It was lying on the tangled sheets and blankets.

"Smith & Wesson .357 Magnum," Jack said. "Powerful enough to blow a hole as big as a fist right through anyone in its way."

Being a revolver instead of a pistol, it wasn't fitted with a silencer, and Rebecca said, "Fired indoors, it'd sound like a cannon. They'd have heard it from one end of this floor to the other."

To Mulgrew, Jack said, "Does it look as if both guns were fired?"

The M.E. nodded. "Yeah. Judging from the expended shell casings, the magazine of the pistol was completely emptied. Ten rounds. The guy with the .357 Magnum managed to get off five shots."

"And didn't hit his assailant," Rebecca said.

"Apparently not," Mulgrew said, "although we're taking blood samples from all over the suite, hoping we'll come up with a type that doesn't belong to one of the three victims."

They had to move to get out of the photographer's way.

Jack noticed two impressive holes in the wall to the left of the bed. "Those from the .357?"

"Yes," Mulgrew said. He swallowed hard; his Adam's apple bobbled. "Both slugs went through the wall, into the next room."

"Jesus. Anyone hurt over there?"

"No. But it was a close thing. The guy in the next room is mad as hell."

"I don't blame him," Jack said.

"Has anyone gotten his story yet?" Rebecca asked.

"He may have talked to the uniforms," Mulgrew said, "but I don't think any detectives have formally questioned him."

Rebecca looked at Jack. "Let's get to him while he's still fresh."

"Okay. But just a second." To Mulgrew, Jack said, "These three victims . . . were they bitten to death?"

"Looks that way."

"Rat bites?"

"I'd rather wait for lab results, the autopsy—"

"I'm only asking for an *unofficial* opinion," Jack said.

"Well . . . unofficially . . . not rats."

"Dogs? Cats?"

"Highly unlikely."

"Find any droppings?"

Mulgrew was surprised. "I thought of that, but it's funny you should. I looked everywhere. Couldn't find a single dropping."

"Anything else strange?"

"You noticed the door, didn't you?"

"Besides that."

"Isn't that enough?" Mulgrew said, astonished. "Listen, the first two bulls on the scene had to break down the door to get in. The suite was locked up tight—from the inside. The windows are locked from the inside, too, and in addition to that, I think they're probably painted shut. So . . . no matter whether they were men or animals, how did the killers get away? You have a locked room mystery on your hands. I think that's pretty strange, don't you?"

Jack sighed. "Actually, it's getting to be downright common."

IX

TED GERNSBY, A telephone company repairman, was working on a junction box in a storm drain not far from Wellton School. He was bracketed by work lights that he and Andy Carnes had brought down from the truck, and the lights were focused on the box; otherwise, the man-high drainage pipe was filled with cool, stagnant darkness.

The lights threw off a small measure of heat, and the air was naturally warmer underground than on the windswept street, although not *much* warmer. Ted shivered. Because the job involved delicate work, he had removed his gloves. Now his hands were growing stiff from the cold.

Although the storm drains weren't connected to the sewer system, and although the concrete conduits were relatively dry after weeks of no precipitation, Ted occasionally got a whiff of a dark, rotten odor that, depending on its intensity, sometimes made him grimace and sometimes made him gag. He wished Andy would hurry back with the circuit board that was needed to finish the repair job.

He put down a pair of needle-nose pliers, cupped his hands over his mouth, and blew warm air into them. He leaned past the work lights in order to see beyond the glare and into the unilluminated length of the tunnel.

A flashlight bobbled in the darkness, coming this way. It was Andy, at last. But why was he running?

Andy Carnes came out of the gloom, breathing fast. He was in his early twenties, about twenty years younger than Ted; they had been working together only a week. Andy was a beachboy type with white-blond hair and a healthy complexion and freckles that were like waterspots on warm, dry sand. He would have looked more at home in Miami or California; in New York, he seemed misplaced. Now, however, he was so pale that, by contrast, his freckles looked like dark holes in his face. His eyes were wild. He was trembling.

"What's wrong?" Ted asked.

"Back there," Andy said shakily. "In the branch tunnel. Just this side of the manhole."

"Something there? What?"

Andy glanced back. "They didn't follow me. Thank God. I was afraid they were after me."

Ted Gernsby frowned. "What're you talking about?"

Andy started to speak, hesitated, shook his head. Looking sheepish, yet still frightened, he said, "You wouldn't believe it. Not in a million years. I don't believe it, and I'm the one who saw it!"

Impatient, Ted unclipped his own flashlight from the tool belt around his waist. He started back toward the branch drain.

"Wait!" Andy said. "It might be . . . dangerous to go back there."

"Why?" Ted demanded, exasperated with him.

"Eyes." Andy shivered. "That's what I saw first. A lot of eyes shining in the dark, there inside the mouth of the branch line."

"Is that all? Listen, you saw a few rats. Nothing to worry about. When you've been on this job a while, you'll get used to them."

"Not rats," Andy said adamantly. "Rats have red eyes, don't they? These were white. Or . . . sort of silvery. Silvery-white eyes. Very bright. It wasn't that they reflected my flashlight. No. I didn't even have the flash on them when I first spotted them. They *glowed*. Glowing eyes, with their own light. I mean . . . like jack-o'-lantern eyes. Little spots of fire, flickering. So then I turned the flash on them, and they were right there, no more than six feet from me, the most incredible damned things. *Right there!*"

"What?" Ted demanded. "You still haven't told me what you saw."

In a tremulous voice, Andy told him.

It was the craziest story Ted had ever heard, but he listened without comment, and although he was sure it couldn't be true, he felt a quiver of fear pass through him. Then, in spite of Andy's protests, he went back to the branch tunnel to have a look for himself. He didn't find anything at all, let alone the monsters he'd heard described. He even went into the tributary for a short distance, probing with the beam of his flashlight. Nothing.

He returned to the work site.

Andy was waiting in the pool of light cast by the big lamps. He eyed the surrounding darkness with suspicion. He was still pale.

"Nothing there," Ted said.

"A minute ago, there was."

Ted switched off his flashlight, snapped it onto his tool belt. He jammed his hands into the fur-lined pockets of his quilted jacket.

He said, "This is the first time you've been sub-street with me."

"So?"

"Ever been in a place like this before?"

Andy said, "You mean in a sewer?"

"It's not a sewer. Storm drain. You ever been underground?"

"No. What's that got to do with it?"

"Ever been in a crowded theater and suddenly felt . . . closed in?"

"I'm not claustrophobic," Andy said defensively.

"Nothing to be ashamed of, you know. I've seen it happen before. A guy is a little uncomfortable in small rooms, elevators, crowded places, though not so uncomfortable that you'd say he was claustrophobic. Then he comes down here on a repair job for the first time, and he starts feeling cramped up, starts to shake, gets short of breath, feels the walls closing in, starts hearing things, imagining things. If that's the case with you, don't worry about it. Doesn't mean you'll be fired or anything like that. Hell, no! They'll just make sure they don't give you another underground assignment; that's all."

"I saw those things, Ted."

"Nothing's there."

"I *saw* them."

X

DOWN THE HALL from the late Dominick Carramazza's hotel suite, the next room was large and pleasant, with a queen-size bed, a writing desk, a bureau, a chest of drawers, and two chairs. The color scheme was coral with turquoise accents.

Burt Wicke, the occupant, was in his late forties. He was about six feet tall, and at one time he'd been solid and strong, but now all the hard meat of him was sheathed with fat. His shoulders were big but round, and his chest was big, and his gut overhung his belt, and as he sat on the edge of the bed, his slacks were stretched tight around his hammy thighs. Jack found it hard to tell if Wicke had ever been good-looking. Too much rich food, too much booze, too many cigarettes, too much of everything had left him with a face that looked partly melted. His eyes protruded just a bit and were bloodshot. In that coral and turquoise room, Wicke looked like a toad on a birthday cake.

His voice was a surprise, higher pitched than Jack expected. He had figured Burt Wicke to be slow-moving, slow-talking, a weary and sedentary man, but Wicke spoke with considerable nervous energy. He couldn't sit still, either. He got up from the bed, paced the room, sat down in a chair, bolted up almost at once, paced, all the while talking, answering questions —and complaining. He was a non-stop complainer.

"This won't take long, will it? I've already had to cancel one business meeting. If this takes long, I'll have to cancel another."

"It shouldn't take long," Jack said.

"I had breakfast here in the room. Not a very good breakfast. The orange juice was too warm, and the coffee wasn't warm enough. I asked for my eggs over well, and they came sunny-side up. You'd think a hotel like this, a hotel with this reputation, a hotel this *expensive,* would be able to give you a decent room service breakfast. Anyway, I shaved and got dressed. I was standing in the bathroom, combing my hair, when I heard somebody shouting. Then screaming. I stepped out of the bathroom and listened, and I was pretty sure it was all coming from next door there. More than one voice."

"What were they shouting?" Rebecca asked.

"Sounded surprised, startled. Scared. Real scared."

"No, what I mean is—do you remember any words they shouted?"

"No words."

"Or maybe names."

"They weren't shouting words or names; nothing like that."

"What were they shouting?"

"Well, maybe it *was* words and names or both, but it didn't come through the wall all that distinctly. It was just noise. And I thought to myself: Christ, not something *else* gone wrong; this has been a rotten trip all the way."

Wicke wasn't only a complainer; he was a whiner. His voice had the power to set Jack's teeth on edge.

"Then what?" Rebecca asked.

"Well, the shouting part didn't last long. Almost right away, the shooting started."

"Those two slugs came through the wall?" Jack asked, pointing to the holes.

"Not right then. Maybe a minute later. And what the hell is this joint made of, anyway, if the walls can't stop a bullet?"

"It was a .357 Magnum," Jack said. "Nothing'll stop that."

"Walls like tissue paper," Wicke said, not wanting to hear anything that might contribute to the hotel's exoneration. He went to the telephone that stood on a nightstand by the bed, and he put his hand on the receiver. "As soon as the shooting started, I scrambled over here, dialed the hotel operator, told her to get the cops. They were a *very* long time coming. Are you always such a long time coming in this city when someone needs help?"

"We do our best," Jack said.

"So I put the phone down and hesitated, not sure what to do, just stood listening to them screaming and shooting over there, and then I realized I might be in the line of fire, so I started toward the bathroom, figuring to hole up in there until it all blew over, and then all of a sudden, Jesus, I *was* in the line of fire. The first shot came through the wall and missed my face by maybe six inches. The second one was even closer. I dropped to the floor and hugged the carpet, but those were the last two shots—and just a few seconds later, there wasn't any more screaming, either."

"Then what?" Jack asked.

"Then I waited for the cops."

"You didn't go into the hall?"

"Why would I?"

"To see what happened."

"Are you crazy? How was I to know who might be out there in the hall? Maybe one of them with a gun was still out there."

"So you didn't see anyone. Or hear anything important, like a name?"

"I already told you. No."

Jack couldn't think of anything more to ask. He looked at Rebecca, and she seemed stymied, too. Another dead end.

They got up from their chairs, and Burt Wicke—still fidgety, still whining—said, "This has been a rotten trip from the beginning, absolutely rotten. First, I have to make the entire flight from Chicago sitting next to a little old lady from Peoria who wouldn't shut up. Boring old bitch. And the plane hit turbulence like you wouldn't believe. Then yesterday, two deals fall through, and I find out my hotel has rats, an *expensive* hotel like this—"

"Rats?" Jack asked.

"Huh?"

"You said the hotel has rats."

"Well, it does."

"You've seen them?" Rebecca asked.

"It's a disgrace," Wicke said. "A place like this, with such an almighty reputation, but crawling with rats."

"Have you seen them?" Rebecca repeated.

Wicke cocked his head, frowned. "Why're you so interested in rats? That's got nothing to do with the murders."

"Have you seen them?" Rebecca repeated in a harsher voice.

"Not exactly. But I heard them. In the walls."

"You heard rats in the walls?"

"Well, in the heating system, actually. They sounded close, like they were right here in these walls, but you know how those hollow metal heating ducts can carry sound. The rats might've been on another floor, even in another wing, but they sure sounded close. I got up on the desk there and put my ear to the vent, and I swear they couldn't've been inches away. Squeaking. A funny sort of squeaking. Chittering, twittering sounds. Maybe half a dozen rats, by the sound of it. I could hear their claws scraping on metal . . . a scratchy, rattly noise that gave me the creeps. I complained, but the management here doesn't bother attending to complaints. From the way they treat their guests, you'd never know this was supposed to be one of the finest hotels in the city."

Jack figured Burt Wicke had lodged an unreasonable number of vociferous, petty complaints prior to hearing the rats. By that time, the management had tagged him as either a hopeless neurotic or a grifter who was trying to establish excuses for not paying his bill.

Having paced to the window, Wicke looked up at the winter sky, down at the street far below. "And now it's snowing. On top of everything else, the weather's got to turn rotten. It isn't fair."

The man no longer reminded Jack of a toad. Now he seemed like a six-foot-tall, fat, hairy, stumpy-legged baby.

Rebecca said, "When did you hear the rats?"

"This morning. Just after I finished breakfast, I called down to the front desk to tell them how terrible their room service food was. After a highly unsatisfactory conversation with the clerk on duty, I put the phone down—

and that's the very moment when I heard the rats. After I'd listened to them a while and was positively sure they *were* rats, I called the manager himself to complain about *that,* again without satisfactory results. That's when I made up my mind to get a shower, dress, pack my suitcases, and find a new hotel before my first business appointment of the day."

"Do you remember the exact time when you heard the rats?"

"Not to the minute. But it must've been around eight-thirty."

Jack glanced at Rebecca. "About one hour before the killing started next door."

She looked troubled. She said, "Weirder and weirder."

XI

IN THE DEATH suite, the three ravaged bodies still lay where they had fallen.

The lab men hadn't finished their work. In the parlor, one of them was vacuuming the carpet around the corpse. The sweepings would be analyzed later.

Jack and Rebecca went to the nearest heating vent, a one-foot-by-eight-inch rectangular plate mounted on the wall, a few inches below the ceiling. Jack pulled a chair under it, stood on the chair, and examined the grille.

He said, "The end of the duct has an inward-bent flange all the way around it. The screws go through the edges of the grille and through the flange."

"From here," Rebecca said, "I see the heads of two screws."

"That's all there are. But anything trying to get out of the duct would have to remove at least one of those screws to loosen the grille."

"And no rat is that smart," she said.

"Even if it was a smart rat, like no other rat God ever put on this earth, a regular Albert Einstein of the rat kingdom, it still couldn't do the job. From inside the duct, it'd be dealing with the pointed, threaded end of the screw. It couldn't grip and turn the damned thing with only its paws."

"Not with its teeth, either."

"No. The job would require fingers."

The duct, of course, was much too small for a man—or even a child—to crawl through it.

Rebecca said. "Suppose a lot of rats, a few dozen of them, jammed up against one another in the duct, all struggling to get out through a ventilation grille. If a real horde of them put enough pressure on the other side of the grille, would they be able to pop the screws through the flange and then shove the grille into the room, out of their way?"

"Maybe," Jack said with more than a little doubt. "Even that sounds too smart for rats. But I guess if the holes in the flange were too much bigger than the screws that passed through them, the threads wouldn't bite on anything, and the grille could be forced off."

He tested the vent plate that he had been examining. It moved slightly back and forth, up and down, but not much.

He said, "This one's pretty tightly fitted."

"One of the others might be looser."

Jack stepped down from the chair and put it back where he'd gotten it.

They went through the suite until they'd found all the vents from the heating system: two in the parlor, one in the bedroom, one in the bath. At each outlet, the grille was fixed firmly in place.

"Nothing got into the suite through the heating ducts," Jack said. "Maybe I can make myself believe that rats could crowd up against the back of the grille and force it off, but I'll never in a million years believe that they left through the same duct and somehow managed to replace the grille behind them. No rat —no animal of any kind you can name—could be that well-trained, that dexterous."

"No. Of course not. It's ridiculous."

"So," he said.

"So," she said. She sighed. "Then you think it's just an odd coincidence that the men here were apparently bitten to death shortly after Wicke heard rats in the walls."

"I don't like coincidences," he said.

"Neither do I."

"They usually turn out not to *be* coincidences."

"Exactly."

"But it's still the most likely possibility. Coincidence, I mean. Unless . . ."

"Unless what?" she asked.

"Unless you want to consider voodoo, black magic—"

"No thank you."

"—demons creeping through the walls—"

"Jack, for God's sake!"

"—coming out to kill, melting back into the walls and just disappearing."

"I won't listen to this."

He smiled. "I'm just teasing, Rebecca."

"Like hell you are. Maybe you think you don't put any credence in that kind of baloney, but deep down inside, there's a part of you that's—"

"Excessively open-minded," he finished.

"If you insist on making a joke of it—"

"I do. I insist."

"But it's true, just the same."

"I may be excessively open-minded, if that's even possible—"

"It is."

"—but at least I'm not inflexible."

"Neither am I."

"Or rigid."

"Neither am I."

"Or frightened."

"What's that supposed to mean?"

"You figure it."

"You're saying I'm frightened?"

"Aren't you, Rebecca?"

"Of what?"

"Last night, for one thing."

"Don't be absurd."

"Then let's talk about it."

"Not now."

He looked at his watch. "Twenty past eleven. We'll break for lunch at twelve. You promised to talk about it at lunch."

"I said *if* we had time for lunch."

"We'll have time."

"I don't think so."

"We'll have time."

"There's a lot to be done here."

"We can do it after lunch."

"People to interrogate."

"We can grill them after lunch."

"You're impossible, Jack."

"Indefatigable."

"Stubborn."

"Determined."

"Damnit."

"Charming, too," he said.

She apparently didn't agree. She walked away from him. She seemed to prefer looking at one of the mutilated corpses.

Beyond the window, snow was falling heavily now. The sky was bleak. Although it wasn't noon yet, it looked like twilight out there.

XII

LAVELLE STEPPED OUT of the back door of the house. He went to the end of the porch, down three steps. He stood at the edge of the dead brown grass and looked up into the whirling chaos of snowflakes.

He had never seen snow before. Pictures, of course. But not the real thing. Until last spring, he had spent his entire life—thirty years—in Haiti, the Dominican Republic, Jamaica, and on several other Caribbean islands.

He had expected winter in New York to be uncomfortable, even arduous, for someone as unaccustomed to it as he was. However, much to his surprise, the experience had been exciting and positive, thus far. If it was only the novelty of winter that appealed to him, then he might feel differently when that novelty eventually wore off, but for the time being, he found the brisk winds and cold air invigorating.

Besides, in this great city he had discovered an enormous reservoir of the power on which he depended in order to do his work: the infinitely useful power of evil. Evil flourished everywhere, of course, in the countryside and in the suburbs, too, not merely within the boundaries of New York City. There was no shortage of evil in the Caribbean, where he had been a practicing *Bocor* —a voodoo priest skilled in the uses of black magic—ever since he was twenty-two. But here, where so many people were crammed into such a relatively small piece of land, here where a score or two of murders were committed every week, here where assaults and rapes and robberies and burglaries numbered in the tens of thousands—even hundreds of thousands—every year, here where there were an army of hustlers looking for an advantage, legions of con men searching for marks, psychos of every twisted sort, perverts, punks, wife-beaters, and thugs almost beyond counting—*this* was where the air was flooded with raw currents of evil that you could see and smell and feel—if, like Lavelle, you were sensitized to them. With each wicked deed, an effluvium of evil rose from the corrupted soul, contributing to the crackling currents in the air, making them stronger, potentially more destructive. Above and through the metropolis, vast tenebrous rivers of evil energy surged and churned. Ethereal rivers, yes. Of no substance. Yet the energy of which they were composed was real, lethal, the very stuff with which Lavelle could achieve virtually any result he wished. He could tap into those midnight tides and twilight pools of malevolent power; he could use them to cast even the most difficult and ambitious spells, curses, and charms.

The city was also crisscrossed by other, different currents of a benign nature, composed of the effluvium arising from good souls engaged in the performance of admirable deeds. These were rivers of hope, love, courage, charity, innocence, kindness, friendship, honesty, and dignity. This, too, was an extremely powerful energy, but it was of absolutely no use to Lavelle. A *Houngon,* a priest skilled at white magic, would be able to tap that benign energy for the purpose of healing, casting beneficial spells, and creating miracles. But Lavelle was a *Bocor,* not a *Houngon.* He had dedicated himself to the black arts, to the rites of *Congo* and *Pétro,* rather than to the various rites of *Rada,* white magic. And dedication to that dark sphere of sorcery also meant confinement to it.

Yet his long association with evil had not given him a bleak, mournful, or even sour aspect; he was a happy man. He smiled broadly as he stood there behind the house, at the edge of the dead brown grass, looking up into the whirling snow. He felt strong, relaxed, content, almost unbearably pleased with himself.

He was tall, six-three. He looked even taller in his narrow-legged black trousers and his long, well-fitted gray cashmere topcoat. He was unusually thin, yet powerful looking in spite of the lack of meat on his long frame. Not even the least observant could mistake him for a weakling, for he virtually radiated confidence and had eyes that made you want to get out of his way in a hurry. His hands were large, his wrists large and bony. His face was noble, not unlike that of the film actor, Sidney Poitier. His skin was exceptionally dark, very black, with an almost purple undertone, somewhat like the skin of a ripe eggplant. Snowflakes melted on his face and stuck in his eyebrows and frosted his wiry black hair.

The house out of which he had come was a three-story brick affair, pseudo-Victorian, with a false tower, a slate-roof, and lots of gingerbread trim, but battered and weathered and grimy. It had been built in the early years of the century, had been part of a really fine residential neighborhood at that time, had still been solidly middle-class by the end of World War Two (though declining in prestige), and had become distinctly lower middle-class by the late 70s. Most of the houses on the street had been converted to apartment buildings. This one had not, but it was in the same state of disrepair as all the others. It wasn't where Lavelle wanted to live; it was where he *had* to live until this little war was finished to his satisfaction; it was his hidey hole.

On both sides, other brick houses, exactly the same as this one, crowded close. Each overlooked its own fenced yard. Not much of a yard: a forty-by-twenty-foot plot of thin grass, now dormant under the harsh hand of winter. At the far end of the lawn was the garage, and beyond the garage was a litter-strewn alley.

In one corner of Lavelle's property, up against the garage wall, stood a corrugated metal utility shed with a white enamel finish and a pair of green metal doors. He'd bought it at Sears, and their workmen had erected it a month ago. Now, when he'd had enough of looking up into the falling snow, he went to the shed, opened one of the doors, and stepped inside.

Heat assaulted him. Although the shed wasn't equipped with a heating system, and although the walls weren't even insulated, the small building—twelve-foot-by-ten—was nevertheless extremely warm. Lavelle had no sooner entered and pulled the door shut behind him than he was obliged to strip out of his nine-hundred-dollar topcoat in order to breathe comfortably.

A peculiar, slightly sulphurous odor hung in the air. Most people would have found it unpleasant. But Lavelle sniffed, then breathed deeply, and smiled. He savored the stench. To him, it was a sweet fragrance because it was the scent of revenge.

He had broken into a sweat.

He took off his shirt.

He was chanting in a strange tongue.

He took off his shoes, his trousers, his underwear.

Naked, he knelt on the dirt floor.

He began to sing softly. The melody was pure, compelling, and he carried it well. He sang in a low voice that could not have been heard by anyone beyond the boundaries of his own property.

Sweat streamed from him. His black body glistened.

He swayed gently back and forth as he sang. In a little while he was almost in a trance.

The lines he sang were lilting, rhythmic chains of words in an ungrammatical, convoluted, but mellifluous mixture of French, English, Swahili, and Bantu. It was partly a Haitian patois, partly a Jamaican patois, partly an African juju chant: the pattern-rich "language" of voodoo.

He was singing about vengeance. About death. About the blood of his enemies. He called for the destruction of the Carramazza family, one member at a time, according to a list he had made.

Finally he sang about the slaughter of that police detective's two children, which might become necessary at any moment.

The prospect of killing children did not disturb him. In fact, the possibility was exciting.

His eyes shone.

His long-fingered hands moved slowly up and down his lean body in a sensuous caress.

His breathing was labored as he inhaled the heavy warm air and exhaled an even heavier, warmer vapor.

The beads of sweat on his ebony skin gleamed with reflected orange light.

Although he had not switched on the overhead light when he'd entered, the interior of the shed wasn't pitch black. The perimeter of the small, windowless room was shrouded in shadows, but a vague orange glow rose from the floor in the center of the chamber. It came out of a hole about five feet in diameter. Lavelle had dug it while performing a complicated, six-hour ritual, during which he had spoken to many of the evil gods—Congo Savanna, Congo Maussai, Congo Moudongue—and the evil angels like the Zandor, the Ibos "je rouge," the Petro Maman Pemba, and Ti Jean Pie Fin.

The excavation was shaped like a meteor crater, the walls sloping inward to form a basin. The center of the basin was only three feet deep. However, if you stared into it long enough, it gradually began to appear much, much deeper than that. In some mysterious way, when you peered at the flickering light for a couple of minutes, when you tried hard to discern its source, your perspective abruptly and drastically changed, and you could see that the bottom of the hole was hundreds if not thousands of feet below. It wasn't merely a hole in the dirt floor of the shed; not anymore; suddenly and magically, it was a doorway into the heart of the earth. But then, with a blink, it seemed only a shallow basin once more.

Now, still singing, Lavelle leaned forward.

He looked at the strange, pulsing orange light.

He looked into the hole.

Looked down.

Down . . .

Down into . . .

Down into the pit.

The Pit.

XIII

SHORTLY BEFORE NOON, Nayva Rooney had finished cleaning the Dawson's apartment.

She had neither seen nor heard anything more of the rat—or whatever it had been—that she had pursued from room to room earlier in the morning. It had vanished.

She wrote a note to Jack Dawson, asking him to call her this evening. He had to be told about the rat, so that he could arrange to have the building superintendent hire an exterminator. She fixed the note to the refrigerator with a magnetic plastic butterfly that was usually used to hold a shopping list in place.

After she put on her rubber boots, coat, scarf, and gloves, she switched off the last light, the hall light. Now, the apartment was lit only by the thin, gray, useless daylight that seemed barely capable of penetrating the windows. The hall, windowless, was not lit at all. She stood perfectly still by the front door for more than a minute—listening.

The apartment remained tomb-silent.

At last, she let herself out and locked the door behind her.

A few minutes after Nayva Rooney had gone, there was movement in the apartment.

Something came out of Penny and Davey's bedroom, into the gloomy hallway. It merged with the shadows. If Nayva had been there, she would have seen only its bright, glowing, fiery white eyes. It stood for a moment, just outside the door through which it had come, and then it moved down the hall toward the living room, its claws clicking on the wooden floor; it made a cold angry, hissing noise as it went.

A second creature came out of the kids' room. It, too, was well-hidden by the darkness in the apartment, just a shadow among shadows—except for its shining eyes.

A third small, dark, hissing beast appeared.

A fourth.

A fifth.

Another. And another . . .

Soon, they were all over the apartment: crouching in corners; perching on furniture or squirming under it; slinking along the baseboard; climbing the walls with insectile skill; creeping behind the drapes; sniffing and hissing; scurrying restlessly from room to room and then back again; ceaselessly growling in what almost sounded like a guttural foreign language; staying, for the most part, in the shadows, as if even the pale winter light coming through the windows was too harsh for them.

Then, suddenly, they all stopped moving and were motionless, as if a command had come to them. Gradually, they began to sway from side to side, their beaming eyes describing small arcs in the darkness. Their metronomic movement was in time with the song that Baba Lavelle sang in another, distant part of the city.

Eventually, they stopped swaying.

They did not become restless again.

They waited in the shadows, motionless, eyes shining.

Soon, they might be called upon to kill.

They were ready. They were eager.

CHAPTER 3

I

CAPTAIN WALTER GRESHAM, of Homicide, had a face like a shovel. Not that he was an ugly man; in fact, he was rather handsome in a sharp-edged sort of way. But his entire face sloped forward, all of his strong features pointing down and out, toward the tip of his chin, so that you were reminded of a garden spade.

He arrived at the hotel a few minutes before noon and met with Jack and Rebecca at the end of the elevator alcove on the sixteenth floor, by a window that looked down on Fifth Avenue.

"What we've got brewing here is a full-fledged gang war," Gresham said. "We haven't seen anything like this in my time. It's like something out of the roaring twenties, for God's sake! Even if it is just a bunch of hoods and scumbags killing one another, I don't like it. Absolutely won't tolerate it in my jurisdiction. I spoke with the Commissioner before I came over here, and he's in full agreement with me: We can't go on treating this as if it were just an ordinary homicide investigation; we've got to put the pressure on. We're forming a special task force. We're converting two interrogation rooms into a task force headquarters, putting in special phone lines and everything."

"Does that mean Jack and I are being pulled off the case?"

"No, no," Gresham said. "I'm putting you in charge of the task force. I want you to head back to the office, work up an attack plan, a strategy, figure out everything you'll need. How many men—both uniforms and detectives? How much clerical support? How many vehicles? Establish emergency liaisons with city, state, and federal drug enforcement agencies, so we don't have to go through the bureaucracy every time we need information. Then meet me in my office at five o'clock."

"We've still got work to do here," Jack said.

"Others can handle that," Gresham said. "And by the way, we've gotten some answers to your queries about Lavelle."

"The phone company?" Jack asked.

"That's one of them. They've no listed or unlisted number for anyone named Baba Lavelle. In the past year, they've had only two new customers named Lavelle. I sent a man around this morning to talk to both of them. Neither is black, like your Lavelle. Neither of them knows anyone named Baba. And neither of them made my man the least bit suspicious."

Driven by a sudden hard wind, snow grated like sand across the window. Below, Fifth Avenue briefly vanished beneath whirling flakes.

"What about the power company?" Jack asked.

"Same situation," Gresham said. "No Baba Lavelle."

"He might've used a friend's name for utility connections."

Gresham shook his head. "Also heard back from the Department of Immigration. No one named Lavelle—Baba or otherwise—applied for any residency permit, either short-term or long-term, in the past year."

Jack frowned. "So he's in the country illegally."

"Or he's not here at all," Rebecca said.

They looked at her, puzzled.

She elaborated: "I'm not convinced there *is* a Baba Lavelle."

"Of course there is," Jack said.

But she said, "We've *heard* a lot about him, and we've seen some smoke. . . . But when it comes to getting hold of physical evidence of his existence, we keep coming up empty-handed."

Gresham was keenly interested, and his interest disheartened Jack. "You think maybe Lavelle is just a red herring? Sort of a . . . paper man behind which the real killer or killers are hiding?"

"Could be," Rebecca said.

"A bit of misdirection," Gresham said, clearly intrigued. "In reality, maybe it's one of the other mafia families making a move on the Carramazzas, trying to take the top rung of the ladder."

"Lavelle exists," Jack said.

Gresham said, "You seem so certain of that. Why?"

"I don't know, really." Jack looked out the window at the snowswept towers of Manhattan. "I won't pretend I've got good reasons. It's just . . . instinct. I feel it in my bones. Lavelle is real. He's out there somewhere. He's out there . . . and I think he's the most vicious, dangerous son of a bitch any of us is ever going to run up against."

II

AT WELLTON SCHOOL, when classes on the third floor recessed for lunch, Penny Dawson wasn't hungry. She didn't even bother to go to her newly assigned locker and get her lunchbox. She stayed at her desk and kept her head down on her folded arms, eyes closed, pretending to nap. A sour, icy ball lay lead-heavy in the pit of her stomach. She was sick—not with any virus, but with fear.

She hadn't told anyone about the silver-eyed goblins in the basement. No one would believe she'd really seen them. And, for sure, no one would believe the goblins were eventually going to attempt to kill her.

But she knew what was coming. She didn't know why it was happening to her, of all people. She didn't know exactly how it would happen or when. She didn't know where the goblins came from. She didn't know if she had a chance of escaping them; maybe there was no way out. But she *did* know what they intended to do to her. Oh, yes.

It wasn't merely her own fate that worried her. She was scared for Davey, too. If the goblins wanted her, they might also want him.

She felt responsible for Davey, especially since their mother had died. After all, she was his big sister. A big sister had an obligation to watch over a little brother and protect him, even if he could be a pain in the neck sometimes.

Right now, Davey was down on the second floor with his classmates and teachers. For the time being, at least, he was safe. The goblins surely wouldn't show themselves when a lot of people were around; they seemed to be very secretive creatures.

But what about later? What would happen when school was out and it was time to go home?

She didn't see how she could protect herself or Davey.

Head down on her arms, eyes closed, pretending to nap, she said a silent prayer. But she didn't think it would do any good.

III

IN THE HOTEL lobby, Jack and Rebecca stopped at the public phones. He tried to call Nayva Rooney. Because of the task force assignment, he wouldn't be able to pick up the kids after school, as planned, and he hoped Nayva would be free to meet them and keep them at her place for a while. She didn't answer her phone, and he thought perhaps she was still at his apartment, cleaning, so he tried his own number, too, but he didn't have any luck.

Reluctantly, he called Faye Jamison, his sister-in-law, Linda's only sister. Faye had loved Linda almost as much as Jack himself had loved her. For that reason he had considerable affection for Faye—although she wasn't always an easy person to like. She was convinced that no one else's life could be well-run without the benefit of her advice. She meant well. Her unsolicited counsel was based on a genuine concern for others, and she delivered her advice in a gentle, motherly voice even if the target of her kibitzing was twice her age. But she was nonetheless irritating for all of her good intentions, and there were times when her soft voice seemed, to Jack, as piercing as a police siren.

Like now, on the telephone, after he asked if she would pick up the kids at school this afternoon, she said, "Of course, Jack, I'll be glad to, but if they expect you to be there and then you don't show, they're going to be disappointed, and if this sort of thing happens too often, they're going to feel worse than just disappointed; they're going to feel abandoned."

"Faye—"

"Psychologists say that when children have already lost one parent, they need—"

"Faye, I'm sorry, but I don't really have time right now to listen to what the psychologists say. I—"

"But you should *make* time for just that sort of thing, dear."

He sighed. "Perhaps I should."

"Every modern parent ought to be well-versed in child psychology."

Jack glanced at Rebecca, who was waiting impatiently by the phones. He raised his eyebrows and shrugged as Faye rattled on:

"You're an old-fashioned, seat-of-the-pants parent, dear. You think you can handle everything with love and cookies. Now, of course, love and cookies are a part of it, but there's a whole lot more to the job than—"

"Faye, listen, nine times out of ten, I *am* there when I tell the kids I will be. But sometimes it isn't possible. This job doesn't have the most regular hours. A homicide detective can't walk away in the middle of pursuing a hot lead just because it's the end of his shift. Besides, there's a crisis here. A big one. Now, will you pick up the kids for me?"

"Of course, dear," she said, sounding slightly hurt.

"I appreciate it, Faye."

"It's nothing."

"I'm sorry if I sounded . . . abrupt."

"You didn't at all. Don't worry about it. Will Davey and Penny be staying for dinner?"

"If it's all right with you—"

"Of course it is. We love having them here, Jack. You know that. And will you be eating with us?"

"I'm not sure I'll be free by then."

"Don't miss too many dinners with them, dear."

"I don't plan to."

"Dinnertime is an important ritual, an opportunity for the family to share the events of the day."

"I know."

"Children need that period of tranquility, of togetherness, at the end of each day."

"I know. I'll try my best to make it. I hardly ever miss."

"Will they be sleeping over?"

"I'm sure I won't be that late. Listen, thanks a lot, Faye. I don't know what I'd do without you and Keith to lean on now and then; really, I don't. But I've got to run now. See you later."

Before Faye could respond with more advice, Jack hung up, feeling both guilty and relieved.

A fierce and bitter wind was stored up in the west. It poured through the cold gray city in an unrelenting flood, harrying the snow before it.

Outside the hotel, Rebecca and Jack turned up their coat collars and tucked their chins down and cautiously negotiated the slippery, snow-skinned pavement.

Just as they reached their car, a stranger stepped up to them. He was tall, dark-complexioned, well-dressed. "Lieutenant Chandler? Lieutenant Dawson? My boss wants to talk to you."

"Who's your boss?" Rebecca asked.

Instead of answering, the man pointed to a black Mercedes limousine that was parked farther along the hotel driveway. He started toward it, clearly expecting them to follow without further question.

After a brief hesitation, they actually did follow him, and when they reached the limousine, the heavily tinted rear window slid down. Jack instantly recognized the passenger, and he saw that Rebecca also knew who the man was: Don Gennaro Carramazza, patriarch of the most powerful mafia family in New York.

The tall man got in the front seat with the chauffeur, and Carramazza, alone in the back, opened his door and motioned for Jack and Rebecca to join him.

"What do you want?" Rebecca asked, making no move to get into the car.

"A little conversation," Carramazza said, with just the vaguest trace of a Sicilian accent. He had a surprisingly cultured voice.

"So talk," she said.

"Not like this. It's too cold," Carramazza said. Snow blew past him, into the car. "Let's be comfortable."

"I am comfortable," she said.

"Well, I'm not," Carramazza said. He frowned. "Listen, I have some extremely valuable information for you. I chose to deliver it myself. *Me.* Doesn't that tell you how important this is? But I'm not going to talk on the street, in public, for Christ's sake."

Jack said, "Get in, Rebecca."

With an expression of distaste, she did as he said.

Jack got into the car after her. They sat in the two seats that flanked the built-in bar and television set, facing the rear of the limousine, where Carramazza sat facing forward.

Up front, Rudy touched a switch, and a thick Plexiglas partition rose between that part of the car and the passenger compartment.

Carramazza picked up an attache case and put it on his lap but didn't open it. He regarded Jack and Rebecca with sly contemplation.

The old man looked like a lizard. His eyes were hooded by heavy, pebbled lids. He was almost entirely bald. His face was wizened and leathery, with sharp features and a wide, thin-lipped mouth. He moved like a lizard, too: very still for long moments, then brief flurries of activity, quick dartings and swivelings of the head.

Jack wouldn't have been surprised if a long, forked tongue had flickered out from between Carramazza's dry lips.

Carramazza swiveled his head to Rebecca. "There's no reason to be afraid of me, you know."

She looked surprised. "Afraid? But I'm not."

"When you were reluctant to get into the car, I thought—"

"Oh, that wasn't fear," she said icily. "I was worried the dry cleaner might not be able to get the stink out of my clothes."

Carramazza's hard little eyes narrowed.

Jack groaned inwardly.

The old man said, "I see no reason why we can't be civil with one another, especially when it's in our mutual interest to cooperate."

He didn't sound like a hoodlum. He sounded like a banker.

"Really?" Rebecca said. "You really see no reason? Please allow me to explain."

Jack said, "Uh, Rebecca—"

She let Carramazza have it: "You're a thug, a thief, a murderer, a dope peddler, a pimp. Is that explanation enough?"

"Rebecca—"

"Don't worry, Jack. I haven't insulted him. You can't insult a pig merely by calling it a pig."

"Remember," Jack said, "he's lost a nephew and a brother today."

"Both of whom were dope peddlers, thugs, and murderers," she said.

Carramazza was startled speechless by her ferocity.

Rebecca glared at him and said, "You don't seem particularly grief-stricken by the loss of your brother. Does he look grief-stricken to you, Jack?"

Without a trace of anger or even any excitement in his voice, Carramazza said, "In the *fratellanza,* Sicilian men don't weep."

Coming from a withered old man, that macho declaration was outrageously foolish.

Still without apparent animosity, continuing to employ the soothing voice of a banker, Carramazza said, "We do *feel,* however. And we do take our revenge."

Rebecca studied him with obvious disgust.

The old man's reptilian hands remained perfectly still on top of the attache case. He turned his cobra eyes on Jack.

"Lieutenant Dawson, perhaps I should deal with you in this matter. You don't seem to share Lieutenant Chandler's . . . prejudices."

Jack shook his head. "That's where you're wrong. I agree with everything she said. I just wouldn't have said it."

He looked at Rebecca.

She smiled at him, pleased by his support.

Looking at her but speaking to Carramazza, Jack said, "Sometimes, my partner's zeal and aggressiveness are excessive and counterproductive, a lesson she seems unable or unwilling to learn."

Her smile faded fast.

With evident sarcasm, Carramazza said, "What do I have here—a couple of self-righteous, holier-than-thou types? I suppose you've never accepted a bribe, not even back when you were a uniformed cop walking a beat and earning barely enough to pay the rent."

Jack met the old man's hard, watchful eyes and said, "Yeah. That's right. I never have."

"Not even one gratuity—"

"No."

"—like a free tumble in the hay with a hooker who was trying to stay out of jail or—"

"No."

"—a little cocaine, maybe some grass, from a pusher who wanted you to look the other way."

"No."

"A bottle of liquor or a twenty-dollar bill at Christmas."

"No."

Carramazza regarded them in silence for a moment, while a cloud of snow swirled around the car and obscured the city. At last he said, "So I've got to deal with a couple of freaks." He spat out the word "freaks" with such contempt that it was clear he was disgusted by the mere thought of an honest public official.

"No, you're wrong," Jack said. "There's nothing special about us. We're not freaks. Not all cops are corrupt. In fact, not even most of them are."

"Most of them," Carramazza disagreed.

"No," Jack insisted. "There're bad apples, sure, and weak sisters. But for the most part, I can be proud of the people I work with."

"Most are on the take, one way or another," Carramazza said.

"That's just not true."

Rebecca said, "No use arguing, Jack. He *has* to believe everyone else is corrupt. That's how he justifies the things he does."

The old man sighed. He opened the attache case on his lap, withdrew a manila envelope, handed it to Jack. "This might help you."

Jack took it with more than a little apprehension. "What is it?"

"Relax," Carramazza said. "It isn't a bribe. It's information. Everything we've been able to learn about this man who calls himself Baba Lavelle. His last-known address. Restaurants he frequented before he started this war and went into hiding. The names and addresses of all the pushers who've distributed his merchandise over the past couple of months—though you won't be able to question some of them, any more."

"Because you've had them killed?" Rebecca asked.

"Maybe they just left town."

"Sure."

"Anyway, it's all there," Carramazza said. "Maybe you already have all that information; maybe you don't; I think you don't."

"Why're you giving it to us?" Jack asked.

"Isn't that obvious?" the old man asked, opening his hooded eyes a bit wider. "I want Lavelle found. I want him stopped."

Holding the nine-by-twelve envelope in one hand, tapping it against his knee, Jack said, "I'd have thought you'd have a much better chance of finding him than we would. He's a drug dealer, after all. He's part of your world. You have all the sources, all the contacts—"

"The usual sources and contacts are of little or no use in this case," the old man said. "This Lavelle . . . he's a loner. Worse than that. It's as if . . . as if he's made of . . . smoke."

"Are you sure he actually exists?" Rebecca asked. "Maybe he's only a straw man. Maybe your *real* enemies created him in order to hide behind him."

"He's real," Carramazza said emphatically. "He entered this country illegally last spring. Came here from Jamaica by way of Puerto Rico. There's a photograph of him in the envelope there."

Jack hastily opened it, rummaged through the contents, and extracted an eight-by-ten glossy.

Carramazza said, "It's an enlargement of a snapshot taken in a restaurant shortly after Lavelle began operating in what has been traditionally our territory."

Traditionally our territory. Good God, Jack thought, he sounds as if he's some British duke complaining about poachers invading his fox-hunting fields!

The photo was a bit fuzzy, but Lavelle's face was sufficiently distinct so that, henceforth, Jack would be able to recognize him if he ever saw him on the street. The man was very black, handsome—indeed, striking—with a broad brow, deepset eyes, high cheekbones, and a wide mouth. In the picture he was smiling at someone who wasn't within the camera's field. He had an engaging smile.

Jack passed the picture to Rebecca.

Carramazza said, "Lavelle wants to take away my business, destroy my reputation within the *fratellanza,* and make me look weak and helpless. *Me.* Me, the man who has controlled the organization with an iron hand for twenty-eight years! *Me!*"

Finally, emotion filled his voice: cold, hard anger. He went on, spitting out the words as if they tasted bad.

"But that isn't the worst of it. No. You see, he doesn't actually want the business. Once he's got it, he'll throw it away, let the other families move in and carve it up among themselves. He just doesn't want me or anyone named Carramazza to have it. This isn't merely a battle for the territory, not just a struggle for control. For Lavelle, this is strictly a matter of revenge. He wants to see me suffer in every way possible. He intends to isolate me and hopes to break my spirit by robbing me of my empire and by killing my nephews, my sons. Yes, all of them, one by one. He threatens to murder my best friends, as well, anyone who has ever meant anything to me. He promises to kill my five precious grandchildren. Can you believe such a thing? He threatens little babies! No vengeance, regardless of how justified it might be, should ever touch innocent children."

"He's actually told you that he'll do all of those things?" Rebecca asked. "When? When did he tell you?"

"Several times."

"You've had face-to-face meetings?"

"No. He wouldn't survive a face-to-face meeting."

The banker image had vanished. There was no veneer of gentility now. The old man looked more reptilian than ever. Like a snake in a thousand-dollar suit. A very poisonous snake.

He said, "This crudball Lavelle told me these things on the phone. My unlisted home number. I keep having the number changed, but the creep gets the new one every time, almost as soon as it's installed. He tells me . . . he says . . . after he has killed my friends, nephews, sons, grandkids, then . . . he says he's going to . . . he says he's going to . . ."

For a moment, recalling Lavelle's arrogant threats, Carramazza was unable to speak; anger locked his jaws; his teeth were clenched, and the muscles in his neck and cheeks were bulging. His dark eyes, always disturbing, now shone with a rage so intense, so inhuman that it communicated itself to Jack and sent a chill up his spine.

Eventually, Carramazza regained control of himself. When he spoke, however, his voice never rose above a fierce, frigid whisper. "This scum, this nigger bastard, this piece of *shit*—he tells me he'll slaughter my wife, my Nina. *Slaughter* was the word he used. And when he's butchered her, he says, he'll then take my daughter from me, too." The old man's voice softened when he spoke of his daughter. "My Rosie. My beautiful Rosie, the light of my life. Twenty-seven, but she looks seventeen. And smart, too. A medical student. Going to be a doctor. Starts her internship this year. Skin like porcelain. The loveliest eyes you've ever seen." He was quiet for a moment, seeing Rosie in his mind's eye, and then his whisper became harsh again: "Lavelle says he'll rape my daughter and then cut her to pieces, dismember her . . . in front of my eyes. He has the balls to say such things to me!" With that last declaration, Carramazza sprayed spittle on Jack's overcoat. For a few seconds, the old man said nothing more; he just took deep, shuddering breaths. His talonlike fingers closed into fists, opened, closed, opened, closed. Then: "I want the bastard stopped."

"You've put all your people into the search for him?" Jack asked. "Used all your sources?"

"Yes."

"But you still can't find him."

"Nooo," Carramazza said, and in the drawing-out of that one word, he revealed a frustration almost as great as his rage. "He's left his place in the Village, gone to ground, hiding out. That's why I'm bringing this information to you. You can put out an APB now that you've got his picture. Then every cop in the city will be looking for him, and that's a lot more men than I've got. You can even put it on the TV news, in the papers, and then virtually everyone in the whole damned city will have an eye out for him. If I can't get to him, then at least I want *you* to nail him and put him away. Once he's behind bars . . ."

"You'll have ways of reaching him in prison," Rebecca said, finishing the thought to which Carramazza would not give voice. "If we arrest him, he'll never stand trial. He'll be killed in jail."

Carramazza wouldn't confirm what she had said, but they all knew it was true.

Jack said, "You've told us Lavelle is motivated by revenge. But for what? What did you do to him that would make him want to exterminate your entire family, even your grandchildren?"

"I won't tell you that. I *can't* tell you because, if I did, I might be compromising myself."

"More likely *incriminating* yourself," Rebecca said.

Jack slipped the photograph of Lavelle back into the envelope. "I've been wondering about your brother Dominick."

Gennaro Carramazza seemed to shrivel and age at the mention of his dead brother.

Jack said, "I mean, he was apparently hiding out, in the hotel here, when Lavelle got to him. But if he knew he was targeted, why didn't he squirrel himself away at his own place or come to you for protection? Under the circumstances, no place in the city would be as safe as your house. With all this going down, surely you must have a fortress out there in Brooklyn Heights."

"It is," the old man said. "My house is a fortress." His eyes blinked once, twice, slow as lizard eyes. "A fortress—but not safe. Lavelle has already struck inside my own house, in spite of the tight security."

"You mean, he's killed in your house—"

"Yes."

"Who?"

"Ginger and Pepper."

"Who're they?"

"My doggies. A matched pair of papillons."

"Ah."

"Little dogs, you know."

"I'm not really sure what they look like," Jack said.

"Toy spaniels," Rebecca said. "Long, silky coats."

"Yes, yes. Very playful," Carramazza said. "Always wrestling with each other, chasing. Always wanting to be held and petted."

"And they were killed in your house."

Carramazza looked up. "Last night. Torn to pieces. Somehow—we *still* don't know how—Lavelle or one of his men got in, killed my sweet little dogs, and got out again without being spotted." He slammed one bony hand down on his attache case. "Damnit, the whole thing's impossible! The house is sealed tight! Guarded by a small army!" He blinked more rapidly than he had done before, and his voice faltered. "Ginger and Pepper were so gentle. They wouldn't bite anyone. Never. They hardly even barked. They didn't deserve to be treated so brutally. Two innocent little creatures."

Jack was astounded. This murderer, this geriatric dope peddler, this ancient racketeer, this supremely dangerous poisonous lizard of a man, who had been unable or unwilling to weep for his dead brother, now seemed on the verge of tears over the slaying of his dogs.

Jack glanced at Rebecca. She was staring at Carramazza, half in wide-eyed wonder, half in the manner of someone watching a particularly loathsome creature as it crawled out from under a rock.

The old man said, "After all, they weren't guard dogs. They weren't attack dogs. They posed no threat. Just a couple of adorable little toy spaniels . . ."

Not quite sure how to handle a maudlin mafia chieftain, Jack tried to get Carramazza off the subject of his dogs before the old man reached that pathetic and embarrassing state of mind on the edge of which he now teetered. He said, "Word on the street is that Lavelle claims to be using voodoo against you."

Carramazza nodded. "That's what he says."

"You believe it?"

"He seems serious."

"But do you think there's anything to this voodoo business?"

Carramazza didn't answer. He gazed out the side window at the wind-whipped snow whirling past the parked limousine.

Although Jack was aware that Rebecca was scowling at him in disapproval, he pressed the point: "You think there's anything to it?"

Carramazza turned his face away from the window. "You mean, do I think it works? A month ago, anybody asked me the same thing, I'd have laughed, but now . . ."

Jack said, "Now you're wondering if maybe . . ."

"Yeah. If maybe . . ."

Jack saw that the old man's eyes had changed. They were still hard, still cold, still watchful, but now there was something new in them. Fear. It was an emotion to which this vicious old bastard was long unaccustomed.

"Find him," Carramazza said.

"We'll try," Jack said.

"Because it's our job," Rebecca said quickly, as if to dispel any notion that they were motivated by concern for Gennaro Carramazza and his blood-thirsty family.

"Stop him," Carramazza said, and the tone of his voice was the closest he would ever come to saying "please" to an officer of the law.

The Mercedes limousine pulled away from the curb and down the hotel driveway, leaving tracks in the quarter-inch skin of snow that now covered the pavement.

For a moment, Jack and Rebecca stood on the sidewalk, watching the car.

The wind had abated. Snow was still falling, even more heavily than before, but it was no longer wind-driven; the lazy, swirling descent of the flakes made it seem, to Jack, as if he were standing inside one of those novelty paperweights that would produce a neatly contained snowstorm anytime you shook it.

Rebecca said, "We better get back to headquarters."

He took the photograph of Lavelle out of the envelope that Carramazza had given him, tucked it inside his coat.

"What're you doing?" Rebecca asked.

He handed her the envelope. "I'll be at headquarters in an hour."

"What are you talking about?"

"Two o'clock at the latest."

"Where are you going?"

"There's something I want to look into."

"Jack, we've got to set up the task force, prepare a—"

"You get it started."

"There's too much work for one—"

"I'll be there by two, two-fifteen at the latest."

"Damnit, Jack—"

"You can handle it on your own for a while."

"You're going up to Harlem, aren't you?"

"Listen, Rebecca—"

"Up to that damned voodoo shop."

He didn't say anything.

She said, "I knew it. You're running up there to see Carver Hampton again. That charlatan. That fraud."

"He's not a fraud. He believes in what he does. I said I'd get back to him today."

"This is crazy."

"Is it? Lavelle *does* exist. We have a photo now."

"So he exists? That doesn't mean voodoo works!"

"I know that."

"If you go up there, how am I supposed to get to the office?"

"You can take the car. I'll get a uniform to drive me."

"Jack, damnit."

"I have a hunch, Rebecca."

"Hell."

"I have a hunch that . . . somehow . . . the voodoo subculture—maybe not any real supernatural stuff —but at least the subculture itself is inextricably entwined with this. I have a strong hunch that's the way to approach the case."

"Christ."

"A smart cop plays his hunches."

"And if you don't get back when you promise, if I'm stuck all afternoon, handling everything myself, and then if I have to go in and face Gresham with—"

"I'll be back by two-fifteen, two-thirty at the latest."

"I'm not going to forgive you for this, Jack."

He met her eyes, hesitated, then said, "Maybe I *could* postpone seeing Carver Hampton until tomorrow if . . ."

"If what?"

"If I knew you'd take just half an hour, just fifteen minutes, to sit down with me and talk about everything that happened between us last night. Where are we going from here?"

Her eyes slid away from his. "We don't have *time* for that now."

"Rebecca—"

"There's a lot of *work* to do, Jack!"

He nodded. "You're right. You've got to get started on the task force details, and I've got to see Carver Hampton."

He walked away from her, toward the uniforms who were standing by the patrol cars.

She said, "No later than two o'clock!"

"I'll make it as fast as I can," he said.

The wind suddenly picked up again. It howled.

IV

THE NEW SNOW had brightened and softened the street. The neighborhood was still seedy, grimy, litter-strewn, and mean, but it didn't look half as bad as it had yesterday, without snow.

Carver Hampton's shop was near the corner. It was flanked by a liquor store with iron bars permanently fixed over the display windows and by a shabby furniture store also huddled behind bars. Hampton's place was the only business on the block that looked prosperous, and there were no bars over its windows, either.

The sign above the door contained only a single word: *Rada.* Yesterday, Jack had asked Hampton what the shop's name signified, and he had learned that there were three great rites or spiritual divisions governing voodoo. Two of those were composed of evil gods and were called *Congo* and *Pétro.* The pantheon of benevolent gods was called the *Rada.* Since Hampton dealt only in substances, implements, and ceremonial clothing necessary for the practice of white (good) magic, that one word above the door was all he needed to attract exactly the clientele he was looking for—those people of the Caribbean and their descendants who, having been transplanted to New York City, had brought their religion with them.

The shop was small, twenty feet wide and thirty deep. In the center were tables displaying knives, staffs, bells, bowls, other implements, and articles of clothing used in various rituals. To the right, low cabinets stood along the entire wall; Jack had no idea what was in them. On the other wall, to the left of the door, there were shelves nearly all the way to the ceiling, and these were crammed full of bottles of every imaginable size and shape, blue and yellow and green and red and orange and brown and clear bottles, each carefully labeled, each filled with a particular herb or exotic root or powdered flower or other substance used in the casting of spells and charms, the brewing of magical potions.

At the rear of the shop, in answer to the bell, Carver Hampton came out of the back room, through a green bead curtain. He looked surprised. "Detective Dawson! How nice to see you again. But I didn't expect you'd come all the way back here, especially not in this foul weather. I thought you'd just call, see if I'd come up with anything for you."

Jack went to the back of the shop, and they shook hands across the sales counter.

Carver Hampton was tall, with wide shoulders and a huge chest, about forty pounds overweight but very formidable; he looked like a pro football lineman who had been out of training for six months. He wasn't a handsome man. There was too much bone in his slablike forehead, and his face was too round for him ever to appear in the pages of *Gentleman's Quarterly;* besides, his nose, broken more than once, now had a distinctly squashlike appearance. But if he wasn't particularly good looking, he *was* very friendly looking, a gentle giant, a perfect black Santa Claus.

He said, "I'm so sorry you came all this way for nothing."

"Then you haven't turned up anything since yesterday?" Jack asked.

"Nothing much. I put the word out. I'm still asking here and there, poking around. So far, all I've been able to find out is that there actually *is* someone around who calls himself Baba Lavelle and says he's a *Bocor.*"

"*Bocor?* That's a priest who practices witchcraft—right?"

"Right. Evil magic. That's all I've learned: that he's real, which you weren't sure of yesterday, so I suppose this is at least of some value to you. But if you'd telephoned—"

"Well, actually, I came to show you something that might be of help. A photograph of Baba Lavelle himself."

"Truly?"

"Yes."

"So you already know he's real. Let me see it, though. It ought to help if I can describe the man I'm asking around about."

Jack withdrew the eight-by-ten glossy from inside his coat and handed it over.

Hampton's face changed the instant he saw Lavelle. If a black man could go pale, that was what Hampton did. It wasn't that the shade of his skin changed so much as that the gloss and vitality went out of it; suddenly it didn't seem like skin at all but like dark brown paper, dry and lifeless. His lips tightened. And his eyes were not the same as they had been a moment ago: haunted, now.

He said, "This *man!*"

"What?" Jack asked.

The photograph quivered as Hampton quickly handed it back. He thrust it at Jack, as if desperate to be rid of it, as if he might somehow be contaminated merely by touching the photographic image of Lavelle. His big hands were shaking.

Jack said, "What is it? What's the matter?"

"I know him," Hampton said. "I've . . . seen him. I just didn't know his name."

"Where have you see him?"

"Here."

"Right in the shop?"

"Yes."

"When?"

"Last September."

"Not since then?"

"No."

"What was he doing here?"

"He came to purchase herbs, powdered flowers."

"But I thought you dealt only in good magic. The *Rada.*"

"Many substances can be used by both the *Bocor* and the *Houngon* to obtain very different results, to work evil magic or good. These were herbs and powdered flowers that were extremely rare and that he hadn't been able to locate elsewhere in New York."

"There are *other* shops like yours?"

"One shop somewhat like this, although not as large. And then there are two practicing *Houngons*—not strong magicians, these two, little more than amateurs, neither of them powerful enough or knowledgeable enough to do well for themselves—who sell the stuff of magic out of their apartments. They have considerable lines of merchandise to offer to other practitioners. But none of those three have scruples. They will sell to either the *Bocor* or the *Houngon.* They even sell the instruments required for a blood sacrifice, the ceremonial hatchets, the razor-edged spoons used to scoop the living eye from the skull. Terrible people, peddling their wares to anyone, anyone at all, even to the most wicked and debased."

"So Lavelle came here when he couldn't get everything he wanted from them."

"Yes. He told me that he'd found most of what he needed, but he said my shop was the only one with a complete selection of even the most seldom-used ingredients for spells and incantations. Which is, of course, true. I pride myself on my selection and on the purity of my goods. But unlike the others, I won't sell to a *Bocor*—if I know what he is. Usually I can spot them. I also won't sell to those amateurs with bad intentions, the ones who want to put a curse of death on a mother-in-law or cause sickness in some man who's a rival for a girl or a job. I'll have none of that. Anyway, this man, this one in the photograph—"

"Lavelle," Jack said.

"But I didn't know his name then. As I was packaging the few things he'd selected, I discovered he was a *Bocor,* and I refused to conclude the sale. He thought I was like all the other merchants, that I'd sell to just anyone, and he was furious when I wouldn't let him have what he wanted. I made him leave the shop, and I thought that was the end of it."

"But it wasn't?" Jack asked.

"No."

"He came back?"

"No."

"Then what happened?"

Hampton came out from behind the sales counter. He went to the shelves where the hundreds upon hundreds of bottles were stored, and Jack followed him.

Hampton's voice was hushed, a note of fear in it: "Two days after Lavelle was here, while I was alone in the shop, sitting at the counter back there, just reading—suddenly, every bottle on those shelves was flung off, to the floor. All in an instant. Such a crash! Half of them broke, and the contents mingled together, all ruined. I rushed over to see what had happened, what had caused it, and as I approached, some of the spilled herbs and powders and ground roots began to . . . well, to *move* . . . to form together . . . and take on life. Out of the debris, composed of several substances, there arose . . . a black serpent, about eighteen inches in length. Yellow eyes. Fangs. A flickering tongue. As real as any serpent hatched from its mother's egg."

Jack stared at the big man, not sure what to think of him or his story. Until this moment, he had thought that Carver Hampton was sincere in his religious beliefs and a perfectly level-headed man, no less rational because his religion was voodoo rather than Catholicism or Judaism. However, it was one thing to believe in a religious doctrine and in the possibility of magic and miracles— and quite another thing altogether to claim to have *seen* a miracle. Those who swore they had seen miracles were hysterics, fanatics, or liars. Weren't they? On the other hand, if you were at all religious—and Jack was not a man without faith—then how could you believe in the possibility of miracles and the existence of the occult without also embracing the claims of at least some of those who said they had been witness to manifestations of the supernatural? Your faith could have no substance if you did not also accept the reality of its effects in this world. It was a thought that hadn't occurred to him before, and now he stared at Carver Hampton with mixed feelings, with both doubt and cautious acceptance.

Rebecca would say he was being excessively open-minded.

Staring at the bottles that now stood on the shelves, Hampton said, "The serpent slithered toward me. I backed across the room. There was nowhere to go. I dropped to my knees. Recited prayers. They were the correct prayers for the situation, and they had their effect. Either that . . . or Lavelle didn't actually intend for the serpent to harm me. Perhaps he only meant it as a warning not to mess with him, a slap in the face for the way I had so unceremoniously ushered him out of my shop. At any rate, the serpent eventually dissolved back into the herbs and powders and ground roots of which it was composed."

"How do you know it was Lavelle who did this thing?" Jack asked.

"The phone rang a moment after the snake . . . decomposed. It was this man, the one I had refused to serve. He told me that it was my prerogative, whether to serve him or not, and that he didn't hold it against me. But he said he wouldn't permit anyone to lay a hand on him as I'd done. So he had smashed my collection of herbs and had conjured up the serpent in retaliation. That's what he said. That's *all* he said. Then he hung up."

"You didn't tell me that you'd actually, physically *thrown* him out of the shop," Jack said.

"I didn't. I merely put a hand on his arm and . . . shall we say . . . *guided* him out. Firmly, yes, but without any real violence, without hurting him. Nevertheless, that was enough to make him angry, to make him seek revenge."

"This was all back in September?"

"Yes."

"And he's never returned?"

"No."

"Never called?"

"No. And it took me almost three months to rebuild my inventory of rare herbs and powders. Many of these items are so very difficult to obtain. You can't imagine. I only recently completed restocking these shelves."

"So you've got your own reasons for wanting to see this Lavelle brought down," Jack said.

Hampton shook his head. "On the contrary."

"Huh?"

"I want nothing more to do with this."

"But—"

"I can't help you any more, Lieutenant."

"I don't understand."

"It should be clear enough. If I help you, Lavelle will send something after me. Something worse than the serpent. And this time it won't be just a warning. No, this time, it'll surely be the death of me."

Jack saw that Hampton was serious—and genuinely terrified. The man believed in the power of voodoo. He was trembling. Even Rebecca, seeing him now, wouldn't be able to claim that he was a charlatan. He *believed.*

Jack said, "But you ought to want him behind bars as much as I do. You ought to want to see him broken, after what he did to you."

"You'll never put him in jail."

"Oh, yes."

"No matter what he does, you'll never be able to touch him."

"We'll get him, all right."

"He's an extremely powerful *Bocor,* Lieutenant. Not an amateur. Not your average spellcaster. He has the power of darkness, the ultimate darkness of death, the darkness of Hell, the darkness of the Other Side. It is a cosmic power, beyond human comprehension. He isn't merely in league with Satan, your Christian and Judaic king of demons. That would be bad enough. But, you see, he is a servant, as well, of *all* the evil gods of the African religions, which go back into antiquity; he has that great, malevolent pantheon behind him. Some of those deities are far more powerful and immeasurably more vicious than Satan has ever been portrayed. A vast legion of evil entities are at Lavelle's beck and call, eager to let him use them because, in turn, *they* use *him* as a sort of doorway into this world. They are eager to cross over, to bring blood and pain and terror and misery to the living, for this world of ours is one into which they are usually denied passage by the power of the benevolent gods who watch over us."

Hampton paused. He was hyperventilating. There was a faint sheen of perspiration on his forehead. He wiped his big hands over his face and took several slow deep breaths. He went on, then, trying to keep his voice calm and reasonable, but only half succeeding.

"Lavelle is a dangerous man, Lieutenant, infinitely more dangerous than you can ever comprehend. I also think he is very probably mad, insane; there was definitely a quality of insanity about him. That is a most formidable combination: evil beyond measure, madness, and the power of a masterfully skilled *Bocor.*"

"But you say you're a *Houngon,* a priest of white magic. Can't you use your power against him?"

"I'm a capable *Houngon,* better than many. But I'm not in this man's league. For instance, with great effort, I might be able to put a curse on his own supply of herbs and powders. I might be able to reach out and cause a few bottles to fall off the shelves in his study or wherever he keeps them—if I had seen the place first, of course. However, I wouldn't be able to cause so much destruction as he did. And I wouldn't be able to conjure up a serpent, as he did. I haven't that much power, that much finesse."

"You could try."

"No. Absolutely not. In any contest of powers, he would crush me. Like a bug."

Hampton went to the door, opened it. The bell above it rang. Hampton stepped aside, holding the door wide open.

Jack pretended not to get the hint. "Listen, if you'll just keep asking around—"

"No. I can't help you any more, Lieutenant. Can't you get that through your head?"

A frigid, blustery wind huffed and moaned and hissed and puffed at the open door, spraying snowflakes like flecks of spittle.

"Listen," Jack said. "Lavelle never has to know that you're asking about him. He—"

"He would find out!" Hampton said angrily, his eyes wide open as the door he was holding. "He knows everything—or can find it out. Everything."

"But—"

"Please go," Hampton said.

"Hear me out. I—"

"Go."

"But—"

"Go, get out, leave, now, damnit, now!" Hampton said in a tone of voice composed of one part anger, one part terror, and one part panic.

The big man's almost hysterical fear of Lavelle had begun to affect Jack. A chill rippled through him, and he found that his hands were suddenly clammy.

He sighed, nodded. "All right, all right, Mr. Hampton. But I sure wish—"

"Now, damnit, *now!*" Hampton shouted.

Jack got out of there.

V

THE DOOR TO *Rada* slammed behind him.

In the snow-quieted street, the sound was like a rifle blast.

Jack turned and looked back, saw Carver Hampton drawing down the shade that covered the glass panel in the center of the door. In bold white letters on the dark canvas, one word was printed: CLOSED.

A moment later the lights went out in the shop.

The snow on the sidewalk was now half an inch deep, twice what it had been when he had gone into Hampton's store. It was still coming down fast, too, out of a sky that was even more somber and more claustrophobically close than it had been twenty minutes ago.

Cautiously negotiating the slippery pavement, Jack started toward the patrol car that was waiting for him at the curb, white exhaust trail pluming up from it. He had taken only three steps when he was stopped by a sound that struck him as being out of place here on the wintry street: a ringing telephone. He looked right, left, and saw a pay phone near the corner, twenty feet behind the waiting black-and-white. In the uncitylike stillness that the muffling snow brought to the street, the ringing was so loud that it seemed to be issuing from the air immediately in front of him.

He stared at the phone. It wasn't in a booth. There weren't many real booths around these days, the kind with the folding door, like a small closet, that offered privacy; too expensive, Ma Bell said. This was a phone on a pole, with a scoop-shaped sound baffle bending around three sides of it. Over the years, he had passed a few other public telephones that had been ringing when there was no one waiting nearby to answer them; on those occasions, he had never given them a second glance, had never been the least bit tempted to lift the receiver and find out who was there; it had been none of his business. Just as *this* was none of his business. And yet . . . this time was somehow . . . different. The ringing snaked out like a lariat of sound, roping him, snaring him, holding him.

Ringing . . .

Ringing . . .

Insistent.

Beckoning.

Hypnotic.

Ringing . . .

A strange and disturbing transformation occurred in the Harlem neighborhood around him. Only three things remained solid and real: the telephone, a narrow stretch of snow-covered pavement leading to the telephone, and Jack himself. The rest of the world seemed to recede into a mist that rose out of nowhere. The buildings appeared to fade away, dissolving as if this were a film in which one scene was fading out to be replaced by another. The few cars progressing hesitantly along the snowy street began to . . . evaporate; they were replaced by the creeping mist, a white-white mist that was like a movie theater screen splashed with brilliant light but with no images. The pedestrians, heads bent, shoulders hunched, struggled against the wind and stinging snow; and gradually they receded and faded, as well. Only Jack was real. And the narrow pathway to the phone. And the telephone itself.

Ringing . . .

He was drawn.

Ringing . . .

Drawn toward the phone.

He tried to resist.

Ringing . . .

He suddenly realized he'd taken a step. Toward the phone.

And another.

A third.

He felt as if he were floating.

Ringing . . .

He was moving as if in a dream or a fever.

He took another step.

He tried to stop. Couldn't.

He tried to turn toward the patrol car. Couldn't.

His heart was hammering.

He was dizzy, disoriented.

In spite of the frigid air, he was sweating along the back of his neck.

The ringing of the telephone was analogous to the rhythmic, glittering, pendulum movement of a hypnotist's pocketwatch. The sound drew him relentlessly forward as surely as, in ancient times, the sirens' songs had pulled unwary sailors to their death upon the reefs.

He knew the call was for him. Knew it without understanding *how* he knew it.

He picked up the receiver. "Hello?"

"Detective Dawson! I'm delighted to have this opportunity to speak with you. My good man, we are most definitely overdue for a chat."

The voice was deep, although not a bass voice, and smooth and elegant, characterized by an educated British accent filtered through the lilting patterns of speech common to tropical zones, so that words like "man" came out as "mon." Clearly a Caribbean accent.

Jack said, "Lavelle?"

"Why, of course! Who else?"

"But how did you know—"

"That you were there? My dear fellow, in an offhanded sort of way, I am keeping tabs on you."

"You're here, aren't you? Somewhere along the street, in one of the apartment buildings here."

"Far from it. Harlem is not to my taste."

"I'd like to talk to you," Jack said.

"We are talking."

"I mean, face-to-face."

"Oh, I hardly think that's necessary."

"I wouldn't arrest you."

"You couldn't. No evidence."

"Well, then—"

"But you'd detain me for a day or two on one excuse or another."

"No."

"And I don't wish to be detained. I've work to do."

"I give you my word we'd only hold you a couple of hours, just for questioning."

"Is that so?"

"You can trust my word when I give it. I don't give it lightly."

"Oddly enough, I'm quite sure that's true."

"Then why not come in, answer some questions, and clear the air, remove the suspicion from yourself?"

"Well, of course, I can't remove the suspicion because, in fact, I'm guilty," Lavelle said. He laughed.

"You're telling me you're behind the murders?"

"Certainly. Isn't that what everyone's been telling you?"

"You've called me to confess?"

Lavelle laughed again. Then: "I've called to give you some advice."

"Yeah?"

"Handle this as the police in my native Haiti would handle it."

"How's that?"

"They wouldn't interfere with a *Bocor* who possessed powers like mine."

"Is that right?"

"They wouldn't dare."

"This is New York, not Haiti. Superstitious fear isn't something they teach at the police academy."

Jack kept his voice calm, unruffled. But his heart continued to bang against his rib cage.

Lavelle said, "Besides, in Haiti, the police would not *want* to interfere if the *Bocor*'s targets were such worthless filth as the Carramazza family. Don't think of me as a murderer, Lieutenant. Think of me as an exterminator, performing a valuable service for society. That's how they'd look at this in Haiti."

"Our philosophy is different here."

"I'm sorry to hear that."

"We think murder is wrong regardless of who the victim is."

"How unsophisticated."

"We believe in the sanctity of human life."

"How foolish. If the Carramazzas die, what will the world lose? Only thieves, murderers, pimps. Other thieves, murderers, and pimps will move in to take their place. Not me, you understand. You may think of me as their equal, as only a murderer, but I am not of their kind. I am a priest. I don't want to rule the drug trade in New York. I only want to take it away from Gennaro Carramazza as part of his punishment. I want to ruin him financially, leave him with no respect among his kind, and take his family and friends away from him, slaughter them, teach him how to grieve. When that is done, when he's isolated, lonely, afraid, when he has suffered for a while, when he's filled with blackest despair, I will at last dispose of him, too, but slowly and with much torture. Then I'll go away, back to the islands, and you won't ever be bothered with me again. I am merely an instrument of justice, Lieutenant Dawson."

"Does justice really necessitate the murder of Carramazza's grandchildren?"

"Yes."

"Innocent little children?"

"They aren't innocent. They carry his blood, his genes. That makes them as guilty as he is."

Carver Hampton was right: Lavelle was insane.

"Now," Lavelle said, "I understand that you will be in trouble with your superiors if you fail to bring someone to trial for at least a few of these killings. The entire police department will take a beating at the hands of the press if something isn't done. I quite understand. So, if you wish, I will arrange to plant a wide variety of evidence incriminating members of one of the city's other mafia families. You can pin the murders of the Carramazzas on some other undesirables, you see, put them in prison, and be rid of yet another troublesome group of hoodlums. I'd be quite happy to let you off the hook that way."

It wasn't only the circumstances of this conversation—the dreamlike quality of the street around the pay phone, the feeling of floating, the fever haze—that made it all seem so unreal; the conversation itself was so bizarre that it would have defied belief regardless of the circumstances in which it had taken place. Jack shook himself, but the world wasn't jarred to life like a stubborn wristwatch; reality didn't begin to tick again.

He said, "You actually think I could take such an offer seriously?"

"The evidence I plant will be irrefutable. It will stand up in any court. You needn't fear you'd lose the case."

"That's not what I mean," Jack said. "Do you really believe I'd conspire with you to frame innocent men?"

"They wouldn't be innocent. Hardly. I'm talking about framing other murderers, thieves, and pimps."

"But they'd be innocent of *these* crimes."

"A technicality."

"Not in my book."

Lavelle was silent for a moment. Then: "You're an interesting man, Lieutenant. Naive. Foolish. But nevertheless interesting."

"Gennaro Carramazza tells us that you're motivated by revenge."

"Yes."

"For what?"

"He didn't tell you that?"

"No. What's the story?"

Silence.

Jack waited, almost asked the question again.

Then Lavelle spoke, at last, and there was a new edge to his voice, a hardness, a ferocity. "I had a younger brother. His name was Gregory. Half brother, really. Last name was Pontrain. He didn't embrace the ancient arts of witchcraft and sorcery. He shunned them. He wouldn't have anything to do with the old religions of Africa. He had no time for voodoo, no interest in it. His was a very modern soul, a machine-age sensibility. He believed in science, not magic; he put his faith in progress and technology, not in the power of ancient gods. He didn't approve of my vocation, but he didn't believe I could really do harm to anyone—or do good, either, for that matter. He thought of me as a harmless eccentric. Yet, for all this misunderstanding, I loved him, and he loved me. We were brothers. *Brothers*. I would have done anything for him."

"Gregory Pontrain . . ." Jack said thoughtfully. "There's something familiar about the name."

"Years ago, Gregory came here as a legal immigrant. He worked very hard, worked his way through college, received a scholarship. He always had writing talent, even as a boy, and he thought he knew what he ought to do with it. Here, he earned a degree in journalism from Columbia. He was first in his class. Went to work for the *New York Times*. For a year or so he didn't even do any writing, just verified research in other reporters' pieces. Gradually, he promoted several writing assignments for himself. Small things. Of no consequence. What you would call 'human interest' stories. And then—"

"Gregory Pontrain," Jack said. "Of course. The crime reporter."

"In time, my brother was assigned a few crime stories. Robberies. Dope busts. He did a good job of covering them. Indeed, he started going after stories that hadn't been handed to him, bigger stories that he'd dug up all by himself. And eventually he became the *Times'* resident expert on narcotics trafficking in the city. No one knew more about the subject, the involvement of the Carramazzas, the way the Carramazza organization had subverted so many vice squad detectives and city politicians; no one knew more than Gregory; no one. He published those articles—"

"I read them. Good work. Four pieces, I believe."

"Yes. He intended to do more, at least half a dozen more articles. There was talk of a Pulitzer, just based on what he'd written so far. Already, he had dug up enough evidence to interest the police and to generate three indictments by the grand jury. He had the sources, you see: insiders in the police and in the Carramazza family, insiders who trusted him. He was convinced he could bring down Dominick Carramazza himself before it was all over. Poor, noble, foolish, brave little Gregory. He thought it was his duty to fight evil wherever he found it. The crusading reporter. He thought he could make a difference, all by himself. He didn't understand that the only way to deal with the powers of darkness is to make peace with them, accommodate yourself to them, as I have done. One night last March, he and his wife, Ona, were on their way to dinner . . ."

"The car bomb," Jack said.

"They were both blown to bits. Ona was pregnant. It would have been their first child. So I owe Gennaro Carramazza for three lives—Gregory, Ona, and the baby."

"The case was never solved," Jack reminded him. "There was no proof that Carramazza was behind it."

"He was."

"You can't be sure."

"Yes, I can. I have my sources, too. Better even than Gregory's. I have the eyes and ears of the Underworld working for me." He laughed. He had a musical, appealing laugh that Jack found unsettling. A madman should have a madman's laugh, not the warm chuckle of a favorite uncle. "The Underworld, Lieutenant. But I don't mean the criminal underworld, the miserable *cosa nostra* with its Sicilian pride and empty code of honor. The Underworld of which I speak is a place much deeper than that which the mafia inhabits, deeper and darker. I have the eyes and ears of the ancient ones, the reports of demons and dark angels, the testimony of those entities who see all and know all."

Madness, Jack thought. The man belongs in an institution.

But in addition to the madness, there was something else in Lavelle's voice that nudged and poked the cop's instincts in Jack. When Lavelle spoke of the supernatural, he did so with genuine awe and conviction; however, when he spoke of his brother, his voice became oily with phony sentiment and unconvincing grief. Jack sensed that revenge was not Lavelle's primary motivation and that, in fact, he might even have hated his straight-arrow brother, might even be glad (or at least relieved) that he was dead.

"Your brother wouldn't approve of this revenge you're taking," Jack said.

"Perhaps he would. You didn't know him."

"But I know enough about him to say with some confidence that he wasn't at all like you. He was a decent man. He wouldn't want all this slaughter. He would be repelled by it."

Lavelle said nothing, but there was somehow a pouting quality to his silence, a smoldering anger.

Jack said, "He wouldn't approve of the murder of anyone's grandchildren, revenge unto the third generation. He wasn't sick, like you. He wasn't crazy."

"It doesn't matter whether he would approve," Lavelle said impatiently.

"I suspect that's because it isn't really revenge that motivates you. Not deep down."

Again, Lavelle was silent.

Pushing, probing for the truth, Jack said, "So if your brother wouldn't approve of murder being done in his name, then why are you—"

"I'm not exterminating these vermin in my brother's name," Lavelle said sharply, furiously. "I'm doing it in my own name. Mine and no one else's. That must be understood. I never claimed otherwise. These deaths accrue to my credit, not to my brother's."

"Credit? Since when is murder a credit, a character reference, a matter of pride? That's insane."

"It isn't insane," Lavelle said heatedly. The madness boiled up in him. "It is the reasoning of the ancient ones, the gods of *Pétro* and *Congo.* No one can take the life of a *Bocor*'s brother and go unpunished. The murder of my brother is an insult to me. It diminishes me. It mocks me. I cannot tolerate that. I will not! My power as a *Bocor* would be weakened forever if I were to forego revenge. The ancient ones would lose respect for me, turn away from me, withdraw their support and power." He was ranting now, losing his cool. "Blood must flow. The floodgates of death must be opened. Oceans of pain must sweep them away, all who mocked me by touching my brother. Even if I despised Gregory, he was of my family; no one can spill the blood of a *Bocor*'s family and go unpunished. If I fail to take adequate revenge, the ancient ones will never permit me to call upon them again; they will not enforce my curses and spells any more. I must repay the murder of my brother with at least a score of murders of my own if I am to keep the respect and patronage of the gods of *Pétro* and *Congo.*"

Jack had probed to the roots of the man's true motivation, but he had gained nothing for his efforts. The true motivation made no sense to him; it seemed just one more aspect of Lavelle's madness.

"You really believe this, don't you?" Jack asked.

"It's the truth."

"It's crazy."

"Eventually, you will learn otherwise."

"Crazy," Jack repeated.

"One more piece of advice," Lavelle said.

"You're the only suspect I've ever known to be so brimming over with advice. A regular Ann Landers."

Ignoring him, Lavelle said, "Remove yourself from this case."

"You can't be serious."

"Get out of it."

"Impossible."

"Ask to be relieved."

"No."

"You'll do it if you know what's good for you."

"You're an arrogant bastard."

"I know."

"I'm a cop, for God's sake! You can't make me back down by threatening me. Threats just make me all the more interested in finding you. Cops in Haiti must be the same. It can't be *that* much different. Besides, what good would it do you if I did ask to be relieved? Someone else would replace me. They'd still continue to look for you."

"Yes, but whoever replaced you wouldn't be broadminded enough to explore the possibility of voodoo's effectiveness. He'd stick to the usual police procedure, and I have no fear of that."

Jack was startled. "You mean my open-mindedness alone is a threat to you?"

Lavelle didn't answer the question. He said, "All right. If you won't step out of the picture, then at least stop your research into voodoo. Handle this as Rebecca Chandler wants to handle it—as if it were an ordinary homicide investigation."

"I don't believe your *gall,*" Jack said.

"Your mind is open, if only a narrow crack, to the possibility of a supernatural explanation. Don't pursue that line of inquiry. That's all I ask."

"Oh, that's all, is it?"

"Satisfy yourself with fingerprint kits, lab technicians, your usual experts, the standard tools. Question all the witnesses you wish to question—"

"Thanks so much for the permission."

"—I don't care about those things," Lavelle continued, as if Jack hadn't interrupted. "You'll never find me that way. I'll be finished with Carramazza and on my way back to the islands before you've got a single lead. Just forget about the voodoo angle."

Astonished by the man's chutzpa, Jack said, "And if I don't forget about it?"

The open telephone line hissed, and Jack was reminded of the black serpent of which Carver Hampton had spoken, and he wondered if Lavelle could somehow send a serpent over the telephone line, out of the earpiece, to bite him on the ear and head, or out of the mouthpiece, to bite him on the lips and on the nose and in the eyes. . . . He held the receiver away from himself, looked at it warily, then felt foolish, and brought it back to his face.

Lavelle said, "If you insist on learning more about voodoo, if you continue to pursue that avenue of investigation . . . then I will have your son and daughter torn to pieces."

Finally, one of Lavelle's threats affected Jack. His stomach twisted, knotted.

Lavelle said, "Do you remember what Dominick Carramazza and his bodyguards looked like—"

And then they were both talking at once, Jack shouting, Lavelle maintaining his cool and measured tone of voice:

"Listen, you creepy son of a bitch—"

"—back there in the hotel, old Dominick, all ripped up—"

"—you stay away from—"

"—eyes torn out, all bloody?"

"—my kids, or I'll—"

"When I'm finished with Davey and Penny—"

"—blow your fuckin' head off!"

"—they'll be nothing but dead meat—"

"I'm warning you—"

"—dog meat, garbage—"

"—I'll find you—"

"—and maybe I'll even rape the girl—"

"—you stinking scumbag!"

"—'cause she's really a tender, juicy little piece. I like them tender sometimes, very young and tender, innocent. The thrill is in the corruption, you see."

"You threaten my kids, you asshole, you just threw away whatever chance you had. Who do you think you *are*? My God, *where* do you think you are? This is America, you dumb shit. You can't get away with that kind of stuff here, threatening my kids."

"I'll give you the rest of the day to think it over. Then, if you don't back off, I'll take Davey and Penny. And I'll make it very painful for them."

Lavelle hung up.

"Wait!" Jack shouted.

He rattled the disconnect lever, trying to reestablish contact, trying to bring Lavelle back. Of course, it didn't work.

He was gripping the receiver so hard that his hand ached and his muscles were bunched up all the way to the shoulder. He slammed the receiver down almost hard enough to crack the earpiece.

He was breathing like a bull that, for some time, had been taunted by the movement of a red cape. He was aware of his own pulse throbbing in his temples, and he could feel the heat in his flushed face. The knots in his stomach had drawn painfully tight.

After a moment, he turned away from the phone. He was shaking with rage. He stood in the falling snow, gradually getting a grip on himself.

Everything would be all right. Nothing to worry about. Penny and Davey were safe at school, where there were plenty of people to watch over them. It was a good, reliable school, with first-rate security. And Faye would pick them up at three o'clock and take them to her place; Lavelle couldn't know about that. If he did decide to hurt the kids this evening, he'd expect to find them at the apartment; when he discovered they weren't at home, he wouldn't know where to look for them. In spite of what Carver Hampton had said, Lavelle couldn't know all and see all. Could he? Of course not. He wasn't God. He

might be a *Bocor,* a priest with real power, a genuine sorceror. But he wasn't
God. So the kids would be safe with Faye and Keith. In fact, maybe it would
be a good idea for them to stay at the Jamison apartment overnight. Or even
for the next few days, until Lavelle was apprehended. Faye and Keith wouldn't
mind; they'd welcome the visit, the opportunity to spoil their only niece and
nephew. Might even be wise to keep Penny and Davey out of school until this
was all over. And he'd talk to Captain Gresham about getting some protection
for them, a uniformed officer to stay in the Jamison apartment when Jack
wasn't able to be there. Not much chance Lavelle would track the kids down.
Highly unlikely. But just in case. . . . And if Gresham didn't take the threat
seriously, if he thought an around-the-clock guard was an unjustified use of
manpower, then something could be arranged with the guys, the other detectives; they'd help him, just as he'd help them if anything like this ever fell in
their direction; each of them would give up a few hours of off-duty time, take a
shift at the Jamisons'; anything for a buddy whose family was marked; it was
part of the code. Okay. Fine. Everything would be all right.

The world, which had strangely receded when the telephone had begun to
ring, now rushed back. Jack was aware of sound, first: a bleating automobile
horn, laughter farther along the street, the clatter-clank of tire chains on the
snowy pavement, the howling wind. The buildings crowded in around him. A
pedestrian scurried past, bent into the wind; and here came three black teenagers, laughing, throwing snowballs at one another as they ran. The mist was
gone, and he didn't feel dizzy or disoriented any longer. He wondered if there
actually had been any mist in the first place, and he decided the eerie fog had
existed only in his mind, a figment of his imagination. What must have happened was . . . he must have had an attack of some kind; yeah, sure, nothing
more than that.

But exactly what kind of attack? And why had he been stricken by it? What
had brought it on? He wasn't an epileptic. He didn't have low blood pressure.
No other physical maladies, as far as he was aware. He had never experienced
a fainting spell in his life; nothing remotely like that. He was in perfect health.
So *why?*

And how had he known the phone call was for him?

He stood there for a while, thinking about it, as thousands of snowflakes
fluttered like moths around him.

Eventually he realized he ought to call Faye and explain the situation to her,
warn her to be certain that she wasn't followed when she picked up the kids at
Wellton School. He turned to the pay phone, paused. No. He wouldn't make
the call here. Not on the very phone Lavelle had used. It seemed ridiculous to
suppose that the man could have a tap on a public phone—but it also seemed
foolish to test the possibility.

Calmer—still furious but less frightened than he had been—he headed back
toward the patrol car that was waiting for him.

Three-quarters of an inch of snow lay on the ground. The storm was turning
into a full-fledged blizzard.

The wind had icy teeth. It bit.

VI

LAVELLE RETURNED TO the corrugated metal shed at the rear of his property.
Outside, winter raged; inside, fierce dry heat made sweat pop out of Lavelle's
ebony skin and stream down his face, and shimmering orange light cast odd

leaping shadows on the ribbed walls. From the pit in the center of the floor, a sound arose, a chilling susurration, as of thousands of distant voices, angry whisperings.

He had brought two photographs with him: one of Davey Dawson, the other of Penny Dawson. He had taken both photographs himself, yesterday afternoon, on the street in front of Wellton School. He had been in his van, parked almost a block away, and he had used a 35-mm Pentax with a telephoto lens. He had processed the film in his own closet-size darkroom.

In order to put a curse on someone and be absolutely certain that it would bring about the desired calamity, a *Bocor* required an icon of the intended victim. Traditionally, the priest prepared a doll, sewed it together from scraps of cotton cloth and filled it with sawdust or sand, then did the best he could to make the doll's face resemble the face of the victim; that done, the ritual was performed with the doll as a surrogate for the real person.

But that was a tedious chore made even more difficult by the fact that the average *Bocor*—lacking the talent and skills of an artist—found it virtually impossible to make a cotton face look sufficiently like *anyone's* real countenance. Therefore, the need always arose to embellish the doll with a lock of hair or a nail clipping or a drop of blood from the victim. Obtaining any one of those items wasn't easy. You couldn't just hang around the victim's barbershop or beauty salon, week after week, waiting for him or her to come in and get a haircut. You couldn't very well ask him to save a few nail clippings for you the next time he gave himself a manicure. And about the only way to obtain a sample of the would-be victim's blood was to assault him and risk apprehension by the police, which was the very thing you were trying to avoid by striking at him with magic rather than with fists or a knife or a gun.

All of those difficulties could be circumvented by the use of a good photograph instead of a doll. As far as Lavelle knew, he was the only *Bocor* who had ever applied this bit of modern technology to the practice of voodoo. The first time he'd tried it, he hadn't expected it to work; however, six hours after the ritual was completed, the intended victim was dead, crushed under the wheels of a runaway truck. Since then, Lavelle had employed photographs in every ceremony that ordinarily would have called for a doll. Evidently, he possessed some of his brother Gregory's machine-age sensibility and faith in progress.

Now, kneeling on the earthen floor of the shed, beside the pit, he used a ballpoint pen to punch a hole in the top of each of the eight-by-ten glossies. Then he strung both photographs on a length of slender cord. Two wooden stakes had been driven into the dirt floor, near the brink of the pit, directly opposite each other, with the void between them. Lavelle tied one end of the cord to one of the wooden stakes, stretched it across the pit, and fastened the other end to the second stake. The pictures of the Dawson children dangled over the center of the hole, bathed in the unearthly orange glow that shone up from the mysterious, shifting bottom of it.

Soon, he would have to kill the children. He was giving Jack Dawson a few hours yet, one last opportunity to back down, but he was fairly sure that Dawson would not relent.

He didn't mind killing children. He looked forward to it. There was a special exhilaration in the murder of the very young.

He licked his lips.

The sound issuing from the pit—the distant susurration that seemed to be composed of tens of thousands of hissing, whispering voices—grew slightly louder when the photographs were suspended where Lavelle wanted them. And there was a new, disquieting tone to the whispers, as well: not merely

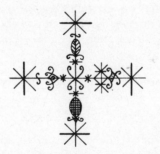

anger; not just a note of menace; it was an elusive quality that, somehow, spoke of monstrous needs, of a hideous voracity, of blood and perversion, the sound of a dark and insatiable *hunger.*

Lavelle stripped out of his clothes.

Fondling his genitals, he recited a short prayer.

He was ready to begin.

To the left of the shed door stood five large copper bowls. Each contained a different substance: white flour, corn meal, red brick powder, powdered charcoal, and powdered tannis root. Scooping up a handful of the red brick powder, allowing it to dribble in a measured flow from one end of his cupped hand, Lavelle began to draw an intricate design on the floor along the northern flank of the pit.

This design was called a *vèvè,* and it represented the figure and power of an astral force. There were hundreds of *vèvès* that a *Houngon* or a *Bocor* must know. Through the drawing of several appropriate *vèvès* prior to the start of a ritual, the priest was forcing the attention of the gods to the *Oumphor,* the temple, where the rites were to be conducted. The *vèvè* had to be drawn freehand, without the assistance of a stencil and most certainly without the guidance of a preliminary sketch scratched in the earth; nevertheless, though done freehand, the *vèvè* had to be symmetrical and properly proportioned if it were to have any effect. The creation of the *vèvès* required much practice, a sensitive and agile hand, and a keen eye.

Lavelle scooped up a second handful of red brick powder and continued his work. In a few minutes he had drawn the *vèvè* that represented Simbi Y-An-Kitha, one of the dark gods of *Pétro:*

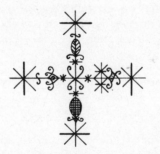

He scrubbed his hand on a clean dry towel, ridding himself of most of the brick dust. He scooped up a handful of flour and began to draw another *vèvè* along the southern flank of the pit. This pattern was much different from the first.

In all, he drew four intricate designs, one on each side of the pit. The third was rendered in charcoal powder. The fourth was done with powdered tannis root.

Then, careful not to disturb the *vèvès,* he crouched, naked, at the edge of the pit.

He stared down.

Down . . .

The floor of the pit shifted, boiled, changed, swirled, oozed, drew close, pulsed, receded. Lavelle had placed no fire or light of any kind inside the hole, yet it glowed and flickered. At first the floor of the pit was only three feet away, just as he had made it. But the longer he stared, the deeper it seemed to become. Now thirty feet instead of three. Now three hundred. Now three miles deep. Now as deep as the center of the earth itself. And deeper, still deeper, deeper than the distance to the moon, the stars, deeper than the distance to the edge of the universe.

When the bottom of the pit had receded to infinity, Lavelle stood up. He broke into a five-note song, a repetitive chant of destruction and death, and he began the ritual by urinating on the photographs that he had strung on the cord.

VII

IN THE SQUAD CAR.

The hiss and crackle of the police-band radio.

Headed downtown. Toward the office.

Chain-rigged tires singing on the pavement.

Snowflakes colliding soundlessly with the windshield. The wipers thumping with metronomic monotony.

Nick Iervolino, the uniformed officer behind the wheel, startled Jack out of a near-trance: "You don't have to worry about my driving, Lieutenant."

"I'm sure I don't," Jack said.

"Been driving a patrol car for twelve years and never had an accident."

"Is that right?"

"Never even put a scratch on one of my cars."

"Congratulations."

"Snow, rain, sleet—nothing bothers me. Never have the least little trouble handling a car. It's a sort of talent. Don't know where I get it from. My mother doesn't drive. My old man does, but he's one of the worst you've ever seen. Scares hell out of me to ride with him. But me—I have a knack for handling a car. So don't worry."

"I'm not worried," Jack assured him.

"You sure *seemed* worried."

"How's that?"

"You were grinding the hell out of your teeth."

"Was I?"

"I expected to hear your molars start cracking apart any second."

"I wasn't aware of it. But believe me, I'm not worried about your driving."

They were approaching an intersection where half a dozen cars were angled everywhichway, spinning their tires in the snow, trying to get reoriented or at least out of the way. Nick Iervolino braked slowly, cautiously, until they were traveling at a crawl, then found a snaky route through the stranded cars.

On the other side of the intersection, he said, "So if you aren't worried about my driving, what *is* eating at you?"

Jack hesitated, then told him about the call from Lavelle.

Nick listened, but without diverting his attention from the treacherous streets. When Jack finished, Nick said, "Jesus Christ Almighty!"

"My sentiments exactly," Jack said.

"You think he can do it? Put a curse on your kids? One that'll actually work?"

Jack turned the question back on him. "What do you think?"

Nick pondered for a moment. Then: "I don't know. It's a strange world we live in, you know. Flying saucers, Big Foot, the Bermuda Triangle, the Abominable Snowman, all sorts of weird things out there. I like to read about stuff like that. Fascinates me. There're millions of people out there who claim to've seen a lot of truly strange things. Not all of it can be bunk—can it? Maybe some of it. Maybe most of it. But not all of it. Right?"

"Probably not all of it," Jack agreed.

"So maybe voodoo works."

Jack nodded.

"Of course, for your sake, and for the kids, I hope to God it *doesn't* work," Nick said.

They traveled half a block in silence.

Then Nick said, "One thing bothers me about this Lavelle, about what he told you."

"What's that?"

"Well, let's just say voodoo *does* work."

"Okay."

"I mean, let's just pretend."

"I understand."

"Well, if voodoo works, and if he wants you off the case, why would he use this magic power of his to kill your kids? Why wouldn't he just use it to kill you? That'd be a lot more direct."

Jack frowned. "You're right."

"If he killed you, they'd assign another detective to the case, and it isn't too likely the new man would be as open-minded as you are about this voodoo angle. So the easiest way for Lavelle to get what he wants is to eliminate you with one of his curses. Now why doesn't he do that—supposing the magic works, I mean?"

"I don't know why."

"Neither do I," Nick said. "Can't figure it. But I think maybe this is important, Lieutenant. Don't you?"

"How?"

"See, even if the guy's a lunatic, even if voodoo doesn't work and you're just dealing with a maniac, at least the rest of his story—all the weird stuff he told you—has its own kind of crazy logic. It's not filled with contradictions. Know what I mean?"

"Yes."

"It hangs together, even if it is bullshit. It's strangely logical. Except for the threat against your kids. That doesn't fit. Illogical. It's too much trouble when he could just put a curse on *you*. So if he has the power, why doesn't he aim it at you if he's going to aim it at anyone?"

"Maybe it's just that he realizes he can't intimidate me by threatening my own life. Maybe he realizes the only way to intimidate me is through my kids."

"But if he just destroyed you, had you chewed to pieces like all these others, then he wouldn't *have* to intimidate you. Intimidation is clumsy. Murder is cleaner. See what I mean?"

Jack watched the snow hitting the windshield, and he thought about what Nick had said. He had a hunch that it *was* important.

VIII

IN THE STORAGE shed, Lavelle completed the ritual. He stood in orange light, breathing hard, dripping sweat. The beads of perspiration reflected the light and looked like droplets of orange paint. The whites of his eyes were stained by the same preternatural glow, and his well-buffed fingernails also gleamed orange.

Only one thing remained to be done in order to assure the deaths of the Dawson children. When the time came, when the deadline arrived for Jack Dawson and he didn't back off as Lavelle wanted, then Lavelle would only have to pick up two pair of ceremonial scissors and cut both ends of the slender cord from which the photographs hung. The pictures would fall into the pit and vanish in the furnacelike glow, and then the demonic powers would be set loose; the curse would be fulfilled. Penny and Davey Dawson wouldn't have a chance.

Lavelle closed his eyes and imagined he was standing over their bloody, lifeless bodies. That prospect thrilled him.

The murder of children was a dangerous undertaking, one which a *Bocor* did not contemplate unless he had no other choice. Before he placed a curse of death upon a child, he had better know how to shield himself from the wrath of the *Rada* gods, the gods of white magic, for they were infuriated by the victimization of children. If a *Bocor* killed an innocent child without knowing the charms and spells that would, subsequently, protect him from the power of the *Rada,* then he would suffer excruciating pain for many days and nights. And when the *Rada* finally snuffed him out, he wouldn't mind dying; indeed, he would be grateful for an end to his suffering.

Lavelle knew how to armor himself against the *Rada.* He had killed other children, before this, and had gotten away with it every time, utterly unscathed. Nevertheless, he was tense and uneasy. There was always the possibility of a mistake. In spite of his knowledge and power, this was a dangerous scheme.

On the other hand, if a *Bocor* used his command of supernatural machinery to kill a child, and if he got away with it, then the gods of *Pétro* and *Congo* were so pleased with him that they bestowed even greater power upon him. If Lavelle could destroy Penny and Davey Dawson and deflect the wrath of *Rada,* his mastery of dark magic would be more awesome than ever before.

Behind his closed eyelids, he saw images of the dead, torn, mutilated bodies of the Dawson children.

He laughed softly.

In the Dawson apartment, far across town from the shed where Baba Lavelle was performing the ritual, two dozen silver-eyed creatures swayed in the shadows, in sympathy with the rhythm of the *Bocor*'s chanting and singing. His voice could not be heard in the apartment, of course. Yet these things with demented eyes were somehow aware of it. Swaying, they stood in the kitchen, the living room—and in the dark hallway, where they watched the door with panting anticipation. When Lavelle reached the end of the ritual, all of the small beasts stopped swaying at exactly the same time, at the very instant Lavelle fell silent. They were rigid now. Watchful. Alert. Ready.

In a storm drain beneath Wellton School, other creatures rocked back and forth in the darkness, eyes gleaming, keeping time with Lavelle's chants, though he was much too far away to be heard. When he ceased chanting, they stopped swaying and were as still, as alert, as ready to attack as were the uninvited guests in the Dawson apartment.

IX

THE TRAFFIC LIGHT turned red, and the crosswalk filled with a river of heavily bundled pedestrians, their faces hidden by scarves and coat collars. They shuffled and slipped and slid past the front of the patrol car.

Nick Iervolino said, "I wonder . . ."

Jack said, "What?"

"Well, just suppose voodoo *does* work."

"We've already been supposing it."

"Just for the sake of argument."

"Yeah, yeah. We've been through this already. Go on."

"Okay. So why does Lavelle threaten your kids? Why doesn't he just put a curse on you, bump you off, forget about them? That's the question."

"That's the question," Jack agreed.

"Well, maybe, for some reason, his magic won't work on you."

"What reason?"

"I don't know."

"If it works on other people—which is what we're supposing—then why wouldn't it work on me?"

"I don't know."

"If it'll work on my kids, why wouldn't it work on me?"

"I don't know. Unless . . . well, maybe there's something different about you."

"Different? Like what?"

"I don't know."

"You sound like a broken record."

"I know."

Jack sighed. "This isn't much of an explanation you've come up with."

"Can you think of a better one?"

"No."

The traffic light turned green. The last of the pedestrians had crossed. Nick pulled into the intersection and turned left.

After a while, Jack said, "Different, huh?"

"Somehow."

As they headed farther downtown, toward the office, they talked about it, trying to figure out what the difference might be.

X

AT WELLTON SCHOOL, the last classes of the day were over at three o'clock. By three-ten, a tide of laughing, jabbering children spilled through the front doors, down the steps, onto the sidewalk, into the driving snow that transformed the gray urban landscape of New York into a dazzling fantasyland. Warmly dressed in knitted caps, earmuffs, scarves, sweaters, heavy coats, gloves, jeans, and high boots, they walked with a slight toddle, arms out at their sides because of all the layers of insulation they were wearing; they looked furry and cuddly and well-padded and stumpy-legged, not unlike a bunch of magically animated teddy bears.

Some of them lived near enough and were old enough to be allowed to walk home, and ten of them piled into a minibus that their parents had bought. But most were met by a mother or father or grandparent in the family car or, because of the inclement weather, by one of those same relatives in a taxi.

Mrs. Shepherd, one of the teachers, had the Dismissal Watch duty this week. She moved back and forth along the sidewalk, keeping an eye on everyone, making sure none of the younger kids tried to walk home, seeing that none of them got into a car with a stranger. Today, she had the added chore of stopping snowball battles before they could get started.

Penny and Davey had been told that their Aunt Faye would pick them up, instead of their father, but they couldn't see her anywhere when they came down the steps, so they moved off to one side, out of the way. They stood in front of the emerald-green wooden gate that closed off the service passageway between Wellton School and the townhouse next door. The gate wasn't flush with the front walls of the two buildings, but recessed eight or ten inches. Trying to stay out of the sharp cold wind that cruelly pinched their cheeks and even penetrated their heavy coats, they pressed their backs to the gate, huddling in the shallow depression in front of it.

Davey said, "Why isn't Dad coming?"

"I guess he had to work."

"Why?"

"I guess he's on an important case."

"What case?"

"I don't know."

"It isn't dangerous, is it?"

"Probably not."

"He won't get shot, will he?"

"Of course not."

"How can you be sure?"

"I'm sure," she said, although she wasn't sure at all.

"Cops get shot all the time."

"Not that often."

"What'll we do if Dad gets shot?"

Immediately after their mother's death, Davey had handled the loss quite well. Better than anyone had expected. Better than Penny had handled it, in fact. *He* hadn't needed to see a psychiatrist. He had cried, sure; he had cried a lot, for a few days, but then he had bounced back. Lately, however, a year and a half after the funeral, he had begun to develop an unnatural fear of losing his father, too. As far as Penny knew, she was the only one who noticed how terribly obsessed Davey was with the dangers—both real and imagined—of his father's occupation. She hadn't mentioned her brother's state of mind to her father, or to anyone else, for that matter, because she thought she could straighten him out by herself. After all, she was his big sister; he was her responsibility; she had certain obligations to him. In the months right after their mother's death, Penny had failed Davey; at least that was how she felt. She had gone to pieces then. She hadn't been there when he'd needed her the most. Now, she intended to make it up to him.

"What'll we do if Dad gets shot?" he asked again.

"He isn't going to get shot."

"But if he *does* get shot. What'll we do?"

"We'll be all right."

"Will we have to go to an orphanage?"

"No, silly."

"Where would we go then? Huh? Penny, where would we go?"

"We'd probably go to live with Aunt Faye and Uncle Keith."

"Yuch."

"They're all right."

"I'd rather go live in the sewers."

"That's ridiculous."

"It'd be neat living in the sewers."

"Neat is the last thing it'd be."

"We could come out at night and steal our food."

"From who—the winos asleep in the gutters?"

"We could have an alligator for a pet!"

"There aren't any alligators in the sewers."

"Of course there are," he said.

"That's a myth."

"A what?"

"A myth. A made-up story. A fairytale."

"You're nuts. Alligators live in sewers."

"Davey—"

"Sure they do! Where *else* would alligators live?"

"Florida, for one place."

"Florida? Boy, you're flako. Florida!"

"Yeah, Florida."

"Only old retired coots and gold-digging bimbos live in Florida."

Penny blinked. "Where'd you hear *that?*"

"Aunt Faye's friend. Mrs. Dumpy."

"Dumphy."

"Yeah. Mrs. Dumpy was talking to Aunt Faye, see. Mrs. Dumpy's husband wanted to retire to Florida, and he went down there by himself to scout around for a place to live, but he never came back 'cause what he did was he ran off with a gold-digging bimbo. Mrs. Dumpy said only old coots and a lot of gold-digging bimbos live down there. And that's another good reason not to live with Aunt Faye. Her friends. They're all like Mrs. Dumpy. Always whining, you know? Jeez. And Uncle Keith smokes."

"A lot of people smoke."

"His clothes stink from the smoke."

"It's not that bad."

"And his breath! Grody!"

"Your breath isn't always like flowers, you know."

"Who'd want breath like flowers?"

"A bumblebee."

"I'm no bumblebee."

"You buzz a lot. You never shut up. Always buzz-buzz-buzz."

"I do not."

"Buzzzzzzzzzz."

"Better watch it. I might sting, too."

"Don't you dare."

"I might sting real bad."

"Davey, don't you dare."

"Anyway, Aunt Faye drives me nuts."

"She means well, Davey."

"She . . . twitters."

"Birds twitter, not people."

"She twitters like a bird."

It was true. But at the advanced age of almost-twelve, Penny had recently begun to feel the first stirrings of comradeship with adults. She wasn't nearly as comfortable ridiculing them as she had been just a few months ago.

Davey said, "And she always nags Dad about whether we're being fed well."

"She just worries about us."

"Does she think Dad would *starve* us?"

"Of course not."

"Then why's she always going on and on about it?"

"She's just . . . Aunt Faye."

"Boy, you can say *that* again!"

An especially fierce gust of wind swept the street, found its way into the recess in front of the green gate. Penny and Davey shivered.

He said, "Dad's got a good gun, doesn't he? They give cops really good guns, don't they? They wouldn't let a cop go out on the street with a half-ass gun, would they?"

"Don't say 'half-ass.' "

"Would they?"

"No. They give cops the best guns there are."

"And Dad's a good shot, isn't he?"

"Yes."

"How good?"

"Very good."

"He's the best, isn't he?"

"Sure," Penny said. "Nobody's better with a gun than Daddy."

"Then the only way he's going to get it is if somebody sneaks up on him and shoots him in the back."

"That isn't going to happen," she said firmly.

"It could."

"You watch too much TV."

They were silent for a moment.

Then he said, "If somebody kills Dad, I want to get cancer and die, too."

"Stop it, Davey."

"Cancer or a heart attack or something."

"You don't mean that."

He nodded emphatically, vigorously: yes, yes, yes; he did mean it; he absolutely, positively did. "I asked God to make it happen that way if it has to happen."

"What do you mean?" she asked, frowning at him.

"Each night. When I say my prayers. I always ask God not to let anything happen to Dad. And then I say, 'Well, God, if you for some stupid reason just *have* to let him get shot, then please let me get cancer and die, too. Or let me get hit by a truck. Something.' "

"That's morbid."

He didn't say anything more.

He looked at the ground, at his gloved hands, at Mrs. Shepherd walking her patrol—everywhere but at Penny. She took hold of his chin, turned his face to her. Tears shimmered in his eyes. He was trying hard to hold them back, squinting, blinking.

He was so small. Just seven years old and not big for his age. He looked fragile and helpless, and Penny wanted to grab hold of him and hug him, but she knew he wouldn't want her to do that when they might be seen by some of the other boys in his class.

She suddenly felt small and helpless herself. But that wasn't good. Not good at all. She had to be strong for Davey's sake.

Letting go of his chin, she said, "Listen, Davey, we've got to sit down and talk. About Mom. About people dying, why it happens, you know, all that stuff, like what it means, how it's not the end for them but maybe only the beginning, up there in Heaven, and how we've got to just go on, no matter what. 'Cause we do. We've got to go on. Mom would be very disappointed in us if we didn't just go on. And if anything happened to Dad—which nothing *is* going to happen to him—but if by some wild chance it *did,* then he'd want us to go on, just the way Mom would want. He'd be very unhappy with us if we—"

"Penny! Davey! Over here!"

A yellow cab was at the curb. The rear window was down, and Aunt Faye leaned out, waved at them.

Davey bolted across the sidewalk, suddenly so eager to be away from any talk of death that he was even glad to see his twittering old Aunt Faye.

Damn! I botched it, Penny thought. I was too blunt about it.

In that same instant, before she followed Davey to the taxi, before she even took one step, a sharp pain lanced through her left ankle. She twitched, yelped, looked down—and was immobilized by terror.

Between the bottom of the green gate and the pavement, there was a four-inch gap. A hand had reached through that gap, from the darkness in the covered serviceway beyond, and it had seized her ankle.

She couldn't scream. Her voice was gone.

It wasn't a human hand, either. Maybe twice the size of a cat's paw. But not a paw. It was a completely—although crudely—formed hand with fingers and a thumb.

She couldn't even whisper. Her throat was locked.

The hand wasn't skin-colored. It was an ugly, mottled gray-green-yellow, like bruised and festering flesh. And it was sort of lumpy, a little ragged looking.

Breathing was no easier than screaming.

The small gray-green-yellow fingers were tapered and ended in sharp claws. Two of those claws had punctured her rubber boot.

She thought of the plastic baseball bat.

Last night. In her room. The thing under the bed.

She thought of the shining eyes in the school basement.

And now *this.*

Two of the small fingers had thrust inside her boot and were scraping at her, digging at her, tearing, gouging.

Abruptly, her breath came to her in a rush. She gasped, sucked in lungsful of frigid air, which snapped her out of the terror-induced trance that, thus far, had held her there by the gate. She jerked her foot away from the hand, tore loose, and was surprised that she was able to do so. She turned and ran to the taxi, plunged inside, and yanked the door shut.

She looked back toward the gate. There was nothing unusual in sight, no creature with small claw-tipped hands, no goblin capering in the snow.

The taxi pulled away from Wellton School.

Aunt Faye and Davey were talking excitedly about the snowstorm which, Faye said, was supposed to dump ten or twelve inches before it was done. Neither of them seemed to be aware that Penny was scared half to death.

While they chattered, Penny reached down and felt her boot. At the ankle, the rubber was torn. A flap of it hung loose.

She unzipped the boot, slipped her hand inside, under her sock, and felt the wound on her ankle. It burned a little. When she brought her hand out of the boot, there was some blood glistening on her fingertips.

Aunt Faye saw it. "What's happened to you, dear?"

"It's okay," Penny said.

"That's blood."

"Just a scratch."

Davey paled at the sight of the blood.

Penny tried to reassure him, although she was afraid that her voice was noticeably shaky and that her face would betray her anxiety: "It's nothing, Davey. I'm all right."

Aunt Faye insisted on changing places with Davey, so she would be next to Penny and could have a closer look at the injury. She made Penny take off the boot, and she peeled down the sock, revealing a puncture wound and several scratches on the ankle. It was bleeding, but not very much; in a couple of minutes, even unattended, it would stop.

"How'd this happen?" Aunt Faye demanded.

Penny hesitated. More than anything, she wanted to tell Faye all about the creatures with shining eyes. She wanted help, protection. But she knew that she couldn't say a word. They wouldn't believe her. After all, she was The Girl Who Had Needed A Psychiatrist. If she started babbling about goblins with shining eyes, they'd think she was having a relapse; they would say she *still* hadn't adjusted to her mother's death, and they would make an appointment with a psychiatrist. While she was off seeing the shrink, there wouldn't be anyone around to keep the goblins away from Davey.

"Come on, come on," Faye said. "Fess up. What were you doing that you shouldn't have been doing?"

"Huh?"

"That's why you're hesitating. What were you doing that you knew you shouldn't be doing?"

"Nothing," Penny said.

"Then how'd you get this cut?"

"I . . . I caught my boot on a nail."

"Nail? Where?"

"On the gate."

"What gate?"

"Back at the school, the gate where we were waiting for you. A nail was sticking out of it, and I got caught up on it."

Faye scowled. Unlike her sister (Penny's mother), Faye was a redhead with sharp features and gray eyes that were almost colorless. In repose, hers was a pretty enough face; however, when she wanted to scowl, she could really do a first-rate job of it. Davey called it her "witch look."

She said, "Was it rusty?"

Penny said, "What?"

"The nail, of course. Was it rusty?"

"I don't know."

"Well, you saw it, didn't you? Otherwise, how'd you know it was a nail?"

Penny nodded. "Yeah. I guess it was rusty."

"Have you had a tetanus shot?"

"Yeah."

Aunt Faye peered at her with undisguised suspicion. "Do you even know what a tetanus shot is?"

"Sure."

"When did you get it?"

"First week of October."

"I wouldn't have imagined that your father would think of things like tetanus shots."

"They gave it to us at school," Penny said.

"Is that right?" Faye said, still doubtful.

Davey spoke up: "They make us take all *kinds* of shots at school. They have a nurse in, and all week we get shots. It's awful. Makes you feel like a pin cushion. Shots for mumps and measles. A flu shot. Other stuff. I *hate* it."

Faye seemed to be satisfied. "Okay. Just the same, when we get home, we'll wash that cut out really good, bathe it in alcohol, get some iodine on it, and a proper bandage."

"It's only a scratch," Penny said.

"We won't take chances. Now put your boot back on, dear."

Just as Penny got her foot in the boot and pulled up the zipper, the taxi hit a pothole. They were all bounced up and thrown forward with such suddenness and force that they almost fell off the seat.

"Young man," Faye said to the driver, even though he was at least forty years old, her own age, "where on earth did you learn to drive a car?"

He glanced in the rearview mirror. "Sorry, lady."

"Don't you *know* the streets of this city are a mess?" Faye demanded. "You've got to keep your eyes open."

"I try to," he said.

While Faye lectured the driver on the proper way to handle his cab, Penny leaned back against the seat, closed her eyes, and thought about the ugly little hand that had torn her boot and ankle. She tried to convince herself that it had been the hand of an ordinary animal of some kind; nothing strange; nothing out of the Twilight Zone. But most animals had paws, not hands. Monkeys had hands, of course. But this wasn't a monkey. No way. Squirrels had hands of a sort, didn't they? And raccoons. But this wasn't a squirrel or a raccoon, either. It wasn't anything she had ever seen or read about.

Had it been trying to drag her down and kill her? Right there on the street?

No. In order to kill her, the creature—and others like it, others with the shining silver eyes—would have had to come out from behind the gate, into the open, where Mrs. Shepherd and others would have seen them. And Penny was pretty sure the goblins didn't want to be seen by anyone but her. They were secretive. No, they definitely hadn't meant to kill her back there at the school; they had only meant to give her a good scare, to let her know they were still lurking around, waiting for the right opportunity. . . .

But *why?*

Why did they want her and, presumably, Davey, instead of some other kids?

What made goblins angry? What did you have to do to make them come after you like this?

She couldn't think of anything she had done that would make anyone terribly angry with her; certainly not goblins.

Confused, miserable, frightened, she opened her eyes and looked out the window. Snow was piling up everywhere. In her heart, she felt as cold as the icy, wind-scoured street beyond the window.

PART TWO

Wednesday, 5:30 P.M.–11:00 P.M.

Darkness devours every shining day.
Darkness demands and always has its way.
Darkness listens, watches, waits.
Darkness claims the day and celebrates.
Sometimes in silence darkness comes.
Sometimes with a gleeful banging of drums.
> —*The Book of Counted Sorrows*

Who is more foolish—
the child afraid of the dark
or the man afraid of the light?
> —Maurice Freehill

CHAPTER 4

I

AT FIVE-THIRTY, JACK and Rebecca went into Captain Walter Gresham's office to present him with the manpower and equipment requirements of the task force, as well as to discuss strategy in the investigation.

During the afternoon, two more members of the Carramazza crime family had been murdered, along with their bodyguards. Already the press was calling it the bloodiest gang war since Prohibition. What the press still didn't know was that the victims (except for the first two) had not been stabbed or shot or garroted or hung on meat hooks in traditional *cosa nostra* style. For the time being, the police had chosen not to reveal that all but the first two victims had been savagely bitten to death. When reporters uncovered that puzzling and grotesque fact, they would realize this was one of the biggest stories of the decade.

"That's when it'll get really bad," Gresham said. "They'll be all over us like fleas on a dog."

The heat was on, about to get even hotter, and Gresham was as fidgety as a toad on a griddle. Jack and Rebecca remained seated in front of the captain's desk, but Gresham couldn't remain still behind it. As they conducted their business, the captain paced the room, went repeatedly to the windows, lit a cigarette, smoked less than a third of it, stubbed it out, realized what he had done, and lit another.

Finally the time came for Jack to tell Gresham about his latest visit to Carver Hampton's shop and about the telephone call from Baba Lavelle. He had never felt more awkward than he did while recounting those events under Gresham's skeptical gaze.

He would have felt better if Rebecca had been on his side, but again they were in adversary positions. She was angry with him because he hadn't gotten back to the office until ten minutes past three, and she'd had to do a lot of the task force preparations on her own. He explained that the snowy streets were choked with crawling traffic, but she was having none of it. She listened to his story, was as angry as he was about the threat to his kids, but was not the least bit convinced that he had experienced anything even remotely supernatural. In fact, she was frustrated by his insistence that a great deal about the incident at the pay phone was just plain uncanny.

When Jack finished recounting those events for Gresham, the captain turned to Rebecca and said, "What do you make of it?"

She said, "I think we can now safely assume that Lavelle is a raving lunatic, not just another hood who wants to make a bundle in the drug trade. This isn't just a battle for territory within the underworld, and we'd be making a big mistake if we tried to handle it the same way we'd handle an honest-to-God gang war."

"What else?" Gresham asked.

"Well," she said. "I think we ought to dig into this Carver Hampton's background, see what we can turn up about him. Maybe he and Lavelle are in this together."

"No," Jack said. "Hampton wasn't faking when he told me he was terrified of Lavelle."

"How did Lavelle know precisely the right moment to call that pay phone?" Rebecca asked. "How did he know *exactly* when you'd be passing by it? One answer is that he was in Hampton's shop the whole time you were there, in the back room, and he knew when you left."

"He wasn't," Jack said. "Hampton's just not that good an actor."

"He's a clever fraud," she said. "But even if he isn't tied to Lavelle, I think we ought to get men up to Harlem this evening and really scour the block with the pay phone . . . and the block across the intersection from it. If Lavelle wasn't in Hampton's shop, then he must have been watching it from one of the other buildings along that street. There's no other explanation."

Unless maybe his voodoo really works, Jack thought.

Rebecca continued: "Have detectives check the apartments along those two blocks, see if Lavelle is holed up in one. Distribute copies of the photograph of Lavelle. Maybe someone up there's seen him around."

"Sounds good to me," Gresham said. "We'll do it."

"And I believe the threat against Jack's kids ought to be taken seriously. Put a guard on them when Jack can't be there."

"I agree," Gresham said. "We'll assign a man right now."

"Thanks, Captain," Jack said. "But I think it can wait until morning. The kids are with my sister-in-law right now, and I don't think Lavelle could find them. I told her to make sure she wasn't being followed when she picked them up at school. Besides, Lavelle said he'd give me the rest of the day to make up my mind about backing off the voodoo angle, and I assume he meant this evening as well."

Gresham sat on the edge of his desk. "If you want, I can remove you from the case. No sweat."

"Absolutely not," Jack said.

"You take his threat seriously?"

"Yes. But I also take my work seriously. I'm on this one to the bitter end."

Gresham lit another cigarette, drew deeply on it. "Jack, do you actually think there could be anything to this voodoo stuff?"

Aware of Rebecca's penetrating stare, Jack said, "It's pretty wild to think maybe there could be something to it. But I just can't rule it out."

"I can," Rebecca said. "Lavelle might believe in it, but that doesn't make it real."

"What about the condition of the bodies?" Jack asked.

"Obviously," she said, "Lavelle's using trained animals."

"That's almost as far-fetched as voodoo," Gresham said.

"Anyway," Jack said, "we went through all of that earlier today. About the only small, vicious, trainable animal we could think of was the ferret. And we've all seen Pathology's report, the one that came in at four-thirty. The teeth impressions don't belong to ferrets. According to Pathology, they don't belong to any other animal Noah took aboard the ark, either."

Rebecca said, "Lavelle's from the Caribbean. Isn't it likely that he's using an animal indigenous to that part of the world, something our forensic experts wouldn't even think of, some species of exotic lizard or something like that?"

"Now you're grasping at straws," Jack said.

"I agree," Gresham said. "But it's worth checking out, anyway. Okay. Anything else?"

"Yeah," Jack said. "Can you explain how I knew that call from Lavelle was for me? Why was I drawn to that pay phone?"

Wind stroked the windows.

Behind Gresham's desk, the ticking of the wall clock suddenly seemed much louder than it had been.

The captain shrugged. "I guess neither of us has an answer for you, Jack."

"Don't feel bad. I don't have an answer for me, either."

Gresham got up from his desk. "All right, if that's it, then I think the two of you ought to knock off, go home, get some rest. You've put in a long day already; the task force is functioning now, and it can get along without you until tomorrow. Jack, if you'll hang around just a couple of minutes, I'll show you a list of the available officers on every shift, and you can handpick the men you want to watch your kids."

Rebecca was already at the door, pulling it open. Jack called to her. She glanced back.

He said, "Wait for me downstairs, okay?"

Her expression was noncommittal. She walked out.

From the window, where he had gone to look down at the street, Walt Gresham said, "It's like the arctic out there."

II

THE ONE THING Penny liked about the Jamisons' place was the kitchen, which was big by New York City apartment standards, almost twice as large as the kitchen Penny was accustomed to, and cozy. A green tile floor. White cabinets with leaded glass doors and brass hardware. Green ceramic-tile counters. Above the double sink, there was a beautiful out-thrusting greenhouse window with a four-foot-long, two-foot-wide planting bed in which a variety of herbs were grown all year long, even during the winter. (Aunt Faye liked to cook with fresh herbs whenever possible.) In one corner, jammed against the wall, was a small butcher's block table, not so much a place to eat as a place to plan menus and prepare shopping lists; flanking the table, there was space for two chairs. This was the only room in the Jamisons' apartment in which Penny felt comfortable.

At twenty minutes past six, she was sitting at the butcher's block table, pretending to read one of Faye's magazines; the words blurred together in front of her unfocused eyes. Actually, she was thinking about all sorts of things she didn't *want* to think about: goblins, death, and whether she'd ever be able to sleep again.

Uncle Keith had come home from work almost an hour ago. He was a partner in a successful stockbrokerage. Tall, lean, with a head as hairless as an egg, sporting a graying mustache and goatee, Uncle Keith always seemed distracted. You had the feeling he never gave you more than two-thirds of his attention when he was talking with you. Sometimes he would sit in his favorite chair for an hour or two, his hands folded in his lap, unmoving, staring at the wall, hardly even blinking, breaking his trance only two or three times an hour in order to pick up a brandy glass and take one tiny sip from it. Other times he would sit at a window, staring and chain-smoking. Secretly, Davey called Uncle Keith "the moon man" because his mind always seemed to be somewhere on the moon. Since coming home today, he'd been in the living room, sipping slowly at a martini, puffing on one cigarette after another, watching TV news and reading the *Wall Street Journal* at the same time.

Aunt Faye was at the other end of the kitchen from the table where Penny sat. She had begun to prepare dinner, which was scheduled for seven-thirty: lemon chicken, rice, and stir-fried vegetables. The kitchen was the only place Aunt Faye was not too much like Aunt Faye. She enjoyed cooking, was very good at it, and seemed like a different person when she was in the kitchen; more relaxed, kinder than usual.

Davey was helping her prepare dinner. At least she was allowing him to think he was helping. As they worked they talked, not about anything important, this and that.

"Gosh, I'm hungry enough to eat a horse!" Davey said.

"That's not a polite thing to say," Faye advised him. "It brings to mind an unpleasant image. You should simply say, 'I'm extremely hungry,' or 'I'm starved,' or something like that."

"Well, naturally, I meant a *dead* horse," Davey said, completely misunderstanding Faye's little lesson in etiquette. "And one that's been cooked, too. I wouldn't want to eat any *raw* horse, Aunt Faye. Yuch and double yuch. But, man-oh-man, I sure could eat a whole lot of just about anything you gimme right now."

"My heavens, young man, you had cookies and milk when we got here this afternoon."

"Only two cookies."

"And you're famished already? You don't have a stomach; what *you* have is a bottomless pit!"

"Well, I hardly had any lunch," Davey said. "Mrs. Shepherd—she's my teacher—she shared some of her lunch with me, but it was really dumb-awful stuff. All she had was yogurt and tuna fish, and I *hate* both of 'em. So what I did, after she gave me a little of each, I nibbled at it, just to make her feel good, and then when she wasn't looking, I threw most of it away."

"But doesn't your father pack a lunch for you?" Faye asked, her voice suddenly sharper than it had been.

"Oh, sure. Or when he doesn't have time, Penny packs it. But—"

Faye turned to Penny. "Did he have a lunch to take to school today? Surely he doesn't have to beg for food!"

Penny looked up from her magazine. "I made his lunch myself, this morning. He had an apple, a ham sandwich, and two big oatmeal cookies."

"That sounds like a fine lunch to me," Faye said. "Why didn't you eat it, Davey?"

"Well, because of the rats, of course," he said.

Penny twitched in surprise, sat up straight in her chair, and stared intently at Davey.

Faye said, "Rats? What rats?"

"Holy-moly, I forgot to tell you!" Davey said. "Rats must've got in my lunchbox during morning classes. Big old ugly rats with yellow teeth, come right up out of the sewers or somewhere. The food was all messed up, torn to pieces, and chewed on. *Grooooooooss,"* he said, drawing the word out with evident pleasure, not disgusted by the fact that rats had been at his lunch, actually excited about it, thrilled by it, as only a young boy could be. At his age, an incident like this was a real adventure.

Penny's mouth had gone as dry as ashes. "Davey? Uh . . . did you see the rats?"

"Nah," he said, clearly disappointed. "They were gone by the time I went to get my lunchbox."

"Where'd you have your lunchbox?" Penny asked.

"In my locker."

"Did the rats chew on anything else in your locker?"

"Like what?"

"Like books or anything."

"Why would they want to chew on books?"

"Then it was just the food?"

"Sure. What else?"

"Did you have your locker door shut?"

"I thought I did," he said.

"Didn't you have it locked, too?"

"I thought I did."

"And wasn't your lunchbox shut tight?"

"It *should* have been," he said, scratching his head, trying to remember.

Faye said, "Well, obviously, it wasn't. Rats can't open a lock, open a door, and pry the lid off a lunchbox. You must have been very careless, Davey. I'm surprised at you. I'll bet you ate one of those oatmeal cookies first thing when you got to school, just couldn't wait, and then forgot to put the lid back on the box."

"But I didn't," Davey protested.

"Your father's not teaching you to pick up after yourself," Faye said. "That's the kind of thing a mother teaches, and your father's just neglecting it."

Penny was going to tell them about how her own locker had been trashed when she'd gone to school this morning. She was even going to tell them about the things in the basement because it seemed to her that what had happened to Davey's lunch would somehow substantiate her story.

But before Penny could speak, Aunt Faye spoke up in her most morally indignant tone of voice: "What *I* want to know is what kind of school this is your father's sent to you. What kind of dirty hole is this place, this Wellton?"

"It's a good school," Penny said defensively.

"With *rats?*" Faye said. "No good school would have rats. No halfway decent school would have rats. Why, what if they'd still been in the locker when Davey went for his lunch? He might've been bitten. Rats are filthy. They carry all kinds of diseases. They're disgusting. I simply can't imagine any school for young children being allowed to remain open if it has rats. The Board of Health has got to be told about this first thing tomorrow. Your father's going to have to do something about the situation immediately. I won't allow him to procrastinate. Not where your health is concerned. Why, your poor dear mother would be appalled by such a place, a school with rats in the walls. Rats! My God, rats carry everything from rabies to the plague!"

Faye droned on and on.

Penny tuned her out.

There wasn't any point in telling them about her own locker and the silver-eyed things in the school basement. Faye would insist they had been rats, too. When that woman got something in her head, there was no way of getting it out again, no way of changing her mind. Now, Faye was looking forward to confronting their father about the rats; she relished the thought of blaming him for putting them in a rat-infested school, and she wouldn't be the least receptive to anything Penny said, to any explanation or any conflicting facts that might put rats completely out of the picture and thereby spare their father from a scolding.

Even if I tell her about the hand, Penny thought, the little hand that came under the green gate, she'll stick to the idea that it's rats. She'll say I was scared and made a mistake about what I saw. She'll say it wasn't really a hand at all, but a rat, a slimy old rat biting at my boot. She'll turn it all around. She'll make it support the story she wants to believe, and it'll just be more ammunition for her to use against Daddy. Damnit, Aunt Faye, why're you so stubborn?

Faye was chattering about the need for a parent to thoroughly investigate a school before sending children to it.

Penny wondered when her father would come to get them, and she prayed he wouldn't be too late. She wanted him to come before bedtime. She didn't want to be alone, just her and Davey, in a dark room, even if it was Aunt Faye's guest room, blocks and blocks away from their own apartment. She was pretty sure the goblins would find them, even here. She had decided to take her father aside and tell him everything. He wouldn't want to believe in goblins, at first. But now there was Davey's lunchbox to consider. And if she went back to their apartment with her father and showed him the holes in Davey's plastic baseball bat, she might be able to convince him. Daddy was a grown-up, like Aunt Faye, sure, but he wasn't stubborn, and he *listened* to kids in a way that few grown-ups did.

Faye said, "With all the money he got from your mother's insurance and from the settlement the hospital made, he could afford to send you to a top-of-the-line school. Absolutely top-of-the-line. I can't imagine why he settled on this Wellton joint."

Penny bit her lip, said nothing.

She stared down at the magazine. The pictures and words swam in and out of focus.

The worst thing was that now she knew, beyond a doubt, that the goblins weren't just after her. They wanted Davey, too.

III

REBECCA HAD NOT waited for Jack, though he had asked her to. While he'd been with Captain Gresham, working out the details of the protection that would be provided for Penny and Davey, Rebecca had apparently put on her coat and gone home.

When Jack found that she had gone, he sighed and said softly, "You sure aren't easy, baby."

On his desk were two books about voodoo, which he had checked out of the library yesterday. He stared at them for a long moment, then decided he needed to learn more about *Bocors* and *Houngons* before tomorrow morning. He put on his coat and gloves, picked up the books, tucked them under one arm, and went down to the subterranean garage, beneath the building.

Because he and Rebecca were now in charge of the emergency task force, they were entitled to perquisites beyond the reach of ordinary homicide detectives, including the full-time use of an unmarked police sedan for each of them, not just during duty hours but around the clock. The car assigned to Jack was a one-year-old, sour-green Chevrolet that bore a few dents and more than a few scratches. It was the totally stripped-down model, without options or luxuries of any kind, just a get-around car, not a racer-and-chaser. The motor pool mechanics had even put the snow chains on the tires. The heap was ready to roll.

He backed out of the parking space, drove up the ramp to the street exit. He stopped and waited while a city truck, equipped with a big snowplow and a salt spreader and lots of flashing lights, passed by in the storm-thrashed darkness.

In addition to the truck, there were only two other vehicles on the street. The storm virtually had the night to itself. Yet, when the truck was gone and the way was clear, Jack still hesitated.

He switched on the windshield wipers.

To head toward Rebecca's apartment, he would have to turn left.

To go to the Jamisons' place, he ought to turn right.

The wipers flogged back and forth, back and forth, left, right, left, right.

He was eager to be with Penny and Davey, eager to hug them, to see them warm and alive and smiling.

Right, left, right.

Of course, they weren't in any real danger at the moment. Even if Lavelle was serious when he threatened them, he wouldn't make his move this soon, and he wouldn't know where to find them even if he *did* want to make his move.

Left, right, left.

They were perfectly safe with Faye and Keith. Besides, Jack had told Faye that he probably wouldn't make it for dinner; she was already expecting him to be late.

The wipers beat time to his indecision.

Finally he took his foot off the brake, pulled into the street, and turned left.

He needed to talk to Rebecca about what had happened between them last night. She had avoided the subject all day. He couldn't allow her to continue to dodge it. She would have to face up to the changes that last night had wrought in both their lives, major changes which he welcomed wholeheartedly but about which she seemed, at best, ambivalent.

Along the edges of the car roof, wind whistled hollowly through the metal beading, a cold and mournful sound.

Crouching in deep shadows by the garage exit, the thing watched Jack Dawson drive away in the unmarked sedan.

Its shining silver eyes did not blink even once.

Then, keeping to the shadows, it crept back into the deserted, silent garage. It hissed. It muttered. It gobbled softly to itself in an eerie, raspy little voice.

Finding the protection of darkness and shadows wherever it wished to go — even where there didn't seem to have been shadows only a moment before — the thing slunk from car to car, beneath and around them, until it came to a drain in the garage floor. It descended into the midnight regions below.

IV

LAVELLE WAS NERVOUS.

Without switching on any lamps, he stalked restlessly through his house, upstairs and down, back and forth, looking for nothing, simply unable to keep still, always moving in deep darkness but never bumping into furniture or doorways, pacing as swiftly and surely as if the rooms were all brightly lighted. He wasn't blind in darkness, never the least disoriented. Indeed, he was at home in shadows. Darkness, after all, was a part of him.

Usually, in either darkness or light, he was supremely confident and self-assured. But now, hour by hour, his self-assurance was steadily crumbling.

His nervousness had bred uneasiness. Uneasiness had given birth to fear. He was unaccustomed to fear. He didn't know quite how to handle it. So the fear made him even more nervous.

He was worried about Jack Dawson. Perhaps it had been a grave mistake to allow Dawson time to consider his options. A man like the detective might put that time to good use.

If he senses that I'm even slightly afraid of him, Lavelle thought, and if he learns more about voodoo, then he might eventually understand why I've got good reason to fear him.

If Dawson discovered the nature of his own special power, and if he learned to use that power, he would find and stop Lavelle. Dawson was one of those rare individuals, that one in ten thousand, who could do battle with even the most masterful *Bocor* and be reasonably certain of victory. If the detective uncovered the secret of himself, then he would come for Lavelle, well-armored and dangerous.

Lavelle paced through the dark house.

Maybe he should strike now. Destroy the Dawson children this evening. Get it over with. Their deaths might send Dawson spiraling down into an emotional collapse. He loved his kids a great deal, and he was already a widower, already laboring under a heavy burden of grief; perhaps the slaughter of Penny and Davey would break him. If the loss of his kids didn't snap his mind, then it would most likely plunge him into a terrible depression that would cloud his thinking and interfere with his work for many weeks. At the very least, Dawson would have to take a few days off from the investigation, in order to arrange the funerals, and those few days would give Lavelle some breathing space.

On the other hand, what if Dawson was the kind of man who drew strength from adversity instead of buckling under the weight of it? What if the murder and mutilation of his children only solidified his determination to find and destroy Lavelle?

To Lavelle, that was an unnerving possibility.

Indecisive, the *Bocor* rambled through the lightless rooms as if he were a ghost come to haunt.

At last, he knew he must consult the ancient gods and humbly request the benefit of their wisdom.

He went to the kitchen and flicked on the overhead light.

From a cupboard, he withdrew a cannister filled with flour.

A radio stood on the counter. He moved it to the center of the kitchen table.

Using the flour, he drew an elaborate *vèvè* on the table, all the way around the radio.

He switched on the radio.

An old Beatles song. *Eleanor Rigby.*

He turned the dial through a dozen stations that were playing every kind of music from pop to rock to country, classical, and jazz. He set the tuner at an unused frequency, where there was no spill-over whatsoever from the stations on either side.

The soft crackle and hiss of the open airwaves filled the room and sounded like the sighing surf-roar of a far-off sea.

He scooped up one more handful of flour and carefully drew a small, simple *vèvè* on top of the radio itself.

At the sink he washed his hands, then went to the refrigerator and got a small bottle full of blood.

It was cat's blood, used in a variety of rituals. Once a week, always at a different pet store or animal pound, he bought or "adopted" a cat, brought it home, killed it, and drained it to maintain a fresh supply of blood.

He returned to the table now, sat down in front of the radio. Dipping his fingers in the cat's blood, he drew certain runes on the table and, last of all, on the plastic window over the radio dial.

He chanted for a while, waited, listened, chanted some more, until he heard an unmistakable yet indefinable change in the sound of the unused frequency. It had been dead just a moment ago. Dead air. Dead, random, meaningless sound. Now it was alive. It was still just the crackle-sputter-hiss of static, a silk-soft sound. But somehow different from what it had been a few seconds ago. *Something* was making use of the open frequency, reaching out from the Beyond.

Staring at the radio but not really seeing it, Lavelle said, "Is someone there?"

No answer.

"Is someone there?"

It was a voice of dust and mummified remains: *"I wait."* It was a voice of dry paper, of sand and splinters, a voice of infinite age, as bitterly cold as the night between the stars, jagged and whispery and evil.

It might be any one of a hundred thousand demons, or a full-fledged god of one of the ancient African religions, or the spirit of a dead man long ago condemned to Hell. There was no way of telling for sure which it was, and Lavelle wasn't empowered to make it speak its name. Whatever it might be, it would be able to answer his questions.

"I wait."

"You know of my business here?"

"Yessss."

"The business involving the Carramazza family."

"Yessss."

If God had given snakes the power of speech, this was what they would have sounded like.

"You know the detective, this man Dawson?"

"Yessss."

"Will he ask his superiors to remove him from the case?"

"Never."

"Will he continue to do research into voodoo?"

"Yessss."

"I've warned him to stop."

"He will not."

The kitchen had grown extremely cold in spite of the house's furnace, which was still operating and still spewing hot air out of the wall vents. The air seemed thick and oily, too.

"What can I do to keep Dawson at bay?"

"You know."

"Tell me."

"You know."

Lavelle licked his lips, cleared his throat.

"You know."

Lavelle said, "Should I have his children murdered now, tonight, without further delay?"

V

REBECCA ANSWERED THE door. She said, "I sort of figured it would be you."

He stood on the landing, shivering. "We've got a raging blizzard out there."

She was wearing a soft blue robe, slippers.

Her hair was honey-yellow. She was gorgeous.

She didn't say anything. She just looked at him.

He said, "Yep, the storm of the century is what it is. Maybe even the start of a new ice age. The end of the world. I asked myself who I'd most like to be with if this actually was the end of the world—"

"And you decided on me."

"Not exactly."

"Oh?"

"I just didn't know where to find Jacqueline Bisset."

"So I was second choice."

"I didn't know Raquel Welch's address, either."

"Third."

"But out of four billion people on earth, third isn't bad."

She almost smiled at him.

He said, "Can I come in? I already took my boots off, see. I won't track up your carpet. And I've got very good manners. I never belch or scratch my ass in public—not intentionally, anyway."

She stepped back.

He went in.

She closed the door and said, "I was about to make something to eat. Are you hungry?"

"What've you got?"

"Drop-in guests can't afford to be choosy."

They went into the kitchen, and he draped his coat over the back of a chair.

She said, "Roast beef sandwiches and soup."

"What flavor soup?"

"Minestrone."

"Homemade?"

"Canned."

"Good."

"Good?"

"I hate homemade stuff."

"Is that so?"

"Too many vitamins in homemade stuff."

"Can there be too many?"

"Sure. Makes me all jumpy with excess energy."

"Ah."

"And there's too much taste in homemade," he said.

"Overwhelms the palate."

"You *do* understand! Give me canned any day."

"Never too much taste in canned."

"Nice and bland, easy to digest."

"I'll set the table and get the soup started."

"Good idea."

"You slice the roast beef."

"Sure."

"It's in the refrigerator, in Saran Wrap. Second shelf, I think. Be careful."

"Why, it is *alive?*"

"The refrigerator's packed pretty full. If you're not careful taking something out, you can start an avalanche."

He opened the refrigerator. On each shelf, there were two or three layers of food, one atop the other. The storage spaces on the doors were crammed full of bottles, cans, and jars.

"You afraid the government's going to outlaw food?" he asked.

"I like to keep a lot of stuff on hand."

"I noticed."

"Just in case."

"In case the entire New York Philharmonic drops in for a nosh?"

She didn't say anything.

He said, "Most supermarkets don't have this much stock."

She seemed embarrassed, and he dropped the subject.

But it was odd. Chaos reigned in the refrigerator, while every other inch of her apartment was neat, orderly, and even Spartan in its decor.

He found the roast beef behind a dish of pickled eggs, atop an apple pie in a bakery box, beneath a package of Swiss cheese, wedged in between two leftover casseroles on one side and a jar of pickles and a leftover chicken breast on the other side, in front of three jars of jelly.

For a while they worked in silence.

Once he had finally cornered her, he had thought it would be easy to talk about what had happened between them last night. But now he felt awkward. He couldn't decide how to begin, what to say first. The direct approach was best, of course. He ought to say, *Rebecca, where do we go from here?* Or maybe, *Rebecca, didn't it mean as much to you as it did to me?* Or maybe even, *Rebecca, I love you.* But everything he might have said sounded, in his own mind, either trite or too abrupt or just plain dumb.

The silence stretched.

She put placemats, dishes, and silverware on the table.

He sliced the beef, then a large tomato.

She opened two cans of soup.

From the refrigerator, he got pickles, mustard, mayonnaise, and two kinds of cheese. The bread was in the breadbox.

He turned to Rebecca to ask how she wanted her sandwich.

She was standing at the stove with her back to him, stirring the soup in the pot. Her hair shimmered softly against her dark blue robe.

Jack felt a tremor of desire. He marveled at how very different she was now from the way she had been when he'd last seen her at the office, only an hour ago. No longer the ice maiden. No longer the Viking woman. She looked smaller, not particularly shorter but narrower of shoulder, slimmer of wrist, overall more slender, more fragile, more girlish than she had seemed earlier.

Before he realized what he was doing, he moved toward her, stepped up behind her, and put his hands on her shoulders.

She wasn't startled. She had sensed him coming. Perhaps she had even *willed* him to come to her.

At first her shoulders were stiff beneath his hands, her entire body rigid.

He pulled her hair aside and kissed her neck, made a chain of kisses along the smooth, sweet skin.

She relaxed, softened, leaned back against him.

He slid his hands down her sides, to the swell of her hips.

She sighed but said nothing.

He kissed her ear.

He slid one hand up, cupped her breast.

She switched off the gas burner on which the pot of minestrone was heating.

His arms were around her now, both hands on her flat belly.

He leaned over her shoulder, kissed the side of her throat. Through his lips, pressed to her supple flesh, he felt one of her arteries throb with her strong pulse; a rapid pulse; faster now and faster still.

She seemed to melt back into him.

No woman, except his lost wife, had ever felt this warm to him.

She pressed her bottom against him.

He was so hard he ached.

She murmured wordlessly, a feline sound.

His hands would not remain still but moved over her in gentle, lazy exploration.

She turned to him.

They kissed.

Her hot tongue was quick, but the kiss was long and slow.

When they broke, drawing back only inches, to take a much-needed breath, their eyes met, and hers were such a fiercely bright shade of green that they didn't seem real, yet he saw a very real longing in them.

Another kiss. This one was harder than the first, hungrier.

Then she pulled back from him. Took his hand in hers.

They walked out of the kitchen. Into the living room.

The bedroom.

She switched on a small lamp with an amber glass shade. It wasn't bright. The shadows retreated slightly but didn't go away.

She took off her robe. She wasn't wearing anything else.

She looked as if she were made of honey and butter and cream.

She undressed him.

Many minutes later, on the bed, when he finally entered her, he said her name with a small gasp of wonder, and she said his. Those were the first words they had spoken since he had put his hands on her shoulders, out in the kitchen.

They found a soft, silken, satisfying rhythm and gave pleasure to each other on the cool, crisp sheets.

VI

LAVELLE SAT AT the kitchen table, staring at the radio.

Wind shook the old house.

To the unseen presence using the radio as a contact point with this world, Lavelle said, "Should I have his children murdered now, tonight, without further delay?"

"Yessss."

"But if I kill his children, isn't there a danger that Dawson will be more determined than ever to find me?"

"Kill them."

"Do you mean killing them might break Dawson?"

"Yessss."

"Contribute to an emotional or mental collapse?"

"Yessss."

"Destroy him?"

"Yessss."

"There is no doubt about that?"

"He lovessss them very muchhhh."

"And there's no doubt what it would do to him?" Lavelle pressed.

"Kill them."

"I want to be sure."

"Kill them. Brutally. It musssst be esssspecccially brutal."

"I see. The brutality of it is the thing that will make Dawson snap. Is that it?"

"Yessss."

"I'll do anything to get him out of my way, but I want to be absolutely sure it'll work the way I want it to work."

"Kill them. Ssssmasssh them. Break their bonessss and tear out their eyessss. Rip out their tonguessss. Gut them assss if they were two pigssss for butchhhhher- ing."

VII

REBECCA'S BEDROOM.

Spicules of snow tapped softly on the window.

They lay on their backs, side by side on the bed, holding hands, in the butterscotch-colored light.

Rebecca said, "I didn't think it would happen again."

"What?"

"This."

"Oh."

"I thought last night was an . . . aberration."

"Really?"

"I was sure we'd never make love again."

"But we did."

"We sure did."

"God, did we ever!"

She was silent.

He said, "Are you sorry we did?"

"No."

"You don't think *this* was the last time, do you?"

"No."

"Can't be the last. Not as good as we are together."

"So good together."

"You can be so soft."

"And you can be so hard."

"Crude."

"But true."

A pause.

Then she said, "What's happened to us?"

"Isn't that clear?"

"Not entirely."

"We've fallen for each other."

"But how could it happen so fast?"

"It wasn't fast."

"All this time, just cops, just partners—"

"More than partners."

"—then all of a sudden—*wham!*"

"It wasn't sudden. I've been falling a long time."

"Have you?"

"For a couple of months, anyway."

"I didn't realize it."

"A long, long, slow fall."

"Why didn't I realize?"

"You realized. Subconsciously."

"Maybe."

"What I wonder is why you resisted it so strenuously."

She didn't reply.

He said, "I thought maybe you found me repellent."

"I find you irresistible."

"Then why'd you resist?"

"It scares me."

"What scares you?"

"This. Having someone. *Caring* about someone."

"Why's that scare you?"

"The chance of losing it."

"But that's silly."

"It is not."

"You've got to risk losing a thing—"

"I know."

"—or else never have it in the first place."

"Maybe that's best."

"Not having it at all?"

"Yes."

"That philosophy makes for a damned lonely life."

"It still scares me."

"We won't lose this, Rebecca."

"Nothing lasts forever."

"That's not what you'd call a good attitude."

"Well, nothing does."

"If you've been hurt by other guys—"

"It isn't that."

"Then what is it?"

She dodged the question. "Kiss me."

He kissed her. Again and again.

They weren't passionate kisses. Tender. Sweet.

After a while he said, "I love you."

"Don't say that."

"I'm not just saying it. I mean it."

"Just don't say it."

"I'm not a guy who says things he doesn't mean."

"I know."

"And I'm not saying it before I'm sure."

She wouldn't look at him.

He said, "I'm sure, Rebecca. I love you."

"I asked you not to say that."

"I'm not asking to hear it from you."

She bit her lip.

"I'm not asking for a commitment," he said.

"Jack—"

"Just say you don't hate me."

"Will you stop—"

"Can't you please just say you don't hate me?"

She sighed. "I don't hate you."

He grinned. "Just say you don't loathe me too much."

"I don't loathe you too much."

"Just say you like me a little bit."

"I like you a little bit."

"Maybe more than a little bit."

"Maybe more than a little bit."

"All right. I can live with that for now."

"Good."

"Meanwhile, *I* love *you.*"

"Damnit, Jack!"

She pulled away from him.

She drew the sheet over herself, all the way up to her chin.

"Don't be cold with me, Rebecca."

"I'm not being cold."

"Don't treat me like you treated me all day today."

She met his eyes.

He said, "I thought you were sorry last night ever happened."

She shook her head: no.

"It hurt me, the way you were, today," he said. "I thought you were disgusted with me, with yourself, for what we'd done."

"No. Never."

"I know that now, but here you are drawing away again, keeping me at arm's length. What's *wrong?*"

She chewed on her thumb. Like a little girl.

"Rebecca?"

"I don't know how to say it. I don't know how to explain. I've never had to put it into words for anyone before."

"I'm a good listener."

"I need a little time to think."

"So take your time."

"Just a little time. A few minutes."

"Take all the time you want."

She stared at the ceiling, thinking.

He got under the sheet with her and pulled the blanket over both of them. They lay in silence for a while.

Outside, the wind sang a two-note serenade.

She said, "My father died when I was six."

"I'm sorry. That's terrible. You never really had a chance to know him, then."

"True. And yet, odd as it seems, I still sometimes miss him so bad, you know, even after all these years—even a father I never really knew and can hardly remember. I miss him, anyway."

Jack thought of his own little Davey, not even quite six when his mother had died.

He squeezed Rebecca's hand gently.

She said, "But my father dying when I was six—in a way, that's not the worst of it. The worst of it is that I saw him die. I was there when it happened."

"God. How . . . how did it happen?"

"Well . . . he and Mama owned a sandwich shop. A small place. Four little tables. Mostly take-out business. Sandwiches, potato salad, macaroni salad, a few desserts. It's hard to make a go of it in that business unless you have two things, right at the start: enough start-up capital to see you through a couple of lean years at the beginning, and a good location with lots of foot traffic passing by or office workers in the neighborhood. But my folks were poor. They had very little capital. They couldn't pay the high rent in a good location, so they started in a bad one and kept moving whenever they could afford to, three times in three years, each time to a slightly better spot. They worked hard, so hard. . . . My father held down another job, too, janitorial work, late at night, after the shop closed, until just before dawn. Then he'd come home, sleep four or five hours, and go open the shop for the lunch trade. Mama cooked a lot of the food that was served, and she worked behind the counter, too, but she also did some house cleaning for other people, to bring in a few extra dollars. Finally, the shop began to pay off. My dad was able to drop his janitorial job, and Mama gave up the house cleaning. In fact, business started getting so good that they were looking for their first employee; they couldn't handle the shop all by themselves any more. The future looked bright. And then . . . one afternoon . . . during the slack time between the lunch and dinner crowds, when Mama was out on an errand and I was alone in the shop with my father . . . this guy came in . . . with a gun . . . ."

"Oh, shit," Jack said. He knew the rest of it. He'd seen it all before, many times. Dead storekeepers, sprawled in pools of their own blood, beside their emptied cash registers.

"There was something strange about this creep," Rebecca said. "Even though I was only six years old, I could tell there was something *wrong* with him the moment he came in, and I went to the kitchen and peeked out at him through the curtain. He was fidgety . . . pale . . . funny around the eyes . . ."

"A junkie?"

"That's the way it turned out, yeah. If I close my eyes now, I can still see his pale face, the way his mouth twitched. The awful thing is . . . I can see it clearer than I can see my own father's face. Those terrible eyes."

She shuddered.

Jack said, "You don't have to go on."

"Yes. I do. I have to tell you. So you'll understand why . . . why I am like I am about certain things."

"Okay. If you're sure—"

"I'm sure."

"Then . . . did your father refuse to hand over the money to this son of a bitch—or what?"

"No. Dad gave him the money. All of it."

"He offered no resistance at all?"

"None."

"But cooperation didn't save him."

"No. This junkie had a bad itch, a real bad need. The need was like something nasty crawling around in his head, I guess, and it made him irritable, mean, crazy-mad at the world. You know how they get. So I think maybe he wanted to kill somebody even more than he wanted the money. So . . . he just . . . pulled the trigger."

Jack put an arm around her, drew her against him.

She said, "Two shots. Then the bastard ran. Only one of the slugs hit my father. But it . . . hit him . . . in the face."

"Jesus," Jack said softly, thinking of six-year-old Rebecca in the sandwich shop's kitchen, peering through the parted curtain, watching as her father's face exploded.

"It was a .45," she said.

Jack winced, thinking of the power of the gun.

"Hollow-point bullets," she said.

"Oh, Christ."

"Dad didn't have a chance at point-blank range."

"Don't torture yourself with—"

"Blew his head off," she said.

"Don't think about it any more now," Jack said.

"Brain tissue . . ."

"Put it out of your mind now."

". . . pieces of his skull . . ."

"It was a long time ago."

". . . blood all over the wall."

"Hush now. Hush."

"There's more to tell."

"You don't have to pour it out all at once."

"I want you to understand."

"Take your time. I'll be here. I'll wait. Take your time."

VIII

IN THE CORRUGATED metal shed, leaning over the pit, using two pair of ceremonial scissors with malachite handles, Lavelle snipped both ends of the cord simultaneously.

The photographs of Penny and Davey Dawson fell into the hole, vanished in the flickering orange light.

A shrill, unhuman cry came from the depths.

"Kill them," Lavelle said.

IX

STILL IN REBECCA'S BED.

Still holding each other.

She said, "The police only had my description to go on."

"A six-year-old child doesn't make the best witness."

"They worked hard, trying to get a lead on the creep who'd shot Daddy. They really worked hard."

"They ever catch him?"

"Yes. But too late. Much too late."

"What do you mean?"

"See, he got two hundred bucks when he robbed the shop."

"So?"

"That was over twenty-two years ago."

"Yeah?"

"Two hundred was a lot more money then. Not a fortune. But a lot more than it is now."

"I still don't see what you're driving at."

"It looked like an easy score to him."

"Not too damned easy. He killed a man."

"But he wouldn't have had to. He *wanted* to kill someone that day."

"Okay. Right. So, twisted as he is, he figures it was easy."

"Six months went by . . ."

"And the cops never got close to him?"

"No. So it looks easier and easier to the creep."

A sickening dread filled Jack. His stomach turned over.

He said, "You don't mean . . . ?"

"Yes."

"He came back."

"With a gun. The same gun."

"But he'd have to've been nuts!"

"All junkies are nuts."

Jack waited. He didn't want to hear the rest of it, but he knew she would tell him; had to tell him; was *compelled* to tell him.

She said, "My mother was at the cash register."

"No," he said softly, as if a protest from him could somehow alter the tragic history of her family.

"He blew her away."

"Rebecca . . ."

"Fired five shots into her."

"You didn't . . . see this one?"

"No. I wasn't in the shop that day."

"Thank God."

"This time they caught him."

"Too late for you."

"Much too late. But it was after that when I knew what I wanted to be when I grew up. I wanted to be a cop, so I could stop people like that junkie, stop them from killing the mothers and fathers of other little girls and boys. There weren't women cops back then, you know, not real cops, just office workers in police stations, radio dispatchers, that sort of thing. I had no role models. But I knew I'd make it someday. I was determined. All the time I was growing up, there was never once when I thought about being anything else but a cop. I never even considered getting married, being a wife, having kids, being a mother, because I knew someone would only come along and shoot my husband or take my kids away from me or take me away from my kids. So what was the point in it? I would be a cop. Nothing else. A cop. And that's what I became. I think I felt guilty about my father's murder. I think I believed that there must've been something I could have done that day to save him. And I *know* I felt guilty about my mother's death. I hated myself for not giving the police a better description of the man who shot my dad, hated myself for being numb and useless, because if I had been of more help to them, maybe they'd have gotten the guy before he killed Mama. Being a cop, stopping other creeps like that junkie, it was a way to atone for my guilt. Maybe that's amateur psychology. But not far off the mark. I'm sure it's part of what motivates me."

"But you haven't any reason at all to feel guilty," Jack assured her. "You did all you possibly could've done. You were only *six!*"

"I know. I understand that. But the guilt is there nevertheless. Still sharp, at times. I guess it'll always be there, fading year by year, but never fading away altogether."

Jack was, at last, beginning to understand Rebecca Chandler—why she was the way she was. He even saw the reason for the overstocked refrigerator; after a childhood filled with so much bad news and unanticipated shocks and instability, keeping a well-supplied larder was one way to buy at least a small measure of security, a way to feel safe. Understanding increased his respect and already deep affection for her. She was a very special woman.

He had a feeling that this night was one of the most important of his life. The long loneliness after Linda's passing was finally drawing to an end. Here, with Rebecca, he was making a new beginning. A good beginning. Few men were fortunate enough to find two good women and be given two chances at happiness in their lives. He was very lucky, and he knew it, and that knowledge made him exuberant. In spite of a day filled with blood and mutilated bodies and threats of death, he sensed a golden future out there ahead of them. Everything was going to work out fine, after all. Nothing could go wrong. Nothing could go wrong now.

X

"KILL THEM, KILL THEM," Lavelle said.

His voice echoed down into the pit, echoed and echoed, as if it had been cast into a deep shaft.

The indistinct, pulsing, shifting, amorphous floor of the pit suddenly became more active. It bubbled, surged, churned. Out of that molten, lavalike sub-

stance—which might have been within arm's reach or, instead, miles below—
something began to take shape.

Something monstrous.

XI

"WHEN YOUR MOTHER was killed, you were only—"

"Seven years old. Turned seven the month before she died."

"Who raised you after that?"

"I went to live with my grandparents, my mother's folks."

"Did that work out?"

"They loved me. So it worked for a while."

"Only for a while?"

"My grandfather died."

"*Another* death?"

"Always another one."

"How?"

"Cancer. I'd seen sudden death already. It was time for me to learn about slow death."

"How slow?"

"Two years from the time the cancer was diagnosed until he finally succumbed to it. He wasted away, lost sixty pounds before the end, lost all his hair from the radium treatments. He looked and acted like an entirely different person during those last few weeks. It was a ghastly thing to watch."

"How old were you when you lost him?"

"Eleven and a half."

"Then it was just you and your grandmother."

"For a few years. Then she died when I was fifteen. Her heart. Not real sudden. Not real slow, either. After that, I was made a ward of the court. I spent the next three years, until I was eighteen, in a series of foster homes. Four of them, in all. I never got close to any of my foster parents; I never allowed myself to get close. I kept asking to be transferred, see. Because by then, even as young as I was, I realized that loving people, depending on them, *needing* them, is just too dangerous. Love is just a way to set you up for a bad fall. It's the rug they pull out from under you at the very moment you finally decide that everything's going to be fine. We're all so ephemeral. So fragile. And life's so unpredictable."

"But that's no reason to insist on going it alone," Jack said. "In fact, don't you see—that's the reason we *must* find people to love, people to share our lives with, to open our hearts and minds to, people to depend on, cherish, people who'll depend on us when *they* need to know they're not alone. Caring for your friends and family, knowing they care for you—that's what keeps our minds off the void that waits for all of us. By loving and letting ourselves be loved, we give meaning and importance to our lives; it's what keeps us from being just another species of the animal kingdom, grubbing for survival. At least for a short while, through love, we can forget about the goddamned darkness at the end of everything."

He was breathless when he finished—and astonished by what he had said, startled that such an understanding had been in him.

She slipped an arm across his chest. She held him fast.

She said, "You're right. A part of me knows that what you've said is true."

"Good."

"But there's another part of me that's afraid of letting myself love or be loved, ever again. The part that can't bear losing it all again. The part that thinks loneliness is preferable to that kind of loss and pain."

"But see, that's just it. Love given or love taken is *never* lost," he said, holding her. "Once you've loved someone, the love is always there, even after they're gone. Love is the only thing that endures. Mountains are torn down, built up, torn down again over millions and millions of years. Seas dry up. Deserts give way to new seas. Time crumbles every building man erects. Great ideas are proven wrong and collapse as surely as castles and temples. But love is a force, an energy, a power. At the risk of sounding like a Hallmark card, I think love is like a ray of sunlight, traveling for all eternity through space, deeper and deeper into infinity; like that ray of light, it never ceases to exist. Love endures. It's a binding force in the universe, like the energy within a molecule is a binding force, as surely as gravity is a binding force. Without the cohesive energy in a molecule, without gravity, without *love*—chaos. We exist to love and be loved, because love seems to me to be the only thing that brings order and meaning and light to existence. It must be true. Because if it isn't true, what purpose *do* we serve? Because if it isn't true—God help us."

For minutes, they lay in silence, touching.

Jack was exhausted by the flood of words and feelings that had rushed from him, almost without his volition.

He desperately wanted Rebecca to be with him for the rest of his life. He dreaded losing her.

But he said no more. The decision was hers.

After a while she said, "For the first time in ages, I'm not so afraid of loving and losing; I'm more afraid of not loving at all."

Jack's heart lifted.

He said, "Don't ever freeze me out again."

"It won't be easy learning to open up."

"You can do it."

"I'm sure I'll backslide occasionally, withdraw from you a little bit, now and then. You'll have to be patient with me."

"I can be patient."

"God, don't I know it! You're the most infuriatingly patient man I've ever known."

"Infuriatingly?"

"There've been times, at work, when I've been so incredibly bitchy, and I knew it, didn't want to be but couldn't seem to help myself. I wished, sometimes, you'd snap back at me, blow up at me. But when you finally responded, you were always so reasonable, so calm, so damned patient."

"You make me sound too saintly."

"Well, you're a good man, Jack Dawson. A nice man. A damned nice man."

"Oh, I know, to you I seem perfect," he said self-mockingly. "But believe it or not, even I, paragon that I am, even *I* have a few faults."

"No!" she said, pretending astonishment.

"It's true."

"Name one."

"I actually like to listen to Barry Manilow."

"No!"

"Oh, I know his music's slick, too smooth, a little plastic. But it sounds good, anyway. I like it. And another thing. I *don't* like Alan Alda."

"Everyone likes Alan Alda!"

"I think he's a phony."

"You disgusting fiend!"

"And I like peanut butter and onion sandwiches."

"Ach! *Alan Alda* wouldn't eat peanut butter and onion sandwiches."

"But I have one great virtue that more than makes up for all of those terrible faults," he said.

She grinned. "What's that?"

"I love you."

This time, she didn't ask him to refrain from saying it.

She kissed him.

Her hands moved over him.

She said, "Make love to me again."

XII

ORDINARILY, NO MATTER how late Davey was allowed to stay up, Penny was permitted one more hour than he was. Being the last to bed was her just due, by virtue of her four-year age advantage over him. She always fought valiantly and tenaciously at the first sign of any attempt to deny her this precious and inalienable right. Tonight, however, at nine o'clock, when Aunt Faye suggested that Davey brush his teeth and hit the sack, Penny feigned sleepiness and said that she, too, was ready to call it a night.

She couldn't leave Davey alone in a dark bedroom where the goblins might creep up on him. She would have to stay awake, watching over him, until their father arrived. Then she would tell Daddy all about the goblins and hope that he would at least hear her out before he sent for the men with the straitjackets.

She and Davey had come to the Jamisons' without overnight bags, but they had no difficulty getting ready for bed. Because they occasionally stayed with Faye and Keith when their father had to work late, they kept spare toothbrushes and pajamas here. And in the guest bedroom closet, there were fresh changes of clothes for them, so they wouldn't have to wear the same thing tomorrow that they'd worn today. In ten minutes, they were comfortably nestled in the twin beds, under the covers.

Aunt Faye wished them sweet dreams, turned out the light, and closed the door.

The darkness was thick, smothering.

Penny fought off an attack of claustrophobia.

Davey was silent awhile. Then: "Penny?"

"Huh?"

"You there?"

"Who do you think just said 'huh?' "

"Where's Dad?"

"Working late."

"I mean . . . really."

"Really working late."

"What if he's been hurt?"

"He hasn't."

"What if he got shot?"

"He didn't. They'd have told us if he'd been shot. They'd probably even take us to the hospital to see him."

"No, they wouldn't, either. They try to protect kids from bad news like that."

"Will you stop worrying, for God's sake? Dad's all right. If he'd been shot or anything, Aunt Faye and Uncle Keith would know all about it."

"But maybe they *do* know."

"We'd know if they knew."

"How?"

"They'd show it, even if they were trying hard not to."

"How would they show it?"

"They'd have treated us different. They'd have acted strange."

"They *always* act strange."

"I mean strange in a different sort of way. They'd have been especially nice to us. They'd have pampered us because they'd have felt sorry for us. And do you think Aunt Faye would have criticized Daddy all evening, the way she did, if she'd known he was shot and in a hospital somewhere?"

"Well . . . no. I guess you're right. Not even Aunt Faye would do that."

They were silent.

Penny lay with her head propped up on the pillow, listening.

Nothing to be heard. Just the wind outside. Far off, the grumble of a snowplow.

She looked at the window, a rectangle of vague snowy luminosity.

Would the goblins come through the window?

The door?

Maybe they'd come out of a crack in the baseboard, come in the form of smoke and then solidify when they had completely seeped into the room. Vampires did that sort of thing. She'd seen it happen in an old Dracula movie.

Or maybe they'd come out of the closet.

She looked toward the darkest end of the room, where the closet was. She couldn't see it; only blackness.

Maybe there was a magical, invisible tunnel at the back of the closet, a tunnel that only goblins could see and use.

That was ridiculous. Or was it? The very idea of goblins was ridiculous, too; yet they were out there; she'd seen them.

Davey's breathing became deep and slow and rhythmic. He was asleep.

Penny envied him. She knew she'd never sleep again.

Time passed. Slowly.

Her gaze moved around and around the dark room. The window. The door. The closet. The window.

She didn't know where the goblins would come from, but she knew, without doubt, that they *would* come.

XIII

LAVELLE SAT IN his dark bedroom.

The additional assassins had risen out of the pit and had crept off into the night, into the storm-lashed city. Soon, both of the Dawson children would be slaughtered, reduced to nothing more than bloody mounds of dead meat.

That thought pleased and excited Lavelle. It even gave him an erection.

The rituals had drained him. Not physically or mentally. He felt alert, fresh, strong. But his *Bocor*'s power had been depleted, and it was time to replenish it. At the moment, he was a *Bocor* in name only; drained like this, he was really just a man—and he didn't like being just a man.

Embraced by the darkness, he reached upward with his mind, up through the ceiling, through the roof of the house, through the snow-filled air, up toward the rivers of evil energy that flowed across the great city. He carefully avoided those currents of benign energy that also surged through the night, for they were of no use whatsoever to him; indeed, they posed a danger to him. He tapped into the darkest, foulest of those ethereal waters and let them pour down into him, until his own reservoirs were full once more.

In minutes he was reborn. Now he was more than a man. Less than a god, yes. But much, much more than just a man.

He had one more act of sorcery to perform this night, and he was happily anticipating it. He was going to humble Jack Dawson. At last he was going to make Dawson understand how awesome was the power of a masterful *Bocor*. Then, when Dawson's children were exterminated, the detective would understand how foolish he had been to put them at such risk, to defy a *Bocor*. He would see how easily he could have saved them—simply by swallowing his pride and walking away from the investigation. Then it would be clear to the detective that he, himself, had signed his own children's death warrants, and *that* terrible realization would shatter him.

XIV

PENNY SAT STRAIGHT up in bed and almost shouted for Aunt Faye.

She had heard something. A strange, shrill cry. It wasn't human. Faint. Far away. Maybe in another apartment, several floors farther down in the building. The cry seemed to have come to her through the heating ducts.

She waited tensely. A minute. Two minutes. Three.

The cry wasn't repeated. There were no other unnatural sounds, either.

But she knew what she had heard and what it meant. They were coming for her and Davey. They were on their way now. Soon, they would be here.

XV

THIS TIME, THEIR love-making was slow, lazy, achingly tender, filled with much nuzzling and wordless murmuring and soft-soft stroking. A series of dreamy sensations: a feeling of floating, a feeling of being composed only of sunlight and other energy, an exhilaratingly weightless tumbling, tumbling. This time, it was not so much an act of sex as it was an act of emotional bonding, a spiritual pledge made with the flesh. And when, at last, Jack spurted deep within her velvet recesses, he felt as if he were fusing with her, melting into her, becoming one with her, and he sensed that she felt the same thing.

"That was wonderful."

"Perfect."

"Better than a peanut butter and onion sandwich?"

"Almost."

"You bastard."

"Hey, peanut butter and onion sandwiches are pretty darned terrific, you know!"

"I love you," he said.

"I'm glad," she said.

That was an improvement.

She still couldn't bring herself to say she loved him, too. But he wasn't particularly bothered by that. He knew she did.

He was sitting on the edge of the bed, dressing.

She was standing on the other side of the bed, slipping into her blue robe.

Both of them were startled by a sudden violent movement. A framed poster from a Jasper Johns art exhibition tore loose of its mountings and flew off the wall. It was a large poster, three-and-a-half-feet-by-two-and-a-half-feet, framed behind glass. It seemed to hang in the air for a moment, vibrating, and then it struck the floor at the foot of the bed with a tremendous crash.

"What the hell!" Jack said.

"What could've done that?" Rebecca said.

The sliding closet door flew open with a bang, slammed shut, flew open again.

The six-drawer highboy tipped away from the wall, toppled toward Jack, and he jumped out of the way, and the big piece of furniture hit the floor with the sound of a bomb explosion.

Rebecca backed against the wall and stood there, rigid and wide-eyed, her hands fisted at her sides.

The air was cold. Wind whirled through the room. Not just a draft, but a wind almost as powerful as the one that whipped through the city streets, outside. Yet there was nowhere that a cold wind could have gained admission; the door and the window were closed tight.

And now, at the window, it seemed as if invisible hands grabbed the drapes and tore them loose of the rod from which they were hung. The drapes dropped in a heap, and then the rod itself was torn out of the wall and thrown aside.

Drawers slid all the way out of the nightstands and fell onto the floor, spilling their contents.

Several strips of wallpaper began to peel off the walls, starting at the top and going down.

Jack turned this way and that, frightened, confused, not sure what he should do.

The dresser mirror cracked in a spiderweb pattern.

The unseen presence stripped the blanket from the bed and pitched it onto the toppled highboy.

"Stop it!" Rebecca shouted at the empty air. *"Stop it!"*

The unseen intruder did not obey.

The top sheet was pulled from the bed. It whirled into the air, as if it had been granted life and the ability to fly; it floated off into a corner of the room, where it collapsed, lifeless again.

The fitted bottom sheet popped loose at two corners.

Jack grabbed it.

The other two corners came loose, as well.

Jack tried to hold on to the sheet. It was a feeble and pointless effort to resist whatever power was wrecking the room, but it was the only thing he could think to do, and he simply *had* to do something. The sheet was quickly wrenched out of his hands with such force that he was thrown off balance. He stumbled and fell to his knees.

On a wheeled TV stand in the corner, the portable television set snapped on of its own accord, the volume booming. A fat woman was dancing the cha-cha with a cat, and a thunderous chorus was singing the praises of Purina Cat Chow.

Jack scrambled to his feet.

The mattress cover was skinned off the bed, lifted into the air, rolled into a ball, and thrown at Rebecca.

On the TV, George Plimpton was shouting like a baboon about the virtues of Intellivision.

The mattress was bare now. The quilted sheath dimpled; a rent appeared in it. The fabric tore right down the middle, from top to bottom, and stuffing erupted along with a few uncoiling springs that rose like cobras to an unheard music.

More wallpaper peeled down.

On the TV, a barker for the American Beef Council was shouting about the benefits of eating meat, while an unseen chef carved a bloody roast on camera.

The closet door slammed so hard that it jumped partially out of its track and rattled back and forth.

The TV screen imploded. Simultaneously with the sound of breaking glass, there was a brief flash of light within the guts of the set, and then a little smoke.

Silence.

Stillness.

Jack glanced at Rebecca.

She looked bewildered. And terrified.

The telephone rang.

The instant Jack heard it, he knew who was calling. He snatched up the receiver, held it to his ear, said nothing.

"You're panting like a dog, Detective Dawson," Lavelle said. "Excited? Evidently, my little demonstration thrilled you."

Jack was shaking so badly and uncontrollably that he didn't trust his voice. He didn't reply because he didn't want Lavelle to hear how scared he was.

Besides, Lavelle didn't seem interested in anything Jack might have to say; he didn't wait long enough to hear a reply even if one had been offered. The *Bocor* said, "When you see your kids—dead, mangled, their eyes torn out, their lips eaten off, their fingers bitten to the bone—remember that you could have saved them. Remember that you're the one who signed their death warrants. You bear the responsibility for their deaths as surely as if you'd seen them walking in front of a train and didn't even bother to call out a warning to them. You threw away their lives as if they were nothing but garbage to you."

A torrent of words spewed from Jack before he even realized he was going to speak: "You fucking sleazy son of a bitch, you'd better not touch one hair on them! You'd better not—"

Lavelle had hung up.

Rebecca said, "Who—"

"Lavelle."

"You mean . . . all of this?"

"You believe in black magic now? Sorcery? Voodoo?"

"Oh, my God."

"*I* sure as hell believe in it now."

She looked around at the demolished room, shaking her head, trying without success to deny the evidence before her eyes.

Jack remembered his own skepticism when Carver Hampton had told him about the falling bottles and the black serpent. No skepticism now. Only terror now.

He thought of the bodies he had seen this morning and this afternoon, those hideously ravaged corpses.

His heart jackhammered. He was short of breath. He felt as if he might vomit.

He still had the phone in his hand. He punched out a number.

Rebecca said, "Who're you calling?"

"Faye. She's got to get the kids out of there, fast."

"But Lavelle can't know where they are."

"He couldn't have known where *I* was, either. I didn't tell anyone I was coming to see you. I wasn't followed here; I'm sure I wasn't. He couldn't have known where to find me—and yet he *knew.* So he probably knows where to find the kids, too. Damnit, why isn't it ringing?"

He rattled the telephone buttons, got another dial tone, tried Faye's number again. This time he got a recording telling him that her phone was no longer in service. Not true, of course.

"Somehow, Lavelle's screwed up Faye's line," he said, dropping the receiver. "We've got to get over there right away. Jesus, we've got to get the kids out!"

Rebecca had stripped off her robe, had yanked a pair of jeans and a pull-over sweater from the closet. She was already half dressed.

"Don't worry," she said. "It'll be all right. We'll get to them before Lavelle does."

But Jack had the sickening feeling that they were already too late.

CHAPTER 5

I

AGAIN, SITTING ALONE in his dark bedroom, with only the phosphoric light of the snowstorm piercing the windows, Lavelle reached up with his mind and tapped the psychic rivers of malignant energy that coursed through the night above the city.

His sorceror's power was not only depleted this time but utterly exhausted. Calling forth a poltergeist and maintaining control over it—as he had done in order to arrange the demonstration for Jack Dawson a few minutes ago—was one of the most draining of all the rituals of black magic.

Unfortunately, it wasn't possible to use a poltergeist to destroy one's enemies. Poltergeists were merely mischievous—at worst, nasty—spirits; they were not evil. If a *Bocor,* having conjured up such an entity, attempted to employ it to murder someone, it would then be able to break free of his controlling spell and turn its energies upon him.

However, when used only as a tool to exhibit a *Bocor*'s powers, a poltergeist produced impressive results. Skeptics were transformed into believers. The bold were made meek. After witnessing the work of a poltergeist, those who were already believers in voodoo and the supernatural were humbled, frightened, and reduced to obedient servants, pitifully eager to do whatever a *Bocor* demanded of them.

Lavelle's rocking chair creaked in the quiet room.

In the darkness, he smiled and smiled.

From the night sky, malignant energy poured down.

Lavelle, the vessel, was soon overflowing with power.

He sighed, for he was renewed.

Before long, the fun would begin.

The slaughter.

II

PENNY SAT ON the edge of her bed, listening.

The sounds came again. Scraping, hissing. A soft thump, a faint clink, and again a thump. A far-off, rattling, shuffling noise.

Far off—but getting closer.

She snapped on the bedside lamp. The small pool of light was warm and welcome.

Davey remained asleep, undisturbed by the peculiar sounds. She decided to let him go on sleeping for the time being. She could wake him quickly if she had to, and one scream would bring Aunt Faye and Uncle Keith.

The raspy cry came again, faint, though perhaps not quite as faint as it had been before.

Penny got up from the bed, went to the dresser, which lay in shadows, beyond the fan of light from her nightstand lamp. In the wall above the dresser, approximately a foot below the ceiling, was a vent for the heating and air-conditioning systems. She cocked her head, trying to hear the distant and furtive noises, and she became convinced that they were being transmitted through the ducts in the walls.

She climbed onto the dresser, but the vent was still almost a foot above her head. She climbed down. She fetched her pillow from the bed and put it on the dresser. She took the thick seat cushions from the two chairs that flanked the window, and she piled those atop her bed pillow. She felt very clever and capable. Once on the dresser again, she stretched, rose up onto her toes, and was able to put her ear against the vent plate that covered the outlet from the ventilation system.

She had thought the goblins were in other apartments or common hallways, farther down in the building; she had thought the ducts were only carrying the sound of them. Now, with a jolt, she realized the ducts were carrying not merely the sound of the goblins but the goblins themselves. *This* was how they intended to get into the bedroom, not through the door or window, not through some imaginary tunnel in the back of the closet. They were in the ventilation network, making their way up through the building, twisting and turning, slithering and creeping, hurrying along the horizontal pipes, climbing laboriously through the vertical sections of the system, but steadily rising nearer and nearer as surely as the warm air was rising from the huge furnace below.

Trembling, teeth chattering, gripped by fear to which she *refused* to succumb, Penny put her face to the vent plate and peered through the slots, into the duct beyond. The darkness in there was as deep and as black and as smooth as the darkness in a tomb.

III

JACK HUNCHED OVER the wheel, squinting at the wintry street ahead.

The windshield was icing up. A thin, milky skin of ice had formed around the edges of the glass and was creeping inward. The wipers were caked with snow that was steadily compacting into lumps of ice.

"Is that damned defroster on full-blast?" he asked, even though he could feel the waves of heat washing up into his face.

Rebecca leaned forward and checked the heater controls. "Full-blast," she affirmed.

"Temperature sure dropped once it got dark."

"Must be ten degrees out there. Colder, if you figure in the wind-chill factor."

Trains of snowplows moved along the main avenues, but they were having difficulty getting the upper hand on the blizzard. Snow was falling in blinding sheets, so thick it obscured everything beyond the distance of one block. Worse, the fierce wind piled the snow in drifts that began to form again and reclaim the pavement only minutes after the plows had scraped it clean.

Jack had expected to make a fast trip to the Jamisons' apartment building. The streets held little or no traffic to get in his way. Furthermore, although his car was unmarked, it had a siren. And he had clamped the detachable red emergency beacon to the metal beading at the edge of the roof, thereby insuring right-of-way over what other traffic there was. He had expected to be holding Penny and Davey in his arms in ten minutes. Now, clearly, the trip was going to take twice that long.

Every time he tried to put on a little speed, the car started to slide, in spite of the snow chains on the tires.

"We could *walk* faster than this!" Jack said ferociously.

"We'll get there in time," Rebecca said.

"What if Lavelle is already there?"

"He's not. Of course he's not."

And then a terrible thought rocked him, and he didn't want to put it into words, but he couldn't stop himself: "What if he *called* from the Jamisons'?"

"He didn't," she said.

But Jack was abruptly obsessed with that horrendous possibility, and he could not control the morbid compulsion to say it aloud, even though the words brought hideous images to him.

"What if he killed all of them—"

(Mangled bodies.)

"—killed Penny and Davey—"

(Eyeballs torn from sockets.)

"—killed Faye and Keith—"

(Throats chewed open.)

"—and then called from right *there*—"

(Fingertips bitten off.)

"—called me from right there in the apartment, for Christ's sake—"

(Lips torn, ears hanging loose.)

"—while he was standing over their bodies!"

She had been trying to interrupt him. Now she shouted at him: "Stop torturing yourself, Jack! We'll make it in time."

"How the hell do you know we'll make it in time?" he demanded angrily, not sure why he was angry with her, just striking out at her because she was a convenient target, because he couldn't strike out at Lavelle or at the weather that was hindering him, and because he *had* to strike out at someone, something, or go absolutely crazy from the tension that was building in him like excess current flowing into an already overcharged battery. "You can't *know*!"

"I know," she insisted calmly. "Just drive."

"Goddamnit, stop patronizing me!"

"Jack—"

"He's got my kids!"

He accelerated too abruptly, and the car immediately began to slide toward the right-hand curb.

He tried to correct their course by pulling on the steering wheel, instead of going along with the slide and turning into the direction of it, and even as he realized his mistake the car started to spin, and for a moment they were traveling sideways—and Jack had the gutwrenching feeling that they were going to slam into the curb at high speed, tip, and roll over—but even as they continued to slide they also continued to swing around on their axis until they were completely reversed from where they had been, a full one hundred and eighty degrees, half the circumference of a circle, now sliding backwards along the street, looking out the icy windshield at where they had been instead of at where they were going, and still they turned, turned like a carousel, until at last the car stopped just short of one entire revolution.

With a shudder engendered by a mental image of what might have happened to them, but aware that he couldn't waste time dwelling on their close escape, Jack started up again. He handled the wheel with even greater caution than before, and he pressed his foot lightly and slowly down on the accelerator.

Neither he nor Rebecca spoke during the wild spin, not even to cry out in surprise or fear, and neither of them spoke for the next block, either.

Then he said, "I'm sorry."

"Don't be."

"I shouldn't have snapped at you like that."

"I understand. You were crazy with worry."

"Still am. No excuse. That was stupid of me. I won't be able to help the kids if I kill us before we ever get to Faye's place."

"I understand what you're going through," she said again, softer than before. "It's all right. And everything'll *be* all right, too."

He knew that she *did* understand all the complex thoughts and emotions that were churning through him and nearly tearing him apart. She understood him better than just a friend could have understood, better than just a lover. They were more than merely compatible; in their thoughts and perceptions and feelings, they were in perfect sympathy, physically and psychologically synchronous. It had been a long time since he'd had anyone that close, that much a part of him. Eighteen months, in fact. Since Linda's death. Not so long, perhaps, considering he had never expected it to happen again. It was good not to be alone any more.

"Almost there, aren't we?" she asked.

"Two or three minutes," he said, hunching over the wheel, peering ahead nervously at the slick, snowy street.

The windshield wipers, thickly crusted with ice, grated noisily back and forth, cleaning less and less of the glass with each swipe they took at it.

IV

LAVELLE GOT UP from his rocking chair.

The time had come to establish psychic bonds with the small assassins that had come out of the pit and were now stalking the Dawson children.

Without turning on any lights, Lavelle went to the dresser, opened one of the top drawers, and withdrew a fistful of silk ribbons. He went to the bed, put the ribbons down, and stripped out of his clothes. Nude, he sat on the edge of the bed and tied a purple ribbon to his right ankle, a white one to his left ankle. Even in the dark, he had no difficulty discerning one color from another. He tied a long scarlet ribbon around his chest, directly over his heart. Yellow around his forehead. Green around his right wrist; black around his left wrist. The ribbons were symbolic ties that would help to put him in intimate contact with the killers from the pit, as soon as he finished the ritual now begun.

It was not his intention to take control of those demonic entities and direct their every move; he couldn't have done so, even if that *was* what he wanted. Once summoned from the pit and sent after their prey, the assassins followed their own whims and strategies until they had dealt with the intended victims; then, murder done, they were compelled to return to the pit. That was all the control he had over them.

The point of this ritual with the ribbons was merely to enable Lavelle to participate, first-hand, in the thrill of the slaughter. Psychically linked to the assassins, he would see through their eyes, hear with their ears, and feel with their golem bodies. When their razor-edged claws slashed at Davey Dawson, Lavelle would feel the boy's flesh rending in his own hands. When their teeth chewed open Penny's jugular, Lavelle would feel her warm throat against his own lips, too, and would taste the coppery sweetness of her blood.

The thought of it made him tremble with excitement.

And if Lavelle had timed it right, Jack Dawson would be there in the Jamison apartment when his children were torn to pieces. The detective ought to arrive just in time to see the horde descend on Penny and Davey. Although he would try to save them, he would discover that the small assassins couldn't be driven back or killed. He would be forced to stand there, powerless, while his children's precious blood spattered over him.

That was the best part.

Yes. Oh, yes.

Lavelle sighed.

He shivered with anticipation.

The small bottle of cat's blood was on the nightstand. He wet two fingertips in it, made a crimson spot on each cheek, wet his fingers again, anointed his lips. Then, still using blood, he drew a very simple *vèvè* on his bare chest.

He stretched out on the bed, on his back.

Staring at the ceiling, he began to chant quietly.

Soon, he was transported in mind and spirit. The real psychic links, which the ribbons symbolized, were successfully achieved, and he was with the demonic entities in the ventilation system of the Jamisons' apartment building. The creatures were only two turns and perhaps twenty feet away from the end of the duct, where it terminated in the wall of the guest bedroom.

The children were near.

The girl was the nearer of the two.

Like the small assassins, Lavelle could sense her presence. Close. Very close. Only another bend in the pipe, then a straightaway, then a final bend.

Close.

The time had come.

V

STANDING ON THE dresser, peering into the duct, Penny heard a voice calling out from within the wall, from another part of the ventilation system, but not far away now. It was a brittle, whispery, cold, hoarse voice that turned her blood to icy slush in her veins. It said, *"Penny? Penny?"*

She almost fell in her haste to get down from the dresser.

She ran to Davey, grabbed him, shook him. "Wake up! Davey, wake up!"

He hadn't been asleep long, no more than fifteen minutes, but he was nevertheless groggy. "Huh? Whaa?"

"They're coming," she said. "They're coming. We've got to get dressed and get out of here. Fast. *They're coming!"*

She screamed for Aunt Faye.

VI

THE JAMISONS' APARTMENT was in a twelve-story building on a cross street that hadn't yet been plowed. The street was mantled with six inches of snow. Jack drove slowly forward and had no trouble for about twenty yards, but then the wheels sank into a hidden drift that had completely filled in a dip in the pavement. For a moment he thought they were stuck, but he threw the car into reverse and then forward and then reverse and then forward again, rocking it, until it broke free. Two-thirds of the way down the block, he tapped the brakes, and the car slid to a stop in front of the right building.

He flung open the door and scrambled out of the car. An arctic wind hit him with sledgehammer force. He put his head down and staggered around the front of the car, onto the sidewalk, barely able to see as the wind picked up crystals of snow from the ground and sprayed them in his face.

By the time Jack climbed the steps and pushed through the glass doors, into the lobby, Rebecca was already there. Flashing her badge and photo ID at the startled doorman, she said, "Police."

He was a stout man, about fifty, with hair as white as the snow outside. He was sitting at a Sheraton desk near the pair of elevators, drinking coffee and taking shelter from the storm. He must have been a day-shift man, filling in for the regular night-shift man (or perhaps new) because Jack had never seen him on the evenings when he'd come here to pick up the kids.

"What is it?" the doorman asked. "What's wrong?"

This wasn't the kind of building where people were accustomed to anything being wrong; it was first-class all the way, and the mere prospect of trouble was sufficient to cause the doorman's face to turn nearly as pale as his hair.

Jack punched the elevator call button and said, "We're going up to the Jamisons' apartment. Eleventh floor."

"I know which floor they're on," the doorman said, flustered, getting up so quickly that he bumped the desk and almost knocked over his coffee cup. "But why—"

One set of elevator doors opened.

Jack and Rebecca stepped into the cab.

Jack shouted back to the doorman: "Bring a passkey! I hope to God we don't need it."

Because if we need it, he thought, that'll mean no one's left alive in the apartment to let us in.

The lift doors shut. The cab started up.

Jack reached inside his overcoat, drew his revolver.

Rebecca pulled her gun, too.

Above the doors, the panel of lighted numbers indicated that they had reached the third floor.

"Guns didn't help Dominick Carramazza," Jack said shakily, staring at the Smith & Wesson in his hand.

Fourth floor.

"We won't need guns anyway," Rebecca said. "We've gotten here ahead of Lavelle. I know we have."

But the conviction had gone out of her voice.

Jack knew why. The journey from her apartment had taken forever. It seemed less and less likely that they were going to be in time.

Sixth floor.

"Why're the elevators so goddamned slow in this building?" Jack demanded.

Seventh floor.

Eighth.

Ninth.

"Move, damnit!" he commanded the lift machinery, as if he thought it would actually speed up if he ordered it to do so.

Tenth floor.

Eleventh.

At last the doors slid open, and Jack stepped through them.

Rebecca followed close behind.

The eleventh floor was so quiet and looked so ordinary that Jack was tempted to hope.

Please, God, please.

There were seven apartments on this floor. The Jamisons had one of the two front units.

Jack went to their door and stood to one side of it. His right arm was bent and tucked close against his side, and the revolver was in his right hand, held close to his face, the muzzle pointed straight up at the ceiling for the moment, but ready to be brought into play in an instant.

Rebecca stood on the other side, directly opposite him, in a similar posture.

Let them be alive. Please. Please.

His eyes met Rebecca's. She nodded. Ready.

Jack pounded on the door.

VII

IN THE SHADOW-CROWDED room, on the bed, Lavelle breathed deeply and rapidly. In fact, he was panting like an animal.

His hands were curled at his sides, fingers hooked and rigid, as if they were talons. For the most part, his hands were still, but now and then they erupted in sudden violent movement, striking at the empty air or clawing frantically at the sheets.

He shivered almost continuously. Once in a while, he jerked and twitched as if an electric current had snapped through him; on these occasions, his entire body heaved up, off the bed, and slammed back down, making the mattress springs squeal in protest.

Deep in a trance, he was unaware of these spasms.

He stared straight up, eyes wide, seldom blinking, but he wasn't seeing the ceiling or anything else in the room. He was viewing other places, in another part of the city, where his vision was held captive by the eager pack of small assassins with which he had established psychic contact.

He hissed.

Groaned.

Gnashed his teeth.

He jerked, flopped, twisted.

Then lay silent, still.

Then clawed the sheets.

He hissed so forcefully that he sprayed spittle into the dark air around him.

His legs suddenly became possessed. He drummed his heels furiously upon the mattress.

He growled in the back of his throat.

He lay silent for a while.

Then he began to pant. He sniffed. Hissed again.

He smelled the girl. Penny Dawson. She had a wonderful scent. Sweet. Young. Fresh. Tender.

He wanted her.

VIII

FAYE OPENED THE door, saw Jack's revolver, gave him a startled look, and said, "My God, what's that for? What're you doing? You know how I hate guns. Put that thing away."

From Faye's demeanor as she stepped back to let them in, Jack knew the kids were all right, and he sagged a little with relief. But he said, "Where's Penny? Where's Davey? Are they okay?"

Faye glanced at Rebecca and started to smile, then realized what Jack was saying, frowned at him, and said, "Okay? Well, of course, they're okay. They're perfectly fine. I might not have kids of my own, but I know how to take care of them. You think I'd let anything happen to those two little monkeys? For heaven's sake, Jack, I don't—"

"Did anyone try to follow you back here from the school?" he asked urgently.

"And just what was all that nonsense about, anyway?" Faye demanded.

"It wasn't nonsense. I thought I made that clear. Did anyone try to follow you? You *did* look out for a tail, like I told you to—didn't you, Faye?"

"Sure, sure, sure. I looked. No one tried to follow me. And I don't think—"

They had moved out of the foyer, into the living room, while they had been talking. Jack looked around, didn't see the kids.

He said, "Faye, where the hell are they?"

"Don't take that tone, for goodness sake. What are you—"

"Faye, damnit!"

She recoiled from him. "They're in the guest room. With Keith," she said, quickly and irritably. "They were put to bed at about a quarter past nine, just as they should have been, and we thought they were just about sound asleep when all of a sudden Penny screamed—"

"Screamed?"

"—and said there were rats in their room. Well, of course, we don't have any—"

Rats!

Jack bolted across the living room, hurried along the short hall, and burst into the guest room.

The bedside lamps, the standing lamp in the corner, and the ceiling light were all blazing.

Penny and Davey were standing at the foot of one of the twin beds, still in their pajamas. When they saw Jack, they cried out happily—"Daddy! Daddy!"—and ran to him, hugged him.

Jack was so overwhelmed at finding them alive and unhurt, so grateful, that for a moment he couldn't speak. He just grabbed hold of them and held them very tightly.

In spite of all the lights in the room, Keith Jamison was holding a flashlight. He was over by the dresser, holding the flash above his head, directing the beam into the darkness beyond the vent plate that covered the outlet in the heating duct. He turned to Jack, frowning, and said, "Something odd's going on here. I—"

"Goblins!" Penny said, clutching Jack. "They're coming, Daddy, they want me and Davey, don't let them, don't let them get us, oh please, I've been waiting for them, waiting and waiting, scared, and now they're almost here!" The words tumbled over one another, flooding out of her, and then she sobbed.

"Whoa," Jack said, holding her close and petting her, smoothing her hair. "Easy now. Easy."

Faye and Rebecca had followed him from the living room.

Rebecca was being her usual cool, efficient self. She was at the bedroom closet, getting the kids' clothes off hangers.

Faye said, "First, Penny shouted that there were rats in her room, and then she started carrying on about goblins, nearly hysterical. I tried to tell her it was only a nightmare—"

"It *wasn't* a nightmare!" Penny shouted.

"Of course it was," Faye said.

"They've been watching me all day," Penny said. "And there was one of them in our room last night, Daddy. And in the school basement today—a whole bunch of them. They chewed up Davey's lunch. And my books, too. I don't know what they want, but they're after us, and they're goblins, real goblins, I swear!"

"Okay," Jack said. "I want to hear all of this, every detail. But later. Now, we have to get out of here."

Rebecca brought their clothes.

Jack said, "Get dressed. Don't bother taking off your pajamas. Just put your clothes on over them."

Faye said, "What on earth—"

"We've got to get the kids out of here," Jack said. "Fast."

"But you act as if you actually believe this goblin talk," Faye said, astonished.

Keith said, "I sure don't believe in goblins, but I sure *do* believe we have some rats."

"No, no, no," Faye said, scandalized. "We can't. Not in *this* building."

"In the ventilation system," Keith said. "I heard them myself. That's why I was trying to see in there with the flashlight when you came busting in, Jack."

"*Sssshhh,*" Rebecca said. "Listen."

The kids continued to get dressed, but no one spoke.

At first Jack heard nothing. Then . . . a peculiar hissing-muttering-growling.

That's no damned rat, he thought.

Inside the wall, something rattled. Then a scratching sound, a furious scrabbling. Industrious noises: clinking, tapping, scraping, thumping.

Faye said, "My God."

Jack took the flashlight from Keith, went to the dresser, pointed the light at the duct. The beam was bright and tightly focused, but it did little to dispel the blackness that pooled beyond the slots in the vent plate.

Another thump in the wall.

More hissing and muted growling.

Jack felt a prickling along the back of his neck.

Then, incredibly, a voice came out of the duct. It was a hoarse, crackling, utterly inhuman voice, thick with menace: *"Penny? Davey? Penny?"*

Faye cried out and stumbled back a couple of steps.

Even Keith, who was a big and rather formidable man, went pale and moved away from the vent. "What the devil was *that?*"

To Faye, Jack said, "Where're the kids' coats and boots? Their gloves?"

"Uh . . . in . . . in the kitchen. D-Drying out."

"Get them."

Faye nodded but didn't move.

Jack put a hand on her shoulder. "Get their coats and boots and gloves, then meet us by the front door."

She couldn't take her eyes off the vent.

He shook her. "Faye! Hurry!"

She jumped as if he'd slapped her face, turned, and ran out of the bedroom.

Penny was almost dressed, and she was holding up remarkably well, scared but in control. Davey was sitting on the edge of the bed, trying not to cry, crying anyway, wiping at the tears on his face, glancing apologetically at Penny and biting his lip and trying very hard to follow her example; his legs were dangling over the side of the bed, and Rebecca was hastily tying his shoes for him.

From the vent: *"Davey? Penny?"*

"Jack, for Christ's sake, what's going on here?" Keith asked.

Not bothering to respond, having no time or patience for questions and answers just now, Jack pointed the flashlight at the vent again and glimpsed movement in the duct. Something silvery lay in there; it glowed and flickered like a white-hot fire—then blinked and was gone. In its place, something dark appeared, shifted, pushed against the vent plate for a moment, as if trying hard to dislodge it, then withdrew when the plate held. Jack couldn't see enough of the creature to get a clear idea of its general appearance.

Keith said, "Jack. The vent screw."

Jack had already seen it. The screw was revolving, slowly coming out of the edge of the vent plate. The creature inside the duct was turning the screw, unfastening it from the other side of the flange to which the plate was attached. The thing was muttering, hissing, and grumbling softly while it worked.

"Let's go," Jack said, striving to keep his voice calm. "Come on, come on. Let's get out of here right now."

The screw popped loose. The vent plate swung down, away from the ventilation outlet, hanging from the one remaining screw.

Rebecca hustled the kids toward the door.

A nightmare crawled out of the duct. It hung there on the wall, with utter disregard for gravity, as if there were suction pads on its feet, although it didn't seem equipped with anything of that sort.

"Jesus," Keith said, stunned.

Jack shuddered at the thought of this repulsive little beast touching Davey or Penny.

The creature was the size of a rat. In shape, at least, its body was rather like that of a rat, too: low-slung, long in the flanks, with shoulders and haunches that were large and muscular for an animal of its size. But there the resemblance to a rat ended, and the nightmare began. This thing was hairless. Its slippery skin was darkly mottled gray-green-yellow and looked more like a slimy fungus than like flesh. The tail was not at all similar to a rat's tail; it was eight or ten inches long, an inch wide at the base, segmented in the manner of a scorpion's tail, tapering and curling up into the air above the beast's hindquarters, like that of a scorpion, although it wasn't equipped with a stinger. The feet were far different from a rat's feet: They were oversize by comparison to the animal itself; the long toes were triple-jointed, gnarly; the curving claws were much too big for the feet to which they were fitted; a razor-sharp, multiply-barbed spur curved out from each heel. The head was even more deadly in appearance and design than were the feet; it was formed over a flattish skull that had many unnaturally sharp angles, unnecessary convexities and concavities, as if it had been molded by an inexpert sculptor. The snout was long and pointed, a bizarre cross between the muzzle of a wolf and that of a crocodile. The small monster opened its mouth and hissed, revealing too many pointed teeth that were angled in various directions along its jaws. A surprisingly long black tongue slithered out of the mouth, glistening like a strip of raw liver; the end of it was forked, and it fluttered continuously.

But the thing's eyes were what frightened Jack the most. They appeared not to be eyes at all; they had no pupils or irises, no solid tissue that he could discern. There were just empty sockets in the creature's malformed skull, crude holes from which radiated a harsh, cold, brilliant light. The intense glow seemed to come from a fire within the beast's own mutant cranium. Which simply could not *be.* Yet was. And the thing wasn't blind, either, as it should have been; there wasn't any question about its ability to see, for it fixed those fire-filled "eyes" on Jack, and he could feel its demonic gaze as surely as he would have felt a knife rammed into his gut. That was the other thing that disturbed him, the very worst aspect of those mad eyes: the death-cold, hate-hot, soul-withering feeling they imparted when you dared to meet them. Looking into the thing's eyes, Jack felt both physically and spiritually ill.

With insectile disregard for gravity, the beast slowly crept head-first down the wall, away from the duct.

A second creature appeared at the opening in the ventilation system. This one wasn't anything like the first. It was in the form of a small man, perhaps ten inches high, crouching up there in the mouth of the duct. Although it possessed the crude form of a man, it was in no other way humanlike. Its hands and feet resembled those of the first beast, with dangerous claws and barbed spurs. The flesh was funguslike, slippery looking, though less green, more yellow and gray. There were black circles around the eyes and patches of corrupted-looking black flesh fanning out from the nostrils. Its head was misshapen, with a toothy mouth that went from ear to ear. And it had those same hellish eyes, although they were smaller than the eyes in the ratlike thing.

Jack saw that the man-form beast was holding a weapon. It looked like a miniature spear. The point was well-honed; it caught the light and glinted along its cutting edge.

Jack remembered the first two victims of Lavelle's crusade against the Carramazza family. They had both been stabbed hundreds of times with a weapon no bigger than a penknife—yet not a penknife. The medical examiner had been perplexed; the lab technicians had been baffled. But, of course, it wouldn't have occurred to them to explore the possibility that those homicides were the work of ten-inch voodoo devils and that the murder weapons were miniature spears.

Voodoo devils? Goblins? Gremlins? What exactly were these things?

Did Lavelle mold them from clay and then somehow invest them with life and malevolent purpose?

Or were they conjured up with the help of pentagrams and sacrifices and arcane chants, the way demons were supposedly called forth by Satanists? *Were* they demons?

Where did they come from?

The man-form thing didn't creep down the wall behind the first beast. Instead, it leaped out of the duct, dropping to the top of the dresser, landing on its feet, agile and quick.

It looked past Jack and Keith, and it said, *"Penny? Davey?"*

Jack pushed Keith across the threshold, into the hall, then followed him and pulled the door shut behind them.

An instant later, one of the creatures—probably the manlike beast—crashed against the other side of the door and began to claw frantically at it.

The kids were already out of the hall, in the living room.

Jack and Keith hurried after them.

Faye shouted, "Jack! Quick! They're coming through the vent out here!"

"Trying to cut us off," Jack said.

Jesus, we're not going to make it, they're everywhere, the damned building's infested with them, they're all around us—

In his mind, Jack quickly slammed the door on those bleak thoughts, closed it tight and locked it and told himself that their worst enemies were their own pessimism and fear, which could enervate and immobilize them.

Just this side of the foyer, in the living room, Faye and Rebecca were helping the kids put on coats and boots.

Snarling, hissing, and eager wordless jabbering issued from the vent plate in the wall above the long sofa. Beyond the slots in that grille, silver eyes blazed in the darkness. One of the screws was being worked loose from inside.

Davey had only one boot on, but time had run out.

Jack picked up the boy and said, "Faye, bring his other boot, and let's get moving."

Keith was already in the foyer. He'd been to the closet and had gotten coats for himself and Faye. Without pausing to put them on, he grabbed Faye by the arm and hurried her out of the apartment.

Penny screamed.

Jack turned toward the living room, instinctively crouching slightly and holding Davey even tighter.

The vent plate was off the duct above the sofa. Something was starting to come out of the darkness there.

But that wasn't why Penny had screamed. Another hideous intruder had come out of the kitchen, and that was what had seized her attention. It was two-thirds of the way through the dining room, scurrying toward the living room archway, coming straight at them. Its coloration was different from that of the other beasts, although no less disgusting; it was a sickly yellow-white with cancerous-looking green-black pockmarks all over it, and like the other beasts Lavelle had sent, this one appeared to be slick, slimy. It was also a lot bigger than any of the others, almost three times the size of the ratlike creature in the bedroom. Somewhat resembling an iguana, although more slender through its body than an iguana, this spawn of nightmares was three to four feet in length, had a lizard's tail, a lizard's head and face. Unlike an iguana, however, the small monster had eyes of fire, six legs, and a body so slinky that it appeared capable of tying itself in knots; it was the very slinkiness and flexibility that made it possible for a creature of this size to slither through the ventilation pipes. Furthermore, it had a pair of batlike wings which were atrophied and surely useless but which unfurled and flapped and fluttered with frightening effect.

The thing charged into the living room, tail whipping back and forth behind it. Its mouth cracked wide, emitting a cold shriek of triumph as it bore down on them.

Rebecca dropped to one knee and fired her revolver. She was at point-blank range; she couldn't miss; she didn't. The slug smashed squarely into its target. The shot lifted the beast off the floor and flung it backwards as if it were a bundle of rags. It landed hard, clear back at the archway to the dining room.

It should have been blown to pieces. It wasn't.

The floor and walls should have been splashed with blood—or with whatever fluid pumped through these creatures' veins. But there was no mess whatsoever.

The thing flopped and writhed on its back for a few seconds, then rolled over and got onto its feet, wobbled sideways. It was disoriented and sluggish, but unharmed. It scuttled around in a circle, chasing its own tail.

Meanwhile, Jack's eyes were drawn to the repulsive thing that had come out of the duct above the sofa. It hung on the wall, mewling, approximately the size of a rat but otherwise unlike a rodent. More than anything else, it resembled a featherless bird. It had an egg-shaped head perched atop a long, thin neck that might have been that of a baby ostrich, and it had a wickedly pointed beak with which it kept slashing at the air. However, its flickering, fiery eyes were not like those of any bird, and no bird on earth possessed stubby tentacles, like these, instead of legs. The beast was an abomination, a mutant horror; just looking at it made Jack queasy. And now, behind it, another similar though not identical creature crept out of the duct.

"Guns aren't any damned use against these things," Jack said.

The iguana-form monstrosity was becoming less disoriented. In a moment it would regain its senses and charge at them again.

Two more creatures appeared at the far end of the dining room, crawling out of the kitchen, coming fast.

A screech drew Jack's attention to the far end of the living room, where the hallway led back to the bedroom and baths. The man-shaped thing was standing there, squealing, holding the spear above its head. It ran toward them, crossing the carpet with shocking speed.

Behind it came a horde of small but deadly creatures, reptilian-serpentine-canine-feline-insectile-rodentlike-arachnoid grotesqueries. In that instant Jack realized that they were, indeed, the Hellborn; they were demonic entities summoned from the depths of Hell by Lavelle's sorcery. That must be the answer, insane as it seemed, for there was no place else from which such gruesome horrors *could* have come. Hissing and chattering and snarling, they flopped and rolled over one another in their eagerness to reach Penny and Davey. Each of them was quite different from the one before it, although all of them shared at least two features: the eyes of silver-white fire, like windows in a furnace—and murderously sharp little teeth. It was as if the gates of Hell had been flung open.

Jack pushed Penny into the foyer. Carrying Davey, he followed his daughter out of the front door, into the eleventh-floor corridor, and hurried toward Keith and Faye, who stood with the white-haired doorman at one of the elevators, keeping the lift open.

Behind Jack, Rebecca fired three shots.

Jack stopped, turned. He wanted to go back for her, but he wasn't sure how he could do that and still protect Davey.

"Daddy! Hurry!" Penny screamed from where she stood half in and half out of the elevator.

"Daddy, let's go, let's go," Davey said, clinging to him.

Much to Jack's relief, Rebecca came out of the apartment, unharmed. She fired one shot into the Jamisons' foyer, then pulled the door shut.

By the time Jack reached the elevators, Rebecca was right behind him. Gasping for breath, he put Davey down, and all seven of them, including the doorman, crowded into the cab, and Keith hit the button that was marked LOBBY.

The doors didn't immediately slide shut.

"They're gonna get in, they're gonna get in," Davey cried, voicing the fear that had just flashed into everyone's mind.

Keith pushed the LOBBY button again, kept his thumb on it this time.

Finally the doors slid shut.

But Jack didn't feel any safer.

Now that he was closed up tight in the cramped cab, he wondered if they would have been wiser to take the stairs. What if the demons could put the lift out of commission, stop it between floors? What if they crept into the elevator shaft and descended onto the stranded cab? What if that monstrous horde found a way to get inside? God in heaven, what if . . . ?

The elevator started down.

Jack looked up at the ceiling of the cab. There was an emergency escape hatch. A way out. And a way *in.* This side of the hatch was featureless: no hinges, no handles. Apparently, it could be pushed up and out—or pulled up and out by rescue workers on the other side. There would be a handle out there on the roof of the cab, which would make it easy for the demons, if they came. But since there wasn't a handle on the inside, the hatch couldn't be held down; the forced entrance of those vicious creatures couldn't be resisted—if they came.

God, please, don't let them come.

The elevator crawled down its long cables as slowly as it had pulled itself up. Tenth floor . . . ninth . . .

Penny had taken Davey's boot from Faye. She was helping her little brother get his foot into it.

Eighth floor.

In a haunted voice that cracked more than once, but still with her familiar imperious tone, Faye said, "What were they, Jack? What were those things in the vents?"

"Voodoo," Jack said, keeping his eyes on the lighted floor indicator above the doors.

Seventh floor.

"Is this some sort of joke?" the doorman asked.

"Voodoo devils, I think," Jack told Faye, "but don't ask me to explain how they got here or anything about them."

Shaken as she was, and in spite of what she'd heard and seen in the apartment, Faye said, "Are you out of your mind?"

"Almost wish I was."

Sixth floor.

"There aren't such things as voodoo devils," Faye said. "There aren't any—"

"Shut up," Keith told her. "You didn't see them. You left the guest room before they came out of the vent in there."

Fifth floor.

Penny said, "And you'd gotten out of the apartment before they started coming through the living room vent, Aunt Faye. You just didn't see them—or you'd believe."

Fourth floor.

The doorman said, "Mrs. Jamison, how well do you know these people? Are they—"

Ignoring and interrupting him, Rebecca spoke to Faye and Keith: "Jack and I have been on a weird case. Psychopathic killer. Claims to waste his victims with voodoo curses."

Third floor.

Maybe we're going to make it, Jack thought. Maybe we won't be stopped between floors. Maybe we'll get out of here alive.

And maybe not.

To Rebecca, Faye said, "Surely *you* don't believe in voodoo."

"I didn't," Rebecca said. "But now . . . yeah."

With a nasty shock, Jack realized the lobby might be teeming with small, vicious creatures. When the elevator doors opened, the nightmare horde might come rushing in, clawing and biting.

"If it's a joke, I don't get it," the doorman said.

Second floor.

Suddenly Jack didn't want to reach the lobby, didn't want the lift doors to open. Suddenly he just wanted to go on descending in peace, hour after hour, on into eternity.

The lobby.

Please, no!

The doors opened.

The lobby was deserted.

They poured out of the elevator, and Faye said, "Where are we going?"

Jack said, "Rebecca and I have a car—"

"In this weather—"

"Snow chains," Jack said, cutting her off sharply. "We're taking the car and getting the kids out of here, keep moving around, until I can figure out what to do."

"We'll go with you," Keith said.

"No," Jack said, ushering the kids toward the lobby doors. "Being with us is probably dangerous."

"We can't go back upstairs," Keith said. "Not with those . . . those demons or devils or whatever the hell they are."

"Rats," Faye said, apparently having decided that she could deal with the uncouth more easily than she could deal with the unnatural. "Only some rats. Of course, we'll go back. Sooner or later, we'll *have* to go back, set traps, exterminate them. The sooner the better, in fact."

Paying no attention to Faye, talking over her head to Keith, Jack said, "I don't think the damned things will hurt you and Faye. Not unless you were to stand between them and the kids. They'll probably kill anyone who tries to protect the kids. That's why I'm getting them away from you. Still, I wouldn't go back there tonight. A few of them might wait around."

"You couldn't drag me back there tonight," Keith assured him.

"Nonsense," Faye said. "Just a few rats—"

"Damnit, woman," Keith said, "it wasn't a rat that called for Davey and Penny from inside that duct!"

Faye was already pale. When Keith reminded her of the voice in the ventilation system, she went pure white.

They all paused at the doors, and Rebecca said, "Keith, is there someone you can stay with?"

"Sure," Keith said. "One of my business partners, Anson Dorset, lives on this same block. On the other side of the street. Up near the avenue. We can spend the night there, with Anson and Francine."

Jack pushed the door open. The wind tried to slam it shut again, almost succeeded, and snow exploded into the lobby. Fighting the wind, turning his face away from the stinging crystals, Jack held the door open for the others and motioned them ahead of him. Rebecca went first, then Penny and Davey, then Faye and Keith.

The doorman was the only one left. He was scratching his white-haired head and frowning at Jack. "Hey, wait. What about me?"

"What about you? You're not in any danger," Jack said, starting through the door, in the wake of the others.

"But what about all that gunfire upstairs?"

Turning to the man again, Jack said, "Don't worry about it. You saw our ID when we came in here, right? We're cops."

"Yeah, but who got shot?"

"Nobody," Jack said.

"Then who were you shooting at?"

"Nobody."

Jack went out into the storm, letting the door blow shut behind him.

The doorman stood in the lobby, face pressed to the glass door, peering out at them, as if he were a fat and unpopular schoolboy who was being excluded from a game.

IX

THE WIND WAS A HAMMER.

The spicules of snow were nails.

The storm was busily engaged on its carpentry work, building drifts in the street.

By the time Jack reached the bottom of the steps in front of the apartment building, Keith and Faye were already angling across the street, heading up toward the avenue, toward the building where their friends lived. Step by step, they were gradually disappearing beyond the phosphorescent curtains of wind-blown snow.

Rebecca and the kids were standing at the car.

Raising his voice above the huffing and moaning of the wind, Jack said, "Come on, come on. Get in. Let's get out of here."

Then he realized something was wrong.

Rebecca had one hand on the door handle, but she wasn't opening the door. She was staring into the car, transfixed.

Jack moved up beside her and looked through the window and saw what she saw. Two of the creatures. Both on the back seat. They were wrapped in shadows, and it was impossible to see exactly what they looked like, but their glowing silver eyes left no doubt that they were kin to the murderous things that had come out of the heating ducts. If Rebecca had opened the door without looking inside, if she hadn't noticed that the beasts were waiting in there, she might have been attacked and overwhelmed. Her throat could have been torn open, her eyes gouged out, her life taken before Jack was even aware of the danger, before he had a chance to go to her assistance.

"Back off," he said.

The four of them moved away from the car, huddled together on the sidewalk, wary of the night around them.

They were the only people on the wintry street, now. Faye and Keith were out of sight. There were no plows, no cars, no pedestrians. Even the doorman was no longer watching them.

It's strange, Jack thought, to feel this isolated and this alone in the heart of Manhattan.

"What now?" Rebecca asked urgently, her eyes fixed on the car, one hand on Davey, one hand inside her coat where she was probably gripping her revolver.

"We keep moving," Jack said, dissatisfied with his answer, but too surprised and too scared to think of anything better.

Don't panic.

"Where?" Rebecca asked.

"Toward the avenue," he said.

Calm. Easy. Panic will finish us.

"The way Keith went?" Rebecca asked.

"No. The other avenue. Third Avenue. It's closer."

"I hope there's people out there," she said.

"Maybe even a patrol car."

And Penny said, "I think we're a whole lot safer around people, out in the open."

"I think so, too, sweetheart," Jack said. "So let's go now. And stay close together."

Penny took hold of Davey's hand.

The attack came suddenly. The thing rushed out from beneath their car. Squealing. Hissing. Eyes beaming silvery light. Dark against the snow. Swift and sinuous. Too damned swift. Lizardlike. Jack saw that much in the storm-diluted glow of the streetlamps, reached for his revolver, remembered that bullets couldn't kill these things, also realized that they were in too close quarters to risk using a gun anyway, and by then the thing was among them, snarling and spitting—all of this in but a single second, one *tick* of time, perhaps even less. Davey shouted. And tried to get out of the thing's way. He couldn't avoid it. The beast pounced on the boy's boot. Davey kicked. It clung to him. Jack lifted-pushed Penny out of the way. Put her against the wall of the apartment building. She crouched there. Gasping. Meanwhile, the lizard had started climbing Davey's legs. The boy flailed at it. Stumbled. Staggered backwards. Shrieking for help. Slipped. Fell. All of this in only one more second, maybe two—*tick, tick*—and Jack felt as if he were in a fever dream, with time distorted as it could be only in a dream. He went after the boy, but he seemed to be moving through air as thick as syrup. The lizard was on the front of Davey's chest now, its tail whipping back and forth, its clawed feet digging at the heavy coat, trying to tear the coat to shreds so that it could then rip open

the boy's belly, and its mouth was wide, its muzzle almost at the boy's face—
no!—and Rebecca got there ahead of Jack. *Tick.* She tore the disgusting thing
off Davey's chest. It wailed. It bit her hand. She cried out in pain. Threw the
lizard down. Penny was screaming: "Davey, Davey, Davey!" *Tick.* Davey had
regained his feet. The lizard went after him again. This time, Jack got hold of
the thing. In his bare hands. On the way up to the Jamisons' apartment, he'd
removed his gloves in order to be able to use his gun more easily. Now,
shuddering at the feel of the thing, he ripped it off the boy. Heard the coat
shredding in its claws. Held it at arm's length. *Tick.* The creature felt repul-
sively cold and oily in Jack's hands, although for some reason he had expected
it to be hot, maybe because of the fire inside its skull, the silvery blaze that now
flickered at him through the gaping sockets where the demon's eyes should
have been. The beast squirmed. *Tick.* It tried to wrench free of him, and it was
strong, but he was stronger. *Tick.* It kicked the air with its wickedly clawed
feet. *Tick. Tick. Tick, tick, tick . . .*

Rebecca said, "Why isn't it trying to bite you?"

"I don't know," he said breathlessly.

"What's different about you?"

"I don't know."

But he remembered the conversation he'd had with Nick Iervolino in the
patrol car, earlier today, on the way downtown from Carver Hampton's shop
in Harlem. And he wondered . . .

The lizard-thing had a second mouth, this one in its stomach, complete with
sharp little teeth. The aperture gaped at Jack, opened and closed, but this
second mouth was no more eager to bite him than was the mouth in the
lizard's head.

"Davey, are you all right?" Jack asked.

"Kill it, Daddy," the boy said. He sounded terrified but unharmed. "Please
kill it. Please."

"I only wish I could," Jack said.

The small monster twisted, flopped, wriggled, did its best to slither out of
Jack's hands. The feel of it revolted him, but he gripped it even tighter than
before, harder, dug his fingers into the cold oily flesh.

"Rebecca, what about your hand?"

"Just a nip," she said.

"Penny?"

"I . . . I'm okay."

"Then the three of you get out of here. Go to the avenue."

"What about you?" Rebecca asked.

"I'll hold onto this thing, give you a head start." The lizard thrashed. "Then
I'll throw it as far as I can before I follow you."

"We can't leave you alone," Penny said desperately.

"Only for a minute or two," Jack said. "I'll catch up. I can run faster than
the three of you. I'll catch up easy. Now go on. Get out of here before another
one of these damned things charges out from somewhere. *Go!*"

They ran, the kids ahead of Rebecca, kicking up plumes of snow as they
went.

The lizard-thing hissed at Jack.

He looked into those eyes of fire.

Inside the lizard's malformed skull, flames writhed, fluttered, flickered, but
never wavered, burned bright and intense, all shades of white and silver, but
somehow it didn't seem like a *hot* fire; it looked cool, instead.

Jack wondered what would happen if he poked a finger through one of those hollow sockets, into the fire beyond. Would he actually find fire in there? Or was it an illusion? If there really was fire in the skull, would he burn himself? Or would he discover that the flames were as lacking in heat as they appeared to be?

White flames. Sputtering.

Cold flames. Hissing.

The lizard's two mouths chewed at the night air.

Jack wanted to see more deeply into that strange fire.

He held the creature closer to his face.

He stared into the empty sockets.

Whirling flames.

Leaping flames.

He had the feeling there was something beyond the fire, something amazing and important, something awesome that he could almost glimpse between those scintillating, tightly contained pyrotechnics.

He brought the lizard even closer.

Now his face was only inches from its muzzle.

He could feel the light of its eyes washing over him.

It was a bitterly cold light.

Incandescent.

Fascinating.

He peered intently into the skull fire.

The flames almost parted, almost permitted him to see what lay beyond them.

He squinted, trying harder to see.

He wanted to understand the great mystery.

The mystery beyond the fiery veil.

Wanted, needed, *had* to understand it.

White flames.

Flames of snow, of ice.

Flames that held a shattering secret.

Flames that beckoned . . .

Beckoned . . .

He almost didn't hear the car door opening behind him. The "eyes" of the lizard-thing had seized him and half mesmerized him. His awareness of the snowswept street around him had grown fuzzy. In a few more seconds, he would have been lost. But they misjudged; they opened the car door one moment too soon, and he heard it. He turned, threw the lizard-thing as far as he could into the stormy darkness.

He didn't wait to see where it fell, didn't look to see what was coming out of the unmarked sedan.

He just ran.

Ahead of him, Rebecca and the kids had reached the avenue. They turned left at the corner, moving out of sight.

Jack pounded through the snow, which was almost over the tops of his boots in some places, and his heart triphammered, and his breath spurted from him in white clouds, and he slipped, almost fell, regained his balance, ran, ran, and it seemed to him that he wasn't running along a real street, that this was only a street in a dream, a nightmare place from which there was no escape.

X

IN THE ELEVATOR, on the way up to the fourteenth floor, where Anson and Francine Dorset had an apartment, Faye said, "Not a word about voodoo or any of that nonsense. You hear me? They'll think you're crazy."

Keith said, "Well, I don't know about voodoo. But I sure as hell saw something strange."

"Don't you *dare* go raving about it to Anson and Francine. He's your business partner, for heaven's sake. You've got to go on working with the man. That's going to be hard to do if he thinks you're some sort of superstitious nut. A broker's got to have an image of stability. A banker's image. Bankers and brokers. People want to see stable, conservative men at a brokerage firm before they trust it with their investments. You can't afford the damage to your reputation. Besides, they were only rats."

"They weren't rats," he said. "I saw—"

"Nothing but rats."

"I know what I saw."

"Rats," she insisted. "But we're not going to tell Anson and Francine we have rats. What would they think of us? I won't have them knowing we live in a building with rats. Why, Francine already looks down on me; she looks down on everyone; she thinks she's such a blueblood, that family she comes from. I won't give her the slightest advantage. I swear I won't. Not a word about rats. What we'll tell them is that there's a gas leak. They can't see our building from their apartment, and they won't be going out on a night like this, so we'll tell them we've been evacuated because of a gas leak."

"Faye—"

"And tomorrow morning," she said determinedly, "I'll start looking for a new place for us."

"But—"

"I won't live in a building with rats. I simply won't do it, and you can't expect me to. You should want out of there yourself, just as fast as it can be arranged."

"But they weren't—"

"We'll sell the apartment. And maybe it's even time we got out of this damned dirty city altogether. I've been half wanting to get out for years. You know that. Maybe it's time we start looking for a place in Connecticut. I know you won't be happy about commuting, but the train isn't so bad, and think of all the advantages. Fresh air. A bigger place for the same money. Our own pool. Wouldn't *that* be nice? Maybe Penny and Davey could come and stay with us for the entire summer. They shouldn't spend their entire childhood in the city. It isn't healthy. Yes, definitely, I'll start looking into it tomorrow."

"Faye, for one thing, everything'll be shut up tight on account of the blizzard—"

"That won't stop me. You'll see. First thing tomorrow."

The elevator doors opened.

In the fourteenth-floor corridor, Keith said, "Aren't you worried about Penny and Davey? I mean, we left them—"

"They'll be fine," she said, and she even seemed to believe it. "It was only rats. You don't think rats are going to follow them out of the building? They're in no danger from a few rats. What I'm most worried about is that father of theirs, telling them it's voodoo, scaring them like that, stuffing their heads full of such nonsense. What's gotten into that man? Maybe he does have a psychotic killer to track down, but voodoo has nothing to do with it. He doesn't sound rational. Honestly, I just can't understand him; no matter how hard I try, I just can't."

They had reached the door to the Dorset apartment. Keith rang the bell.

Faye said, "Remember, not a word!"

Anson Dorset must have been waiting with his hand on the doorknob ever since they phoned up from downstairs, for he opened up at once, just as Faye issued that warning to Keith. He said, "Not a word about what?"

"Rats," Keith said. "All of a sudden, it seems as if our building is infested with rats."

Faye cast a murderous look at him.

He didn't care. He wasn't going to spin an elaborate story about a gas leak. They could be caught too easily in a lie like that, and then they'd look like fools. So he told Anson and Francine about a plague of vermin, but he didn't mention voodoo or say anything about the weird creatures that had come out of the guest room vent. He conceded that much to Faye because she was absolutely right on that score: A stockbroker had to maintain a conservative, stable, level-headed image at all times—or risk ruin.

But he wondered how long it would be before he could forget what he had seen.

A long time.

A long, long time.

Maybe never.

XI

SLIDING A LITTLE, then stomping through a drift that put snow inside his boots, Jack turned the corner, onto the avenue. He didn't look back because he was afraid he'd discover the goblins—as Penny called them—close at his heels.

Rebecca and the kids were only a hundred feet ahead. He hurried after them.

Much to his dismay, he saw that they were the only people on the broad avenue. There were only a few cars, all deserted and abandoned after becoming stuck in the snow. Nobody out walking. And who, in his right mind, *would* be out walking in gale-force winds, in the middle of a blinding snowstorm? Nearly two blocks away, red taillights and revolving red emergency beacons gleamed and winked, barely visible in the sheeting snow. It was a train of plows, but they were headed the other way.

He caught up with Rebecca and the kids. It wasn't difficult to close the gap. They were no longer moving very fast. Already, Davey and Penny were flagging. Running in deep snow was like running with lead weights on the feet; the constant resistance was quickly wearing them down.

Jack glanced back the way they had come. No sign of the goblins. But those lantern-eyed creatures would show up, and soon. He couldn't believe they had given up this easily.

When they *did* come, they would find easy prey. The kids would have slowed to a weary, shambling walk in another minute.

Jack didn't feel particularly spry himself. His heart was pounding so hard and fast that it seemed as if it would tear loose of its moorings. His face hurt from the cold, biting wind, which also stung his eyes and brought tears to them. His hands hurt and were somewhat numb, too, because he hadn't had time to put on his gloves again. He was breathing hard, and the arctic air cracked his throat, made his chest ache. His feet were freezing because of all the snow that had gotten into his boots. He wasn't in any condition to provide much protection to the kids, and that realization made him angry and fearful, for he and Rebecca were the only people standing between the kids and death.

As if excited by the prospect of their slaughter, the wind howled louder, almost gleefully.

The winter-bare trees, rising from cut-out planting beds in the wide sidewalk, rattled their stripped limbs in the wind. It was the sound of animated skeletons.

Jack looked around for a place to hide. Just ahead, five brownstone apartment houses, each four stories tall, were sandwiched between somewhat higher and more modern (though less attractive) structures. To Rebecca, he said, "We've got to get out of sight," and he hurried all of them off the sidewalk, up the snow-covered steps, through the glass-paneled front doors, into the security foyer of the first brownstone.

The foyer wasn't well-heated; however, by comparison with the night outside, it seemed wonderfully tropical. It was also clean and rather elegant, with brass mailboxes and a vaulted wooden ceiling, although there was no doorman. The complex mosaic-tile floor—which depicted a twining vine, green leaves, and faded yellow flowers against an ivory background—was highly polished, and not one piece of tile was missing.

But, even as pleasant as it was, they couldn't stay here. The foyer was also brightly lighted. They would be spotted easily from the street.

The inner door was also glass paneled. Beyond it lay the first-floor hall, the elevator and stairs. But the door was locked and could be opened only with a key or with a lock-release button in one of the apartments.

There were sixteen apartments in all, four on each floor. Jack stepped to the brass mailboxes and pushed the call button for a Mr. and Mrs. Evans on the fourth floor.

A woman's voice issued tinnily from the speaker at the top of the mailbox. "Who is it?"

"Is this the Grofeld apartment?" Jack asked, knowing full well that it wasn't.

"No," the unseen woman said. "You've pressed the wrong button. The Grofelds' mailbox is next to ours."

"Sorry," he said as Mrs. Evans broke the connection.

He glanced toward the front door, at the street beyond.

Snow. Naked, blackened trees shaking in the wind. The ghostly glow of storm-shrouded streetlamps.

But nothing worse than that. Nothing with silvery eyes. Nothing with lots of pointed little teeth.

Not yet.

He pressed the Grofelds' button, asked if this were the Santini apartment, and was curtly told that the Santinis' mailbox was the next one.

He rang the Santinis and was prepared to ask if theirs was the Porterfield apartment. But the Santinis apparently expected someone and were considerably less cautious than their neighbors, for they buzzed him through the inner door without asking who he was.

Rebecca ushered the kids inside, and Jack quickly followed, closing the foyer door behind them.

He could have used his police ID to get past the foyer, but it would have taken too long. With the crime rate spiraling upward, most people were more suspicious these days than they'd once been. If he had been straightforward with Mrs. Evans, right there at the start, she wouldn't have accepted his word that he was a cop. She would have wanted to come down—and rightly so—to examine his badge through the glass panel in the inner door. By that time, one of Lavelle's demonic assassins might have passed by the building and spotted them.

Besides, Jack was reluctant to involve other people, for to do so would be to put their lives at risk if the goblins should suddenly arrive and attack.

Apparently, Rebecca shared his concern about dragging strangers into it, for she warned the kids to be especially quiet as she escorted them into a shadowy recess under the stairs, to the right of the main entrance.

Jack crowded into the nook with them, away from the door. They couldn't be seen from the street or from the stairs above, not even if someone leaned out over the railing and looked down.

After less than a minute had passed, a door opened a few floors overhead. Footsteps. Then someone, apparently Mr. Santini, said, "Alex? Is that you?"

Under the stairs, they remained silent, unmoving.

Mr. Santini waited.

Outside, the wind roared.

Mr. Santini descended a few steps. "Is anyone there?"

Go away, Jack thought. You haven't any idea what you might be walking into. *Go away.*

As if he were telepathic and had received Jack's warning, the man returned to his apartment and closed the door.

Jack sighed.

Eventually, speaking in a tremulous whisper, Penny said, "How will we know when it's safe to go outside again?"

"We'll just give it a little time, and then when it seems right . . . I'll slip out there and take a peek," Jack said softly.

Davey was shaking as if it were colder in here than it was outside. He wiped his runny nose with the sleeve of his coat and said, "How much time will we wait?"

"Five minutes," Rebecca told him, also whispering. "Ten at most. They'll be gone by then."

"They will?"

"Sure. They might already be gone."

"You really think so?" Davey asked. "Already?"

"Sure," Rebecca said. "There's a good chance they didn't follow us. But even if they did come after us, they won't hang around this area all night."

"Won't they?" Penny asked doubtfully.

"No, no, no," Rebecca said. "Of course they won't. Even goblins get bored, you know."

"Is that what they are?" Davey asked. "Goblins? Really?"

"Well, it's hard to know exactly what we ought to call them," Rebecca said.

"Goblins was the only word I could think of when I saw them," Penny said. "It just popped into my mind."

"And it's a pretty darned good word," Rebecca assured her. "You couldn't have thought of anything better, so far as I'm concerned. And, you know, if you think back to all the fairytales you ever heard, goblins were always more bark than bite. About all they ever really did to anyone was scare them. So if we're patient and careful, really careful, then everything will be all right."

Jack admired and appreciated the way Rebecca was handling the children, alleviating their anxiety. Her voice had a soothing quality. She touched them continually as she spoke to them, squeezed and stroked them, gentled them down.

Jack pulled up his sleeve and looked at his watch.

Ten-fourteen.

They huddled together in the shadows under the stairs, waiting. Waiting.

CHAPTER 6

I

FOR A WHILE Lavelle lay on the floor of the dark bedroom, stunned, breathing only with difficulty, numb with pain. When Rebecca Chandler shot a few of those small assassins in the Jamisons' apartment, Lavelle had been in psychic contact with them, and he'd felt the impact of the bullets on their golem bodies. He hadn't been injured, not any more than the demonic entities themselves had been injured. His skin wasn't broken. He wasn't bleeding. In the morning, there would be no bruises, no tenderness of flesh. But the impact of those slugs had been agonizingly real and had rendered him briefly unconscious.

He wasn't unconscious now. Just disoriented. When the pain began to subside a little, he crawled around the room on his belly, not certain what he was searching for, not even certain where he was. Gradually he regained his senses. He crept back to the bed, levered himself onto the mattress, and flopped on his back, groaning.

Darkness touched him.

Darkness healed him.

Snow tapped the windows.

Darkness breathed over him.

Roof rafters creaked in the wind.

Darkness whispered to him.

Darkness.

Eventually, the pain was gone.

But the darkness remained. It embraced and caressed him. He suckled on it. Nothing else soothed as completely and as deeply as the darkness.

In spite of his unsettling and painful experience, he was eager to reestablish the psychic link with the creatures that were in pursuit of the Dawsons. The ribbons were still tied to his ankles, wrists, chest, and head. The spots of cat's blood were still on his cheeks. His lips were still anointed with blood. And the blood *vèvè* was still on his chest. All he had to do was repeat the proper chants, which he did, staring at the tenebrous ceiling. Slowly, the bedroom faded around him, and he was once again with the silver-eyed horde, relentlessly stalking the Dawson children.

II

TEN-FIFTEEN.

Ten-sixteen.

While they huddled under the stairs, Jack looked at the bite on Rebecca's left hand. Three puncture marks were distributed over an area as large as a nickel, on the meatiest part of her palm, and there was a small tear in the skin, as well, but the lizard-thing hadn't bitten deeply. The flesh was only slightly puffy. The wound no longer wept; there was only dried blood.

"How does it feel?"

"Burns a bit," she said.

"That's all?"

"It'll be fine. I'll put my glove on; that ought to help prevent it from breaking open and bleeding again."

"Keep a watch on it, okay? If there's any discoloration, any more swelling, anything at all odd about it, maybe we ought to get you to a hospital."

"And when I talk to the doctor, what'll I say happened to me?"

"Tell him you were bitten by a goblin. What else?"

"Might be worth it just to see his expression."

Ten-seventeen.

Jack examined Davey's coat, at which the lizard had clawed in a murderous frenzy. The garment was heavy and well-made; the fabric was sturdy. Nevertheless, the creature's claws had sliced all the way through in at least three places—and through the quilted lining, too.

It was a miracle that Davey was unharmed. Although the claws had pierced the coat as if it were so much cheesecloth, they hadn't torn the boy's sweater or his shirt; they hadn't left even one shallow scratch on his skin.

Jack thought about how close he had come to losing both Davey and Penny, and he was acutely aware that he might still lose them before this case was closed. He put one hand to his son's fragile face. An icy premonition of dreadful loss began to blossom within him, spreading frozen petals of terror and despair. His throat clenched. He struggled to hold back tears. He must not cry. The kids would come apart if he cried. Besides, if he gave in to despair now, he would be surrendering—in some small but significant way—to Lavelle. Lavelle was evil, not just another criminal, not merely corrupted, but *evil,* the very essence and embodiment of it, and evil thrived on despair. The best weapons against evil were hope, optimism, determination, and faith. Their chances of survival depended on their ability to keep hoping, to believe that life (not death) was their destiny, to believe that good could triumph over evil, simply to *believe.* He would not lose his kids. He would not allow Lavelle to have them.

"Well," he said to Davey, "it's too well-ventilated for a winter coat, but I think we can fix that." He took off his long neckscarf, wound it overtop the boy's damaged coat, twice around his small chest, and knotted it securely at his waist. "There. That ought to keep the gaps closed. You okay, skipper?"

Davey nodded and tried very hard to look brave. He said, "Dad, do you think maybe what you need here is a magic sword?"

"A magic sword?" Jack said.

"Well, isn't that what you've got to have if you're going to kill a bunch of goblins?" the boy asked earnestly. "In all the stories, they usually have a magic sword or a magic staff, see, or maybe just some magic powder, and that's what always does in the goblins or the witches or ogres or whatever it is that has to be done in. Oh, and sometimes, what it is they have . . . it's a magic jewel, you know, or a sorcerer's ring. So, since you and Rebecca are detectives, maybe this time it's a goblin gun. Do you know if the police department has anything like that? A goblin gun?"

"I don't really know," Jack said solemnly, wanting to hug the boy very close and very tight. "But it's a darned good suggestion, son. I'll look into it."

"And if they don't have one," Davey said, "then maybe you could just ask a priest to sort of bless your own gun, the one you already have, and then you could load it up with lots and lots of silver bullets. That's what they do with werewolves, you know."

"I know. And that's a good suggestion, too. I'm real glad to see you're thinking about ways to beat these things. I'm glad you aren't giving up. That's what's important—not giving up."

"Sure," Davey said, sticking his chin out. "I know *that.*"

Penny was watching her father over Davey's shoulder. She smiled and winked.

Jack winked back at her.

Ten-twenty.

With every minute that passed uneventfully, Jack felt safer.

Not *safe*. Just safer.

Penny gave him a very abbreviated account of her encounters with the goblins.

When the girl finished, Rebecca looked at Jack and said, "He's been keeping a watch on them. So he'd always know exactly where to find them when the time came."

To Penny, Jack said, "My God, baby, why didn't you wake me last night when the thing was in your room?"

"I didn't really see it—"

"But you heard it."

"That's all."

"And the baseball bat—"

"Anyway," Penny said with a sudden odd shyness, unable to meet his eyes, "I was afraid you'd think I'd gone . . . crazy . . . again."

"Huh? Again?" Jack blinked at her. "What on earth do you mean—*again?*"

"Well . . . you know . . . like after Mama died, the way I was then . . . when I had my . . . trouble."

"But you weren't crazy," Jack said. "You just needed a little counseling; that's all, honey."

"That's what you called him," the girl said, barely audible. "A counselor."

"Yeah. Dr. Hannaby."

"Aunt Faye, Uncle Keith, everyone called him a counselor. Or sometimes a doctor."

"That's what he was. He was there to counsel you, to show you how to deal with your grief over your mom's death."

The girl shook her head: no. "One day, when I was in his office, waiting for him . . . and he didn't come in to start the session right away . . . I started to read the college degrees on his wall."

"And?"

With evident embarrassment, Penny said, "I found out he was a psychiatrist. Psychiatrists treat crazy people. That's when I knew I was a little bit . . . crazy."

Surprised and dismayed that such a misconception could have gone uncorrected for so long, Jack said, "No, no, no. Sweetheart, you've got it all wrong."

Rebecca said, "Penny, for the most part, psychiatrists treat ordinary people with ordinary problems. Problems that we all have at one time or another in our lives. Emotional problems, mostly. That's what yours were. *Emotional* problems."

Penny looked at her shyly. She frowned. Clearly, she wanted to believe.

"They treat some mental problems, too, of course," Rebecca said. "But in their offices, among their regular patients, they hardly ever see anyone who's really, really insane. Truly crazy people are hospitalized or kept in institutions."

"Sure," Jack said. He reached for Penny's hands, held them. They were small, delicate hands. The fragility of her hands, the vulnerability of an eleven-year-old who liked to think of herself as grown-up—it made his heart ache. "Honey, you were never crazy. Never even close to crazy. What a terrible thing to've been worrying about all this time."

The girl looked from Jack to Rebecca to Jack again. "You really mean it? You really mean lots of ordinary, everyday people go to psychiatrists?"

"Absolutely," he said. "Honey, life threw you a pretty bad curve, what with your mom dying so young, and I was so broken up myself that I wasn't much good at helping you handle it. I guess . . . I should have made an extra-special effort. But I was feeling so bad, so lost, so helpless, so darned sorry for myself that I just wasn't able to heal both of us, you and me. That's why I sent you to Dr. Hannaby when you started having your problems. Not because you were crazy. Because you needed to talk to someone who wouldn't start crying about your mom as soon as *you* started crying about your mom. Understand?"

"Yeah," Penny said softly, tears shining in her eyes, brightly suspended but unspilled.

"Positive?"

"Yeah. I really do, Daddy. I understand now."

"So you should have come to me last night, when the thing was in your room. Certainly after it poked holes in that plastic baseball bat. I wouldn't have thought you were crazy."

"Neither would I," Davey said. "I never-ever thought you were crazy, Penny. You're probably the least craziest person I know."

Penny giggled, and Jack and Rebecca couldn't help grinning, but Davey didn't know what was so funny.

Jack hugged his daughter very tight. He kissed her face and her hair. He said, "I love you, peanut."

Then he hugged Davey and told him he loved him, too.

And then, reluctantly, he looked at his wristwatch.

Ten-twenty-four.

Ten minutes had elapsed since they had come into the brownstone and had taken shelter in the space under the big staircase.

"Looks like they didn't follow us," Rebecca said.

"Let's not be too hasty," he said. "Give it another couple of minutes."

Ten-twenty-five.

Ten-twenty-six.

He didn't relish going outside and having a look around. He waited one more minute.

Ten-twenty-seven.

Finally he could delay no longer. He eased out from the staircase. He took two steps, put his hand on the brass knob of the foyer door—and froze.

They were here. The goblins.

One of them was clinging to the glass panel in the center of the door. It was a two-foot-long, wormlike thing with a segmented body and perhaps two dozen legs. Its mouth resembled that of a fish: oval, with the teeth set far back from the writhing, sucking lips. Its fiery eyes fixed on Jack.

He abruptly looked away from that white-hot gaze, for he recalled how the eyes of the lizard had nearly hypnotized him.

Beyond the worm-thing, the security foyer was crawling with other, different devils, all of them small, but all of them so incredibly vicious and grotesque in appearance that Jack began to shake and felt his bowels turn to jelly. There were lizard-things in various sizes and shapes. Spider-things. Rat-things. Two of the man-form beasts, one of them with a tail, the other with a sort of cock's comb on its head and along its back. Dog things. Crablike, feline, snakelike, beetle-form, scorpionlike, dragonish, clawed and fanged, spiked and spurred and sharply horned *things*. Perhaps twenty of them. No. More than twenty. At least thirty. They slithered and skittered across the mosaic-tile floor, and they crept tenaciously up the walls, their foul tongues darting and fluttering ceaselessly, teeth gnashing and grinding, eyes shining.

Shocked and repelled, Jack snatched his hand away from the brass doorknob. He turned to Rebecca and the kids. "They've found us. They're here. Come on. Got to get out. Hurry. Before it's too late."

They came away from the stairs. They saw the worm-thing on the door and the horde in the foyer beyond. Rebecca and Penny stared at the Hellborn pack without speaking, both of them driven beyond the need—and perhaps beyond the ability—to scream. Davey was the only one who cried out. He clutched at Jack's arm.

"They must be inside the building by now," Rebecca said. "In the walls."

They all looked toward the hallway's heating vents.

"How do we get out?" Penny asked.

How, indeed?

For a moment no one spoke.

In the foyer other creatures had joined the worm-thing on the glass of the inner door.

"Is there a rear entrance?" Rebecca wondered.

"Probably," Jack said. "But if there is, then these things will be waiting there, too."

Another pause.

The silence was oppressive and terrifying—like the unspent energy in the raised blade of a cocked guillotine.

"Then we're trapped," Penny said.

Jack felt his own heart beating. It shook him.

Think.

"Daddy, don't let them get me, please don't let them," Davey said miserably.

Jack glanced at the elevator, which was opposite the stairs. He wondered if the devils were already in the elevator shaft. Would the doors of the lift suddenly open, spilling out a wave of hissing, snarling, snapping death?

Think!

He grabbed Davey's hand and headed toward the foot of the stairs.

Following with Penny, Rebecca said, "Where are you going?"

"This way."

They climbed the steps toward the second floor.

Penny said, "But if they're in the walls, they'll be all through the building."

"Hurry," was Jack's only answer. He led them up the steps as fast as they could go.

III

IN CARVER HAMPTON'S apartment above his shop in Harlem, all the lights were on. Ceiling lights, reading lamps, table lamps, and floor lamps blazed; no room was left in shadow. In those few corners where the lamplight didn't reach, candles had been lit; clusters of them stood in dishes and pie pans and cake tins.

Carver sat at the small kitchen table, by the window, his strong brown hands clamped around a glass of Chivas Regal. He stared out at the falling snow, and once in a while he took a sip of the Scotch.

Fluorescent bulbs glowed in the kitchen ceiling. The stove light was on. And the light above the sink, too. On the table, within easy reach, were packs of matches, three boxes of candles, and two flashlights—just in case the storm caused a power failure.

This was not a night for darkness.

Monstrous things were loose in the city.

They *fed* on darkness.

Although the night-stalkers had not been sent to get Carver, he could sense them out there in the stormy streets, prowling, hungry; they radiated a palpable evil, the pure and ultimate evil of the Ancient Ones. The creatures now loose in the storm were foul and unspeakable presences that couldn't go unnoticed by a man of Carver Hampton's powers. For one who was gifted with the ability to detect the intrusion of otherworldly forces into this world, their mere existence was an intolerable abrasion of the nerves, the soul. He assumed they were Lavelle's hellish emissaries, bent on the brutal destruction of the Carramazza family, for to the best of his knowledge there was no other *Bocor* in New York who could have summoned such creatures from the Underworld.

He sipped his Scotch. He wanted to get roaring drunk. But he wasn't much of a drinking man. Besides, this night of all nights, he must remain alert, totally in control of himself. Therefore, he allowed himself only small sips of whiskey.

The Gates had been opened. The very Gates of Hell. Just a crack. The latch had barely been slipped. And through the application of his formidable powers as a *Bocor*, Lavelle was holding the Gates against the crush of demonic entities that sought to push forth from the other side. Carver could sense all of those things in the currents of the ether, in the invisible and soundless tides of benign and malevolent energies that ebbed and flowed over the great metropolis.

Opening the Gates was a wildly dangerous step to have taken. Few *Bocors* were even capable of doing it. And of those few, fewer still would have dared such a thing. Because Lavelle evidently was one of the most powerful *Bocors* who had ever drawn a *vèvè*, there was good reason to believe that he would be able to maintain control of the Gates and that, in time, when the Carramazzas were disposed of, he would be able to cast back the creatures that he had permitted out of Hell. But if he lost control for even a moment . . .

Then God help us, Carver thought.

If He *will* help us.

If He *can* help us.

A hurricane-force gust of wind slammed into the building and whined through the eaves.

The window rattled in front of Carver, as if something more than the wind was out there and wanted to get in at him.

A whirling mass of snow pressed to the glass. Incredibly, those hundreds upon hundreds of quivering, suspended flakes seemed to form a leering face that glared at Hampton. Although the wind huffed and hammered and whirled and shifted directions and then shifted back again, that impossible face did not dissolve and drift away on the changing air currents; it hung there, just beyond the pane, unmoving, as if it were painted on canvas.

Carver lowered his eyes.

In time the wind subsided a bit.

When the howling of it had quieted to a moan, he looked up once more. The snow-formed face was gone.

He sipped his Scotch. The whiskey didn't warm him. Nothing could warm him this night.

Guilt was one reason he wished he could get drunk. He was eaten by guilt because he had refused to give Lieutenant Dawson any more help. That had been wrong. The situation was too dire for him to think only about himself. The Gates were open, after all. The world stood at the brink of Armageddon— all because one *Bocor,* driven by ego and pride and an unslakeable thirst for blood, was willing to take any risk, no matter how foolish, to settle a personal grudge. At a time like this, a *Houngon* had certain responsibilities. Now was an hour for courage. Guilt gnawed at him because he kept remembering the midnight-black serpent that Lavelle had sent, and with that memory tormenting him, he couldn't find the courage he required for the task that called.

Even if he dared get drunk, he would still have to carry that burden of guilt. It was far too heavy—immense—to be lifted by booze alone.

Therefore, he was now drinking in hope of finding courage. It was a peculiarity of whiskey that, in moderation, it could sometimes make heroes of the very same men of whom it made buffoons on other occasions.

He must find the courage to call Detective Dawson and say, *I want to help.*

More likely than not, Lavelle would destroy him for becoming involved. And whatever death Lavelle chose to administer, it would not be an easy one.

He sipped his Scotch.

He looked across the room at the wall phone.

Call Dawson, he told himself.

He didn't move.

He looked at the blizzard-swept night outside.

He shuddered.

IV

BREATHLESS, JACK AND REBECCA and the kids reached the fourth-floor landing in the brownstone apartment house.

Jack looked down the stairs they'd just climbed. So far, nothing was after them.

Of course, something could pop out of one of the walls at any moment. The whole damned world had become a carnival funhouse.

Four apartments opened off the hall. Jack led the others past all four of them without knocking, without ringing any doorbells.

There was no help to be found here. These people could do nothing for them. They were on their own.

At the end of the hall was an unmarked door. Jack hoped to God it was what he thought it was. He tried the knob. From this side, the door was unlocked. He opened it hesitantly, afraid that the goblins might be waiting on the other side. Darkness. Nothing rushed at him. He felt for a light switch, half expecting to put his hand on something hideous. But he didn't. No goblins. Just the switch. *Click.* And, yes, it was what he hoped: a final flight of steps, considerably steeper and narrower than the eight flights they had already conquered, leading up to a barred door.

"Come on," he said.

Following him without question, Davey and Penny and Rebecca clumped noisily up the stairs, weary but still too driven by fear to slacken their pace.

At the top of the steps, the door was equipped with two deadbolt locks, and it was braced by an iron bar. No burglar was going to get into this place by way of the roof. Jack snapped open both deadbolts and lifted the bar out of its braces, stood it to one side.

The wind tried to hold the door shut. Jack shouldered it open, and then the wind caught it and pulled on it instead of pushing, tore it away from him, flung it outward with such tremendous force that it banged against the outside wall. He stepped across the threshold, onto the flat roof.

Up here, the storm was a living thing. With a lion's ferocity, it leapt out of the night, across the parapet, roaring and sniffing and snorting. It tugged at Jack's coat. It stood his hair on end, then plastered it to his head, then stood it on end again. It expelled its frigid breath in his face and slipped cold fingers under the collar of his coat.

He crossed to that edge of the roof which was nearest the next brownstone. The crenelated parapet was waist-high. He leaned against it, looked out and down. As he had expected, the gap between the buildings was only about four feet wide.

Rebecca and the kids joined him, and Jack said, "We'll cross over."

"How do we bridge it?" Rebecca asked.

"Must be something around that'll do the job."

He turned and surveyed the roof, which wasn't entirely cast in darkness; in fact, it possessed a moon-pale luminescence, thanks to the sparkling blanket of snow that covered it. As far as he could see, there were no loose pieces of lumber or anything else that could be used to make a bridge between the two buildings. He ran to the elevator housing and looked on the other side of it, and he looked on the far side of the exit box that contained the door at the head of the stairs, but he found nothing. Perhaps something useful lay underneath the snow, but there was no way he could locate it without first shoveling off the entire roof.

He returned to Rebecca and the kids. Penny and Davey remained hunkered down by the parapet, sheltering against it, keeping out of the biting wind, but Rebecca rose to meet him.

He said, "We'll have to jump."

"What?"

"Across. We'll have to jump across."

"We can't," she said.

"It's less than four feet."

"But we can't get a running start."

"Don't need it. Just a small gap."

"We'll have to stand on this wall," she said, touching the parapet, "and jump from there."

"Yeah."

"In this wind, at least one of us is sure as hell going to lose his balance even before he makes the jump—get hit by a hard gust of wind and just fall right off the wall."

"We'll make it," Jack said, trying to pump up his own enthusiasm for the venture.

She shook her head. Her hair blew in her face. She pushed it out of her eyes. She said, "Maybe, with luck, both you and I could do it. Maybe. But not the kids."

"Okay. So one of us will jump on the other roof, and one of us will stay here, and between us we'll hand the kids across, from here to there."

"Pass them over the gap?"

"Yeah."

"Over a fifty-foot drop?"

"There's really not much danger," he said, wishing he believed it. "From these two roofs, we could reach across and hold hands."

"Holding hands is one thing. But transferring something as heavy as a child—"

"I'll make sure you have a good grip on each of them before I let go. And as you haul them in, you can brace yourself against the parapet over there. No sweat."

"Penny's getting to be a pretty big girl."

"Not that big. We can handle her."

"But—"

"Rebecca, those *things* are in this building, right under our feet, looking for us right this very minute."

She nodded. "Who goes first?"

"You."

"Gee, thanks."

He said, "I can help you get up on top of the wall, and I can hold you until just a split second before you jump. That way, there's hardly any chance you could lose your balance and fall."

"But after I'm over there and after we've passed the kids across, who's going to help *you* get on top of the wall and keep your balance up there?"

"Let me worry about that when the time comes," he said.

Wind like a freight train whistled across the roof.

V

SNOW DIDN'T CLING to the corrugated metal storage shed at the rear of Lavelle's property. The falling flakes melted when they touched the roof and walls of that small structure. Wisps of steam were actually rising from the leeward slope of the roof; those pale snakes of vapor writhed up until they came within range of the wind's brisk broom; then they were swept away.

Inside, the shed was stifling hot.

Nothing moved except the shadows. Rising out of the hole in the floor, the irregularly pulsing orange light was slightly brighter than it had been earlier. The flickering of it caused the shadows to quiver, giving an illusion of movement to every inanimate object in the dirt-floored room.

The cold night air wasn't the only thing that failed to penetrate these metal walls. Even the shrieking and soughing of the storm was inaudible herein. The atmosphere within the shed was unnatural, uncanny, disquieting, as if the room had been lifted out of the ordinary flow of time and space, and was now suspended in a void.

The only sound was that which came from deep within the pit. It was a distant hissing-murmuring-whispering-growling, like ten thousand voices in a far-off place, the distance-muffled roar of a crowd. An angry crowd.

Suddenly, the sound grew louder. Not a great deal louder. Just a little.

At the same moment, the orange light beamed brighter than ever before. Not a lot brighter. Just a little. It was as if a furnace door, already ajar, had been pushed open another inch.

The interior of the shed grew slightly warmer, too.

The vaguely sulphurous odor became stronger.

And something strange happened to the hole in the floor. All the way around the perimeter, bits of earth broke loose and fell inward, away from the rim, vanishing into the mysterious light at the bottom. Like the increase in the brilliance of that light, this alteration in the rim of the hole wasn't major; only an incremental change. The diameter was increased by less than one inch. The dirt stopped falling away. The perimeter stabilized. Once more, everything in the shed was perfectly still.

But now the pit was bigger.

VI

THE TOP OF the parapet was ten inches wide. To Rebecca it seemed no wider than a tightrope.

At least it wasn't icy. The wind scoured the snow off the narrow surface, kept it clean and dry.

With Jack's help, Rebecca balanced on the wall, in a half crouch. The wind buffeted her, and she was sure that she would have been toppled by it if Jack hadn't been there.

She tried to ignore the wind and the stinging snow that pricked her exposed face, ignored the chasm in front of her, and focused both her eyes and her mind on the roof of the next building. She had to jump far enough to clear the parapet over there and land on the roof. If she came down a bit short, on top of that waist-high wall, on that meager strip of stone, she would be unbalanced for a moment, even if she landed flat on both feet. In that instant of supreme vulnerability, the wind would snatch at her, and she might fall, either forward onto the roof, or backward into the empty air between the buildings. She didn't dare let herself think about *that* possibility, and she didn't look down.

She tensed her muscles, tucked her arms in against her sides, and said, "Now," and Jack let go of her, and she jumped into the night and the wind and the driving snow.

Airborne, she knew at once that she hadn't put enough power into the jump, knew she was not going to make it to the other roof, knew she would crash into the parapet, knew she would fall backwards, knew that she was going to die.

But what she *knew* would happen *didn't* happen. She cleared the parapet, landed on the roof, and her feet slipped out from under her, and she went down on her backside, hard enough to hurt but not hard enough to break any bones.

As she got to her feet, she saw the dilapidated pigeon coop. Pigeon-keeping was neither a common nor an unusual hobby in this city; in fact, this coop was smaller than some, only six feet long. At a glance she was able to tell that it hadn't been used for years. It was so weathered and in such disrepair that it would soon cease to be a coop and would become just a pile of junk.

She shouted to Jack, who was watching from the other building: "I think maybe I've found our bridge!"

Aware of how fast time was running out, she brushed some of the snow from the roof of the coop and saw that it appeared to be formed by a single six-foot sheet of one-inch plywood. That was even better than she had hoped; now they wouldn't have to deal with two or three loose planks. The plywood had been painted many times over the years, and the paint had protected it from rot once the coop was abandoned and maintenance discontinued; it seemed sturdy enough to support the kids and even Jack. It was loose along one entire side, which was a great help to her. Once she brushed the rest of the snow off the coop roof, she gripped it by the loose end, pulled it up and back. Some of the nails popped out, and some snapped off because they were rusted clear through. In a few seconds she had wrenched the plywood free.

She dragged it to the parapet. If she tried to lever it onto the wall and shove it out toward Jack, the strong wind would get under it, treat it like a sail, lift it, tear it out of her hands, and send it kiting off into the storm. She had to wait for a lull. One came fairly soon, and she quickly heaved the plywood up, balanced it on top of the parapet, slid it out toward Jack's reaching hands. In a moment, as the wind whipped up once more, they had the bridge in place. Now, with the two of them holding it, they would be able to keep it down even if a fierce wind got under it.

Penny made the short journey first, to show Davey how easily it could be done. She wriggled across on her belly, gripping the edges of the board with her hands, pulling herself along. Convinced it could be done, Davey followed safely after her.

Jack came last. As soon as he was on the bridge, there was, of course, no one holding the far end of it. However, his weight held it in place, and he didn't scramble completely off until there was another lull in the wind. Then he helped Rebecca drag the plywood back onto the roof.

"Now what?" she asked.

"One building's not enough," he said. "We've got to put more distance between us and them."

Using the plywood, they crossed the gulf between the second and third apartment houses, went from the third roof to the fourth, then from the fourth to the fifth. The next building was ten or twelve stories higher than this one. Their roof-hopping had come to an end, which was just as well, since their arms were beginning to ache from dragging and lifting the heavy sheet of plywood.

At the rear of the fourth brownstone, Rebecca leaned over the parapet and looked down into the alley, four stories below. There was some light down there: a streetlamp at each end of the block, another in the middle, plus the glow that came from all the windows of the first-floor apartments. She couldn't see any goblins in the alley, or any other living creatures for that matter—just snow in blankets and mounds, snow twirling in small and short-lived tornadoes, snow in vaguely phosphorescent sheets like the gowns of ghosts racing in front of the wind. Maybe there were goblins crouching in the shadows somewhere, but she didn't really think so because she couldn't see any glowing white eyes.

A black, iron, switchback fire escape descended to the alley in a zig-zag path along the rear face of the building. Jack went down first, stopping at each landing to wait for Penny and Davey; he was prepared to break their fall if they slipped on the cold, snow-covered, and occasionally ice-sheathed steps.

Rebecca was the last off the roof. At each landing on the fire escape, she paused to look down at the alley, and each time she expected to see strange, threatening creatures loping through the snow toward the foot of the iron steps. But each time, she saw nothing.

When they were all in the alley, they turned right, away from the row of brownstones, and ran as fast as they could toward the cross street. When they reached the street, already slowing from a run to a fast walk, they turned away from Third Avenue and headed back toward the center of the city.

Nothing followed them.

Nothing came out of the dark doorways they passed.

For the moment they seemed safe. But more than that . . . they seemed to have the entire metropolis to themselves, as if they were the only four survivors of doomsday.

Rebecca had never seen it snow this hard. This was a rampaging, lashing, hammering storm more suitable to the savage polar ice fields than to New York. Her face was numb, and her eyes were watering, and she ached in every joint and muscle from the constant struggle required to resist the insistent wind.

Two-thirds of the way to Lexington Avenue, Davey stumbled and fell and simply couldn't find the energy to continue on his own. Jack carried him.

From the look of her, Penny was rapidly using up the last of her reserves, as well. Soon, Rebecca would have to take Davey, so Jack could then carry Penny.

And how far and how fast could they expect to travel under those circumstances? Not far. Not very damned fast. They needed to find transportation within the next few minutes.

They reached the avenue, and Jack led them to a large steel grate which was set in the pavement and from which issued clouds of steam. It was a vent from one sort of underground tunnel or another, most likely from the subway system. Jack put Davey down, and the boy was able to stand on his own feet. But it was obvious that he would still have to be carried when they started out again. He looked terrible; his small face was drawn, pinched, and very pale except for enormous dark circles around his eyes. Rebecca's heart went out to him, and she wished there was something she could do to make him feel better, but she didn't feel so terrific herself.

The night was too cold and the heated air rising out of the street wasn't heated enough to warm Rebecca as she stood at the edge of the grate and allowed the wind to blow the foul-smelling steam in her face; however, there was an illusion of warmth, if not the real thing, and at the moment the mere illusion was sufficiently spirit-lifting to forestall everyone's complaints.

To Penny, Rebecca said, "How're you doing, honey?"

"I'm okay," the girl said, although she looked haggard. "I'm just worried about Davey."

Rebecca was amazed by the girl's resilience and spunk.

Jack said, "We've got to get a car. I'll only feel safe when we're in a car, rolling, moving; they can't get at us when we're moving."

"And it'll b-b-be warm in a c-car," Davey said.

But the only cars on the street were those that were parked at the curb, unreachable beyond a wall of snow thrown up by the plows and not yet hauled away. If any cars had been abandoned in the middle of the avenue, they had already been towed away by the snow emergency crews.

None of those workmen were in sight now. No plows, either.

"Even if we could find a car along here that wasn't plowed in," Rebecca said, "it isn't likely there'd be keys in it—or snow chains on the tires."

"I wasn't thinking of these cars," Jack said. "But if we can find a pay phone, put in a call to headquarters, we could have them send out a department car for us."

"Isn't that a phone over there?" Penny asked, pointing across the broad avenue.

"Snow's so thick, I can't be sure," Jack said, squinting at the object that had drawn Penny's attention. "It *might* be a phone."

"Let's go have a look," Rebecca said.

Even as she spoke, a small but sharply clawed hand came out of the grating, from the space between two of the steel bars.

Davey saw it first, cried out, stumbled back, away from the rising steam.

A goblin's hand.

And another one, scrabbling at the toe of Rebecca's boot. She stomped on it, saw shining silver-white eyes in the darkness under the grate, and jumped back.

A third hand appeared, and a fourth, and Penny and Jack got out of the way, and suddenly the entire steel grating rattled in its circular niche, tilted up at one end, slammed back into place, but immediately tilted up again, a little farther than an inch this time, but fell back, rattled, bounced. The horde below was trying to push out of the tunnel.

Although the grating was large and immensely heavy, Rebecca was sure the creatures below would dislodge it and come boiling out of the darkness and steam. Jack must have been equally convinced, for he snatched up Davey and ran. Rebecca grabbed Penny's hand, and they followed Jack, fleeing down the blizzard-pounded avenue, not moving as fast as they should, not moving very fast at all. None of them dared to look back.

Ahead, on the far side of the divided thoroughfare, a Jeep station wagon turned the corner, tires churning effortlessly through the snow. It bore the insignia of the city department of streets.

Jack and Rebecca and the kids were headed downtown, but the Jeep was headed uptown. Jack angled across the avenue, toward the center divider and the other lanes beyond it, trying to get in front of the Jeep and cut it off before it was past them.

Rebecca and Penny followed.

If the driver of the Jeep saw them, he didn't give any indication of it. He didn't slow down.

Rebecca was waving frantically as she ran, and Penny was shouting, and Rebecca started shouting, too, and so did Jack, all of them shouting their fool heads off because the Jeep was their only hope of escape.

VII

AT THE TABLE in the brightly lighted kitchen above *Rada,* Carver Hampton played a few hands of solitaire. He hoped the game would take his mind off the evil that was loose in the winter night, and he hoped it would help him overcome his feelings of guilt and shame, which plagued him because he hadn't done anything to stop that evil from having its way in the world. But the cards couldn't distract him. He kept looking out the window beside the table, sensing something unspeakable out there in the dark. His guilt grew stronger instead of weaker; it chewed on his conscience.

He was a *Houngon.*

He had certain responsibilities.

He could not condone such monstrous evil as this.

Damn.

He tried watching television. *Quincy.* Jack Klugman was shouting at his stupid superiors, crusading for Justice, exhibiting a sense of social compassion greater than Mother Teresa's, and otherwise comporting himself more like Superman than like a real medical examiner. On *Dynasty,* a bunch of rich people were carrying on in the most licentious, vicious, Machiavellian manner, and Carver asked himself the same question he always asked himself when he was unfortunate enough to catch a few minutes of *Dynasty* or *Dallas* or one of their clones: If *real* rich people in the *real* world were this obsessed with sex, revenge, back-stabbing, and petty jealousies, how could any of them ever have had the time and intelligence to make any money in the first place? He switched off the TV.

He was a *Houngon*.

He had certain responsibilities.

He chose a book from the living room shelf, the new Elmore Leonard novel, and although he was a big fan of Leonard's, and although no one wrote stories that moved faster than Leonard's stories, he couldn't concentrate on this one. He read two pages, couldn't remember a thing he'd read, and returned the book to the shelf.

He was a *Houngon*.

He returned to the kitchen, went to the telephone. He hesitated with his hand on it.

He glanced at the window. He shuddered because the vast night itself seemed to be demonically alive.

He picked up the phone. He listened to the dial tone for a while.

Detective Dawson's office and home numbers were on a piece of notepaper beside the telephone. He stared at the home number for a while. Then, at last, he dialed it.

It rang several times, and he was about to give up, when the receiver was lifted at the other end. But no one spoke.

He waited a couple of seconds, then said, "Hello?"

No answer.

"Is someone there?"

No response.

At first he thought he hadn't actually reached the Dawson number, that there was a problem with the connection, that he was listening to dead air. But as he was about to hang up, a new and frightening perception seized him. He sensed an evil presence at the other end, a supremely malevolent entity whose malignant energy poured back across the telephone line.

He broke out in a sweat. He felt soiled. His heart raced. His stomach turned sour, sick.

He slammed the phone down. He wiped his damp hands on his pants. They still felt unclean, merely from holding the telephone that had temporarily connected him with the beast in the Dawson apartment. He went to the sink and washed his hands thoroughly.

The thing at the Dawsons' place was surely one of the entities that Lavelle had summoned to do his dirty work for him. But what was it doing there? What did this mean? Was Lavelle crazy enough to turn loose the powers of darkness not only on the Carramazzas but on the police who were investigating those murders?

If anything happens to Lieutenant Dawson, Hampton thought, I'm responsible because I refused to help him.

Using a paper towel to blot the cold sweat from his face and neck, he considered his options and tried to decide what he should do next.

VIII

THERE WERE ONLY two men in the street department's Jeep station wagon, which left plenty of room for Penny, Davey, Rebecca, and Jack.

The driver was a merry-looking, ruddy-faced man with a squashed nose and big ears; he said his name was Burt. He looked closely at Jack's police ID and, satisfied that it was genuine, was happy to put himself at their disposal, swing the Jeep around, and run them back to headquarters, where they could get another car.

The interior of the Jeep was wonderfully warm and dry.

Jack was relieved when the doors were all safely shut and the Jeep began to pull out.

But just as they were making a U-turn in the middle of the deserted avenue, Burt's partner, a freckle-faced young man named Leo, saw something moving through the snow, coming toward them from across the street. He said, "Hey, Burt, hold on a sec. Isn't that a cat out there?"

"So what if it is?" Burt asked.

"He shouldn't be out in weather like this."

"Cats go where they want," Burt said. "You're the cat fancier; you should know how independent they are."

"But it'll freeze to death out there," Leo said.

As the Jeep completed the turn, and as Burt slowed down a bit to consider Leo's statement, Jack squinted through the side window at the dark shape loping across the snow; it moved with feline grace. Farther back in the storm, beyond several veils of falling snow, there might have been other things coming this way; perhaps it was even the entire nightmare pack moving in for the kill, but it was hard to tell for sure. However, the first of the goblins, the catlike thing that had caught Leo's eye, was undeniably out there, only thirty or forty feet away and closing fast.

"Stop just a sec," Leo said. "Let me get out and scoop up the poor little fella."

"No!" Jack said. "Get the hell out of here. That's no damned cat out there."

Startled, Burt looked over his shoulder at Jack.

Penny began to shout the same thing again and again, and Davey took up her chant: "Don't let them in, don't let them in here, don't let them in!"

Face pressed to the window in his door, Leo said, "Jesus, you're right. It isn't any cat."

"Move!" Jack shouted.

The thing leaped and struck the side window in front of Leo's face. The glass cracked but held.

Leo yelped, jumped, scooted backwards across the front seat, crowding Burt.

Burt tramped down on the accelerator, and the tires spun for a moment.

The hideous cat-thing clung to the cracked glass.

Penny and Davey were screaming. Rebecca tried to shield them from the sight of the goblin.

It probed at them with eyes of fire.

Jack could almost feel the heat of that inhuman gaze. He wanted to empty his revolver at the thing, put half a dozen slugs into it, though he knew he couldn't kill it.

The tires stopped spinning, and the Jeep took off with a lurch and a shudder.

Burt held the steering wheel with one hand and used the other hand to try to push Leo out of the way, but Leo wasn't going to move even an inch closer to the fractured window where the cat-thing had attached itself.

The goblin licked the glass with its black tongue.

The Jeep careened toward the divider in the center of the avenue, and it started to slide.

Jack said, "Damnit, don't lose control!"

"I can't steer with him on my lap," Burt said.

He rammed an elbow into Leo's side, hard enough to accomplish what all the pushing and shoving and shouting hadn't managed to do; Leo moved—although not much.

The cat-thing grinned at them. Double rows of sharp and pointed teeth gleamed.

Burt stopped the sliding Jeep just before it would have hit the center divider. In control again, he accelerated.

The engine roared.

Snow flew up around them.

Leo was making odd gibbering sounds, and the kids were crying, and for some reason Burt began blowing the horn, as if he thought the sound would frighten the thing and make it let go.

Jack's eyes met Rebecca's. He wondered if his own gaze was as bleak as hers.

Finally, the goblin lost its grip, fell off, tumbled away into the snowy street.

Leo said, "Thank God," and collapsed back into his own corner of the front seat.

Jack turned and looked out the rear window. Other dark beasts were coming out of the whiteness of the storm. They loped after the Jeep, but they couldn't keep up with it. They quickly dwindled.

Disappeared.

But they were still out there. Somewhere.

Everywhere.

IX

THE SHED.

The hot, dry air.

The stench of Hell.

Again, the orange light abruptly grew brighter than it had been, not a lot brighter, just a little, and at the same time the air became slightly hotter, and the noises coming out of the pit grew somewhat louder and angrier, although they were still more of a whisper than a shout.

Again, around the perimeter of the hole, the earth loosened of its own accord, dropped away from the rim, tumbled to the bottom and vanished in the pulsing orange glow. The diameter had increased by more than two inches before the earth became stable once more.

And the pit was bigger.

PART THREE

Wednesday 11:20 P.M.—*Thursday,* 2:30 A.M.

You know, Tolstoy, like myself, wasn't taken
in by superstitions—like science and medicine.
—George Bernard Shaw

There is superstition in avoiding superstition.
—Francis Bacon

CHAPTER 7

I

AT HEADQUARTERS, THE underground garage was lighted but not very brightly lighted. Shadows crouched in corners; they spread like a dark fungus on the walls; they lay in wait between the rows of cars and other vehicles; they clung to the concrete ceilings and watched all that went on beneath them.

Tonight, Jack was scared of the garage. Tonight, the omnipresent shadows themselves seemed to be alive and, worse, seemed to be creeping closer with great cleverness and stealth.

Rebecca and the kids evidently felt the same way about the place. They stayed close together, and they looked around worriedly, their faces and bodies tense.

It's all right, Jack told himself. The goblins can't have known where we were going. For the time being, they've lost track of us. For the moment, at least, we're safe.

But he didn't *feel* safe.

The night man in charge of the garage was Ernie Tewkes. His thick black hair was combed straight back from his forehead, and he wore a pencil-thin mustache that looked odd on his wide upper lip.

"But each of you already signed out a car," Ernie said, tapping the requisition sheet on his clipboard.

"Well, we need two more," Jack said.

"That's against regulations, and I—"

"To hell with the regulations," Rebecca said. "Just give us the cars. *Now.*"

"Where're the two you already got?" Ernie asked. "You didn't wrack them up, did you?"

"Of course not," Jack said. "They're bogged down."

"Mechanical trouble?"

"No. Stuck in snow drifts," Jack lied.

They had ruled out going back for the car at Rebecca's apartment, and they had also decided they didn't dare return to Faye and Keith's place. They were sure the devil-things would be waiting at both locations.

"Drifts?" Ernie said. "Is that all? We'll just send a tow truck out, get you loose, and put you on the road again."

"We don't have time for that," Jack said impatiently, letting his gaze roam over the darker portions of the cavernous garage. "We need two cars right now."

"Regulations say—"

"Listen," Rebecca said, "weren't a number of cars assigned to the Carramazza task force?"

"Sure," Ernie said. "But—"

"And aren't some of those cars still here in the garage, right now, unused?"

"Well, at the moment, nobody's using them," Ernie admitted. "But maybe—"

"And who's in charge of the task force?" Rebecca demanded.

"Well . . . you are. The two of you."

"This is an emergency related to the Carramazza case, and we need those cars."

"But you've already got cars checked out, and regulations say you've got to fill out breakdown or loss reports on them before you can get—"

"Forget the bullshit bureaucracy," Rebecca said angrily. "Get us new wheels now, this minute, or so help me God I'll rip that funny little mustache out of your face, take the keys off your pegboard there, and get the cars myself."

Ernie stared wide-eyed at her, evidently stunned by both the threat and the vehemence with which it was delivered.

In this particular instance, Jack was delighted to see Rebecca revert to a nail-eating, hard-nosed Amazon.

"Move!" she said, taking one step toward Ernie.

Ernie moved. Fast.

While they waited by the dispatcher's booth for the first car to be brought around, Penny kept looking from one shadowy area to another. Again and again, she thought she saw things moving in the gloom: darkness slithering through darkness; a ripple in the shadows between two patrol cars; a throbbing in the pool of blackness that lay behind a police riot wagon; a shifting, malevolent shape in the pocket of darkness in that corner over there; a watchful, hungry shadow hiding among the ordinary shadows in that other corner; movement just beyond the stairway and more movement on the other side of the elevators and something scuttling stealthily across the dark ceiling and—

Stop it!

Imagination, she told herself. If the place was crawling with goblins, they'd have attacked us already.

The garage man returned with a slightly battered blue Chevrolet that had no police department insignia on the doors, though it did have a big antenna because of its police radio. Then he hurried away to get the second car.

Daddy and Rebecca checked under the seats of the first one, to be sure no goblins were hiding there.

Penny didn't want to be separated from her father, even though she knew separation was part of the plan, even though she had heard all the good reasons why it was essential for them to split up, and even though the time to leave had now come. She and Davey would go with Rebecca and spend the next few hours driving slowly up and down the main avenues, where the snowplows were working the hardest and where there was the least danger of getting stuck; they didn't dare get stuck because they were vulnerable when they stayed in one place too long, safe only while they were on wheels and moving, where the goblins couldn't get a fix on them. In the meantime her father would go to Harlem to see a man named Carver Hampton, who would probably be able to help him find Lavelle. Then he was going after that witchdoctor. He was sure he wouldn't be in terrible danger. He said that, for some reason he really didn't understand, Lavelle's magic had no effect on him. He said putting the cuffs on Lavelle wouldn't be any more difficult or dangerous than putting them on any other criminal. He meant it, too. And Penny wanted to believe that he was absolutely right. But deep in her heart, she was certain she would never see him again.

Nevertheless, she didn't cry too much, and she didn't hang on him too much, and she got into the car with Davey and Rebecca. As they drove out of the garage, up the exit ramp, she looked back. Daddy was waving at them. Then they reached the street and turned right, and he was out of sight. From that moment, it seemed to Penny that he was already as good as dead.

II

A FEW MINUTES after midnight, in Harlem, Jack parked in front of *Rada.* He knew Hampton lived above the store, and he figured there must be a private entrance to the apartment, so he went around to the side of the building, where he found a door with a street number.

There were a lot of lights on the second floor. Every window glowed brightly.

Standing with his back to the pummeling wind, Jack pushed the buzzer beside the door but wasn't satisfied with just a short ring; he held his thumb there, pressing down so hard that it hurt a little. Even through the closed door, the sound of the buzzer swiftly became irritating. Inside, it must be five or six times louder. If Hampton looked out through the fisheye security lens in the door and saw who was waiting and decided not to open up, then he'd better have a damned good pair of earplugs. In five minutes the buzzer would give him a headache. In ten minutes it would be like an icepick probing in his ears. If that didn't work, however, Jack intended to escalate the battle; he'd look around for a pile of loose bricks or several empty bottles or other hefty pieces of rubbish to throw through Hampton's windows. He didn't care about being charged with reckless use of authority; he didn't care about getting in trouble and maybe losing his badge. He was past the point of polite requests and civilized debate.

To his surprise, in less than half a minute the door opened, and there was Carver Hampton, looking bigger and more formidable than Jack remembered him, not frowning as expected but smiling, not angry but delighted.

Before Jack could speak, Hampton said, "You're all right! Thank God for that. Thank God. Come in. You don't know how glad I am to see you. Come in, come in." There was a small foyer beyond the door, then a set of stairs, and Jack went in, and Hampton closed the door but didn't stop talking. "My God, man, I've been worried half to death. Are you all right? You look all right. Will you please, for God's sake, tell me you're all right?"

"I'm okay," Jack said. "Almost wasn't. But there's so much I have to ask you, so much I—"

"Come upstairs," Hampton said, leading the way. "You've got to tell me what's happened, all of it, every detail. It's been an eventful and momentous night; I know it; I sense it."

Pulling off his snow-encrusted boots, following Hampton up the narrow stairs, Jack said, "I should warn you—I've come here to demand your help, and by God you're going to give it to me, one way or the other."

"Gladly," Hampton said, further surprising him. "I'll do whatever I possibly can; anything."

At the top of the stairs, they came into a comfortable-looking, well-furnished living room with a great many books on shelves along one wall, an Oriental tapestry on the wall opposite the books, and a beautiful Oriental carpet, predominantly beige and blue, occupying most of the floor space. Four blown-glass table lamps in striking blues and greens and yellows were placed with such skill that you were drawn by their beauty no matter which way you were facing. There were also two reading lamps, more functional in design, one by each of the big armchairs. Both of those and all four of the blown-glass lamps were on. However, their light didn't fully illuminate every last corner of the room, and in those areas where there otherwise might have been a few thin shadows, there were clusters of burning candles, at least fifty of them in all.

Hampton evidently saw that he was puzzled by the candles, for the big man said, "Tonight there are two kinds of darkness in this city, Lieutenant. First, there's that darkness which is merely the absence of light. And then there's that darkness which is the physical presence—the very manifestation—of the ultimate, Satanic evil. That second and malignant form of darkness feeds upon and cloaks itself in the first and more ordinary kind of darkness, cleverly disguises itself. *But it's out there!* Therefore, I don't wish to have shadows close to me this night, if I can avoid it, for one never knows when an innocent patch of shade might be something more than it appears."

Before this investigation, even as excessively open-minded as Jack had always been, he wouldn't have taken Carver Hampton's warning seriously. At best, he would have thought the man eccentric; at worst, a bit mad. Now, he didn't for a moment doubt the sincerity or the accuracy of the *Houngon*'s statements. Unlike Hampton, Jack wasn't afraid that the shadows themselves would suddenly leap at him and clutch him with insubstantial yet somehow deadly hands of darkness; however, after the things he had seen tonight, he couldn't rule out even that bizarre possibility. Anyway, because of what might be hiding within the shadows, he, too, preferred bright light.

"You look frozen," Hampton said. "Give me your coat. I'll hang it over the radiator to dry. Your gloves, too. Then sit down, and I'll bring you some brandy."

"I don't have time for brandy," Jack said, leaving his coat buttoned and his gloves on. "I've got to find Lavelle. I—"

"To find and stop Lavelle," Hampton said, "you've got to be properly prepared. That's going to take time. Only a fool would go rushing back out into that storm with only a half-baked idea of what to do and where to go. And you're no fool, Lieutenant. So give me your coat. I can help you, but it's going to take longer than two minutes."

Jack sighed, struggled out of his heavy coat, and gave it to the *Houngon.*

Minutes later, Jack was ensconced in one of the armchairs, holding a glass of Remy Martin in his cupped hands. He had taken off his shoes and socks and had put them by the radiator, too, for they had gotten thoroughly soaked by the snow that had gotten in over the tops of his boots as he'd waded through the drifts. For the first time all night, his feet began to feel warm.

Hampton opened the gas jets in the fireplace, poked a long-stemmed match in among the ceramic logs, and flames *whooshed* up. He turned the gas high. "Not for the heat so much as to chase the darkness from the flue," he said. He shook out the match, dropped it into a copper scuttle that stood on the hearth. He sat down in the other armchair, facing Jack across a coffee table on which were displayed two pieces of Lalique crystal—a clear bowl with green lizards for handles, and a tall frosted vase with a graceful neck. "If I'm to know how to proceed, you'll have to tell me everything that—"

"First, I've got some questions," Jack said.

"All right."

"Why wouldn't you help me earlier today?"

"I told you. I was scared."

"Aren't you scared now?"

"More than ever."

"Then why're you willing to help me now?"

"Guilt. I was ashamed of myself."

"It's more than that."

"Well, yes. As a *Houngon,* you see, I routinely call upon the gods of *Rada* to perform feats for me, to fulfill blessings I bestow on my clients and on others I wish to help. And, of course, it's the gods who make my magic potions work as intended. In return, it is incumbent upon me to resist evil, to strike against the agents of *Congo* and *Pétro* wherever I encounter them. Instead, for a while, I tried to hide from my responsibilities."

"If you had refused again to help me . . . would these benevolent gods of *Rada* continue to perform their feats for you and fulfill the blessings you bestow? Or would they abandon you and leave you without power?"

"It's highly unlikely they would abandon me."

"But possible?"

"Remotely, yes."

"So, at least in some small degree, you're also motivated by self-interest. Good. I like that. I'm comfortable with that."

Hampton lowered his eyes, stared into his brandy for a moment, then looked at Jack again and said, "There's another reason I must help. The stakes are higher than I first thought when I threw you out of the shop this afternoon. You see, in order to crush the Carramazzas, Lavelle has opened the Gates of Hell and has let out a host of demonic entities to do his killing for him. It was an insane, foolish, terribly prideful, stupid thing for him to have done, even if he is perhaps the most masterful *Bocor* in the world. He could have conjured up the spiritual essence of a demon and could have sent *that* after the Carramazzas; then there would have been no need to open the Gates at all, no need to bring those hateful creatures to this plane of existence in *physical* form. Insanity! Now, the Gates are open only a crack, and at the moment Lavelle is in control. I can sense that much through the cautious application of my own power. But Lavelle is a madman and, in some lunatic fit, might decide to fling the Gates wide, just for the fun of it. Or perhaps he'll grow weary and weaken; and if he weakens enough, the forces on the other side will surely burst the Gates against Lavelle's will. In either case, vast multitudes of monstrous creatures will come forth to slaughter the innocent, the meek, the good, and the just. Only the wicked will survive, but they'll find themselves living in Hell on Earth."

III

REBECCA DROVE UP the Avenue of the Americas, almost to Central Park, then made an illegal U-turn in the middle of the deserted intersection and headed downtown once more, with no cause to worry about other drivers. There actually was some traffic—snow removal vehicles, an ambulance, even two or three radio cabs—but for the most part the streets were bare of everything but snow. Twelve or fourteen inches had fallen, and it was still coming down fast. No one could see the lane markings through the snow; even where the plows scraped, they didn't make it all the way down to bare pavement. And no one was paying any attention to one-way signs or to traffic signals, most of which were on the blink because of the storm.

Davey's exhaustion had eventually proved greater than his fear. He was sound asleep on the back seat.

Penny was still awake, although her eyes were bloodshot and watery looking. She was clinging resolutely to consciousness because she seemed to have a compulsive need to talk, as if continual conversation would somehow keep the goblins away. She was also staying awake because, in a round-about fashion, she seemed to be leading up to some important question.

Rebecca wasn't sure what was on the girl's mind, and when, at last, Penny got to it, Rebecca was surprised by the kid's perspicacity.

"Do you like my father?"

"Of course," Rebecca said. "We're partners."

"I mean, do you like him more than just as a partner?"

"We're friends. I like him very much."

"More than just friends?"

Rebecca glanced away from the snowy street, and the girl met her eyes. "Why do you ask?"

"I just wondered," Penny said.

Not quite sure what to say, Rebecca returned her attention to the street ahead.

Penny said, "Well? Are you? More than just friends?"

"Would it upset you if we were?"

"Gosh, no!"

"Really?"

"You mean, maybe I might be upset because I'd think you were trying to take my mother's place?"

"Well, that's sometimes a problem."

"Not with me, it isn't. I loved my Mom, and I'll never forget her, but I know she'd want me and Davey to be happy, and one thing that'll make us real happy is if we could have another mom before we're too old to enjoy her."

Rebecca almost laughed in delight at the sweet, innocent, and yet curiously sophisticated manner in which the girl expressed herself. But she bit her tongue and remained straight-faced because she was afraid that Penny might misinterpret her laughter. The girl was so *serious.*

Penny said, "I think it would be terrific—you and Daddy. He needs some-one. You know . . . someone . . . to love."

"He loves you and Davey very much. I've never known a father who loved his children—who *cherished* them—as much as Jack loves and cherishes the two of you."

"Oh, I know that. But he needs more than us." The girl was silent for a moment, obviously deep in thought. Then: "See, there're basically three types of people. First, you've got your givers, people who just give and give and give and never expect to take anything in return. There aren't many of those. I guess that's the kind of person who sometimes ends up being made a saint a hundred years after he dies. Then there're your givers-and-takers, which is what most people are; that's what I am, I guess. And way down at the bottom, you've got your takers, the scuzzy types who just take and take and never-ever give anything to anyone. Now, I'm not saying Daddy's a complete giver. I know he isn't a saint. But he's not exactly a giver-and-taker, either. He's somewhere in between. He gives a whole lot more than he takes. You know? He enjoys giving more than he enjoys getting. He needs more than just Davey and me to love . . . because he's got a lot more love in him than just that." She sighed and shook her head in evident frustration. "Am I making any sense at all?"

"A lot of sense," Rebecca said. "I know exactly what you mean, but I'm amazed to be hearing it from an eleven-year-old girl."

"Almost twelve."

"Very grown up for your age."

"Thank you," Penny said gravely.

Ahead, at a cross street, a roaring river of wind moved from east to west and swept up so much snow that it almost looked as if the Avenue of the Americas terminated there, in a solid white wall. Rebecca slowed down, switched the headlights to high beam, drove through the wall and out the other side.

"I love your father," she told Penny, and she realized she hadn't yet told Jack. In fact, this was the first time in twenty years, the first time since the death of her grandfather, that she had admitted loving anyone. Saying those words was easier than she had thought it would be. "I love him, and he loves me."

"That's fabulous," Penny said, grinning.

Rebecca smiled. "It is rather fabulous, isn't it?"

"Will you get married?"

"I suspect we will."

"Double fabulous."

"Triple."

"After the wedding, I'll call you Mom instead of Rebecca—if that's all right."

Rebecca was surprised by the tears that suddenly rose in her eyes, and she swallowed the lump in her throat and said, "I'd like that."

Penny sighed and slumped down in her seat. "I was worried about Daddy. I was afraid that witchdoctor would kill him. But now that I know about you and him . . . well, that's one more thing he has to live for. I think it'll help. I think it's real important that he's got not just me and Davey but you to come home to. I'm still afraid for him, but I'm not so afraid as I was."

"He'll be all right," Rebecca said. "You'll see. He'll be just fine. We'll all come through this just fine."

A moment later, when she glanced at Penny, she saw that the girl was asleep.

She drove on through the whirling snow.

Softly, she said, "Come home to me, Jack. By God, you'd better come home to me."

IV

JACK TOLD CARVER HAMPTON everything, beginning with the call from Lavelle on the pay phone in front of *Rada,* and concluding with the rescue by Burt and Leo in their Jeep, the trip to the garage for new cars, and the decision to split up and keep the kids safely on the move.

Hampton was visibly shocked and distressed. He sat very still and rigid throughout the story, not even once moving to sip his brandy. Then, when Jack finished, Hampton blinked and shuddered and downed his entire glassful of Remy Martin in one long swallow.

"And so you see," Jack said, "when you said these things came from Hell, maybe some people might've laughed at you, but not me. I don't have any trouble believing you, even though I'm not too sure how they made the trip."

After sitting rigidly for long minutes, Hampton suddenly couldn't keep still. He got up and paced. "I know something of the ritual he must have used. It would only work for a master, a *Bocor* of the first rank. The ancient gods wouldn't have answered a less powerful sorcerer. To do this thing, the *Bocor* must first dig a pit in the earth. It's shaped somewhat like a meteor crater, sloping to a depth of two or three feet. The *Bocor* recites certain chants . . . uses certain herbs. . . . And he pours three types of blood into the hole—cat, rat, and human. As he sings a final and very long incantation, the bottom of the pit is miraculously transformed. In a sense . . . in a way that is impossible to explain or understand, the pit becomes far deeper than two or three feet; it interfaces with the Gates of Hell and becomes a sort of highway between this world and the Underworld. Heat rises from the pit, as does the stench of Hell, and the bottom of it appears to become molten. When the *Bocor* finally summons the entities he wants, they pass out through the Gates and then up through the bottom of the pit. On their way, these spiritual beings acquire physical bodies, golem bodies composed of the earth through which they pass; clay bodies that are nevertheless flexible and fully animated and *alive.* From your vivid descriptions of the creatures you've seen tonight, I'd say they were the incarnations of minor demons and of evil men, once mortal, who were condemned to Hell and are its lowest residents. Major demons and the ancient evil gods themselves would be considerably larger, more vicious, more powerful, and infinitely more hideous in appearance."

"Oh, these damned things were plenty hideous enough," Jack assured him.

"But, supposedly, there are many Ancient Ones whose physical forms are so repulsive that the mere act of looking at them results in instant death for he who sees," Hampton said, pacing.

Jack sipped his brandy. He needed it.

"Furthermore," Hampton said, "the small size of these beasts would seem to support my belief that the Gates are currently open only a crack. The gap is too narrow to allow the major demons and the dark gods to slip out."

"Thank God for that."

"Yes," Carver Hampton agreed. "Thank *all* the benevolent gods for that."

V

PENNY AND DAVEY were still asleep. The night was lonely without their company.

The windshield wipers flogged the snow off the glass.

The wind was so fierce that it rocked the sedan and forced Rebecca to grip the steering wheel more firmly than she had done before.

Then something made a noise beneath the car. *Thump, thump.* It knocked against the undercarriage hard enough to startle her, though not loud enough to wake the kids.

And again. *Thump, thump.*

She glanced in the rearview mirror, trying to see if she'd run over anything. But the car's back window was partially frosted, limiting her view, and the tires churned up plumes of snow so thick that they cast everything behind the car into obscurity.

She nervously scanned the lighted instrument panel in the dashboard, but she couldn't see any indication of trouble. Oil, fuel, alternator, battery—all seemed in good shape; no warning lights, no plunging needles on the gauges. The car continued to purr along through the blizzard. Apparently, the disconcerting noise hadn't been related to a mechanical problem.

She drove half a block without a recurrence of the sound, then an entire block, then another one. She began to relax.

Okay, okay, she told herself. Don't be so damned jumpy. Stay calm and be cool. That's what the situation calls for. Nothing's wrong now, and nothing's going to *go* wrong, either. I'm fine. The kids are fine. The car's fine.

Thump-thump-thump.

VI

THE GAS FLAMES licked the ceramic logs.

The blown-glass lamps glowed softly, and the candles flickered, and the special darkness of the night pressed against the windows.

"Why wouldn't those creatures bite me? Why can't Lavelle's sorcery harm me?"

"There can be only one answer," Hampton said. "A *Bocor* has no power whatsoever to harm a righteous man. The righteous are well-armored."

"What's that supposed to mean?"

"Just what I said. You're righteous, virtuous. You're a man whose soul bears the stains of only the most minor sins."

"You've got to be kidding."

"No. By the manner in which you've led your life, you've earned immunity to the dark powers, immunity to the curses and charms and spells of sorcerers like Lavelle. You cannot be touched."

"That's just plain ridiculous," Jack said, feeling uncomfortable in the role of a righteous man.

"Otherwise, Lavelle would have had you murdered by now."

"I'm no angel."

"I didn't say you were. Not a saint, either. Just a righteous man. That's good enough."

"Nonsense. I'm not righteous or—"

"If you thought of yourself as righteous, that would be a sin—a sin of *self*-righteousness. Smugness, an unshakable conviction of your own moral superiority, a self-satisfied blindness to your own faults—none of those qualities is descriptive of you."

"You're beginning to embarrass me," Jack said.

"You see? You aren't even guilty of the sin of excessive pride."

Jack held up his brandy. "What about this? I drink."

"To excess?"

"No. But I swear and curse. I sure do my own share of that. I take the Lord's name in vain."

"A very minor sin."

"I don't attend church."

"Church-going has nothing to do with righteousness. The only thing that really counts is how you treat your fellow human beings. Listen, let's pin this down; let's be absolutely sure this is why Lavelle can't touch you. Have you ever stolen from anyone?"

"No."

"Have you ever cheated someone in a financial transaction?"

"I've always looked out for my own interests, been aggressive in that regard, but I don't believe I've ever cheated anyone."

"In your official capacity, have you ever accepted a bribe?"

"No. You can't be a good cop if you've got your hand out."

"Are you a gossiper, a slanderer?"

"No. But forget about that small stuff." He leaned forward in his armchair and locked eyes with Hampton and said, "What about murder? I've killed two men. Can I kill two men and still be righteous? I don't think so. That strains your thesis more than a little bit."

Hampton looked stunned but only for a moment. He blinked and said, "Oh. I see. You mean that you killed them in the line of duty."

"Duty is a cheap excuse, isn't it? Murder is murder. Right?"

"What crimes were these men guilty of?"

"The first was a murderer himself. He robbed a series of liquor stores and always shot the clerks. The second was a rapist. Twenty-two rapes in six months."

"When you killed these men, was it necessary? Could you have apprehended them without resorting to a gun?"

"In both cases they started shooting first."

Hampton smiled, and the hard lines of his battered face softened. "Self-defense isn't a sin, Lieutenant."

"Yeah? Then why'd I feel so dirty after I pulled the trigger? Both times. I felt soiled. Sick. Once in a while, I still have a nightmare about those men, bodies torn apart by bullets from my own revolver . . ."

"Only a righteous man, a very virtuous man, would feel remorse over the killing of two vicious animals like the men you shot down."

Jack shook his head. He shifted in his chair, uncomfortable with this new vision of himself. "I've always seen myself as a fairly average, ordinary guy. No worse and no better than most people. I figure I'm just about as open to temptation, just about as corrupt as the next joe. And in spite of everything you've said, I *still* see myself that way."

"And you always will," Hampton said. "Humility is part of being a righteous man. But the point is, to deal with Lavelle, you don't have to *believe* you're really a righteous man; you just have to *be* one."

"Fornication," Jack said in desperation. "That's a sin."

"Fornication is a sin only if it is obsessive, adulterous, or an act of rape. An obsession is sinful because it violates the moral precept 'All things in moderation.' Are you obsessed with sex?"

"I like it a lot."

"Obsessed?"

"No."

"Adultery is a sin because it is a violation of the marriage vows, a betrayal of trust, and a conscious cruelty," Hampton said. "When your wife was alive, did you ever cheat on her?"

"Of course not. I was in love with Linda."

"Before your marriage or after your wife's death, did you ever go to bed with somebody else's wife? No? Then you aren't guilty of either form of adultery, and I know you're incapable of rape."

"I just can't buy this righteousness stuff, this idea that I'm one of the chosen or something. It makes me queasy. Look, I didn't cheat on Linda, but while we were married I saw other women who turned me on, and I fantasized, and I *wanted* them, even if I didn't do anything about it. My *thoughts* weren't pure."

"Sin isn't in the thought but in the deed."

"I am *not* a saintly character," Jack said adamantly.

"As I told you, in order to find and stop Lavelle, you don't need to *believe*— you only need to *be.*"

VII

REBECCA LISTENED TO the car with growing dread. Now, there were other sounds coming from the undercarriage, not just the odd thumping, but rattling and clanking and grating noises, as well. Nothing loud. But worrisome.

We're only safe as long as we keep moving.

She held her breath, expecting the engine to go dead at any moment.

Instead, the noises stopped again. She drove four blocks with only the normal sounds of the car and the overlaid moan and hiss of the storm wind.

But she didn't relax. She knew something was wrong, and she was sure it would start acting up again. Indeed, the silence, the anticipation, was almost worse than the strange noises.

VIII

STILL PSYCHICALLY LINKED with the murderous creatures he had summoned from the pit, Lavelle drummed his heels on the mattress and clawed at the dark air. He was pouring sweat; the sheets were soaked, but he was not aware of that.

He could smell the Dawson children. They were very close.

The time had almost come. Just minutes now. A short wait. And then the slaughter.

IX

JACK FINISHED HIS brandy, put the glass on the coffee table, and said, "There's a big hole in your explanation."

"And what's that?" Hampton asked.

"If Lavelle can't harm me because I'm a righteous man, then why can he hurt my kids? They're not wicked, for God's sake. They're not sinful little wretches. They're damned good kids."

"In the view of the gods, children can't be considered righteous; they're simply innocent. Righteousness isn't something we're born with; it's a state of grace we achieve only through years of virtuous living. We become righteous people by consciously choosing good over evil in thousands of situations in our day-to-day lives."

"Are you telling me that God—or all the benevolent gods, if you'd rather put it that way—protects the righteous but not the innocent?"

"Yes."

"Innocent little children are vulnerable to this monster Lavelle, but I'm not? That's outrageous, unfair, just plain wrong."

"You have an overly keen sense of injustice, both real and imagined. That's because you're a righteous man."

Now it was Jack who could no longer sit still. While Hampton slumped contentedly in an armchair, Jack paced in his bare feet. "Arguing with you is goddamned frustrating!"

"This is my field, not yours. I'm a theologist, not legitimized by a degree from any university, but not merely an amateur, either. My mother and father were devout Roman Catholics. In finding my own beliefs, I studied every religion, major and minor, before becoming convinced of the truth and efficacy of voodoo. It's the only creed that has always accommodated itself to other faiths; in fact, voodoo absorbs and uses elements from every religion with which it comes into contact. It is a synthesis of many doctrines that usually war against one another—everything from Christianity and Judaism to sun-worship and pantheism. I am a man of religion, Lieutenant, so it's to be expected that I'll tie you in knots on this subject."

"But what about Rebecca, my partner? She was bitten by one of these creatures, but she's not, by God, a wicked or corrupt person."

"There are degrees of goodness, of purity. One can be a good person and not yet truly righteous, just as one can be righteous and not yet be a saint. I've met Miss Chandler only once, yesterday. But from what I saw of her, I suspect she keeps her distance from people, that she has, to some degree, withdrawn from life."

"She had a traumatic childhood. For a long time, she's been afraid to let herself love anyone or form any strong attachments."

"There you have it," Hampton said. "One can't earn the favor of the *Rada* and be granted immunity to the powers of darkness if one withdraws from life and avoids a lot of those situations that call for a choice between good and evil, right and wrong. It is the making of those choices that enables you to achieve a state of grace."

Jack was standing at the hearth, warming himself in the heat of the gas fire —until the leaping flames suddenly reminded him of the goblins' eye sockets. He turned away from the blaze. "Just supposing I *am* a righteous man, how does that help me find Lavelle?"

"We must recite certain prayers," Hampton said. "And there's a purification ritual you must undergo. When you've done those things, the gods of *Rada* will show you the way to Lavelle."

"Then let's not waste any more time. Come on. Let's get started."

Hampton rose from his chair, a mountain of a man. "Don't be too eager or too fearless. It's best to proceed with caution."

Jack thought of Rebecca and the kids in the car, staying on the move to avoid being trapped by the goblins, and he said, "Does it matter whether I'm cautious or reckless? I mean, Lavelle can't harm me."

"It's true that the gods have provided you with protection from sorcery, from all the powers of darkness. Lavelle's skill as a *Bocor* won't be of any use to him. But that doesn't mean you're immortal. It doesn't mean you're immune to the dangers of *this* world. If Lavelle is willing to risk being caught for the crime, willing to risk standing trial, then he could still pick up a gun and blow your head off."

X

REBECCA WAS ON Fifth Avenue when the thumping and rattling in the car's undercarriage began again. It was louder this time, loud enough to wake the kids. And it wasn't just beneath them, any more; now, it was also coming from the front of the car, under the hood.

Davey stood up in back, holding onto the front seat, and Penny sat up straight and blinked the sleep out of her eyes and said, "Hey, what's that noise?"

"I guess we're having some sort of mechanical trouble," Rebecca said, although the car was running well enough.

"It's the goblins," Davey said in a voice that was half filled with terror and half with despair.

"It can't be them," Rebecca said.

Penny said, "They're under the hood."

"No," Rebecca said. "We've been moving around steadily since we left the garage. There's no way they could have gotten into the car. No way."

"Then they were there even in the garage," Penny said.

"No. They'd have attacked us right there."

"Unless," Penny said, "maybe they were afraid of Daddy."

"Afraid he could stop them," Davey said.

"Like he stopped the one that jumped on you," Penny said to her brother, "the one outside Aunt Faye's place."

"Yeah. So maybe the goblins figured to hang under the car and just wait till we were alone."

"Till Daddy wasn't here to protect us."

Rebecca knew they were right. She didn't want to admit it, but she *knew*.

The clattering in the undercarriage and the thumping-rattling under the hood increased, became almost frantic.

"They're tearing things apart," Penny said.

"They're gonna stop the car!" Davey said.

"They'll get in," Penny said. "They'll get in at us, and there's no way to stop them."

"Stop it!" Rebecca said. "We'll come out all right. They won't get us."

On the dashboard, a red warning light came on. In the middle of it was the word OIL.

The car had ceased to be a sanctuary.

Now it was a trap.

"They won't get us. I swear they won't," Rebecca said again, but she said it as much to convince herself as to reassure the children.

Their prospects for survival suddenly looked as bleak as the winter night around them.

Ahead, through the sheeting snow, less than a block away, St. Patrick's

Cathedral rose out of the raging storm, like some great ship on a cold night sea. It was a massive structure, covering one entire city block.

Rebecca wondered if voodoo devils would dare enter a church. Or were they like vampires in all the novels and movies? Did they shy away in terror and pain from the mere sight of a crucifix?

Another red warning light came on. The engine was overheating.

In spite of the two gleaming indicators on the instrument panel, she tramped on the accelerator, and the car surged forward. She angled across the lanes, toward the front of St. Patrick's.

The engine sputtered.

The cathedral offered small hope. Perhaps false hope. But it was the only hope they had.

XI

THE RITUAL OF purification required total immersion in water prepared by the *Houngon.*

In Hampton's bathroom, Jack undressed. He was more than a little surprised by his own new-found faith in these bizarre voodoo practices. He expected to feel ridiculous as the ceremony began, but he didn't feel anything of the sort because he had *seen* those Hellborn creatures.

The bathtub was unusually long and deep. It occupied more than half the bathroom. Hampton said he'd had it installed expressly for ceremonial baths.

Chanting in an eerily breathless voice that sounded too delicate to be coming from a man of his size, reciting prayers and petitions in a patois of French and English and various African tribal languages, Hampton used a bar of green soap—Jack thought it was Irish Spring—to draw *vèvès* all over the inside of the tub. Then he filled it with hot water. To the water, he added a number of substances and items that he had brought upstairs from his shop: dried rose petals; three bunches of parsley; seven vine leaves; one ounce of orgeat, which is a syrup made from almonds, sugar, and orange blossoms; powdered orchid petals; seven drops of perfume; seven polished stones in seven colors, each from the shore of a different body of water in Africa; three coins; seven ounces of seawater taken from within the territorial limits of Haiti; a pinch of gunpowder; a spoonful of salt; lemon oil; and several other materials.

When Hampton told him that the time had come, Jack stepped into the pleasantly scented bath. The water was almost too hot to bear, but he bore it. With steam rising around him, he sat down, pushed the coins and stones and other hard objects out of his way, then slid onto his tailbone, until only his head remained above the waterline.

Hampton chanted for a few seconds, then said, "Totally immerse yourself and count to thirty before coming up for air."

Jack closed his eyes, took a deep breath, and slid flat on his back, so that his entire body was submerged. He had counted only to ten when he began to feel a strange tingling from head to foot. Second by second, he felt somehow . . . *cleaner* . . . not just in body but in mind and spirit, as well. Bad thoughts, fear, tension, anger, despair—all were leeched out of him by the specially treated water.

He was getting ready to confront Lavelle.

XII

THE ENGINE DIED. A snowbank loomed.

Rebecca pumped the brakes. They were extremely soft, but they still worked. The car slid nose-first into the mounded snow, hitting with a *thunk* and a crunch, harder than she would have liked, but not hard enough to hurt anyone.

Silence.

They were in front of the main entrance to St. Patrick's.

Davey said, "Something's inside the seat! It's coming through!"

"What?" Rebecca asked, baffled by his statement, turning to look at him.

He was standing behind Penny's seat, pressed up against it, but facing the other way, looking at the backrest of the rear seat where he had been sitting just a short while ago. Rebecca squinted past him and saw movement under the upholstery. She heard an angry, muffled snarling, too.

One of the goblins must have gotten into the trunk. It was chewing and clawing through the seat, burrowing toward the interior of the car.

"Quick," Rebecca said. "Come up here with us, Davey. We'll all go out through Penny's door, one after the other, real quick, and then straight into the church."

Making desperate wordless sounds, Davey climbed into the front seat, between Rebecca and Penny.

At the same moment, Rebecca felt something pushing at the floorboards under her feet. A second goblin was tearing its way into the car from that direction.

If there were only two of the beasts, and if both of them were busily engaged in boring holes into the car, they might not immediately realize that their prey was making a run for the cathedral. It was at least something to hope for; not much, but something.

At a signal from Rebecca, Penny flung open the door and went out, into the storm.

Heart hammering, gasping in shock when the bitterly cold wind hit her, Penny scrambled out of the car, slipped on the snowy pavement, almost fell, windmilled her arms, and somehow kept her balance. She expected a goblin to rush out from beneath the car, expected to feel teeth sinking through one of her boots and into her ankle, but nothing like that happened. The streetlamps, shrouded and dimmed by the storm, cast an eerie light like that in a nightmare. Penny's distorted shadow preceded her as she clambered up the ridge of snow that had been formed by passing plows. She struggled all the way to the top, panting, using her hands and knees and feet, getting snow in her face and under her gloves and inside her boots, and then she jumped down to the sidewalk, which was buried under a smooth blanket of virgin snow, and she headed toward the cathedral, never looking back, never, afraid of what she might see behind her, pursued (at least in her imagination) by all the monsters she had seen in the foyer of that brownstone apartment house earlier tonight. The cathedral steps were hidden under deep snow, but Penny grabbed the brass handrail and used it as a guide, stomped all the way up the steps, suddenly wondering if the doors would be unlocked at this late hour. Wasn't a cathedral always open? If it was locked now, they were dead. She went to the centermost portal, gripped the handle, pulled, thought for a moment that it *was* locked, then realized it was just a very heavy door, seized the handle with both hands, pulled harder than before, opened the door, held it wide, turned, and finally looked back the way she'd come.

Davey was two-thirds of the way up the steps, his breath puffing out of him in jets of frost-white steam. He looked so small and fragile. But he was going to make it.

Rebecca came down off the ridge of snow at the curb, onto the sidewalk, stumbled, fell to her knees.

Behind her, two goblins reached the top of the piled-up snow.

Penny screamed. "They're coming! Hurry!"

When Rebecca fell to her knees, she heard Penny scream, and she got up at once, but she took only one step before the two goblins dashed past her, Jesus, as fast as the wind, a lizard-thing and a cat-thing, both of them screeching. They didn't attack her, didn't nip at her or hiss, didn't even pause. They weren't interested in her at all; they just wanted the kids.

Davey was at the cathedral door now, standing with Penny, and both of them were shouting at Rebecca.

The goblins reached the steps and climbed half of them in what seemed like a fraction of a second, but then they abruptly slowed down, as if they had realized they were rushing toward a holy place, although that realization didn't stop them altogether. They crept slowly and cautiously from step to step, sinking half out of sight in the snow.

Rebecca yelled at Penny—"Get in the church and close the door!"—but Penny hesitated, apparently hoping that Rebecca would somehow make it past the goblins and get to safety herself (if the cathedral actually *was* safe), but even at their slower pace the goblins were almost to the top of the steps. Rebecca yelled again. And again Penny hesitated. Now, moving slower by the second, the goblins were within one step of the top, only a few feet away from Penny and Davey . . . and now they *were* at the top, and Rebecca was shouting frantically, and at last Penny pushed Davey into the cathedral. She followed her brother and stood just inside the door for a moment, holding it open, peering out. Moving slower still, but still moving, the goblins headed for the door. Rebecca wondered if maybe these creatures *could* enter a church when the door was held open for them, just as (according to legend) a vampire could enter a house only if invited or if someone held the door for him. It was probably crazy to think the same rules that supposedly governed mythical vampires would apply to these very *real* voodoo devils. Nevertheless, with new panic in her voice, Rebecca shouted at Penny again, and she ran halfway up the steps because she thought maybe the girl couldn't hear her above the wind, and she screamed at the top of her voice, "Don't worry about me! Close the door! Close the door!" And finally Penny closed it, although reluctantly, just as the goblins arrived at the threshold.

The lizard-thing threw itself at the door, rebounded from it, and rolled onto its feet again.

The cat-thing wailed angrily.

Both creatures scratched at the portal, but neither of them showed any determination, as if they knew that, for them, this was too great a task. Opening a cathedral door—opening the door to *any* holy place—required far greater power than they possessed.

Frustrated, they turned away from the door. Looked at Rebecca. Their fiery eyes seemed brighter than the eyes of the other creatures she had seen at the Jamisons' and in the foyer of that brownstone apartment house.

She backed down one step.

The goblins started toward her.

She descended all the other steps, stopping only when she reached the sidewalk.

The lizard-thing and the cat-thing stood at the top of the steps, glaring at her.

Torrents of wind and snow raced along Fifth Avenue, and the snow was falling so heavily that it almost seemed she would drown in it as surely as she would have drowned in an onrushing flood.

The goblins descended one step.

Rebecca backed up until she encountered the ridge of snow at the curb.

The goblins descended a second step, a third.

CHAPTER 8

I

THE BATH OF purification lasted only two minutes. Jack dried himself on three small, soft, highly absorbent towels which had strange runes embroidered in the corners; they were of a material not quite like anything he had ever seen before.

When he had dressed, he followed Carver Hampton into the living room and, at the *Houngon*'s direction, stood in the center of the room, where the light was brightest.

Hampton began a long chant, holding an *asson* over Jack's head, then slowly moving it down the front of him, then around behind him and up along his spine to the top of his head once more.

Hampton had explained that the *asson*—a gourd rattle made from a cala-bash plucked from a liana of a *calebassier courant* tree—was the symbol of office of the *Houngon*. The gourd's natural shape provided a convenient han-dle. Once hollowed out, the bulbous end was filled with eight stones in eight colors because that number represented the concept of eternity and life ever-lasting. The vertebrae of snakes were included with the stones, for they were symbolic of the bones of ancient ancestors who, now in the spirit world, might be called upon for help. The *asson* was also ringed with brightly colored porcelain beads. The beads, stones, and snake vertebrae produced an unusual but not unpleasant sound.

Hampton shook the rattle over Jack's head, then in front of his face. For almost a minute, singing hypnotically in some long-dead African language, he shook the *asson* over Jack's heart. He used it to draw figures in the air over each of Jack's hands and over each of his feet.

Gradually, Jack became aware of numerous appealing odors. First, he de-tected the scent of lemons. Then chrysanthemums. Magnolia blossoms. Each fragrance commanded his attention for a few seconds, until the air currents brought him a new odor. Oranges. Roses. Cinnamon. The scents grew more intense by the second. They blended together in a wonderfully harmonious fashion. Strawberries. Chocolate. Hampton hadn't lit any sticks of incense; he hadn't opened any bottles of perfume or essences. The fragrances seemed to occur spontaneously, without source, without reason. Black walnuts. Lilacs.

When Hampton finished chanting, when he put down the *asson,* Jack said, "Those terrific smells—where are they coming from?"

"They're the olfactory equivalents of visual apparitions," Hampton said.

Jack blinked at him, not sure he understood. "Apparitions? You mean . . . *ghosts?*"

"Yes. Spirits. Benign spirits."

"But I don't see them."

"You're not meant to see them. As I told you, they haven't materialized visually. They've manifested themselves as fragrances, which isn't an unheard of phenomenon."

Mint.

Nutmeg.

"Benign spirits," Hampton repeated, smiling. "The room is filled with them, and that's a very good sign. They're messengers of the *Rada.* Their arrival here, at this time, indicates that the benevolent gods support you in your battle against Lavelle."

"Then I'll find Lavelle and stop him?" Jack asked. "Is that what this means —that I'll win out in the end? Is it all predetermined?"

"No, no," Hampton said. "Not at all. This means only that you've got the support of the *Rada.* But Lavelle has the support of the dark gods. The two of you are instruments of higher forces. One will win, and one will lose; that's all that's predetermined."

In the corners of the room, the candle flames shrank until they were only tiny sparks at the tips of the wicks. Shadows sprang up and writhed as if they were alive. The windows vibrated, and the building shook in the grip of a sudden, tremendous wind. A score of books flew off the shelves and crashed to the floor.

"We have evil spirits with us, as well," Hampton said.

In addition to the pleasant fragrances that filled the room, a new odor assaulted Jack. It was the stench of corruption, rot, decay, death.

II

THE GOBLINS HAD descended all but the last two of the cathedral steps. They were within only a dozen feet of Rebecca.

She turned and bolted away from them.

They shrieked with what might have been anger or glee or both—or neither. A cold, alien cry.

Without looking back, she knew they were coming after her.

She ran along the sidewalk, the cathedral at her right side, heading toward the corner, as if she intended to flee to the next block, but that was only a ruse. After she'd gone ten yards, she made a sharp right turn, toward the cathedral, and mounted the steps in a snow-kicking frenzy.

The goblins squealed.

She was halfway up the steps when the lizard-thing snared her left leg and sank claws through her jeans, into her right calf. The pain was excruciating.

She screamed, stumbled, fell on the steps. But she continued upward, crawling on her belly, with the lizard hanging on her leg.

The cat-thing leaped onto her back. Clawed at her heavy coat. Moved quickly to her neck. Tried to nip her throat. It got only a mouthful of coat collar and knitted scarf.

She was at the top of the steps.

Whimpering, she grabbed the cat-thing and tore it loose.

It bit her hand.

She pitched it away.

The lizard was still on her leg. It bit her thigh a couple of inches above her knee.

She reached down, clutched it, was bitten on the other hand. But she ripped the lizard loose and pitched it down the steps.

Eyes shining silver-white, the cat-form goblin was already coming back at her, squalling, a windmill of teeth and claws.

Energized by desperation, Rebecca gripped the brass handrail and lurched to her feet in time to kick out at the cat. Fortunately, the kick connected solidly, and the goblin tumbled end over end through the snow.

The lizard rushed toward her again.

There was no end to it. She couldn't possibly keep both of them at bay. She was tired, weak, dizzy, and wracked with pain from her wounds.

She turned and, trying hard to ignore the pain that flashed like an electric current through her leg, she flung herself toward the door through which Penny and Davey had entered the cathedral.

The lizard-thing caught the bottom of her coat, climbed up, around her side, onto the front of the coat, clearly intending to go for her face this time.

The catlike goblin was back, too, grabbing at her foot, squirming up her leg.

She reached the door, put her back to it.

She was at the end of her resources, heaving each breath in and out as if it were an iron ingot.

This close to the cathedral, right up against the wall of it, the goblins became sluggish, as she had hoped they would, just as they had done when pursuing Penny and Davey. The lizard, its claws hooked in the front of her coat, let go with one deformed hand and swiped at her face. But the creature was no longer too fast for her. She jerked her head back in time and felt the claws trace only light scratches on the underside of her chin. She was able to pull the lizard off without being bitten; she threw it as hard as she could, out toward the street. She pried the cat-thing off her leg, too, and pitched it away from her.

Turning quickly, she yanked open the door, slipped inside St. Patrick's Cathedral, and pushed the door shut after her.

The goblins thumped against the other side of it, once, and then were silent.

She was safe. Amazingly, thankfully safe.

She limped away from the door, out of the dimly lighted vestibule in which she found herself, past the marble holy water fonts, into the vast, vaulted, massively-columned nave with its rows and rows of polished pews. The towering stained-glass windows were dark and somber with only night beyond them, except in a few places where an errant beam from a streetlamp outside managed to find and pierce a cobalt blue or brilliant red piece of glass. Everything here was big and solid-looking—the huge pipe organ with its thousands of brass pipes soaring up like the spires of a smaller cathedral, the great choir loft above the front portals, the stone steps leading up to the high pulpit and the brass canopy above it—and that massiveness contributed to the feeling of safety and peace that settled over Rebecca.

Penny and Davey were in the nave, a third of the way down the center aisle, talking excitedly to a young and baffled priest. Penny saw Rebecca first, shouted, and ran toward her. Davey followed, crying with relief and happiness at the sight of her, and the cassocked priest came, too.

They were the only four in the immense chamber, but that was all right. They didn't need an army. The cathedral was an inviolable fortress. Nothing could harm them there. Nothing. The cathedral was safe. It *had* to be safe, for it was their last refuge.

III

IN THE CAR IN front of Carver Hampton's shop, Jack pumped the accelerator and raced the engine, warming it.

He looked sideways at Hampton and said, "You sure you really want to come along?"

"It's the last thing I want to do," the big man said. "I don't share your immunity to Lavelle's powers. I'd much rather stay up there in the apartment, with all the lights on and the candles burning."

"Then stay. I don't believe you're hiding anything from me. I really believe you've done everything you can. You don't owe me anything more."

"I owe *me*. Going with you, helping you if I can—that's the right thing to do. I owe it to myself not to make another wrong choice."

"All right then." Jack put the car in gear but kept his foot on the brake pedal. "I'm still not sure I understand how I'm going to find Lavelle."

"You'll simply *know* what streets to follow, what turns to make," Hampton said. "Because of the purification bath and the other rituals we performed, you're now being guided by a higher power."

"Sounds better than a Three-A map, I guess. Only . . . I sure don't feel anything guiding me."

"You will, Lieutenant. But first, we've got to stop at a Catholic church and fill these jars"—he held up two small, empty jars that would hold about eight ounces each—"with holy water. There's a church straight ahead, about five blocks from here."

"Fine," Jack said. "But one thing."

"What's that?"

"Will you drop the formality, stop calling me Lieutenant? My name's Jack."

"You can call me Carver, if you like."

"I'd like."

They smiled at each other, and Jack took his foot off the brake, switched on the windshield wipers, and pulled out into the street.

They entered the church together.

The vestibule was dark. In the deserted nave there were a few dim lights burning, plus three or four votive candles flickering in a wrought iron rack that stood on this side of the communion railing and to the left of the chancel. The place smelled of incense and furniture polish that had evidently been used recently on the well-worn pews. Above the altar, a large crucifix rose high into the shadows.

Carver genuflected and crossed himself. Although Jack wasn't a practicing Catholic, he felt a sudden strong compulsion to follow the black man's example, and he realized that, as a representative of the *Rada* on this special night, it was incumbent upon him to pay obeisance to all the gods of good and light, whether it was the Jewish god of the old testament, Christ, Buddha, Mohammed, or any other deity. Perhaps this was the first indication of the "guidance" of which Carver had spoken.

The marble font, just this side of the narthex, contained only a small puddle of holy water, insufficient for their needs.

"We won't even be able to fill one jar," Jack said.

"Don't be so sure," Carver said, unscrewing the lid from one of the containers. He handed the open jar to Jack. "Try it."

Jack dipped the jar into the font, scraped it along the marble, scooped up some water, didn't think he'd gotten more than two ounces, and blinked in surprise when he held the jar up and saw that it was full. He was even more surprised to see just as much water left in the font as had been there before he'd filled the jar.

He looked at Carver.

The black man smiled and winked. He screwed the lid on the jar and put it in his coat pocket. He opened the second jar and handed it to Jack.

Again, Jack was able to fill the container, and again the small puddle of water in the font appeared untouched.

IV

LAVELLE STOOD BY the window, looking out at the storm.

He was no longer in psychic contact with the small assassins. Given more time, time to marshal their forces, they might yet be able to kill the Dawson children, and if they did he would be sorry he'd missed it. But time was running out.

Jack Dawson was coming, and no sorcery, regardless of how powerful it might be, would stop him.

Lavelle wasn't sure how everything had gone wrong so quickly, so completely. Perhaps it had been a mistake to target the children. The *Rada* was always incensed at a *Bocor* who used his power against children, and they always tried to destroy him if they could. Once committed to such a course, you had to be extremely careful. But, damnit, he *had* been careful. He couldn't think of a single mistake he might have made. He was well-armored; he was protected by all the power of the dark gods.

Yet Dawson was coming.

Lavelle turned away from the window.

He crossed the dark room to the dresser.

He took a .32 automatic out of the top drawer.

Dawson was coming. Fine. Let him come.

V

REBECCA SAT DOWN in the aisle of the cathedral and pulled up the right leg of her jeans, above her knee. The claw and fang wounds were bleeding freely, but she was in no danger of bleeding to death. The jeans had provided some protection. The bites were deep but not too deep. No major veins or arteries had been severed.

The young priest, Father Walotsky, crouched beside her, appalled by her injuries. "How did this happen? What did this to you?"

Both Penny and Davey said, *"Goblins,"* as if they were getting tired of trying to make him understand.

Rebecca pulled off her gloves. On her right hand was a fresh, bleeding bite mark, but no flesh was torn away; it was just four small puncture wounds. The gloves, like her jeans, had provided at least some protection. Her left hand bore two bite marks; one was bleeding and seemed no more serious than the wound on her right hand, painful but not mortal, while the other was the old bite she'd received in front of Faye's apartment building.

Father Walotsky said, "What's all that blood on your neck?" He put a hand to her face, gently pressed her hand back, so he could see the scratches under her chin.

"Those're minor," she said. "They sting, but they're not serious."

"I think we'd better get you some medical attention," he said. "Come on."

She pulled down the leg of her jeans.

He helped her to her feet. "I think it would be all right if I took you to the rectory."

"No," she said.

"It's not far."

"We're staying here," she said.

"But those look like animal bites. You've got to have them attended to. Infection, rabies. . . . Look, it's not far to the rectory. We don't have to go out in the storm, either. There's an underground passage between the cathedral and—"

"No," Rebecca said firmly. "We're staying here, in the cathedral, where we're protected."

She motioned for Penny and Davey to come close to her, and they did, eagerly, one on each side of her.

The priest looked at each of them, studied their faces, met their eyes, and his face darkened. "What *are* you afraid of?"

"Didn't the kids tell you some of it?" Rebecca asked.

"They were babbling about goblins, but—"

"It wasn't just babble," Rebecca said, finding it odd to be the one professing and defending a belief in the supernatural, she who had always been anything *but* excessively open-minded on the subject. She hesitated. Then, as succinctly as possible, she told him about Lavelle, the slaughter of the Carramazzas, and the voodoo devils that were now after Jack Dawson's children.

When she finished, the priest said nothing and couldn't meet her eyes. He stared at the floor for long seconds.

She said, "Of course, you don't believe me."

He looked up and appeared to be embarrassed. "Oh, I don't think you're lying to me . . . exactly. I'm sure *you* believe everything you've told me. But, to me, voodoo is a sham, a set of primitive superstitions. I'm a priest of the Holy Roman Church, and I believe in only one Truth, the Truth that Our Savior—"

"You believe in Heaven, don't you? And Hell?"

"Of course. That's part of Catholic—"

"These things have come straight up from Hell, Father. If I'd told you that it was a *Satanist* who had summoned these demons, if I'd never mentioned the word voodoo, then maybe you still wouldn't have believed me, but you wouldn't have dismissed the possibility so fast, either, because your religion encompasses Satan and Satanists."

"I think you should—"

Davey screamed.

Penny said, "They're here!"

Rebecca turned, breath caught in her throat, heart hanging in mid-beat.

Beyond the archway through which the center aisle of the nave entered the vestibule, there were shadows, and in those shadows were silver-white eyes glowing brightly. Eyes of fire. Lots of them.

VI

JACK DROVE THE snow-packed streets, and as he approached each intersection, he somehow sensed when a right turn was required, when he should go left instead, and when he should just speed straight through. He didn't know *how* he sensed those things; each time, a feeling came over him, a feeling he couldn't put into words, and he gave himself to it, followed the guidance that was being given to him. It was certainly unorthodox procedure for a cop accustomed to employing less exotic techniques in the search for a suspect. It was also creepy, and he didn't like it. But he wasn't about to complain, for he desperately wanted to find Lavelle.

Thirty-five minutes after they had collected the two small jars of holy water, Jack made a left turn into a street of pseudo-Victorian houses. He stopped in front of the fifth one. It was a three-story brick house with lots of gingerbread trim. It was in need of repairs and painting, as were all the houses in the block, a fact that even the snow and darkness couldn't hide. There were no lights in the house; not one. The windows were perfectly black.

"We're here," Jack told Carver.

He cut the engine, switched off the headlights.

VII

FOUR GOBLINS CREPT out of the vestibule, into the center aisle, into the light that, while not bright, revealed their grotesque forms in more stomach-churning detail than Rebecca would have liked.

At the head of the pack was a foot-tall, man-form creature with four fire-filled eyes, two in its forehead. Its head was the size of an apple, and in spite of the four eyes, most of the misshapen skull was given over to a mouth crammed full and bristling with teeth. It also had four arms and was carrying a crude spear in one spike-fingered hand.

It raised the spear above its head in a gesture of challenge and defiance.

Perhaps because of the spear, Rebecca was suddenly possessed of a strange but unshakable conviction that the man-form beast had once been—in very ancient times—a proud and blood-thirsty African warrior who had been condemned to Hell for his crimes and who was now forced to endure the agony and humiliation of having his soul embedded within a small, deformed body.

The man-form goblin, the three even more hideous creatures behind it, and the other beasts moving through the dark vestibule (and now seen only as pairs of shining eyes) all moved slowly, as if the very air inside this house of worship was, for them, an immensely heavy burden that made every step a painful labor. None of them hissed or snarled or shrieked, either. They just approached silently, sluggishly, but implacably.

Beyond the goblins, the doors to the street still appeared to be closed. They had entered the cathedral by some other route, through a vent or a drain that was unscreened and offered them an easy entrance, a virtual invitation, the equivalent of the "open door" that they, like vampires, probably needed in order to come where evil wasn't welcome.

Father Walotsky, briefly mesmerized by his first glimpse of the goblins, was the first to break the silence. He fumbled in a pocket of his black cassock, withdrew a rosary, and began to pray.

The man-form devil and the three things immediately behind it moved steadily closer, along the main aisle, and other monstrous beings crept and slithered out of the dark vestibule, while new pairs of glowing eyes appeared in the darkness there. They still moved too slowly to be dangerous.

But how long will that last? Rebecca wondered. Perhaps they'll somehow become conditioned to the atmosphere in the cathedral. Perhaps they'll gradually become bolder and begin to move faster. What then?

Pulling the kids with her, Rebecca began to back up the aisle, toward the altar. Father Walotsky came with them, the rosary beads clicking to his hands.

VIII

THEY SLOGGED THROUGH the snow to the foot of the steps that led up to Lavelle's front door.

Jack's revolver was already in his hand. To Carver Hampton, he said, "I wish you'd wait in the car."

"No."

"This is police business."

"It's more than that. You know it's more than that."

Jack sighed and nodded.

They climbed the steps.

Obtaining an arrest warrant, pounding on the door, announcing his status as an officer of the law—none of that usual procedure seemed necessary or sensible to Jack. Not in this bizarre situation. Still, he wasn't comfortable or happy about just barging into a private residence.

Carver tried the doorknob, twisted it back and forth several times. "Locked."

Jack could see that it was locked, but something told him to try it for himself. The knob turned under his hand, and the latch clicked softly, and the door opened a crack.

"Locked for me," Carver said, "but not for you."

They stepped aside, out of the line of fire.

Jack reached out, pushed the door open hard, and snatched his hand back.

But Lavelle didn't shoot.

They waited ten or fifteen seconds, and snow blew in through the open door. Finally, crouching, Jack moved into the doorway and crossed the threshold, his gun thrust out in front of him.

The house was exceptionally dark. Darkness would work to Lavelle's advantage, for he was familiar with the place, while it was all strange territory to Jack.

He fumbled for the light switch and found it.

He was in a broad entrance hall. To the left were inlaid oak stairs with an ornate railing. Directly ahead, beyond the stairs, the hall narrowed and led all the way to the rear of the house. A couple of feet ahead and to the right, there was an archway, beyond which lay more darkness.

Jack edged to the brink of the arch. A little light spilled in from the hall, but it showed him only a section of bare floor. He supposed it was a living room.

He reached awkwardly around the corner, trying to present a slim profile, feeling for another light switch, found and flipped it. The switch operated a ceiling fixture; light filled the room. But that was just about the only thing in it —light. No furniture. No drapes. A film of gray dust, a few balls of dust in the corners, a lot of light, and four bare walls.

Carver moved up beside Jack and whispered, "Are you sure this is the right place?"

As Jack opened his mouth to answer, he felt something whiz past his face and, a fraction of a second later, he heard two loud shots, fired from behind him. He dropped to the floor, rolled out of the hall, into the living room.

Carver dropped and rolled, too. But he had been hit. His face was contorted by pain. He was clutching his left thigh, and there was blood on his trousers.

"He's on the stairs," Carver said raggedly. "I got a glimpse."

"Must've been upstairs, then came down behind us."

"Yeah."

Jack scuttled to the wall beside the archway, crouched there. "You hit bad?"

"Bad enough," Carver said. "Won't kill me, though. You just worry about getting him."

Jack leaned around the archway and squeezed off a shot right away, at the staircase, without bothering to look or aim first.

Lavelle was there. He was halfway down the final flight of stairs, hunkered behind the railing.

Jack's shot tore a chunk out of the bannister two feet from the *Bocor*'s head.

Lavelle returned the fire, and Jack ducked back, and shattered plaster exploded from the edge of the archway.

Another shot.

Then silence.

Jack leaned out into the archway again and pulled off three shots in rapid succession, aiming at where Lavelle had been, but Lavelle was already on his way upstairs, and all three shots missed him, and then he was out of sight.

Pausing to reload his revolver with the loose bullets he carried in one coat pocket, Jack glanced at Carver and said, "Can you make it out to the car on your own?"

"No. Can't walk with this leg. But I'll be all right here. He only winged me. You just go get him."

"We should call an ambulance for you."

"Just get him!" Carver said.

Jack nodded, stepped through the archway, and went cautiously to the foot of the stairs.

IX

PENNY, DAVEY, REBECCA, and Father Walotsky took refuge in the chancel, behind the altar railing. In fact, they climbed up onto the altar platform, directly beneath the crucifix.

The goblins stopped on the other side of the railing. Some of them peered between the ornate supporting posts. Others climbed onto the communion rail itself, perched there, eyes flickering hungrily, black tongues licking slowly back and forth across their sharp teeth.

There were fifty or sixty of them now, and more were still coming out of the vestibule, far back at the end of the main aisle.

"They w-won't come up here, w-w-will they?" Penny asked. "Not this c-close to the crucifix. *Will they?*"

Rebecca hugged the girl and Davey, held them tight and close. She said, "You can see they've stopped. It's all right. It's all right now. They're afraid of the altar. They've stopped."

But for how long? she wondered.

X

JACK CLIMBED THE stairs with his back flat against the wall, moving sideways, trying to be utterly silent, nearly succeeding. He held his revolver in his left hand, with his arm rigidly extended, aiming at the top of the steps, his aim never wavering as he ascended, so he'd be ready to pull the trigger the instant Lavelle appeared. He reached the landing without being shot at, climbed three steps of the second flight, and then Lavelle leaned out around the corner above, and both of them fired—Lavelle twice, Jack once.

Lavelle pulled the trigger without pausing to take aim, without even knowing exactly where Jack was. He just took a chance that two rounds, placed down the center of the stairwell, would do the job. Both missed.

On the other hand, Jack's gun was aimed along the wall, and Lavelle leaned right into its line of fire. The slug smashed into his arm at the same moment he finished pulling the trigger of his own gun. He screamed, and the pistol flew out of his hand, and he stumbled back into the upstairs hall where he'd been hiding.

Jack took the stairs two at a time, jumping over Lavelle's pistol as it came tumbling down. He reached the second-floor hallway in time to see Lavelle enter a room and slam the door behind him.

Downstairs, Carver lay on the dust-filmed floor, eyes closed. He was too weary to keep his eyes open. He was growing wearier by the second.

He didn't feel like he was lying on a hard floor. He felt as if he were floating in a warm pool of water, somewhere in the tropics. He remembered being shot, remembered falling; he knew the floor really was there, under him, but he just couldn't feel it.

He figured he was bleeding to death. The wound didn't *seem* that bad, but maybe it was worse than he thought. Or maybe it was just shock that made him feel this way. Yeah, that must be it, shock, just shock, not bleeding to death after all, just suffering from shock, but of course shock could kill, too.

Whatever the reasons, he floated, oblivious of his own pain, just bobbing up and down, drifting there on the hard floor that wasn't hard at all, drifting on some far-away tropical tide . . . until, from upstairs, there was the sound of gunfire and a shrill scream that snapped his eyes open. He had an out-of-focus, floor-level view of the empty room. He blinked his eyes rapidly and squinted until his clouded vision cleared, and then he wished it *hadn't* cleared because he saw that he was no longer alone.

One of the denizens of the pit was with him, its eyes aglow.

Upstairs, Jack tried the door that Lavelle had slammed. It was locked, but the lock probably didn't amount to much, just a privacy set, flimsy as they could be made, because people didn't want to put heavy and expensive locks *inside* a house.

"Lavelle?" he shouted.

No answer.

"Open up. No use trying to hide in there."

From inside the room came the sound of a shattering window.

"Shit," Jack said.

He stepped back and kicked at the door, but there was more to the lock than he'd expected, and he had to kick it four times, as hard as he could, before he finally smashed it open.

He switched on the light. An ordinary bedroom. No sign of Lavelle.

The window in the opposite wall was broken out. Drapes billowed on the in-rushing wind.

Jack checked the closet first, just to be sure this wasn't a bit of misdirection to enable Lavelle to get behind his back. But no one waited in the closet.

He went to the window. In the light that spilled past him, he saw footprints in the snow that covered the porch roof. They led out to the edge. Lavelle had jumped down to the yard below.

Jack squeezed through the window, briefly snagging his coat on a shard of glass, and went onto the roof.

In the cathedral, approximately seventy or eighty goblins had come out of the vestibule. They were lined up on the communion rail and between the supporting posts under the rail. Behind them, other beasts slouched up the long aisle.

Father Walotsky was on his knees, praying, but he didn't seem to be doing any good, so far as Rebecca could see.

In fact, there were some bad signs. The goblins weren't as sluggish as they had been. Tails lashed. Mutant heads whipped back and forth. Tongues flickered faster than before.

Rebecca wondered if they could, through sheer numbers, overcome the benign power that held sway within the cathedral and that had, so far, prevented them from attacking. As each of the demonic creatures entered, it brought its own measure of malignant energy. If the balance of power tipped in the other direction . . .

One of the goblins hissed. They had been perfectly silent since entering the cathedral, but now one of them hissed, and then another, and then three more, and in seconds all of them were hissing angrily.

Another bad sign.

Carver Hampton.

When he saw the demonic entity in the hallway, the floor suddenly seemed a bit more solid to him. His heart began to pound, and the real world came swimming back to him out of the tropical hallucination—although this part of the real world contained, at this time, something from a nightmare.

The thing in the hall skittered toward the open arch and the living room. From Carver's perspective, it looked enormous, at least his own size, but he realized it wasn't really as large as it seemed from his peculiar floor-level point of view. But big enough. Oh, yes. Its head was the size of his fist. Its sinuous, segmented, wormlike body was half again as long as his arm. Its crablike legs ticked against the wooden floor. The only features on its misshapen head were an ugly suckerlike mouth full of teeth and those haunting eyes of which Jack Dawson had spoken, those eyes of silver-white fire.

Carver found the strength to move. He hitched himself backwards across the floor, gasping in exhaustion and wincing with rediscovered pain, leaving a trail of blood in his wake. He came up against the wall almost at once, startling himself; he'd thought the room was bigger than that.

With a thin, high-pitched keening, the worm-thing came through the archway and scurried toward him.

* * *

When Lavelle jumped off the porch roof, he didn't land on his feet. He slipped in the snow and crashed onto his wounded arm. The explosion of pain almost blew him into unconsciousness.

He couldn't understand why everything had gone so wrong. He was confused and angry. He felt naked, powerless; that was a new feeling for him. He didn't like it.

He crawled a few feet through the snow before he could find the strength to stand, and when he stood he heard Dawson shouting at him from the edge of the porch roof. He didn't stop, didn't wait passively to be captured, not Baba Lavelle the great *Bocor*. He headed across the rear lawn toward the storage shed.

His source of power lay beyond the pit, with the dark gods on the other side. He would demand to know why they were failing him. He would demand their aid.

Dawson fired one shot, but it must have been just a warning because it didn't come anywhere close to Lavelle.

The wind battered him and threw snow in his face, and with blood pouring out of his shattered arm he wasn't easily able to resist the storm, but he stayed on his feet and reached the shed and pulled open the door—and cried out in shock when he saw that the pit had grown. It now occupied the entire small building, from one corrugated wall to the other, and the light coming from it wasn't orange any longer but blood-red and so bright it hurt his eyes.

Now he knew why his malevolent benefactors were letting him go down to defeat. They had allowed him to use them only as long as they could use him, in turn. He had been their conduit to this world, a means by which they could reach out and claw at the living. But now they had something better than a conduit; now they had a doorway to this plane of existence, a *real* doorway that would permit them to leave the Underworld. And it was thanks to him that they'd been given it. He had opened the Gates just a crack, confident that he could hold them to that narrow and insignificant breach, but he had lost control without knowing it, and now the Gates were surging wide. The Ancient Ones were coming. They were on their way. They were almost here. When they arrived, Hell would have relocated to the surface of the earth.

In front of his feet, the rim of the pit was continuing to crumble inward, faster and faster.

Lavelle stared in horror at the beating heart of hate-light within the pit. He saw something dark at the bottom of that intense red glow. It rippled. It was huge. And it was rising toward him.

Jack jumped from the roof, landed on both feet in the snow, and started after Lavelle. He was halfway across the lawn when Lavelle opened the door to the corrugated metal shed. The brilliant and eerie crimson light that poured forth was sufficient to stop Jack in his tracks.

It was the pit, of course, just as Carver had described it. But it surely wasn't as small as it was supposed to be, and the light wasn't soft and orange. Carver's worst fear was coming true: the Gates of Hell were swinging open all the way.

As that mad thought struck Jack, the pit suddenly grew larger than the shed that had once contained it. The corrugated metal walls fell away into the void. Now there was only a hole in the ground. Like a giant searchlight, the red beams from the pit speared up into the dark and storm-churned sky.

Lavelle staggered back a few steps, but he was evidently too terrified to be able to turn and run.

The earth trembled.

Within the pit, something roared. It had a voice that shook the night. The air stank of sulphur.

Something snaked up from the depths. It was like a tentacle but not exactly a tentacle, like a chitinous insect leg but not exactly an insect leg, sharply jointed in several places and yet as sinuous as a serpent. It soared up to a height of fifteen feet. The tip of the thing was equipped with long whiplike appendages that writhed around a loose, drooling, toothless mouth large enough to swallow a man whole. Worse, it was in some ways exceedingly clear that this was only a minor feature of the huge beast rising from the Gates; it was as small, proportionately, as a human finger compared to an entire human body. Perhaps this was the only thing that the escaping Lovecraftian entity had thus far been able to extrude between the opening Gates—this one finger.

The giant, insectile, tentacular limb bent toward Lavelle. The whiplike appendages at the tip lashed out, snared him, and lifted him off the ground, into the blood-red light. He screamed and flailed, but he could do nothing to prevent himself from being drawn into that obscene, drooling mouth. And then he was gone.

In the cathedral, the last of the goblins had reached the communion railing. At least a hundred of them turned blazing eyes on Rebecca, Penny, Davey, and Father Walotsky.

Their hissing was now augmented with an occasional snarl.

Suddenly the four-eyed, four-armed manlike demon leaped off the rail, into the chancel. It took a few tentative steps forward and looked from side to side; there was an air of wariness about it. Then it raised its tiny spear, shook it, and shrieked.

Immediately, all of the other goblins shrieked, too.

Another one dared to enter the chancel.

Then a third. Then four more.

Rebecca glanced sideways, toward the sacristy door. But it was no use running in there. The goblins would only follow. The end had come at last.

The worm-thing reached Carver Hampton where he sat on the floor, his back pressed to the wall. It reared up, until half its disgusting body was off the floor.

He looked into those bottomless, fiery eyes and knew that he was too weak a *Houngon* to protect himself.

Then, out behind the house, something roared; it sounded enormous and very much alive.

The earth quaked, and the house rocked, and the worm-demon seemed to lose interest in Carver. It turned half away from him and moved its head from side to side, began to sway to some music that Carver could not hear.

With a sinking heart, he realized what had temporarily enthralled the thing: the sound of other Hell-trapped souls screeching toward a long-desired freedom, the triumphant ululation of the Ancient Ones at last breaking their bonds.

The end had come.

Jack advanced to the edge of the pit. The rim was dissolving, and the hole was growing larger by the second. He was careful not to stand at the very brink.

The fierce red glow made the snowflakes look like whirling embers. But now there were shafts of bright white light mixed in with the red, the same silvery-white as the goblins' eyes, and Jack was sure this meant the Gates were opening dangerously far.

The monstrous appendage, half insectile and half like a tentacle, swayed above him threateningly, but he knew it couldn't touch him. Not yet, anyway. Not until the Gates were all the way open. For now, the benevolent gods of *Rada* still possessed some power over the earth, and he was protected by them.

He took the jar of holy water from his coat pocket. He wished he had Carver's jar, as well, but this would have to do. He unscrewed the lid and threw it aside.

Another menacing shape was rising from the depths. He could see it, a vague dark presence rushing up through the nearly blinding light, howling like a thousand dogs.

He had accepted the reality of Lavelle's black magic and of Carver's white magic, but now he suddenly was able to do more than accept it; he was able to understand it in concrete terms, and he knew he now understood it better than Lavelle or Carver ever had or ever would. He looked into the pit and he *knew.* Hell was not a mythical place, and there was nothing supernatural about demons and gods, nothing holy or unholy about them. Hell—and consequently Heaven—were as real as the earth; they were merely other dimensions, other planes of physical existence. Normally, it was impossible for a living man or woman to cross over from one plane to the other. But religion was the crude and clumsy science that had theorized ways in which to bring the planes together, if only temporarily, and magic was the tool of that science.

After absorbing that realization, it seemed as easy to believe in voodoo or Christianity or any other religion as it was to believe in the existence of the atom.

He threw the holy water, jar and all, into the pit.

The goblins surged through the communion rail and up the steps toward the altar platform.

The kids screamed, and Father Walotsky held his rosary out in front of him as if certain it would render him impervious to the assault. Rebecca drew her gun, though she knew it was useless, took careful aim on the first of the pack—

And all one hundred of the goblins turned to clumps of earth which cascaded harmlessly down the altar steps.

The worm-thing swung its hateful head back toward Carver and hissed and struck at him.

He screamed.

Then gasped in surprise as nothing more than dirt showered over him.

The holy water disappeared into the pit.

The jubilant squeals, the roars of hatred, the triumphant screams all ceased as abruptly as if someone had pulled the plug on a stereo. The silence lasted only a second, and then the night was filled with cries of anger, rage, frustration, and anguish.

· The earth shook more violently than before.

Jack was knocked off his feet, but he fell backwards, away from the pit.

He saw that the rim had stopped dissolving. The hole wasn't getting any larger.

The mammoth appendage that towered over him, like some massive fairytale serpent, did not take a swipe at him as he had been afraid it might.

Instead, its disgusting mouth sucking ceaselessly at the night, it collapsed back into the pit.

Jack got to his feet again. His overcoat was caked with snow.

The earth continued to shake. He felt as if he were standing on an egg from which something deadly was about to hatch. Cracks radiated out from the pit, half a dozen of them—four, six, even eight inches wide and as much as ten feet long. Jack found himself between the two largest gaps, on an unstable island of rocking, heaving earth. The snow melted into the cracks, and light shone up from the strange depths, and heat rose in waves as if from an open furnace door, and for one ghastly moment it seemed as if the entire world would shatter underfoot. Then quickly, mercifully, the cracks closed up again, sealed tight, as if they had never been.

The light began to fade within the pit, changing from red to orange around the edges.

The hellish voices were fading, too.

The gates were easing shut.

With a flush of triumph, Jack inched closer to the rim, squinting into the hole, trying to see more of the monstrous and fantastic shapes that writhed and raged beyond the glare.

The light suddenly pulsed, grew brighter, startling him. The screaming and bellowing became louder.

He stepped back.

The light dimmed once more, then grew brighter again, dimmed, grew brighter. The immortal entities beyond the Gates were struggling to keep them open, to force them wide.

The rim of the pit began to dissolve again. Earth crumbled away in small clods. Then stopped. Then started. In spurts, the pit was still growing.

Jack's heart seemed to beat in concert with the crumbling of the pit's perimeter. Each time the dirt began to fall away, his heart seemed to stop; each time the perimeter stabilized, his heart began to beat again.

Maybe Carver Hampton had been wrong. Maybe holy water and the good intentions of a righteous man had not been sufficient to put an end to it. Perhaps it had gone too far. Perhaps nothing could prevent Armageddon now.

Two glossy black, segmented, whiplike appendages, each an inch in diameter, lashed up from the pit, snapped in front of Jack, snaked around him. One wound around his left leg from ankle to crotch. The other looped around his chest, spiraled down his left arm, curled around his wrist, snatched at his fingers. His leg was jerked out from under him. He fell, thrashing, flailing desperately at the attacker but to no avail; it had a steel grip; he couldn't free himself, couldn't pry it loose. The beast from which the tentacles sprouted was hidden far down in the pit, and now it tugged at him, dragged him toward the brink, a demonic fisherman reeling in its catch. A serrated spine ran the length of each tentacle, and the serrations were sharp; they didn't immediately cut through his clothes, but where they crossed the bare skin of his wrist and hand, they sliced open his flesh, cut deep.

He had never known such pain.

He was suddenly scared that he would never see Davey, Penny, or Rebecca again.

He began to scream.

In St. Patrick's Cathedral, Rebecca took two steps toward the piles of now-ordinary earth that had, only a moment ago, been living creatures, but she stopped short when the scattered dirt trembled with a current of impossible, perverse life. The stuff wasn't dead after all. The grains and clots and clumps of soil seemed to draw moisture from the air; the stuff became damp; the separate pieces in each loose pile began to quiver and strain and draw laboriously toward the others. This evilly enchanted earth was apparently trying to regain its previous forms, struggling to reconstitute the goblins. One small lump, lying apart from all the others, began to shape itself into a tiny, wickedly clawed foot.

"Die, damnit," Rebecca said. *"Die!"*

Sprawled on the rim of the pit, certain that he was going to be pulled into it, his attention split between the void in front of him and the pain blazing in his savaged hand, Jack screamed—

—and at that same instant the tentacle around his arm and torso abruptly whipped free of him. The second demonic appendage slithered away from his left leg a moment later.

The hell-light dimmed.

Now, the beast below was wailing in pain and torment of its own. Its tentacles lashed erratically at the night above the pit.

In that moment of chaos and crisis, the gods of *Rada* must have visited a revelation upon Jack, for he knew—without understanding *how* he knew— that it was his blood that had made the beast recoil from him. In a confrontation with evil, perhaps the blood of a righteous man was (much like holy water) a substance with powerful magical qualities. And perhaps his blood could accomplish what holy water alone could not.

The rim of the pit began to crumble again. The hole grew wider. The Gates were again rolling open. The light rising out of the earth turned from orange to crimson once more.

Jack pushed up from his prone position and knelt at the brink. He could feel the earth slowly—and then not so slowly—coming apart beneath his knees. Blood was streaming off his torn hand, dripping from all five fingertips. He leaned out precariously, over the pit, and shook his hand, flinging scarlet droplets into the center of the seething light.

Below, the shrieking and keening swelled to an even more ear-splitting pitch than it had when he'd tossed the holy water into the breach. The light from the devil's furnace dimmed and flickered, and the perimeter of the pit stabilized.

He cast more of his blood into the chasm, and the tortured cries of the damned faded but only slightly. He blinked and squinted at the pulsing, shifting, mysteriously indefinable bottom of the hole, leaned out even farther to get a better look—

—and with a *whoosh* of blisteringly hot air, a huge face rose up toward him, ballooning out of the shimmering light, a face as big as a truck, filling most of the pit. It was the leering face of all evil. It was composed of slime and mold and rotting carcasses, a pebbled and cracked and lumpy and pock-marked face, dark and mottled, riddled with pustules, maggot-rich, with vile brown foam dripping from its ragged and decaying nostrils. Worms wriggled in its night-black eyes, and yet it could see, for Jack could feel the terrible weight of its hateful gaze. Its mouth broke open—a vicious, jagged slash large enough to swallow a man whole—and bile-green fluid drooled out. Its tongue was long and black and prickled with needle-sharp thorns that punctured and tore its own lips as it licked them.

Dizzied, dispirited, and weakened by the unbearable stench of death that rose from the gaping mouth, Jack shook his wounded hand above the apparition, and a rain of blood fell away from his weeping stigmata. "Go away," he told the thing, choking on the tomb-foul air. "Leave. Go. *Now.*"

The face receded into the furnace glow as his blood fell upon it. In a moment it vanished into the bottom of the pit.

He heard a pathetic whimpering. He realized he was listening to himself.

And it wasn't over yet. Below, the multitude of voices became louder again, and the light grew brighter, and dirt began to fall away from the perimeter of the hole once more.

Sweating, gasping, squeezing his sphincter muscles to keep his bowels from loosening in terror, Jack wanted to run away from the pit. He wanted to flee into the night, into the storm and the sheltering city. But he knew that was no solution. If he didn't stop it now, the pit would widen until it grew large enough to swallow him no matter where he hid.

With his uninjured right hand, he pulled and squeezed and clawed at the wounds in his left hand until they had opened farther, until his blood was flowing much faster. Fear had anesthetized him; he no longer felt any pain. Like a Catholic priest swinging a sacred vessel to cast holy water or incense in a ritual of sanctification, he sprayed his blood into the yawning mouth of Hell.

The light dimmed somewhat but pulsed and struggled to maintain itself. Jack prayed for it to be extinguished, for if this did not do the trick, there was only one other course of action: He would have to sacrifice himself entirely; he would have to go down into the pit. And if he went down there . . . he knew he would never come back.

The last evil energy seemed to have drained out of the clumps of soil on the altar steps. The dirt had been still for a minute or more. With each passing second, it was increasingly difficult to believe that the stuff had ever really been alive.

At last Father Walotsky picked up a clod of earth and broke it between his fingers.

Penny and Davey stared in fascination. Then the girl turned to Rebecca and said, "What happened?"

"I'm not sure," she said. "But I think your daddy accomplished what he set out to do. I think Lavelle is dead." She looked out across the immense cathedral, as if Jack might come strolling in from the vestibule, and she said softly, "I love you, Jack."

The light faded from orange to yellow to blue.

Jack watched tensely, not quite daring to believe that it was finally finished.

A grating-creaking sound came out of the earth, as if enormous gates were swinging shut on rusted hinges. The faint cries rising from the pit had changed from expressions of rage and hatred and triumph to pitiful moans of despair.

Then the light was extinguished altogether.

The grating and creaking ceased.

The air no longer had a sulphurous stench.

No sounds at all came from the pit.

It wasn't a doorway any longer. Now, it was just a hole in the ground.

The night was still bitterly cold, but the storm seemed to be passing.

Jack cupped his wounded hand and packed it full of snow to slow the bleeding now that he no longer *needed* blood. He was still too high on adrenaline to feel any pain.

The wind was barely blowing now, but to his surprise it brought a voice to him. Rebecca's voice. Unmistakable. And four words that he much wanted to hear: "I love you, Jack."

He turned, bewildered.

She was nowhere in sight, yet her voice seemed to have been at his ear.

He said, "I love you, too," and he knew that, wherever she was, she heard him as clearly as he had heard her.

The snow had slackened off. The flakes were no longer small and hard but big and fluffy, as they had been at the beginning of the storm. They fell lazily now, in wide, swooping spirals.

Jack turned away from the pit and went back into the house to call an ambulance for Carver Hampton.

> *We can embrace love; it's not too late.*
> *Why do we sleep, instead, with hate?*
> *Belief requires no suspension*
> *to see that Hell is our invention.*
> *We make Hell real; we stoke its fires.*
> *And in its flames our hope expires.*
> *Heaven, too, is merely our creation.*
> *We can grant ourselves our own salvation.*
> *All that's required is imagination.*
> —The Book of Counted Sorrows

PHANTOMS

*This book is dedicated to
the one who is always there,
the one who always cares
the one who always understands,
the one like whom there is no other:*

Gerda,

my wife and my best friend.

PART ONE

VICTIMS

Fear came upon me, and trembling
—*The Book of Job,* 4:14

The civilized human spirit . . . cannot
get rid of a feeling of the uncanny.
—*Dr. Faustus,*
Thomas Mann

CHAPTER 1

THE TOWN JAIL

THE SCREAM WAS distant and brief. A woman's scream.

Deputy Paul Henderson looked up from his copy of *Time*. He cocked his head, listening.

Motes of dust drifted lazily in a bright shaft of sunlight that pierced one of the mullioned windows. The thin, red second hand of the wall clock swept soundlessly around the dial.

The only noise was the creak of Henderson's office chair as he shifted his weight in it.

Through the large front windows, he could see a portion of Snowfield's main street, Skyline Road, which was perfectly still and peaceful in the golden afternoon sunshine. Only the trees moved, leaves aflutter in a soft wind.

After listening intently for several seconds, Henderson was not sure he had actually heard anything.

Imagination, he told himself. Just wishful thinking.

He almost would have preferred that someone *had* screamed. He was restless.

During the off season, from April through September, he was the only full-time sheriff's deputy assigned to the Snowfield substation, and the duty was dull. In the winter, when the town was host to several thousand skiers, there were drunks to be dealt with, fistfights to be broken up, and room burglaries to be investigated at the inns, lodges, and motels where the skiers stayed. But now, in early September, only the Candleglow Inn, one lodge, and two small motels were open, and the natives were quiet, and Henderson—who was just twenty-four years old and concluding his first year as a deputy—was bored.

He sighed, looked down at the magazine that lay on his desk—and heard another scream. As before, it was distant and brief, but this time it sounded like a man's voice. It wasn't merely a shriek of excitement or even a cry of alarm; it was the sound of terror.

Frowning, Henderson got up and headed toward the door, adjusting the holstered revolver on his right hip. He stepped through the swinging gate in the railing that separated the public area from the bull pen, and he was halfway to the door when he heard movement in the office behind him.

That was impossible. He had been alone in the office all day, and there hadn't been any prisoners in the three holding cells since early last week. The rear door was locked, and that was the only other way into the jail.

When he turned, however, he discovered that he wasn't alone any more. And suddenly he wasn't the least bit bored.

CHAPTER 2

COMING HOME

/////

DURING THE TWILIGHT hour of that Sunday in early September, the mountains were painted in only two colors: green and blue. The trees—pine, fir, spruce—looked as if they had been fashioned from the same felt that covered billiard tables. Cool, blue shadows lay everywhere, growing larger and deeper and darker by the minute.

Behind the wheel of her Pontiac Trans Am, Jennifer Paige smiled, buoyed by the beauty of the mountains and by a sense of homecoming. This was where she belonged.

She turned the Trans Am off the three-lane state road, onto the county-maintained, two-lane blacktop that twisted and climbed four miles through the pass to Snowfield.

In the passenger seat, her fourteen-year-old sister, Lisa, said, "I love it up here."

"So do I."

"When will we get some snow?"

"Another month, maybe sooner."

The trees crowded close to the roadway. The Trans Am moved into a tunnel formed by overhanging boughs, and Jenny switched on the headlights.

"I've never seen snow, except in pictures," Lisa said.

"By next spring, you'll be sick of it."

"Never. Not me. I've always dreamed about living in snow country, like you."

Jenny glanced at the girl. Even for sisters, they looked remarkably alike: the same green eyes, the same auburn hair, the same high cheekbones.

"Will you teach me to ski?" Lisa asked.

"Well, honey, once the skiers come to town, there'll be the usual broken bones, sprained ankles, wrenched backs, torn ligaments . . . I'll be pretty busy then."

"Oh," Lisa said, unable to conceal her disappointment.

"Besides, why learn from me when you can take lessons from a real pro?"

"A pro?" Lisa asked, brightening somewhat.

"Sure. Hank Sanderson will give you lessons if I ask him."

"Who's he?"

"He owns Pine Knoll Lodge, and he gives skiing lessons, but only to a handful of favored students."

"Is he your boyfriend?"

Jenny smiled, remembering what it was like to be fourteen years old. At that age, most girls were obsessively concerned about boys, boys above all else. "No, Hank isn't my boyfriend. I've known him for two years, ever since I came to Snowfield, but we're just good friends."

They passed a green sign with white lettering: SNOWFIELD—3 MILES.

"I'll bet there'll be lots of really neat guys my age."

"Snowfield's not a very big town," Jenny cautioned. "But I suppose you'll find a couple of guys who're neat enough."

"Oh, but during the ski season, there'll be dozens!"

"Whoa, kid! You won't be dating out-of-towners—at least not for a few years."

"Why won't I?"

"Because I said so."

"But why not?"

"Before you date a boy, you should know where he comes from, what he's like, what his family is like."

"Oh, I'm a terrific judge of character," Lisa said. "My first impressions are completely reliable. You don't have to worry about me. I'm not going to hook up with an ax murderer or a mad rapist."

"I'm sure you won't," Jenny said, slowing the Trans Am as the road curved sharply, "because you're only going to date local boys."

Lisa sighed and shook her head in a theatrical display of frustration. "In case you haven't noticed, Jenny, I passed through puberty while you've been gone."

"Oh, that hasn't escaped my attention."

They rounded the curve. Another straightaway lay ahead, and Jenny accelerated again.

Lisa said, "I've even got boobs now."

"I've noticed that, too," Jenny said, refusing to be rattled by the girl's blunt approach.

"I'm not a child any more."

"But you're not an adult, either. You're an adolescent."

"I'm a young woman."

"Young? Yes. Woman? Not yet."

"Jeez."

"Listen, I'm your legal guardian. I'm responsible for you. Besides, I'm your sister, and I love you. I'm going to do what I think—what I *know*—is best for you."

Lisa sighed noisily.

"Because I love you," Jenny stressed.

Scowling, Lisa said, "You're going to be just as strict as Mom was."

Jenny nodded. "Maybe worse."

"Jeez."

Jenny glanced at Lisa. The girl was staring out the passenger-side window. Her face was only partly visible, but she didn't appear to be angry; she wasn't pouting. In fact, her lips seemed to be gently curved in a vague smile.

Whether they realize it or not, Jenny thought, all kids want to have rules put down for them. Discipline is an expression of concern and love. The trick is not to be too heavy-handed about it.

Looking at the road again, flexing her hands on the steering wheel, Jenny said, "I'll tell you what I *will* let you do."

"What?"

"I'll let you tie your own shoes."

Lisa blinked. "Huh?"

"And I'll let you go to the bathroom whenever you want."

Unable to maintain a pose of injured dignity any longer, Lisa giggled. "Will you let me eat when I'm hungry?"

"Oh, absolutely." Jenny grinned. "I'll even let you make your own bed every morning."

"Positively permissive!" Lisa said.

At that moment the girl seemed even younger than she was. In tennis shoes, jeans, and a Western-style blouse, unable to stifle her giggles, Lisa looked sweet, tender, and terribly vulnerable.

"Friends?" Jenny asked.

"Friends."

Jenny was surprised and pleased by the ease with which she and Lisa had been relating to each other during the long drive north from Newport Beach. After all, in spite of their blood tie, they were virtually strangers. At thirty-one, Jenny was seventeen years older than Lisa. She had left home before Lisa's second birthday, six months before their father had died. Throughout her years in medical school and during her internship at Columbia Presbyterian Hospital in New York, Jenny had been too over-worked and too far from home to see either her mother or Lisa with any regularity. Then, after completing her residency, she returned to California to open an office in Snowfield. For the past two years, she had worked extremely hard to establish a viable medical practice that served Snowfield and a few other small towns in the mountains. Recently, her mother had died, and only then had Jenny begun to miss not having had a closer relationship with Lisa. Perhaps they could begin to make up for all the lost years—now that there were only the two of them left.

The county lane rose steadily, and the twilight temporarily grew brighter as the Trans Am ascended out of the shadowed mountain valley.

"My ears feel like they're stuffed full of cotton," Lisa said, yawning to equalize the pressure.

They rounded a sharp bend, and Jenny slowed the car. Ahead lay a long, up-sloping straightaway, and the county lane became Skyline Road, the main street of Snowfield.

Lisa peered intently through the streaked windshield, studying the town with obvious delight. "It's not at all what I thought it would be!"

"What did you expect?"

"Oh, you know, lots of ugly little motels with neon signs, too many gas stations, that sort of thing. But this place is really, really neat!"

"We have strict building codes," Jenny said. "Neon isn't acceptable. Plastic signs aren't allowed. No garish colors, no coffee shops shaped like coffee pots."

"It's super," Lisa said, gawking as they drove slowly into town.

Exterior advertising was restricted to rustic wooden signs bearing each

store's name and line of business. The architecture was somewhat eclectic—
Norwegian, Swiss, Bavarian, Alpine-French, Alpine-Italian—but every building was designed in one mountain-country style or another, making liberal use
of stone, slate, bricks, wood, exposed beams and timbers, mullioned windows,
stained and leaded glass. The private homes along the upper end of Skyline
Road were also graced by flower-filled window boxes, balconies, and front
porches with ornate railings.

"Really pretty," Lisa said as they drove up the long hill toward the ski lifts
at the high end of the town. "But is it always this quiet?"

"Oh, no," Jenny said. "During the winter, the place really comes alive
and . . ."

She left the sentence unfinished as she realized that the town was not merely
quiet. It looked *dead.*

On any other mild Sunday afternoon in September, at least a few residents
would have been strolling along the cobblestone sidewalks and sitting on the
porches and balconies that overlooked Skyline Road. Winter was coming, and
these last days of good weather were to be treasured. But today, as afternoon
faded into evening, the sidewalks, balconies, and porches were deserted. Even
in those shops and houses where there were lights burning, there was no sign of
life. Jenny's Trans Am was the only moving car on the long street.

She braked for a stop sign at the first intersection. St. Moritz Way crossed
Skyline Road, extending three blocks east and four blocks west. She looked in
both directions, but she could see no one.

The next block of Skyline Road was deserted, too. So was the block after
that.

"Odd," Jenny said.

"There must be a terrific show on TV," Lisa said.

"I guess there must be."

They passed the Mountainview Restaurant at the corner of Vail Lane and
Skyline. The lights were on inside and most of the interior was visible through
the big corner windows, but there was no one to be seen. Mountainview was a
popular gathering place for locals both in the winter and during the off season,
and it was unusual for the restaurant to be completely deserted at this time of
day. There weren't even any waitresses in there.

Lisa already seemed to have lost interest in the uncanny stillness, even
though she had noticed it first. She was again gawking at and delighting in the
quaint architecture.

But Jenny couldn't believe that everyone was huddled in front of TV sets, as
Lisa had suggested. Frowning, perplexed, she looked at every window as she
drove farther up the hill. She didn't see a single indication of life.

Snowfield was six blocks long from top to bottom of its sloping main street,
and Jenny's house was in the middle of the uppermost block, on the west side
of the street, near the foot of the ski lifts. It was a two-story, stone and timber
chalet with three dormer windows along the street side of the attic. The many-
angled, slate roof was a mottled gray-blue-black. The house was set back
twenty feet from the cobblestone sidewalk, behind a waist-high evergreen
hedge. By one corner of the porch stood a sign that read JENNIFER PAIGE,
M.D.; it also listed her office hours.

Jenny parked the Trans Am in the short driveway.

"What a nifty house!" Lisa said.

It was the first house Jenny had ever owned; she loved it and was proud of it.
The mere sight of the house warmed and relaxed her, and for a moment she
forgot about the strange quietude that blanketed Snowfield. "Well, it's some-

what small, especially since half of the downstairs is given over to my office and waiting room. And the bank owns more of it than I do. But it sure does have character, doesn't it?"

"Tons," Lisa said.

They got out of the car, and Jenny discovered that the setting sun had given rise to a chilly wind. She was wearing a long-sleeved, green sweater with her jeans, but she shivered anyway. Autumn in the Sierras was a succession of mild days and contrastingly crisp nights.

She stretched, uncramping muscles that had knotted up during the long drive, then pushed the door shut. The sound echoed off the mountain above and through the town below. It was the *only* sound in the twilight stillness.

At the rear of the Trans Am, she paused for a moment, staring down Skyline Road, into the center of Snowfield. Nothing moved.

"I could stay here forever," Lisa declared, hugging herself as she happily surveyed the town below.

Jenny listened. The echo of the slammed car door faded away—and was replaced by no other sound except the soft soughing of the wind.

There are silences and silences. No one of them is like another. There is the silence of grief in velvet-draped rooms of a plushly carpeted funeral parlor, which is far different from the bleak and terrible silence of grief in a widower's lonely bedroom. To Jenny, it seemed curiously as if there were cause for grieving in Snowfield's silence; however, she didn't know why she felt that way or even why such a peculiar thought had occurred to her in the first place. She thought of the silence of a gentle summer night, too, which isn't actually a silence at all, but a subtle chorus of moth wings tapping on windows, crickets moving in the grass, and porch swings ever-so-faintly sighing and creaking. Snowfield's soundless slumber was imbued with some of that quality, too, a hint of fevered activity—voices, movement, struggle—just beyond the reach of the senses. But it was more than that. There is also the silence of a winter night, deep and cold and heartless, but containing an expectation of the bustling, growing noises of spring. *This* silence was filled with expectation, too, and it made Jenny nervous.

She wanted to call out, ask if anyone was here. But she didn't because her neighbors might come out, startled by her cry, all of them safe and sound and bewildered by her apprehension, and then she would look foolish. A doctor who behaved foolishly in public on Monday was a doctor without patients on Tuesday.

". . . stay here forever and ever and ever," Lisa was saying, still swooning over the beauty of the mountain village.

"It doesn't make you . . . uneasy?" Jenny asked.

"What?"

"The silence."

"Oh, I love it. It's so peaceful."

It *was* peaceful. There was no sign of trouble.

So why am I so damned jumpy? Jenny wondered.

She opened the trunk of the car and lifted out one of Lisa's suitcases, then another.

Lisa took the second suitcase and reached into the trunk for a book bag.

"Don't overload yourself," Jenny said. "We've got to make a couple of more trips, anyway."

They crossed the lawn to a stone walkway and followed that to the front porch, where, in response to the amber-purple sunset, shadows were rising and opening petals as if they were night-blooming flowers.

Jenny opened the front door, and stepped into the dark foyer. "Hilda, we're home!"

There was no answer.

The only light in the house was at the far end of the hall, beyond the open kitchen door.

Jenny put down the suitcase and switched on the hall light. "Hilda?"

"Who's Hilda?" Lisa asked, dropping her suitcase and the book bag.

"My housekeeper. She knew what time we expected to arrive. I thought she'd be starting dinner about now."

"Wow, a housekeeper! You mean, a live-in?"

"She has the apartment above the garage," Jenny said, putting her purse and car keys on the small foyer table that stood beneath a large, brass-framed mirror.

Lisa was impressed. "Hey, are you rich or something?"

Jenny laughed. "Hardly. I can't really afford Hilda—but I can't afford to be without her, either."

Wondering why the kitchen light was on if Hilda wasn't here, Jenny headed down the hall, with Lisa following close behind.

"What with keeping regular office hours and making emergency house calls to three other towns in these mountains, I'd never eat more than cheese sandwiches and doughnuts if it wasn't for Hilda."

"Is she a good cook?" Lisa asked.

"Marvelous. *Too* good when it comes to desserts."

The kitchen was a large, high-ceilinged room. Pots, pans, ladles, and other utensils hung from a gleaming, stainless-steel utility rack above a central cooking island with four electric burners, a grill, and a work area. The countertops were ceramic tile, and the cabinets were dark oak. On the far side of the room were double sinks, double ovens, a microwave oven, and the refrigerator.

Jenny turned left as soon as she stepped through the door, and she went to the built-in secretary where Hilda planned menus and composed shopping lists. It was there she would have left a note. But there was no note, and Jenny was turning away from the small desk when she heard Lisa gasp.

The girl had walked around to the far side of the central cooking island. She was standing by the refrigerator, staring down at something on the floor in front of the sinks. Her face was flour-white, and she was trembling.

Filled with sudden dread, Jenny stepped quickly around the island.

Hilda Beck was lying on the floor, on her back, dead. She stared at the ceiling with sightless eyes, and her discolored tongue thrust stiffly between swollen lips.

Lisa looked up from the dead woman, stared at Jenny, tried to speak, could not make a sound.

Jenny took her sister by the arm and led her around the island to the other side of the kitchen, where she couldn't see the corpse. She hugged Lisa.

The girl hugged back. Tightly. Fiercely.

"Are you okay, honey?"

Lisa said nothing. She shook uncontrollably.

Just six weeks ago, coming home from an afternoon at the movies, Lisa had found her mother lying on the kitchen floor of the house in Newport Beach, dead of a massive cerebral hemorrhage. The girl had been devastated. Never having known her father, who had died when she was only two years old, Lisa had been especially close to her mother. For a while, that loss had left her deeply shaken, bewildered, depressed. Gradually, she had accepted her mother's death, had discovered how to smile and laugh again. During the past few days, she had seemed like her old self. And now this.

Jenny took the girl to the secretary, urged her to sit down, then squatted in front of her. She pulled a tissue from the box of Kleenex on the desk and blotted Lisa's damp forehead. The girl's flesh was not only as pale as ice; it was ice-cold as well.

"What can I do for you, Sis?"

"I'll b-be okay," Lisa said shakily.

They held hands. The girl's grip was almost painfully tight.

Eventually, she said, "I thought . . . When I first saw her there . . . on the floor like that . . . I thought . . . crazy, but I thought . . . that it was Mom." Tears shimmered in her eyes, but she held them back. "I kn-know Mom's gone. And this woman here doesn't even look like her. But it was . . . a surprise . . . such a shock . . . and so confusing."

They continued to hold hands, and slowly Lisa's grip relaxed.

After a while, Jenny said, "Feeling better?"

"Yeah. A little."

"Want to lie down?"

"No." She let go of Jenny's hand in order to pluck a tissue from the box of Kleenex. She wiped at her nose. She looked at the cooking island, beyond which lay the body. "Is it Hilda?"

"Yes," Jenny said.

"I'm sorry."

Jenny had liked Hilda Beck enormously. She felt sick at heart about the woman's death, but right now she was more concerned about Lisa than about anything else. "Sis, I think it would be better if we got you out of here. How about waiting in my office while I take a closer look at the body. Then I've got to call the sheriff's office and the county coroner."

"I'll wait here with you."

"It would be better if—"

"No!" Lisa said, suddenly breaking into shivers again. "I don't want to be alone."

"All right," Jenny said soothingly. "You can sit right here."

"Oh, Jeez," Lisa said miserably. "The way she looked . . . all swollen . . . all black and b-blue. And the expression on her face—" She wiped at her eyes with the back of one hand. "Why's she all *dark* and puffed up like that?"

"Well, she's obviously been dead for a few days," Jenny said. "But listen, you've got to try not to think about things like—"

"If she's been dead for a few days," Lisa said quaveringly, "why doesn't it stink in here? Wouldn't it stink?"

Jenny frowned. Of course, it should stink in here if Hilda Beck had been dead long enough for her flesh to grow dark and for her body tissues to bloat as much as they had. It *should* stink. But it didn't.

"Jenny, what *happened* to her?"

"I don't know yet."

"I'm scared."

"Don't be scared. There's no reason to be scared."

"That expression on her face," Lisa said. "It's awful."

"However she died, it must have been quick. She doesn't seem to have been sick or to have struggled. She couldn't have suffered much pain."

"But . . . it looks like she died in the middle of a scream."

CHAPTER 3

THE DEAD WOMAN

JENNY PAIGE HAD never seen a corpse like this one. Nothing in medical school or in her own practice of medicine had prepared her for the peculiar condition of Hilda Beck's body. She crouched beside the corpse and examined it with sadness and distaste—but also with considerable curiosity and with steadily increasing bewilderment.

The dead woman's face was swollen; it was now a round, smooth, and somewhat shiny caricature of the countenance she had worn in life. Her body was bloated, too, and in some places it strained against the seams of her gray and yellow housedress. Where flesh was visible—the neck, lower arms, hands, calves, ankles—it had a soft, overripe look. However, this did not appear to be the gaseous bloat that was a natural consequence of decomposition. For one thing, the stomach should have been grossly distended with gas, far more bloated than any other part of the body, but it was only moderately expanded. Besides, there was no odor of decay.

On close inspection, the dark, mottled skin did not appear to be the result of tissue deterioration. Jenny couldn't locate any certain, visible signs of ongoing decomposition: no lesions, no blistering, no weeping pustules. Because they were composed of comparatively soft tissue, a corpse's eyes usually bore evidence of physical degeneration before most other parts of the body. But Hilda Beck's eyes—wide open, staring—were perfect specimens. The whites of her eyes were clear, neither yellowish nor discolored by burst blood vessels. The irises were clear as well; there were not even milky, postmortem cataracts to obscure the warm, blue color.

In life, there had usually been merriment and kindness in Hilda's eyes. She had been sixty-two, a gray-haired woman with a sweet face and a grandmotherly way about herself. She spoke with a slight German accent and had a surprisingly lovely singing voice. She had often sung while cleaning house or cooking, and she had found joy in the most simple things.

Jenny was stricken by a sharp pang of grief as she realized how very much she would miss Hilda. She closed her eyes for a moment, unable to look at the corpse. She collected herself, suppressed her tears. Finally, when she had reestablished her professional detachment, she opened her eyes and went on with the examination.

The longer she looked at the body, the more the skin seemed *bruised.* The coloration was indicative of severe bruising: black, blue, and a deep sour yellow, the colors blending in and out of one another. But this was unlike any contusion Jenny had ever seen. As far as she could tell, it was *universal;* not even one square inch of visible skin was free of it. She carefully took hold of one sleeve of the dead woman's housedress and pulled it up the swollen arm as far as it would easily slide. Under the sleeve, the skin was also dark, and Jenny suspected that the entire body was covered with an incredible series of contiguous bruises.

She looked again at Mrs. Beck's face. Every last centimeter of skin was contusive. Sometimes, a victim of a serious auto accident sustained injuries that left him with bruises over *most* of his face, but such a severe condition was always accompanied by worse trauma, such as a broken nose, split lips, a broken jaw . . . How could Mrs. Beck have acquired bruises as grotesque as these without also suffering other, more serious injuries?

"Jenny?" Lisa said. "Why're you taking so long?"

"I'll only be a minute. You stay there."

So . . . perhaps the contusions that covered Mrs. Beck's body were not the result of externally administered blows. Was it possible that the discoloration of the skin was caused, instead, by internal pressure, by the swelling of subcutaneous tissue? That swelling was, after all, vividly present. But surely, in order to have caused such thorough bruising, the swelling would have had to have taken place suddenly, with incredible violence. Which didn't make sense, damn it. Living tissue couldn't swell that fast. Abrupt swelling was symptomatic of certain allergies, of course; one of the worst was severe allergic reaction to penicillin. But Jenny was not aware of anything that could cause critical swelling with such suddenness that hideously ugly, universal bruising resulted.

And even if the swelling wasn't simply classic postmortem bloat—which she was sure it wasn't—and even if it was the cause of the bruising, what in the name of God had caused the swelling in the first place? She had ruled out allergic reaction.

If a poison was responsible, it was an extremely exotic variety. But where would Hilda have come into contact with an exotic poison? She had no enemies. The very idea of murder was absurd. And whereas a child might be expected to put a strange substance into his mouth to see if it tasted good, Hilda wouldn't do anything so foolish. No, not poison.

Disease?

If it was disease, bacterial or viral, it was not like anything that Jenny had been taught to recognize. And what if it proved to be contagious?

"Jenny?" Lisa called.

Disease.

Relieved that she hadn't touched the body directly, wishing that she hadn't even touched the sleeve of the housedress, Jenny lurched to her feet, swayed, and stepped back from the corpse.

A chill rippled through her.

For the first time, she noticed what lay on the cutting board beside the sink. There were four large potatoes, a head of cabbage, a bag of carrots, a long knife, and a vegetable peeler. Hilda had been preparing a meal when she had dropped dead. Just like that. *Bang.* Apparently, she hadn't been ill, hadn't had any warning. Such a sudden death sure as hell wasn't indicative of disease.

What disease resulted in death without first progressing through ever more debilitating stages of illness, discomfort, and physical deterioration? None. None that was known to modern medicine.

"Jenny, can we get out of here?" Lisa asked.

"Sssshhh! In a minute. Let me think," Jenny said, leaning against the island, looking down at the dead woman.

In the back of her mind, a vague and frightening thought had been stirring: *plague.* The plague—bubonic and other forms—was not a stranger to parts of California and the Southwest. In recent years, a couple of dozen cases had been reported; however, it was rare that anyone died of the plague these days, for it could be cured by the administration of streptomycin, chloramphenicol, or any of the tetracyclines. Some strains of the plague were characterized by the appearance of petechiae; these were small, purplish, hemorrhagic spots on the skin. In extreme cases, the petechiae became almost black and spread until large areas of the body were afflicted by them; in the Middle Ages, it had been known, simply, as the Black Death. But could petechiae arise in such abundance that the victim's body would turn as completely dark as Hilda's?

Besides, Hilda had died suddenly, while cooking, without first suffering vomiting, fever, incontinence—which ruled out the plague. And which, in fact, ruled out every other known infectious disease, too.

Yet there were no blatant signs of violence. No bleeding gunshot wounds. No stab wounds. No indications that the housekeeper had been beaten or strangled.

Jenny stepped around the body and went to the counter by the sink. She touched the head of cabbage and was startled to find that it was still chilled. It hadn't been here on the cutting board any longer than an hour or so.

She turned away from the counter and looked down at Hilda again, but with even greater dread than before.

The woman had died within the past hour. The body might even still be warm to the touch.

But what had killed her?

Jenny was no closer to an answer now than she had been before she'd examined the body. And although disease didn't seem to be the culprit here, she couldn't rule it out. The possibility of contagion, though remote, was frightening.

Hiding her concern from Lisa, Jenny said, "Come on, honey. I can use the phone in my office."

"I'm feeling better now," Lisa said, but she got up at once, obviously eager to go.

Jenny put an arm around the girl, and they left the kitchen.

An unearthly quiet filled the house. The silence was so deep that the whisper of their footsteps on the hall carpet was thunderous by contrast.

Despite overhead fluorescent lights, Jenny's office wasn't a stark, impersonal room like those that many physicians preferred these days. Instead, it was an old-fashioned, country doctor's office, rather like a Norman Rockwell painting in the *Saturday Evening Post.* Bookshelves were overflowing with books and medical journals. There were six antique wooden filing cabinets that Jenny had gotten for a good price at an auction. The walls were hung with diplomas, anatomy charts, and two large watercolor studies of Snowfield. Beside the locked drug cabinet, there was a scale, and beside the scale, on a small table, was a box of inexpensive toys—little plastic cars, tiny soldiers, miniature dolls —and packs of sugarless chewing gum that were dispensed as rewards—or bribes—to children who didn't cry during examinations.

A large, scarred, dark pine desk was the centerpiece of the room, and Jenny guided Lisa into the big leather chair behind it.

"I'm sorry," the girl said.

"Sorry?" Jenny said, sitting on the edge of the desk and pulling the telephone toward her.

"I'm sorry I flaked out on you. When I saw . . . the body . . . I . . . well . . . I got hysterical."

"You weren't hysterical at all. Just shocked and frightened, which is understandable."

"But *you* weren't shocked or frightened."

"Oh, yes," Jenny said. "Not just shocked; *stunned.*"

"But you weren't scared, like I was."

"I was scared, and I still am." Jenny hesitated, then decided that, after all, she shouldn't hide the truth from the girl. She told her about the disturbing possibility of contagion. "I don't think it *is* a disease that we're dealing with here, but I could be wrong. And if I'm wrong . . ."

The girl stared at Jenny with wide-eyed amazement. "You were scared, like me, but you still spent all that time examining the body. Jeez, I couldn't do that. Not me. Not ever."

"Well, honey, I'm a *doctor*. I'm trained for it."

"Still . . ."

"You didn't flake out on me," Jenny assured her.

Lisa nodded, apparently unconvinced.

Jenny lifted the telephone receiver, intending to call the sheriff's Snowfield substation before contacting the coroner over in Santa Mira, the county seat. There was no dial tone, just a soft hissing sound. She jiggled the disconnect buttons on the phone's cradle, but the line remained dead.

There was something sinister about the phone being out of order when a dead woman lay in the kitchen. Perhaps Mrs. Beck *had* been murdered. If someone cut the telephone line and crept into the house, and if he sneaked up on Hilda with care and cunning . . . well . . . he could have stabbed her in the back with a long-bladed knife that had sunk deep enough to pierce her heart, killing her instantly. In that case, the wound would have been where Jenny couldn't have seen it—unless she had turned the corpse completely over, onto its stomach. That didn't explain why there wasn't any blood. And it didn't explain the universal bruising, the swelling. Nevertheless, the wound could be in the housekeeper's back, and since she had died within the past hour, it was also conceivable that the killer—if there *was* a killer—might still be here, in the house.

I'm letting my imagination run away with me, Jenny thought.

But she decided it would be wise for her and Lisa to get out of the house right away.

"We'll have to go next door and ask Vince or Angie Santini to make the calls for us," Jenny said quietly, getting up from the edge of the desk. "Our phone is out of order."

Lisa blinked. "Does that have anything to do with . . . what happened?"

"I don't know," Jenny said.

Her heart was pounding as she crossed the office toward the half-closed door. She wondered if someone was waiting on the other side.

Following Jenny, Lisa said, "But the phone being out of order *now* . . . it's kind of strange, isn't it?"

"A little."

Jenny half-expected to encounter a huge, grinning stranger with a knife. One of those sociopaths who seemed to be in such abundant supply these days. One of those Jack the Ripper imitators whose bloody handiwork kept the TV reporters supplied with grisly film for the six o'clock news.

She looked into the hall before venturing out there, prepared to jump back and slam the door if she saw anyone. It was deserted.

Glancing at Lisa, Jenny saw the girl had quickly grasped the situation.

They hurried along the hall toward the front of the house, and as they approached the stairs to the second floor, which lay just this side of the foyer, Jenny's nerves were wound tighter than ever. The killer—if there is a killer, she reminded herself exasperatedly—might be on the stairs, listening to them as they moved toward the front door. He might lunge down the steps as they passed him, a knife raised high in his hand . . .

But no one waited on the stairs.

Or in the foyer. Or on the front porch.

Outside, the twilight was fading rapidly into night. The remaining light was purplish, and shadows—a zombie army of them—were rising out of tens of thousands of places in which they had hidden from the sunlight. In ten minutes, it would be dark.

CHAPTER 4

THE HOUSE NEXT DOOR

//////

THE SANTINIS' STONE and redwood house was of more modern design than Jenny's place, all rounded corners and gentle angles. It thrust up from the stony soil, conforming to the contours of the slope, set against a backdrop of massive pines; it almost appeared to be a natural formation. Lights were on in a couple of the downstairs rooms.

The front door was ajar. Classical music was playing inside.

Jenny rang the bell and stepped back a few paces, where Lisa was waiting. She believed that the two of them ought to keep some distance between themselves and the Santinis; it was possible they had been contaminated merely by being in the kitchen with Mrs. Beck's corpse.

"Couldn't ask for better neighbors," she told Lisa, wishing the hard, cold lump in her stomach would melt. "Nice people."

No one responded to the doorbell.

Jenny stepped forward, pressed the button again, and returned to Lisa's side. "They own a ski shop and a gift store in town."

The music swelled, faded, swelled. Beethoven.

"Maybe no one's home," Lisa said.

"Must be someone here. The music, the lights . . ."

A sudden, sharp whirlwind churned under the porch roof, blades of air chopping up the strains of Beethoven, briefly transforming that sweet music into irritating, discordant sound.

Jenny pushed the door all the way open. A light was on in the study, to the left of the foyer. Milky luminescence spilled out of the open study doors, across the oak-floored foyer, to the brink of the dark living room.

"Angie? Vince?" Jenny called.

No answer.

Just Beethoven. The wind abated, and the torn music was knitted together again in the windless calm. The Third Symphony, *Eroica.*

"Hello? Anybody home?"

The symphony reached its stirring conclusion, and when the last note faded, no new music began. Apparently, the stereo had shut itself off.

"Hello?"

Nothing. The night behind Jenny was silent, and the house before her was now silent, too.

"You aren't going in there?" Lisa asked anxiously.

Jenny glanced at the girl. "What's the matter?"

Lisa bit her lip. "Something's wrong here. You feel it, too, don't you?"

Jenny hesitated. Reluctantly, she said, "Yes. I feel it, too."

"It's as if . . . as if we're alone here . . . just you and me . . . and then again . . . *not* alone."

Jenny *did* have the strangest feeling that they were being watched. She turned and studied the lawn and the shrubs, which had been almost completely swallowed by the darkness. She looked at each of the blank windows that faced onto the porch. There was light in the study, but the other windows were flat, black, and shiny. Someone could be standing just beyond any of those panes of glass, cloaked in shadow, seeing but unseen.

"Let's go, please," Lisa said. "Let's get the police or somebody. Let's go *now*. Please."

Jenny shook her head. "We're overwrought. Our imagination is getting the best of us. Anyway, I should take a look in there, just in case someone's hurt —Angie, Vince, maybe one of the kids . . ."

"Don't." Lisa grabbed Jenny's arm, restraining her.

"I'm a doctor. I'm obligated to help."

"But if you picked up a germ or something from Mrs. Beck, you might infect the Santinis. You said so yourself."

"Yes, but maybe they're already dying of the same thing that killed Hilda. What then? They might need medical attention."

"I don't think it's a disease," Lisa said bleakly, echoing Jenny's own thoughts. "It's something worse."

"What could be worse?"

"I don't know. But I . . . I *feel* it. Something worse."

The wind rose up again and rustled the shrubs along the porch.

"Okay," Jenny said. "You wait here while I go have a look at—"

"No," Lisa said quickly. "If you're going in there, so am I."

"Honey, you wouldn't be flaking out on me if you—"

"I'm going," the girl insisted, letting go of Jenny's arm. "Let's get it over with."

They went into the house.

Standing in the foyer, Jenny looked through the open door on the left.

"Vince?"

Two lamps cast warm golden light into every corner of Vince Santini's study, but the room was deserted.

"Angie? Vince? Is anyone here?"

No sound disturbed the preternatural silence, although the darkness itself seemed somehow alert, watchful—as if it were an immense, crouching animal.

To Jenny's right, the living room was draped with shadows as thick as densely woven black bunting. At the far end, a few splinters of light gleamed at the edges and at the bottom of a set of doors that closed off the dining room, but that meager glow did nothing to dispel the gloom on this side.

She found a wall switch that turned on a lamp, revealing the unoccupied living room.

"See," Lisa said, "no one's home."

"Let's have a look in the dining room."

They crossed the living room, which was furnished with comfortable beige sofas and elegant, emerald-green Queen Anne wing chairs. The stereo phonograph and tape deck were nestled inconspicuously in a corner wall unit. That's where the music had been coming from; the Santinis had gone out and left it playing.

At the end of the room, Jenny opened the double doors, which squeaked slightly.

No one was in the dining room, either, but the chandelier shed light on a curious scene. The table was set for an early Sunday supper: four placemats; four clean dinner plates; four matching salad plates, three of them shiny-clean, the fourth holding a serving of salad; four sets of stainless-steel flatware; four glasses—two filled with milk, one with water, and one with an amber liquid that might be apple juice. Ice cubes, only partly melted, floated in both the juice and the water. In the center of the table were serving dishes: a bowl of salad, a platter of ham, a potato casserole, and a large dish of peas and carrots. Except for the salad, from which one serving had been taken, all of the food was untouched. The ham had grown cold. However, the cheesy crust on top of the potatoes was unbroken, and when Jenny put one hand against the casserole, she found that the dish was still quite warm. The food had been put on the table within the past hour, perhaps only thirty minutes ago.

"Looks like they had to go somewhere in an awful hurry," Lisa said.

Frowning, Jenny said, "It almost looks as if they were taken away against their will."

There were a few unsettling details. Like the overturned chair. It was lying on one side, a few feet from the table. The other chairs were upright, but on the floor beside one of them lay a serving spoon and a two-pronged meat fork. A balled-up napkin was on the floor, too, in a corner of the room, as if it had not merely been dropped but *flung* aside. On the table itself, a salt shaker was overturned.

Small things. Nothing dramatic. Nothing conclusive.

Nevertheless, Jenny worried.

"Taken away against their will?" Lisa asked, astonished.

"Maybe." Jenny continued to speak softly, as did her sister. She still had the disquieting feeling that someone was lurking nearby, hiding, watching them— or at least listening.

Paranoia, she warned herself.

"I've never heard of anyone kidnapping an entire family," Lisa said.

"Well . . . maybe I'm wrong. What probably happened was that one of the kids took ill suddenly, and they had to rush to the hospital over in Santa Mira. Something like that."

Lisa surveyed the room again, cocked her head to listen to the tomblike silence in the house. "No. I don't think so."

"Neither do I," Jenny admitted.

Walking slowly around the table, studying it as if expecting to discover a secret message left behind by the Santinis, her fear giving way to curiosity, Lisa said, "It sort of reminds me of something I read about once in a book of strange facts. You know—*The Bermuda Triangle* or a book like that. There was this big sailing ship, the *Mary Celeste* . . . this is back in 1870 or around then . . . Anyway, the *Mary Celeste* was found adrift in the middle of the Atlantic, with the table set for dinner, but the entire crew was missing. The ship hadn't been damaged in a storm, and it wasn't leaking or anything like that. There wasn't any reason for the crew to abandon her. Besides, the lifeboats were all still there. The lamps were lit, and the sails were properly rigged, and the food was on the table like I said; everything was exactly as it should have been, except that every last man aboard had vanished. It's one of the great mysteries of the sea."

"But I'm sure there's no great mystery about *this,*" Jenny said uneasily. "I'm sure the Santinis haven't vanished forever."

Halfway around the table, Lisa stopped, raised her eyes, blinked at Jenny. "If they *were* taken against their will, does that have something to do with your housekeeper's death?"

"Maybe. We just don't know enough to say for sure."

Speaking even more quietly than before, Lisa said, "Do you think we ought to have a gun or something?"

"No, no." She looked at the untouched food congealing in the serving dishes. The spilled salt. The overturned chair. She turned away from the table. "Come on, honey."

"Where now?"

"Let's see if the phone works."

They went through the door that connected the dining room to the kitchen, and Jenny turned on the light.

The phone was on the wall by the sink. Jenny lifted the receiver, listened, tapped the disconnect buttons, but could get no dial tone.

This time, however, the line wasn't actually dead, as it had been at her own house. It was an open line, filled with the soft hiss of electronic static. The number of the fire department and the sheriff's substation were on a sticker on the base of the phone. In spite of having no dial tone, Jenny punched out the seven digits for the sheriff's office, but she couldn't make a connection.

Then, even as Jenny put her fingers on the disconnect buttons to jiggle them again, she began to suspect that someone was on the line, listening to her.

Into the receiver, she said, "Hello?"

Far-away hissing. Like eggs on a griddle.

"Hello?" she repeated.

Just distant static. What they called "white noise."

She told herself there was nothing except the ordinary sounds of an open phone line. But what she *thought* she could hear was someone listening intently to her while she listened to him.

Nonsense.

A chill prickled the back of her neck, and, nonsense or not, she quickly put down the receiver.

"The sheriff's office can't be far in a town this small," Lisa said.

"A couple of blocks."

"Why don't we walk there?"

Jenny had intended to search the rest of the house, in case the Santinis were lying sick or injured somewhere. Now she wondered if someone *had* been on the telephone line with her, listening on an extension phone in another part of the house. That possibility changed everything. She didn't take her medical vows lightly; actually, she enjoyed the special responsibilities that came with her job, for she was the kind of person who needed to have her judgment, wits, and stamina put to the test on a regular basis; she thrived on challenge. But right now, her first responsibility was to Lisa and to herself. Perhaps the wisest thing to do was to get the deputy, Paul Henderson, return here with him, and *then* search the rest of the house.

Although she wanted to believe it was only her imagination, she still sensed inquisitive eyes; someone watching . . . waiting.

"Let's go," she said to Lisa. "Come on."

Clearly relieved, the girl hurried ahead, leading the way through the dining room and living room to the front door.

Outside, night had fallen. The air was cooler than it had been at dusk, and soon it would get downright cold—forty-five or forty degrees, maybe even a bit colder—a reminder that autumn's tenancy in the Sierras was always brief and that winter was eager to move in and take up residency.

Along Skyline Road, the streetlamps had come on automatically with the night's descent. In several store windows, after-hours lights also had come on, activated by light-sensing diodes that had responded to the darkening world outside.

On the sidewalk in front of the Santinis' house, Jenny and Lisa stopped, struck by the sight below them.

Shelving down the mountainside, its peaked and gabled roofs thrusting into the night sky, the town was even more beautiful now than it had been at twilight. A few chimneys issued ghostly plumes of wood smoke. Some windows glowed with light from within, but most, like dark mirrors, cast back the beams of the streetlamps. The mild wind made the trees sway gently, in a lullaby rhythm, and the resultant susurration was like the soft sighs and dreamy murmurs of a thousand peacefully slumbering children.

However, it wasn't just the beauty that was arresting. The perfect stillness, the silence—*that* was what made Jenny pause. On their arrival, she had found it strange. Now she found it ominous.

"The sheriff's substation is on the main street," she told Lisa. "Just two and a half blocks from here."

They hurried into the unbeating heart of town.

CHAPTER 5

THREE BULLETS

/////

A SINGLE FLUORESCENT lamp shone in the gloom of the town jail, but the flexible neck of it was bent sharply, focusing the light on the top of a desk, revealing little else of the big main room. An open magazine lay on the desk blotter, directly in the bar of hard, white light. Otherwise, the place was dark except for the pale luminescence that filtered through the mullioned windows from the streetlights.

Jenny opened the door and stepped inside, and Lisa followed close behind her.

"Hello? Paul? Are you here?"

She located a wall switch, snapped on the overhead lights—and physically recoiled when she saw what was on the floor in front of her.

Paul Henderson. Dark, bruised flesh. Swollen. Dead.

"Oh, Jesus!" Lisa said, quickly turning away. She stumbled to the open door, leaned against the jamb, and sucked in great shuddering breaths of the cool night air.

With considerable effort, Jenny quelled the primal fear that began to rise within her, and she went to Lisa. Putting a hand on the girl's slender shoulder, she said, "Are you okay? Are you going to be sick?"

Lisa seemed to be trying hard not to gag. Finally she shook her head. "No. I w-won't be sick. I'll be all right. L-let's get out of here."

"In a minute," Jenny said. "First I want to take a look at the body."

"You can't *want* to look at that."

"You're right. I don't want to, but maybe I can get some idea what we're up against. You can wait here in the doorway."

The girl sighed with resignation.

Jenny went to the corpse that was sprawled on the floor, knelt beside it.

Paul Henderson was in the same condition as Hilda Beck. Every visible inch of the deputy's flesh was bruised. The body was swollen: a puffy, distorted face; the neck almost as large as the head; fingers that resembled knotted links of sausage; a distended abdomen. Yet Jenny couldn't detect even the vaguest odor of decomposition.

Unseeing eyes bulged from the mottled, storm-colored face. Those eyes, together with the gaping and twisted mouth, conveyed an unmistakable emotion: *fear.* Like Hilda, Paul Henderson appeared to have died suddenly—and in the powerful, icy grip of terror.

Jenny hadn't been a close friend of the dead man's. She had known him, of course, because everyone knew everyone else in a town as small as Snowfield. He had seemed pleasant enough, a good law officer. She felt wretched about what had happened to him. As she stared at his contorted face, a rope of nausea tied itself into a knot of dull pain in her stomach, and she had to look away.

The deputy's sidearm wasn't in his holster. It was on the floor, near the body. A .45-caliber revolver.

She stared at the gun, considering the implications. Perhaps it had slipped out of the leather holster as the deputy had fallen to the floor. Perhaps. But she doubted it. The most obvious conclusion was that Henderson had drawn the revolver to defend himself against an attacker.

If that were the case, then he hadn't been felled by a poison or a disease.

Jenny glanced behind her. Lisa was still standing at the open door, leaning against the jamb, staring out at Skyline Road.

Getting off her knees, turning away from the corpse, Jenny crouched over the revolver for long seconds, studying it, trying to decide whether or not to touch it. She was not as worried about contagion as she had been immediately after finding Mrs. Beck's body. This was looking less and less like a case of some bizarre plague. Besides, if an exotic disease *was* stalking Snowfield, it was frighteningly virulent, and Jenny almost surely was contaminated by now. She had nothing to lose by picking up the revolver and studying it more closely. What most concerned her was that she might obliterate incriminating fingerprints or other important evidence.

But even if Henderson *had* been murdered, it wasn't likely that his killer had used the victim's own gun, conveniently leaving fingerprints on it. Furthermore, Paul didn't appear to have been shot; on the contrary, if any shooting had been done, he was probably the one who had pulled the trigger.

She picked up the gun and examined it. The cylinder had a six-round capacity, but three of the chambers were empty. The sharp odor of burnt gunpowder told her that the weapon had been fired recently; sometime today; maybe even within the past hour.

Carrying the .45, scanning the blue tile floor, she rose and walked to one end of the reception area, then to the other end. Her eye caught a glint of brass, another, then another: three expended cartridges.

None of the shots had been fired downward, into the floor. The highly polished blue tiles were unmarred.

Jenny pushed through the swinging gate in the wooden railing, moving into the area that TV cops always called the "bull pen." She walked down an aisle between facing pairs of desks, filing cabinets, and work tables. In the center of the room, she stopped and let her gaze travel slowly over the pale green walls and the white acoustic-tile ceiling, looking for bullet holes. She couldn't find any.

That surprised her. If the gun hadn't been discharged into the floor, and if it hadn't been aimed at the front windows—which it hadn't; no broken glass—

then it had to have been fired with the muzzle pointing into the room, waist-high or higher. So where had the slugs gone? She couldn't see any ruined furniture, no splintered wood or torn sheet-metal or shattered plastic, although she knew that a .45-caliber bullet would do considerable damage at the point of impact.

If the expended rounds weren't in this room, there was only one other place they could be: in the man or men at whom Paul Henderson had taken aim.

But if the deputy had wounded an assailant—or two or three assailants—with three shots from a .45 police revolver, three shots so squarely placed in the assailant's body trunk that the bullets had been stopped and had not passed through, then there would have been blood everywhere. But there wasn't a drop.

Baffled, she turned to the desk where the gooseneck fluorescent lamp cast light on an open issue of *Time.* A brass nameplate read SERGEANT PAUL J. HENDERSON. This was where he had been sitting, passing an apparently dull afternoon, when whatever happened had . . . happened.

Already sure of what she would hear, Jenny lifted the receiver from the telephone that stood on Henderson's desk. No dial tone. Just the electronic, insect-wing hiss of an open line.

As before, when she had attempted to use the telephone in the Santinis' kitchen, she had the feeling that she wasn't the only one on the line.

She put the receiver down—too abruptly, too hard.

Her hands were trembling.

Along the back wall of the room, there were two bulletin boards, a photocopier, a locked gun cabinet, a police radio (a home base set), and a teletype link. Jenny didn't know how to operate the teletype. Anyway, it was silent and appeared to be out of order. She couldn't make the radio come to life. Although the power switch was in the on-position, the indicator lamp didn't light. The microphone remained dead. Whoever had done in the deputy had also done in the teletype and the radio.

Heading back to the reception area at the front of the room, Jenny saw that Lisa was no longer standing in the doorway, and for an instant her heart froze. Then she saw the girl hunkered down beside Paul Henderson's body, peering intently at it.

Lisa looked up as Jenny came through the gate in the railing. Indicating the badly swollen corpse, the girl said, "I didn't realize skin could stretch as much as this without splitting." Her pose—scientific inquisitiveness, detachment, studied indifference to the horror of the scene—was as transparent as a window. Her darting eyes betrayed her. Pretending she didn't find it stressful, Lisa looked away from the deputy and stood up.

"Honey, why didn't you stay by the door?"

"I was disgusted with myself for being such a coward."

"Listen, Sis, I told you—"

"I mean, I'm afraid something's going to happen to us, something bad, right here in Snowfield, tonight, any minute maybe, something really awful. But I'm not ashamed of *that* fear because it's only common sense to be afraid after what we've seen. But I was even afraid of the deputy's body, and that was just plain childish."

When Lisa paused, Jenny said nothing. The girl had more to say, and she needed to get it off her mind.

"He's dead. He can't hurt me. There's no reason to be so scared of him. It's wrong to give in to irrational fears. It's wrong and weak and stupid. A person should face up to fears like that," Lisa insisted. "Facing up to them is the only way to get over them. Right? So I decided to face up to *this.*" With a tilt of her head, she indicated the dead man at her feet.

There's such anguish in her eyes, Jenny thought.

It wasn't merely the situation in Snowfield that was weighing heavily on the girl. It was the memory of finding her mother dead of a stroke on a hot, clear afternoon in July. Suddenly, because of all of *this,* all of *that* was coming back to her, coming back hard.

"I'm okay now," Lisa said. "I'm still afraid of what might happen to us, but I'm not afraid of *him.*" She glanced down at the corpse to prove her point, then looked up and met Jenny's eyes. "See? You can count on me now. I won't flake out on you again."

For the first time, Jenny realized that she was Lisa's role model. With her eyes and face and voice and hands, Lisa revealed, in countless subtle ways, a respect and an admiration for Jenny that was far greater than Jenny had imagined. Without resorting to words, the girl was saying something that deeply moved Jenny: *I love you, but even more than that, I* like *you; I'm proud of you; I think you're terrific, and if you're patient with me, I'll make you proud and happy to have me for a kid sister.*

The realization that she occupied such a lofty position in Lisa's personal pantheon was a surprise to Jenny. Because of the difference in their ages and because Jenny had been away from home almost constantly since Lisa was two, she had thought that she was virtually a stranger to the girl. She was both flattered and humbled by this new insight into their relationship.

"I know I can count on you," she assured the girl. "I never thought I couldn't."

Lisa smiled self-consciously.

Jenny hugged her.

For a moment, Lisa clung to her fiercely, and when they pulled apart, she said, "So . . . did you find any clue to what happened here?"

"Nothing that makes sense."

"The phone doesn't work, huh?"

"No."

"So they're out of order all over town."

"Probably."

They walked to the door and stepped outside, onto the cobblestone sidewalk.

Surveying the hushed street, Lisa said, "Everyone's dead."

"We can't be sure."

"Everyone," the girl insisted softly, bleakly. "The whole town. All of them. You can *feel* it."

"The Santinis were missing, not dead," Jenny reminded her.

A three-quarter moon had risen above the mountains while she and Lisa had been in the sheriff's substation. In those night-clad places where the streetlamps and shop lights did not reach, the silvery light of the moon limned the edges of shadowed forms. But the moonglow revealed nothing. Instead, it fell like a veil, clinging to some objects more than to others, providing only vague hints of their shapes, and, like all veils, somehow managing to make all things beneath it more mysterious and obscure than they would have been in total darkness.

"A graveyard," Lisa said. "The whole town's a graveyard. Can't we just get in the car and go for help?"

"You know we can't. If a disease has—"

"It's not disease."

"We can't be absolutely sure."

"I am. I'm sure. Anyway, you said you'd almost ruled it out, too."

"But as long as there's the slightest chance, however remote, we've got to consider ourselves quarantined."

Lisa seemed to notice the gun for the first time. "Did that belong to the deputy?"

"Yes."

"Is it loaded?"

"He fired it three times, but that leaves three bullets in the cylinder."

"Fired at what?"

"I wish I knew."

"Are you keeping it?" Lisa asked, shivering.

Jenny stared at the revolver in her right hand and nodded. "I guess maybe I should."

"Yeah. Then again . . . it didn't save *him,* did it?"

CHAPTER 6

NOVELTIES AND NOTIONS

THEY PROCEEDED ALONG Skyline Road, moving alternately through shadows, yellowish sodium-glow from the streetlamps, darkness, and phosphoric moonlight. Regularly spaced trees grew from curbside planters on the left. On the right, they passed a gift shop, a small cafe, and the Santinis' ski shop. At each establishment, they paused to peer through the windows, searching for signs of life, finding none.

They also passed townhouses that faced directly onto the sidewalk. Jenny climbed the steps at each house and rang the bell. No one answered, not even at those houses where light shone beyond the windows. She considered trying a few doors and, if they were unlocked, going inside. But she didn't do it because she suspected, just as Lisa did, that the occupants (if they could be found at all) would be in the same grotesque condition as Hilda Beck and Paul Henderson. She needed to locate living people, survivors, witnesses. She couldn't learn anything more from corpses.

"Is there a nuclear power plant around here?" Lisa asked.

"No. Why?"

"A big military base?"

"No."

"I thought maybe . . . radiation."

"Radiation doesn't kill this suddenly."

"A really *strong* blast of radiation?"

"Wouldn't leave victims who look like these."

"No?"

"There'd be burns, blisters, lesions."

They came to the Lovely Lady Salon, where Jenny always had her hair cut. The shop was deserted, as it would have been on any ordinary Sunday. Jenny wondered what had happened to Madge and Dani, the beauticians who owned the place. She liked Madge and Dani. She hoped to God they'd been out of town all day, visiting their boyfriends over in Mount Larson.

"Poison?" Lisa asked as they turned away from the beauty shop.

"How could the entire town be poisoned simultaneously?"

"Bad food of some kind."

"Oh, maybe if everyone had been at the town picnic, eating the same tainted potato salad or infected pork or something like that. But they weren't. There's only one town picnic, and that's on the Fourth of July."

"Poisoned water supply?"

"Not unless everyone just happened to take a drink at precisely the same moment, so that no one had a chance to warn anyone else."

"Which is just about impossible."

"Besides, this doesn't look much like any kind of poison-reaction I've ever heard about."

Liebermann's Bakery. It was a clean, white building with a blue-and-white-striped awning. During the skiing season, tourists lined up halfway down the block, all day long, seven days a week, just to buy the big flaky cinnamon wheels, the sticky buns, chocolate-chip cookies, almond cupcakes with gooey mandarin-chocolate centers, and other goodies that Jakob and Aida Liebermann produced with tremendous pride and delicious artistry. The Liebermanns enjoyed their work so much that they even chose to live near it, in an apartment above the bakery (no light visible up there now), and although there wasn't nearly as much profit in the April-to-October trade as there was the rest of the year, they remained open Monday through Saturday in the off season. People drove over from all the outlying mountain towns—Mount Larson, Shady Roost, and Pineville—to purchase bags and boxes full of the Liebermanns' treats.

Jenny leaned close to the big window, and Lisa put her forehead against the glass. In the rear of the building, back in the part where the ovens were, light poured brightly through an open door, splashing one end of the sales room and indirectly illuminating the rest of the place. Small cafe tables stood to the left, each with a pair of chairs. The white enamel display cases with glass fronts were empty.

Jenny prayed that Jakob and Aida had escaped the fate that appeared to have befallen the rest of Snowfield. They were two of the gentlest, kindest people she had ever met. People like the Liebermanns made Snowfield a good place to live, a haven from the rude world where violence and unkindness were disconcertingly common.

Turning away from the bakery window, Lisa said, "How about toxic waste? A chemical spill. Something that would've sent up a cloud of deadly gas."

"Not here," Jenny said. "There aren't any toxic waste dumps in these mountains. No factories. Nothing like that."

"Sometimes it happens whenever a train derails and a tank car full of chemicals splits open."

"Nearest railroad tracks are twenty miles away."

Her brow creasing with thought, Lisa started walking away from the bakery.

"Wait. I want to take a look in here," Jenny said, stepping to the front door of the shop.

"Why? No one's there."

"We can't be sure." She tried the door but couldn't open it. "The lights are on in the back room, the kitchen. They could be back there, getting things ready for the morning's baking, unaware of what's happened in the rest of the town. This door's locked. Let's go around back."

Behind a solid wood gate, a narrow covered serviceway led between Liebermann's Bakery and the Lovely Lady Salon. The gate was held shut by a single sliding bolt, which yielded to Jenny's fumbling fingers. It shuddered open with a squeal and a rasp of unoiled hinges. The tunnel between the buildings was forbiddingly dark; the only light lay at the far end, a dim gray patch in the shape of an arch, where the passageway ended at the alley.

"I don't like this," Lisa said.

"It's okay, honey. Just follow me and stay close. If you get disoriented, trail one hand along the wall."

Although Jenny didn't want to contribute to her sister's fear by revealing her own doubts, the unlighted walkway made her nervous, too. With each step, the passage seemed to grow narrower, crowding her.

A quarter of the way into the tunnel, she was stricken by the uncanny feeling that she and Lisa weren't alone. An instant later, she became aware of something moving in the darkest space, under the roof, eight or ten feet overhead. She couldn't say exactly *how* she became aware of it. She couldn't hear anything other than her own and Lisa's echoing footsteps; she couldn't see much of anything, either. She just suddenly sensed a hostile presence, and as she squinted ahead at the coal-black ceiling of the passageway, she was sure the darkness was . . . *changing.*

Shifting. Moving. Moving up there in the rafters.

She told herself she was imagining things, but by the time she was halfway along the tunnel, her animal instincts were screaming at her to get out, to run. Doctors weren't supposed to panic; equanimity was part of the training. She did pick up her pace a bit, but only a little, not much, not in panic; then after a few steps, she picked up the pace a bit more, and a bit *more,* until she was running in spite of herself.

She burst into the alley. It was gloomy there, too, but not as dark as the tunnel had been.

Lisa came out of the passageway in a stumbling run, slipped on a wet patch of blacktop, and nearly fell.

Jenny grabbed her and prevented her from going down.

They backed up, watching the exit from the lightless, covered passage. Jenny raised the revolver that she'd taken from the sheriff's substation.

"Did you feel it?" Lisa asked breathlessly.

"Something up under the roof. Probably just birds or maybe, at worst, several bats."

Lisa shook her head. "No, no. N-not under the roof. It was c-crouched up against the w-wall."

They kept watching the mouth of the tunnel.

"I saw something in the rafters," Jenny said.

"No," the girl insisted, shaking her head vigorously.

"What did *you* see then?"

"It was against the wall. On the left. About halfway through the tunnel. I almost stumbled into it."

"What was it?"

"I . . . I don't know exactly. I couldn't actually see it."

"Did you hear anything?"

"No," Lisa said, eyes riveted on the passageway.

"Smell something?"

"No. But . . . the darkness was . . . Well, at one place there, the darkness was . . . different. I could sense something moving . . . or sort of moving . . . shifting . . ."

"That's like what I thought I saw—but up in the rafters."

They waited. Nothing came out of the passageway.

Gradually, Jenny's heartbeat slowed from a wild gallop to a fast trot. She lowered the gun.

Their breathing grew quiet. The night silence poured back in like heavy oil.

Doubts surfaced. Jenny began to suspect that she and Lisa simply had succumbed to hysteria. She didn't like that explanation one damn bit, for it didn't fit the image she had of herself. But she was sufficiently honest with herself to face the unpleasant fact that, just this one time, she might have panicked.

"We're just jumpy," she told Lisa. "If there were anything or anyone dangerous in there, they'd have come out after us by now—don't you think?"

"Maybe."

"Hey, you know what it might have been?"

"What?" Lisa asked.

The cold wind stirred up again and soughed softly through the alleyway.

"It could have been cats," Jenny said. "A few cats. They like to hang out in those covered walkways."

"I don't think it was cats."

"Could be. A couple of cats up there in the rafters. And one or two down on the floor, along the wall, where you saw something."

"It seemed bigger than a cat. It seemed a *lot* bigger than a cat," Lisa said nervously.

"Okay, so maybe it wasn't cats. Most likely, it wasn't anything at all. We're keyed up. Our nerves are wound tight." She sighed. "Let's go see if the rear door of the bakery is open. That's what we came back here to check out—remember?"

They headed toward the rear of Liebermann's Bakery, but they glanced repeatedly behind them, at the mouth of the covered passage.

The service door at the bakery was unlocked, and there was light and warmth beyond it. Jenny and Lisa stepped into a long, narrow storage room.

The inner door led from the storage room to the huge kitchen, which smelled pleasantly of cinnamon, flour, black walnuts, and orange extract. Jenny inhaled deeply. The appetizing fragrances that wafted through the kitchen were so homey, so natural, so pungently and soothingly reminiscent of normal times and normal places that she felt some of her tension fading.

The bakery was well-equipped with double sinks, a walk-in refrigerator, several ovens, several immense white enamel storage cabinets, a dough-kneading machine, and a large array of other appliances. The middle of the room was occupied by a long, wide counter, the primary work area; one end of it had a shiny stainless-steel top, and the other end had a butcher's-block surface. The stainless-steel portion—which was nearest the store-room door, where Jenny and Lisa had entered—was stacked high with pots, cupcake and cookie trays, baking racks, bundt pans, regular cake pans, and pie tins, all clean and bright. The entire kitchen gleamed.

"Nobody's here," Lisa said.

"Looks that way," Jenny said, her spirits rising as she walked farther into the room.

If the Santini family had escaped, and if Jakob and Aida had been spared, perhaps most of the town wasn't dead. Perhaps—

Oh, God.

On the other side of the piled cookware, in the middle of the butcher's-block counter, lay a large disk of pie dough. A wooden rolling pin rested on the dough. Two hands gripped the ends of the rolling pin. Two severed, human hands.

Lisa backed up against a metal cabinet with such force that the stuff inside rattled noisily. "What the *hell* is going on? What the *hell?*"

Drawn by morbid fascination and by an urgent need to understand what was happening here, Jenny moved closer to the counter and stared down at the disembodied hands, regarding them with equal measures of disgust and disbelief—and with fear as sharp as razor blades. The hands were not bruised or swollen; they were pretty much flesh-colored, though gray-pale. Blood—the first blood she had seen so far—trailed wetly from the raggedly torn wrists and glistened in streaks and drops, midst a fine film of flour dust. The hands were strong; more precisely—they had once been strong. Blunt fingers. Large knuckles. Unquestionably a man's hands, with white hair curled crisply on the backs of them. Jakob Liebermann's hands.

"Jenny!"

Jenny looked up, startled.

Lisa's arm was raised, extended; she was pointing across the kitchen.

Beyond the butcher's-block counter, set in the long wall on the far side of the room, were three ovens. One of them was huge, with a pair of solid, over-and-under, stainless-steel doors. The other two ovens were smaller than the first, though still larger than the conventional models used in most homes; there was one door in each of these two, and each door had a glass portal in the center of it. None of the ovens was turned on at the moment, which was fortunate, for if the smaller ones had been in operation, the kitchen would have been filled with a sickening stench.

Each one contained a severed head.

Jesus.

Ghastly, dead faces gazed out into the room, noses pressed to the inside of the oven glass.

Jakob Liebermann. White hair spattered with blood. One eye half shut, the other glaring. Lips pressed together in a grimace of pain.

Aida Liebermann. Both eyes open. Mouth gaping as if her jaws had come unhinged.

For a moment Jenny couldn't believe the heads were real. Too much. Too shocking. She thought of expensive, lifelike Halloween masks peering out of the cellophane windows in costume boxes, and she thought of the grisly novelties sold in joke shops—those wax heads with nylon hair and glass eyes, those gruesome things that young boys sometimes found wildly amusing (and surely that's what *these* were)—and, crazily, she thought of a line from a TV commercial for cake mixes—*Nothin' says lovin' like somethin' from the oven!*

Her heart thudded.

She was feverish, dizzy.

On the butcher's-block counter, the severed hands were still poised on the rolling pin. She half-expected them to skitter suddenly across the counter as if they were two crabs.

Where were the Liebermanns' decapitated bodies? Stuffed in the big oven, behind steel doors that had no windows? Lying stiff and frosted in the walk-in refrigerator?

Bitterness rose in her throat, but she choked it back.

The .45 revolver now seemed an ineffectual defense against this incredibly violent, unknown enemy.

Again, Jenny had the feeling of being watched, and the drumbeat of her heart was no longer snare but timpani.

She turned to Lisa. "Let's get out of here."

The girl headed for the storeroom door.

"Not that way!" Jenny said sharply.

Lisa turned, blinking, confused.

"Not the alley," Jenny said. "And not that dark passage again."

"God, no," Lisa agreed.

They hurried across the kitchen and through the other door, into the sales room. Past the empty pastry cases. Past the cafe tables and chairs.

Jenny had some trouble with the deadbolt lock on the front door. It was stiff. She thought they might have to leave by way of the alley, after all. Then she realized she was trying to turn the thumb-latch the wrong way. Twisted the proper direction, the bolt slipped back with a *clack,* and Jenny yanked the door open.

They rushed out into the cool, night air.

Lisa crossed the sidewalk to a tall pine tree. She seemed to need to lean against something.

Jenny joined her sister, glancing back apprehensively at the bakery. She wouldn't have been surprised to see two decapitated bodies shambling toward her with demonic intent. But nothing moved back there except the scalloped edge of the blue-and-white-striped awning, which undulated in the inconstant breeze.

The night remained silent.

The moon had risen somewhat higher in the sky since Jenny and Lisa had entered the covered passageway.

After a while the girl said, "Radiation, disease, poison, toxic gas—boy, we sure were on the wrong track. Only other people, sick people, do that kind of weird stuff. Right? Some weird psycho did all of this."

Jenny shook her head. "One man can't have done it all. To overwhelm a town of nearly five hundred people, it would take an *army* of psychopathic killers."

"Then that's what it was," Lisa said, shivering.

Jenny looked nervously up and down the deserted street. It seemed imprudent, even reckless, to be standing here, in plain sight, but she couldn't think of anywhere else that would be safer.

She said, "Psychopaths don't join clubs and plan mass murders as if they were Rotarians planning a charity dance. They almost always act alone."

Flicking her eyes from shadow to shadow as if she expected one of them to have substance and malevolent intentions, Lisa said, "What about the Charles Manson commune, back in the sixties, those people who killed the movie star —what was her name?"

"Sharon Tate."

"Yeah. Couldn't this be a group of nuts like that?"

"At most, there were half a dozen people in the core of the Manson family, and that was a *very* rare deviation from the lone-wolf pattern. Anyway, half a dozen couldn't do this to Snowfield. It would take fifty, a hundred, maybe more. That many psychopaths just couldn't act together."

They were both silent for a while. Then Jenny said, "There's another thing that doesn't figure. Why wasn't there more blood in the kitchen?"

"There was some."

"Hardly any. Just a few smears on the counter. There should've been blood all over the place."

Lisa rubbed her hands briskly up and down her arms, trying to generate some heat. Her face was waxen in the yellowish glow of the nearest streetlamp. She seemed years older than fourteen. Terror had matured her.

The girl said, "No signs of a struggle, either."

Jenny frowned. "That's right; there weren't."

"I noticed it right away," Lisa said. "It seemed so odd. They don't seem to've fought back. Nothing thrown. Nothing broken. The rolling pin would've made a pretty good weapon, wouldn't it? But he didn't use it. Nothing was knocked over, either."

"It's as if they didn't resist at all. As if they . . . willingly put their heads on the chopping block."

"But why would they do that?"

Why *would* they do that?

Jenny stared up Skyline Road toward her house, which was less than three blocks away, then looked down toward Ye Olde Towne Tavern, Big Nickle Variety Shop, Patterson's Ice Cream Parlor, and Mario's Pizza.

There are silences and silences. No one of them is quite like another. There is the silence of death, found in tombs and deserted graveyards and in the cold-storage room in a city morgue and in hospital rooms on occasion; it is a flawless silence, not merely a hush but a void. As a physician who had treated her share of terminally ill patients, Jenny was familiar with that special, grim silence.

This was it. This was the silence of death.

She hadn't wanted to admit it. That was why she had not yet shouted "hello" into the funereal streets. She had been afraid no one would answer.

Now she didn't shout because she was afraid someone *would* answer. Someone or something. Someone or something dangerous.

At last she had no choice but to accept the facts. Snowfield was indisputably dead. It wasn't really a town any more; it was a cemetery, an elaborate collection of stone-timber-shingle-brick-gabled-balconied tombs, a graveyard fashioned in the image of a quaint alpine village.

The wind picked up again, whistling under the eaves of the buildings. It sounded like eternity.

CHAPTER 7

THE COUNTY SHERIFF

/////

THE COUNTY AUTHORITIES, headquartered in Santa Mira, were not yet aware of the Snowfield crisis. They had their own problems.

Lieutenant Talbert Whitman entered the interrogation room just as Sheriff Bryce Hammond switched on the tape recorder and started informing the suspect of his constitutional rights. Tal closed the door without making a sound. Not wanting to interrupt just as the questioning was about to get underway, he didn't take a chair at the big table, where the other three men were seated. Instead, he went to the big window, the only window, in the oblong room.

The Santa Mira County Sheriff's Department occupied a Spanish-style structure that had been erected in the late 1930s. The doors were all solid and solid-sounding when you closed them, and the walls were thick enough to provide eighteen-inch-deep windowsills like the one on which Tal Whitman settled himself.

Beyond the window lay Santa Mira, the county seat, with a population of eighteen thousand. In the mornings, when the sun at last topped the Sierras and burned away the mountain shadows, Tal sometimes found himself looking around in amazement and delight at the gentle, forested foothills on which Santa Mira rose, for it was an exceptionally neat, clean city that had put down its concrete and iron roots with some respect for the natural beauty in which it had grown. Now night was settled in. Thousands of lights sparkled on the rolling hills below the mountains, and it looked as if the stars had fallen here.

For a child of Harlem, black as a sharp-edged winter shadow, born in poverty and ignorance, Tal Whitman had wound up, at the age of thirty, in a most unexpected place. Unexpected but wonderful.

On *this* side of the window, however, the scene was not so special. The interrogation room resembled countless others in police precinct houses and sheriffs' stations all over the country. A cheap linoleum-tile floor. Battered filing cabinets. A round conference table and five chairs. Institutional-green walls. Bare fluorescent bulbs.

At the conference table in the center of the room, the current occupant of the suspect's chair was a tall, good-looking, twenty-six-year-old real estate agent named Fletcher Kale. He was working himself into an impressive state of righteous indignation.

"Listen, Sheriff," Kale said, "can we just cut this crap? You don't have to read me my rights *again,* for Christ's sake. Haven't we been through this a dozen times in the past three days?"

Bob Robine, Kale's attorney, quickly patted his client's arm to make him be quiet. Robine was pudgy, round-faced, with a sweet smile but with the hard eyes of a casino pit boss.

"Fletch," Robine said, "Sheriff Hammond knows he's held you on suspicion just about as long as the law allows, and he knows that *I* know it, too. So what he's going to do—he's going to settle this one way or the other within the next hour."

Kale blinked, nodded, and changed his tactics. He slumped in his chair as if a great weight of grief lay on his shoulders. When he spoke, there was a faint tremor in his voice. "I'm sorry if I sort of lost my head there for a minute, Sheriff. I shouldn't have snapped at you like that. But it's so hard . . . so very, very hard for me." His face appeared to cave in, and the tremor in his voice became more pronounced. "I mean, for God's sake, I've lost my family. My wife . . . my son . . . both gone."

Bryce Hammond said, "I'm sorry if you think I've treated you unfairly, Mr. Kale. I only try to do what I think is best. Sometimes, I'm right. Maybe I'm wrong this time."

Apparently deciding that he wasn't in too much trouble after all, and that he could afford to be magnanimous now, Fletcher Kale dabbed at the tears on his face, sat up straighter in his chair, and said, "Yeah . . . well, uh . . . I guess I can see your position, Sheriff."

Kale was underestimating Bryce Hammond.

Bob Robine knew the sheriff better than his client did. He frowned, glanced at Tal, then stared hard at Bryce.

In Tal Whitman's experience, most people who dealt with the sheriff underestimated him, just as Fletcher Kale had done. It was an easy thing to do. Bryce didn't look impressive. He was thirty-nine, but he seemed a lot younger than that. His thick sandy hair fell across his forehead, giving him a mussed, boyish appearance. He had a pug nose with a spatter of freckles across the bridge of it and across both cheeks. His blue eyes were clear and sharp, but they were hooded with heavy lids that made him seem bored, sleepy, maybe even a little bit dull-witted. His voice was misleading, too. It was soft, melodic, gentle. Furthermore, he spoke slowly at times, and always with measured deliberation, and some people took his careful speech to mean that he had difficulty forming his thoughts. Nothing could have been further from the truth. Bryce Hammond was acutely aware of how others perceived him, and when it was to his advantage, he reinforced their misconceptions with an ingratiating manner, with an almost witless smile, and with a further softening of speech that made him seem like the classic hayseed cop.

Only one thing kept Tal from fully enjoying this confrontation: He knew the Kale investigation had affected Bryce Hammond on a deep, personal level. Bryce was hurting, sick at heart about the pointless deaths of Joanna and Danny Kale, because in a curious way this case echoed events in his own life. Like Fletcher Kale, the sheriff had lost a wife and a son, although the circumstances of his loss were considerably different from Kale's.

A year ago, Ellen Hammond had died instantly in a car crash. Seven-year-old Timmy, sitting on the front seat beside his mother, had suffered serious head injuries and had been in a coma for the past twelve months. The doctors didn't give Timmy much chance of regaining consciousness.

Bryce had nearly been destroyed by the tragedy. Only recently had Tal Whitman begun to feel that his friend was moving away from the abyss of despair.

The Kale case had opened Bryce Hammond's wounds again, but he hadn't allowed grief to dull his senses; it hadn't caused him to overlook anything. Tal Whitman had known the precise moment, last Thursday evening, when Bryce had begun to suspect that Fletcher Kale was guilty of two premeditated murders, for suddenly something cold and implacable had come into Bryce's heavy-lidded eyes.

Now, doodling on a yellow note pad as if only half his mind was on the interrogation, the sheriff said, "Mr. Kale, rather than ask you a lot of questions that you've already answered a dozen times, why don't I summarize what you've told us? If my summary sounds pretty much right to you, then we can get on with these new items I'd like to ask you about."

"Sure. Let's get it over with and get out of here," Kale said.

"Okay then," Bryce said. "Mr. Kale, according to your testimony, your wife, Joanna, felt she was trapped by marriage and motherhood, that she was too young to have so much responsibility. She felt she had made a terrible mistake and was going to have to pay for it for the rest of her life. She wanted some kicks, a way to escape, so she turned to dope. Would you say that's how you've described her state of mind?"

"Yes," Kale said. "Exactly."

"Good," Bryce said. "So she started smoking pot. Before long, she was stoned almost continuously. For two and a half years, you lived with a pothead, all the while hoping you could change her. Then a week ago she went berserk, broke a lot of dishes and threw some food around the kitchen, and you had hell's own time calming her down. That was when you discovered she'd recently begun using PCP—what's sometimes called 'angel dust' on the street. You were shocked. You knew that some people became maniacally violent while under the influence of PCP, so you made her show you where she kept her stash, and you destroyed it. Then you told her that if she ever used drugs around little Danny again, you'd beat her within an inch of her life."

Kale cleared his throat. "But she just laughed at me. She said I wasn't a woman-beater and I shouldn't pretend to be Mr. Macho. She said, 'Hell, Fletch, if I kicked you in the balls, you'd thank me for livening up your day.' "

"And that was when you broke down and cried?" Bryce asked.

Kale said, "I just . . . well, I realized I didn't have any influence with her."

From his window seat, Tal Whitman watched Kale's face twist with grief — or with a reasonable facsimile. The bastard was *good*.

"And when she saw you cry," Bryce said, "that sort of brought her to her senses."

"Right," Kale said. "I guess it . . . affected her . . . a big ox like me bawling like a baby. She cried, too, and she promised not to take any more PCP. We talked about the past, about what we had expected from marriage, said a lot of things maybe we should have said before, and we felt closer than we had in a couple of years. At least *I* felt closer. I thought she did, too. She swore she'd start cutting down on the pot."

Still doodling, Bryce said, "Then last Thursday you came home early from work and found your little boy, Danny, dead in the master bedroom. You heard something behind you. It was Joanna, holding a meat cleaver, the one she'd used to kill Danny."

"She was stoned," Kale said. "PCP. I could see it right away. That wildness in her eyes, that animal look."

"She screamed at you, a lot of irrational stuff about snakes that lived inside people's heads, about people being controlled by evil snakes. You circled away from her, and she followed. You didn't try to take the cleaver away from her—"

"I figured I'd be killed. I tried to talk her down."

"So you kept circling until you reached the nightstand where you kept a .38 automatic."

"I warned her to drop the cleaver. I *warned* her."

"Instead, she rushed at you with the cleaver raised. So you shot her. Once. In the chest."

Kale was leaning forward now, his face in his hands.

The sheriff put down his pen. He folded his hands on his stomach and laced his fingers. "Now, Mr. Kale, I hope you can bear with me a little bit longer. Just a few more questions, and then we can all get out of here and get on with our lives."

Kale lowered his hands from his face. It was clear to Tal Whitman that Kale figured "getting on with our lives" meant he would be released at last. "I'm all right, Sheriff. Go ahead."

Bob Robine didn't say a word.

Slouched in his chair, looking loose and boneless, Bryce Hammond said, "While we've been holding you on suspicion, Mr. Kale, we've come up with a few questions we need to have answered, so we can set our minds to rest about this whole terrible thing. Now, some of these things may seem awful trivial to you, hardly worth my time or yours. They *are* little things. I admit that. The reason I'm putting you through more trouble . . . well, it's because I want to get reelected next year, Mr. Kale. If my opponents catch me out on one technicality, on even one tiny little damned thing, they'll huff and puff and blow it into a scandal; they'll say I'm slipping or lazy or something." Bryce grinned at Kale—actually *grinned* at him. Tal couldn't believe it.

"I understand, Sheriff," Kale said.

On his window seat, Talbert Whitman tensed and leaned forward.

And Bryce Hammond said, "First thing is—I was wondering why you shot your wife *and then did a load of laundry* before calling us to report what had happened."

CHAPTER 8

BARRICADES

SEVERED HANDS. SEVERED HEADS.

Jenny couldn't get those gruesome images out of her mind as she hurried along the sidewalk with Lisa.

Two blocks east of Skyline Road, on Vail Lane, the night was as still and as quietly threatening as it was everywhere else in Snowfield. The trees here were bigger than those on the main street; they blocked out most of the moonlight. The streetlamps were more widely spaced, too, and the small pools of amber light were separated by ominous lakes of darkness.

Jenny stepped between two gateposts, onto a brick walk that led to a one-story English cottage set on a deep lot. Warm light radiated through leaded glass windows with diamond-shaped panes.

Tom and Karen Oxley lived in the deceptively small-looking cottage, which actually had seven rooms and two baths. Tom was the accountant for most of the lodges and motels in town. Karen ran a charming French cafe during the season. Both were amateur radio operators, and they owned a shortwave set, which was why Jenny had come here.

"If someone sabotaged the radio at the sheriff's office," Lisa said, "what makes you think they didn't get this one, too?"

"Maybe they didn't know about it. It's worth taking a look."

She rang the bell, and when there was no response, she tried the door. It was locked.

They went around to the rear of the property, where brandy-hued light flowed out through the windows. Jenny looked warily at the rear lawn, which was left moonless by tree shadows. Their footsteps echoed hollowly on the wooden floor of the back porch. She tried the kitchen door and found it was locked, too.

At the nearest window, the curtains were drawn aside. Jenny looked in and saw only an ordinary kitchen: green counters, cream-colored walls, oak cabinets, gleaming appliances, no signs of violence.

Other casement windows faced onto the porch, and one of these, Jenny knew, was a den window. Lights were on, but the curtains were drawn. Jenny rapped on the glass, but no one responded. She tested the window, found that it was latched. Gripping the revolver by the barrel, she smashed a diamond-shaped pane adjacent to the center post. The sound of shattering glass was jarringly loud. Although this was an emergency, she felt like a thief. She reached through the broken pane, threw open the latch, pulled the halves of the window apart, and went over the sill, into the house. She fumbled through the drapes, then drew them aside, so that Lisa could enter more easily.

Two bodies were in the small den. Tom and Karen Oxley.

Karen was lying on the floor, on her side, legs drawn up toward her belly, shoulders curled forward, arms crossed over her breasts—a fetal position. She was bruised and swollen. Her bulging eyes stared in terror. Her mouth hung open, frozen forever in a scream.

"Their faces are the worst thing," Lisa said.

"I can't understand why the facial muscles didn't relax upon death. I don't see how they can remain taut like that."

"What did they *see?*" Lisa wondered.

Tom Oxley was sitting in front of the shortwave radio. He was slumped over the radio, his head turned to one side. He was sheathed in bruises and swollen hideously, just as Karen was. His right hand was clenched around a table-model microphone, as if he had perished while refusing to relinquish it. Evidently, however, he had not managed a call for help. If he had gotten a message out of Snowfield, the police would have arrived by now.

The radio was dead.

Jenny had figured as much as soon as she had seen the bodies.

However, neither the condition of the radio nor the condition of the corpses was as interesting as the barricade. The den door was closed and, presumably, locked. Karen and Tom had dragged a heavy cabinet in front of it. They had pushed a pair of easy chairs hard against the cabinet, then had wedged a television set against the chairs.

"They were determined to keep something from getting in here," Lisa said.

"But it got in anyway."

"How?"

They both looked at the window through which they'd come.

"It was locked from the inside," Jenny said.

The room had only one other window.

They went to it and pulled back the drapes.

It was also latched securely on the inside.

Jenny stared out at the night, until she felt that something hidden in the darkness was staring back at her, getting a good look at her as she stood unprotected in the lighted window. She quickly closed the drapes.

"A locked room," Lisa said.

Jenny turned slowly around and studied the den. There was a small outlet from a heating duct, covered with a metal vent plate full of narrow slots, and there was perhaps a half-inch of air space under the barricaded door. But there was no way anyone could have gained access to the room.

She said, "As far as I can see, only bacteria or toxic gas or some kind of radiation could've gotten in here to kill them."

"But none of those things killed the Liebermanns."

Jenny nodded. "Besides, you wouldn't build a barricade to keep out radiation, gas, or germs."

How many of Snowfield's people had locked themselves in, thinking they had found defensible havens—only to die as suddenly and mysteriously as those who'd had no time to run? And what was it that could enter locked rooms without opening doors or windows? What had passed through this barricade without disturbing it?

The Oxleys' house was as silent as the surface of the moon.

Finally, Lisa said, "Now what?"

"I guess maybe we have to risk spreading a contagion. We'll drive out of town only as far as the nearest pay phone, call the sheriff in Santa Mira, tell him the situation, and let him decide how to handle it. Then we'll come back here to wait. We won't have any direct contact with anyone, and they can sterilize the telephone booth if they think that's necessary."

"I hate the idea of coming back here once we've gotten out," Lisa said anxiously.

"So do I. But we've got to act responsibly. Let's go," Jenny said, turning toward the open window through which they had entered.

The phone rang.

Startled, Jenny turned toward the strident sound.

The phone was on the same table as the radio.

It rang again.

She snatched up the receiver. "Hello?"

The caller didn't respond.

"Hello?"

Icy silence.

Jenny's hand tightened on the receiver.

Someone was listening intently, remaining utterly silent, waiting for her to speak. She was determined not to give him that satisfaction. She just pressed the receiver to her ear and strained to hear something, anything, if even nothing more than the faint sealike ebb and flow of his breathing. He didn't make the slightest sound, but still she could *feel,* at the other end of the line, the presence that she had felt when she'd picked up the phone in the Santinis' house and in the sheriff's substation.

Standing in the barricaded room, in that silent house where Death had crept in with impossible stealth, Jenny Paige felt an odd transformation overtaking her. She was well-educated, a woman of reason and logic, not even mildly superstitious. Thus far, she had attempted to solve the mystery of Snowfield by applying the tools of logic and reason. But for the first time in her life, they had utterly failed her. Now deep in her mind, something . . . *shifted,* as if an enormously heavy iron cover were being slid off a dark pit in her subconscious. In that pit, within ancient chambers of the mind, there lay a host of primitive sensations and perceptions, a superstitious awe that was new to her. Virtually on the level of racial memory stored in the genes, she sensed what was happening in Snowfield. The knowledge was within her; however, it was so alien, so fundamentally illogical, that she resisted it, fighting hard to suppress the superstitious terror that boiled up within her.

Clutching the telephone receiver, she listened to the silent presence on the line, and she argued with herself:

—It isn't a man; it's a *thing.*

—Nonsense.

—It's not human, but it's aware.

—You're hysterical.

—Unspeakably malevolent; perfectly, purely evil.

—Stop it, stop it, *stop it!*

She wanted to slam down the phone. She couldn't do it. The thing on the other end of the line had her mesmerized.

Lisa stepped close. "What's wrong? What's happening?"

Shaking, drenched with sweat, feeling tainted merely by listening to the despicable presence, Jenny was about to tear the receiver away from her ear when she heard a hiss, a click—and then a dial tone.

For a moment, stunned, she couldn't react.

Then, with a whimper, she jabbed at the 0 button on the phone.

There was a ringing on the line. It was a wonderful, sweet, reassuring sound.

"Operator."

"Operator, this is an emergency," Jenny said. "I've got to reach the county sheriff's office in Santa Mira."

CHAPTER 9

A CALL FOR HELP

"LAUNDRY?" KALE ASKED. "What laundry?"

Bryce could see that Kale was jolted by the question and was only pretending not to understand.

"Sheriff, where is this supposed to lead?" Bob Robine asked.

Bryce's hooded eyes remained hooded, and he kept his voice calm, slow. "Gee, Bob, I'm just trying to get to the bottom of things, so we can all get out of here. I swear, I don't like working on Sundays, and here this one is almost shot to hell already. I have these questions, and Mr. Kale doesn't have to answer a one of them, but I *will* ask, so that I can go home and put my feet up and have a beer."

Robine sighed. He looked at Kale. "Don't answer unless I say it's okay."

Worried now, Kale nodded.

Frowning at Bryce, Robine said, "Go ahead."

Bryce said, "When we arrived at Mr. Kale's house last Thursday, after he phoned in to report the deaths, I noticed that one cuff of his slacks and the thick bottom edge of his sweater both looked slightly damp, so as you'd hardly notice. I got the notion he'd laundered everything he was wearing and just hadn't left his clothes in the dryer quite long enough. So I had a look in the laundry room, and I found something interesting. In the cupboard right there beside the washer, where Mrs. Kale kept all of her soaps and detergents and fabric softeners, there were two bloody fingerprints on the big box of Cheer. One was smeared, but the other was clear. The lab says it's Mr. Kale's print."

"Whose blood was on the box?" Robine asked sharply.

"Both Mrs. Kale and Danny were type O. So is Mr. Kale. That makes it a little more difficult for us to—"

"The blood on the box of detergent?" Robine interrupted.

"Type O."

"Then it could have been my client's own blood! He could have gotten it on the box on a previous occasion, maybe after he cut himself gardening last week."

Bryce shook his head. "As you know, Bob, this whole blood-typing business is getting highly sophisticated these days. Why, they can break down a sample into so many enzymes and protein signatures that a person's blood is almost as unique as his fingerprints. So they could tell us unequivocally that the blood on the box of Cheer—the blood on Mr. Kale's hand when he made those two prints—was little Danny Kale's blood."

Fletcher Kale's gray eyes remained flat and unexpressive, but he turned quite pale. "I can explain," he said.

"Hold it!" Robine said. "Explain it to me first—in private." The attorney led his client to the farthest corner of the room.

Bryce slouched in his chair. He felt gray. Washed out. He'd been that way since Thursday, since seeing Danny Kale's pathetic, crumpled body.

He had expected to take considerable pleasure in watching Kale squirm. But there was no pleasure in it.

Robine and Kale returned. "Sheriff, I'm afraid my client did a stupid thing."

Kale tried to look properly abashed.

"He did something that could be misinterpreted—just as you *have* misinterpreted it. Mr. Kale was frightened, confused, and grief-stricken. He wasn't thinking clearly. I'm sure any jury would sympathize with him. You see, when he found the body of his little boy he picked it up—"

"He told us he never touched it."

Kale met Bryce's gaze forthrightly and said, "When I first saw Danny lying on the floor . . . I couldn't *really* believe that he was . . . dead. I picked him up . . . thinking I should rush him to the hospital . . . Later, after I'd shot Joanna, I looked down and saw that I was covered with . . . with Danny's blood. I *had* shot my wife, but suddenly I realized it might look as if I'd killed my own son, too."

"There was still the meat cleaver in your wife's hand," Bryce said. "And Danny's blood was all over *her,* too. And you could've figured the coroner would find PCP in her bloodstream."

"I realize that now," Kale said, pulling a handkerchief from his pocket and wiping his eyes. "But at the time, I was afraid I'd be accused of something I'd never done."

The word "psychopath" wasn't exactly right for Fletcher Kale, Bryce decided. He wasn't crazy. Nor was he a sociopath, exactly. There wasn't a word that described him properly. However, a good cop would recognize the type and see the potential for criminal activity and, perhaps, the talent for brute violence, as well. There is a certain kind of man who has a lot of vitality and likes plenty of action, a man who has more than his share of shallow charm, whose clothes are more expensive than he can afford, who owns not a single book (as Kale did not), who seems to have no well-thought-out opinions about politics or art or economics or any issue of real substance, who is not religious except when misfortune befalls him or when he wishes to impress someone with his piety (as Kale, member of no church, now read the Bible in his cell for at least four hours every day), who has an athletic build but who seems to loathe any pursuit as healthy as physical exercise, who spends his leisure time in bars and cocktail lounges, who cheats on his wife as a matter of habit (as did Kale, by all reports), who is impulsive, who is unreliable and always late for appointments (as was Kale), whose goals are either vague or unrealistic ("Fletcher Kale? He's a dreamer."), who frequently overdraws his checking account and lies about money, who is quick to borrow and slow to pay back, who exaggerates, who *knows* he's going to be rich one day but who has no specific plan for acquiring that wealth, who never doubts or thinks about next year, who worries only about himself and only when it's too late. There was such a man, such a type, and Fletcher Kale was a prime example of the animal in question.

Bryce had seen others like him. Their eyes were always flat; you couldn't see into their eyes at all. Their faces expressed whatever emotion seemed required, although every expression was a shade too *right.* When they expressed concern for anyone but themselves, you could detect a bell-clear ring of insincerity. They were not burdened by remorse, morality, love, or empathy. Often, they led lives of acceptable destruction, ruining and embittering those who loved them, shattering the lives of friends who believed them and relied on them, betraying trusts, but never quite crossing the line into outright criminal behavior. Now and then, however, such a man went too far. And because he was the type who never did things by halves, he always went much, *much* too far.

Danny Kale's small, torn, bloody body lying in a heap.

The grayness enveloping Bryce's mind grew thicker, until it seemed like a cold, oily smoke. To Kale, he said, "You've told us that your wife was a heavy marijuana smoker for two and a half years."

"That's right."

"At my direction, the coroner looked for a few things that wouldn't ordinarily have interested him. Like the condition of Joanna's lungs. She wasn't a smoker at all, let alone a pothead. Lungs were clean."

"I said she smoked pot, not tobacco," Kale said.

"Marijuana smoke and ordinary tobacco smoke both damage the lungs," Bryce said. "In Joanna's case, there was no damage whatsoever."

"But I—"

"Quiet," Bob Robine advised his client. He pointed a long, slim finger at Bryce, waggled it, and said, "The important thing is—was there PCP in her blood or wasn't there?"

"There was," Bryce said. "It was in her blood, but she didn't *smoke* it. Joanna took the PCP orally. There was still a lot of it in her stomach."

Robine blinked in surprise but recovered quickly. "There you go," he said. "She took it. Who cares how?"

"In fact," Bryce said, "there was more of it in her stomach than in her bloodstream."

Kale tried to look curious, concerned, and innocent—all at the same time; even his elastic features were strained by that expression.

Scowling, Bob Robine said, "So there was more in her stomach than in her bloodstream. So what?"

"Angel dust is highly absorbable. Taken orally, it doesn't remain in the stomach for very long. Now, while Joanna had swallowed enough dope to freak out, there hadn't been time for it to affect her. You see, she took the PCP with ice cream. Which coated her stomach and retarded the absorption of the drug. During the autopsy, the coroner found partially digested chocolate fudge ice cream. So there hadn't been time for the PCP to cause hallucinations or to send her into a berserk rage." Bryce paused, took a deep breath. "There was chocolate fudge ice cream in Danny's stomach, too, but no PCP. When Mr. Kale told us he came home from work early on Thursday, he didn't mention bringing an afternoon treat for the family. A half-gallon of chocolate fudge ice cream."

Fletcher Kale's face had gone blank. At last, he seemed to have used up his collection of human expressions.

Bryce said, "We found a partly empty container of ice cream in Kale's freezer. Chocolate fudge. What I think happened, Mr. Kale, is that you dished out some ice cream for everyone. I think you secretly laced your wife's serving with PCP, so you could later claim she was in a drug-induced frenzy. You didn't figure the coroner would catch you out."

"Wait just one goddamned minute!" Robine shouted.

"Then, while you washed your bloody clothes," Bryce said to Kale, "you cleaned up the ice-cream-smeared dishes and put them away because your story was that you had come home from work to find little Danny already dead and his mother already freaked out on PCP."

Robine said, "That's only supposition. Have you forgotten motive? Why in God's name would my client do such a hideous thing?"

Watching Kale's eyes, Bryce said, "High Country Investments."

Kale's face remained impassive, but his eyes flickered.

"High Country Investments?" Robine asked. "What's that?"

Bryce stared at Kale. "Did you buy ice cream before you went home last Thursday?"

"No," Kale said flatly.

"The manager of the 7-Eleven store over on Calder Street says you did."

The muscles in Kale's jaws bulged as he clenched his teeth in anger.

"What about High Country Investments?" Robine asked.

Bryce fired another question at Kale. "Do you know a man named Gene Terr?"

Kale only stared.

"People sometimes just call him 'Jeeter.' "

Robine said, "Who is he?"

"Leader of the Demon Chrome," Bryce said, watching Kale. "It's a motorcycle gang. Jeeter deals drugs. Actually, we've never been able to catch him at it himself; we've only been able to jail some of his people. We leaned on Jeeter about this, and he steered us to someone who admitted supplying Mr. Kale with grass on a regular basis. Not Mrs. Kale. She never bought."

"Who says?" Robine demanded. "This motorcycle creep? This social reject? This drug pusher? He's not a reliable witness!"

"According to our source, Mr. Kale didn't just buy grass last Tuesday. Mr. Kale bought angel dust, too. The man who sold the drugs will testify in return for immunity."

With animal cunning and suddenness, Kale bolted up, seized the empty chair beside him, threw it across the table at Bryce Hammond, and ran for the door of the interrogation room.

By the time the chair had left Kale's hands and was in the air, Bryce was already up and moving, and it sailed harmlessly past his head. He was around the table when the chair crashed to the floor behind him.

Kale pulled open the door and plunged into the corridor.

Bryce was four steps behind him.

Tal Whitman had come off the window ledge as if he'd been blown off by an explosive charge, and he was one step behind Bryce, shouting.

Reaching the corridor, Bryce saw Fletcher Kale heading for a yellow exit door about twenty feet away. He went after the son of a bitch.

Kale hit the crashbar and flung the metal door open.

Bryce reached him a fraction of a second later, as Kale was setting foot onto the macadamed parking lot.

Sensing Bryce close behind him, Kale turned with catlike fluidity and swung one huge fist.

Bryce ducked the blow, threw a punch of his own, connecting with Kale's hard, flat belly. Then he swung again, hitting him in the neck.

Kale stumbled back, putting his hands to his throat, gagging and choking. Bryce moved in.

But Kale wasn't as badly stunned as he pretended to be. He leaped forward as Bryce approached and grabbed him in a bear hug.

"Bastard," Kale said, spraying spittle.

His gray eyes were wide. His lips were skinned back from his teeth in a fierce snarl. He looked lupine.

Bryce's arms were pinned, and although he was a strong man himself, he couldn't break Kale's iron hold on him. They staggered a few steps backwards, stumbled, and went down, with Kale on top. Bryce's head thumped hard against the pavement, and he thought he was going to black out.

Kale punched him once, ineffectively, then rolled off him and crawled away fast.

Warding off the darkness that rose behind his eyes, surprised that Kale had surrendered the advantage, Bryce pushed up onto his hands and knees. He shook his head—and then saw what the other man had gone after.

A revolver.

It lay on the macadam, a few yards away, gleaming darkly in the glow of the yellowish sodium-vapor lights.

Bryce felt his holster. Empty. The revolver on the ground was his own. Apparently, it had slipped out of his holster and had spun across the pavement when he'd fallen.

The killer's hand closed on the weapon.

Tal Whitman stepped in and swung a nightstick, striking Kale across the back of the neck. The big man collapsed on top of the gun, unconscious.

Crouching, Tal rolled Kale over and checked his pulse.

Holding the back of his own throbbing skull, Bryce hobbled over to them. "Is he all right, Tal?"

"Yeah. He'll be coming around in a few minutes." He picked up Bryce's gun and got to his feet.

Accepting the revolver, Bryce said, "I owe you one."

"Not at all. How's your head?"

"I should be so lucky to own an aspirin company."

"I didn't expect him to run."

"Neither did I," Bryce said. "When things get worse and worse for a man like that, he usually just gets calmer, cooler, more careful."

"Well, I guess this one saw the walls closing in."

Bob Robine was standing in the open doorway, staring out at them, shaking his head in consternation.

A few minutes later, as Bryce Hammond sat at his desk, filling out the forms charging Fletcher Kale with two homicides, Bob Robine rapped on the open door.

Bryce looked up. "Well, counselor, how's your client?"

"He's okay. But he's not my client any more."

"Oh? His decision or yours?"

"Mine. I can't handle a client who lies to me about *everything*. I don't *like* being made a fool of."

"So does he want to call another attorney tonight?"

"No. When he's arraigned, he's going to ask the judge for a public defender."

"That'll be the first thing in the morning."

"Not wasting any time, huh?"

"Not with this one," Bryce said.

Robine nodded. "Good. He's a *very* bad apple, Bryce. You know, I've been a lapsed Catholic for fifteen years," Robine said softly. "I made up my mind long ago that there weren't such things as angels, demons, miracles. I thought I was too well educated to believe that Evil—with a capital E—stalks the world on cloven hooves. But back there in the cell, Kale suddenly whirled on me and said, 'They won't get me. They won't destroy me. Nobody can. I'll walk away from this.' When I warned him against excessive optimism, he said, 'I'm not afraid of your kind. Besides, I didn't commit murder; I just disposed of some garbage that was stinking up my life.' "

"Jesus," Bryce said.

They were both silent. Then Robine sighed. "What about High Country Investments? How's it provide a motive?"

Before Bryce could explain, Tal Whitman rushed in from the hall. "Bryce, could I have a word with you?" He glanced at Robine. "Uh, this better be in private."

"Sure," Robine said.

Tal closed the door behind the lawyer. "Bryce, do you know Dr. Jennifer Paige?"

"She set up practice in Snowfield sometime back."

"Yeah. But what kind of person would you say she is?"

"I've never met her. I heard she's a fine doctor, though. And folks up in those little mountain towns are glad they don't have to drive all the way in to Santa Mira for a doctor any more."

"I've never met her either. I was just wondering if maybe you'd heard anything about . . . about whether she drinks. I mean . . . booze."

"No, I haven't heard any such thing. Why? What's going on?"

"She called a couple of minutes ago. She says there's been a disaster up in Snowfield."

"Disaster? What's she mean?"

"Well, she says she doesn't know."

Bryce blinked. "Did she sound hysterical?"

"Frightened, yeah. But not hysterical. She doesn't want to say much of anything to anyone but you. She's on line three right now."

Bryce reached for the phone.

"One more thing," Tal said, worry lines creasing his forehead.

Bryce paused, hand on the receiver.

Tal said: "She did tell me one thing, but it doesn't make sense. She said . . ."

"Yes?"

"She said that everyone's dead up there. Everyone in Snowfield. She said she and her sister are the only ones alive."

CHAPTER 10

SISTERS AND COPS

JENNY AND LISA left the Oxley house the same way they had entered: through the window.

The night was growing colder. The wind had risen once more.

They walked back to Jenny's house at the top of Skyline Road and got jackets to ward off the chill.

Then they went downhill again to the sheriff's substation. A wooden bench was bolted to the cobblestones by the curb in front of the town jail, and they sat waiting for help from Santa Mira.

"How long will it take them to get here?" Lisa asked.

"Well, Santa Mira is more than thirty miles away, over some pretty twisty roads. And they've got to take some unusual precautions." Jenny looked at her wristwatch. "I guess they'll be here in another forty-five minutes. An hour at most."

"Jeez."

"It's not so long, honey."

The girl turned up the collar of her fleece-lined, denim jacket. "Jenny, when the phone rang at the Oxley place and you picked it up . . ."

"Yes?"

"Who was calling?"

"No one."

"What did you hear?"

"Nothing," Jenny lied.

"From the look on your face, I thought someone was threatening you or something."

"Well, I was upset, of course. When it rang, I thought the phones were working again, but when I picked it up and it was only another dead line, I felt . . . crushed. That was all."

"Then you got a dial tone?"

"Yes."

She probably doesn't believe me, Jenny thought. She thinks I'm trying to protect her from something. And, of course, I am. How can I explain the feeling that something evil was on that phone with me? I can't even begin to understand it myself. Who or what *was* on that telephone? Why did he—or *it* —finally let me have a dial tone?

A scrap of paper blew along the street. Nothing else moved.

A thin rag of cloud passed over one corner of the moon.

After a while, Lisa said, "Jenny, in case something happens to me tonight—"

"Nothing's going to happen to you, honey."

"But in case something *does* happen to me tonight," Lisa insisted, "I want you to know that I . . . well . . . I really am . . . proud of you."

Jenny put an arm around her sister's shoulders, and they moved even closer together. "Sis, I'm sorry that we never had much time together over the years."

"You got home as often as you could," Lisa said. "I know it wasn't easy. I must've read a couple of dozen books about what a person has to go through to become a doctor. I always knew there was a lot on your shoulders, a lot you had to worry about."

Surprised, Jenny said, "Well, I still could've gotten home more often."

She had stayed away from home on some occasions because she had not been able to cope with the accusation in her mother's sad eyes, an accusation which was even more powerful and affecting because it was never bluntly put into words: *You killed your father, Jenny; you broke his heart, and that killed him.*

Lisa said, "And Mom was always so proud of you, too."

That statement not only surprised Jenny: It rocked her.

"Mom was always telling people about her daughter the doctor." Lisa smiled, remembering. "I think there were times her friends were ready to throw her out of her bridge club if she said just one more word about your scholarships or your good grades."

Jenny blinked. "Are you serious?"

"Of course, I'm serious."

"But didn't Mom . . . ."

"Didn't she what?" Lisa asked.

"Well . . . didn't she ever say anything about . . . about Dad? He died twelve years ago."

"Jeez, I know that. He died when I was two and a half." Lisa frowned. "But what're you talking about?"

"You mean you never heard Mom blame me?"

"Blame you for what?"

Before Jenny could respond, Snowfield's graveyard tranquillity was snuffed out. All the lights went off.

Three patrol cars set out from Santa Mira, headed into the night-en-shrouded hills, toward the high, moon-bathed slopes of the Sierras, toward Snowfield, their red emergency lights flashing.

Tal Whitman drove the car at the head of the speeding procession, and Sheriff Hammond sat beside him. Gordy Brogan was in the back seat with another deputy, Jake Johnson.

Gordy was scared.

He knew his fear wasn't visible, and he was thankful for that. In fact, he looked as if he didn't know *how* to be afraid. He was tall, large-boned, slab-muscled. His hands were strong and as large as the hands of a professional basketball player; he looked capable of slam-dunking anyone who gave him trouble. He knew that his face was handsome enough; women had told him so. But it was also a rather rough-looking face, dark. His lips were thin, giving his mouth a cruel aspect. Jake Johnson had said it best: *Gordy, when you frown, you look like a man who eats live chickens for breakfast.*

But in spite of his fierce appearance, Gordy Brogan was scared. It wasn't the prospect of disease or poison that occasioned fear in Gordy. The sheriff had said that there were indications that the people in Snowfield had been killed not by germs or by toxic substances but *by other people.* Gordy was afraid that he would have to use his gun for the first time since he had become a deputy, eighteen months ago; he was afraid he would be forced to shoot someone—either to save his own life, the life of another deputy, or that of a victim.

He didn't think he could do it.

Five months ago, he had discovered a dangerous weakness in himself when he had answered an emergency call from Donner's Sports Shop. A disgruntled former employee, a burly man named Leo Sipes, had returned to the store two weeks after being fired, had beaten up the manager, and had broken the arm of the clerk who had been hired to replace him. By the time Gordy arrived on the scene, Leo Sipes—big and dumb and drunk—was using a woodsman's hatchet to smash and splinter all of the merchandise. Gordy was unable to talk him into surrendering. When Sipes started after him, brandishing the hatchet, Gordy had pulled his revolver. And then found he couldn't use it. His trigger finger became as brittle and inflexible as ice. He'd had to put the gun away and risk a physical confrontation with Sipes. Somehow, he'd gotten the hatchet away from him.

Now, five months later, as he sat in the rear of the patrol car and listened to Jake Johnson talking to Sheriff Hammond, Gordy's stomach clenched and turned sour at the thought of what a .45-caliber hollow-nose bullet would do to a man. It would *literally* take off his head. It would smash a man's shoulder into rags of flesh and broken needles of bone. It would rip open a man's chest, shattering the heart and everything else in its path. It would blow off a leg if it struck a kneecap, would turn a face to bloody slush. And Gordy Brogan, God help him, was just not capable of doing such a thing to anyone.

That was his terrible weakness. He knew there were people who would say that his inability to shoot another being was not a weakness but a sign of moral superiority. However, he knew that was not always true. There were times when shooting was a moral act. An officer of the law was sworn to protect the public. For a cop, the inability to shoot (when shooting was clearly justified) was not only weakness but madness, perhaps even sinful.

During the past five months, following the unnerving episode at Donner's Sports Shop, Gordy had been lucky. He'd drawn only a few calls involving violent suspects. And fortunately, he had been able to bring his adversaries to heel by using his fists or his nightstick or threats—or by firing warning shots into the air. Once, when it had seemed that shooting someone was unavoidable, the other officer, Frank Autry, had fired first, winging the gunman, before Gordy had been confronted with the impossible task of pulling the trigger.

But now something unimaginably violent had transpired up in Snowfield. And Gordy knew all too well that violence frequently had to be met with violence.

The gun on his hip seemed to weigh a thousand pounds.

He wondered if the time was approaching when his weakness would be revealed. He wondered if he would die tonight—or if he would cause, by his weakness, the unnecessary death of another.

He ardently prayed that he could beat this thing. Surely, it was possible for a man to be peaceful by nature and still possess the nerve to save himself, his friends, his kind.

Red emergency beacons flashing on their roofs, the three white and green squad cars followed the winding highway into the night-cloaked mountains, up toward the peaks where the moonlight created the illusion that the first snow of the season had already fallen.

Gordy Brogan was scared.

The streetlamps and all other lights went out, casting the town into darkness.

Jenny and Lisa bolted up from the wooden bench.

"What happened?"

"Ssshh!" Jenny said. *"Listen!"*

But there was only continued silence.

The wind had stopped blowing, as if startled by the town's abrupt blackout. The trees waited, boughs hanging as still as old clothes in a closet.

Thank God for the moon, Jenny thought.

Heart thudding, Jenny turned and studied the buildings behind them. The town jail. A small cafe. The shops. The townhouses.

All the doorways were so clotted with shadows that it was difficult to tell if the doors were open or closed—or if, just now, they were slowly, slowly coming open to release the hideous, swollen, demonically reanimated dead into the night streets.

Stop it! Jenny thought. The dead don't come back to life.

Her eyes came to rest on the gate in front of the covered serviceway between the sheriff's substation and the gift shop next door. It was exactly like the cramped, gloomy passageway beside Liebermann's Bakery.

Was something hiding in this tunnel, too? And, with the lights out, was it creeping inexorably toward the far side of the gate, eager to come out onto the dark sidewalk?

That primitive fear again.

That sense of evil.

That superstitious terror.

"Come on," she said to Lisa.

"Where?"

"In the street. Nothing can get us out there—"

"—without our seeing it coming," Lisa finished, understanding.

They went into the middle of the moonlit roadway.

"How long until the sheriff gets here?" Lisa asked.

"At least fifteen or twenty minutes yet."

The town's lights all came on at once. A brilliant shower of electric radiance stung their eyes with surprise—then darkness again.

Jenny raised the revolver, not knowing where to point it.

Her throat was fear-parched, her mouth dry.

A blast of sound—an ungodly wail—slammed through Snowfield.

Jenny and Lisa both cried out in shock and turned, bumping against each other, squinting at the moon-tinted darkness.

Then silence.

Then another shriek.

Silence.

"What?" Lisa asked.

"The firehouse!"

It came again: a short burst of the piercing siren from the east side of St. Moritz Way, from the Snowfield Volunteer Fire Company stationhouse.

Bong!

Jenny jumped again, twisted around.

Bong! Bong!

"A church bell," Lisa said.

"The Catholic church, west on Vail."

The bell tolled once more—a loud, deep, mournful sound that reverberated in the blank windows along the dark length of Skyline Road and in other, unseen windows throughout the dead town.

"Someone has to pull a rope to ring a bell," Lisa said. "Or push a button to set off a siren. So there *must* be someone else here beside us."

Jenny said nothing.

The siren sounded again, whooped and then died, whooped and then died, and the church bell began to toll again, and the bell and the siren cried out at the same time, again and again, as if announcing the advent of someone of tremendous importance.

In the mountains, a mile from the turnoff to Snowfield, the night landscape was rendered solely in black and moon-silver. The looming trees were not green at all; they were somber shapes, mostly shadows, with albescent fringes of vaguely defined needles and leaves.

In contrast, the shoulders of the highway were blood-colored by the light that splashed from the revolving beacons atop the three Ford sedans which all bore the insignia of the Santa Mira County Sheriff's Department on their front doors.

Deputy Frank Autry was driving the second car, and Deputy Stu Wargle was slouched down on the passenger's seat.

Frank Autry was lean, sinewy, with neatly trimmed salt-and-pepper hair. His features were sharp and economical, as if God hadn't been in the mood to waste anything the day that He had edited Frank's genetic file: hazel eyes under a finely chiseled brow; a narrow, patrician nose; a mouth that was neither too parsimonious nor too generous; small, nearly lobeless ears tucked flat against the head. His mustache was most carefully groomed.

He wore his uniform precisely the way the service manual said he should: black boots polished to a mirrored shine, brown slacks with a knife-edge crease, leather belt and holster kept bright and supple with lanolin, brown shirt crisp and fresh.

"It isn't fucking fair," Stu Wargle said.

"Commanding officers don't always have to be fair—just right," Frank said.

"What commanding officer?" Wargle asked querulously.

"Sheriff Hammond. Isn't that who you mean?"

"I don't think of him as no commanding officer."

"Well, that's what he is," Frank said.

"He'd like to break my ass," Wargle said. "The bastard."

Frank said nothing.

Before signing up with the county constabulary, Frank Autry had been a career military officer. He had retired from the United States Army at the age of forty-four, after twenty-five years of distinguished service, and had moved back to Santa Mira, the town in which he'd been born and raised. He had intended to open a small business of some kind in order to supplement his pension and to keep himself occupied, but he hadn't been able to find anything that looked interesting. Gradually, he had come to realize that, for him at least, a job without a uniform and without a chain of command and without an element of physical risk and without a sense of public service was just not a job worth having. Three years ago, at the age of forty-six, he had signed up with the sheriff's department, and in spite of the demotion from major, which was the rank he'd held in the service, he had been happy ever since.

That is, he had been happy except for those occasions, usually one week a month, when he'd been partnered with Stu Wargle. Wargle was insufferable. Frank tolerated the man only as a test of his own self-discipline.

Wargle was a slob. His hair often needed washing. He always missed a patch of bristles when he shaved. His uniform was wrinkled, and his boots were never shined. He was too big in the gut, too big in the hips, too big in the butt.

Wargle was a bore. He had absolutely no sense of humor. He read nothing, knew nothing—yet he had strong opinions about every current social and political issue.

Wargle was a creep. He was forty-five years old, and he still picked his nose in public. He belched and farted with aplomb.

Still slumped against the passenger-side door, Wargle said, "I'm supposed to go off duty at ten o'clock. Ten goddamned *o'clock!* It's not fair for Hammond to pull me for this Snowfield crap. And me with a hot number all lined up."

Frank didn't take the bait. He didn't ask who Wargle had a date with. He just drove the car and kept his eyes on the road and hoped that Wargle wouldn't tell him who this "hot number" was.

"She's a waitress over at Spanky's Diner," Wargle said. "Maybe you seen her. Blond broad. Name's Beatrice; they call her Bea."

"I seldom stop at Spanky's," Frank said.

"Oh. Well, she don't have a half-bad face, see. One hell of a set of knockers. She's got a few extra pounds on her, not much, but she thinks she looks worse than she does. Insecurity, see? So if you play her right, if you kind of work on her doubts about herself, see, and then if you say you want her, anyway, in spite of the fact that she's let herself get a little pudgy—why, hell, she'll do any damned thing you want. *Anything.*"

The slob laughed as if he had said something unbearably funny.

Frank wanted to punch him in the face. Didn't.

Wargle was a woman-hater. He spoke of women as if they were members of another, lesser species. The idea of a man happily sharing his life and innermost thoughts with a woman, the idea that a woman could be loved, cherished, admired, respected, valued for her wisdom and insight and humor—that was an utterly alien concept to Stu Wargle.

Frank Autry, on the other hand, had been married to his lovely Ruth for twenty-six years. He adored her. Although he knew it was a selfish thought, he sometimes prayed that he would be the first to die, so that he wouldn't have to handle life without Ruth.

"That fuckin' Hammond wants my ass nailed to a wall. He's always needling me."

"About what?"

"Everything. He don't like the way I keep my uniform. He don't like the way I write up my reports. He told me I should try to improve my attitude. Christ, my *attitude!* He wants my ass, but he won't get it. I'll hang in five more years, see, so I can get my thirty-year pension. That bastard won't squeeze me out of my pension."

Almost two years ago, voters in the city of Santa Mira approved a ballot initiative that dissolved the metropolitan police, putting law enforcement for the city into the hands of the county sheriff's department. It was a vote of confidence in Bryce Hammond, who had built the county department, but one provision of the initiative required that no city officers lose their jobs or pensions because of the transfer of power. Thus, Bryce Hammond was stuck with Stewart Wargle.

They reached the Snowfield turnoff.

Frank glanced in the rearview mirror and saw the third patrol car pull out of the three-car train. As planned, it swung across the entrance to Snowfield Road, setting up a blockade.

Sheriff Hammond's car continued on toward Snowfield, and Frank followed it.

"Why the hell did we have to bring water?" Wargle asked.

Three five-gallon bottles of water stood on the floor in the back of the car. Frank said, "The water in Snowfield might be contaminated."

"And all that food we loaded into the trunk?"

"We can't trust the food up there, either."

"I don't believe they're all dead."

"The sheriff couldn't raise Paul Henderson at the substation."

"So what? Henderson's a jerk-off."

"The doctor up there said Henderson's dead, along with—"

"Christ, the doctor's off her nut or drunk. Who the hell would go to a woman doctor, anyway? She probably screwed her way through medical school."

"What?"

"No broad has what it takes to *earn* a degree like that!"

"Wargle, you never cease to amaze me."

"What's eating you?" Wargle asked.

"Nothing. Forget it."

Wargle belched. "Well, I don't believe they're all dead."

Another problem with Stu Wargle was that he didn't have any imagination.

"What a lot of crap. And me lined up with a hot number."

Frank Autry, on the other hand, had a very good imagination. Perhaps too good. As he drove higher into the mountains, as he passed a sign that read SNOWFIELD—3 MILES, his imagination was humming like a well-lubricated machine. He had the disturbing feeling—Premonition? Hunch?—that they were driving straight into Hell.

* * *

The firehouse siren screamed.

The church bell tolled faster, faster.

A deafening cacophony clattered through the town.

"Jenny!" Lisa shouted.

"Keep your eyes open! Look for movement!"

The street was a patchwork of ten thousand shadows; there were too many dark places to watch.

The siren wailed, and the bell rang, and now the lights began to flash again —house lights, shop lights, streetlights—on and off, on and off so rapidly that they created a strobelike effect. Skyline Road flickered; the buildings seemed to jump toward the street, then fall back, then jump forward; the shadows danced jerkily.

Jenny turned in a complete circle, the revolver thrust out in front of her.

If something was approaching under cover of the stroboscopic light show, she couldn't see it.

She thought: What if, when the sheriff arrives, he finds two severed heads in the middle of the street? Mine and Lisa's.

The church bell was louder than ever, and it banged away continuously, madly.

The siren swelled into a teeth-jarring, bone-piercing screech. It seemed a miracle that windows didn't shatter.

Lisa had her hands over her ears.

Jenny's gun hand was shaking. She couldn't keep it steady.

Then, as abruptly as the pandemonium had begun, it ceased. The siren died. The church bell stopped. The lights stayed on.

Jenny scanned the street, waiting for something more to happen, something worse.

But nothing happened.

Again, the town was as tranquil as a graveyard.

A wind sprang out of nowhere and caused the trees to sway, as if responding to ethereal music beyond the range of human hearing.

Lisa shook herself out of a daze and said, "It was almost as if . . . as if they were *trying* to scare us . . . teasing us."

"Teasing," Jenny said. "Yes, that's exactly what it was like."

"Playing with us."

"Like a cat with mice," Jenny said softly.

They stood in the middle of the silent street, afraid to go back to the bench in front of the town jail, lest their movement should start the siren and the bell again.

Suddenly, they heard a low grumbling. For an instant, Jenny's stomach tightened. She raised the gun once more, although she could see nothing at which to shoot. Then she recognized the sound: automobile engines laboring up the steep mountain road.

She turned and looked down the street. The grumble of engines grew louder. A car appeared around the curve, at the bottom of town.

Flashing red roof lights. A police car. Two police cars.

"Thank God," Lisa said.

Jenny quickly led her sister to the cobblestone sidewalk in front of the substation.

The two white and green patrol cars came slowly up the deserted street and angled to the curb in front of the wooden bench. The two engines were cut off simultaneously. Snowfield's deathlike hush took possession of the night once more.

A rather handsome black man in a deputy's uniform got out of the first car, letting his door stand open. He looked at Jenny and Lisa but didn't immediately speak. His attention was captured by the preternaturally silent, unpeopled street.

A second man got out of the front seat of the same vehicle. He had unruly, sandy hair. His eyelids were so heavy that he looked as if he were about to fall asleep. He was dressed in civilian clothing—gray slacks, a pale blue shirt, a dark blue nylon jacket—but there was a badge pinned to the jacket.

Four other men got out of the cruisers. All six newcomers stood there for a long moment without speaking, eyes moving over the quiet stores and houses.

In that strange, suspended bubble of time, Jenny had an icy premonition that she didn't want to believe. She was certain—she sensed; she *knew*—that not all of them would leave this place alive.

CHAPTER 11

EXPLORING

BRYCE KNELT ON one knee beside the body of Paul Henderson.

The other seven—his own men, Dr. Paige, and Lisa—crowded into the reception area, outside the wooden railing, in the Snowfield substation. They were quiet in the presence of Death.

Paul Henderson had been a good man with decent instincts. His death was a terrible waste.

Bryce said, "Dr. Paige?"

She crouched down at the other side of the corpse. "Yes?"

"You didn't move the body?"

"I didn't even touch it, Sheriff."

"There was no blood?"

"Just as you see it now. No blood."

"The wound might be in his back," Bryce said.

"Even if it was, there'd still be some blood on the floor."

"Maybe." He stared into her striking eyes—green flecked with gold. "Ordinarily, I wouldn't disturb a body until the coroner had seen it. But this is an extraordinary situation. I'll have to turn this man over."

"I don't know if it's safe to touch him."

"Someone has to do it," Bryce said.

Dr. Paige stood up, and everyone moved back a couple of steps.

Bryce put a hand to Henderson's purple-black, distorted face. "The skin is still slightly warm," he said in surprise.

Dr. Paige said, "I don't think they've been dead very long."

"But a body doesn't discolor and bloat in just a couple of hours," Tal Whitman said.

"*These* bodies did," the doctor said.

Bryce rolled the corpse over, exposing the back. No wound.

Hoping to find an unnatural depression in the skull, Bryce thrust his fingers into the dead man's thick hair, testing the bone. If the deputy had been struck hard on the back of the head . . . But that wasn't the case, either. The skull was intact.

Bryce got to his feet. "Doctor, these two decapitations you mentioned . . .
I guess we'd better have a look at those."

"Do you think one of your men could stay here with my sister?"

"I understand your feelings," Bryce said. "But I don't really think it would
be wise for me to split up my men. Maybe there isn't any safety in numbers;
then on the other hand, maybe there *is.*"

"It's okay," Lisa assured Jenny. "I don't want to be left behind, anyway."

She was a spunky kid. Both she and her older sister intrigued Bryce Hammond. They were pale, and their eyes were alive with dervish shadows of shock
and horror—but they were coping a great deal better than most people would
have in this bizarre, waking nightmare.

The Paiges led the entire group out of the substation and down the street to
the bakery.

Bryce found it difficult to believe that Snowfield had been a normal, bustling
village only a short while ago. The town felt as dry and burnt-out and dead as
an ancient lost city in a far desert, off in a corner of the world where even the
wind often forgot to go. The hush that cloaked the town seemed a silence of
countless years, of decades, of centuries, a silence of unimaginably long epochs
piled on epochs.

Shortly after arriving in Snowfield, Bryce had used an electric bullhorn to
call for a response from the silent houses. Now it seemed foolish ever to have
expected an answer.

They entered Liebermann's Bakery through the front door and went into
the kitchen at the rear of the building.

On the butcher's-block table, two severed hands gripped the handles of a
rolling pin.

Two severed heads peered through two oven doors.

"Oh, my God," Tal said quietly.

Bryce shuddered.

Clearly in need of support, Jake Johnson leaned against a tall white cabinet.

Wargle said, "Christ, they were butchered like a couple of goddamned
cows," and then everyone was talking at once.

"—why the hell anyone would—"

"—sick, twisted—"

"—so where are the bodies?"

"Yes," Bryce said, raising his voice to override the babble, "where are the
bodies? Let's find them."

For a couple of seconds, no one moved, frozen by the thought of what they
might find.

"Dr. Paige, Lisa—there's no need for you to help us," Bryce said. "Just
stand aside."

The doctor nodded. The girl smiled in gratitude.

With trepidation, they searched all the cupboards, opened all the drawers
and doors. Gordy Brogan looked inside the big oven that wasn't equipped with
a porthole, and Frank Autry went into the walk-in refrigerator. Bryce inspected the small, spotless lavatory off one end of the kitchen. But they
couldn't find the bodies—or any other pieces of the bodies—of the two elderly
people.

"Why would the killers cart away the bodies?" Frank asked.

"Maybe we're dealing with some sort of cultists," Jake Johnson said.
"Maybe they wanted the bodies for some weird ritual."

"If there was any ritual," Frank said, "it looks to me like it was conducted
right here."

Gordy Brogan bolted for the lavatory, stumbling and weaving, a big gangling kid who seemed to be composed solely of long legs and long arms and elbows and knees. Retching sounds came through the door that he had slammed behind himself.

Stu Wargle laughed and said, "Jesus, what a ninny."

Bryce turned on him and scowled. "What in God's name do you find so funny, Wargle? People are dead here. Seems to me that Gordy's reaction is a lot more natural than any of ours."

Wargle's pig-eyed, heavy-jowled face clouded with anger. He didn't have the wit to be embarrassed.

God, I despise that man, Bryce thought.

When Gordy came back from the bathroom, he looked sheepish. "Sorry, Sheriff."

"No reason to be, Gordy."

They trooped through the kitchen, across the sales room, out onto the sidewalk.

Bryce went immediately to the wooden gate between the bakery and the shop next door. He stared over the top of the gate, into the lightless, covered passageway. Dr. Paige moved to his side, and he said, "Is this where you thought something was in the rafters?"

"Well, Lisa thought it was crouched along the wall."

"But it was *this* serviceway?"

"Yes."

The tunnel was utterly black.

He took Tal's long-handled flashlight, opened the creaking gate, drew his revolver, and stepped into the passage. A vague, dank odor clung to the place. The squeal of the rusty gate hinges and then the sound of his own footsteps echoed down the tunnel ahead of him.

The beam of the flash was powerful; it carried over half the length of the passageway. However, he focused it close at hand, swept it back and forth over the immediate area, studying the concrete walls, then looking up at the ceiling, which was eight or ten feet overhead. In this part of the serviceway, at least, the rafters were deserted.

With each step, Bryce grew increasingly certain that drawing his revolver had been unnecessary—until he was almost halfway through the tunnel. Then he suddenly felt . . . something odd . . . a tingle, a cold augural quiver along the spine. He sensed that he wasn't alone any longer.

He was a man who trusted his hunches, and he didn't discount this one. He stopped advancing, brought the revolver up, listened more closely than before to the silence, moved the flashlight rapidly over the walls and ceiling, squinted with special care at the rafters, looked ahead into the gloom almost as far as the mouth of the alleyway, and even glanced back to see if something had crept magically around behind him. Nothing waited in the darkness. Yet he continued to feel that he was being watched by unfriendly eyes.

He started forward again, and his light caught something. Covered by a metal grille, a foot-square drain opening was set in the floor of the serviceway. Inside the drain, something indefinable glistened, reflecting the flashlight beam; it *moved*.

Cautiously, Bryce stepped closer and directed the light straight down into the drain. Whatever had glistened was gone now.

He squatted beside the drain and peered between the ribs of the grille. The light revealed only the walls of a pipe. It was a storm drain, about eighteen inches in diameter, and it was dry, which meant he had not merely seen water.

A rat? Snowfield was a resort that catered to a relatively affluent crowd; therefore, the town took unusually stringent measures to keep itself free of all manner of pests. Of course, in spite of Snowfield's diligence in such matters, the existence of a rat or two certainly wasn't impossible. It *could* have been a rat. But Bryce didn't believe that it *had* been.

He walked all the way to the alley, then retraced his steps to the gate where Tal and the others waited.

"See anything?" Tal asked.

"Not much," Bryce said, stepping onto the sidewalk and closing the gate behind him. He told them about his feeling of being watched and about the movement in the drain.

"The Liebermanns were killed by people," Frank Autry said. "Not by something small enough to crawl through a drain."

"That certainly would seem to be the case," Bryce agreed.

"But you did *feel* it in there?" Lisa asked anxiously.

"I felt something," Bryce told the girl. "It apparently didn't affect me as strongly as you said it did you. But it was definitely . . . strange."

"Good," Lisa said. "I'm glad you don't think we're just hysterical women."

"Considering what you've been through, you two are about as *un*hysterical as you could get."

"Well," the girl said, "Jenny's a doctor, and I think maybe I'd like to be a doctor someday, and doctors simply can't afford to get hysterical."

She was a cute kid—although Bryce couldn't help noticing that her older sister was even better looking. Both the girl and the doctor had the same lovely shade of auburn hair; it was the dark red-brown of well-polished cherry wood, thick and lustrous. Both of them had the same golden skin, too. But because Dr. Paige's features were more mature than Lisa's, they were also more interesting and appealing to Bryce. Her eyes were a shade greener than her sister's, too.

Bryce said, "Dr. Paige, I'd like to see that house where the bodies were barricaded in the den."

"Yeah," Tal said. "The locked room murders."

"That's the Oxley place over on Vail." She led them down the street toward the corner of Vail Lane and Skyline Road.

The dry shuffle of their footsteps was the only sound, and it made Bryce think of desert places again, of scarabs swarming busily across stacks of ancient, brittle papyrus scrolls in desert tombs.

Rounding the corner onto Vail Lane, Dr. Paige halted and said, "Tom and Karen Oxley live . . . uh . . . *lived* two blocks farther along here."

Bryce studied the street. He said, "Instead of walking straight to the Oxleys', let's have a look in all the houses and shops between here and there — at least on this side of the street. I think it's safe to split up into two squads, four to a group. We won't be going off entirely in different directions. We'll be close enough to help each other if there's trouble. Dr. Paige, Lisa—you stay with Tal and me. Frank, you're in charge of the second team."

Frank nodded.

"The four of you stick together," Bryce warned them. "And I mean *together.* Each of you remain within sight of the other three at all times. Understood?"

"Yes, Sheriff," Frank Autry said.

"Okay, you four have a look in the first building past the restaurant here, and we'll take the place next door to that. We'll hopscotch our way along the street and compare notes at the end of the block. If you come across something really interesting, something more than just additional bodies, come get me. If you need help, fire two or three rounds. We'll hear the gunshots even if we're inside another building. And you listen for gunfire from us."

"May I make a suggestion?" Dr. Paige asked.

"Sure," Bryce said.

To Frank Autry, she said, "If you come across any bodies that show signs of hemorrhaging from the eyes, ears, nose, or mouth, let me know at once. Or any indications of vomiting or diarrhea."

"Because those things might indicate disease?" Bryce asked.

"Yes," she said. "Or poisoning."

"But we've ruled that out, haven't we?" Gordy Brogan asked.

Jake Johnson, looking older than his fifty-seven years, said, "It wasn't a disease that cut off those people's heads."

"I've been thinking about that," Dr. Paige said. "What if this is a disease or a chemical toxin that we've never encountered before—a mutant strain of rabies, say—that kills some people but merely drives others stark raving mad? What if the mutilations were done by those who were driven into a savage madness?"

"Is such a thing likely?" Tal Whitman asked.

"No. But then again, maybe not impossible. Besides, who's to say what's likely or unlikely any more? Is it *likely* that this would have happened to Snowfield in the first place?"

Frank Autry tugged at his mustache and said, "But if there are packs of rabid maniacs roaming around out there . . . where *are* they?"

Everyone looked at the quiet street. At the deepest pools of shadow spilling over lawns and sidewalks and parked cars. At unlighted attic windows. At dark basement windows.

"Hiding," Wargle said.

"Waiting," Gordy Brogan said.

"No, that doesn't make sense," Bryce said. "Rabid maniacs just wouldn't hide and wait and *plan.* They'd charge us."

"Anyway," Lisa said quietly, "it isn't rabid people. It's something a lot stranger."

"She's probably right," Dr. Paige said.

"Which somehow doesn't make me feel any better," Tal said.

"Well, if we find any indications of vomiting, diarrhea, or hemorrhaging," Bryce said, "then we'll know. And if we don't . . . ."

"I'll have to come up with a new hypothesis," Dr. Paige said.

They were silent, not eager to begin the search because they didn't know what they might find—or what might find them.

Time seemed to have stopped.

Dawn, Bryce Hammond thought, will never come unless we move.

"Let's go," he said.

The first building was narrow and deep, with a combination art gallery and crafts shop on the first floor. Frank Autry broke a pane of glass in the front door, reached inside, and released the lock. He entered and switched on the lights.

Motioning the others to follow, he said, "Spread out. Don't stay too close together. We don't want to offer an easy target."

As Frank spoke, he was reminded of the two tours of duty he served in Vietnam almost twenty years ago. This operation had the nerve-twisting quality of a search-and-destroy mission in guerrilla territory.

They prowled cautiously through the gallery's display but found no one. Likewise, there was no one in the small office at the rear of the showroom. However, a door in that office opened onto stairs that led to the second floor.

They took the stairs in military fashion. Frank climbed to the top alone, gun drawn, while the others waited. He located the light switch at the head of the stairs, snapped it on, and saw that he was in one corner of the living room of the gallery owner's apartment. When he was certain the room was deserted, he motioned for his men to come up. As the others climbed the stairs, Frank moved into the living room, staying close to the wall, watchful.

They searched the rest of the apartment, treating every doorway as a potential point of ambush. The den and dining room were both deserted. No one was hiding in the closets.

On the kitchen floor, however, they found a dead man. He was wearing only blue pajama bottoms, propping the refrigerator door open with his bruised and swollen body. There were no visible wounds. There was no look of horror on his face. Apparently, he had died too suddenly to have gotten a glimpse of his assailant—and without the slightest warning that death was near. The makings of a sandwich were scattered on the floor around him: a broken jar of mustard, a package of salami, a partially squashed tomato, a package of Swiss cheese.

"It sure wasn't no illness killed him," Jake Johnson said emphatically. "How sick could he have been if he was gonna eat salami?"

"And it happened real fast," Gordy said. "His hands were full of the stuff he got out of the refrigerator, and as he turned around . . . it just happened. *Bang:* just like that."

In the bedroom they discovered another corpse. She was in bed, naked. She was no younger than about twenty, no older than forty; it was difficult to guess her age because of the universal bruising and swelling. Her face was contorted in terror, precisely as Paul Henderson's had been. She had died in the middle of a scream.

Jake Johnson took a pen from his shirt pocket and slipped it through the trigger of a .22 automatic that was lying on the rumpled sheets beside the body.

"I don't think we have to be careful with that," Frank said. "She wasn't shot. There aren't any wounds; no blood. If anybody used the gun, it was her. Let me see it."

He took the automatic from Jake and ejected the clip. It was empty. He worked the slide, pointed the muzzle at the bedside lamp, and squinted into the barrel; there was no bullet in the chamber. He put the muzzle to his nose, sniffed, smelled gunpowder.

"Fired recently?" Jake asked.

"Very recently. Assuming the clip was full when she used it, that means she fired off ten rounds."

"Look here," Wargle said.

Frank turned and saw Wargle pointing to a bullet hole in the wall opposite the foot of the bed. It was at about the seven-foot level.

"And here," Gordy Brogan said, drawing their attention to another bullet lodged in the splintered wood of the dark pine highboy.

They found all ten of the brass shell casings in or around the bed, but they couldn't find where the other eight bullets were lodged.

"You don't think she scored eight hits?" Gordy asked Frank.

"Christ, she can't have!" Wargle said, hitching his gun belt up on his fat hips. "If she'd hit somebody eight times, she wouldn't be the only damned corpse in the room."

"Right," Frank said, though he disliked having to agree with Stu Wargle about anything. "Besides, there's no blood. Eight hits would mean a lot of blood."

Wargle went to the foot of the bed and stared at the dead woman. She was propped up by a couple of plump pillows, and her legs were spread in a grotesque parody of desire. "The guy in the kitchen must've been in here, screwing this broad," Wargle said. "When he was finished with her, he went into the kitchen to get them somethin' to eat. While they was separated, someone came in and killed her."

"They killed the man in the kitchen first," Frank said. "He couldn't have been taken by surprise if he'd been attacked *after* she fired ten shots."

Wargle said, "Man, I sure wish *I'd* spent all day in the sack with a broad like that."

Frank gaped at him. "Wargle, you're disgusting. Are you even turned on by a bloated corpse—just because it's naked?"

Wargle's face reddened, and he looked away from the corpse. "What the hell's the matter with you, Frank? What d'ya think I *am*—some kind of pervert? Huh? Hell, *no.* I seen that picture over on the nightstand." He pointed to a silver-framed photograph beside the lamp. "See, she's wearin' a bikini. You can see she was a hell of a nice-lookin' broad. Big jugs on her. Great legs, too. *That's* what turned me on, pal."

Frank shook his head. "I'm just amazed that anything could turn you on in the midst of *this,* in the midst of so much death."

Wargle thought it was a compliment. He winked.

If I get out of this business alive, Frank thought, I won't ever let Bryce Hammond partner me with Wargle. I'll quit first.

Gordy Brogan said, "How could she have made eight hits and not have stopped something? How come there's not one drop of blood?"

Jake Johnson pushed a hand through his white hair again. "I don't know, Gordy. But one thing I *do* know—I sure wish Bryce'd never picked me to come up here."

Next to the art gallery, the sign on the front of the quaint, two-story building read:

BROOKHART'S
BEER WINE LIQUOR TOBACCO
MAGAZINES NEWSPAPERS BOOKS

The lights were on, and the door was unlocked. Brookhart's stayed open until nine even on Sunday evenings during the off season.

Bryce went in first, followed by Jennifer and Lisa Paige. Tal entered last. When choosing a man to protect his back in a dangerous situation, Bryce always preferred Tal Whitman. He trusted no one else as much as he trusted Tal, not even Frank Autry.

Brookhart's was a cluttered place, but curiously warm and pleasing. There were tall glass-doored coolers filled with cans and bottles of beer, shelves and racks and bins laden with bottles of wine and liquor, and other racks brimming with paperbacks, magazines, and newspapers. Cigars and cigarettes were stacked in boxes and cartons, and tins of pipe tobacco were displayed in haphazard mounds on several countertops. A variety of goodies were tucked in wherever there was space: candy bars, Life-Savers, chewing gum, peanuts, popcorn, pretzels, potato chips, corn twisties, tortilla chips.

Bryce led the way through the deserted store, looking for bodies in the aisles. But there were none.

There was, however, an enormous puddle of water, about an inch deep, that covered half the floor. They stepped gingerly around it.

"Where'd all this water come from?" Lisa wondered.

"Must be a leak in the condensation pan under one of the beer coolers," Tal Whitman said.

They came around the end of a wine bin and got a good look at all of the coolers. There was no water anywhere near those softly humming appliances.

"Maybe there's a leak in the plumbing," Jennifer Paige said.

They continued their exploration, descending into the cellar, which was used for the storage of wine and booze in cardboard cases, then going up to the top floor, above the store, where there was an office. They found nothing out of the ordinary.

In the store again, heading toward the front door, Bryce stopped and hunkered down for a closer look at the puddle on the floor. He moistened one fingertip in the stuff; it *felt* like water, and it was odorless.

"What's wrong?" Tal asked.

Standing again, Bryce said, "It's odd—all this water here."

Tal said, "Most likely, it's what Dr. Paige said—only a leak in the plumbing."

Bryce nodded. However, although he couldn't say why, the big puddle seemed significant to him.

Tayton's Pharmacy was a small place that served Snowfield and all of the outlying mountain towns. An apartment occupied two floors above the pharmacy; it was decorated in shades of cream and peach, with emerald-green accent pieces, and with a number of fine antiques.

Frank Autry led his men through the entire building, and they found nothing remarkable—except for the sodden carpet in the living room. It was literally soaking wet; it squished beneath their shoes.

The Candleglow Inn positively radiated charm and gentility: the deep eaves and elaborately carved cornices, the mullioned windows flanked by carved white shutters. Two carriage lamps were fixed atop stone pilasters, bracketing the short stone walkway. Three small spotlights spread dramatic fans of light across the face of the inn.

Jenny, Lisa, the sheriff, and Lieutenant Whitman paused on the sidewalk in front of the Candleglow, and Hammond said, "Are they open this time of year?"

"Yes," Jenny said. "They manage to stay about half full during the off season. But then they have a marvelous reputation with discriminating travelers—and they only have sixteen rooms."

"Well . . . let's have a look."

The front doors opened onto a small, comfortably appointed lobby: an oak floor, a dark oriental carpet, light beige sofas, a pair of Queen Anne chairs upholstered in a rose-colored fabric, cherry wood end tables, brass lamps.

The registration desk was off to the right. A bell rested on the wooden counter, and Jenny struck it several times, rapidly, expecting no response and getting none.

"Dan and Sylvia keep an apartment behind this office area," she said, indicating the cramped business quarters beyond the counter.

"They own the place?" the sheriff asked.

"Yes. Dan and Sylvia Kanarsky."

The sheriff stared at her for a moment. "Friends?"

"Yes. Close friends."

"Then maybe we'd better not look in their apartment," he said.

Warm sympathy and understanding shone in his heavy-lidded blue eyes. Jenny was surprised by a sudden awareness of the kindness and intelligence that informed his face. During the past hour, watching him operate, she had gradually realized that he was considerably more alert and efficient than he had at first appeared to be. Now, looking into his sensitive, compassionate eyes, she realized he was perceptive, interesting, formidable.

"We can't just walk away," she said. "This place has to be searched sooner or later. The whole town has to be searched. We might as well get this part of it out of the way."

She lifted a hinged section of the wooden countertop and started to push through a gate into the office space beyond.

"Please, Doctor," the sheriff said, "always let me or Lieutenant Whitman go first."

She backed out obediently, and he preceded her into Dan's and Sylvia's apartment, but they didn't find anyone. No dead bodies.

Thank God.

Back at the registration desk, Lieutenant Whitman paged through the guest log. "Only six rooms are being rented right now, and they're all on the second floor."

The sheriff located a passkey on a pegboard beside the mailboxes.

With almost monotonous caution, they went upstairs and searched the six rooms. In the first five, they found luggage and cameras and half-written postcards and other indications that there actually were guests at the inn, but they didn't find the guests themselves.

In the sixth room, when Lieutenant Whitman tried the door to the adjoining bath, he found it locked. He hammered on it and shouted, "Police! Is anyone there?"

No one answered.

Whitman looked at the doorknob, then at the sheriff. "No lock button on this side, so someone must be in there. Break it down?"

"Looks like a solid-core door," Hammond said. "No use dislocating your shoulder. Shoot the lock."

Jenny took Lisa's arm and drew the girl aside, out of the path of any debris that might blow back.

Lieutenant Whitman called a warning to anyone who might be in the bathroom, then fired one shot. He kicked the door open and went inside fast. "Nobody's here."

"Maybe they climbed out a window," the sheriff said.

"There aren't any windows in here," Whitman said, frowning.

"You're sure the door was locked?"

"Positive. And it could only be done from the inside."

"But how—if no one was in there?"

Whitman shrugged. "Besides that, there's something you ought to have a look at."

They all had a look at it, in fact, for the bathroom was large enough to accommodate four people. On the mirror above the sink, a message had been hastily printed in bold, greasy, black letters:

TIMOTHY FLYTE THE ANCIENT ENEMY

* * *

In another apartment above another shop, Frank Autry and his men found another water-soaked carpet that squished under their feet. In the living room, dining room, and bedrooms, the carpet was dry, but in the hallway leading to the kitchen, it was saturated. And in the kitchen itself, three-quarters of the vinyl-tile floor was covered with water up to a depth of one inch in places.

Standing in the hallway, staring into the kitchen, Jake Johnson said, "Must be a plumbing leak."

"That's what you said at the other place," Frank reminded him. "Seems coincidental, don't you think?"

Gordy Brogan said, "It *is* just water. I don't see what it could have to do with . . . all the murders."

"Shit," Stu Wargle said, "we're wastin' time. There's nothin' here. Let's go."

Ignoring them, Frank stepped into the kitchen, treading carefully through one end of the small lake, heading for a dry area by a row of cupboards. He opened several cupboard doors before he found a small plastic tub used for storing leftovers. It was clean and dry, and it had a snap-on lid that made an airtight seal. In a drawer he found a measuring spoon, and he used it to scoop water into the plastic container.

"What're you doing?" Jake asked from the doorway.

"Collecting a sample."

"Sample? Why? It's only water."

"Yeah," Frank said, "but there's something funny about it."

The bathroom. The mirror. The bold, greasy, black letters.

Jenny stared at the five printed words.

Lisa said, "Who's Timothy Flyte?"

"Could be the guy who wrote this," Lieutenant Whitman said.

"Is the room rented to Flyte?" the sheriff asked.

"I'm sure I didn't see that name on the registry," the lieutenant said. "We can check it out when we go downstairs, but I'm really sure."

"Maybe Timothy Flyte is one of the killers," Lisa said. "Maybe the guy renting this room recognized him and left this message."

The sheriff shook his head. "No. If Flyte's got something to do with what's happened to this town, he wouldn't leave his name on the mirror like that. He would've wiped it off."

"Unless he didn't know it was there," Jenny said.

The lieutenant said, "Or maybe he knew it was there, but he's one of the rabid maniacs you talked about, so he doesn't care whether we catch him or not."

Bryce Hammond looked at Jenny. "Anyone in town named Flyte?"

"Never heard of him."

"Do you know everyone in Snowfield?"

"Yeah."

"All five hundred?"

"Nearly everyone," she said.

"*Nearly* everyone, huh? Then there *could* be a Timothy Flyte here?"

"Even if I'd never met him, I'd still have heard someone mention him. It's a *small* town, Sheriff, at least during the off season."

"Could be someone from over in Mount Larson, Shady Roost, or Pineville," the lieutenant suggested.

She wished they could go somewhere else to discuss the message on the mirror. Outside. In the open. Where nothing could creep close to them without revealing itself. She had the uncanny, unsupported, but undeniable feeling that something—something damned strange—was moving about in another part of the inn right this minute, stealthily carrying out some dreadful task of which she and the sheriff and Lisa and the deputy were dangerously unaware.

"What about the second part of it?" Lisa asked, indicating THE ANCIENT ENEMY.

Jenny finally said, "Well, we're back to what Lisa first said. It looks as if the man who wrote this was telling us that Timothy Flyte was his enemy. Our enemy, too, I guess."

"Maybe," Bryce Hammond said dubiously. "But it seems like an unusual way to put it—'the ancient enemy.' Kind of awkward. Almost archaic. If he locked himself in the bathroom to escape Flyte and then wrote a hasty warning, why wouldn't he say, 'Timothy Flyte, my old enemy,' or something straightforward?"

Lieutenant Whitman agreed. "In fact, if he wanted to leave a message accusing Flyte, he'd have written, 'Timothy Flyte did it,' or maybe 'Flyte killed them all.' The *last* thing he'd want is to be obscure."

The sheriff began sorting through the articles on the deep shelf that was above the sink, just under the mirror: a bottle of Mennen's Skin Conditioner, lime-scented aftershave, a man's electric razor, a pair of toothbrushes, toothpaste, combs, hairbrushes, a woman's makeup kit. "From the looks of it, there were two people in this room. So maybe they both locked themselves in the bath—which means *two* of them vanished into thin air. But what did they write on the mirror with?"

"It looks as if it must've been an eyebrow pencil," Lisa said.

Jenny nodded. "I think so, too."

They searched the bathroom for a black eyebrow pencil. They couldn't find it.

"Terrific," the sheriff said exasperatedly. "So the eyebrow pencil disappeared along with maybe two people who locked themselves in here. Two people kidnapped out of a locked room."

They went downstairs to the front desk. According to the guest register, the room in which the message had been found was occupied by a Mr. and Mrs. Harold Ordnay of San Francisco.

"None of the other guests was named Timothy Flyte," Sheriff Hammond said, closing the register.

"Well," Lieutenant Whitman said, "I guess that's about all we can do here right now."

Jenny was relieved to hear him say that.

"Okay," Bryce Hammond said. "Let's catch up with Frank and the others. Maybe they've found something we haven't."

They started across the lobby. After only a couple of steps, Lisa stopped them with a scream.

They all saw it a second after it caught the girl's attention. It was on an end table, directly in the fall of light from a rose-shaded lamp, so prettily lit that it seemed almost like a piece of artwork on display. A man's hand. A severed hand.

Lisa turned away from the macabre sight.

Jenny held her sister, looking over Lisa's shoulder with ghastly fascination. The hand. The damned, mocking, impossible hand.

It was holding an eyebrow pencil firmly between its thumb and first two fingers. *The* eyebrow pencil. The same one. It *had* to be.

Jenny's horror was as great as Lisa's, but she bit her lip and suppressed a scream. It wasn't merely the sight of the hand that repelled and terrified her. The thing that made the breath catch and burn in her chest was the fact that this hand hadn't been on this end table a short while ago. Someone had placed it here while they were upstairs, knowing that they would find it; someone was mocking them, someone with an extremely twisted sense of humor.

Bryce Hammond's hooded eyes were open farther than Jenny had yet seen them. "Damn it, this thing wasn't here before—was it?"

"No," Jenny said.

The sheriff and deputy had been carrying their revolvers with the muzzles pointed at the floor. Now they raised their weapons as if they thought the severed hand might drop the eyebrow pencil, launch itself off the table toward someone's face, and gouge out someone's eyes.

They were speechless.

The spiral patterns in the oriental carpet seemed to have become refrigeration coils, casting off waves of icy air.

Overhead, in a distant room, a floorboard or an unoiled door creaked, groaned, creaked.

Bryce Hammond looked up at the ceiling of the lobby.

Creeeeeaaak.

It could have been only a natural settling noise. Or it could have been something else.

"There's no doubt now," the sheriff said.

"No doubt about what?" Lieutenant Whitman asked, looking not at the sheriff but at other entrances to the lobby.

The sheriff turned to Jenny. "When you heard the siren and the church bell just before we arrived, you said you realized that whatever had happened to Snowfield might still *be* happening."

"Yes."

"And now we know you're right."

CHAPTER 12
BATTLEGROUND

JAKE JOHNSON WAITED with Frank, Gordy, and Stu Wargle at the end of the block, on a brightly lighted stretch of sidewalk in front of Gilmartin's Market, a grocery store.

He watched Bryce Hammond coming out of the Candleglow Inn, and he wished to god the sheriff would move faster. He didn't like standing here in all this light. Hell, it was like being on stage. Jake felt vulnerable.

Of course, a few minutes ago, while conducting a search of some of the buildings along the street, they'd had to pass through dark areas where the shadows had seemed to pulse and move like living creatures, and Jake had looked with fierce longing toward this very same stretch of brightly lighted pavement. He had feared the darkness as much as he now feared the light.

He nervously combed one hand through his thick white hair. He kept his other hand on the butt of his holstered revolver.

Jake Johnson not only believed in caution: He worshiped it; caution was his god. *Better safe than sorry; a bird in the hand is worth two in the bush; fools rush in where angels fear to tread* . . . He had a million maxims. They were, to him, lightposts marking the one safe route, and beyond those lights lay only a cold void of risk, chance, and chaos.

Jake had never married. Marriage meant taking on a lot of new responsibilities. It meant risking your emotions and your money and your entire future.

Where finances were concerned, he had also lived a cautious, frugal existence. He had put away a rather substantial nest egg, spreading his funds over a wide variety of investments.

Jake, now fifty-eight, had worked for the Santa Mira County Sheriff's Department for over thirty-seven years. He could have retired and claimed a pension a long time ago. But he had worried about inflation, so he had stayed on, building his pension, putting away more and more money.

Becoming an officer of the law was perhaps the only incautious thing that Jake Johnson had ever done. He hadn't *wanted* to be a cop. God, no! But his father, Big Ralph Johnson, had been county sheriff in the 1940s and 50s, and he had expected his son to follow in his footsteps. Big Ralph never took no for an answer. Jake had been pretty sure that Big Ralph would disinherit him if he didn't go into police work. Not that there was a vast fortune in the family; there wasn't. But there had been a nice house and respectable bank accounts. And behind the family garage, buried three feet below the lawn, there had been several big mason jars filled with tightly rolled wads of twenty- and fifty- and hundred-dollar bills, money that Big Ralph had taken in bribes and had set aside against bad times. So Jake had become a cop like his daddy, who had finally died at the age of eighty-two, when Jake was fifty-one. By then Jake was stuck with being a cop for the rest of his working life because it was the only thing he knew.

He was a *cautious* cop. For instance, he avoided taking domestic disturbance calls because policemen sometimes got killed by stepping between hot-tempered husbands and wives; passions ran too high in confrontations of that sort. Just look at this real estate agent, Fletcher Kale. A year ago, Jake had bought a piece of mountain property through Kale, and the man had seemed as normal as anyone. Now he had killed his wife and son. If a cop had stepped into that scene, Kale would have killed him, too. And when a dispatcher alerted Jake to a robbery-in-progress, he usually lied about his location, putting himself so far from the scene of the crime that other officers would be closer to it; then he showed up later, when the action was over.

He wasn't a coward. There had been times when he'd found himself in the line of fire, and on those occasions he'd been a tiger, a lion, a raging bear. He was just cautious.

There was some police work he actually enjoyed. The traffic detail was okay. And he positively delighted in paperwork. The only pleasure he took in making an arrest was the subsequent filling out of numerous forms that kept him safely tied up at headquarters for a couple of hours.

Unfortunately, this time, the trick of dawdling over paperwork had backfired on him. He'd been at the office, filling out forms, when Dr. Paige's call had come in. If he'd been out on the street, driving patrol, he could have avoided the assignment.

But now here he was. Standing in bright light making a perfect target of himself. Damn.

To make matters worse, it was obvious that something extremely violent had transpired inside Gilmartin's Market. Two of the five large panes of glass along the front of the market had been broken from inside; glass lay all over the sidewalk. Cases of canned dog food and six-packs of Dr Pepper had crashed through the windows and now lay scattered across the pavement. Jake was afraid the sheriff was going to make them go into the market to see what had happened, and he was afraid that someone dangerous was still in there, waiting.

The sheriff, Tal Whitman, and the two women finally reached the market, and Frank Autry showed them the plastic container that held the sample of water. The sheriff said he'd found another enormous puddle back at Brookhart's, and they agreed it might mean something. Tal Whitman told them about the message on the mirror—and about the severed hand; sweet Jesus!—at the Candleglow Inn, and no one knew what to make of that, either.

Sheriff Hammond turned toward the shattered front of the market and said what Jake was afraid he would say: "Let's have a look."

Jake didn't want to be one of the first through the doors. Or one of the last either. He slipped into the middle of the procession.

The grocery store was a mess. Around the three cash registers, black metal display stands had been toppled. Chewing gum, candy, razor blades, paperback books, and other small items spilled over the floor.

They walked across the front of the store, looking into each aisle as they passed it. Goods had been pulled off the shelves and thrown to the floor. Boxes of cereal were smashed, torn open, the bright cardboard poking up through drifts of cornflakes and Cheerios. Smashed bottles of vinegar produced a pungent stench. Jars of jam, pickles, mustard, mayonnaise, and relish were tumbled in a jagged, glutinous heap.

At the head of the last aisle, Bryce Hammond turned to Dr. Paige. "Would the store have been open this evening?"

"No," the doctor said, "but I think sometimes they stock the shelves on Sunday evenings. Not often, but sometimes."

"Let's have a look in the back," the sheriff said. "Might find something interesting."

That's what I'm afraid of, Jake thought.

They followed Bryce Hammond down the last aisle, stepping over and around five-pound bags of sugar and flour, a few of which had split open.

Waist-high coolers for meat, cheese, eggs, and milk were lined up along the rear of the store. Beyond the coolers lay the sparkling-clean work area where the meat was cut, weighed, and wrapped for sale.

Jake's eyes nervously flicked over the porcelain and butcher's-block tables. He sighed with relief when he saw that nothing lay on any of them. He wouldn't have been surprised to see the store manager's body neatly chopped into steaks, roasts, and cutlets.

Bryce Hammond said, "Let's have a look in the storeroom."

Let's not, Jake thought.

Hammond said, "Maybe we—"

The lights went out.

The only windows were at the front of the store, but even up there it was dark; the streetlights had gone out, too. Here, the darkness was complete, blinding.

Several voices spoke at once:

"Flashlights!"

"Jenny!"

"Flashlights!"

Then a lot happened very fast.

Tal Whitman switched on a flashlight, and the bladelike beam stabbed down at the floor. In the same instant, something struck him from behind, something unseen that had approached with incredible speed and stealth under the cover of darkness. Whitman was flung forward. He crashed into Stu Wargle.

Autry was pulling the other long-handled flashlight from the utility loop on his gun belt. Before he could switch it on, however, both Wargle and Tal Whitman fell against him, and all three went down.

As Tal fell, the flashlight flew out of his hand.

Bryce Hammond, briefly illuminated by the airborne light, grabbed for it; missed.

The flashlight struck the floor and spun away, casting wild and leaping shadows with each revolution, illuminating nothing.

And something cold touched the back of Jake's neck. Cold and slightly moist—yet something that was *alive*.

He flinched at the touch, tried to pull away and turn.

Something encircled his throat with the suddenness of a whip.

Jake gasped for breath.

Even before he could raise his hands to grapple with his assailant, his arms were seized and pinned.

He was being lifted off his feet as if he were a child.

He tried to scream, but a frigid hand clamped over his mouth. At least he *thought* it was a hand. But it felt like the flesh of an eel, cold and damp.

It stank, too. Not much. It didn't send out clouds of stink. But the odor was so different from anything Jake had ever smelled before, so bitter and sharp and unclassifiable that even in small whiffs it was nearly intolerable.

Waves of revulsion and terror broke and foamed within him, and he sensed he was in the presence of something unimaginably strange and unquestionably evil.

The flashlight was still spinning across the floor. Only a couple of seconds had passed since Tal had dropped it, although to Jake it seemed much longer than that. Now it spun one last time and clanged against the base of the milk cooler; the lens burst into countless pieces, and they were denied even that meager, erratic light. Although it had illuminated nothing, it had been better than total darkness. Without it, hope was extinguished, too.

Jake strained, twisted, flexed, jerked, and writhed in an epileptic dance of panic, a spasmodic fandango of escape. But he couldn't free even one hand. His unseen adversary merely tightened its grip.

Jake heard the others calling to one another; they sounded far away.

CHAPTER 13
SUDDENLY

JAKE JOHNSON HAD DISAPPEARED.

Before Tal could locate the unbroken flashlight, the one that Frank Autry had dropped, the market's lights flickered and then came on bright and steady. The darkness had lasted no longer than fifteen or twenty seconds.

But Jake was gone.

They searched for him. He wasn't in the aisles, the meat locker, the storeroom, the office, or the employees' bathroom.

They left the market—only seven of them now—following Bryce, moving with extreme caution, hoping to find Jake outside, in the street. But he wasn't there, either.

Snowfield's silence was a mute, mocking shout of ridicule.

Tal Whitman thought the night seemed infinitely darker now than it had been a few minutes ago. It was an enormous maw into which they had stepped, unaware. This deep and watchful night was hungry.

"Where could he have gone?" Gordy asked, looking a little savage, as he always did when he frowned, even though, right now, he was actually just scared.

"He didn't go anywhere," Stu Wargle said. "He was *taken.*"

"He didn't call for help."

"Never had a chance."

"You think he's alive . . . or dead?" the young Paige girl asked.

"Little doll," Wargle said, rubbing the beard stubble on his chin, "I wouldn't get my hopes up if I was you. I'll bet my last buck we'll find Jake somewheres, stiff as a board, all swelled up and purple like the rest of 'em."

The girl winced and sidled closer to her sister.

Bryce Hammond said, "Hey, let's not write Jake off that quickly."

"I agree," Tal said. "There *are* a lot of dead people in this town. But it seems to me that most of them *aren't* dead. Just missing."

"They're all deader than napalmed babies. Isn't that right, Frank?" Wargle said, never missing a chance to needle Autry about his service in Vietnam. "We just haven't found 'em yet."

Frank didn't rise to the bait. He was too smart and too self-controlled for that. Instead, he said, "What I don't understand is why it didn't take all of us when it had the chance? Why did it just knock Tal down?"

"I was switching on the flashlight," Tal said. "It didn't want me to do that."

"Yes," Frank said, "but why was Jake the only one of us it grabbed, and why did it do a fast fade right after?"

"It's teasing us," Dr. Paige said. The streetlamp made her eyes flash with green fire. "It's like I said about the church bell and the fire siren. It's like a cat playing with mice."

"But *why?*" Gordy asked exasperatedly. "What's it get out of all this? What's it want?"

"Hold on a minute," Bryce said. "How come everyone's all of a sudden saying 'it'? Last time I took an informal survey, seems to me the general consensus was that only a pack of psychopathic killers could've done this. Maniacs. *People.*"

They regarded one another with uneasiness. No one was eager to say what was on his mind. Unthinkable things were now thinkable. They were things that reasonable people could not easily put into words.

The wind gusted out of the darkness, and the obeisant trees bent reverently. The streetlamps flickered.

Everyone jumped, startled by the lights' inconstancy. Tal put his hand on the butt of his holstered revolver. But the lights did not go out.

They listened to the cemeterial town. The only sound was the whisper of the wind-stirred trees, which was like the last long exhalation of breath before the grave, an extended dying sigh.

Jake *is* dead, Tal thought. Wargle is right for once. Jake is dead and maybe the rest of us are, too, only we don't know it yet.

To Frank Autry, Bryce said, "Frank, why'd you say 'it' instead of 'they' or something else?"

Frank glanced at Tal, seeking support, but Tal wasn't sure why he, himself, had said "it." Frank cleared his throat. He shifted his weight from one foot to the other and looked at Bryce. He shrugged. "Well, sir, I guess maybe I said 'it' because . . . well . . . a soldier, a *human* adversary, would have blown us away right there in the market when he had the opportunity, all of us at once, in the darkness."

"So you think—what?—that this adversary isn't human?"

"Maybe it could be some kind of . . . animal."

"Animal? Is that really what you think?"

Frank looked exceedingly uncomfortable. "No, sir."

"What *do* you think?" Bryce asked.

"Hell, I don't *know* what to think," Frank said in frustration. "I'm military-trained, as you know. A military man doesn't like to plunge blindly into any situation. He likes to plan his strategy carefully. But good, sound strategic planning depends on a reliable body of experience. What happened in comparable battles in other wars? What have other men done in similar circumstances? Did they succeed or fail? But this time there just *aren't* any comparable battles; there's no experience to draw upon. This is so strange, I'm going to go right on thinking of the enemy as a faceless, neutral 'it.' "

Turning to Dr. Paige, Bryce said, "What about you? Why did you use the word 'it'?"

"I'm not sure. Maybe because Officer Autry used it."

"But you were the one who advanced the theory about a mutant strain of rabies that could create a pack of homicidal maniacs. Are you ruling that out now?"

She frowned. "No. We can't rule out anything at this point. But, Sheriff, I never meant that that was the only possible theory."

"Do you have any others?"

"No."

Bryce looked at Tal. "What about you?"

Tal felt every bit as uncomfortable as Frank had looked. "Well, I guess I used 'it' because I can't accept the homicidal-maniac theory any more."

Bryce's heavy eyelids lifted higher than usual. "Oh? Why not?"

"Because of what happened at the Candleglow Inn," Tal said. "When we came downstairs and found that hand on the table in the lobby, holding the eyebrow pencil we'd been looking for . . . well . . . that just didn't seem like something a homicidal nut case would *do.* We've all been cops long enough to've dealt with our share of unbalanced people. Have any of you ever encountered one of those types who had a sense of humor? Even an ugly, twisted sense of humor? They're humorless people. They've lost the ability to laugh at *anything,* which is probably part of the reason they're crazy. So when I saw that hand on the lobby table it just didn't seem to fit. I agree with Frank; for now I'm going to think of our enemy as a faceless 'it.' "

"Why won't any of you admit what you're feeling?" Lisa Paige said softly. She was fourteen, an adolescent, on her way to being a lovely young lady, but she gazed at each of them with the unselfconscious directness of a child. "Somehow, deep down inside where it really counts, we all *know* it wasn't people who did these things. It's something really awful—Jeez, just *feel* it out there—something strange and disgusting. Whatever it is, we all *feel* it. We're all scared of it. So we're all trying hard not to admit it's there."

Only Bryce returned the girl's stare; he studied her thoughtfully. The others looked away from Lisa. They didn't want to meet one another's eyes, either.

We don't want to look inside ourselves, Tal thought, and that's exactly what the girl's telling us to do. We don't want to look inward and find primitive superstition. We're all civilized, reasonably well-educated *adults,* and adults aren't supposed to believe in the boogeyman.

"Lisa's right," Bryce said. "The only way we're going to solve this one— maybe the only way we're going to avoid becoming victims ourselves—is to keep our minds open and let our imaginations have free rein."

"I agree," Dr. Paige said.

Gordy Brogan shook his head. "But what are we supposed to think, then? *Anything?* I mean, aren't there any limits? Are we supposed to start worrying about ghosts and ghouls and werewolves and . . . and vampires? There's got to be *some* things we can rule out."

"Of course," Bryce said patiently. "Gordy, no one's saying we're dealing with ghosts and werewolves. But we've got to realize that we're dealing with the unknown. That's all. *The unknown.*"

"I don't buy it," Stu Wargle said sullenly. "The unknown, my ass. When it's all said and done, what we'll find is that it's the work of some pervert, some stinkin' scumbag pretty much like all the stinkin' scumbags we've dealt with before."

Frank said, "Wargle, your kind of thinking is exactly what'll cause us to overlook important evidence. And it's also the kind of thinking that'll get us killed."

"You just wait," Wargle told them. "You'll find out I'm right." He spat on the sidewalk, hooked his thumbs in his gun belt, and tried to give the impression that he was the only levelheaded man in the group.

Tal Whitman saw through the macho posturing; he saw terror in Wargle, too. Though he was one of the most insensitive men Tal had ever known, Stu was not unaware of the primitive response of which Lisa Paige had spoken. Whether he admitted it or not, he clearly felt the same bone-deep chill that shivered through all of them.

Frank Autry also saw that Wargle's imperturbability was a pose. In a tone of exaggerated, insincere admiration, Frank said, "Stu, by your fine example, you fortify us. You inspire us. What would we do without you?"

"Without me," Wargle said sourly, "you'd go right down the old toilet, Frank."

With mock dismay, Frank looked around at Tal, Gordy, and Bryce. "Does that sound like a swelled head?"

"Sure does. But don't blame Stu. In his case," Tal said, "a swelled head is just a result of Nature's frenzied efforts to fill a vacuum."

It was a small joke, but the laugh it elicited was large. Although Stu enjoyed wielding the needle, he despised being on the pricking end of it; yet even he managed to dredge up a smile.

Tal knew they were not laughing at the joke as much as they were laughing at Death, laughing in its skeletal face.

But when the laughter faded, the night was still dark.

The town was still unnaturally silent.

Jake Johnson was still missing.

And *it* was still out there.

Dr. Paige turned to Bryce Hammond and said, "Are you ready to take a look at the Oxley house?"

Bryce shook his head. "Not right now. I don't think it's wise for us to do any more exploring until we get some reinforcements. I'm not going to lose another man. Not if I can help it."

Tal saw anguish pass through Bryce's eyes at the mention of Jake.

He thought: Bryce, my friend, you always take too much of the responsibility when something goes wrong, just like you're always too quick to share the credit for successes that have been entirely yours.

"Let's go back to the substation," Bryce said. "We've got to plan our moves carefully, and I've got calls to make."

They returned along the route by which they had come. Stu Wargle, still determined to prove his fearlessness, insisted on being the rear guard this time, and he swaggered along behind them.

As they reached Skyline Road, a church bell tolled, startling them. It tolled again, slowly, again, slowly, again . . .

Tal felt the metallic sound reverberating in his teeth.

They all stopped at the corner, listening to the bell and staring west, toward the other end of Vail Lane. Only a little more than one block away, a brick church tower rose above the other buildings; there was one small light at each corner of the peaked, slate belfry roof.

"The Catholic church," Dr. Paige informed them, raising her voice to compete with the bell. "It serves all the towns around here. Our Lady of the Mountains."

The pealing of a church bell could be a joyous music. But there was nothing joyous about this one, Tal decided.

"Who's ringing it?" Gordy wondered aloud.

"Maybe nobody's ringing it," Frank said. "Maybe it's hooked up to a mechanical device of some kind; maybe it's on a timer."

In the lighted belfry, the bell swung, casting off a glint of brass along with its one clear note.

"Does it usually ring this time on a Sunday night?" Bryce asked Dr. Paige.

"No."

"Then it's not on a timer."

A block away, high above the ground, the bell wink-flashed and rang again.

"So who's pulling the rope?" Gordy Brogan asked.

A macabre image crept into Tal Whitman's mind: Jake Johnson, bruised and bloated and stone-cold dead, standing in the bell-ringer's chamber at the bottom of the church tower, the rope gripped in his bloodless hands, dead but demonically animated, dead but nevertheless pulling on the rope, pulling and pulling, dead face turned up, grinning the wide mirthless grin of a corpse, protuberant eyes staring at the bell that swung and clanged under the peaked roof.

Tal shuddered.

"Maybe we should go over to the church and see who's there," Frank said.

"No," Bryce said instantly. "That's what it wants us to do. It wants us to come have a look. It wants us to go inside the church, and then it'll turn out the lights again . . ."

Tal noticed that Bryce, too, was now using the pronoun "it."

"Yeah," Lisa Paige said. "It's over there right this minute, waiting for us."

Even Stu Wargle wasn't prepared to encourage them to visit the church tonight.

In the open belfry, the visible bell swung, splintering off another shard of brassy light, swung, gleamed, swung, winked, as if it were flashing out a semaphoric message of hypnotic power at the same time that it issued its monotonous clang: *You are growing drowsy, even drowsier, sleepy, sleepy . . . you are deep asleep, in a trance . . . you are under my power . . . you will come to the church . . . you will come now, come, come, come to the church and see the wonderful surprise that awaits you here . . . come . . . come . . .*

Bryce shook himself as if casting off a dream. He said, "If it wants us to come to the church, that's a good reason not to go. No more exploring until daylight."

They all turned away from Vail Lane and went north on Skyline Road, past the Mountainview Restaurant, toward the substation.

They had gone perhaps twenty feet when the church bell stopped tolling.

Once more, the uncanny silence poured like viscous fluid through the town, coating everything.

When they reached the substation, they discovered that Paul Henderson's corpse was gone. It seemed as if the dead deputy had simply gotten up and walked away. Like Lazarus.

CHAPTER 14

CONTAINMENT

BRYCE WAS SITTING at the desk that had belonged to Paul Henderson. He had pushed aside the open issue of *Time* that Paul apparently had been reading when Snowfield had been wiped out. A yellow sheet of note paper lay on the blotter, filled with Bryce's economical handwriting.

Around him, the six others were busily carrying out tasks that he had assigned to them. A wartime atmosphere prevailed in the stationhouse. Their grim determination to survive had caused a fragile but steadily strengthening camaraderie to spring up among them. There was even guarded optimism, perhaps based on the observation that they were still alive while so many others were dead.

Bryce quickly scanned the list he had made, trying to determine if he had overlooked anything. Finally, he pulled the telephone to him. He got a dial tone immediately, and he was grateful for it, considering Jennifer Paige's difficulties in that regard.

He hesitated before placing the first call. A sense of the immense importance of the moment weighed heavily on him. The savage obliteration of Snowfield's entire population was like nothing that had ever happened before. Within hours, journalists would be coming to Santa Mira County by the scores, by the hundreds, from all over the world. By morning, the Snowfield story would have pushed all other news off the front pages. CBS, ABC, and NBC would all be interrupting regularly scheduled broadcasts for updates and bulletins throughout the duration of the crisis. The media coverage would be intense. Until the world knew whether or not some mutated germ had a role in the events here, hundreds of millions of people would wait breathlessly, wondering if their own death notices had been issued in Snowfield. Even if disease were ruled out, the world's attention wouldn't be diverted from Snowfield until the mystery had been explained. The pressure to find a solution was going to be unbearable.

On a personal level, Bryce's own life would be forever changed. He was in charge of the police contingent; therefore, he would be featured in all the news stories. That prospect appalled him. He wasn't the kind of sheriff who liked to grandstand. He preferred to keep a low profile.

But he couldn't just walk away from Snowfield now.

He dialed the emergency number at his own offices in Santa Mira, bypassing the switchboard operator. The desk sergeant on duty was Charlie Mercer, a good man who could be counted on to do precisely what he was told to do.

Charlie answered the phone halfway through the second ring. "Sheriff's Department." He had a flat, nasal voice.

"Charlie, this is Bryce Hammond."

"Yes, sir. We've been wondering what's happening up there."

Bryce succinctly outlined the situation in Snowfield.

"Good God!" Charlie said. "Jake's dead, too?"

"We don't know for sure that he's dead. We can hope not. Now listen, Charlie, there are a lot of things we've got to do in the next couple of hours, and it would be easier for all of us if we could maintain secrecy until we've established our base here and secured the perimeters. *Containment,* Charlie. That's the key word. Snowfield has to be sealed off tight, and that'll be a lot easier to accomplish if we can do it before the newsmen start tramping through the mountains. I know I can count on you to keep your mouth shut, but there are a few of the men . . ."

"Don't worry," Charlie said. "We can hold it close to the vest for a couple of hours."

"All right. First thing I want is twelve more men. Two more on the roadblock at the Snowfield turnoff. Ten here with me. Wherever you can, select single men without families."

"It really looks that bad?"

"It really does. And better select men who don't have relatives in Snowfield. Another thing: They'll have to bring a couple of days' worth of drinking water and food. I don't want them consuming anything in Snowfield until we know for sure that the stuff is safe here."

"Right."

"Every man should bring his sidearm, a riot gun, and tear gas."

"Got it."

"This'll leave you shorthanded, and it'll get worse when the media people start pouring in. You'll have to call in some of the auxiliary deputies for directing traffic and crowd control. Now, Charlie, you know this part of the county pretty well—don't you?"

"I was born and raised in Pineville."

"That's what I thought. I've been looking at the county map, and so far as I can see, there are only two passable routes into Snowfield. First, there's the highway, which we've already blockaded." He swiveled on his chair and stared at the huge, framed map on the wall.

"Then there's an old fire trail that leads about two-thirds of the way up the other side of the mountain. Where the fire trail leaves off, an established wilderness trail seems to pick up. It's just a footpath from that point, but from the way it looks on the map, it comes out smack-dab at the top of the longest ski-run on this side of the mountain, up here above Snowfield."

"Yeah," Charlie said. "I've backpacked through that neck of the woods. It's officially the Old Mount Greentree Wilderness Trail. Or as we locals used to call it—the Muscle Liniment Highway."

"We'll have to station a couple of men at the bottom of the fire trail and turn back anyone who tries to come in that way."

"It would take one hell of a determined reporter to try it."

"We can't take chances. Are you aware of any other route that isn't on the map?"

"Nope," Charlie said. "Otherwise, you'd have to come into Snowfield straight overland, making your own trail every damned step of the way. That *is* wilderness out there; it's not just a playground for weekend campers, by God. No experienced backpacker would try to come overland. That'd be plain stupid."

"All right. Something else I need is a phone number from the files. Remember that law enforcement seminar I went to in Chicago . . . oh . . . about sixteen months ago. One of the speakers was an army man. Copperfield, I think. General Copperfield."

"Sure," Charlie said. "The Army Medical Corps' CBW Division."

"That's it."

"I think they call Copperfield's office the Civilian Defense Unit. Hold on." Charlie was off the line less than a minute. He came back with the number, read it to Bryce. "That's out in Dugway, Utah. Jesus, do you think this could be something that'd bring those boys running? That's scary."

"Real scary," Bryce agreed. "A couple of other things. I want you to put a name on the teletype. Timothy Flyte." Bryce spelled it. "No description. No known address. Find out if he's wanted anywhere. Check with the FBI, too. Then find out all you can about a Mr. and Mrs. Harold Ordnay of San Francisco." He gave Charlie the address that had been in the Candleglow Inn's guest register. "One more thing. When those new men come up here, have them bring some plastic body bags from the county morgue."

"How many?"

"To start with . . . two hundred."

"Uh . . . two . . . *hundred?*"

"We might need a great many more than that before we're through. We might have to borrow from other counties. Better check into that. A lot of people seem just to've disappeared, but their bodies may still turn up. There were about five hundred people living here. We could possibly need that many body bags."

And maybe even more than five hundred, Bryce thought. Because we might need a few bags for ourselves, too.

Although Charlie had listened attentively when Bryce told him that the entire town had been wiped out, and although there was no doubt that he believed Bryce, he obviously hadn't fully, *emotionally* comprehended the awful dimensions of the disaster until he'd heard the request for two hundred body bags. An image of all those corpses, sealed in opaque plastic, stacked atop one another in Snowfield's streets—that was what had finally pierced him.

"Holy Mother of God," Charlie Mercer said.

While Bryce Hammond was on the telephone with Charlie Mercer, Frank and Stu started to dismantle the hulking, police-band radio that stood against the back wall of the room. Bryce had told them to find out what was wrong with the set, for there weren't any visible signs of damage.

The front plate was fastened down by ten tightly turned screws. Frank worked them loose one at a time.

As usual, Stu wasn't much help. He kept glancing around at Dr. Paige, who was at the other end of the room, working with Tal Whitman on another project.

"She's sure a sweet piece of meat," Stu said, casting a covetous look at the doctor and picking his nose at the same time.

Frank said nothing.

Stu looked at what he'd pried out of his nose, inspecting it as if it were a pearl found in an oyster. He glanced back at the doctor again. "Look at the way she fills out them jeans. Christ, I'd love to dip my wick in that."

Frank stared at the three screws he'd removed from the radio and counted to ten, resisting the urge to drive one of the screws straight into Stu's thick skull. "You aren't stupid enough to make a pass at her, I hope."

"Why not? That's a hot number if ever I did see one."

"You try it, and the sheriff'll kick your ass."

"He don't spook me."

"You amaze me, Stu. How can you be thinking about sex right now? Hasn't it occurred to you that we all might die here, tonight, maybe even in the next minute or two?"

"All the more reason to make a play for her if I get a chance," Wargle said. "I mean, shit, if we're livin' on borrowed time, who cares? Who wants to die limp? Right? Even the other one's nice."

"The other what?"

"The girl, the kid," Stu said.

"She's only fourteen."

"Sweet stuff."

"She's a *child*, Wargle."

"She's plenty old enough."

"That's sick."

"Wouldn't you like to have her firm little legs wrapped around you, Frank?"

The screwdriver slipped out of the notch on the head of the screw and skidded across the metal cover plate with a stuttering screech.

In a voice which was nearly inaudible but which nevertheless froze Wargle's grin, Frank said, "If I ever hear of you laying one filthy finger on that girl or on any other young girl, anywhere, any time, I won't just help press charges against you; *I'll come after you.* I know how to go after a man, Wargle. I wasn't just a desk jockey in Nam. I was in the field. And I still know how to handle myself. I know how to handle *you*. You hear me? You believe me?"

For a moment Wargle was unable to speak. He just stared into Frank's eyes.

Conversations drifted over from other parts of the big room, but none of the words were clear. Still, it was obvious that no one realized what was happening at the radio.

Wargle finally blinked and licked his lips and looked down at his shoes and then looked up and put on an aw-shucks grin. "Hey, gee, Frank, don't get sore. Don't get so riled up. I didn't *mean* it."

"You believe me?" Frank insisted.

"Sure, sure. But I tell you I didn't mean nothin'. I was just shootin' off at the mouth. Locker room talk. You know how it is. You know I didn't mean it. Am I some kind of pervert, for God's sake? Hey, come on, Frank, lighten up. Okay?"

Frank stared at him a moment longer, then said, "Let's get this radio dismantled."

Tal Whitman opened the tall metal gun locker.

Jenny Paige said, "Good heavens, it's a regular arsenal."

He passed the weapons to her, and she lined them up on a nearby work table.

The locker seemed to contain an excessive amount of firepower for a town like Snowfield. Two high-powered rifles with sniper scopes. Two semiautomatic shotguns. Two nonlethal riot guns, which were specially modified shotguns that fired only soft plastic pellets. Two flare guns. Two rifles that fired tear gas grenades. Three handguns: a pair of .38s and a big Smith & Wesson .357 Magnum.

As the lieutenant piled boxes of ammunition on the table, Jenny gave the Magnum a close inspection. "This is a real monster, isn't it?"

"Yeah. You could stop a Brahman bull with that one."

"Looks as if Paul kept everything in first-rate condition."

"You handle guns like you know all about them," the lieutenant said, putting more ammunition on the table.

"Always hated guns. Never thought I'd own one," she said. "But after I'd been living up here three months, we started having trouble with a motorcycle gang that decided to set up a sort of summer retreat on some land out along the Mount Larson Road."

"The Demon Chrome."

"That's them," Jenny said. "Rough-looking crowd."

"That's putting it kindly."

"A couple of times, when I was making a house call at night, over to Mount Larson or Pineville, I got an unwanted motorcycle escort. They rode on each side of the car, too close for safety, grinning in the side windows at me, shouting at me, waving, being foolish. They didn't actually try anything, but it sure was . . ."

"Threatening."

"You said it. So I bought a gun, learned how to shoot it, and got a permit to carry."

The lieutenant began to open the boxes of ammunition. "Ever have occasion to use it?"

"Well," she said, "I never had to shoot anyone, thank God. But I did have to show it once. It was just after dark. I was on my way to Mount Larson, and the Demons gave me another escort, but this time it was different. Four of them boxed me in, and they all started slowing down, forcing me to slow down, too. Finally, they brought me to a complete stop in the middle of the road."

"That must've given your heart a good workout."

"Did it ever! One of the Demons got off his bike. He was big, maybe six feet three or four, with long curly hair and a beard. He wore a bandanna around his head. And one gold earring. He looked like a pirate."

"Did he have a red and yellow eye tattooed on the palm of each hand?"

"Yes! Well, at least on the palm he put against the car window when he was looking in at me."

The lieutenant leaned against the table on which they had placed the guns. "His name's Gene Terr. He's the leader of the Demon Chrome. They don't come much meaner. He's been in the slammer two or three times but never for anything serious and never for long. Whenever it looks as if Jeeter's going to have to do hard time, one of his people takes the blame for all the charges. He has an incredible hold on his followers. They'll do anything he wants; it's almost as if they worship him. Even after they're in jail, Jeeter takes care of them, smuggling money and drugs in to them, and they stay faithful to him. He knows we can't touch him, so he's always infuriatingly polite and helpful to us, pretending to be an upstanding citizen; it's a big joke to him. Anyway, Jeeter came over to your car and looked in at you?"

"Yes. He wanted me to get out, and I wouldn't. He said I should at least roll down the window, so we wouldn't have to shout to hear each other. I said I didn't mind shouting a little. He threatened to smash the window if I didn't roll it down. I knew if I did, he'd reach right inside and unlock the door, so I figured it was better to get out of the car willingly. I told him I'd come out if he'd back off a little. He stepped away from the door, and I snatched the gun from under the seat. As soon as I opened the door and got out, he tried to move in on me. I jammed the muzzle into his belly. The hammer was pulled back, fully cocked; he saw that right away."

"God, I wish I'd seen the look on his face!" Lieutenant Whitman said, grinning.

"I was scared to death," Jenny said, remembering. "I mean, I was scared of him, of course, but, I was also scared I might have to pull the trigger. I wasn't even sure I *could* pull the trigger. But I knew I couldn't let Jeeter see I had any doubts."

"If he'd seen, he'd have eaten you alive."

"That's what I thought. So I was very cold, very firm. I told him that I was a doctor, that I was on my way to see a very sick patient, and that I didn't intend to be detained. I kept my voice low. The other three men were still on their bikes, and from where they were, they couldn't see the gun or hear exactly what I was saying. This Jeeter looked like the type who'd rather die than let anyone see him take any orders from a woman, so I didn't want to embarrass him and maybe make him do something foolish."

The lieutenant shook his head. "You sure had him pegged right."

"I also reminded him that *he* might need a doctor some day. What if he took a spill off that bike of his and was lying on the road, critically injured, and *I* was the doctor who showed up—after he'd hurt me and given me good reason to hurt him in return? I told him there are things a doctor can do to complicate injuries, to make sure the patient has a long and painful recovery. I asked him to think about that."

Whitman gaped at her.

She said, "I don't know if that unsettled him or whether it was simply the gun, but he hesitated, then made a big scene for the benefit of his three buddies.

He told them I was a friend of a friend. He said he'd met me once, years ago, but hadn't recognized me at first. I was to be given every courtesy the Demon Chrome could extend. No one would ever bother me, he said. Then he climbed back on his Harley and rode away, and the other three followed him."

"And you just went on to Mount Larson?"

"What else? I still had a patient to see."

"Incredible."

"I will admit, though, I had the sweats and the shakes all the way to Mount Larson."

"And no biker has ever bothered you since?"

"In fact, when they pass me on the roads around here, they all smile and wave."

Whitman laughed.

Jenny said, "So there's the answer to your question: Yes, I know how to use a gun, but I hope I never have to shoot anyone."

She looked at the .357 Magnum in her hand, scowled, opened a box of ammunition, and began to load the revolver.

The lieutenant took a couple of shells from another carton and loaded a shotgun.

They were silent for a moment, and then he said, "Would you have done what you told Gene Terr?"

"What? Shoot him?"

"No. I mean, if he'd hurt you, maybe raped you, and then if you'd later had a chance to treat him as a patient . . . would you have . . . ?"

Jenny finished loading the Magnum, clicked the cylinder into place, and put the gun down. "Well, I'd be tempted. But on the other hand, I have enormous respect for the Hippocratic Oath. So . . . well . . . I suppose this means I'm just a wimp at heart—but I'd give Jeeter the best medical care I could."

"I knew you'd say that."

"I talk tough, but I'm just a marshmallow inside."

"Like hell," he said. "The way you stood up to him took about as much toughness as *anybody* has. But if he'd hurt you, and if you'd later abused your trust as a doctor just to get even with him . . . well, that would be different."

Jenny looked up from the .38 that she'd just taken from the array of weapons on the table, and she met the black man's eyes. They were clear, probing eyes.

"Dr. Paige, you have what we call 'the right stuff.' If you want, you can call me Tal. Most people do. It's short for Talbert."

"All right, Tal. And you can call me Jenny."

"Well, I don't know about that."

"Oh? Why not?"

"You're a doctor and all. My Aunt Becky—she's the one who raised me—always had great respect for doctors. It just seems funny to be calling a doctor by his . . . by *her* first name."

"Doctors are people too, you know. And considering that we're all in sort of a pressure cooker here—"

"Just the same," he said, shaking his head.

"If it bothers you, then call me what most of my patients call me."

"What's that?"

"Just plain Doc."

"Doc?" He thought about it, and a slow smile spread over his face. "Doc. It makes you think of one of those grizzled, cantankerous old coots that Barry Fitzgerald used to play in the movies, way back in the thirties and forties."

"Sorry I'm not grizzled."

"That's okay. You're not an old coot, either."

She laughed softly.

"I like the irony of it," Whitman said. "Doc. Yeah, and when I think of you jamming that revolver in Gene Terr's belly, it fits."

They loaded two more guns.

"Tal, why all these weapons for a little substation in a town like Snowfield?"

"If you want to get state and federal matching funds for the county law enforcement budget, you've got to meet their requirements for all sorts of ridiculous things. One of the specifications is for minimal arsenals in substations like this. Now . . . well . . . maybe we should be glad we've got all this hardware."

"Except so far we haven't seen anything to shoot at."

"I suspect we will," Tal said. "And I'll tell you something."

"What's that?"

His broad, dark, handsome face could look unsettlingly dour. "I don't think you'll have to worry about having to shoot other people. Somehow, I don't believe it's *people* we have to worry about."

Bryce dialed the private, unlisted number at the governor's residence in Sacramento. He talked to a maid who insisted the governor couldn't come to the phone, not even to take a life-and-death call from an old friend. She wanted Bryce to leave a message. Then he talked to the chief of the household staff, who also wanted him to leave a message. Then, after being put on hold, he talked to Gary Poe, Governor Jack Retlock's chief political aide and advisor.

"Bryce," Gary said. "Jack just can't come to the phone right now. There's an important dinner underway here. The Japanese trade minister and the consul general from San Francisco."

"Gary—"

"We're trying damned hard to get that new Japanese-American electronics plant for California, and we're afraid it's going to go to Texas or Arizona or maybe even New York. Jesus, New York!"

"Gary—"

"Why would they even consider New York, with all the labor problems and the tax rates what they are back there? Sometimes I think—"

"Gary, shut up."

"Huh?"

Bryce never snapped at anyone. Even Gary Poe—who could talk faster and louder than a carnival barker—was shocked into silence.

"Gary, this is an emergency. Get Jack for me."

Sounding hurt, Poe said, "Bryce, I'm authorized to—"

"I've got a hell of a lot to do in the next hour or two, Gary. If I live long enough to do it, that is. I can't spend fifteen minutes laying this whole thing out for you and then another fifteen laying it out again for Jack. Listen, I'm in Snowfield. It appears as if everyone who lived here is dead, Gary."

"What?"

"Five hundred people."

"Bryce, if this is some sort of joke or—"

"Five hundred dead. And that's the least of it. Now will you for Christ's sake get Jack?"

"But Bryce, five hundred—"

"Get Jack, damn it!"

Poe hesitated, then said, "Old buddy, this better be the straight shit." He dropped the phone and went for the governor.

Bryce had known Jack Retlock for seventeen years. When he joined the Los Angeles police, he had been assigned to Jack for his rookie year. At that time, Jack was a seven-year veteran of the force, a seasoned hand. Indeed, Jack had seemed so savvy and streetwise that Bryce had despaired of ever being even half as good at the job. In a year, however, he was better. They voted to stay together, partners. But eighteen months later, fed up with a legal system that regularly turned loose the punks he worked so hard to imprison, Jack quit police work and went into politics. As a cop, he'd collected a fistful of citations for bravery. He parlayed his hero image into a seat on the L.A. city council, then ran for mayor, winning in a landslide. From there, he'd jumped into the governor's chair. It was a far more impressive career than Bryce's own halting progress to the sheriff's post in Santa Mira, but Jack always was the more aggressive of the two.

"Doody? Is that you?" Jack asked, picking up the phone in Sacramento.

Doody was his nickname for Bryce. He'd always said that Bryce's sandy hair, freckles, wholesome face, and marionette eyes made him look like Howdy Doody.

"It's me, Jack."

"Gary's raving some lunatic nonsense—"

"It's true," Bryce said.

He told Jack all about Snowfield.

After listening to the entire story, Jack took a deep breath and said, "I wish you were a drinking man, Doody."

"This isn't booze talking, Jack. Listen, the first thing I want is—"

"National Guard?"

"No!" Bryce said. "That's exactly what I want to avoid as long as we have any choice."

"If I don't use the Guard and every agency at my disposal, and then if it later turns out I should've sent them in first thing, my ass will be grass, and there'll be a herd of hungry cows all around me."

"Jack, I'm counting on you to make the right decisions, not just the right *political* decisions. Until we know more about the situation, we don't want hordes of Guardsmen tramping around up here. They're great for helping out in a flood, a postal strike, that sort of thing. But they're not full-time military men. They're salesmen and attorneys and carpenters and schoolteachers. This calls for a tightly controlled, efficient little police action, and that sort of thing can be conducted only by real cops, full-time cops."

"And if your men can't handle it?"

"Then I'll be the first to yell for the Guard."

Finally Retlock said, "Okay. No Guardsmen. For now."

Bryce sighed. "And I want to keep the State Health Department out of here, too."

"Doody, be reasonable. How can I do that? If there's any chance that a contagious disease has wiped out Snowfield—or some kind of environmental poisoning—"

"Listen, Jack, Health does a fine job when it comes to tracking down and controlling vectors for outbreaks of plague or mass food poisoning or water contamination. But essentially, they're bureaucrats; they move slowly. We can't *afford* to move slowly on this. I have the gut feeling that we're living strictly on borrowed time. All hell could break loose at any time; in fact, I'll be surprised if it doesn't. Besides, the Health Department doesn't have the equipment to handle it, and they don't have a contingency plan to cover the death of an entire town. But there's someone who does, Jack. The Army Medical Corps' CBW Division has a relatively new program they call the Civilian Defense Unit."

"CBW Division?" Retlock asked. There was a new tension in his voice. "You don't mean the chemical and biological warfare boys?"

"Yes."

"Christ, you don't think it has anything to do with nerve gas or germ war—"

"Probably not," Bryce said, thinking of the Liebermanns' severed heads, of the creepy feeling that had overcome him inside the covered passageway, of the incredible suddenness with which Jake Johnson had vanished. "But I don't know enough about it to rule out CBW or anything else."

A hard edge of anger had crystallized in the governor's voice. "If the damned army has been careless with one of its fucking doomsday viruses, I'm going to have their heads!"

"Easy, Jack. Maybe it's not an accident. Maybe it's the work of terrorists who got their hands on a sample of some CBW agent. Or maybe it's the Russians running a little test of our CBW analysis and defense system. It was to handle those kinds of situations that the Army Medical Corps instructed its CBW Division to create General Copperfield's office."

"Who's Copperfield?"

"General Galen Copperfield. He's the commanding officer of the Civilian Defense Unit of the CBW Division. This is precisely the kind of situation they want to be notified about. Within hours, Copperfield can put a team of well-trained scientists into Snowfield. First-rate biologists, virologists, bacteriologists, pathologists with training in the very latest forensic medicine, at least one immunologist and biochemist, a neurologist—and even a neuropsychologist. Copperfield's department has designed elaborate mobile field laboratories. They've got them garaged at depots all over the country, so there must be one relatively close to us. Hold off the State Health gang, Jack. They don't have people of the caliber that Copperfield can provide, and they don't have state-of-the-art diagnostic equipment as mobile as Copperfield's. I want to call the general; I *am* going to call him, in fact, but I'd prefer to have your agreement and your guarantee that state bureaucrats won't be tramping around here, interfering."

After a brief hesitation, Jack Retlock said, "Doody, what kind of world have we let it become when things like Copperfield's department are even necessary?"

"You'll hold off Health?"

"Yes. What else do you need?"

Bryce glanced down at the list in front of him. "You could approach the telephone company about pulling the Snowfield circuits off automatic switching. When the world finds out what's happened up here, every phone in town will be ringing off the hook, and we won't be able to maintain essential communications. If they could route all calls to and from Snowfield through a few special operators and weed out the crank stuff and—"

"I'll handle it," Jack said.

"Of course, we could lose the phones at any time. Dr. Paige had trouble getting a call out when she first tried, so I'll need a shortwave set. The one here at the substation seems to've been sabotaged."

"I can get you a mobile shortwave unit, a van that has its own gasoline generator. The Office of Earthquake Preparedness has a couple. Anything else?"

"Speaking of generators, it'd be nice if we didn't have to depend on the public power supply. Evidently, our enemy here can tamper with it at will. Could you get two big generators for us?"

"Can do. Anything else?"

"If I think of anything, I won't hesitate to ask."

"Let me tell you, Bryce, as a friend, I hate like hell to see you in the middle of this one. But as a governor, I'm damned glad it fell in your jurisdiction, whatever the hell it is. There are some prize assholes out there who'd already have screwed it up if it'd fallen in *their* laps. By now, if it was a disease, they'd have spread it to half the state. We sure can use you up there."

"Thanks, Jack."

They were both silent for a moment.

Then Retlock said, "Doody?"

"Yeah, Jack?"

"Watch out for yourself."

"I will, Jack," Bryce said. "Well, I've got to get on to Copperfield. I'll call you later."

The governor said, "Please do that, Bryce. Call me later. Don't *you* vanish, old buddy."

Bryce put down the phone and looked around the substation. Stu Wargle and Frank were removing the front access plate from the radio. Tal and Dr. Paige were loading guns. Gordy Brogan and young Lisa Paige, the biggest and the smallest of the group, were making coffee and putting food on one of the worktables.

Even in the midst of disaster, Bryce thought, even here in the Twilight Zone, we have to have our coffee and supper. Life goes on.

He picked up the receiver to call Copperfield's number out at Dugway, Utah.

There was no dial tone. He jiggled the disconnect button.

"Hello," he said.

Nothing.

Bryce sensed someone or something listening. He could feel the presence, just as Dr. Paige had described it.

"Who is this?" he asked.

He didn't really expect an answer, but he got one. It wasn't a voice. It was a peculiar yet familiar sound: the cry of birds, perhaps gulls; yes, sea gulls shrieking high above a windswept shoreline.

It changed. It became a clattering sound. A rattle. Like beans in a hollow gourd. The warning sound of a rattlesnake. Yes, no doubt about it. The very distinct sound of a rattlesnake.

And then it changed again. Electronic buzzing. No, not electronic. Bees. Bees buzzing, swarming.

And now the cry of gulls once more.

And the call of another bird, a trilling musical voice.

And panting. Like a tired dog.

And snarling. Not a dog. Something larger.

And the hissing and spitting of fighting cats.

Although there was nothing especially menacing about the sounds themselves—except, perhaps, for the rattlesnake and the snarling—Bryce was chilled by them.

The animal noises ceased.

Bryce waited, listened, said, "Who is this?"

No answer.

"What do you want?"

Another sound came over the wire, and it pierced Bryce as if it were a dagger of ice. Screams. Men and women and children. More than a few of them. Dozens, scores. Not stage screams; not make-believe terror. They were the stark, shocking cries of the damned: screams of agony, fear and soul-searing despair.

Bryce felt sick.

His heart raced.

It seemed to him that he had an open line to the bowels of Hell.

Were these the cries of Snowfield's dead, captured on a recording tape? By whom? Why? Is it live or is it Memorex?

One final scream. A child. A little girl. She cried out in terror, then in pain, then in unimaginable suffering, as if she were being torn apart. Her voice rose, spiraled up and up—

Silence.

The silence was even worse than the screaming because the unnameable presence was still on the line, and Bryce could feel it more strongly now. He was stricken by an awareness of pure, unrelenting evil.

It was there.

He quickly put down the phone.

He was shaking. He had not been in any danger—yet he was shaking.

He looked around the bull pen. The others were still busy with the tasks he had assigned to them. Apparently, no one had noticed that his most recent session on the phone had been far different from those that had gone before it.

Sweat trickled down the back of his neck.

Eventually, he would have to tell the others what had happened. But not right now. Because right now he couldn't trust his voice. They would surely hear the nervous flutter, and they would know that this strange experience had badly shaken him.

Until reinforcements arrived, until their foothold in Snowfield was more firmly established, until they all felt less afraid, it wasn't wise to let the others see him shaking with dread. They looked to him for leadership, after all; he didn't intend to disappoint them.

He took a deep, cleansing breath.

He picked up the receiver and immediately got a dial tone.

Immensely relieved, he called the CBW Civilian Defense Unit in Dugway, Utah.

Lisa liked Gordy Brogan.

At first he had seemed menacing and sullen. He was such a big man, and his hands were so enormous they made you think of the Frankenstein monster. His face was rather handsome, actually, but when he frowned, even if he wasn't angry, even if he was just worrying about something or thinking especially hard, his brows knitted together in a fierce way, and his black-black eyes grew even blacker than usual, and he looked like doom itself.

A smile transformed him. It was the most astonishing thing. When Gordy smiled, you knew right away that you were seeing the *real* Gordy Brogan. You knew that the other Gordy—the one you *thought* you saw when he frowned or when his face was in repose—was purely a figment of your imagination. His warm, wide smile drew your attention to the kindness shining in his eyes, the gentleness in his broad brow.

When you got to know him, he was like a big puppy, eager to be liked. He was one of those rare adults who could talk to a kid without being self-conscious or condescending or patronizing. He was even better in that regard than Jenny. And even under the current circumstances, he could laugh.

As they put the food on the table—lunch meat, bread, cheese, fresh fruit, doughnuts—and brewed coffee, Lisa said, "You just don't seem like a cop to me."

"Oh?" Gordy said. "What's a cop supposed to seem like?"

"Whoops. Did I say the wrong thing? Is 'cop' an offensive word?"

"In some quarters, it is. Like in prisons, for instance."

She was amazed that she still could laugh after everything that had happened this evening. She said, "Seriously. What do officers of the law prefer to be called? Policemen?"

"It doesn't matter. I'm a deputy, policeman, cop—whatever you like. Except you think I don't really look the part."

"Oh, you look the part all right," Lisa said. "Especially when you scowl. But you don't *seem* like a cop."

"What do I seem like to you?"

"Let me think." She took an immediate interest in this game, for it diverted her mind from the nightmare around her. "Maybe you seem like . . . a young minister."

"Me?"

"Well, in the pulpit, you'd be just fantastic delivering a fire-and-brimstone sermon. And I can see you sitting in a parsonage, an encouraging smile on your face, listening to people's problems."

"Me, a minister," he said, clearly astonished. "With that imagination of yours, you should be a writer when you grow up."

"I think I should be a doctor like Jenny. A doctor can do so much good." She paused. "You know why you don't seem like a cop? It's because I can't picture you using *that.*" She pointed at his revolver. "I can't picture you shooting someone. Not even if he deserved it."

She was startled by the expression that came over Gordy Brogan's face. He was visibly shocked.

Before she could ask what was wrong, the lights flickered.

She looked up.

The lights flickered again. And again.

She glanced at the front windows. Outside, the streetlights were blinking, too.

No, she thought. No, please, God, not again. Don't throw us into darkness again; please, *please!*

The lights went out.

CHAPTER 15
THE THING AT THE WINDOW

BRYCE HAMMOND HAD spoken to the night-duty officer manning the emergency line at the CBW Civilian Defense Unit at Dugway, Utah. He hadn't needed to say much before he'd been patched through to General Galen

Copperfield's home number. Copperfield had listened, but he hadn't said much. Bryce wanted to know whether it seemed at all likely that a chemical or biological agent had caused Snowfield's agony and obliteration. Copperfield said, "Yes." But that was all he *would* say. He warned Bryce that they were speaking on an unsecured telephone line, and he made vague but stern references to classified information and security clearances. When he'd heard all of the essentials but only a few details, he cut Bryce off rather curtly and suggested they discuss the rest of it when they met face to face. "I've heard enough to be convinced that my organization should be involved." He promised to send a field lab and a team of investigators into Snowfield by dawn or shortly thereafter.

Bryce was putting down the receiver when the lights flickered, dimmed, flickered, wavered—and went out.

He fumbled for the flashlight on the desk in front of him, found it, and switched it on.

Upon returning to the substation a while ago, they had located two additional, long-handled police flashlights. Gordy had taken one; Dr. Paige had taken the other. Now, both of those lights flicked on simultaneously, carving long bright wounds in the darkness.

They had discussed a plan of action, a routine to follow if the lights went off again. Now, as planned, everyone moved to the center of the room, away from the doors and windows, and clustered together in a circle, facing outward, their backs turned to one another, reducing their vulnerability.

No one said much of anything. They were all listening intently.

Lisa Paige stood to the left of Bryce, her slender shoulders hunched, her head tucked down.

Tal Whitman stood at Bryce's right. His teeth were bared in a silent snarl as he studied the darkness beyond the sweeping scythe of the flashlight beam.

Tal and Bryce were holding revolvers.

The three of them faced the rear half of the room, while the other four—Dr. Paige, Gordy, Frank, and Stu—faced the front.

Bryce played the beam of his flashlight over everything, for even the shadowy outlines of the most mundane objects suddenly seemed threatening. But nothing hid or moved among the familiar pieces of furniture and equipment.

Silence.

Set in the back wall, toward the right-hand corner of the room, were two doors. One led to the corridor that served the three holding cells. They had searched that part of the building earlier; the cells, the interrogation room, and the two bathrooms that occupied that half of the ground floor were all deserted. The other door led to stairs that went up to the deputy's apartment; those rooms, too, were unoccupied. Nevertheless, Bryce repeatedly brought the beam of light back to the half-open doors; he was uneasy about them.

In the darkness, something thumped softly.

"What was that?" Wargle asked.

"It came from over this way," Gordy said.

"No, from over this way," Lisa Paige said.

"Quiet!" Bryce said sharply.

Thump . . . thump-thump.

It was the sound of a padded blow. Like a dropped pillow striking the floor.

Bryce swept his light rapidly back and forth.

Tal tracked the beam with his revolver.

Bryce thought: What do we do if the lights are out for the rest of the night?

What do we do when the flashlight batteries finally go dead? What happens *then?*

He had not been afraid of darkness since he'd been a small child. Now he remembered what it was like.

Thump-thump . . . thump . . . thump-thump.

Louder. But not closer.

Thump!

"The windows!" Frank said.

Bryce swung around, probing with his flashlight.

Three bright beams found the front windows at the same time, transforming the mullioned squares of glass into mirrors that hid whatever lay beyond them.

"Turn your lights toward the floor or ceiling," Bryce said.

One beam swung up, two down.

The backsplash of light revealed the windows, but it didn't turn them into reflective silver surfaces.

Thump!

Something struck a window, rattled a loose pane, and rebounded into the night. Bryce had an impression of wings.

"What was it?"

"—bird—"

"—not a bird of any kind I ever—"

"—something—"

"—awful—"

It returned, battering itself against the glass with greater determination than before: *Thump-thump-thump-thump-thump!*

Lisa screamed.

Frank Autry gasped, and Stu Wargle said, "Holy shit!"

Gordy made a strangled, wordless sound.

Staring at the window, Bryce felt as if he had lurched through the curtain of reality, into a place of nightmare and illusion.

With the streetlamps extinguished, Skyline Road was dark except for the luminous moonfall; however, the thing at the window was vaguely illuminated.

Even vague illumination of that fluttering monstrosity was too much. What Bryce saw on the other side of the glass—what he *thought* he saw in the kaleidoscopic multiplicity of light, shadow, and shimmering moonlight—was something out of a fever dream. It had a three- or four-foot wingspan. An insectoid head. Short, quivering antennae. Small, pointed, and ceaselessly working mandibles. A segmented body. The body was suspended between the pale gray wings and was approximately the size and shape of two footballs placed end to end; it, too, was gray, the same shade as the wings—a moldy, sickly gray—and fuzzy and moist-looking. Bryce glimpsed eyes, as well: huge, ink-black, multifaceted, protuberant lenses that caught the light, refracting and reflecting it, gleaming darkly and hungrily.

If he was seeing what he thought he was seeing, the thing at the window was a moth as large as an eagle. Which was madness.

It bashed itself against the windows with new fury, in a frenzy now, its pale wings beating so fast that it became a blur. It moved along the dark panes, repeatedly rebounding into the night, then returning, trying feverishly to crash through the window. *Thumpthumpthumpthump.* But it didn't have the strength to smash its way inside. Furthermore, it didn't have a carapace; its body was entirely soft, and in spite of its incredible size and formidable appearance, it was incapable of cracking the glass.

Thumpthumpthump.

Then it was gone.

The lights came on.

It's like a damned stage play, Bryce thought.

When they realized that the thing at the window wasn't going to return, they all moved, by unspoken consent, to the front of the room. They went through the gate in the railing, into the public area, to the windows, gazing out in stunned silence.

Skyline Road was unchanged.

The night was empty.

Nothing moved.

Bryce sat down in the creaking chair at Paul Henderson's desk. The others gathered around.

"So," Bryce said.

"So," Tal said.

They looked at one another. They fidgeted.

"Any ideas?" Bryce asked.

No one said anything.

"Any theories about what it might have been?"

"Gross," Lisa said, and shuddered.

"It was that, all right," Dr. Paige said, putting a comforting hand on her younger sister's shoulder.

Bryce was impressed with the doctor's emotional strength and resiliency. She seemed to be taking every shock that Snowfield threw at her. Indeed, she seemed to be holding up better than his own men. Hers were the only eyes that didn't slide away when he met them; she returned his stare forthrightly.

This, he thought, is a special woman.

"Impossible," Frank Autry said. "That's what it was. Just plain impossible."

"Hell, what's the matter with you people?" Wargle asked. He screwed up his meaty face. "It was only a bird. That's all it was out there. Just a goddamned bird."

"Like hell it was," Frank said.

"Just a lousy bird," Wargle insisted. When the others disagreed, he said, "The bad light and all them shadows out there sort of give you a false impression. You didn't see what you all think you seen."

"And what do *you* think we saw?" Tal asked him.

Wargle's face became flushed.

"Did we see the same thing you saw, the thing you don't want to believe?" Tal pressed. "A moth? Did you see one goddamned big, ugly impossible moth?"

Wargle looked down at his shoes. "I seen a bird. Just a bird."

Bryce realized that Wargle was so utterly lacking in imagination that the man couldn't encompass the possibility of the impossible, not even when he had witnessed it with his own eyes.

"Where did it come from?" Bryce asked.

No one had any ideas.

"What did it want?" he asked.

"It wanted *us,*" Lisa said.

Everyone seemed to agree with that assessment.

"But the thing at the window wasn't what got Jake," Frank said. "It was weak, lightweight. It couldn't carry off a grown man."

"Then what got Jake?" Gordy asked.

"Something bigger," Frank said. "Something a whole lot stronger and meaner."

Bryce decided that, after all, the time had come to tell them about the things he had heard—and sensed—on the telephone, between his calls to Governor Retlock and General Copperfield: the silent presence; the forlorn cries of sea gulls; the warning sound of a rattlesnake; worst of all, the agonizing and despairing screams of men, women, and children. He hadn't intended to mention any of that until morning, until the arrival of daylight and reinforcements. But they might spot something important that he had missed, some scrap, some clue that would be of help. Besides, now that they had all seen the thing at the window, the phone incident was, by comparison, no longer very shocking.

The others listened to Bryce, and this new information had a negative effect on their demeanor.

"What kind of degenerate would tape-record the screams of his victims?" Gordy asked.

Tal Whitman shook his head. "It could be something else. It could be that . . ."

"Yes?"

"Well, maybe none of you wants to hear this right now."

"Since you've started it, finish it," Bryce insisted.

"Well," Tal said, "what if it wasn't a recording you heard? I mean, we know people have disappeared from Snowfield. In fact as far as we've seen, more have vanished than died. So . . . what if the missing are being held somewhere? As hostages? Maybe the screams were coming from people who were still alive, who were being tortured and maybe killed right *then,* right then while you were on the phone, listening."

Remembering those terrible screams, Bryce felt his marrow slowly freezing.

"Whether it was tape-recorded or not," Frank Autry said, "it's probably a mistake to think in terms of hostages."

"Yes," Dr. Paige said. "If Mr. Autry means that we've got to be careful not to narrow our thinking to conventional situations, then I wholeheartedly agree. This just doesn't feel like a hostage drama. Something damned peculiar is happening here, something that no one's ever encountered before, so let's not start backsliding just because we'd be more comfortable with cozy, familiar explanations. Besides, if we're dealing with terrorists, how does that fit with the thing we saw at the window? It doesn't."

Bryce nodded. "You're right. But I don't believe Tal meant that people were being held for conventional motives."

"No, no," Tal said. "It doesn't have to be terrorists or kidnappers. Even if people are being held hostage, that doesn't necessarily mean *other people* are holding them. I'm even willing to consider that they're being held by something that isn't human. How's *that* for remaining open-minded? Maybe *it* is holding them, the *it* that none of us can define. Maybe it's holding them just to prolong the pleasure it takes from snuffing the life out of them. Maybe it's holding them just to tease us with their screams, the way it teased Bryce on the phone. Hell, if we're dealing with something truly extraordinary, truly unhuman, its reasons for holding hostages—if it *is* holding any—are bound to be incomprehensible."

"Christ, you're talking like lunatics," Wargle said.

Everyone ignored him.

They had stepped through the looking glass. The impossible was possible. The enemy was the unknown.

Lisa Paige cleared her throat. Her face was pasty. In a barely audible voice, she said, "Maybe it spun a web somewhere, down in a dark place, in a cellar or a cave, and maybe it tied all the missing people into its web, sealed them up in cocoons, alive. Maybe it's just saving them until it gets hungry again."

If absolutely nothing lay beyond the realm of possibility, if even the most outrageous theories could be true, then perhaps the girl was right, Bryce thought. Perhaps there *was* an enormous web vibrating softly in some dark place, hung with a hundred or two hundred or even more man- and woman- and child-size tidbits, wrapped in individual packages for freshness and convenience. Somewhere in Snowfield, were there living human beings who had been reduced to the awful equivalent of foil-wrapped Pop Tarts, waiting only to provide nourishment for some brutal, unimaginably evil, darkly intelligent, other-dimensional horror.

No. Ridiculous.

On the other hand: maybe.

Jesus.

Bryce crouched in front of the shortwave radio and squinted at its mangled guts. Circuit boards had been snapped. Several parts appeared to have been crushed in a vice or hammered flat.

Frank said, "They had to take off the cover plate to get at all this stuff, just the way we did."

"So after they smashed the crap out of it," Wargle said, "why'd they bother to put the plate back on?"

"And why go to all that trouble to begin with?" Frank wondered. "They could've put the radio out of commission just by ripping the cord loose."

Lisa and Gordy appeared as Bryce was turning away from the radio. The girl said, "Food and coffee's ready if anyone wants anything."

"I'm starved," Wargle said, licking his lips.

"We should all eat something, even if we don't feel like it," Bryce said.

"Sheriff," Gordy said, "Lisa and I have been wondering about the animals, the pets. What made us think about it was when you said you heard dog and cat sounds over the phone. Sir, what's happened to all the pets?"

"Nobody's seen a dog or cat," Lisa said. "Or heard barking."

Thinking of the silent streets, Bryce frowned and said, "You're right. It's strange."

"Jenny says there were some pretty big dogs in town. A few German shepherds. One Doberman that she knows of. Even a Great Dane. Wouldn't you think they'd have fought back? Wouldn't you think some of the dogs would've gotten away?" the girl asked.

"Okay," Gordy said quickly, anticipating Bryce's response, "so maybe *it* was big enough to overwhelm an ordinary, angry dog. Okay, so we also know that bullets didn't stop it, which says that maybe nothing can. It's apparently big, and it's strong. But, sir, big and strong don't necessarily count for much with a *cat.* Cats are greased lightning. It'd take something real damned sneaky to slip up on every cat in town."

"Real sneaky and real *fast,*" Lisa said.

"Yeah," Bryce said uneasily. *"Real* fast."

Jenny had just begun eating a sandwich when Sheriff Hammond sat down in a chair beside the desk, balancing his plate on his lap. "Mind some company?"

"Not at all."

"Tal Whitman's been telling me you're the scourge of our local motorcycle gang."

She smiled. "Tal's exaggerating."

"That man doesn't know how to exaggerate," the sheriff said. "Let me tell you something about him. Sixteen months ago, I was away for three days at a law enforcement conference in Chicago, and when I got back, Tal was the first person I saw. I asked him if anything special had happened while I'd been gone, and he said it was just the usual business with drunk drivers, bar fights, a couple of burglaries, various CITs—"

"What's a CIT?" Jenny asked.

"Oh, it's just a cat-in-tree report."

"Policemen don't really rescue cats, do they?"

"Do you think we're heartless?" he asked, feigning shock.

"CITs? Come on now."

He grinned. He had a marvelous grin. "Once every couple of months, we *do* have to get a cat out of a tree. But a CIT doesn't mean *just* cats in trees. It's our shorthand for any kind of nuisance call that takes us away from more important work."

"Ah."

"So anyway, when I came back from Chicago that time, Tal told me it'd been a pretty ordinary three days. And then, almost as an afterthought, he said there'd been an attempted robbery at a 7-Eleven. Tal had been a customer, out of uniform, when it went down. But even off duty, a cop's required to carry his gun, and Tal had a revolver in an ankle holster. He told me one of the punks had been armed; he said he'd been forced to kill him, and he said I wasn't to worry about whether it was a justified shooting or not. He said it was as justified as they come. When I got concerned about *him,* he said, 'Bryce. It was really just a cakewalk.' Later, I found out the two punks had intended to shoot everyone. Instead, Tal shot the gunman—although not before he was shot himself. The punk put a bullet through Tal's left arm, and just about a split second after that, Tal killed him. Tal's wound wasn't serious, but it bled like hell, and it must've hurt something awful. Of course, I hadn't seen the bandage because it was under the shirt-sleeve, and Tal hadn't bothered to mention it. So anyway, there's Tal in the 7-Eleven, bleeding all over the place, and he discovers he's out of ammo. The second punk, who grabbed the gun the first one dropped, is also out of ammo, and he decides to run. Tal goes after him, and they have themselves a knock-down-drag-out fight from one end of that little grocery store to the other. The guy was two inches taller and twenty pounds heavier than Tal, and *he* wasn't wounded. But you know what the backup officer told me they found when they arrived? They said Tal was sitting up on the counter by the cash register, his shirt off, sipping a complimentary cup of coffee, while the clerk tried to stanch the flow of blood. One suspect was dead. The other one was unconscious, sprawled in a sticky mess of Hostess Twinkies and Fudge Fantasies and coconut cupcakes. Seems they'd knocked over a rack of lunchbox cakes right in the middle of the fight. About a hundred packages of snack stuff spilled onto the floor, and Tal and this other guy stepped all over them while they were grappling. Most of the packages broke open. There was icing and crumbled cookies and smashed Twinkies all over one aisle. Staggered footprints were pressed right into the garbage, so that you could follow the progress of the battle just by looking at the sticky trail."

The sheriff finished his story and looked at Jenny expectantly.

"Oh! Yes, he told you it'd been an easy arrest—just a cakewalk."

"Yeah. A cakewalk." The sheriff laughed.

Jenny glanced at Tal Whitman, who was across the room, eating a sandwich, talking to Officer Brogan and to Lisa.

"So you see," the sheriff said, "when Tal tells me you're the scourge of the Demon Chrome, I know he's not exaggerating. Exaggeration just isn't his style."

Jenny shook her head, impressed. "When I told Tal about my little encounter with this man he calls Gene Terr, he acted as if he thought it was one of the bravest things anyone had ever done. Compared to that 'cakewalk' of his, my story must've seemed like a dispute on a kindergarten playground."

"No, no," Hammond said. "Tal wasn't just humoring you. He really does think you did a damned brave thing. So do I. Jeeter's a snake, Dr. Paige. Poisonous variety."

"You can call me Jenny if you like."

"Well, Jenny-if-you-like, you can call me Bryce."

He had the bluest eyes she had ever seen. His smile was defined as much by those luminous eyes as it was by the curve of his mouth.

As they ate, they talked about inconsequential things, as if this were an ordinary evening. He possessed an impressive ability to put people at ease regardless of the circumstances. He brought with him an aura of tranquillity. She was grateful for the calm interlude.

When they finished eating, however, he guided the conversation back to the crisis at hand. "You know Snowfield better than I do. We've got to find a suitable headquarters for this operation. This place is too small. Soon, I'll have ten more men here. And Copperfield's team in the morning."

"How many is he bringing?"

"At least a dozen people. Maybe as many as twenty. I need an HQ from which every aspect of the operation can be coordinated. We might be here for days, so there'll have to be a room where off-duty people can sleep, and we'll need a cafeteria arrangement to feed everyone."

"One of the inns might be just the place," Jenny said.

"Maybe. But I don't want people sleeping two by two in a lot of different rooms. They'd be too vulnerable. We've got to set up a single dormitory."

"Then the Hilltop Inn is your best bet. It's about a block from here, on the other side of the street."

"Oh, yeah, of course. Biggest hotel in town, isn't it?"

"Yeah. The Hilltop has a large lobby because it doubles as the hotel bar."

"I've had a drink there once or twice. If we change the lobby furniture, it could be set up as a work area to accommodate everyone."

"There's also a large restaurant divided into two rooms. One part could be a cafeteria, and we could carry mattresses down from the rooms and use the other half of the restaurant as a dorm."

Bryce said, "Let's have a look at it."

He put his empty paper plate on the desk and got to his feet.

Jenny glanced at the front windows. She thought of the strange creature that had flown into the glass, and in her mind she heard the soft yet frenzied *thumpthumpthumpthump.*

She said, "You mean . . . have a look at it now?"

"Why not?"

"Wouldn't it be wise to wait for the reinforcements?" she asked.

"They probably won't arrive for a while yet. There's no point in just sitting around, twiddling our thumbs. We'll all feel better if we're doing something constructive; it'll take our minds off . . . the worst things we've seen."

Jenny couldn't free herself from the memory of those black insect eyes, so malevolent, so hungry. She stared at the windows, at the night beyond. The town no longer seemed familiar. It was utterly alien now, a hostile place in which she was an unwelcome stranger.

"We're not one bit safer in here than we would be out there," Bryce said gently.

Jenny nodded, remembering the Oxleys in their barricaded room. As she got up from the desk, she said, "There's no safety anywhere."

CHAPTER 16

OUT OF THE DARK

BRYCE HAMMOND LED the way out of the stationhouse. They crossed the moonlight-mottled cobblestones, stepped through a fall of amber light from a streetlamp, and headed into Skyline Road. Bryce carried a shotgun as did Tal Whitman.

The town was breathless. The trees stood unrespiring, and the buildings were like vapor-thin mirages hanging on walls of air.

Bryce moved out of the light, walked on moon-dappled pavement, crossing the street, finding shadows scattered in the middle of it. Always shadows.

The others came silently behind him.

Something crunched under Bryce's foot, startling him. It was a withered leaf.

He could see the Hilltop Inn farther up Skyline Road. It was a four-story, gray stone building almost a block away, and it was very dark. A few of the fourth-floor windows reflected the nearly full moon, but within the hotel not a single light burned.

They had all reached or passed the middle of the street when something came out of the dark. Bryce was aware, first, of a moon shadow that fluttered across the pavement, like a ripple passing through a pool of water. Instinctively, he ducked. He heard wings. He felt something brush lightly over his head.

Stu Wargle screamed.

Bryce shot up from his crouch and whirled around.

The moth.

It was fixed firmly to Wargle's face, holding on by some means not visible to Bryce. Wargle's entire head was hidden by the thing.

Wargle wasn't the only one screaming. The others cried out and fell back in surprise. The moth was squealing, too, making a high-pitched, keening sound.

In the moon's silvery beams, the impossible insect's huge pale velvety wings flapped and folded and spread with horrible grace and beauty, buffeting Wargle's head and shoulders.

Wargle staggered away, veering downhill, moving blindly, clawing at the outrageous thing that clung to his face. His screams quickly grew muffled; within a couple of seconds, they were silenced altogether.

Bryce, like the others, was paralyzed by disgust and disbelief.

Wargle began to run, but he only went a few yards before coming to an abrupt halt. His hands dropped away from the thing on his face. His knees were buckling.

Snapping out of his brief trance, Bryce dropped his useless shotgun and ran toward Stu.

Wargle didn't crumple to the ground, after all. Instead, his shaky knees locked, and he snapped erect. His shoulders jerked back. His body twitched and shuddered as if an electric current had flashed through him.

Bryce tried to grab the moth and tear it away from Wargle. But the deputy began to weave and thrash in a St. Vitus dance of pain and suffocation, and Bryce's hands closed on empty air. Wargle moved erratically across the street, jerked this way and that, heaved and writhed and spun, as if he were attached to strings that were being manipulated by a drunken puppeteer. His hands hung slackly at his sides, which made his frantic and spasmodic capering seem especially eerie. His hands flopped and fluttered weakly, but they did not rise to tear at his assailant. It was almost as if, now, he were in the grip of ecstasy rather than the clutch of pain. Bryce followed him, tried to move in on him, but couldn't get close.

Then Wargle collapsed.

In that same instant, the moth rose and turned, suspended in the air, hovering on rapidly beating wings, eye night-black and hateful. It swooped at Bryce.

He stumbled backwards and threw his arms across his face. He fell.

The moth sailed over his head.

Bryce twisted around, looked up.

The kite-size insect glided soundlessly across the street, toward the buildings on the other side.

Tal Whitman raised his shotgun. The blast was like cannonfire in the silent town.

The moth pitched sideways in midair. It tumbled in a loop, dropped almost to the ground, then it swooped up again and flew on, disappearing over a rooftop.

Stu Wargle was sprawled on the pavement, flat on his back. Unmoving.

Bryce scrambled to his feet and went to Wargle. The deputy lay in the middle of the street, where there was just enough light to see that his face was gone. Jesus. *Gone.* As if it had been torn off. His hair and ragged ribbons of his scalp bristled over the white bone of his forehead. A skull peered up at Bryce.

CHAPTER 17

THE HOUR BEFORE MIDNIGHT

/////

TAL, GORDY, FRANK, and Lisa sat in red leatherette armchairs in a corner of the lobby of the Hilltop Inn. The inn had been closed since the end of the past skiing season, and they had removed the dusty white dropcloths from the chairs before collapsing into them, numb with shock. The oval coffee table was still covered by a dropcloth; they stared at that shrouded object, unable to look at one another.

At the far end of the room, Bryce and Jenny were standing over the body of Stu Wargle, which lay on a long, low sideboard against the wall. No one in the armchairs could bring himself to look over that way.

Staring at the covered coffee table, Tal said, "I shot the damned thing. I hit it. I know I did."

"We all saw it take the buckshot," Frank agreed.

"So why wasn't it blown apart?" Tal demanded. "Hit dead-on by a blast from a 20-gauge. It should've been torn to pieces, damn it."

"Guns aren't going to save us," Lisa said.

In a distant, haunted voice, Gordy said, "It could've been any of us. That thing could've gotten me. I was right behind Stu. If he had ducked or jumped out of the way . . ."

"No," Lisa said. "No. It wanted Officer Wargle. Nobody else. Just Officer Wargle."

Tal stared at the girl. "What do you mean?"

Her flesh had taken paleness from her bones. "Officer Wargle refused to admit he'd seen it when it was battering against the window. He insisted it was just a bird."

"So?"

"So it wanted him. Him especially," she said. "To teach him a lesson. But mostly to teach *us* a lesson."

"It couldn't have heard what Stu said."

"It did. It heard."

"But it couldn't have understood."

"It did."

"I think you're crediting it with too much intelligence," Tal said. "It was big, yes, and like nothing any of us has ever seen before. But it was still only an insect. A moth. Right?"

The girl said nothing.

"It's not omniscient," Tal said, trying to convince himself more than anyone else. "It's not all-seeing, all-hearing, all-knowing."

The girl stared silently at the covered coffee table.

Suppressing nausea, Jenny examined Wargle's hideous wound. The lobby lights were not quite bright enough, so she used a flashlight to inspect the edges of the injury and to peer into the skull. The center of the dead man's demolished face was eaten away clear to the bone; all the skin, flesh, and cartilage were gone. Even the bone itself appeared to be partially dissolved in places, pitted, as if it had been splashed with acid. The eyes were gone. There was, however, normal flesh on all sides of the wound; smooth untouched flesh lay along both sides of the face, from the outer points of the jawbones to the cheekbones, and there was unmarked skin from the midpoint of the chin on down, and from the midpoint of the forehead on up. It was as if some torture artist had designed a frame of healthy skin to set off the gruesome exhibition of bone on display in the center of the face.

Having seen enough, Jenny switched off the flashlight. Earlier, they had covered the body with a dropcloth from one of the chairs. Now Jenny drew the sheet over the dead man's face, relieved to be covering that skeletal grin.

"Well?" Bryce asked.

"No teeth marks," she said.

"Would a thing like that have teeth?"

"I know it had a mouth, a small chitinous beak. I saw its mandibles working when it bashed itself against the substation windows."

"Yeah. I saw them, too."

"A mouth like that would mark the flesh. There'd be slashes. Bite marks. Indications of chewing and tearing."

"But there were none?"

"No. The flesh doesn't look as if it was ripped off. It seems to've been . . . dissolved. Along the edges of the wound, the remaining flesh is even sort of cauterized, as if it has been seared by something."

"You think that . . . that insect . . . secreted an acid?"

She nodded.

"And dissolved Stu Wargle's face?"

"And sucked up the liquefied flesh," she said.

"Oh, Jesus."

"Yes."

Bryce was as pale as an untinted deathmask, and his freckles seemed, by contrast, to burn and shimmer on his face. "That explains how it could've done so much damage in only a few seconds."

Jenny tried not to think of the bony face peering out of the flesh—like a monstrous visage that had removed a mask of normality.

"I think the blood is gone," she said. "All of it."

"What?"

"Was the body lying in a pool of blood?"

"No."

"There's no blood on the uniform, either."

"I noticed that."

"There should be blood. He should've spouted like a fountain. The eye sockets should be pooled with it. But there's not a drop."

Bryce wiped one hand across his face. He wiped so hard, in fact, that some color rose in his cheeks.

"Take a look at his neck," she said. "The jugular."

He didn't move toward the corpse.

She said, "And look at the insides of his arms and the backs of his hands. There's no blueness of veins anywhere, no tracery."

"Collapsed blood vessels?"

"Yeah. I think all the blood is drained out of him."

Bryce took a deep breath. He said, "I killed him. I'm responsible. We should have waited for reinforcements before leaving the substation—just like you said."

"No, no. You were right. It was no safer there than in the street."

"But he died in the street."

"Reinforcements wouldn't have made a bit of difference. The way that damned thing dropped out of the sky . . . hell, not even an army could've stopped it. Too quick. Too surprising."

Bleakness had taken up tenancy in his eyes. He felt his responsibility far too keenly. He was going to insist on blaming himself for his officer's death.

Reluctantly, she said, "There's worse."

"Couldn't be."

"His brain . . ."

Bryce waited. Then he said, "What? What about his brain?"

"Gone."

"Gone?"

"His cranium is empty. Utterly empty."

"How can you possibly know that without opening—"

She held out the flashlight, interrupting him: "Take this and shine it into the eye sockets."

He made no move to act upon her suggestion. His eyes were not hooded now. They were wide, startled.

She noticed that she couldn't hold the flashlight steady. Her hand was shaking violently.

He noticed, too. He took the flash away from her and put it down on the sideboard, next to the shrouded corpse. He took both of her hands and held them in his own large, leathery, cupped hands; he warmed them.

She said, "There's nothing beyond the eye sockets, nothing at all, nothing, nothing whatsoever, except the back of his skull."

Bryce rubbed her hands soothingly.

"Just a damp, reamed-out cavity," she said. As she spoke, her voice rose and cracked: "It ate through his face, right through his eyes, probably about as fast as he could blink, for God's sake, ate into his mouth and took his tongue out by the roots, stripped the gums away from his teeth, then ate up through the roof of his mouth, Jesus, just consumed his brain, consumed all of the blood in his body, too, probably just sucked it up and out of him and—"

"Easy, easy," Bryce said.

But the words rattle-clanked out of her as if they were links in a chain that bound her to an albatross: "—consumed all of that in no more than ten or twelve seconds, which is impossible, damn it to hell, plain impossible! It devoured—do you understand?—*devoured* pounds and pounds and pounds of tissue—the brain alone weighs six or seven pounds—devoured all of that in ten or twelve *seconds!*"

She stood gasping, hands trapped in his.

He led her to a sofa that lay under a dusty white drape. They sat side by side.

Across the room, none of the others was looking this way.

Jenny was glad for that. She didn't want Lisa to see her in this condition.

Bryce put a hand on her shoulder. He spoke to her in a low, reassuring voice.

She gradually grew calmer. Not less disturbed. Not less afraid. Just calmer.

"Better?" Bryce asked.

"As my sister says—I guess I flaked out on you, huh?"

"Not at all. Are you kidding or what? I couldn't even take the flashlight from you and look in those eyes like you wanted me to. *You're* the one who had the nerve to examine him."

"Well, thanks for getting me back together. You sure know how to knit up raveled nerves."

"Me? I didn't do anything."

"You sure have a comforting way of doing nothing."

They sat in silence, thinking of things they didn't want to think about.

Then he said, "That moth . . ."

She waited.

He said, "Where'd it *come* from?"

"Hell?"

"Any other suggestions?"

Jenny shrugged. "The Mesozoic era?" she said half-jokingly.

"When was that?"

"The age of dinosaurs."

His blue eyes flickered with interest. "Did moths like that exist back then?"

"I don't know," she admitted.

"I *can* sort of picture it soaring through prehistoric swamps."

"Yeah. Preying on small animals, bothering a *Tyrannosaurus rex* about the same way our own tiny summer moths bother us."

"But if it's from the Mesozoic, where's it been hiding for the last hundred million years?" he asked.

More seconds, ticking.

"Could it be . . . something from a genetic engineering lab?" she wondered. "An experiment in recombinant DNA?"

"Have they gone that far? Can they produce whole new species? I only know what I read in the papers, but I thought they were years away from that sort of thing. They're still working with bacteria."

"You're probably right," she said. "But still . . ."

"Yeah. Nothing's impossible because the moth is *here*."

After another silence, she said, "And what else is crawling or flying around out there?"

"You're thinking about what happened to Jake Johnson?"

"Yeah. What took him? Not the moth. Even as deadly as it is, it couldn't kill him silently, and it couldn't carry him away." She sighed. "You know, at first I wouldn't try to leave town because I was afraid we'd spread an epidemic. Now I wouldn't try to leave because I know we wouldn't make it out alive. We'd be stopped."

"No, no. I'm sure we could get you out," Bryce said. "If we can prove there's no disease-related aspect to this, if General Copperfield's people can rule that out, then, of course, you and Lisa will be taken to safety right away."

She shook her head. "No. There's something out there, Bryce, something more cunning and a whole lot more formidable than the moth, and it doesn't want us to leave. It wants to play with us before it kills us. It won't let any of us go, so we'd damned well better find it and figure out how to deal with it before it gets tired of the game."

In both rooms of the Hilltop Inn's large restaurant, chairs were stacked upside-down atop the tables, all covered with green plastic dropcloths. In the first room, Bryce and the others removed the plastic sheeting, took the chairs off the tables, and began to prepare the place to serve as a cafeteria.

In the second room, the furniture had to be moved out to make way for the mattresses that would later be brought down from upstairs. They had only just begun emptying that part of the restaurant when they heard the faint but unmistakable sound of automobile engines.

Bryce went to the French windows. He looked left, down the hill, toward the foot of Skyline Road. Three county squad cars were coming up the street, red beacons flashing.

"They're here," Bryce told the others.

He had been thinking of the reinforcements as a reassuringly formidable replenishment of their own decimated contingent. Now he realized that ten more men were hardly better than one more.

Jenny Paige had been right when she'd said that Stu Wargle's life probably wouldn't have been saved by waiting for reinforcements before leaving the substation.

All the lights in the Hilltop Inn and all the lights along the main street flickered. Dimmed. Went out. But they came back on after only a second of darkness.

It was 11:15, Sunday night, counting down toward the witching hour.

CHAPTER 18
LONDON, ENGLAND

WHEN MIDNIGHT CAME to California, it was eight o'clock Monday morning in London.

The day was dreary. Gray clouds melted across the city. A steady, dismal drizzle had been falling since before dawn. The drowned trees hung limply, and the streets glistened darkly, and everyone on the sidewalks seemed to have black umbrellas.

At the Churchill Hotel in Portman Square, rain beat against the windows and streamed down the glass, distorting the view from the dining room. Occasionally, brilliant flashes of lightning, passing through the water-beaded windowpanes, briefly cast shadowy images of raindrops onto the clean white tablecloths.

Burt Sandler, in London on business from New York, sat at one of the window tables, wondering how in God's name he was going to justify the size of this breakfast bill on his expense account. His guest had begun by ordering a bottle of good champagne: Mumm's Extra Dry, which didn't come cheap. With the champagne, his guest wanted caviar—champagne and caviar for breakfast!—and two kinds of fresh fruit. And the old fellow clearly was not finished ordering.

Across the table, Dr. Timothy Flyte, the object of Sandler's amazement, studied the menu with childlike delight. To the waiter, he said, "And I should like an order of your croissants."

"Yes, sir," the waiter said.

"Are they very flaky?"

"Yes, sir. Very."

"Oh, good. And eggs," Flyte said. "Two lovely eggs, of course, rather soft, with buttered toast."

"Toast?" the waiter asked. "Is that in addition to the two croissants, sir?"

"Yes, yes," Flyte said, fingering the slightly frayed collar of his white shirt. "And a rasher of bacon with the eggs."

The waiter blinked. "Yes, sir."

At last Flyte looked up at Burt Sandler. "What's breakfast without bacon? Am I right?"

"I'm an eggs-and-bacon man myself," Burt Sandler agreed, forcing a smile.

"Wise of you," Flyte said sagely. His wire-rimmed spectacles had slipped down his nose and were now perched on the round, red tip of it. With a long, thin finger, he pushed them back into place.

Sandler noticed that the bridge of the eyeglasses had been broken and soldered. The repair job was so distinctly amateurish that he suspected Flyte had soldered the frames himself, to save money.

"Do you have good pork sausages?" Flyte asked the waiter. "Be truthful with me. I'll send them back straightaway if they aren't of the highest quality."

"We've quite good sausages," the waiter assured him. "I'm partial to them myself."

"Sausages, then."

"Is that in place of the bacon, sir?"

567

"No, no, no. In addition," Flyte said, as if the waiter's question was not only curious but a sign of thick-headedness.

Flyte was fifty-eight but looked at least a decade older. His bristly white hair curled thinly across the top of his head and thrust out around his large ears as if crackling with static electricity. His neck was scrawny and wrinkled; his shoulders were slight; his body favored bone and cartilage over flesh. There was some legitimate doubt whether he could actually eat all that he had ordered.

"Potatoes," Flyte said.

"Very well, sir," the waiter said, scribbling it down on his order pad, on which he had very nearly run out of room to write.

"Do you have suitable pastries?" Flyte inquired.

The waiter, a model of deportment under the circumstances, having made not the slightest allusion to Flyte's amazing gluttony, looked at Burt Sandler as if to say: *Is your grandfather hopelessly senile, sir, or is he, at his age, a marathon runner who needs the calories?*

Sandler merely smiled.

To Flyte, the waiter said, "Yes, sir, we have several pastries. There's a delicious—"

"Bring an assortment," Flyte said. "At the end of the meal, of course."

"Leave it to me, sir."

"Good. Very good. Excellent!" Flyte said, beaming. Finally, with a trace of reluctance, he relinquished his menu.

Sandler almost sighed with relief. He asked for orange juice, eggs, bacon, and toast, while Professor Flyte adjusted the day-old carnation pinned to the lapel of his somewhat shiny blue suit.

As Sandler finished ordering, Flyte leaned toward him conspiratorially. "Will you be having some of the champagne, Mr. Sandler?"

"I believe I might have a glass or two," Sandler said, hoping the bubbly would liberate his mind and help him formulate a believable explanation for this extravagance, a likely tale that would convince even the parsimonious clerks in accounting who would be poring over this bill with an electron microscope.

Flyte looked at the waiter. "Then perhaps you'd better bring *two* bottles."

Sandler, who was sipping ice-water, nearly choked.

The waiter left, and Flyte looked out through the rain-streaked window beside their table. "Nasty weather. Is it like this in New York in autumn?"

"We have our share of rainy days. But autumn can be beautiful in New York."

"Here, too," Flyte said. "Though I rather imagine we have more days like this than you. London's reputation for soggy weather isn't entirely undeserved."

The professor insisted on small talk until the champagne and caviar were served, as if he feared that, once business had been discussed, Sandler would quickly cancel the rest of the breakfast order.

He's a character out of Dickens, Sandler thought.

As soon as they had proposed a toast, wishing each other good fortune, and had sipped the Mumm's, Flyte said, "So you've come all the way from New York to see me, have you?" His eyes were merry.

"To see a number of writers, actually," Sandler said. "I make the trip once a year. I scout out books in progress. British authors are popular in the States, especially thriller writers."

"MacLean, Follett, Forsythe, Bagley, that crowd?"

"Yes, very popular, some of them."

The caviar was superb. At the professor's urging, Sandler tried some of it with chopped onions. Flyte piled gobs on small wedges of dry toast and ate it without benefit of condiments.

"But I'm not only scouting for thrillers," Sandler said. "I'm after a variety of books. Unknown authors, too. And I suggest projects on occasion, when I have a subject for a particular author."

"Apparently, you have something in mind for me."

"First, let me say I read *The Ancient Enemy* when it was first published, and I found it fascinating."

"A number of people found it fascinating," Flyte said. "But most found it infuriating."

"I hear the book created problems for you."

"Virtually nothing *but* problems."

"Such as?"

"I lost my university position fifteen years ago, at the age of forty-three, when most academics are achieving job security."

"You lost your position because of *The Ancient Enemy?*"

"They didn't put it quite that bluntly," Flyte said, popping a morsel of caviar into his mouth. "That would have made them seem too closeminded. The administrators of my college, the head of my department, and most of my distinguished colleagues chose to attack indirectly. My dear Mr. Sandler, the competition among power-mad politicians and the Machiavellian backstabbing of junior executives in a major corporation are as nothing, in terms of ruthlessness and spitefulness, when compared to the behavior of academic types who suddenly see an opportunity to climb the university ladder at the expense of one of their own. They spread rumors without foundation, scandalous tripe about my sexual preferences, suggestions of intimate fraternization with my female students. And with my male students, for that matter. None of those slanders was openly discussed in a forum where I could refute them. Just rumors. Whispered behind the back. Poisonous. More openly, they made polite suggestions of incompetence, overwork, mental fatigue. I was eased out, you see; that's how they thought of it, though there was nothing easy about it from my point of view. Eighteen months after the publication of *The Ancient Enemy,* I was gone. And no other university would have me, ostensibly because of my unsavory reputation. The true reason, of course, was that my theories were too bizarre for academic tastes. I stood accused of attempting to make a fortune by pandering to the common man's taste for pseudoscience and sensationalism, of selling my credibility."

Flyte paused to take some champagne, savoring it.

Sandler was genuinely appalled by what Flyte had told him. "But that's outrageous! Your book was a scholarly treatise. It was never aimed at the bestseller lists. The common man would've had enormous difficulty wading through *The Ancient Enemy.* Making a fortune from that kind of work is virtually impossible."

"A fact to which my royalty statements can attest," Flyte said. He finished the last of the caviar.

"You were a respected archaeologist," Sandler said.

"Oh, well, never really all *that* respected," Flyte said self-deprecatingly. "Though I was certainly never an embarrassment to my profession, as was so often suggested later on. If my colleagues' conduct seems incredible to you, Mr. Sandler, that's because you don't understand the nature of the animal. I mean, the scientist animal. Scientists are educated to believe that all new knowledge comes in tiny increments, grains of sand piled one on another. Indeed, that *is* how most knowledge is gained. Therefore, they are never prepared for those visionaries who arrive at new insights which, overnight, utterly transform an entire field of inquiry. Copernicus was ridiculed by his contemporaries for believing that the planets revolved around the sun. Of course, Copernicus was proved right. There are countless examples in the history of science." Flyte blushed and drank some more champagne. "Not that I compare myself to Copernicus or any of those other great men. I'm simply trying to explain why my colleagues were conditioned to turn against me. I should have seen it coming."

The waiter came to take away the caviar dish. He also served Sandler's orange juice and Flyte's fresh fruit.

When he was alone with Flyte again, Sandler said, "Do you still believe your theory had validity?"

"Absolutely!" Flyte said. "I *am* right; or at least there's an awfully good chance I am. History is filled with mysterious mass disappearances for which historians and archaeologists can provide no viable explanation."

The professor's rheumy eyes became sharp and probing beneath his bushy white eyebrows. He leaned over the table, fixing Burt Sandler with a hypnotic stare.

"On December 10, 1939," Flyte said, "outside the hills of Nanking, an army of three thousand Chinese soldiers, on its way to the front lines to fight the Japanese, simply vanished without a trace before it got anywhere near the battle. Not a single body was ever found. Not one grave. Not one witness. The Japanese military historians have never found any record of having dealt with that particular Chinese force. In the countryside through which the missing soldiers passed, no peasants heard gunfire or other indications of conflict. An *army* evaporated into thin air. And in 1711, during the Spanish War of Succession, four thousand troops set out on an expedition into the Pyrenees. Every last man disappeared on familiar and friendly ground, before the first night's camp was established!"

Flyte was still as gripped by his subject as he had been when he had written the book, seventeen years ago. His fruit and champagne were forgotten. He stared at Sandler as if daring him to challenge the infamous Flyte theories.

"On a grander scale," the professor continued, "consider the great Mayan cities of Copán, Piedras Negras, Palenque, Menché, Seibal, and several others which were abandoned overnight. Tens of thousands, *hundreds* of thousands of Mayans left their homes, approximately in A.D. 610, perhaps within a single week, even within one *day.* Some appear to have fled northward, to establish new cities, but there is evidence that countless thousands just disappeared. All within a shockingly brief span of time. They didn't bother to take many of their pots, tools, cooking utensils . . . My learned colleagues say the land around those Mayan cities became infertile, thus making it essential that the people move north, where the land would be more productive. But if this great exodus was planned, why were belongings left behind? Why was precious seed corn left behind? Why didn't a single survivor ever return to loot those cities of their abandoned treasures?" Flyte softly struck the table with one fist. "It's irrational! Emigrants don't set out on long, arduous journeys without preparation, without taking every tool that might assist them. Besides, in some of the homes in Piedras Negras and Seibal, there is evidence that families departed after preparing elaborate dinners—*but before eating them.* This would surely seem to indicate that their leaving was sudden. No current theories adequately answer these questions—except mine, bizarre as it is, odd as it is, *impossible* as it is."

"Frightening as it is," Sandler added.

"Exactly," Flyte said.

The professor sank back in his chair, breathless. He noticed his champagne glass, seized it, emptied it, and licked his lips.

The waiter appeared and refilled their glasses.

Flyte quickly consumed his fruit, as if afraid the waiter might spirit it away while the hothouse strawberries remained untouched.

Sandler felt sorry for the old bird. Evidently, it had been quite some time since the professor had been treated to an expensive meal served in an elegant atmosphere.

"I was accused of trying to explain *every* mysterious disappearance from the Mayans to Judge Crater and Amelia Earhart, all with a single theory. That was most unfair. I never mentioned the judge or the luckless aviatrix. I am interested only in unexplained *mass* disappearances of both humankind and animals, of which there have been literally hundreds throughout history."

The waiter brought croissants.

Outside, lightning stepped quickly down the somber sky and put its spiked foot to the earth in another part of the city; its blazing descent was accompanied by a terrible crash and roar that echoed across the entire firmament.

Sandler said, "If subsequent to the publication of your book, there had been a new, startling mass disappearance, it would have lent considerable credibility—"

"Ah," Flyte interrupted, tapping the table emphatically with one stiff finger, "but there *have* been such disappearances!"

"But surely they would have been splashed all over the front page—"

"I am aware of two instances. There may be others," Flyte insisted. "One of them involved the disappearance of masses of lower lifeforms—specifically, *fish*. It was remarked on in the press, but not with any great interest. Politics, murder, sex, and two-headed goats are the only things newspapers care to report about. You have to read scientific journals to know what's really happening. That's how I know that, eight years ago, marine biologists noted a dramatic decrease in fish population in one region of the Pacific. Indeed, the numbers of some species had been cut in half. Within certain scientific circles, there was panic at first, some fear that ocean temperatures might be undergoing a sudden change that would depopulate the seas of all but the hardiest species. But that proved not to be the case. Gradually, sea life in that area—which covered hundreds of square miles—replenished itself. In the end no one could explain what had happened to the millions upon millions of creatures that had vanished."

"Pollution," Sandler suggested, between alternating sips of orange juice and champagne.

Dabbing marmalade on a piece of croissant, Flyte said, "No, no, no. No, sir. It would have required the most massive case of water pollution in history to cause such a devastating depopulation over that wide an area. An accident on that scale could not go unnoticed. But there were no accidents, no oil spills — nothing. Indeed, a mere oil spill could not have accounted for it; the affected region and the volume of water was too vast for that. And dead fish did *not* wash up on the beaches. They merely vanished without a trace."

Burt Sandler was excited. He could smell money. He had hunches about some books, and none of his hunches had ever been wrong. (Well, except for that diet book by the movie star who, a week before publication day, died of malnutrition after subsisting for six months on little more than grapefruit, papaya, raisin toast, and carrots.) There was a surefire best-seller in this: two or three hundred thousand copies in hardcover, perhaps even more; two million in paperback. If he could persuade Flyte to popularize and update the dry academic material in *The Ancient Enemy,* the professor would be able to afford his own champagne for many years to come.

"You said you were aware of *two* mass disappearances since the publication of your book," Sandler said, encouraging him to continue.

"The other was in Africa in 1980. Between three and four thousand primitive tribesmen—men, women, and children—vanished from a relatively remote area of central Africa. Their villages were found empty; they had abandoned all their possessions, including large stores of food. They seemed to have just run off into the bush. The only signs of violence were a few broken pieces of pottery. Of course, mass disappearances in that part of the world are dismayingly more frequent than they once were, primarily due to political violence. Cuban mercenaries, operating with Soviet weaponry, have been assisting in the liquidation of whole tribes that are unwilling to put their ethnic identities second to the revolutionary purpose. But when entire villages are slaughtered for political purposes, they are always looted, then burned, and the bodies are always interred in mass graves. There was no looting in this instance, no burning, no bodies to be found. Some weeks later, game wardens in that district reported an inexplicable decrease in the wildlife population. No one connected it to the missing villagers; it was reported as a separate phenomenon."

"But you know differently."

"Well, I *suspect* differently," Flyte said, putting strawberry jam on a last bit of croissant.

"Most of these disappearances seem to occur in remote areas," Sandler said. "Which makes verification difficult."

"Yes. That was thrown in my face as well. Actually, most incidents probably occur at sea, for the sea covers the largest part of the earth. The sea can be as remote as the moon, and much of what takes place beneath the waves is beyond our notice. Yet don't forget the two armies I mentioned—the Chinese and Spanish. *Those* disappearances took place within the context of modern civilization. And if tens of thousands of Mayans fell victim to the ancient enemy whose existence I've theorized, then that was a case in which entire cities, hearts of civilization, were attacked with frightening boldness."

"You think it could happen now, today—"

"No question about it!"

"—in a place like New York or even here in London?"

"Certainly! It could happen virtually anywhere that has the geological underpinnings I outlined in my book."

They both sipped champagne, thinking.

The rain hammered on the windows with greater fury than before.

Sandler was not certain that he believed in the theories Flyte had propounded in *The Ancient Enemy.* He knew they could form the basis for a wildly successful book written in a popular vein, but that didn't mean he had to believe in them. He didn't really *want* to believe. Believing was like opening the door to Hell.

He looked at Flyte, who was straightening his wilted carnation again, and he said, "It gives me the chills."

"It should," Flyte said, nodding. "It should."

The waiter came with the eggs, bacon, sausages, and toast.

CHAPTER 19

THE DEAD OF NIGHT

THE INN WAS A FORTRESS. Bryce was satisfied with the preparations that had been made.

At last, after two hours of arduous labor, he sat down at a table in the cafeteria, sipping decaffeinated coffee from a white ceramic mug on which was emblazoned the blue crest of the hotel.

By one-thirty in the morning, with the help of the ten deputies who had arrived from Santa Mira, much had been accomplished. One of the two rooms had been converted into a dormitory; twenty mattresses were lined up on the floor, enough to accommodate any single shift of the investigative team, even after General Copperfield's people arrived. In the other half of the restaurant, a couple of buffet tables had been set up at one end, where a cafeteria line could be formed at mealtimes. The kitchen had been cleaned and put in order. The large lobby had been converted into an enormous operations center, with desks, makeshift desks, typewriters, filing cabinets, bulletin boards, and a big map of Snowfield.

Furthermore, the inn had been given a thorough security inspection, and steps had been taken to prevent a break-in by the enemy. The two rear entrances—one through the kitchen, one through the lobby—were locked, and additionally secured with slanted two-by-fours, which were wedged under the crash-bars and nailed to the frames; Bryce had ordered that extra precaution to avoid wasting guards at those entrances. The door to the emergency stairs was similarly sealed off; nothing could enter the higher floors of the hotel and come down upon them by surprise. Now, only a pair of small elevators connected the lobby level to the three upper floors, and two guards were stationed there. Another guard stood at the front entrance. A detail of four men had ascertained that all upstairs rooms were empty. Another detail had determined that all of the ground-floor windows were locked; most of them were painted shut, as well. Nevertheless, the windows were points of weakness in their fortifications.

At least, Bryce thought, if anything tries to get inside through a window, we'll have the sound of breaking glass to warn us.

A host of other details had been attended to. Stu Wargle's mutilated corpse had been temporarily stored in a utility room that adjoined the lobby. Bryce had drawn up a duty roster, and had structured twelve-hour work shifts for the next three days, should the crisis last that long. Finally, he couldn't think of anything more that could be done until first light.

Now he sat alone at one of the round tables in the dining room, sipping Sanka, trying to make sense of the night's events. His mind kept circling back to one unwanted thought:

His brain was gone. His blood was sucked out of him—every damned drop.

He shook off the sickening image of Wargle's ruined face, got up, went for more coffee, then returned to the table.

The inn was very quiet.

At another table, three of the nightshift men—Miguel Hernandez, Sam Potter, and Henry Wong—were playing cards, but they weren't talking much. When they did speak, it was almost in whispers.

The inn was very quiet.

The inn was a fortress.

The inn *was* a fortress, damn it.

But was it safe?

Lisa chose a mattress in a corner of the dormitory, where her back would be up against a blank wall.

Jenny unfolded one of the two blankets stacked at the foot of the mattress, and draped it over the girl.

"Want the other one?"

"No," Lisa said. "This'll be enough. It feels funny, though, going to bed with all my clothes on."

"Things'll get back to normal pretty soon," she said, but even as she spoke she realized how inane that statement was.

"Are you going to sleep now?"

"Not quite yet."

"I wish you would," Lisa said. "I wish you'd lay down right there on the next mattress."

"You're not alone, honey." Jenny smoothed the girl's hair.

A few deputies—including Tal Whitman, Gordy Brogan, and Frank Autry —had bedded down on other mattresses. There were also three heavily armed guards who would watch over everyone throughout the night.

"Will they turn the lights down any farther?" Lisa asked.

"No. We can't risk darkness."

"Good. They're dim enough. Will you stay with me until I fall asleep?" Lisa asked, seeming much younger than fourteen.

"Sure."

"And talk to me."

"Sure. But we'll talk softly, so we don't disturb anyone."

Jenny lay down beside her sister, her head propped up on one hand. "What do you want to talk about?"

"I don't care. Anything. Anything except . . . tonight."

"Well, there is something I want to ask you," Jenny said. "It's not about tonight, but it's about something you said tonight. Remember when we were sitting on the bench in front of the jail, waiting for the sheriff? Remember how we were talking about Mom, and you said Mom used to . . . used to brag about me?"

Lisa smiled. "Her daughter, the doctor. Oh, she was *so* proud of you, Jenny."

As it had done before, that statement unsettled Jenny.

"And Mom never blamed me for Dad's stroke?" she asked.

Lisa frowned. "Why would she blame you?"

"Well . . . because I guess I caused him some heartache there for a while. Heartache and a lot of worry."

"*You?*" Lisa asked, astonished.

"And when Dad's doctor couldn't control his high blood pressure and then he had a stroke—"

"According to Mom, the only thing you ever did bad in your entire life was when you decided to give the calico cat a black dye job for Halloween and you got Clairol all over the sun porch furniture."

Jenny laughed with surprise. "I'd forgotten that. I was only eight years old."

They smiled at each other, and in that moment they felt more than ever like sisters.

Then Lisa said, "Why'd you think Mom blamed you for Daddy's dying? It was natural causes, wasn't it? A stroke. How could it possibly have been your fault?"

Jenny hesitated, thinking back thirteen years to the start of it. That her mother had never blamed her for her father's death was a profoundly liberating realization. She felt free for the first time since she'd been nineteen.

"Jenny?"

"Mmmm?"

"Are you crying?"

"No, I'm okay," she said, fighting back tears. "If Mom didn't hold it against me, I guess I've been wrong to hold it against myself. I'm just happy, honey. Happy about what you've told me."

"But what was it you thought you did? If we're going to be good sisters, we shouldn't keep secrets. Tell me, Jenny."

"It's a long story, Sis. I'll tell you about it eventually, but not now. Now I want to hear all about you."

They talked about trivialities for a few minutes, and Lisa's eyes grew steadily heavier.

Jenny was reminded of Bryce Hammond's gentle, hooded eyes.

And of Jakob and Aida Liebermann's eyes, glaring out of their severed heads.

And Deputy Wargle's eyes. Gone. Those burnt-out, empty sockets in that hollow skull.

She tried to force her thoughts away from that gruesomeness, from that too-well-remembered, grim reaper's gaze. But her mind kept circling back to that image of monstrous violence and death.

She wished there were someone to talk her to sleep as she was doing for Lisa. It was going to be a restless night.

In the utility room that adjoined the lobby and backed up against the elevator shaft, the light was off. There were no windows.

A faint odor of cleaning fluids clung to the place. Pinesol. Lysol. Furniture polish. Floor wax. Janitorial supplies were stored on shelves along one wall.

In the right-hand corner, farthest from the door, was a large metal sink. Water dripped from a leaky faucet—one drop every ten or twelve seconds. Each pellet of water struck the metal basin with a soft, hollow *ping*.

In the center of the room, as shrouded in utter blackness as was everything else, the faceless body of Stu Wargle lay on a table, covered by a dropcloth. All was still. Except for the monotonous *ping* of the dripping water.

A breathless anticipation hung in the air.

Frank Autry huddled under the blanket, his eyes closed, and he thought about Ruth. Tall, willowy, sweet-faced Ruthie. Ruthie with the quiet yet crisp voice, Ruthie with the throaty laugh that most people found infectious, his wife of twenty-six years: She was the only woman he had ever loved; he still loved her.

He had spoken with her by telephone for a few minutes, just before turning in for the night. He had not been able to tell her much about what was happening—just that there was a siege situation underway in Snowfield, that it was being kept quiet as long as possible, and that by the look of it he wouldn't be home tonight. Ruthie hadn't pressed him for details. She had been a good army wife through all his years in the service. She still was.

Thinking of Ruth was his primary psychological defense mechanism. In times of stress, in times of fear and pain and depression, he simply thought of Ruth, concentrated solely on her, and the strife-filled world faded. For a man who had spent so much of his life engaged in dangerous work—for a man whose occupations had seldom allowed him to forget that death was an intimate part of life, a woman like Ruth was indispensable medicine, an inoculation against despair.

Gordy Brogan was afraid to close his eyes again. Each time that he *had* closed them, he had been plagued by bloody visions that had rolled up out of his own private darkness. Now he lay under his blanket, eyes open, staring at Frank Autry's back.

In his mind, he composed his letter of resignation to Bryce Hammond. He wouldn't be able to type and submit that letter until after this Snowfield business was settled. He didn't want to leave his buddies in the middle of a battle; that didn't seem right. He might actually be of some help to them, considering that it didn't appear as if he would be required to shoot at *people*. However, as soon as this thing was settled, as soon as they were back in Santa Mira, he would write the letter and hand-deliver it to the sheriff.

He had no doubt about it now: police work was not—and never had been—for him.

He was still a young man; there was time to change careers. He had become a cop partly as an act of rebellion against his parents, for it had been the last thing they had wanted. They'd noted his uncanny way with animals, his ability to win the trust and friendship of any creature on four legs within about half a minute flat, and they had hoped he would become a veterinarian. Gordy had always felt smothered by his mother's and father's unflagging affection, and when they had nudged him toward a career in veterinary medicine, he had rejected the possibility. Now he saw that they were right and that they only wanted what was best for him. Indeed, deep down, he had always known they were right. He was a healer, not a peacekeeper.

He had also been drawn to the uniform and the badge because being a cop had seemed a good way of proving his masculinity. In spite of his formidable size and muscles, in spite of his acute interest in women, he had always believed that others thought of him as androgynous. As a boy, he had never been interested in sports, which had obsessed all of his male contemporaries. And endless talk about hotrods had simply bored him. His interests lay elsewhere and, to some, seemed effete. Although his talent was only average, he enjoyed painting. He played the French horn. Nature fascinated him, and he was an avid bird-watcher. His abhorrence of violence had not been acquired as an adult; even as a child, he had avoided confrontations. His pacifism, when considered with his reticence in the company of girls, had made him appear, at least to himself, somewhat less than manly. But now, at long last, he saw that he did not need to prove anything.

He would go to school, become a vet. He would be content. His folks would be happy, too. His life would be on the right track again.

He closed his eyes, sighing, seeking sleep. But out of darkness came nightmarish images of the severed heads of cats and dogs, flesh-crawling images of dismembered and tortured animals.

He snapped his eyes open, gasping.

What *had* happened to all the pets in Snowfield?

The utility room, off the lobby.

Windowless, lightless.

The monotonous *ping* of water dropping into the metal sink had stopped.

But there wasn't silence now. Something moved in the darkness. It made a soft, wet, stealthy sound as it crept around the pitch-black room.

Not yet ready to sleep, Jenny went into the cafeteria, poured a cup of coffee, and joined the sheriff at a corner table.

"Lisa sleeping?" he asked.

"Like a rock."

"How're you holding up? This must be hard on you. All your neighbors, friends . . ."

"It's hard to grieve properly," she said. "I'm just sort of numb. If I let myself react to every death that's had an effect on me, I'd be a blubbering mess. So I've just let my emotions go numb."

"It's a normal, healthy response. That's how we're all dealing with it."

They drank some coffee, chatted a bit. Then:

"Married?" he asked.

"No. You?"

"I was."

"Divorced?"

"She died."

"Oh, Christ, of course. I read about it. I'm sorry. A year ago, wasn't it? A traffic accident?"

"A runaway truck."

She was looking into his eyes, and she thought they clouded and became less blue than they had been. "How's your son doing?"

"He's still in a coma. I don't think he'll ever come out of it."

"I'm sorry, Bryce. I really am."

He folded his hands around his mug and stared down at the coffee. "With Timmy like he is, it'll be a blessing, really, when he just finally lets go. I was numb about it for a while. I couldn't feel anything, not just emotionally but physically, as well. At one point I cut my finger while I was slicing an orange, and I bled all over the damned kitchen and even ate a few bloody sections of the orange before I noticed that something was wrong. Even then I never felt any pain. Lately, I've been coming around to an understanding, to an acceptance." He looked up and met Jenny's eyes. "Strangely enough, since I've been here in Snowfield, the grayness has gone away."

"Grayness?"

"For a long time, the color has been leached out of everything. It's all been gray. But tonight—just the opposite. Tonight, there's been so much excitement, so much tension, so much *fear,* that everything has seemed extraordinarily vivid."

Then Jenny spoke of her mother's death, of the surprisingly powerful effect it had had on her, despite the twelve years of partial estrangement that should have softened the blow.

Again, Jenny was impressed by Bryce Hammond's ability to make her feel at ease. They seemed to have known each other for years.

She even found herself telling him about the mistakes she had made in her eighteenth and nineteenth years, about her naive and stubbornly wrongheaded behavior that had grievously hurt her parents. Toward the end of her first year in college, she had met a man who had captivated her. He was a graduate student—Campbell Hudson; she called him Cam—five years her senior. His attentiveness, charm, and passionate pursuit of her had swept her away. Until then, she had led a sheltered life; she had never tied herself down to one steady boyfriend, had never really dated heavily at all. She was an easy target. Having fallen for Cam Hudson, she then became not only his lover but his rapt student and disciple and, very nearly, his devoted slave.

"I can't see you subjugating yourself to anyone," Bryce said.

"I was young."

"Always an acceptable excuse."

She had moved in with Cam, taking insufficient measures to conceal her sinning from her mother and father; and *sinning* was how they saw it. Later, she decided—rather, she allowed Cam to decide for her—that she would drop out of college and work as a waitress, helping pay his bills until he was finished with his master's and doctoral work.

Once trapped in Cam Hudson's self-serving scenario, she gradually found him less attentive and less charming than he had once been. She learned he had a violent temper. Then her father died while she was still with Cam, and at the funeral she sensed that her mother blamed her for his untimely passing. Within a month of the day that her father was consigned to the grave, she learned she was pregnant. She had been pregnant when he'd died. Cam was furious and insisted on a quick abortion. She asked for a day to consider, but he became enraged at even a twenty-four-hour delay. He beat her so severely that she had a miscarriage. It was over then. The foolishness was over. She grew up suddenly—although her abrupt coming of age was too late to please her father.

"Since then," she told Bryce, "I've spent my life working hard—maybe too hard—to prove to my mother that I was sorry and that I was, after all, worthy of her love. I've worked weekends, turned down countless party invitations, skipped most vacations for the past twelve years, all in the name of bettering myself. I didn't go home as often as I should have done. I couldn't face my mother. I could see the accusation in her eyes. And then tonight, from Lisa, I learned the most amazing thing."

"Your mother never blamed you," Bryce said, displaying that uncanny sensitivity and perception that she had seen in him before.

"Yes!" Jenny said. "She never held anything against me."

"She was probably even proud of you."

"Yes, again! She never blamed me for Dad's death. It was *me* doing all the blaming. The accusation I thought I saw in her eyes was only a reflection of my own guilty feelings." Jenny laughed softly and sourly, shaking her head. "It'd be funny if it wasn't so damned sad."

In Bryce Hammond's eyes, she saw the sympathy and understanding for which she had been searching ever since her father's funeral.

He said, "We're a lot alike in some ways, you and I. I think we both have martyr complexes."

"No more," she said. "Life's too short. That's something that's been brought home to me tonight. From now on I'm going to live, really live—if Snowfield will let me."

"We'll get through this," he said.

"I wish I could feel sure of that."

Bryce said, "You know, having something to look forward to will help us make it. So how about giving *me* something to look forward to?"

"Huh?"

"A date." He leaned forward. His thick, sandy hair fell into his eyes. "Gervasio's Ristorante in Santa Mira. Minestrone. Scampi in garlic butter. Some good veal or maybe a steak. A side dish of pasta. They make a wonderful vermicelli al pesto. Good wine."

She grinned. "I'd love it."

"I forgot to mention the garlic bread."

"Oh, I love garlic bread."

"Zabaglione for dessert."

"They'll have to carry us out," she said.

"We'll arrange for wheelbarrows."

They chatted for a couple of minutes, relieving tension, and then both of them were finally ready to sleep.

Ping.

In the dark utility room where Stu Wargle's body lay on a table, water had begun to drop into the metal sink again.

Ping.

Something continued to move stealthily in the darkness, around and around the table. It made a slick, wet, slithering-through-the-mud noise.

That wasn't the only sound in the room; there were many other noises, all soft and low. The panting of a weary dog. The hiss of an angry cat. Quiet, silvery, haunting laughter; the laughter of a small child. Then a woman's pained whimpering. A moan. A sigh. The chirruping of a swallow, rendered clearly but softly, so as not to draw the attention of any of the guards posted out in the lobby. The warning of a rattlesnake. The humming of bumblebees. The higher-pitched, sinister buzzing of wasps. A dog growling.

The noises ceased as abruptly as they had begun.

Silence returned.

Ping.

The quiet lasted, unbroken except for the regularly spaced notes of the falling water, for perhaps a minute.

Ping.

There was a rustle of cloth in the lightless room. The shroud over Wargle's corpse. The shroud had slipped off the dead man and had fallen to the floor.

Slithering again.

And a dry-wood splintering sound. A brittle, muffled but violent sound. A hard, sharp bonecrack.

Silence again.

Ping.

Silence.

Ping. Ping. Ping.

While Tal Whitman waited for sleep, he thought about fear. That was the key word; it was the foundry emotion that had forged him. Fear. His life was one long vigorous denial of fear, a refutation of its very existence. He refused to be affected by—humbled by, driven by—fear. He would not admit that anything could scare him. Early in his life, hard experience had taught him that even acknowledgment of fear could expose him to its voracious appetite.

He had been born and raised in Harlem, where fear was everywhere: fear of street gangs, fear of junkies, fear of random violence, fear of economic privation, fear of being excluded from the mainstream of life. In those tenements, along those gray streets, fear waited to gobble you up the instant you gave it the slightest nod of recognition.

In childhood, he had not been safe even in the apartment that he had shared with his mother, one brother, and three sisters. Tal's father had been a sociopath, a wife-beater, who had shown up once or twice a month merely for the pleasure of slapping his woman senseless and terrorizing his children. Of course, Mama had been no better than the old man. She drank too much wine, tooted too much dope, and was nearly as ruthless with her children as their father was.

When Tal was nine, on one of the rare nights when his father was home, a fire swept the tenement house. Tal was his family's sole survivor. Mama and the old man had died in bed, overcome by smoke in their sleep. Tal's brother, Oliver, and his sisters—Heddy, Louisa, and baby Francesca—were lost, and now all these years later it was sometimes difficult to believe that they had ever really existed.

After the fire, he was taken in by his mother's sister, Aunt Rebecca. She lived in Harlem, too. Becky didn't drink. She didn't use dope. She had no children of her own, but she did have a job, and she went to night school, and she believed in self-sufficiency, and she had high hopes. She often told Tal that there was nothing to fear but Fear Itself and that Fear Itself was like the boogeyman, just a shadow, not worth fearing at all. "God made you healthy, Talbert, and he gave you a good brain. Now if you mess up, it's nobody's fault but your own." With Aunty Becky's love, discipline, and guidance, young Talbert had eventually come to think of himself as virtually invincible. He was not scared of anything in life; he was not scared of dying, either.

That was why, years later, after surviving the shoot-out in the 7-Eleven store over in Santa Mira, he was able to tell Bryce Hammond that it had been a mere cakewalk.

Now, for the first time in a long, long string of years, he had come across a knot of fear.

Tal thought of Stu Wargle, and the knot of fear pulled tighter, squeezing his guts.

The eyes were eaten right out of his skull.

Fear Itself.

But this boogeyman was real.

Half a year from his thirty-first birthday, Tal Whitman was discovering that he could still be afraid, regardless of how strenuously he denied it. His fearlessness had brought him a long way in life. But, in opposition to all that he had believed before, he realized that there were also times when being afraid was merely being smart.

Shortly before dawn, Lisa woke from a nightmare she couldn't recall.

She looked at Jenny and the others who were sleeping, then turned toward the windows. Outside, Skyline Road was deceptively peaceful as the end of night drew near.

Lisa had to pee. She got up and walked quietly between two rows of mattresses. At the archway, she smiled at the guard, and he winked.

One man was in the dining room. He was paging through a magazine.

In the lobby, two guards were stationed by the elevator doors. The two polished oak front doors of the inn, each with an oval of beveled glass in the center of it, were locked, but a third guard was positioned by that entrance. He was holding a shotgun and staring out through one of the ovals, watching the main approach to the building.

A fourth man was in the lobby. Lisa had met him earlier—a bald, florid-faced deputy named Fred Turpner. He was sitting at the largest desk, monitoring the telephone. It must have rung frequently during the night, for a couple of legal-size sheets of paper were filled with messages. As Lisa passed by, the phone rang again. Fred raised one hand in greeting, then snatched up the receiver.

Lisa went directly to the restrooms, which were tucked into one corner of the lobby:

SNOW BUNNIES   SNOW BUCKS

That cuteness was out of sync with the rest of the Hilltop Inn.

She pushed through the door marked SNOW BUNNIES. The restrooms had been judged safe territory because they had no windows and could be entered only through the lobby, where there were always guards. The women's room was large and clean, with four stalls and sinks. The floor and walls were covered with white ceramic tile bordered by dark blue tile around the edge of the floor and around the top of the walls.

Lisa used the first stall and then the nearest sink. As she finished washing her hands and looked up at the mirror above the sink, she saw him. *Him.* The dead deputy. Wargle.

He was standing behind her, eight or ten feet away, in the middle of the room. Grinning.

She swung around, sure that somehow it was a flaw in the mirror, a trick of the looking glass. Surely he wasn't really there.

But he *was* there. Naked. Grinning obscenely.

His face had been restored: the heavy jowls, the thick-lipped and greasy-looking mouth, the piggish nose, the little quick eyes. The flesh was magically whole again.

Impossible.

Before Lisa could react, Wargle stepped between her and the door. His bare feet made a flat, slapping sound against the tile floor.

Someone was pounding on the door.

Wargle seemed not to hear it.

Pounding and pounding and pounding . . .

Why didn't they just open the door and come in?

Wargle extended his arms and made come-to-me motions with his hands. Grinning.

From the moment Lisa had met him, she hadn't liked Wargle. She had caught him looking at her when he thought her attention was elsewhere, and the expression in his eyes had been unsettling.

"Come here, sweet stuff," he said.

She looked at the door and realized no one was pounding on it. She was only hearing the frantic thump of her own heart.

Wargle licked his lips.

Lisa suddenly gasped, surprising herself. She had been so totally paralyzed by the man's return from the dead that she had forgotten to breathe.

"Come here, you little bitch."

She tried to scream. Couldn't.

Wargle touched himself obscenely.

"Bet you'd like a taste of this, huh?" he said, grinning, his lips moist from his hungrily licking tongue.

Again, she tried to scream. Again, she couldn't. She could barely wrench each badly needed breath into her burning lungs.

He's not real, she told herself.

If she closed her eyes for a few seconds, squeezed them tightly shut and counted to ten, he wouldn't be there when she looked again.

"Little bitch."

He was an illusion. Maybe even part of a dream. Maybe her coming to the bathroom was really just another part of her nightmare.

But she didn't test her theory. She didn't close her eyes and count to ten. She didn't *dare*.

Wargle took a step toward her, still fondling himself.

He isn't real. He's an illusion.

Another step.

He isn't real, he's an illusion.

"Come on, sweet stuff, let me nibble on them titties of yours."

He isn't real he's an illusion he isn't real he's—

"You're gonna love it, sweet stuff."

She backed away from him.

"Cute little body you got, sweet stuff. Real cute."

He continued to advance.

The light was behind him now. His shadow fell on her.

Ghosts didn't throw shadows.

In spite of his laugh and in spite of his fixed grin, his voice became steadily harsher, nastier. "You stupid little slut. I'm gonna use you real good. Real damned good. Better than any of them high school boys ever used you. You ain't gonna be able to walk right for a week when I'm through with you, sweet stuff."

His shadow had completely engulfed her.

Her heart slamming so hard that it seemed about to tear loose, Lisa backed up farther, farther—but soon collided with the wall. She was in a corner.

She looked around for a weapon, something she could at least throw at him. There was nothing.

Each breath was harder to draw than the one before it. She was dizzy and weak.

He isn't real. He's an illusion.

But she couldn't delude herself any longer; she couldn't believe in the dream any more.

Wargle stopped just an arm's length from her. He glared at her. He swayed from side to side, and he rocked back and forth on the balls of his bare feet, as if some mad-dark-private music swelled and ebbed and swelled within him.

He closed his hateful eyes, swaying dreamily.

A second passed.

What's he doing?

Two seconds, three, six, ten.

Still, his eyes remained closed.

She felt herself carried away in a whirlpool of hysteria.

Could she slip past him? While his eyes were closed? Jesus. No. He was too close. To get away, she would have to brush against him. Jesus. Brush against him? No. God, that would snap him out of his trance or whatever this was, and he would seize her, and his hands would be cold, dead-cold. She could not bring herself to touch him. No.

Then she noticed something odd happening behind his eyes. Wriggling movement. The lids themselves no longer conformed to the curvature of his eyeballs.

He opened his eyes.

They were gone.

Beneath the lids lay only empty black sockets.

She finally screamed, but the cry she brought forth was beyond human hearing. Breath passed out of her in an express-train rush, and she felt her throat working convulsively, but there was absolutely no sound that would bring help.

His eyes.

His empty eyes.

She was certain that those hollow sockets could still see her. They sucked at her with their emptiness.

His grin had not faded.

"Little pussy," he said.

She screamed her silent scream.

"Little pussy. Kiss me, little pussy."

Somehow, dark as midnight, those bone-rimmed sockets still held a glimmer of malevolent awareness.

"Kiss me."

No!

Let me die, she prayed. God, please let me die first.

"I want to suck on your juicy tongue," Wargle said urgently, bursting into a giggle.

He reached for her.

She pressed hard against the unyielding wall.

Wargle touched her cheek.

She flinched and tried to pull away.

His fingertips trailed lightly down her cheek.

His hand was icy and slick.

She heard a thin, dry, eerie groan—*"Uh-uh-uh-uh-uhhhhhhh"*— and realized that she was listening to herself.

She smelled something strange, acrid. His breath? The stale breath of a dead man, expelled from rotting lungs? Did the walking dead breathe? The stench was faint but unbearable. She gagged.

He lowered his face toward hers.

She stared into his eaten-away eyes, into the swarming blackness beyond, and it was like peering through two peepholes into the deepest chambers of Hell.

His hand tightened on her throat.

He said, "Give us—"

She heaved in a hot breath.

"—a little kiss."

She heaved out another scream.

This time the scream wasn't silent. This time she pealed forth a sound that seemed loud enough to shatter the restroom mirrors and to crack the ceramic tile.

As Wargle's dead, eyeless face slowly, slowly descended toward her, as she heard her scream echoing off the walls, the whirlpool of hysteria in which she'd been spinning became, now, a whirlpool of darkness, and she was drawn down into oblivion.

CHAPTER 20
BODYSNATCHERS

IN THE LOBBY of the Hilltop Inn, on a rust-colored sofa, against that wall which was farthest from the restrooms, Jennifer Paige sat beside her sister, holding the girl.

Bryce squatted in front of the sofa, holding Lisa's hand, which he couldn't seem to make warm again no matter how firmly he pressed and rubbed it.

Except for the guards on duty, everyone had gathered behind Bryce, in a semicircle around the front of the sofa.

Lisa looked terrible. Her eyes were sunken, guarded, haunted. Her face was as white as the tile floor in the ladies' room, where they had found her unconscious.

"Stu Wargle is dead," Bryce assured her yet again.

"He wanted me t-t-to . . . kiss him," the girl repeated, clinging resolutely to her bizarre story.

"There was no one in the restroom but you," Bryce said. "Just you, Lisa."

"He was *there,*" the girl insisted.

"We came running as soon as you screamed. We found you alone—"

"He was there."

"—on the floor, in the corner, out cold."

"He was there."

"His body is in the utility room," Bryce said, gently squeezing her hand. "We put it there earlier. You remember, don't you?"

"Is it *still* there?" the girl asked. "Maybe you'd better look."

Bryce met Jenny's eyes. She nodded. Remembering that *anything* was possible tonight, Bryce got to his feet, letting go of the girl's hand. He turned toward the utility room.

"Tal?"

"Yeah?"

"Come with me."

Tal drew his revolver.

Pulling his own sidearm from his holster, Bryce said, "The rest of you stay back."

With Tal at his side, Bryce crossed the lobby to the utility room door and paused in front of it.

"I don't think she's the kind of kid who makes up wild stories," Tal said.

"I know she's not."

Bryce thought about how Paul Henderson's corpse had vanished from the substation. Damn it, though, that had been very different from this. Paul's body had been accessible, unguarded. But no one could have gotten to Wargle's corpse—and it couldn't have gotten up and walked away of its own accord—without being seen by one of the three deputies posted in the lobby. Yet no one and nothing *had* been seen.

Bryce moved to the left of the door and motioned Tal over to the right of it.

They listened for several seconds. The inn was silent. There was no sound from within the utility room.

Keeping his body out of the doorway, Bryce leaned forward and reached across the door, took hold of the knob, turned it slowly and silently until it had gone as far as it would go. He hesitated. He glanced over at Tal, who indicated his own readiness. Bryce took a deep breath, threw the door inward, and jumped back, out of the way.

Nothing rushed from the unlighted room.

Tal inched to the edge of the jamb, reached around with one arm, fumbled for the light switch, and found it.

Bryce was crouched down, waiting. The instant the light came on, he launched himself through the doorway, his revolver poked out in front of him.

Stark fluorescent light spilled down from the twin ceiling panels and glinted off the edges of the metal sink and off the bottles and cans of cleaning materials.

The shroud, in which they had wrapped the body, lay in a pile on the floor, beside the table.

Wargle's corpse was missing.

Deke Coover had been the guard stationed at the front doors of the inn. He wasn't much help to Bryce. He had spent a lot of time looking out at Skyline Road, with his back to the lobby. Someone could have carted Wargle's body away without Coover being the wiser.

"You told me to watch the front approach, Sheriff," Deke said. "As long as he didn't accompany himself with a song, Wargle could've come out of there all by his lonesome, doing an old soft-shoe routine and waving a flag in each hand, and he mightn't have attracted my notice."

The two men stationed by the elevators, near the utility room, were Kelly MacHeath and Donny Jessup. They were two of Bryce's younger men, in their mid-twenties, but they were both able, trustworthy, and reasonably experienced.

MacHeath, a blond and beefy fellow with a bull's neck and heavy shoulders, shook his head and said, "Nobody went in or out of the utility room all night."

"Nobody," Jessup agreed. He was a wiry, curly-haired man with eyes the color of tea. "We would've seen them."

"The door's right *there,*" MacHeath observed.

"And we were here all night."

"You know us, Sheriff," MacHeath said.

"You know we aren't slackers," Jessup said.

"When we're supposed to be on duty—"

"—we *are* on duty," Jessup finished.

"Damn it," Bryce said. "Wargle's body is *gone.* It didn't just climb off that table and walk through a wall!"

"It didn't just climb off that table and walk through that door, either," MacHeath insisted.

"Sir," Jessup said, "Wargle was dead. I didn't see the body myself, but from what I hear, he was *very* dead. Dead men stay where you put them."

"Not necessarily," Bryce said. "Not in this town. Not tonight."

In the utility room with Tal, Bryce said, "There's just not another way out of here but the door."

They walked slowly around the room, studying it.

The leaky faucet drooled out a drop of water that struck the pan of the metal sink with a soft *ping.*

"The heating vent," Tal said, pointing to a grille in one wall, directly under the ceiling. "What about that?"

"Are you serious?"

"Better have a look."

"It's not big enough for a man to pass through."

"Remember the burglary at Krybinsky's Jewelry Store?"

"How could I forget? It's still unsolved, as Alex Krybinsky so pointedly reminds me every time we meet."

"That guy entered Krybinsky's basement through an unlocked window almost as small as that grille."

Bryce knew, as did any cop who handled burglaries, that a man of ordinary build required a surprisingly small opening to gain entrance to a building. Any hole large enough to accept a man's head was also large enough to provide an entrance for his entire body. The shoulders were wider than the head, of course, but they could be collapsed forward or otherwise contorted enough to be squeezed through; likewise, the breadth of the hips was nearly always sufficiently alterable to follow where the shoulders had gone. But Stu Wargle hadn't been a man of ordinary build.

"Stu's belly would've stuck in there like a cork in a bottle," Bryce said.

Nevertheless, he pulled up a stepstool that had been standing in one corner, climbed onto it, and took a closer look at the vent.

"The grille's not held in place by screws," he told Tal. "It's a spring-clip model, so it could conceivably have been snapped into place from inside the duct, once Wargle went through, so long as he wriggled in feet-first."

He pulled the grille off the wall.

Tal handed him a flashlight.

Bryce directed the beam into the dark heating duct and frowned. The narrow, metal passageway ran only a short distance before taking a ninety-degree upward turn.

Switching off the flashlight and passing it down to Tal, Bryce said, "Impossible. To get through there, Wargle would have to've been no bigger than Sammy Davis, Jr., and as flexible as the rubber man in a carnival sideshow."

Frank Autry approached Bryce Hammond at the central operations desk in the middle of the lobby, where the sheriff was seated, reading over the messages that had come in during the night.

"Sir, there's something you ought to know about Wargle."

Bryce looked up. "What's that?"

"Well . . . I don't like to have to speak ill of the dead . . ."

"None of us cared much for him," Bryce said flatly. "Any attempt to honor his memory would be hypocritical. So if you know something that'll help me, spill it, Frank."

Frank smiled. "You'd have done real well for yourself in the army." He sat on the edge of the desk. "Last night, when Wargle and I were dismantling the radio over at the substation, he made several disgusting remarks about Dr. Paige and Lisa."

"Sex stuff?"

"Yeah."

Frank recounted the conversation that he'd had with Wargle.

"Christ," Bryce said, shaking his head.

Frank said, "The thing about the girl was what bothered me most. Wargle was half serious when he talked about maybe making a move on her if the opportunity arose. I don't think he'd have gone as far as rape, but he was capable of making a *very* heavy pass and using his authority, his badge, to coerce her. I don't think that kid could be coerced; she's too spunky. But I think Wargle might've tried it."

The sheriff tapped a pencil on the desk, staring thoughtfully into the air.

"But Lisa couldn't have known," Frank said.

"She couldn't have overheard any of your conversation?"

"Not a word."

"She might have suspected what kind of man Wargle was from the way he looked at her."

"But she couldn't have *known,*" Frank said. "Do you see what I'm driving at?"

"Yes."

"Most kids," Frank said, "if they were going to make up a tall tale, they would be satisfied just to say they'd been chased by a dead man. They wouldn't ordinarily embellish it by saying the dead man wanted to molest them."

Bryce tended to agree. "Kids' minds aren't that baroque. Their lies are usually simple, not elaborate."

"Exactly," Frank said. "The fact that she said Wargle was naked and wanted to molest her . . . well . . . to me, that seems to add credibility to her story. Now, we'd all like to believe that someone sneaked into the utility room and stole Wargle's body. And we'd like to believe they put the body in the ladies' room, that Lisa saw it, that she panicked, and that she imagined all the rest. And we'd like to believe that after she fainted, someone got the corpse out of there by some incredibly clever means. But that explanation is full of holes. What happened was a lot stranger than that."

Bryce dropped his pencil and leaned back in his chair. "Shit. You believe in ghosts, Frank? The living dead?"

"No. There's a real explanation for this," Frank said. "Not a bunch of superstitious mumbo-jumbo. A *real* explanation."

"I agree," Bryce said. "But Wargle's face was . . ."

"I know. I saw it."

"How could his face have been put back together?"

"I don't know."

"And Lisa said his eyes . . ."

"Yeah. I heard what she said."

Bryce sighed. "You ever worked Rubik's Cube?"

Frank blinked. "No. I never did."

"Well, I did," the sheriff said. "The damned thing almost drove me crazy, but I stuck with it, and eventually I solved it. Everybody thinks that's a hard puzzle, but compared to this case, Rubik's Cube is a kindergarten game."

"There's another difference," Frank said.

"What's that?"

"If you fail to solve Rubik's Cube, the punishment isn't death."

In Santa Mira, in his cell in the county jail, Fletcher Kale, slayer of wife and son, woke before dawn. He lay motionless on the thin foam mattress and stared at the window, which presented a rectangular slab of the predawn sky for his inspection.

He would not spend his life in prison. Would *not.*

He had a magnificent destiny. That was the thing no one understood. They saw the Fletcher Kale who existed *now,* without being able to see what he would become. He was destined to have it all: money beyond counting, power beyond imagining, fame, respect.

Kale knew he was different from the ruck of mankind, and it was this knowledge that kept him going in the face of all adversity. The seeds of greatness within him were already sprouting. In time, he would make them all see how wrong they had been about him.

Perception, he thought as he stared up at the barred window, perception is my greatest gift. I'm extraordinarily perceptive.

He saw that, without exception, human beings were driven by self-interest. Nothing wrong with that. It was the nature of the species. That was how humankind was *meant* to be. But most people could not bear to face the truth. They dreamed up so-called inspiring concepts like love, friendship, honor, truthfulness, faith, trust, and individual dignity. They claimed to believe in all those things and more; however, at heart, they knew it was all bullshit. They just couldn't admit it. And so, they stupidly hobbled themselves with a smarmy, self-congratulatory code of conduct, with noble but hollow senti- ments, thus frustrating their true desires, dooming themselves to failure and unhappiness.

Fools. God, he despised them.

From his unique perspective, Kale saw that mankind was, in reality, the most ruthless, dangerous, unforgiving species on earth. And he *reveled* in that knowledge. He was proud to be a member of such a race.

I'm ahead of my own time, Kale thought as he sat up on the edge of his bunk and put his bare feet on the cold floor of his cell. I am the next step of evolution. I've evolved beyond the need to believe in morality. That's why they look at me with such loathing. Not because I killed Joanna and Danny. They hate me because I'm better than they are, more completely in touch with my true human nature.

He'd had no choice but to kill Joanna. She had refused to give him the money, after all. She had been prepared to humiliate him professionally, ruin him financially, and wreck his entire future.

He'd *had* to kill her. She was in his way.

It was too bad about Danny. Kale sort of regretted that part. Not always. Just now and then. Too bad. Necessary, but too bad.

Anyway, Danny had always been a regular mama's boy. In fact, he was actually downright distant toward his father. That was Joanna's handiwork. She had probably been brainwashing the kid, turning him against his old man. In the end, Danny really hadn't been Kale's son at all. He'd become a stranger.

Kale got down on the floor of his cell and began to do pushups.

One-two, one-two, one-two.

He intended to keep himself in shape for that moment when an opportunity for escape presented itself. He knew exactly where he would go when he escaped. Not west, not out of the county, not over toward Sacramento. That's what they would expect him to do.

One-two, one-two.

He knew of a perfect hideout. It was right here in the county. They wouldn't be looking for him under their noses. When they couldn't find him in a day or so, they'd decide he had already split, and they'd stop actively looking in this neighborhood. When several more weeks passed, when they weren't thinking about him any longer, *then* he would leave the hideout, double back through town, and head west.

One-two.

But first, he would go up into the mountains. That's where the hideout was. The mountains offered him the best chance of eluding the cops once he'd escaped. He had a hunch about it. The mountains. Yeah. He felt *drawn* to the mountains.

* * *

Dawn came to the mountains, spreading like a bright stain across the sky, soaking into the darkness and discoloring it.

The forest above Snowfield was quiet. Very quiet.

In the underbrush, the leaves were beaded with morning dew. The pleasant odor of rich humus rose up from the spongy forest floor.

The air was chilly, as if the last exhalation of the night still lay upon the land.

The fox stood motionless on a limestone formation that thrust up from an open slope, just below the treeline. The wind gently ruffled his gray fur.

His breath made a small phosphoric plume in the crisp air.

The fox was not a night hunter, yet he had been on the prowl since an hour before dawn. He had not eaten in almost two days.

He had been unable to find game. The woods had been unnaturally silent and devoid of the scent of prey.

In all his seasons as a hunter, the fox had never encountered such barren quietude as this. The most bitter days of midwinter were filled with more promise than this. Even in the wind-whipped snows of January, there was always the blood scent, the game scent.

Not now.

Now there was nothing.

Death seemed to have claimed all the creatures in this part of the forest—except for one small, hungry fox. Yet there was not even the scent of death, not even the ripe stench of a carcass moldering in the underbrush.

But at last, as he had scampered across the low limestone formation, being careful not to set foot in one of the crevices or flute holes that dropped down into the caves beneath, the fox had seen something move on the slope ahead of him, something that had not merely been stirred by the wind. He had frozen on the low rocks, staring uphill at the shadowy perimeter of this new arm of the forest.

A squirrel. Two squirrels. No, there were even more of them than that—five, ten, twenty. They were lined up side by side in the dimness along the treeline.

At first there had been no game whatsoever. Now there was an equally strange abundance of it.

The fox sniffed.

Although the squirrels were only five or six yards away, he could not get their scent.

The squirrels were looking directly at him, but they didn't seem frightened.

The fox cocked his head, suspicion tempering his hunger.

The squirrels moved to their left, all at once, in a tight little group, and then came out of the shadows of the trees, away from the protection of the forest, onto open ground, straight toward the fox. They roiled over and under and around one another, a frantic confusion of brown pelts, a blur of motion in the brown grass. When they came to an abrupt halt, all at the same instant, they were only three or four yards from the fox. And they were no longer squirrels.

The fox twitched and made a hissing sound.

The twenty small squirrels were now four large raccoons.

The fox growled softly.

Ignoring him, one of the raccoons stood on its hind feet and began washing its paws.

The fur along the fox's back bristled.

He sniffed the air.

No scent.

He put his head low and watched the raccoons closely. His sleek muscles grew even more tense than they had been, not because he intended to spring, but because he intended to flee.

Something was very wrong.

All four raccoons were sitting up now, forepaws tucked against their chests, tender bellies exposed.

They were watching the fox.

The raccoon was not usually prey for the fox. It was too aggressive, too sharp of tooth, too quick with its claws. But though it was safe from foxes, the raccoon never enjoyed confrontation; it never flaunted itself as these four were doing.

The fox licked the cold air with his tongue.

He sniffed again and finally *did* pick up a scent.

His ears snapped back flat against his skull, and he snarled.

It wasn't the scent of raccoons. It wasn't the scent of any denizen of the forest that he had ever encountered before. It was an unfamiliar, sharp, unpleasant odor. Faint. But repellent.

This vile odor wasn't coming from any of the four raccoons that posed in front of the fox. He wasn't quite able to make out where it *was* coming from.

Sensing grave danger, the fox whipped around on the limestone, turning away from the raccoons, although he was reluctant to put his back to them.

His paws scraped and his claws clicked on the hard surface as he launched himself down the slope, across the flat weatherworn rock, his tail streaming out behind him. He leaped over a foot-wide crevice in the stone—

—and in midleap he was snatched from the air by something dark and cold and pulsing.

The thing burst up out of the crevice with brutal, shocking force and speed.

The agonized squeal of the fox was sharp and brief.

As quickly as the fox was seized, it was drawn down into the crevice. Five feet below, at the bottom of the miniature chasm, there was a small hole that led into the caves beneath the limestone outcropping. The hole was too small to admit the fox, but the struggling creature was dragged through anyway, its bones snapping as it went.

Gone.

All in the blink of an eye. Half a blink.

Indeed, the fox had been *sucked* into the earth before the echo of its dying cry had even pealed back from a distant hillside.

The raccoons were gone.

Now, a flood of field mice poured onto the smooth slabs of limestone. Scores of them. At least a hundred.

They went to the edge of the crevice.

They stared down into it.

One by one, the mice slipped over the edge, dropped to the bottom, and then went through the small natural opening into the cavern below.

Soon, all the mice were gone, too.

Once again, the forest above Snowfield was quiet.

PART TWO

PHANTOMS

Evil is not an abstract concept. It lives.
It has a form. It stalks. It is too real.
—Dr. Tom Dooley

Phantoms! Whenever I think I fully
understand mankind's purpose on
earth, just when I foolishly imagine
that I have seized upon the meaning of
life . . . suddenly I see phantoms
dancing in the shadows, mysterious
phantoms performing a gavotte that
says, as pointedly as words, "What
you know is nothing, little man; what
you have to learn, immense."
—Charles Dickens

CHAPTER 21

THE BIG STORY

Santa Mira.

Monday—1:02 A.M.

"Hello?"

"Is this the *Santa Mira Daily News?*"

"Yeah."

"The newspaper?"

"Lady, the paper's closed. It's after one in the morning."

"Closed? I didn't know a newspaper ever closed."

"This isn't the *New York Times.*"

"But aren't you printing tomorrow's edition now?"

"The printing's not done here. These are the business and editorial offices. Did you want the printer or what?"

"Well . . . I have a story."

"If it's an obituary or a church bake sale or something, what you do is you call back in the morning, after nine o'clock, and you—"

"No, no. This is a *big* story."

"Oh, a garage sale, huh?"

"What?"

"Never mind. You'll just have to call back in the morning."

"Wait, listen, I work for the phone company."

"That's not such a big story."

"No, see, it's because I work for the phone company that I found out about this thing. Are you the editor?"

"No. I'm in charge of selling ad space."

"Well . . . maybe you can still help me."

"Lady. I'm sitting here on a Sunday night—no, a Monday morning now—all alone in a dreary little office, trying to figure out how the devil to drum up enough business to keep this paper afloat. I am tired. I am irritable—"

"How awful."

"—and I am afraid you'll have to call back in the morning."

"But something terrible has happened in Snowfield. I don't know exactly what, but I know people are dead. There might even be a *lot* of people dead or at least in danger of dying."

"Christ, I must be tireder than I thought. I'm getting interested in spite of myself. Tell me."

"We've rerouted Snowfield's phone service, pulled it off the automatic dialing system, and restricted all ingoing calls. You can only reach two numbers up there now, and both of them are being answered by the sheriff's men. The reason they've set it up that way is to seal the place off before the reporters find out something's up."

"Lady, what've you been drinking?"

"I don't drink."

"Then what've you been smoking?"

"Listen, I know a little bit more. They're getting calls from the Santa Mira sheriff's office all the time, and from the governor's office, and from some military base out in Utah, and they—"

San Francisco.
Monday—1:40 A.M.

"This is Sid Sandowicz. Can I help you?"

"I keep tellin' them I want to talk to a *San Francisco Chronicle* reporter, man."

"That's me."

"Man, you guys have hung up on me three times! What the fuck's the matter with you guys?"

"Watch your language."

"Shit."

"Listen, do you have any idea how many kids like you call up newspapers, wasting our time with silly-ass gags and hot tip hoaxes?"

"Huh? How'd you even know I was a kid?"

" 'Cause you sound twelve."

"I'm fifteen!"

"Congratulations."

"Shit!"

"Listen, son, I've got a boy your age, which is why I'm bothering to listen to you when the other guys wouldn't. So if you've really got something of interest, spill it."

"Well, my old man's a professor at Stanford. He's a virologist and an epidemiologist. You know what that means, man?"

"He studies viruses, disease, something like that."

"Yeah. And he's let himself be corrupted."

"How's that?"

"He accepted a grant from the fuckin' military. Man, he's involved with some biological warfare outfit. It's supposed to be a peaceful application of his research, but you know that's a lot of horseshit. He sold his soul, and now they're finally claimin' it. The shit's hit the fan."

"The fact that your father sold out—if he *did* sell out—might be big news in your family, son, but I'm afraid it wouldn't be of much interest to our readers."

"Hey, man, I didn't call up just to jerk you off. I've got a real *story.* Tonight they came for him. There's a crisis of some kind. I'm supposed to think he had to fly back East on business. I snuck upstairs and listened at their bedroom door while he was layin' it all out for the old lady. There's been some kind of contamination in Snowfield. A big emergency. Everyone's tryin' to keep it secret."

"Snowfield, California?"

"Yeah, yeah. What I figure, man, is that they were secretly runnin' a test of some germ weapon *on our own people* and it got out of hand. Or maybe it was an accidental spill. Somethin' real heavy's goin' down, for sure."

"What's your name, son?"

"Ricky Bettenby. My old man's name is Wilson Bettenby."

"Stanford, you said?"

"Yeah. You gonna follow up on this, man?"

"Maybe there's something to it. But before I start calling people at Stanford, I need to ask you a lot more questions."

"Fire away. I'll tell you whatever I can. I want to blast this wide open, man. I want him to *pay* for sellin' out."

Throughout the night, the leaks sprung one by one. At Dugway, Utah, an army officer, who should have known better, used a pay phone off the base to call New York and spill the story to a much-loved younger brother who was a cub reporter for the *Times.* In bed, after sex, an aide to the governor told his lover, a woman reporter. Those and other holes in the dam caused the flow of information to grow from a trickle to a flood.

By three o'clock in the morning, the switchboard at the Santa Mira County Sheriff's Office was overloaded. By dawn, the newspaper, television, and radio reporters were swarming into Santa Mira. Within a few hours of first light, the street in front of the sheriff's offices was crowded with press cars, camera vans bearing the logos of TV stations in Sacramento and San Francisco, reporters, and curiosity seekers of all ages.

The deputies gave up trying to keep people from congregating in the middle of the street, for there were too many of them to be herded onto the sidewalks. They sealed off the block with sawhorses and turned it into a big open-air press compound. A couple of enterprising kids from a nearby apartment building starting selling Tang, cookies, and—with the aid of the longest series of extension cords anyone could remember seeing—hot coffee. Their refreshment stand became the rumor center, where reporters gathered to share theories and hearsay while they waited for the latest official information handouts.

Other newsmen spread out through Santa Mira, seeking people who had friends or relatives living up in Snowfield, or who were in some way related to the deputies now stationed there. Out at the junction of the state route and Snowfield Road, still other reporters were camping at the police roadblock.

In spite of all this hurly-burly, fully half of the press had not yet arrived.

Many representatives of the Eastern media and the foreign press were still in transit. For the authorities who were trying hard to deal with the mess, the worst was yet to come. By Monday afternoon, it would be a circus.

CHAPTER 22

MORNING IN SNOWFIELD

NOT LONG AFTER dawn, the shortwave radio and the two gasoline-powered electric generators arrived at the roadblock that marked the perimeter of the quarantine zone. The two small vans which bore them were driven by California Highway Patrolmen. They were permitted to pass through the blockade, to a point midway along the four-mile Snowfield Road, where they were parked and abandoned.

When the CHiP officers returned to the roadblock, county deputies radioed a situation report to headquarters in Santa Mira. In turn, headquarters put through a go-ahead call to Bryce Hammond at the Hilltop Inn.

Tal Whitman, Frank Autry, and two other men took a squad car to the midpoint of the Snowfield Road and picked up the abandoned vans. Containment of any possible disease vectors was thus maintained.

The shortwave was set up in one corner of the Hilltop lobby. A message sent to headquarters in Santa Mira was received and answered. Now, if something happened to the telephones, they wouldn't be entirely isolated.

Within an hour, one of the generators had been wired into the circuitry of the streetlamps on the west side of the Skyline Road. The other was spliced into the hotel's electrical system. Tonight, if the main power supply was mysteriously cut off, the generators would kick in automatically. Darkness would last only one or two seconds.

Bryce was confident that not even their unknown enemy could snatch away a victim *that* fast.

Jenny Paige began the morning with an unsatisfactory sponge bath, followed by a completely satisfactory breakfast of eggs, sliced ham, toast, and coffee.

Then, accompanied by three heavily armed men, she went up the street to her house, where she got some fresh clothes for herself and for Lisa. She also stopped in her office, where she gathered up a stethoscope, a sphygmomanometer, tongue depressors, cotton pads, gauze, splints, bandages, tourniquets, antiseptics, disposable hypodermic syringes, painkillers, antibiotics, and other instruments and supplies that she would need in order to establish an emergency infirmary in one corner of the Hilltop Inn's lobby.

The house was quiet.

The deputies kept looking around nervously, entering each new room as if they suspected a guillotine was rigged above the door.

As Jenny was finishing packing up supplies in her office, the telephone rang. They all stared at it.

They knew only two phones in town were working, and both were at the Hilltop Inn.

The phone rang again.

Jenny lifted the receiver. She didn't say hello.

Silence.

She waited.

After a second, she heard the distant cries of sea gulls. The buzzing of bees. The mewling of a kitten. A weeping child. Another child: laughing. A panting dog. The *chicka-chicka-chicka-chicka* sound of a rattlesnake.

Bryce had heard similar things on the phone last night, in the substation, just before the moth had come tapping at the windows. He had said that the sounds had been perfectly ordinary, familiar animal noises. They had nonetheless, unsettled him. He hadn't been able to explain why.

Now Jenny knew exactly what he meant.

Birds singing.

Frogs croaking.

A cat purring.

The purr became a hiss. The hiss became a cat-shriek of anger. The shriek became a brief but terrible squeal of pain.

Then a voice: "I'm gonna shove my big prick into your succulent little sister."

Jenny recognized the voice. Wargle. The dead man.

"You hear me, Doc?"

She said nothing.

"And I don't give a rat's ass which end of her I stick it in." He giggled.

She slammed the phone down.

The deputies looked at her expectantly.

"Uh . . . no one on the line," she said, deciding not to tell them what she had heard. They were already too jumpy.

From Jenny's office, they went to Tayton's Pharmacy on Vail Lane, where she stocked up on more drugs: additional painkillers, a wide spectrum of antibiotics, coagulants, anticoagulants, and anything else she might conceivably need.

As they were finishing in the pharmacy, the phone rang.

Jenny was closest to it. She didn't want to answer, but she couldn't resist.

And *it* was there again.

Jenny waited a moment, then said, "Hello?"

Wargle said, "I'm gonna use your little sister so hard she won't be able to walk for a week."

Jenny hung up.

"Dead line," she told the deputies.

She didn't think they believed her. They stared at her trembling hands.

Bryce sat at the central operations desk, talking by telephone to headquarters in Santa Mira.

The APB on Timothy Flyte had turned up nothing whatsoever. Flyte wasn't wanted by any police agency in the United States or Canada. The FBI had never heard of him. The name on the bathroom mirror at the Candleglow Inn was still a mystery.

The San Francisco police had been able to supply background on the missing Harold Ordnay and wife, in whose room Timothy Flyte's name had been found. The Ordnays owned two bookstores in San Francisco. One was an ordinary retail outlet. The other was an antiquarian and rare book dealership; apparently, it was by far the more profitable of the two. The Ordnays were well known and respected in collecting circles. According to their family, Harold and Blanche had gone to Snowfield for a four-day weekend to celebrate their thirty-first anniversary. The family had never heard of Timothy Flyte. When police were granted permission to look through the Ordnays' personal address book, they found no listing for anyone named Flyte.

The police had not yet been able to locate any of the bookstores' employees; however, they expected to do so as soon as both shops opened at ten o'clock this morning. It was hoped that Flyte was a business acquaintance of the Ordnays' and would be familiar to the employees.

"Keep me posted," Bryce told the morning desk man in Santa Mira. "How're things there?"

"Pandemonium."

"It'll get worse."

As Bryce was putting down the receiver, Jenny Paige returned from her safari in search of drugs and medical equipment. "Where's Lisa?"

"With the kitchen detail," Bryce said.

"She's all right?"

"Sure. There are three big, strong, well-armed men with her. Remember? Is something wrong?"

"Tell you later."

Bryce assigned Jenny's three armed guards to new duties, then helped her establish an infirmary in one corner of the lobby.

"This is probably wasted effort," she said.

"Why?"

"So far no one's been injured. Just killed."

"Well, that could change."

"I think *it* only strikes when it intends to kill. It doesn't take halfway measures."

"Maybe. But with all these men toting guns, and with everyone so damned jumpy, I wouldn't be half surprised if someone accidentally winged someone else or even shot himself in the foot."

Arranging bottles in a desk drawer, Jenny said, "The telephone rang at my place and again over at the pharmacy. It was Wargle." She told him about both calls.

"You're sure it was really him?"

"I remember his voice clearly. An unpleasant voice."

"But, Jenny, he was—"

"I know, I know. His face was eaten away, and his brain was gone, and all the blood was sucked out of him. I know. And it's driving me crazy trying to figure it out."

"Someone doing an impersonation?"

"If it was, then there's someone out there who makes Rich Little look like an amateur."

"Did he sound as if he—"

Bryce broke off in midsentence, and both he and Jenny turned as Lisa ran through the archway.

The girl motioned to them. "Come on! Quick! Something weird is happening in the kitchen."

Before Bryce could stop her, she ran back the way she had come.

Several men started after her, drawing their guns as they went, and Bryce ordered them to halt. "Stay here. Stay on the job."

Jenny had already sprinted after the girl.

Bryce hurried into the dining room, caught up with Jenny, moved ahead of her, drew his revolver, and followed Lisa through the swinging doors into the hotel kitchen.

The three men assigned to this shift of kitchen duty—Gordy Brogan, Henry Wong, and Max Dunbar—had put down their can openers and cooking utensils in favor of their service revolvers, but they didn't know what to aim at. They glanced up at Bryce, looking disconcerted and baffled.

> *"Here we go 'round the mulberry bush,*
> *the mulberry bush, the mulberry bush."*

The air was filled with a child's singing. A little boy. His voice was clear and fragile and sweet.

> *"Here we go 'round the mulberry bush,*
> *so early in the moooorrrrninnnggg!"*

"The sink," Lisa said, pointing.

Puzzled, Bryce went to the nearest of three double sinks. Jenny came close behind him.

The song had changed. The voice was the same:

> *"This old man, he plays one;*
> *he plays nick-nack on my drum.*
> *With a nick-nack, paddywack,*
> *give a dog a bone—"*

The child's voice was coming out of the drain in the sink, as if he were trapped far down in the pipes.

> *"—this old man goes rolling home."*

For metronomic seconds, Bryce listened with spellbound intensity. He was speechless.

He glanced at Jenny. She gave him the same astonished stare that he had seen on his men's faces when he had first pushed through the swinging doors.

"It just started all of a sudden," Lisa said, raising her voice above the singing.

"When?" Bryce asked.

"A couple of minutes ago," Gordy Brogan said.

"I was standing at the sink," Max Dunbar said. He was a burly, hairy, rough-looking man with warm, shy brown eyes. "When the singing started up . . . Jesus, I must've jumped two feet!"

The song changed again. The sweetness was replaced by a cloying, almost mocking piety:

> *"Jesus loves me, this I know,*
> *for the Bible tells me so."*

"I don't like this," Henry Wong said. "How can it be?"

> *"Little ones to Him are drawn.*
> *They are weak, but He is strong."*

Nothing about the singing was overtly threatening; yet, like the noises Bryce and Jenny had heard on the telephone, the child's tender voice, issuing from such an unlikely source, was unnerving. Creepy.

> *"Yes, Jesus loves me.*
> *Yes, Jesus loves me.*
> *Yes, Jesus—"*

The singing abruptly ceased.

"Thank God!" Max Dunbar said with a shudder of relief, as if the child's melodic crooning had been unbearably harsh, grating, off-key. "That voice was drilling right through to the roots of my teeth!"

After several seconds had passed in silence, Bryce began to lean toward the drain, to peer into it—

—and Jenny said maybe he shouldn't—

—and something exploded out of that dark, round hole.

Everyone cried out, and Lisa screamed, and Bryce staggered back in fear and surprise, cursing himself for not being more careful, jerking his revolver up, bringing the muzzle to bear on the thing that came out of the drain.

But it was only water.

A long, high-pressure stream of exceptionally filthy, greasy water shot almost to the ceiling and rained down over everything. It was a short burst, only a second or two, spraying in every direction.

Some of the foul droplets struck Bryce's face. Dark blotches appeared on the front of his shirt. The stuff stank.

It was exactly what you would expect to gush out of a backed-up drain: dirty brown water, threads of gummy sludge, bits of this morning's breakfast scraps which had been run through the garbage disposal.

Gordy got a roll of paper towels, and they all scrubbed at their faces and blotted at the stains on their clothes.

They were still wiping at themselves, still waiting to see if the singing would begin again, when Tal Whitman pushed open one of the swinging doors. "Bryce, we just got a call. General Copperfield and his team reached the roadblock and were passed through a couple of minutes ago."

CHAPTER 23

THE CRISIS TEAM

SNOWFIELD LOOKED FRESHLY scrubbed and tranquil in the crystalline light of morning. A breeze stirred the trees. The sky was cloudless.

Coming out of the inn, with Bryce and Frank and Doc Paige and a few of the others behind him, Tal glanced up at the sun, the sight of which unlocked a memory of his childhood in Harlem. He used to buy penny candy at Boaz's Newsstand, which was at the opposite end of the block from his Aunt Becky's apartment. He favored the lemondrops. They were the prettiest shade of yellow he had ever seen. And now this morning, he saw that the sun was precisely *that* shade of yellow, hanging up there like an enormous lemondrop. It brought back the sights and sounds and smells of Boaz's with surprising force.

Lisa moved up beside Tal, and they all stopped on the sidewalk, facing downhill, waiting for the arrival of the CBW Defense Unit.

Nothing moved at the bottom of the hill. The mountainside was silent. Evidently, Copperfield's team was some distance away.

Waiting in the lemon sunshine, Tal wondered if Boaz's Newsstand was still doing business at its old location. Most likely, it was now just another empty store, filthy and vandalized. Or maybe it was selling magazines, tobacco, and candy only as a front for pushing dope.

As he grew older, he became ever more acutely aware of a tendency toward degeneration in all things. Nice neighborhoods somehow became shabby neighborhoods; shabby neighborhoods became seedy neighborhoods; seedy neighborhoods became slums. Order giving way to chaos. You saw it everywhere these days. More homicides this year than last. Greater and greater abuse of drugs. Spiraling rates of assault, rape, burglary. What saved Tal from being a pessimist about mankind's future was his fervent conviction that good people—people like Bryce, Frank, and Doc Paige; people like his Aunt Becky —could stem the tide of devolution and maybe even turn it back now and then.

But his faith in the power of good people and responsible actions was facing a severe test here in Snowfield. This evil seemed unbeatable.

"Listen!" Gordy Brogan said. "I hear engines."

Tal looked at Bryce. "I thought they weren't expected until around noon. They're three hours early."

"Noon was the latest possible arrival time," Bryce said. "Copperfield wanted to make it sooner if he could. Judging from the conversation I had with him, he's a tough taskmaster, the kind of guy who usually gets exactly what he wants out of his people."

"Just like you, huh?" Tal asked.

Bryce regarded him from under sleepy, drooping eyelids. "Me? Tough? Why, I'm a pussycat."

Tal grinned. "So's a panther."

"Here they come!"

At the bottom of Skyline Road, a large vehicle hove into view, and the sound of its laboring engine grew louder.

There were three large vehicles in the CBW Civilian Defense Unit. Jenny watched them as they crawled slowly up the long, sloped street toward the Hilltop Inn.

Leading the procession was a gleaming, white motor home, a lumbering thirty-six foot behemoth that had been somewhat modified. It had no doors or windows along its flank. The only entrance evidently was at the back. The curved, wraparound windshield of the cab was tinted very dark, so you couldn't see inside, and it appeared to be made of much thicker glass than that used in ordinary motor homes. There was no identification on the vehicle, no project name, no indication that it was army property. The license plate was standard California issue. Anonymity during transport was clearly part of Copperfield's program.

Behind the first motor home came a second. Bringing up the rear was an unmarked truck pulling a thirty-foot, plain gray trailer. Even the truck's windows were tinted, armor-thick glass.

Not certain that the driver of the lead vehicle had seen their group standing in front of the Hilltop, Bryce stepped into the street and waved his arms over his head.

The payloads in the motor homes and in the truck were obviously quite heavy. Their engines strained hard, and they ground their way up the street, moving slower than ten miles an hour, then slower than five, inching, groaning, grinding. When at last they reached the Hilltop, they kept on going, made a right-hand turn at the corner, and swung into the cross street that flanked the inn.

Jenny, Bryce, and the others went around to the side of the inn as the motorcade pulled up to the curb and parked. All of the east-west streets in Snowfield ran across the broad face of the mountain, so that most of them were level. It was much easier to park and secure the three vehicles there than on the steeply sloped Skyline Road.

Jenny stood on the sidewalk, watching the rear door of the first motor home, waiting for someone to come out.

The three overheated engines were switched off, one after the other, and silence fell in with a weight of its own.

Jenny's spirits were higher than they had been since she'd driven into Snowfield last night. The specialists had arrived. Like most Americans, she had enormous faith in specialists, in technology, and in science. In fact, she probably had more faith than most, for she was a specialist herself, a woman of science. Soon, they would understand what had killed Hilda Beck and the Liebermanns and all the others. The specialists had arrived. The cavalry had ridden in at last.

The back door of the truck opened first, and men jumped down. They were dressed for operations in a biologically contaminated atmosphere. They were wearing the white, airtight vinyl suits of the type developed for NASA, with large helmets that had oversize, plexiglass faceplates. Each man carried his own air supply tank on his back, as well as a briefcase-size waste purification and reclamation system.

Curiously, Jenny did not, at first, think of the men as resembling astronauts. They seemed like followers of some strange religion, resplendent in their priestly raiments.

Half a dozen agile men had scrambled out of the truck. More were still coming when Jenny realized that they were heavily armed. They spread out around both sides of their caravan and took up positions between their transport and the people on the sidewalk, facing away from the vehicles. These men weren't scientists. They were support troops. Their names were stenciled on their helmets, just above their faceplates: SGT. HARKER, PVT. FODOR, PVT. PASCALLI, LT. UNDERHILL. They brought up their guns and aimed outward, securing a perimeter in a determined fashion that brooked no interference.

To her shock and confusion, Jenny found herself staring into the muzzle of a submachine gun.

Taking a step toward the troops, Bryce said, "What the hell is the meaning of this?"

Sergeant Harker, nearest to Bryce, swung his gun toward the sky and fired a short burst of warning shots.

Bryce stopped abruptly.

Tal and Frank reached automatically for their own sidearms.

"No!" Bryce shouted. "No shooting, for Christ's sake! We're on the same side."

One of the soldiers spoke. Lieutenant Underhill. His voice issued tinnily from a small radio amplifier in a six-inch-square box on his chest. "Please stay back from the vehicles. Our first duty is to guard the integrity of the labs, and we will do so at all costs."

"Damn it," Bryce said, "we're not going to cause any trouble. I'm the one who called for you in the first place."

"Stay back," Underhill insisted.

The rear door of the first motor home finally opened. The four individuals who came out were also dressed in airtight suits, but they were not soldiers. They moved unhurriedly. They were unarmed. One of them was a woman; Jenny caught a glimpse of a strikingly lovely, female, oriental face. The names on their helmets weren't preceded by designation of rank: BETTENBY, VALDEZ, NIVEN, YAMAGUCHI. These were the civilian physicians and scientists who, in an extreme chemical-biological warfare emergency, walked away from their private lives in Los Angeles, San Francisco, Seattle, and other Western cities, putting themselves at Copperfield's disposal. According to Bryce, there was one such team in the West, one in the East, and one in the Southern-Gulf states.

Six men came out of the second motor home. GOLDSTEIN, ROBERTS, COPPERFIELD, HOUK. The last two were in unmarked suits, no names above their faceplates. They moved up the line, staying behind the armed soldiers, and joined up with Bettenby, Valdez, Niven, and Yamaguchi.

Those ten conducted a brief conversation among themselves, by way of intersuit radio. Jenny could see their lips moving behind their plexiglass visors, but the squawk boxes on their chests did not transmit a word, which meant they had the capability to conduct both public and strictly private discussions. For the time being, they were opting for privacy.

But why? Jenny wondered. They don't have anything to hide from us. Do they?

General Copperfield, the tallest of the twenty, turned away from the group at the rear of the first motor home, stepped onto the sidewalk, and approached Bryce.

Before Copperfield took the initiative, Bryce stepped up to him. "General, I demand to know why we're being held at gunpoint."

"Sorry," Copperfield said. He turned to the stone-faced troopers and said, "Okay, men. It's a no-sweat situation. Parade rest."

Because of the air tanks they were carrying, the soldiers couldn't comfortably assume a classic parade rest position. But, moving with the fluid harmony of a precision drill team, they immediately slung their submachine guns from their shoulders, spread their feet precisely twelve inches apart, put their arms straight down at their sides, and stood motionless, facing forward.

Bryce had been correct when he'd told Tal that Copperfield sounded like a tough taskmaster. It was obvious to Jenny that there was no discipline problem in the general's unit.

Turning to Bryce again, smiling through his faceplate, Copperfield said, "That better?"

"Better," Bryce said. "But I still want an explanation."

"Just SOP," Copperfield said. "Standard Operating Procedure. It's part of the normal drill. We don't have anything against you or your people, Sheriff. You *are* Sheriff Hammond, aren't you? I remember you from the conference in Chicago last year."

"Yes, sir, I'm Hammond. But you *still* haven't given me a suitable explanation. SOP just isn't good enough."

"No need to raise your voice, Sheriff." With one gloved hand, Copperfield tapped the squawk box on his chest. "This thing's not just a speaker. It's also equipped with an extremely sensitive microphone. You see, going into a place where there might be serious biological or chemical contamination, we've got to consider the possibility that we might be overwhelmed by a lot of sick and dying people. Now, we simply aren't equipped to administer cures or even amelioratives. We're a *research* team. Strictly pathology, not treatment. It's our job to find out all we can about the nature of the contaminant, so that properly equipped medical teams can come in right behind us and deal with the survivors. But dying and desperate people might not understand that we can't treat them. They might attack the mobile labs out of anger and frustration."

"And fear," Tal Whitman said.

"Exactly," the general said, missing the irony. "Our psychological stress simulations indicate that it's a very real possibility."

"And if sick and dying people *did* try to disrupt your work," Jenny said, "would you kill them?"

Copperfield turned to her. The sun flashed off his faceplate, transforming it into a mirror, and for a moment she could not see him. Then he shifted slightly, and his face emerged into view again, but not enough of it for her to see what he really looked like. It was a face out of context, framed in the transparent portion of his helmet.

He said, "Dr. Paige, I presume?"

"Yes."

"Well, Doctor, if terrorists or agents of a foreign government committed an act of biological warfare against an American community, it would be up to me and my people to isolate the microbe, identify it, and suggest measures to contain it. That is a sobering responsibility. If we allowed anyone, even the suffering victims, to deter us, the danger of the plague spreading would increase dramatically."

"So," Jenny said, still pressing him, "if sick and dying people *did* try to disrupt your work, you'd kill them."

"Yes," he said flatly. "Even decent people must occasionally choose between the lesser of two evils."

Jenny looked around at Snowfield, which was as much of a graveyard in the morning sun as it had been in the gloom of night. General Copperfield was right. *Anything* he might have to do to protect his team would only be a little evil. The big evil was what had been done—what was still being done—to this town.

She wasn't quite sure why she had been so testy with him.

Maybe it was because she had thought of him and his people as the cavalry, riding in to save the day. She had wanted all the problems to be solved, all the ambiguities cleared up instantly upon Copperfield's arrival. When she'd realized that it wasn't going to work out that way, when they had actually pulled guns on *her*, the dream had faded fast. Irrationally, she had blamed the general.

That wasn't like her. Her nerves must be more badly frayed than she had thought.

Bryce began to introduce his men to the general, but Copperfield interrupted. "I don't mean to be rude, Sheriff, but we don't have time for introductions. Later. Right now, I want to *move*. I want to see all those things you told me about on the phone last night, and then I want to get an autopsy started."

He wants to skip introductions because it doesn't make sense to be chummy with people who may be doomed, Jenny thought. If we develop disease symptoms in the next few hours, if it turns out to be a brain disease, and if we go berserk and try to rush the mobile labs, it'll be easier for him to have us shot if he doesn't know us very well.

Stop it! she told herself angrily.

She looked at Lisa and thought: Good heavens, kid, if I'm this frazzled, what a state *you* must be in. Yet you've kept as stiff an upper lip as anyone. What a damned fine kid to have for a sister.

"Before we show you around," Bryce told Copperfield, "you ought to know about the thing we saw last night and what happened to—"

"No, no," Copperfield said impatiently. "I want to go through it step by step. Just the way you found things. There'll be plenty of time to tell me what happened last night. Let's get moving."

"But, you see, it's beginning to look as if it can't possibly be a disease that's wiped out this town," Bryce protested.

The general said, "My people have come here to investigate possible CBW connections. We'll do that first. *Then* we can consider other possibilities. SOP, Sheriff."

Bryce sent most of his men back into the Hilltop Inn, keeping only Tal and Frank with him.

Jenny took Lisa's hand, and they, too, headed back to the inn.

Copperfield called out to her. "Doctor! Wait a moment. I want you with us. You were the first physician on the scene. If the condition of the corpses has changed, you're the one most likely to notice."

Jenny looked at Lisa. "Want to come along?"

"Back to the bakery? No, thanks." The girl shuddered.

Thinking of the eerily sweet, childlike voice that had come from the sink drain, Jenny said, "Don't go in the kitchen. And if you have to go to the bathroom, ask someone to go along with you."

"Jenny, they're all guys!"

"I don't care. Ask Gordy. He can stand outside the stall with his back turned."

"Jeez, that'd be embarrassing."

"You want to go into that bathroom by yourself again?"

The color drained out of the girl's face. "No way."

"Good. Keep close to the others. And I mean *close.* Not just in the same room. Stay in the same *part* of the room. Promise?"

"Promise."

Jenny thought about the two telephone calls from Wargle this morning. She thought of the gross threats he'd made. Although they had been the threats of a dead man and should have been meaningless, Jenny was frightened.

"You be careful, too," Lisa said.

She kissed the girl on the cheek. "Now hurry and catch up with Gordy before he turns the corner."

Lisa ran, calling ahead: "Gordy! Wait up!"

The tall young deputy stopped at the corner and looked back.

Watching Lisa sprint along the cobblestone sidewalk, Jenny felt her heart tightening.

She thought: What if, when I come back, she's gone? What if I never see her alive again?

CHAPTER 24

COLD TERROR

LIEBERMANN'S BAKERY.

Bryce, Tal, Frank, and Jenny entered the kitchen. General Copperfield and the nine scientists on his team followed closely, and four soldiers, toting submachine guns, brought up the rear.

The kitchen was crowded. Bryce felt uncomfortable. What if they were attacked while they were all jammed together? What if they had to get out in a hurry?

The two heads were exactly where they had been last night: in the ovens, peering through the glass. On the worktable the severed hands still clutched the rolling pin.

Niven, one of the general's people, took several photographs of the kitchen from various angles, then about a dozen closeups of the heads and hands.

The others kept edging around the room to get out of Niven's way. The photographic record had to be completed before the forensic work could begin, which was not unlike the routine policemen followed at the scene of a crime.

As the spacesuited scientists moved, their rubberized clothing squeaked. Their heavy boots scraped noisily on the tile floor.

"You still think it looks like a simple incident of CBW?" Bryce asked Copperfield.

"Could be."

"Really?"

Copperfield said, "Phil, you're the resident nerve gas specialist. Are you thinking what I'm thinking?"

The question was answered by the man whose helmet bore the name HOUK. "It's much too early to tell anything for certain, but it seems as if we could be dealing with a neuroleptic toxin. And there are some things about this—most notably, the extreme psychopathic violence—that lead me to wonder if we've got a case of T-139."

"Definitely a possibility," Copperfield said. "Just what I thought when we walked in."

Niven continued to snap photographs, and Bryce said, "So what's this T-139?"

"One of the primary nerve gases in the Russian arsenal," the general said. "The full moniker is Timoshenko-139. It's named after Ilya Timoshenko, the scientist who developed it."

"What a lovely monument," Tal said sarcastically.

"Most nerve gases cause death within thirty seconds to five minutes after skin contact," Houk said. "But T-139 isn't that merciful."

"Merciful!" Frank Autry said, appalled.

"T-139 isn't just a killer," Houk said. "That *would* be merciful by comparison. T-139 is what military strategists call a demoralizer."

Copperfield said, "It passes through the skin and enters the bloodstream in ten seconds or less, then migrates to the brain and almost instantly causes irreparable damage to cerebral tissues."

Houk said, "For a period of about four to six hours, the victim retains full use of his limbs and a hundred percent of his normal strength. At first, it's only his mind that suffers."

"Dementia paranoides," Copperfield said. "Intellectual confusion, fear, rage, loss of emotional control, and a very strongly held feeling that everyone is plotting against him. This is combined with a fierce compulsion to commit violent acts. In essence, Sheriff, T-139 turns people into mindless killing machines for four to six hours. They prey on one another and on unaffected people outside the area of the gas attack. You can see what an extremely demoralizing effect it would have on an enemy."

"Extremely," Bryce said. "And Dr. Paige theorized just such a disease last night, a mutant rabies that would kill some people while turning others into demented murderers."

"T-139 isn't a disease," Houk said quickly. "It's a nerve gas. And if I had my choice, I'd rather this *was* a nerve gas attack. Once gas has dissipated, the threat is over. A biological threat is considerably harder to contain."

"If it was gas," Copperfield said, "it'll have dissipated long ago, but there'll be traces of it on almost everything. Condensative residue. We'll be able to identify it in no time at all."

They backed against a wall to make way for Niven and his camera.

Jenny said, "Dr. Houk, in regards to this T-139, you mentioned that the ambulatory stage lasts four to six hours. Then what?"

"Well," Houk said, "the second stage is the terminal stage, too. It lasts anywhere from six to twelve hours. It begins with the deterioration of the efferent nerves and escalates to paralysis of the cardiac, vasomotor, and respiratory reflex centers in the brain."

"Good God," Jenny said.

Frank said, "Once more for us laymen."

Jenny said, "It means that during the second stage of the illness, over a period of six to twelve hours, T-139 gradually reduces the brain's ability to regulate the automatic functions of the body—such as breathing, heartbeat, blood vessel dilation, organ function . . . The victim starts experiencing an irregular heartbeat, extreme difficulty in breathing, and the gradual collapse of every gland and organ. Twelve hours might not seem gradual to you, but it would seem like an eternity to the victim. There would be vomiting, diarrhea, uncontrollable urination, continuous and violent muscle spasms . . . And if only the efferent nerves were damaged, if the rest of the nervous system remained intact, there would be excruciating, unrelenting pain."

"Six to twelve hours of hell," Copperfield confirmed.

"Until the heart stops," Houk said, "or until the victim simply stops breathing and suffocates."

For long seconds, as Niven clicked the last of his photographs, no one spoke.

Finally, Jenny said, "I still don't think a nerve gas could've played any part in this, not even something like T-139 that would explain these beheadings. For one thing, none of the victims we found showed any signs of vomiting or incontinence."

"Well," Copperfield said, "we could be dealing with a derivative of T-139 that doesn't produce those symptoms. Or some other gas."

"No gas can explain the moth," Tal Whitman said.

"Or what happened to Stu Wargle," Frank said.

Copperfield said, "Moth?"

"You didn't want to hear about that until you'd seen these other things," Bryce reminded Copperfield. "But now I think it's time you—"

Niven said, "Finished."

"All right," Copperfield said. "Sheriff, Dr. Paige, deputies, if you will please maintain silence until we've completed the rest of our tasks here, your cooperation will be much appreciated."

The others immediately set to work. Yamaguchi and Bettenby transferred the severed heads into a pair of porcelain-lined specimen buckets with locking, airtight lids. Valdez carefully pried the hands away from the rolling pin and put them in a third specimen bucket. Houk scraped some flour off the table and into a small plastic jar, evidently because dry flour would have absorbed— and would still contain—traces of the nerve gas—if, in fact, there had *been* any nerve gas. Houk also took a sample of the pie crust dough that lay under the rolling pin. Goldstein and Roberts inspected the two ovens from which the heads had been removed, and then Goldstein used a small, battery-powered vacuum cleaner to sweep out the first oven. When that was done, Roberts took the bag of sweepings, sealed it, and labeled it, while Goldstein used the vacuum to collect minute and even microscopic evidence from the second oven.

All of the scientists were busy except for the two men who were wearing the suits that had no names on the helmets. They stood to one side, merely watching.

Bryce watched the watchers, wondering who they were and what function they performed.

As the others worked, they described what they were doing and made comments about what they found, always speaking in a jargon that Bryce couldn't follow. No two of them spoke at once; that fact—when coupled with Copperfield's request for silence from those who were not team members— made it seem as if they were speaking for the record.

Among the items that hung from the utility belt around Copperfield's waist there was a tape recorder wired directly into the communications system of the general's suit. Bryce saw that the reels of tape were moving.

When the scientists had gotten everything they wanted from the bakery kitchen, Copperfield said, "All right, Sheriff. Where now?"

Bryce indicated the tape recorder. "Aren't you going to switch that off until we get there?"

"Nope. We started recording from the moment we were allowed past the roadblock, and we'll keep recording until we've found out what's happened to this town. That way, if something goes wrong, if we all die before we find the solution, the new team will know every step we took. They won't have to start from scratch, and they might even have a detailed record of the fatal mistake that got *us* killed."

The second stop was the arts and crafts gallery into which Frank Autry had led the three other men last night. Again, he led the way through the showroom, into the rear office, and up the stairs to the second-floor apartment.

It seemed to Frank that there was almost something comic about the scene: all these spacemen lumbering up the narrow stairs, their faces theatrically grim behind plexiglass faceplates, the sound of their breathing amplified by the closed spaces of their helmets and projected out of the speakers on their chests at an exaggerated volume, an ominous sound. It was like one of those 1950s science fiction movies—*Attack of the Alien Astronauts* or something equally corny—and Frank couldn't help smiling.

But his vague smile vanished when he entered the apartment kitchen and saw the dead man again. The corpse was where it had been last night, lying at the foot of the refrigerator, wearing only blue pajama bottoms. Still swollen, bruised, staring wide-eyed at nothing.

Frank moved out of the way of Copperfield's people and joined Bryce beside the counter where the toaster oven stood.

As Copperfield again requested silence from the uninitiated, the scientists stepped carefully around the sandwich fixings that were scattered across the floor. They crowded around the corpse.

In a few minutes they were finished with a preliminary examination of the body.

Copperfield turned to Bryce and said, "We're going to take this one for an autopsy."

"You still think it looks as if we're dealing with just a simple incident of CBW?" Bryce asked, as he had asked before.

"It's entirely possible, yes," the general said.

"But the bruising and swelling," Tal said.

"Could be allergic reactions to a nerve gas," Houk said.

"If you'll slide up the leg of the pajamas," Jenny said, "I believe you'll find that the reaction extends even to unexposed skin."

"Yes, it does," Copperfield said. "We've already looked."

"But how could the skin react even where no nerve gas came into contact with it?"

"Such gases usually have a high penetration factor," Houk said. "They'll pass right through most clothes. In fact, about the only thing that'll stop many of them is vinyl or rubber garments."

Just what you're wearing, Frank thought, and just what we're not.

"There's another body here," Bryce told the general. "Do you want to have a look at that one, too?"

"Absolutely."

"It's this way, sir," Frank said.

He led them out of the kitchen and down the hall, his gun drawn.

Frank dreaded entering the bedroom where the dead woman lay naked in the rumpled sheets. He remembered the crude things that Stu Wargle had said about her, and he had the terrible feeling that Stu was going to be there now, coupled with the blonde, their dead bodies locked in cold and timeless passion.

But only the woman was there. Sprawled on the bed. Legs still spread wide. Mouth open in an eternal scream.

When Copperfield and his people had finished a preliminary examination of the corpse and were ready to go, Frank made sure they had seen the .22 automatic which she had apparently emptied at her killer. "Do you think she would have shot at just a cloud of nerve gas, General?"

"Of course not," Copperfield said. "But perhaps she was already affected by the gas, already brain damaged. She could have been shooting at hallucinations, at phantoms."

"Phantoms," Frank said. "Yes, sir, that's just about what they would've had to've been. Because, see, she fired all ten shots in the clip, yet we found only two expended slugs—one in that highboy over there, one in the wall where you see the hole. That means she mostly hit whatever she was shooting at."

"I knew these people," Doc Paige said, stepping forward. "Gary and Sandy Wechlas. She was something of a markswoman. Always target shooting. She won several competitions at the county fair last year."

"So she had the skill to make eight hits out of ten," Frank said. "And even eight hits didn't stop the thing she was trying to stop. Eight hits didn't even make it bleed. Of course, phantoms don't bleed. But, sir, would a phantom be able to walk out of here *and take those eight slugs with it?*"

Copperfield stared at him, frowning.

All the scientists were frowning, too.

The soldiers weren't only frowning, they were looking around uneasily.

Frank could see that the condition of the two bodies—especially the woman's nightmarish expression—had had an effect on the general and his people. The fear in everyone's eyes was sharper now. Although they didn't want to admit it, they had encountered something beyond their experience. They were still clinging to explanations that made sense to them—nerve gas, virus, poison —but they were beginning to have doubts.

Copperfield's people had brought a zippered plastic body bag with them. In the kitchen, they slipped the pajama-clad corpse into the bag, then carried it out of the building and left it on the sidewalk, intending to pick it up again on the way back to the mobile labs.

Bryce led them to Gilmartin's Market. Inside, back by the milk coolers where it had happened, he told them about Jake Johnson's disappearance. "No screams. No sound at all. Just a few seconds of darkness. *A few seconds.* But when the lights came on again, Jake was gone."

Copperfield said, "You looked—"

"Everywhere."

"He could have run away," Roberts said.

"Yes," Dr. Yamaguchi said. "Maybe he deserted. Considering the things he'd seen . . ."

"My God," Goldstein said, "what if he left Snowfield? He might be beyond the quarantine line, carrying the infection—"

"No, no, no. Jake wouldn't desert," Bryce said. "He wasn't exactly the most aggressive officer on the force, but he wouldn't run out on me. He wasn't irresponsible."

"Definitely not," Tal agreed. "Besides, Jake's old man was once county sheriff, so there's a lot of family pride involved."

"And Jake was a cautious man," Frank said. "He didn't do anything on impulse."

Bryce nodded. "Anyway, even if he was spooked enough to run, he'd have taken a squad car. He sure wouldn't have *walked* out of town."

"Look," Copperfield said, "he'd have known they wouldn't let him past the roadblock, so he'd have avoided the highway altogether. He might have gone off through the woods."

Jenny shook her head. "No, General. The land is *wild* out there. Deputy Johnson would've known he'd get lost and die."

"And," Bryce said, "would a frightened man plunge pell-mell into a strange forest at night? I don't think so, General. But I *do* think it's time you heard about what happened to my other deputy."

Leaning against a cooler full of cheese and lunchmeat, Bryce told them about the moth, about the attack on Wargle and the bloodcurdling condition of the corpse. He told them about Lisa's encounter with a resurrected Wargle and about the subsequent discovery that the body was missing.

Copperfield and his people expressed astonishment at first, then confusion, then fear. But during most of Bryce's tale, they stared at him in wary silence and glanced at one another knowingly.

He finished by telling them about the child's voice that had come from the kitchen drain just moments before their arrival. Then, for the third time, he said, "Well, General, do you *still* think it looks like a simple incident of CBW?"

Copperfield hesitated, looked around at the littered market, finally met

Bryce's eyes, and said, "Sheriff, I want Dr. Roberts and Dr. Goldstein to give complete physical examinations to you and to everyone who saw this . . . uh . . . moth."

"You don't believe me."

"Oh, I believe that you genuinely, sincerely *think* you saw all of those things."

"Damn," Tal said.

Copperfield said, "Surely, you can understand that, to us, it sounds as if you've all been contaminated, as if you're suffering from hallucinations."

Bryce was weary of their disbelief and frustrated by their intellectual rigidity. As scientists, they were supposed to be receptive to new ideas and unexpected possibilities. Instead, they appeared determined to *force* the evidence to conform to their preconceived notions of what they would find in Snowfield.

"You think we all could've had the *same* hallucination?" Bryce asked.

"Mass hallucinations aren't unknown," Copperfield said.

"General," Jenny said, "there was absolutely nothing hallucinatory about what we saw. It had the gritty texture of reality."

"Doctor Paige, I would ordinarily accord considerable weight to any observation you cared to make. But as one of those who claim to have *seen* this moth, your medical judgment in the matter simply isn't objective."

Scowling at Copperfield, Frank Autry said, "But, sir, if it was all just something we hallucinated—then where is Stu Wargle?"

"Maybe both he *and* this Jake Johnson ran out on you," Roberts said. "And maybe you've merely incorporated their disappearances into your delusions."

From long experience, Bryce knew that a debate was always lost the moment you became emotional. He forced himself to remain in a relaxed position, leaning against the cooler. Keeping his voice soft and slow, he said, "General, from the things you and your people have said, someone could get the idea that the Santa Mira County Sheriff's Department is staffed exclusively by cowards, fools, and goldbrickers."

Copperfield made placating gestures with his rubber-sheathed hands. "No, no, no. We're not saying anything of the kind. Please, Sheriff, try to understand. We're only being straightforward with you. We're telling you how the situation looks to us—how it would look to *anyone* with any specialized knowledge of chemical and biological warfare. Hallucination is one of the things we expect to find in survivors. It's one of the things we *have* to look for. Now, if you could offer us a logical explanation for the existence of this eagle-size moth . . . well, maybe then we could come to believe in it ourselves. But you can't. Which leaves our suggestion—that you merely hallucinated it—as the only explanation that makes sense."

Bryce noticed the four soldiers staring at him in a much different way now that he was thought to be a victim of nerve gas. After all, a man suffering from bizarre hallucinations was obviously unstable, dangerous, perhaps even violent enough to cut off people's heads and pop them into bakery ovens. The soldiers raised their submachine guns an inch or two, although they didn't actually aim at Bryce. They regarded him—and Jenny and Tal and Frank—with a new and unmistakable air of suspicion.

Before Bryce could respond to Copperfield, he was startled by a loud noise at the back of the market, beyond the butcher's-block tables. He stepped away from the cooler, turned toward the source of the commotion, and put his right hand on his holstered revolver.

Out of the corner of his eye, he saw two soldiers reacting to him rather than to the noise. When he had put his hand on his revolver, they had instantly raised their submachine guns.

It was a hammering sound that had drawn his attention. And a voice. Both were coming from within the walk-in meat locker, on the other side of the butcher's work area, no more than fifteen feet away, almost directly opposite the point at which Bryce and the others were gathered. The thick, insulated door of the locker muffled the blows that were being rained on it, but they were still loud. The voice was muffled, too, the words unclear, but Bryce thought he could hear someone shouting for help.

"Somebody's trapped in there," Copperfield said.

"Can't be," Bryce said.

Frank said, "Can't be locked in because the door opens from both sides."

The hammering and shouting ceased abruptly.

A clatter.

A rattle of metal on metal.

The handle on the large, burnished-steel door moved up, down, up, down, up . . .

The latch clicked. The door swung open. But only a couple of inches. Then it stopped.

The refrigerated air inside the locker rushed out, mixing with the warmer air in the market. Tendrils of frosty vapor rose along the length of the open door.

Although the light was on in the room beyond the door, Bryce couldn't see anything through the narrow gap. Nevertheless, he knew what the refrigerated meat locker looked like. During last night's search for Jake Johnson, Bryce had been in there, poking around. It was a frigid, windowless, claustrophobic place, about twelve by fifteen feet. There was one other door—equipped with two deadbolt locks—that opened onto the alley for the easy receival of meat deliveries. A painted concrete floor. Sealed concrete walls. Fluorescent lights. Vents in three of the walls circulated cold air around the sides of beef, veal, and slabs of pork that hung from the ceiling racks.

Bryce could hear nothing except the amplified breathing of the scientists and soldiers in the decontamination suits, and even that was subdued; some of them seemed to be holding their breath.

Then from within the locker came a groan of pain. A pitifully weak voice cried out for help. Rebounding from the cold concrete walls, carried on the spiraling thermals of air that escaped through the narrowly opened door, the voice was shaky, echo-distorted, yet recognizable.

"Bryce . . . Tal . . . ? Who's out there? Frank? Gordy? Is somebody out there? Can . . . somebody . . . help me?"

It was Jake Johnson.

Bryce, Jenny, Tal, and Frank stood very still, listening.

Copperfield said, "Whoever it is, he needs help badly."

"Bryce . . . please . . . somebody . . ."

"You know him?" Copperfield asked. "He's calling your name—isn't he, Sheriff?"

Without waiting for an answer, the general ordered two of his men—Sergeant Harker and Private Pascalli—to look in the meat locker.

"Wait!" Bryce said. "Nobody goes back there. We're keeping these coolers between us and that locker until we know more."

"Sheriff, while I fully intend to cooperate with you as far as possible, you have no authority over my men or me."

"Bryce . . . it's me . . . Jake . . . For God's sake, help me. I broke my damned leg."

"Jake?" Copperfield asked, squinting curiously at Bryce. "You mean that man in there is the same one you said was snatched away from here last night?"

"Somebody . . . help . . . Jesus, it's c-cold . . . so c-c-cold."

"It sounds like him," Bryce admitted.

"Well, there you are!" Copperfield said. "Nothing mysterious about it, after all. He's been right here all this time."

Bryce glared at the general. "I told you we searched everywhere last night. Even in the goddamned meat locker. He wasn't there."

"Well, he is now," the general said.

"Hey, out there! I'm c-cold. Can't m-m-move this . . . damned leg!"

Jenny touched Bryce's arm. "It's wrong. It's all wrong."

Copperfield said, "Sheriff, we can't just stand here and allow an injured man to suffer."

"If Jake had really been in there all night," Frank Autry said, "he would've frozen to death by now."

"Well, if it's a meat locker," Copperfield said, "then the air inside isn't freezing. It's just cold. If the man was warmly dressed he might easily have survived this long."

"But how'd he get in there in the first place?" Frank asked. "What the devil's he been *doing* in there?"

"And he wasn't in there last night," Tal said impatiently.

Jake Johnson called for help again.

"There's danger here," Bryce told Copperfield. "I sense it. My men sense it. Dr. Paige senses it."

"I don't," Copperfield said.

"General, you just haven't been in Snowfield long enough to understand that you've got to expect the utterly unexpected."

"Like moths the size of eagles?"

Biting back his anger, Bryce said, "You haven't been here long enough to understand that . . . well . . . nothing's quite what it seems."

Copperfield studied him skeptically. "Don't get mystical on me, Sheriff."

In the meat locker, Jake Johnson began to cry. His whimpering pleas were awful to hear. He sounded like a pain-racked, terrified old man. He didn't sound the least bit dangerous.

"We've got to help that man *now,* " Copperfield said.

"I'm not risking my men," Bryce said. "Not yet."

Copperfield again ordered Sergeant Harker and Private Pascalli to look in the meat locker. Although it was obvious from his demeanor that he didn't think there was much danger for men armed with submachine guns, he told them to proceed with caution. The general still believed the enemy was something as small as a bacterium or molecule of nerve gas.

The two soldiers hurried along the rows of coolers toward the gate that led into the butcher's work area.

Frank said, "If Jake could open the door, why couldn't he push it *completely* open and let us see him?"

"He probably used up the last of his strength just getting the door unlatched," Copperfield said. "You can hear it in his voice, for God's sake. Utter exhaustion."

Harker and Pascalli went through the gate, behind the coolers.

Bryce's hand tightened on the butt of his holstered revolver.

Tal Whitman said, "There's too much wrong with this setup, damn it. If it's really Jake, if he needs help, why did he wait until *now* to open the door?"

"The only way we'll find out is to ask him," the general said.

"No, I mean, there's an outside entrance to that locker," Tal said. "He could've opened the door earlier and shouted out into the alley. As quiet as this town is, we'd have heard him all the way over at the Hilltop."

"Maybe he's been unconscious until now," Copperfield said.

Harker and Pascalli were moving past the worktables and the electric meat saw.

Jake Johnson called out again: *"Is someone . . . coming? Is someone . . . coming now?"*

Jenny began to raise another objection, but Bryce said, "Save your breath."

"Doctor," Copperfield said, "can you actually expect us to just ignore the man's cries for help?"

"Of course not," she said. "But we ought to take time to think of a *safe* way of having a look in there."

Shaking his head, Copperfield interrupted her: "We've got to attend to him without delay. *Listen* to him, Doctor. He's hurt bad."

Jake was moaning in pain again.

Harker moved toward the meat locker door.

Pascalli dropped back a couple of paces and over to one side, covering his sergeant as best he could.

Bryce felt the muscles bunching with tension in his back, across his shoulders, and in his neck.

Harker was at the door.

"No," Jenny said softly.

The locker door was hinged to swing inward. Harker reached out with the barrel of his submachine gun and shoved the door all the way open. The cold hinges rasped and squealed.

That sound sent a shiver through Bryce.

Jake wasn't sprawled in the doorway. He wasn't anywhere in sight.

Past the sergeant, nothing could be seen except the hanging sides of beef: dark, fat-mottled, bloody.

Harker hesitated—

(Don't do it! Bryce thought.)

—and then plunged through the doorway. He crossed the threshold in a crouch, looking left and swinging the gun that way, then almost instantly looking right and bringing the muzzle around.

To his right, Harker saw something. He jerked upright in surprise and fear. Stumbling hastily backwards, he collided with a side of beef. *"Holy shit!"*

Harker punctuated his cry with a short burst of fire from his submachine gun.

Bryce winced. The boom-rattle of the weapon was thunderous.

Something pushed against the far side of the meat locker door and slammed it shut.

Harker was trapped in there with it. *It.*

"Christ!" Bryce said.

Not wasting the time it would have taken to run to the gate, Bryce clambered up onto the waist-high cooler in front of him, stepping on packets of Kraft Swiss cheese and wax-encased gouda. He scrambled across and dropped off the other side, into the butcher's area.

Another burst of gunfire. Longer this time. Maybe even long enough to empty the gun's magazine.

Pascalli was at the locker door, struggling frantically with the handle.

Bryce rounded the worktables. "What's wrong?"

Private Pascalli looked too young to be in the army—and very scared.

"Let's get him the hell out of there!" Bryce said.

"Can't! This fucker won't open!"

Inside the meat locker, the gunfire stopped.

The screaming began.

Pascalli wrenched desperately at the unrelenting handle.

Although the thick, insulated door muffled Harker's screams, they were nevertheless loud, and they swiftly grew even louder. Coming through the walkie-talkie built into Pascalli's suit, the agonized wailing must have been deafening, for the private suddenly put a hand to his helmeted head as if trying to block out the sound.

Bryce pushed the soldier aside. He gripped the long, lever-action door handle with both hands. It wouldn't budge up or down.

In the locker, the piercing screams rose and fell and rose, getting louder and shriller and more horrifying.

What in the hell is it *doing* to Harker? Bryce wondered. Skinning the poor bastard alive?

He looked toward the coolers. Tal had scrambled over the display case and was coming on the double. The general and another soldier, Private Fodor, were rushing through the gate. Frank had jumped onto one of the coolers but was facing out toward the main part of the store, guarding against the possibility that the commotion at the meat locker was just a diversion. Everyone else was still standing in a group, in the aisle beyond the coolers.

Bryce shouted, "Jenny!"

"Yeah?"

"Does this store have a hardware section?"

"Odds and ends."

"I need a screwdriver."

"Can do." She was already running.

Harker screamed.

Jesus, what a terrible cry it was. Out of a nightmare. Out of a lunatic asylum. Out of Hell.

Just listening to it caused Bryce to break out in a cold sweat.

Copperfield reached the locker. "Let me at that handle."

"It's no use."

"Let me at it!"

Bryce got out of the way.

The general was a big brawny man—the biggest man here, in fact. He looked strong enough to uproot century-old oaks. Straining, cursing, he moved the door handle no farther than Bryce had done.

"The goddamned latch must be broken or bent," Copperfield said, panting.

Harker screamed and screamed.

Bryce thought of Liebermann's Bakery. The rolling pin on the table. The hands. The severed hands. This was the way a man might scream while he watched his hands being cut off at the wrists.

Copperfield pounded on the door in rage and frustration.

Bryce glanced at Tal. This was a first: Talbert Whitman visibly frightened.

Calling to Bryce, Jenny came through the gate. She had three screwdrivers, each of them sealed in a brightly colored cardboard and plastic package.

"Didn't know which size you needed," she said.

"Okay," Bryce said, reaching for the tools, "now get out of here fast. Go back with the others."

Ignoring his command, she gave him two of the screwdrivers, but she held on to the third.

Harker's screams had become so shrill, so awful, that they no longer sounded human.

As Bryce ripped open one package, Jenny tore the third bright yellow container to shreds and extracted the screwdriver from it.

"I'm a doctor. I stay."

"He's beyond any doctor's help," Bryce said, frantically tearing open the second package.

"Maybe not. If you thought there wasn't a chance, you wouldn't be trying to get him out of there."

"Damn it, Jenny!"

He was worried about her, but he knew he wouldn't be able to persuade her to leave if she had already made up her mind to stay.

He took the third screwdriver from her, shouldered past General Copperfield, and returned to the door.

He couldn't remove the door's hinge pins. It swung into the locker, so the hinges were on the inside.

But the lever-action handle fitted through a large cover plate behind which lay the lock mechanism. The plate was fastened to the face of the door by four screws. Bryce hunkered down in front of it, selected the most suitable screwdriver, and removed the first screw, letting it drop to the floor.

Harker's screaming stopped.

The ensuing silence was almost worse than the screams.

Bryce removed the second, third, and fourth screws.

There was still no sound from Sergeant Harker.

When the cover plate was loose, Bryce slid it along the handle, pulled it free, and discarded it. He squinted at the guts of the lock, probed at the mechanism with the screwdriver. In response, ragged bits of torn metal popped out of the lock; other pieces rattled down through a hollow space in the interior of the door. The lock had been thoroughly mangled *from within the door.* He found the manual release slot in the shaft of the latch bolt, slid the screwdriver through it, pulled to the right. The spring seemed to have been badly bent or sprung, for there was very little play left in it. Nevertheless, he drew the bolt back far enough to bring it out of the hole in the jamb, then pushed inward. Something clicked; the door started to swing open.

Everyone, including Bryce, backed out of the way.

The door's own weight contributed sufficiently to its momentum, so that it continued to swing slowly, slowly inward.

Private Pascalli was covering it with his submachine gun, and Bryce drew his own handgun, as did Copperfield, although Sergeant Harker had conclusively proved that such weapons were useless.

The door swung all the way open.

Bryce expected something to rush out at them. Nothing did.

Looking through the doorway and across the locker, he could see that the outer door was open, too, which it definitely hadn't been when Harker had gone inside a couple of minutes ago. Beyond it lay the sun-splashed alleyway.

Copperfield ordered Pascalli and Fodor to secure the locker. They went through the door fast, one turning to the left, the other to the right, out of sight.

In a few seconds, Pascalli returned. "It's all clear, sir."

Copperfield went into the locker, and Bryce followed.

Harker's submachine gun was lying on the floor.

Sergeant Harker was hanging from the ceiling meat rack, next to a side of beef—hanging on an enormous, wickedly pointed, two-pronged meat hook that had been driven through his chest.

Bryce's stomach heaved. He started to turn away from the hanging man—and then realized it wasn't really Harker. It was only the sergeant's decontamination suit and helmet, hanging slack, empty. The tough vinyl fabric was slashed. The plexiglass faceplate was broken and torn half out of the rubber gasket into which it had been firmly set. Harker had been pulled from the suit before it had been impaled.

But where was Harker?

Gone.

Another one. Just gone.

Pascalli and Fodor were out on the loading platform, looking up and down the alleyway.

"All that screaming," Jenny said, stepping up beside Bryce, "yet there's no blood on the floor or on the suit."

Tal Whitman scooped up several expended shell casings that had been spat out by the submachine gun; scores of them littered the floor. The brass casings gleamed in his open palm. "Lots of these, but I don't see many slugs. Looks like the sergeant hit what he was shooting at. Must've scored at least a hundred hits. Maybe two hundred. How many rounds are in one of those big magazines, General?"

Copperfield stared at the shiny casings but didn't answer.

Pascalli and Fodor came back in from the loading platform, and Pascalli said, "There's no sign of him out there, sir. You want us to search farther along the alley?"

Before Copperfield could respond, Bryce said, "General, you've got to write off Sergeant Harker, painful as that might be. He's dead. Don't hold out any hope for him. Death is what this is all about. *Death.* Not hostage-taking. Not terrorism. Not nerve gas. There's nothing halfway about this. We're playing for all the marbles. I don't know exactly what the hell's out there or where it came from, but I do know that it's Death personified. Death is out there in some form we can't even imagine yet, driven by some purpose we might never understand. The moth that killed Stu Wargle—that wasn't even the true appearance of this thing. I *feel* it. The moth was like the reanimation of Wargle's body, when he went after Lisa in the restroom: It was a bit of misdirection . . . sleight-of-hand."

"A phantom," Tal said, using the word that Copperfield had introduced with somewhat different meaning.

"A phantom, yes," Bryce said. "We haven't yet encountered the real enemy. It's something that just plain likes to kill. It can kill quickly and silently, the way it took Jake Johnson. But it killed Harker more slowly, hurting him real bad, making him scream. Because it wanted us to hear those screams. Harker's murder was sort of like what you said about T-139: It was a demoralizer. This thing didn't carry Sergeant Harker away. It got him, General. *It* got him. Don't risk the lives of more men searching for a corpse."

Copperfield was silent for a moment. Then he said, "But the voice we heard. It was *your* man, Jake Johnson."

"No," Bryce said. "I don't think it really was Jake. It sounded like him, but now I'm beginning to suspect we're up against something that's a terrific mimic."

"Mimic?" Copperfield said.

Jenny looked at Bryce. "Those animal sounds on the telephone."

"Yeah. The cats, dogs, birds, rattlesnakes, the crying child . . . It was almost like a performance. As if it were bragging: 'Hey, look what I can do; look how clever I am.' Jake Johnson's voice was just one more impersonation in its repertoire."

"What are you proposing?" Copperfield asked. "Something supernatural?"

"No. This is real."

"Then what? Put a name to it," Copperfield demanded.

"I *can't*, damn it," Bryce said. "Maybe it's a natural mutation or even something that came out of a genetic engineering lab somewhere. You know anything about that, General? Maybe the army's got an entire goddamned division of geneticists creating biological fighting machines, man-made monsters designed to slaughter and terrorize, creatures stitched together from the DNA of half a dozen animals. Take some of the genetic structure of the tarantula and combine it with some of the genetic structure of the crocodile, the cobra, the wasp, maybe even the grizzly bear, and then insert the genes for human intelligence just for the hell of it. Put it all in a test tube; incubate it; nurture it. What would you get? What would it look like? Do I sound like a raving lunatic for even proposing such a thing? Frankenstein with a modern twist? Have they actually gone that far with recombinant DNA research? Maybe I shouldn't even have ruled out the supernatural. What I'm trying to say, General, is that it could be *anything*. That's why I can't put a name to it. Let your imagination run wild, General. No matter what hideous thing you conjure up, we can't rule it out. We're dealing with the unknown, and the unknown encompasses all our nightmares."

Copperfield stared at him, then looked up at Sergeant Harker's suit and helmet which hung from the meat hook. He turned to Pascalli and Fodor. "We won't search the alley. The sheriff is probably right. Sergeant Harker is lost, and there's nothing we can do for him."

For the fourth time since Copperfield had arrived in town, Bryce said, "Do you *still* think it looks as if we're dealing with just a simple incident of CBW?"

"Chemical or biological agents might be involved," Copperfield said. "As you observed, we can't rule out anything. But it's not a simple case. You're right about that, Sheriff. I'm sorry for suggesting you were only hallucinating and—"

"Apology accepted," Bryce said.

"Any theories?" Jenny asked.

"Well," Copperfield said, "I want to start the first autopsy and pathology tests right away. Maybe we won't find a disease or a nerve gas, but we still might find something that'll give us a clue."

"You'd better do that, sir," Tal said. "Because I have a hunch that time is running out."

CHAPTER 25
QUESTIONS

🌠////🌠

CORPORAL BILLY VELAZQUEZ, one of General Copperfield's support troops, climbed down through the manhole, into the storm drain. Although he hadn't exerted himself, he was breathing hard. Because he was scared.

What had happened to Sergeant Harker?

The others had come back, looking stunned. Old man Copperfield said Harker was dead. He said they weren't quite sure what had killed Sarge, but they intended to find out. Man, that was bullshit. They must know what killed him. They just didn't want to say. That was typical of the brass, making secrets of everything.

The ladder descended through a short section of vertical pipe, then into the main horizontal drain. Billy reached the bottom. His booted feet made hard, flat sounds when they struck the concrete floor.

The tunnel wasn't high enough to allow him to stand erect. He crouched slightly and swept his flashlight around.

Gray concrete walls. Telephone and power company pipes. A little moisture. Some fungus here and there. Nothing else.

Billy stepped away from the ladder as Ron Peake, another member of the support squad, came down into the drain.

Why hadn't they at least brought Harker's body back with them when they'd returned from Gilmartin's Market?

Billy kept shining his flashlight around and glancing nervously behind him.

Why had old Iron Ass Copperfield kept stressing the need to be watchful and careful down here?

Sir, what're we supposed to be on the lookout for? Billy had asked.

Copperfield had said, *Anything. Everything. I don't know if there's any danger or not. And even if there is, I don't know exactly what to tell you to look for. Just be damned cautious. And if anything moves down there, no matter how innocent it looks, even if it's just a mouse, get your asses out of there fast.*

Now what the hell kind of answer was that?

Jesus.

It gave him the creeps.

Billy wished he'd had a chance to talk to Pascalli or Fodor. They weren't the damned brass. They would give him the whole story about Harker—if he ever got a chance to ask them about it.

Ron Peake reached the bottom of the ladder. He looked anxiously at Billy.

Velazquez directed the flashlight all the way around them in order to show the other man there was nothing to worry about.

Ron switched on his own flash and smiled self-consciously, embarrassed by his jumpiness.

The men above began to feed a power cable through the open manhole. It led back to the two mobile laboratories, which were parked a few yards from the entrance to the drain.

Ron took the end of the cable, and Billy, shuffling forward in a crouch, led the way east. On the street above, the other men paid out more cable into the drain.

This tunnel should intersect an equally large or perhaps larger conduit under the main street, Skyline Road. At that point there ought to be a power company junction box where several strands of the town's electrical web were joined together. As Billy proceeded with all the caution that Copperfield had suggested, he played the beam of his flashlight over the walls of the tunnel, looking for the power company's insignia.

The junction box was on the left, five or six feet this side of the intersection of the two conduits. Billy walked past it, to the Skyline Road drain, leaned out into the passageway, and pointed his light to the right and to the left, making sure there was nothing lurking around. The Skyline Road pipe was the same size as the one in which he now stood, but it followed the slope of the street above it, plunging down the mountainside. There was nothing in sight.

Looking downhill, into the dwindling gray bore of the tunnel, Billy Velazquez was reminded of a story he'd read years ago in a horror comic. He'd forgotten the title of it. The tale was about a bank robber who killed two people during a holdup and then, fleeing police, slipped into the city's storm drain system. The villain had taken a downward-sloping tunnel, figuring it would lead to the river, but where it had led, instead, was to Hell. That was what the Skyline Road drain looked like as it fell down, down, down: a road to Hell.

Billy turned to peer uphill again, wondering if it would look like a road to Heaven. But it looked the same both ways. Up or down, it looked like a road to Hell.

What had happened to Sergeant Harker?

Would the same thing happen to everyone, sooner or later?

Even to William Luis Velazquez, who had always been so sure (until now) that he would live forever?

His mouth was suddenly dry.

He turned his head inside his helmet and put his parched lips on the nipple of the nutrient tube. He sucked on it, drawing a sweet, cool, carbohydrate-packed, vitamin-and-mineral-rich fluid into his mouth. What he wanted was a beer. But until he could get out of this suit, the nutrient solution was the only thing available. He carried a forty-eight-hour supply—if he didn't take more than two ounces an hour.

Turning away from the road to Hell, he went to the junction box. Ron Peake was at work already. Moving efficiently despite their bulky decon suits and the cramped quarters, they tapped into the power supply.

The unit had brought its own generator, but it would be used only if the more convenient municipal power were lost.

In a few minutes, Velazquez and Peake were finished. Billy used his suit-to-suit radio to call up to the surface. "General, we've made the tap. You should have power now, sir."

The response came at once: "We do. Now get your asses out of there on the double!"

"Yes, sir," Billy said.

Then he heard . . . something.

Rustling.

Panting.

And Ron Peake grabbed Billy's shoulder. Pointed. Past him. Back toward the Skyline drain.

Billy whirled around, crouched down even farther, and shone his flashlight out into the intersection, where Peake's flash was focused.

Animals were streaming down the Skyline Road tunnel. Dozens upon dozens. Dogs. White and gray and black and brown and rust-red and golden, dogs of all sizes and descriptions: mostly mutts but also beagles, toy poodles, full-size poodles, German shepherds, spaniels, two Great Danes, a couple of Airedales, a schnauzer, a pair of coal-black Dobermans with brown-trimmed muzzles. And there were cats, too. Big and small. Lean cats and fat cats. Black and calico and white and yellow and ring-tailed and brown and spotted and striped and gray cats. None of the dogs barked or growled. None of the cats meowed or hissed. The only sounds were their panting and the soft padding and scraping of their paws on the concrete. The animals poured down through the drain with a curious intensity, all of them looking straight ahead, none of them even glancing into the intersecting drain, where Billy and Peake stood.

"What're they doing down here?" Billy wanted to know. "How'd they get here?"

From the street above, Copperfield radioed down: "What's wrong, Velazquez?"

Billy was so amazed by the procession of animals that he didn't immediately respond.

Other animals began to appear, mixed in among the cats and dogs. Squirrels. Rabbits. A gray fox. Raccoons. More foxes and more squirrels. Skunks. All of them were staring straight ahead, oblivious of everything except the need to keep moving. Possums and badgers. Mice and chipmunks. Coyotes. All rushing down the road to Hell, swarming over and around and under one another, yet never once stumbling or hesitating or snapping at one another. This strange parade was as swift, continuous, and harmonious as flowing water.

"Velazquez! Peake! Report in!"

"Animals," Billy told the general. "Dogs, cats, raccoons, all kinds of things. A river of 'em."

"Sir, they're running down the Skyline tunnel, just beyond the mouth of the pipe," Ron Peake said.

"Underground," Billy said, baffled. "It's crazy."

"Retreat, goddamnit!" Copperfield said urgently. "Get out of there now. *Now!*"

Billy remembered the general's warning, issued just before they had descended through the manhole: *If anything moves down there . . . even if it's just a mouse, get your asses out of there fast.*

Initially, the subterranean parade of animals had been startling but not particularly frightening. Now, the bizarre procession was suddenly eerie, even threatening.

And now there were snakes among the animals. Scores of them. Long blacksnakes, slithering fast, with their heads raised a foot or two above the floor of the storm drain. And there were rattlers, their flat and evil heads held lower than those of the longer blacksnakes, but moving just as fast and just as sinuously, swarming with mysterious purpose toward a dark and equally mysterious destination.

Although the snakes paid no more attention to Velazquez and Peake than the dogs and cats did, their slithering arrival was enough to snap Billy out of his trance. He hated snakes. He turned back the way he had come, prodded Peake. "Go. Go on. Get out of here. Run!"

Something shrieked-screamed-roared.

Billy's heart pounded with jackhammer ferocity.

The sound came from the Skyline drain, from back there on the road to Hell. Billy didn't dare look back.

It was neither a human scream nor like any animal sound, yet it was unquestionably the cry of a living thing. There was no mistaking the raw emotions of that alien, blood-freezing bleat. It wasn't a scream of fear or pain. It was a blast of rage, hatred, and feverish blood-hunger.

Fortunately, that malevolent roar didn't come from nearby, but from farther up the mountain, toward the uppermost end of the Skyline conduit. The beast —whatever in God's name it was—was at least not already upon them. But it was coming fast.

Ron Peake hurried back toward the ladder, and Billy followed. Encumbered by their bulky decontamination suits, slowed by the curved floor of the pipe, they ran in a lurching shuffle. Although they hadn't far to go, their progress was maddeningly slow.

The thing in the tunnel cried out again.

Closer.

It was a whine and a snarl and a howl and a roar and a petulant squeal all tangled together, a barbed-wire sound that punctured Billy's ears and raked cold metal spikes across his heart.

Closer.

If Billy Velazquez had been a God-fearing Nazarene or a Bible-thumping, fire-and-brimstone, fundamentalist Christian, he would have known what beast might make such a cry. If he had been taught that the Dark One and His wicked minions stalked the earth in fleshy forms, seeking unwary souls to devour, he would have identified this beast at once. He would have said, "It's Satan." The roar echoing through the concrete tunnels was truly *that* terrible.

And closer.

Getting closer.

Coming fast.

But Billy was a Catholic. Modern Catholicism tended to downplay the sulphurous-pits-of-Hell stories in favor of emphasizing God's great mercy and infinite compassion. Extremist Protestant fundamentalists saw the hand of the Devil in everything from television programming to the novels of Judy Blume to the invention of the push-up bra. But Catholicism struck a quieter, more light-hearted note than that. The Church of Rome now gave the world such things as singing nuns, Wednesday Night Bingo, and priests like Andrew Greeley. Therefore, Billy Velazquez, raised a Catholic, did not immediately associate supernatural Satanic forces with the chilling cry of this unknown beast—not even though he so vividly remembered that old road-to-Hell comic book story. Billy just knew that the bellowing creature approaching through the bowels of the earth was a *bad thing*. A *very* bad thing.

And it was getting closer. Much closer.

Ron Peake reached the ladder, started up, dropped his flashlight, didn't bother to return for it.

Peake was too slow, and Billy shouted at him: "Move your ass!"

The scream of the unknown beast had become an eerie ululation that filled the subterranean warren of storm drains as completely as floodwater. Billy couldn't even hear himself shouting.

Peake was halfway up the ladder.

There was almost enough room for Billy to slip in under him and start up. He put one hand on the ladder.

Peake's foot slipped. He dropped down a rung.

Billy cursed and snatched his hand out of the way.

The banshee keening grew louder.

Closer, closer.

Peake's fallen flashlight was pointing off toward the Skyline drain, but Billy didn't look back that way. He stared only up toward the sunlight. If he glanced behind and saw something hideous, his strength would flee him, and he would be unable to move, and it would get him, by God, it would get him.

Peake scrambled upwards again. His feet stayed on the rungs this time.

The concrete drain was transmitting vibrations that Billy could feel through the soles of his boots. The vibrations were like heavy, lumbering, yet lightning-quick footsteps.

Don't look, don't look!

Billy grabbed the sides of the ladder and clawed his way up as rapidly as Peake's progress would allow. One rung. Two. Three.

Above, Peake passed through the manhole and into the street.

With Peake out of the way, a fall of autumn sunlight splashed down over Billy Velazquez, and there was something about it that was like light piercing a church window—maybe because it represented hope.

He was halfway up the ladder.

Going to make it, going to make it, definitely going to make it, he told himself breathlessly.

But the shrieking and howling, Jesus, like being in the center of a cyclone!

Another rung.

And another one.

The decontamination suit felt heavier than it had ever felt before. A ton. A suit of armor. Weighing him down.

He was in the vertical pipe now, moving out of the horizontal drain that ran beneath the street. He looked up longingly at the light and the faces peering down at him, and he kept moving.

Going to make it.

His head rose through the manhole.

Someone reached out, offering a hand. It was Copperfield himself.

Behind Billy, the shrieking stopped.

He climbed another rung, let go of the ladder with one hand, and reached for the general—

—but something seized his legs from below before he could grasp Copperfield's hand.

"No!"

Something grabbed him, wrenched his feet off the ladder, and yanked him away. Screaming—strangely, he heard himself screaming for his mother— Billy went down, cracking his helmet against the wall of the pipe and then against a rung of the ladder, stunning himself, smashing his elbows and knees, trying desperately to catch hold of a rung but failing, finally collapsing into the powerful embrace of an unspeakable something that began to drag him backwards toward the Skyline conduit.

He twisted, kicked, struck out with his fists, to no effect. He was held tightly and dragged deeper into the drains.

In the backsplash of light coming through the manhole, then in the rapidly dimming beam of Peake's discarded flashlight, Billy saw a bit of the thing that had him in its grasp. Not much. Fragments looming out of the shadows, then vanishing into darkness again. He saw just enough to make his bowels and bladder loosen. It was lizardlike. But not a lizard. Insectlike. But not an insect. It hissed and mewled and snarled. It snapped and tore at his suit as it pulled him along. It had cavernous jaws and teeth. Jesus, Mary, and Joseph—the teeth! A double row of razor-edge spikes. It had claws, and it was huge, and its eyes were smoky red with elongated pupils as black as the bottom of a grave. It had scales instead of skin, and two horns, thrusting from its brow above its baleful eyes, curving out and up, as sharply pointed as daggers. A snout rather than a nose, a snout that oozed snot. A forked tongue that flickered in and out and in and out across all those deadly fangs, and something that looked like the stinger on a wasp or maybe a pincer.

It dragged Billy Velazquez into the Skyline conduit. He clawed at the concrete, desperately seeking something to hold on to, but he only succeeded in abrading away the fingers and palms of his gloves. He felt the cool underground air on his hands, and he realized he might now be contaminated, but that was the least of his worries.

It dragged him into the hammering heart of darkness. It stopped, held him tightly. It tore at his suit. It cracked his helmet. It pried at his plexiglass faceplate. It was after him as if he were a delicious morsel of nut meat in a hard shell.

His hold on sanity was tenuous at best, but he struggled to keep his wits about him, tried to understand. At first, it seemed to him that this was a prehistoric creature, something millions of years old that had somehow dropped through a time warp into the storm drains. But that was crazy. He felt a silvery, high-pitched, lunatic giggle coming over him, and he knew he would be lost if he gave voice to it. The beast tore away most of his decontamination suit. It was on him now, pressing hard, a cold and disgustingly slick thing that seemed to pulse and somehow to *change* when it touched him. Billy, gasping and weeping, suddenly remembered an illustration in an old catechism text. A drawing of a demon. That was what *this* was. Like the drawing. Yes, exactly like it. The horns. The dark, forked tongue. The red eyes. A demon risen from Hell. And then he thought: No, no; that's crazy, too! And all the while that those thoughts raced through his mind, the ravenous creature stripped him and pulled his helmet almost completely apart. In the unrelieved darkness, he sensed its snout pressing through the halves of the broken helmet, toward his face, sniffing. He felt its tongue fluttering against his mouth and nose. He smelled a vague but repellent odor, like nothing he had ever smelled before. The beast gouged at his belly and thighs, and then he felt a strange and brutally painful fire eating into him; acid fire. He writhed, twisted, bucked, strained—all to no avail. Billy heard himself cry out in terror and pain and confusion: "It's the Devil, it's the Devil!" He realized he had been shouting and screaming things almost continuously, from the moment he had been dragged off the ladder. Now, unable to speak as the flameless fire burned his lungs to ash and churned into his throat, he prayed in a silent singsong chant, warding off fear and death and the terrible feeling of smallness and worthlessness that had come over him: *Mary, Mother of God, Mary, hear my plea . . . hear my plea, Mary, pray for me . . . pray, pray for me, Mary, Mother of God, Mary, intercede for me and—*

His question had been answered.

He knew what had happened to Sergeant Harker.

Galen Copperfield was an outdoorsman, and he knew a great deal about the wildlife of North America. One of the creatures he found most interesting was the trap-door spider. It was a clever engineer, constructing a deep, tubular nest in the ground with a hinged lid at the top. The lid blended so perfectly with the soil in which it was set that other insects wandered across it, unaware of the danger below, and were instantly snatched into the nest, dragged down, and devoured. The suddenness of it was horrifying and fascinating. One instant, the prey was there, standing atop the trap-door, and the next instant it was gone, as if it had never been.

Corporal Velazquez's disappearance was as sudden as if he had stepped upon the lid of a trap-door spider's lair.

Gone.

Copperfield's men were already edgy about Harker's disappearance and were frightened by the nightmarish howling that ceased just before Velazquez was dragged down. When the corporal was taken, they all stumbled back across the street, afraid that something was about to launch itself out of the manhole.

Copperfield, in the act of reaching for Velazquez when he was snatched, jumped back. Then froze. Indecisive. That was not like him. He had never before been indecisive in a crisis.

Velazquez was screaming through the suit-to-suit radio.

Breaking the ice that locked his joints, Copperfield went to the manhole and looked down. Peake's flashlight lay on the floor of the drain. But there was nothing else. No sign of Velazquez.

Copperfield hesitated.

The corporal continued to scream.

Send other men down after the poor bastard?

No. It would be a suicide mission. Remember Harker. Cut the losses here, now.

But, good God, the screaming was terrible. Not as awful as Harker's. Those had been screams born of excruciating pain. These were screams of mortal terror. Not as bad, perhaps, but bad enough. As bad as anything Copperfield had heard on the battlefield.

There were words among the screams, spat out in explosive gasps. The corporal was making a desperate, babbling attempt to explain to those above-ground—and maybe to himself—just what he was seeing.

". . . lizard . . ."

". . . bug . . ."

". . . dragon . . ."

". . . prehistoric . . ."

". . . demon . . ."

And finally, with both physical pain and anguish of the soul in his voice, the corporal cried out, "It's the Devil, it's the Devil!"

After that, the screams were every bit as bad as Harker's. At least these didn't last as long.

When there was only silence, Copperfield slid the manhole cover back into place. Because of the power cable, the metal plate didn't fit tightly and was tilted up at one end, but it covered most of the hole.

He stationed two men on the sidewalk, ten feet from the entrance to the drain, and ordered them to shoot anything that came out.

Because a gun had been of no help to Harker, Copperfield and a few other men collected everything needed to manufacture Molotov cocktails. They got a couple of dozen bottles of wine from Brookhart's liquor store on Vail Lane, emptied them, put an inch of soap powder in the bottom of each, filled them with gasoline, and twisted rag fuses into the necks of them until they were snugly stoppered.

Would fire succeed where bullets had failed?

What had happened to Harker?

What had happened to Velazquez?

What will happen to me? Copperfield wondered.

The first of the two mobile field laboratories had cost more than three million dollars, and the Defense Department had gotten its money's worth.

The lab was a marvel of technological microminiaturization. For one thing, its computer—based on a trio of Intel 432 micromainframes; 690,000 transistors squeezed onto only nine silicon chips—took up no more room than a couple of suitcases, yet it was a highly sophisticated system that was capable of complex medical analyses. In fact, it was a more elaborate system—with greater logic and memory capacities—than could be found in most major university hospitals' pathology labs.

There was a great deal of diagnostic equipment in the motor home, all of it designed and positioned for maximum utilization of the limited space. In addition to a pair of computer access terminals along one wall, there were a number of devices and machines: a centrifuge that would be used to separate the major components of blood, urine, and other fluid samples; a spectrophotometer; a spectrograph; an electron microscope with an image interpretation-enhancement read-out link to one of the computer screens; a compact appliance that would quick-freeze blood and tissue samples for storage and for use in tests in which element extractions were more easily performed on frozen materials; and much, much more.

Toward the front of the vehicle, behind the drivers' compartment, was an autopsy table that collapsed into the wall when not in use. At the moment, the table was down, and the body of Gary Wechlas—male, thirty-seven, Caucasian—lay on the stainless-steel surface. The blue pajama bottoms had been scissored away from the corpse and set aside for later examination.

Dr. Seth Goldstein, one of the three leading forensic medicine specialists on the West Coast, would perform the autopsy. He stood at one side of the table with Dr. Daryl Roberts, and General Copperfield stood at the other side, facing them across the dead body.

Goldstein pressed a button on a control panel that was set in the wall to his right. A recording would be made of every word spoken during the autopsy; this was common procedure in even ordinary postmortems. A visual record was also being made: two ceiling-mounted videotape cameras were focused on the corpse; they, too, were activated when Dr. Goldstein pressed the button on the wall panel.

Goldstein began by closely examining and describing the corpse: the unusual facial expression, the universal bruising, the curious swelling. He was especially searching for punctures, abrasions, localized contusions, cuts, lesions, blisters, fractures, and other indications of specific points of injury. He could not find any.

With his gloved hand poised over the instrument tray, Goldstein hesitated, not quite sure where to start. Usually, at the beginning of an autopsy, he already had a pretty good idea of the cause of death. When the deceased had been wasted by a disease, Goldstein usually had seen the hospital report. If death had resulted from an accident, there were visible trauma. If it was death at the hand of another, there were signs of violence. But in this case, the conditions of the corpse raised more questions than it answered, strange questions unlike any he had ever faced before.

As if sensing Goldstein's thoughts, Copperfield said, "You've got to find some answers for us, Doctor. Our lives very probably depend on it."

The second motor home had many of the same diagnostic machines and instruments that were in the lead vehicle—a test tube centrifuge, an electron microscope, and so forth—in addition to several pieces of equipment that were not duplicated in the other vehicle. It contained no autopsy table, however, and only one videotape system. There were three computer terminals instead of two.

Dr. Enrico Valdez was sitting at one of the programming boards, in a deep-seated chair designed to accommodate a man in a decontamination suit complete with air tank. He was working with Houk and Niven on chemical analysis of samples of various substances collected from several business places and dwellings along Skyline Road and Vail Lane—such as the flour and dough taken from the table in Liebermann's Bakery. They were seeking traces of nerve gas condensate or other chemical substances. Thus far, they had found nothing out of the ordinary.

Dr. Valdez didn't believe that nerve gas or disease would turn out to be the culprit.

He was beginning to wonder if this whole thing might actually be in Isley's and Arkham's territory. Isley and Arkham, the two men without names on their decontamination suits, were not even members of the Civilian Defense Unit. They were from a different project altogether. Just this morning, before dawn, when Dr. Valdez had been introduced to them at the team rendezvous point in Sacramento, when he had heard what kind of research they were doing, he had almost laughed. He had thought their project was a waste of taxpayers' money. Now he wasn't so sure. Now he wondered . . .

He wondered . . . and he worried.

Dr. Sara Yamaguchi was also in the second motor home.

She was preparing bacteria cultures. Using a sample of blood taken from the body of Gary Wechlas, she was methodically contaminating a series of growth media, jellied compounds filled with nutrients on which bacteria generally thrived: horse blood agar, sheep blood agar, simplex, chocolate agar, and many others.

Sara Yamaguchi was a geneticist who had spent eleven years in recombinant DNA research. If it developed that Snowfield had been stricken by a man-made microorganism, Sara's work would become central to the investigation. She would direct the study of the microbe's morphology, and when that was completed, she would have a major role in attempting to determine the function of the bug.

Like Dr. Valdez, Sara Yamaguchi had begun to wonder if Isley and Arkham might become more essential to the investigation than she had thought. This morning, their area of expertise had seemed as exotic as voodoo. But now, in light of what had taken place since the team's arrival in Snowfield, she was forced to admit that Isley's and Arkham's specialty seemed increasingly pertinent.

And like Dr. Valdez, she was worried.

Dr. Wilson Bettenby, chief of the civilian scientific arm of the CBW Civilian Defense Unit's West Coast team, sat at a computer terminal, two seats away from Dr. Valdez.

Bettenby was running an automated analysis program on several water samples. The samples were inserted into a processor that distilled the water, stored the distillate, and subjected the filtered-out substances to spectrographic analysis and other tests. Bettenby was not searching for microorganisms; that would require different procedures than these. This machine only identified and quantified all mineral and chemical elements present in the water; the data was displayed on the cathode ray tube.

All but one of the water samples had been taken from taps in the kitchens and bathrooms of houses and businesses along Vail Lane. They proved to be free of dangerous chemical impurities.

The other water sample was the one that Deputy Autry had collected from the kitchen floor of the apartment on Vail Lane, sometime last night. According to Sheriff Hammond, puddles of water and saturated carpets had been discovered in several buildings. By this morning, however, the water had pretty much evaporated, except for a couple of damp carpets from which Bettenby wouldn't have been able to obtain a clean sample. He put the deputy's sample into the processor.

In a few minutes, the computer flashed up the complete chemical-mineral analysis of the water and of the residue that remained after all of the liquid in the sample had been distilled:

PERCENT OF SOLUTION		PERCENT OF RESIDUE	PERCENT OF SOLUTION		PERCENT OF RESIDUE
H	11.188	00.00	HE	00.00	00.00
LI	00.00	00.00	BE	00.00	00.00
B	00.00	00.00	C	00.00	00.00
N	00.00	00.00	O	88.812	00.00
NA	00.00	00.00	MG	00.00	00.00
AL	00.00	00.00	SI	00.00	00.00
P	00.00	00.00	S	00.00	00.00
CL	00.00	00.00	K	00.00	00.00

The computer went on at considerably greater length, flashing up the findings for every substance that might ordinarily be detected. The results were the same. In its undistilled state, the water contained absolutely no traces of any elements other than its two components, hydrogen and oxygen. And complete distillation and filtration had left behind no residue whatsoever, not even any trace elements. Autry's sample couldn't have come from the town's water supply, for it was neither chlorinated nor fluoridated. It wasn't bottled water, either. Bottled water would have had a normal mineral content. Perhaps there was a filtration system underneath the kitchen sink in that apartment—a Culligan unit—but even if there was, the water that passed through it would still possess more mineral content than this. What Autry had collected was the purest laboratory grade of distilled and multiply filtered water.

So . . . what was it doing all over that kitchen floor?

Bettenby stared at the computer screen, frowning.

Was the small lake at Brookhart's liquor store also composed of this ultrapure water?

Why would anyone go around town emptying out gallons and gallons of distilled water?

And where would they find it in such quantity to begin with?

Strange.

Jenny, Bryce, and Lisa were at a table in one corner of the dining room at the Hilltop Inn.

Major Isley and Captain Arkham, who wore the decontamination suits that had no names on the helmets, were sitting on two stools, across the table. They had brought the news about Corporal Velazquez. They had also brought a tape recorder, which was now in the center of the table.

"I still don't see why this can't wait," Bryce said.

"We won't take long," Major Isley said.

"I've got a search team ready to go," Bryce said. "We've got to go through every building in this town, take a body count, find out how many are dead and how many are missing, and look for some clue as to what the hell killed all these people. There's several days of work ahead of us, especially since we can't continue with the search past sundown. I won't let my men go prowling around at night, when the power might go off at any second. Damned if I will."

Jenny thought of Wargle's eaten face. The hollow eye sockets.

Major Isley said, "Just a few questions."

Arkham switched on the tape recorder.

Lisa was staring hard at the major and at the captain.

Jenny wondered what was on the girl's mind.

"We'll start with you, Sheriff," Major Isley said. "In the forty-eight hours prior to these events, did your office receive any reports of power failures or telephone service interruptions?"

"If there were problems of that nature," Bryce said, "people would generally call the utility companies, not the sheriff."

"Yes, but wouldn't the utilities notify you? Aren't power and telephone outages contributory to criminal activity?"

Bryce nodded. "Of course. And to the best of my knowledge, we didn't receive any such alerts."

Captain Arkham leaned forward. "What about difficulties with television and radio reception in this area?"

"Not that I'm aware of," Bryce said.

"Any reports of unexplainable explosions?"

"Explosions?"

"Yes," Isley said. "Explosions or sonic booms or any unusually loud and untraceable noises."

"No. Nothing like that."

Jenny wondered what in the devil they were driving at.

Isley hesitated and said, "Any reports of unusual aircraft in the vicinity?"

"No."

Lisa said, "You guys aren't part of General Copperfield's team, are you? That's why you don't have names on your helmets."

Bryce said, "And your decontamination suits don't fit as well as everyone else's. Theirs are custom tailored. Yours are strictly off the rack."

"Very observant," Isley said.

"If you aren't with the CBW project," Jenny said, "what *are* you doing here?"

"We didn't want to bring it up at the start," Isley said. "We thought we might get straighter answers from you if you weren't immediately aware of what we were looking for."

Arkham said, "We're not Army Medical Corps. We're Air Force."

"Project Skywatch," Isley said. "We're not exactly a secret organization, but . . . well . . . let's just say we discourage publicity."

"Skywatch?" Lisa said, brightening. "Are you talking about UFOs? Is that it? Flying saucers?"

Jenny saw Isley wince at the words "flying saucers."

Isley said, "We don't go around checking out every crackpot report of little green men from Mars. For one thing, we don't have the funds to do that. Our job is planning for the scientific, social, and military aspects of mankind's first encounter with an alien intelligence. We're really more of a think tank than anything else."

Bryce shook his head. "No one around here's been reporting flying saucers."

"But that's just what Major Isley means," Arkham said. "You see, our studies indicate the first encounter might start out in such a bizarre way that we wouldn't even recognize it as a first encounter. The popular concept of spaceships descending from the sky . . . well, it might not be like that. If we find ourselves dealing with *truly* alien intelligences, their ships might be so different from our concept of a ship that we wouldn't even be aware they'd landed."

"Which is why we check into strange phenomena that don't seem to be UFO related at first glance," Arkham said. "Like last spring, up in Vermont, there was a house in which an extremely active poltergeist was at work. Furniture was levitated. Dishes flew across the kitchen and smashed against the wall. Streams of water burst from walls in which there were no water pipes. Balls of flame erupted out of empty air—"

"Isn't a poltergeist supposed to be a ghost?" Bryce asked. "What could ghosts have to do with your area of interest?"

"Nothing," Isley said. "We don't believe in ghosts. But we wondered if perhaps poltergeist phenomena might result from an attempt at interspecies communication gone awry. If we were to encounter an alien race that communicated only by telepathy, and if we were unable to receive those telepathic thoughts, maybe the unreceived psychic energy would produce destructive phenomena of the sort sometimes attributed to malign spirits."

"And what did you finally decide about the poltergeist up there in Vermont?" Jenny asked.

"Decide? Nothing," Isley said.

"Just that it was . . . interesting," Arkham said.

Jenny glanced at Lisa and saw that the girl's eyes were very wide. *This* was something Lisa could grasp, accept, and cling to. This was a fear she had been thoroughly prepared for, thanks to movies and books and television. Monsters from outer space. Invaders from other worlds. It didn't make the Snowfield killings any less gruesome. But it was a *known* threat, and that made it infinitely preferable to the unknown. Jenny strongly doubted this was mankind's first encounter with creatures from the stars, but Lisa seemed eager to believe.

"And what about Snowfield?" the girl asked. "Is that what's going on? Has something landed from . . . *out there?*"

Arkham looked uneasily at Major Isley.

Isley cleared his throat: As translated by the squawk box on his chest, it was a racheting, machinelike sound. "It's much too soon to make any judgment about that. We *do* believe there's a small chance the first contact between man and alien might involve the danger of biological contamination. That's why we've got an information-sharing arrangement with Copperfield's project. An inexplicable outbreak of an unknown disease might indicate an unrecognized contact with an extraterrestrial presence."

"But if it *is* an extraterrestrial creature we're dealing with," Bryce said, obviously doubtful, "it seems damned savage for a being of 'superior' intelligence."

"The same thought occurred to me," Jenny said.

Isley raised his eyebrows. "There's no guarantee that a creature with greater intelligence would be pacifistic and benevolent."

"Yeah," Arkham said. "That's a common conceit: the notion that aliens would've learned how to live in complete harmony among themselves and with other species. As that old song says . . . it ain't necessarily so. After all, mankind is considerably further along the road of evolution than gorillas are, but as a species we're definitely more warlike than gorillas at their most aggressive."

"Maybe one day we *will* encounter a benevolent alien race that'll teach us how to live in peace," Isley said. "Maybe they'll give us the knowledge and technology to solve all our earthly problems and even to reach the stars. Maybe."

"But we can't rule out the alternative," Arkham said grimly.

CHAPTER 26

LONDON, ENGLAND

ELEVEN O'CLOCK MONDAY morning in Snowfield was seven o'clock Monday evening in London.

A miserably wet day had flowed into a miserably wet night. Raindrops drummed on the window in the cubbyhole kitchen of Timothy Flyte's two-room, attic apartment.

The professor was standing in front of a cutting board, making a sandwich.

After partaking of that magnificent champagne breakfast at Burt Sandler's expense, Timothy hadn't felt up to lunch. He had forgone afternoon tea, as well.

He'd met with two students today. He was tutoring one of them in hiero-glyphics analysis and the other in Latin. Surfeited with breakfast, he had nearly fallen asleep during both sessions. Embarrassing. But, as little as his pupils were paying him, they could hardly complain too strenuously if, just once, he dozed off in the middle of a lesson.

As he put a thin slice of boiled ham and a slice of Swiss cheese on mustard-slathered bread, he heard the telephone ringing down in the front hall of the rooming house. He didn't think it was for him. He received few calls.

But seconds later, there was a knock at the door. It was the young Indian fellow who rented a room on the first floor. In heavily accented English, he told Timothy the call was for him. And urgent.

"Urgent? Who is it?" Timothy asked as he followed the young man down the stairs. "Did he give his name?"

"Sand-leer," the Indian said.

Sandler? Burt Sandler?

Over breakfast, they had agreed on terms for a new edition of *The Ancient Enemy,* one that was completely rewritten to appeal to the average reader. Following the original publication of the book, almost seventeen years ago, he had received several offers to popularize his theories about historical mass disappearances, but he had resisted the idea; he had felt that the issuance of a popularized version of *The Ancient Enemy* would be playing into the hands of all those who had so unfairly accused him of sensationalism, humbug, and money grubbing. Now, however, years of want had made him more amenable to the idea. Sandler's appearance on the scene and his offer of a contract had come at a time when Timothy's ever-worsening poverty had reached a critical stage; it was truly a miracle. This morning, they had settled on an advance (against royalties) of fifteen thousand dollars. At the current rate of exchange, that amounted to a little more than eight thousand pounds sterling. It wasn't a fortune, but it was more money than Timothy had seen in a long, long time, and at the moment it seemed like wealth beyond counting.

As he went down the narrow stairs, toward the front hall, where the telephone stood on a small table beneath a cheap print of a bad painting, Timothy wondered if Sandler was calling to back out of the agreement.

The professor's heart began to pound with almost painful force.

The young Indian gentleman said, "I hope is no trouble, sir."

Then he returned to his own room and closed the door.

Flyte picked up the phone. "Hello?"

"My God, do you get an evening newspaper?" Sandler asked. His voice was shrill, almost hysterical.

Timothy wondered if Sandler was drunk. Was *this* what he considered urgent business?

Before Timothy could respond, Sandler said, "I think it's happened! By God, Dr. Flyte, I think it's actually happened! It's in the newspaper tonight. And on the radio. Not many details yet. But it sure looks as if it's happened."

The professor's worry about the book contract was now compounded by exasperation. "Could you please be more specific, Mr. Sandler?"

"The ancient enemy, Dr. Flyte. One of those creatures has struck again. Just yesterday. A town in California. Some are dead. Most are missing. Hundreds. An entire town. Gone."

"God help them," Flyte said.

"I've got a friend in the London office of the Associated Press, and he's read me the latest wire service reports," Sandler said. "I know things that aren't in the papers yet. For one thing, the police out there in California have put out an all-points bulletin for you. Apparently, one of the victims had read your book. When the attack came, he locked himself in a bathroom. It got him anyway. But he gained enough time to scrawl your name and the title of your book on the mirror!"

Timothy was speechless. There was a chair beside the telephone. He suddenly needed it.

"The authorities in California don't understand what's happened. They don't even realize *The Ancient Enemy* is the title of a book, and they don't know what part you play in all this. They think it was a nerve gas attack or an act of biological warfare or even extraterrestrial contact. But the man who wrote your name on that mirror knew better. And so do we. I'll tell you more in the car."

"Car?" Timothy said.

"My God, I hope you have a passport!"

"Uh . . . yes."

"I'm coming by with a car to take you to the airport. I want you to go to California, Dr. Flyte."

"But—"

"Tonight. There's an available seat on a flight from Heathrow. I've reserved it in your name."

"But I can't afford—"

"Your publisher is paying all expenses. Don't worry. You *must* go to Snowfield. You won't be writing just a popularization of *The Ancient Enemy.* Not any more. Now, you're going to write a well-rounded human story about Snowfield, and all of your material on historical mass disappearances and your theories about the ancient enemy will be supportive of that narrative. Do you see? Won't it be great?"

"But would it be right for me to rush in there now?"

"What do you mean?" Sandler asked.

"Would it be proper?" Timothy asked worriedly. "Wouldn't it appear as if I were attempting to cash in on a terrible tragedy?"

"Listen, Dr. Flyte, there are going to be a hundred hustlers in Snowfield, all with book contracts in their back pockets. They'll rip off your material. If you don't write *the* book on the subject, one of them will write it at your expense."

"But hundreds are dead," Timothy said. He felt ill. "Hundreds. The pain, the tragedy . . ."

Sandler was clearly impatient with the professor's hesitancy. "Well . . . okay, okay. Maybe you're right. Maybe I haven't really stopped to think about the horror of it. But don't you see—that's why you *must* be the one to write the ultimate book on the subject. No one else can bring your erudition or compassion to the project."

"Well . . ."

Seizing on Timothy's hesitation, Sandler said, "Good. Pack a suitcase fast. I'll be there in half an hour."

Sandler hung up, and Timothy sat for a moment, holding the receiver, listening to the dead line. Stunned.

In the taxi's headlights, the rain was silvery. It slanted on the wind, like thousands of thin streamers of glittering Christmas tinsel. On the pavement, it puddled in quicksilver pools.

The cabdriver was reckless. The car careened along the slick streets. With one hand, Timothy held tightly to the safety bar on the door. Evidently Burt Sandler had promised a very large tip as a reward for speed.

Sitting next to the professor, Sandler said, "There'll be a layover in New York, but not too long. One of our people will meet you and shepherd you through. We won't alert the media in New York. We'll save the press conference for San Francisco. So be prepared to face an army of eager reporters when you get off the plane there."

"Couldn't I just go quietly to Santa Mira and present myself to the authorities there?" Timothy asked unhappily.

"No, no, no!" Sandler said, clearly horrified by the very thought. "We've got to have a press conference. You're the only one with the *answer,* Dr. Flyte. We've got to let everyone know that you're the one. We've got to start beating the drum for your next book before Norman Mailer puts aside his latest study of Marilyn Monroe and jumps into this thing with both feet!"

"I haven't even begun to write the book yet."

"God, I know. And by the time we publish, the demand will be phenomenal!"

The cab turned a corner. Tires squealed. Timothy was thrown against the door.

"A publicist will meet you at the plane in San Francisco. He'll guide you through the press conference," Sandler said. "One way or another he'll get you to Santa Mira. It's a fairly long drive, so maybe it can be done by helicopter."

"Helicopter?" Timothy said, astonished.

The taxi sped through a deep puddle, casting up plumes of silvery water. The airport was within sight.

Burt Sandler had been talking nonstop since Timothy had gotten into the cab. Now he said, "One more thing. At your press conference, tell them the stories you told me this morning. About the disappearing Mayans. And three thousand Chinese infantrymen who vanished. And be sure to make any references you possibly can to mass disappearances that took place in the U.S.— even before there *was* a United States, even in previous geological eras. That'll appeal to the American press. Local ties. That always helps. Didn't the first British colony in America vanish without a trace?"

"Yes. The Roanoke Island colony."

"Be sure to mention it."

"But I can't say conclusively that the disappearance of the Roanoke colony is connected with the ancient enemy."

"Is there any chance whatsoever that it might've been?"

Fascinated, as always, by this subject, Timothy was able, for the first time, to wrench his mind away from the suicidal behavior of the cabdriver. "When a British expedition, funded by Sir Walter Raleigh, returned to the Roanoke colony in March of 1590, they found everyone gone. One hundred and twenty people had vanished without a trace. Countless theories have been advanced regarding their fate. For example, the most popular theory holds that the people at Roanoke Island fell victim to the Croatoan Indians, who lived nearby. The only message left by the colonists was the name of that tribe, hastily slashed into the bark of a tree. But the Croatoans professed to know nothing about the disappearance. And they were peaceful Indians. Not the least bit warlike. Indeed, they had initially helped the colonists settle in. Furthermore, there were no signs of violence at the settlement. No bodies were ever found. No bones. No graves. So you see, even the most widely accepted theory raises a greater number of questions than it answers."

The taxi swept around another curve, braked abruptly to avoid colliding with a truck.

But now Timothy was only passingly aware of the driver's daredevil conduct. He continued:

"It occurred to me that the word the colonists had carved into that tree—*Croatoan*—might not have been intended to point an accusing finger. It might have meant that the Croatoans would know what had happened. I read the journals of several British explorers who later talked with the Croatoans about the colony's disappearance, and there's evidence the Indians did, indeed, have some idea of what had happened. Or *thought* they knew. But they were not taken seriously when they tried to explain to the white man. The Croatoans reported that, simultaneously with the disappearance of the colonists, there was a great depletion of game in the forests and fields in which the tribe hunted. Virtually all species of wildlife had abruptly dwindled drastically in numbers. A couple of the more perceptive explorers noted in their journals that the Indians regarded the subject with superstitious dread. They seemed to have a religious explanation for the disappearance. But unfortunately, the white men who talked with them about the missing colonists were not interested in Indian superstitions and did not pursue that avenue of enquiry."

"I gather you've researched Croatoan religious beliefs," Burt Sandler said.

"Yes," Timothy said. "Not an easy subject, for the tribe has been extinct itself for many, many years. What I've found is that the Croatoans were spiritualists. They believed that the spirit endured and walked the earth even after the death of the body, and they believed there were 'greater spirits' that manifested themselves in the elements—wind, earth, fire, water, and so forth. Most important of all—as far as we're concerned—they also believed in an *evil* spirit, a source of *all* evil, an equivalent to the Christians' Satan. I forget the exact Indian word for it, but it translates roughly as He Who Can Be Anything Yet is Nothing."

"My God," Sandler said. "That's not a bad description of the ancient enemy."

"Sometimes there are truths hidden in superstitions. The Croatoans believed that both the wildlife and the colonists had been taken away by He Who Can Be Anything Yet is Nothing. So . . . while I cannot say conclusively that the ancient enemy had something to do with the disappearance of the Roanoke Islanders, it seems to me sufficient reason to consider the possibility."

"Fantastic!" Sandler said. "Tell them all of that at the press conference in San Francisco. Just the way you've told me."

The taxi squealed to a stop in front of the terminal.

Burt Sandler shoved a few five-pound notes into the driver's hand. He glanced at his watch. "Dr. Flyte, let's get you on that plane."

From his window seat, Timothy Flyte watched the city lights disappearing beneath the storm clouds. The jet speared upward through the thin rain. Soon, they rose above the overcast; the storm was below them, clear sky overhead. The rays of the moon bounced off the churning tops of the clouds, and the night beyond the plane was filled with soft, eerie light.

The seatbelt sign winked off.

He unbuckled but couldn't relax. His mind was churning just as the storm clouds were.

The stewardess came around, offering drinks. He asked for Scotch.

He felt like a coiled spring. Overnight, his life had changed. There had been more excitement in this one day than in the entire past year.

The tension that gripped him was not unpleasant. He was more than happy to slough off his dreary existence; he was putting on a new and better life as quickly as he might have put on a new suit of clothes. He was risking ridicule and all the old familiar accusations by going public with his theories again. But there was also a chance that he would at last be able to prove himself.

The Scotch came, and he drank it. He ordered another. Slowly, he relaxed.

Beyond the plane, the night was vast.

CHAPTER 27

ESCAPE

FROM THE BARRED window of the temporary holding cell, Fletcher Kale had a good view of the street. All morning he watched the reporters congregating. Something really big had happened.

Some of the other inmates were sharing news cell to cell, but none of them would share anything with Kale.

They hated him. Frequently, they taunted him, called him a baby killer. Even in jail, there were social classes, and no one was farther down the ladder than child killers.

It was almost funny. Even car thieves, muggers, burglars, holdup men, and embezzlers needed to feel morally superior to someone. So they reviled and persecuted anyone who had harmed a child, and somehow that made them feel like priests and bishops by comparison.

Fools. Kale despised them.

He didn't ask anyone to share information with him. He wouldn't give them the satisfaction of freezing him out.

He stretched out on his bunk and daydreamed about his magnificent destiny: fame, power, wealth . . .

At eleven-thirty, he was still lying on his bunk when they came to take him to the courthouse for arraignment on two counts of murder. The cellblock guard unlocked the door. Another man—a gray-haired, pot-bellied deputy—came in and put handcuffs on Kale.

"We're shorthanded today," he told Kale. "I'm the only one detailed for this. But don't you get some damn-fool idea that you'd have a chance to make a break for it. You're cuffed, and I've got the gun, and nothing would please me as much as shooting your ass off."

In both the guard's and the deputy's eyes, there was loathing.

At last, the possibility of spending the rest of his life in prison became real to Kale. To his surprise, he began to cry as they led him out of the cell.

The other prisoners hooted and laughed and called him names.

The potbellied man prodded Kale in the ribs. "Get a move on."

Kale stumbled along the corridor on weak legs, through a security gate that rolled open for them, out of the cellblock, into another hall. The guard remained behind, but the deputy prodded Kale toward the elevators, prodded him too often and too hard, even when it wasn't necessary. Kale felt his self-pity giving way to anger.

In the small, slowly descending elevator, he realized that the deputy no longer saw any threat in his prisoner. He was disgusted, impatient, embarrassed by Kale's emotional collapse.

By the time the doors opened, a change had occurred in Kale, as well. He was still weeping quietly, but the tears were no longer genuine, and he was shaking with excitement rather than with despair.

They went through another checkpoint. The deputy presented a set of papers to another guard who called him Joe. The guard looked at Kale with unconcealed disdain. Kale averted his face as if he were ashamed of himself. And continued to cry.

Then he and Joe were outside, crossing a large parking lot toward a row of green and white police cruisers that were lined up in front of a cyclone fence. The day was warm and sunny.

Kale continued to cry and to pretend that his legs were rubbery. He kept his shoulders hunched and his head low. He shuffled along listlessly, as if he were a broken, beaten man.

Except for him and the deputy, the parking lot was deserted. Just the two of them. Perfect.

All the way to the car, Kale looked for the right moment in which to make his move. For a while he thought it wouldn't come.

Then Joe shoved him against a car and half-turned away to unlock the door —and Kale struck. He threw himself at the deputy as the man bent to insert a key into the lock. The deputy gasped and swung a fist at him. Too late. Kale ducked under the blow and came up fast and slammed him against the car, pinning him. Joe's face went white with pain as the door handle rammed hard against the base of his spine. The ring of keys flew out of his hand, and even as they were falling, he was using the same hand to grab for his holstered revolver.

Kale knew, with his hands cuffed, he couldn't wrestle the gun away. As soon as the revolver was drawn, the fight was finished.

So Kale went for the other man's throat. Went for it with his teeth. He bit deep, felt blood gushing, bit again, pushed his mouth into the wound, like an attack dog, and bit again, and the deputy screamed, but it was only a yelp-rattle-sigh that no one could have heard, and the gun fell out of the holster and out of the deputy's spasming hand, and both men went down hard, with Kale on top, and the deputy tried to scream again, so Kale rammed a knee into his crotch, and blood was pump-pump-pumping out of the man's throat.

"Bastard," Kale said.

The deputy's eyes froze. The blood stopped spurting from the wound. It was over.

Kale had never felt so powerful, so *alive.*

He looked around the parking lot. Still no one in sight.

He scrambled to the ring of keys, tried them one by one until he unlocked his handcuffs. He threw the cuffs under the car.

He rolled the dead deputy under the cruiser, too, out of sight.

He wiped his face on his sleeve. His shirt was spotted and stained with blood. There was nothing he could do about that. Nor could he change the fact that he was wearing baggy, blue, coarsely woven institutional clothing and a pair of canvas and rubber slip-on shoes.

Feeling conspicuous, he hurried along the fence, through the open gate. He crossed the alley and went into another parking lot behind a large, two-story apartment complex. He glanced up at all the windows and hoped no one was looking.

There were perhaps twenty cars in the lot. A yellow Datsun had keys in the ignition. He got behind the wheel, closed the door, and sighed with relief. He was out of sight, and he had transportation.

A box of Kleenex stood on the console. Using paper tissues and spit, he cleaned his face. With the blood removed, he looked at himself in the rearview mirror—and grinned.

CHAPTER 28

BODY COUNT

//////

WHILE GENERAL COPPERFIELD'S unit was conducting the autopsy and tests in the mobile field lab, Bryce Hammond formed two search teams and began a building-by-building inspection of the town. Frank Autry led the first group, and Major Isley went along as an observer for Project Skywatch. Likewise, Captain Arkham joined Bryce's group. Block by block and street by street, the two teams were never more than one building apart, remaining in close touch with walkie-talkies.

Jenny accompanied Bryce. More than anyone else, she was familiar with Snowfield's residents, and she was the one most likely to identify any bodies that were found. In most cases, she could also tell them who had lived in each house and how many people had been in each family—information they needed to compile a list of the missing.

She was troubled about exposing Lisa to more gruesome scenes, but she couldn't refuse to assist the search team. She couldn't leave her sister behind at the Hilltop Inn, either. Not after what had happened to Harker. And to Velazquez. But the girl coped well with the tension of the house-to-house search. She was still proving herself to Jenny, and Jenny was increasingly proud of her.

They didn't find any bodies for a while. The first businesses and houses they entered were deserted. In several houses, tables were set for Sunday dinner. In others, tubs were filled with bathwater that had grown cold. In a number of places, television sets were still playing, but there was no one to watch them.

In one kitchen they discovered Sunday dinner on the electric stove. The food in the three pots had cooked for so many hours that all of the water content had evaporated. The remains were dry, hard, burnt, blistered, and unidentifiable. The stainless-steel pots were ruined; they had turned bluish-black both inside and out. The plastic handles of the pots had softened and partially melted. The entire house reeked with the most acrid, nauseating stench Jenny had ever encountered.

Bryce switched off the burners. "It's a miracle the whole place wasn't set on fire."

"It probably would've been if that were a gas stove," Jenny said.

Above the three pots, there was a stainless-steel range hood with an exhaust fan. When the food had burned, the hood had contained the short-lived flash of flames and had prevented the fire from spreading to the surrounding cabinetry.

Outside again, everyone (except Major Arkham in his decontamination suit) took deep breaths of the clean mountain air. They needed a couple of minutes to purge their lungs of the vile stuff they had breathed inside that house.

Then, next door, they found the first body of the day. It was John Farley, who owned the Mountain Tavern, which was open only during the ski season. He was in his forties. He had been a striking man, with salt-and pepper hair, a large nose, and a wide mouth that had frequently curved into an immensely engaging smile. Now he was bloated and bruised, his eyes bulging out of his skull, his clothes bursting at the seams as his body swelled.

Farley was sitting at the breakfast table, at one end of his big kitchen. On a plate before him was a meal of cheese-filled ravioli and meatballs. There was also a glass of red wine. On the table, beside the plate, there was an open magazine. Farley was sitting up straight in his chair. One hand lay palm-up in his lap. His other arm was on the table, and in that hand was clenched a crust of bread. Farley's mouth was partly open, and there was a bite of bread trapped between his teeth. He had perished in the act of chewing; his jaw muscles had never even relaxed.

"Good God," Tal said, "he didn't have time to spit the stuff out or swallow it. Death must've been instantaneous."

"And he didn't see it coming, either," Bryce said. "Look at his face. There's no expression of horror or surprise or shock as there is with most of the others."

Staring at the dead man's clenched jaws, Jenny said, "What I don't understand is why death doesn't bring any relaxation of the muscles whatsoever. It's weird."

In Our Lady of the Mountains Church, sunlight streamed through the stained-glass windows, which were composed predominantly of blues and greens. Hundreds of irregularly shaped patches of royal blue, sky blue, turquoise, aquamarine, emerald green, and many other shades dripped across the polished wooden pews, puddled in the aisles, and shimmered on the walls.

It's like being underwater, Gordy Brogan thought as he followed Frank Autry into the strangely and beautifully illuminated nave.

Just beyond the narthex, a stream of crimson light splashed across the white marble font that contained the holy water. It was the crimson of Christ's blood. The sun pierced a stained-glass image of Christ's bleeding heart and sprayed sanguineous rays upon the water that glistened in the pale marble bowl.

Of the five men in the search team, only Gordy was a Catholic. He moistened two fingers in the holy water, crossed himself, and genuflected.

The church was solemn, silent, still.

The air was softened by a pleasant trace of incense.

In the pews, there were no worshipers. At first it appeared as if the church was deserted.

Then Gordy looked more closely at the altar and gasped.

Frank saw it, too. "Oh, my God."

The chancel was cloaked in more shadows than was the rest of the church, which was why the men hadn't immediately noticed the hideous—and sacrilegious—thing above the altar. The altar candles had burned down all the way and had gone out.

However, as the men in the search team progressed hesitantly down the center aisle, they got a clearer and clearer view of the life-size crucifix that rose up from the center of the altar, along the rear wall of the chancel. It was a wooden cross, with an exquisitely detailed, hand-painted, glazed plaster figure of Christ fixed to it. At the moment, much of the godly image was obscured by another body that hung in front of it. A real body, not another plaster corpus. It was the priest in his robes; he was nailed to the cross.

Two altarboys knelt on the floor in front of the altar. They were dead, bruised, bloated.

The flesh of the priest had begun to darken and to show other signs of imminent decomposition: His body was not in the same bizarre condition as all the others that had been found thus far. In his case, the discoloration was what you would expect of a day-old corpse.

Frank Autry, Major Isley, and the other two deputies continued through the gate in the altar railing and stepped up into the chancel.

Gordy wasn't able to go with them. He was too badly shaken and had to sit in the front pew to keep from collapsing.

After inspecting the chancel and glancing through the sacristy door, Frank used his walkie-talkie to call Bryce Hammond in the building next door. "Sheriff, we've found three here in the church. We need Doc Paige for positive IDs. But it's especially grisly, so better leave Lisa in the vestibule with a couple of the guys."

"We'll be there in two minutes," the sheriff said.

Frank came down from the chancel, through the gate in the railing, and sat down beside Gordy. He was holding the walkie-talkie in one hand and a gun in the other. "You're a Catholic."

"Yeah."

"Sorry you had to see this."

"I'll be okay," Gordy said. "It's no easier for you just because you're not a Catholic."

"You know the priest?"

"I think his name's Father Callahan. I didn't go to this church, though. I attended St. Andrew's, down in Santa Mira."

Frank put the walkie-talkie down and scratched his chin. "From all the other indications we've had, it looked like the attack came yesterday evening, not long before Doc and Lisa came back to town. But now this . . . If these three died in the morning, during Mass—"

"It was probably during Benediction," Gordy said. "Not Mass."

"Benediction?"

"The Benediction of the Blessed Sacrament. The Sunday evening service."

"Ah. Then it fits right in with the timing of the others." He looked around at the empty pews. "What happened to the parishioners? Why are only the altarboys and the priest here?"

"Well, not an awful lot of people come to Benediction," Gordy said. "There were probably at least two or three others. But *it* took them."

"Why didn't it just take everyone?"

Gordy didn't answer.

"Why did it have to do something like *this?*" Frank pressed.

"To ridicule us. To mock us. To steal our hope," Gordy said miserably.

Frank stared at him.

Gordy said, "Maybe some of us have been counting on God to get us through this alive. Probably most of us have. I know I've sure been praying a lot since we came here. Probably you have, too. It knew we would do that. It knew we would ask God for help. So this is its way of letting us know that God *can't* help us. Or at least that's what it would like us to believe. Because that's its way. To instill doubt about God. That's always been its way."

Frank said, "You sound as if you know exactly what we're up against here."

"Maybe," Gordy said. He stared at the crucified priest, then turned to Frank again. "Don't you know? Don't you really, Frank?"

After they left the church and went around the corner onto the cross street, they found two wrecked cars.

A Cadillac Seville had run across the front lawn of the church rectory, mowing down the shrubbery in its path, and had collided with a porch post at one corner of the house. The post was nearly splintered in two. The porch roof was sagging.

Tal Whitman squinted through the side window of the Caddy. "There's a woman behind the wheel."

"Dead?" Bryce asked.

"Yeah. But not from the accident."

At the other side of the car, Jenny tried to open the driver's door. It was locked. All of the doors were locked, and all of the windows were rolled up tight.

Nevertheless, the woman behind the wheel—Edna Gower; Jenny knew her —was like the other corpses. Darkly bruised. Swollen. A scream of terror frozen on her twisted face.

"How could it get in there and kill her?" Tal wondered aloud.

"Remember the locked bathroom at the Candleglow Inn," Bryce said.

"And the barricaded room at the Oxleys'," Jenny said.

Captain Arkham said, "It's almost an argument for the general's nerve gas theory."

Then Arkham unclipped a miniaturized geiger counter from his utility belt and carefully examined the car. But it wasn't radiation that had killed the woman inside.

The second car, half a block away, was a pearl-white Lynx. On the pavement behind it were black skid marks. The Lynx was angled across the street, blocking it. The front end was punched into the side of a yellow Chevy van. There wasn't a lot of damage because the Lynx had almost braked to a stop before hitting the parked vehicle.

The driver was a middle-aged man with a bushy mustache. He was wearing cut-off jeans and a Dodgers T-shirt. Jenny knew him, too. Marty Sussman. He had been Snowfield's city manager for the past six years. Affable, earnest Marty Sussman. Dead. Again, the cause of death was clearly not related to the collision.

The doors of the Lynx were locked. The windows were rolled up tight, just as they had been on the Cadillac.

"Looks like they both were trying to escape from something," Jenny said.

"Maybe," Tal said. "Or they might just have been out for a drive or going somewhere on an errand when the attack came. If they were trying to escape, something sure stopped them cold, forced them right off the street."

"Sunday was a warm day. Warm but not *too* warm," Bryce said. "Not hot enough to ride around with the windows closed and the air conditioner on. It was the kind of day when most people keep the windows down, taking advantage of the fresh air. So it looks to me as if, after they were forced to stop, they put up the windows and locked themselves in, trying to keep something out."

"But it got them anyway," Jenny said.

It.

Ned and Sue Marie Bischoff owned a lovely Tudor-style home set on a double lot, nestled among huge pine trees. They lived there with their two boys. Eight-year-old Lee Bischoff could already play the piano surprisingly well, in spite of the smallness of his hands, and once told Jenny he was going to be the next Stevie Wonder "only not blind." Six-year-old Terry looked exactly like a black-skinned Dennis the Menace, but he had a sweet temper.

Ned was a successful artist. His oil paintings sold for as much as six and seven thousand dollars, and his limited edition prints went for four or five hundred dollars apiece.

He was a patient of Jenny's. Although he was only thirty-two and was already a success in life, she had treated him for an ulcer.

The ulcer wouldn't be bothering him any more. He was in his studio, lying on the floor in front of an easel, dead.

Sue Marie was in the kitchen. Like Hilda Beck, Jenny's housekeeper, and like many other people all over town, Sue Marie had died while preparing dinner. She had been a pretty woman. Not any more.

They found the two boys in one of the bedrooms.

It was a wonderful room for kids, large and airy, with bunk beds. There were built-in bookshelves full of children's books. On the walls were paintings that Ned had done just for his kids, whimsical fantasy scenes quite unlike the pieces for which he was well known: a pig in a tuxedo, dancing with a cow in an evening gown; the interior of a spaceship command chamber, where all the astronauts were toads; an eerie yet charming scene of a school playground at night, bathed in the light of a full moon, no kids around, but with a huge and monstrous-looking werewolf having a grand and giddy time on a set of swings.

The boys were in one corner, beyond an array of overturned Tonka Toys. The younger boy, Terry, was behind Lee, who seemed to have made a valiant effort to protect his smaller brother. The boys were staring out into the room, eyes bulging, their dead gazes still fixed upon whatever had threatened them yesterday. Lee's muscles had locked, so that his thin arms were in the same position now as they had been in the last seconds of his life: raised in front of him, shielding him, palms spread, as if warding off blows.

Bryce knelt in front of the kids. He put one trembling hand against Lee's face, as if unwilling to believe that the child was actually dead.

Jenny knelt beside him.

"Those are the Bischoffs' two boys," she said, unable to keep her voice from breaking. "So now the whole family's accounted for."

Tears were streaming down Bryce's face.

Jenny tried to remember how old his own son was. Seven or eight? About the same age as Lee Bischoff. Little Timmy Hammond was lying in the hospital in Santa Mira this very minute, comatose, just as he had been for the past year. He was pretty much a vegetable. Yes, but even that was better than this. Anything was better than *this*.

Eventually, Bryce's tears dried up. There was rage in him now. "I'll get them for this," he said. "Whoever did this . . . I'll make them pay."

Jenny had never met a man quite like him. He had considerable masculine strength and purpose, but he was also capable of tenderness.

She wanted to hold him. And be held.

But, as always, she was far too guarded about expressing her own emotional state. If she had possessed his openness, she would never have become estranged from her mother. But she wasn't that way, not yet, although she wanted to be. So, in response to his vow to get the killers of the Bischoffs' children, she said, "But what if it isn't anything human that killed them? Not all evil is in men. There's evil in nature. The blind maliciousness of earthquakes. The uncaring evil of cancer. This thing here could be like that—remote and unaccountable. There'll be no taking it to court if it isn't even human. What then?"

"Whoever or whatever the hell it is, I'll get it. I'll stop it. I'll make it pay for what's been done here," he said stubbornly.

Frank Autry's search team prowled through three deserted houses after leaving the Catholic church. The fourth house wasn't empty. They found Wendell Hulbertson, a high school teacher who worked in Santa Mira but who chose to live here in the mountains, in a house that had once belonged to his mother. Gordy had been in Hulbertson's English class only five years ago. The teacher was not swollen or bruised like the other corpses; he had taken his own life. Backed into a corner of his bedroom, he had put the barrel of a .32 automatic in his mouth and had pulled the trigger. Evidently, death by his own hand had been preferable to whatever *it* had been about to do to him.

After leaving the Bischoff residence, Bryce led his group through a few houses without finding any bodies. Then, in the fifth house, they discovered an elderly husband and wife locked in a bathroom, where they had tried to hide from their killer. She was sprawled in the tub. He was in a heap on the floor.

"They were patients of mine," Jenny said. "Nick and Melina Papandrakis."

Tal wrote their names down on a list of the dead.

Like Harold Ordnay and his wife in the Candleglow Inn, Nick Papandrakis had attempted to leave a message that would point a finger at the killer. He had taken some iodine from the medicine cabinet and had used it to paint on the wall. He hadn't had a chance to finish even one word. There were only two letters and part of a third:

PR(

"Can anyone figure out what he intended to write?" Bryce asked.

They all took turns squeezing into the bathroom and stepped over Nick Papandrakis's corpse to have a look at the orange-brown letters on the wall, but none of them had any flashes of inspiration.

Bullets.

In the house next to the Papandrakis's, the kitchen floor was littered with expended bullets. Not entire cartridges. Just dozens of lead slugs, sans their brass casings.

The fact that there were no ejected casings anywhere in the room indicated that no gunfire had taken place here. There was no odor of gunpowder. No bullet holes in the walls or cabinets.

There were just bullets all over the floor, as if they had rained magically out of thin air.

Frank Autry scooped up a handful of the gray lumps of metal. He wasn't a ballistics expert, but, oddly, none of the bullets was fragmented or badly deformed, and that enabled him to see that they had come from a variety of weapons. Most of them—*scores* of them—appeared to be the type and caliber of ammunition that was spat out by the submachine guns with which General Copperfield's support troops were armed.

Are these slugs from Sergeant Harker's gun? Frank wondered. Are these the rounds Harker fired at his killer in the meat locker at Gilmartin's Market?

He frowned, perplexed.

He dropped the bullets, and they clattered on the floor. He plucked several other slugs off the tiles. There were a .22 and a .32 and another .22 and a .38. There were even a lot of shotgun pellets.

He picked up a single .45-caliber bullet and examined it with special interest. It was exactly the ammunition that his own revolver handled.

Gordy Brogan hunkered down beside him.

Frank didn't look at Gordy. He continued to stare intently at the slug. He was wrestling with an eerie thought.

Gordy scooped a few bullets off the kitchen tiles. "They aren't deformed at all."

Frank nodded.

"They had to've hit *something,*" Gordy said. "So they should be deformed. Some of them should be, anyway." He paused, then said, "Hey, you're a million miles away. What're you thinking about?"

"Paul Henderson." Frank held the .45 slug in front of Gordy's face. "Paul fired three like this last night, over at the substation."

"At his killer."

"Yeah."

"So?"

"So I have this crazy hunch that if we asked the lab to run ballistics tests on it, they'd find it came from Paul's revolver."

Gordy blinked at him.

"And," Frank said, "I also think that if we searched through all of the slugs on the floor here, we'd find exactly two more like this one. Not just one more, mind you. And not three more. Just two more with precisely the same markings as this one."

"You mean . . . the same three Paul fired last night."

"Yeah."

"But how'd they get from there to here?"

Frank didn't answer. Instead, he stood and thumbed the send button on the walkie-talkie. "Sheriff?"

Bryce Hammond's voice issued crisply from the small speaker. "What is it, Frank?"

"We're still here at the Sheffield house. I think you'd better come over. There's something you ought to see."

"More bodies?"

"No, sir. Uh . . . something sort of weird."

"We'll be there," the sheriff said.

Then, to Gordy, Frank said, "What I think is . . . sometime within the past couple of hours, sometime after Sergeant Harker was taken from Gilmartin's Market, *it* was here, right in this room. It got rid of all the bullets it'd taken last night and this morning."

"The hits it took?"

"Yes."

"Got *rid* of them? Just like that?"

"Just like that," Frank said.

"But how?"

"Looks like it just sort of . . . expelled them. Looks like it shed those bullets the way a dog shakes off loose hairs."

CHAPTER 29

ON THE RUN

DRIVING THROUGH SANTA MIRA in the stolen Datsun, Fletcher Kale heard about Snowfield on the radio.

Although it had captured the rest of the country's attention, Kale wasn't very interested. He was never particularly concerned about other people's tragedies.

He reached out to switch off the radio, already weary of hearing about Snowfield when he had so many problems of his own—and then he caught a name that *did* mean something to him. Jake Johnson. Johnson was one of the deputies who had gone up to Snowfield last night. Now he was missing and might even be dead.

Jake Johnson . . .

A year ago, Kale had sold Johnson a solidly built log cabin on five acres in the mountains.

Johnson had professed to be an avid hunter and had pretended to want the cabin for that purpose. However, from a number of things the deputy let slip,

Kale decided that Johnson was actually a survivalist, one of those doomsayers who believed the world was rushing toward Armageddon and that society was going to collapse either because of runaway inflation or nuclear war or some other catastrophe. Kale became increasingly convinced that Johnson wanted the cabin for a hiding place that could be stocked with food and ammunition— and then easily defended in times of social upheaval.

The cabin was certainly remote enough for that purpose. It was on Snowtop Mountain, all the way around the other side from the town of Snowfield. To get to the place, you had to go up a county fire road, a narrow dirt track that was passable virtually only to a four-wheel-drive vehicle, then switch to another, even tougher track. The final quarter-mile had to be covered on foot.

Two months after Johnson purchased the mountain property, Kale sneaked up there on a warm June morning when he knew the deputy was on duty in Santa Mira. He wanted to see if Johnson was turning the place into a wilderness fortress, as he suspected.

He found the cabin untouched, but he discovered that Johnson was doing extensive work in some of the limestone caves to which there was an entrance on his land. Outside the caves, there were sacks of cement and sand, a wheelbarrow, and a pile of stones.

Just inside the mouth of the first cave, there had been two Coleman gas lanterns standing on the stone floor, by the wall. Kale had picked up one of the lanterns and had gone deeper into the subterranean chambers.

The first cave was long and narrow, little more than a tunnel. At the end of it, he followed a series of doglegs, twisting through irregular limestone antechambers, before he came into the first roomlike cave.

Stacked against one wall were cases of five-pound, vacuum-sealed cans of nitrogen-preserved milk powder, freeze-dried fruits and vegetables, freeze-dried soup, powdered eggs, cans of honey, drums of whole grain. An air mattress. And much more. Jake had been busy.

The first underground room led to another. In this one, there was a naturally formed hole in the floor, about ten inches in diameter, and odd noises were rising out of it. Whispering voices. Menacing laughter. Kale almost turned and ran, but then he realized that he was hearing nothing more sinister than the chuckling of running water. An underground stream. Jake Johnson had lowered one-inch rubber tubing into the natural well and had rigged a hand pump beside it.

All the comforts of home.

Kale decided that Johnson was not merely cautious. The man was *obsessed*.

On another day at the end of that same summer, late in August, Kale returned to the mountain property. To his surprise, the cave mouth—which was about four feet high and five feet wide—was no longer visible. Johnson had created an effective barrier of vegetation to conceal the entrance to his hideaway.

Kale pushed through the brush, careful not to trample it.

He had brought his own flashlight this time. He crawled through the mouth of the cave, stood up once he was inside, followed the tunnel through three doglegs—and suddenly came up against an unexpected dead end. He knew there should be one more short doglegged passageway and then the first of the large caves. Instead, there was only a wall of limestone, a flat face of it that sealed off the rest of the caverns.

For a moment Kale stared at the barrier, confused. Then he examined it closely, and in a few minutes he found the hidden release. The rock was actually a thin façade that had been bonded with epoxy to a door that Johnson had cleverly mounted in the natural frame between the final dogleg and the first of the room-size caves.

That day in August, marveling over the hidden door, Kale decided that he would take the retreat for his own if the need ever arose. After all, maybe these survivalists were on to something. Maybe they were right. Maybe the fools out there would try to blow up the world some day. If so, Kale would get to this retreat first, and when Johnson came through his cleverly hidden door, Kale would simply blow him away.

That thought pleased him.

It made him feel shrewd. Superior.

Thirteen months later, he had, much to his surprise and horror, seen the end of the world coming. The end of *his* world. Locked up in the county jail, charged with murder, he knew where he could go if he could only manage to escape: into the mountains, to the caves. He could stay up there for several weeks, until the cops finally stopped looking for him in and around Santa Mira County.

Thank you, Jake Johnson.

Jake Johnson . . .

Now, in the stolen yellow Datsun, with the county jail only a few minutes behind him, Kale heard about Johnson on the radio. As he listened, he began to smile. Fate was on his side.

After escaping, his biggest problem was disposing of his jail clothes and getting properly outfitted for the mountains. He hadn't been quite sure how he would do that.

As soon as he heard the radio reporter say that Jake Johnson was dead—or at least out of the way, up there in Snowfield—Kale knew he would go straight to Johnson's house, here in Santa Mira. Johnson had no family. It was a safe, temporary hiding place. Johnson wasn't exactly Kale's size, but they were close enough so that Kale could swap his jail uniform for the most suitable items in the deputy's closet.

And guns. Jake Johnson, survivalist that he was, would surely have a gun collection somewhere in the house.

The deputy lived in the same one-story, three-bedroom house that he had inherited from his father, Big Ralph Johnson. It wasn't what you would call a showplace. Big Ralph hadn't spent his bribe and graft money with reckless abandon; he had known how to keep a low profile when it came to anything that might draw the attention of a passing IRS agent. Not that the Johnson place was a shack. It was in the center block of Pine Shadow Lane, a well-established neighborhood of mostly larger homes, oversized lots, and mature trees. The Johnson house, one of the smaller ones, had a large Jacuzzi sunk in the tile floor of its rear sun porch, an enormous game room with an antique pool table, and a number of other creature comforts not visible from outside.

Kale had been there twice during the course of selling Johnson the mountain property. He had no difficulty finding the house again.

He pulled the Datsun into the driveway, cut the engine, and got out. He hoped no neighbors were watching.

He went around toward the back of the house, broke a kitchen window, and clambered inside.

He went directly to the garage. It was big enough for two cars, but only a four-wheel-drive Jeep station wagon was there. He had known Johnson owned the Jeep, and he had hoped to find it here. He opened the garage door and drove the stolen Datsun inside. When the door was closed again and the Datsun could not be seen from the street, he felt safer.

In the master bedroom, he went through Johnson's closet and found a pair of sturdy hiking boots only half a size larger than he required. Johnson was a couple of inches shorter than Kale, so the pants weren't the right length, but tucked into the boots, they looked good enough. The waist was too large for Kale, but he cinched it in with a belt. He selected a sports shirt and tried it on. Good enough.

Once dressed, he studied himself in the full-length mirror.

"Looking good," he told his reflection.

Then he went through the house, looking for guns. He couldn't find any.

All right, then they were hidden somewhere. He'd tear the joint to pieces to find them, if it came to that.

He started in the master bedroom. He emptied out the contents of the bureau and dresser drawers. No guns. He went through both nightstands. No guns. He took everything out of the walk-in closet: clothes, shoes, suitcases, boxes, a steamer trunk. No guns. He pulled up the edges of the carpet and searched under it for a hidden storage area. He found nothing.

Half an hour later, he was sweating but not tired. Indeed, he was exhilarated. He looked around at the destruction he had wrought, and he was strangely pleased. The room appeared to have been bombed.

He went into the next room—probing, ripping, overturning, and smashing everything in his path.

He wanted very much to find those guns.

But he was also having fun.

CHAPTER 30

SOME ANSWERS
MORE QUESTIONS

//////

THE HOUSE WAS EXCEPTIONALLY neat and clean, but the color scheme and the unrelenting frilliness made Bryce Hammond nervous. Everything was either green or yellow. *Everything.* The carpets were green, and the walls were pale yellow. In the living room, the sofas were done in a yellow and green floral print that was bright enough to send you running for an ophthalmologist. The two armchairs were emerald green, and the two side chairs were canary yellow. The ceramic lamps were yellow with green swirls, and the shades were chartreuse with tassels. On the walls were two big prints—yellow daisies in a verdant field. The master bedroom was worse: floral wallpaper brighter than the fabric on the living room sofas, searingly yellow drapes with a scalloped valance. A dozen accent pillows were scattered across the upper end of the bed; some of them were green with yellow lace trim, and some were yellow with green lace trim.

According to Jenny, the house was occupied by Ed and Theresa Lange, their three teenagers, and Theresa's seventy-year-old mother.

None of the occupants could be found. There were no bodies, and Bryce was thankful for that. Somehow, a bruised and swollen corpse would have looked especially terrible here, in the midst of this almost maniacally cheerful decor.

The kitchen was green and yellow, too.

At the sink, Tal Whitman said, "Here's something. Better have a look at this, Chief."

Bryce, Jenny, and Captain Arkham went to Tal, but the other two deputies remained back by the doorway with Lisa between them. It was hard to tell what might turn up in a kitchen sink in this town, in the middle of this Lovecraftian nightmare. Someone's head, maybe. Or another pair of severed hands. Or worse.

But it wasn't worse. It was merely odd.

"A regular jewelry store," Tal said.

The double sink was filled with jewelry. Mostly rings and watches. There were both men's and women's watches: Timex, Seiko, Bulova, even a Rolex; some of them were attached to flexible bands; some with no bands at all; none of them was attached to a leather or plastic band. Bryce saw scores of wedding and engagement rings; the diamonds glittered brilliantly. Birthstone rings, too: garnet, amethyst, bloodstone, topaz, tourmaline; rings with ruby and emerald chips. High school and college rings. Junk jewelry was all mixed up with the high-priced pieces. Bryce dug his hands into one of the piles of valuables the way a pirate, in the movies, always drenched his hands in the contents of a treasure chest. He stirred up the shining baubles and saw other kinds of jewelry: earrings, charm bracelets, loose pearls from a broken necklace or two, gold chains, a lovely cameo pendant . . .

"This stuff can't all belong to the Langes," Tal said.

"Wait," Jenny said. She snatched a watch from the pile and examined it closely.

"Recognize that one?" Bryce asked.

"Yes. Cartier. A tank watch. Not the classic tank with Roman numerals. This has no numerals and a black face. Sylvia Kanarsky gave it to her husband, Dan, for their fifth wedding anniversary."

Bryce frowned. "Where do I know that name from?"

"They own the Candleglow Inn," Jenny said.

"Oh, yes. Your friends."

"Among the missing," Tal said.

"Dan loved this watch," Jenny said. "When Sylvia bought it for him, it was a terrible extravagance. The inn was still on rather shaky financial footing, and the watch cost three hundred and fifty dollars. Now of course, it's worth considerably more. Dan used to joke that it was the best investment they'd ever made."

She held the watch up, so Tal and Bryce could see the back. At the top of the gold case, above the Cartier logo, was engraved: TO MY DAN. At the bottom, under the serial number, was LOVE, SYL.

Bryce looked down at the sinkful of jewelry. "So the stuff probably belongs to people from all over Snowfield."

"Well, I'd say it belongs to those who're missing, anyway," Tal said. "The victims we've found so far were still wearing their jewelry."

Bryce nodded. "You're right. So those who're missing were stripped of all their valuables before they were taken to . . . to . . . well, to wherever the hell they were taken."

"Thieves wouldn't let the loot lie around like this," Jenny said. "They wouldn't collect it and then just dump it in someone's kitchen sink. They'd pack it up and take it with them."

"Then what's all this stuff doing here?" Bryce said.

"Beats me," Jenny said.

Tal shrugged.

In the two sinks, the jewelry gleamed and flashed.

The cries of sea gulls.

Dogs barking.

Galen Copperfield looked up from the computer terminal, where he had been reading data. He was sweaty inside his decon suit, tired and achy. For a moment, he wasn't sure he was really hearing the birds and dogs.

Then a cat squealed.

A horse whinnied.

The general glanced around the mobile lab, frowning.

Rattlesnakes. A lot of them. The familiar, deadly sound: *chicka-chicka-chicka-chicka.*

Buzzing bees.

The others heard it, too. They looked at one another uneasily.

Roberts said, "It's coming through the suit-to-suit radio."

"Affirmative," Dr. Bettenby said from over in the second motor home. "We hear it here, too."

"Okay," Copperfield said, "let's give it a chance to perform. If you want to speak to one another, use your external com systems."

The bees stopped buzzing.

A child—the sex indeterminate; androgynous—began to sing very softly, far away:

> *"Jesus loves me, this I know,*
> *for the Bible tells me so.*
> *Little ones to Him are drawn.*
> *They are weak, but He is strong."*

The voice was sweet. Melodic.

Yet it was also blood-freezing.

Copperfield had never heard anything quite like it. Although it was a child's voice, tender and fragile, it nevertheless contained . . . something that shouldn't be in a child's voice. A profound lack of innocence. Knowledge, perhaps. Yes. Too much knowledge of too many terrible things. Menace. Hatred. Scorn. It wasn't audible on the surface of the lilting song, but it was there beneath the surface, pulsing and dark and immeasurably disturbing.

> *"Yes, Jesus loves me.*
> *Yes, Jesus loves me.*
> *Yes, Jesus loves me—*
> *the Bible tells me so."*

"They told us about this," Goldstein said. "Dr. Paige and the sheriff. They heard it on the phone and coming out of the kitchen drains at the inn. We didn't believe them; it sounded so ridiculous."

"Doesn't sound ridiculous now," Roberts said.

"No," Goldstein said. Even inside his bulky suit, his shivering was visible.

"It's broadcasting on the same wavelength as our suit radios," Roberts said.

"But how?" Copperfield wondered.

"Velazquez," Goldstein said suddenly.

"Of course," Roberts said. "Velazquez's suit had a radio. It's broadcasting through Velazquez's radio."

The child stopped singing. In a whispery voice, it said, *"Better say your prayers. Everyone say your prayers. Don't forget to say your prayers."* Then it giggled.

They waited for something more.

There was only silence.

"I think it was threatening us," Roberts said.

"Damn it, put a lid on that kind of talk right now," Copperfield said. "Let's not panic ourselves."

"Have you noticed we're saying *it* now?" Goldstein asked.

Copperfield and Roberts looked at him and then at each other, but they said nothing.

"We're saying *it* the same way that Dr. Paige and the sheriff and the deputies do. So . . . have we come completely around to their way of thinking?"

In his mind, Copperfield could still hear the child's haunting, human-yet-not-human voice.

It.

"Come on," he said gruffly. "We've still got a lot of work to get done."

He turned his attention back to the computer terminal, but he had difficulty concentrating.

It.

By 4:30 Monday afternoon, Bryce called off the house-to-house search. A couple of hours of daylight remained, but everyone was bone weary. Weary from climbing up and down stairs. Weary of grotesque corpses. Weary of nasty surprises. Weary of the extent of the human tragedy, of horror that numbed the senses. Weary of the fear knotted in their chests. Constant tension was as tiring as heavy manual labor.

Besides, it had become apparent to Bryce that the job was simply too big for them. In five and a half hours, they had covered only a small portion of the town. At that rate, confined to a daylight schedule, and with their limited numbers, they would need at least two weeks to give Snowfield a thorough inspection. Furthermore, if the missing people didn't turn up by the time the last building was explored, and if a clue to their whereabouts could not be found, then an even more difficult search of the surrounding forest would have to be undertaken.

Last night, Bryce hadn't wanted the National Guard tramping through town. But now he and his people had had the town to themselves for the better part of a day, and Copperfield's specialists had collected their samples and had begun their work. As soon as Copperfield could certify that the town had not been stricken by a bacteriological agent, the Guard could be brought in to assist Bryce's own men.

Initially, knowing little about the situation here, he had been reluctant to surrender any of his authority over a town in his jurisdiction. But now, although not willing to surrender authority, he was certainly willing to share it. He needed more men. Hour by hour, the responsibility was becoming a crushing weight, and he was ready to shift some of it to other shoulders.

Therefore, at 4:30 Monday afternoon, he took his two search teams back to the Hilltop Inn, placed a call to the governor's office, and spoke with Jack Retlock. It was agreed that the Guard would be placed on standby for a call-up, pending an all-clear signal from Copperfield.

He had no sooner hung up the phone than Charlie Mercer, the desk-sergeant at HQ in Santa Mira, rang through. He had news. Fletcher Kale had escaped while being taken to the county courthouse for arraignment on two charges of murder in the first degree.

Bryce was furious.

Charlie let him rage on for a while, and when Bryce quieted down, Charlie said, "There's worse. He killed Joe Freemont."

"Aw, shit," Bryce said. "Has Mary been told?"

"Yeah. I went over there myself."

"How's she taking it?"

"Bad. They were married twenty-six years."

More death.

Death everywhere.

Christ.

"What about Kale?" Bryce asked Charlie.

"We think he took a car from the apartment complex across the alley. One's been stolen from that lot. So we put up the roadblocks as soon as we knew Kale slipped, but I figure he had almost an hour's lead on us."

"Long gone."

"Probably. If we don't nab the son of a bitch by seven o'clock, I want to call the blocks off. We're so shorthanded—what with everything that's going on— we can't keep tying men up on roadblocks."

"Whatever you think's best," Bryce said wearily. "What about the San Francisco police? You know—about that message Harold Ordnay left on the mirror up here?"

"That was the other thing I called about. They finally got back to us."

"Anything useful?"

"Well, they talked to the employees at Ordnay's bookstores. You remember, I told you one of the shops deals strictly in out-of-print and rare books. The assistant manager at that store, name of Celia Meddock, recognized the Timothy Flyte moniker."

"He's a customer?" Bryce asked.

"No. An author."

"Author? Of what?"

"One book. Guess the title."

"How the devil could I . . . Oh. Of course. *The Ancient Enemy.*"

"You got it," Charlie Mercer said.

"What's the book about?"

"That's the best part. Celia Meddock says she thinks it's about mass disappearances throughout history."

For a moment, Bryce was speechless. Then: "Are you serious? You mean there've been a lot of others?"

"I guess so. At least a bookful of 'em."

"Where? When? How come I've never heard about them?"

"Meddock said something about the disappearance of ancient Mayan populations—"

(Something stirred in Bryce's mind. An article he had read in an old science magazine. Mayan civilizations. Abandoned cities.)

"—and the Roanoke Colony, which was the first British settlement in North America," Charlie finished.

"*That* I've heard about. It's in the schoolbooks."

"I guess maybe a lot of the other disappearances go back to ancient times," Charlie said.

"Christ!"

"Yeah. Flyte apparently has some theory to account for such things," Charlie said. "The book explains it."

"What's the theory?"

"The Meddock woman didn't know. She hasn't read the book."

"But Harold Ordnay must've read it. And what he saw happening here in Snowfield must've been exactly what Flyte wrote about. So Ordnay printed the title on the bathroom mirror."

"So it seems."

With a rush of excitement, Bryce said, "Did the San Francisco P.D. get a copy of the book?"

"Nope. Meddock didn't have one. The only reason she knew about it was because Ordnay recently sold a copy—two, three weeks ago."

"Can *we* get a copy?"

"It's out of print. In fact, it never was in print in this country. The copy they sold was British, which is evidently the only edition there ever was—and a small one. It's a *rare* book."

"What about the person Ordnay sold it to? The collector. What's his name and address?"

"Meddock doesn't remember. She says the guy's not a heavy customer of theirs. She says Ordnay would probably know."

"Which doesn't do us one damned bit of good. Listen, Charlie, I've *got* to get a copy of that book."

"I'm working on it," Charlie said. "But maybe you won't need it. You'll be able to get the whole story from the horse's mouth. Flyte's on his way here from London right now."

Jenny was sitting on the edge of the central operations desk in the middle of the lobby, gaping at Bryce as he leaned back in his chair; she was amazed by what he had told her. "He's on his way here from London? Now? Already? You mean he *knew* this was going to happen?"

"Probably not," Bryce said. "But I guess the minute he heard the news, he knew it was a case that fit his theory."

"Whatever it is."

"Whatever."

Tal was standing in front of the desk. "When's he due in?"

"He'll be in San Francisco shortly after midnight. His U.S. publisher has arranged a news conference for him at the airport. Then he'll come straight to Santa Mira."

"U.S. publisher?" Frank Autry said. "I thought you told us his book was never in print over here."

"It wasn't," Bryce said. "Evidently, he's writing a new one."

"About Snowfield?" Jenny asked.

"I don't know. Maybe. Probably."

"He sure works fast," Jenny said, frowning. "Less than a day after it happens, he's got a contract to write a book about it."

"I wish he worked even faster. I wish to God he was here right now."

Tal said, "I think what Doc means is that this Flyte character might just be another sharp hustler out to make a fast buck."

"Exactly," Jenny said.

"Could be," Bryce admitted. "But don't forget Ordnay wrote Flyte's name on that mirror. In a way, Ordnay's the only witness we have. And from his message, we have to deduce that what happened was very much like the thing Timothy Flyte wrote about."

"Damn," Frank said. "If Flyte's really got some information that could help us, he should've called. He shouldn't have made us wait."

"Yeah," Tal said. "We could all be dead by midnight. He should have called to tell us what we can do."

"There's the rub," Bryce said.

"What do you mean?" Jenny asked.

Bryce sighed. "Well, I have a hunch that Flyte *would* have called if he could've told us how to protect ourselves. Yeah, I think maybe he knows exactly what sort of creature or force we're dealing with, but I strongly suspect he doesn't have the faintest idea what to do about it. Regardless of how much he can tell us, I suspect he won't be able to tell us the one thing we need to know the most—*how to save our asses.*"

Jenny and Bryce were having coffee at the operations desk. They were talking about what they had discovered during today's search, trying to make sense of senseless things: the mocking crucifixion of the priest; the bullets all over the kitchen floor of the Sheffield house; the bodies in the locked cars . . .

Lisa was sitting nearby. She appeared to be totally involved in a crossword puzzle magazine, which she had picked up somewhere along the search route. Suddenly she looked up and said, "I know why the jewelry was piled in those two sinks."

Jenny and Bryce looked at her expectantly.

"First," the girl said, leaning forward on her chair, "you've got to accept that all the people who're missing are really dead. And they are. Dead. No question about that."

"But there *is* some question about that, honey," Jenny said.

"They're dead," Lisa said softly. "I know it. So do you." Her vivid green eyes were almost feverish. "It took them, and it *ate* them."

Jenny recalled Lisa's response last night, at the substation, after Bryce had told them about hearing tortured screams on the phone, when *it* had been in control of the line. Lisa had said, *Maybe it spun a web somewhere, down in a dark place, in a cellar or a cave, and maybe it tied all the missing people into its web, sealed them up in cocoons, alive. Maybe it's just saving them until it gets hungry again.*

Last night, everyone had stared at the girl, wanting to laugh, but realizing there could be a crazy sort of truth to what she said. Not necessarily a web or cocoons or a giant spider. But something. None of them had wanted to admit it, but the possibility was there. The unknown. The unknown *thing*. The unknown thing that ate people.

And now Lisa returned to the same theme. "It *ate* them."

"But how does that explain the jewelry?" Bryce asked.

"Well," Lisa said, "after it ate the people, maybe it . . . maybe it just spit out all that jewelry . . . the same way you would spit out cherry pits."

Dr. Sara Yamaguchi walked into the Hilltop Inn, paused to answer a question from one of the guards at the front door, and came across the lobby toward Jenny and Bryce. She was still dressed in her decontamination suit, but she was no longer wearing the helmet, the tank of compressed air, or the waste recycling unit. She was carrying some folded clothes and a thick sheaf of pale green papers.

Jenny and Bryce rose to meet her, and Jenny said, "Doctor, has the quarantine been lifted already?"

"Already? Seems like I've been trapped inside this suit for *years*." Dr.

Yamaguchi's voice was different from what it had sounded like through the squawk box. It was fragile and sweet. Her voice was even more diminutive than she was. "It feels good to breathe air again."

"You've run bacteria cultures, haven't you?" Jenny asked.

"Started to."

"Well, then . . . doesn't it take twenty-four to forty-eight hours to get results?"

"Yes. But we've decided it's pointless to wait for the cultures. We're not going to grow any bacteria on them—neither benign bacteria nor otherwise."

Neither benign bacteria nor otherwise. That peculiar statement intrigued Jenny, but before she could ask about it, the geneticist said:

"Besides, Meddy told us it was safe."

"Meddy?"

"That's shorthand for Medanacomp," Dr. Yamaguchi said. "Which is itself short for Medical Analysis and Computation Systems. Our computer. After Meddy assimilated all the data from the autopsies and tests, she gave us a probability figure for biological causation. Meddy says there's a zero point zero chance that a biological agent is involved here."

"And you trust a computer's analysis enough to breathe real air," Bryce said, clearly surprised.

"In over eight hundred trial runs, Meddy's never been wrong."

"But this isn't just a trial run," Jenny said.

"Yes. But after what we found in the autopsies and in all pathology tests . . ." The geneticist shrugged and handed the sheaf of green papers to Jenny. "Here. It's all in the results. General Copperfield thought you'd like to see them. If you have any questions, I'll explain. Meanwhile, all the men are up at the field lab, changing out of their decon suits, and I'm itching to do the same. And I do mean *itching.*" She smiled and scratched her neck. Her gloved fingers left faint red marks on her porcelain-smooth skin. "Is there some way I could wash?"

Jenny said, "We've got soap, towels, and a washbasin set up in one corner of the kitchen. It doesn't offer much privacy, but we're willing to sacrifice a little privacy rather than be alone."

Dr. Yamaguchi nodded. "Understandable. How do I get to this washbasin?"

Lisa jumped up from her chair, casting aside the crossword puzzle. "I'll show you. And I'll make sure the guys who're working in the kitchen keep their backs turned and their eyes to themselves."

The pale green papers were computer print-outs that had been cut into eleven-inch pages, numbered, and clipped together along the left-hand margin with plastic pressure binding.

With Bryce looking over her shoulder, Jenny leafed through the first section of the report, which was a computer transcription of Seth Goldstein's autopsy notes. Goldstein noted indications of possible suffocation, as well as even more evident signs of severe allergic reaction to an unidentified substance, but he could not fix a cause of death.

Then her attention came to rest on one of the first pathology tests. It was a light microscopy examination of unstained bacteria in a long series of hanging-drop preparations that had been contaminated by tissue and fluid samples from Gary Wechlas's body; darkfield illumination had been used to identify even the smallest microorganisms. They had been searching for bacteria that were still thriving in the cadaver. What they found was startling.

HANGING-DROP PREPARATIONS
AUTO SCAN - MEDANACOMP
EYE VERIFICATION - BETTENBY
FREQUENCY OF EYE VERIFICATION - 20% OF
SAMPLES
PRINT

SAMPLE 1
ESCHERICHIA GENUS
  FORMS PRESENT:
    NO FORMS PRESENT
NOTE: ABNORMAL DATA.
NOTE: IMPOSSIBLE VARIANT - NO ANIMATE E.
COLI IN BOWEL - CONTAMINATE SAMPLE.
  ↓

CLOSTRIDIUM GENUS
  FORMS PRESENT:
    NO FORMS PRESENT
NOTE: ABNORMAL DATA.
NOTE: IMPROBABLE VARIANT - NO ANIMATE C.
WELCHII IN BOWEL - CONTAMINATE SAMPLE.
  ↓

PROTEUS GENUS
  FORMS PRESENT:
    NO FORMS PRESENT
NOTE: ABNORMAL DATA.
NOTE: IMPROBABLE VARIANT - NO ANIMATE P.
VULGARIS IN BOWEL - CONTAMINATE SAMPLE.

The print-out continued to list bacteria for which the computer and Dr. Bettenby had searched, all with the same results.

Jenny remembered what Dr. Yamaguchi had said, the statement that she had wondered about and about which she had wanted to inquire: *neither benign bacteria nor otherwise.* And here was the data, every bit as abnormal as the computer said it was.

"Strange," Jenny said.

Bryce said, "It doesn't mean a thing to me. Translation?"

"Well, you see, a cadaver is an excellent breeding ground for all sorts of bacteria—at least for the short run. This many hours after death, Gary Wechlas's corpse ought to be teeming with *Clostridium welchii,* which is associated with gas gangrene."

"And it isn't?"

"They couldn't find even one lonely, living *C. welchii* in the water droplet that had been contaminated with bowel material. And that is precisely the sample that ought to be swimming with it. It should be teeming with *Proteus vulgaris,* too, which is a saprophytic bacterium."

"Translation?" he asked patiently.

"Sorry. Saprophytic means it flourishes in dead or decaying matter."

"And Wechlas is unquestionably dead."

"Unquestionably. Yet there's no *P. vulgaris.* There should be other bacteria, too. Maybe *Micrococcus albus* and *Bacillus mesentericus.* Anyway, there aren't any of the microorganisms that're associated with decomposition, not any of the forms you'd expect to find. Even stranger, there's no living *Escherichia coli* in the body. Now, damn it, that would've been there, thriving, even before Wechlas was killed. And it should be there now, still thriving. *E. coli* inhabits the colon. Yours, mine, Gary Wechlas's, everyone's. As long as it's contained within the bowel, it's generally a benign organism." She paged through the report. "Now, here. Here, look at this. When they used general and differential stains to search for dead microorganisms, they found plenty of *E. coli*. But all the specimens were dead. There are no living bacteria in Wechlas's body."

"What's that supposed to tell us?" Bryce asked. "That the corpse isn't decomposing as it should be?"

"It isn't decomposing *at all*. Not only that. Something a whole lot stranger. The reason it isn't decomposing is because it's apparently been injected with a massive dose of a sterilizing and stabilizing agent. A preservative, Bryce. The corpse seems to have been injected with an extremely effective preservative."

Lisa brought a tray to the table. There were four mugs of coffee, spoons, napkins. The girl passed coffee to Dr. Yamaguchi, Jenny, and Bryce; she took the fourth mug for herself.

They were sitting in the dining room at the Hilltop, near the windows. Outside, the street was bathed in the orange-gold sunlight of late afternoon.

In an hour, Jenny thought, it'll be dark again. And then we'll have to wait through another long night.

She shivered. She sure needed the hot coffee.

Sara Yamaguchi was now wearing tan corduroy jeans and a yellow blouse. Her long, silky, black hair spilled over her shoulders. "Well," she was saying, "I guess everyone's seen enough of those old Walt Disney wildlife documentaries to know that some spiders and mud wasps—and certain other insects—inject a preservative into their victims and put them aside for consumption later or to feed their unhatched young. The preservative distributed through Mr. Wechlas's tissues is vaguely similar to those substances but far more potent and sophisticated."

Jenny thought of the impossibly large moth that had attacked and killed Stewart Wargle. But that wasn't the creature that had depopulated Snowfield. Definitely not. Even if there were hundreds of those things lurking somewhere in town, they couldn't have gotten at everyone. No moth that size could have found its way into locked cars, locked houses, and barricaded rooms. Something *else* was out there.

"Are you saying it was an insect that killed these people?" Bryce asked Sara Yamaguchi.

"Actually, the evidence doesn't point that way. An insect would employ a stinger to kill and to inject the preservative. There would be a puncture wound, however minuscule. But Seth Goldstein went over the Wechlas corpse with a magnifying glass. Literally. Over every square inch of skin. Twice. He even used a depilatory cream to remove all the body hair in order to examine the skin more closely. Yet he couldn't find a puncture or any other break in the skin through which an injection might have been administered. We were afraid we had atypical or inaccurate data. So a second postmortem was performed."

"On Karen Oxley," Jenny said.

"Yes." Sara Yamaguchi leaned toward the windows and peered up the street, looking for General Copperfield and the others. When she turned back to the table, she said, "However, everything tested out the same. No animate bacteria in the corpse. Decomposition unnaturally arrested. Tissues saturated with preservative. It was bizarre data again. But we were satisfied that it wasn't atypical or inaccurate data."

Bryce said, "If the preservative wasn't injected, how was it administered?"

"Our best guess is that it's highly absorbable and enters the body by skin contact, then circulates through the tissues within seconds."

Jenny said, "Could it be a nerve gas, after all? Maybe the preservative aspect is only a side effect."

"No," Sara Yamaguchi said. "There aren't any traces on the victims' clothes, as there would absolutely have to be if we're dealing here with gas saturation. And although the substance has a toxic effect, chemical analysis shows it isn't primarily a toxin, which a nerve gas would be; primarily, it's a preservative."

"But was it the cause of death?" Bryce asked.

"It contributed. But we can't pinpoint the cause. It was partly the toxicity of the preservative, but other factors lead us to believe death also resulted from oxygen deprivation. The victims suffered either a prolonged constriction or a complete blockage of the trachea."

Bryce leaned forward. "Strangulation? Suffocation?"

"Yes. But we don't know precisely which."

"But how can it be either one?" Lisa asked. "You're talking about things that took a minute or two to happen. But these people died *fast*. In just a second or two."

"Besides," Jenny said, "as I remember the scene in the Oxleys' den, there weren't any signs of struggle. People being smothered to death will generally thrash like hell, knock things over—"

"Yes," the geneticist said, nodding. "It doesn't make sense."

"Why are all the bodies swollen?" Bryce asked.

"We think it's a toxic reaction to the preservative."

"The bruising, too?"

"No. That's . . . different."

"How?"

Sara didn't answer right away. Frowning, she stared down at the coffee in her mug. Finally: "Skin and subcutaneous tissue from both corpses clearly indicate that the bruising was caused by compression *from an external source;* they were classic contusions. In other words, the bruising wasn't due to the swelling, and it wasn't a separate allergic reaction to the preservative. It seems as if something struck the victims. Hard. Repeatedly. Which is just crazy. Because to cause that much bruising, there would have to be at least a fracture, one fracture, somewhere. Another crazy thing: The degree of bruising is the same all over the body. The tissues are damaged to precisely the same degree on the thighs, on the hands, on the chest, everywhere. Which is impossible."

"Why?" Bryce asked.

Jenny answered him. "If you were to beat someone with a heavy weapon, some areas of the body would be more severely bruised than others. You wouldn't be able to deliver every blow with precisely the same force and at precisely the same angle as all the other blows, which is what you would've *had* to've done to create the kind of contusions on these bodies."

"Besides," Sara Yamaguchi said, "they're bruised even in places where a club wouldn't land. In their armpits. Between the cheeks of the buttocks. And on the soles of their feet! Even though, in the case of Mrs. Oxley, she had her shoes on."

"Obviously," Jenny said, "the tissue compression that resulted in bruising was caused by something other than blows to the body."

"Such as?" Bryce asked.

"I've no idea."

"And they died fast," Lisa reminded everyone.

Sara leaned back in her chair, tilting it onto its rear legs, and looked out the window again. Up the hill. Toward the labs.

Bryce said, "Dr. Yamaguchi, what's your opinion? Not your professional opinion. Personally, informally, what do you think's going on here? Any theories?"

She turned to him, shook her head. Her black hair tossed, and the beams of the late-afternoon sunlight played upon it, sending brief ripples of red and green and blue through it the same way that light, shimmering on the black surface of oil, creates short-lived, wriggling rainbows. "No. No theories, I'm afraid. No coherent thought. Just that . . ."

"What?"

"Well . . . now I believe Isley and Arkham were wise to come along."

Jenny was still skeptical about extraterrestrial connections, but Lisa continued to be intrigued. The girl said, "You really think it's from a different world?"

"There may be other possibilities," Sara said, "but at the moment, it's difficult to see what they are." She glanced at her wristwatch and scowled and fidgeted and said, "What's taking them so long?" She turned her attention to the window again.

Outside, the trees were motionless.

The awnings in front of the stores hung limp.

The town was dead-still.

"You said they were packing away the decon suits."

Sara said, "Yes, but that just wouldn't take this long."

"If there'd been any trouble, we'd have heard gunfire."

"Or explosions," Jenny said. "Those firebombs they made."

"They should've been here at least five . . . maybe ten minutes ago," the geneticist insisted. "And still no sign of them."

Jenny remembered the incredible stealth with which *it* had taken Jake Johnson.

Bryce hesitated, then pushed his chair back. "I suppose it won't hurt if I take a few men to have a look."

Sara Yamaguchi swung away from the window. The front legs of her chair came down hard against the floor, making a sharp, startling sound. She said, "Something's wrong."

"No, no. Probably not," Bryce said.

"You feel it, too," Sara said. "I can tell you do. Jesus."

"Don't worry," Bryce said calmly.

However, his eyes were not as calm as his voice. During the past twenty-some hours, Jenny had learned to read those hooded eyes quite well. Now they were expressing tension and icy, needle-sharp dread.

"It's much too soon to be worried," he said.

But they all knew.

They didn't want to believe it, but they *knew.*

The terror had begun again.

Bryce chose Tal, Frank, and Gordy to accompany him to the lab.

Jenny said, "I'm going, too."

Bryce didn't want her to come. He was more afraid for her than he was for Lisa or for his own men or even for himself.

An unexpected and rare connection had taken place between them. He felt *right* with her, and he believed she felt the same. He didn't want to lose her.

And so he said, "I'd rather you didn't go."

"I'm a doctor," Jenny said, as if that were not only a calling but an armor that would shield her from all harm.

"It's a regular fortress here," he said. "It's safer here."

"It's not safe anywhere."

"I didn't say safe. I said *safer.*"

"They might need a doctor."

"If they've been attacked, they're either dead or missing. We haven't found anyone just wounded, have we?"

"There's always a first time." Jenny turned to Lisa and said, "Get my medical bag, honey."

The girl ran toward the makeshift infirmary.

"She stays here for sure," Bryce said.

"No," Jenny said. "She stays with me."

Exasperated, Bryce said, "Listen, Jenny, this is virtually a martial law situation. I can *order* you to stay here."

"And enforce the order—how? At gunpoint?" she asked, but with no antagonism.

Lisa returned with the black leather bag.

Standing by the front doors of the inn, Sara Yamaguchi called to Bryce: "Hurry. Please hurry."

If *it* had struck at the field lab, there was probably no use hurrying.

Looking at Jenny, Bryce thought: I can't protect you, Doc. Don't you see? Stay here where the windows are locked and the doors are guarded. Don't rely on me to protect you because, sure as hell, I'll fail. Like I failed Ellen . . . and Timmy.

"Let's go," Jenny said.

Agonizingly aware of his limitations, Bryce led them out of the inn and up the street toward the corner—beyond which *it* might very well be waiting for them. Tal walked at the head of the procession, beside Bryce. Frank and Gordy brought up the rear. Lisa, Sara Yamaguchi, and Jenny were in the middle.

The warm day was beginning to turn cool.

In the valley below Snowfield, a mist had begun to form.

Less than three-quarters of an hour remained before nightfall. The sun spilled a final flood of bloody light through the town. Shadows were extremely long, distorted. Windows blazed with reflected solar fire, reminding Bryce of eyeholes in Halloween jack-o'-lanterns.

The street seemed even more ominously silent than it had been last night. Their footsteps echoed as if they were crossing the floor of a vast, abandoned cathedral.

They rounded the corner cautiously.

Three decontamination suits lay tangled and untenanted in the middle of the street. Another empty suit lay half in the gutter and half on the sidewalk. Two of the helmets were cracked.

Submachine guns were scattered around, and unused Molotov cocktails were lined up along the curb.

The back of the truck was open. More empty decontamination suits and submachine guns were piled in there. No people.

Bryce shouted: "General? General Copperfield?"

Graveyard silence.

Surface-of-the-moon silence.

"Seth!" Sara Yamaguchi cried. "Will? Will Bettenby? Galen? Somebody, please answer me."

Nothing. No one.

Jenny said, "They didn't even manage to fire one shot."

Tal said, "Or scream. The guards at the front door of the inn would've heard them even if they'd just screamed."

Gordy said, "Oh, shit."

The rear doors on both labs were ajar.

Bryce had the feeling that something was waiting for them inside.

He wanted to turn and walk away. Couldn't. He was the leader here. If he panicked, they would all panic. Panic was an invitation to death.

Sara started toward the rear of the first lab.

Bryce stopped her.

"They're my friends, damn it," she said.

"I know. But let me look first," he said.

For a moment, however, he couldn't move.

He was immobilized by fear.

Couldn't move an inch.

But then at last, of course, he did.

CHAPTER 31

COMPUTER GAMES

BRYCE'S SERVICE REVOLVER was drawn and cocked. He seized the door with his other hand and threw it wide open. At the same time, he jumped back, pointing his gun into the lab.

It was deserted. Two crumpled decon suits lay on the floor, and another was draped over a swivel chair in front of a computer terminal.

He went to the rear of the second lab.

Tal said, "Let me do this one."

Bryce shook his head. "You stay back there. Protect the women; they don't have guns. If anything comes out of here when I open the door, run like hell."

Heart pounding, Bryce hesitated behind the second field lab. Put his hand on the door. Hesitated again. Then pulled it open even more carefully than he had opened the first.

It was deserted, too. Two decontamination suits. Nothing else.

As Bryce peered into the lab, all the ceiling lights winked out, and he jerked in surprise at the sudden darkness. In a second, however, light sprang up once more, although not from the ceiling bulbs; this was an unusual light, a green flash that startled him. Then he saw it was only the three video display terminals, which had all come on at once. Now they went off. And came on. Off, on, off, on, off . . . At first they flashed simultaneously, then in sequence, around and around. Finally they all came on and stayed on, filling the other-wise unlighted work area with an eerie glow.

"I'm going in," Bryce said.

The others protested, but he was already up the step and through the door.

He went to the first terminal screen, where six words burned in pale green letters across a dark green background.

JESUS LOVES ME - THIS I KNOW.

Bryce glanced at the other two screens. They bore the same words.

Blink. Now there were new words:

FOR THE BIBLE TELLS ME SO.

Bryce frowned.

What sort of program was this? These were the words to one of the songs that had come out of the kitchen drain at the inn.

THE BIBLE IS FULL OF SHIT, the computer told him.

Blink.

JESUS FUCKS DOGS.

The latest three words remained on the screen for several seconds. It seemed to Bryce as if the green light from the display terminals was cold. As fireplace light carries a dry heat with it, so this radiance carried a chill that pierced him.

This was no ordinary program being run on these displays. This was nothing General Copperfield's people had put into the computer, no form of code, no exercise of logic, no systems test of any kind.

Blink.

JESUS IS DEAD. GOD IS DEAD.

Blink.

I AM ALIVE.

Blink.

DO YOU WANT TO PLAY 20 QUESTIONS?

Gazing at the screen, Bryce felt a primitive, superstitious terror rising within him; terror and awe, twisting his gut and clutching his throat. But he didn't know why. On a deep, almost subconscious level, he sensed that he was in the presence of something evil, ancient, and . . . familiar. But how could it be familiar? He didn't even know what *it* was. And yet . . . And yet perhaps he did know. Deep down. Instinctively. If only he could reach inside himself, down past his civilized veneer which embodied so much skepticism, if he could reach into his racial memory, he might find the truth about the thing that had seized and slaughtered the people of Snowfield.

Blink.

SHERIFF HAMMOND?

Blink.

DO YOU WANT TO PLAY 20 QUESTIONS WITH ME?

The use of his name jolted him. And then a far bigger and more disturbing surprise followed.

ELLEN

The name burned on the screen, the name of his dead wife, and every muscle in his body grew tense, and he waited for something more to flash up, but for long seconds, there was only the precious name, and he could not take his eyes away from it, and then—

ELLEN ROTS.

He couldn't breathe.

How could it know about Ellen?

Blink.

ELLEN FEEDS THE WORMS.

What kind of shit was this? What was the point of this?

TIMMY WILL DIE.

The prophecy glowed, green on green.

He gasped. "No," he said softly. For the past year, he had thought it would be better if Timmy succumbed. Better than a slow wasting away. Only yesterday, he would have said that his son's swift death would be a blessing. But not any longer. Snowfield had taught him that nothing was worse than death. In the arms of death, there was no hope. But as long as Timmy lived, there was a possibility of recovery. After all, the doctors said the boy hadn't suffered massive brain damage. Therefore, if Timmy ever woke from his unnatural sleep, he had a good chance of retaining his normal faculties and functions. Chance, promise, hope. So Bryce said, "No," to the computer. "No."

Blink.

TIMMY WILL ROT. ELLEN ROTS. ELLEN ROTS IN HELL.

"Who *are* you?" Bryce demanded.

The moment he spoke, he felt foolish. He couldn't just talk to a computer as if it were another human being. If he wanted to ask a question, he would have to type it out.

SHALL WE HAVE A LITTLE CHAT?

Bryce turned away from the terminal. He went to the door and leaned outside.

The others looked relieved to see him.

Clearing his throat, trying to conceal the fact that he was badly shaken, he said, "Dr. Yamaguchi, I need your help here."

Tal, Jenny, Lisa, and Sara Yamaguchi stepped into the field lab. Frank and Gordy remained outside, by the door, nervously surveying the street, where the daylight was fading fast.

Bryce showed Sara the computer screens.

SHALL WE HAVE A LITTLE CHAT?

He told them what had flashed onto the video displays, and before he was finished, Sara interrupted him to say, "But that's not possible. This computer has no program, no vocabulary that would enable it to—"

"Something has control of your computer," he said.

Sara scowled. "Control? How?"

"I don't know."

"Who?"

"Not *who,*" Jenny said, putting an arm around her sister. "More like *what.*"

"Yeah," Tal said. "This thing, this killer, whatever the hell it is, *it* has control of your computer, Dr. Yamaguchi."

Obviously doubtful, the geneticist sat down at one of the display terminals and threw a switch on an automatic typewriter. "Might as well have a printout just in case we actually get something from this." She hesitated with her delicate, almost childlike hands poised above the keyboard. Bryce watched over her shoulder. Tal, Jenny, and Lisa turned to the other two screens—just as all the displays went blank. Sara stared at the smooth field of green light in front of her, and then finally keyed in the access code and typed a question.

IS SOMEONE THERE?

The automatic typewriter chattered, beginning the print-out, and the answer came at once. YES.

WHO ARE YOU?

COUNTLESS.

"What's it mean?" Tal asked.

"I don't know," the geneticist said.

Sara tapped out the question again and received the same obscure response: COUNTLESS.

"Ask it for a name," Bryce said.

Sara typed, and the words she composed appeared instantly on all three of the display screens: DO YOU HAVE A NAME?

YES.

WHAT IS YOUR NAME?

MANY.

YOU HAVE MANY NAMES?

YES.

WHAT IS ONE OF YOUR NAMES?

CHAOS.

WHAT OTHER NAMES DO YOU HAVE?

YOU ARE A BORING, STUPID CUNT. ASK ANOTHER QUESTION.

Visibly shocked, the geneticist glanced up at Bryce. *"That* is definitely not a word you're going to find in any computer language."

Lisa said, "Don't ask it *who* it is. Ask it *what* it is."

"Yeah," Tal said. "See if it'll give you a physical description."

"It'll think we're asking it to run diagnostic tests on itself," Sara said. "It'll start flashing up circuitry diagrams."

"No, it won't," Bryce said. "Remember, it's not the computer you're having a dialogue with. It's something else. The computer is only the means of communication."

"Oh. Of course," Sara said. "In spite of the word it just used, I still want to think of it as good old Meddy."

After a moment's thought, she typed: PROVIDE A PHYSICAL DESCRIPTION OF YOURSELF.

I AM ALIVE.

BE MORE SPECIFIC, Sara directed.

I AM BY NATURE UNSPECIFIC.

ARE YOU HUMAN?

I ENCOMPASS THAT POSSIBILITY ALSO.

"It's just playing with us," Jenny said. "Amusing itself."

Bryce wiped a hand over his face, "Ask it what happened to Copperfield."

WHERE IS GALEN COPPERFIELD?

DEAD.

WHERE IS HIS BODY?

GONE.

WHERE HAS IT GONE?

BORING BITCH.

WHERE ARE THE OTHERS WHO WERE WITH GALEN COP-PERFIELD?

DEAD.

DID YOU KILL THEM?

YES.

WHY DID YOU KILL THEM?

YOU

Sara tapped the keyboard: CLARIFY.

YOU ARE

CLARIFY.

YOU ARE ALL DEAD.

Bryce saw that the woman's hands were shaking. Yet they moved across the keys with skill and accuracy: WHY DO YOU WANT TO KILL US?

THAT IS WHAT YOU ARE FOR.

ARE YOU SAYING WE EXIST ONLY TO BE KILLED?

YES. YOU ARE CATTLE. YOU ARE PIGS. YOU ARE WORTHLESS.

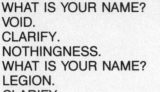

WHAT IS YOUR NAME?
VOID.
CLARIFY.
NOTHINGNESS.
WHAT IS YOUR NAME?
LEGION.
CLARIFY.
CLARIFY MY COCK, YOU BORING BITCH.
Sara blushed and said, "This is madness."
"You can almost feel it in here with us now," Lisa said.
Jenny squeezed her sister's shoulder encouragingly and said, "Honey? What do you mean by that?"
The girl's voice was strained, tremulous. "You can almost feel its presence." Her gaze roamed over the lab. "The air seems thicker—don't you think? And colder. It's as if something's going to . . . materialize right here in front of us."
Bryce knew what she meant.
Tal caught Bryce's eye and nodded. He felt it, too.
However, Bryce was certain that what they felt was entirely a subjective sensation. Nothing was really going to materialize. The air wasn't actually thicker than it had been a minute ago; it just seemed thicker because they were all tense, and when you were rigid with tension, it was just naturally somewhat more difficult to draw your breath. And if the air was colder . . . well, that was only because the night was coming.
The computer screens went blank. Then: WHEN IS HE COMING?
Sara typed, CLARIFY.
WHEN IS THE EXORCIST COMING?
"Christ," Tal said. "What *is* this?"
CLARIFY, Sara typed.
TIMOTHY FLYTE.
"I'll be damned," Jenny said.
"It knows this Flyte character," Tal said. "But how? And is it afraid of him —or what?"
ARE YOU AFRAID OF FLYTE?
STUPID BITCH.
ARE YOU AFRAID OF FLYTE? she persisted, undeterred.
I AM AFRAID OF NOTHING.
WHY ARE YOU INTERESTED IN FLYTE?
I HAVE DISCOVERED THAT HE KNOWS.
WHAT DOES HE KNOW?
ABOUT ME.
"Evidently," Bryce said, "we can rule out the possibility that Flyte is just another hustler."
Sara tapped the keys: DOES FLYTE KNOW WHAT YOU ARE?
YES. I WANT HIM HERE.
WHY DO YOU WANT HIM HERE?
HE IS MY MATTHEW.
CLARIFY.
HE IS MY MATTHEW, MARK, LUKE AND JOHN.
Frowning, Sara paused, glanced at Bryce. Then her fingers flew over the keys again: DO YOU MEAN THAT FLYTE IS YOUR APOSTLE?
NO. HE IS MY BIOGRAPHER. HE CHRONICLES MY WORK. I WANT HIM TO COME HERE.

DO YOU WANT TO KILL HIM TOO?

NO. I WILL GRANT HIM SAFE PASSAGE.

CLARIFY.

YOU WILL ALL DIE. BUT FLYTE WILL BE ALLOWED TO LIVE. YOU MUST TELL HIM. IF HE DOES NOT KNOW THAT HE HAS SAFE PASSAGE, HE WILL NOT COME.

Sara's hands were shaking worse than ever. She missed a key, hit a wrong letter, had to cancel out and start over again. She asked: IF WE BRING FLYTE TO SNOWFIELD, WILL YOU LET US LIVE?

YOU ARE MINE.

WILL YOU LET US LIVE?

NO.

Thus far, Lisa had been braver than her years. However, seeing her fate spelled out so bluntly on a computer display was too much for her. She began to cry softly.

Jenny comforted the girl as best she could.

"Whatever it is," Tal said, "it sure is arrogant."

"Well, we're not dead yet," Bryce told them. "There's hope. There's always hope as long as we're still alive."

Sara used the keyboard again: WHERE ARE YOU FROM?

TIME IMMEMORIAL.

CLARIFY.

BORING BITCH.

ARE YOU EXTRATERRESTRIAL?

NO.

"So much for Isley and Arkham," Bryce said, before realizing that Isley and Arkham were already dead and gone.

"Unless it's lying," Jenny said.

Sara returned to a question she had posed earlier: WHAT ARE YOU?

YOU BORE ME.

WHAT ARE YOU?

STUPID SLUT.

WHAT ARE YOU?

FUCK OFF.

WHAT ARE YOU? She typed again, pounding at the keys so hard that Bryce thought she might break them. Her anger appeared to have outgrown her fear.

I AM GLASYALABOLAS.

CLARIFY.

THAT IS MY NAME. I AM A WINGED MAN WITH THE TEETH OF A DOG. I FOAM AT THE MOUTH. I HAVE BEEN CONDEMNED TO FOAM AT THE MOUTH FOR ALL ETERNITY.

Bryce stared at the display, uncomprehending. Was it serious? A winged man with the teeth of a dog? Surely not. It must be playing with them, amusing itself again. But what was so amusing about this?

The screen went blank.

A pause.

New words appeared, even though Sara had asked no question.

I AM HABORYM. I AM A MAN WITH THREE HEADS—ONE HUMAN, ONE CAT, ONE SERPENT.

"What's this crap all about?" Tal asked, frustrated.

The air in the room was definitely colder.

Only the wind, Bryce told himself. The wind at the door, bringing the coolness of the oncoming night.

I AM RANTAN.

Blink.

I AM PALLANTRE.

Blink.

I AM AMLUTIAS, ALFINA, EPYN, FUARD, BELIAL, OMGORMA, NEBIROS, BAAL, ELIGOR, AND MANY OTHERS.

The strange names glowed on all three screens for a moment, then winked off.

I AM ALL AND NONE. I AM NOTHING. I AM EVERYTHING.

Blink.

The trio of video displays shone brightly, greenly, blankly for a second, two, three. Then went dark.

The overhead lights came on.

"End of interview," Jenny said.

Belial. That was one of the names it had given itself.

Bryce was not an ardently religious man, but he was sufficiently well-read to know that Belial was either another name for Satan or the name of one of the other fallen angels. He wasn't sure which it was.

Gordy Brogan was the most religious one among them, a devout Roman Catholic. When Bryce came out of the field lab, the last to leave it, he asked Gordy to look at the names toward the end of the print-out.

They stood on the sidewalk by the lab, in the dwindling light of day, while Gordy read the pertinent lines. In twenty minutes, perhaps less, it would be dark.

"Here," Gordy said. "This name. Baal." He pointed to it on the accordion-folded length of computer paper. "I don't know exactly where I've seen it before. Not in church or catechism. Maybe I read it in a book somewhere."

Bryce detected an odd tone and rhythm in Gordy's speech. It was more than just nervousness. He spoke too slowly for a few words, then much to fast, then slowly again, then almost frenetically.

"A book?" Bryce asked. "The *Bible?*"

"No, I don't think so. I'm not much of a Bible reader. Should be. Should read it regular. But where I saw this name was in an ordinary book. A novel. I can't quite remember."

"So who is this Baal?" Bryce asked.

"I think he's supposed to be a very powerful demon," Gordy said. And something was definitely wrong with his voice; with *him.*

"What about the other names?" Bryce asked.

"They don't mean anything to me."

"I thought they might be the names of other demons."

"Well, you know, the Catholic Church doesn't go in much for fire-and-brimstone preaching," Gordy said, still speaking oddly. "Maybe it should. Yeah. Maybe it should. 'Cause I think you're right. I think those are the names of demons."

Jenny sighed wearily. "So it was just playing another one of its games with us."

Gordy shook his head vigorously. "No. Not a game. Not at all. It was telling the truth."

Bryce frowned. "Gordy, you don't actually think it's a demon or Satan himself or anything like that—do you?"

"That's all nonsense," Sara Yamaguchi said.

"Yes," Jenny said. "The entire performance on the computer, this demonic image it wants to project—all of that's only more misdirection. It's never going to tell us the truth about itself because if we knew the truth, then we might be able to think of a way to beat it."

"How do you explain the priest who was crucified above the altar at Our Lady of the Mountains?" Gordy asked.

"But that was just one more part of the charade," Tal said.

Gordy's eyes were strange. It wasn't just fear. They were the eyes of a man who was in spiritual distress, even agony.

I should've noticed this coming sooner, Bryce berated himself.

Speaking softly but with spellbinding intensity, Gordy said, "I think maybe the time has come. The end. The time of the ending. At last. Just like the Bible says. That was something I never believed. I believed in everything else the Church taught. But not that. Not judgment day. I just sort of thought everything would go on like this forever. But now it's here, isn't it? Yes. The judgment. Not just for the people who live in Snowfield. For all of us. The end. So I've been asking myself how I'll be judged. And I'm scared. I mean, I was given a gift, a very special gift, and I threw it away. I was given the gift of St. Francis. I've always had a way with animals. It's true. No dog ever barks at me. Did you know that? No cat has ever scratched me. Animals respond to me. They trust me. Maybe they even love me. Never met one that didn't. I've coaxed some wild squirrels to eat right out of my hand. It's a gift. So my folks wanted me to be a veterinarian. But I turned my back on them and on my gift. Became a cop instead. Picked up a gun. A *gun.* I wasn't meant to pick up a gun. Not me. Not ever. I did it partly 'cause I knew it would bother my folks. I was expressing my independence, see? But I forgot. I forgot about where it tells you in the Bible to honor thy father and thy mother. What I did instead was hurt them. And I turned my back on God's gift to me. More than that. Worse than that. What I did was to spit on the gift. Last night I made up my mind to quit the force, put away the gun, and become a vet. But I think I was too late. Judgment was already underway, and I didn't realize it. I've spit on the gift God gave me, and now . . . I'm afraid."

Bryce didn't know what to say to Gordy. His imagined sins were so far removed from genuine evil that it was almost laughable. If there was anyone here who was destined for Heaven, it was Gordy. Not that Bryce believed the judgment day had come. He didn't. But he couldn't think of a thing to say to Gordy, for the big, rawboned kid was too far gone to be talked out of his delusion.

"Timothy Flyte is a scientist, not a theologian," Jenny said firmly. "If Flyte's got an explanation for what's happening here, it's strictly scientific, not religious."

Gordy wasn't listening to her. Tears were streaming down his face. His eyes looked glazed. When he tilted his head and stared up at the sky, he was not seeing the sunset; he was apparently seeing, instead, some grand celestial highway on which the archangels and hosts of Heaven would soon descend in their chariots of fire.

He was in no condition to be entrusted with a loaded gun. Bryce slipped the revolver out of Gordy's holster and took possession of it. The deputy didn't even seem to notice.

Bryce saw that Gordy's bizarre soliloquy had had a serious effect on Lisa. She looked as if she had been hit very hard, stunned.

"It's all right," Bryce told her. "It's not really the end of the world. It's not

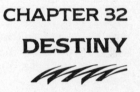

judgment day. Gordy's just . . . disturbed. We're going to come through this just fine. Do you believe me, Lisa? Can you keep that pretty chin of yours lifted? Can you be brave for just a little while longer?"

She didn't immediately respond. Then she reached into herself and found yet another reserve of strength and nerve. She nodded. She even managed a weak, uncertain smile.

"You're a hell of a kid," he said. "A lot like your big sister."

Lisa glanced at Jenny, then brought her eyes back to Bryce again. "You're a hell of a sheriff," she said.

He wondered if his own smile was as shaky as hers.

He was embarrassed by her trust, for he wasn't worthy of it.

I lied to you, girl, he thought. Death is still with us. It'll strike again. Maybe not for an hour. Maybe not even for a whole day. But sooner or later, it *will* strike again.

In fact, although he couldn't possibly have known it, one of them would die in the next minute.

CHAPTER 32

DESTINY

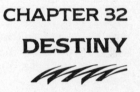

IN SANTA MIRA, Fletcher Kale spent the greatest part of Monday afternoon tearing apart Jake Johnson's house, room by room. He thoroughly enjoyed himself.

In the walk-in pantry, off the kitchen, he at last located Johnson's cache. It wasn't on the shelves, which were crammed full of at least a year's supply of canned and bottled food, or on the floor with stacks of other supplies. No, the *real* treasure was *under* the pantry floor: under the loose linoleum, under the subflooring, in a secret compartment.

A small, carefully selected, formidable collection of guns was hidden there; each of the weapons was individually wrapped in watertight plastic. Feeling as if it were Christmas morning, Kale unwrapped all of them. There were a pair of Smith & Wesson Combat Magnums, perhaps the best and most powerful handgun in the world. Loaded with .357s, it was the deadliest piece a man could carry, with enough punch to stop a grizzly bear; and with light-loaded .38s, it was an equally useful and extremely accurate gun for small game. One shotgun: a Remington 870 Brushmaster 12-gauge with adjustable rifle sights, a folding stock, a pistol grip, magazine extension, and sling. Two rifles. An M-1 semiautomatic. But far better than that, there was a Heckler & Koch HK91, a superb assault rifle, complete with eight thirty-round magazines, already loaded, and a couple of thousand rounds of additional ammunition.

For almost an hour, Kale sat examining and playing with the rifles. Fondling them. If the cops happened to spot him on his way to the mountains, they would wish they had looked the other way.

The hole beneath the pantry also contained money. A lot of it. The bills were tightly rolled wads, encircled by rubber bands, and then stuffed into five large, well-sealed mason jars; there were anywhere from three to five rolls in each container.

He took the jars out to the kitchen and stood them on the table. He looked in the refrigerator for a beer, had to settle for a can of Pepsi, sat down at the table, and began to count his treasure.

$63,440.

One of the most enduring modern legends of Santa Mira County was the one that concerned Big Ralph Johnson's secret fortune, amassed (so it was rumored) through graft and bribe-taking. Obviously, this was what remained of Big Ralph's ill-gotten stash. Just the kind of grubstake Kale needed to start on a new life.

The ironic thing about finding the stash was that he wouldn't have had to kill Joanna and Danny if only he'd had this money in his hands last week. This was more than he had needed to bail himself out of his difficulties with High Country Investments.

A year and a half ago, when he had become a partner in High Country, he couldn't have foreseen that it would lead to disaster. Back then, it had seemed like the golden opportunity that he knew was destined to come his way sooner or later.

Each of the partners in High Country Investments had put up one-seventh of the necessary funds to acquire, subdivide, and develop a thirty-acre parcel over at the eastern edge of Santa Mira, on top of Highline Ridge. To get in on the ground floor, Kale had been forced to commit every available dollar he could lay his hands on, but the potential return had seemed well worth the risk.

However, the Highline Ridge project turned out to be a money-eating monster with a voracious appetite.

The way the deal was set up, each partner was liable for additional assessments if the initial pool of capital proved inadequate to the task. If Kale (or any other partner) failed to meet an assessment, he was out of High Country Investments, immediately, without any compensation for what he had already paid in, thank you very much and goodbye. Then the remaining partners became liable for equal portions of his assessment—and acquired equal fractions of his share of the project. It was the sort of arrangement that facilitated the financing of the project by enticing (usually) only those investors who had a lot of liquidity—but it also required an iron stomach and steel nerves.

Kale hadn't thought there would be any assessments. The original capital pool had looked more than adequate to him. But he was wrong.

When the first of the special assessments was levied for thirty-five thousand dollars, he had been shocked but not defeated. He figured they could borrow ten thousand from Joanna's parents, and there was sufficient equity in their house to arrange refinancing to free another twenty. The last five thousand could be pieced together.

The only problem was Joanna.

Right from the start, she hadn't wanted him to become involved in High Country Investments. She had said the deal was too rich for him, that he should stop trying to play the big-shot wheeler-dealer.

He had gone ahead anyway, and then the assessment had come, and she reveled in his desperation. Not openly, of course. She was too clever for that. She knew she could play the martyr more effectively than she could play the harpy. She never said I-told-you-so, not directly, but that smug accusation was in her eyes, humiliatingly evident in the way she treated him.

Finally he talked her into refinancing the house and taking a loan from her parents. It had not been easy.

He had smiled and nodded and taken all their smarmy advice and snide criticism, but he had promised himself he would eventually rub their faces in all the crap they'd thrown at him. When he hit it big with High Country, he'd make them crawl, Joanna most of all.

Then, to his consternation, the second special assessment had been levied on the seven partners. It was forty thousand dollars.

He could have met that obligation, too, if Joanna had sincerely wanted him to succeed. She could have tapped the trust fund for it. When Joanna's grandmother had died, five months after Danny was born, the old hag had left almost half her estate—fifty thousand dollars—in trust for her only great-grandson. Joanna was appointed the chief administrator of the fund. So when the second assessment came from High Country, she could have taken forty thousand of the trust fund money and paid the bill. But Joanna had refused. She had said, "What if there's *another* assessment? You lose everything, Fletch, everything, and Danny loses most of his trust fund, too." He had tried to make her see that there wouldn't be a third assessment. But, of course, she would not listen to him because she didn't really want him to succeed, because she wanted to see him lose everything and be humiliated, because she wanted to ruin him, break him.

He'd had no choice but to kill her and Danny. The way the trust was set up, if Danny were to die before his twenty-first birthday, the fund would be dissolved. The money, after taxes, would become Joanna's property. And if Joanna died, all of her estate went to her husband; that's what her will said. So if he got rid of both of them, the proceeds of the trust fund—plus a twenty-thousand-dollar bonus in the form of Joanna's life insurance policy—wound up in his hands.

The bitch had left him no choice.

It wasn't his fault she was dead.

She had done it to herself, really. She had arranged things so that there wasn't any other way out for him.

He smiled, remembering her expression when she had seen the boy's body—and when she'd seen him point the gun at her.

Now, sitting at Jake Johnson's kitchen table, Kale looked at all the money, and his smile grew even broader.

$63,440.

A few hours ago, he had been in jail, virtually penniless, facing a trial that could result in a death penalty. Most men would have been immobilized by despair. But Fletcher Kale had not been beaten. He knew he was destined for great things. And here was proof. In an incredibly short time, he had gone from jail to freedom, from penury to $63,440. He now had money, guns, transportation, and a safe hideout in the nearby mountains.

It had begun at last.

His special destiny had begun to unfold.

CHAPTER 33
PHANTOMS

BRYCE SAID, "We'd better get back to the inn."

Within the next quarter of an hour, night would take possession of the town.

Shadows were growing with cancerous speed, oozing out of hiding places, where they had slept the day away. They spread toward one another, forming pools of darkness.

The sky was painted in carnival colors—orange, red, yellow, purple—but it cast only meager light upon Snowfield.

They turned away from the field lab, where they'd recently had a conversation with *it,* by way of computer, and they headed toward the corner as the streetlamps came on.

At the same moment, Bryce heard something. A whimper. A mewling. And then a bark.

The whole group turned as one and looked back.

Behind them, a dog was limping along the sidewalk, past the field lab, trying hard to catch up with them. It was an Airedale. Its left foreleg appeared to be broken. Its tongue was lolling. Its hair was lank and knotted; it looked disheveled, whipped. It took another lurching step, paused to lick its wounded leg, and whined pitifully.

Bryce was riveted by the sudden appearance of the dog. This was the first survivor they had found, not in very good shape, but *alive.*

But *why* was it alive? What was different about him that had saved him when everything else had perished?

If they could discover the answer, it might help them save themselves.

Gordy was the first to act.

The sight of the injured Airedale affected him more strongly than it affected any of the others. He couldn't bear to see an animal in pain. He would rather suffer himself. His heart started beating faster. This time, the reaction was even stronger than usual, for he knew that this was no ordinary dog needing help and comfort. This Airedale was a sign from God. Yes. A sign that God was giving Gordon Brogan one more chance to accept His gift. He had the same way with animals that St. Francis of Assisi had, and he must not spurn it or take it lightly. If he turned his back on God's gift, as he had done before, he would be damned for sure this time. But if he chose to help this dog . . . Tears burned in the corners of Gordy's eyes; they trickled down his cheeks. Tears of relief and happiness. He was overwhelmed by the mercy of God. There was no doubt what he must do. He hurried toward the Airedale, which was about twenty feet away.

At first, Jenny was dumbstruck by the dog. She gaped at it. And then a fierce joy began to swell within her. Life had somehow triumphed over death. *It* hadn't gotten every living thing in Snowfield, after all. This dog (which sat down wearily when Gordy started toward it) had survived, which meant maybe they, themselves, would manage to leave this town alive—

—and then she thought of the moth.

The moth had been a living thing. But it hadn't been friendly.

And Stu Wargle's reanimated corpse.

Back there on the sidewalk, at the edge of shadows, the dog put its head down on the pavement and whimpered, begging to be comforted.

Gordy approached it, crouching, speaking in encouraging, loving tones: "Don't be afraid, boy. Easy, boy. Easy now. What a nice dog you are. Everything'll be okay. Everything'll be all right, boy. Easy . . ."

Horror rose in Jenny. She opened her mouth to scream, but others beat her to it.

"Gordy, *no!*" Lisa cried.

"Get back!" Bryce shouted, as did Frank Autry.

Tal shouted: "Get away from it, Gordy!"

But Gordy didn't seem to hear them.

As Gordy drew near the Airedale, it lifted its chin off the sidewalk, raised its square head, and made soft, ingratiating noises. It was a fine specimen. With its leg mended, with its coat washed and brushed and shining, it would be beautiful.

He put a hand out to the dog.

It nuzzled him but didn't lick.

He stroked it. The poor thing was cold, incredibly cold, and slightly damp.

"Poor baby," Gordy said.

The dog had an odd smell, too. Acrid. Nauseating, really. Gordy had never smelled anything quite like it.

"Where on earth have you been?" he asked the dog. "What kind of muck have you been rolling around in?"

The pooch whined and shivered.

Behind him, Gordy heard the others shouting, but he was much too involved with the Airedale to listen. He got both hands around the dog, lifted it off the pavement, stood up, and held it close to his chest, with its injured leg dangling.

He had never felt an animal this cold. It wasn't just that its coat was wet, and therefore, cold; there didn't seem to be any heat rising from beneath the coat, either.

It licked his hand.

Its *tongue* was cold.

Frank stopped shouting. He just stared. Gordy had picked up the mutt, had begun cuddling it and fussing over it, and nothing terrible had happened. So maybe it was just a dog, after all. Maybe it—

Then.

The dog licked Gordy's hand, and a strange expression crossed Gordy's face, and the dog began to . . . change.

Christ.

It was like a lump of putty being reshaped under an invisible sculptor's swiftly working hands. The matted hair appeared to melt and change color, then the texture changed, too, until it looked more like scales than anything else, greenish scales, and the head began to sink back into the body, which wasn't really a body any more, just a shapeless *thing,* a lump of writhing tissue, and the legs shortened and grew thicker, and all this happened in just five or six seconds, and then—

Gordy stared in shock at the thing in his hands.

A lizard head with wicked yellow eyes began to take form in the amorphous mass into which the dog had degenerated. The lizard's mouth appeared in the puddinglike tissue, and a forked tongue flickered, and there were lots of pointy little teeth.

Gordy tried to throw the thing down, but it clung to him, Jesus, clung tight to him, as if it had reshaped itself around his hands and arms, as if his hands were actually *inside* of it now.

Then it ceased to be cold. Suddenly it was warm. And then hot. Painfully hot.

Before the lizard had completely risen out of the throbbing mass of tissue, it began to dissolve, and a new animal started to take shape, a fox, but the fox quickly degenerated before it was entirely formed, and it became squirrels, a pair of them, their bodies joined like Siamese twins but swiftly separating, and—

Gordy began to scream. He shook his arms up and down, trying to throw the thing off.

The heat was like a fire now. The pain was unbearable.

Jesus, *please.*

Pain ate its way up his arms, across his shoulders.

He screamed and sobbed and staggered forward one step, shook his arms again, tried to pull his hands apart, but the thing clung to him.

The half-formed squirrels melted away, and a cat began to appear in the amorphous tissue that he held and that held him, and then the cat swiftly faded, and something else arose—Jesus, no, no, Jesus, no—something insectile, big as an Airedale but with six or eight eyes across the top of its hateful head and a lot of spiky legs and—

Pain roared through him. He stumbled sideways, fell to his knees, then onto his side. He kicked and thrashed in agony, writhed and heaved on the sidewalk.

Sara Yamaguchi stared in disbelief. The beast attacking Gordy seemed to have total control of its DNA. It could change its shape at will and with astonishing speed.

No such creature could exist. She should know; she was a biologist, a geneticist. Impossible. Yet here it was.

The spider form degenerated, and no new phantom shape took its place. In a natural state, the creature seemed to be simply a mass of jellied tissue, mottled gray-maroon-red, a cross between an enlarged amoeba and some disgusting fungus. It oozed up over Gordy's arms—

—and suddenly, one of Gordy's hands poked through the slime that had sheathed it. But it wasn't a hand any more. God, no. It was only bones. Skeletal fingers, stiff and white, picked clean. The flesh had been eaten away.

She gagged, stumbled backwards, turned to the gutter, vomited.

Jenny pulled Lisa two steps back, farther away from the thing with which Gordy was grappling.

The girl was screaming.

The slime oozed around the bony hand, reclaimed those denuded fingers, enfolded them, sheathed them in a glove of pulsing tissue. In a couple of seconds, the bones were gone as well, dissolved, and the glove folded up into a ball and melted back into the main body of the organism. The thing writhed obscenely, churned within itself, swelled, bulged here, formed a concavity there, now a concavity where the bulge had been, now a swelling nodule where the concavity had been, feverishly changing, as if even a moment's stillness meant death. It pulled itself up Gordy's arms, and he struggled desperately to rid himself of it, and as it progressed toward his shoulders, it left nothing behind it, nothing, no stumps, no bones; it devoured everything. It began to spread across his chest, too, and wherever it went, Gordy simply disappeared into it and did not come out, as if he were sinking into a vat of fiercely corrosive acid.

Lisa looked away from the dying man and clung to Jenny, sobbing.

Gordy's screams were unbearable.

Tal's revolver was already in his hand. He hurried toward Gordy.

Bryce stopped him. "Are you crazy? Tal, damn it, there's nothing we can do."

"We can put him out of his misery."

"Don't get too close to that damned thing!"

"We don't have to get *too* close to get a good shot."

Gordy's eyes became more tortured by the second, and now he began to scream for Jesus's help, and he drummed his heels on the pavement, arched his back, vibrated with the strain, trying to push up from under the growing weight of the nightmarish assailant.

Bryce winced. "All right. Quickly."

They both edged nearer to the thrashing, dying deputy and opened fire. Several shots struck him. His screaming stopped.

They quickly backed off.

They didn't try to kill the thing that was feeding on Gordy. They knew bullets had no effect on it, and they were beginning to understand why. Bullets killed by destroying vital organs and essential blood vessels. But from the look of it, this thing had no organs and no conventional circulatory system. No skeleton, either. It seemed to be a mass of undifferentiated—yet highly sophisticated—protoplasm. A bullet would pierce it, but the amazingly malleable flesh would flow into the channel carved by the bullet, and the wound would heal in an instant.

The beast fed more frantically than before, in a silent frenzy, and in seconds there was no sign of Gordy at all. He had ceased to exist. There was only the shape-changer, grown larger, much bigger than the dog that it had been, even bigger than Gordy, whose substance it now incorporated.

Tal and Bryce rejoined the others, but they didn't run for the inn. As the twilight was slowly squeezed out of the sky in a vise of darkness, they watched the amoeboid thing on the sidewalk.

It began to take a new shape. In only seconds, all of the free-form protoplasm had been molded into a huge, menacing timber wolf, and the creature threw its head back and howled at the sky.

Then its face rippled, and elements of its ferocious countenance shifted, and Tal could see human features trying to rise up through the image of a wolf. Human eyes replaced the animal's eyes, and there was part of a human chin. Gordy's eyes? Gordy's chin? The lycanthropic metamorphosis lasted only seconds, and then the thing's features flowed back into the wolf form.

Werewolf, Tal thought.

But he knew it wasn't anything like that. It wasn't *anything*. The wolf identity, as real and frightening as it looked, was as false as all the other identities.

For a moment it stood there, confronting them, baring its enormous and wickedly sharp teeth, far greater in size than any wolf that had ever stalked the plains and forests of this world. Its eyes blazed with the muddy-bloody color of the sunset.

It's going to attack, Tal thought.

He fired at it. The bullets penetrated but left no visible wound, drew no blood, caused no apparent pain.

The wolf turned away from Tal, with a sort of cool indifference to the gunfire, and trotted toward the open manhole, into which the field lab's electric power cables disappeared.

Abruptly, something rose out of that hole, came from the storm drain below the street, rose and rose into the twilight, shuddering, smashing up into the air with tremendous power, a dark and pulsating mass, like a flood of sewage, except that it was not a fluid but a jellied substance that formed itself into a column almost as wide as the hole from which it continued to extrude itself in an obscene, rhythmic gush. It grew and grew: four feet high, six feet, eight . . .

Something struck Tal across the back. He jumped, tried to turn, and realized that he had only collided with the wall of the inn. He hadn't been aware he'd been backing away from the towering thing that had soared out of the manhole.

He saw now that the pulsing, rippling column was another body of freeform protoplasm like the Airedale that had become a timber wolf; however, this thing was considerably larger than the first creature. Immense. Tal wondered how much of it was still hidden below the street, and he had a hunch that the storm drain was filled with it, that what they were seeing here was only a small portion of the beast.

When it reached a height of ten feet, it stopped rising and began to change. The upper half of the column broadened into a hood, a mantle, so that the thing now resembled the head of a cobra. Then more of the amorphous flesh flowed out of the oozing, glistening, shifting column and poured into the hood, so that the hood rapidly grew wider, wider, until it was not a hood at all any more; now it was a pair of gigantic wings, dark and membranous, like a bat's wings, sprouting out of the central (and still shapeless) trunk. And then the body segment between the wings began to acquire a texture—coarse, overlapping scales—and small legs and clawed feet began to form. It was becoming a winged serpent.

The wings flapped.

The sound was like a whip cracking.

Tal pressed back against the wall.

The wings flapped.

Lisa's grip on Jenny tightened.

Jenny held the girl close, but her eyes, mind, and imagination were fixed upon the monstrous thing that had risen out of the storm drain. It flexed and throbbed and writhed in the twilight and seemed like nothing so much as a shadow that had come to life.

The wings flapped again.

Jenny felt a cold, wing-stirred breeze.

This new phantom looked as if it would detach itself from whatever additional protoplasm lay within the storm drain. Jenny expected it to leap into the darkening air and soar away—or come straight at them.

Her heart thumped; slammed.

She knew escape was impossible. Any movement she made would only draw unwanted attention from *it*. There was no point wasting energy in flight. There was nowhere to hide from a thing like this.

More streetlamps came on, and shadows slunk in with ghostly stealth.

Jenny watched in awe as a serpent's head took shape at the top of the ten-foot-high column of mottled tissue. A pair of hate-filled green eyes swelled out of the shapeless flesh; it was like viewing time-lapse photography of the growth of two malignant tumors. Cloudy eyes, obviously blind, milky green ovals; they quickly cleared, and the elongated black pupils became visible, and the eyes glared down at Jenny and the others with malevolent intent. A foot-wide, slitted mouth sprang open; a row of sharp white fangs grew from the black gums.

Jenny thought of the demonic names that had glowed on the video display terminals, the Hell-born names the thing had given itself. The mass of amorphous flesh, forming itself into a winged serpent, *was* like a demon summoned from beyond.

The phantom wolf, which incorporated the substance of Gordy Brogan, approached the base of the towering serpent. It brushed against the column of pulsing flesh—and simply melted into it. In less than a blink of an eye, the two creatures became as one.

Evidently, the first shape-changer wasn't a separate individual. It was now, and perhaps always had been, part of the gargantuan creature that moved within the storm drains, under the streets. Apparently, that massive mother-body could detach pieces of itself and dispatch them on tasks of their own— such as the attack on Gordy Brogan—and then recall them at will.

The wings flapped, and the whole town reverberated with the sound. Then they began to melt back into the central column, and the column grew thicker as it absorbed that tissue. The serpent's face dissolved, too. *It* had grown tired of this performance. The legs and three-toed feet and vicious talons withdrew into the column, until there was nothing left but a churning, oozing mass of darkly mottled tissue, as before. For several seconds, it posed in the gloomy dusk, a vision of evil, then began to shrink down into the drains under it, down through the manhole.

Soon it was gone.

Lisa had stopped screaming. She was gasping for air and crying.

Some of the others were nearly as shaken as the girl. They looked at one another, but none of them spoke.

Bryce looked as if he had been clubbed.

At last he said, "Come on. Let's get back to the inn before it gets any darker."

There was no guard at the front entrance of the inn.

"Trouble," Tal said.

Bryce nodded. He stepped through the double doors with caution and almost put his foot on a gun. It was lying on the floor.

The lobby was deserted.

"Damn," Frank Autry said.

They searched the place, room by room. No one in the cafeteria. No one in the makeshift dormitory. The kitchen was deserted, too.

Not a shot had been fired.

No one had cried out.

No one had escaped, either.

Ten more deputies were gone.

Outside, night had fallen.

CHAPTER 34

SAYING GOODBYE

THE SIX SURVIVORS—Bryce, Tal, Frank, Jenny, Lisa, and Sara—stood at the windows in the lobby of the Hilltop Inn. Outside, Skyline Road was still and silent, rendered in stark patterns of night-shadow and streetlamp-glow. The night seemed to tick softly, like a bomb clock.

Jenny was remembering the covered passageway beside Liebermann's Bakery. Last night, she had thought something was in the rafters of the service tunnel, and Lisa had believed something was crouching along the wall; very likely they had both been right. The shape-changer—or at least a part of it—had been there, slithering soundlessly through the rafters and down the wall. Later, when Bryce had caught a glimpse of something in the drain inside that passage, he had surely seen a dark glob of protoplasm creeping through the pipe, either keeping tabs on them or engaged upon some alien and unfathomable task.

Thinking, also, of the Oxleys in their barricaded den, Jenny said, "The locked-room mysteries suddenly aren't very mysterious any more. That thing could ooze under the door or through a heating duct. The smallest hole or crack would be big enough. As for Harold Ordnay . . . after he locked himself in the bathroom at the Candleglow Inn, the thing probably got at him through the sink and bathtub drains."

"The same for the locked cars with victims in them," Frank said. "It could surround a car, envelope it, and squeeze in through the vents."

"If it wanted to," Tal said, "it could move real quietly. That's why so many people were caught by surprise. It was behind them, oozing under a door or out of a heating vent, getting bigger and bigger, but they didn't *know* it was there until it attacked."

Outside, a thin fog was coming up the street, rising out of the valley below. Misty auras began to form around the streetlights.

"How big do you think it is?" Lisa asked.

No one responded for a moment. Then Bryce said, "Big."

"Maybe the size of a house," Frank said.

"Or as big as this entire inn," Sara said.

"Or even bigger," Tal said. "After all, it struck in every part of town, apparently simultaneously. It could be like . . . like an underground lake, a lake of living tissue, beneath most of Snowfield."

"Like God," Lisa said.

"Huh?"

"It's everywhere," Lisa said. "It sees all and knows all. Just like God."

"We've got five patrol cars," Frank said. "If we split up, take all five cars, and drive out of here at exactly the same time—"

"It would stop us," Bryce said.

"Maybe it wouldn't be able to stop all of us. Maybe one car would get through."

"It stopped a whole town."

"Well . . . yeah," Frank said reluctantly.

676

Jenny said, "Anyway, it's probably listening to us right this minute. It would stop us before we even reached the cars."

They all looked at the heating ducts near the ceiling. There was nothing to be seen beyond the metal grilles. Nothing but darkness.

They gathered around a table in the dining room of the fortress that was no longer a fortress. They pretended to want coffee because, somehow, sharing coffee gave them a sense of community and normality.

Bryce didn't bother putting a guard on the front doors. Guards were useless. If *it* wanted them, it would surely get them.

Beyond the windows, the fog was getting thicker. It pressed against the glass.

They were compelled to talk about what they had seen. They were all aware that death was coming for them, and they needed to understand why and how they were meant to die. Death was terrifying, yes; however, senseless death was the worst of all.

Bryce knew about senseless death. A year ago, a runaway truck had taught him everything he needed to know about that subject.

"The moth," Lisa said. "Was that like the Airedale, like the thing that . . . that got Gordy?"

"Yes," Jenny said. "The moth was just a phantom, a small piece of the shape-changer."

To Lisa, Tal said, "When Stu Wargle came after you last night, it wasn't actually him. The shape-changer probably absorbed Wargle's body after we left it in the utility room. Then, later, when it wanted to terrorize you, it assumed his appearance."

"Apparently," Bryce said, "the damned thing can impersonate anyone or any animal that it's previously fed upon."

Lisa frowned. "But what about the moth? How could it have fed on anything like the moth? Nothing like that *exists.*"

"Well," Bryce said, "maybe insects that size thrived a long time ago, tens of millions of years ago, back in the age of dinosaurs. Maybe that's when the shape-changer fed on them."

Lisa's eyes widened. "You mean the thing that came out of the manhole might've been millions of years old?"

"Well," Bryce said, "it certainly doesn't conform to the rules of biology as we know them—does it, Dr. Yamaguchi?"

"No," the geneticist said.

"So why shouldn't it also be immortal?"

Jenny looked dubious.

Bryce said, "You have an objection?"

"To the possibility that it's immortal? Or the next thing to immortal? No. I'll accept that. It might be something out of the Mesozoic, all right, something so self-renewing that it's virtually immortal. But how does the winged serpent fit? I find it damned hard to believe that anything like *that* has ever existed. If the shape-changer becomes only those things it has previously ingested, then how could it become something like the winged serpent?"

"There've been animals like that," Frank said. "Pterodactyls were winged reptiles."

"Reptiles, yes," Jenny said. "But not serpents. Pterodactyls were the ancestors of birds. But that thing was clearly a serpent, which is very different. It looked like something out of a fairy tale."

"No," Tal said. "It was straight out of voodoo."

Bryce turned to Tal, surprised. "Voodoo? What would you know about voodoo?"

Tal didn't seem to be able to look at Bryce, and he spoke with evident reluctance. "In Harlem, when I was a kid, there was this enormous fat lady, Agatha Peabody, in our apartment building, and she was a *boko*. That's a sort of witch who uses voodoo for immoral or evil purposes. She sold charms and spells, helped people strike back at their enemies, that sort of thing. All nonsense. But to a kid, it seemed exciting and spooky. Mrs. Peabody ran an open apartment, with clients and hangers-on going in and out all day and night. For a few months I spent a lot of time there, listening and watching. And there were quite a few books on the black arts. In a couple of them, I saw drawings of Haitian and African versions of Satan, voodoo and juju devils. One of them was a giant, winged serpent. Black, with bat wings. And terrible green eyes. It was *exactly* like the thing we saw tonight."

In the street, beyond the windows, the fog was very thick now. It churned sluggishly through the diffused glow of the streetlamps.

Lisa said, "Is it *really* the Devil? A demon? Something from Hell?"

"No," Jenny said. "That's just a . . . pose."

"But then why does it take the shape of the Devil?" Lisa asked. "And why does it call itself the names of demons?"

"I figure the Satanic mumbo-jumbo is just something that amuses it," Frank said. "One more way to tease us and demoralize us."

Jenny nodded. "I suspect it isn't limited to the forms of its victims. It can assume the shape of anything it has absorbed *and* anything it can imagine. So if one of the victims was somebody familiar with voodoo, then *that's* where it got the idea of becoming a winged serpent."

That thought startled Bryce. "Do you mean it not only absorbs and incorporates the *flesh* of its victims *but their knowledge and memories as well?*"

"It sure looks that way," Jenny said.

"Biologically, that's not unheard of," Sara Yamaguchi said, combing her long black hair with both hands and nervously tucking it behind her delicate ears. "For instance . . . If you put a certain kind of flatworm through a maze often enough, with food at one end, eventually it'll learn to negotiate the maze more quickly than it did at first. Then, if you grind it up and feed it to another flatworm, the new worm will negotiate the maze quickly, too, even though it's never been put through the test before. Somehow, it ate the knowledge and experience of its cousin when it ate the flesh."

"Which is how the shape-changer knows about Timothy Flyte," Jenny said. "Harold Ordnay knew about Flyte, so now *it* knows about him, too."

"But how in the name of God did Flyte know about *it?*" Tal asked.

Bryce shrugged. "That's a question only Flyte can answer."

"Why didn't it take Lisa last night in the restroom? For that matter, why hasn't it taken all of us?"

"It's just toying with us."

"Having fun. A sick kind of fun."

"There's that. But I think it's also kept us alive so we could tell Flyte what we've seen and lure him here."

"It wants us to pass along the offer of safe conduct to Flyte."

"We're just bait."

"Yes."

"And when we've served our purpose . . ."

"Yes."

* * *

Something thumped solidly against the outside of the inn. The windows rattled, and the building seemed to shake.

Bryce stood so fast that he knocked over his chair.

Another crash. Harder, louder. Then a scraping noise.

Bryce listened intently, trying to get a fix on the sound. It seemed to be coming from the north wall of the building. It started at ground level but swiftly began to move up, away from them.

A clattering-rattling sound. A bony sound. Like the skeletons of long-dead men clawing their way out of a sepulcher.

"Something big," Frank said. "Pulling itself up the side of the inn."

"The shape-changer," Lisa said.

"But not in its jellied form," Sara said. "In its natural state, it would just flow up the wall silently."

They all stared at the ceiling, listening, waiting.

What phantom form has it assumed this time? Bryce wondered.

Scrape. Tick. Clatter.

The sound of death.

Bryce's hand was colder than the butt of his revolver.

The six of them went to the window and looked out. The fog swirled everywhere.

Then, down the street, almost a block away, at the penumbra of a sodium-vapor lamp, something moved. Half-seen. A menacing shadow, distorted by the fog. Bryce got an impression of a crab as large as a car. He glimpsed arachnoid legs. A monstrous claw with saw-toothed edges flashed into the light, immediately into darkness again. And there: the febrile, quivering, seeking length of antennae. Then the thing scuttled off into the night again.

"That's what's climbing the building," Tal said. "Another damned crab thing like that one. Something straight out of an alky's DTs."

They heard it reach the roof. Its chitinous limbs tapped and scraped across the slate shingles.

"What's it up to?" Lisa asked worriedly. "Why's it pretending to be what it isn't?"

"Maybe it just enjoys mimicry," Bryce said. "You know . . . the same way some tropical birds like to imitate sounds just for the pleasure of it, just to hear themselves."

The noises on the roof stopped.

The six waited.

The night seemed to be crouched like a wild thing, studying its prey, timing its attack.

They were too restless to sit down. They continued to stand by the windows. Outside, only the fog moved.

Sara Yamaguchi said, "The universal bruising is understandable now. The shape-changer enfolded its victims, squeezed them. So the bruising came from a brutal, sustained, universally applied pressure. That's how they suffocated, too—wrapped up inside the shape-changer, totally encapsulated in it."

"I wonder," Jenny said, "if maybe it produces its preservative while squeezing its victims."

"Yes, probably," Sara said. "That's why there's no visible point of injection in either body we studied. The preservative is most likely applied to every square inch of the body, squeezed into every pore. Sort of an osmotic application."

Jenny thought of Hilda Beck, her housekeeper, the first victim she and Lisa had found.

She shuddered.

"The water," Jenny said.

"What?" Bryce said.

"Those pools of distilled water we found. The shape-changer expelled that water."

"How do you figure?"

"The human body is mostly water. So after the thing absorbed its victims, after it used every milligram of mineral content, every vitamin, every usable calorie, it expelled what it didn't need: excess amounts of absolutely pure water. Those pools and puddles we found were all the remains we'll ever have of the hundreds who're missing. No bodies. No bones. Just water . . . which has already evaporated."

The noises on the roof did not resume; silence reigned. The phantom crab was gone.

In the dark, in the fog, in the sodium-yellow light of the streetlamps, nothing moved.

They turned away from the windows at last and went back to the table.

"Can the damned thing be killed?" Frank wondered.

"We know for sure that bullets won't do the job," Tal said.

"Fire?" Lisa said.

"The soldiers had firebombs they'd made," Sara reminded them. "But the shape-changer evidently struck so suddenly, so unexpectedly, that no one had time to grab the bottles and light the fuses."

"Besides," Bryce said, "fire most likely won't do the trick. If the shape-changer caught fire, it could just . . . well . . . *detach* itself from that part of it that was aflame and move the bulk of itself to a safe place."

"Explosives are probably useless, too," Jenny said. "I have a hunch that, if you blew the thing into a thousand pieces, you'd wind up with a thousand smaller shape-changers, and they'd all flow together again, unharmed."

"So can the thing be killed or not?" Frank asked again.

They were silent, considering.

Then Bryce said, "No. Not so far as I can see."

"But then what can we do?"

"I don't know," Bryce said. "I just don't know."

Frank Autry phoned his wife, Ruth, and spoke with her for nearly half an hour. Tal called a few friends on the other telephone. Later, Sara Yamaguchi tied up one of the lines for almost an hour. Jenny called several people, including her aunt in Newport Beach, to whom Lisa talked, as well. Bryce spoke with several men at headquarters in Santa Mira, deputies with whom he had worked for years and with whom he shared a bond of brotherhood; he spoke with his parents in Glendale and with Ellen's father in Spokane.

All six survivors were upbeat in their conversations. They talked about whipping this thing, about leaving Snowfield soon.

However, Bryce knew that they were all just putting the best possible face on a bad situation. He knew these weren't ordinary phone calls; in spite of their optimistic tone, these calls had only one grim purpose; the six survivors were saying goodbye.

CHAPTER 35

PANDEMONIUM

SAL CORELLO, THE publicity agent who had been hired to meet Timothy Flyte at San Francisco International Airport, was a small yet hard-muscled man with corn-yellow hair and purple-blue eyes. He looked like a leading man. If he had been six foot two instead of just five foot one, his face might have been as famous as Robert Redford's. However, his intelligence, wit, and aggressive charm compensated for his lack of height. He knew how to get what he wanted for himself and for his clients.

Usually, Corello could even make newsmen behave so well that you might mistake them for civilized people; but not tonight. This story was too big and much too hot. Corello had never seen anything like it: Hundreds of reporters and curious civilians rushed at Flyte the instant they saw him, pulling and tugging at the professor, shoving microphones in his face, blinding him with batteries of camera lights, and frantically shouting questions. "Dr. Flyte . . ." "Professor Flyte . . ." ". . . Flyte!" *Flyte, Flyte, Flyte-Flyte-Flyte, Flyte-FlyteFlyteFlyte* . . . The questions were reduced to meaningless gabble by the roar of competing voices. Sal Corello's ears hurt. The professor looked bewildered, then scared. Corello took the old man's arm and held it tightly and led him through the surging flock, turning himself into a small but highly effective battering ram. By the time they reached the small platform that Corello and airport security officers had set up at one end of the passengers' lounge, Professor Flyte looked as if he might expire of fright.

Corello took the microphone and quickly silenced the throng. He urged them to let Flyte deliver a brief statement, promised that a few questions would be permitted later, introduced the speaker, and stepped out of the way.

When everyone got a good, clear look at Timothy Flyte, they couldn't conceal a sudden attack of skepticism. It swept the crowd; Corello saw it in their faces: a very visible apprehension that Flyte was hoaxing them. Indeed, Flyte appeared to be a tad maniacal. His white hair was frizzed out from his head, as if he had just stuck a finger in an electric socket. His eyes were wide, both with fear and with an effort to stave off fatigue, and his face had the dissipated look of a wino's grizzled visage. He needed a shave. His clothes were rumpled, wrinkled; they hung like shapeless bags. He reminded Corello of one of those street corner fanatics declaring the imminence of Armageddon.

Earlier in the day, on the telephone from London, Burt Sandler, the editor from Wintergreen and Wyle, had prepared Corello for the possibility that Flyte would make a negative impression on the newsmen, but Sandler needn't have worried. The newsmen grew restless as Flyte cleared his throat half a dozen times, loudly, into the microphone, but when he began to speak at last, they were enthralled within a minute. He told them about the Roanoke Island colony, about vanishing Mayan civilizations, about mysterious depletions of marine populations, about an army that disappeared in 1711. The crowd grew hushed. Corello relaxed.

Flyte told them about the Eskimo village of Anjikuni, five hundred miles northwest of the Royal Canadian Mounted Police outpost at Churchill. On a snowy afternoon in November of 1930, a French-Canadian trapper and trader, Joe LaBelle, stopped at Anjikuni—only to discover that everyone who lived there had disappeared. All belongings, including precious hunting rifles, had been left behind. Meals had been left half-eaten. The dogsleds (but no dogs) were still there, which meant there was no way the entire village could have moved overland to another location. The settlement was, as LaBelle put it later, "as eerie as a graveyard in the very dead of night." LaBelle hastened to the Mounted Police Station at Churchill, and a major investigation was launched, but no trace was ever found of the Anjikunians.

As the reporters took notes and aimed tape recorder microphones at Flyte, he told them about his much-maligned theory: the ancient enemy. There were gasps of surprise, incredulous expressions, but no noisy questioning or blatantly expressed disbelief.

The instant Flyte finished reading his prepared statement, Sal Corello reneged on his promise of a question-and-answer session. He took Flyte by the arm and hustled him through a door behind the makeshift platform on which the microphones stood.

The newsmen howled with indignation at this betrayal. They rushed the platform, trying to follow Flyte.

Corello and the professor entered a service corridor where several airport security men were waiting. One of the guards slammed and locked the door behind them, cutting off the reporters, who howled even louder than before.

"This way," a security man said.

"The chopper's here," another said.

They hurried along a maze of hallways, down a flight of concrete stairs, through a metal fire door, and outside, onto a windswept expanse of tarmac, where a sleek, blue helicopter waited. It was a plush, well-appointed, executive craft, a Bell JetRanger II.

"It's the governor's chopper," Corello told Flyte.

"The governor?" Flyte said. "He's here?"

"No. But he's put his helicopter at your disposal."

As they climbed through the door, into the comfortable passengers' compartment, the rotors began to churn overhead.

Forehead pressed to the cool window, Timothy Flyte watched San Francisco fall away into the night.

He was excited. Before the plane had landed, he had felt dopey and bedraggled; not any more. He was alert and eager to learn more about what was happening in Snowfield.

The JetRanger had a high cruising speed for a helicopter, and the trip to Santa Mira took less than two hours. Corello—a clever, fast-talking, amusing man—helped Timothy prepare another statement for the media people who were waiting for them. The journey passed quickly.

They touched down with a thump in the middle of the fenced parking lot behind the county sheriff's headquarters. Corello opened the door of the passengers' compartment even before the chopper's rotors had stopped whirling; he plunged out of the craft, turned to the door again, buffeted by the wind from the blades, and lent a hand to Timothy.

An aggressive contingent of newsmen—even more of them than in San Francisco—filled the alleyway. They were pressed against the chain-link fence, shouting questions, aiming microphones and cameras.

"We'll give them a statement later, at *our* convenience," Corello told him, shouting in order to be heard above the din. "Right now, the police here are waiting to put you on the phone to the sheriff up in Snowfield."

A couple of deputies hustled Timothy and Corello into the building, along the hallway, and into an office where another uniformed man was waiting for them. His name was Charlie Mercer. He was husky, with the bushiest eyebrows that Timothy had ever seen—and the briskly efficient manner of a first-rate executive secretary.

Timothy was escorted to the chair behind the desk.

Mercer dialed a number in Snowfield, making the connection with Sheriff Hammond. The call was put on a conference speaker, so that Timothy didn't have to hold a receiver, and so that everyone in the room could hear both sides of the conversation.

Hammond delivered the first shocker as soon as he and Timothy had exchanged greetings: "Dr. Flyte, we've seen the ancient enemy. Or at least I guess it's the thing you had in mind. A massive . . . amoeboid thing. A shape-changer that can mimic anything."

Timothy's hands were shaking; he gripped the arms of his chair. "My God."

"Is that your ancient enemy?" Hammond asked.

"Yes. A survivor from another era. Millions of years old."

"You can tell us more when you get here," Hammond said. "If I can persuade you to come."

Timothy only heard half of what the sheriff was saying. He was thinking of the ancient enemy. He had written about it; he had truly believed in it; yet, somehow, he had not been prepared to actually have his theory confirmed. It rocked him.

Hammond told him about the hideous death of a deputy named Gordy Brogan.

Besides Timothy himself, only Sal Corello looked stunned and horrified by Hammond's story. Mercer and the others had evidently heard all about it hours ago.

"You've seen it *and lived?*" Timothy said, amazed.

"It had to leave some of us alive," Hammond said, "so that we'd try to convince you to come. It has guaranteed your safe conduct."

Timothy chewed thoughtfully on his lower lip.

Hammond said, "Dr. Flyte? Are you still there?"

"What? Oh . . . yes. Yes, I'm still here. What do you mean by saying it *guaranteed* my safe passage?"

Hammond told him an astonishing story about communication with the ancient enemy by way of a computer.

As the sheriff talked, Timothy broke into a sweat. He saw a box of Kleenex on one corner of the desk in front of him; he grabbed a handful of tissues and mopped his face.

When the sheriff finished, the professor drew a deep breath and spoke in a strained voice. "I never anticipated . . . I mean . . . well, it never occurred to me that . . ."

"What's wrong?" Hammond asked.

Timothy cleared his throat. "It never occurred to me that the ancient enemy would possess *human-level* intelligence."

"I suspect it may even be a *superior* intelligence," Hammond said.

"But I always thought of it as just a dumb animal, of distinctly limited self-awareness."

"It's not."

"That makes it a lot more dangerous. My God. A *lot* more dangerous."

"Will you come up here?" Hammond asked.

"I hadn't intended to come any closer than I am now," Timothy said. "But if it's *intelligent* . . . and if it's offering me safe passage . . ."

On the telephone, a child's voice piped up, the sweet voice of a young boy, perhaps five or six years old: "Please, please, please come play with me, Dr. Flyte. Please. We'll have lots of fun. Please?"

And then, before Timothy could respond, there came a woman's soft and musical voice: "Yes, dear Dr. Flyte, by all means, do come pay us a visit. You're more than welcome. No one will harm you."

Finally, the voice of an old man came over the line, warm and tender: "You have so much to learn about me, Dr. Flyte. So much wisdom to acquire. Please come and begin your studies. The offer of safe passage is sincere."

Silence.

Confused, Timothy said, "Hello? Hello? Who's this?"

"I'm still here," Hammond answered.

The other voices did not return.

"Just me now," Hammond said.

Timothy said, "But who were those people?"

"They're not actually people. They're just phantoms. Mimicry. Don't you get it? In three different voices, *it* just offered you safe passage again. The ancient enemy, Doctor."

Timothy looked at the other four men in the room. They were all staring intently at the black conference box from which Hammond's voice—and the voices of the creature—had issued.

Clutching a wad of already sodden paper tissues in one hand, Timothy wiped his sweat-slick face again. "I'll come."

Now, everyone in the room looked at him.

On the telephone, Sheriff Hammond said, "Doctor, there's no good reason to believe that it'll keep its promise. Once you're here, you may very well be a dead man, too."

"But if it's intelligent . . ."

"That doesn't mean it plays fair," Hammond said. "In fact, all of us up here are certain of one thing: This creature is the very essence of evil. Evil, Dr. Flyte. Would you trust in the Devil's promise?"

The child's voice came on the line again, still lilting and sweet: "If you come, Dr. Flyte, I'll not only spare you, but these six people who're trapped here. I'll let them go if you come play with me. But if you don't come, I'll take these pigs. I'll crush them. I'll squeeze the blood and shit out of them, squeeze them into pulp, and use them up."

Those words were spoken in light, innocent, childlike tones—which somehow made them far more frightening than if they had been shouted in a basso profundo rage.

Timothy's heart was pounding.

"That settles it," he said. "I'll come. I have no choice."

"Don't come on our account," Hammond said. "It might spare you because it calls you its Saint Matthew, its Mark, its Luke and John. But it sure as hell won't spare us, no matter what it says."

"I'll come," Timothy insisted.

Hammond hesitated. Then: "Very well. I'll have one of my men drive you to the Snowfield roadblock. From there, you'll have to come alone. I can't risk another man. Do you drive?"

"Yes, sir," Timothy said. "You provide the car, and I'll get there by myself."

The line went dead.

"Hello?" Timothy said. "Sheriff?"

No answer.

"Are you there? Sheriff Hammond?"

Nothing.

It had cut them off.

Timothy looked up at Sal Corello, Charlie Mercer, and the two men whose names he didn't know.

They were all staring at him as if he were already dead and lying in a casket.

But if I die in Snowfield, if the shape-changer takes me, he thought, there'll be no casket. No grave. No everlasting peace.

"I'll drive you as far as the roadblock," Charlie Mercer said. "I'll drive you myself."

Timothy nodded.

It was time to go.

CHAPTER 36

FACE TO FACE

〃〃〃〃

AT 3:12 A.M., SNOWFIELD'S church bells began to clang.

In the lobby of the Hilltop Inn, Bryce got up from his chair. The others rose, too.

The firehouse siren wailed.

Jenny said, "Flyte must be here."

The six of them went outside.

The streetlamps were flashing off and on, casting leaping marionette shadows through the shifting banks of fog.

At the foot of Skyline Road, a car turned the corner. Its headlights speared upward, imparting a silvery sheen to the mist.

The streelamps stopped blinking, and Bryce stepped into the soft cascade of yellow light beneath one of them, hoping that Flyte would be able to see him through the veils of fog.

The bells continued to peal, and the siren shrieked, and the car crawled slowly up the long hill. It was a green and white sheriff's department cruiser. It pulled to the curb and stopped ten feet from where Bryce stood; the driver extinguished the headlights.

The driver's door opened, and Flyte got out. He wasn't what Bryce had expected. He was wearing thick glasses that made his eyes appear abnormally large. His fine, white, tangled hair bristled in a halo around his head. Someone at headquarters had lent him an insulated jacket with the Santa Mira County Sheriff's Department seal on the left breast.

The bells stopped ringing.

The siren groaned to a throaty finish.

The subsequent silence was profound.

Flyte gazed around the fog-shrouded street, listening and waiting.

At last Bryce said, "Apparently, it's not ready to show itself."

Flyte turned to him. "Sheriff Hammond?"

"Yes. Let's go inside and be comfortable while we wait."

The inn's dining room. Hot coffee.

Shaky hands clattered china mugs against the tabletop. Nervous hands curled and clamped around the warm mugs in order to make themselves be still.

The six survivors leaned forward, hunched over the table, the better to listen to Timothy Flyte.

Lisa was clearly enthralled by the British scientist, but at first Jenny had serious doubts. He seemed to be an outright caricature of the absent-minded professor. But when he began to speak about his theories, Jenny was forced to discard her initial, unfavorable opinion, and soon she was as fascinated as Lisa.

He told them about vanishing armies in Spain and China, about abandoned Mayan cities, the Roanoke Island colony.

And he told them of Joya Verde, a South American jungle settlement that had met a fate similar to Snowfield's. Joya Verde, which means Green Jewel, was a trading post on the Amazon River, far from civilization. In 1923, six hundred and five people—every man, woman, and child who lived there— vanished from Joya Verde in a single afternoon, sometime between the morning and evening visits of regularly scheduled riverboats. At first it was thought that nearby Indians, who were normally peaceful, had become inexplicably hostile and had launched a surprise attack. However, there were no bodies found, no indications of fighting, and no evidence of looting. A message was discovered on the blackboard at the mission school: *It has no shape, yet it has every shape.* Many who investigated the Joya Verde mystery were quick to dismiss those nine chalk-scrawled words as having no connection with the disappearances. Flyte believed otherwise, and after listening to him, so did Jenny.

"A message of sorts was also left in one of those ancient Mayan cities," Flyte said. "Archaeologists have unearthed a portion of a prayer, written in hieroglyphics, dating from the time of the great disappearance." He quoted from memory: " 'Evil gods live in the earth, their power asleep in rock. When they awake, they rise up as lava rises, but cold lava, flowing, and they assume many shapes. Then proud men know that we are only voices in the thunder, faces on the wind, to be dispersed as if we never lived.' " Flyte's glasses had slid down his nose. He pushed them back into place. "Now, some say that particular part of the prayer refers to the power of earthquakes and volcanoes. I think it's about the ancient enemy."

"We found a message here, too," Bryce said. "Part of a word."

"We can't make anything of it," Sara Yamaguchi said.

Jenny told Flyte about the two letters—P and R—that Nick Papandrakis had painted on his bathroom wall, using a bottle of iodine. "There was a portion of a third letter, too. It might have been the beginning of a U or an O."

"Papandrakis," Flyte said, nodding vigorously. "Greek. Yes, yes, yes— here's confirmation of what I'm telling you. Was this fellow Papandrakis proud of his heritage?"

"Yes," Jenny said. "Extremely proud of it. Why?"

"Well, if he was proud of being Greek," Flyte said, "he might well have known Greek mythology. You see, in ancient Greek myth, there was a god named Proteus. I suspect that was the word your Mr. Papandrakis was trying to write on the wall. Proteus. A god who lived in the earth, crawled through its bowels. A god who was without any shape of his own. A god who could take any form he wished—and who fed upon everything and everyone that he desired."

With frustration in his voice, Tal Whitman said, "What *is* all this supernatural stuff? When we communicated with it through the computer, it insisted on giving itself the names of demons."

Flyte said, "The amorphous demon, the shapeless and usually evil god that can assume any form it wishes—those are relatively common figures in most ancient myth systems and in most if not all of the world's religions. Such a mythological creature appears under scores of names, in all of the world's cultures. Consider the Old Testament of the Bible, for example. Satan first appears as a serpent, later as a goat, a ram, a stag, a beetle, a spider, a child, a beggar, and many other things. He is called, among other names: Master of Chaos and Formlessness, Master of Deceit, the Beast of Many Faces. The Bible tells us that Satan is 'as changeable as shadows' and 'as clever as water, for as water can become steam or ice, so Satan can become that which he wishes to become.' "

Lisa said, "Are you saying the shape-changer here in Snowfield *is* Satan?"

"Well . . . in a way, yes."

Frank Autry shook his head. "No. I'm not a man who believes in spooks, Dr. Flyte."

"Nor am I," Flyte assured him. "I'm not arguing that this thing is a super-natural being. It isn't. It's real, a creature of flesh—although not flesh like ours. It's not a spirit or a devil. Yet . . . in a way . . . I believe it *is* Satan. Because, you see, I believe it was this creature—or another like it, another monstrous survivor from the Mesozoic Era—that inspired the myth of Satan. In prehistoric times, men must have encountered one of these things, and some of them must have lived to tell about it. They naturally described their experiences in the terminology of myth and superstition. I suspect most of the demonic figures in the world's various religions are actually reports of these shape-changers, reports passed down through countless generations before they were at last committed to hieroglyphics, scrolls, and then print. They were reports of a very rare, very real, very dangerous beast . . . but described in the language of religious myth."

Jenny found this part of Flyte's thesis to be both crazy and brilliant, unlikely yet convincing. "The thing somehow absorbs the knowledge and memories of those on whom it feeds," she said, "so it knows that many of its victims see it as the Devil, and it gets some sort of perverse pleasure out of playing that role."

Bryce said, "It seems to enjoy mocking us."

Sara Yamaguchi tucked her long hair behind her ears and said, "Dr. Flyte, how about explaining this in scientific terms. How can such a creature exist? How can it function biologically? What's your scientific rationalization, your theory?"

Before Flyte could answer her, *it* came.

High on one wall, near the ceiling, a metal grille covering a heating duct suddenly popped from its screws. It flew into the room, crashed into an empty table, slid off the table, clattered-rattled-banged onto the floor.

Jenny and the others leapt up from their chairs.

Lisa screamed, pointed.

The shape-changer bulged out of the duct. It hung there on the wall. Dark. Wet. Pulsing. Like a mass of glistening, bloody snot suspended from the edge of a nostril.

Bryce and Tal reached for their revolvers, then hesitated. There was nothing whatsoever that they could do.

The thing continued to surge out of the duct, swelling, rippling, growing into an obscene, gnarled, shifting lump the size of a man. Then, still flowing out of the wall, it began to slide down. It formed into a mound on the floor. Much bigger than a man now, still oozing out of the duct. Growing, growing.

Jenny looked at Flyte.

The professor's face could not settle on a single expression. It tried wonder, then terror, then awe, then disgust, then awe and terror and wonder again.

The viscous, ever-churning mass of dark protoplasm was now as large as three or four men, and still more of the vile stuff gushed from the heating duct in a revolting, vomitous flow.

Lisa gagged and averted her face.

But Jenny couldn't take her eyes from the thing. There was a grotesque fascination that couldn't be denied.

In the already enormous agglomeration of shapeless tissue that had extruded itself into the room, limbs began to form, although none of them maintained its shape for more than a few seconds. Human arms, both male and female, reached out as if seeking help. The thin, flailing arms of children were formed from the jellied tissue, some of them with their small hands open in a silent, pathetic plea. It was difficult to keep in mind that these were not the arms of children trapped within the shape-changer; they were imitation, phantom arms, a part of *it,* not a part of any child. And claws. A startling, frightening variety of claws and animal limbs appeared out of the protoplasmic soup. There were insect parts, too, enormous, hugely exaggerated, terrifyingly frenetic and grasping. But all of these swiftly melted back into the formless protoplasm almost as soon as they took shape.

The shape-changer bulged across the width of the room. It was now larger than an elephant.

As the thing engaged upon a continuous, relentless, mysterious pattern of apparently purposeless change, Jenny and the others edged back toward the windows.

Outside, in the street, the fog roiled in its own formless dance, as if it were a ghostly reflection of the shape-changer.

Flyte spoke with a sudden urgency, answering the questions that Sara Yamaguchi had posed, as if he felt he didn't have much time left to explain. "About twenty years ago, it occurred to me that there might be a connection between mass disappearances and the unexplained extinction of certain species in pre-human geological eras. Like the dinosaurs, for instance."

The shape-changer pulsed and throbbed, towering almost to the ceiling, filling the entire far end of the room.

Lisa clung to Jenny.

A vague but repellent odor laced the air. Slightly sulphurous. Like a draft from Hell.

"There are a host of theories purporting to explain the demise of the dinosaurs," Flyte said. "But no single theory answers all the questions. So I wondered . . . what if the dinosaurs were exterminated by another creature, a natural enemy, that was a superior hunter and fighter? It would have to have been something large. And it would have been something with a very frail skeleton or perhaps with no skeleton whatsoever, for we've never found a fossil record of any species that would have given those great saurians a real battle."

A shudder passed through the entire bulk of tenebrous, churning slime. Across the oozing mass, dozens of faces began to appear.

"And what if," Flyte said, "several of those amoeboid creatures had survived through millions of years . . ."

Human and animal faces arose from the amorphous flesh, shimmered in it.

". . . living in subterranean rivers or lakes . . ."

There were faces that had no eyes. Others had no mouths. But then the eyes appeared, blinked open. They were achingly real, penetrating eyes, filled with pain and fear and misery.

". . . or in deep ocean trenches . . ."

And mouths cracked into existence on those previously seamless countenances.

". . . thousands of feet below the surface of the sea . . ."

Lips formed around the gaping mouths.

". . . preying on marine life . . ."

The phantom faces were screaming, yet they made no sounds.

". . . infrequently rising to feed . . ."

Cat faces. Dog faces. Prehistoric reptile visages. Ballooning up from the slime.

". . . and even less frequently feeding on human beings . . ."

To Jenny, the human faces looked as if they were peering out from the far side of a smoky mirror. None of them ever quite finished taking shape. They *had* to melt away, for there were countless new faces surging and coalescing beneath them. It was an endlessly flickering shadow show of the lost and the damned.

Then the faces stopped forming.

The huge mass was quiescent for a moment, slowly and almost imperceptibly pulsing, but otherwise still.

Sara Yamaguchi was groaning softly.

Jenny held Lisa close.

No one spoke. For several seconds, no one even dared breathe.

Then, in a new demonstration of its plasticity, the ancient enemy abruptly sprouted a score of tentacles. Some of them were thick, with the suction pads of a squid or an octopus. Others were thin and ropy; some of these were smooth, and some were segmented; they were even more obscene than the fat, moist-looking tentacles. Some of the appendages slid back and forth across the floor, knocking over chairs and pushing tables aside, while others wriggled in the air, like cobras swaying to the music of a snake charmer.

Then it struck. It moved fast, gushed forward.

Jenny stumbled back one step. She was at the end of the room.

The many tentacles snapped toward them, whiplike, cutting the air with a hiss.

Lisa could no longer keep from looking. She gasped at what she saw.

In just a fraction of a second, the tentacles grew dramatically.

A rope of cold, slick, utterly alien flesh fell across the back of Jenny's hand. It curled around her wrist.

No!

With a shudder of relief, she pulled loose. It hadn't taken much effort to free herself. Evidently, the thing really wasn't interested in her; not now; not yet.

She crouched as tentacles lashed the air above her head, and Lisa huddled with her.

In his haste to get out of the creature's way, Flyte tripped and fell.

A tentacle moved toward him.

Flyte scooted backwards across the floor, came to the wall.

The tentacle followed, hovered over him, as if it would smash him. Then it moved away. It wasn't interested in Flyte, either.

Although the gesture was pointless, Bryce fired his revolver.

Tal shouted something Jenny couldn't understand. He moved in front of her and Lisa, between them and the shape-changer.

After passing over Sara, the thing seized Frank Autry. *That* was whom it wanted. Two thick tentacles snapped around Frank's torso and dragged him away from the others.

Kicking, flailing with his fists, clawing at the thing that held him, Frank cried out wordlessly, face contorted with horror.

Everyone was screaming now—even Bryce, even Tal.

Bryce went after Frank. Clutched his right arm. Tried to pull him away from the beast, which was relentlessly reeling him in.

"Get it off me! Get it off me!" Frank shouted.

Bryce tried peeling one of the tentacles away from the deputy.

Another of the thick, slimy appendages swept up from the floor, whirled, whipped, struck Bryce with tremendous force, sent him sprawling.

Frank was lifted off the floor and held in midair. His eyes bulged as he looked down at the dark, oozing, changing bulk of the ancient enemy. He kicked and fought to no avail.

Yet another pseudopod erupted from the central mass of the shape-changer and rose into the air, trembling with savage eagerness. Along part of the tentacle's repulsive length, the mottled gray-maroon-red-brown skin seemed to dissolve. Raw, weeping tissue appeared.

Lisa gagged.

It wasn't just the sight of the suppurating flesh that was loathsome and sickening. The foul odor had gotten stronger, too.

A yellowish fluid began to drip from the open wound in the tentacle. Where the drops struck the floor, they sizzled and foamed and ate into the tile.

Jenny heard someone say, "Acid!"

Frank's screaming became a desperate, piercing shriek of terror and despair.

The acid-dripping tentacle slipped sinuously around the deputy's neck and drew as tight as a garrote.

"Oh, Jesus, no!"

"Don't look," Jenny told Lisa.

The shape-changer was showing them how it had beheaded Jakob and Aida Liebermann. Like a child showing off.

Frank Autry's scream died in a bubbling, mucous-thick, blood-choked gurgle. The flesh-eating tentacle cut through his neck with startling quickness. Only a second or two after Frank was silenced, his head popped loose and fell to the floor, smashed into the tiles.

Jenny tasted bile in the back of her throat, choked it down.

Sara Yamaguchi was sobbing.

The thing still held Frank's headless body in midair. Now, in the mass of shapeless tissue from which the tentacles sprouted, a huge toothless maw opened hungrily. It was more than large enough to swallow a man whole. The tentacles drew the deputy's decapitated corpse into the gaping, ragged mouth. The dark flesh oozed around the body. Then the mouth closed up tight and ceased to exist.

Frank Autry had ceased to exist, too.

Bryce stared in shock at Frank's severed head. The sightless eyes gazed at him, through him.

Frank was gone. Frank, who had survived several wars, who had survived a life of dangerous work, had not survived this.

Bryce thought of Ruth Autry. His heart, already jackhammering, twisted with grief as he pictured Ruth alone. She and Frank had been exceptionally close. Breaking the news to her would be painful.

The tentacles shrank back into the pulsing glob of shapeless tissue; in a second or two, they were gone.

The formless, rippling hulk filled a third of the room.

Bryce could imagine it oozing swiftly through prehistoric swamps, blending with the muck, creeping up on its prey. Yes, it would have been more than a match for the dinosaurs.

Earlier, he had believed that the shape-changer had spared him and a few of the others so that they could entice Flyte to Snowfield. Now he realized that wasn't the case. It could have consumed them and then imitated their voices on the telephone, and Flyte would have been coaxed to Snowfield just as easily. It had saved them for some other reason. Perhaps it had spared them only in order to kill them, one at a time, in front of Flyte, so that Flyte would be able to see precisely how it functioned.

Christ.

The shape-changer towered over them, quivering gelatinously, its entire grotesque bulk pulsating as if with the unsynchronized beats of a dozen hearts.

In a voice even shakier than Bryce felt, Sara Yamaguchi said, "I wish there was some way we could get a tissue sample. I'd give anything to be able to study it under a microscope . . . get some idea of the cell structure. Maybe we could find a weakness . . . a way to deal with it, maybe even a way to defeat it."

Flyte said, "I'd like to study it . . . just to be able to understand . . . just to *know.*"

An extrusion of tissue oozed out from the center of the shapeless mass. It began to acquire a human form. Bryce was shocked to see Gordy Brogan coalescing in front of him. Before the phantom was entirely realized, while the body was still lumpy and half detailed, and although the face wasn't finished, the mouth nevertheless opened and the replica of Gordy spoke, though not with Gordy's voice. It was Stu Wargle's voice, instead, a supremely disconcerting touch.

"Go to the lab," it said, its mouth only half formed, yet speaking with perfect clarity. "I will show you everything you want to see, Dr. Flyte. You are my Matthew. My Luke. Go to the lab. Go to the lab."

The unfinished image of Gordy Brogan dissolved almost as if it had been composed of smoke.

The extruded man-size lump of gnarled tissue flowed back into the larger bulk behind it.

The entire pulsating, heaving mass began to surge back through the umbilical that led up the wall and into the heating duct.

How much more of it lies there within the walls of the inn? Bryce wondered uneasily. How much more of it waits down in the storm drains? How large *is* the god Proteus?

As the thing oozed away from them, oddly shaped orifices opened all over it, none bigger than a human mouth, a dozen of them, two dozen, and noises issued forth: the chirruping of birds, the cries of sea gulls, the buzzing of bees, snarling, hissing, child-sweet laughter, distant singing, the hooting of an owl, the maracalike warning of a rattlesnake. Those noises, all ringing out simultaneously, blended into an unpleasant, irritating, decidedly ominous chorus.

Then the shape-changer was gone back through the wall vent. Only Frank's severed head and the bent grille from the heating duct remained as proof that something Hell-born had been here.

According to the electric wall clock, the time was 3:44.

The night was nearly gone.

How long until dawn? Bryce wondered. An hour and a half? An hour and forty minutes or more?

He supposed it didn't matter.

He didn't expect to live to see the sunrise, anyway.

CHAPTER 37

EGO

/////

THE DOOR OF the second lab stood wide open. The lights were on. The computer screens glowed. Everything was ready for them.

Jenny had been trying to hold to the belief that they could still somehow resist, that they still had a chance, however small, of influencing the course of events. Now that fragile, cherished belief was blown away. They were powerless. They would do only what *it* wanted, go only where *it* allowed.

The six of them crowded inside the lab.

"Now what?" Lisa asked.

"We wait," Jenny said.

Flyte, Sara, and Lisa sat down at the three bright video display terminals. Jenny and Bryce leaned against a counter, and Tal stood by the open door, looking out.

Fog foamed past the door.

We wait, Jenny had told Lisa. But waiting wasn't easy. Each second was an ordeal of tense and morbid expectations.

Where would death come from next?

And in what fantastic form?

And to whom would it come this time?

At last Bryce said, "Dr. Flyte, if these prehistoric creatures have survived for millions of years in underground lakes and rivers, in the deepest sea trenches . . . or wherever . . . and if they surface to feed . . . then why aren't mass disappearances more common?"

Flyte pulled at his chin with one thin, long-fingered hand and said, "Because it seldom encounters human beings."

"But why seldom?"

"I doubt that more than a handful of these beasts have survived. There may have been a climatic change that killed off most and drove the few remaining into a subterranean and suboceanic existence."

"Nevertheless, even a few of them—"

"A rare few," Flyte stressed, "scattered over the earth. And perhaps they feed only infrequently. Consider the boa constrictor, for example. That snake takes nourishment only once every few weeks. So perhaps this thing feeds irregularly, as seldom as once every several months or even once every couple of years. Its metabolism is so utterly different from ours that almost anything may be possible."

"Could its life cycle include periods of hibernation," Sara asked, "lasting not just a season or two, but years at a time?"

"Yes, yes," Flyte said, nodding. "Very good. Very good, indeed. That would also help explain why the thing only infrequently encounters men. And let me remind you that mankind inhabits less than one percent of the planet's surface.

Even if the ancient enemy did feed with some frequency, it would hardly ever run up against us."

"And when it *did,*" Bryce said, "it would very likely encounter us at sea because the largest part of the earth is covered with water."

"Exactly," Flyte said. "And if it seized everyone aboard a ship, there wouldn't be witnesses, we'd never know about *those* contacts. The history of the sea *is* replete with stories of vanished ships and ghost ships from which the crews disappeared."

"The *Mary Celeste,*" Lisa said, glancing at Jenny.

Jenny remembered when her sister had first mentioned the *Mary Celeste.* It had been early Sunday evening, when they had gone next door to the Santinis' house and had found the table set for dinner.

"The *Mary Celeste* is a famous case," Flyte agreed. "But it's not unique. Literally hundreds upon hundreds of ships have vanished under mysterious circumstances ever since reliable nautical records have been kept. In good weather, in peacetime, with no 'logical' explanation. In aggregate, the missing crews must surely number in the tens of thousands."

From his post by the open door of the lab, Tal said, "That area of the Caribbean where so many ships have disappeared . . ."

"The Bermuda Triangle," Lisa said quickly.

"Yeah," Tal said. "Could that be . . . ?"

"The work of a shape-changer?" Flyte said. "Yes. Possibly. Over the years, there have been a few mysterious depletions of fish populations in that area, too, so the ancient enemy theory is applicable."

Data flashed up on the video displays: I SEND YOU A SPIDER.

"What's that supposed to mean?" Flyte asked.

Sara tapped the keys: CLARIFY.

The same message repeated: I SEND YOU A SPIDER.

CLARIFY.

LOOK AROUND YOU.

Jenny saw it first. It was poised on the work surface to the left of the VDT that Sara was using. A black spider. Not as big as a tarantula, but much bigger than an ordinary spider.

It curled into a lump, retracting its long legs. It changed. First, it shimmered dully. The black coloration was replaced by the familiar gray-maroon-red of the shape-changer. The spider form melted away. The lump of amorphous flesh assumed another, longer shape: It became a cockroach, a hideously ugly, unrealistically large cockroach. And then a small mouse, with twitching whiskers.

New words appeared on the video displays.

HERE IS THE TISSUE SAMPLE THAT YOU REQUESTED, DR. FLYTE.

"It's so damned cooperative all of a sudden," Tal said.

"Because it knows that nothing we find out about it will help us destroy it," Bryce said morosely.

"There must be a way," Lisa insisted. "We can't lose hope. We just can't."

Jenny stared in wonder as the mouse dissolved into a wad of shapeless tissue.

THIS IS MY SACRED BODY, WHICH I GIVE UNTO THEE, it told them, continuing to mock them with religious references.

The lump rippled and churned within itself, formed minute concavities and convexities, nodules and holes. It was unable to remain entirely still, just as the larger mass, which had killed Frank Autry, had seemed unable or unwilling to remain motionless for even a second.

BEHOLD THE MIRACLE OF MY FLESH, FOR IT IS ONLY IN ME THAT THOU CANST ACHIEVE IMMORTALITY. NOT IN GOD. NOT IN CHRIST. ONLY IN ME.

"I see what you mean about it taking pleasure in mockery and ridicule," Flyte said.

The screen blinked. A new message flashed up:
YOU MAY TOUCH IT.
Blink.
YOU WILL NOT BE HARMED IF YOU TOUCH IT.

No one moved toward the quivering wad of strange flesh.
TAKE SAMPLES FOR YOUR TESTS. DO WITH IT WHAT YOU WISH.
Blink.
I WANT YOU TO UNDERSTAND ME.
Blink.
I WANT YOU TO KNOW THE WONDERS OF ME.

"It isn't only self-aware; it appears to possess a well-developed ego, too," Flyte said.

Finally, hesitantly, Sara Yamaguchi reached out, put the tip of one finger against the small glob of protoplasm.

"It's not warm like our flesh. Cool. Cool and a little . . . greasy."

The small piece of the shape-changer quivered agitatedly.

Sara quickly pulled her hand away. "I'll need to section it."

"Yeah," Jenny said. "We'll need one or two thin cross-sections for light microscopy."

"And another one for the electron miscroscope," Sara said. "And a larger piece for analysis of the chemical and mineral composition."

Through the computer, the ancient enemy encouraged them.
PROCEED, PROCEED, PROCEED, PROCEED
                                        PROCEED
                                        PROCEED
                                        PROCEED

CHAPTER 38

A FIGHTING CHANCE

//////

Tendrils of fog slipped through the open door, into the lab.

Sara was seated at a work counter, hunched over a microscope. "Incredible," she said softly.

Jenny was seated at another microscope, beside Sara, examining another slide of the shape-changer's tissue. "I've never seen cellular structure like this."

"It's impossible . . . yet here it is," Sara said.

Bryce stood behind Jenny. He was eager for her to let him have a look at the slide. It wouldn't mean much to him, of course. He wouldn't know the difference between normal and abnormal cellular structure. Nevertheless, he *had* to have a look at it.

Although Dr. Flyte was a scientist, he wasn't a biologist; cell structure would mean little more to him than it would to Bryce. Yet he, too, was eager to take a peek. He hung over Sara's shoulder, waiting. Tal and Lisa remained nearby, equally anxious to get a look at the Devil on a glass slide.

Still peering intently into the microscope, Sara said, "Most of the tissue is *without* cell structure."

"The same with this sample," Jenny said.

"But all organic matter must have cell structure," Sara said. "Cell structure is virtually a definition of organic matter, a requisite of all living tissue, plant or animal."

"Most of this stuff looks inorganic to me," Jenny said, "but of course it can't be."

Bryce said, "Yeah. We know all too well how alive it is."

"I do see cells here and there," Jenny said. "Not many; a few."

"A few in this sample, too," Sara said. "But each cell appears to exist independently of the others."

"They're widely separated, all right," Jenny said. "They're just sort of swimming in a sea of undifferentiated matter."

"Very flexible cell walls," Sara said. "A trifurcated nucleus. That's odd. And it occupies about half the interior cell space."

"What's that mean?" Bryce asked. "Is it important?"

"I don't know if it's important or not," Sara said, leaning away from the microscope and scowling. "I just don't know what to make of it."

On all three computer screens, a question flashed up: DID YOU NOT EX-PECT THE FLESH OF SATAN TO BE MYSTERIOUS?

The shape-changer had sent them a mouse-size sample of its flesh, but thus far not all of it had been needed for the various tests. Half remained in a petri dish on the counter.

It quivered gelatinously.

It became a spider again and circled the dish restlessly.

It became a cockroach and darted back and forth for a while.

It became a slug.

A cricket.

A green beetle with a lacy red pattern on its shell.

Bryce and Dr. Flyte were seated in front of the microscopes now, while Lisa and Tal waited their turn.

Jenny and Sara stood in front of a VDT, where a computer-enhanced representation of an electron microscope autoscan was underway. Sara had directed the system to zero in and fix upon the nucleus in one of the shape-changer's widely scattered cells.

"Any ideas?" Jenny asked.

Sara nodded but didn't look away from the screen. "At this point, I can only make an educated guess. But I'd say the undifferentiated matter, which is clearly the bulk of the creature, is the stuff that can imprint any cell structure it wants; it's the tissue that mimics. It can form itself into dog cells, rabbit cells, human cells . . . But when the creature is at rest, that tissue has no cellular structure of its own. As for the few scattered cells we see . . . well, they must somehow control the amorphous tissue. The cells give the orders; they produce enzymes or chemical signals which tell the unstructured tissue what it should become."

"So those scattered cells would remain unchanged at all times, regardless of what form the creature took."

"Yes. So it would seem. If the shape-changer became a dog, for instance, and if we took a sample of the dog's tissue, we'd see dog cells. But here and there, spread throughout the sample, we'd come across these flexible cells with their trifurcated nuclei, and we'd have proof that it wasn't really a dog at all."

"So does this tell us anything that'll help us save ourselves?" Jenny asked.

"Not that I can see."

In the petri dish, the scrap of amorphous flesh had assumed the identity of a spider once again. Then the spider dissolved, and there were dozens of tiny ants, swarming across the floor of the dish and across one another. The ants rejoined to form a single creature—a worm. The worm wriggled for a moment and became a very large sow bug. The sow bug became a beetle. The pace of the changes seemed to be speeding up.

"What about a brain?" Jenny wondered aloud.

Sara said, "What do you mean?"

"The thing must have a center of intellect. Surely, its memory, knowledge, reasoning abilities aren't stored in those scattered cells."

"You're probably right," Sara said. "Somewhere in the creature there's most likely an organ that's analogous to the human brain. Not the same as our brain, of course. Very, very different. But with similar functions. It probably controls the cells we've seen, and they in turn control the formless proto-plasm."

With growing excitement, Jenny said, "The brain cells would have at least one important thing in common with the scattered cells in the amorphous tissue: They would *never* change form themselves."

"That's most likely true. It's hard to imagine how memory, logical function, and intelligence could be stored in any tissue that didn't have a relatively rigid, permanent cell structure."

"So the brain would be vulnerable," Jenny said.

Hope crept into Sara's eyes.

Jenny said, "If the brain's not amorphous tissue, then it can't repair itself when it's damaged. Punch a hole in it, and the hole will *stay* there. The brain will be permanently damaged. If it's damaged extensively enough, it won't be able to control the amorphous tissue that forms its body, and the body will die, too."

Sara stared at her. "Jenny, I think maybe you've got something."

Bryce said, "If we could locate the brain and fire a few shots into it, we'd stop the thing. But how do we locate it? Something tells me the shape-changer keeps its brain well protected, hidden far away from us, underground."

Jenny's excitement faded. Bryce was right. The brain might be its weak spot, but they'd have no opportunity to test that theory.

Sara pored over the results of the mineral and chemical analyses of the tissue sample.

"An extremely varied list of hydrocarbons," she said. "And some of them are more than trace elements. A very high hydrocarbon content."

"Carbons are a basic element of all living tissue," Jenny said. "What's different about this?"

"Degree," Sara said. "There's such an abundance of carbon in such various forms . . ."

"Does that help us somehow?"

"I don't know," Sara said thoughtfully. She riffled through the print-out, looking at the rest of the data.

* * *

Sow bug.

Grasshopper.

Caterpillar.

Beetle. Ants. Caterpillar. Sow bug.

Spider, earwig, cockroach, centipede, spider.

Beetle-worm-spider-snail-earwig.

Lisa stared at the lump of tissue in the petri dish. It was going through a rapid series of changes, much faster than before, faster and faster by the minute.

Something was wrong.

"Petrolatum," Sara said.

Bryce said, "What's that?"

"Petroleum jelly," Jenny said.

Tal said, "You mean . . . like Vaseline?"

And Flyte said to Sara, "But surely you're not saying the amorphous tissue is anything as simple as petrolatum."

"No, no, no," Sara said quickly. "Of course not. This is living tissue. But there are similarities in the ratio of hydrocarbons. The composition of the tissue is far more complex than the composition of petrolatum, of course. An even longer list of minerals and chemicals than you'd find in the human body. An array of acids and alkalines . . . I can't begin to figure out how it makes use of nourishment, how it respires, how it functions without a circulatory system, without any apparent nervous system, or how it builds new tissue without using a cellular format. But these extremely high hydrocarbon values . . ."

Her voice trailed away. Her eyes appeared to swim out of focus, so that she was no longer actually looking at the test results.

Watching the geneticist, Tal had the feeling that she was suddenly excited about something. It didn't show in her face or in any aspect of her body or posture. Nevertheless, there was definitely a new air about her that told him she was onto something important.

Tal glanced at Bryce. Their eyes met. He saw that Bryce, too, was aware of the change in Sara.

Almost unconsciously, Tal crossed his fingers.

"Better come look at this," Lisa said urgently.

She was standing by the petri dish that contained the portion of the tissue sample they hadn't yet used.

"Hurry, come here!" Lisa said when they didn't immediately respond.

Jenny and the others gathered around and stared at the thing in the petri dish.

Grasshopper-worm-centipede-snail-earwig.

"It just goes faster and faster and faster," Lisa said.

Spider-worm-centipede-spider-snail-spider-worm-spider-worm . . .

And then even faster.

. . . spiderwormspiderwormspiderwormspider . . .

"It's only half-changed into a worm before it starts changing back into a spider again," Lisa said. "Frantic like. See? Something's happening to it."

"Looks as if it's lost control, gone crazy," Tal said.

"Having some sort of breakdown," Flyte said.

Abruptly, the composition of the small wad of amorphous tissue changed. A milky fluid seeped from it; the wad collapsed into a runny pile of lifeless mush.

It didn't move.

It didn't take on another form.

Jenny wanted to touch it; didn't dare.

Sara picked up a small lab spoon, poked at the stuff in the dish.

It still didn't move.

She stirred it.

The tissue liquefied even further, but otherwise did not respond.

"It's dead," Flyte said softly.

Bryce seemed electrified by this development. He turned to Sara. "What was in the petri dish before you put the tissue sample there?"

"Nothing."

"There must've been a residue."

"No."

"Think, damn it. Our lives depend on this."

"There was nothing in the dish. I took it from the sterilizer."

"A trace of some chemical . . ."

"It was perfectly clean."

"Wait, wait, wait. Something in the dish must've reacted with the shape-changer's tissue," Bryce said. "Right? Isn't that clear?"

"And whatever was in the dish," Tal said, *"that's* our weapon."

"It's the stuff that'll kill the shape-changer," Lisa said.

"Not necessarily," Jenny said, hating to shatter the girl's hopes.

"Sounds too easy," Flyte agreed, combing his wild white hair with a trembling hand. "Let's not leap to conclusions."

"Especially when there're other possibilities," Jenny said.

"Such as?" Bryce asked.

"Well . . . we know that the main mass of the creature can shed pieces of itself in about any form it chooses, can direct the activities of those detached parts, and can summon them back the way it summoned the part of itself that it sent to kill Gordy. But now suppose that a detached portion of the shape-changer can only survive for a relatively short period of time on its own, away from the mother-body. Suppose the amorphous tissue needs a steady supply of a particular enzyme in order to maintain its cohesiveness, an enzyme that *isn't* manufactured in those independently situated control cells that're scattered throughout the tissue—"

"—an enzyme that's produced only by the shape-changer's brain," Sara said, picking up on Jenny's chain of thought.

"Exactly," Jenny said. "So . . . any detached portion would have to reintegrate itself with the main mass in order to replenish its supply of that vital enzyme, or whatever the substance may be."

"That's not unlikely," Sara said. "After all, the human brain produces enzymes and hormones without which our own bodies wouldn't be able to survive. Why shouldn't the shape-changer's brain fulfill a similar function?"

"All right," Bryce said. "What does this discovery mean to us?"

"If it *is* a discovery and not just a wrongheaded guess," Jenny said, "then it means we could definitely destroy the entire shape-changer if we could destroy the brain. The creature wouldn't be able to separate into several parts and crawl away and go on living in other incarnations. Without the essential brain-manufactured enzymes—or hormones or whatever—the separate parts would all eventually dissolve into lifeless mush, the way the thing in the petri dish has done."

Bryce sagged with disappointment. "We're back at square one. We have to locate its brain before we have any chance of striking a death blow, but the thing's never going to let us do that."

"We're *not* back to square one," Sara said. Pointing to the lifeless slime in the petri dish: "This tells us something else that's important."

"What?" Bryce asked, his voice heavy with frustration. "Is it something useful, something that could save us—or is it just another item of bizarre information?"

Sara said, "We now know the amorphous tissue exists in a delicate chemical balance *that can be disrupted.*"

She let that sink in.

The deep worry lines in Bryce's face softened a bit.

Sara said, "The flesh of the shape-changer can be damaged. It can be killed. Here's proof in the petri dish."

"How do we use that knowledge?" Tal asked. "How do we disrupt the chemical balance?"

"That's what we've got to find out," Sara said.

"Do you have any ideas?" Lisa asked the geneticist.

"No," Sara said. "None."

But Jenny suddenly had the feeling that Sara Yamaguchi was lying.

Sara wanted to tell them about the plan that had occurred to her, but she couldn't say a word. For one thing, her strategy offered only a fragile thread of hope. She didn't want to raise their hopes unrealistically and then see them dashed again. More importantly, if she told them what was on her mind, and if by some miracle she actually had found a way to destroy the shape-changer, *it* would hear what she said, and it would know her plans, and it would stop her. There was no place where she could safely discuss her thoughts with Jenny and Bryce and the others. Their best hope was to keep the ancient enemy smug and complacent.

But she had to buy some time, several hours, in which to set her plan in motion. The shape-changer was millions and millions of years old, virtually immortal. What were a few hours to this creature? Surely, it would comply with her request. Surely.

She sat down at one of the computer terminals, her eyes burning with weariness. She needed sleep. They all needed sleep. The night was nearly gone. She wiped one hand across her face, as if she could slough off her weariness. Then she typed: ARE YOU THERE?

YES.

WE HAVE COMPLETED A NUMBER OF TESTS, she typed as the others crowded around her.

I KNOW, it replied.

WE ARE FASCINATED. THERE IS MORE WE WISH TO KNOW.

OF COURSE.

THERE ARE OTHER TESTS WE WANT TO CONDUCT.

WHY?

IN ORDER THAT WE CAN KNOW MORE ABOUT YOU.

CLARIFY, it answered teasingly.

Sara thought for a moment, then typed: DR. FLYTE NEEDS ADDITIONAL DATA IF HE IS TO WRITE ABOUT YOU WITH AUTHORITY.

HE IS MY MATTHEW.

HE NEEDS MORE DATA TO TELL YOUR STORY AS IT SHOULD BE TOLD.

It flashed back a three-line response in the center of the video display:
—A FLOURISH OF TRUMPETS—
THE GREATEST STORY EVER TOLD
—A FLOURISH OF TRUMPETS—

Sara couldn't be sure if it was merely mocking them or whether its ego was actually so large that it could seriously equate its own story with the story of Christ.

The screen blinked. New words appeared: PROCEED WITH YOUR TESTS.

WE WILL NEED TO SEND FOR MORE LAB EQUIPMENT.

WHY? YOU HAVE A FULLY EQUIPPED LAB.

Sara's hands were moist. She blotted them on her jeans before tapping out her answer.

THIS LAB IS FULLY EQUIPPED ONLY FOR A NARROW AREA OF SCIENTIFIC INQUIRY: THE ANALYSIS OF CHEMICAL AND BIOLOGICAL WARFARE AGENTS. WE DID NOT ANTICIPATE ENCOUNTERING A BEING OF YOUR NATURE. WE MUST HAVE OTHER LAB EQUIPMENT IN ORDER TO DO A PROPER JOB.

PROCEED.

IT WILL TAKE SEVERAL HOURS TO HAVE THE EQUIPMENT SENT HERE, she told it.

PROCEED.

She stared at the word, green on green, hardly daring to believe that gaining more time would be this easy.

She tapped the keys: WE WILL NEED TO RETURN TO THE INN AND USE THE TELEPHONE THERE.

PROCEED, YOU BORING BITCH. PROCEED, PROCEED, PROCEED, PROCEED.

Her hands were damp again. She wiped them on her jeans and stood up.

From the way the others were looking at her, she realized that they knew she was hiding something, and they understood why she was remaining silent about it.

But how did they know? Was she that obvious? And if they knew, did *it* know, too?

She cleared her throat. "Let's go," she said shakily.

"Let's go," Sara Yamaguchi said shakily, but Timothy said, "Wait. Just a minute or two, please. There's something I've got to try."

He sat down at a computer terminal. Although he had gotten some sleep on the airliners, his mind was not as sharp as it ought to be. He shook his head and took several deep breaths, then typed: THIS IS TIMOTHY FLYTE.

I KNOW.

WE MUST HAVE A DIALOGUE.

PROCEED.

MUST WE DO IT THROUGH THE COMPUTER?

IT IS BETTER THAN A BURNING BUSH.

For a second or two, Timothy didn't understand what it meant. When he got the joke, he almost laughed aloud. The damned thing had its own perverse sense of humor. He typed: YOUR SPECIES AND MINE SHOULD LIVE IN PEACE.

WHY?

BECAUSE WE SHARE THE EARTH.

AS THE FARMER SHARES THE FARM WITH HIS CATTLE. YOU ARE MY CATTLE.

WE ARE THE ONLY TWO INTELLIGENT SPECIES ON EARTH.

YOU THINK YOU KNOW SO MUCH. IN FACT YOU KNOW SO LITTLE.

WE SHOULD COOPERATE, Flyte persisted doggedly.

YOU ARE INFERIOR TO ME.

WE HAVE MUCH TO LEARN FROM EACH OTHER.

I HAVE NOTHING TO LEARN FROM YOUR KIND.

WE MAY BE MORE CLEVER THAN YOU BELIEVE.

YOU ARE MORTAL. IS THAT NOT TRUE?

YES.

TO ME, YOUR LIVES ARE AS BRIEF AND UNIMPORTANT AS THE LIVES OF MAYFLIES SEEM TO YOU.

IF THAT IS THE WAY YOU FEEL, WHY DO YOU CARE WHETHER OR NOT I WRITE ABOUT YOU?

IT AMUSES ME THAT ONE OF YOUR SPECIES HAS THEORIZED MY EXISTENCE. IT IS LIKE A PET MONKEY LEARNING A DIFFICULT TRICK.

I DO NOT BELIEVE WE ARE YOUR INFERIORS, Flyte typed gamely.

CATTLE.

I BELIEVE YOU WANT TO BE WRITTEN ABOUT BECAUSE YOU HAVE ACQUIRED A VERY HUMAN EGO.

YOU ARE WRONG.

I BELIEVE THAT YOU WERE NOT AN INTELLIGENT CREATURE UN- TIL YOU BEGAN FEEDING UPON INTELLIGENT CREATURES, UPON MEN.

YOUR IGNORANCE DISAPPOINTS ME.

Timothy continued to challenge it. I BELIEVE THAT ALONG WITH KNOWLEDGE AND MEMORY THAT WAS ABSORBED FROM YOUR HU- MAN VICTIMS, YOU ALSO ACQUIRED INTELLIGENCE. YOU OWE US FOR YOUR OWN EVOLUTION.

It did not reply.

Timothy cleared the screen and typed more: YOUR MIND SEEMS TO HAVE A VERY HUMAN STRUCTURE—EGO, SUPEREGO, AND SO FORTH.

CATTLE, it replied.

Blink.

PIGS, it said.

Blink.

GROVELING ANIMALS, it said.

Blink.

YOU BORE ME, it said.

And then all the screens went dark.

Timothy leaned back in his chair and sighed.

Sheriff Hammond said, "Nice try, Dr. Flyte."

"Such arrogance," Timothy said.

"Befitting a god," Dr. Paige said. "And that's more or less how it thinks of itself."

"In a way," Lisa Paige said, "that's what it really *is.*"

"Yeah," Tal Whitman said, "for all intents and purposes, it might as well *be* a god. It has all the powers of a god, doesn't it?"

"Or a devil," Lisa said.

* * *

Beyond the streetlamps and above the fog, the night was gray now. The first vague glow of dawn had sparked the far end of the sky.

Sara wished Dr. Flyte hadn't challenged the shape-changer so boldly. She was worried that he had antagonized it, and that now it would renege on its promise to give them more time.

During the short walk from the field lab to the Hilltop Inn, she kept expecting a grotesque phantom to lope or scuttle at them from out of the fog. It must not take them now. Not now. Not when there was, at long last, a glimmer of hope.

Elsewhere in town, off in the fog and shadows, there were strange animal sounds, eerie ululating cries like nothing that Sara had ever heard before. *It* was still engaged upon its ceaseless mimicry. A hellish shriek, uncomfortably close at hand, caused the survivors to bunch together.

But they were not attacked.

The streets, although not silent, were still. There was not even a breeze; the mist hung motionless in the air.

Nothing waited for them inside the inn, either.

At the central operations desk, Sara sat down and dialed the number of the CBW Civilian Defense Unit's home base in Dugway, Utah.

Jenny, Bryce, and the others gathered around to listen.

Because of the ongoing crisis in Snowfield, there was not just the usual night-duty sergeant at the Dugway headquarters. Captain Daniel Tersch, a physician in the Army Medical Corps, a specialist in containing contagious disease, third in charge of the unit, was standing by to direct any support operations that might become necessary.

Sara told him about their latest discoveries—the microscopic examinations of the shape-changer's tissue, the results of the various mineral and chemical analyses—and Tersch was fascinated, though this was well beyond his field of expertise.

"Petrolatum?" he asked at one point, surprised by what she had told him.

"The amorphous tissue resembles petrolatum only in that it has a somewhat similar mix of hydrocarbons that register very high values. But of course it's much more complex, much more sophisticated."

She stressed this particular discovery, for she wanted to be certain that Tersch passed it along to other scientists on the CBW team at Dugway. If another geneticist or a biochemist were to consider this data and then look at the list of materials she was going to ask for, he would almost certainly know what her plan was. If someone in the CBW unit *did* get her message, he would assemble the weapon for her before it was sent into Snowfield, sparing her the time-consuming and dangerous job of assembling it with the shape-changer looking over her shoulder.

She couldn't just tell Tersch what she had in mind, for she was certain the ancient enemy was listening in. There was an odd, faint hissing on the line . . .

Finally she spoke of her need for additional laboratory equipment. "Most of this stuff can be borrowed from university and industry labs right here in Northern California," she told Tersch. "I just need you to use the army's manpower, transportation, and authority to put together the package and get it to me as quickly as possible."

"What do you need?" Tersch asked. "Just tell me, and you'll have it in five or six hours."

She recited a list of equipment in which she actually had no real interest, and then she finished by saying, "I will also need as much of the fourth generation of Dr. Chakrabarty's little miracle as it's feasible to send. And I'll need two or three compressed-air dispersal units, too."

"Who's Chakrabarty?" Tersch asked, puzzled.

"You wouldn't know him."

"What's his little miracle? What do you mean?"

"Just write down Chakrabarty, fourth generation." She spelled the name for him.

"I haven't the vaguest idea what this is," he said.

Good, Sara thought with considerable relief. Perfect.

If Tersch had known what Dr. Ananda Chakrabarty's little miracle was, he might have blurted something before she could stop him. And the ancient enemy would have been forewarned.

"It's outside your area of specialization," she said. "There's no reason you should recognize the name or know the device." She spoke hurriedly now, trying to move away from the subject as smoothly and as rapidly as possible. "I don't have time to explain it, Dr. Tersch. Other people in the CBW program will definitely know what it is I need. Let's get moving on this. Dr. Flyte very much wants to continue his studies of the creature, and he needs all the items on my list just as soon as he can get them. Five or six hours, you said?"

"That should do it," Tersch said. "How should we deliver?"

Sara glanced at Bryce. He wouldn't want to risk yet another of his men in order to have the cargo driven into town. To Captain Tersch, she said, "Can it be brought in by army helicopter?"

"Will do."

"Better tell the pilot not to try landing. The shape-changer might think we were attempting to escape. It would almost certainly attack the crew and kill all of us the moment the chopper touched down. Just have them hover and lower the package on a cable."

"This could be quite a large bundle," Tersch said.

"I'm sure they can lower it," she said.

"Well . . . all right. I'll get on it right away. And good luck to you."

"Thanks," Sara said. "We'll need it."

She hung up.

"All of a sudden, five or six hours seems like a long time," Jenny said.

"An eternity," Sara said.

They were all clearly eager to hear about her scheme but knew it couldn't be discussed. However, even in their silence, Sara detected a new note of optimism.

Don't get your hopes too high, she thought anxiously.

There was a chance that her plan had no merit. In fact, the odds were stacked against them. And if the plan failed, the shape-changer would know what they had intended to do, and it would wipe them out in some especially brutal fashion.

Outside, dawn had come.

The fog had lost its pale glow. Now the mist was dazzling, white-white, shining with refractions of the morning sunlight.

CHAPTER 39
THE APPARITION

FLETCHER KALE WOKE in time to see the first light of dawn.

The forest was still mostly dark. Milky daylight speared down in shafts, through scattered holes in the green canopy that was formed by the densely interlaced branches of the mammoth trees. The sunshine was diffused by the fog, muted, revealing little.

He had passed the night in the Jeep station wagon that belonged to Jake Johnson. Now he got out and stood beside the Jeep, listening to the woods, alert for the sounds of pursuit.

Last night, a few minutes after eleven o'clock, headed for Jake Johnson's secret retreat, Kale had driven up the Mount Larson Road, had swung the Jeep onto the unpaved fire lane that led up the wild north slopes of Snowtop— and had run smack into trouble. Within twenty feet, his headlights picked up signs posted on both sides of the roadway; large red letters on a white background read QUARANTINE. Going too fast, he swung around a bend, and directly ahead of him was a police blockade, one county cruiser angled across the road. Two deputies started getting out of the car.

He remembered hearing about a quarantine zone encircling Snowfield, but he'd thought it was in effect only on the other side of the mountain. He hit the brakes, wishing that, for once, he'd paid more attention to the news.

There was an APB circulating with his photograph. These men would recognize him, and within an hour he'd be back in jail.

Surprise was his only hope. They wouldn't be expecting trouble. Maintaining a quarantine checkpoint would be easy, lulling duty.

The HK91 assault rifle was on the seat beside Kale, covered with a blanket. He grabbed the gun, got out of the Jeep, and opened fire on the cops. The semiautomatic weapon chattered, and the deputies did a brief, erratic dance of death, spectral figures in the fog.

He rolled the bodies into a ditch, pulled the patrol car out of the way, and drove the Jeep past the checkpoint. Then he went back and repositioned the car, so that it would appear that the deputies' killer hadn't continued up the mountain.

He drove three miles up the rugged fire lane, until he came to an even more rugged, overgrown track. A mile later, at the end of that trail, he parked the Jeep in a tunnel of brush and climbed out.

In addition to the HK91, he had a sackful of other guns from Johnson's closet, plus the $63,440, which was distributed through the seven zippered pockets in the hunting jacket he wore. The only other thing he carried was a flashlight, and that was really all he needed because the limestone caves would be well stocked with other supplies.

The last quarter of a mile had to be covered on foot, and he had intended to finish the journey right away, but he had quickly found that even with the flashlight the forest was confusing at night, in the fog. Getting lost was almost a certainty. Once lost in this wilderness, you could wander in circles, within yards of your destination, never discovering how close you were to salvation. After only a few paces, Kale had turned back to the Jeep to wait for daylight.

Even if the two dead deputies at the blockade were discovered before morning, and even if the cops figured the killer had come onto the mountain, they wouldn't launch a manhunt until first light. By the time the posse reached here tomorrow, Kale would be snug in the caves.

He had slept on the front seat of the Jeep. It wasn't the Plaza Hotel, but it was more comfortable than jail.

Now, standing beside the Jeep in the wan light of early morning, he listened for the sounds of a search party. He heard nothing. He hadn't really expected to hear anything. It wasn't his destiny to rot in prison. His future was golden. He was sure of that.

He yawned, stretched, then pissed against the trunk of a big pine.

Thirty minutes later, when there was more light, he followed the foot-path he hadn't been able to find last night. And he saw something that hadn't been obvious in the dark: The brush was extensively trampled. People had been through here recently.

He proceeded with caution, cradling the HK91 in his right arm, ready to blow away anyone who might try to rush him.

In less than half an hour, he came out of the trees, into the clearing around the log cabin—and saw why the footpath had been trampled. Eight motorcycles were lined up alongside the cabin, big Harleys, all emblazoned with the name DEMON CHROME.

Gene Terr's bunch of misfits. Not all of them. About half the gang, by the looks of it.

Kale crouched against an outcropping of limestone and studied the mist-wrapped cabin. No one was in sight. He quietly fished in the laundry bag, located a fresh magazine for the HK91, rammed it in place.

How had Terr and his vicious playmates gotten here? A two-wheel trip up the mountain would have been difficult, wildly dangerous, a nerve-twisting bit of motocross. Of course, those crazy bastards thrived on danger.

But what the devil were they *doing* here? How had they found the cabin, and why had they come?

As he listened for a voice, for some indication of where the cyclists were and what they were up to, Kale realized there weren't even any animal or insect sounds. No birds. Absolutely nothing. Spooky.

Then, behind him, a rustle in the brush. A soft sound. In the preternatural silence, it might as well have been a cannon shot.

Kale had been kneeling on the ground. With catlike quickness, he fell on his side, rolled onto his back, brought up the HK91.

He was prepared to kill, but he wasn't prepared for what he saw. It was Jake Johnson, about twenty-five feet away, coming out of the trees and fog, grinning. Naked. Utterly bareassed.

Other movement. To the left of Johnson. Farther along the treeline.

Kale caught it from the corner of his eye and whipped his head around, swung the rifle in that direction.

Another man came out of the woods, through the mist, with the tall grass fluttering around his bare legs. He was also naked. And grinning broadly.

But that wasn't the worst of it. The worst part was that the second man was also Jake Johnson.

Kale looked from one to the other, startled and baffled. They were as perfectly alike as a set of identical twins.

But Jake was an only child—wasn't he? Kale had never heard anything about a twin.

A third figure advanced from the shadows beneath the spreading boughs of a huge spruce. This one, too, was Jake Johnson.

Kale couldn't breathe.

Maybe there was an outside chance that Johnson had a twin, but he damned well wasn't one of triplets.

Something was horribly wrong. Suddenly, it wasn't just the impossible triplets that frightened Kale. Suddenly, everything seemed menacing: the forest, the mist, the stony contours of the mountainside . . .

The three look-alikes walked slowly up the slope on which Kale was sprawled, closing in from different angles. Their eyes were strange, and their mouths were cruel.

Kale scrambled to his feet, heart lurching. "Stop right there!"

But they didn't stop, even though he brandished the assault rifle.

"Who are you? What are you? What *is* this?" Kale demanded.

They didn't answer. Kept coming. Like zombies.

He grabbed the bag that was filled with guns, and he backed rapidly and clumsily away from the nightmarish trio.

No. Not a trio any more. A quartet. Downslope, a fourth Jake Johnson came out of the trees, stark naked like the rest.

Kale's fear trembled on the edge of panic.

The four moved toward Kale with hardly a sound; dried leaves underfoot; nothing else. They made no complaint about the stones and sharp weeds and prickly burrs that must have hurt their feet. One of them began to lick his lips hungrily. The others immediately began to lick their lips, too.

A quiver of icy dread went through Kale's bowels, and he wondered if he had lost his mind. But that thought was short-lived. Unfamiliar with self-doubt, he didn't know how to entertain it for long.

He dropped the laundry bag, clutched the HK91 in both hands, and opened fire, describing an arc with the spurting muzzle of the gun. The bullets hit. He saw them tear into the four men, saw the wounds burst open. But there was no blood. And as soon as the wounds blossomed, they withered; they healed, vanished within seconds.

The men kept coming.

No. Not men. Something else.

Hallucinations? Years ago, in high school, Kale had dropped a lot of acid. Now he remembered that flashbacks could plague you months—even years—after you stopped using LSD. He'd never had acid flashbacks before, but he'd heard about them. Was that what was happening here? Hallucinations?

Perhaps.

On the other hand . . . all four of the men were glistening, as if the morning mists were condensing on their bare skin, and that wasn't the sort of detail you usually noticed in a hallucination. And this entire situation was *very* different from any drug experience he'd ever known.

Still grinning, the nearest Doppelganger raised one arm, pointed at Kale. Incredibly, the flesh of that hand split and peeled away from the fingers, from the palm. The flesh actually appeared to *ooze* bloodlessly back into the arm, as if it were wax melting and running from a flame; the wrist became thicker with this tissue, and then the hand was nothing but bones, white bones. One skeletal finger pointed at Kale.

Pointed with anger, scorn, and accusation.

Kale's mind reeled.

The other three look-alikes had undergone even more macabre changes. One had lost the flesh from part of his face: A cheekbone shone through, a row of teeth; the right eye, deprived of a lid and of all surrounding tissue, gleamed wetly in the calcimine socket. The third man was missing a chunk of flesh from his torso; you could see his sharp ribs and slick wet organs pulsing darkly inside. The fourth walked on one normal leg and one leg that was only bones and tendons.

As they closed on Kale, one of them spoke: "Baby killer."

Kale screamed, dropped the HK91, and ran. Stopped short when he saw two more Johnson look-alikes approaching from behind, from the cabin. Nowhere to run. Except up toward the high limestone outcroppings above the cabin. He bolted that way, gasping and wheezing, reached the brush, whimpering, waded through it to the mouth of the cave, glanced behind, saw that the six were still coming after him, and he plunged into the cave, into darkness, wishing he'd held onto his flashlight, and he put one hand against the wall, shuffled along, feeling his way, trying to recall the layout, remembering it was more or less a long tunnel ending in a series of doglegs—and suddenly he realized this might not be a safe place; it might be a trap, instead; yes, he was sure of it; they *wanted* him to come here—and he looked back, saw two decomposing men at the entrance, heard himself wail, and hurried faster, faster, into the deep blackness because there was nowhere else to go, even if it was a trap, and he scraped his hand on a sharp projection of rock, stumbled, flailed, charged on, reached the doglegs, one after the other, and then the door, and he went through, slammed it behind him, but he knew it wouldn't keep them out, and then he was aware of light, in the next chamber, toward which he now began to move in a dreamlike haze of terror, passing stacks of supplies and equipment.

The light came from a Coleman lantern.

Kale stepped into the third chamber.

In the frost-pale glow, he saw something that made him freeze. It had risen from the subterranean river, up through the cave floor, out of the hole in which Jake Johnson had rigged a water pump. It writhed. It churned, pulsated, rippled. Dark, blood-mottled flesh. Shapeless.

Wings began to form. Then melted away.

A sulphurous odor, not strong yet nauseating.

Eyes opened all over the seven-foot column of slime. They focused on Kale.

He shrank from them, backed into a wall, held on to the stone as if it were reality, a last place to grip on the precipice of madness.

Some of the eyes were human. Some were not. They fixed on him—then closed and disappeared.

Mouths opened where no mouths had been. Teeth. Fangs. Forked tongues lolled over black lips. From other mouths, wormlike tentacles erupted, wriggled in the air, withdrew. Like the wings and eyes, the mouths eventually vanished into the formless flesh.

A man sat on the floor. He was a few feet from the pulsing thing that had come up from beneath the cave, and he was seated in the penumbra of the lantern's glow, his face in shadow.

Aware that Kale had noticed him, the man leaned forward slightly, putting his face in the light. He was six feet four or taller, with long curly hair and a beard. He wore a rolled bandanna around his head. One gold earring dangled. He smiled the most peculiar smile Kale had ever seen, and he raised one hand in greeting, and on the palm of the hand was a red and yellow tattoo of an eyeball.

It was Gene Terr.

CHAPTER 40

BIOLOGICAL WARFARE

THE ARMY HELICOPTER arrived three and a half hours after Sara spoke to Daniel Tersch in Dugway, two hours earlier than promised. Evidently, it had been dispatched from a base in California, and evidently her colleagues in the CBW program had figured out her war plan. They had realized she didn't actually need most of the equipment she had asked for, and they had collected only what she required for the attack on the shape-changer. Otherwise, they wouldn't have been so quick.

Please, God, let it be true, Sara thought. They must have brought the right stuff. They *must* have.

It was a large, camouflage-painted chopper with two full sets of whirling blades. Hovering sixty to seventy feet above Skyline Road, it stirred the morning air, created a turbulent downdraft, and sliced up what little mist remained. It sent waves of hard sound crashing through the town.

A door slid open on the side of the helicopter, and a man leaned out of the cargo hold, looked down. He made no attempt to call to them, for the chattering rotors and roaring engines would have scattered his words. Instead, he used a series of incomprehensible hand signals.

Finally Sara realized that the crew was waiting for some indication that this was the drop spot. With hand signals of her own, she urged everyone to form a circle with her, in the middle of the street. They didn't join hands, but stood with a couple of yards between each of them. The circle had a diameter of twelve to fifteen feet.

A canvas-wrapped bundle, somewhat larger than a man, was pushed out of the chopper. It was attached to a cable, which was reeled out by an electric winch. Initially, the bundle descended slowly, then slower still, at last settling to the pavement in the center of the circle, so gently that it seemed the chopper crewmen thought they were delivering raw eggs.

Bryce broke out of the formation before the package touched down and was the first to reach it. He located the snaplink and released the cable by the time Sara and the others joined him.

As the chopper reeled in the line, it swung toward the valley below, moved off, out of the danger zone, gaining altitude as it went.

Sara crouched beside the bundle and started loosening the nylon rope that was threaded through the eyelets in the canvas. She worked feverishly and, in a few seconds, unpacked the contents.

There were two blue cannisters bearing white stenciled words and numbers. She sighed with relief when she saw them. Her message had been properly interpreted. There were also three aerosol tank sprayers similar in size and appearance to those used to spread weed killer and insecticide on a lawn, except that these were not powered by a hand pump but by cylinders of compressed air. Each tank was equipped with a harness that made it easy to carry on the back. A flexible rubber hose, ending in a four-foot metal extension with a high-pressure nozzle, made it possible to stand twelve to fourteen feet from the target that you wished to spray.

Sara lifted one of the pressurized tanks. It was heavy, already filled with the same fluid that was in the two spare, blue cannisters.

The helicopter dwindled into the Western sky, and Lisa said, "Sara, this isn't everything you asked for—is it?"

"This is everything we need," Sara said evasively.

She looked around nervously, expecting to see the shape-changer rushing toward them. But there was no sign of it.

She said, "Bryce, Tal, if you'd take two of these tanks . . ."

The sheriff and his deputy grabbed two of the units, slipped their arms through the harness loops, buckled the chest straps, shrugged their shoulders to settle the tanks as comfortably as possible.

Without having been told, both men clearly realized the tanks contained a weapon that might destroy the shape-changer. Sara knew they must be eaten by curiosity, and she was impressed that they asked no questions.

She had intended to handle the third sprayer herself, but it was considerably heavier than she'd expected. Straining, she would be able to carry it, but she wouldn't be able to maneuver quickly. And during the next hour or so, survival would depend on speed and agility.

Someone else would have to use the third unit. Not Lisa; she was no bigger than Sara. Not Flyte; he had some arthritis in his hand, of which he'd complained last night, and he seemed frail. That left Jenny. She was only three or four inches taller than Sara, only fifteen or twenty pounds heavier, but she appeared to be in excellent physical condition. She almost certainly would be able to handle the sprayer.

Flyte protested but then relented after trying to heft the tank. "I must be older than I think," he said wearily.

Jenny agreed that she was the one best suited, and Sara helped her get into the harness, and they were ready for the battle.

Still no sign of the shape-changer.

Sara wiped sweat from her brow. "All right. The instant it shows itself, spray it. Don't waste a second. Spray it, saturate it, keep backing away if possible, try to draw more of it out of hiding, and spray, spray, spray."

"Is this some sort of acid—or what?" Bryce asked.

"Not acid," Sara said. "Although the effect will be something very like acid —if it works at all."

"So if it's not an acid," Tal said, "what is it?"

"A unique, highly specialized microorganism," Sara said.

"Germs?" Jenny asked, eyes widening in surprise.

"Yes. They're suspended in a liquid growth culture."

"We're gonna make the shape-changer *sick?*" Lisa asked, frowning.

"I sure to God hope so," Sara said.

Nothing moved. Nothing. But something was out there, and it was probably listening. With the ears of the cat. With the ears of the fox. With highly sensitive ears of its own special design.

"Very, very sick, if we're lucky," Sara said. "Because disease would seem to be the only way to kill it."

Now their lives were at risk because *it* knew they had tricked it.

Flyte shook his head. "But the ancient enemy's so utterly alien, so different from man and animals . . . diseases dangerous to other species would have no effect whatsoever on it."

"Right," Sara said. "But this microbe isn't an ordinary disease. In fact, it isn't a disease-causing organism at all."

Snowfield shelved down the mountain, still as a postcard painting.

Looking around uneasily, alert for movement in and around the buildings, Sara told them about Ananda Chakrabarty and his discovery.

In 1972, on behalf of Dr. Chakrabarty, his employer—the General Electric Corporation—applied for the first-ever patent on a man-made bacterium. Using sophisticated cell fusion techniques, Chakrabarty had created a microorganism that could feed upon, digest, and thereby transform the hydrocarbon compounds of crude oil.

Chakrabarty's bug had at least one obvious commercial application: It could be used to clean up oil spills at sea. The bacteria literally *ate* an oil slick, rendering it harmless to the environment.

After a series of vigorous legal challenges from many sources, General Electric won the right to patent Chakrabarty's discovery. In June, 1980, the Supreme Court handed down a landmark decision, ruling that Chakrabarty's discovery was "not nature's handiwork, but his own; accordingly, it's patentable subject matter."

"Of course," Jenny said, "I read about the case. It was a big story that June —man competing with God and all that."

Sara said, "Originally, GE didn't intend to market the bug. It was a fragile organism that couldn't survive outside of strictly controlled lab conditions. They applied for a patent to test the legal question, to settle the matter before other experiments in genetic engineering produced more usable and more valuable discoveries. But after the court's decision, other scientists spent a few years working with the organism, and now they have a hardier strain that'll stand up outside the lab for twelve to eighteen hours. In fact it's been on the market under the trade name Biosan-4, and it's been used successfully to clean up oil slicks all over the world."

"And that's what's in these tanks?" Bryce asked.

"Yes. Biosan-4. In a sprayable solution."

The town was funereal. The sun beat down from an azure sky, but the air remained chilly. In spite of the uncanny silence, Sara had the unshakable feeling that *it* was coming, that it had heard and was coming and was very, very near, indeed.

The others felt it, too. They looked around uneasily.

Sara said, "Do you remember what we discovered when we studied the shape-changer's tissue?"

"You mean the high hydrocarbon values," Jenny said.

"Yes. But not just hydrocarbons. All forms of carbon. Very high values all across the board."

Tal said, "You told us something about it being like petrolatum."

"Not the same. But reminiscent of petrolatum in some respects," Sara said. "What we have here is living tissue, very alien but complex and alive. And with such extraordinarily high carbon content . . . Well, what I mean is, this thing's tissue seems like an organic, metabolically active cousin of petrolatum. So I'm hoping Chakrabarty's bug will . . ."

Something is coming.

Jenny said, "You're hoping it'll eat into the shape-changer the same way it would eat into an oil slick."

Something . . . something . . .

"Yes," Sara said nervously. "I'm hoping it'll attack the carbon and break down the tissue. Or at least interfere with the delicate chemical balance enough to—"

Coming, coming . . .

". . . uh, enough to destabilize the entire organism," Sara finished, weighed down by a sense of impending doom.

Flyte said, "Is that the best chance we have? Is it really?"

"I think it is."

Where is it? Where's it coming from? Sara wondered, looking at the deserted buildings, the empty street, the motionless trees.

"Sounds awfully thin to me," Flyte said doubtfully.

"It *is* awfully thin," Sara said. "It's not much of a chance, but it's the only one we've got."

A noise. A chittering, hissing, hair-raising sound.

They froze. Waited.

But, again, the town pulled a cloak of silence around itself.

The morning sun cast its fiery reflection in some windows and glinted off the curved glass of the streetlamps. The black slate roofs looked as if they had been polished during the night; the last of the mist had condensed on those smooth surfaces, leaving a moist sheen.

Nothing moved. Nothing happened. The noise did not resume.

Bryce Hammond's face clouded with worry. "This Biosan . . . I gather it isn't harmful to us."

"Utterly harmless," Sara assured him.

The noise again. A short burst. Then silence.

"Something's coming," Lisa said softly.

God help us, Sara thought.

"Something's coming," Lisa said softly, and Bryce felt it, too. A sense of onrushing horror. A thickening and cooling of the air. A new predatory quality to the stillness. Reality? Imagination? He could not be certain. He only knew that he *felt* it.

The noise burst forth again, a sustained squeal, not just a short blast. Bryce winced. It was piercingly shrill. Buzzing. Whining. Like a power drill. But he knew it wasn't anything as harmless and ordinary as that.

Insects. The coldness of the sound, the metallic quality made him think of insects. Bees. Yes. It was the greatly amplified buzzing-screeching of hornets.

He said, "The three of you who aren't armed with sprayers, get in the middle here."

"Yeah," Tal said. "We'll circle around, give you a little protection."

Very damned little if this Biosan doesn't work, Bryce thought.

The strange noise grew louder.

Sara, Lisa, and Dr. Flyte stood together, while Bryce and Jenny and Tal ringed them, facing outward.

Then, down the street, near the bakery, something monstrous appeared in the sky, skimming over the tops of the buildings, hovering for a few seconds above Skyline Road. A wasp. A phantom the size of a German shepherd. Nothing remotely like this insect had ever existed during the tens of millions of years that the shape-changer had been alive. This was surely something that had sprung from its vicious imagination, a horrible invention. Six-foot, opalescent wings beat furiously upon the air, glimmered with rainbow color. The multifaceted black eyes were slant-set in the narrow, pointed, wicked head. There were four twitching legs with pincered feet. The curled, segmented, mold-white body terminated in a foot-long stinger with a needle-sharp point.

Bryce felt as if his intestines were turning to ice water.

The wasp stopped hovering. It struck.

Jenny screamed as the wasp streaked toward them, but she didn't run. She aimed the nozzle of the sprayer and squeezed the pressure-release lever. A cone-shaped, milky mist erupted for a distance of about six feet.

The wasp was twenty feet away and closing fast.

Jenny squeezed the lever all the way down. The mist became a stream, arcing fifteen or sixteen feet out from the nozzle.

Bryce loosed a stream from his sprayer. The two trails of Biosan played across each other, steadied, took the same aim, flowed together in midair.

The wasp came within range. The high-pressure streams struck it, dulled the rainbow color of the wings, soaked the segmented body.

The insect stopped abruptly, hesitated, dipped lower, as if unable to maintain altitude. Hovered. Its attack had been arrested, although it still regarded them with hate-filled eyes.

Jenny felt a surge of relief and hope.

"It works!" Lisa cried.

Then the wasp came at them again.

Just when Tal thought they were safe, the wasp came at them again, through the mist of Biosan-4, flying slow but still flying.

"Down!" Bryce shouted.

They crouched, and the wasp swept over them, dripping milky fluid from its grotesque legs and from the tip of its stinger.

Tal stood again, so that he could give the thing a long squirt now that it was within range.

It swung toward him, but before he could give it a shot, the wasp faltered, fluttered wildly, then plummeted to the pavement. It flopped and buzzed angrily. It tried to rise up. Couldn't. Then it changed.

It changed.

With the others, Timothy Flyte edged closer to the wasp and watched as it melted into a shapeless mass of protoplasm. The hind legs of a dog began to form. And the snout. It was going to be a Doberman, judging by that snout. One eye began to open. But the shape-changer couldn't complete the transformation; the dog's features vanished. The amorphous tissue shuddered and pulsed in a manner unlike anything that Timothy had seen it do before.

"It's dying," Lisa said.

Timothy stared in awe as the strange flesh convulsed. This heretofore immortal being now knew the meaning and the fear of death.

The unformed mass broke out in pustulelike sores, leaking a thin yellow fluid. The thing spasmed violently. Additional sores opened in hideous profusion, lesions of all shapes and sizes that split and cracked and popped across the pulsating surface. Then, just as the tiny wad of tissue in the petri dish had done, this phantom degenerated into a lifeless pool of stinking, watery mush.

"By God, you've done it!" Timothy said, turning toward Sara.

Tentacles. Three of them. Behind her.

They rose out of a drain grating in the gutter, fifteen feet away. Each was as big around as Timothy's wrist. Already, the questing tips of them had slithered across the pavement, within a yard of Sara.

Timothy shouted a warning, but he was too late.

Flyte shouted, and Jenny whirled. *It* was among them.

Three tentacles whipped up from the pavement with shocking speed, surged forward with sinuous malevolence, and dropped onto Sara. In an instant, one lashed around the geneticist's legs, one around her waist, and the third around her slender neck.

Christ, it's too fast, too fast for us! Jenny thought.

She pointed the nozzle of her sprayer even as she turned, cursing, squeezing the lever, spewing Biosan-4 over Sara and the tentacles.

Bryce and Tal stepped in, using their sprayers, but they were all too slow, too late.

Sara's eyes widened; her mouth opened in a silent scream. She was lifted into the air and—

No! Jenny prayed.

—flung back and forth as if she were a doll—

No!

—and then her head fell from her shoulders and struck the street with a hard, sickening crack.

Gagging, Jenny stumbled back.

The tentacles rose twelve feet into the air. They writhed and twisted and foamed, broke open in sores as the bacteria destroyed the binding structure of the amorphous tissue. As Sara had hoped, Biosan affected the shape-changer almost the way sulphuric acid affected human tissue.

Tal darted past Jenny, heading straight toward the three tentacles, and she screamed at him to stop.

What in God's name was he doing?

Tal ran through the weaving shadows cast by the moving tentacles and prayed that none of them would fall on him. When he reached the drain from which the things were extruded, he could see that the three appendages were separating from the main body of dark, throbbing protoplasm in the drainpipe below. The shape-changer was shedding the infected tissue before the bacteria could reach into the main body mass. Tal poked the nozzle of the sprayer through the grate and released Biosan-4 into the drain below.

The tentacles tore loose from the rest of the creature. They flopped and wriggled in the street. Down in the drain, oozing slime retreated from the spray, shedding another piece of itself, which began to foam and spasm and die.

Even the Devil could be wounded. Even Satan was vulnerable.

Exhilarated, Tal shot more of the fluid into the drain.

The amorphous tissue withdrew, out of sight, creeping deeper into the subterranean passageways, no doubt shedding more pieces of itself.

Tal turned away from the drain and saw the severed tentacles had lost their definition; they were now just long, tangled ropes of suppurating tissue. They lashed themselves and one another in apparent agony and rapidly degenerated into stinking, lifeless slop.

He looked at another gutter drain, at the silent buildings, at the sky, wondering from where the next attack would come.

Suddenly the pavement rumbled and heaved under his feet. In front of him, Flyte was thrown to the ground; his glasses shattered. Tal staggered sideways, nearly trampling Flyte.

The street leaped and shuddered again, harder than before, as if earthquake shockwaves had passed beneath it. But this was not a quake. *It* was coming— not just a fragment, not just another phantom, but the largest part of it, perhaps the entire great bulk, surging toward the surface with unimaginable destructive power, rising like a god betrayed, bringing its unholy wrath and vengeance to the men and women who had dared to strike at it, forming itself into an enormous mass of muscle fiber and pushing, pushing, until the macadam bulged and cracked.

Tal was thrown to the ground. His chin snapped hard against the street; he was dazed. He tried to get up, so that he could use the sprayer when the creature appeared. He got as far as his hands and knees. The street was still rocking too much. He lay down again to wait it out.

We're going to die, he thought.

Bryce was flat on his face, hugging the pavement.

Lisa was beside him. She might have been crying or screaming. He couldn't hear her; there was too much noise.

Along this entire block of Skyline Road, an atonal symphony of destruction reached an ear-shattering crescendo: squealing, grinding, cracking, splitting sounds; the world itself coming asunder. The air was filled with dust that spurted up from widening fissures in the pavement.

The roadbed tilted with tremendous force. Chunks of it spewed into the air. Most were the size of gravel, but some were as large as a fist. A few were even larger than that, fifty- and hundred- and two-hundred-pound blocks of concrete, leaping five or ten feet into the air as the protean creature below rammed relentlessly toward the surface.

Bryce pulled Lisa against him and tried to shield her. He could feel the violent tremors passing through her.

The earth under them lifted. Fell with a crash. Lifted and fell again. Gravel-size debris rained down, clanked off the tank sprayer strapped to Bryce's back, thumped off his legs, snapped against his head, making him wince.

Where was Jenny?

He looked around in sudden desperation.

The street had hoved up; a ridge had formed down the middle of Skyline. Apparently, Jenny was on the other side of the hump, clinging to the street over there.

She's alive, he thought. She's alive. Damn it, she *has* to be!

A huge slab of concrete erupted from the roadbed to their left and was flung eight or ten feet into the air. He was sure it was going to crash down on them, and he hugged Lisa as tight as he could, although nothing he could do would save them if the slab struck. But it hit Timothy Flyte instead. It slammed across the scientist's legs, breaking them, pinning Flyte, who howled in pain, howled so loudly that Bryce could hear him above the roar of the disintegrating pavement.

Still, the shaking continued. The street heaved up farther. Ragged teeth of macadam-coated concrete bit at the morning air.

In seconds, *it* would break through and be upon them before they had a chance to stand and fight back.

A baseball-size missile of concrete, spat into the air by the shape-changer's volcanic emergence from the storm drain, now slammed back to the pavement, impacting two or three inches from Jenny's head. A splinter of concrete pierced her cheek, drew a trickle of blood.

Then the ridge-forming pressure from below was suddenly withdrawn. The street ceased shaking. Ceased rising.

The sounds of destruction faded. Jenny could hear her own raspy, harried breathing.

A few feet away, Tal Whitman started getting to his feet.

On the far side of the hoved-up pavement, someone wailed in agony. Jenny couldn't see who it was.

She tried to stand, but the street shuddered once more, and she was pitched flat on her face again.

Tal went down again, too, cursing loudly.

Abruptly, the street began caving in. It made a tortured sound, and pieces broke loose along the fracture lines. Slabs tumbled into the emptiness below. Too much emptiness: it sounded as if things were falling into a chasm, not just a drain. Then the entire hoved-up section collapsed with a thunderous roar, and Jenny found herself at the brink.

She lay belly-down, head lifted, waiting for something to rise up from the depths, dreading to see what form the shape-changer would assume this time.

But it didn't come. Nothing rose out of the hole.

The pit was ten feet across, at least fifty feet long. On the far side, Bryce and Lisa were trying to get to their feet. Jenny almost cried out in happiness at the sight of them. They were alive!

Then she saw Timothy. His legs were pinned under a massive hunk of concrete. Worse than that—he was trapped on a precarious piece of roadbed that thrust over the rim of the hole, with no support beneath it. At any moment, it might crack loose and fall into the pit, taking him with it.

Jenny edged forward a few inches and stared into the hole. It was at least thirty feet deep, probably a lot deeper in places; she couldn't gauge it accurately because there were many shadows along its fifty-foot length. Apparently, the ancient enemy hadn't merely surged up from the storm drains; it had risen from some previously stable, limestone caves far below the solid ground on which the street was built.

But what degree of phenomenal strength, what unthinkably huge *size* must it possess in order to shift not only the street but the natural rock formations below? And where had it gone?

The pit appeared untenanted, but Jenny knew *it* must be down there somewhere, in the deeper regions, in the subterranean warrens, hiding from the Biosan spray, waiting, listening.

She looked up and saw Bryce making his way toward Flyte.

A crisp, cracking noise split the air. Flyte's concrete perch shifted. It was going to break loose and tumble into the chasm.

Bryce saw the danger. He clambered over a tilted slab of pavement, trying to reach Flyte in time.

Jenny didn't think he'd make it.

Then the pavement under her groaned, trembled, and she realized that she, too, was on treacherous territory. She started to get up. Beneath her, the concrete snapped with a bomb blast of sound.

CHAPTER 41

LUCIFER

/////

THE SHADOWS ON the cave walls were ever-changing; so was the shadow-maker. In the moon-strange glow of the gas lantern, the creature was like a column of dense smoke, writhing, formless, blood-dark.

Although Kale wanted to believe it *was* only smoke, he knew better. Ecto-plasm. That's what it must be. The otherworldly stuff of which demons, ghosts, and spirits were said to be composed.

Kale had never believed in ghosts. The concept of life after death was a crutch for weaker men, not for Fletcher Kale. But now . . .

Gene Terr sat on the floor, staring at the apparition. His one gold earring glittered.

Kale stood with his back pressed to a cool limestone wall. He felt as if he were fused to the rock.

The repellent, sulphurous odor still hung on the dank air.

To Kale's left, a man came through the opening from the first room of the underground retreat. No; not a man. It was one of the Jake Johnson look-alikes. The one that had called him a baby killer.

Kale made a small, desperate sound.

This was the demonic version of Johnson whose skull was half-stripped of flesh. One wet, lidless eye peered out of a bony socket, glaring malevolently at Kale. Then the demon turned toward the oozing monstrosity in the center of the chamber. It walked to the column of roiling slime, spread its arms, embraced the gelatinous flesh—and simply melted into it.

Kale stared uncomprehendingly.

Another Jake Johnson entered. The one that lacked flesh along his flank. Beyond the exposed rib cage, the bloody heart throbbed; the lungs expanded; yet, somehow, the organs didn't spill through the gaps between the ribs. Such a thing was impossible. Except that this was an apparition, a Hell-born presence that had swarmed up from the Pit—just smell the sulphur, the scent of Satan! —and therefore *anything* was possible.

Kale *believed* now.

The only alternative to belief was madness.

One by one, the remaining four Johnson look-alikes entered, glanced at Kale, then were absorbed by the oozing, rippling slime.

The Coleman lantern made a soft, continuous hissing.

The jellied flesh of the netherworld visitor began to sprout black, terrible wings.

The hissing of the lantern echoed sibilantly off the stone walls.

The half-formed wings degenerated into the column of slime from which they had sprung. Insectile limbs started to take shape.

Finally, Gene Terr spoke. He might have been in a trance—except that there was a lively sparkle in his eyes. "We come up here, me and some of my guys, two or maybe three times a year. You know? What it is . . . this here's a perfect place for a fuck an' waste party. Nobody to hear nothin'. Nobody to see. You know?"

At last Jeeter looked away from the creature and met Kale's eyes.

Kale said, "What the hell's a . . . a fuck and waste party?"

"Oh, every couple months, sometimes more often, a chick shows up and wants to join the Chrome, wants to be somebody's old lady, you know, doesn't care whose, or maybe she'll settle for bein' an all-purpose bitch that all the guys can hack at when they want a little variety in their pussy. You know?" Jeeter sat with his legs crossed in a yoga position. His hands lay unmoving in his lap. He looked like an evil Buddha. "Sometimes, one of us happens to be lookin' for a new main squeeze, or maybe the chick is really foxy, so we make room for her. But it don't happen like that very often. Most of the time we tell them to beat it."

In the center of the cave, the insectile legs melted back into the oozing column of muck. Dozens of hands began to form, the fingers opening like petals of strange blossoms.

Jeeter said, "But then once in a while, a chick shows up, and she's damned good-lookin', but we don't happen to need or want her with us, and what we want instead is to have fun with her. Or maybe we see a kid who's run away from home, you know, sweet sixteen, some hitchhiker, and we pick her up, no matter whether she wants to come along or not. We give her some nose candy or hash, get her feelin' good, then we bring her up here where it's real remote, and what we do is we fuck her brains out for a couple days, turn her inside out, and then when none of us can get it up any more, we waste her in really interestin' ways."

The demonic presence in the center of the room changed yet again. The multitude of hands melted away. A score of mouths opened along the dark length of it, every one filled with razor-edged fangs.

Gene Terr glanced at this latest manifestation but didn't seem frightened. In fact, Jeeter smiled at it.

"Waste them?" Kale said. "You kill them?"

"Yeah," Jeeter said. "In interestin' ways. We bury 'em around here, too. Who's ever gonna find the bodies in the middle of nowhere like this? It's always a kick. Thrills. Until Sunday. Sunday afternoon late, we was out there in the grass by the cabin, drinkin' and gangin' a chick, and all of a sudden Jake Johnson comes out of the woods, bare-assed, like he figured on fuckin' the bitch, too. At first I thought we'd have some fun with him. I figured, well, we'll waste him when we waste the girl, get rid of the witness, you know, but before we can grab him, another Jake comes out of the woods, then a third—"

"Just like what happened to me," Kale said.

"—and another one and another. We shot 'em, hit 'em square in the chest, in the face, but they didn't go down, didn't even pause, just kept comin'. So Little Willie, one of my main men, rushes the nearest one and uses a knife, but it doesn't do no good. Instead, *that* Johnson grabs Willie, and he can't break loose, and then all of a sudden like . . . well . . . Johnson isn't Johnson any more. He's just this *thing,* this bloody-lookin' thing without no shape at all. The thing eats Willie . . . eats into him like . . . well, hell, it just sort of *dissolves* Willie, man. And the thing gets bigger, and then it turns into the craziest damn big wolf—"

"Jesus," Kale said.

"—biggest wolf you ever saw, and then the other Jakes turn into other things, like big lizards with the nastiest jaws, but one of them wasn't a lizard or a wolf but somethin' I just can't describe, and they all come after us. We can't get to our bikes, man, 'cause these things are between us and them, and so they kill a couple more of my guys, and then they start to herd us up the hill."

"Toward the caves," Kale said. "That's what they did to me."

"We never even knew about these caves," Terr said. "So we get in here, way in here in the dark, and the things start killin' more of us, man, killin' us in the dark—"

The fang-filled mouths vanished.

"—and there's all this screamin', you know, and I couldn't see where I was, so I crawled into a corner to hide, hoped they wouldn't smell me out, though I figured for sure they would."

The blood-streaked tissue pulsed, rippled.

"—and after a while the screamin' stops. Everyone's dead. It's real quiet . . . and then I hear somethin' movin' around."

Kale was listening to Terr but staring at the column of slime. A different kind of mouth appeared, a sucker, like you might see on an exotic fish. It sucked greedily at the air, as if seeking flesh.

Kale shuddered. Terr smiled.

Other sucker-mouths began to form all over the creature.

Still smiling, Jeeter said, "So I'm there in the dark, and I hear movement, but nothin' comes at me. Instead, a light comes on. Faint at first, then brighter. It's one of the Jakes, lightin' a Coleman. He tells me to come with him. I don't want to go. He grabs my arm, and his hand's cold, man. *Strong.* He won't let go, makes me come here, where that thing's pushing up out of the floor, and I never seen anythin' like *that* before; never, nowhere. I almost shit. He makes me sit down, sets the lantern with me, then just walks into the oozin' crud over there, melts into it, and I'm left alone with the thing, which starts right away goin' through all kinds of changes."

It was still going through changes, Kale saw. The suckerlike mouths vanished. Viciously pointed horns formed along the churning flanks of the creature; dozens of horns, barbed and unbarbed, in a variety of textures and colors, rising from the gelatinous mass.

"So for about a day and a half now," Terr said, "I've been sittin' here, watchin' it, except when I doze off or go into the other room for somethin' to eat. Now and then it talks to me, you know. It seems to know almost everythin' there is to know about me, things that only my closest brother bikers ever knew. It knows all about the bodies buried up here, and it knows about the Mex bastards we wasted when we took the drug business away from them, and it knows about the cop we chopped to pieces two years ago, and like, see, not even the other cops suspect we had anythin' to do with *that* one. This thing here, this beautiful strange thing, it knows all my little secrets, man. And what it doesn't know about, it asks to hear, and it listens real good. It approves of me, man. I never thought I'd really meet up with it. I always hoped, but I never thought I would. I been worshipin' it for years, man, and the whole gang used to hold these black masses once a week, but I never thought it would ever really appear to me. We've given it sacrifices, even human sacrifices, and chanted all the right chants, but we never were able to conjure up anythin'. So this here's a miracle." Jeeter laughed. "I been doin' its work all my life, man. Prayin' to it all my life, prayin' to the Beast. Now here it is. It's a fuckin' miracle."

Kale didn't want to understand. "You've lost me."

Terr stared at him. "No, I haven't. You know what I'm talkin' about, man. You *know.*"

Kale said nothing.

"You've been thinkin' this must be a demon, somethin' from Hell. And it *is* from Hell, man. But it's no demon. It's *Him. Him.* Lucifer."

Among the dozens of sharply pointed horns, small red eyes opened in the tenebrous flesh. A multitude of piercing little eyes glowed crimson with hatred and evil knowledge.

Terr motioned for Kale to come closer. "He's allowin' me to go on livin' because He knows I'm His true disciple."

Kale didn't move. His heart boomed. It wasn't fear that loosed the adrenaline in him. Not fear alone. There was another emotion that shook him, overwhelmed him, an emotion he couldn't quite identify . . .

"He let me live," Jeeter repeated, "because He knows I always do His work. Some of the others . . . maybe they weren't as purely devoted to His work as I am, so He destroyed them. But me . . . I'm different. He's lettin' me live to do His work. Maybe He'll let me live forever, man."

Kale blinked.

"And he's lettin' you live for the same reason, you know," Jeeter said. "Sure. Must be. Sure. Because you do *His* work."

Kale shook his head. "I've never been a . . . a Devil worshiper. I never believed."

"Don't matter. You still do His work, and you enjoy it."

The red eyes watched Kale.

"You killed your wife," Jeeter said.

Kale nodded dumbly.

"Man, you even killed your own little baby boy. If that isn't *His* work, then what is?"

None of the shining eyes blinked, and Kale began to identify the emotion surging within him. Elation, awe . . . religious rapture.

"Who knows what *else* you've done over the years," Jeeter said. "Must've done lots of stuff that was His work. Maybe almost everthin' you ever done was His work. You're like me, man. You were born to follow Lucifer. You and me . . . it's in our genes. In our *genes,* man."

At last Kale moved away from the wall.

"That's it," Jeeter said. "Come here. Come close to Him."

Kale was overwhelmed with emotion. He had always known he was different from other men. Better. Special. He had always *known,* but he had never expected *this.* Yet here it was, undeniable proof that he was chosen. A fierce, heart-swelling joy suffused him.

He knelt beside Jeeter, near the miraculous presence.

He had arrived at last.

His moment had come.

Here, Kale thought, is my destiny.

CHAPTER 42

THE OTHER SIDE OF HELL

🖋🖋

BENEATH JENNY, THE concrete roadbed snapped with a sound like a cannon shot.

Wham!

She scrambled back but wasn't fast enough. The pavement shifted and began to drop out from under her.

She was going into the pit, *Christ,* no, if she wasn't killed by the fall then *it* would come out of hiding and get her, drag her down, out of sight; it would devour her before anyone could attempt to save her—

Tal Whitman grabbed her ankles and held on. She was dangling in the pit, head down. The concrete tumbled into the hole and landed with a crash. The pavement under Tal's feet shook, started to give way, and he almost lost his grip on Jenny. Then he moved back, hauling her with him, away from the crumbling brink. When she was on solid ground once more, he helped her stand.

Even though she knew it wasn't biologically possible for her heart to rise into her throat, she swallowed it anyway.

"My God," she said breathlessly, "thank you! Tal, if you hadn't—"

"All in a day's work," he said, although he had nearly followed her into the spider's trap.

Just a cakewalk, Jenny thought, remembering the story about Tal that she had heard from Bryce.

She saw that Timothy Flyte, on the far side of the pit, wasn't going to be as fortunate as she had been. Bryce wasn't going to reach him in time.

The pavement beneath Flyte gave way. An eight-foot-long, four-foot-wide slab descended into the pit, carrying the archaeologist with it. It didn't crash to the bottom as the concrete had done on Jenny's side. Over there, the pit had a sloped wall, and the slab scooted down, slid thirty feet to the base, and came to rest against other rubble.

Flyte was still alive. He was screaming in pain.

"We've got to get him out of there fast," Jenny said.

"No use even trying," Tal said.

"But—"

"Look!"

It came for Flyte. It exploded out of one of the tunnels that pocked the floor of the pit and apparently led down into deep caverns. A massive pseudopod of amorphous protoplasm rose ten feet into the air, quivered, dropped to the ground, broke free of the mother-body hiding below, and formed itself into an obscenely fat black spider the size of a pony. It was only ten or twelve feet from Timothy Flyte, and it clambered through the shattered blocks of pavement, heading toward him with murderous intent.

Sprawled helplessly on the concrete sled that had brought him into the pit, Timothy saw the spider coming. His pain was washed away by a wave of terror.

The black spindly legs found easy purchase in the angled ruins, and the thing progressed far more swiftly than a man would have done. There were thousands of bristling, wirelike black hairs on those brittle legs. The bulbous belly was smooth, glossy, pale.

Ten feet away. Eight feet.

It was making a blood-freezing sound, half-squeal, half-hiss.

Six feet. Four.

It stopped in front of Timothy. He found himself looking up into a pair of huge mandibles, sharp-edged chitinous jaws.

The door between madness and sanity began to open in his mind.

Suddenly, a milky rain fell across Timothy. For an instant he thought the spider was squirting venom at him. Then he realized it was Biosan-4. They were standing above, on the rim of the pit, pointing their sprayers down.

The fluid spattered over the spider, too. White spots began to speckle its black body.

Bryce's sprayer had been damaged by a chunk of debris. He couldn't get a drop of fluid from it.

Cursing, he unbuckled the harness and shrugged out of it, dropping the tank on the street. While Tal and Jenny shot Biosan down from the other side of the pit, Bryce hurried to the gutter and collected the two spare cannisters of bacteria-rich solution. They had rolled across the pavement, away from the erupting concrete, and had come to rest against the curb. Each cannister had a handle, and Bryce clutched both of them. They were heavy. He rushed back to the brink of the pit, hesitated, then plunged over the side, down the slope, all the way to the bottom. Somehow, he managed to stay on his feet, and he kept a firm grip on both cannisters.

He didn't go to Flyte. Jenny and Tal were doing all that could be done to destroy the spider. Instead, Bryce wound through and clambered over the rubble, heading toward the hole out of which the shape-changer had dispatched this latest phantom.

Timothy Flyte watched in horror as the spider, looming over him, metamorphosed into an enormous hound. It wasn't merely a dog; it was a Hellhound with a face that was partly canine and partly human. Its coat (where it wasn't spattered with Biosan) was far blacker than the spider, and its big paws had barbed claws, and its teeth were as large as Timothy's fingers. Its breath stank of sulphur and of something worse.

Lesions began to appear on the hound as the bacteria ate into the amorphous flesh, and hope sparked in Timothy.

Looking down at him, the hound spoke in a voice like gravel rolling on a tin chute: "I thought you were my Matthew, but you were my Judas."

The mammoth jaws opened.

Timothy screamed.

Even as the thing succumbed to the degenerative effects of the bacteria, it snapped its teeth together and savagely bit his face.

As he stood at the edge of the pit, looking down, Tal Whitman's attention was torn between the gruesome spectacle of Flyte's murder and Bryce's suicidal mission with the cannisters.

Flyte. Although the phantom dog was dissolving as the bacteria had its acidlike effect, it was not dying fast enough. It bit Flyte in the face, then in the neck.

Bryce. Twenty feet from the Hellhound, Bryce had reached the hole out of which the protoplasm had erupted a couple of minutes ago. He started unscrewing the lid of one of the cannisters.

Flyte. The hound tore viciously at Flyte's head. The hindquarters of the beast had lost their shape and were foaming as they decomposed, but the phantom struggled hard to retain its shape, so that it could slash and chew at Flyte as long as possible.

Bryce. He got the lid off the first cannister. Tal heard it ring off a piece of concrete as Bryce tossed it aside. Tal was sure something was going to leap out of the hole, up from the caverns below, and seize Bryce in a deadly embrace.

Flyte. He had stopped screaming.

Bryce. He tipped the cannister and poured the bacterial solution into the subterranean warren under the floor of the pit.

Flyte was dead.

The only thing that remained of the hound was its large head. Although it was disembodied, although it was blistering and suppurating, it continued to snap at the dead archaeologist.

Below, Timothy Flyte lay in bloody ruins.

He had seemed like a nice old man.

Shuddering with revulsion, Lisa, who was alone on her side of the pit, backed away from the edge. She reached the gutter, sidled along it, finally stopped, stood there, shaking—

—until she realized she was standing on a drain grate. She remembered the tentacles that had slithered out of the drain, snaring and killing Sara Yamaguchi. She quickly hopped up onto the sidewalk.

She glanced at the buildings behind her. She was near one of the covered serviceways between two stores. She stared at the closed gate with apprehension.

Was something lurking in this passageway? Watching her?

Lisa started to step into the street again, saw the drain grate, and stayed on the sidewalk.

She took a tentative step to the left, hesitated, moved to the right, hesitated again. Doorways and serviceway gates lay in both directions. There was no sense in moving. No other place was any safer.

Just as he began to pour the Biosan-4 out of the blue cannister, into the hole in the floor of the pit, Bryce thought he saw movement in the gloom below. He expected a phantom to launch itself up and drag him down into its subterranean lair. But he emptied the entire contents of the cylinder into the hole, and nothing came after him.

Lugging the second cannister, pouring sweat, he made his way through the angled slabs and spires of concrete and broken pipe. He stepped gingerly around a torn and sputtering electric power line, leaped across a small puddle that had formed beside a leaking water main. He passed Flyte's mangled body and the stinking remains of the decomposed phantom that had killed him.

When Bryce reached the next hole in the pit floor, he crouched, unscrewed the lid from the second cannister, and dumped the contents into the chamber below. Empty. He discarded it, turned away from the hole, and ran. He was anxious to get out of the pit before a phantom came after him the way one had gone after Flyte.

He was a third of the way up the sloped wall of the pit, finding the climb considerably more difficult than he had anticipated, when he heard something terrible behind him.

Jenny was watching Bryce claw his way up toward the street. She held her breath, afraid that he wasn't going to make it.

Suddenly her eyes were drawn to the first hole into which he had dumped Biosan. The shape-changer surged up from underground, gushed out onto the floor of the pit. It looked like a tide of thick, congealed sewage; except for where it was stained by the bacterial solution, it was now darker than it had been before. It rippled, writhed, and churned more agitatedly than ever, which was perhaps a sign of degeneration. The milky stain of infection was spreading visibly through the creature: Blisters formed, swelled, popped; ugly sores broke open and wept a watery yellow fluid. Within only a few seconds, at least a ton of the amorphous flesh had spewed out of the hole. All of it was apparently afflicted with disease, and still it came, ever faster, a lavalike outpouring, a wild spouting of living, gelatinous tissue. Even more of the beast began to issue from another hole. The great oozing mass lapped across the rubble, formed pseudopods—shapeless, flailing arms—that rose into the air but quickly fell back in foaming, spasming seizures. And then, from still other holes, there came a ghastly sound: the voices of a thousand men, women, children, and animals, all crying out in pain, horror, and bleak despair. It was an agonized wail of such heartbreak that Jenny could not bear it—especially when a few voices sounded uncannily familiar, like old friends and good neighbors. She put her hands to her ears, but to no avail; the roar of the suffering multitude still penetrated. It was, of course, the death-cry of only one creature, the shape-changer, but since *it* had no voice of its own, it was forced to employ the voices of its victims, expressing its inhuman emotions and unhuman terror in intensely human terms.

It surged across the rubble. Toward Bryce.

Halfway up the slope, Bryce heard the noise behind him change from the wailing of a thousand lonely voices to a roar of rage.

He dared to look back. He saw that three or four tons of amorphous tissue had fountained into the pit, and more was still gushing forth, as if the bowels of the earth were emptying. The ancient enemy's flesh was shuddering, leaping, bursting with leprous lesions. It tried to create winged phantoms, but it was too weak or unstable to competently mimic anything; the half-realized birds and enormous insects either decomposed into a sludge that resembled pus or collapsed back into the pool of tissue beneath them. The ancient enemy was coming toward Bryce nonetheless, coming in a quivering-churning frenzy; it had flowed almost to the base of the slope, and now it was sending degenerating yet still powerful tentacles toward his heels.

He turned away from it and redoubled his efforts to reach the rim of the pit.

The two big windows of the Towne Bar and Grille, in front of which Lisa was standing, exploded out onto the sidewalk. A shard nicked her forehead, but she was otherwise unhurt, for most of the fragments landed on the sidewalk between her and the building.

An obscene, shadowy mass bulged through the broken windows.

Lisa stumbled backwards and nearly fell off the curb.

The foul, oozing flesh appeared to fill the entire building out of which it extruded itself.

Something snaked around Lisa's ankle.

Tendrils of amorphous flesh had slithered out of the drain grate in the gutter behind her. They had taken hold of her.

Screaming, she tried to pull free of them—and found that it was surprisingly easy to do so. The thin, wormlike tentacles fell away. Lesions broke out along the length of them; they split open, and in seconds they were reduced to inanimate slime.

The disgusting mass that burgeoned out of the barroom was also succumbing to the bacteria. Gobs of foaming tissue fell away and splattered the sidewalk. Still, it continued to gush forth, forming tentacles, and the tentacles weaved through the air, seeking Lisa, but with the tentative groping of something sick and blind.

Tal saw the Towne Bar and Grille's windows explode on the other side of the street, but before he could take one step to help Lisa, windows shattered behind him, too, in the lobby and dining room of the Hilltop Inn, and he turned in surprise, and the front doors of the inn flew open, and from both the doors and the windows came tons of protoplasm that pulsated (Oh, Jesus, how big *was* the goddamned thing? As big as the whole town? As big as the mountain out of which it had come? Infinite?) and roiled, sprouting a score of lashing tentacles as it surged forth, marked by disease but noticeably more active than the extension of itself that it had sent after Bryce in the pit, and before Tal could raise the nozzle of his sprayer and depress the pressure-release lever, the cold tentacles found him, gripped him with dismaying strength, and then he was being dragged across the pavement, toward the inn, toward the oozing wall of slime that was still rupturing through the shattered windows, and the tentacles began to burn through his clothing, he felt his skin burning, blistering, he howled, the digestive acids were eating into his flesh, he felt brands of fire across his arms, he felt one fiery line along his left thigh, he remembered how a tentacle had beheaded Frank Autry by eating swiftly through the man's neck, he thought of his Aunt Becky, he—

Jenny dodged a tentacle that took a swipe at her.

She sprayed Tal and all the snaky appendages—three of them—that had hold of him.

Decomposing tissue sloughed off the tentacles, but they didn't degenerate entirely.

Even where she hadn't sprayed, the creature's flesh broke out in new sores. The entire beast was contaminated; it was being eaten up from within. It couldn't last much longer. Maybe just long enough to kill Tal Whitman.

He was screaming, thrashing.

Frantic, Jenny let go of the sprayer's hose and moved in closer to Tal. She grabbed one of the tentacles that gripped him, and she tried to pry it loose.

Another tentacle clutched at her.

She twisted out of its fumbling grip and realized that, if she could evade it so easily, it must be swiftly losing its battle with the bacteria.

In her hands, pieces of the tentacle came away, chunks of dead tissue that stank horribly.

Gagging, she clawed harder than ever, and the tentacle finally dropped away from Tal, and then so did the other two, and he collapsed in a heap on the pavement, gasping and bleeding.

The blind, groping tentacles never touched Lisa. They receded into the vomitous mass that had poured out of the front of the Towne Bar and Grille. Now, that heaving monstrosity spasmed and flung off foaming, infected gobbets of itself.

"It's dying," Lisa said aloud, although no one was close enough to hear her. "The Devil is dying."

Bryce crawled on his belly for the last few, almost vertical feet of the pit wall. He reached the rim at last and pulled himself out.

He looked down the way he had come. The shape-changer hadn't gotten close to him. An incredibly large, gelatinous lake of amorphous tissue lay at the bottom of the pit, pooling over and around the debris, but it was virtually inactive. A few human and animal forms still tried to rise up, but the ancient enemy was losing its talent for mimicry. The phantoms were imperfect and sluggish. The shape-changer was slowly disappearing under a layer of its own dead and decomposing tissue.

Jenny knelt beside Tal.

His arms and chest were marked by livid wounds. A raw, weeping wound extended the length of his left thigh, as well.

"Pain?" she asked.

"When it had me, yeah, a lot. Not so much now," he said, although his expression left no doubt that he was still suffering.

The enormous bulk of slime that had erupted from the Hilltop Inn now began to withdraw, retreating into the plumbing from which it had risen, leaving behind the steaming residue of its decomposing flesh.

A Mephistophelian retreat. Back to the netherworld. Back to the other side of Hell.

Satisfied that they weren't in any immediate danger, Jenny looked more closely at Tal's wounds.

"Bad?" he asked.

"Not as bad as I would've thought." She forced him to lie back. "The skin's eaten away in places. And some of the fatty tissue underneath."

"Veins? Arteries?"

"No. It was weak when it took hold of you, too weak to burn that deep. A lot of ruined capillaries in the surface tissue. That's the cause of the bleeding. But there's not even as much blood as you'd expect. I'll get my bag as soon as it seems safe to go inside, and I'll treat you for infection. I think maybe you ought to be in the hospital for a couple of days, for observation, just to be sure there's no delayed allergic reaction to the acid or any toxins. But I really think you'll be just fine."

"You know what?" he said.

"What?"

"You're talking like it's all over."

Jenny blinked.

She looked up at the inn. She could see through the smashed windows, into the dining room. There was no sign of the ancient enemy.

She turned and looked across the street. Lisa and Bryce were making their way around to this side of the pit.

"I think it is," she said to Tal. "I think it's all over."

CHAPTER 43

APOSTLES

FLETCHER KALE WAS no longer afraid. He sat beside Jeeter and watched the Satanic flesh metamorphose into ever more bizarre forms.

Gradually, he became aware that the calf of his right leg itched. He scratched continuously, absentmindedly, while he watched the truly miraculous transformation of the demonic visitor.

Restricted to the caves since Sunday, Jeeter knew nothing about what had happened in Snowfield. Kale recounted what little he knew, and Jeeter was thrilled. "You know, what it is, it's a *sign*. What He did in Snowfield is like a sign tellin' the world His time is comin'. His reign is gonna begin soon. He'll rule the earth for a thousand years. That's what the Bible itself says, man—a thousand years of Hell on earth. Everyone'll suffer—except you and me and others like us. 'Cause we're the chosen ones, man. We're His apostles. We'll rule the world with Lucifer, and it'll belong to us, and we'll be able to do any fuckin' outrageous thing to anybody we happen to want to do it to. *Anybody*. And no one'll touch us, no one, ever. You understand?" Terr demanded, gripping Kale's arm, voice rising with excitement, trembling with evangelical passion, a passion that was easily communicated to Kale and stirred in him a dizzying, unholy rapture.

With Jeeter's hand on his arm, Kale imagined he could feel the hot gaze of the red and yellow eye tattoo. It was a magical eye that peered into his soul and recognized a certain dark kinship.

Kale cleared his throat, scratched his ankle, scratched his calf. He said, "Yeah. Yeah, I understand. I really do."

The column of slime in the center of the room began to form a whiplike tail. Wings emerged, spread, flapped once. Arms grew, large and sinewy. The hands were enormous, with powerful fingers that tapered into talons. At the top of the column, a face took shape in the oozing mass: chin and jaws like chiseled granite; a gash of a mouth with thin lips, crooked yellow teeth, viperous fangs; a nose like the snout of a pig; mad, crimson eyes, not remotely human, like the prismed eyes of a fly. Horns sprouted on the forehead, a concession to Christian myth-conceptions. The hair appeared to be worms; they glistened, fat and green-black, writhing continuously in tangled knots.

The cruel mouth opened. The Devil said, "Do you believe?"

"Yes," Terr said in adoration. "You are my lord."

"Yes," Kale said shakily. "I believe." He scratched at his right calf. "I do believe."

"Are you mine?" the apparition asked.

"Yes, always," Terr said, and Kale agreed.

"Will you ever forsake me?" it asked.

"No."

"Never."

"Do you wish to please me?"

"Yes," Terr said, and Kale said, "Whatever you want."

"I will be leaving soon," the manifestation said. "It is not yet my time to rule. That day is coming. Soon. But there are conditions that must be met, prophesies to be fulfilled. Then I will come again, not merely to deliver a sign to all mankind, but to stay for a thousand years. Until then, I will leave you with the protection of my power, which is vast; no one will be able to harm or thwart you. I grant you life everlasting. I promise that, for you, Hell will be a place of great pleasure and immense rewards. In return, you must complete five tasks."

He told them what He would have them do to prove themselves and please Him. As He spoke, He broke out in pustules, hives, and lesions that wept a thin yellow fluid.

Kale wondered what significance these sores might have, then realized Lucifer was the father of all disease. Perhaps this was a not-so-subtle reminder of the terrible plagues He could visit upon them if they were unwilling to undertake the five tasks.

The flesh foamed, dissolved. Gobs of it dropped to the floor; a few were flung against the walls as the figure heaved and writhed. The Devil's tail dropped from the main body and wriggled on the floor; in seconds, it was reduced to inanimate muck that stank of death.

When he finished telling them what He wanted of them, He said, "Do we have a bargain?"

"Yes," Terr said, and Kale said, "Yes, a bargain."

The face of Lucifer, covered with running sores, melted away. The horns and wings melted, too. Churning, seeping a puslike paste, the thing sank down into the floor, disappeared into the river below.

Strangely, the odorous dead tissue did not vanish. Ectoplasm was supposed to disappear when the supernatural presence had departed, but this stuff remained: foul, nauseating, glistening in the gaslight.

Gradually, Kale's rapture faded. He began to feel the cold radiating from the limestone, through the seat of his pants.

Gene Terr coughed. "Well . . . well now . . . wasn't that somethin'?"

Kale scratched his itchy calf. Beneath the itchiness, there was now a dull little spot of pain, throbbing.

It had reached the end of its feeding period. In fact, it had overfed. It had intended to move toward the sea later today, through a series of caverns, subterranean channels, and underground watercourses. It had wanted to travel out beyond the edge of the continent, into the ocean trenches. Countless times before, it had passed its lethargic periods—sometimes lasting many years—in the cool, dark depths of the sea. Down there where the pressure was so enormous that few forms of life could survive, down there where absolute lightlessness and silence provided little stimulation, the ancient enemy was able to slow down its metabolic processes; down there, it could enter a much-desired dreamlike state, in which it could ruminate in perfect solitude.

But it would never reach the sea. Never again. It was dying.

The concept of its own death was so new that it had not yet adjusted to the grim reality. In the geological substructure of Snowtop Mountain, the shapechanger continued to slough off diseased portions of itself. It crept deeper, deeper, across the underworld river that flowed in Stygian darkness, deeper still, farther down into the infernal regions of the earth, into the chambers of Orcus, Hades, Osiris, Erebus, Minos, Loki, Satan. Each time that it believed itself free of the devouring microorganism, a peculiar tingling sensation arose at some point in the amorphous tissue, a wrongness, *and then there came a pain quite unlike human pain, and it was forced to rid itself of even more infected flesh. It went deeper, down into jahanna, into Gehenna, into Sheol, Abbadon, into the Pit. Over the centuries it had eagerly assumed the role of Satan and other evil figures, which men had attributed to it, had amused itself by catering to their superstitions. Now, it was condemned to a fate consistent with the mythology it had helped create. It was bitterly aware of the irony. It had been cast down. It had been damned. It would dwell in darkness and despair for the rest of its life—which could be measured in hours.*

At least it had left behind two apostles. Kale and Terr. They would do its work even after it had ceased to exist. They would spread terror and take revenge. They were perfectly suited to the job.

Now, reduced to only a brain and minimal supporting tissue, the shapechanger cowered in a chthonian niche of densely packed rock and waited for the end. It spent its last minutes seething with hatred, raging at all mankind.

Kale rolled up his trousers and looked at the calf of his right leg. In the lantern light, he saw two small red spots; they were swollen, itchy, and very tender.

"Insect bites," he said.

Gene Terr looked. "Ticks. They burrow under the skin. The itchin' won't stop until you get 'em out. Burn 'em out with a cigarette."

"Got any?"

Terr grinned. "Couple joints of grass. They'll work just as well, man. And the ticks'll die happy."

They smoked the joints, and Kale used the glowing tip of his to burn out the ticks. It didn't hurt much.

"In the woods," Terr said, "keep your pants tucked in your boots."

"They *were* tucked into my boots."

"Yeah? Then how'd them ticks get underneath?"

"I don't know."

After they had smoked more grass, Kale frowned and said, "He promised us no one could hurt or stop us. He said we'd be under His protection."

"That's right, man. Invincible."

"So how come I've got to put up with tick bites?" Kale asked.

"Hey, man, it's no big thing."

"But if we're really protected—"

"Listen, maybe the tick bites are sort of like His way of sealing the bargain you made with Him. With a little blood. Get it?"

"Then why don't you have tick bites?"

Jeeter shrugged. "Ain't important, man. Besides, the fuckin' ticks bit you *before* you struck your bargain—didn't they?"

"Oh." Kale nodded, fuzzy-headed from dope. "Yeah. That's right."

They were silent for a while.

Then Kale said, "When do you think we can leave here?"

"They're probably still lookin' for you pretty hard."

"But if they can't hurt me—"

"No sense makin' the job harder for ourselves," Terr said.

"I guess so."

"We'll lay low for like a few days. Worst of the heat will be off by then."

"Then we do the five like he wants. And after that?"

"Head on out, man. Move on. Make tracks."

"Where?"

"Somewhere. He'll show us the way." Terr was silent for a while. Then he said, "Tell me about it. About killin' your wife and kid."

"What do you want to know?"

"Everythin' there is to know, man. Tell me what it felt like. What was it like to off your old lady. Mostly, tell me about the kid. What'd it feel like, wastin' a kid? Huh? I never did one that young, man. You kill him fast or drag it out? Did it feel different than killin' her? What exactly did you *do* to the kid?"

"Only what I had to do. They were in my way."

"Draggin' you down, huh?"

"Both of them."

"Sure. I see how it was. But what did you *do?*"

"Shot her."

"Shoot the kid, too?"

"No. I chopped him. With a meat cleaver."

"No shit?"

They smoked more joints, and the lantern hissed, and the whisper-chuckle of the underground river came up through the hole in the floor, and Kale talked about killing Joanna, Danny, and the county deputies.

Every once in a while, punctuating his words with a little marijuana giggle, Jeeter said, "Hey, man, are we gonna have some fun? Are we gonna have some fun together, you and me? Tell me more. Tell me. Man, are we gonna have some fun?"

CHAPTER 44

VICTORY?

BRYCE STOOD ON the sidewalk, studying the town. Listening. Waiting. There was no sign of the shape-changer, but he was reluctant to believe it was dead. He was afraid it would spring at him the moment he relaxed his guard.

Tal Whitman was stretched out on the pavement. Jenny and Lisa cleaned the acid burns, dusted them with antibiotic powder, and applied temporary bandages.

And Snowfield remained as silent as if it were at the bottom of the sea.

Finished ministering to Tal, Jenny said, "We should get him to the hospital right away. The wounds aren't deep, but there might be a delayed allergic reaction to one of the shape-changer's toxins. He might suddenly start having respiratory difficulties or blood pressure problems. The hospital is equipped for the worst possibilities; I'm not."

Sweeping the length of the street with his eyes, Bryce said, "What if we get in the car, trap ourselves in a moving car, and then *it* comes back?"

"We'll take a couple of sprayers with us."

"There might not be time to use them. It could come up out of a manhole, overturn the car, and kill us that way, without ever touching us, without giving us a chance to use the sprayers."

They listened to the town. Nothing. Just the breeze.

Lisa finally said, "It's dead."

"We can't be sure," Bryce said.

"Don't you feel it?" Lisa insisted. "Feel the difference. It's gone! It's dead. You can *feel* the change in the air."

Bryce realized the girl was right. The shape-changer had not been merely a physical presence, but a spiritual one as well; he had been able to sense the evil of it, an almost tangible malevolence. Apparently, the ancient enemy had emitted subtle emanations—Vibrations? Psychic waves?—that couldn't be seen or heard but which were registered on an instinctual level. They left a stain on the soul. And now those vibrations were gone. There was no menace in the air.

Bryce took a deep breath. The air was clean, fresh, sweet.

Tal said, "If you don't want to get in a car just yet, don't worry about it. We can wait awhile. I'm okay. I'll be fine."

"I've changed my mind," Bryce said. "We can go. Nothing's going to stop us. Lisa's right. It's dead."

In the patrol car, as Bryce started the engine, Jenny said, "You remember what Flyte said about the creature's intelligence? When he was speaking to it, through the computer, he told it that it had probably acquired its intelligence and self-awareness only after it had begun consuming intelligent creatures."

"I remember," Tal said from the back seat, where he sat with Lisa. "It didn't like hearing that."

"And *so?*" Bryce asked. "What's your point, Doc?"

"Well, if it acquired its intelligence by absorbing our knowledge and cognitive mechanisms . . . then did it also acquire its cruelty and viciousness from us, from mankind?" She saw that the question made Bryce uneasy, but she plunged on. "When you come right down to it, maybe the only real devils are human beings; not all of us; not the species as a whole; just the ones who're twisted, the ones who somehow never acquire empathy or compassion. If the shape-changer *was* the Satan of mythology, perhaps the evil in human beings isn't a reflection of the Devil; perhaps the Devil is only a reflection of the savagery and brutality of our own kind. Maybe what we've done is . . . create the Devil in our own image."

Bryce was silent. Then: "You may be right. I suspect you are. There's no use wasting energy being afraid of devils, demons, and things that go bump in the night . . . because, ultimately, we'll never encounter anything more terrifying than the monsters among us. Hell is where we make it."

They drove down Skyline Road.

Snowfield looked serene and beautiful.

Nothing tried to stop them.

CHAPTER 45
GOOD AND EVIL

ON SUNDAY EVENING, one week after Jenny and Lisa found Snowfield in its graveyard silence, five days after the death of the shape-changer, they were at the hospital in Santa Mira, visiting Tal Whitman. He had, after all, suffered a toxin reaction to some fluid secreted by the shape-changer and had also developed a mild infection, but he had never been in serious danger. Now he was almost as good as new—and eager to go home.

When Lisa and Jenny stepped into Tal's room, he was seated in a chair by the window, reading a magazine. He was dressed in his uniform. His gun and holster were lying on a small table beside the chair.

Lisa hugged him before he could get up, and Tal hugged her back.

"Lookin' good," she told him.

"Lookin' fine," he told her.

"Like a million bucks."

"Like two million."

"You'll turn the ladies' heads."

"And you'll make the boys do back-flips."

It was a ritual they went through every day, a small ceremony of affection that always elicited a smile from Lisa. Jenny loved to see it; Lisa didn't smile often these days. In the past week, she hadn't laughed at all, not once.

Tal stood up, and Jenny hugged him, too. She said, "Bryce is with Timmy. He'll be up in a little while."

"You know," Tal said, "he seems to be handling that situation a whole lot better. All this past year, you could see how Timmy's condition was killing him. Now he seems able to cope with it."

Jenny nodded. "He'd gotten it in his head that Timmy would be better off dead. But up in Snowfield, he had a change of heart. I think he decided that, after all, there *wasn't* a fate worse than death. Where there's life, there's hope."

"That's what they say."

"In another year, if Timmy's still in a coma, Bryce might change his mind again. But for the moment, he seems grateful just to be able to sit down there for a while each day, holding his little boy's warm hand." She looked Tal over and demanded: "What's with the street clothes?"

"I'm being discharged."

"Fantastic!" Lisa said.

Timmy's roommate these days was an eighty-two-year-old man who was hooked up to an IV, a beeping cardiac monitor, and a wheezing respirator.

Although Timmy was attached only to an IV, he was in the embrace of an oblivion as complete as the octogenarian's coma. Once or twice an hour, never more often, never for longer than a minute at a time, the boy's eyelids fluttered or his lips twitched or a muscle ticked in his cheek. That was all.

Bryce sat beside the bed, his hand through the railing, gently gripping his son's hand. Since Snowfield, just this meager contact was enough to satisfy him. Each day he left the room feeling better.

There wasn't much light now that evening had come. On the wall at the head of the bed, there was a dim lamp that cast a soft glow only as far as Timmy's shoulders, leaving his sheet-covered body in shadow. In that wan illumination, Bryce could see how his boy had withered, losing weight in spite of the IV solution. The cheekbones were too prominent. There were dark circles around his eyes. The chin and jawline looked pathetically fragile. His son had always been small for his age. But now the hand Bryce held seemed to belong to a much younger child than Timmy; it seemed like the hand of an infant.

But it was warm. It was warm.

After a while, Bryce reluctantly let go. He smoothed the boy's hair, straightened the sheet, fluffed the pillow.

It was time to leave, but he couldn't go; not yet. He was crying. He didn't want to step into the hall with tears on his face.

He pulled a few Kleenex from the box on the nightstand, got up, went to the window, and looked out at Santa Mira.

Although he wept every day when he came here, these were different tears from those he had cried before. These scalded, washed away the misery, and healed. Bit by bit, slowly, they healed him.

"Discharged?" Jenny said, scowling. "Says who?"

Tal grinned. "Says me."

"Since when have you become your own doctor?"

"I just thought a second opinion seemed called for, so I asked myself in for consultation, and I recommended to me that I go home."

"Tal—"

"Really, Doc, I feel great. The swelling's gone. Haven't run a temperature in two days. I'm a prime candidate for release. If you try to make me stay here any longer, my death will be on your hands."

"Death?"

"The hospital food is sure to kill me."

"He looks ready to go dancing," Lisa said.

"And when'd you get *your* medical degree?" Jenny asked. To Tal she said, "Well . . . let me have a look. Take off your shirt."

He slipped out of it quickly and easily, not nearly as stiff as he'd been yesterday. Jenny carefully untaped the bandages and found that he was right: no swelling, no breaks in the scabs.

"We've beaten it," he assured her.

"Usually, we don't discharge a patient in the evening. Orders are written in the morning; release comes between ten o'clock and noon."

"Rules are made to be broken."

"What an awful thing for a policeman to say," she teased. "Look, Tal, I'd prefer you stayed here one more night, just in case—"

"And I'd prefer I *didn't,* just in case I go *stir* crazy."

"You're really determined?"

"He's really determined," Lisa said.

Tal said, "Doc, they had my gun in a safe, along with their drug supply. I had to wheedle, beg, plead, and tease a sweet nurse named Paula, so she'd get it for me this afternoon. I told her you'd let me out tonight for sure. Now, see, Paula's a soul sister, a very attractive lady, single, eligible, delicious—"

"Don't get too steamy," Lisa said. "There's a minor present."

"I'd like to have a date with Paula," Tal said. "I'd like to spend eternity with Paula. But now, Doc, if you say I can't go home, then I'll have to put my revolver back in the safe, and maybe Paula's supervisor'll find out she let me have it before my discharge was final, and then Paula might lose her job, and if she loses it because of me, I'll never get a date with her. If I don't get a date with her, I'm not going to be able to marry her, and if I don't marry her, there won't be any little Tal Whitmans running around, not ever, because I'll go away to a monastery and become celibate, seeing as how I've made up my mind that Paula's the *only* woman for me. So if you won't discharge me, then you'll not only be ruining my life but depriving the world of a little black Einstein or maybe a little black Beethoven."

Jenny laughed and shook her head. "Okay, okay. I'll write a discharge order, and you can leave tonight."

He hugged her and quickly began putting on his shirt.

"Paula better watch out," Lisa said. "You're too smooth to be left loose among women without a bell around your neck."

"Me? Smooth?" He buckled his holster around his waist. "I'm just good old Tal Whitman, sort of bashful. Been shy all my life."

"Oh, sure," Lisa said.

Jenny said, "If you—"

And suddenly Tal went berserk. He shoved Jenny aside, knocked her down. She struck the footboard of the bed with her shoulder and hit the floor hard. She heard gunfire and saw Lisa falling and didn't know if the girl had been hit or was just diving for cover; and for an instant she thought Tal was shooting at them. Then she saw he was still pulling his revolver out of his holster.

Even as the sound of the shot slammed through the room, glass shattered. It was the window behind Tal.

"Drop it!" Tal shouted.

Jenny turned her head, saw Gene Terr standing in the doorway, silhouetted by the brighter light in the hospital corridor behind him.

Standing in the deep shadows by the window, Bryce finished drying his tears and wadded up the damp Kleenex. He heard a soft noise in the room behind him, thought it was a nurse, turned—and saw Fletcher Kale. For a moment Bryce was frozen by disbelief.

Kale was standing at the foot of Timmy's bed, barely identifiable in the weak light. He hadn't seen Bryce. He was watching the boy—and grinning. Madness knotted his face. He was holding a gun.

Bryce stepped away from the window, reaching for his own revolver. Too late, he realized he wasn't in uniform, wasn't wearing a sidearm. He had an off-duty snubnose .38 in an ankle holster; he stooped to get it.

But Kale had seen him. The gun in Kale's hand snapped up, barked once, twice, three times in rapid succession.

Bryce felt a sledgehammer hit him high and on the left side, and pain flashed across his entire chest. As he crumpled to the floor, he heard the killer's gun roar three more times.

"Drop it!" Tal shouted, and Jenny saw Jeeter, and another shot ricocheted off the bed rail and must have gone through the ceiling because a couple of squares of acoustic tile fell down.

Crouching, Tal fired two rounds. The first shot took Jeeter in the left thigh. The second struck him in the gut, lifted him, and threw him backwards, into the corner, where he landed in a spray of blood. He didn't move.

Tal said, "What the *hell?*"

Jenny cried for Lisa and scrambled on all fours around the bed, wondering if her sister was alive.

Kale had been sick for a couple of hours. He was running a fever. His eyes burned and felt grainy. It had come on him suddenly. He had a headache, too, and standing there at the foot of the boy's bed, he began to feel nauseated. His legs became weak. He didn't understand; he was supposed to be protected, invincible. Of course, maybe Lucifer was impatient with him for waiting five days before leaving the caves. Maybe this illness was a warning to get on with His work. The symptoms would probably vanish the moment the boy was dead. Yeah. That was probably what would happen. Kale grinned at the comatose child, began to raise his revolver, and winced as a cramp twisted his guts.

Then he saw movement in the shadows. Swung away from the bed. A man. Coming at him. Hammond. Kale opened fire, squeezing off six rounds, taking no chances. He was dizzy, and his vision was blurry, and his arm felt weak, and he could hardly keep a grip on the gun; even in those close quarters, he couldn't trust his aim.

Hammond went down hard and lay very still.

Although the light was dim, and although Kale's eyes wouldn't focus properly, he could see spots of blood on the wall and floor.

Laughing happily, wondering when the illness would leave him now that he'd completed one of the tasks Lucifer had given him, Kale weaved toward the body, intending to deliver the *coup de grâce.* Even if Hammond was stone-cold dead, Kale wanted to put a bullet in that snide, smug face, wanted to mess it up real good.

Then he would deal with the boy.

That was what Lucifer wanted. Five deaths. Hammond, the boy, Whitman, Dr. Paige, and the girl.

He reached Hammond, started to bend down to him—

—and the sheriff moved. His hand was lightning quick. He snatched a gun from an ankle holster, and before Kale could respond, there was a muzzle flash.

Kale was hit. He stumbled, fell. His revolver flew out of his hand. He heard it clang against the leg of one of the beds.

This can't be happening, he told himself. I'm protected. No one can harm me.

* * *

Lisa was alive. When she'd fallen behind the bed, she hadn't been shot; she'd just been diving for cover. Jenny held her tightly.

Tal was crouched over Gene Terr. The gang leader was dead, a gaping hole in his chest.

A crowd had gathered: nurses, nurses' aides, a couple of doctors, a patient or two in bathrobe and slippers.

A red-haired orderly hurried up. He looked shell-shocked. "There's been a shooting on the second floor, too!"

"Bryce," Jenny said, and a cold blade of fear pierced her.

"What's going *on* here?" Tal said.

Jenny ran for the exit door at the end of the hall, slammed through it, went down the stairs two at a time. Tal caught up with her by the time she reached the bottom of the second flight. He pulled open the door, and they rushed out into the second-floor corridor.

Another crowd had gathered outside Timmy's room. Her heart beating twenty to the dozen, Jenny rammed through the onlookers.

A body was on the floor. A nurse stooped beside it.

Jenny thought it was Bryce. Then she saw him in a chair. Another nurse was cutting the shirt away from his shoulder. He was just wounded.

Bryce forced a smile. "Better be careful, Doc. If you always arrive on the scene this soon, they'll start calling you an ambulance chaser."

She wept. She couldn't help it. She had never been so glad to hear anything as she was to hear his voice.

"Just a scratch," he said.

"Now you sound like Tal," she said, laughing through her tears. "Is Timmy okay?"

"Kale was going to kill him. If I hadn't been here . . ."

"This is Kale?"

"Yeah."

Jenny wiped her eyes with her sleeves and examined Bryce's shoulder. The bullet had passed through, in the front and out the back. There was no reason to think it had fragmented, but she intended to order X-rays anyway. The wound was bleeding freely, although it wasn't spurting, and she directed the nurse to staunch the flow with gauze pads soaked in boric acid.

He was going to be all right.

Sure of Bryce's condition, Jenny turned to the man on the floor. He was in more serious condition. The nurse had torn open his jacket and shirt; he'd been shot in the chest. He coughed, and bright blood sputtered over his lips.

Jenny sent the nurse for a stretcher and put in an emergency call for a surgeon. Then she noticed Kale was running a fever. His forehead was hot, face flushed. When she took his wrist to check his pulse, she saw it was covered with fiery red spots. She pushed up his sleeve and found the spots extended halfway up his arm. They were on his other wrist, too. None on his face or neck. She had noticed pale red marks on his chest but had mistaken them for blood. Looking again, more closely than before, she saw they were like the spots on his wrists.

Measles? No. Something else. Something worse than measles.

The nurse returned with two orderlies and a wheeled stretcher, and Jenny said, "We'll have to quarantine this floor. And the one above. We've got some disease here, and I'm not entirely sure what it is."

After X-rays and after his wound had been dressed, Bryce was put in a room down the hall from Timmy. The ache in his shoulder got worse, not better, as the shocked nerves began to regain their function. He refused painkillers, intending to keep a clear head until he knew what had happened and why.

Jenny came to see him half an hour after he was put to bed. She looked exhausted, yet her weariness didn't diminish her beauty. The sight of her was all the medicine he needed.

"How's Kale?" he asked.

"The bullet didn't damage his heart. It collapsed one lung, nicked an artery. Ordinarily, the prognosis would be fair. But he's not only got surgery to recuperate from; he's also got to deal with a case of Rocky Mountain spotted fever."

Bryce blinked. "Spotted fever?"

"There're two cigarette burns on his right calf, or rather the scars of two burns, where he got rid of the ticks. Wood ticks transmit the disease. Judging from the look of the scars, I'd say he was bitten five or six days ago, which is just about the incubation period for spotted fever. The symptoms must've hit him within the past several hours. He must've been dizzy, chilled, weak in the joints . . ."

"That's why his aim was so bad!" Bryce said. "He fired three times at close range and only winged me once."

"You'd better thank God for sending that tick up his pants leg."

He thought about that and said, "It almost *does* seem like an act of God, doesn't it? But what were he and Terr up to? Why'd they risk coming here with guns? I can understand Kale might want to kill me and even Timmy. But why Tal and you and Lisa?"

"You're not going to believe this," she said. "Since last Tuesday morning, Kale's been keeping a written record of what he calls 'The Events After the Epiphany.' It seems that Kale and Terr made a bargain with the Devil."

Four o'clock Monday morning, only six days after the epiphany of which Kale had written, he died in the county hospital. Before he passed out of this life, he opened his eyes, stared wildly at a nurse, then looked past her, saw something that terrified him, something the nurse couldn't see. He somehow found the strength to raise his hands, as if trying to protect himself, and he cried out; it was a thin, death-rattle scream. When the nurse tried to calm him, he said, "But *this* isn't my destiny." And then he was gone.

On October 31, more than six weeks after the events in Snowfield, Tal Whitman and Paula Thorne (the nurse he'd been dating) held a Halloween costume party at Tal's house in Santa Mira. Bryce went as a cowboy. Jenny was a cowgirl. Lisa was dressed as a witch, with a tall pointed hat and lots of black mascara.

Tal opened the door and said, "Cluck, cluck." He was wearing a chicken suit.

Jenny had never seen a more ridiculous costume. She laughed so hard that, for a while, she didn't realize Lisa was laughing, too.

It was the first laugh the girl had given voice to in the past six weeks. Previously, she'd managed only a smile. Now she laughed until tears ran down her face.

"Well, hey, just a minute here," Tal said, pretending to be offended. "You make a pretty silly-looking witch, too."

He winked at Jenny, and she knew he'd chosen the chicken suit for the effect it would have on Lisa.

"For God's sake," Bryce said, "get out of the doorway and let us inside, Tal.

If the public sees you in that getup, they'll lose what little respect they have left for the sheriff's department."

That night, Lisa joined in the conversation and the games, and she laughed a great deal. It was a new beginning.

In August of the following year, on the first day of their honeymoon, Jenny found Bryce on the balcony of their hotel room, overlooking Waikiki Beach. He was frowning.

"You aren't worried about being so far away from Timmy, are you?" she asked.

"No. But it's Timmy I'm thinking about. Lately . . . I've had this feeling everything's going to be all right, after all. It's strange. Like a premonition. I had a dream last night. Timmy woke up from his coma, said hello to me, and asked for a Big Mac. Only . . . it wasn't like any dream I've ever had before. It was so *real.*"

"Well, you've never lost hope."

"Yes. For a while I lost it. But I've got it back again."

They stood in silence for a while, letting the warm sea wind wash over them, listening to the waves breaking on the beach.

Then they made love again.

That night they had dinner at a good Chinese restaurant in Honolulu. They drank champagne all evening, even though the waiter politely suggested they switch to tea with the meal, so their palates would not be "stained."

Over dessert, Bryce said, "There was something else Timmy said in that dream. When I was surprised he'd awakened from his coma, he said, 'But, Daddy, if there's a Devil, then there's got to be a God, too. Didn't you already figure that out when you met the Devil? God wouldn't let me sleep my whole life away.' "

Jenny stared at him uncertainly.

He smiled. "Don't worry. I'm not flaking out on you. I'm not going to start sending money to those charlatan preachers on TV, asking them to pray for Timmy. Hell, I'm not even going to start attending church. Sunday's the only day I can sleep in! What I'm talking about isn't your standard, garden variety religion . . ."

"Yes, but it wasn't *really* the Devil," she said.

"Wasn't it?"

"It was a prehistoric creature that—"

"Couldn't it be *both?*"

"What're we getting into here?"

"A philosophical discussion."

"On our honeymoon?"

"I married you partly for your mind."

Later, in bed, just before sleep took them, he said, "Well, all I know is that the shape-changer made me realize there's a lot more mystery in this world than I once thought. I just won't rule anything out. And looking back on it, considering what we survived in Snowfield, considering how Tal had just strapped on his gun when Jeeter walked in, considering how the spotted fever screwed up Kale's aim . . . well, it seems to me like we were *meant* to survive."

They slept, woke toward dawn, made love, slept again.

In the morning, she said, "I know one thing for *sure.*"

"What's that?"

"We were *meant* to be married."

"Definitely."

"No matter what, fate would've run us headlong into each other sooner or later."

That afternoon, as they strolled along the beach, Jenny thought the waves sounded like huge, rumbling wheels. The sound called to mind an old saying about the mill wheels of Heaven grinding slowly. The rumble of the waves enforced that image, and in her mind she could see immense stone mill wheels turning against each other.

She said, "You think it has a meaning, then? A purpose?"

He didn't have to ask what she meant. "Yes. Everything, every twist and turn of life. A meaning, a purpose."

The sea foamed on the sand.

Jenny listened to the mill wheels and wondered what mysteries and miracles, what horrors and joys were being ground out at this very moment, to be served up in times to come.

A NOTE TO THE READER

Like all the characters in this novel, Timothy Flyte is a fictional person, but many of the mass disappearances to which he refers are not merely figments of the author's imagination. They really happened. The disappearance of the Roanoke Island colony, the mysteriously deserted Eskimo village of Anjikuni, the vanished Mayan populations, the unexplained loss of thousands of Spanish soldiers in 1711, the equally mystifying loss of the Chinese battalions in 1939, and certain other cases mentioned in *Phantoms* are actually well-documented, historical events.

Likewise, there is a *real* Dr. Ananda Chakrabarty. In *Phantoms,* the details of his development of the first patented microorganism are drawn from public record. Dr. Chakrabarty's bacterium was, as stated in the book, too fragile to survive outside of the laboratory. Biosan-4, the trade name of a supposedly hardier strain of Chakrabarty's bug, is a fictional device; to the best of my knowledge, no effort has been made to refine and improve Dr. Chakrabarty's discovery, and it remains a laboratory oddity of note, primarily, because of its role in the precedent-setting Supreme Court decision.

And of course the ancient enemy is a product of the author's imagination. But what if . . .

ABOUT THE AUTHOR

Dean R. Koontz, author of the national bestsellers WATCHERS, LIGHTNING, MIDNIGHT, and COLD FIRE, won an *Atlantic Monthly* fiction competition in 1965 at the age of twenty and has been writing ever since. Dean Koontz and his wife, Gerda, live in southern California.